Praise for *Against the Day*

"Pynchon here offers his most successful and cogent articulation of the concerns that have haunted his work from the start."

—Christopher Sorrentino, *Los Angeles Times*

"Welcome back to Pynchonland, where wormholes in time are as common as potholes, and the real world overlaps with the imaginary in a most colorful weave."

—*The Seattle Times*

"The most audacious and boisterous epic novel of the year."

—*The Providence Journal*

"Pynchon's gift for language remains undiminished, a roiling, imaginative flood that makes his voice utterly unique, and his latest a must-read."

—*Time Out New York*

"Large, extravagant, wildly inventive and harboring everywhere in it—in the vast shoals of prodigal imagination and fantasy—hard, brittle and dark diamonds of hard life and hard science, collapsed light and bitter, dangerous truths. . . . A crackling good read."

—*Rocky Mountain News*

"It is brilliant . . . if you slow down, let the author entertain you at his own speed, then it all opens up. He's having fun one page at a time, no reason you shouldn't, too."

—*Newsweek*

"*Against the Day* may well be his best yet."

—*The San Diego Union-Tribune*

"*Against the Day* . . . vibrates with the wacky humor, highbrow ideas, and imaginative aliveness we have come to expect from an encyclopedically minded author."

—*The Miami Herald*

"Pynchon, with all his ambition intact, rails against the day that freedom might ever be curtailed."

—*The Village Voice*

"An immensely rich, extraordinarily imaginative, intellectually affecting epic of wonder and depravity that seeks to illuminate the hidden dimensions of life and the mind by bedazzling and bedeviling the reader with rampant humor, cosmic amplitude and dark radiance."

—*The Atlanta Journal-Constitution*

"Funny, wise, poetic, and always over the top."

—*The Denver Post*

"A luminous novel that sets off an anarchic explosion of the imagination to demolish our simple myths of progress, which would only strand us in the dark, and carry careful and faithful readers further into the light."

—*Los Angeles Citybeat*

"Pynchon's ability . . . goes beyond the extraordinary into the miraculous." —*O, The Oprah Magazine*

"At turns hilarious in its absurdity and gut-wrenching in its descriptiveness, Pynchon's latest is enormous, beautiful, frustrating and wry." —*Relevance*

"The breadth of Pynchon's intellect and literary lexicography is astounding; readers follow the offspring of Traverse on strange tangents as they explore the nature of time, theoretical mathematics, familial vendetta and bizarre sexual fetishes in the context of laissez-faire macroeconomics conflict."

—Drew Toal, *New York Press*

"Pynchon is both wordsmith and world-smith. He's Dickens with degrees in chemistry and mathematics, Dostoevesky with a fondness for dumb jokes and awful puns, Faulkner with an even more pronounced apocalyptic imagination. Master of the knowledge he has acquired and the worlds he surveys, he challenges us to envision with him an opaque and threatening future, while mourning perversions of humanity's accomplishments and aspirations, fearing the worst, and laughing all the way." —Bruce Allen, *Kirkus Reviews*

"Pick up another book for a break, and it will seem relentlessly ordinary." —Barbara Hoffert, *Library Journal*

"Psychological truth keeps pace with phantasmagorical invention throughout. . . . Pynchon is still the archpoet of death from above, comedy from below and sex from all sides."
—*Publishers Weekly* (starred review)

PENGUIN BOOKS

AGAINST THE DAY

Thomas Pynchon is the author of *V.*; *The Crying of Lot 49*; *Gravity's Rainbow*; *Slow Learner*, a collection of short stories; *Vineland*; and, most recently, *Mason and Dixon*. He received the National Book Award for *Gravity's Rainbow* in 1974.

Thomas Pynchon

Against the Day

PENGUIN BOOKS

PENGUIN BOOKS
Published by Penguin Group
Penguin Group (USA) Inc., 375 Hudson Street, New York, New York 10014, USA
Penguin Group (Canada), 90 Eglinton Avenue East, Suite 700, Toronto,
Ontario, Canada M4P 2Y3 (a division of Pearson Penguin Canada Inc.)
Penguin Books Ltd., 80 Strand, London WC2R 0RL, England
Penguin Ireland, 25 St. Stephen's Green, Dublin 2, Ireland (a division of Penguin Books Ltd)
Penguin Group (Australia), 250 Camberwell Road, Camberwell,
Victoria 3124, Australia (a division of Pearson Australia Group Pty Ltd)
Penguin Books India Pvt. Ltd., 11 Community Centre,
Panchsheel Park, New Delh – 110 017, India
Penguin Group (NZ), 67 Apollo Drive, Rosedale, North Shore 0745,
Auckland, New Zealand (a division of Pearson New Zealand Ltd)
Penguin Books (South Africa) (Pty) Ltd, 24 Sturdee Avenue,
Rosebank, Johannesburg 2196, South Africa

Penguin Books Ltd, Registered Offices: 80 Strand, London WC2R 0RL, England

First published in the United States of America by The Penguin Press,
a member of Penguin Group (USA) Inc. 2006
Published in Penguin Books 2007

1 3 5 7 9 10 8 6 4 2

PUBLISHER'S NOTE
This is a work of fiction. Names, characters, places, and incidents either are the product of the author's imagination or are used fictitiously, and any resemblance to actual persons, living or dead, business establishments, events, or locales is entirely coincidental.

THE LIBRARY OF CONGRESS HAS CATALOGED THE HARDCOVER EDITION AS FOLLOWS:
Pynchon, Thomas
Against the day / Thomas Pynchon.
p. cm.
Novel.
ISBN 1-59420-120-X (hc.)
ISBN 978-0-14-311256-3 (pbk.)
I. Title.
PS3566.Y55A73 2006
813'.54—dc22 2006050714

Printed in the United States of America
Designed by Claire Vaccaro and Amanda Dewey

Contents

It's always night, or we wouldn't need light.

—THELONIOUS MONK

One

The Light Over the Ranges

"Now single up all lines!"

"Cheerly now . . . handsomely . . . very well! Prepare to cast her off!"

"Windy City, here we come!"

"Hurrah! Up we go!"

It was amid such lively exclamation that the hydrogen skyship *Inconvenience,* its gondola draped with patriotic bunting, carrying a five-lad crew belonging to that celebrated aeronautics club known as the Chums of Chance, ascended briskly into the morning, and soon caught the southerly wind.

When the ship reached cruising altitude, those features left behind on the ground having now dwindled to all but microscopic size, Randolph St. Cosmo, the ship commander, announced, "Now secure the Special Sky Detail," and the boys, each dressed neatly in the summer uniform of red-and-white-striped blazer and trousers of sky blue, spiritedly complied.

They were bound this day for the city of Chicago, and the World's Columbian Exposition recently opened there. Since their orders had come through, the "scuttlebutt" among the excited and curious crew had been of little besides the fabled "White City," its great Ferris wheel, alabaster temples of commerce and industry, sparkling lagoons, and the thousand more such wonders, of both a scientific and an artistic nature, which awaited them there.

"Oh, boy!" cried Darby Suckling, as he leaned over the lifelines to watch the national heartland deeply swung in a whirling blur of green far below, his tow-colored locks streaming in the wind past the gondola like a banner to leeward. (Darby, as my faithful readers will remember, was the "baby" of the crew, and served as both factotum and mascotte, singing as well the difficult treble parts whenever these adolescent aeronauts found it impossible to contain song of some kind.) "I can't hardly wait!" he exclaimed.

"For which you have just earned five more demerits!" advised a stern voice close to his ear, as he was abruptly seized from behind and lifted clear of the lifelines. "Or shall we say ten? How many times," continued Lindsay Noseworth, second-in-command here and known for his impatience with all manifestations of the slack, "have you been warned, Suckling, against informality of speech?" With the deftness of long habit, he flipped Darby upside down, and held the flyweight lad dangling by the ankles out into empty space—"terra firma" by now being easily half a mile below—proceeding to lecture him on the many evils of looseness in one's expression, not least among them being the ease with which it may lead to profanity, and worse. As all the while, however, Darby was screaming in terror, it is doubtful how many of the useful sentiments actually found their mark.

"Say, that is enough, Lindsay," advised Randolph St. Cosmo. "The lad has work to do, and if you frighten him that way, he sure won't be of much use."

"All right, short-stuff, turn to," muttered Lindsay, reluctantly setting the terrified Darby back on his feet. As Master-at-Arms, in charge of discipline aboard the ship, he went about his job with a humorless severity which might, to the impartial observer, easily have suggested a form of monomania. But considering the ease with which this high-spirited crew were apt to find pretexts for skylarking—resulting more than once in the sort of "close call" which causes aeronauts to freeze with horror—Randolph usually allowed his second-in-command to err on the side of vehemence.

From the far end of the gondola now came a prolonged crash, followed by an intemperate muttering that caused Randolph, as always, to frown and reach for his stomach. "I have only tripped over one of these picnic baskets," called out Handyman Apprentice Miles Blundell, "the one all the crockery was in, 's what it looks like. . . . I guess I did not see it, Professor."

"Perhaps its familiarity," Randolph suggested plaintively, "rendered it temporarily invisible to you." His reproof, though approaching the caustic, was well founded, for Miles, while possessed of good intentions and the kindest heart in the little band, suffered at times from a confusion in his motor processes, often producing lively results, yet as frequently compromising the crew's physical safety. As Miles now went about picking up pieces of the damaged porcelain, he evoked the mirth of one Chick Counterfly, the newest member of the crew, who was leaning against a stay, observing him.

"Ha, ha," cried young Counterfly, "say, but if you ain't the most slob-footed chap I ever seen! Ha, ha, ha!" An angry retort sprang to Miles's lips, but he suppressed it, reminding himself that, as insult and provocation came naturally to the class from which the newcomer sprang, it was upon his unhealthy past that one must blame the lad's habits of speech.

"Why don't you give me some of that fancy silverware, Blundell?" young Counterfly now continued. "And when we get to Chicago we'll find us a 'hock shop' a-and—"

"I recall to your attention," replied Miles politely, "that all tableware bearing the Chums of Chance Insignia is Organizational property, to be kept aboard ship for use during official meal periods."

"Like Sunday school around here," muttered the picklesome youth.

At one end of the gondola, largely oblivious to the coming and going on deck, with his tail thumping expressively now and then against the planking, and his nose among the pages of a volume by Mr. Henry James, lay a dog of no particular breed, to all appearances absorbed by the text before him. Ever since the Chums, during a confidential assignment in Our Nation's Capital (see *The Chums of Chance and the Evil Halfwit*), had rescued Pugnax, then but a pup, from a furious encounter in the shadow of the Washington Monument between rival packs of the District's wild dogs, it had been his habit to investigate the pages of whatever printed material should find its way on board *Inconvenience,* from theoretical treatments of the aeronautical arts to often less appropriate matter, such as the "dime novels"—though his preference seemed more for sentimental tales about his own species than those exhibiting extremes of human behavior, which he appeared to find a bit lurid. He had learned with the readiness peculiar to dogs how with the utmost delicacy to turn pages using nose or paws, and anyone observing him thus engaged could not help noting the changing expressions of his face, in particular the uncommonly articulate eyebrows, which contributed to an overall effect of interest, sympathy, and—the conclusion could scarce be avoided—comprehension.

An old aerostat hand by now, Pugnax had also learned, like the rest of the crew, to respond to "calls of nature" by proceeding to the downwind side of the gondola, resulting in surprises among the surface populations below, but not often enough, or even notably enough, for anyone to begin to try to record, much less coördinate reports of, these lavatorial assaults from the sky. They entered rather the realm of folklore, superstition, or perhaps, if one does not mind stretching the definition, the religious.

Darby Suckling, having recovered from his recent atmospheric excursion, addressed the studious canine. "I say, Pugnax—what's that you're reading now, old fellow?"

"Rr Rff-rff Rr-rr-*rff*-rrf-rrf," replied Pugnax without looking up, which Darby, having like the others in the crew got used to Pugnax's voice—easier, really, than some of the regional American accents the boys heard in their travels—now interpreted as, "*The Princess Casamassima.*"

"Ah. Some sort of . . . Italian romance, I'll bet?"

"Its subject," he was promptly informed by the ever-alert Lindsay Noseworth, who had overheard the exchange, "is the inexorably rising tide of World Anarchism, to be found peculiarly rampant, in fact, at our current destination—a sinister affliction to which I pray we shall suffer no occasion for exposure more immediate than that to be experienced, as with Pugnax at this moment, safely within the fictional leaves of some book." Placing upon the word "book" an emphasis whose level of contempt can be approached perhaps only by Executive Officers. Pugnax sniffed briefly in Lindsay's direction, trying to detect that combination of olfactory "notes" he had grown accustomed to finding in other humans. But as always this scent eluded him. There might be an explanation, though he was not sure he should insist upon one. Explanations did not, as far as he could tell, appear to be anything dogs either sought or even were entitled to. Especially dogs who spent as much time as Pugnax did up here, in the sky, far above the inexhaustible complex of odors to be found on the surface of the planet below.

The wind, which till now had been steady on their starboard quarter, began to shift. As their orders had directed them to proceed to Chicago without delay, Randolph, after studying an aeronautical chart of the country below them, called out, "Now, Suckling—aloft with the anemometer—Blundell and Counterfly, stand by the Screw," referring to an aerial-propulsion device, which the more scientific among my young readers may recall from the boys' earlier adventures (*The Chums of Chance at Krakatoa, The Chums of Chance Search for Atlantis*), for augmenting the cruising speed of the *Inconvenience*—invented by their longtime friend Professor Heino Vanderjuice of New Haven, and powered by an ingenious turbine engine whose boiler was heated by burning surplus hydrogen gas taken from the envelope through special valve arrangements—though the invention had been predictably disparaged by Dr. Vanderjuice's many rivals as no better than a perpetual-motion machine, in clear violation of thermodynamical law.

Miles, with his marginal gifts of coördination, and Chick, with a want of alacrity fully as perceptible, took their stations at the control-panels of the apparatus, as Darby Suckling, meantime, went scrambling up the ratlines and shrouds of the giant ellipsoidal envelope from which the gondola depended, to the very top, where the aery flux was uninterrupted, in order to read, from an anemometer of the Robinson's type, accurate wind measurements, as an index of how rapidly the ship was proceeding, conveying these down to the bridge by means of a written note inside a tennis-ball lowered on a length of line. It will be recalled that this method of passing information had been adopted by the crew during their brief though inconclusive sojourn "south of the border," where they had observed it among the low elements who dissipate their lives in placing wagers on the outcomes of *pelota* games. (For readers here making their first acquaintance with our band of young adventurers, it must be emphasized at once that—perhaps excepting the as yet insufficiently known Chick Counterfly—none would e'er have entered the morally poisonous atmosphere of the "*frontón,*" as such haunts are called down there, had it not been essential to the intelligence-gathering activities the Chums had contracted to render at that time to the Interior Ministry of President Porfirio Díaz. For details of their exploits, see *The Chums of Chance in Old Mexico.*)

Though the extreme hazard was obvious to all, Darby's enthusiasm for the task at hand created, as ever, a magical cloak about his elfin form that seemed to protect him, though not from the sarcasm of Chick Counterfly, who now called after the ascending mascotte, "Hey! Suckling! Only a *saphead* would risk his life to see how fast the wind's blowing!"

Hearing this, Lindsay Noseworth frowned in perplexity. Even allowing for his irregular history—a mother, so it was said, vanished when he was yet a babe—a father, disreputably adrift somewhere in the Old Confederacy—Counterfly's propensity for gratuitous insult had begun to pose a threat to his probationary status with the Chums of Chance, if not, indeed, to group morale.

Two weeks previous, beside a black-water river of the Deep South, with the Chums attempting to negotiate a bitter and unresolved "piece of business" from the Rebellion of thirty years previous—one still not advisable to set upon one's page—Chick had appeared one night at their encampment in a state of extreme fright, pursued by a band of night-riders in white robes and sinister pointed hoods, whom the boys recognized immediately as the dreaded "Ku Klux Klan."

His story, as clearly as could be made out among the abrupt changes of register which typify the adolescent voice, exacerbated by the perilousness of the situation, was as follows. Chick's father, Richard, commonly known as "Dick," originally from the North, had for several years been active in the Old Confederacy trying his hand at a number of business projects, none of which, regrettably, had proven successful, and not a few of which, in fact, had obliged him, as the phrase went, to approach the gates of the Penitentiary. At length, upon the imminent arrival of a posse comitatus who had learned of his attempted scheme to sell the state of Mississippi to a mysterious Chinese consortium based in Tijuana, Mexico, "Dick" Counterfly had absquatulated swiftly into the night, leaving his son with only a pocketful of specie and the tender admonition, "Got to 'scram,' kid—write if you get work." Since then Chick had lived from hand to mouth, until, at the town of Thick Bush, not far from the Chums' encampment, someone, recognizing him as the son of a notorious and widely sought "carpetbagger," had suggested an immediate application of tar and feathers to his person.

"Much as we might be inclined to offer our protection," Lindsay had informed the agitated youth, "here upon the ground we are constrained by our Charter, which directs us never to interfere with legal customs of any locality down at which we may happen to have touched."

"You ain't from these parts," replied Chick, somewhat sharply. "When they're after a fellow, legal ain't got nothing to do with it—it's run, Yankee, run, and Katie bar the door."

"In polite discourse," Lindsay hastened to correct him, "'isn't' is preferable to 'ain't.'"

"Noseworth, for mercy's sake!" cried Randolph St. Cosmo, who had been glancing anxiously out at the robed and hooded figures at the perimeter of the camp, the blazing torches they carried lighting each fold and wrinkle of their rude drapery with almost theatrical precision and casting weird shadows among the tupelo, cypress, and hickory. "There is nothing further to discuss—this fellow is to be granted asylum and, if he wishes, provisional membership in our Unit. There certainly remains to him no future down here."

It had been a night of sleepless precaution lest sparks from the torches of the mob drift anywhere near the hydrogen-generating apparatus and devastation result. In time, however, the ominously cloaked rustics, perhaps in superstitious fear of that very machinery, had dispersed to their homes and haunts. And Chick Counterfly, for better or worse, had remained. . . .

The Screw device soon accelerated the ship to a speed which, added to that of the wind from directly astern, made it nearly invisible from the ground. "We're doing a way better than a mile a minute," remarked Chick Counterfly from the control-console, unable to eliminate from his voice a certain awe.

"That could put us in Chicago before nightfall," reckoned Randolph St. Cosmo. "Feeling all right, Counterfly?"

"Crackerjack!" exclaimed Chick.

Like most "rookies" in the organization, Chick had found his initial difficulties to lie not so much with velocity as with altitude, and the changes in air-pressure and temperature that went along with it. The first few times aloft, he did his duty without complaint but one day was discovered unauthorizedly rummaging through a locker containing various items of arctic gear. When confronted by Lindsay Noseworth, the lad in his defense could only chatter, "C-c-cold!"

"Do not imagine," Lindsay instructed, "that in coming aboard *Inconvenience* you have escaped into any realm of the counterfactual. There may not be mangrove swamps or lynch law up here, but we must nonetheless live with the constraints of the given world, notable among them the decrease of temperature with altitude. Eventually your sensitivities in that regard should moderate, and in the meantime"—tossing him a foul-weather cloak of black Japanese goatskin with C. OF C. PROPERTY stenciled in bright yellow on the back—"this is to be considered as a transitional garment only, until such time as you adapt to these altitudes and, if fortunate, learn the lessons of unpremeditated habitude among them."

"Here it is in a nutshell," Randolph confided later. "Going up is like going north." He stood blinking, as if expecting comment.

"But," it occurred to Chick, "if you keep going far enough north, eventually you pass over the Pole, and then you're heading south again."

"Yes." The skyship commander shrugged uncomfortably.

"So . . . if you went up high enough, you'd be going *down* again?"

"Shh!" warned Randolph St. Cosmo.

"Approaching the surface of *another planet,* maybe?" Chick persisted.

"Not exactly. No. Another 'surface,' but an earthly one. Often to our regret, all too earthly. More than that, I am reluctant—"

"These are mysteries of the profession," Chick supposed.

"You'll see. In time, of course."

As they came in low over the Stockyards, the smell found them, the smell and the uproar of flesh learning its mortality—like the dark conjugate of some daylit fiction they had flown here, as appeared increasingly likely, to help promote. Somewhere down there was the White City promised in the Columbian Exposition brochures, somewhere among the tall smokestacks unceasingly vomiting black grease-smoke, the effluvia of butchery unremitting, into which the buildings of the leagues of city lying downwind retreated, like children into sleep which bringeth not reprieve from the day. In the Stockyards, workers coming off shift, overwhelmingly of the Roman faith, able to detach from earth and blood for a few precious seconds, looked up at the airship in wonder, imagining a detachment of not necessarily helpful angels.

Beneath the rubbernecking Chums of Chance wheeled streets and alleyways in a Cartesian grid, sketched in sepia, mile on mile. "The Great Bovine City of the World," breathed Lindsay in wonder. Indeed, the backs of cattle far outnumbered the tops of human hats. From this height it was as if the Chums, who, out on adventures past, had often witnessed the vast herds of cattle adrift in ever-changing cloudlike patterns across the Western plains, here saw that unshaped freedom being rationalized into movement only in straight lines and at right angles and a progressive reduction of choices, until the final turn through the final gate that led to the killing-floor.

Close to sundown, south of the city, as the *Inconvenience* bobbed in fitful breezes above a sweeping stretch of prairie which was to be the site this week of the great international gathering of aeronauts being held in conjunction with the World's Fair, "Professor" St. Cosmo, spying at length a clear patch of meadow among the vast population of airships already berthed below, had given the order, "Prepare to descend." The state of reduced attention into which he seemed then to have drifted was broken soon enough by Lindsay, advising, biliously, "As I am sure it has not escaped your attention, Blundell's ineptness with the Main Valve, grown I fear habitual, has increased the speed of our descent to a notable, if not in fact alarming, degree."

Indeed, the well-meaning but far from dextrous Miles Blundell had somehow contrived to wrap the pull-rope leading to the valve mechanism around his foot, and could be seen moving that extremity to and fro, a bewildered look on his wide, honest face, in hopes that the spring-loaded valve would thus, somehow, close again—for it had already allowed an enormous quantity of hydrogen gas to escape the envelope in a sudden rush, causing the ship to plummet toward the lakeside like a toy dropped by some cosmic urchin.

"Blundell, what in Heaven's name!" Randolph exclaimed. "Why, you will destroy us all!"

"Say, it just got tangled up, Professor," declared Miles, plucking ineffectually at the coils of hemp, which only grew more snarled as his efforts continued.

With an inadvertent yet innocuous oath, Lindsay had sprung to the side of young Blundell, grasping him about his ample waist, in an attempt to lift him, in hopes that this would relieve the tautness in the pull-rope and allow the valve to close. "Here, Counterfly," the second-in-command snapped at Chick, who, jeeringly amused, had been lounging against a gear locker, "do rouse yourself for a moment and bear a hand with Blundell," that awkward fellow, disposed to ticklishness, meanwhile having begun to scream and thrash about in his efforts to escape Lindsay's grasp. Chick Counterfly rose indolently and approached the lurching pair with some caution, unsure of which part of Miles to take hold of, lest it but increase his agitation.

As the vital gas continued to stream in unsettling shriek from the valve overhead, and the airship to plunge ever more rapidly Earthward, Randolph, gazing at the feckless struggling of his crew, understood too well that the responsibility for the disaster nearly upon them was, as always, none but his own, this time for having delegated duties to those unskilled in them. . . .

His broodful reflections were interrupted by Darby, running over to tug at the sleeve of his blazer—"Professor, Professor! Lindsay has just now made a defamatory remark about Miles's mother, yet he's forever after me about using 'slang,' and is that fair, I ask you?"

"Insubordinate drivel, Suckling," sternly declared Lindsay, "will earn you someday what is known among the lower seafaring elements as a 'Liverpool Kiss,' long before you ever receive one of the more conventional variety, save perhaps for those rare occasions upon which *your* mother, no doubt in some spell of absentmindedness, has found herself able to bestow that astonishing yet, I fear (unhappy woman), misplaced, sign of affection."

"You see, you see?" squealed Darby, "going after a fellow's mother—"

"Not now!" screamed Randolph, flinging off the young mascotte's importunate grasp and frightening him nearly out of his wits. "Counterfly, the ballast, man! leave that spastical oaf be, and jettison our sandbags, or we are done for!"

Chick shrugged and released his grip on Miles, proceeding lackadaisically to the nearest gunwale to unlash the ballast bags there, leaving Lindsay, with no time to adjust to the increased burden, to crash to the deck with a panicked cry, and the now all but hysterical Miles Blundell on top of him. With a loud twang that may as well have been the Crack of Doom, the line around his foot was yanked free of its attachment to the Main Valve, though not before pulling beyond its elastic limit the spring meant to restore it to a safely-closed position. The valve now remained ajar—the very mouth of Hell!

"Suckling! aloft, and quickly!"

The ready little fellow scurried up the lines, as Randolph, preoccupied with the crisis and staggering across the deck, somehow tripped over Lindsay Noseworth attempting to extricate himself from beneath the squirming mass of Miles Blundell, and abruptly joined his horizontal shipmates. Looking up, he observed Darby Suckling gazing down at him, inquisitively.

"What is it that I am to do up here, Professor?" called the ingenuous mascotte.

As tears of frustration began to gather in Randolph's eyes, Lindsay, sensing in his chief a familiar inertia, his speech only temporarily muffled by Miles's elbow, rushed, or more accurately crawled, into the vacuum of authority. "Return the valve manually," he shouted up at Darby, "to its closed position," adding, "you little fool," in a barely audible tone. Darby, his uniform fluttering in the outrush of gas, gallantly hastened to comply.

"Like me to break out some of them parachute rigs, Noseworth?" drawled Chick.

"*Mr.* Noseworth," Lindsay corrected him. "No, Counterfly, I think not, there scarcely being time—moreover, the complexities that would attend rigging Blundell in the necessary paraphernalia would tax the topological genius of Herr Riemann himself." This irony was lost, however, on Chick as well as its object, who, having at last somehow regained his feet, now went stumbling with serene insouciance over to the rail, apparently to have a look at the scenery. Above him, Darby, with a triumphant "Hurrah!" succeeded in closing the valve, and the huge airship accordingly slackened in its downward hurtling to a velocity no more ominous than that of a leaf in autumn.

"Well, we certainly scared those chaps down there, Professor," commented Miles, gazing over the side. "Dropping all those sandbags, I'll wager."

"Eh?" Randolph beginning to regain his air of phlegmatic competence. "How's that?"

"Well, they're running just lickety-split," Miles continued, "a-and say, one of them hasn't even got any clothes on, that's sure what it looks like all right!" From an instrument locker nearby, he produced a powerful spyglass, and trained it upon the objects of his curiosity.

"Come, Blundell," Randolph arising from where he had fallen, "there is quite enough to be done at the moment without more idle shenanigans—" He was interrupted by a gasp of terror from Miles.

"Professor!" cried that lad, peering incredulously through the burnished cylinder, "the unclad figure I reported—it is not that of a chap, after all, but rather of . . . *a lady!*"

There was an "eager stampede" to the rail, and a joint attempt to wrest the telescope from Miles, who, however, clung to it stubbornly. All meanwhile stared or squinted avidly, attempting to verify the reported apparition.

Across the herbaceous nap below, in the declining light, among the brighter star-shapes of exploded ballast-bags, running heedless, as across some earthly firmament, sped a stout gentleman in a Norfolk jacket and plus-fours, clutching a straw "skimmer" to the back of his head with one hand while with the other keeping balanced upon his shoulder a photographic camera and tripod. Close behind him came the female companion Blundell had remarked, carrying a bundle of ladies' apparel, though clad at the moment in little beyond a floral diadem of some sort, charmingly askew among masses of fair hair. The duo appeared to be making for a nearby patch of woods, now and then casting apprehensive looks upward at the enormous gasbag of the descending *Inconvenience,* quite as if it were some giant eyeball, perhaps that of Society itself, ever scrutinizing from above, in a spirit of constructive censure. By the time Lindsay could remove the optical instrument from the moist hands of Miles Blundell, and induce the consequently disgruntled youth to throw out grapnels and assist Darby in securing the great airship to "Mother Earth," the indecorous couple had vanished among the foliage, as presently would this sector of the Republic into the falling darkness.

· · ·

DARBY SWUNG LIKE a regular little monkey hand over hand down the anchor line, gained the ground and, tripping briskly about beneath *Inconvenience,* adroitly caught each of the mooring lines flung down to him by Miles Blundell. With a mallet driving home, one by one, sturdy wooden pegs through the eye-splices at the ends of the hempen strands, he soon had the giant vehicle, as if charmed into docility by some diminutive beast-wrangler, tethered motionless above him.

The Jacob's-ladder now came clattering over the side, and upon it, presently, in uncertain descent, Miles, surmounted by a giant sack of soiled laundry. There remained in the western sky only an after-glow of deep crimson, against which could be seen Miles's silhouette, as well as those of the heads of the other boys above the curved rim of the gondola.

Since that morning, before the first light, a gay, picnic-going throng of aeromaniacs of one sort and another had been continuing all day now to *vol-à-voile* in, till long after sundown, through the midwestern summer evening whose fading light they were most of them too busy quite to catch the melancholy of, their wings both stationary and a-flap, gull and albatross and bat-styled wings, wings of gold-beaters' skin and bamboo, wings laboriously detailed with celluloid feathers, in a great heavenwide twinkling they came, bearing all degrees of aviator from laboratory skeptic to Jesus-rapt ascensionary, accompanied often by sky-dogs, who had learned how to sit still, crowded next to them in the steering-cabins of their small airships, observing the instrument panels and barking if they noticed something the pilot had failed to—though others could be observed at gunwales and flying bridges, their heads thrust out into the passing airflow, looks of bliss on their faces. From time to time, the aeronauts hailed one another through megaphones, and the evening was thus atwitter, like the trees of many a street in the city nearby, with aviatory pleasantries.

In short order, the boys had set up their mess-tent, gathered wood, and ignited a small fire in the galley stove, well downwind of *Inconvenience* and its hydrogen-generating apparatus. Miles busied himself in the miniature galley, and soon had fried them up a "mess" of catfish, caught that morning and kept all day on ice whose melting had been retarded by the frigidity of altitude. Around them the other groups of sky-brothers were busy at their own culinary arrangements, and roasting meat, frying onions, and baking bread sent delicious odors creeping everywhere about the great encampment.

After dinner and Evening Quarters, the boys dedicated a few moments to song, as a group differently engaged might have to prayer. Since their Hawaiian escapades a few years previous (*The Chums of Chance and the Curse of the Great Kahuna*), Miles had become an enthusiastic ukulelist, and tonight, after securing the scullery and restoring the mess decks to their usual spotless state, he produced one of many of the four-stringed instruments which he kept in his sky-chest, and, after strumming a brief introduction, accompanied the boys as they sang,

There's fellows live in little towns,
And those who live on farms,
And never seem to wander far
From smiles and loving arms—
They always know just who they are
And how their lives will go—
And then there's boys like us, who say
Good-bye before hello,
For we're the
Aces of the Altitudes
Vagabonds of the Void. . . .
When some folks shrink with terror, say,
We scarcely get annoyed.
Let the winds blow clear off the Beaufort Scale,
And the nights grow dark as can be,
Let the lightning lash,
And the thunder thrash,
Only cheerful young hearts have we!
For . . .
the Chum of Chance is a pluc-ky soul,
Who shall neither whine nor ejac-u-late,
For his blood's as red and his mind's as pure
As the stripes of his bla-a-zer immac-u-late!

That evening Chick and Darby, as the port section of the crew, had watch-duty, while Miles and Lindsay were to be allowed "ground-leave" in Chicago. Each in his own way excited at the prospect of attending the Exposition, the two lads shifted rapidly into dress uniform, although Miles encountered such difficulty in lacing his leggings, knotting his neckerchief with the needed symmetry, and securing correctly the forty-four buttons of his dickey, one for each State of the Union, that Lindsay, after having applied a few drops of Macassar oil to his own locks and combing them carefully, was obliged to go to his unskillful shipmate's assistance.

When Miles had been rendered as fit to be seen by the populace of "The Windy City" as he would ever be, the two boys came smartly to attention, dressing right at close interval in the circle of firelight, to await inspection. Pugnax joined them, tail still, gaze expectant. Randolph emerged from his tent in mufti, every bit as spruce as his liberty section, for he, too, was bound for earthly chores, his Chums of Chance flight uniform having been replaced by a tastefully checked Kentucky hemp suit and Ascot tie, with a snappy fedora topping off the *ensemble.*

"Say, Randolph," called Darby, "you look like you're going over to meet a girl!"

As his bantering tone, however, was not unmixed with manly admiration, Randolph chose not to respond to the *innuendo* with the *pique* it would otherwise have merited, instead riposting, "I had not been aware that fellows of your years recognized any distinction between the sexes," drawing from Lindsay an appreciative chuckle, before promptly returning to moral seriousness.

"About the fringes," Randolph reminded the liberty-goers, "of any gathering on the scale of this Exposition, are apt to lurk vicious and debased elements, whose sole aim is to take advantage of the unwary. I will not dignify it by naming that sinister quarter where such dangers are most probably to be encountered. The very vulgarity of its aspect, particularly by night, will speak for itself, disinclining all but the most reckless of their well-being to linger in contemplation upon, much less actually investigate, the unprofitable delights offered therein. A word to the wise . . . or, in this case . . . hrrumph, hmmm, howsoever . . . good liberty, boys, I say, and good luck." Wherewith Randolph saluted, turned, and vanished soundlessly into the great fragrant darkness.

"You have the watch, Suckling," Lindsay advised before departing. "You know the penalties for falling asleep—be sure that you impress them upon your watchmate Counterfly, who inclines, I suspect, toward sloth. Perimeter check once every hour, as well as a reading of the tension of the gas within the envelope, corrected, I need scarcely add, for the lower temperatures of the nighttime." He turned and strode away to join Miles, while Pugnax, whose tail had regained its customary animation, was left to scout the bounds of the encampment, searching for evidence of other dogs and their humans who might seek unauthorized entry.

Darby, left solitary in the glow of the watch-fire, applied himself, with his customary vivacity, to the repair of the main hydrogen valve whose mechanical disruption earlier had nearly spelt their doom. That unpleasant memory, like the damage beneath Darby's nimble fingers, would soon be quite unmade . . . as if it were something the stripling had only read about, in some boys' book of adventures . . . as if that page of their chronicles lay turned and done, and the order "About-face" had been uttered by some potent though invisible Commandant of Earthly Days, toward whom Darby, in amiable obedience, had turned again. . . .

He had just completed his repairs when, looking up, he noticed Chick Counterfly by the fire, brewing a pot of coffee.

"Care for some?" Chick offered. "Or don't they let you drink this stuff yet?"

Something in his tone suggested that this was only the sort of friendly teasing a fellow Darby's age had to expect and put up with. "Thanks, wouldn't mind a cup at all."

They sat by the fire for a while, silent as a pair of drovers camping out on the western prairie. Finally, to Darby's surprise, "I sure do miss my Pop," Chick confided, abruptly.

"I guess that must be awful tough for you, Chick. I don't think I even remember mine."

Chick gazed dolefully into the fire. After a moment, "Thing is, I believe he would have hung on. If he could have. We were partners, see? Always had something going. Some swell little moneymaker. Not always to the sheriff's liking, but enough to keep beans in the pot. Didn't mind all the midnight relocations, but those small-town courtrooms, I never could get used to them. Judge'd take one look at us, up went that hammer, whiz! we were usually out the door and on the main road before it came back down again."

"Good exercise, I bet."

"Well, but it seemed like Pop was starting to slow down some. Wondered if it was me somehow. You know, the extra trouble or something."

"Sounds more like it was all that Chinese foofooraw you mentioned," said Darby, "nothing you caused. Here, do you smoke these?" lighting up a species of cigarette and offering one to Chick.

"My Great-Aunt Petunia!" exclaimed Chick, "what is that smell?"

"Say, it's cubebs. Medicinal use only. No tobacco allowed on board, as you might recall from your Chums of Chance Membership Oath."

"Did I swear off? I must've been all confused in my mind. No tobacco! Say, it's the goldurn Keeley Cure around here. How do you people get through your day?"

Suddenly what sounded like a whole kennelful of dogs began to bark furiously. "Pugnax," explained Darby, noting Chick's alarmed expression.

"Him and what else?"

"Just ol' Pugnax. One of his many talents. Guess we'd better go have a look."

They found Pugnax up on his feet, clenched and alert, watching the outer darkness intently—from what the boys could tell, poised to launch a massive counter-assault on whatever was now approaching their perimeter.

"Here you go," called an invisible voice, "nice doggy!" Pugnax stood his ground but had ceased barking, apparently judging the visitors nasally acceptable. As Darby and Chick watched, out of the evening came a giant beefsteak, soaring in an arc, slowly rotating, and hit the dirt almost exactly between Pugnax's front paws, where he regarded it for a while, a single eyebrow raised, one would have to say, disdainfully.

"Hey, anybody home?" Into the firelight emerged two boys and a girl, carrying picnic baskets and wearing flight uniforms of indigo mohair brilliantine with scarlet pinstripes, and headgear which had failed to achieve the simpler geometry of the well-known Shriner fez, being far more ornate and, even for its era, arguably not in the best of taste. There was an oversize spike, for example, coming out the top, German style, and a number of plumes dyed a pale eclipse green. "Howdy, Darb! What's up and what's down?"

Darby, recognizing them as members of Bindlestiffs of the Blue A.C., a club of ascensionaries from Oregon, with whom the Chums of Chance had often flown on joint manœuvres, broke into a welcoming smile, especially for Miss Penelope ("Penny") Black, whose elfin appearance disguised an intrepid spirit and unfaltering will, and on whom he had had a "case" for as long as he could remember. "Hello, Riley, Zip . . . Penny," he added shyly.

"That's 'Captain' to you." She held up a sleeve to display four gold stripes, at whose edges could be seen evidence of recent needlework. The Bindlestiffs were known and respected for granting the loquacious sex membership on a strictly equal footing with boys, including full opportunities for promotion. "Yeahp," Penny grinned, "they gave me the *Tzigane*—just brought the old tub in here from Eugene, got her berthed down past that little grove of trees there, nobody worse for wear."

"W-wow! Your first command! That's champion!" He found himself shuffling nervously, and with no idea what to do about his hands.

"You better kiss me," she said, "it's tradition and all."

Even with the chorus of hoots it evoked from the other boys, Darby found the fleeting brush of her freckled cheek against his lips more than worth the aggravation. After introductions, Chick and Darby brought out folding camp chairs, the Bindlestiffs opened their baskets of delectables, and the colleagues settled down to an evening of gossip, shop talk, and sky-stories.

"Coming in over 'Egypt,' downstate Illinois to you, Darb, we caught us an upriser off a cornfield by Decatur, thought we'd be onto the dang moon by now—'scuse me"—pausing to sneeze—"icicles o' snot down to our belt buckles, goin all blue from the light of that electric fluid, 's whirlpoolin round our heads—ahh-pffeugghh!"

"Oh, Gesundheit, Riley," said Zip, "but last time you told that one, it was strange voices and so forth—"

"We'd picked up a little galvanic halo ourselves by the time we got here," said Chick, "what with the speed and all."

"A-aw that's nothin," cried Riley, "next to dodgin tornadoes all day! You boys want real electricity, git on out to Oklahoma sometime, get a treat for your ears into the bargain that will sure's hell drownd out any strange voices in your neighborhood."

"Speaking of voices," said Penny, "what have you heard about these . . . 'sightings' that keep getting reported in? Not just from crews up in the air but sometimes even from civilians on the ground?"

"You mean aside from the usual," Darby said, "fata morgana, northern lights, and so forth?"

"Different," Zip in a low, ominous voice. "There's lights, but there's sound, too. Mostly in the upper altitudes, where it gets that dark blue in the daytime? Voices calling out together. All directions at once. Like a school choir, only no tune, just these—"

"Warnings," said Riley.

Darby shrugged. "News to me. *Inconvenience,* we're only the runts of the Organization, last at the trough, nobody ever tells us anything—they keep cutting our orders, we follow 'em, is all."

"Well we were over by Mount Etna there back in the spring," Penny said, "and you remember those Garçons de '71, I expect." For Chick's benefit, Darby explained that this outfit had first been formed over twenty years ago, during the Sieges of Paris, when manned balloons were often the only way to communicate in or out of the city. As the ordeal went on, it became clear to certain of these balloonists, observing from above and poised ever upon a cusp of mortal danger, how much the modern State depended for its survival on maintaining a condition of *permanent siege*—through the systematic encirclement of populations, the starvation of bodies and spirits, the relentless degradation of civility until citizen was turned against citizen, even to the point of committing atrocities like those of the infamous *pétroleurs* of Paris. When the Sieges ended, these balloonists chose to fly on, free now of the political delusions that reigned more than ever on the ground, pledged solemnly only to one another, proceeding as if under a world-wide, never-ending state of siege.

"Nowadays," Penny said, "they'll fly wherever they're needed, far above fortress walls and national boundaries, running blockades, feeding the hungry, sheltering the sick and persecuted . . . so of course they make enemies everyplace they go, they get fired at from the ground, all the time. But this was different. We happened to be up with them that one day, and it was just the queerest thing. Nobody saw any projectiles, but there was . . . a kind of force . . . energy we could feel, directed personally at us. . . ."

"Somebody out there," Zip said solemnly. "Empty space. But inhabited."

"This making you nervous, Chick?" teased Darby.

"Nawh. Thinking about who wants that last apple fritter there."

Meantime Miles and Lindsay were off to the Fair. The horse-drawn conveyance they had boarded took them through the swarming streets of southern Chicago. Miles gazed with keen curiosity, but Lindsay regarded the scene with a peevish stare.

"You look kind of glum, Lindsay."

"I? no, not at all—beyond an unavoidable apprehension at the thought of Counterfly with full run of the ship and no one to supervise him, I am as cheerful as a finch."

"But Darby's there with him."

"Please. Any influence Suckling could exert on a character that depraved would be negligible at best."

"Oh, but say," reckoned the kind-hearted Miles, "Counterfly does seem a good skate, and I bet you he'll soon get the hang of things."

"As Master-at-Arms," muttered Lindsay, perhaps only to himself, "my own view of human nature is necessarily less hopeful."

At length the car deposited them at a street-corner from which, the conductor assured them, it would be but a short walk to the Fairgrounds—or, as he chuckled, "depending how late in the evening, a brisk run," and went on its way in metal-to-metal clangor and clopping. At a distance the boys could see in the sky the electrical glow of the Fair, but hereabouts all was in shadow. Presently they found a gap in the fence, and an admissions gate with something of the makeshift about it, lit by a single candle-stub, whose attendant, a scowling Asiatic midget of some sort, though eager enough to take their proffered fifty-cent pieces, had to be pressed by the scrupulous Lindsay for a duly executed receipt. The diminutive sentinel then held out his palm as if for a gratuity, which the boys ignored. "Deadbeats!" he screamed, by way of introducing them to the quatercentennial celebration of Columbus's advent upon our shores.

From somewhere ahead too dark to see came music from a small orchestra, unusually syncopated, which grew louder, till they could make out a small outdoor dance-floor, all but unlit, where couples were dancing, and about which crowds were streaming densely everywhere, among odors of beer, garlic, tobacco smoke, inexpensive perfume, and, from Buffalo Bill's Wild West Show, somewhere up ahead, the unmistakable scent of massed livestock.

Observers of the Fair had remarked how, as one moved up and down its Midway, the more European, civilized, and . . . well, frankly, *white* exhibits located closer to the center of the "White City" seemed to be, whereas the farther from that alabaster Metropolis one ventured, the more evident grew the signs of cultural darkness and savagery. To the boys it seemed that they were making their way through a separate, lampless world, out beyond some obscure threshold, with its own economic life, social habits, and codes, aware of itself as having little if anything to do with the official Fair. . . . As if the half-light ruling this perhaps even unmapped periphery were not a simple scarcity of streetlamps but deliberately provided in the interests of mercy, as a necessary veiling for the faces here, which held an urgency somehow too intense for the full light of day and those innocent American visitors with their Kodaks and parasols who might somehow happen across this place. Here in the shadows, the faces moving by smiled, grimaced, or stared directly at Lindsay and Miles as if somehow they knew them, as if in the boys' long career of adventure in exotic corners of the world there had been accumulating, unknown to them, a reserve of mistranslation, offense taken, debt entered into, here being re-expressed as a strange Limbo they must negotiate their way through, expecting at any moment a "run-in" with some enemy from an earlier day, before they might gain the safety of the lights in the distance.

Armed "bouncers," drawn from the ranks of the Chicago police, patrolled the shadows restlessly. A Zulu theatrical company re-enacted the massacre of British troops at Isandhlwana. Pygmies sang Christian hymns in the Pygmy dialect, Jewish klezmer ensembles filled the night with unearthly clarionet solos, Brazilian Indians allowed themselves to be swallowed by giant anacondas, only to climb out again, undigested and apparently with no discomfort to the snake. Indian swamis levitated, Chinese boxers feinted, kicked, and threw one another to and fro.

Temptation, much to Lindsay's chagrin, lurked at every step. Pavilions here seemed almost to represent not nations of the world but Deadly Sins.

Pitchmen in their efforts at persuasion all but seized the ambulant youths by their lapels.

"Exotic smoking practices around the world, of great anthropological value!"

"Scientific exhibit here boys, latest improvements to the hypodermic syringe and its many uses!"

Here were Waziris from Waziristan exhibiting upon one another various techniques for waylaying travelers, which reckoned in that country as a major source of income. . . . Tarahumara Indians from northern Mexico crouched, apparently in total nakedness, inside lath-and-plaster replicas of the caves of their native Sierra Madre, pretending to eat vision-producing cacti that sent them into dramatic convulsions scarcely distinguishable from those of the common "geek" long familiar to American carnival-goers. . . . Tungus reindeer herders stood gesturing up at a gigantic sign reading SPECIAL REINDEER SHOW, and calling out in their native tongue to the tip gathered in front, while a pair of young women in quite revealing costumes—who, being blonde and so forth, did not, actually, appear to share with the Tungus many racial characteristics—gyrated next to a very patient male reindeer, caressing him with scandalous intimacy, and accosting passersby with suggestive phrases in English, such as "Come in and learn dozens ways to have fun in Siberia!" and "See what really goes on during long winter nights!"

"This doesn't seem," Lindsay adrift between fascination and disbelief, "quite . . . authentic, somehow."

"Come over here, boys, first time for free, find the red get a pat on the head, find the black, get nothin back!" cried a cheerful Negro in a "pork-pie" hat, who was standing behind a folding table nearby, setting down and picking up playing-cards.

"If I didn't know better, I'd say that was one of those monte games," murmured Lindsay, politely suppressing his disapproval.

"No, boss, it's an ancient African method of divination, allows you to change your fate." The sharper who had addressed them now began to move cards around with bewildering speed. At times there were too many cards to count, at others none at all were visible, seeming to have vanished into some dimension well beyond the third, though this could have been a trick of what light there was.

"O.K.! maybe it's your lucky night, just tell us where that red is, now." Three cards lay face-down before them.

After a moment of silence, it was Miles who announced in a clear and firm voice, "The cards you have put down there all happen to be black—your 'red' is the nine of diamonds, the curse of Scotland, and it's right here," reaching to lift the sharper's hat, and to remove from atop his head, and exhibit, the card at issue.

"Lord have mercy, last time that happened I ended up in the Cook County jail for a nice long vacation. A tribute to your sharp eyes, young man, and no hard feelings," holding out a ten-dollar banknote.

"Oh, that is . . ." Lindsay began tentatively, but Miles had already pocketed the offering, amiably calling out, "Evening, sir," as they strolled away.

A surprised expression could be noted on Lindsay's face. "That was . . . well executed, Blundell. How did you know where that card was?"

"Sometimes," Miles with a strangely apprehensive note in his voice, "these peculiar feelings will surround me, Lindsay . . . like the electricity coming on—as if I can see everything just as clear as day, how . . . how everything fits together, connects. It doesn't last long, though. Pretty soon I'm just back to tripping over my feet again."

Presently they had come within view of the searchlight beams sweeping the skies from the roof of the immense Manufactures and Liberal Arts Building—a miniature city, nested within the city-within-a-city which was the Fair itself—and began to see caped Columbian Guards on patrol, a reassuring sight, to Lindsay at least.

"Come on, Lindsay," Miles flourishing the banknote they had acquired so unexpectedly. "Long as we have this windfall, let's go get us some root beer, and some of that 'Cracker Jack,' too. Say, what do you know! We're here! We're at the Fair!"

MEANWHILE RANDOLPH ST. COSMO, though out of uniform, was still on duty. The detective agency he sought was located in a seedy block of the New Levee district, between a variety saloon and a manufacturer of exploding cigars. The sign read WHITE CITY INVESTIGATIONS. Randolph tugged the brim of his hat a bit lower, looked swiftly up and down the littered and shadowy street, and sidled in the entrance. A young lady typewriter who managed to act prim and bold at the same time glanced up from her florally-appliquéd machine. "It's after bedtime, sonny."

"The door was open—"

"Yeah, and maybe this ain't the Epworth League."

"I was supposed to see Mr. Privett?"

"Nate!" she screamed, causing Randolph to jump. Her smile was not unmischievous. "You bring a note from your parents, kid?"

In Nate's office were a combination sideboard, bookcase, and filing cabinet with assorted bottles of whiskey, a bed-lounge over in the corner, a couple of cane-bottom chairs, a curtain desk with about a thousand pigeonholes, a window with a view of the German saloon across the street, local-business awards and testimonials on the dark-paneled walls, along with photos of notable clients, some of them posed with Nate himself, including Doc Holliday, out in front of the Occidental Saloon in Tombstone, Doc and Nate each pointing a .44 Colt at the other's head and pretending to scowl terribly. The picture was inscribed, *More of a shotgun man myself, regards, Doc.*

"Since the Haymarket bomb," Nate was explaining, "we've had more work than we can handle, and it's about to get even more hectic, if the Governor decides to pardon that gang of anarchistic murderers. Heaven knows what *that's* gonna let loose on Chicago, the Fair in particular. Antiterrorist security now more than ever will be of the essence here. And, well, you boys enjoy the one perspective that all us in the 'spotter' community long for—namely, a view from overhead. We can't pay you as well as the Pinkertons might, but maybe we could work out a deferred arrangement, small percent of profits down the line instead of cash right now. Not to mention what tips or other off-the-books revenue might come your way."

"That is between you and our National Office," Randolph supposed. "For here at Unit level, our compensation may not exceed legitimate expenses."

"Sounds crazy. But, we'll have our legal folks draw up some language we can all live with, how's that?" He was peering at Randolph now with that mixture of contempt and pity which the Chums in their contact with the ground population were sooner or later sure to evoke. Randolph was used to it, but determined to proceed in a professional manner.

"Of what exactly would our services consist?"

"Got room on your ship for an extra passenger?"

"We have carried up to a dozen well-fed adults with no discernible loss of lift," replied Randolph, his glance not quite able to avoid lingering upon Mr. Privett's embonpoint.

"Take our man up on a short trip or two's about all it'll amount to," the sleuth-officer now, it seemed, grown a bit shifty. "Out to the Fair, maybe down to the Yards, duck soup."

Strolling among the skyships next morning, beneath a circus sky which was slowly becoming crowded as craft of all sorts made their ascents, renewing acquaintance with many in whose company, for better or worse, they had shared adventures, the Chums were approached by a couple whom they were not slow to recognize as the same photographer and model they had inadvertently bombarded the previous evening.

The sportive lensman introduced himself as Merle Rideout. "And my fair companion here is . . . give me a minute—"

"You bean-brain." The young woman directed a graceful kick which was not, however, altogether lacking in affection, and said, "I'm Chevrolette McAdoo, and mighty pleased to meet you fellows, even if you did nearly sandbag us into the beyond yesterday." Fully attired, she seemed to have just stepped out of a ladies' magazine, her ensemble this forenoon right at the vanguard of summer fashion, the current revival of the leg-of-mutton sleeve having resulted in a profusion of shirtwaists with translucent shoulders "big as balloons, all over town"—as Chick Counterfly, a devoted observer of the female form, would express it—in Miss McAdoo's case, saturated in a vivid magenta, and accompanied by a long ostrich-feather boa dyed the same shade. And her hat, roguishly atilt, egret plumes swooping each time she moved her head, would have charmed even the most zealous of conservationist bird-lovers.

"Nice put-together," Chick nodded admiringly.

"And you haven't seen the turn she does down to that South Seas Pavilion yet," declared Merle Rideout gallantly. "Makes Little Egypt look like a church lady."

"You are an artiste, Miss McAdoo?"

"I perform the Dance of Lava-Lava, the Volcano Goddess," she replied.

"I greatly admire the music of the region," said Miles, "the ukulele in particular."

"There are several ukulelists in my pit-band," said Miss McAdoo, "tenor, baritone, and soprano."

"And is it authentic native music?"

"More of a medley, I believe, encompassing Hawaiian and Philippino motifs, and concluding with a very tasteful adaptation of Monsieur Saint-Saëns's wonderful 'Bacchanale,' as recently performed at the Paris Opera."

"I am only an amateur, of course," Miles, though long a member of the prestigious International Academy of Ukulelists, said modestly, "and get lost now and then. But if I promised to go back to the tonic and wait, do you think they'd let me come and sit in?"

"I'll certainly put in a good word," said Chevrolette.

Merle Rideout had brought a hand camera with him, and was taking "snaps" of the flying machines, aloft and parked on the ground, which were continuing to arrive and take off with no apparent letup. "Some social, ain't it! Why, every durn professor of flight from here to Timbuctoo's flying in, 's what it looks like."

The smoke from breakfast campfires rose fragrantly through the air. Babies could be heard in both complaint and celebration. Far-off sounds of railway traffic and lake navigation came in on the wind. Against the sun as yet low across the Lake, wings cast long shadows, their edges luminous with dew. There were steamers, electrics, Maxim whirling machines, ships powered by guncotton reciprocators and naphtha engines, and electrical lifting-screws of strange hyperboloidal design for drilling upward through the air, and winged aerostats, of streamlined shape, and wing-flapping miracles of ornithurgy. A fellow scarcely knew after a while where to look—

"Pa!" An attractive little girl of four or five with flaming red hair was running toward them at high speed. "Say, Pa! I need a drink!"

"Dally, ya little weasel," Merle greeted her, "the corn liquor's all gone, I fear, it'll have to be back to the old cow juice for you, real sorry," as he went rummaging in a patent dinner pail filled with ice. The child, meanwhile, having caught sight of the Chums in their summer uniforms, stood gazing, her eyes wide, as if deciding how well behaved she ought to be.

"You have been poisoning this *helpless angel* with strong drink?" cried Lindsay Noseworth. "Sir, one must protest!" Dally, intrigued, ran over and stood in front of him, peering up, as if waiting for the next part of some elaborate joke.

Lindsay blinked. "This cannot be," he muttered. "Small children hate me."

"A fine-looking little girl, sir," Randolph, brimming with avuncularity. "You are the proud grandfather, of course."

"Ha! D'ye hear that, Carrot-head? Thinks I'm your grandpa. Thank you, lad, but this here is my daughter Dahlia, I'm proud to say. Her mother, alas—" He sighed, gazing upward and into the distance.

"Our deepest sympathies," Randolph hastily, "yet Heaven, in its inscrutability—"

"Heaven, hell," cackled Merle Rideout. "She's out there in the U.S.A. someplace with the mesmerizin variety artist she run away with, a certain Zombini the Mysterious."

"Know him, by gosh!" Chick Counterfly, nodding vigorously. "Makes his molly disappear down a common kitchen funnel! *'Imbottigliata!'* ain't it? then he twirls his cape? Seen it down in New Orleans with my own peepers! some awesome turn, you bet!"

"The very customer," Merle beamed, "and that beauteous conjuror's assistant you saw'd likely be ol' Erlys herself, and say, you'll want to close your mouth there, Buck, 'fore somethin flies into it?"—the casual mention of adultery having produced in Randolph's face a degree of stupefaction one regrets to term characteristic. Chick Counterfly, less affected, was alert enough to offer, "Well—an entirely admirable lady, whoever she was."

"Admiration noted—and you might examine little Dahlia here, who's the spit of her Ma, fulminate me if she ain't, fact if you're ramblin by some ten, twelve years hence, why ride on over, have another look, make an offer, no price too small or too insulting I wouldn't consider. Or if you're willing to wait, take an option now to buy, got her on special, today and tomorrow only, dollar ninety-eight takes her away, heartbreakin smile and all. Yehp—there, lookit, just like 'at. Throw you in an extra bonnet, I'm a reasonable sort, 'n' the minute she blows that sweet-sixteenth birthday candle out, why she's on them rails, express to wherever you be."

"Seems a little long to wait, don't it?" leered Chick Counterfly.

"—I could go age fifteen, I guess," Merle went on, twinkling directly at Lindsay Noseworth strangling with indignation, "but you'd have to pay in gold, and come fetch her on your own ticket. . . . But say now would you mind if I got a snap of you all in front of this Trouvé-screw unit over here?"

The boys, fascinated as always with modern sciences such as the photographic, were of course happy to comply. Chevrolette managed to mollify even Lindsay by borrowing his "skimmer" and holding it coyly in front of their faces, as if to conceal a furtive kiss, while the frolicsome Darby Suckling, without whose spirited "clowning" no group snapshot would have been complete, threatened the pair with a baseball bat and a comical expression meant to convey his ingenuous notion of jealous rage.

Lunch-time arrived, and with it Lindsay's announcement of early liberty.

"Hurrah!" cried Chick Counterfly, "me and old Suckling here being starboard liberty section will just head on over to that Midway Plaisance, to have us a peep at Little Egypt and that Polynesian exhibit, and if we can fit it in, why some of those African Amazons too—oh, and don't worry, lad, anything you need explained, just ask me!"

"Come on, boys," Chevrolette McAdoo gesturing with a cigarette in a rhinestone-encrusted holder, "I'm headed in for work now, I can show you backstage at the South Seas, too."

"Oboy, oboy," Darby's nose beginning to run.

"Suck*linggg*?" screamed Lindsay, but to no avail. Crowds of colorfully-dressed aeronauts had swept between them, as ships arrived and took off, and the great makeshift aerodrome seethed with distractions and chance meetings. . . .

In fact, just about then who should arrive, aboard a stately semirigid craft of Italian design, but the boys' longtime friend and mentor Professor Heino Vanderjuice of Yale University, a look of barely suppressed terror on his features, desperately preoccupied during the craft's descent with keeping secured to his head a stovepipe hat whose dents, scars, and departures from the cylindrical spoke as eloquently as its outdated style of a long and adventuresome history.

"Galloping gasbags, but it's just capital to see you fellows again!" the Professor greeted them. "Last I heard, you'd come to grief down in New Orleans, no doubt from packing away more alligator *à l'étouffée* than that old *Inconvenience* quite had the lift for!"

"Oh, an anxious hour or two, perhaps," allowed Randolph, his facial expression suggesting gastric memories. "Tell us, Professor, how is your work coming along? What recent marvels emerging from the Sloane Laboratory?"

"Well now, there's a student of Professor Gibbs whose work really bears looking into, young De Forest, a regular wizard with the electricity . . . along with a Japanese visitor, Mr. Kimura—but say, where can a starving pedagogue and his pilot get a couple of those famous Chicago beefsteaks around here? Boys, like you to meet Ray Ipsow, without whom I'd still be back in Outer Indianoplace, waiting for some interurban that never comes."

"Just missed you boys once, over there in that Khartoum business," the genial skyfarer informed them, "trying to make it out of town a couple steps ahead of the Mahdi's army—saw you sailing overhead, wished I could've been on board, had to settle for jumpin in the river and waiting till the clambake subsided a little."

"As it happened," Lindsay, the Unit Historian, recalled, "we caught a contrary wind, and ended up in the middle of some unpleasantness in Oltre Giubba, instead of down at Alex, where we had counted upon some weeks of educational diversion, not to mention a more salubrious atmosphere."

"Why and bless me," the Professor cried, "if that isn't Merle Rideout I see!"

"Still up to no good," Merle beamed.

"No need for introductions, then," Lindsay calculated.

"Nah, we're partners in crime, from back in the olden days in Connecticut, long before your time, fellows, I used to do some tinkering for him now and then. Don't suppose one of you boys could get a snap of us together?"

"Sure!" volunteered Miles.

They went off to a steak house nearby for lunch. Though reunions with the Professor were always enjoyable, this time something different, some autumnal disquiet behind the climate of warm celebration, produced psychogastric twinges Randolph had learned from experience he could ignore only at his peril.

Having attended several useful symposia for airship commanders on techniques for avoiding the display of hurt feelings, Randolph could detect now that something was preying on the Professor's mind. In a curious departure from the good-hearted old fellow's usual "style," his luncheon comments today were increasingly brief, indeed on occasion approaching the terse, and no sooner had the pie *à la mode* made its appearance than he had called for the check.

"Sorry boys," he frowned, making a show of pulling out and consulting his old-fashioned railroad watch. "I'd love to stay and chat some more, but I've a little business to take care of." He rose abruptly, as did Ray Ipsow, who, shrugging sympathetically to the boys and murmuring to Randolph, "I'll keep an eye on him," followed the eminent Yale savant, who, once outside, lost no time hailing a carriage, holding out a greenback and requesting top speed, and just like that they were off, arriving at the Palmer House, where the functionary at the desk tipped a salute from a nonexistent hat brim. "Penthouse suite, Professor, take the elevator over there, it only makes one stop. They're expecting you." If there was a note of amused contempt in his voice, Professor Vanderjuice was too preoccupied to notice.

It swiftly became evident to Ray Ipsow that his friend was in town to conclude a bargain with forces that might be described, with little risk of overstatement, as evil. In the suite upstairs, they found heavy curtains drawn against the festive town, lamps sparsely distributed in a perpetual twilight of tobacco smoke, no cut flowers or potted plants, a silence punctuated only rarely by speech, and that generally telephonic.

One could hardly have expected a widely celebrated mogul like Scarsdale Vibe not to attend the World's Columbian Exposition. Along with the obvious appeal of its thousands of commercial possibilities, the Chicago Fair also happened to provide a vast ebb and flow of anonymity, where one could meet and transact business without necessarily being observed. Earlier that day Vibe had stepped out of his private train, "The Juggernaut," onto a personally reserved platform at the Union Station, having only the night before departed from the Grand Central depot in New York. As usual, he was in disguise, accompanied by bodyguards and secretaries. He carried an ebony stick whose handle was a gold and silver sphere chased so as to represent an accurate and detailed globe of the world, and inside of whose shaft was concealed a spring, piston, and cylinder arrangement for compressing a charge of air to propel small-caliber shot at any who might offend him. A sealed motor conveyance awaited him, and he was translated as if by supernatural agency to the majestic establishment defined by State, Monroe, and Wabash. On the way into the lobby, an elderly woman, respectably though not sumptuously dressed, approached him, crying, "If I were your mother I would have strangled you in your cradle." Calmly Scarsdale Vibe nodded, raised his ebony air-cane, cocked it, and pressed the trigger. The old woman tilted, swayed, and went down like a tree.

"Tell the house physician the bullet is only in her leg," said Scarsdale Vibe helpfully.

NO ONE HAD offered to take Professor Vanderjuice's hat, so he held it in his lap, as an insecure young actor might a "prop."

"They treating you all right over at the Stockmen's Hotel?" the magnate inquired.

"Well actually, it's the Packer's Inn, Forty-seventh and Ashland. Right in the middle of the Stockyards and all—"

"Say," it occurred to a large and criminal-looking individual who had been whittling an image of a locomotive from a piece of firewood with one of those knives known throughout the prisons of our land as an *Arkansas toothpick,* "you're not of the vegetarian persuasion, I hope."

"This is Foley Walker," said Scarsdale Vibe, "in whom his mother claims to find virtues not immediately apparent to others."

"Guess you can hear that whole hootenanny from where you are," Foley went on. "Bet you there's even guests known to catch insomnia from it, eh?

but there's equally as many find it strangely soothing. No different here at the Palmer House, if you think about it. Racket level runs about the same."

"Same kind of activities as well," muttered Ray Ipsow. They were gathered at a marble table in a sort of parlor, over cigars and whiskey. The small-talk had turned to surplus wealth. "I know this fellow back in New Jersey," said Scarsdale Vibe, "who collects railroads. Not just rolling stock, mind, but stations, sheds, rails, yards, personnel, the whole shebang."

"Expensive hobby," marveled the Professor. "Are there such people?"

"You have to have some idea of the idle money out here. It can't all be endowments to the church of one's choice, mansions and yachts and dog-runs paved with gold or what have you, can it. No, at some point that's all over with, has to be left behind . . . and still here's this huge mountain of wealth unspent, piling up higher every day, and dear oh dear, whatever's a businessman to do with it, you see."

"Hell, send it on to me," Ray Ipsow put in. "Or even to somebody who really needs it, for there's sure enough of those."

"That's not the way it works," said Scarsdale Vibe.

"So we always hear the plutocracy complaining."

"Out of a belief, surely fathomable, that merely to need a sum is not to deserve it."

"Except that in these times, 'need' arises directly from criminal acts of the rich, so it 'deserves' whatever amount of money will atone for it. Fathomable enough for you?"

"You are a socialist, sir."

"As anyone not insulated by wealth from the cares of the day is obliged to be. Sir."

Foley paused in his whittling and looked over as if in suddenly piqued interest.

"Now, Ray," admonished the Professor, "we're here to discuss electromagnetism, not politics."

Vibe chuckled soothingly. "The Professor's afraid you're going to chase me off with radical talk like that. But I am not that sensitive a soul, I am guided, as ever, by Second Corinthians." He had a careful look around the table, estimating the level of Scriptural awareness.

"Suffering fools is unavoidable," said Ray Ipsow, "but don't ask me to be 'glad' about it."

The guards lounging by the doorway seemed to grow more alert. Foley got to his feet and strolled over to the window. Scarsdale squinted, not sure if this should be taken as an affront to his faith.

Ray gathered his hat and stood. "It's all right, I'll be down at the bar," as he went through the door, adding, "praying for wisdom."

Down in the elegant Pump Room, Ray ran into Merle Rideout and Chevrolette McAdoo, who were "out on the town," owing to a fortunate wager Merle had made earlier that day.

Couples in boutonnières and ostrich-plume hats paraded self-composedly among the dwarf palms or paused by the Italian Fountain as if thinking about jumping in. Somewhere a small string orchestra was playing an arrangement of "Old Zip Coon."

Ray Ipsow regarded the surface of his beer. "He seems different these days. You notice anything?"

Merle nodded. "Something missing. He used to get so fired up about everything—we'd be designing something, run out of paper, he'd take his shirt collar off and just use that to scribble on."

"Lately he's been keeping those ideas pretty much to himself, like he's finally learned how much they might be worth. Seen that happen enough, Lord knows. This big parade of modern inventions, all spirited march tunes, public going ooh and aah, but someplace lurking just out of sight is always some lawyer or accountant, beating that 2/4 like clockwork and runnin the show."

"Anybody feel like dancing?" offered Chevrolette.

UP IN HIS PENTHOUSE SUITE, Scarsdale had moved on to the business at hand. "Back in the spring, Dr. Tesla was able to achieve readings on his transformer of up to a million volts. It does not take a prophet to see where this is headed. He is already talking in private about something he calls a 'World-System,' for producing huge amounts of electrical power that anyone can tap in to for free, anywhere in the world, because it uses the planet as an element in a gigantic resonant circuit. He is naïve enough to think he can get financing for this, from Pierpont, or me, or one or two others. It has escaped his mighty intellect that no one can make any money off an invention like that. To put up money for research into a system of free power would be to throw it away, and violate—hell, betray—the essence of everything modern history is supposed to be."

The Professor was literally having an attack of nausea. Every time Tesla's name came up, this was the predictable outcome. Vomit. The audacity and scope of the inventor's dreams had always sent Heino Vanderjuice staggering back to his office in Sloane Lab feeling not so much a failure as someone who has taken a wrong turn in the labyrinth of Time and now cannot find his way back to the moment he made it.

"If such a thing is ever produced," Scarsdale Vibe was saying, "it will mean the end of the world, not just 'as we know it' but as anyone knows it. It is a weapon, Professor, surely you see that—the most terrible weapon the world has seen, designed to destroy not armies or matériel, but the very nature of exchange, our Economy's long struggle to evolve up out of the fish-market anarchy of all battling all to the rational systems of control whose blessings we enjoy at present."

"But," too much smoke in the air, not much time before he'd have to excuse himself, "I'm not sure how I can help."

"Speak bluntly may I? Invent us a counter-transformer. Some piece of equipment that will detect one of these Tesla rigs in operation, and then broadcast something equal and opposite that'll nullify its effects."

"Hmm. It would help to see Dr. Tesla's drawings and calculations."

"Precisely why Pierpont's in on this. That and his arrangement with Edison—but there I go again spilling secrets. Bankrolling Tesla has given Morgan's access to all Tesla's engineering secrets. And he has operatives on the spot, ready day and night to rush us photographed copies of anything we need to know."

"Well in theory, I don't see any great obstacle. It's a simple phase inversion, though there may be non-linear phenomena of scale we cannot predict till we build a working Device—"

"Tell me the details later. Now—how much do you reckon something like that would actually, um," lowering his voice, "cost?"

"Cost? Oh, I couldn't really—that is, I shouldn't—"

"Come now, Professor," boomed Foley Walker, holding a hotel whiskey decanter as if he meant to drink from it, "to the nearest million or so, just a rough guess?"

"Hmm . . . well . . . as a figure to start from . . . if only for symmetry's sake . . . say about what Brother Tesla's getting from Mr. Morgan?"

"Well, ring-tailed rutabagas." Vibe's eyes with a contemptuous twinkle which colleagues had learned meant he had what he wanted. "Here I figured you fellows spend your time wandering around with your thoughts all far, far away, and Professor, why, you're just a damn horse trader without mercy's what it is. Guess I should summon the legal staff, before I find myself hanging in a poultry-shop window, two bits away from getting fricasseed. Foley, would you just crank us up long distance there on the telephone—get us Somble, Strool & Fleshway, if you'd be so kind? Could be they'd share some ideas on how best to 'spring' for a project of this scale."

The call went through immediately, and Scarsdale, excusing himself, withdrew to an instrument in another part of the suite. The Professor was left to stare into the depths of his ancient hat, as if it were a vestiary expression of his present situation. More and more in recent weeks, he had found himself approaching likewise the condition of an empty cylinder, only intermittently occupied by intelligent thought. Was this the right thing to do? Should he even be here? The criminality in the room was almost palpable. Ray certainly didn't care for any it, and the boys today, even in their usual unworldliness, had regarded him with something like apprehension. Would any sum the New York lawyers might be suggesting now be worth the loss of that friendship?

The Chums of Chance could have been granted no more appropriate form of "ground-leave" than the Chicago Fair, as the great national celebration possessed the exact degree of fictitiousness to permit the boys access and agency. The harsh nonfictional world waited outside the White City's limits, held off for this brief summer, making the entire commemorative season beside Lake Michigan at once dream-like and real.

If there were any plots afoot to commit bomb or other outrages upon the Fair, the *Inconvenience* was ideal not only for scanning the grounds fence to fence, but also for keeping an eye out against any sea-borne assaults contemplated from the Lake side. Fairgoers would see the ship overhead and yet not see it, for at the Fair, where miracles were routinely expected, nothing this summer was too big, too fast, too fantastically rigged out to impress anybody for more than a minute and a half, before the next marvel appeared. *Inconvenience* would fit right in, as one more effect whose only purpose was to entertain.

The boys began regular surveillance runs the next day. The "spotter" from White City Investigations showed up at dawn, packing a small observatory's worth of telescopic gear. "Broke these in on the Ferris wheel," he said, "but couldn't figure out how to compensate for the movement. Gets blurry and so forth."

Lew Basnight seemed a sociable enough young man, though it soon became obvious that he had not, until now, so much as heard of the Chums of Chance.

"But every boy knows the Chums of Chance," declared Lindsay Noseworth perplexedly. "What could you've been reading, as a youth?"

Lew obligingly tried to remember. "Wild West, African explorers, the usual adventure stuff. But you boys—you're not storybook characters." He had a thought. "Are you?"

"No more than Wyatt Earp or Nellie Bly," Randolph supposed. "Although the longer a fellow's name has been in the magazines, the harder it is to tell fiction from non-fiction."

"I guess I read the sports pages mostly."

"Good!" declared Chick Counterfly, "at least we won't have to get on to the Anarchist question."

Fine with Lew, who wasn't even sure what Anarchists were, exactly, though the word was sure in the air. He was not in the detective business out of political belief. He had just sort of wandered into it, by way of a sin he was supposed once to have committed. As to the specifics of this lapse, well, good luck. Lew couldn't remember what he'd done, or hadn't done, or even when. Those who didn't know either still acted puzzled, as if he were sending out rays of iniquity. Those who did claim to remember, all too well, kept giving him sad looks which soon—it being Illinois—soured into what was known as moral horror.

He was denounced in the local newspapers. Newsboys made up lurid headlines about him, which they shouted all through the civic mobilities morning and evening, making a point of pronouncing his name disrespectfully. Women in intimidating hats glared at him with revulsion.

He became known as the Upstate-Downstate Beast.

It would've helped if he could remember, but all he could produce was this peculiar haze. The experts he went to for advice had little to tell him. "Past lives," some assured him. "Future lives," said other confident swamis. "Spontaneous Hallucination," diagnosed the more scientific among them. "Perhaps," one beaming Oriental suggested, "*it* was hallucinating *you*."

"Very helpful, thanks," Lew murmured, and tried to leave, only to find that the door would not open.

"A formality. Too many bank drafts have come back unhonored."

"Here's cash. Can I go?"

"When your anger has cooled, consider what I have told you."

"It's no use to me."

He fled in among the skyscrapers of Chicago, leaving a note at work suggesting he'd be back shortly. No use. A close business associate followed, confronted, and publicly denounced him, knocking his hat off and kicking it into the middle of Clark Street, where it was run over by a beer wagon.

"I don't deserve this, Wensleydale."

"You have destroyed your name." And without speaking further, turned, there, right out among the city traffic, and walked away, soon vanishing into the summertime clutter of noise and light.

Worst of all, Lew's adored young wife, Troth, when she found his breezy note, headed straight for the interurban and up to Chicago, intending to plead with him to come back, though by the time she got off at Union Station, reflection to the pulse of the rails had done its work.

"Never more Lewis, do you understand, never under the same roof, ever."

"But what are they saying I did? I swear, Troth, I can't remember."

"If I told you, I would have to hear it once again, and once has already been more than enough."

"Where'll I live, then?" All through their long discussion they had been walking, walkers in the urban unmappable, and had reached a remote and unfamiliar part of the city—in fact, an enormous district whose existence neither, till now, had even suspected.

"I don't care. Go back to one of your other wives."

"God! How many are there supposed to be?"

"Stay here in Chicago if you like, it's all the same to me. This neighborhood we're in right now might suit you perfectly, and I know *I'll* never come here again."

In an ignorance black as night, he understood only that he had struck at her grievously, and that neither his understanding nor his contrition would save them. By now he could not bear her woundedness—the tears, through some desperate magic, kept gelid at her lower lids, because she would not let them fall, not till he had left her sight.

"Then I'll look for a place here in town, good suggestion Troth, thank you. . . ." But she had hailed a hansom-cab, and climbed in without looking back, and was quickly borne away.

Lew looked around. Was it still Chicago? As he began again to walk, the first thing he noticed was how few of the streets here followed the familiar grid pattern of the rest of town—everything was on the skew, narrow lanes radiating starwise from small plazas, tramlines with hairpin turns that carried passengers abruptly back the way they'd been coming, increasing chances for traffic collisions, and not a name he could recognize on any of the street-signs, even those of better-traveled thoroughfares . . . foreign languages, it seemed. Not for the first time, he experienced a kind of *waking swoon*, which not so much propelled as allowed him entry into an urban setting, *like* the world he had left but differing in particulars which were not slow to reveal themselves.

Occasionally a street would open up into a small plaza, or a convergence with other streets, where pitches had been set up by puppeteers, music and dance acts, and vendors of everything—divination books, grilled squabs on toast, ocarinas and kazoos, roast ears of corn, summer caps and straw hats, lemonade and lemon ice, something new everyplace he turned to look. In a small courtyard within a courtyard, he came upon a group of men and women, engaged in slow ritual movement, a country dance, almost—though Lew, pausing to watch, was not sure what country. Soon they were gazing back, as if in some way they knew him, and all about his troubles. When their business was done, they invited him over to a table under an awning, where all at once, over root beer and Saratoga chips, Lew found himself confessing "everything," which in fact wasn't much—"What I need is some way to atone for whatever it is I've done. I can't keep on with this life. . . ."

"We can teach you," said one of them, who seemed to be in charge, introducing himself only as Drave.

"Even if—"

"Remorse without an object is a doorway to deliverance."

"Sure, but I can't pay you for it, I don't even have a place to live."

"Pay for it!" The tableful of adepts was amused at this. "Pay! Of course you can pay! Everyone can!"

"You will have to remain not only until you learn the procedure," Lew was informed, "but until *we* are sure of you as well. There is a hotel close to here, the Esthonia, which penitents who come to us often make use of. Mention us, they will give you a good discount."

Lew went to register at the tall, rickety Esthonia Hotel. The lobby clerks and the bellmen on duty all acted like they'd been expecting him. The form he was given to fill out was unusually long, particularly the section headed "Reasons for Extended Residence," and the questions quite personal, even intimate, yet he was urged to be as forthcoming as possible—indeed, according to a legal notice in large type at the top of the form, anything less than total confession would make him *liable to criminal penalties.* He tried to answer honestly, despite a constant struggle with the pen they insisted he use, which was leaving blotches and smears all over the form.

When the application, having been sent off to some invisible desk up the other end of a pneumatic house-tube, at length came thumping back hand-stamped "Approved," Lew was told that one of the bellmen must conduct him to his room. He couldn't be expected to find it on his own.

"But I didn't bring anything, no luggage, not even money—which reminds me, how will I be paying for this?"

"Arrangements are in place, sir. Please go with Hershel now, and try to remember the way, for he won't want to show it to you again."

Hershel was large for one of his calling, looking less like a uniformed jockey than an ex-pugilist. The two of them scarcely fit into the tiny electric elevator, which turned out to be more frightening than the worst carnival ride Lew had ever been on. The blue arcing from loosely dangling wires, whose woven insulation was frayed and thick with greasy dust, filled the little space with a strong smell of ozone. Hershel had his own notions of elevator etiquette, trying to start conversations about national politics, labor unrest, even religious controversy, any of which it might take an ascent of hours, into lofty regions no high-iron pioneer had yet dared, even to begin to discuss. More than once they were obliged to step out into refuse-filled corridors, negotiate iron ladders, cross dangerous catwalks not visible from the streets, only to reboard the fiendish conveyance at another of its stops, at times traveling not even vertically, until at last reaching a floor with a room somehow cantilevered out in the wind, autumnal today and unremitting, off Lake Michigan.

When the door swung open, Lew noted a bed, a chair, a table, a resonant absence of other furnishing which in different circumstances he would have called sorrowful, but which here he was able, in the instant, to recognize as perfect.

"Hershel, I don't know how I'm supposed to tip you."

Hershel holding out a banknote, "Reverse tip. Bring me a bottle of Old Gideon and some ice. If there's any change, keep it. Learn frugality. Begin to see the arrangement?"

"Service?"

"That, maybe some conjuring too. You disappear like an elf into the woodwork, the more professionally the better, and when you reappear, you've got the hooch, not to mention the ice, see."

"Where will you be?"

"I'm a bellhop, Mr. Basnight, not a guest. There ain't that many places a guest can be, though a bellhop can be just about anywhere in the establishment."

Finding bourbon for Hershel was a breeze, they sold it here out of every street-door from dry-goods shops to dentist's offices, and they all waved away Hershel's greenback, being strangely happy for Lew just to start a tab. By the time he tracked down the bellhop again, the ice had all melted. Somehow this got back to Drave, who, deeply though perhaps unhealthily amused, struck Lew repeatedly with a "remembrance stick." Taking this as acceptance, Lew continued to perform chores assigned him, some commonplace, others strange beyond easy reckoning, transacted in languages he didn't always understand, until he began to feel some approach, out at the fringe of his awareness, like a streetcar in the city distance, and some fateful, perhaps dangerous, invitation to climb aboard and be taken off to parts unknown. . . .

Through the winter, though it seemed like any Chicago winter, that is a sub-zero-degrees version of Hell, Lew lived as economically as possible, watching his bank account dwindle toward nothing, haunted both sleeping and waking by unusually vivid reveries of Troth, all stricken with a tenderness he had never noticed in their actual life together. Out the window in the distance, contradicting the prairie, a mirage of downtown Chicago ascended to a kind of lurid acropolis, its light as if from nightly immolation warped to the red end of the spectrum, smoldering as if always just about to explode into open flames.

Now and then, unannounced, Drave showed up to review Lew's progress.

"First of all," he advised, "I can't speak for God, but your wife is not going to forgive you. She's never coming back. If that's what you thought the payoff here was going to be, you need to re-evaluate."

The soles of Lew's feet began to ache, as if wanting to be taken all the way to the center of the Earth.

"What if I didn't care what it took to bring her back?"

"Penance? You'll do that anyway. You're not Catholic, Mr. Basnight?"

"Presbyterian."

"Many people believe that there is a mathematical correlation between sin, penance, and redemption. More sin, more penance, and so forth. Our own point has always been that there is no connection. All the variables are independent. You do penance not because you have sinned but because it is your destiny. You are redeemed not through doing penance but because it happens. Or doesn't happen.

"It's nothing supernatural. Most people have a wheel riding up on a wire, or some rails in the street, some kind of guide or groove, to keep them moving in the direction of their destiny. But you keep bouncing free. Avoiding penance and thereby definition."

"Going off my trolley. And you're trying to help me get back to the way most people live, 's that it?"

" 'Most people,' " not raising his voice, though something in Lew jumped as if he had, "are dutiful and dumb as oxen. Delirium literally means going out of a furrow you've been plowing. Think of this as a productive sort of delirium."

"What do I do with that?"

"It's something you don't want?"

"Would you?"

"Not sure. Maybe."

. . .

SPRING ARRIVED, wheelfolk appeared in the streets and parks, in gaudy striped socks and long-billed "Scorcher" caps. Winds off the lake moderated. Parasols and sidelong glances reappeared. Troth was long gone, remarried it seemed the minute the decree came down, and rumored now to be living on Lake Shore Drive someplace up north of Oak Street. Some vice-president or something.

One mild and ordinary work-morning in Chicago, Lew happened to find himself on a public conveyance, head and eyes inclined nowhere in particular, when he entered, all too briefly, a condition he had no memory of having sought, which he later came to think of as grace. Despite the sorry history of rapid transit in this city, the corporate neglect and high likelihood of collision, injury, and death, the weekday-morning overture blared along as usual. Men went on grooming mustaches with gray-gloved fingers. A rolled umbrella dented a bowler hat, words were exchanged. Girl amanuenses in little Leghorn straw hats and striped shirtwaists with huge shoulders that took up more room in the car than angels' wings dreamed with contrary feelings of what awaited them on upper floors of brand-new steel-frame "skyscrapers." The horses stepped along in their own time and space. Passengers snorted, scratched, and read the newspaper, sometimes all at once, while others imagined that they could get back to some kind of vertical sleep. Lew found himself surrounded by a luminosity new to him, not even observed in dreams, nor easily attributable to the smoke-inflected sun beginning to light Chicago.

He understood that things were exactly what they were. It seemed more than he could bear.

He must have descended to the sidewalk and entered a cigar store. It was that early hour in cigar stores all over town when boys are fetching in bricks that have been soaking all night in buckets of water, to be put into the display cases to keep the inventory humidified. A plump and dapper individual was in buying domestic cheroots. He watched Lew for a while, just short of staring, before asking, with a nod at the display, "That box on the bottom shelf—how many colorado-claros left in it? Without looking, I mean."

"Seventeen," said Lew without any hesitation the other man could detect.

"You know not everybody can do that."

"What?"

"Notice things. What was that just went by the window?"

"Shiny black little trap, three springs, brass fittings, bay gelding about four years old, portly gent in a slouch hat and a yellow duster, why?"

"Amazing."

"Not really. Just, nobody ever asks."

"You had breakfast?"

In the cafeteria next door, the early crowd had been and gone. Everybody here knew Lew, usually, knew his face, but this morning, being transfigured and all, it was like he passed unidentified.

His companion introduced himself as Nate Privett, personnel director at White City Investigations, a detective agency.

In the near and far distance, explosions, not always to be identified in the next day's newspapers, now and then sent leisurely rips through the fabric of the day, to which Nate Privett pretended to be listening. "Ironworkers' Union," he nodded. "After enough of 'em, a man begins to develop an ear." He poured syrup on a towering stack of pancakes out of which butter melted and ran. "See, it's not safecrackers, embezzlers, murderers, spouses on the run, none of the dime-novel stuff, put all that out of your head. Here in Chi, this year of our Lord, it's all about the labor unions, or as we like to call them, anarchistic scum," said Nate Privett.

"No experience with any of that."

"You appear qualified, I should say." Nate's mouth went sly for a second. "Can't believe you haven't been approached about Pinkerton work, pay over there's almost too good for a man *not* to sign up."

"Don't know. Too much of the modern economics for me, for there's surely more to life than just wages."

"Oh? What?"

"Well, give me a few minutes with that one."

"You think working for the Eye's a life of moral squalor, you ought to have a look at our shop."

Lew nodded and took him up on it. Next thing he knew, he was on the payroll, noticing how every time he entered a room somebody was sure to remark, ostensibly to somebody else, "Gravy, a man could get *killed* out there!" By the time he got that pleasantry all decoded, Lew found he was more than able to shrug it off. His office and field skills weren't the worst in the shop, but he knew that what distinguished him was a keen sympathy for the invisible.

At White City Investigations, invisibility was a sacred condition, whole darn floors of office buildings being given over to its art and science—resources for disguise that outdid any theatrical dressing room west of the Hudson, rows of commodes and mirrors extending into the distant shadows, acres of costumes, forests of hatracks bearing an entire Museum of Hat History, countless cabinets stuffed full of wigs, false beards, putty, powder, kohl and rouge, dyes for skin and hair, adjustable gaslight at each mirror that could be taken from a lawn party at a millionaire's cottage in Newport to a badlands saloon at midnight with just a tweak to a valve or two. Lew enjoyed wandering around, trying on different rigs, like every day was Hallowe'en, but he understood after a while that he didn't have to. He had learned to step to the side of the day. Wherever it was he stepped to had its own vast, incomprehensible history, its perils and ecstasies, its potential for unannounced romance and early funerals, but when he was there, it was apparently not as easy for anyone in "Chicago" to be that certain of his whereabouts. Not exactly invisibility. Excursion.

Nate showed up at Lew's desk one day with a thick folder that had some kind of royal crest on it, featuring a two-headed eagle.

"Not me," Lew edging away.

"Austrian Archduke is in town, we need somebody to keep an eye on him."

"Fellows like that don't have bodyguards of their own?"

"Sure do, they call em 'Trabants' over there, but have a lawyer explain civil liability to you, Lew, I'm just an old gumshoe guy, all's I know is there's a couple a thousand hunkies down to the Yards come over here with hate in their hearts for this bird and his family, maybe with good reason, too. If it was just the wholesome educational exhibits on the Fairgrounds and all why I wouldn't be too concerned, but the book on young Francis Ferdinand is, is he prefers our own New Levee and high-life neighborhoods like that. So every alleyway down here, every shadow big enough to hide a shive artist with a grudge, is a warm invitation to rewrite history."

"I get any backup on this, Nate?"

"I can spare Quirkel."

"Somebody get Rewrite!" Lew pretended to cry, affably enough.

F.F., as he was termed in his dossier, was out on a world tour whose officially stated purpose was to "learn about foreign peoples." How Chicago fit the bill was about to become clearer. The Archduke had put in an appearance at the Austrian Pavilion, sat through Buffalo Bill's Wild West Show with a certain amount of impatience, and lingered at the Colorado Silver Camp exhibit, where, imagining that camps must necessarily include camp-followers, he proceeded to lead his entourage on a lively search after ladies of flagrant repute that would have taxed the abilities of even a seasoned spotter, let alone a greenhorn like Lew—running up and down and eventually out into the Midway, accosting amateur actors who had never been west of Joliet with untranslatable ravings in Viennese dialect and gesticulations which could easily be—well, were—taken the wrong way. Uniformed handlers, fooling elaborately with their whiskers, gazed anywhere but at the demented princeling. Lew slid like a snake from one architectural falsehood to the next, his working suits by the end of each day smudged white from rubbing against so much "staff," a mixture of plaster and hemp fibers, ubiquitous at the White City that season, meant to counterfeit some deathless white stone.

"What I am really looking for in Chicago," the Archduke finally got around to confessing, "is something new and interesting to kill. At home we kill boars, bears, stags, the usual—while here in America, so I am told, are enormous *herds of bison, ja?*"

"Not around Chicago anymore, Your Highness, I'm sorry to say," Lew replied.

"Ah. But, at present, working here in your famous slaughterhouse district . . . *are* many . . . Hungarians, not true?"

"Y— maybe. I'd have to go look up the figures," Lew trying not to get into eye contact with this customer.

"In Austria," the Archduke was explaining, "we have forests full of game, and hundreds of beaters who drive the animals toward the hunters such as myself who are waiting to shoot them." He beamed at Lew, as if mischievouly withholding the final line of a joke. Lew's ears began to itch. "Hungarians occupy the lowest level of brute existence," Francis Ferdinand declared—"the wild swine by comparison exhibits refinement and nobility—do you think the Chicago Stockyards might possibly be rented out to me and my friends, for a weekend's amusement? We would of course compensate the owners for any loss of revenue."

"Your Royal Highness, I'll sure ask about that, and somebody'll get back to you."

Nate Privett thought this was just a knee-slapper. "Gonna be Emperor one of these days, can you beat that!"

"Like there ain't enough Hungarians back home to keep him busy?" Lew was wondering.

"Well, not that he wouldn't be doing *us* a favor."

"How's that, boss?"

"With more them damned anarchistic foreign-born south of Forty-seventh than you could point a Mannlicher at," chuckled Nate, "sure'd be a few less of em to worry about, wouldn't it?"

Curious himself about who might be his opposite number on the Austrian side of this exercise, Lew nosed around and picked up an item or two. Young Max Khäutsch, newly commissioned a captain in the Trabants, was here on his first overseas assignment, as field chief of "K&K Special Security," having already proven himself useful at home as an assassin, an especially deadly one, it seemed. Standard Habsburg procedure would have been to put him out of the way at some agreed-upon point of diminishing usefulness, but nobody was willing to try. Despite his youth he was said to give an impression of access to resources beyond his own, of being comfortable in the shadows and absolutely unprincipled, with an abiding contempt for any distinction between life and death. Sending him to America seemed appropriate.

Lew found him sympathetic . . . the oblique planes of his face revealing an origin somewhere in the Slavic vastnesses of Europe as yet but lightly traveled by the recreational visitor. . . . They got into the habit of early-morning coffee at the Austrian Pavilion, accompanied by a variety of baked goods. "And *this* might be of particular interest to you, Mr. Basnight, considering the widely known *Kuchenteigs-Verderbtheit* or pastry-depravity of the American detective. . . ."

"Well we . . . we try not to talk about that."

"*So?* in Austria it is widely remarked upon."

Despite young Khäutsch's police skills, somehow the Archduke kept giving him the slip. "Perhaps I am too clever to deal efficiently with Habsburg stupidity," mused Khäutsch. One night when it seemed Franz Ferdinand had dropped off the map of greater Chicago, Khäutsch got on the telephone and began calling around town, eventually reaching White City Investigations.

"I'll go have a look," said Lew.

After a lengthy search including obvious favorites like the Silver Dollar and Everleigh House, Lew found the Archduke at last in the Boll Weevil Lounge, a Negro bar down on South State in the Thirties, the heart of the vaudeville and black entertainment district in those days, hollering his way into an evening which promised at least a troublesome moment or two. Barrelhouse piano, green beer, a couple of pool tables, girls in rooms upstairs, smoke from two-for-a-penny cigars. "Squalid!" screamed the Archduke. "I love it!"

Lew kind of enjoyed it himself in this part of town, unlike some of the ops at White City, who seemed skittish around Negroes, who'd been arriving lately in ever-increasing numbers from down South. Something about the neighborhood drew him, maybe the food—surely the only place in Chicago a man could find a decent orange phosphate—although right at the moment you could not call the atmosphere welcoming.

"What here are you looking at, you wish to steal *eine . . . Wassermelone,* perhaps?"

"Ooooo," went several folks in earshot. The insultee, a large and dangerous-looking individual, could not believe he was hearing this. His mouth began to open slowly as the Austrian prince continued—

"Something about . . . your . . . wait . . . *deine Mutti,* as you would say, your . . . *your mama,* she plays third base for the Chicago White Stockings, *nicht wahr?*" as customers begin tentatively to move toward the egresses, "a quite unappealing woman, indeed she is so fat, that to get from her tits to her ass, one has to take the 'El'! Tried once to get into the Exposition, they say, no, no, lady, this is the World's Fair, not the World's Ugly!"

"Whatchyou doin, you fool, you can get y'ass killed talking like that, what are you, from *England* or some shit?"

"Um, Your Royal Highness?" Lew murmured, "if we could just have a word—"

"It is all right! I know how to talk to these people! I have studied their culture! Listen—*'st los, Hund?* Boogie-boogie, *ja?*"

Lew, supposed to be disciplined in the ways of the East, would not allow himself the luxury of panic, but at times, like now, could've used maybe a homeopathic dose, just to keep his immunity up. "Hopelessly insane," he announced, waving a thumb F.F.'s way, "escaped in his time from some of the fanciest bughouses of Europe, very little remaining of the brains he was born with, except possibly," lowering his voice, "how much money you bring with you, there, Highness?"

"Ah, I understand," murmured the imperial scapegrace. Turning to the room, "When Franz Ferdinand drinks," he cried, "everybody drinks!"

Which helped to restore a level of civility in the room, and soon even of cheer, as smart neckties were soaked in suds, the piano player came back out from under the bar, and people in the room resumed dancing syncopated two-steps. After a while somebody started singing "All Pimps Look Alike to Me," and half the room joined in. Lew, however, noticing the way the Archduke seemed to keep inching stealthily but unmistakably toward the street door, thought it wise to do the same. Sure enough, just before sliding out the door, Der F.F. with a demonic grin screamed, "And when Franz Ferdinand pays, everybody pays!" whereupon he disappeared, and it was a near thing that Lew got out with his keester intact.

Outside they found Trabant Khäutsch ready with a two-horse hack poised for instant departure, and the Archduke's own double-barreled Mannlicher resting nonchalantly but visibly on one shoulder. As they were speeding along dodging grip cars, private carriages, police patrol wagons with their gongs banging, and so forth, Khäutsch casually offered, "If you're ever in Vienna, and for any reason need a favor, please do not hesitate."

"Soon's I learn to waltz, I'm on my way."

The Archduke, pouting like a child whose mischief has been interrupted, did not offer comment.

LEW WAS JUST HEADED out to Kinsley's for a late steak when Nate called him into the office, reaching to fetch down a new folder. "Old F.F.'ll be out of town in just a couple more days, Lew, but meantime here's somethin for you tonight."

"Thought I might grab some sleep."

"Anarchy never sleeps, son. They're meeting right down the El line a couple-three stops, and you might want to take a look in. Even get educated, maybe."

At first Lew took it for a church—something about the echoes, the smell—though in fact, on weekends anyway, it was a small variety theater. Up on the stage now was a lectern flanked by a pair of gas lamps with Welsbach mantles, at which stood a tall individual in workmen's overalls, identified presently as the traveling Anarchist preacher the Reverend Moss Gatlin. The crowd—Lew had been expecting only a handful of malcontents—was numerous, after a while in fact spilling into the street. Unemployed men from out of town, exhausted, unbathed, flatulent, sullen . . . collegians having a look in at possibilities for hell-raising . . . Women in surprising numbers, bearing the marks of their trades, scars from the blades of the meatpacking floors, squints from needlework carried past the borderlands of sleep in clockless bad light, women in head-scarves, crocheted fascinators, extravagantly flowered hats, no hats at all, women just looking to put their feet up after too many hours of lifting, fetching, walking the jobless avenues, bearing the insults of the day . . .

There was an Italian with an accordion. The company began to sing, from the *Workers' Own Songbook,* though mostly without the aid of the text, choral selections including Hubert Parry's recent setting of Blake's "Jerusalem," taken not unreasonably as a great anticapitalist anthem disguised as a choir piece, with a slight adjustment to the last line—"In *this our* green and pleasant land."

And another which went,

Fierce as the winter's tempest
Cold as the smoth'ring snow

On grind the mills of Avarice
High rides the cruel-eyed foe. . . .
Where is the hand of mercy,
Where is the kindly face,
Where in this heedless slaughter
Find we the promis'd place?
Sweated, despised and hearthless,
Scorned 'neath the banker's boot,
We freeze by their frost-bound windows—
As they fondle their blood-bought loot—
Love never spared a sinner,
Hate never cured a saint,
Soon is the night of reckoning,
Then let no heart be faint,
Teach us to fly from shelter
Teach us to love the cold,
Life's for the free and fearless—
Death's for the bought and sold!

. . . moving from the minor mode it had been in throughout into the major, ending with a Picardy third cadence that, if it did not break Lew's heart exactly, did leave a fine crack that in time was to prove unmendable. . . .

For something here was striking him as what you'd have to call odd. Nate Privett, everybody else at W.C.I., needless to say most of the Agency's clients, none had too good of a word to say about the labor unions, let alone Anarchists of any stripe, that's if they even saw a difference. There was a kind of general assumption around the shop that laboring men and women were all more or less evil, surely misguided, and not quite American, maybe not quite human. But here was this hall full of Americans, no question, even the foreign-born, if you thought about where they had come from and what they must've been hoping to find over here and so forth, American in their prayers anyway, and maybe a few hadn't shaved for a while, but it was hard to see how any fit the bearded, wild-eyed, bomb-rolling Red description too close, in fact give them a good night's sleep and a square meal or two, and even a veteran detective'd have a hard time telling the difference from regular Americans. Yet here they were expressing the most subversive thoughts, as ordinary folks might discuss crops, or last night's ball game. Lew understood that this business would not end with him walking out the door tonight and over to the El and on to some next assignment.

. . .

IT MUST HAVE BEEN that Austrian Archduke. Look after one royal, everybody starts making assumptions. Anarchists and heads of state being defined these days as natural enemies, Lew by this logic became the natural gumshoe to be taking aim at Anarchists, wherever they happened to pop up in the shooting gallery of day-to-day history. Anarchist-related tickets began landing on his desk with some regularity. He found himself out by factory fences breathing coal-smoke, walking picket lines in various of W.C.I.'s thousand disguises, learning enough of several Slavic tongues to be plausible down in the deadfalls where the desperate malcontents convened, fingerless slaughterhouse veterans, irregulars in the army of sorrow, prophesiers who had seen America as it might be in visions America's wardens could not tolerate.

Soon, along with dozens of file drawers stuffed with the information he brought back, Lew had moved into his own office, at whose doorsill functionaries of government and industry presently began to appear, having surrendered their hats in the outer office, to ask respectfully for advice which Nate Privett kept a keen eye on the market value of. Of course this provoked some grumbling in the business, mainly from Pinkerton's, who, having assumed American Anarchism was their own personal cookie jar, wondered how an upstart like White City dared aspire to more than crumbs. The discontent became evident in the White City shop as well, as The Unsleeping Eye began to lure away personnel, soon more of them than Nate could afford to lose. One day he came bounding into Lew's office surrounded by a nimbus of cheer phony as nickel-a-quart bay rum—"Good news, Agent Basnight, another step up your personal career ladder! How does . . . 'Regional Director' sound?"

Lew looked up, poker-faced. "What 'region' is it I'm being packed off to, Nate?"

"Lew, you card! Be serious!" W.C.I. had decided to open a Denver office, Nate explained, and with more Anarchists per square foot out there than a man could begin to count, who better than Lew to ramrod the operation?

As if this were a real question, Lew began to recite names of plausible colleagues, all of them with an edge on him in seniority, till Nate's frown had grown deep enough. "O.K., boss, I get the drift. It's not up to you, that what you're about to say?"

"Lew, it's gold and silver mining out there. Nuggets for the picking up. Favors that you can name your own price."

Lew reached for a panatela and lit up. After a couple-three slow puffs,

"Ever come out of work in this town when the light's still in the sky and the lamps are just being lit along the big avenues and down by the Lake, and the girls are all out of the offices and shops and heading home, and the steak houses are cranking up for the evening trade, and the plate-glass windows are shining, with the rigs all lined up by the hotels, and—"

"No," Nate staring impatiently, "not too often, I work too late for that."

Lew blew a smoke ring, and a few more concentrically. "Well now shit, there, Nate."

FOR SOME REASON Lew felt uncomfortable telling the Chums of Chance about his transfer. In the short time he'd been riding with them, he'd almost come to feel more at home up in the *Inconvenience* than he did at the Agency.

The visibility today was unlimited, the Lake sparkling with a million highlights, the little electric launches and gondolas, the crowds in the plazas adjoining the mammoth exhibition buildings, the whiteness of the place nearly unbearable. . . . Faint janglings of music ascended from the Midway pavilions, a bass drum thumped like the pulse of some living collective creature down there.

Professor Vanderjuice was along for the day, having completed whatever business had detained him in Chicago. Lew's detective reflexes warned him of something deeply evasive about this personable academic, which he guessed the boys were aware of, too, though it was their business what to make of it. His presence made it no easier for Lew to impart his news, but he did manage at last to blurt, "Doggone but I'm going to miss this."

"Still some weeks till the fair closes," said Randolph.

"I'll be gone by then. They're sending me west, fellows, and I guess it's so long."

Randolph had a sympathetic look. "At least they tell you where it is you'll be sent off to. After the closing-day ceremonies here, our future's all a blank."

"It may not be quite the West you're expecting," Professor Vanderjuice put in. "Back in July my colleague Freddie Turner came out here from Harvard and gave a speech before a bunch of anthro people who were all in town for their convention and of course the Fair. To the effect that the Western frontier we all thought we knew from song and story was no longer on the map but gone, absorbed—a dead duck."

"To show you what he means," said Randolph, putting the helm over and causing the *Inconvenience* to veer inland, bearing northwest, toward the Union Stockyards.

"Yes here," continued the Professor, nodding down at the Yards as they began to flow by beneath, "here's where the Trail comes to its end at last, along with the American Cowboy who used to live on it and by it. No matter how virtuous he's kept his name, how many evildoers he's managed to get by undamaged, how he's done by his horses, what girls he has chastely kissed, serenaded by guitar, or gone out and raised hallelujah with, it's all back there in the traildust now and none of it matters, for down there you'll find the wet convergence and finale of his drought-struck tale and thankless calling, Buffalo Bill's Wild West Show stood on its head—spectators invisible and silent, nothing to be commemorated, the only weapons in view being Blitz Instruments and Wackett Punches to knock the animals out with, along with the blades everybody is packing, of course, and the rodeo clowns jabber on in some incomprehensible lingo not to distract the beast but rather to heighten and maintain its attention to the single task at hand, bringing it down to those last few gates, the stunning-devices waiting inside, the butchering and blood just beyond the last chute—and the cowboy with him. Here." He handed Lew a pair of field-glasses. "That little charabanc down there just making the turn off Forty-seventh?"

As the airship descended closer, Lew watched the open vehicle pull up inside the Halstead Street gate to discharge its passengers, and understood, with some perplexity, that it was an excursion group, in town for a tour among the killing-floors and sausage rooms, an instructive hour of throat-slashing, decapitation, skinning, gutting, and dismemberment—"Say, Mother, come have a look at *these* poor bastards!" following the stock in their sombre passage from arrival in rail cars, into the smells of shit and chemicals, old fat and tissue diseased, dying, and dead, and a rising background choir of animal terror and shouting in human languages few of them had heard before, till the moving chain brought in stately parade the hook-hung carcasses at last to the chilling-rooms. At the exit the visitors would find a souvenir-shop, where they could purchase stereopticon slides, picture-postcards, and cans of "Top Gourmet Grade" souvenir luncheon meat, known to include fingers and other body parts from incautious workmen.

"Don't think I'll give up steaks just yet," Lew said, "but it does make a man wonder how disconnected those folks down there'd have to be."

"That's about it," the Professor nodded. "The frontier ends and disconnection begins. Cause and effect? How the dickens do I know? I spent my earlier hob-raising years out where you're headed, Denver and Cripple Creek and Colorado Springs, while there was still a frontier, you always knew where it was and how to get there, and it wasn't always just between natives and strangers or Anglos and Mexicans or cavalry and Indians. But you could feel it, unmistakeably, like a divide, where you knew you could stand and piss would flow two ways at once."

But if the Frontier was gone now, did that mean Lew was about to be disconnected, too, from himself? sent off into exile, into some silence beyond silence as retribution for a remote and ancient vice always just about to be remembered, half stunned, in a half dream like a surgeon's knot taken swiftly in the tissue of time and pulled snug, delivered into the control of potent operatives who did not wish him well?

THE BOYS GAVE Lew a gold-and-enamel Chums of Chance honorary membership pin to be worn beneath his lapel, which, upon being revealed at any branch anyplace in the world, would entitle him to all visitors' privileges provided for in the C. of C. Charter. Lew in return gave them a miniature spotter's telescope disguised as a watch fob, also holding a single .22 round which it was able to fire in an emergency. The boys thanked him sincerely enough, but that night after Evening Quarters argued late over the recurring question of introducing firearms aboard the *Inconvenience.* In the matter of Lew's gift, the solution was easy enough—keep it unloaded. But the broader issue remained. "As of this moment we are all friends and brothers," Randolph supposed, "but historically any ship's armory is a free-standing volume of potential trouble—an attraction to would-be mutineers, and little else. There it sits, waiting its moment, taking up space that might, particularly on an airship, be more usefully assigned." The other danger was less easy to speak of, and everyone—except possibly Pugnax, whose thoughts were difficult of access—found themselves speaking in euphemisms. For cases were known and whispered through the service, more certain than idle rumors or skystories, of extended duty so terrible in its demands on morale that now and then, unable to continue, some unfortunate Chum of Chance had decided to end his life, the overwhelming choice among methods being the "midnight plunge"—simply rolling over the gunwale during a night flight—yet, for those who might prefer less dependence on altitude, any gun on board would present an irresistible appeal.

Cheerfulness, once taken as a condition of life on the *Inconvenience,* was in fact being progressively revealed to the boys as a precarious commodity, these days. They seemed held here, as if under some unconfided spell. Autumn deepened among the desolate city blocks, an edge appeared to the hum of life here, invisible sometimes and furtive as worn boot-heels vanishing round the corners of the stately arcades where the boys resorted, in great shabby rooms, among the smells of stale animal fat and ammonia on the floor, with glass-roofed steam-tables offering three choices of sandwich, lamb, ham, or beef, all heavy on the fat and gristle, stale odors, frown-lined women slapping together meat and bread, a shaken spoon that smacked the flour-heavy gravy on like plaster, eyes cast downward all day long, behind them in front of the mirror rising a pyramid of cheap miniature bottles, known hereabouts as "Mickeys," holding three choices of wine, red, white, and muscatel.

When not reeling about quite as uncontrollably as drunkards, the boys would gather to dine on these horrible wet-and-dry sandwiches, drinking the low-priced wine and noting with clogged humor how swiftly each seemed to fatten before the gazes of the others. "Hang it, fellows," Randolph expostulated, "we've got to try to pull out of this!" They began to imagine, jointly and severally, some rescuer entering the crew spaces, moving among them, weighing, choosing, a creature of fantasy to bring them back each to his innocence, to lead him out of his unreliable body and his unique loss of courage, so many years in the making—though, much as he enjoyed unanimous admiration from the crew, it had not turned out to be Lew Basnight. He had moved on, as had so many in their lives, and they continued in a fragmented reverie which, they had learned, often announced some change in the works.

And sure enough, one morning the boys found, wedged casually between two strands of mooring cable, as always unconnected with any action they might've been contemplating, orders silently delivered in the night.

"Bear east is pretty much all it says," Randolph in quiet consternation. "East by south."

Lindsay pulled out charts. Speculation began to fill the day. Once it had been enough to know the winds, and how they blew at each season of the year, to get a rough idea of where they might be headed. Presently, as the *Inconvenience* began to acquire its own sources of internal power, there would be other global streamings to be taken into account—electromagnetic lines of force, Æther-storm warnings, movements of population and capital. Not the ballooning profession as the boys had learned it.

LATER, after closing day, as autumn deepened over the corrupted prairie, as the ill-famed Hawk, miles aloft, invisibly rehearsed its Arctic repertoire of swift descent, merciless assault, rapture of souls—the abandoned structures of the Fair would come to house the jobless and hungry who had always been there, even at the height of the season of miracle just concluded. The Colorado Silver Mining Camp, like the other former exhibits, was occupied now by drifters, squatters, mothers with nursing infants, hell-raisers hired for the run of the Fair, now, their market value having vanished, returned to the consolations of drink, dogs and cats who preferred the company of their own species, some who still bore memories of Pugnax and his conversation, and excursions they had been out on. All moving in closer to the fires of Fair debris, once the substance of wonder, as the temperature headed down.

Not long after Erlys had gone off with Zombini the Mysterious, Merle Rideout dreamed he was in a great museum, a composite of all possible museums, among statues, pictures, crockery, folk-amulets, antiquated machinery, stuffed birds and animals, obsolete musical instruments, and whole corridors of stuff he would not get to see. He was there with a small party of people he didn't know, but in the dream was supposed to know. Abruptly, in front of a display of Japanese weapons, an official person in ragged plainclothes, unshaven, mistrusting and bitterly humorless, who may or may not have been a museum guard, grabbed hold of him on suspicion of having stolen some small art object, and demanded that he empty out his pockets, including a bulging and dilapidated old cowhide wallet, which the "guard" indicated was to be emptied, too. A crowd had gathered around, including the familiar-unfamiliar group he'd come here with, all silently staring. The wallet was itself a sort of museum, on a smaller scale—a museum of his life, overstuffed with old ticket stubs, receipts, notes to himself, names and addresses of half- or sometimes totally forgotten folks from his past. In the midst of all this biographical litter, a *miniature portrait of her* appeared. He woke up, understanding at once that the whole purpose of the dream was to remind him, with diabolical roundaboutness, of Erlys Mills.

Her name was never far from the discourse of the day. Since about the minute she could talk, Dally had been good for all kinds of interesting questions.

"And, so, what first attracted you to her?"

"Didn't run away screaming when I told her how I felt."

"Love at first sight, something like that?"

"Figured there was no point trying to hide it. Minute and a half longer, she'd've figured it out anyway."

"And . . ."

"What was I doing in Cleveland in the first place?"

Which usually was how Dally got to hear about her mother, in these bits and pieces. One day Merle had read in the *Hartford Courant* about a couple of professors at the Case Institute in Cleveland who were planning an experiment to see what effect, if any, the motion of the Earth had on the speed of light through the luminiferous Æther. He had already heard in some dim way about the Æther, though being more on the practical side of things, he couldn't see much use for it. Exists, doesn't exist, what's it got to do with the price of turnips basically. And anything that happened at the speed of light would have too many unknowables attached to begin with—closer to religion than science. He discussed it one day with his friend at Yale, Professor Vanderjuice, who, having just emerged from another of the laboratory mishaps for which he was widely known, carried as always a smell of sal ammoniac and singed hair.

"Small confrontation with the Töpler Influence Machine, nothing to worry about."

"Guess I'd better go take a look. Probably that gear train again."

They strolled among the elm-shadows, eating sandwiches and apples out of paper bags, "a peripatetic picnic," as the Professor called it, slipping thereupon into his lecture-hall style.

"You're quite right, of course, the Æther has always been a religious question. Some don't believe in it, some do, neither will convince the other, it's all faith at the moment. Lord Salisbury said it was only a noun for the verb 'to undulate.' Sir Oliver Lodge defined it as 'one continuous substance filling all space, which can vibrate light . . . be sheared into positive and negative electricity,' and so on in a lengthy list, almost like the Apostles' Creed. It certainly depends on a belief in the waviness of light—if light were particulate, it could just go blasting through empty space with no need for any Æther to carry it. Indeed one finds in the devout Ætherist a propensity of character ever toward the continuous as against the discrete. Not to mention a vast patience with all those tiny whirlpools the theory has come to require."

"Think this is worth going out to Cleveland for?"

"Mr. Rideout, we wander at the present moment through a sort of vorticalist twilight, holding up the lantern of the Maxwell Field Equations and squinting to find our way. Michelson's done this experiment before, in Berlin, but never so carefully. This new one could be the giant arc-lamp we need to light our way into the coming century. I don't know the man personally, but I'll write you a letter of introduction anyway, it can't hurt."

Merle had been born and raised in northwest Connecticut, a region of clockmakers, gunsmiths and inspired tinkers, so his trip out to the Western Reserve was just a personal expression of Yankee migration generally. This strip of Ohio due west of Connecticut had for years, since before American independence, been considered part of Connecticut's original land grant. So despite days and nights of traveling, Merle had an eerie sense of not having left Connecticut—same plain gable-front houses, white Congregational church steeples, even stone fences—more Connecticut, just shifted west, was all.

Merle arrived to find the "Forest City" obsessed by the pursuit of genial desperado Blinky Morgan, who was being sought for allegedly murdering a police detective while trying to rescue a member of his gang who'd been picked up on a fur-robbery charge. Newsboys cried the tale, and rumors flew like bugs in summer. Detectives swaggered everywhere, their black stiff hats shining like warrior helmets of old. Chief Schmitt's bravos in blue were detaining and subjecting to lengthy and mostly aimless questioning anybody whose looks they didn't care much for, which took in a wide piece of the population, including Merle, who was stopped on Rockville Street as he was heading out toward the Case Institute.

"What's in the wagon, son?"

"Nothin much. You're sure welcome to look."

"Well this is refreshing, usually we get Blinky jokes."

Merle went off into a long and confused description of the Michelson-Morley experiment, and his interest in it, which was not shared by the policemen, who began to grow distant, and presently truculent.

"Another candidate for Newburgh here, looks like."

"Well, let's do a check. Crossed eyes, protruding tongue, Napoleon hat?" They were talking about the Northern Ohio Insane Asylum, a few miles southeast of town, in which currently were lodged some of the more troublesome of the scientific cranks Cleveland these days had been filling up rapidly with, enthusiasts from everywhere in the nation and abroad for that matter, eager to bathe in the radiance of the celebrated Æther-drift experiment in progress out at Case. Some were inventors with light-engines that could run a bicycle all day but at nightfall stopped abruptly, causing the bike to fall over with you on it, if you weren't careful. Some claimed that light had a consciousness and personality and could even be chatted with, often revealing its deeper secrets to those who approached it in the right way. Groups of these could be observed in Monumental Park at sunrise, sitting in the dew in uncomfortable positions, their lips moving inaudibly. There were diet faddists who styled themselves Lightarians, living on nothing but light, even setting up labs they thought of as kitchens and concocting meals from light recipes, fried light, fricaseed light, light *à la mode,* calling for different types of lamp filament and colors of glass envelope, the Edison lamp being brand new in those days but certainly not the only design under study. There were light addicts who around sunset began to sweat and itch and seclude themselves in toilets with portable electric lanterns. Some spent most of their time at telegraph offices squinting at long scrolls of mysteriously arrived "weather reports," about weather not in the atmosphere but in the luminiferous Æther. "Yes it's all here," said Ed Addle, one of the regulars at the Oil Well Saloon, "Æther-wind speed, Ætheric pressure, there are instruments to measure those, even an analogy to temperature, which depends on the ultramicroscopic vortices and how energetically they interact. . . ."

Merle came back with another round of beers. "How about humidity?"

"Controversial," said Ed. "What, in the Æther, would occupy the place of water-vapor in the air? Some of us believe it is Vacuum. Minute droplets of nothing at all, mixed in with the prevailing Ætheric medium. Until the saturation point is reached, of course. Then there is condensation, and storms in which not rain but precipitated nothingness sweeps a given area, cyclones and anticyclones of it, abroad not only locally at the planetary surface but outside it, through cosmic space as well."

"There's a U.S. Bureau in charge of reporting all this?" wondered Roswell Bounce, who was gainfully self-employed as a photographer, "a network of stations? Ships and balloons?"

Ed became guarded. "Is this just your usual wet-blanket talk, or do you really want to know?"

"If there was a reliable light-meter," said Roswell, "it might make a difference to know about how the light was being transmitted, is all."

It was a sort of small Ætherist community, maybe as close as Merle ever came to joining a church. They hung out in the saloons of Whiskey Hill and were tolerated by though not especially beloved of the regulars, who were mill hands with little patience for extreme forms of belief, unless it was Anarchism, of course.

Merle by then was also spending a lot of time, not to mention money, on a couple of sisters named Madge and Mia Culpepper, who worked at the Hamilton Street establishment of Blinky Morgan's lady friend Nelly Lowry. He had actually glimpsed the flashily turned-out Blinky a couple of times coming and going, as had the police, most likely, because the place was under close surveillance, but attentiveness to duty being negotiable in those days, there were intervals of invisibility for anybody who could afford it.

Merle found himself more often than not the monkey in the middle, trying to calm the dangerously fervid, find work for those who ran short, put people up in the wagon when landlords got mean, trying meantime to stay reasonably unentangled with moneymaking schemes which, frankly, though plentiful as fungi after the rain, verged all too often on the unworkably eccentric, ". . . amount of light in the universe being finite, and diminishing fast enough so that damming, diversion, rationing, not to mention pollution, become possibilities, like water rights, only different, and there's sure to be an international scramble to *corner light.* We have the know-how, the world's most inventive engineers and mechanics, all's we need is to get far enough out to catch the prevailing flows. . . ."

"Airships?"

"Better. Psychical anti-gravity." Ætherists possessed to this degree usually ended up for a stay in Newburgh, from which it became necessary to break them out, Merle after a while becoming known as the fellow to see, once he'd developed a relationship with elements of the staff out there who did not mind an escapee now and then, the work-load being what it was.

"Escaped!"

"Ed, they'll hear you, try not to holler quite so—"

"Free! Free as a bird!"

"Shh! Will you just—" By which point uniformed guards were approaching at a clip you could call moderate.

SOMEHOW MERLE GOT the idea in his head that the Michelson-Morley experiment and the Blinky Morgan manhunt were connected. That if Blinky were ever caught, there would also turn out to be no Æther. Not that one would cause the other, exactly, but that both would be different utterances of the same principle.

"This is primitive hoodoo," objected Roswell Bounce. "You might as well head for the deep jungle and talk this over with the trees, for in this town that kind of thinking won't go, nosir not at all."

"But you've seen his picture in the papers." Each of Blinky's eyes, according to press accounts, saw the world differently, the left one having undergone an obscure trauma, either from a premature detonation during a box job or from a naval howitzer while fighting in the Rebellion. Blinky gave out a number of stories.

"A walking interferometer, as you'd say," suggested Ed Addle.

"A double-refractor, for that matter."

"There you go. An asymmetry with respect to light anyway." One day Merle had seen the astonishing truth of the case, though admittedly he had been most of the night working his way from one Whiskey Hill saloon to the next, drinking. Why hadn't he seen it before? It was so obvious! Professor Edward Morley and Charles "Blinky" Morgan were one and the same person! Separated by a couple-three letters in name as if alphabetically double-refracted, you could say. . . .

"And they've both of 'em got long shaggy hair and big red mustaches—"

"No, no couldn't be, Blinky's a natty dresser, whereas Professor Morley's attire is said to exhibit a certain tendency to the informal. . . ."

"Yes yes but suppose, suppose when they split that light beam, that one half of it is Michelson's and the other is his partner Morley's, which turns out to be the half that comes back with the phases perfectly matched up—but under slightly different conditions, alternative axioms, there could be another pair that *don't* match up, see, in fact millions of pairs, that sometimes you could blame it on the Æther, sure, but other cases maybe the light *goes someplace else,* takes a detour and that's why it shows up late and out of phase, because it went where Blinky was when he was invisible, and—"

In late June, just about when Michelson and Morley were making their final observations, Blinky Morgan was apprehended in Alpena, Michigan, a resort town built on the site of an Indian graveyard. "Because Blinky *emerged from invisibility,* and the moment he reentered the world that contained Michelson and Morley, the experiment was fated to have a negative outcome, the Æther was doomed. . . ."

For word was circulating that Michelson and Morley had found no difference in the speed of light coming, going, or sideways relative to the Earth speeding along in its orbit. If the Æther was there, in motion or at rest, it was having no effect on the light it carried. The mood in the saloons frequented by Ætherists grew sombre. As if it possessed the substance of an invention or a battle, the negative result took its place in the history of Cleveland, as another of the revealed mysteries of light.

"It's like these cults who believe the world will end on such and such a day," Roswell opined, "they get rid of all their earthly possessions and head off in a group for some mountaintop and wait, and then the end of the world doesn't happen. The world keeps going on. What a disappointment! Everybody has to troop back down the mountain with their spiritual tails dragging, except for one or two incurably grinning idiots who see it as a chance to start a new life, fresh, without encumbrances, to be reborn, in fact.

"So with this Michelson-Morley result. We've all had a lot of faith invested. Now it looks like the Æther, whether it's moving or standing still, just doesn't exist. What do we do now?"

"Taking a contrary view," said O. D. Chandrasekhar, who was here in Cleveland all the way from Bombay, India, and didn't say much, but when he did, nobody could figure out what he meant, "this null result may as easily be read as *proving the existence* of the Æther. Nothing is there, yet light travels. The absence of a light-bearing medium is the emptiness of what my religion calls *akasa,* which is the ground or basis of all that we imagine 'exists.' "

Everybody took a moment of silence, as if considering this. "What I worry about," said Roswell at last, "is that the Æther will turn out to be something like God. If we can explain everything we want to explain without it, then why keep it?"

"Unless," Ed pointed out, "it *is* God." Somehow this escalated into a general free-for-all, in which furniture and glassware didn't come out much better than the human participants, a rare sort of behavior among Ætherists, but everybody had been feeling at loose ends lately.

For Merle it had been a sort of directionless drift, what Mia Culpepper, who was devoted to astrology, called "void of course," which went on till mid-October, when there was a fire at the Newburgh asylum, where Merle happened to be that night, taking advantage of an inmates' dance to break out Roswell Bounce, who had offended a policeman by snapping his picture just as he emerged from the wrong sporting establishment. The asylum was in chaos. Lunatics and keepers alike ran around screaming. This was the second major fire at Newburgh in fifteen years, and the horror of the first had not yet faded. Crowds of onlookers from the neighborhood had gathered to see the show. Sparks and coals blew and fell. Gusts of hot red light swept the grounds, reflecting brightly off desperately rolling eyeballs, as shadows darted everywhere, changing shape and size. Merle and Roswell went down to the creek and joined a bucket brigade, hoses were run from hydrants, and later some engines showed up from Cleveland. By the time the fire was under control, the exhaustion and confusion were too advanced for anyone to notice as Merle and Roswell slipped away.

Back in Whiskey Hill, they made a beeline for Morty Vicker's Saloon. "What a hell of a night," Roswell said. "I could've been in the chapel at that dance where the fire broke out. Guess you saved my fundament, there."

"Buy the next round, we'll call it even."

"Better than that, my apprentice ran off when the coppers showed up. How'd you like to learn the deepest secrets of the photographer's trade?"

Since Roswell had only been in the asylum for a day or two, they found his equipment untouched by local scavengers or the landlord. Merle was no hoosier on the subject, he had seen cameras before, even had himself snapped once or twice. It had always seemed like an idiot's game, line them up, squeeze the bulb, take the money. Like anybody, of course, he had wondered what happened during the mysteriously guarded transition from plate to print, but never enough to step across any darkroom's forbidden doorsill to have a look. As a mechanic he respected any straightforward chain of cause and effect you could see or handle, but chemical reactions like this went on down in some region too far out of anyone's control, they were something you had to stand around and just let happen, which was about as interesting as waiting for corn to grow.

"O.K., here we go." Roswell lit a ruby darkroom lamp. Took a dry plate from a carrying case. "Hold this a minute." Started measuring out liquids from two or three different bottles, keeping up a sort of patter meantime, hardly any of which Merle could follow—"Pyrogallic, mumblemumble citric, potassium bromide . . . ammonia . . ." Stirring it all in a beaker, he put the plate in a developing tray and poured the mixture over it. "Now watch." And Merle saw the image appear. Come from nothing. Come in out of the pale Invisible, down into this otherwise explainable world, clearer than real. It happened to be the Newburgh asylum, with two or three inmates standing in the foreground, staring. Merle peered uneasily. Something was wrong with the faces. The whites of their eyes were dark gray. The sky behind the tall, jagged roofline was nearly black, windows that should have been light-colored were dark. As if light had been witched somehow into its opposite. . . .

"What is it? They look like spirits, or haunts or something."

"It's a negative. When we print this, it'll all flip back to normal. First we have to fix it. Reach me that bottle of hypo there."

So the night went on, spent mostly washing things in different solutions and then waiting for them to dry. By the time the sun rose over Shaker Heights, Roswell Bounce had introduced Merle to photography. "Photography, this is Merle, Merle—"

"All right, all right. And you swear this is made of silver?"

"Just like what's in your pocket."

"Not lately."

Damn.

"Do one more." He knew he sounded like some rube at the fair but couldn't help it. Even if it was only some conjuring trick, purely secular, he wanted to learn it.

"Just what people have been noticing ever since the first sunburn," Roswell shrugged, “which is that light makes things change color. The professors call it ‘photochemistry.’ ”

Merle’s all-night illumination prolonged itself into an inescapable glow that began to keep him awake. He parked the wagon out on a vacant patch in Murray Hill and set in to study the mysteries of light-portraiture as then understood, gathering information dip-fingered and without shame from everyplace he could, from Roswell Bounce to the Cleveland Library, which as Merle soon discovered had taken the revolutionary step some ten years before of opening up its stacks, so anybody could walk in and spend all day reading what they needed to know for whatever it was they had in mind to do.

After going through all the possible silver compounds, Merle moved on to salts of gold, platinum, copper, nickel, uranium, molybdenum, and antimony, abandoning metallic compounds after a while for resins, squashed bugs, coal-tar dyes, cigar smoke, wildflower extracts, urine from various critters including himself, reinvesting what little money came in from portrait work into lenses, filters, glass plates, enlarging machines, so that soon the wagon was just a damn rolling photography lab. He grabbed images of anything that came in range, never mind focus—streets aswarm with townsfolk, cloud-lit hillsides where nothing seemed to move, grazing cows who ignored him, insane squirrels who made a point of coming right up to the lens and making faces, picnickers out at Rocky River, abandoned wheelbarrows, patent bobwire stretchers left to rust under the sky, clocks on walls, stoves in kitchens, streetlamps lit and unlit, policemen running at him waving day clubs, girls arm in arm window-shopping on their lunch hours or strolling after work in the lakeside breezes, electric runabouts, flush toilets, 1,200-volt trolley dynamos and other wonders of the modern age, the new Viaduct under construction, weekend funseekers up by the reservoir, and next thing he knew, winter and spring had passed and he was out on his own, trying to make a living as a circuit-riding photographer, sometimes taking the wagon, sometimes just traveling light, a hand camera and a dozen plates, keeping to the interurbans, Sandusky to Ashtabula, Brooklyn out to Cuyahoga Falls and Akron, playing a lot of railroad euchre as a result, and posting a modest profit each trip out.

In August he happened to be in Columbus, where the papers were full of Blinky Morgan’s impending execution at the state pen and various last-ditch efforts to prevent it. A sweltering somnambulism possessed the town. It was impossible to get a decent meal, or even snack, anywhere, burned flapjacks and vulcanized steaks being as appetizing as things got. It also quickly became evident—horribly evident—that no one in the city knew how to make coffee, as if there were some sort of stultified consensus, or even city ordinance, about never waking up. Bridge-rails were crowded with people watching the Scioto move sluggishly along. Saloons were full of silent drinkers, who drank very slowly till they collapsed, typically around eight in the evening, which appeared to be closing time here. Day and night, thousands of petitioners milled at the gates of the Capitol seeking admission to the hanging. Souvenir stands enjoyed a remunerative trade in Blinky poker decks and board games, watch-fobs and cigar cutters, Blinky lockets and charms, commemorative china and wallpaper, Blinky toys including stuffed Blinky dolls which each came suspended by the neck from its own little toy gallows, and a great favorite, Blinky thumb-books, whose pages, showing full-color artist's renderings of the bloody murders in Ravenna, if flipped rapidly with your thumb appeared actually to be in motion. For a while, fascinated, Merle wandered the booths and pitches, setting up his camera and taking plate after plate of these Blinky Morgan keepsakes, displayed by the identical dozens, until somebody asked him why he wasn't trying to get in to photograph the execution. "Why, you know," as if coming to his senses, "I don't know." There were people at the *Plain Dealer* he could have wired, he supposed, cashed in a favor maybe. . . . Alarmed at what seemed a dangerously morbid lapse, he uncovered all the plates he'd taken and left them out in a vacant lot under the daylight, to return to blankness and innocence.

As if the light of Heaven had performed a similar service for his brain, Merle understood that he must never if he could avoid it set foot within the limits of this place again. "If the U.S. was a person," he later became fond of saying, "and it *sat down*, Columbus, Ohio would instantly be plunged into darkness."

MERLE NEVER DID get to use Professor Vanderjuice's letter of introduction to Michelson. By the time he got what he would have called back on track, the Æther-drift experiment was all written up in the science journals and Michelson was away teaching at Clark University, and too famous to be giving itinerant technicals the time of day.

Just like that, as if some period of youthful folly had expired, it seemed time to move on—Madge and Mia had both found rich beaux, the police had turned their attention to Anarchism in the streetcar workers' union, the Blinkyites had left town, many of them bound for Lorain County, where it was rumored Blinky and his gang had buried a huge treasure, the Ætherists and otherwise light-obsessed had dispersed to resume whatever lapses of balance had brought them here—including Roswell Bounce, who had been subpœnaed to appear in Pittsburgh regarding some patent dispute. And it was exactly in this blessed lull in the daily discombobulation that Merle met Erlys Mills Snidell, and found himself unexpectedly miles up some unfamiliar road, as if in the dark he had encountered an unmapped fork. "The Æther might've still been an open question," he told Dally, years later, "but there was never no doubt about that Erlys."

"Then—"

"Why'd she leave? Say, my little eggplant, how would I know? come back one day, she's just up and gone, was all. You on the bed blissfully deep in the first colic-free sleep of your young life—"

"Wait. *She made* me have the colic?"

"Didn't say that. Did I say that? Just a coincidence, I'm sure. Your Ma stuck as long as she could, Dally, brave of her, too, considering the life we were trying to lead, deputies with court orders way before breakfast, patent lawyers, vigilantes with shotguns, and worst of all those town ladies, herds o' locusts, no end to em, torchlight rallies waving signs on sticks, 'Beast Without Shame,' so forth—she could soldier on when it was just the men after me, but them sisters in indignation, why, she couldn't bear much of that, it's women beware women when *that* starts rolling down the pike. Oh but beg pardon, you're all but about to be one yourself ain't you, so sorry there—"

"Wait, wait, go back a little, tell me how that Zombini bird fits in to this again?"

"Oh, him. Wish I could say he's this evil interloper come swooping in and made off with her, alienation of affections and all, but I figure you're old enough to hear the truth, that's o' course if I knew what that was, seein's I'd have to speak for your Ma as far as inner feelings and them, which'd be not only unfair to her but also impossible for me—"

"All right, Pa. Don't go gettin tongue-tied, I can wait to ask her in person someday."

"I mean—"

"It's O.K. Really. Someday."

Piece by piece, though, she got some of the story. Luca Zombini back then had been pursuing a modest career in stage magic, playing local variety circuits in the Midwest. One day in East Fullmoon, Iowa, his regular stage-assistant Roxana ran off with a tenor sax player from the pit band at the local opera house, with little hope on the horizon of this remote town for any replacement. Then, just to make the day complete, one of Luca's magnetic stage gadgets broke down. At his wit's end, ready for anything like a piece of luck, he spotted Merle's wagon parked out at the edge of town. Erlys looked up from darning a sock to see him perched on the doorsill, holding his hat. "I don't suppose you'd have a spare electrical coil around?"

Merle had been down to the opera house and recognized him. "Look around, take what you need—what's it for?"

"Hong Kong Mystery Effect. Show you the work if you like."

"Rather be puzzled. Just having lunch if you'd care to sit."

"Smells like minestrone."

"Think that's what they called it back in Cleveland, when they were showing me how to do it. Fry everything first, basically."

"Murray Hill? Eh, I got cousins there."

Both men were aware of a silence audibly fallen over Erlys, though each interpreted it in his own way. It never occurred to Merle that Zombini the Mysterious might be the cause, especially as he showed none of those classic Italian warning signs, ringlets, dark flashing eyes, oily courtesies—none of that, just an average-looking gent who as far as anybody could tell hadn't even noticed Erlys till the matter of the magician's-assistant vacancy came up, when he abruptly turned to her, simmering like a pot of soup down the end of the table—"Excuse me, signora, what may seem a peculiar question, but . . . have you ever felt that you wished to suddenly disappear, even from a room full of people, just"—tossing his hands to suggest smoke vanishing—"gone?"

"Me? All the time, why?"

"Could you stand perfectly still while somebody throws knives at you?"

"Been known to hold still for worse'n that," flicking a glance, then, in Merle's direction. At which point Dally woke up, as if she'd been keeping track and chosen just that moment.

"I'll see to her." Merle brushing past, voice in a mumble, painfully aware of the beauty that had swept upon the young woman, as it did now and then, always unexpected, like a galvanic shadow, her face, that is, while her long body did not brighten but took on a vibrant dark density, a dimension you had to observe directly, with care, when that might've been the last thing you were ready just then to do. He didn't know what was happening. He did know.

Roxana, possibly at the urging of the sax player, had taken her costume along with her, so for that night's performance Erlys had to put one together, borrowing tights from one of the dancers and a short sequined dress from one of the acrobats. When she appeared in the stage-light, Merle felt himself hollow out from neck to groin with desire and desperation. It might have been only the lip-rouge, but he thought he saw a smile, almost cruel, he hadn't much noticed before, self-sufficient to be sure, but determined enough now, no denying it, on a separate fate. From her eyes, the lids and lashes darkened elaborately with chimney soot and petrolatum, he could read nothing. Next day, without mystical words or special equipment, she and the magician had vanished, and Dally stayed behind with a note pinned to her blanket, *I'll be back for her when I can.* No "Good luck" or "Love always, Erlys," nothing like that.

Merle waited in East Fullmoon as long as he could, waited for mail, a telegram, a rider, a carrier pigeon circling in from the winter skies, and in the meantime learned how straightforward it would all be, taking care of this baby here, long as he didn't fret about the time or any need he might've thought he had to get on with some larger plan—with Erlys gone, anything like that was out the window and down the turnpike anyway—and that long as he just kept breathing smoothly in and out, just staying within the contours of the chore of the moment, life with young Dahlia would provide precious little occasion for complaint, bitter or otherwise.

After the closing of the Columbian Fair, once out of Chicago and into the land again, Dally and Merle began to catch sight of refugees from the "national" exhibits which had lined the Midway Plaisance, all these non-midwestern varieties of human, some teamed up together, some going it alone. Merle would run for a camera trying to grab a snap, but by the time he set up they were usually gone. Through the falling snow, Dally thought she saw dog teams and Eskimos in silent recessional ever northward. She invited Merle's attention to Pygmies looking out at them from among the trunks of birch forests. Down in the riverfront saloons of the towns, South Sea Island tattoo artists whose faces seemed to her obscurely familiar inscribed the biceps of riverboat men with hieratic images that someday when least expected would be good for small but crucial acts of magic. Dally assumed these wanderers had all been banished for no good reason from the White City, too, making her and her Pa just some different kind of Eskimo, was all, and the country they moved through never about to be better than a place of exile. Rolling into city after city, St. Louis, Wichita, Denver, she caught herself each time hoping that somewhere in it, some neighborhood down the end of some electric line, it'd be there waiting for her, the real White City again, lit up all spectral and cool at night and shimmering by day in the bright humidity of its webwork of canals, the electric launches moving silently through the waterways with their parasoled ladies and straw-hatted men and little kids with Cracker Jack pieces stuck in their hair.

As years piled on, it came to seem more like the memory of some previous life, deformed, disguised, stretches of it missing, this capital of dream she had once lived in, maybe was even numbered among the rightful nobility of. At first she begged Merle, tearfully as she knew how, to please bring them back, please, and he never quite found the way to tell her that the fairground was most of it surely burned down by now, pulled to pieces, taken away to salvage yards, sold off, crumbled away, staff and scantlings at the mercy of the elements, of the man-made bad times that had come upon Chicago and the nation. After a while her tears only reflected light but did not flow, and she dropped into silences, and then these, too, gradually lost their resentful edges.

Planted rows went turning past like giant spokes one by one as they ranged the roads. The skies were interrupted by dark gray storm clouds with a flow like molten stone, swept and liquid, and light that found its way through them was lost in the dark fields but gathered shining along the pale road, so that sometimes all you could see was the road, and the horizon it ran to. Sometimes she was overwhelmed by the green life passing in such high turbulence, too much to see, all clamoring to have its way. Leaves sawtooth, spade-shaped, long and thin, blunt-fingered, downy and veined, oiled and dusty with the day—flowers in bells and clusters, purple and white or yellow as butter, star-shaped ferns in the wet and dark places, millions of green veilings before the bridal secrets in the moss and under the deadfalls, went on by the wheels creaking and struck by rocks in the ruts, sparks visible only in what shadow it might pass over, a busy development of small trailside shapes tumbling in what had to be deliberately arranged precision, herbs the wildcrafters knew the names and market prices of and which the silent women up in the foothills, counterparts whom they most often never got even to meet, knew the magic uses for. They lived for different futures, but they were each other's unrecognized halves, and what fascination between them did come to pass was lit up, beyond question, with grace.

Merle had put in some time at this thankless job, argued with botanical jobbers out on warehouse docks, learned a couple of the indications but never found in himself the gift the true wildcrafters had, the unerring feet, the sure nose.

"There. Smell that?"

A scent at the edge of her memory, ghostly as if a presence from a former life had just passed through . . . Erlys. "Lily of the valley. Sort of."

"It's 'seng. Fetches top dollar, so we're gonna eat for a while. Look. Little red berries there?"

"Why are we whispering?" Peering up from under her flowered bonnet-brim.

"Chinese believe the root is a small person, who can hear you coming and so forth."

"We're Chinese?"

He shrugged as if he wasn't sure. "Don't mean it ain't the truth."

"And cash crop here or whatever, we still aren't going to use the money to try and find Mama, are we?"

Should've seen that coming. "No."

"When then?"

"You'll get your turn, Trooper. Sooner than you think."

"Promise?"

"Ain't mine to promise. Just how it works."

"Well, don't sound so happy about it."

They pushed out into morning fields that went rolling all the way to every horizon, the Inner American Sea, where the chickens schooled like herring, and the hogs and heifers foraged and browsed like groupers and codfish, and the sharks tended to operate out of Chicago or Kansas City—the farmhouses and towns rising up along the journey like islands, with girls in every one, Merle couldn't help but notice, the extravagantly kept promises of island girls, found riding the electric trolley-lines that linked each cozy city to each, or serenely dealing cards in the riverside saloons, slinging hash in cafeterias you walked downstairs into out of the redbrick streets, gazing through doorscreens in Cedar Rapids, girls at fences in front of long fields in yellow light, Lizas and Chastinas, girls of the plains and of profusely-flowered seasons that may never quite have been, cooking for threshers far into and sometimes all through the nights of harvest, watching the streetcars come and go, dreaming of cavalry boys ridden off down the pikes, sipping the local brain tonic, tending steaming washtubs full of corn ears at the street corners with radiant eyes ever on the move, out in the yard in Ottumwa beating a rug, waiting in the mosquito-thick evenings of downstate Illinois, waiting by the fencepost where the bluebirds were nesting for a footloose brother to come back home after all, looking out a window in Albert Lea as the trains went choiring by.

In the towns, iron-rimmed carriage wheels rang loud on the paving stones, and Dally one day would recall how the horses had turned their heads to wink at her. Brown creepers strolled whistling up and down the tree trunks in the parks. Underneath bridges, struts rang when the riverboats whistled. Sometimes they stayed for a while, sometimes they were on their way again before the sun had moved a minute of arc, having shone down on soot-black trolley tracks and bridge rails, clockfaces high on the fronts of buildings, everything they needed to know—though after a while she didn't mind even the big towns, was even ready to forgive them for not being Chicago, enjoyed the downtown stores smelling like yard goods and carbolic soap, black linoleum parquetry, went down sandstone steps to have her hair cut in fragrant barbershops in the basements of hotels, brightly lit against the stormy days, smelling of every grade of cigar, witch hazel brewed and distilled in the back rooms, leather-cushioned chairs with elaborate old footrests wrought in the rosebuds-and-bluebirds intertwining of the century about to pass, as if poised among the thorned helixes of vines. . . . Next thing you knew, the haircut was done, a whisk-broom all over her back, and clouds of scented powder in the air. A palm out for a tip.

As Merle watched her sleep, an unmanly warmth about the eyeballs would surprise him. Her hearth-colored hair in a careless child's snarl. She was somewhere off wandering those dangerous dark fields, maybe even finding there some version of himself, of Erlys, that he'd never get to hear about, among the sorrowful truths, being lost, being found, flying, journeying to places too detailed to be anything but real, meeting the enemy, dying, being born over and over. . . . He wanted to find a way in, to look out for her at least, keep her from the worst if he could. . . .

Waiting out there for them each daybreak, green and wet or leafless and frozen, was always that map crisscrossed with pikes and highways and farm-to-market roads, for their scratchy eyelids to open and regard as if from above, as if having risen into the orange dawn skies and hovered, scanning like journeyman hawks for the next day's work, which more and more turned out to be some street-corner picture operation in another little prairie town to get them through a couple more meals. As years went along, the film got faster, the exposure times shorter, the cameras lighter. Premo came out with a celluloid film pack allowing you to shoot twelve at a time, which sure beat glass plates, and Kodak started selling its "Brownie," a little box camera that weighed practically nothing. Merle could bring it anywhere as long as he held everything steady in the frame, and by then—the old glass-plate folding models having weighed in at three pounds plus plates—he had learned to breathe, calm as a sharpshooter, and the images showed it, steady, deep, sometimes, Dally and Merle agreed, more real, though they never got into "real" that far.

There was always plenty of bell-hanger work—a sudden huge demand was spreading throughout the Midwest for electric bells, doorbells, hotel annunciators, elevator bells, fire and burglar alarms—you sold and installed them on the spot, walked away down the front path counting out your commission while the customer stood there with her finger on the buzzer like she couldn't get enough of the sound. And shingle-weaving, and mending some fence, and always frog-bonding work in the towns big enough to have streetcars, and plenty of machinery to see to in the powerhouses and car barns. . . . One summer Merle put in a hitch as a lightning-rod salesman, which he quit after finding himself at last unable to misrepresent as shamefully as his colleagues the nature of electricity.

"Any type of lightning, friends—fork, chain, heat and sheet, you name it, we'll send it back to ground right where it belongs."

"Ball lightning," somebody said after a silence. "That's the kind we worry about here. What've you got for that?"

Merle immediately grew sober. "You've had ball lightning out this way?"

"Nothing but, we specialize in it, we're the ball-lightning capital of the U.S."

"Thought that was East Moline."

"You fixin to be around for a while?"

Before the week was out, Merle had his first, and as it turned out only, ball-lightning job. It was haunting the upstairs of a farmhouse, persistent as a ghost anyway. He brought in all the equipment he could think of, copper grounding spikes, cabling, an insulated cage run up on the spot and hooked to a sal ammoniac battery to try and trap the critter in.

It moved around the rooms, up and down the hallway, and he watched carefully and patiently. He made no threatening moves. It reminded him of some wild night-animal that was being extra wary around humans. Little by little it came closer, till at last it was right up in his face, spinning slowly, and then they stayed like that awhile, in the small wood house, close, as if they were learning to trust each other. Out the curtained window, long grass blew just like every day. Chickens pecked around the yard and compared notes. Merle thought he could feel a little heat, and of course his hair was standing on end. He was of two minds about starting a conversation, since it didn't seem like this ball lightning could talk, or not the way a human does. Finally he took a chance and said, "Look, I'm not about to do you any harm, and I hope you'll return the favor."

To his surprise, the ball lightning replied, though not exactly out loud, "Sounds fair. My name is Skip, what's yours?"

"Pleasure, Skip, I'm Merle," said Merle.

"Just don't send me to ground, it's no fun there."

"O.K."

"And forget that cage."

"Deal."

Slowly they became sidekicks. From then on the ball lightning, or "Skip," was never far from Merle's side. Merle understood that he was now committed to a code of behavior as to whose details he was almost completely in the dark. Any small violation that displeased Skip could send the electrical phenomenon away, maybe for good, maybe not before first frying Merle in his tracks, Merle had no way to tell. It seemed to Dally at first he'd finally slipped his trolley in some fashion she could see no way back from.

"Other kids have sisters and brothers," she pointed out carefully. "What's this?"

"Sort of the same, only—"

"Different, yes but—"

"If you'd give him a chance—"

"'Him'? Sure, of course, you always wanted a boy."

"Foul ball, Dahlia. And you got no idea what I always wanted."

She had to admit Skip was an obliging little cuss, got their cookfires going in a snap, lit Merle's cigars for him, climbed inside the railroad lantern hanging off the back of the wagon when they had to travel in the dark. After a while, some nights, when she was up late reading, there'd be Skip up next to her, lighting the page, bobbing gently, as if reading along.

Until one night, during a fierce lightning storm out in Kansas someplace,

"They're calling me," Skip said. "I have to go."

"Your family," Dally guessed.

"Hard to explain."

"Just getting to like you, too. Any chance—"

"Of coming back? You get sort of gathered back into it all, 's how it works, so it wouldn't be me anymore, really."

"Guess I better just blow you a kiss, huh?"

In the months that followed, she found herself thinking more than she ever had about brothers and sisters, and whether Erlys and Zombini the Mysterious had had any more children, and how many, and what kind of a home situation that might be like to live in. It never occurred to her not to share these thoughts with her Pa.

"Here," Merle producing a pickling jar and dropping in two bits. "Now, every time I act like a damn fool, I'll drop in another one. Some point we'll have you the fare to wherever she is."

"No more'n a couple days, I calculate."

One of their last days in unbroken country, the wind was blowing in the high Indian grass, and her father said, "There's your gold, Dahlia, the real article." As usual, she threw him a speculative look, knowing by then roughly what an alchemist was, and that none of that shifty crew ever spoke straight—their words always meant something else, sometimes even because the "something else" really was beyond words, maybe in the way departed souls are beyond the world. She watched the invisible force at work among the million stalks tall as a horse and rider, flowing for miles under the autumn suns, greater than breath, than tidal lullabies, the necessary rhythms of a sea hidden far from any who would seek it.

They found themselves presently across the Colorado line, moving on into coal country, over toward the Sangre de Cristos—and they kept bearing westward until one day they were in the San Juans and Dally came walking in through some doorway or other and Merle looked up and saw this transformed young woman and knew it was only a matter of time now before she was out the chute and making life complicated for every rodeo clown that crossed her path.

AND AS IF that wasn't enough, one day in Denver Merle had happened to go in a cigar store and noticed there in a rack of magazines a *Dishforth's Illustrated Weekly* from back east and months ago, with an article in it about the celebrated magician Luca Zombini and his lovely bride, formerly his stage assistant, and their children and their warm and wonderful home in New York. There wasn't a hell of a lot of silver in Merle's pocket at the moment but he found enough to buy the magazine, forgot about the Cuban panatela he was fixing to smoke and settled for a three-cent domestic instead, lit it up and went outside to read the story. Most of the photographs, printed by what looked to be some new kind of gravure process, in a grain so fine that squint as he might he could find no evidence of screenwork, featured Erlys, surrounded by what looked like a dozen or so kids. He stood there in the corner of an alleyway, just out of a wind meaner than any he could remember since Chicago, full of ice crystals and hostile intent, and imagined it was telling him to wake up. He had no illusions about what could be done in the darkroom to enhance a human image, but Erlys, who had always been beautiful, was way beyond all that now. Years of bitterness about how little she had loved him sloughed away and Merle understood, miles down the line, the simple truth that Erlys had no more been "his" than the unfortunate Bert Snidell's, and that to persist in that belief anymore was to approach the gates of the laughing academy.

His next thought was, Dally better not see this, and then immediately, sure

Merle, good luck. And when he caught sight of her just about then coming up the street to find him, her hair in the wind a banner flown by the only force he had ever sworn allegiance to, he added, reluctantly, and it'll have to be me that tells her.

She was a sport about the whole thing, stepped careful around his feelings, read the whole article through, and though he never saw it again he understood she'd put the magazine away safely among her possessions. And from then on, like a charge slowly building up on a condenser plate, it was going to be only a matter of time before she was off to New York in a great irresistible surge of energy.

In Colorado they found a farm outbuilding, forgotten years earlier after the farm went under and the farmhouse burned down, leaving this overgrown shed, which Merle managed to fill up to the rafters with photographer's or, if you like, alchemist's stuff—containers ranging from banged-up vegetable cans to jugs and bottles holding liquids or powders of different colors, to gigantic glazed crocks, fifty gallons and more, that you might be able to lift empty but wouldn't necessarily want to, carefully bent glass tubes and copper coils running everyplace, a small forge over in one corner, an electric generator hooked to an old bicycle, battery cells dry and wet, electromagnets, burners, an annealing oven, a workbench littered with lenses, developing tanks, exposure meters, printing frames, magnesium flash-lamps, a gas-heated rotary burnishing machine, and other stuff Merle had almost forgotten he had. Berry vines crept in the crevices, and spiders adorned the sashwork with webs that when the early daylight was right could cause you to stand there just stupefied. Most folks who showed up thought he was running a still, Sheriff's boys liked to come by at odd hours, and sometimes, depending how the day was proceeding, Merle would bring out the heavier science talk, which hypnotized them into going away, disappointed as always. Other days the visitors were as likely to be polarized the other way, legally speaking.

"Couldn't help smellin what you're cookin in here. Back over the ridgeline and across the creek, 's a matter of fact. It's 'at there nitro, ain't it?"

Merle had seen enough back-country insanity by now to keep a piece of his eye on the shotgun under the table. "Almost. In the nitro family. Distant relative, the kind you pay to stay out of town."

"Run into it in my work, time to time."

"That'd be . . ."

"Sort of mine engineer. Not as well paid as that, but same idea. Little Hellkite works over by Telluride?"

He was on the abbreviated side, packing no firearms Merle could see, and got around to introducing himself as Webb Traverse.

Dally came in scowling, some encounter out in the brush having put her in a mood. "Why Father, I'd no idea there were guests. Let me go and see to the tea and biscuits. I'll only be a moment."

"But say," Webb giving her a wary look, "what was I thinkin here, you must be kind of occupied at the moment—"

"Bloviating, getting in the quota for the week. Stick around, I can see you have a legitimate curiosity." Merle beaming like a tent-meeting preacher at a promising sinner.

Webb nodded at a jug of store-bought quicksilver on the table. "See a lot of that up at the assay office." Carefully, as if expecting a countersign.

"The old-timers," Merle as well feeling his way, "used to believe that if you took away from mercury everything not essential, the liquid-metal business, the shine, the greasy feel, the weight, all the things that make it 'mercury,' see, you'd be left with this unearthly pure form of it the cupel ain't been made that can hold it, somethin that would make this stuff here seem dull as traprock. Philosophic Mercury, 's what they called it, which you won't find anyplace among the metals of metallurgy, the elements of the periodic table, the catalogues of industry, though many say it's really more of a figure of speech, like the famous Philosopher's Stone—supposed to really mean God, or the Secret of Happiness, or Union with the All, so forth. Chinese talk. But in fact these things, they've been out there all along, real material things, just not easy to get to, though alchemists keep tryin, it's what we do."

" 'Alchemist' work, that's what you're doin up here? Well but mercury now, there is this one interesting compound I keep runnin into, fulminate I believe it's called. . . ."

"Basic ingredient of the du Pont blasting cap, not to mention our everyday well-known .44 round. There's also silver fulminate, not quite the same thing as 'fulminating silver,' which'll blow up if you touch it with a feather. Fulminating gold, too, if your tastes happen to be more expensive."

"Hard to cook up?"

"Basically you take gold and ammonia, or silver and nitric acid, or mercury ore and fulminic acid, which is just good old prussic acid, the suicide's friend, patriarch of the cyanide family with an oxygen tacked on, and just as poisonous to breathe the fumes of."

Webb shook his head as if in dismay at the world and its ironies, but Merle had seen some unguarded-henhouse gleam in his eye. "You mean to say gold, silver, these shinin and wonderful metals, basis of all the world's economies, you go in a laboratory, fool with em a little, acid and so on, and you get a high explosive that all you got to do's sneeze at the wrong time and it's adios, muchachos?"

Merle, with a fair idea where this was going, nodded. "Sort of the *infernal* side to the story, you could say."

"Almost makes you think, if there's a Philosopher's Stone, there might not also be—"

"Careful," said Merle.

Webb peered at him, almost amused. "Somethin you fellas don't talk about?"

"Can't. Or that's the tradition."

"Easier that way, I guess."

"For who?"

Webb may have caught some wariness in his tone but went ahead. "Case a man ever did get tempted . . ."

"Hmmn. Who says men never do?"

"Wouldn't know." A moment of reflection, then, as if unable not to pursue the thought, "But if the one's a figure of speech for God and salvation and all that good stuff, why then the other—"

"All right. But do everybody a favor, say 'Anti-Stone.' It has another name, but we'd just get into trouble sayin it out loud. Sure, there's probably as many lost souls out lookin for that as regular alchemists. You think of the power you stand to gain, why the payoff's way too hard to resist."

"You're resistin, ain't you?"

"Am I."

"Nothin personal." Webb let his eyes slide around the little shed.

"This is temporary," Merle explained, "the mansion's got mice and our agents are out looking for a new one."

"And if a nightshirt for a elephant cost two cents," Dally put in, "we couldn't buy a baby bonnet for a piss ant."

"You know your way around quicksilver? Ever done any amalgamator work?"

"Time to time," Merle said carefully. "Leadville, couple other places, fun while it lasts, not sure it's much of a career."

"Little Hellkite they're lookin for an amalgamator, seein 's how with the altitude and breathin in those fumes, the current one's got it into his head he's the President."

"Oh. Of . . . ?"

"Put it this way, he has this nipper with a harmonica foll'n him around everwhere playin 'Hail to the Chief.' Out of tune. Goes off into long speeches nobody can understand, declared war on the state of Colorado last week.

Needs to be replaced and quick, but nobody wants to use force, bein that these cases are said to have superhuman powers."

"How true. That'd be up by Telluride, you say."

"Dandy little town, churches, schools, wholesome environment for the young lady."

Dally snorted. "Hell with electric lights is more like it, and school ain't exactly my glass of beer either, mister, if I wanted to waste my time I'd be lookin more for powder-monkey work, wouldn't I."

"Sure they can fix you up with that," said Webb. "But no need to mention my name around the Little Hellkite, O.K.? I ain't exactly no miner of the month up there right now."

"Sure thing," said Merle, "long as the alchemy part of it don't come up either."

The two men looked at each other, each pretty sure who the other was. "Mine engineers take a dim view," Merle pretended to explain, "old-time superstition from back in the Dark Ages, nowhere near's scientific as modern-day metallurgy." He paused, as if to catch his breath. "But if you look at the history, modern chemistry only starts coming in to replace alchemy around the same time capitalism really gets going. Strange, eh? What do you make of that?"

Webb nodded agreeably. "Maybe *capitalism* decided it didn't need the old magic anymore." An emphasis whose contempt was not meant to escape Merle's attention. "Why bother? Had their own magic, doin just fine, thanks, instead of turning lead into gold, they could take poor people's sweat and turn it into greenbacks, and save that lead for enforcement purposes."

"And the gold and silver . . ."

"More of a curse than they know, maybe. Sittin right there in the vault, just waitin for—"

"Don't say it!"

But Webb rode away with the grand possibility repeating in his mind like a heartbeat—the Anti-Stone. The Anti-Stone. Useful magic that might go one better on the widely admired Mexican principle of politics through chemistry. Not that life wasn't peculiar enough up in these mountains already, but here was this fast-talking quicksilver wizard in with fresh news that maybe, with luck, it was fixing to get even more so, and the day of commonwealth and promise, temples of Mammon all in smithereens—poor folks on the march, bigger than Coxey's Army, through the rubble—that much closer. Or he'd turn out as crazy as the present amalgamator at Little Hellkite—soon to be former amalgamator, because next time Webb was up that way, he found "the President" had been replaced, sure enough, by Merle Rideout.

Which was how Merle and Dally, after a long spell of drifting job to job, happened to roll to a stop in San Miguel County for the next couple of years—as it would turn out, some of the worst years in the history of those unhappy mountains. Lately Merle had been visited by a strange feeling that "photography" and "alchemy" were just two ways of getting at the same thing—redeeming light from the inertia of precious metals. And maybe his and Dally's long road out here was not the result of any idle drift but more of a secret imperative, like the force of gravity, from all the silver he'd been developing out into the pictures he'd been taking over these years—as if silver were alive, with a soul and a voice, and he'd been working for it as much as it for him.

July Fourth started hot and grew hotter, early light on the peaks descending, occupying, the few clouds bright and shapely and unpromising of rain, nitro beginning to ooze out of dynamite sticks well before the sun had cleared the ridge. Among stockmen and rodeo riders, today was known as "Cowboy's Christmas," but to Webb Traverse it was more like Dynamite's National Holiday, though you found many of the Catholic faith liked to argue that that ought to be the Fourth of December, feast of St. Barbara, patron saint of artillerymen, gunsmiths, and by not that big of a stretch, dynamiters too.

Everybody today, drovers and barkeeps, office clerks and hardcases, gentle elderly folks and openmouth reckless youth, would be seized sooner or later by the dynamitic mania prevailing. They would take little fractions of a stick, attach cap and fuse, light them up and throw them at each other, drop it in reservoirs and have all-day fish fries, blast picturesque patterns in the landscape that'd be all but gone next day, put it lit into empty beer barrels to be rolled down mountainsides, and take bets on how close to town before it all blew to bits—a perfect day all round for some of that good Propaganda of the Deed stuff, which would just blend right in with all the other percussion.

Webb staggered up out of his bedroll after one of those nights when he did not so much sleep as become intermittently conscious of time. Already warm-up blasts could be heard up and down the valley. Today's would be a fairly routine job, and Webb was looking forward to a little saloon time at the end of it. Zarzuela was out by the fence waiting, having known Webb long enough to have an idea that whatever the day held in store, it would include explosion, which the colt was used to and even looked forward to.

Webb rode up the valley and then up over Red Mountain Pass, cicadas going by like prolonged ricochets. Pausing after a while for water, he ran into a skinner in gauntlets and chaps and a hat with the brim turned down, with his dog and an unroped train of little burros, known hereabouts as "Rocky Mountain canaries." The winsome animals, packed with boxes of dynamite, detonator caps, and fuse, were browsing around eating wildflowers. Webb felt a shortness of breath and a wandering in his head that had little to do with the altitude. Glory, could he smell that nitro. No Chinaman and his opium could be any more intimate than Webb and the delicately poised chemistry there. He let his horse have some water, but in the unsettling presence of nasal desire, unwilling to trust his own voice too far, stayed up in the saddle, straight-faced and yearning. The burro-puncher was just as happy to do no more than nod, preferring to save his voice for his string. After Webb had gone on, the dog stood and barked for a while, not warning or angry, just being professional.

Veikko was waiting as they'd arranged by a waste pile from the old Eclipse Union mine. Webb, who could judge from a hundred yards away how crazy the Finn was apt to be feeling on a given day, noticed a two-gallon canteen sure to be full of that home-brewed potato spirits they all tended to go for, hung from the pommel of his saddle. There also seemed to be flames issuing out of his head, but Webb put that down to some trick of the light. From the look on his face, Webb could see signs of an oncoming dynamite headache after hanging around too long snorting nitro fumes.

"You're late, Brother Traverse."

"Rather be at a picnic, myself," said Webb.

"I'm in a really bad mood."

"What's that got to do with me?"

"You are what usually makes it worse."

They had some such exchange once or twice a week. Helped them get along, annoyance, for both of them, working as a social lubricant.

Veikko was a veteran of the Cour d'Alene bullpens and the strike in Cripple Creek for an eight-hour day. He had quickly become known to all levels of the law up here, being a particular favorite of state militia, who liked to see how much pounding he could take. Finally he'd been picked up in a general sweep and with about two dozen other union miners sealed in a side-door pullman and taken south on the Denver & Rio Grande across the invisible border into New Mexico. Guardsmen sat up top with machine guns, and the prisoners had to pretty much piss where they could, sometimes, in the dark, on each other. In the middle of the night, deep in the southern San Juans, the train came to a halt, there was metallic thumping overhead, the door slid open. "End of the line for you all," called an unfriendly voice, and few there were ready to hear it in any but the worst way. But they were only going to be left to walk, their boots in a further act of meanness taken away, and told to stay out of Colorado unless they wanted to leave it next time in a box. It turned out they were near an Apache reservation, and the Indians were kind enough to take Veikko and a few others in for a while, not to mention share a bottomless supply of cactus beer. They thought it was funny that white men should act quite so disagreeably toward other whites, treating them indeed almost as if they were Indians, some of them already believing that Colorado, because of its shape, had actually been created as a reservation for whites. Somebody brought out an old geography schoolbook with a map of the state in it, including their own reservation boundaries, which showed Colorado as a rectangle, seven degrees of longitude wide by four degrees of latitude high—four straight lines on paper made up the borders Veikko had been forbidden to cross—not like there were rivers or ridgelines where the militia might lie in wait to shoot at him the minute he stepped over—from which he reasoned that, if exile from Colorado was that abstract, then as long as he stayed off the roads, he could come back into the state anytime and just keep soldiering on same as before.

Mostly with Veikko you had your choice of two topics, techniques of detonation or Veikko's distant country and its beleaguered constitution, Webb never having seen him raise a glass, for example, that wasn't dedicated to the fall of the Russian Tsar and his evil viceroy General Bobrikoff. But sometimes Veikko went on and got philosophical. He'd never seen much difference between the Tsar's regime and American capitalism. To struggle against one, he figured, was to struggle against the other. Sort of this world-wide outlook. "Was a little worse for us, maybe, coming to U.S.A. after hearing so much about 'land of the free.'" Thinking he'd escaped something, only to find life out here just as mean and cold, same wealth without conscience, same poor people in misery, army and police free as wolves to commit cruelties on behalf of the bosses, bosses ready to do anything to protect what they had stolen. The main difference he could see was that the Russian aristocracy, after centuries of believing in nothing but its own entitlement, had grown weak, neuræsthenic. "But American aristocracy is not even a century old, in peak of fighting condition, strong from efforts it took to acquire its wealth, more of a challenge. Good enemy."

"You think they're too strong for the workers?"

At which Veikko's eyes would grow pale and illuminated from within, his voice issuing from an abundant and unkempt beard which suggested even on his calmest days an insane fanaticism. "We are their strength, without us they are impotent, we are they," and so forth. Webb had learned that if you stayed quiet and just waited, these spells passed, and pretty soon the Finn would be back to his usual self, stolid as ever, reaching sociably for the vodka.

At the moment, however, Webb noticed that Veikko had been sitting reading over and over to himself a withered postcard from Finland, a troubled look on his face, a slow flush gathering around his eyes.

"Look. These aren't real stamps here," Veikko said. "They are pictures of stamps. The Russians no longer allow Finnish stamps, we have to use Russian ones. These postmarks? They're not real either. Pictures of postmarks. This one, August fourteen, 1900, was the last day we could use our own stamps for overseas mail."

"So this is a postcard with a picture of what a postcard used to look like before the Russians. That's what '*Minneskort*' means?"

"Memory card. A memory of a memory." It was a card from his sister back in Finland. "Nothing in particular. They censor everything. Nothing that would get anybody in trouble. Family news. My crazy family." He gestured toward Webb with the vodka canteen.

"I'll wait."

"I won't."

Veikko, being the sort of blaster who likes to watch it happen, had brought along an oak magneto box and a big spool of wire, whereas Webb, more circumspect and preferring to be well out of the area, tended to go for the two-dollar Ingersoll or time-delay method. Their target was a railroad bridge across a little canyon, on a spur between the main line and Relámpagos, a mining town up northeast of Silverton. Fairly straightforward, four wood trestles of different heights holding up some iron Fink trusses. Webb and Veikko got into the usual argument about whether to blast the 'sucker now or wait till a train came. "You know how owners are," Veikko said, "lazy sons of bitches can't be bothered to saddle up, they take trains wherever they go. We blow train, maybe get a couple of them with it."

"I ain't about to sit out here all day waitin for some train that likely won't be runnin anyhow, it bein a three-day holiday."

"Aitisi nai poroja," replied Veikko, a pleasantry long grown routine, meaning, "Your mother fucks reindeer."

The tricky patch, it had seemed to Webb for a while now, came in choosing the targets, it being hard enough just to find time to think any of it through, under the daily burdens of duty and hard labor and, more often than you'd think, grief. Lord knew that owners and mine managers deserved to be blown up, except that they had learned to keep extra protection around them—not that going after their property, like factories or mines, was that much better of an idea, for, given the nature of corporate greed, those places would usually be working three shifts, with the folks most likely to end up dying being miners, including children working as nippers and swampers—the same folks who die when the army comes charging in. Not that any owner ever cared rat shit about the lives of workers, of course, except to define them as Innocent Victims in whose name uniformed goons could then go out and hunt down the Monsters That Did the Deed.

And even worse, the sort of thing that can get a true bomber mighty irritated, some of these explosions, the more deadly of them, in fact, were really set off to begin with not by Anarchists but by the owners themselves. Imagine that. Here was nitro, the medium of truth, being used by these criminal bastards to tell their lies with. Damn. The first time Webb saw hard proof of this going on, he felt like a kid about to cry. That the world should know so little about what was good for it.

Which left precious few targets except for the railroad. Fair enough, to Webb's way of thinking, for the railroad had always been the enemy, going back generations. Farmers, stockmen, buffalo-hunting Indians, track-laying Chinamen, passengers in train wrecks, whoever you were out here, sooner or later you had some bad history with the railroad. He had worked as a section hand just enough over the years to at least know where to spot the charges so they'd do the most good.

They took cord and bundled the sticks together. Webb was far more partial to gelatin, which let you shape the charge some and direct the blast better, but that made sense only in the cooler weather. Keeping an eye out for snakes, they worked their way along the wash, placing the charges in the shade when they could and piling rocks and dirt around. The day was quiet, windless. A redtail hawk hung up there and seemed to be looking at them, which would put them in the same category as field rodents. Which in turn would put the hawk in the same category as a mine manager. . . . Webb shook his head irritably. He did not much admire himself when he drifted off this way. It was always minute to minute, step to step, and he had seen too many good brothers and sisters end up in the dirt or in the fathomless dark at the bottom of some shaft as the price of inattention. Fact, if he'd known what it cost, the total cost, spread over a lifetime, he wondered sometimes if he would've ever signed on.

Webb's trajectory toward the communion of toil which had claimed his life had begun right out in the middle of Cripple Creek, blooming in those days like a flower of poisonous delight among its spoil heaps, cribs, parlor houses and gambling saloons. It was a time in Cripple and Victor, Leadville and Creede, when men were finding their way to the unblastable seams of their own secret natures, learning the true names of desire, which spoken, so they dreamed, would open the way through the mountains to all that had been denied them. In the broken and soon-enough-interrupted dreams close to dawn in particular, Webb would find himself standing at some divide, facing west into a great flow of promise, something like wind, something like light, free of the damaged hopes and pestilent smoke east of here—sacrificial smoke, maybe, but not ascending to Heaven, only high enough to be breathed in, to sicken and cut short countless lives, to change the color of the daylight and deny to walkers of the night the stars they remembered from younger times. He would wake to the day and its dread. The trail back to that high place and the luminous promise did not run by way of Cripple, though Cripple would have to serve, hopes corroded to fragments—overnight whiskey, daughters of slaves, rigged faro games, the ladies who work on the line.

One night in Shorty's Billiard Saloon, some poolplayer had propelled his cue ball on the break perhaps too forcefully and with scarcely any draw onto it into the triangle of shiny balls, which happened to be made of some newly patented variety of celluloid. Upon being struck, the first ball exploded, initiating a chain of similar explosions across the table. Mistaking these for gunshots, several among the clientele drew their pistols and began, with some absence of thought, to contribute in their own ways to the commotion. "Nice break," somebody was heard to say before the noise got too loud. Webb, frozen in terror, delayed diving for cover until it was all over, realizing after a while that he had been standing in a roomful of flying lead without being hit once. How could this be? He found himself in the street wandering hatless and confused, colliding presently with the Reverend Moss Gatlin, who was stumbling down a long flight of wood stairs from a sojourn up at Fleurette's Cloudtop Retreat, not exactly at the moment looking for uninstructed souls, which didn't keep Webb, in a torrent of speech, from telling the Rev all about his miraculous escape. "Brother, we are stripes and solids on the pool table of earthly existence," the Rev explained, "and God and his angels are the sharpers who keep us ever in motion." Instead of dismissing this for the offhanded preacherly drivel it almost certainly was, Webb, in what you'd have to call a state of heightened receptivity, stood there as if professionally sapped for another quarter of an hour after the Rev had moved on, ignored by the pernicious bustle of Myers Street, and the following Sunday could be observed in the back room of the faro establishment where Reverend Gatlin preached his ministry, listening as if much, maybe all, depended on it, to the sermon, which happened to take as its text Matthew 4:18 and 19, "And Jesus, walking by the Sea of Galilee, saw two brethren, Simon called Peter, and Andrew his brother, casting a net into the sea: for they were fishers.

"And he saith unto them, Follow me, and I will make you fishers of men."

"And Jesus," elaborated Moss, "walking out by some American lake, some reservoir in the mountains—here's Billy and his brother Pete, casting quarter-sticks of dynamite into the lake, for they are dynamiters—and harvesting whatever floats to the surface. What does Jesus think of this, and what does he say unto them? What will he make them fishers of?

"For dynamite is both the miner's curse, the outward and audible sign of his enslavement to mineral extraction, and the American working man's equalizer, his agent of deliverance, if he would only dare to use it. . . . Every time a stick goes off in the service of the owners, a blast convertible at the end of some chain of accountancy to dollar sums no miner ever saw, there will have to be a corresponding entry on the other side of God's ledger, convertible to human freedom no owner is willing to grant.

"You've heard the suggestion that there are no innocent bourgeoisie. One of those French Anarchists, some say Emile Henry as he was going to the guillotine, others say Vaillant when they tried him for bombing the Chamber of Deputies. Answering the question, how can anyone set off a bomb that will take innocent lives?"

"Long fuse," somebody hollered helpfully.

"Easier with a timer!"

"Think about it," when the remarks had faded some, "like Original Sin, only with exceptions. Being born into this don't automatically make you innocent. But when you reach a point in your life where you understand who is fucking who—beg pardon, Lord—who's taking it and who's not, that's when you're obliged to choose how much you'll go along with. If you are not devoting every breath of every day waking and sleeping to destroying those who slaughter the innocent as easy as signing a check, then how innocent are you willing to call yourself? It must be negotiated with the day, from those absolute terms."

It would have been almost like being born again, except that Webb had never been particularly religious, nor had any of his family, an old ridegerunning clan from southern Pennsylvania, close to the Mason-Dixon. The Civil War, which ate up a good part of Webb's boyhood, split the family as well, so that shortly before it was over, he found himself in the back of a wagon heading west, about the same time other Traverse Irreconcilables were choosing to head for Mexico. But, hell—same thing.

Across the Ohio in a hill town whose name he soon couldn't remember, there was a dark-haired girl Webb's age whose name, Teresa, he would never forget. They were out walking the wagon ruts, just beyond a fenceline the hills went rushing away, the sky was clouded over, it might've been between rain showers, and young Webb was all ready to unburden his heart, which like the sky was about to reveal something beyond itself. He almost did tell her. They both seemed to see it coming, and later, heading west, he carried with him that silence that had stretched on between them until there was no point anymore. He might have stayed, otherwise, snuck off from the wagons, headed back to her. She might have found a way to come after him, too, but that was a dream, really, he didn't know, would never know, how she felt.

It took maybe nine or ten years more of westward drift, over the rolling prairie, through the cheatgrass, the sage grouse exploding skyward, the dread silences when skies grow black in the middle of all that country, outracing cyclones and rangefires, switchbacking up the eastern slope of the Rockies through meadows of mule-ear and sneezeweed, on over the great torn crestline, to be delivered at last into these unholy mountains Webb grew to manhood in and had not left since, into whose depths he had ventured after silver and gold, up on whose heights he had struggled, always, for breath.

By that time both his parents were gone, and he was left with not much more than his Uncle Fletcher's old twelve-cylinder Confederate Colt, whose brasswork he took care to keep shined, for whose sake he'd put up with remarks like "Thing's bigger'n you are, Webbie," though he kept practicing whenever he could, and the day did come finally when he found he was hitting more than half of any given row of bean cans with it.

In Leadville, the year the gaslight went in, he saw Mayva Dash, dancing up on top of the bar of Pap Wyman's Saloon in high boots and jet beads while freightmen, roustabouts, and grease-bearded ten-dayers hollered for every kick and twirl, even to taking their cigars out of their mouths before they did.

"Yes children, strange to tell, your Ma was a saloon girl when first we met."

"You're giving em the wrong idea," she pretended to object. "I always worked for myself."

"You were paying off that bartender."

"We all were."

"Way he saw it, that meant working for him."

"He tell you that?"

"Not Adolph. But the other one, Ernst?"

"With the real weedy mustache, talked sort of foreign?"

"That's him."

"Just lonely. Thought we 's all gonna be his concubines, which was a common arrangement, accordin to him, wherever that was he was from."

The town, only recently founded, was already being turned black with slag, up every alley all the way out into open country you saw it towering in great poisoned mountains. Not a place where you'd expect romance to blossom, but next thing either of them knew, they were hitched and living up East Fifth in Finntown among the waste piles. One night just off shift, Webb heard a tremendous uproar in the narrow alley known as St. Louis Avenue, and there was Veikko Rautavaara, carefully holding a vodka jug in one hand while battling a number of camp guards with the other. For a weedy little customer, Webb could be formidable in these affairs, though by the time he got into it, most of the hard work was done, Veikko bleeding but solid on his feet and the hirelings either flat on the pavement or limping away. When Webb brought him back to the house, Mayva might have raised an eyebrow. "Nice to see this married life ain't slowing you down, Honey."

She kept her job at Pap Wyman's till she was sure Reef was on the way. The kids were all silver-boom babies, up and running just in time for Repeal. "Been dealt a full house here," Webb liked to say, "Jacks and Queens—'less you count your Ma as the Ace o' Spades."

"Death card," she'd mutter, "thanks a lot."

"But Dearest," Webb in all innocence, "I meant it as a compliment!"

They had maybe a year or two where it wasn't too desperate. Webb took them all to Denver and bought Mayva a fancy briar pipe to replace the beat-up old corncob she usually smoked. They ate ice cream at a soda fountain. They went to Colorado Springs and stayed at the Antlers Hotel and took the cog railway up Pike's Peak.

Though maybe for a couple of years off and on with the railroad Webb might've seen some ray of daylight, he always ended up back down some hole in some mountain, mucking, timbering, whatever he could get. Leadville, thinking itself God's own beneficiary when the old lode was rediscovered in '92, got pretty much done in by Repeal, and Creede the same, sucker-punched right after the big week-long wingding on the occasion of Bob Ford's funeral. The railroad towns, Durango, Grand Junction, Montrose, and them, were pretty stodgy by comparison, what Webb mostly remembered being the sunlight. Telluride was in the nature of an outing to a depraved amusement resort, whose electric lighting at night in its extreme and unmerciful whiteness produced a dream-silvered rogues' district of non-stop poker games, erotic practices in back-lot shanties, Chinese opium dens most of the Chinese in town had the sense to stay away from, mad foreigners screaming in tongues apt to come skiing down the slopes in the dark with demolition in mind.

After 1893, after the whole nation, one way or another, had been put through a tiresome moral exercise over repeal of the Silver Act, ending with the Gold Standard reclaiming its ancient tyranny, it was slow times for a while, and Webb and the family moved around a lot, down to Huerfano County for a while to dig coal, while Ed Farr was still sheriff, before he got shot by train robbers over near Cimarron, and Webb would come home black-faced and unrecognizable enough that the kids either fell down laughing or ran away screaming. Later, in Montrose, they all lived in some little part-tent, part-shed on the lot out back of a boarding house that was hardly more than a shack itself, Lake helping with chores, Reef and Frank bringing potato sacks from the wagon, sometimes pulling third-shift scullery duty or, as the gold camps began to pick up some of the slack, back down into one or another of those mountainside workings, Reef, before he got out of the house for good, working a spell same shift as his father, picking up the loose ore and loading it on to the cars and pushing them to the hoist, over and over. He got to hate it pretty quick, and Webb, seeing his point, never held it against him. When Webb and the boys were on different shifts, Mayva had nothing but round-the-clock work, cooking Cornish pasties by the dozens for them to take down in the hole—she'd learned from the Cornish wives in Jacktown to put apple slices in along with the meat and potatoes. Then something else hot to feed each of them again when they come back up, hungrier than bears.

By the time Webb had worked his way from hoistman through singlejacker to assistant foreman, he was intimate with the deepest arcana of dynamite. Or acted like he was. Even on his own time, he loved to play with that miserable stuff, it drove Mayva just damn crazy, but nothing she ever said had any effect, he was always out in some high meadow or back of some waste dump, crouched down behind a rock with that fox's gleam in his eye, trembling, waiting for one of his old explosions. When he thought they were the right age, he brought the children into it one by one, each taking to it different. No way to tell from just watching of course who might grow up into a decent bomber. Fact, Webb wasn't sure he wanted to let any of them all the way in.

Reef didn't say much, but his eyes got a squint into them that when you saw it, you learned to take care. Frank was more curious, in a kid-engineer kind of way, trying to blow up every form of terrain he could talk Webb around to, just to see if there was a general rule to any of it. When it came little Kit's turn, he already had it in his mind from a carnival show down at Olathe, where he'd seen a dynamited carny jump up out of the blast good as new, that you could blow up anybody over and over and the worst they'd ever get'd be comically inconvenienced, so after one lesson he was set to run out and dynamite schoolteachers, shift bosses, storekeepers, anybody happened to offend him on a particular day, and it took extra vigilance all around to keep him out of Webb's string of personal blasting sheds. Lake, bless her heart, did not make faces, or plug her ears, or sigh in boredom, or anything else the boys had assumed she'd do. She picked up the process right away, first time touching off a fine high-radius concussion, creating several tons of traprock . . . maybe smiling some to herself, the way she had begun to do.

The question of where his loyalties should—as against "did"—lie had been gnawing at Webb a good part of his life since Shorty's Billiard Saloon in Cripple, one he never was able to get sorted out, really. If there'd only been the simple luxury of time, maybe to do nothing but put his feet up on some wood porchrail, roll a cigarette, gaze at the hills, let the breezes slide over him—sure—but as it was, he never saw a minute that didn't belong to somebody else. Any discussion of deeper topics such as what to keep hammering at, what to let go, how much he owed who, had to be done on the run, with people he hoped were not going to fink him out.

"Not so sure sometimes I wouldn't be better off without all these family obligations," he admitted once to Reverend Moss, who, though lacking the authority to remit the sins of his flock of dynamiters, made up for that with a bottomless appetite for listening to complaints. "Just to be workin solo," Webb muttered, "some room to move."

"Maybe not." And the Rev set out his theory and practice of resistance to power. "You live any kind of a covert life at all, and they are going to come after you. They hate loners. They can smell it. Best disguise is no disguise. You must belong to this everyday world—be in it, be of it. A man like you, with a wife, children—last ones they tend to suspect, too much to lose, no one could be that hard of a hardcase, they think, no one is willing to risk losing that."

"Well, they'd be right, I'm not."

He shrugged. "Then better be no more than what you seem."

"But I can't just—"

The Rev, who hardly ever so much as smiled, was close to it now. "No, you can't." He nodded. "And God bless you for it, class brother."

"Mind telling me when I'm supposed to sleep?"

"Sleep? is when you sleep. That all you're worried about?"

"Only that I wouldn't want it out where anybody can get to me—I'd sure need a safe bedroll someplace."

"Someplace secret. But there's 'at word again—you can't be having too many them secrets, can you, if you're trying to look normal."

And yet the Normal World of Colorado, how safe was that to be relying on, with death around every corner, when all could be gone in an uncaught breath, quick as an avalanche? Not as if the Rev wanted Heaven, he'd have been content with someplace the men didn't have to be set on each other like dogs in a dogfight for lung-destroying jobs that paid at best $3-blessed-.50 a day—there had to be a living wage and some right to organize, because alone a man was a mule dropping on the edge of life's mountain trail, ready to be either squashed flat or kicked into the void.

Turned out the Rev was yet another casualty of the Rebellion. "So this is how we found our dear lost South again, maybe not exactly the redemption we had in mind. Instead of the old plantation, this time it was likely to be a silver camp, and the Negro slaves turned out to be us. Owners found they could work us the same way, if anything with even less mercy, they ridiculed and feared us as much as our folks done the slaves a generation before—the big difference being if we should run away, they sure 's hell wouldn't come chasing after us, no fugitive laws for them, they'd just say fine, good riddance, there's always more where they come from that'll work cheaper. . . ."

"That's wicked, Rev."

"Maybe, but we got just what we deserved."

The atmosphere in Colorado those days had become so poisoned that the owners were ready to believe anything about anybody. They hired what they called "detectives," who started keeping dossiers on persons of interest. The practice quickly became commonplace. As bureaucratic technique went, it wasn't that much of a radical step even the first time, and sooner than anybody would've thought, it became routine and all but invisible.

Webb was presently thus recorded, though what on the face of it was so dangerous about him, really? No more than a rank-and-filer in the Western Federation of Miners—but maybe those anarchistic bastards were hiding their records. He might be conspiring *in secret.* Midnight oaths, invisible ink. Wouldn't be the first or only. And he seemed to move around a lot, too much for a family man, you'd think, always had money too, not a lot, but more than you'd expect from somebody working at miners' wages . . . good worker, ain't like that he kept getting fired, no, it was always him 's the one quitting, moving on camp to camp, and somehow always bringing trouble with him. Well, not always. But how many times did it take to stop being a coincidence and start being a pattern?

So they started poking. Just little things. Advisements from the shift boss. Summonses to interviews up at the office. Humiliation routines over short weight or docked hours. Saloon ejections and tabs abruptly discontinued. Assignment to less hopeful, even dangerous rockfaces and tunnels. The kids grew up seeing Webb thrown out of places, more and more as time went on, often being right there with him, Frank especially, when it happened. Picking up his hat for him, helping him get vertical. Long as he knew there was an audience, Webb tried to make it look as funny as he could.

"Why do they do that, Pa?"

"Oh . . . maybe some educational point to it. You been keeping score like I asked, on who it is 't's doin it?"

"Stores, saloons, eating houses, mostly."

"Names, faces?" And they'd tell him what they could remember. "And you notice how that some are makin up these fancy excuses, and others are just sayin get the hell out?"

"Yeah but—"

"Well, it's deservin of your close attention, children. Varieties of hypocrite, see. Like learning the different kinds of poison plants out here, some'll kill the stock, some'll kill you, but use em right and some, believe it or not, will cure you instead. Nothing vegetable or human that ain't of some use, 's all I'm sayin. Except mine owners, maybe, and their got-damned finks."

He was trying to pass on what he thought they should know, when he had a minute, though there was never the time. "Here. The most precious thing I own." He took his union card from his wallet and showed them, one by one. "These words right here"—pointing to the slogan on the back of the card—"is what it all comes down to, you won't hear it in school, maybe the Gettysburg Address, Declaration of Independence and so forth, but if you learn nothing else, learn this by heart, what it says here—'Labor produces all wealth. Wealth belongs to the producer thereof.' Straight talk. No double-talking you like the plutes do, 'cause with them what you always have to be listening for is the opposite of what they say. 'Freedom,' then's the time to watch your back in particular—start telling you how free you are, somethin's up, next thing you know the gates have slammed shut and there's the Captain givin you them looks. 'Reform'? More new snouts at the trough. 'Compassion' means the population of starving, homeless, and dead is about to take another jump. So forth. Why, you could write a whole foreign phrase book just on what Republicans have to say."

Frank had always taken Webb for what he appeared to be—an honest, dedicated miner, exploited to the last, who never got but a fraction of what his labor was worth. He had resolved himself pretty early on to do better, maybe someday get licensed as an engineer, able to call at least a few more of his own shots, at least not have to work quite as unremittingly. He could find nothing wrong with this approach, and Webb couldn't quite summon up the heart to argue with him.

Reef, on the other hand, had seen pretty early through that amiable pose of working-stiff family man and down into the anger behind it, which he was no stranger to himself, wishing, as the insults multiplied, wishing desperately, for the ability to destroy, purely through the force of his desire, to point or stare furiously enough at any of these owners' creatures to make them go up in bright, preferably loud, bursts of flame. Somehow he convinced himself that Webb possessed, if not exactly this power of instant justice, at least a secret life, in which, when night fell, he could put on, say, a trick hat and duster which would make him invisible, and take to the trails, grim and focused, to do the people's work, if not God's, the two forces according to Reverend Gatlin having the same voice. Or even some supernormal power, such as multiplying himself so he could be in several places at once. . . . But Reef couldn't figure a way to bring any of it up with Webb. He would have begged to work as his father's apprentice and sidekick, any kind of drudgery necessary, but Webb was immune—sometimes, indeed, pretty harshly so. "Don't beg, you hear me? Don't any of you ever, fucking, beg, me or nobody, for nothin." A timely cussword to drive in the lesson being part of Webb's theory of education. But standing even more in the way of Reef ever getting to be his Pop's midnight compadre was his own reluctance to trigger one of those towering conniption fits allowed as a privilege to fathers only, which he could recognize sometimes as a form of bad playacting, deployed for convenience, but, knowing the true depths of Webb's rage, was still not about to put himself in the way of. So he settled instead for what confidences might accidentally leak through now and then.

"There is a master list," Webb announced one day, "in Washington, D.C., of everybody they think is up to no good, maintained by the U.S. Secret Service."

"Thought those boys 's there to keep the President from gettin shot," Reef said.

"By law, that and go after counterfeiters. But there's no law says they can't loan their agents out to anybody who needs well, say a secret type of individual. So these federal gumshoes're really all over the place, and noplace thicker on the slopes than Colorado."

"Come on, Pop, where are we, Russia?"

"Say, open up em peepers 'fore you walk over a cliff someplace."

It was more than the usual teasing around. Webb was worried, and Reef guessed it was about being on that list. When Webb didn't smile, which more and more got to be days on end, he looked years older. Of course, when he did smile, the pointed ears, nose, and chin, the furrows from here to there, the cheerily snarled eyebrows, all revealed a foxlike charm that extended to confidences kept safe, advice offered, rounds stood without hesitation. But always, Reef noted, that part withheld that you felt you couldn't get to. The other Webb who rode by night, invisible. He wanted to say, don't it get you crazy, Pop, don't you want to just kill some of em, and keep on killing, and how can everybody out here just allow em to get away with what they do? He started hanging around with known recreational blasters his age and a little older, whose ideas of amusement included loitering out by the tailings, drinking jug whiskey, and tossing among themselves a lit stick of dynamite, timing it all so as not to be too close when it went off.

Alarmed, Mayva brought up the practice with Webb, who only shrugged. "Just good old dynamite rounders, every sheriff has at least a dozen in his county. Reef knows enough to be careful with the stuff, I trust him."

"Just to set my own mind at rest, though—"

"Sure, I'll have a word if you like."

He caught up with Reef out by one of the lesser avalanche sites near Ouray, just sitting there as if he was waiting for something. "Hear you and Otis and them've discovered Holdin-the-Bag. Fun ain't it?"

"So far." Reef's grin was so fake even Webb could see it.

"And it don't scare you, son?"

"No. Some. Not enough, maybe," with one of those insane adolescent laughs at his own stumbling tongue.

"It scares *me.*"

"Oh, sure it does." He looked at his father, waiting for the rest of the joke. Webb understood that regardless of how seriously Reef might someday come to take the subject, he himself would never find a way to take dynamite as lightly as his son did. He gazed at Reef in almost unconcealed envy, failing completely to recognize the darker thing, the desire, the desperate need to create a radius of annihilation that, if it could not include the ones who deserved it, might as well include himself.

Webb was no professor, he could only doggedly repeat to his kids the same old lessons, point to the same obvious injustices, hope some of it managed to sprout, and just continue with his own work all dummied up, poker-faced and unaccompanied, letting his anger build a head of pressure till it was ready to do some useful work. If dynamite was what it took, well, so be it—and if it took growing into a stranger to those kids and looking like some kind of screaming fool whenever he did show up at home, and then someday sooner or later losing them, their clean young gazes, their love and trust, the unquestioning way they spoke his name, all that there is to break a father's heart, well, children grow up, and that would have to be reckoned into the price, too, along with jail time, bullpens, beatings, lockouts, and the rest. The way it happens. Webb would have to set aside his feelings, not just the sentimental baby stuff but the terrible real ballooning of emptiness at the core of his body when he paused to consider all that losing them would mean. When he did get to pause. Good kids, too. All he knew how to do was smash around the place, helpless, and risk them thinking it was aimed at them, no counting on Mayva to get him out of it, being she was the target, too, often as not, and no way he knew of to tell any of them otherwise. Not that they'd believe it if he did. Not, after too short a while, not anymore.

"WE READY?"

Veikko shrugged, reaching for the plunger handle on the magneto box.

"Let's do 'er."

Four closely set blasts, cracks in the fabric of air and time, merciless, bone-strumming. Breathing seemed beside the point. Rising dirt-yellow clouds full of wood splinters, no wind to blow them anyplace. Track and trusswork went sagging into the dust-choked arroyo.

Webb and Veikko watched across a meadow of larkspur and Indian paint-brush, and behind them a little creek rushed down the hillside. "Seen worse," Webb nodded after a while.

"Was beautiful! what do you want, end of the world?"

"Sufficient unto the day," Webb shrugged. "Course."

Veikko was pouring vodka. "Happy Fourth of July, Webb."

For years after, there were tales told in Colorado of the amazing, world-reversing night of Fourth of July Eve 1899. Next day'd be full of rodeos, marching bands, and dynamite explosions—but that night there was man-made lightning, horses gone crazy for miles out into the prairie, electricity flooding up through the iron of their shoes, shoes that when they finally came off and got saved to use for cowboy-quoits, including important picnic tourneys from Fruita to Cheyenne Wells, why they would fly directly and stick on to the spike in the ground, or to anything else nearby made of iron or steel, that's when they weren't collecting souvenirs on their way through the air—gunmen's guns came right up out of their holsters and buck knives out from under pants legs, keys to traveling ladies' hotel rooms and office safes, miners' tags, fence-nails, hairpins, all seeking the magnetic memory of that long-ago visit. Veterans of the Rebellion fixing to march in parades were unable to get to sleep, metallic elements had so got to humming through their bloodmaps. Children who drank the milk from the dairy cows who grazed nearby were found leaning against telegraph poles listening to the traffic speeding by through the wires above their heads, or going off to work in stockbrokers' offices where, unsymmetrically intimate with the daily flow of prices, they were able to amass fortunes before anyone noticed.

Young Kit Traverse happened to be in on the high-voltage experiment that had caused it all, working as a matter of fact that summer in Colorado Springs, for Dr. Tesla himself. By now Kit thought of himself as a Vectorist, having arrived at that mathematical persuasion not by any abstract route but, as most had up till then, by way of the Electricity, and its practical introduction, during his own early years, at an increasingly hectic clip, into lives previously innocent of it.

In those days, he was a roving electrical apprentice—"Could call me a *circuit* rider, I guess"—journeying one mountain valley to the next, looking to keep from ever going down into another mine, taking any job that happened to be open, long as it was something, anything, to do with electricity. Electricity was all the go then in southwest Colorado, nearly every stream intersecting sooner or later with some small private electrical plant for running mine or factory machinery or lighting up towns—basically a turbine generator located underneath a waterfall, which given the altitudes out here could be pretty near anyplace a fellow might want to look. Kit was big enough for his age, and foremen were willing to go along with whatever age he filled in on the forms, when there were forms at all.

Something, some devotedness or need that in those days among less credentialed working stiffs was finding its expression in union loyalty, disposed slightly older kid engineering students, out here usually for the summer from back east, Cornell, Yale, so forth, to help Kit out, to lend him books he needed, Maxwell's *Treatise on Electricity and Magnetism* of 1873, Heaviside's more recent *Electromagnetic Theory* (1893), and so forth. Once Kit had the knack of the notation, which didn't take long, he was off to the races.

It could have been a religion, for all he knew—here was the god of Current, bearing light, promising death to the falsely observant, here were Scripture and commandments and liturgy, all in this priestly Vectorial language whose texts he had to get his head around as they came, study when he ought to be sleeping, by miners' candles or coal-oil light and often enough by the actual incandescence from the same electrical mystery he was studying, growing hit-or-miss into an understanding, out of his hankering in the course of a day's work just to *see* in some way—directly, without equations, the way Faraday had, according to the folklore anyway—what was going on inside the circuits he was obliged to work with. Which seemed fair enough. After a while, now and then, he found it was him explaining things to the collegiate hotshots—not everything, of course, they knew everything—but maybe a detail here and there, manipulating vector symbols that stood for unseen—though easily enough and sometimes dangerously felt—electrical events being a chore not too different when you came to it from situating the wheelcases under the falls, getting the turbines leveled and solidly supported, tweaking the shapes of their blades, wrestling together the penstocks, suction pipes and wheelcases and so forth, all or most of it sweat and sore muscles and arguing with foremen, struggling up and down the terrain finding purchases and setting up tackle, not to mention when necessary some bricklaying, carpentry, riveting, and welding—going without sleep and being yelled at, but none of it too mysterious until one night out west of Rico someplace a window opened for him into the Invisible, and a voice, or something like a voice, whispered unto him, saying, "Water falls, electricity flows—one flow becomes another, and thence into light. So is altitude transformed, continuously, to light." Words to that effect, well, maybe not words exactly. . . . And he found himself staring into the ordinarily blinding glow of a lamp filament, which he found instead unaccountably lambent, like light through the crack of a door left open, inviting him into a friendly house. With the stream in question roaring in sovereign descent just a few feet away. It had not been a dream, nor the sort of illumination he would someday learn that Hamilton had experienced at Brougham Bridge in Ireland in 1845—but it represented a jump from one place to another with who knew what perilous æther opening between and beneath. He saw it. The vectorial expressions in the books, surface integrals and potential functions and such, would henceforth figure as clumsier repetitions of the truth he now possessed in his personal interior, certain and unshakable.

WORD ONE DAY was out on the electricians' grapevine that the renowned Dr. Nikola Tesla was on his way out to Colorado Springs, to set up an experimental station. Kit's sidekick Jack Gigg was unable to sit still. He kept running in and out of Kit's vicinity. "Hey Kit, ain't you ready yet, come on, Kit, we'll camp out up there, there's got to be plenty of jobs just waiting for a couple of old hands like us."

"Jack, we're seventeen."

"Is what I'm sayin. Pike's Peak or Bust!"

Kit remembered visiting Colorado Springs as a youngster. Streetcars and a seven-story building. Violent red sunsets behind Pike's Peak. The cog-railway car with its roof the same color. The station at the summit and the spidery observation deck on top of it, that Frank got so nervous about climbing up on he was kidded mercilessly about it forever after.

They found the Tesla operation set up about a mile out of town, near the Union Printers' Home. They were greeted by a blunt individual with some way of the Cañon City alumnus about him, who introduced himself as Foley Walker. Kit and Jack assumed he was in charge of hiring. Later they found out he was special assistant to famed financier Scarsdale Vibe, and out here to keep an eye on how the money, much of it Mr. Vibe's, was being spent.

Next day, on his way to the mess tent, Kit was accosted by Foley. "You are crazy, as I see it," this deputy of Wealth suggested, "to get out of the house, and be doing somethin besides the swamping, am I close?"

Kind of a line you used on girls, it occurred to Kit—tried it himself, never worked. "I've been out of the house," he muttered, "as you call it, for a few years now."

"Nothin' personal," said Foley. "Only wonderin if you've heard of Mr. Vibe's Lieutenants of Industry Scholarship Program."

"Sure. Last barrelhouse I was in, 'at's all they talked about."

Foley patiently explained that the Program was always scouting around for kids with potential engineering talent to finance through college.

"School of Mines, something like that?" Kit interested despite himself.

"Even better," said Foley. "How does Yale College sound to you?"

"Like 'Mr. Merriwell, we really need this touchdown,'" said Kit in a passable back-east voice.

"Seriously."

"Tuition? Room and board?"

"All included."

"Automobile? Champagne deliveries day or night? Sweater with a big *Y* on it?"

"I can do that," said Foley.

"Horsefeathers. Only Scarsdale Vibe his mighty self can do that, mister."

"I am he."

"You're not 'he.' I read the papers and look at the magazines, you ain't even 'him.'"

"If I may elucidate." Foley once again was obliged to tell his Civil War Substitute story, a chore growing, with the years, ever more wearying. During the Rebellion, shortly after Antietam, just as he was beginning his sophomore year at New Haven, Scarsdale Vibe, having turned the right age for it, had received a notice of conscription. Following the standard practice, his father had purchased for him a substitute to serve in his place, assuming that upon obtaining a properly executed receipt for the three hundred dollars, why that would be that. Imagine everyone's surprise when, a couple of decades later, Foley appeared early one day in the outer offices of the Vibe Corporation, claiming to've been this very substitute conscriptee and producing documents to back it up. "I'm a busy man," Scarsdale might have said, or "How much does he want, and will he take a check?" Instead, curious, he decided to have a look personally.

Foley was ordinary-enough looking, not having yet taken on the more menacing aspect that the years in their peculiar mercy would provide him—what might've been exceptional was his idea of social or phatic conversation. "Took a Reb bullet for you, sir," was the first thing out of his mouth. "Pleased to meet you, of course."

"A bullet. Where?"

"Cold Harbor."

"Yes, but where?"

Foley tapped his head beside the left temple. "Pretty spent by the time it got to me—didn't make it all the way through, and nobody has ever known how to get it out. They used to stand around like I wasn't there, discussing the Brain and Its Mysteries. If a fellow could keep his ears open, why it was like going to medical school on the cheap. Fact is, guided only by what I remember of those bedside conferences, I did go on to perform a few minor head surgeries in my time."

"So it's still in there?"

"Minié ball, judging from everybody else's wounds around that time."

"Giving you any trouble?"

His smile, in its satisfaction, struck even Scarsdale as terrible. "Wouldn't call it trouble. You'd be amazed what I get to see."

"And . . . hear?"

"Call em communications from far, far away."

"Is your army pension taking care of this? Anything you need that you're not getting?"

Foley watched Scarsdale's hands getting ready to reach, for either a pistol or a checkbook. "You know what the Indians out west believe? That if you save the life of another, he becomes your responsibility forever."

"That's all right. I can take care of myself. I have all the bodyguards I need."

"Isn't exactly your *physical* well-being I'm instructed to look after."

"Oh. Of course, those voices you hear. Well, what are they saying to you, Mr. Walker?"

"You mean lately? A lot of talk about some kerosene company out in Cleveland. Fact, not a day goes by there isn't something. You'd know better'n me. 'The Standard Oil'? Supposed to be 'expanding their capital,' whatever that means. Voices say now'd be a good time to buy in?"

"Everything all right in here, Mr. Vibe?"

"Fine, Bruno, just fine, thanks. Let's indulge this gentleman, shall we. Let's just buy a hundred shares of this kerosene stock, if it exists, and see what happens."

"Voices say five hundred'd be better."

"Had your breakfast yet, Mr. Walker? show him the company mess hall, Bruno, if you'd be so kind."

Foley Walker's advice that day provided critical acceleration in the growth of the legendary Vibe fortune. He polished off a side of bacon and the day's output of the Company henhouse up on the H.Q.'s roof, plus a loaf of bread and ten gallons of coffee, give or take a cup, before Bruno, expecting never to lay eyes on him again, was able to usher him into the street puffing on one of a fistful of Scarsdale's second-best Havanas. A week later, after a frantic search of various opium joints and concert saloons, he was located and hired on as an "investigative consultant," and thenceforward Scarsdale grew increasingly reluctant to make any move of a business nature without him, expanding that definition, in the course of time, to include the outcomes of boxing matches, baseball games, and especially horse races, as to which Foley's advice was seldom in error.

The Twin Vibes, as they soon came to be known, were sighted together often at Monmouth Park and Sheepshead Bay as well as tracks farther afield, togged out in matching sport ensembles of a certain canary-and-indigo check, screaming and waving fistfuls of betting slips—when they were not careering at excessive speeds up and down the avenues of Manhattan in a maroon phæton whose brass and nickelwork were kept rubbed to a blinding shine, side by side in their pale dusters, appearing to the unwary spectator as ineluctable as any other Apocalyptic Riders.

"So you could make a case," Foley concluded, "for me being more Scarsdale Vibe than Scarsdale Vibe himself."

Kit was respectful but not convinced. "You see the problem for me, I hope. Supposed to believe that some remittance'll show up every month, on time, for three or four years straight? With that kind of personal faith, I could be out in some tent handling snakes and *really* making a name for myself."

The famed inventor was at this moment observed passing swiftly left to right. "*Izvinite,* there, Dr. Tesla!" Foley cried out, "—mind if we use your telegraph?"

"In the office," the reedy Serb called over his shoulder, breezing on to meet the day's next intractable difficulty.

"*Hvala!* Come on along, buckaroo, prepare to be amazed."

Once in Tesla's shack, Foley lost no time getting onto the telegraph key and in touch with the Vibe offices back East. A few moments later, as if remembering Kit's existence, "How much earnest money on this deal would you be thinking?"

"Pardon?"

"Would five hundred dollars take care of it for the moment?" Foley's finger starting in again with the beetle-banter, faster than eyes could follow—then an attentive stillness as the other end chattered back. "O.K., all set. It'll be there tomorrow at the Bank of Colorado Springs, made out to you personally. Just go on in and sign."

Kit kept a poker face. "Long night ahead."

Longer than expected. Around eight o'clock, a secondary winding on one of the transmitters blew up, having been repeatedly charged at, somewhere out along the miles of coil length required by the low frequencies of the waves in use, by a maddened elk. Near midnight a couple of prairie tornadoes roared by as if seeking in the two-hundred-foot transmission tower a companion in electrical debauchery, and about the middle of the midwatch a couple of stimulated freightmen down from Leadville got in a dispute and exchanged shots, which, as usual, nothing came of, owing to the magnetic fields around here being so strong and erratic they kept pulling the pistol barrels off target. Lurid bursts of blue, red, and green light, with their man-made thunderclaps, kept the skies busy till dawn. Kids at the adjoining Deaf and Blind School reported hearing and seeing frequencies hitherto unaccounted for in the medical science of the day.

In the morning, after a pot of trail coffee, Kit saddled up and rode in to the bank, where all was just as Foley had promised. A teller with some green celluloid rig across his brow peered up at Kit with an interest few had ever shown. "Another one of Doc Tesla's boys, eh?" Kit, sleepless after thirty-six hours of voltaic frenzy and odd behavior human and animal, took it as a message from perhaps farther beyond where it'd actually come from. Somewhere along East Platte Street on the way back, guiding on the tower with its three-foot copper sphere on top catching the sun across the prairie, Kit was assaulted all at once by a yearning, or that's how he'd think of it later—a clarity of desire—to belong to that band of adventurers into the Æther and its mysteries, to become, *por vida,* one of Doc Tesla's boys. Well inside the mile or so back to the test station, he found himself, unaccountably, ready to sign up with Foley's plan for his life.

"After I finish college I come work for Mr. Vibe till the debt's paid off, that right?"

"Right—and if you'll sign this one here, too, just a standard release . . . Sure, think of it as paid conscription. Us geezers from the days of the Rebellion, we tend to take it for the way of the world, one element in society wishing to keep clear of some spell of unpleasantness—your case, having to learn all that college stuff—paying another element to take it on instead. Basic arrangement. Those above get their piece of time untroubled and free, us below get our cash right away, and depending on the job, maybe even a thrill now and then."

"But after the War, as you tell it, you thought your man still owed you."

"Might've been from observing how Mr. Vibe and other notable ransomed souls of his era had been left free to behave. Not to mention the profit curve that resulted for them, while they just went waltzing on, some of them even today unable to imagine any form of real trouble. We that went and found more of that than we could bear felt like that we ought to be seeking reparations, our damages to body and spirit being the debit side of all their good fortune, you could say."

"If you were a socialist, you could," Kit supposed.

"Sure, and isn't that just the class system for ya? Eternal youth bought with the sickness and death of others. Call it what you like. If you go back East, you may run into more thinking along these same lines, so if it offends you now, better speak up, we'll go make other arrangements."

"No, no, I'll be all right."

"That's also what Mr. Vibe thinks."

"He doesn't know me."

"That will change."

Later in the shack, Kit came upon Tesla, frowning at a pencil sketch. "Oh. Sorry, I was looking for—"

"This toroid is the wrong shape," said Tesla. "Come, look at this a moment."

Kit had a look. "Maybe there's a vector solution."

"How's that?

"We know what we want the field to look like at each point, don't we. Well, maybe we can generate a surface shape that'll give us that field."

"You see it," Tesla half-inquired, looking at Kit with some curiosity.

"I see something," Kit shrugged.

"The same began to happen to me also at your age," Tesla recalled. "When I could find the time to sit still, the images would come. But it's always finding the time, isn't it."

"Sure, always something. . . . Chores, something."

"Tithing," Tesla said, "giving back to the day."

"Not complainin about the hours here, nothin like that, sir."

"Why not? I complain all the time. Not enough of them, basically."

When Kit got back from Colorado Springs all on fire with the news of Foley's offer, Webb would have none of it. "You crazy? I'll get somebody to write em, tell em no."

"Wasn't you they asked."

"It's me they're after, son."

"They don't know you down there," Kit argued.

"They own the mines here. You think I'm not on their list? I'm on everbody else's. They're tryin to buy my family away. And if gold don't work, sooner or later they get around to lead."

"I don't think you understand this."

"Everbody's ignorant about somethin. Me, it's the electricity. You, looks like it's rich folks."

"They can afford this so easily. Can you?"

It was falling apart. Webb could feel himself losing this argument, losing his son. Too fast, he said, "And what's the payback?"

"I go to work for the Vibe Corp. when I graduate. Anything wrong with that?"

Webb shrugged. "They own you."

"It'll mean steady work. Not like . . ."

"Like around here." Kit just stared back. It was over, Webb guessed. "O.K., well. You're either my boy or theirs, can't be both."

"That's the choice?"

"You're not goin, Kit."

"Oh ain't I." It was out, just that tone of voice, before the boy could think, nor did he register too deeply then what sorrow came flooding into Webb's face, usually a little upturned these days owing to Kit's still-increasing height.

"That case," Webb pretending to look at some kind of shift-boss paperwork, "leave just when you want. Jake with me." They would make a practice from there on of not letting their eyes meet, which as things turned out was never to happen again, not here on the desolate lee shore whose back country is death.

"Being a little hard with him," it seemed to Mayva.

"You too? You look at him lately, May, he ain't exactly some damn baby anymore, you can't just keep girlyin onto him till he's no damn good for nothing."

"But he is our baby, Webb."

"Baby's ass. He's old enough and sure big enough to see what this is, now. How the deal works."

It took a while, till Kit had left and the emotions had lost some of that knife edge, before Webb began to remember times him and his own father, Cooley, had gone round and round, and just as loud, and just as senseless, and he couldn't even remember what it had been about, not every time. And though Webb was younger when Cooley died, it had never occurred to him, from that day to this, how Cooley might have been feeling the same way Webb felt now. He wondered if it would stay this way for the rest of his life—he had never made it right between him and his Pa, and the same thing now, like some damn curse, was happening between him and Kit. . . .

Mayva saw Kit off at the depot, but it was a chilly parting, and not too long on hope. He was pretending not to understand why nobody else had showed up, none of the men. She was wearing her church hat—"church" having been conducted often as not out under the sky, the old maroon velvet had picked up some years of trail dust and grown sun-faded along its many miniature ridgetops. Wasn't too long ago that he'd still been too short to look down and notice that. She fussed in and out of the depot, making sure its clock was working all right, learning what she could of the train's whereabouts from the lady telegraph operator and her assistant, asking Kit more than once if he thought she'd packed him enough food for the journey. Cornish pasties and so forth.

"Not like it's forever, Ma."

"No. Course not. Only me, just being, I don't know . . ."

"Might not even work out. Easy to see that happening, in fact."

"Just so you mind that, that penmanship. In school you always wrote so neatly."

"I'll be writing to you, Ma, regular, so you can keep an eye on that."

Some stirring now along the line of town trainwatchers, as if they'd caught signals from the invisible distance in that joint waking dream of theirs, or maybe, as some swore, like that they'd seen the track shift, just a hair, long before the first smoke over the rise or steam whistles in the distance.

"I'll never see you again." No. She didn't say that. But she might've, so easy. A look from him. Any small gesture of collapse from his careful, young man's posture back into the boy she wanted, after all, to keep.

The call had come just a week before, in the midwatch, which the Chums, even in this era of desuetude, nonetheless continued, every night, to stand. A boy with the face of an angel in an old painting under a baggy cap with its bill turned sidewise had appeared with a telephone set whose cord trailed out the door into the scarcely lit darkness. It could've been someone up too late, playing a practical joke. Opinion next morning, over watery oatmeal and fatback and the dregs of the previous day's coffee, was in fact divided. There were no navigational charts to help them to find the way. Their only instructions were to steer southwest and await course correction from a station unnamed, at a distance indeterminate, which would be calling in via the airship's new Tesla device, which had remained silent since the day it was installed, though kept ever electrified and flawlessly calibrated.

The voices which arrived over the next few days were difficult to credit with any origin in the material sphere. Even the unimaginative Lindsay Noseworth reported feeling a fine sustained chill across his shoulders whenever the instrument began its hoarse whispering.

Presently they had picked up the westerlies which would convey them with all-but-geometrical precision to the uninhabited and little-known Indian Ocean islands of Amsterdam and St. Paul, recently annexed by France.

They were borne scant dozens of feet above a high and hostile sea scattered with islands of bare black rock, unpopulated, without vegetation. "At one time," related Miles Blundell, "in the days of the first explorers, each one of these islands, no matter how small, was given its own name, so amazing was their abundance in the sea, so grateful to God were their discoverers for any sort of landfall . . . but nowadays the names are being lost, this sea is lapsing back into anonymity, each island rising from it only another dark desert." As, no longer named, one by one the islets vanished from the nautical charts, and one day from the lighted world as well, to rejoin the Invisible.

On certain of these wind-haunted rocks, the Chums could observe work details, rigged with safety lines, scrambling over wet surfaces scarcely big enough to hold them all, moving swiftly and purposefully, though there was nothing evident, not even guano, worth risking their safety for. The ships anchored close by were of the latest design and appeared to be carrying armament available only to the European Powers. Their presence in these waters, not so much as hinted at in any of the extensive communiqués reaching the boys from Chums Headquarters, was a mystery dark as the storm-lit seascape.

The last island where they could take on perishable supplies, such as milk, was St. Masque, which at first, as they landed, appeared to be uninhabited. Then, slowly, in ones and twos, people began to appear, until soon the Chums were surrounded by a considerable population and a city to go with it, as if it had been there all along, waiting for their arrival . . . a city of some size, English-speaking, so clean and litter-free that everyone walked around barefoot, no matter how formally they might be dressed otherwise—town suits, tea gowns, no matter—it was the visitor wearing shoes who was stared at. In the center of town, some huge underground construction venture was in progress, citizens stood on overpasses and catwalks gazing down into concrete pits full of steam-machinery, draft animals, and debris. When asked its purpose, they frowned, puzzled, as if they had not quite heard the visitors. "Home," some said, "it's home. What is home where you come from?" But wandered away before any of the lads could answer.

In a seamen's tavern down by the docks, one of those low haunts he had a sure instinct for finding wherever in the world the boys happened to go, Chick Counterfly met up with a shadowy sea-derelict who claimed to be a survivor of the frigate H.M.S. *Megaera* which had been wrecked on Amsterdam Island nearly thirty years before. "Miserable place. Took months for us to be rescued. No different from sea duty . . . oh, that absence of motion of course, bit more fish in the diet as you'd imagine. . . . One continued to stand watch, and share space with the same people one had already learned to tolerate, or hate, or both at the same time, which taken from the standpoint of pure survival proved a great blessing—imagine if the old *Meg* had been a passenger ship full of strangers—half of us would have murdered the other half within the first week and perhaps eaten them as well. But four hundred of us made it."

"Curious," Chick said. "That's about what I estimated the population of St. Masque to be."

· · ·

And only hours after leaving behind these de-christened fragments in the sea's reasserted emptiness, they had raised the volcano, dark and ruinous, which was their destination. The assignment was to observe what would happen at the point on the Earth antipodal to Colorado Springs, during Dr. Tesla's experiments there. They had been provided via Chums of Chance Logistical Services, never questioned, always on time, an expensive array of electrical instrumentation, reflecting everything within the current state of technical knowledge, delivered uninvoiced by Oriental laborers who trooped in and out of the encampment, shift after shift, beneath often quite staggering burdens. Pallets and nails from opened crates soon littered the area. Thatch debris fallen bit by bit from coolie hats drifted here and there ankle deep. Vermin brought ashore with the cargo, sometimes all the way from California, scrambled off and soon had found homes on the slopes of the volcano, venturing down to the camp only on late-night galley raids.

The stevedoring at length done with, the itinerant work crews were rowed away silently, out to the flagless vessel lying offshore, to be body-jobbed away somewhere else in the hemisphere. South Africa, most likely. Leaving the boys to gather closely, beneath the mephitically seeping volcano which rose nearly a thousand feet overhead, on a beach so intensely sunlit as to appear almost colorless, the blindness at the heart of a diamond for all they knew, while ocean waves came towering in one by one, arriving measured as the breath of some local god. No one at first had anything to say, even if it had been possible to hear above the battery of the surf.

Mealtimes lately had been fraught with political instability, owing to an ongoing dispute over the choice of a new figurehead for the ship. The previous one, representing the head of President McKinley, had been seriously damaged in an unpremeditated collision with a Chicago skyscraper building which had not, as far as any of the boys knew, been there the day before.

Chick Counterfly and Darby Suckling had been lobbying for a naked woman, "A-and th' more curvaceous, the better!" as Darby demanded at each of their frequent *ad hoc* gatherings on the subject, bringing to the lips of Lindsay Noseworth a reproof by now all but reflexive—"Suckling, Suckling . . . your list of demerits grows at a dishearteningly vertiginous rate."

"And not one of em that ain't just danged shipboard politics," expostulated Darby, with a red-faced scowl. Since his voice had changed, its charmingly insubordinate tone, once tolerable, had darkened to something more considered and, to that degree, disquieting. The once cheery mascotte had passed from political innocence, through a short period of adolescent uncertainty, into a distrust of authority approaching the very slopes of Nihilism. His shipmates, even the reliably humorous Chick Counterfly, now reflected at length before uttering even the most routine of jocularities in Suckling's hearing, lest he take offense.

Randolph St. Cosmo had continued, in the matter of choosing a figurehead, to promote the National Bird, as a safe and patriotic choice. Miles Blundell, for his part, didn't care what the figurehead represented, as long as it was something to eat—while Lindsay, as if offended by the worldliness of these choices, argued as always for pure abstraction—"One of the Platonic polyhedra, perhaps."

"That jasper," sniggered Darby, "never pulled out his 'dummy' for nothing but pissing, I bet you!"

"No takers!" Chick scornfully guffawed.

The figurehead debate, at first no deeper than varying decorative tastes might account for, had grown bitter and complex, swiftly reaching an intensity that astonished them all. Old injuries "kicked up," pretexts were found to exchange shoves and, not infrequently, blows. A sign in very large Clarendons appeared in the mess area—

FUNDAMENT-SEIZING ACTIVITIES IN THE "CHOW LINE"
WILL NOT BE TOLERATED!!!
VIOLATIONS WILL DRAW TEN WEEKS' EXTRA DUTY!!! EACH!!!
By order of the Executive Officer.
P.S.—Yes, that's WEEKS!!!

Nonetheless, they went on shuffling and muttering, sneaking finger-size globs out of the asparagus mousse, Creole-Style Gumbo, or mashed turnips, whenever they thought the Master-at-Arms wasn't looking—not actually to eat but surreptitiously to *flick at one another,* hoping for a response. Miles Blundell, as Ship's Commissary, looked on in genial bewilderment. "Zumbledy bongbong," he called encouragingly, as the food flew. "Vamble, vamble!"

Wandering corridors of the spectral, Miles had begun, increasingly, to alarm his shipmates. Mealtimes too often were apt to revert to exercises in deep, even mortal, uncertainty, depending where Miles had been that day to procure his ingredients. Sometimes his cooking was pure *cordon bleu,* sometimes it was inedible, due to excursions of spirit whose polarity was never entirely predictable from one day to the next. Not that Miles would deliberately set out to wreck the soup or burn the meat loaves—he seldom got that overt, tending more to forgetful omissions, or misreadings of quantity and timing. "If anything's an irreversible process, cooking is!" lectured Thermodynamics Officer Chick Counterfly, meaning to be helpful, though unavoidably in some agitation. "You can't de-roast a turkey, or unmix a failed sauce—time is intrinsic in every recipe, and one shrugs it off at one's peril."

Sometimes Miles would reply, "Thank you, Chick, it is wise counsel . . . fellows . . . you are all so amazingly patient with me, and I will endeavor as best I can to improve," and sometimes he would cry, "Of the metawarble of blibfloth zep!" gesturing violently with his chef's toque, his face illuminated by an enigmatic smile.

The one diner in the company who had never suffered disappointment, however, was Pugnax, whose fastidiousness of diet Miles, regardless of his moods, had always honored. Along with a range of human preferences that included vintage Champagnes, terrapin stew, and asparagus hollandaise, Pugnax insisted upon separate courses served in separate dishes, which must be of bone china of a certain age and authenticated origin, bringing new import to the expression "dog's dinner."

IN THE U.S.A., it was almost the Fourth of July, which meant that tonight, by standing orders, there had to be a shipboard celebration out here, too, like it or not.

"Lights and noise, just to keep us hoppin like trained baboons," was Darby's opinion.

"Anyone at all educated," protested Lindsay, "knows that Fourth of July fireworks are the patriotic symbols of noteworthy episodes of military explosion in our nation's history, deemed necessary to maintain the integrity of the American homeland against threats presented from all sides by a benightedly hostile world."

"Explosion without an objective," declared Miles Blundell, "is politics in its purest form."

"If we don't take care," opined Scientific Officer Counterfly, "folks will begin to confuse us with the Anarcho-syndicalists."

"About time," snarled Darby. "I say let's set off our barrage tonight in honor of the Haymarket bomb, bless it, a turning point in American history, and the only way working people will ever get a fair shake under that miserable economic system—through the wonders of chemistry!"

"Suckling!" the astounded Lindsay Noseworth struggling to maintain his composure. "But, that is blatant anti-Americanism!"

"Eehhyyhh, and your mother's a Pinkerton, too."

"Why you communistic little—"

"I wish I knew what they were arguing about," complained Randolph St. Cosmo, to no one in particular. Perhaps, in this remoteness, to the wind.

Yet tonight's pyrotechnics amounted after all to more than simple explosion. As one by one their violent candles bloomed deafeningly above the ruined volcano, Miles bade the company consider, in tones of urgency they seldom heard from him, the nature of a skyrocket's ascent, in particular that unseen extension of the visible trail, after the propellant charge burns out, yet before the slow-match has ignited the display—that implied moment of ongoing passage upward, in the dark sky, a linear continuum of points invisible yet present, just before lights by the hundreds appear—

"Stop, stop!" Darby clutching his ears comically, "it sounds like Chinese!"

"Who invented fireworks," Miles agreed, "but what does this suggest to you about the trajectories of your own lives? Anybody? Think, bloviators, think!"

The hour of the great experiment on the other side of the world approached. Smells not quite of mess-cooking collected in the lee of the wrecked volcano, as if some lengthy chemical procedure had repeatedly failed to provide an unambiguous result. Electrodes sputtered and flared, and giant transformer coils droned afflictedly, almost in human accents, fed by electrical generators whose steam was being supplied by the local hot springs. Transmitting and receiving antennas for the wireless equipment had been run up the sides of the lava-cone, and communication had commenced, while, almost exactly on the other side of Earth, Chums of Chance monitoring personnel waited in a weather-proofed shack at the top of Pike's Peak, though beliefs varied as to the nature of the strange link—was the signal going around the planet, or through it, or was linear progression not at all the point, with everything instead happening simultaneously at every part of the circuit?

BY THE TIME *Inconvenience* was ready to take once more to the sky, the figurehead dispute had been resolved amicably—the boys had compromised on a draped female personage, perhaps more maternal than erotic—apologies were exchanged, reiterated, eventually at tiresome length, new apologies for these reiterations then became necessary, and the working days became saturated in sky-punctilio. After a while the boys would come to think of the episode as others might remember a time of illness, or youthful folly. As Lindsay Noseworth was there to remind them all, such difficulties always arose for good reason—namely, to provide cautionary lessons.

"Like what," sneered Darby, "'be nice'?"

"We were always supposed—by whom it is less clear—to be above such behavior," asserted the "X.O." somberly. "Literally above. That sort of bickering may be for ground people, but it is not for us."

"Oh, I don't know, I kind of enjoyed it," said Darby.

"Despite which, we must ever strive to minimize contamination by the secular," declared Lindsay.

Each of the boys in his way agreed. "We have had a narrow escape, fellows," said Randolph St. Cosmo.

"Let us develop protocols," added Chick Counterfly, "to avoid its happening again."

"Gloymbroognitz thidfusp," nodded Miles, vigorously.

Was it any wonder that when the opportunity did arise, as it would shortly, the boys would grasp unreflectively at a chance to transcend "the secular," even at the cost of betraying their organization, their country, even humankind itself?

THE ORDERS HAD ARRIVED with the usual lack of ceremony or even common courtesy, by way of the Oyster Stew traditionally prepared each Thursday as the Plat du Jour by Miles Blundell, who, that morning, well before sunup, had visited the shellfish market in the teeming narrow lanes of the old town in Surabaya, East Java, where the boys were enjoying a few days of ground-leave. There, Miles had been approached by a gentleman of Japanese origin and unusual persuasiveness, who had sold him, at what did seem a remarkably attractive price, two buckets full of what he repeatedly described as "Special Japanese Oyster," these being in fact the only English words Miles would recall him having spoken. Miles had thought no more about it until the noon mess was interrupted by an agonized scream from Lindsay Noseworth, followed by a half minute of uncharacteristic profanity. On the mess-tray before him, where he had just vigorously expelled it from his mouth, lay a pearl of quite uncommon size and iridescence, seeming indeed to glow from within, which the boys, gathered about, recognized immediately as a communication from the Chums of Chance Upper Hierarchy.

"Don't suppose you happened to get that oyster merchant's name or address," said Randolph St. Cosmo.

"Only this." Miles produced a small business card covered with Japanese text, which, regrettably, none of the boys had ever learned to read.

"Mighty helpful," sneered Darby Suckling. "But heck, we all know the story by now." Chick Counterfly had already brought out of its storage locker a peculiar-looking optical contraption of prisms, lenses, Nernst lamps, and adjustment screws, into an appropriate receptacle of which he now carefully placed the pearl. Lindsay, still clutching his jaw in dental discomfort and muttering aggrievedly, lowered the shades in the dining saloon against the tropical noontide, and the boys directed their attention to a reflective screen set on one bulkhead, where presently, like a photographic image emerging from its solution, a printed message began to appear.

Through a highly secret technical process, developed in Japan at around the same time Dr. Mikimoto was producing his first cultured pearls, portions of the original aragonite—which made up the nacreous layers of the pearl—had, through "induced paramorphism," as it was known to the artful sons of Nippon, been selectively changed here and there to a different form of calcium carbonate—namely, to microscopic crystals of the doubly-refracting calcite known as Iceland spar. Ordinary light, passing through this mineral, was divided into two separate rays, termed "ordinary" and "extraordinary," a property which the Japanese scientists had then exploited to create an additional channel of optical communication wherever in the layered structure of the pearl one of the thousands of tiny, cunningly-arranged crystals might occur. When illuminated in a certain way, and the intricately refracted light projected upon a suitable surface, any pearl so modified could thus be made to yield a message.

To the fiendishly clever Oriental mind, it had been but a trivial step to combine this paramorphic encryption with the Mikimoto process, whereupon every oyster at the daily markets of the world suddenly became a potential carrier of secret information. If pearls so modified were then further incorporated into jewelry, reasoned the ingenious Nipponese, the necks and earlobes of rich women in the industrial West might provide a medium even less merciful than the sea into whose brute flow messages of yearning or calls for help sealed in bottles were still being dropped and abandoned. What deliverance from the limitless mischief of pearls, what votive offering in return for it, would be possible?

The message from Upper Hierarchy directed the crew to get up buoyancy immediately and proceed by way of the Telluric Interior to the north polar regions, where they were to intercept the schooner *Étienne-Louis Malus* and attempt to persuade its commander, Dr. Alden Vormance, to abandon the expedition he was currently engaged upon, using any means short of force—which, though not prohibited outright to the Chums of Chance, did create a strong presumption of Bad Taste, which every Chum by ancient tradition was sworn, if not indeed at pains, to avoid.

Some of the greatest minds in the history of science, including Kepler, Halley, and Euler, had speculated as to the existence of a so-called "hollow Earth." One day, it was hoped, the technique of intra-planetary "short-cutting" about to be exercised by the boys would become routine, as useful in its way as the Suez or the Panama Canal had proved to surface shipping. At the time we speak of, however, there still remained to our little crew occasion for stunned amazement, as the *Inconvenience* left the South Indian Ocean's realm of sunlight, crossed the edge of the Antarctic continent, and began to traverse an immense sweep of whiteness broken by towering black ranges, toward the vast and tenebrous interior which breathed hugely miles ahead of them.

Something did seem odd, however. "The navigation's not as easy this time," Randolph mused, bent over the chart table in some perplexity. "Noseworth, you can remember the old days. We knew for hours ahead of time." Skyfarers here had been used to seeing flocks of the regional birds spilling away in long helical curves, as if to escape being drawn into some vortex inside the planet sensible only to themselves, as well as the withdrawal, before the advent of the more temperate climate within, of the eternal snows, to be replaced first by tundra, then grassland, trees, plantation, even at last a settlement or two, just at the Rim, like border towns, which in former times had been the sites of yearly markets, as dwellers in the interior came out to trade luminous fish, giant crystals with geomantic properties, unrefined ores of various useful metals, and mushrooms unknown to the fungologists of the surface world, who had once journeyed regularly hither in high expectation of discovering new species with new properties of visionary enhancement.

On this trip, however, the polar ice persisted until quite close to the great portal, which itself seemed to have become *noticeably smaller,* with a strange sort of ice-mist, almost the color of the surface landscape, hovering over it and down inside, soon becoming so thick that for a short while the crew of the *Inconvenience* were in effect flying blind, guided only by their sense of smell, among odors of sulfurous combustion, fungus harvesting, and the resinous transpiration of the vast forests of sprucelike conifers which began fitfully to emerge out of the mist.

Its engines humming strenuously, the airship entered the planet's interior. The antennas and rigging were soon outlined in a pale blue radiance much more noticeable than on previous transits. "Even with the Southern winter," reported Chick Counterfly, who had been taking photometric readings, "it is much darker in here than previously, which is certainly consistent with a smaller entrance-way admitting less light from the surface."

"I wonder what could be responsible," frowned Randolph. "Can't say I like it, much."

"Inordinate attention from the middle latitudes," proclaimed Miles, with a sort of vatic swoon in his voice. "When the interior feels itself under threat, this is a self-protective reflex, all living creatures possess it in one form or another. . . ."

Far "below," through the intraplanetary dusk, they could make out upon the great inner concavity, spreading into the distances, the phosphorescent chains and webs of settlement crossing lightless patches of wilderness still unvisited by husbandry, as, silently as the ship's nitro-lycopodium engines would allow, the skyfarers made their passage. "Do you think they know we're here?" whispered Lindsay, as he always did on this passage, peering through his night-glass.

"Absent any signs as yet of other airborne traffic," shrugged Randolph, "it seems an academic point."

"If any of them down there were to possess long-range armament," suggested Chick mischievously, "—destructive rays, perhaps, or lenses for focusing the auroral energy upon our all-too-vulnerable envelope—they may only be waiting for us to come in range."

"Perhaps, then, we ought to implement heightened alert status," proposed Lindsay Noseworth.

"Eenhhyhh, nervous Nellies the bunch o' yih," scoffed Darby Suckling. "Keep chinnin about it, ladies, maybe you can worry us into a real disaster."

"There is traffic on the Tesla device," Miles, who had been attending *Inconvenience*'s wireless apparatus, now advised in hushed tones.

"How do you know, Bug-brains?"

"Listen." Miles, smiling calmly at what might, by someone more engaged with the earthly, easily be read as provocation, reached for and threw a set of knife-switches on the console before him, and an electrical sound-magnifier nearby sputtered into life.

At first the "noise" seemed no more than the ensemble of magneto-atmospheric disturbances which the boys had long grown used to, perhaps here intensified by the vastly resonant space into which they were moving ever deeper. But presently the emission began to coalesce into human timbres and rhythms—not speech so much as music, as if the twilit leagues passing below were linked by means of song.

Lindsay, who was Communications Officer, had his ear close to the Tesla device, squinting attentively, but at last withdrew, shaking his head. "Gibberish."

"They are calling for help," declared Miles, "clear as day and quite desperately, too. They claim to be under attack by a horde of hostile gnomes, and have set out red signal lamps, arranged in concentric circles."

"There they are!" called Chick Counterfly, pointing over the starboard quarter.

"Then there is nothing to discuss," declared Randolph St. Cosmo. "We must put down and render aid."

They descended over a battlefield swarming with diminutive combatants wearing pointed hats and carrying what proved to be electric crossbows, from which they periodically discharged bolts of intense greenish light, intermittently revealing the scene with a morbidity like that of a guttering star.

"We cannot attack these fellows," protested Lindsay, "for they are shorter than we, and the Rules of Engagement clearly state—"

"In an emergency, that choice lies at the Commander's discretion," replied Randolph.

They were soaring now close above the metallic turrets and parapets of a sort of castle, where burned the crimson lights of distress. Figures could be discerned below gazing up at the *Inconvenience.* Peering at them through a night-glass, Miles stood at the conning station, transfixed by the sight of a woman poised upon a high balcony. "My word, she's lovely!" he exclaimed at last.

Their fateful decision to land would immediately embroil them in the byzantine politics of the region, and eventually they would find themselves creeping perilously close to outright violation of the Directives relating to Noninterference and Height Discrepancy, which might easily have brought an official hearing, and perhaps even disfellowshipment from the National Organization. For a detailed account of their subsequent narrow escapes from the increasingly deranged attentions of the Legion of Gnomes, the unconscionable connivings of a certain international mining cartel, the sensual wickedness pervading the royal court of Chthonica, Princess of Plutonia, and the all-but-irresistible fascination that subterranean monarch would come to exert, Circe-like, upon the minds of the crew of *Inconvenience* (Miles, as we have seen, in particular), readers are referred to *The Chums of Chance in the Bowels of the Earth*—for some reason one of the less appealing of this series, letters having come in from as far away as Tunbridge Wells, England, expressing displeasure, often quite intense, with my harmless little intraterrestrial scherzo.

After their precipitate escape from the ill-disposed hordes of thick-set indigenous, over another night and day, as time is reckoned on the surface, the Chums swept through the interior of the Earth and at last out her Northern portal, which they beheld as a tiny circle of brightness far ahead. As before, all remarked the diminished size of the planetary exit. It was a tricky bit of steering, as they emerged, to locate the exact spot, on the swiftly dilating luminous circumference, where they might with least expenditure of time find themselves in the vicinity of the schooner *Étienne-Louis Malus,* carrying the Vormance Expedition toward a fate few of its members would willingly have chosen.

Two
Iceland Spar

Besides keeping a sharp eye out himself from the flying bridge, Randolph St. Cosmo had also posted lookouts forward and aft with the most powerful binoculars on the ship. Here, north of the Arctic Circle, the standing directive to all Chums of Chance vessels was, "Unfamiliar sky-traffic is to be presumed hostile until proven otherwise." Daily skirmishes were now being fought, no longer for territory or commodities but for electro-magnetic information, in an international race to measure and map most accurately the field-coefficients at each point of that mysterious mathematical lattice-work which was by then known to surround the Earth. As the Era of Sail had depended upon the mapping of seas and seacoasts of the globe and winds of the wind-rose, so upon the measurement of newer variables would depend the history that was to pass up here, among reefs of magnetic anomaly, channels of least impedance, storms of rays yet unnamed lashing out of the sun. There was a "Ray-rush" in progress—light and magnetism, as well as all manner of extra-Hertzian rays, were there for the taking, and prospectors had come flooding in, many of them professional claim-jumpers aiming to get by on brute force, a very few genuinely able to dowse for rays of all frequencies, most neither gifted nor unscrupulous, simply caught up in everybody else's single-minded flight from reason, diseased as the gold and silver seekers of earlier days. Here at the high edge of the atmosphere was the next untamed frontier, pioneers arriving in airships instead of wagons, setting in motion property disputes destined to last generations. The Northern Lights which had drawn them from their childhood beds in lower latitudes on so many deep winter nights, while summoning in their parents obscure feelings of dread, could now be viewed up here at any time from within, at altitude, in heavenwide pulses of color, dense sheets and billows and colonnades of light and current, in transfiguration unceasing.

In small, remote corners of the planet nobody was paying much attention to, between factions nobody knew much about, the undeclared and largely imperceptible war had been under way for years. All up and down the Northern latitudes, clandestine transmitters had been deployed amid pinnacles of ice, in abandoned mining works, in the secret courtyards of ancient Iron-Age fortresses, manned and unmanned, lonely and unearthly in the iceblink. On sky-piercing crags as likely to be frozen seabird guano as rock, scouts of Earth's Field, desperate, insomniac, interrogated horizons as to any signs of their relief, who were often years late. . . . And indeed for some, the Polar night would last forever—they would pass from the Earth amid unreportable splendor, the aurora in the sky raging up and down spectra visible and invisible. Souls bound to the planetary lines of force, swept pole to pole and through the fabled interior regions as well. . . .

Manœuvring in vessels camouflaged in naval-style "dazzle painting," whereby areas of the structure could actually disappear and reappear in clouds of chromatic twinkling, scientist-skyfarers industriously gathered their data, all of deepest interest to the enterprisers convened leagues below, at intelligence centers on the surface such as the Inter-Group Laboratory for Opticomagnetic Observation (I.G.L.O.O.), a radiational clearing-house in Northern Alaska, which these days was looking more like some Lloyd's of the high spectrum, with everyone waiting anxiously for the next fateful Lutine announcement.

"Dangerous conditions lately."

"Hell, some days you'd give the world for a nice easygoing Indian attack."

"I tell you it can't go on like this."

A few heads turned, though the plangent note was long familiar. "Presumptuous whelp, what would you know, you weren't even around for the last eclipse."

It was a dark assembly-room, its windows shuttered in iron, illuminated in patches by green-shaded lamps gas and electric, a gloom relieved only by the brief glittering of watch-chains across dark vests, pen-nibs, coins, dining utensils, glasses, and bottles. Outside, in streets of beaten snow, wolves, foraging far from home, howled all but eloquently.

"Yes—these days in the business too many people your age altogether. Unreflective steps, harmful consequences, no attention to history or the sacrifices of those who've gone before, so forth. . . ."

"Ever thus, old-timer."

"You like to fricasseed a bunch of my boys the other day. D' you care to address that?"

"The area was posted. They had ample warning. You know you don't send a ship out on test-days."

"Assbackwards as usual. You don't test when there's ships out, not even if it's one defenseless little cutter—"

"Defenseless! She was fully rigged up as an assault ship, sir."

"—cruising along innocent as any pleasure craft, till you assaulted *her,* with your infernal rays."

"She made a Furtive Movement. We kept to procedure."

"Here—this furtive enough for you?"

"Boys, boys!"

Such disputes had become so common that it hardly surprised Randolph now when the gong of the after lookout telegraph, whose sender was attached to Pugnax's tail, began to clamor.

"Quickly, the field-glasses. . . . Now, what in blazes have we here?" The ship in the distance was distinguished by an envelope with the onionlike shape—and nearly the dimensions, too—of a dome on an Eastern Orthodox church, against whose brilliant red surface was represented, in black, the Romanoff crest, and above it, in gold Cyrillic lettering, the legend BOL'SHAIA IGRA, or, "The Great Game." It was readily recognized by all as the flagship of Randolph's mysterious Russian counterpart—and, far too often, nemesis—Captain Igor Padzhitnoff, with whom previous "run-ins" (see particularly *The Chums of Chance and the Ice Pirates, The Chums of Chance Nearly Crash into the Kremlin*) evoked in the boys lively though anxious memories.

"What's up with old Padzhy, I wonder?" murmured Randolph. "They're sure closing awfully rapidly."

The parallel organization at St. Petersburg, known as the Tovarishchi Slutchainyi, was notorious for promoting wherever in the world they chose a program of mischief, much of its motivation opaque to the boys, Padzhitnoff's own specialty being to arrange for bricks and masonry, always in the four-block fragments which had become his "signature," to fall on and damage targets designated by his superiors. This lethal debris was generally harvested from the load-bearing walls of previous targets of opportunity.

"We certainly have cause to steer clear of these fellows," Lindsay nodded, sourly. "They will no doubt imagine us to be trespassing upon their 'sky-space' again. Given the far from trifling degree of nasal dislocation over that Polish contretemps—though certainly owing to no fault of our own—nevertheless, upon this occasion we had better get our story straight *before* they intercept us, which, it appears, could be at any moment—um, in fact—" Abruptly, a violent thump shook *Inconvenience* throughout her structure as the Russian craft came none too politely alongside.

"Oh, gravy," muttered Randolph.

"Ahoy! Balloon boys!" Captain Padzhitnoff was flaxen-haired, athletic, and resolutely chirpy—indeed, far more than ordinary sky-business usually demanded. "Getting jump on me once again! What happened? Am I too old for this?" His smile, while perhaps unremarkable down on Earth's surface among, say, a gathering of the insane, here, thousands of feet in the air and far from any outpost of Reason, seemed even more ominous than the phalanx of rifles, apparently late-model Turkish Mausers, as well as weapons less readily identifiable, which his crew were now pointing at *Inconvenience.*

"Na sobrat' ya po nebo!" Randolph greeted them, as nonchalantly as possible.

"Where are you headed?" boomed the Russian commander through a gigantic speaking-trumpet of Chinese silver.

"South, as you see."

"Zone of Emergency has just been declared by authorities," Padzhitnoff sweeping his arm to indicate a wide sector of the frozen terrain below. "You may wish to divert."

"Authorities?" Lindsay inquired, keenly, as if he had recognized the name of an intimate acquaintance.

"I.G.L.O.O.," The Russian commander shrugged. "We pay no attention to them, but you might."

"What sort of emergency," inquired Randolph, "did they say?"

The Muscovite skyfarers grew convulsive with sinister merriment. "In part of Russia where I grew up," Captain Padzhitnoff was able to say at last, "all animals, no matter how large or dangerous, had names—bears, wolves, Siberian tigers. . . . All except for one. One creature that other animals, including humans, were afraid of, because if it found them it would eat them, without necessarily killing them first. It appreciated pain. Pain was like . . . salt. Spices. That creature, we did not have name for. Ever. Do you understand?"

"Goodness," whispered Lindsay to his chief, "all we did was ask."

"Thank you," Randolph replied. "We shall proceed with particular caution. May we help you with any problem of resupply? anything you may have begun to run short of?"

"Respect for your blind innocence," smiled his opposite number—not for the first time, for it had become a ritual exchange. The *Bol'shaia Igra* began to drift away, its captain and senior officers remaining at the rail of the bridge and conferring together as they gazed after *Inconvenience.* When the ships were nearly out of earshot, Captain Padzhitnoff waved and called, "Bon voyage!" his voice tiny and plaintive in the immensity of Arctic sky.

"Well, what was all that about? If they were trying to warn us off . . ."

"No mention of the Vormance party, you notice."

"It was something else," said Miles Blundell, the only one of the crew who seemed to have taken the warning to heart, returning, as the other boys resumed their own activities, to his preparation of the midday meal, and Pugnax re-inserted his nose among the pages of a *roman-feuilleton* by M. Eugène Sue, which he appeared to be reading in the original French.

So they proceeded into the Zone of Emergency, keeping an alert ear to the Tesla device and scanning carefully the colorless wastes below. And for hours, well past suppertime, their enigmatic rival the *Bol'shaia Igra* hung distant but dogged upon their starboard quarter, red as a cursed ruby representing a third eye in the brow of some idol of the incomprehensible.

HAVING JUST MISSED intercepting the Expedition steamer at Isafjörðr the boys turned north again, continuing their pursuit yet somehow at each step just missing the vessel, now owing to a contrary wind, now an erroneous report over the wireless or a delay in port because of the late return of some crew member who proved to be spectral at best, the "extra man" of Arctic myth. A familiar story up here. But no less unsettling, for there seemed, now and then, to be an extra member of the *Inconvenience*'s crew, though this was never recorded at the morning roll call. At times one of the boys would understand, too late of course, that the face he thought he was dealing with was not in any way the true face—or even one he recognized.

One day the *Inconvenience* arrived over a little settlement whose streets and lanes seemed crowded with wax figures, so still were they in their attention to the gigantic vehicle creeping above them.

Randolph St. Cosmo decided to grant ground-leave. "These are a Northern people, remember," he advised. "They're not likely to mistake us for gods or anything, not like those customers back in the East Indies that time."

"Wasn't that a paradise!" cried Darby Suckling.

After the ship had landed and tied up, the boys barged ashore, eager to spend their pay on anything at all.

"Is this turquoise?"

"We call it Blue Ivory. Preserved bones of real prehistoric mammoths, not the tinted bonzoline you see further south."

"This one—"

"This is a miniature copy of an inukshuk that actually stands up on a ridgeline far away in the interior, rocks piled in roughly the shape of a human, not to threaten the stranger but to guide him in country where landmarks are either too few or too many to keep straight."

"Sounds like my average day."

"Perhaps why these copies are sold in such numbers. For any day, even in the cities of the South, can turn in a moment to wilderness."

From time to time in the difficult days ahead, each of the boys was to gaze at the enigmatic miniature he had purchased, representing a faraway disposition of rocks he would probably never get to see, and try to glimpse, even at this degree of indirectness, some expression of a truth beyond the secular.

THE *ÉTIENNE-LOUIS MALUS* was named for the Napoleonic army engineer and physicist who, in late 1808, looking though a piece of Iceland spar at the sunset reflected from a window of the Luxembourg Palace, discovered polarized light. She was built of oak and iron, 376 feet, 6 inches long, with shelter and boat decks, two masts, two cargo booms, and a single tall black smokestack. The guy wires of dozens of transmitting and receiving antennas descended to fittings everywhere around the weather decks. Her prow was raked back from the waterline a little aft of vertical, as if she were expecting to cut through ice.

As she sailed north on her long voyage to the coasts of "Iceland," to the inhabited cliffs of ice, those not actually on watch or asleep sat out on the fantail, watching the lower latitudes drop away from them, and played mandolins and little mahogany concertinas, and sang,

No more girls,
But the girls of Iceland,
No more nights,
But the nights of cold . . .
For we sail
With no sure returning,
Into winds
That will freeze the soul. . . .

They passed around rumors—the Captain was insane again, ice-pirates were hunting the *Malus* like whalers and if caught, her crew would be shown even less mercy—some believed they were on an expedition to find a new source of Iceland spar pure as the legendary crystals of Helgustaðir, purer than anything being pulled these days out of Missouri or Guanajuato . . . but that was only one suspicion among many. It might not be about Iceland spar after all.

One day walls of green ice, nearly invisible off in the Northern dusk, began to slide by. The ship approached a green headland, sheer green walls of ice, the greenness nearest the water figuring also as a *scent,* a sea-smell of deep decay and reproduction.

From her ancestral home on an island just the other side of the promontory from town, Constance Penhallow, now passed into legend, though not herself ambitious for even local respect, watched the arrival of the *Malus.* When required she could pose with the noblest here against the luminous iceblink, as if leaning anxiously out of some portrait-frame, eyes asking not for help but understanding, cords of her neck edged in titanium white, a three-quarters view from behind, showing the face only just crescent, the umbra of brushed hair and skull-heft, the brass shadow amiably turned toward an open shelf of books with no glass cover there arranged to throw back images of a face, only this dorsal finality. So had her grandson Hunter painted her, standing in a loose, simple dress in a thousand-flower print in green and yellow, viewed as through dust, dust of another remembered country observed late in the day, risen by way of wind or horses from a lane beyond a walled garden . . . in the background a half-timbered house, steep gabling of many angles, running back into lizard imbrication of gray slatework, shining as with rain . . . wilds of rooftops, unexplored reaches, stretching as to sunset. . . .

Tales survived here from the first millennium, the first small pack of outlaws on the run, not yet come to be haunted by any promise of Christ's return, thinking only of the ax-bearing avengers at their backs, setting off westward, suicidally cheerful, almost careless . . . tales of Harald the Ruthless, son of King Sigurd, sailing north, drawn by inexplicable desire, farther away each sunset from all comfort, all kindness, to the awful brink, scant oarstrokes away from falling into Ginnungagap the lightless abyss, glimpsed through the Northern obscurities and reported on over the years by lost fisherfolk, marauders, God-possessed fugitives. . . . Harald threw over his tiller, the men backed their oars, the fateful circumference wheeling past them through the fog, and Harald Hårdråde, having come about just in time, understood, from that moment of unsought mercy, with the end of the world now at his back, more than perhaps he cared to about desire, and the forsaking of desire in submission to one's duties to history and blood. Something had called to him out of that vaporous immensity, and he had answered, in a dream, and at the last instant had awakened, and turned. For in the ancient

Northmen's language, *"Gap"* meant not only this particular chasm, the ice-chaos from which arose, through the giant Ymir, the Earth and everything in it, but also a wide-open human mouth, mortal, crying, screaming, calling out, calling back.

So relates Adam of Bremen in the *Historia Hammaburgensis Ecclesiæ.*

And this current expedition, if not by its official remit bound all the way to Ginnungagap, must nonetheless acknowledge its presence up there ahead in the fog, in the possible darkening of some day's water-sky to the reflection of a mythical Interior, the chance, in this day and age, of sailing off the surface of the World, drawn into another, toroidal dispensation, more up-to-date topologically than any simple disk or spheroid.

Already, by the time of Harald Hårdråde, the once terrible void was scarcely a remnant, a vaporous residue of the world's creation and the high drama of the Ymir-Audumla era, no longer the intersection of Niflheim's ice and Muspellheim's fire but the debris from a calamitous birth.

Though Penhallow forebears might have undertaken some similar expedition, all, until now, had found reasons not to. There was even some suggestion of a conspiracy of ancestors, against the future, certainly against this voyage. . . . The Penhallow money came from Iceland spar—they owned extensive deposits all over the Arctic, having been crystal tycoons since the first Penhallows arrived in Iceland late in the seventeenth century as part of a calcite rush set off by the famous arrival of the double-refracting mineral in Copenhagen by way of a sailor who'd discovered some near the Bay of Röerford.

When the Vormance Expedition arrived, Constance's grandson, Hunter Penhallow, was off on the ferry to the mainland every day in delirious truancy, abandoning his easel and brushes, working whatever odd quayside jobs he could for these scientific folk with their strange lower-eighties accents. His parents, one day too early in his life for him to remember, had "withdrawn" southward to that region of sailors' yarns and oddities unconfirmed, and Constance—headlong, unable to withhold, even knowing, in the oracular way expected of her, that as soon as he could he would follow their example if not their exact tracks—had become all his home. Of course he would leave—that was only fortune-telling—it could not interfere with her love. He would stow away on the *Malus,* sail off to sea with the Vormance Expedition, as Constance had known and feared that one day, on some ship, he must. No one in the crew or among the scientists tried to prevent him—hadn't it become a custom on these expeditions for trustworthy natives to tag along, often in just some mascotte capacity? When he finally did go round the Point and out to sea, it was to bear away with him, first northward and then back down into the lower latitudes, the curse of the great silent struggle which was the ground for the history of this place, since at least the discovery of the first crystal-choked cave.

BUILT ONLY A FEW YEARS BEFORE, in clapboard siding of a vivid cream color, roofed in gray shakes a shade or two lighter than the outcroppings and stone walls that surrounded it, the Hotel Borealis, where the Expedition had set up headquarters, presented at one corner a curious sort of open turret, whose slender white columns supported semicircular balconies on the first and second floors, and above them held up a conical roof, almost a steeple, with a high finial that carried a weather vane and some wireless antennas as well. In back of the hotel rose a steep green mountainside. Mist seethed and glided everywhere. At the end of the lane began the fjord, sudden and deep.

Hunter set up his easel outside across the road and began to try to paint the place, though microscopic droplets of salt fog inevitably got folded though not mixed in with the Payne's gray and Naples yellow, and in years to come, as the small canvases from this period traveled the world increasing in value, this introduced modelings, shadows, redefinitions of space, which, though they were physically there, Hunter had not seen at the time—would have to wait for his later "Venice" and "London" phases even to recognize.

All night, out in the great fjord, they heard the ice, they woke, they dozed again, the voices of the ice entered their dreams, dictated what they would see, what would happen to each dreaming eye as, helpless, it gazed. Just to the north loomed a far-spreading glacier, the only one in this entire domain of ice that had never been named, as if in fearful acknowledgment of its ancient nobility, its seemingly conscious pursuit of a project. . . .

"We can't afford to winter here, we'll have to move while we can still get out to sea."

"Fine with me. I'm not sure I can take even another week here. The food—"

"Not a Meat Olaf fancier, I gather."

"Can anything be done?"

"Well, it's supposed to be for emergencies, but I guess this qualifies as one." Unlocking a black valise and gazing inside for a moment. "Here you go," handing over an ancient hand-blown bottle whose label, carefully engraved and printed in an unfaded spectrum of tropical colors, showed an erupting volcano, a parrot with a disdainful smile and the legend *¡Cuidado Cabrón! Salsa Explosiva La Original.* "Couple of drops is all you'll need really to light that Meat Olaf right up, not that I'm being stingy, understand. My father handed this on to me, as did his father to him, and it isn't down by even a quarter of an inch yet, so do exercise caution's all I'm saying."

As expected, this advice was ignored, and next mealtime the bottle got passed around and everybody slopped on the salsa. The evening that resulted was notable for hysteria and recrimination.

The luxuriant world of the parrot on the label, though seemingly as remote from this severe ice-scape as could be imagined, in fact was separated from it by only the thinnest of membranes. To get from one to the other one had only to fill one's attention unremittingly with the bird's image, abasing oneself meantime before his contempt, and repeat "*¡Cuidado cabrón!*" preferably with a parrot accent, until the phrase no longer had meaning—though in practice, of course, the number of repetitions was known to run into the millions, even as it ran listeners' forbearance into the ground. In thus acquiring some of the force of a Tibetan prayer-wheel, the practice was thought to serve as an open-sesame to the Tsangpo-Brahmaputra country as well, a point which old Expedition hands were not reluctant to bring up.

At first glance a roomful merely of bearded gentlemen in dark suits and matching waistcoats, these scientists actually made up an international spectrum of motive and eccentricity. Dr. Vormance was on sabbatical from Candlebrow University, where he ordinarily headed the Department of Mineralogy. The noted Quaternionist Dr. V. Ganesh Rao of Calcutta University was seeking a gateway to the Ulterior, as he liked to phrase it, having come to recognize the wisdom of simply finding silence and allowing Mathematics and History to proceed as they would. The American bucket-shop desperado Dodge Flannelette, on the other hand, was chiefly up here for the practical uses any discoveries could be put to, having been privately informed, for instance, that Iceland spar was central to the development of means to send moving images thousands of miles, if not in fact everywhere in the world. And young Mr. Fleetwood Vibe was here at the behest of his father, Wall Street eminence Scarsdale Vibe, who was effectively bankrolling the Expedition. One of Fleetwood's chores was to observe and write down instances of money recklessly spent, enabling the elder Vibe someday to exact an appropriate revenge.

"The main thing to be looking at, though," the tycoon gazing off into various distances which failed to include his son, a tell that Fleetwood and his brothers had learned quite early meant that Scarsdale did not fully trust them and was not providing the full story, not by a damn sight, "is the railworthiness of the terrain. As we speak, Brother Harriman is out buying up scientists by the shipload, mobilizing some kind of Alaskan junket. Him and old Schiff as usual, hand in glove. Almost certainly suggesting a scheme for a rail link across the Bering Strait, Alaska to Siberia, hooking on into the Trans-Sib, and from there God knows. Setting aside of course the unholy conditions any train trying to cross a railroad bridge over the Bering Strait would likely encounter."

This had the appearance of an open sharing of deep business confidences, but all it meant was that important data were being withheld, which Fleetwood, if he wished further enlightenment, must inquire after on his own. "So . . . you want to beat him to it."

"Them," Scarsdale corrected him. "A climber plus a Jew. Any wonder the world's going to hell."

THE TRANSNOCTIAL DISCUSSION GROUP met in one of the lounges in the basement of the hotel, located well out of the earshot of other guests who might have wished, for example, to sleep. Tonight's announced topic was "The Nature of Expeditions."

"We learned once how to break horses and ride them for long distances, with oceangoing ships we left flat surfaces and went into Riemann space, we crossed solid land and deep seas, and colonized what we found," said Dr. Vormance. "Now we have taken the first few wingbeats of what will allow us to begin colonizing the Sky. Somewhere in it, God dwells in His Heavenly City. How far into that unmapped wilderness shall we journey before we find Him? Will He withdraw before our advance, continue to withdraw into the Infinite? Will He send back to us divine Agents, to help, to deceive, to turn us away? Will we leave settlements in the Sky, along our invasion routes, or will we choose to be wanderers, striking camp each morning, content with nothing short of Zion? And what of colonizing additional dimensions beyond the third? Colonize Time. Why not?"

"Because, sir," objected Dr. Templeton Blope, of the University of the Outer Hebrides, "—we are limited to three."

"Quaternionist talk," shouted his collegial nemesis Hastings Throyle. "Everything, carnal and spiritual, invested in the given three dimensions—for what use, as your Professor Tate famously asked, are any more than three?"

"Ever so frightfully sorry. The given world, in case you hadn't noticed. Planet Earth."

"Which not so long ago was believed to be a plane surface."

So forth. A recurring argument. Quaternionism in this era still enjoyed the light and warmth of a cheerful noontide. Rival systems might be acknowledged now and then, usually for some property considered bothersome, but those of the Hamiltonian faith felt an immunity to ever being superseded, children imagining they would live forever—though the sizable bloc of them aboard the *Malus* were not quite certain what the closely guarded Mission Document meant when it described the present journey as being taken "at right angles to the flow of time."

"Time moves on but one axis," advised Dr. Blope, "past to future—the only turnings possible being turns of a hundred and eighty degrees. In the Quaternions, a ninety-degree direction would correspond to an *additional axis* whose unit is $\sqrt{-1}$. A turn through any other angle would require for its unit a complex number."

"Yet mappings in which a linear axis becomes curvilinear—functions of a complex variable such as $w=e^z$, where a straight line in the z-plane maps to a circle in the w-plane," said Dr. Rao, "do suggest the possibility of linear time becoming circular, and so achieving eternal return as simply, or should I say complexly, as that."

Inexpensive cigar smoke thickened the air, and the fifteen-cent bottles of imported Danish aquavit ran out, to be replaced by a locally distilled product stored in somewhat larger earthen crocks. Out in the dark, the ancient ice went creaking, as if trying to express some argument of its own.

As if the hour itself in growing later had exposed some obscure fatality, the discussion moved to the subject of the luminiferous Æther, as to which exchanges of opinion—relying, like Quaternions, largely on faith—often failed to avoid a certain vehemence.

"Bloody idiots!" screamed Dr. Blope, who belonged to that British school, arisen in the wake of the Michelson-Morley Experiment, of belief in some secret Agency in Nature which was conspiring to prevent all measurement of the Earth's velocity through the Æther. If such velocity produced, as Fitzgerald maintained, a shrinkage of dimension in the same direction, it was impossible to measure it, because the measuring device would shrink as well. "It's obvious Something doesn't want us to know!"

"About what I'd expect from the Brits," thoughtfully countered Dr. Vormance. "Half the dwelling units of that island have been visibly haunted at some time or other. They see ghosts, they see fairies under every fungus, edible and otherwise. They believe in astral projection, foreknowledge, reincarnation, and other proofs of immunity to Time."

"You're talking about me, aren't you?"

"Why no, Blope, no not at all."

Everyone chuckled condescendingly, except of course for Dr. Blope.

"What cannot be resolved inside the psyche," put in the Expedition alienist, Otto Ghloix, "must enter the outside world and become physically, objectively 'real.' For example, one who cannot come to terms with the, one must say *sinister unknowability* of Light, projects an Æther, real in every way, except for its being detectable."

"Seems like an important property to be missing, don't you think? Puts it in the same class as God, the soul—"

"Fairies under mushrooms," from a heckler somewhere in the group, whom nobody, strangely, seemed quite able to locate.

Icelanders, however, had a long tradition of ghostliness that made the Brits appear models of rationalism. Earlier members of the Expedition had visited the great Library of Iceland behind the translucent green walls facing the sunlit sea. Some of these spaces were workshops or mess-halls, some centers of operation, stacked to the top of the great cliff, easily a dozen levels, probably more. Among the library shelves could be found *The Book of Iceland Spar,* commonly described as "like the *Ynglingasaga* only different," containing family histories going back to the first discovery and exploitation of the eponymic mineral up to the present, including a record of each day of this very Expedition now in progress, even of *days not yet transpired.*

"Fortune-telling! Impossible!"

"Unless we can allow that certain texts are—"

"Outside of time," suggested one of the Librarians.

"Holy Scripture and so forth."

"In a different relation to time anyhow. Perhaps even to be read through, mediated by, a lens of the very sort of calcite which according to rumor you people are up here seeking."

"Another Quest for another damned Magic Crystal. Horsefeathers, I say. Wish I'd known before I signed on. Say, you aren't one of these Sentient Rocksters, are you?"

Mineral consciousness figured even back in that day as a source of jocularity—had they known what was waiting in that category . . . waiting to move against them, grins would have frozen and chuckles turned to dry-throated coughing.

"Of course," said the Librarian, "you'll find Iceland spar everywhere in the world, often in the neighborhood of zinc, or silver, some of it perfectly good for optical instruments. But up here it's of the essence, found in no other company but its own. It's the genuine article, and the sub-structure of reality. The doubling of the Creation, each image clear and believable. . . . And you being mathematical gentlemen, it can hardly have escaped your attention that its curious advent into the world occurred within only a few years of the discovery of Imaginary Numbers, which also provided a doubling of the mathematical Creation.

"For this is not *only* the geographical Iceland here, it is also one of several convergences among the worlds, found now and then lying behind the apparent, like these subterranean passages beneath the surface, which lead among the caves of Iceland spar, blindly among crystals untouched, perhaps never to be touched, by light. Down where the 'Hidden People' live, inside their private rock dwellings, where humans who visit them can be closed in and never find a way out again. Iceland spar is what hides the Hidden People, makes it possible for them to move through the world that thinks of itself as 'real,' provides that all-important ninety-degree twist to *their* light, so they can exist alongside our own world but not be seen. They and others as well, visitors from elsewhere, of non-human aspect.

"They have been crossing here, crossing over, between the worlds, for generations. Our ancestors knew them. Looking back over a thousand years, there is a time when their trespassings onto our shores at last converge, as in a vanishing-point, with those of the first Norse visitors.

"They arrive here in criminal frames of mind, much like those early Norsemen, who were either fleeing retribution for offenses committed back where they came from or seeking new coastlines to pillage. Who in our excess of civilization strike us now as barbaric, incapable of mercy. Compared to these other Trespassers, however, they are the soul of civility."

THE SUN CAME UP a baleful smear in the sky, not quite shapeless, in fact able to assume the appearance of a device immediately recognizable yet unnamable, so widely familiar that the inability to name it passed from simple frustration to a felt dread, whose intricacy deepened almost moment to moment . . . its name a word of power, not to be spoken aloud, not even to be remembered in silence. All around lay ambushes of the bad ice, latent presences, haunting all transaction, each like the infinitesimal circle converging toward zero that mathematicians now and then find use for. A silver-gray, odorless, silent exit from the upper world. . . . The sun might be visible from time to time, with or without clouds, but the sky was more neutral-density gray than blue. Out on the promontory grew some even-textured foliage, in this light a blazing, virtually shadowless green, and breaking down at the base of the headland was the sea-green sea, the ice-green, glass-green sea.

Hunter had been out with his sketchbook all day, taking down as much as he could, to bring away with him. That night was the last he and Constance would have before his departure. "I wanted this to be a bon voyage party," she said, "but there's nothing here to eat."

"I can go over to Narvik's."

"It's late. Bad ice after midnight."

"It isn't that dark tonight, Grandmother. Won't take me long."

There were usually boatmen down at the shore, who would bring passengers over after the regular ferries had docked for the night—they could count on a steady, if not brisk, all-night traffic, as if over on the mainland were a darkly glamorous resort known only to the discerning few. With winter in the offing, leads of open water were harder to find. The sleek little steam craft throbbed to and fro in the accents of frustrated hunting dogs, and the pilots called to each other over the drifting floes. Something phosphorescent in the ice kept the night well illuminated.

But tonight the town was a melancholy place. Not much going on. The impending departure of the *Malus* seemed to have put everyone at loose ends. Lights burned everywhere, as if invisible receptions of some kind were in progress. Insomnia wrapped the town like a sweaty blanket. Gangs of petty criminals swept by from time to time, committing no offense more serious than staring. Like temporary innkeepers, the unsleeping residents brought the newly arrived in to their own parlors, sitting without speaking, seldom offering alcohol because of its exorbitant price, paid in the dark and in banknotes only, as the noise of specie traveled too far, undiminished, in the vast silences.

The only eating place open this time of night was Narvik's Mush-It-Away Northern Cuisine, crowded at all hours, usually with a queue out the door. Hunter foresaw a long wait. Not only was the line intolerably slow—often it did not move, for fifteen minutes—but when it did move, it ratcheted ahead only *a fraction of the space* a single body would occupy. As if some of those waiting were, somehow, only fractionally present.

Alongside the creeping queue, in the opposite direction, an ingenious steam-driven train of pot-size wheeled conveyances passed continuously, to remind those waiting of today's menu, the braised blubber with cloudberries, skua eggs any style, walrus chops, and snow parfaits, not to mention the widely praised Meat Olaf, which was This Week's—in fact Every Week's—Special, all cranking along behind the display glass, inches away from the drooling clientele, though, given the absence of impulse-control locals were notorious for, not securely protected. Along with episodes of snack theft, the waiting was enlivened as well by queue-jumping, food-throwing, mother defamation, and unpremeditated excursions off the end of Narvik's pier.

Narvik himself, rumored never to sleep, continued to fidget to and fro as he had all through the night, greeting customers, bringing out orders from the kitchen, taking money, in general attempting with Arctic humor to cheer those too long in line. "Canadian walks into a bar—goes, 'Ouch, eh?' Two

Italians prospecting in the Yukon, one comes running into camp. 'I found gold!'—the other one says, 'Eh, a fangool-a *you* and-a you mother, too.' What's the favorite pickup line in Alaska? 'Woof, woof.'"

"Couple of those Meat Olafs, I guess," Hunter said at last, "some root slaw, too, with that, oh and can I get the Mystery Sauce on the side?"

He returned to the island through the middle of a night now cold and unpopulated as a promise of the winter to come, in perilous transit through icefields which sought as if with conscious malevolence to take the unwary down like quicksand, without warning.

And in the ceaseless drift of the ice, the uncountable translations and rotations, meltings and freezings, there would come a moment, maybe two, when the shapes and sizes of the masses here at this "Venice of the Arctic" would be exactly the same as those of secular Venice and its own outlying islands. Not all of these shapes would be dry land, of course, some would be ice, but, considered as multiply-connected spaces, the two would be the same, Murano, Burano, San Michele, the Grand Canal, each small waterway in painstaking detail, and for that brief instant it would be possible to move from one version to the other. All through his boyhood, Hunter Penhallow had watched for the fateful moment, prayed for its thunderous assault on his sensorium, for immediate translation miles and years away from here, to the City of Silence and Queen of the Adriatic herself. He would "wake," though it was more like having arrived after an unsensed journey, in a room in the Bauer-Grünewald with a tenor in full heartbreaking cry accompanied by a concertina just beneath the window, and the sun going down behind Mestre.

But ice always crept back into his nighttime dreaming. The frozen canals. The security of the ice. To return each night to the ice, as to home. To recline, horizontal as ice, beneath the surface, to enter the lockless, the unbreachable, the long-sought sleep. . . . Down in the other world of childhood and dreams, where polar bears no longer lumber and kill but once in the water and swimming beneath the ice become great amphibious white sea-creatures, graceful as any dolphin.

When his grandmother was a girl, she told him once, the sisters announced in school one day that the topic of study would be Living Creatures. "I suggested ice. They threw me out of class."

ABOUT MID-MORNING, Constance went to the ridgetop, looked down the long declivity, down the shorn hills, and saw that the miniature ship that had once lain waiting there, secured only by the lightest of kedgework to the Harbor bed, seeming sometimes to tremble with its desire to be away, had gone at last, bound for seas more emerald, aromatic winds, hammocks out on deck. Up here the view of the sea continued as gray as ever, the wind no colder than usual, perhaps a minimum austerity of growth, all in shades of white, buff, and gray, pale grasses, failing by a visible margin to be green, bending to the wind together, a million stalks all held to the same exact angle, which no scientific instrument would measure. She looked to every horizon, taking her time, saving south for last. Not a wisp of smoke, not the last, wind-muted cry of a steam siren, only the good-bye letter waiting this morning on her work-table, held now like a crushed handkerchief in her pocket, in which he had given her his heart—but which she could not open again and read for fear that through some terrible magic she had never learned to undo, it might have become, after all, a blank sheet.

From the Journals of Mr. Fleetwood Vibe—

It wasn't any Rapture of the North. Ask anybody who was there. They landed. They conversed. They shared their picnic baskets. Jellied pâté de foie gras, truffled pheasant, Nesselrode pudding, a '96 Champagne which they had frappéd in local ice . . .

It was the singing we became aware of first. In such cases the first thing that has to be ruled out is collective dementia, though none in the party could agree even on *what was being sung*. Only after prolonged sweeps with field-glasses in the direction of that shrill and unfamiliar music did any of us detect a dark dot, poised low in a frozen sky, which slowly grew in size, even as the witless chorale, paradoxically yet mercifully, seemed to abate, though not before the song was engraved upon every brain. Dating from about 1897, it commemorated the reappearance on the north coast of Norway of Fridtjof Nansen and Frederik Hjalmar Johansen, back after three years' journey into the Polar silence, within weeks of the ship they'd set off in, the doughty *Fram*. If only for the sake of scientific objectivity, I feel obliged to include it here.

The world's gone crazy,
Romancin'
Over Nansen and Johansen,
Those sturdy young Pals of the Po-o-o-le!

Oh, my, there's legions
Besiegin'

These darin' Norwegians,
Where'er in the region they ro-o-o-ll!

Three years ago
They sailed off in the *Fram,*
Now that they're back,
Life's just muffins and jam!

They've all got ants in
Their pants, 'n'
For Nansen and Johansen
They're dancin' right out of contro-o-ol!

We were stunned at the immensity of the vehicle which finally came to stand above us. There were scarcely enough of us to handle the lines they threw down. We must have looked to them like interchangeable insects, scurrying beneath.

"We are neither in danger," we assured them repeatedly, "nor, in fact, in need of any assistance."

"You are in *mortal* danger," declared their Scientific Officer, Dr. Counterfly, a scholarly sort, bearded and bundled like the rest of them, his eyes concealed by a pair of ingenious goggles, whose lenses proved to be matched pairs of Nicol prisms which could be rotated so as to control precisely the amount of light admitted to each eye. "Maybe you've been too close to see it. . . . We, on the other hand, have seen little else, since clearing the Eightieth Parallel. A Zone of Emergency has been declared for hundreds of miles' radius. The peak in whose lee you have chosen to set up your command post is far too regular in shape to be the *nunatak* you imagine it. Did none of you suspect an artificial structure? In fact it was not situated here by accident, and you could have chosen no site more perilous."

"Ah," twinkled Dr. Vormance, "and you can see right down through the snow at the base of it, I suppose."

"Nowadays, as you know, sir, there are Rays, and there are Rays, and it can be readily contrived for wave-lengths other than those of light to travel all the way through even the most obstinate of media."

Nunatak, in the Eskimo tongue literally "land connected," refers to a mountain peak tall enough to rise above the wastes of ice and snow that otherwise cover the terrain. Each, believed to have its own guardian spirit, is alive, an ark sheltering whatever lichens, mosses, flowers, insects, or even birds may be borne to it by the winds of the Region. During the last Ice Age, many of our own mountains in the U.S., familiar and even famous now, were *nunataks* then, rising in the same way above that ancient frozen expanse, keeping the flames of species aglow till such time as the ice should recede and life resume its dominion.

At their invitation we crowded into the spacious control cabin of the great airship, where scientific gear occupied every available cubic—perhaps hypercubic—inch. Among the fantastical glass envelopes and knottings of gold wire as unreadable to us as the ebonite control panels scrupulously polished and reflecting the Arctic sky, we were able here and there to recognize more mundane items—here Manganin resistance-boxes and Tesla coils, there Leclanché cells and solenoidal magnets, with electrical cables sheathed in commercial-grade Gutta Percha running everywhere.

Inside, the overhead was much higher than expected, and the bulkheads could scarcely be made out in the muted light through three hanging Fresnel lenses, the mantle behind each glowing a different primary color, from sensitive-flames which hissed at different frequencies. Strange sounds, complex harmonies and dissonances, resonant, sibilant, and percussive at once, being monitored from someplace far Exterior to this, issued from a large brass speaking-trumpet, with brass tubing and valvework elaborate as any to be found in an American marching band running back from it and into an extensive control panel on which various metering gauges were ranked, their pointers, with exquisite Breguet-style arrowheads, trembling in their rise and fall along the arcs of italic numerals. The glow of electrical coils seeped beyond the glass cylinders which enclosed them, and anyone's hands that came near seemed dipped in blue chalk-dust. A Poulsen's Telegraphone, recording the data being received, moved constantly to and fro along a length of shining steel wire which periodically was removed and replaced.

"Ætheric impulses," Dr. Counterfly was explaining. "For vortex stabilization we need a membrane sensitive enough to respond to the slightest eddies. We use a human caul—a 'veil,' as some say."

"Isn't a child born with a veil believed to have powers of second sight?" Dr. Vormance inquired.

"Correct. And a ship with a veil aboard it will never sink—or, in our case, crash."

"Things have been done to obtain a veil," darkly added a junior officer, Mr. Suckling, "that may not even be talked about."

"Interesting. How'd you come by yours?"

"A long history, of some complexity." At this point Science Officer Counterfly advised us that the Special Ray Generator had come up to speed, enabling us to view the "*nunatak*" in a different light, so to speak. He led us into an adjoining compartment, where translucent screens glowed at various colors and intensities, and over to a panel, before which he seated himself.

"Now, let's adjust the gain here. . . . Good. Can you see it? Look on the reflecting-sheet, there, just below the quartz-work."

It took some moments to interpret what the curious *camera lucida* was revealing. At first all was a blurry confusion of strange yellowish green, in which areas of light and dark moved in a squirming restlessness, seeming in their slow boil to penetrate, while at the same time to envelop, one another. But once taken into that serpentine hypnosis, we became aware that the frame of visibility was moving ever downward, even as the glaucous turmoil began, here and there, to coalesce into a series of inscriptions, rushing by, that is, upward, too fast to read, even had the language been familiar.

"We believe them to be warnings," remarked the airship Commander, Professor St. Cosmo, "perhaps regarding the site of some sacred burial . . . a tomb of some sort. . . ."

"Uneasy reference," chuckled Dr. Vormance, "I take it, to the recent misfortunes of certain Egyptologists imprudent enough to have penetrated *those* realms of eternal rest?"

"More like due diligence," replied Dr. Counterfly, "and a respect for probabilities." He gestured toward the image transmitted by the prisms of the instrument, which had been growing steadily clearer, like a fateful dawn none await with any eagerness. Too soon we discovered that we could not look away. Though details were still difficult to make out, the Figure appeared to recline on its side, an odalisque of the snows—though to what pleasures given posed a question far too dangerous—with as little agreement among us as to its "facial" features, some describing them as "Mongoloid," others as "serpent-like." Its eyes, for the most part, if eyes be what they were, remained open, its gaze as yet undirected—though we were bound in a common terror of that moment at which it might *become aware of our interest* and smoothly pivot its awful head to stare us full in the face.

Oddly, questions of its being "alive" or "conscious" never figured in our decision to recover it. How deep did it lie? we wanted to know. Was there snow all the way down there, or would we run into rock of some kind? Practical matters. A muscular approach. Not a dreamer in the lot of us, to be honest, much less any dreamer of nightmares—the presence of at least one of whom, on any expedition of this sort, ought in future to be required by statute. Whatever we thought we had seen upon the viewing instrument, we had already, in mute fear, dismissed.

Scholars of the Eddas, recently having perused them in original form in the Library of Iceland, were to suggest later—too late—comparison to Buri, grandfather of Odin and the first gods, frozen in the ice of Niflheim for uncounted ages, till being licked awake by the tongue of the mythic cow Audumla. Which of us then, mindlessly as children at a fairground, had not performed the analogous service for our own frozen Visitant? What gods, what races, what worlds were about to be born?

Alpinists among us were to describe the recovery as no more arduous than a descent into a crevasse. The crew of the great airship, having warned us as much as they felt they could, now held aloof. Their charge appeared to go no further than warning—they shook their heads ruefully, they gazed down at us from the rail of their gondola, but they neither interfered nor lifted a finger to help. And we, intrepid innocents, we climbed down into those shadows, leaving abruptly the wind, as the scentless snow walls rose about us, and we followed the all-too-regular slope of what we foolishly continued to call the "*nunatak,*" down to meet our destiny. The Eskimos had seemed eager, at times unnaturally so, to speed our work. But whenever we happened upon a group of them conversing, they fell silent and did not resume till we had passed from earshot. Soon, one by one, on some private schedule we could not decipher, they departed, muttering, gliding away over the ice and into the yellowed glare forever.

We entered a period of uncritical buoyancy, borne along by submission to a common fate of celebrity and ease. We exchanged formulaic sentiments—"Even the weather is cooperating." "Glad we've all got contracts." "Vibes will sell it, whatever it is, the minute they see it." We labored in the polar darkness, our faces beaten at by the terrible orange flame-light of the Aurora. From time to time, the dogs went crazy—rigid, staring in fear, they ran away and tried to hide or to bite anything that got close. Sometimes there were real-life explanations—some polar bear or walrus scented from miles away. But sometimes no explanation could be found. Whatever it was, it was invisible.

And on occasion they did not bark when they should have. One day there came walking to us over the white plain a figure in bearskins not of the region, strangely, unsettlingly, *approaching from the north.* Mr. Dodge Flannelette was impulsively reaching for his rifle, when Mr. Hastings

Throyle, I believe it was, called out in Tungus, adding, "Damned if it isn't old Magyakan. Knew him in Siberia."

"He can't have come all this way on foot," said Dr. Vormance skeptically.

"Actually, most likely he flew here, and not only is he here visiting with us but also and simultaneously, I've no doubt, back in the Yenisei watershed with his people as well."

"You are beginning to worry me, Throyle."

Throyle explained about the mysterious shamanic power known as bilocation, which enables those with the gift literally to be in two or more places, often widely separated, at the same time. "He says he has a message for us."

"He seems afraid of something."

"Arctic hysteria," said Dr. Ghloix, the Expedition's psychomedical officer. "A sort of Northern melancholia, all too often a foreshadowing of suicide."

Magyakan declined food but took a cup of tea and a Havana cigar, sat, half-closed his eyes, and began to speak, with Throyle translating.

"They may not wish to harm us. They may even in some way love us. But they have no more choice than your own sled dogs, in the terrible, to them empty, land upon which they have chosen to trespass, where humans are the only source of food. We are allowed to live and work until we fall from exhaustion. But they are suffering as much as we. Their voices will be gentle, they will administer the pain only when they must, and when they bring out the weapons, objects we've never seen before, we stare, wordless as dogs, we don't recognize them, perhaps we think they are toys or something else to amuse us. . . ." He fell silent, sat and smoked and presently slept. Sometime after midnight he woke, rose, and walked away into the Arctic emptiness.

"It was some sort of a prophecy, then?" asked Dr. Vormance.

"Not quite as we're used to thinking of it," Throyle replied. "For us it's simple ability to see into the future, based on our linear way of regarding time, a simple straight line from past, through present, into the future. Christian time, as you might say. But shamans see it differently. Their notion of time is spread out not in a single dimension but over many, which all exist in a single, timeless instant."

We found ourselves watching the dogs more closely. Often they were observed in the company of another large, otherwise nondescript dog, who had flown here with the airship crew. The sled dogs were usually gathered round him in an orderly circle, as if he were in some way addressing them.

What bothered them particularly was the task of pulling the improvised sled we used to transport the object over the ice to the ship. It might as well have been a canine labor union. Perhaps, under the guidance of Pugnax, for that was the airship dog's name, that is what it was.

Bringing what we had recovered back to the ship proved to be only the first of our trials. Stowing the object in the hold was cursed from the beginning. One failure followed another—if a purchase did not give way, then some hawser, regardless of size, was sure to strand—yet each time, mysteriously, the object was rescued from falling to its possible destruction . . . as if it were somehow *meant to survive* our worst efforts. Trying to get it to fit inside the ship, we measured, and remeasured, and each time the dimensions kept coming out different—not just slightly so but drastically. There seemed no way to get the object through any of the ship's hatches. We had finally to resort to our cutting-torches. All the while the thing regarded us with what, later, when we had begun to appreciate the range of its emotions, we might too easily have recognized as contempt. With its "eyes" set closely side by side like those of humans and other binocular predators, its gaze had remained directed solely, personally, to each of us, no matter where we stood or moved.

Of the journey south again, we ought to have remembered more, our waking watches speeding by, the melodic whispering of a crewman's ocarina down a passageway framed in steel-bolted timbers, the smell of the coffee at breakfast, the gibbous presence of the airship which had come to warn us, persistent off the starboard quarter, like a misplaced moon, until at last, as if given up on our common sense, they took their leave with a salute of Bengal lights from which irony may not have been entirely absent.

Which of us was willing to turn, to look the future in the face, to mutiny if necessary and oblige the Captain to put about, return the thing to where we had found it? The last of our mean innocence tolled away ship's bell after bell. Even if we could not predict in detail what was about to happen, there could have been no one among us, not even the most literal-minded, who did not feel that something, down there, below our feet, below the waterline where it lay patient and thawing, was terribly, and soon to be more terribly, amiss.

Returned to harbor at last, we felt little alarm when those first deep metal-to-metal groans began. Here in this as in any great seaport, being invisible, so we thought, was the same as being safe, invisible amid all these impersonal momenta of the Commercial, the coming and going of Whitehall gigs, the bristling masts and funnels, the jungles of rigging, the bills of lading, the routine attendances of fitters, chandlers, insurance men, port officials, longshoremen, and at last a delegation from the Museum, to take delivery of what we had brought, and by whom we were ignored, nearly unsensed.

Perhaps in their haste to be rid of us, they had missed seeing, as had we, how *imperfectly contained* the object really was. As if it were the embodiment of a newly-discovered "field" as yet only roughly calculated, there lay our original sin—the repeated failure, back there up north, to determine the distribution of its weight in ordinary space, which should have offered a strong hint, to any of us willing to devote a moment's thought, that some fraction of the total must necessarily have escaped confinement. That this unbounded part had been neither detected nor measured was equivalent to saying that *no* part of it had *ever* been contained—and that thus had we, in our cloud of self-deluding and dream, brought it home *already at large.*

Those who claim to have heard it speak as it made its escape are now safely away in the upstate security of Matteawan, receiving the most modern care. "Nothing voiced—all hisses, a serpent, vengeful, relentless," they raved. Others attested to languages long dead to the world, though of course known to their reporters. "The man-shaped light shall not deliver you," it allegedly declared, and, "Flames were always your destiny, my children." *Its* children— Is it worth anyone's while now to journey out those starfish corridors where they suffer, each behind his door of oak and iron, the penance they bear as a condition of that awful witness?

My own part in the fateful transmittal, as I imagined, being discharged, I had intended to entrain at once for the Nation's Capital, leaving others to dispute credit and compensation. As, in any case, it was a Washingtonian Entity to which I was obliged to report, I foresaw no difficulty in completing for them at least a précis during the journey south. Vain dream! Once the terror had commenced, even reaching the depot would prove an Odyssey.

For the streets were in mad disorder. A troop of irregulars in red Zouave-style hats and trousers, their mounts confused and terrified, wheeled helplessly, with who knew what negligible increase of anxiety surely enough to start them shooting at one another, not to mention at innocent civilians. The shadows of the tall buildings swooped in the fire-reddened light. Ladies, and in many cases gentlemen, screamed without ceasing, to no apparent effect. Street-vendors, the only ones to show any composure at all, ran about trying to sell restoratives alcoholic and ammoniac, ingenious respirator helmets to protect against inhalation of smoke, illustrated maps purporting to show secret tunnels, sub-basements and other arks of safety, as well as secure routes out of town. The omnibus I had taken seemed scarcely to move, the distant flagpoles atop the station ever to linger against the sky, unattainable as Heaven. Newsboys ran to and fro alongside, waving late editions jagged with exclamatory headlines.

Arrived at last at the depot, I joined a mass of citizens all trying to get aboard any outbound trains they could find. At the entrance the ungoverned mass of us was somehow spun into single-file, proceeding then with ominous slowness to thread the marble maze inside, its ultimate destination impossible to see. Non-uniformed monitors, street toughs in soiled work-clothes by the look of them, made sure none of us violated the rules, of which there seemed already too many. Outside, gunfire continued intermittently.

Clocks high overhead told us sweep after sweep how late, increasingly late, we would be.

AT THE EXPLORERS' CLUB TODAY, the less fashionable one, seeking refuge from the pestilential rains of the District, everyone mingling in the anterooms, waiting for the liveried Pygmies bearing their Chinese bronze dinner gongs to announce the famed Gratuitous Midday Repast. If anyone observed me shaking from time to time, they assumed it was the usual bush fever.

"Afternoon, General . . . ma'am . . ."

"But I say, old 'Wood! Haven't the wogs killed you yet? Thought you were in Africa."

"So did I. Can't imagine what I'm doing here."

"Since Dr. Jim's little adventure it's all been Queer Street out there, hasn't it. War any moment, shouldn't wonder." He began to quote the British poet-laureate's commemorative verse, with its questionable rhyme of "pelt" and "veldt."

I have begun to notice, among southern Africa hands in particular, this vernacular of unease and hallucination. Is it the growing political tension in the Transvaal, and the huge amounts of money changing hands from the traffic in gold and diamonds? Should I put some money in Rand shares?

During luncheon got into a funny sort of confab about civilized evil in far-off lands.

"Maybe the tropics," somebody, probably the General said, "but never the Polar Region, it's too white, too mathematical up there."

"But always in our business there are natives, and then there are natives, don't you see? Us and natives. Any particular tribe, the details of it, get lost in the general question—who is laboring to whose benefit, sort of thing."

"There's never a question. The machines, the buildings, all the industrial structures we've put in out there. They see these things, they learn to operate them, they come to understand how powerful they are. How deadly. How deadly *we* are. Machinery can crush them. Trains can run them over. In the Rand some of the shafts go down four thousand feet."

"I say, 'Wood, isn't there a story about you out there, dispatching a coolie or something with a Borchardt?"

"He was looking at me strangely," I said. It is as far as I have ever gone with that story.

"How's that, 'Wood? 'Strangely'? What's that?"

"Well I didn't exactly ask him what it meant, did I? He was Chinese."

The company, fitful, uneasy, half of them down with fever of some kind, shrugged and went jittering on to other topics.

"Back in '95, Nansen's plan on his final northward journey was eventually, as the total load grew lighter, to kill sled dogs one by one and feed them to the rest. At first, he reported, the other dogs refused to eat dog-flesh, but slowly they came to accept it.

"Suppose it were to happen to us, in the civilized world. If 'another form of life' decided to use humans for similar purposes, and being out on *a mission of comparable desperation,* as its own resources dwindled, we human beasts would likewise simply be slaughtered one by one, and those still alive obliged to, in some sense, eat their flesh."

"Oh, dear." The General's wife put down her utensils and gazed at her plate.

"Sir, that is disgusting."

"Not literally, then . . . but we do use one another, often mortally, with the same disablement of feeling, of conscience . . . each of us knowing that at some point it will be our own turn. Nowhere to run but into a hostile and lifeless waste."

"You refer to present world conditions under capitalism and the Trusts."

"There appears to be little difference. How else could we have come to it?"

"Evolution. Ape evolves to man, well, what's the next step—human to what? Some *compound organism,* the American Corporation, for instance, in which even the Supreme Court has recognized legal personhood—a new living species, one that can out-perform most anything an individual can do by himself, no matter how smart or powerful he is."

"If that brings you comfort, believe it. I believe in incursion from elsewhere. They've swept upon us along a broad front, we don't know 'when' they first came, Time itself was disrupted, a thoroughgoing and merciless forswearing of Time as we had known it, as it had gone safely ticking for us moment into moment, with an innocence they knew how to circumvent. . . ."

It was understood at some point by all the company that they were speaking of the unfortunate events to the north, the bad dream I still try to wake from, the great city brought to sorrow and ruin.

Leaving the Arctic wastes, *Inconvenience* pressed southward, using as much fuel as they dared, jettisoning all the weight they could afford to, in a desperate attempt to reach the city before the steamer *Étienne-Louis Malus*.

"I cannot but wonder what is to become of those unfortunate devils," brooded Chick Counterfly.

The sombre brown landscape of north Canada, perforated with lakes by the uncountable thousands, sped by, a league below them. "Great place to buy lakefront property!" cried Miles.

The scientists of the Vormance Expedition had continued to believe it was a meteorite they were bringing back, like Peary and other recent heroes of science. Given the long history of meteor strikes in the Northern regions, more than one reputation had been made with rented ships and deferred payrolls, and a few wishfully storm-free weeks up there cruising some likely iceblink. Just before the discovery, the Vormance team, scrutinizing the sky, had certainly been shown signs enough. But who could have foreseen that the far-fallen object would prove to harbor not merely a consciousness but an ancient purpose as well, and a plan for carrying it out?

"It deceived us into *classifying* it as a meteorite, you see. . . ."

"The object?"

"The visitor."

"Your whole Expedition got hypnotized by a rock? that what you're asking us to believe?" The Board of Inquiry was meeting in upper rooms of the Museum of Museumology, dedicated to the history of institutional collecting, classifying, and exhibiting. A decision to ration the whiskey supply had managed only to hasten a descent into incivility, which all the newspapers, whatever their arrangements with power, would comment upon in days to follow. From these turret windows, one might view some good-size wedges of the city, here and there all the way to the horizon—charred trees still quietly smoking, flanged steelwork fallen or leaning perilously, streets near the bridges and ferry slips jammed with the entangled carriages, wagons, and streetcars which the population had at first tried to flee in, then abandoned, and which even now lay unclaimed, overturned, damaged by collision and fire, hitched to animals months dead and yet unremoved.

Before the disaster the whiskered faces at this long curved table, expressing such offended righteousness, belonged merely to appointees of a Mayor no more dishonest than the standards of the time provided for—Tammanoid creatures, able to deliver votes when required on a scale suitable to membership on this upstart museum's Board of Overseers. Unlike those who sat on the boards of more exalted institutions, none here possessed a fortune or a family pedigree—city folk, few of them had observed so much as a stationary star, let alone one of the falling sort. Eminent scientific witnesses, who before the Events might have held these politicos in light regard, now could not meet their steady, and from time to time inquisitorial, gazes. Today to a man they were become Archangels of municipal vengeance, chiefly because no one else was available for the task—the Mayor and most of the City Council having been among the incendiary Figure's first victims, the great banks and trading houses in severe disarray even yet, the National Guard broken in spirit and fled, vowing to re-group, into New Jersey. The only organized units to brave the immediate aftermath were the White Wings, who with exemplary grit continued to go wading into the inconceivable cleanup job with never less than their usual cheer and discipline. Today, in fact, the only signs of human movement in all the desolate post-urban tract one could see from here were a small party of the pith-helmeted warriors, accompanied by a refuse wagon and one of the last live horses in the Metropolitan area.

Sometimes this inquiry board held night sessions, striding in the side entrance, where the enfeebled and unprotected had learned to come and wait for as long as they must. The Museum at night presented a vista of earthbound buttresses, unlighted and towering, secret doorways between bays, several miniature street-level beer gardens within, remaining open until late, through the kindness and wisdom of the precinct police—block after block of sloping masonry, a sooty yellow in this growing dark, indistinct, as if printed out of register.

"The Eskimo believe that every object in their surroundings has its invisible ruler—in general not friendly—an enforcer of ancient, indeed pre-human, laws, and thus a Power that must be induced not to harm men, through various forms of bribery." At mention of the time-honored practice, Commissional ears were observed to develop sharp points and to tilt forward. "It was thus not so much the visible object we sought and wished to deliver to the Museum as its invisible *ruling component.* In the Eskimo view, someone of our party, by failing to perform the due observances, showed deep disrespect, causing the Power to follow its nature, in exacting an appropriate vengeance."

"Appropriate? given the great loss of property, not to mention innocent life . . . appropriate to what, sir?"

"To urban civilization. Because we took the creature out of its home territory. The usual sanctions—bad ice, blizzards, malevolent ghosts—were no longer available. So the terms of retribution assumed a character more suitable to the new surroundings—fire, damage to structures, crowd panic, disruption to common services."

It had become quite unpleasant that night. This city, even on the best of days, had always been known for its background rumble of anxiety. Anyone who wittingly dwelt here gambled daily that whatever was to happen would proceed slowly enough to allow at least one consultation with somebody—that "there would always be time," as citizens liked to put it. But that quarterless nightfall, events were moving too fast even to take in, forget about examine, or analyze, or in fact do much of anything but run from, and hope you could avoid getting killed. That's about as closely as anybody was thinking it through—everyone in town, most inconveniently at the same time, suffering that Panic fear. Down the years of boom and corruption, they'd been warned, repeatedly, about just such a possibility. The city more and more vertical, the population growing in density, all hostages to just such an incursion. . . . Who outside the city would have imagined them as victims taken by surprise—who, for that matter, inside it? though many in the aftermath did profit briefly by assuming just that affecting pose.

They had established few facts. Deep downtown, where a narrow waterway from long ago still ran up into the city, a cargo ship had arrived, in whose hold, kept in restraints more hopeful than effective, stirred a Figure with supernatural powers, which no one in its as-yet-unwritten history had ever known how to stop. Everyone in town seemed to know what the creature was—to have known all along, a story taken so for granted that its coming-true was the last thing anybody expected—including what its pitiless gifts would mean for any populace they might be unleashed upon—whereas, oddly, none of the men of science who had brought it here, the old polar hands, living only a few metal corridors away, all of its journey south, had so much as guessed.

Now, knowing perfectly the instant of arrival, having willed itself up to the necessary temperature, it began, methodical and unrelenting, to burn its way out of its enclosure. Those who had chosen to stay aboard ship for as long as possible, one by one, as in a kind of moral exhaustion, let go, tumbled into flight, up the ladders, out the hatches, away over the brow and down into the thoroughfares of the city. But with only dwindling moments of normal history remaining, where could any of them have found refuge in time? No escort of Tenderloin toughs, no chamber of privilege however deep within the anchors of any of the great bridges, no train- or water-tunnel could have preserved even one of these impure refugees from what was to come.

Fire and blood were about to roll like fate upon the complacent multitudes. Just at the peak of the evening rush-hour, electric power failed everywhere throughout the city, and as the gas mains began to ignite and the thousand local winds, distinct at every street-corner, to confound prediction, cobblestones erupted skyward, to descend blocks away in seldom observed yet beautiful patterns. All attempts to counter-attack or even to avoid the Figure would be defeated. Later, fire alarms would go unanswered and the firemen on the front lines find themselves too soon without reinforcement, or the hope of any. The noise would be horrific and unrelenting, as it grew clear even to the willfully careless that there was no refuge.

The mobilization was city-wide as reports flew of negotiations with visitors unnamed, military leaves canceled, opera performances cut in half—arias, even famous ones, omitted altogether—to allow for early audience dismissal, railway stations echoing with troop movement, card and dice games up Tenderloin alleyways rudely interrupted and usually at critical moments, fear among the populace of twilight hours too abruptly extended, of indistinct faces, of high windows and what might, for the first time in civic memory, plausibly enter there. . . .

There was debate in the aftermath about what had happened to the Mayor. Fled, dead, not right in the head, the theories proliferated in his absence. His face appeared on bills posted all over the wood fences around vacant lots, the rear ends of streetcars, its all-too-familiar bone structure shining with the unforgiving simplicity of a skull. "Remain indoors," warned bulletins posted on the carbonized walls over his signature. "This night you will not be welcome in my streets, whether there be too many of you or too few."

As the daylight left the city that night, the streetlamps were not up to anything like their usual candle-power. It was difficult to make out anything clearly. Ordinary social restraints were apt to be defective or not there at all. The screaming that went on all night, ignored as background murmur during the day, now, absent the clamor of street traffic, had taken on urgency and despair—a chorale of pain just about to pass from its realm of the invisible into something that might actually have to be dealt with. Figures which late at night appeared only in levels of gray were now seen to possess color, not the fashionable shades of daytime but blood reds, morgue yellows, poison greens.

In a metropolis where Location was often the beginning, end, and entire story in between, the presence of an underground spring beneath the Cathedral of the Prefiguration, feeding its three baptismal fonts, had until this unaccountable advent been thought a sufficient, if not to everyone miraculous, defense. But now, in arc-light, at the church's highest point, authorities had begun to project a three-dimensional image in full color, not exactly of Christ but with the same beard, robes, ability to emit light—as if, should the worst happen, they could deny all-out Christian allegiance and so make that much easier whatever turnings of heart might become necessary in striking a deal with the invader. Each night at dusk, the luminous declaration was tested for electrical continuity, power level, accuracy of colors, and so on. Spare lamps were kept ready, for the possibility haunted everyone that the projection device might fail at a critical moment. "No one would venture at night into a neighborhood of known vampires without carrying along a cross," as the Archbishop had declared, "would they now? no, and so with this Our Protector," who remained, guardedly, unnamed.

Despite the recent incorporation, the outer boroughs would be allowed a few more honorable years of wilderness and pastoral calm, having escaped at least for a while the stultified scrawling of builders and developers that was passing in those days for dream. Though what future could there've been for the "territory across the bridge" but sooner or later a suburban history and culture to be undergone?

So the city became the material expression of a particular loss of innocence—not sexual or political innocence but somehow a shared dream of what a city might at its best prove to be—its inhabitants became, and have remained, an embittered and amnesiac race, wounded but unable to connect through memory to the moment of the injury, unable to summon the face of their violator.

Out of that night and day of unconditional wrath, folks would've expected to see any city, if it survived, all newly reborn, purified by flame, taken clear beyond greed, real-estate speculating, local politics—instead of which, here was this weeping widow, some one-woman grievance committee in black, who would go on to save up and lovingly record and mercilessly begrudge every goddamn single tear she ever had to cry, and over the years to come would make up for them all by developing into the meanest, cruelest bitch of a city, even among cities not notable for their kindness.

To all appearance resolute, adventurous, manly, the city could not shake that terrible all-night rape, when "he" was forced to submit, surrendering, inadmissably, blindly feminine, into the Hellfire embrace of "her" beloved. He spent the years afterward forgetting and fabulating and trying to get back some self-respect. But inwardly, deep inside, "he" remained the catamite of Hell, the punk at the disposal of all the denizens thereof, the bitch in men's clothing.

So, in hopes of being spared further suffering, as demonstrations of loyalty to the Destroyer, in the spirit of the votive shrine, the city had put up a number of propitiatory structures. Many of these were deliberately burned, attempts being made to blacken the stylized wreckage in aesthetic and interesting ways. Attention was directed Downtown, kept wrapped in a plasma of protective ignorance, extending at last to the enormous rampart of silence along its edge, one limit of the known world, beyond which lay a realm the rest of the city could not speak of, as if having surrendered, as part of some Plutonian bargain, even the language to do so. It being the grand era of arch-building in the City, usually of the triumphal sort, it was decided to put up, at some transition point into the forbidden realm, another great Portal, inscribed I AM THE WAY INTO THE DOLEFUL CITY—DANTE, above which, on each anniversary of that awful event, spanning the sky over the harbor, would appear a night panorama—not quite a commemorative reenactment—more an abstract array of moving multicolored lights against a blue, somehow maritime, darkness, into which the viewer might read what he chose.

On the night in question, Hunter Penhallow had been on his way out of town but, feeling something at his back, had turned to witness the tragedy unfolding along the horizon, stricken into remembering a nightmare too ancient to be his alone, eyeballs ashine with mercilessly sharp images in flame tones, so over-bright that his orbits and cheekbones gathered some of the fiery excess.

He was abruptly lost in an unfamiliar part of town—the grid of numbered streets Hunter thought he'd understood made no sense anymore. The grid in fact had been distorted into an expression of some other history of civic need, streets no longer sequentially numbered, intersecting now at unexpected angles, narrowing into long, featureless alleyways to nowhere, running steeply up and down hills which had not been noticed before. He pushed on, assuming that far enough along he would come out at an intersection he could recognize, but everything only got less familiar. At some point he must have come indoors, entering a sort of open courtyard, a ruined shell of rust-red and yellowish debris towering ten or twelve stories overhead. A sort of monumental gateway, unaccountably more ancient and foreign than anything in the known city. The streets had by now grown intimate, more like corridors. Without intending to, he soon was walking through inhabited rooms. At one end of a mostly empty hallway, he found a meeting in progress. People were sitting clustered about a fireplace, with cups and glasses, ashtrays and spittoons, but the occasion was more than social. Both the men and women had kept their coats and hats on. Hunter approached tentatively.

"I think we're agreed we all have to get out of the city."

"Everyone's packed up? The children are ready?"

People were getting to their feet, preparing to leave. Someone noticed Hunter. "There's room, if you'd like to come."

How stupefied he must have looked. He followed the group dumbly down a flight of winding metal steps to an electric-lit platform where others, quite a few others in fact, were boarding a curious mass conveyance, of smooth iron painted a dark shade of industrial gray, swept and sleek, with the pipework of its exhaust manifold led outside the body, running lights all up and down its length. He got on, found a seat. The vehicle began to move, passing among factory spaces, power generators, massive installations of machinery whose purpose was less certain—sometimes wheels spun, vapors burst from relief valves, while other plants stood inert, in unlighted mystery—entering at length a system of tunnels and, once deep inside, beginning to accelerate. The sound of passage, hum and wind-rush, grew louder, somehow more comforting, as if confident in its speed and direction. There seemed no plan to stop, only to continue at increasing velocity. Occasionally, through the windows, inexplicably, there were glimpses of the city above them, though how deep beneath it they were supposed to be traveling was impossible to tell. Either the track was rising here and there to break above the surface or the surface was making deep, even heroic, excursions downward to meet them. The longer they traveled, the more "futuristic" would the scenery grow. Hunter was on his way to refuge, whatever that might have come to mean anymore, in this world brought low.

Kit didn't get to meet his benefactor until the weekend of the Yale-Harvard game, on a clouded and windless late-November day, in a side room of the Taft Hotel. They were introduced officially by Foley Walker, who was wearing a sporting suit in some horse-blanket plaid of vibrant orange and indigo, and a top hat *that matched*, while the magnate was dressed more like a feed-company clerk from parts considerably south of here, and likely west as well. He also had on smoked "specs" and a straw hat whose brim width unavoidably suggested disguise, with Irish pennants flying head to toe. "You'll do," he greeted Kit.

Load off *my* mind, Kit supposed to himself.

It was a less than intimate tête-à-tête. Alumni of both persuasions were milling everywhere in and out of the lobby, gesturing carelessly with foaming beer steins, sporting hats, spats, and ulsterettes vividly dyed in varying densities of the rival school hues. Every five minutes a page came briskly through, calling, "Mr. Rinehart! Call for Mr. Rinehart! Oh, Mr. Rinehart!"

"Popular fellow, this Rinehart," Kit remarked.

"A Harvard pleasantry from a few years back," explained Scarsdale Vibe, "which shows no sign of abating. Uttered in repetition, like this, it's exhausting enough, but chorused by a hundred male voices on a summer's evening, with Harvard Yard for an echo chamber? well . . . on the Tibetan prayer-wheel principle, repeat it enough and at some point something unspecified but miraculous will come to pass. Harvard in a nutshell, if you really want to know."

"They teach Quaternions there instead of Vector Analysis," Kit helpfully put in.

Pre-game passions were running high. Venerable professors of Linguistics who had never so much as picked up a football had been earnestly reminding their classes that, by way of the ancient Sanskrit *krimi* and the later Arabic *qirmiz,* both names for the insect from which the color was once derived, "crimson" is cognate with "worm." Young men in striped mufflers knitted by sweethearts who had dutifully included rows of flask-size pockets ran clanking to and fro, getting a head start on the alcoholic merriment sure to prevail in the stands.

"I was hoping my son would deign to stop in for a moment, but I fear it is not to be. Detained by an orgy, no doubt. It is surely among the more compelling forms of human sadness to watch one's alma mater decline into this Saturnalian swamp of iniquity."

"I think he's playing in some intramural freshman game this morning," Kit said. "He really should be on the varsity."

"Yes and a shame there's no professional football, for his career would be assured. Colfax is the last of a litter that, love 'em all as I must, promise despite me to redefine fecklessness for generations to come. It is the old capitalist's curse—the aptitudes that matter most, such as a head for business, can't be passed on."

"Oh, but on the field, sir, he's as go-ahead a fellow as any captain of industry could wish."

"Let me tell you. Colfax used to work for me down at the Pearl Street offices, summer vacations, fifty cents an hour, far more than he deserved. I would send him out on grease runs—'Here—bring this to Councilman So-and-so. Don't look inside.' The young idiot, literal as well as obedient, *never looked inside.* Hopeful, though increasingly desperate, I kept sending him out, again and again, making it more obvious each time, even to leaving corners of greenbacks sticking out of the satchel and so forth, but the pup's naïveté withstood that, too. At last, God help me, I brought in the police, hoping to shock my imbecile son back into some relation with the World of Reality. He would still be languishing in the Tombs today had I not given up the struggle and begun, in the matter of an heir, to search outside the immediate bloodlines. You following this?"

"All respect, sir, think I read it in a dime novel once, wait, what am I saying, more than once, and you know how that stuff pickles your brain for you. . . ."

"Less so, I pray, than the crockful of cucumbers I have sired. What I'm working up to here is a fairly grand offer."

"What I was afraid of, sir." Kit found himself steady on his feet and able to gaze back calmly into Scarsdale's increasingly perplexed stare.

"Drawing against a hefty trust fund, inheriting uncounted millions when I'm dead, not up your alley, young man?"

"Apologies, but with no idea how you've gone about earning it, I couldn't add much to it—more likely be spending the rest of my life in courtrooms fighting off the turkey buzzards, not how I was fixing to occupy my adult years, exactly."

"Oh? You have an alternative plan. Admirable, Mr. Traverse. Tell me, I'm really interested."

Kit ran silently through the list of topics better not gone into with Scarsdale, beginning with Tesla and his project of free universal power for everybody, proceeding through the enchantments of Vectorism, the kindness and genius of Willard Gibbs. . . . Didn't leave much they could talk about. And there was something. . . . The man had been looking at him strangely. Not a fatherly or even foster-fatherly expression. No, it was—Kit almost blushed at the thought—it was desire. He was desired, for reasons that went beyond what little he could make of this decadent East Coast swamp of lust in idleness to begin with.

Despite having gone in with a determination to cut the place some slack, Kit had seen Yale almost immediately for what it was. The book-learning part of it, two or three good companions not yet quite crippled into the reflexive and humorless caution which leading the nation would require—that was all just swell, and almost made up for the rest of it. Kit was presently cranked up, bright-eyed and zealous, accosting as-yet-unintroduced Saturday-night shopgirls out on Chapel Street to lecture to on the subject of Vectorism—Gibbsian, Hamiltonian, and beyond—for this most miraculous of systems seemed to him bound to improve the lives of anybody he could acquaint with it—even if the girls were not always so sure.

"You chase them away, Kit." 'Fax, about to go meet a "date," was inspecting his turnout in the mirror of the rooms they shared. "My cousin knows any number of girls who wouldn't mind playing a little parcheesi with you now and then, except you're too intimidating with all this arithmetic business."

"It isn't 'arithmetic.'"

"There. Just what I'm talking about. Girls don't know the difference and, more important, don't care."

"As usual, 'Fax, I defer to your wisdom in all matters of sport."

No sarcasm intended here, or even possible. By the age of eighteen, Colfax Vibe had already developed into a classic "Corinthian" of the day, recognized as an expert—occasionally champion—skier, polo player, distance runner, pistol and rifle shot, huntsman, aeronaut—the list ran on to a length quite depressing indeed to any observer with merely everyday skills. When at last he did make his first appearance on an Ivy League gridiron, in the waning minutes of the Yale-Princeton game, 'Fax took the ball from deep in his own end zone and ran it back for a winning touchdown against and through the best defensive efforts of the opposition, not to mention a certain amount of unwitting interference from his own team. Walter Camp was to call it "the most splendid display of broken-field running in Yale football history," and Negro folks who lived in Princeton slept a little easier that Saturday night, knowing they'd been spared at least a week free of Princeton-boy posses come hollering down Witherspoon Street to rip porches off the houses for the victory bonfire. "Oh, hell, I'd been feeling cooped up," 'Fax would explain. "Just needed a good run."

As 'Fax's ideas about leisure-time, not surprisingly, tended to converge in the more life-threatening areas, he and Kit over this first year of their acquaintance would find themselves well matched, Kit grasping at any piece of the outer and solid world as to flotsam in a furious turbulence of symbols, operations, and abstractions, and 'Fax, chirping daily hymns to Rooseveltian strenuosity, finding in Kit's semi-religious attachment to Vectorism a gravity and, for all 'Fax knew, even a chance at deliverance from what he might have feared to be an idling and shallow life, in which the motif of failure was all too apt to break in.

It had been often commented upon that Vibe offspring tended to be crazy as bedbugs. 'Fax's brother Cragmont had run away with a trapeze girl, then brought her back to New York to get married, the wedding being actually performed *on trapezes,* groom and best man, dressed in tails and silk opera hats held on with elastic, swinging upside down by their knees in perfect synchrony across the perilous æther to meet the bride and her father, a carnival "jointee" or concessionaire, in matched excursion from their own side of the ring, bridesmaids observed at every hand up twirling by their chins in billows of spangling, forty feet above the faces of the guests, feathers dyed a deep acid green sweeping and stirring the cigar smoke rising from the crowd. Cragmont Vibe was but thirteen that circus summer he became a husband and began what would become, even for the day, an enormous family.

The third brother, Fleetwood, best man at this ceremony, had also got out of the house early, fast-talking his way onto an expedition heading for Africa. He kept as clear of political games as of any real scientific inquiry, preferring to take the title of "Explorer" literally, and do nothing but explore. It did not hurt Fleetwood's chances that a hefty Vibe trust fund was there to pick up the bills for bespoke pith helmets and meat lozenges and so forth. Kit met him one spring weekend out at the Vibe manor on Long Island.

"Say, but you've never seen our cottage," 'Fax said one day after classes. "What are you doing this weekend? Unless there's another factory girl or pizza princess or something in the works."

"Do I use that tone of voice about the Seven Sisters material you specialize in?"

"I've nothing against the newer races," 'Fax protested. "But you might like to meet Cousin Dittany anyway."

"The one at Smith."

"Mount Holyoke, actually."

"Can't wait."

They arrived under a dourly overcast sky. Even in cheerier illumination, the Vibe mansion would have registered as a place best kept clear of—four stories tall, square, unadorned, dark stone facing looking much older than the known date of construction. Despite its aspect of abandonment, an uneasy tenancy was still pursued within, perhaps by some collateral branch of Vibes . . . it was unclear. There was the matter of the second floor. Only the servants were allowed there. It "belonged," in some way nobody was eager to specify, to previous occupants.

"Someone's living there?"

"Someone's there."

. . . from time to time, a door swinging shut on a glimpse of back stairway, a muffled footfall . . . an ambiguous movement across a distant doorframe . . . a threat of somehow being obliged to perform a daily search through the forbidden level, just at dusk, so detailed that contact with the unseen occupants, in some form, at some unannounced moment, would be inevitable . . . all dustless and tidy, shadows in permanent possession, window-drapes and upholstery in deep hues of green, claret, and indigo, servants who did not speak, who would or could not meet one's gaze . . . and in the next room, the next instant, waiting . . .

"Real nice of you to have me here, folks," chirped Kit at breakfast. "Fellow sleeps like a top. Well, except . . ."

Pause in the orderly gobbling and scarfing. Interest from all around the table.

"I mean, who came in the room in the middle of the night like that?"

"You're sure," said Scarsdale, "it wasn't just the wind, or the place settling."

"They were walking around, like they were looking for something."

Glances were exchanged, failed to be exchanged, were sent out but not returned. "Kit, you haven't seen the stables yet," Cousin Dittany offered at last. "Wouldn't you like to go riding?"

Before Kit could reply, there was a great commotion outside the entrance to the breakfast room. Later he would swear he had heard a symphonic brass section play a lengthy fanfare. "Mother!" cried 'Fax. "Aunt Eddie!" exclaimed Cousin Dittany. And in, making a rare appearance, swept Mrs. Vibe, the former Edwarda Beef of Indianapolis. She sang mezzo-soprano and had married almost shockingly young, the boys coming along in close order, "the way certain comedians make their entrances in variety acts," it seemed to her, and about the time Colfax shot his first brace of pheasant, she had abruptly one day packed a scant six trunksful of clothes and with her maid, Vaseline, reinstalled herself in Greenwich Village in a town house floridly faced in terra-cotta imported from far away, designed inside by Elsie de Wolfe, adjoining that of her husband's younger brother, R. Wilshire Vibe, who for some years had been living in his own snug spherelet of folly and decadence, squandering his share of the family money on ballet girls and the companies they performed for, especially those that could be induced to mount productions of the horrible "musical dramas" he kept composing, fake, or as he preferred, *faux,* European operettas on American subjects—*Roscoe Conkling, Princess of the Badlands, Mischief in Mexico,* and so many others. The town was briefly amused by Edwarda's change of domicile but re-focused soon enough upon varieties of scandal having more to do with money than with passion, a subject more fit for opera in languages they did not speak. As Scarsdale had by then grown adept at covering his financial tracks, and as Edwarda was perfectly content not only to get laced in and decked out to appear at functions as his titular wife but also, as her fame in the theatrical world grew, to sit on boards of a cultural nature and serve as hostess to any number of memorable gatherings, Scarsdale actually began to look on her more as an asset than any possible source of marital distress.

Her brother-in-law, R. Wilshire Vibe, delighted to have her for a neighbor—for "Eddie" was nothing if not a handsome length of goods—soon found amusement in fixing her up with the artists, musicians, actors, writers, and other specimens of low-life to be found in his milieu in such plentiful supply. By force of what were her undoubted dramatic gifts, she soon managed to convince the impresario that, as it was in the nature of a great personal favor to *him* for her even to be seen with these unsuitable wretches, she wished no recompense other than to . . . well not *star* perhaps, not at first anyway, but at least to have a go at some second-soubrette part, for example the lively *bandida* Consuelo in *Mischief in Mexico,* then in rehearsal—though this did require considerable and often quite frankly disgusting interaction with a trained pig, Tubby, for whom more often than not she found she was there to act as stooge or straight person, "laying pipe," as the actors said, so that it would always be the ill-behaved porker who got the laughs. By the end of the run, however, she and Tubby were "closest friends," as she confided to the theatrical gazettes, which were taking by then a keen interest in her career.

Bigger parts followed, presently with Edwarda's arias or "numbers" so expanded as to require earlier curtain times to accommodate them. "Spellbindingly incomparable!" proclaimed the reviewers, "transcendently splendiferous!" too, and soon she was christened in Champagne "The Diva of Delmonico's." The adjoining town houses, ever a scene of license and drollery, shimmered within a permanent and agreeable fog of smoke from recreational sources, including hemp and opium, as well as the mists arising from seltzer bottles discharged sometimes into drinking vessels but more usually at companions in what seemed eternal play. Young women attired often in nothing more than ostrich-feather aigrettes dyed in colors of doubtful taste ran nubilely up and down the marble staircases, chased by young men in razor-toed ball shoes of patent-leather. In the middle of the bacchanalian goings-on night after night was ever-merry Edwarda, drinking Sillery from the bottle and exclaiming "Ha, ha, ha!"—not always at anyone in particular.

Thus Edwarda and Scarsdale found themselves together every day and yet leading almost entirely unsynchronized lives, inhabiting each his and her own defective city, like partial overlays in some new color-printing process, Scarsdale's in gray tones, Edwarda's in mauve. Puce sometimes.

Kit had wandered down to the stables, where he was presently joined by Dittany Vibe, her eyes sparkling from beneath the brim of an all-but-irresistible hat. In the tackroom she pretended to inspect a sizable inventory of harness, halters, bridles, collars, traces, quirts, crops, buggy whips, and so on. "I do love the way it smells in here," she whispered. She took down a braided stallion whip and snapped it once or twice. "You must have used these in Colorado, Kit."

"Few choice words is all we need usually," Kit said. "Our horses behave themselves pretty good, I guess."

"Not at all like eastern horses," she murmured. "You see how many whips and things there are here. Our horses are very, very naughty." She handed him the whip. "I imagine this one must sting just terribly." Before he knew it, she had turned, and lifted the skirt of her riding habit, and presented herself, gazing back over her shoulder with what you'd have to call a mischievous expectancy.

He looked at the whip. It was about four feet long, maybe a finger's thickness. "Seems kind of professional-weight—sure you wouldn't be happier with something lighter?"

"We could leave my drawers on."

"Hmm, let's see . . . if I remember right, it's how you plant your feet—"

"On second thought," said Cousin Dittany, "your gloved hand should do quite nicely."

"My pleasure," beamed Kit, and, as it turned out, Dittany's as well, though things got noisy after a while, and they decided to move to an adjoining hayloft.

He tried for the rest of the day to find a moment with 'Fax to have a word about this matter of his cousin, but, as if the others were conspiring to prevent it, there were always unexpected visitors, calls on the telephone, impromptu lawn-tennis games. Kit began to feel fretful, the way that working on a vector problem for too long could bring him to a state much like drunkenness, whereupon his other or co-conscious mind would emerge at last to see what it could do.

Later that evening, after another breathless ten minutes with Dittany inside a striped palmetto tent during an afternoon croquet party, most of the company having retired, Kit was wandering through the house when he heard piano music coming, he supposed, from the music room. He followed the sound, the unresolved phrases that gave rise to new ones equally unfulfilled, chords he had himself hit by accident, sitting on piano keyboards and so forth, but had never considered music, exactly. . . . He moved through a darkening amber light as if the electric current in the house were being drained away, smoothly diminishing like gaslight beneath a hand at a hidden valve. He looked around for wall switches but could see none. Far down at the end of one of the corridors, he thought he saw a dark figure receding into the invisible wearing one of those pith helmets explorers were said to wear. Kit realized it must be the widely discussed black sheep Fleetwood Vibe, in from one of his expeditions.

R. Wilshire Vibe had not endeared himself to his nephew with his current "show" *African Antics,* featuring the catchy

When those na-tives, run amuck!
When your life-ain't, worth a buck!
Eyes all poppin, goin ber-serk,
Might even make you late for work, say
Tell me, what-cha gon-na do,
When they come screamin, after you?
Runnin through those jungle trees,
Tryin not to be the, gro-ce-ries! well,

Out there, in that, distant land,
You won't find no "hot-dog" stand (uh-uh!)
What- they- like- to- eat- in- stead, is
Barbecued brains straight-outa-your-head, so

If you're trav'lin, out that way,
Listen up to, what I say,
Don't wan-na be no-body's meal? Bet-
-ter bring along a real fast
Automo-bile!

Which everybody liked to gather around the Steinway in the parlor to sing along with. All great fun for everybody except Fleetwood, who spent at least thirty-two bars a night trying not to take offense.

"They don't actually know I'm here," he confided to Kit. "If they do, it's only in the way some can detect ghosts—though you may have noticed already these are not the most spiritual of people. I once had hopes that Dittany could escape the general corruption, but not so much lately."

"She seems straightforward enough to me."

"I'm less and less qualified to judge anyway. In fact, you shouldn't trust anything I have to say about this family."

Kit laughed. "Oh, good. Logical paradoxes. Them I understand O.K."

They had reached the top of a steep hill, emerging from a stand of maples and black walnuts, some of them already old when Europeans first arrived—the mansion hidden in foliage somewhere below. "We all used to come up here in the winter and bobsled down this thing. Back then it seemed damned near vertical. And look at that out there." He nodded westward. Through the miles of coalsmoke and salt haze, Kit could make out a few semivisible towers of the city of New York, descended upon by radial shafts of late sunlight from behind and among clouds that seemed almost their own heavenly prototypes, what photographers called a "two-minute sky," destined rapidly to cloud over and maybe even start dropping some rain. "When I came up here by myself, it was to look at the city—I thought there had to be some portal into another world. . . . I couldn't imagine any continuous landscape that would ever lead naturally from where I was to what I was seeing. Of course it was Queens, but by the time I had that sorted out, it was too late, I was possessed by the dream of a passage through an invisible gate. It could have been a city, but it didn't have to be a city. It was more a matter of the invisible taking on substance."

Kit nodded. "And . . ."

Fleetwood stood with his hands in his pockets, shaking his head slowly. "There are stories, like maps that agree . . . too consistent among too many languages and histories to be only wishful thinking. . . . It is always a hidden place, the way into it is not obvious, the geography is as much spiritual as physical. If you should happen upon it, your strongest certainty is not that you have discovered it but returned to it. In a single great episode of light, you remember everything."

"Home."

"Oh . . ." Following Kit's glance, downhill, toward the invisible "big house," the late sun on the trees. "There's home, and there's home, you know. And these days—all my colleagues care about is finding waterfalls. The more spectacular the falls, the better the chance for an expensive hotel. . . . It seems all I'm looking for now is movement, just for its own sake, what you fellows call the vector, I guess. . . . Are there such things as vectorial unknowns?"

"Vectors . . . can be solved for. Sure. But maybe you mean something else."

"This one always points away from here, but that"—indicating the shimmering metropolis with a sidewise lift of his head—"is where the money is." He did not pause then so much as wait, as one might before a telegraph sounder, for some affirmation from the far invisible.

"You know," he continued, "out there you run into some queer characters. You see them go in, they don't come out again till months later, sometimes never. Missionaries, deserters, citizens of the trail, for that always turned out to be what they'd sworn their allegiance to—trail, track, river, whatever could carry them to the next ridgeline, the next bend in the river emerging from that strange humid light. 'Home,' what could that possibly mean, what claim could it have on them? I'll tell you a story about the Heavenly City. About Zion."

One night in eastern Africa, he was no longer sure where, exactly, Fleetwood met Yitzhak Zilberfeld, a Zionist agent, out traveling in the world scouting possibilities for a Jewish homeland. They promptly got into discussion about the homeless condition vis-à-vis the ownership of property. Fever, abuse of local drugs, tribal blood-warfare ubiquitous and never-ending, the thousand threats to white intrusion here, many of them invisible, turned the colloquy increasingly deranged.

"What is the modern state," Yitzhak declared, "but a suburban house-lot taken up to a larger scale? Anti-Semitism flows directly from the suburban fear of those who are always on the move, who set up camp for a night, or pay rent, unlike the Good Citizen who believes he 'owns' his home, although it is more likely to be owned by a bank, perhaps even a Jewish bank. Everyone must live in a simply-connected space with an unbroken line around it. Some put hair ropes, to keep snakes out. Any who live outside property-lines of any scale are automatically a threat to the suburban order and by extension the State. Conveniently, Jews have this history of statelessness."

"It's not dishonorable to want your own piece of land, is it?" Fleetwood objected.

"Of course not. But no Jewish homeland will ever end hatred of the unpropertied, which is a given element of the suburban imperative. The hatred gets transferred to some new target, that's all."

And would there ever actually prove to be, right in the middle of the worst of the jungle, some peaceful expanse of rangeland, unsettled as yet, free of all competing claims, high, fertile, disease-free, naturally defensible, so forth? Would they come around a bend in the trail, or over a ridge, and abruptly be taken through the previously hidden passage, into the pure land, into Zion?

They sat as the sun declined over the blessed possibility. "Is this real?"

A shrug. "Yes. . . . Or, no."

"Or we're both feverish."

They set up camp in a clearing, near a small waterfall, and built a cookfire. Night began, as if declared.

"What was that?"

"An elephant," Fleetwood said. "How long did you say you'd been out here?"

"It sounds kind of close, don't you think?" When Fleetwood shrugged, "I mean, you've had . . . encounters with elephants?"

"Now and then."

"You have an elephant *gun* with you?"

"No. You?"

"So, this one charges us, what do we do?"

"Depends how much he's charging—try to talk him down a little?"

"Anti-Semitic!"

The elephant in the darkness let loose with another fanfare, this time joined by another. In harmony. Whether by way of commentary or not, who knew?

"What, they don't sleep at night?"

Fleetwood exhaled audibly. "I don't mean to offend, but . . . if this sort of elephant-related anxiety is at all common among your people, perhaps Africa is not the most promising site for a Zionist settlement."

Through their feet they could feel percussion on the jungle floor, consistent with an adult elephant approaching at high speed.

"Well, it's been nice chatting," said Yitzhak, "and now I think I'll just—"

"Suggest you stand your ground, actually."

"And what?"

"Look him straight in the eyes."

"Stare down some murderous elephant."

"Ancient wisdom of the bush," Fleetwood advised, "never run. Run, you'll get trampled."

The elephant, standing about twelve feet high, emerged from the perimeter of forest, heading straight for Fleetwood and Yitzhak, his displeasure clear. He had his trunk lifted and curled back, a precaution elephants are known to observe just before using their tusks against some particular target of their spite.

"O.K., to review this—we stand here, maintain eye contact, and you absolutely guarantee me, this elephant will just . . . stop? Turn around, walk away, no hard feelings?"

"Watch."

The headline in next week's *Bush Gazette* would read SAVES JEW FROM INSANE ELEPHANT. Yitzhak was so grateful he passed along a number of investment tips, plus the names of useful banking contacts all over Europe, that eventually would have done quite nicely for Fleetwood had he not by then been pursuing less financial goals. He tried to explain.

"I used to read Dickens as a child. The cruelty didn't surprise me, but I did wonder at the moments of uncompensated kindness, which I had never observed outside the pages of fiction. In any world I knew, it was a time-honored principle to do nothing for free."

"Just so," said Yitzhak. "Trust me. Buy Rand shares."

"South Africa? But there's a war going on there."

"Wars end, there's fifty thousand Chinese coolies all lined up, sleeping on the docks from Tientsin to Hong Kong, waiting to be shipped into the Transvaal the minute the shooting stops. . . ."

As it happened, it was not too long before the markets of the Earth were being swamped with gold, not only Rand gold but also proceeds from the Australian gold rush then ebulliently in progress—exactly the sort of "unfairly earned" revenue which sent the Vibe patriarch into mouth-foaming episodes of unseemly behavior.

"I don't understand it. This money is coming from nowhere."

"But it's real," Foley Walker pointed out. "What they're buying with it is real."

"I feel myself turning goddamned socialist," said Scarsdale. "Communist, even. Like you know when you're coming down with a cold? My mind—or the part of it I use for thinking about business matters—aches."

"But Mr. V., you hate socialists."

"I hate these climber sons of bitches worse."

· · ·

HE WAS ONLY faintly visible in the dark, at a window on the haunted floor of the house, almost a fixture in the room from some previous era, there for some outdated domestic purpose. It was the one part of the house no one would come near, dedicated to exile, departure, unquiet journeying, reserved for any who could not reside there. He was remembering, declining into a sickbed of remembrance.

In Africa he had known saintly lieutenants who were fated to die young, fugitives from all across the wreck of the Eastern Question, traders in flesh or firearms indifferent to the nature of the goods they handled, who would emerge from the green otherworld after months, their cargo vanished not only from possession but from memory as well, sick, poisoned, too often dying, cursed by shamans, betrayed by magnetic anomalies, racked by Guinea worm and malaria, who, despite all, wished only to return to the embrace of the interior. . . . Fleetwood wanted to be like them. . . . He prayed to become one of them. He went out into country even the local European insane knew was too dangerous, hoping to be invaded by whatever it had to be. . . . Nothing "took." No one had the bad taste to suggest that it was his money keeping away the spirits whose intercession he sought—that even those agents of mischief somehow knew better than to get too close to unregulated funds whose source lay in criminal acts, however fancifully defined.

At Massawa, Fleetwood had found a coaster heading south. Debarking at Lourenço Marques, he spent a week in various local *cantinhas,* gathering information, as he liked to think of it. This required a tidy lakeful of Portuguese colonial-market wine, the rotgut rejectamenta of Bucelas and Dão, among puzzled looks from the locals who by tradition were its devotees.

When it felt to Fleetwood that every bit of American predisposition had been leached away at last, he got on a train for the Transvaal. But in the handful of minutes between Ressano Garcia and Komati Poort, something rearranged itself in his thoughts. The moment he crossed the frontier, he understood what he was supposed to be doing out here—he was headed for Johannesburg to make his own personal fortune, in that hell of chronic phthisis, scabbed veldt, shopkeepers' avarice, seething rickshaw traffic, desperately too few white women, a town belonging to the unhistoried . . . "like Baku with giraffes," as he wrote home. The Veldt went on far too long, without a tree in sight, only smokestacks and stamp mills, which pounded in a hellish uproar audible for miles, day and night, sending up an inescapable, vile white dust that either remained in the air for one to breathe or descended to coat housing, clothing, vegetation, skins of all colors. At any given time in the world, there would be enough towns like Johannesburg to keep occupied a certain type of energetic young fortune seeker. It would be necessary to plunge in, from whatever condition of bourgeois stultification, whatever prevailing weather, market narrative, fluctuations in harvests—including Death's—might have defined his average day, to leap as stoically as possible into the given fever and conduct himself as survival and profit might direct in the way of intoxication, betrayal, brutality, risk (deep descents into the abysses of the gold reef proving minor next to the moral plunges available, indeed beckoning, at every hand), sexual obsession, gambling for epical stakes, seduction into the haunts of the *dagga rooker* and opium slave. Everyone white was in some way caught up in this, it was a no-limit game, though the Witwatersrand high court provided a locus of public conscience, in practice one could be back on the Lourenço Marques train and into Portuguese jurisdiction in a day and a half, for good if one liked, the money itself gone on ahead, deposited in safety, already seeming to have proceeded from dream, unsoiled as any figures inked in any ledger neatly as you please. . . . Little to prevent one's turning up one day back at the old local saloon, standing rounds till closing time. "No, not fantastically wealthy, but you know . . . a tickey here, a tickey there, after a while it adds up. . . ."

The Kaffirs called it eGoli, "The City of Gold." Soon after his arrival at Johannesburg, Fleetwood was well aboard what the smokers of *dagga* called the Ape Train. There was a story that he had shot a coolie, but the other story was that it was a Kaffir he had caught stealing a diamond, and that he had given the Kaffir a choice, to be shot or to step into a mine shaft half a mile deep. He was a thief, after all, though the stone was not so grand as diamonds go, to Fleetwood's admittedly untrained eye perhaps less than three carats when Amsterdam was done with it. "I did not steal this," the black man was saying. But did as he was told, and relinquished it into the white man's hand. Fleetwood gestured him with the Borchardt toward his fate and felt a queer euphoria expanding to fill his body, amazed to see, moreover, that the Kaffir not only recognized the state but was entering it himself. The American stain, after all, would not be eradicated. The two stood for a pulsebeat by the edge of the terrible steep void, and Fleetwood understood too late that he could have made the Kaffir do anything but somehow had come up with nothing better than this.

Though legal pretense would have taken the merciless honed edge from the joy of the deed itself, it scarcely mattered whether or not the Kaffir had stolen the stone, and perhaps had only been waiting for the right moment to take it out of the compound, where the chances were good that within minutes someone else would have stolen it from him, some other Kaffir half a lungful of *dagga* smoke more capable for the moment, at which point matters would have become far more ugly and painful for him than this relatively humane long descent into the abyss through the blue ground, the side-tunnels whistling by faster and faster—rather pleasant, Fleetwood imagined, for as one fell, it would grow warmer, wouldn't it—perhaps even feel like being taken back into a dark womb. . . .

That came later, in the dreams, along with the unavoidable face of the dead man, dust-whitened, looming close. As if looking out through holes in a mask, the eyes moved and gleamed, shockingly alive in flesh that might as well have been artificial. Seemed to be whispering advice. Warning that there was some grave imbalance in the structure of the world, which would have to be corrected.

Then each time Fleetwood would be not so much overcome by remorse as bedazzled at having been shown the secret backlands of wealth, and how sooner or later it depended on some act of murder, seldom limited to once. He learned to wait for this revelation, though sometimes he woke too soon.

It comforted him to imagine that on the karmic ledger the Kaffir and the Jew balanced out. But in fact, as Fleetwood was informed in these lucid dreams close to dawn, all the gold in the Transvaal could not buy the remission of a single minute of whatever waited for him. He laughed angrily. "Purgatory? A higher law? Kaffir next of kin, chasing me across the world? Be serious."

Pygmies at the Club stared at him with unspoken loathing. Chinese in the street cursed him, and, knowing only a few words, he still thought he could recognize "kill," "mother," and "fuck." Word was about that Alden Vormance was getting up a party to go north and recover a meteorite. There would be no gold, no diamonds, no women, no dream-inducing smoke, no coolies or blacks, though possibly the odd Eskimo. And the purity, the geometry, the cold.

Taking quick looks behind him on the trail, Lew Basnight was apt to see things that weren't necessarily there. Mounted figure in a black duster and hat, always still, turned sidewise in the hard, sunlit distance, horse bent to the barren ground. No real beam of attention, if anything a withdrawal into its own lopsided star-shaped silhouette, as if that were all it had ever aspired to. It did not take long to convince himself that the presence behind him now, always just out of eyeball range, belonged to one and the same subject, the notorious dynamiter of the San Juans known as the Kieselguhr Kid.

The Kid happened to be of prime interest to White City Investigations. Just around the time Lew was stepping off the train at the Union Station in Denver, and the troubles up in the Coeur d'Alene were starting to bleed over everywhere in the mining country, where already hardly a day passed without an unscheduled dynamite blast in it someplace, the philosophy among larger, city-based detective agencies like Pinkerton's and Thiel's began to change, being as they now found themselves with far too much work on their hands. On the theory that they could look at their unsolved cases the way a banker might at instruments of debt, they began selling off to less-established and accordingly hungrier outfits like White City their higher-risk tickets, including that of the long-sought Kieselguhr Kid.

It was the only name anybody seemed to know him by, "Kieselguhr" being a kind of fine clay, used to soak up nitroglycerine and stabilize it into dynamite. The Kid's family had supposedly come over as refugees from Germany shortly after the reaction of 1849, settling at first near San Antonio, which the Kid-to-be, having developed a restlessness for higher ground, soon left, and then after a spell in the Sangre de Cristos, so it went, heading west again, the San Juans his dream, though not for the silver-mine money, nor the trouble he could get into, both of those, he was old enough by then to appreciate, easy enough to come by. No, it was for something else. Different tellers of the tale had different thoughts on what.

"Don't carry pistols, don't own a shotgun nor a rifle—no, his trade-mark, what you'll find him packing in those tooled holsters, is always these twin sticks of dynamite, with a dozen more—"

"Couple dozen, in big bandoliers across his chest."

"Easy fellow to recognize, then."

"You'd think so, but no two eyewitnesses have ever agreed. It's like all that blasting rattles it loose from everybody's memory."

"But say, couldn't even a slow hand just gun him before he could get a fuse lit?"

"Wouldn't bet on it. Got this clever wind-proof kind of striker rig on to each holster, like a safety match, so all's he has to do's draw, and the 'sucker's all lit and ready to throw."

"Fast fuses, too. Some boys down the Uncompahgre found out about that just last August, nothin left to bury but spurs and belt buckles. Even old Butch Cassidy and them'll begin to coo like a barn full of pigeons whenever the Kid's in the county."

Of course, nobody ever'd been sure about who was in Butch Cassidy's gang either. No shortage of legendary deeds up here, but eyewitnesses could never swear beyond a doubt who in each case, exactly, had done which, and, more than fear of retaliation—it was as if physical appearance *actually shifted,* causing not only aliases to be inconsistently assigned but identity itself to change. Did something, something essential, happen to human personality above a certain removal from sea level? Many quoted Dr. Lombroso's observation about how lowland folks tended to be placid and law-abiding while mountain country bred revolutionaries and outlaws. That was over in Italy, of course. Theorizers about the recently discovered subconscious mind, reluctant to leave out any variable that might seem helpful, couldn't avoid the altitude, and the barometric pressure that went with it. This was spirit, after all.

Right at the moment Lew was out in the field, in Lodazal, Colorado, chatting with Burke Ponghill, the editor of *Lodazal Weekly Tidings,* the newspaper of record for a town which as yet was little more than a wishful real-estate venture. It was young Ponghill's job to fill empty pages with phantom stories, in hopes that readers far away would be intrigued enough to come and visit, and maybe even settle.

"But so far all we've really got's a mining town that ain't built yet."

"Silver? Gold?"

"Well, ore anyway . . . containing this metallic element that ain't exactly been—"

"Discovered?"

"Maybe discovered, but not quite refined out?"

"Useful for . . . ?"

"Applications yet to be devised?"

"Well, say, sounds good to me. Where could a fellow get a room for the night?"

"Hot bath? home-cooked meal?"

"There you go." The wind swept through the brittlebush, and both men lit cigars. Lew tried not to succumb to the weariness of the trail.

"The voice in these letters," Ponghill tapping the pile of loose sheets in front of him, "far from belongin to some crazy passionate South European or semieducated Peter specialist, it suggests instead an hombre who knows full well that *something has happened to him,* but for the life of him he just can't figure what—you know that feeling?—sure, who don't?—and he's tryin to work 'at through, here on paper, how it was done to him, and better yet who did it. But by damn, look at his targets. You notice he always identifies them by name and address, without getting all general as some of the bombers do, none of that 'Wall Street,' or 'Mine Owners Association,'—no, see, these evildoers're all clearly indicted, one by one."

"'Evildoers'?"

"He ain't in it for no fun, Mr. Basnight, nor the thrill of the blast, nope, got us a man of principle here. Somewhat removed from the workaday world . . . not to mention lack of exposure to the fair sex, all that civilizing influence they're known for. . . ."

"Too much time alone, jizzmatic juices backin up, putting pressure onto the brain— oh but hell, wouldn't that qualify half of these mountains? Fact, it's kind of a naïve theory, isn't it Mr. Ponghill, not your own, I hope?"

"A lady of my acquaintance. She feels like that if he'd get out more—"

"Now you mention it, every day back down to the Denver office, we do see letters for this bird, all but a couple of em from women, strange but true, and most of those proposing marriage. Now and then there's a fellow will pop the question, too, but that goes in a different file."

"You open and read his mail?"

"Not like that he has any name or fixed address—not like that we're some *damn forwarding service,* is it?"

"Don't mean he ain't got a right to his privacy."

"His . . . Oh. Well, glory, if this isn't just rejuvenating, a discussion about rights of the criminal, takes a man back to the campfires of his youth, only then it was God didn't have a name or address."

The brown jug came out, and Burke Ponghill grew confessional. The search for the mysterious dynamiter had in its relentlessness begun to affect families entirely unconnected with the case, including Ponghill's own, putting them under unaccustomed pressures either to turn various black sheep in as likely candidates or to protect them from the law. The conflict was explicit, between the State and one's blood loyalties. The Ponghill residence became a house divided. "It's moral idiocy, Ma, examine his skull, the lobes for social feeling just aren't there."

"Buddy, he's your own brother."

"They're going to catch him and shoot him down, don't you know by now what these got-damn people are like?"

"And if you turn him in, they'll hang him."

"Not with a good lawyer."

"*Those* sons of bitches don't work for free."

"Sometimes they work for conscience."

"Oh, Buddy." A lifetime of attending to his rosy expectations and wild-goose schemes in that sigh, but he went right on as if he hadn't heard it.

"So Buddy turned in our little brother," Burke told Lew, "and now the best Brad can hope for is stay alive long enough to get the trial moved down to Denver, where our local junta don't cut that much of a figure, and the papers back east can get to the story. . . ."

LEW LEFT the little rough-milled shed of a printer's office and headed back down the valley. So far this trip, he had not been shot at, or not for verifiably sure, but the foreboding that he would be had grown, in recent days, almost to a gastric condition. He had learned early on the job to attend to land- and townscapes only out as far as the range of the firearms most likely to be in the hands of possible harmdoers—past that radius all those mountains and sunsets'd have to get along without the admiring eyes of Lew Basnight.

As the evening crept across the valley, and farm stoves were poked up to working heat, and lamps lit indoors whose light soon filled the windowframes, outshining the departing sunlight on the spruce siding around them and draining down among the rows of the vegetable patches, the sawn ends of logs in woodpiles dyed the same intense orange yellow, the bark nearly black, silvered, full of shadows . . . Lew found himself, as usual this time of day, growing a little short-tempered with all this spirit-squeezing, horse-abusing sleuth exercise denying him even this hour, for everybody else a chance at some domestic ease. But the choice was this or Denver, behind his desk, blowing dust off of files too outdated to need to saddle up for anymore.

At the next convenient rise, he paused and regarded the peaceful valley. Maybe he had not yet seen it all, but Lew would be reluctant to wager more than a glass of beer that Chicago, for all its urban frenzy, had much on this country out here. He guessed that every cabin, outbuilding, saloon, and farmhouse in his field of sight concealed stories that were anything but peaceful—horses of immoderate beauty had gone crazy, turned like snakes and taken from their riders chunks of body flesh that would never grow back, wives had introduced husbands to the culinary delights of mushrooms that would turn a silver coin to black, vegetable farmers had shot sheepherders over some unguarded slide of the eye, sweet little girls had turned overnight into whooping, hollering brides of the multitude, obliging men in the family to take actions not always conducive to public calm, and, as boilerplate to the contract with its fate, the land held the forever unquiet spirits of generations of Utes, Apaches, Anasazi, Navajo, Chirakawa, ignored, betrayed, raped, robbed, and murdered, bearing witness at the speed of the wind, saturating the light, whispering over the faces and in and out the lungs of the white trespassers in a music toneless as cicadas, unforgiving as any grave marked or lost.

When he left Chicago, nobody had come to see him off, not even Nate Privett, who you might've expected would've been there just to make sure he left. Thinking back over how he'd got to this point in his life, Lew guessed it was close enough to leaving under a cloud.

Not so long ago, he wouldn't have known how to take sides. In the course of his Anarchist-hunting days in Chicago, Lew had found his way to a convenient insulation, for a while anyhow, from too much sympathy for either victim or perpetrator. How could you walk into the aftermath of a bombing and get anywhere by going all to pieces over the senseless waste of life, the blood and pain? Only slowly would it occur to his ultra-keen detective's reasoning that these bombs could have been set by anybody, including those who would clearly benefit if "Anarchists," however loosely defined, could be blamed for it. Neither, in the course of long pursuits down back of the Yards and beyond, was it escaping his attention how desperately miserable were the lives found among the realities of Anarchist communion, though it promised a man his only redemption from a captivity often cruel as the old Negro slavery. Crueler, sometimes. Lew began to find himself entertaining seductive daydreams about picking up some surrogate bomb, a chunk of ice or, better, a frozen pile of horse-droppings, to sling at the next silk hat he saw serenely borne along in the street, the next mounted policeman beating on an unprotected striker.

It was most obvious at the Yards, but there was the Pullman plant, too, and the steel mills and McCormick Reaper, and not only Chicago—he'd bet you could find this same structure of industrial Hells wrapped in public silence everyplace. There was always some Forty-seventh Street, always some legion of invisible on one side of the account book, set opposite a handful on the other who were getting very, if not incalculably, rich at their expense.

The altitude, the scale of the country out here, put a balloonheaded clarity onto vision when directed at mine owners and workers alike, revealing the Plutonic powers as they daily sent their legions of gnomes underground to hollow out as much of that broken domain as they could before the overburden collapsed, often as not on top of their heads, though what did it matter to the Powers, who always had more dwarves waiting, even eagerly, to be sent below. Scabs and Union men, Union and scabs, round and round, changing sides, changing back again, sure didn't help with what he felt no embarrassment in thinking of as a contest for his soul.

Nevertheless he soldiered along in Denver, getting to know who was who, becoming a regular at Pinhorn's Manhattan steak house, running tabs at every other bar along Seventeenth Street, making friends among crime reporters who hung out at Tortoni's up on Arapahoe and Gahan's saloon across the street from City Hall, paid off enough of his losses at Ed's Arcade to stay friendly with associates of Ed Chase, the boss of the red-light district, went whole days at a time without thinking much of Chicago or comparing the two cities but was unable somehow to stay cooped up in town for more than a week or two before finding himself back on the Denver & Rio Grande, headed up into mining country. Couldn't keep away, though each time he went out, it seemed relations between owners and miners had worsened. It got like practically every day out here saw another little Haymarket, dynamite in these hard-rock mountains not being quite the exotic substance it had been in Chicago. Pretty soon he was meeting posse-size units on the trail, armed to the teeth, calling themselves Citizens' Alliances or Proprietors' Auxiliaries. They were carrying, some of them, quite-sophisticated firearms, army-issue Krag-Jørgensen rifles, repeating shotguns, field howitzers disassembled and packed along on strings of mules. At first he was able to ride by with no more trouble than a nod and salute off his hatbrim, but each time the atmosphere was a little more tense, and soon they were stopping him and asking what they must have figured were pointed questions. He learned to bring along his Illinois and Colorado licenses after a while, though many of these jaspers couldn't read too well.

By now he had been slowly pushed out of half his office space by an accumulation of files on Anarchists professional and amateur, labor organizers, bombers, potential bombers, hired guns, and so on—girls he kept hiring to help him out with the typewriting and office-tending lasted on average a month before they ran off, exasperated, to the comforting simplicities of marriage, a parlor house on The Row, schoolteaching, or some other office or shop in town where a person could at least slip off her shoes and have a good chance of finding them again.

Lew had too much trouble even locating jackets on individual cases to be able to stand back and put any of it together, but what he could begin to see was that both sides in this were organized, it wasn't just unconnected skirmishing, a dynamite blast here and there, a few shots from ambush—it was a war between two full-scale armies, each with its chain of command and long-term strategic aims—civil war again, with the difference now being the railroads, which ran out over all the old boundaries, redefining the nation into exactly the shape and size of the rail network, wherever it might run to.

He had felt it as early as the Pullman strike back in Chicago, federal troops patrolling the streets, the city at the center of twenty or thirty railway lines, radiating with their interconnections out to the rest of the continent. In crazier moments it seemed to Lew that the steel webwork was a living organism, growing by the hour, answering some invisible command. He found himself out lying at suburban tracksides in the deep nighttime hours, between trains, with his ear to the rails, listening for stirrings, quickening, like some anxious father-to-be with his ear to the abdomen of a beloved wife. Since then American geography had gone all peculiar, and what was he supposed to be doing stuck out here in Colorado, between the invisible forces, half the time not knowing who hired him or who might be fixing to do him up. . . .

Nearly every workday, in neighborhood saloons, eating-houses, and cigar stores, he found he was running across and even getting in conversations with folks, from both the Union and the Owners Associations, who previously had been only names in field reports. The really odd thing he began to notice was that the names of owners' operatives were also turning up among his files on the mine workers. Some were wanted by authorities in distant states for crimes against owners, and not always trivial offenses either—union outlaws, even Anarchist bombers, yet here they were at the same time on the payroll of the Owners Association. "Strange," Lew muttered, puffing energetically on a cigar and grinding the mouth end of it to shreds with his teeth, because he was getting a sick feeling, not all from swallowing tobacco juice, that somebody might be playing him for a sap. Who were these birds—dynamiters pretending to work for the owners while they planned more outrages? owners' stooges infiltrating the W.F.M. to betray their brothers? Were some of them, God help him, both—greedy pikers playing both sides and loyal only to U.S. currency?

"Here's what you do," suggested Tansy Wagwheel, whom this job in just a few short weeks would drive screaming down Fifteenth Street and on into the embrace of the Denver County public-school system, "It's in this wonderful book I keep close to me all the time, *A Modern Christian's Guide to Moral Perplexities*. Right here, on page eighty-six, is your answer. Do you have your pencil? Good, write this down—'Dynamite Them All, and Let Jesus Sort Them Out.'"

"Uh . . ."

"Yes, I know. . . ." The dreamy look on her face could not possibly be for Lew.

"Does it do horse races?" Lew asked after a while.

"Mr. Basnight, you card."

NEXT TIME LEW got up into the embattled altitudes of the San Juans, he noticed out on the trail that besides the usual strikebreaking vigilantes there were now cavalry units of the Colorado National Guard, in uniform, out ranging the slopes and creeksides. He had thought to obtain, through one of the least trustworthy of his contacts in the Mine Owners Association, a safe-passage document, which he kept in a leather billfold along with his detective licenses. More than once he ran into ragged groups of miners, some with deeply bruised or swelling faces, coatless, hatless, shoeless, being herded toward some borderline by mounted troopers. Or the Captain said some borderline. Lew wondered what he should be doing. This was wrong in so many ways, and bombings might help but would not begin to fix it.

It wasn't long before one day he found himself surrounded—one minute aspen-filtered shadows, the next a band of Ku Klux Klan night-riders, and here it was still daytime. Seeing these sheet-sporting vigilantes out in the sunlight, their attire displaying all sorts of laundering deficiencies, including cigar burns, food spills, piss blotches, and shit streaks, Lew found, you'd say, a certain de-emphasis of the sinister, pointy hoods or not. "Howdy, fellers!" he called out, friendly enough.

"Don't look like no nigger," commented one.

"Too tall for a miner," said another.

"Heeled, too. Think I saw him on a poster someplace."

"What do we do? Shoot him? Hang him?"

"Nail his dick to a stump, and, and then, set him on *fahr,*" eagerly accompanied by a quantity of drool visibly soaking the speaker's hood.

"You all are doing a fine job of security here," Lew beamed, riding through them easy as a herd of sheep, "and I'll be sure to pass that along to Buck Wells when next I see him." The name of the mine manager and cavalry commander at Telluride worked its magic.

"Don't forget my name!" hollered the drooler, "Clovis Yutts!"

"Shh! Clovis, you hamhead, you ain't supposed to tell em your name."

What in Creation could be going on up here, Lew couldn't figure. He had a distinct, sleep-wrecking impression that he ought to just be getting his backside to the trackside, head on down to Denver, and not come up here again till it was all over. Whatever it was. It sure 's hell looked like war, and that must be what was keeping him here, he calculated, that possibility. Something like wanting to find out which side he was on without all these doubts. . . .

BACK IN DENVER AGAIN, Lew returned late to his room, discovering from all the way down the hall that the day wasn't close to being over yet, for through the transom came drifting the scent of a burning leaf that stirred in him, as always, mixed feelings. It would be Nate Privett, with one of his trademark Key West cheroots, way out here from Chicago on his yearly tour of inspection, though how it could be a year already since the last visit was beyond Lew.

Downstairs in the Anarchists' saloon, they were whooping it up, starting early as usual. Singing in so many different tempos and keys, like a bunch of Congregationalists, you couldn't even tell what the song was. Girls whose audible high notes bore a component of amateur cheeriness, as if they would rather be dancing than practicing even routine deception. Boots stomping in strange, un-American rhythms. Lew had fallen into the habit of dropping in for a sociable beer at the end of the day, and little by little found himself being seduced in a political and maybe also a romantic way, for there were any number of Anarchist chickadees hanging around who liked nothing better than to see what was up with these gruff Pinkertonian types. Today he'd have to pass that up for Nate, a dubious exchange.

Wearily, Lew put on a face and opened his door. "Well, Nate, good evening. Hope I haven't kept you waiting."

"Always another report to go through. Time is never wasted, Lew, if you remember to bring along something to read."

"See you found the Valley Tan."

"Thorough search, only bottle in the room. When'd you switch to Mormon whiskey?"

"When your checks started coming back from the bank. That bottle does seem to be down by six fingers or more, since last I looked."

"A desperate man will console himself with anything, Lew."

"How desperate's that, Nate?"

"Been reading your last report on the Kieselguhr Kid ticket. Read it over twice in fact, strongly reminded me of that legendary Butch Cassidy and his Hole-in-the-Wall Gang? though you never brought those names up, exactly."

Lew sure had had a long day. Nate Privett was one of these desk operatives with an irrational belief that somewhere in the endless heaps of subpoenaed account books, itineraries, operating logs, and so forth, shining out sudden as a vision, answers would just reveal themselves, Heaven forfend anybody should actually have to saddle up and get out there and into country a little more twilit.

"Funny," trying to keep the annoyance out of his voice, "but Butch Cassidy situations've been growing not that uncommon here o' late—mind conveying over that bottle, thanks—fiendish acts of semi-imaginary badmen—maybe even more than just any one lone Kid here, maybe *multiple conspiracies* of bombers, not to mention that small army of laughing-academy material ever with us, just itching to commit acts, or not commit acts but be blamed for 'em anyway, in the Kid's name—"

"Lew?"

"This case, frankly, it's a bitch, and growing more difficult every day. I'm workin' it all alone out here, and there's times I wouldn't even mind if The Unsleepin Eye with all its corporate resources just took the whole damn ticket back again—"

"Whoa, whoa just a minute, Lew, not how it works, and besides, the clients are still payin *in,* you see, every month—oh, they're happy, I tell you, no reason not to just keep going along, exactly the way we—" He stopped, as if aware of having been indiscreet.

"Ah! So *that's* it." Making believe he had just figured it all out. "Why, you buzzards."

"Well . . . no need to . . ."

"All this time out here, so far, far from the lights of Michigan Avenue, and never once suspecting . . . why it was just some damn opium-pipe special's all it ever was—"

"Sure wouldn't want any hard feelings, Lew—"

"I'm smiling, ain't I?"

"See, back in Chicago we're only as good as our credibility, which is what Regional Operative-in-Charge Lew Basnight's been giving us here, what with the kind of respect you enjoy in the business—"

"Oh, your mother's ass, Nate. Your own, for that matter. No hard feelings."

"Now, Lew—"

"Good luck, Nate."

Next night in Walker's on Arapahoe, inhaling one twenty-five-cent pony of bourbon after another, wedged in with five other fast drinkers, which was as many as the vest-pocket establishment would hold, he understood in an all-but-religious way that this was supposed to have happened years ago, that he or whatever was living his life had been taking their sweet time with it, that he could have been working for the right side years before this, and now it might be too late, already past the point where anybody stood a chance against the juggernaut that had rolled down on the country and flat stolen it.

Later he made it back to the Anarchists' saloon, and there, as he'd half expected, was this customer giving him one of those unfinished-business looks. Probably not the Kieselguhr Kid, but Lew by now being in an experimental frame of mind decided to go ahead on the assumption that he was. "Buy you a beer?"

"Depends if you've come to your senses yet."

"Let's say I have."

"Pretty soon, then, everybody'll know, and it'll be run Anarchist run for you, Brother Basnight."

"Mind if I ask something? Not that I'm about to just yet, but you must've set off a stick or two of dynamite in a what they call purposeful way. Any regrets about that?"

"Only if there was innocent lives caught into it. But none ever was, not by me."

"But if 'there are no innocent bourgeoisie,' as many Anarchist folks believe—"

"You follow the topic, I see. Well. I might not know a bourgeoisie 'f one ran up and bit me, for there's not been a hell of a lot of them back where I've been, more like you'd call 'em peasantry and proletariat. Mostly, doing my work, it comes down to remembering to be careful."

"Your work." Lew wrote himself a lengthy note on his shirt cuff, then, looking up again guilelessly, "Well what about me? me or somebody in the same line, getting hurt?"

"You think you're *innocent*? Hell, man, you're working for them—you'd've killed me if it ever came up."

"I'd've brought you in."

"Maybe, but it wouldn't've been alive."

"Getting me confused with Pat Garrett, Wyatt Earp, hardcases of the frontier never cared nor maybe knew which side they were on. Not having had that luxury, I wouldn't've done you in then any more than now, when I know better."

"That's sure a relief. Here, you're dry. Herman, give this screamin Red threat to society another of them."

Little by little the place filled up and turned into a hoedown of sorts, and the Kid, or whoever he was, sort of faded into the mobility, and Lew didn't see him again for a while.

BACK IN CHICAGO, Nate, in his own paper homeland again, kept wasting Agency money rattling off one telegram after another. Figuring nothing had changed, regional office on the job, all serene. But now there might as well be hired roughnecks with wire-cutters up on every pole in the thousand miles between them, for all Nate was ever going to find out from Lew anymore.

It was about then that what Lew came to regard as his Shameful Habit began. He was in the pleasant little desert oasis of Los Fatzos, handling explosives most of the day, must have had his gloves off (though some were never to buy that story), P.E.T.N. as best he could recall—well, maybe something a little more experimental, for he'd been visiting widely-respected mad scientist Dr. Oyswharf, a possible unwitting supply source for Kieselguhr Kid–related bomb outrages, recently rumored to be working on different mixtures of nitro compounds and polymethylenes. Lethally tricky stuff. Somehow the afternoon just drifted on into the dinner hour, and Lew must've forgot to wash his hands, because next thing he knew, he was experiencing the hotel dining room in a range of colors, not to mention cultural references, which had not been there when he came in. The wallpaper in particular presented not a repeating pattern at all but a single view, in the French "panoramic" style, of a land very far away indeed, perhaps not even on our planet as currently understood, in which beings who resembled—though not compellingly—humans went about their lives—*in motion,* understand—beneath the gigantic looming of a nocturnal city full of towers, domes, and spidery catwalks, themselves edged by an eerie illumination proceeding not entirely from municipal sources.

Presently Lew's "food" arrived, and immediately caught his attention—the details of his "steak," the closer he looked at that, seeming to suggest not the animal origins a fellow might reasonably expect so much as the further realms of crystallography, each section he made with his knife in fact revealing new vistas, among the intricately disposed axes and polyhedra, into the hivelike activities of a race of very small though perfectly visible inhabitants who as they seethed and bustled about, to all appearances unaware of his scrutiny, sang miniature though harmonically complex little choruses in tiny, speeded-up voices whose every word chimed out with ever-more-polycrystalline luminosities of meaning—

Yes we're Beavers of the Brain,
Just as busy as you please
Though we're frequently reported
To behave like lit-tle bees
Keep that Bulldog in your pocket
Do not bother to complain
Or you might get *into trouble*
With the Beavers of the Brain. . . .

Exactly, puzzled Lew, a-and now what about— "*Everything all right,* Mr. B.?" Curly the waiter standing over Lew with an anxious and, it appeared to Lew, ominous look. It was Curly, of course, but in some more profound sense it was not. "You were looking at your food funny."

"Well that's 'cause it *is* funny," Lew replied reasonably, or so he thought, until noticing everybody in the room now all frantically trying to get out the door at the same time. Was it something he'd said? done? Perhaps he should inquire. . . .

"He's insane!" screamed a woman. "Emmett, now don't let him near me!"

Lew came to in the town pokey, in the company of one or two regulars who were conferring together indignantly while casting that judgmental alcoholic eye Lew's way. Soon as the Marshal had had a look in and deemed him street-safe, Lew was back out at the Doctor's lab, looking you'd say a little sheepish. "About that— I forget its name—"

"Sure. Being more or less cyclopropane plus dynamite," grinned the Doc, mischievously it seemed to Lew, "no reason we shouldn't call it 'Cyclomite,' eh? go ahead, free samples today, take as much 's you like, it's pretty stable, so if it was blasting work you wanted it for, you'd have to use detonator caps, DuPont number sixes seem to work as good as any. Though *you* might also want some plasticerator for it, some say it helps with the . . . allover effect." He did not quite add, "Easier on the old choppers as well," but Lew somehow sensed that was coming, so he shook his head vigorously no, grabbed the goods, muttered his thanks, and left as quick as he could.

"And have your ticker looked at now and then," the Doc called after him.

Lew paused. "How's that?"

"A croaker could explain it to you maybe, but there's a strange chemical relation between these nitro explosives and the human heart."

From then on, whenever a dynamite blast went off, even far away out of earshot, something concurrent was triggered somewhere in Lew's consciousness . . . after a while even if one was only *about* to go off. Anywhere. Soon he was pursuing a Cyclomite habit, you'd have to say energetically.

First dynamite blast Lew had ever witnessed was at a county fair in Kankakee. There were motorcycle daredevils snarling round and round half blind from their own exhaust smoke inside a Wall of Death. There were young women in carnival attire, to view whom in anything less would cost an extra nickel and into whose fenced-off vicinity kids could only hope to sneak. There was the Astounding Galvanic Grandpa, who sprouted electric plumes of many colors from his toetips to his ears while hanging on to a generator being cranked by some lucky local kid. And there was the attraction known as the Dynamite Lazarus, where an ordinary-looking workhand in cap and overalls climbed inside a pine casket painted black, which a crew then solemnly proceeded to stuff with a shedful of dynamite and attach a piece of vivid orange fuse to that didn't look nearly long enough. After they'd nailed down the lid, their foreman flourished a strike-anywhere match, ignited it dramatically on the seat of his pants, and lit the fuse, whereupon everybody ran like hell. Somewhere a drummer began a drumroll that grew louder, rough-ins overlapping faster and faster as the fuse burned ever shorter—Lew, in the grandstand, was far enough away to see the box begin to explode a split-second before he heard the blast, time enough to think maybe nothing would happen after all, and then the front of that compression wave hit. It was the end of something—if not his innocence, at least of his faith that things would always happen gradually enough to afford time to do something about it in. It wasn't just the loudness, mind, it was the *shape.*

He had run across a homeopathic doctor or two and was aware of the theory that you could cure an ailment with very small doses of some specific chemical which, if swallowed full strength, would produce the same symptoms. Maybe eating Cyclomite had been helping him build up an immunity to explosions. Or maybe it was dumb luck. But wouldn't you know, the minute Lew had brought up with Nate Privett his doubts about the Kieselguhr Kid—in effect quitting the case—that's just when *whatever it was* decided to have a crack at him. He'd left his horse back upstream and was quietly pissing into a small arroyo when the world turned all inside out. Lew knew the carnival theory, which was to throw yourself into the middle of the blast the second it went off, so that the shock-wave would already be outside of and heading away from you, leaving you safe inside the vacuum at the center—maybe knocked out for a little, but all in one piece. But when it came right to *doing* it, with no choice left but to dive at the sparks of the too-short fuse, into that radiant throatway leading to who knew what, in the faith that there would be something there, and not just Zero and blackness . . . well if there'd been time to think about it, he might have hesitated, and that would've done him for certain.

Wherever he was when he came to, it didn't seem like Colorado anymore, nor these creatures ministering to him your usual run of trail scum either—more like visitors from elsewhere, and far away, too. Through it all, as he began now to recall, he had stayed awake, out of his body, gliding above the scene without a care in the world—whatever "the world" meant right at the moment—trying to keep it just like that, non-mental and serene, for as long as possible—till he saw they were about to give up, pile a few rocks over him and leave him there for the critters, which is what at last obliged him to make a hasty jump back into his carcass—by now, he couldn't help noticing, strangely aglow.

"I say Nigel, he is at least *breathing*, isn't he?"

"Honestly Neville, however should I know, isn't one supposed to hold a mirror or something?"

"Wait! I've one in my kit. . . ."

"Vain creature!"

So the New Lew's first sight of the world reconstituted was his own astonished, hair-clogged nostrils, bobbing around in some fancy oval traveler's mirror framed by silver lady's tresses, or maybe weeds in the water, expensive no doubt, and being rhythmically blurred by breathing, apparently his own.

"Here." One of them had produced a flask. Lew didn't recognize what was inside, some kind of brandy he guessed, but he took a long pull anyhow and was soon on his feet. The boys had even found his horse close by and physically undamaged, though mentally could be a different story.

"Thanks, fellows, guess I'll be on my way."

"Wouldn't dream of it!" cried Neville.

"Whoever tried to blow you up back there might want another go," said Nigel.

Lew had a look at the two of them. His rescuers did not on first inspection seem to offer much deterrent to further bomb-roller interest in his person. Trilby hats, velvet knee-britches, fringe haircuts, gunbelts adorned with avalanche lilies and wild primrose. The Oscar Wilde influence, he guessed. Since the famous poet had returned to England from his excursion to America, brimming with enthusiasm for the West and Leadville in particular, all kinds of flamboyant adventurers had been showing up in these mountains.

Then again, where else did he have to go to anymore, now that he'd crossed over what had just been revealed with such clarity as the terrible American divide, between hunter and prey?

By nightfall they were among old Anasazi ruins up west of Dolores Valley someplace.

"Like a Red Indian Stonehenge!"

"Only different!"

They sat in a "mystic triangle" and lit aromatic candles and some hand-rolled cigarettes of local *grifa,* and one of them produced a strange, though not all that strange, deck of cards.

"What are these—they're Mex, ain't they?"

"British, actually. Well, Miss Colman-Smith is West Indian. . . ."

"These *espadas* here I recognize, and these are *copas,* but what's with this customer hangin' upside down with his leg bent in a figure four—"

"It's the Hanged Man, of course. . . . Oh, I say, do you mean you've *never* seen a Tarot pack before?"

"Every chartomancer's dream!" and "Whizzo!" and so forth, including an embarrassingly long examination of Lew's face. "Yes, well, dark hair and eyes, that's usually the Knight of Swords—"

"What you must do now, Lewis, as Querent, if you don't mind, is to ask the cards for the answer to a specific question."

"Sure. How many Chinese living in South Dakota?"

"No, no—something about your life, that you need to know. Something personal."

"Like, 'What in hell's going on here,' would that do it?"

"It might. Let's inquire, shall we." And sure enough, the last card to turn up in the layout, the one these birds kept saying really mattered, was that Hanged Man again.

Overhead every few seconds, arcs of light went falling in all directions. It was the Perseid meteor shower, a seasonal event, but for a while it seemed like that the whole firmament was coming unstitched. Not to mention Indian ghosts sweeping by all night, as amused as Indians ever got with the mysteries of the white man.

Next morning the trio rode south, looking to pick up the train in New Mexico—Neville and Nigel being on the way back to their native England—and within the week found themselves aboard a strangely luxurious string of oversize parlor, dining, and club cars, even the crew's caboose turning out to be fancier than the average Chicago hotel suite. The payback for all this lavish appointment was a rumor, inescapable as engine soot, of a mysterious plot to blow the train up. "Probably gonna all have to get out and walk," opined Mr. Gilmore, the senior conductor.

"Not a cozy situation, Chief," Lew reverting to his former identity, which seemed more and more lately to be off on an extended vacation, or maybe even world tour. "What've we got here, reds? Wops? some gang of box-blowers?"

Mr. Gilmore produced a handkerchief the size of a saloon towel to mop off his brow. "You name it, and there's at least one story. Only part they all have in common is it's gonna be a hell of a blow-up. Bigger than dynamite. Whole stretch of Texas, maybe New Mexico, turned to badlands quick as a maiden's sigh."

So they proceeded from one depot to the next, waiting for the terrible moment, palatial towers of carved stone and fancy millwork coming up over the edge of the brushland, looming out of early-morning thunderstorms, then, presently, shining in the downpours, roads and shacks, fences and crossroads saloons . . . passing down main streets of towns, attended as they crept in and through by riders in trail slickers who galloped alongside for miles, small boys who jumped on and off whenever the train slowed for grades or curves, elderly humorists who pretended to lie down on the track to catch a snooze only to roll out of the way cackling at the last minute, lines of drovers at trackside who just stood and watched the leisurely trundling, no telling what was on their minds, reflections of clouds in the sky blowing smoothly across their eyeballs, horses patiently hitched nearby, exchanging looks now and then, all of whom seemed to be in on the story, which, however, varied. Sometimes whatever was on the way might resemble a tornado the size of a county, a night-bringing presence at the horizon, moving across the plain, while for others it might be lights in the sky, "A second Moon, that you can't tell how close or how dangerous. . . ." What Lew had been trying not to think about was the Kieselguhr Kid or somebody who'd decided to call themselves that, because sometimes it was like he was out there, a spirit hovering just over the nearest ridgeline, the embodiment of a past obligation that would not let him go but continued to haunt, to insist.

Lew, bewildered, sat and watched and mostly just smoked cigars and covertly nibbled at his dwindling Cyclomite supply, trying to make sense of the alterations proceeding inside his brain, eyes gleaming with unaccustomed emotional dew.

They arrived in Galveston without incident but with whatever was nearly upon them hanging, waiting to descend. Neville and Nigel booked transatlantic passage on a louche-looking freighter whose flag neither of them recognized, and spent the rest of the day attempting to communicate with a Chinese gentleman who they had somehow convinced themselves was a retailer of opiates.

"Good heavens, Nigel, we nearly forgot! The others are going to be ever so frightfully upset if we don't bring them back some *Wild West souvenirs,* if not an actual *scalp* or something."

"Well, don't look at me," said Lew.

"Yes, but you'd be perfect!" cried Neville.

"For what?"

"We'll bring *you* to England," Nigel declared. "That's what we'll do."

"Don't have a ticket."

"It's all right, we'll stow you away."

"Don't I need a passport?"

"Not for England. Just don't forget your *cowboy sombrero.* It is authentic, isn't it?"

Lew had a close look at them. The boys were flushed around the eyeballs, their pupils were tiny pinpoints you could hardly make out, and they were giggling so much you had to ask them to repeat things more than once.

He ended up down in a cargo hold for the next two weeks, inside a steamer trunk with a couple-three discreet airholes bored into it. From time to time, one of the N's crept down with food stolen from the mess decks, though Lew didn't have an appetite.

"This tub's been rocking around some," he stopped vomiting long enough to mention.

"They say there's some sort of dreadful storm blowing up from the south," Nigel said.

Only when they got to England did they learn of the disastrous hurricane that had struck Galveston the day after they left—135-mile-per-hour winds, the city underwater, six thousand dead.

"We got out just in time," said Nigel.

"Yes what frightfully good luck."

"Oh, but I say, look at Lewis, he's gone all neuræsthenic."

"Why Lewis, whatever is the matter?"

"Six thousand people," said Lew, "to begin with."

"Happens out in India all the time," said Nigel. "It is the world, after all."

"Yes Lewis, wherever could you have been living, before that frightful bomb brought you to us?"

By the end, Webb Traverse had worked his way up to shift boss at the Little Hellkite workings. Veikko and his squarehead compadres gave him a party to celebrate, and as usual it reminded him that drinking potato spirits all night is not for everyone. Luckily, the snow was still a while off, or there might've been a repeat of last winter when he let some Finns talk him into putting on a pair of skis, up past Smuggler, by the giant pre-avalanche buildup known as the Big Elephant—scared the bejeezus out of him, as it would've anybody in their right mind, all present being mightily relieved when he fell down safely in the snow without breaking any bones or starting a slide.

It seemed he could get along with everybody these days except the two women in his own family, the ones that ought to've mattered most, as if with the boys all out in the wind his place was now out there too, as if the chances of running into each other again somehow were better out there than in some domestic interior. When he did put his nose in the door, things would rapidly go sour. Once, Lake took off and didn't come back. He waited a day and a night, and finally, just around third shift, she showed up out of the dark with a bundle of U.S. currency.

"Where you been, miss? Where'd you get that?"

"Just over to Silverton. Bettin on a fight."

"Betting with what?"

"Saved up from doin laundry."

"And who was fighting again?"

"Fireman Jim Flynn."

"And who?"

"Andy Malloy?"

"Save it, kid, listen, Andy could never fight worth beans, no more'n his brother Pat. Fireman and him'd be too much of a mismatch to ever happen, and maybe you want to try another story?"

"Or do I mean Mexican Pete Everett?"

"Who were you with?"

"Rica Treemorn."

"The Floradora Girls. Her people know about this?"

Lake shrugged. "Think what you like." Face inclined, eyes turned away as if in some incommunicable sorrow in no way congruent with the rosy appearance that had probably got him going to begin with.

"Child of the storm," nearly a whisper in the general noise level. A desperate look on his face. As if possessed by something she had known and feared since before things had names.

"Pa, what 'n the hell's that mean?" She wanted to sound more confident, but she was getting scared now, saw him turning in front of her into somebody else—

"See how long you can stay out in it alone. *Child of the storm.* Well. Let the god-damned storm protect you." What was he talking about? He wouldn't explain, though it was nothing so mysterious. Not that long ago, one of their spells up at Leadville, during one of those Leadville blue northers, with the lightning that never stopped, that came gusting like the winter wind . . . her young face just so clear to him, the way the fierce light had struck her hair nearly white, streaming back from her small face as if from that wind, though the air in the little shack was still. Under the black apocalyptic sky. He had got something down his spine that he thought meant he was about to be hit by lightning.

Only understood later it was fear. Fear of this young female spirit who only yesterday would come wriggling dirty-faced into his arms.

"You gone crazy, Pa?"

"Don't run no shelter for whores here." At the top of his voice and almost shaking with the pleasure of knowing there was nothing he could do to stop this.

Just as happy to oblige. "Shelter? Who did you ever shelter? you can't *shelter* your family, you can't even *shelter* yourself, you sorry son of a bitch."

"Oh! fine, well that's it—" And his hand was up and ready in a fist.

May had just got her pipe going, and had to put it aside and once more haul her weary bones into the rodeo chute. "Webb, please hold it, now, Lake, you get over there a minute— can't you see, she's done nothin wrong."

"Stays in Silverton a week, comes back with a year's rent, what fertilizer wagon you think I fell off of here, wife? Got us a damn Blair Street debutante, looks like."

He did go after her then, and Mayva had to pick up a shovel, and finally for different reasons they were both yelling at Lake to get out of the house. By which point, hell, she was all for it.

I'm so bad, she kept telling herself but couldn't believe it till she was in Silverton again, where a badgirl could find her own true self, like coming home to her real family. Just a little grid of streets set in a green flat below the mountain peaks, but for wickedness it was one of the great metropolises of the fallen earth. . . . Jittering Jesus. Sixty or seventy saloons and twenty parlor houses just on Blair Street alone. Drinking gambling fucking twenty-four hours a day. Repeal? What repeal? Smoking opium with the Chinaman who came and did the girls' laundry. Handled by foreign visitors from far across the sea with dangerous tastes, as well as domestic American child-corruptors, wife-cripplers, murderers, Republicans, hard to say which of them, her or Rica, had less sense about who she went upstairs with. Somehow they glided through the nights as if under supernatural protection. Learned not to let their eyes meet, because they always started laughing, and some customers got violent about that. Sometimes they woke up in the little jailhouse and heard the usual from a sheriff's wife with an ineradicable frown. It went on till winter began to make itself felt and the prospect of snow up to the eaves got all the ladies on the Line to making those seasonal readjustments.

Lake came back to the cabin once to get some of her things. The place echoed with desertion. Webb was on shift, Mayva was out running chores. All her brothers were long gone, the one she missed most being Kit, for they were the two youngest and had shared a kind of willfulness, a yearning for the undreamt-of destiny, or perhaps no more than a stubborn aversion to settling for the everyday life of others.

She imagined taking a stick of dynamite, waiting for Webb someday out on some trail. Drop it on him, while she'd be up safe, cradled in a niche of mountain wall, and him tiny, unprotected, far below. Put on the cap, light the fuse, and release the stick in a long, swooping curve, trailing sparks behind, down out of the sunlight into a well of shadow, and the old sumbitch would be obliterated in a flower of dirt, stone, and flame and a deep rolling cry of doom.

MAYVA KNEW SHE'D been there. Maybe her store-bought perfume, maybe something out of place, maybe just that she knew. What was clear to her was that she had to try and save at least one of her children.

"Webb, I've got to stick with her. A while longer anyway."

"Let her go."

"How can I leave her out there, out in all that?"

"She's nearly twenty, she can take care of her damn self by now."

"Sakes, it's war up here, nobody can do much more'n stay out of the way."

"She don't need you, May."

"It's you she don't need."

They looked at each other, confounded.

"Sure, you go ahead then, too. And that'll be the whole fuckin poker hand. I'll just do for myself, ain't like that I don't know how. You and that bitch go have a real good time down there."

"Webb."

"You're goin, go."

"It'll only be—"

"You decide to come back, don't send no telegrams, I still got to show my face around here, just surprise me. Or don't, more likely." The stamps beating somewhere in the distance. A mule string heehawing away down the hillside. National Guard up by the pass shooting off their cannon to keep the natives in line. Webb was standing in the middle of the place, lines of his face set like stone, patch of sunlight just touching his foot, so still. "So still," Mayva remembered later, "it wasn't him at all, really, it was somethin he'd gotten to be and from then on wouldn't be nothing else, anymore, and I should have known then, oh, daughter, I should have. . . ."

"Nothing you could've done." Lake squeezed her shoulder. "It was already on the way."

"No. You, me, and him could've got back together, Lake, left town, gone someplace those people don't go, don't even know about, down out of these god-damned mountains, might've found us a patch of land—"

"And he still would've found some way to wreck it," Lake's face puffy, as if just risen from dreams she could tell no one about, older than her mother was used to seeing it. Emptier.

"I know you say you don't miss him. But God help you. How can you stay like this? unforgivin and all?"

"We were never that important to him, Mamma. He had his almighty damn Union, that's what he loved. If he loved anything."

If it was love, it was less than two-way. With no more respectable family-man dodge to hide behind, Webb sought the embrace of Local 63, which, alarmed at the vehemence of his need, decided there ought to be some distance between him and the Union, and suggested he shift over into the Uncompahgre for a while, to the Torpedo workings. Which is where he ran into Deuce Kindred, who, having departed Grand Junction in some haste, had just hired on at the Torpedo, as if working for wages underground would hide him from some recently exhibited legal interest in his person.

Deuce had been one of these Sickly Youths who was more afraid of the fate all too obviously in store for weaklings in this country than of the physical exertion it would take to toughen up and avoid it. However self-schooled in the ways of Strenuosity, he had still absorbed enough early insult to make inevitable some later re-emission, at a different psychical frequency—a fluorescence of vindictiveness. He thought of it usually as the need to prevail over every challenge that arose *regardless of scale,* from cutting a deck to working a rock face.

"Rather be workin fathoms," Deuce muttered.

"No contract system around here," said Webb, who happened to be single-jacking alongside. "Not since the aught-one strike, and it took some good men dyin to get that."

"Nothin personal. Seems more like work somehow is all."

They were interrupted by the arrival of a sepulchral figure in a three-dollar sack suit. Deuce flashed Webb a look.

"What's this?" Webb said.

"Don't know. Stares at me funny, and everybody says step careful with him."

"Him? 'At's just ol' Avery."

"Company spy's what they say."

"Another name for Inspector around here. Don't worry too much—all 'em boys act nervous, never more than a step away from going down a shaft. . . . But you know all that, didn't you say you worked up in Butte?"

"Not me." A wary look. "Who told you that?"

"Oh, you know, you're a new fella, there's all kinds of stories," Webb laying a reassuring hand on the kid's shoulder, and not feeling or choosing to ignore Deuce's flinch. Having succeeded one way or another in driving away his whole family, Webb was joining the company of those who, with their judgment similarly impaired, had allowed themselves to be charmed by Deuce Kindred, to their great consequent sorrow.

Couple-three nights later, he ran into young Kindred down at the Beaver Saloon, playing poker with a tableful of notoriously unprincipled gents. Webb waited till the boy took a break, and stood a couple of short bits.

"How you doin tonight?"

"About even."

"Night's young. Wouldn't want you to be the fish at that table."

"I ain't. It's that little guy there with the specs."

"The Colonel? Lord, son, he's up on vacation from Denver 'cause they don't let him play down there no more."

"Didn't notice that many chips in front of him."

"He's rat-holin em. Watch his cigar, he'll put up a big cloud of smoke, and— there, see that?"

"Huh, what do you know."

"Your money, o' course."

"Thanks, Mr. Traverse."

"Webb's O.K."

"YOU'VE DONE THESE before, Mr. Kindred?"

"If you mean persuading them more into line with the client's thinking—"

"Say this one time they wanted to take it further."

"They said that?"

"They said, suppose there was an animal—dog, mule, bites or kicks all the time—what do you do?"

"Me, I'd pass the critter on to somebody can't tell the difference between that and all broke in."

"Everybody up here knows the difference," said the company rep, quietly, though with some impatience.

"You are . . . not fixing to tell me out loud what you want, 's that it?"

"Maybe we're interested in how much you can figure out on your own, Mr. Kindred."

"Sure, what they call 'initiative.' That case there'd have to be some Initiative Fee connected onto it."

"Oh? Running in the neighborhood of . . . ?"

It turned out Deuce knew more than the rep expected about how much the company might be ready to let go of. "Course if you don't have the spendin authority, we could put him onto the stub instead, leave him off up on Dallas Divide, say, cost of the ticket to Montrose plus my percent, or for a little bit more, clear on out of the state and you'd never see him again. Save you some money, maybe trouble later on—"

"Done right, there isn't any trouble."

Deuce could appreciate that. "I'm listenin."

"Nerve and initiative, Mr. Kindred, two separate things." They settled on a sum.

. . .

Deuce's sidekick, Sloat Fresno, was about twice his size and thought that Deuce was *his* sidekick. It wasn't the first time they'd made themselves useful to the Owners Association. Mine security, sort of thing. They'd picked up a reputation for being steady, for not talking to people they didn't know. In saloon engagements they tended to fight back to back, each thinking he was protecting the other, which made them that much harder to go after.

They got together first in Cripple Creek during the earlier troubles, 1895 or thereabouts. Sloat had just begun a career as a wanted man for practicing to flagrant excess what in those days was known as "copping the borax"—enlisting in the Army, collecting the bonus, deserting, showing up at another post, enlisting, collecting the bonus, deserting again, all through the occupied West, eventually becoming for the military as much of an annoyance as Geronimo himself, with unflattering likenesses tacked up in dayrooms from Fort Bliss to the Coeur d'Alenes. The strike in Cripple may have looked to Sloat like some harebrained chance to reingratiate himself with the forces of law and order. It must've worked, because from then on he and Deuce were considered reliable enough for steady work and even train fare sometimes to vicinities aswarm with anarchistic heads yet unbroken.

"Just keep back of me now, li'l buddy, watch careful back there, 'cause if they ever get me, what'll become o' you?" sorts of remarks Deuce had learned to ignore, though sometimes just barely. With particular reference to Webb Traverse, "You do the old men, just leave the younger meat to the Big S., he'll have it all dressed out with no fuss 'fore y'even know it." Though Sloat was frankly in it for the feelings of passionate alertness that grew in him while he was inflicting damage (though not necessarily pain, for hell, any ordinary day is pain ain't it), Deuce for his part had found sport, and eventually respect, in the field of mental domination, being known to intimidate whole posses without taking his hands out of his pockets. . . . Some called it hypnotism, whatever—folks said that until you had seen those two snake's eyes lit up so bright in the shadow of his hatbrim, zeroing in on you alone, why, you had not yet run into a really dedicated badman.

But the difference between Deuce and the common gunhand was, was that for Deuce it always got emotional somehow. If it wasn't to begin with, before the end of the assignment there'd always be something he could find either contemptible or desirable enough to prod him through it. He envied the more professional shootists of the time, even Sloat with his enlisted-man's approach, dreading the day he might have to walk out there in cold blood, with nothing else to crank him up.

Deuce came to imagine himself as "on assignment," for the owners, a sort of undercover "detective" keeping an eye on agitators, including Webb Traverse. Webb half-consciously imagined he'd found a replacement son, and Deuce did nothing to tell him any different. Knowing there was seldom a clear moment in these matters when the deceiver thinks his task is accomplished, any more than the deceived stops worrying how solid the friendship is, Deuce eased snakewise into the subject of Union activities, to see how far he could get while pretending every appearance of openness—something he thought he knew how to do by now, this sympathetic-young-man performance.

Webb had got into the practice of dropping by the Torpedo boardinghouse, usually around 4:00 A.M. when the night shift came off, and they talked late into the night, beneath the unnatural, hard moonlight of electric lamps up and down the trails and pipelines and out from the dormitory windows, to the coming and going of the third-shifters. Shadows blacker somehow than they ought to be. Two of them sitting there drinking red liquor like it was sadness medicine. Stupid. Thinking he saw something wistful on Deuce's face, though it could've been end-of-shift exhaustion, Webb said, "Too bad my daughter's flown the nest, I could've introduced you two."

No he couldn't. What was he thinking anyway? She was gone. Bitch was gone. . . .

"Thanks. Single life ain't that bad . . ." Deuce trailed off, as if it was something he didn't want to get into.

"It's a mixed blessing, son. Enjoy it while it's there."

When Deuce eventually understood he was in the presence of an honest-to-God dynamite-happy Anarchist, he wondered if he should have charged more. He sought out the company rep. "Got us a definite time and place, oh and by the way—"

"Are you out of your godforsaken mind? I don't know you, we never spoke, get the hell away from me before somebody sees us."

Deuce shrugged. Worth a shot anyway.

THE COMPANY INSPECTOR SAID, "You've been high-grading, Webb."

"Who don't walk out of here with rocks in their dinner pail?"

"Maybe over in Telluride, but not in this mine."

Webb looked at the "evidence" and said, "You know this was planted onto me. One of your finks over here. Maybe even you, Cap'n—"

"Watch what you say."

"—no damned inspector yet ain't taken a nugget when he thought he could." Teeth bared, almost smiling.

"Oh? seen a lot of that in your time?"

"Everybody has. What're we bullshittin' about, here, really?"

The first blow came out of the dark, filling Webb's attention with light and pain.

IT WAS TO BE a trail of pain, Deuce trying to draw it out, Sloat, closer to the realities of pain, trying to move it along.

"Thought we 's just gonna shoot him simple and leave him where he fell."

"No, this one's a special job, Sloat. Special handling. You might say we're in the big time now."

"Looks like just some of the usual ten-day trash to me, Deuce."

"Well that's where you'd be wrong. It turns out Brother Traverse here is a major figure in the world of criminal Anarchism."

"Of what's that again?"

"Apologies for my associate, the bigger words tend to throw him. You better get a handle on 'Anarchism' there, Sloat, because it's the coming thing in our field. Piles of money to be made."

Webb just kept quiet. It didn't look like these two were fixing to ask him any questions, because neither had spared him any pain that he could tell, pain and information usually being convertible, like gold and dollars, practically at a fixed rate. He didn't know how long he'd hold out in any case if they really wanted to start in. But along with the pain, worse, he guessed, was how stupid he felt, what a hopeless damn fool, at just how deadly wrong he'd been about this kid.

Before, Webb had only recognized it as politics, what Veikko called "procedure"—accepting that it might be necessary to lay down his life, that he was committed as if by signed contract to die for his brothers and sisters in the struggle. But now that the moment was upon him . . .

Since teaming up, the partners had fallen into a division of labor, Sloat tending to bodies, Deuce specializing more in harming the spirit, and thrilled now that Webb was so demoralized that he couldn't even look at them.

Sloat had a railroad coupling pin he'd taken from the D.&R.G. once, figuring it would come in handy. It weighed a little over seven pounds, and Sloat at the moment was rolling it in a week-old copy of the *Denver Post.* "We done both your feet, how about let's see your hands there, old-timer." When he struck, he made a point of not looking his victim in the face but stayed professionally focused on what it was he was aiming to damage.

Webb found himself crying out the names of his sons. From inside the pain, he was distantly surprised at a note of reproach in his voice, though not sure if it had been out loud or inside his thoughts. He watched the light over the ranges slowly draining away.

After a while he couldn't talk much. He was spitting blood. He wanted it over with. He sought Sloat's eyes with his one undamaged one, looking for a deal. Sloat looked over at Deuce.

"Where we headed for, li'l podner?"

"Jeshimon." With a malignant smile, meant to wither what spirit remained to Webb, for Jeshimon was a town whose main business was death, and the red adobe towers of Jeshimon were known and feared as the places you ended up on top of when nobody wanted you found. "You're going over into Utah, Webb. We happen to run across some Mormon apostles in time, why you can even get baptised, get a bunch of them proxy wives what they call sealed on to you, so's you'll enjoy some respect among the Saints, how's that, while you're all waiting for that good bodily resurrection stuff." Webb kept gazing at Sloat, blinking, waiting for some reaction, and when none came, he finally looked away.

As THEY WERE passing through Cortez, the notorious local gunhand Jimmy Drop happened to be out in back of the Four Corners Saloon pissing in the alley, when next thing he knew, there were Deuce and Sloat with Webb slung over a packhorse between them, on the way out of town. There was still light enough for Jimmy to recognize Deuce, who had ridden briefly with his outfit. "Hey!"

"Shit and what next," Sloat taking out his pistol and firing a couple of well-meaning rounds back in Jimmy's direction.

"No time," Deuce agreed, using his spurs, yanking on the lead of the horse carrying Webb.

"Can't have none of this," Jimmy observed to himself. He had checked his revolver at the door. Damn. Buttoning up his pants, he went running back into the saloon. "Apologies, miss, just need to borrow this a minute," searching energetically beneath the skirts of the nearest unoccupied fandango girl.

She was holding a buck knife and for the moment smiling. "Sir, please relocate your hand or I shall be obliged to do so myself."

"Hoping you might be packing a Derringer of some make—"

"Not down there, dude rancher." She reached into her decolletage and came up with a small over-under .22. "And it's for rent, payable in advance." By which time Webb and his murderers had vanished from the streets of Cortez, and shadow had taken the immeasurable plain.

To help him through mine school, Frank had borrowed some money from his brother Reef, who in those days was known for promoting quick cash out of the air.

"Don't know when I can pay this back, old Reefer."

"Whenever that is, if I'm still alive, that would be payback enough for me, so don't worry." As usual, Reef wasn't thinking that closely about what he was saying, finding it in fact impossible to imagine any kind of a future in which being dead was preferable to living. Part of the same rooster-in-the-morn attitude that kept him winning at games of chance. Or winning enough. Or he thought it did.

One day out of the usual nowhere, Reef showed up in Golden to find Frank with his nose in a metallurgy book.

"I have a chore to run, sort of romantic chore, nothing too difficult, you want to come along?"

"Where to? Being's I've got this exam?" Flapping the book pages at his brother for emphasis.

"Well you look like you could use a break. Why don't we go up Castle Rock to that amusement park and have us a few beers."

Why didn't they? Frank had no idea. Next thing he knew it was daytime again, Reef had squared everything with the Professor, and they were headed for Nevada.

After what seemed like a week on the train, "What did you need me along for, again?"

"Cover my back."

"She that dangerous?"

“Yehp, and she ain’t all that’s there.” After a couple of slow, wheeling changes of landscape, “You might like it, Francisco, why, there’s a church, a schoolhouse, any number of those back-east vegetarian restaurants—”

“Oh I’ll find something to do.”

“Don’t be mopin’ now.”

“Whoa, you think I’m mopin, I ain’t mopin about this, how can you think such a thing?”

“Don’t know, if it was me, I might be.”

“You, Reefer, you don’t know your heart from your hatband.”

“Put it this way—everybody has to have somebody to make em look good, which just happens to be you in this case.”

“Course, but wait a minute, now which one . . . is making the other one look good, again?”

Well, it was sure another world they were riding through, a waking dream. Saltflats in the rain, no horizon, mountains and their mirage-reflections like skulls of animals from other times, washed in a white shimmer . . . sometimes you could see all the way to a planetary horizon warped into an arc. Eastbound storms were likely to carry snow with some thunder and lightning thrown in, and the valley fog was the same color as the snow.

THE DEPOT at Nochecita had smooth stuccoed apricot walls, trimmed in a somehow luminous shade of gray—around the railhead and its freight sheds and electrical and machine shops, the town had grown, houses and businesses painted vermilion, sage, and fawn, and towering at the end of the main street, a giant sporting establishment whose turquoise and crimson electric lamps were kept lit all night and daytime, too, for the place never closed.

There was an icehouse and a billiard parlor, a wine room, a lunch and eating counter, gambling saloons and taquerías. In the part of town across the tracks from all that, Estrella Briggs, whom everybody called Stray, was living upstairs in what had been once the domestic palace of a mine owner from the days of the first great ore strikes around here, now a dimly illicit refuge for secret lives, dark and in places unrepainted wood rearing against a sky which since this morning had been threatening storm. Walkways in from the street were covered with corrugated snow-shed roofing. The restaurant and bar on the ground-floor corner had been there since the boom times, offering two-bit all-you-can-eat specials, sawdust on the floor, heavy-duty crockery, smells of steaks, chops, venison chili, coffee and beer and so on worked into the wood of the wall paneling, old trestle tables, bar and barstools. At all hours the place'd be racketing with gambling-hall workers on their breaks, big-hearted winners and bad losers, detectives, drummers, adventuresses, pigeons, and sharpers. A sunken chamber almost like a natatorium at some hot-springs resort, so cool and dim that you forgot after a while about the desert waiting out there to resume for you soon as you stepped back into it. . . .

STRAY, as it turned out, was real pregnant. Not only showing it, but also that other composed and dreamy thing you couldn't help noticing right away when the rest of the neighborhood was anything but. Through the upper rooms, insomnia ruled. It happened to be a week of convergences from all over. Everybody but Stray was nearly crazy already, Reef and Frank showing up was just one more problem. There were also her friend Sage's Mormon ex–foster parents from olden times, "sacred arrangements" going back in history to her Ma's problems with these people, Sage's own promise to join the faith, her latest beau, and maybe even another ex-beau, who might or might not be also about to show up, or even be in town already, along with newer influences, not so much personal it seemed as almost public, a set of born-again "friends"—though more in this official, maybe even sheriff's-office way—"friends" more newly made than these Mormons but no less clamoring for the girl's time, uneasy, in fact desperate to see her safe and married, who would stand literally *in a circle* around the couple as if enforcing the choice and allowing them no other. . . .

Frank came quickly to understand that Stray and his brother had had a dustup, and Reef had taken off but was now repentant, and what he needed Frank along for seemed to be muscle. Maybe. Almost as if he didn't really know what he was doing, and meant to consult Frank about it. Or as if two piss-ignorant rounders would turn out to be smarter than one.

"Nice that you got around to tellin me anyhow."

"Frank, meet Stray."

Oh-oh, Frank thought. "Family idiot," he introduced himself, "taggin along case anybody needs some emergency droolin done, or whatever."

At any given time, two or three girls were either packing or unpacking, just back from trips or just about to leave, so there were clothes new bought and not yet put on, sewing patterns and scraps of material, provisions in cans or jars or sacks, all as yet unstashed, strewn about the rooms. No claims of female tidiness around here it seemed. Though all of these girl bunkmates—how many and what their names were he never got straight either—were pleasant enough, letting Frank right into the kitchen and eventually the pantry, assigning him one of the dozen or so empty beds, he couldn't be sure they weren't a little wary of him for being Reef's brother. Ready, at anybody's first funny move, to protect Stray. There was also a possibility in the air that Stray and Sage would just fling up their hands and go vamoose town together if the beau situation got much more complicated.

One of these semi-awaited young gents—Cooper—when he did show up, turned out to be blond, shy, scaled about seven-eighths the size you'd expect, pleasant-faced enough except for something about his upper lip, which tucked over his teeth in a protective way, as if there was deep injury of some kind in his past, long enough ago at least for this defense to have worked in and set. Wouldn't come in the house, just sat out there astride his machine, a black and gold V-twin with white rubber tires and a brass headlamp, beaming his own blue-heaven luminaries at those who passed—with whom, despite the lip held so neutral, this tended to register as a smile.

Cooper and his rig were parked across the street. Frank, trying to be helpful, went down there to look them both over. "How you doin?"

The scaled-down motor badman nodded back, beaming away.

"Lookin for Sage?" coming out harsher than it should. Maybe this got Cooper to dim down a little, though given the eyeball diameter here, it wasn't much as flinches go. "'Cause I think she went to the depot, 's all I meant."

"Meetin somebody, or leavin town?"

"Didt'n hear no more'n 'at."

"Will anybody mind some pickin?" Now producing a "Cornell" model Acme guitar, Grand Concert size, mail-ordered from Sears and Roebuck, whose notes, as he began to play, rang like schoolbells from end to dusty end of the desert town. Lunchtime customers came squinting out of the gloom of the Double Jack or detouring down the alley to see what this might be. As he sang, the newcomer had his way-too-readable eyes locked on the upstairs windows across the street, waiting for faces there, or a particular face, to be drawn by the music, which now and then found strange notes added into the guitar chords, as though Cooper had hit between the wrong frets, only somehow it sounded right. Little kids from the schoolhouse next door came piling out into shade under cottonwood trees or onto porch steps to eat or play with their lunch, some of the moodier even to sing along—

Out on the wind . . .
Durango dove,
Ride the sky,
Dare the storm. . . .
We never once
Did speak of love,

Or I'd be free,
And a long time gone. . . .
When the lamplight
Comes on in town,
Rings and rouge,
Satin gown . . .
Oh, but my
Lost . . .
Durango dove,
Do they believe it all,
The way I do?
Would they fall
Into your sky,
Even die,
Dove, for you. . . .

The small, vibratoless voices, wind in cottonwoods. Cooper's fingers squeaking along the wire-wrapped strings, creaky percussion of wagon traffic in the dirt streets. The onset of siesta time. The pearl and windless sky. And who meanwhile had materialized at the upstairs window? The boy's ironclad lip slid up into the most unexpected of smiles, not very controlled, way too longing. Sage appeared on the outside stairs in some saloon-dancer's practice concern of palest gray, all legs and sobriety, coming down to him so smoothly, without a thought for step-by-step details of her entrance, all as easy and light as a breath, that before the young motor-wheelman could so much as blink, she had slipped a bare forearm into his shirtsleeve up alongside of his own arm, and he was trying to focus 'em baby blues, was how close she was standing, though she still hadn't quite looked him in the face.

Reef couldn't believe it. "Three weeks' wages for one those things? Might be worth it. Couldn't be that hard to learn how to play."

"You think it'd help *you*?" inquired Frank, innocently.

In the middle of the night, the schoolteacher next door was out on the second-floor veranda preparing meals for the next day. Frank couldn't sleep. He stumbled out onto the hardpan and happened to look up. "You still working?"

"You still loitering down there?"

"I could loiter up there, I guess."

"Have to put you to work."

"Sure."

Up close, in the light from the streetlamps, he couldn't help noticing how pretty she was—her cheeks, beneath dark eyes and eyebrows, showing just the beginnings of some weathering in, desert influence, no doubt. . . .

"Here, do these peas. Have you known Estrella for long?"

"Well . . . it's her and my brother—"

"*Oh* Lord. That was 'at Reef Traverse?"

"Was last time I looked—I'm Frank . . . the one that ain't Reef?"

"Linnet Dawes." A desert lady's hand, a square handshake that didn't choose to linger. Or, he guessed, loiter.

"Reef's well known around town here, is he?"

"Estrella has mentioned him once or twice. Not that we're confidantes or anything."

A midnight breeze had risen, bringing with it the sound of a creek not far away. As if Linnet's own serenity might be catching, he felt content to just sit there and shell peas, without much need to be chinning away, though he did slide his eyeballs over now and then to see what she might be up to in the fractional moonlight, and even found her looking at him once or twice in the same sidelong way.

Was it just this country? Something to do with the relative humidity, maybe? Frank had been noticing some kind of deadman switch or shutdown mechanism at work which, every time an interesting or even interested woman appeared, immediately doomed all possibility of romance. Men in this era not being known to sigh, he exhaled expressively. A fellow could rely on Market Street only so far, and then even that began to get discouraging, plagal cadences on parlor pianos, bright lights, and mirrors to the contrary notwithstanding.

Linnet, done with her chores, stood, shook out her apron. Frank handed her the bowl of loose peas. "Thanks. Your brother has his work cut out for him."

"Well I'll pass that on." No, wait—wrong answer, he bet.

She was shaking her head, lips pursed in a lopsided way. "I'm not worried about either of *them,* much."

He figured he should let it go at that, instead of ask who else she might be worried about. She was watching him as if following along as these thoughts occurred. Over her shoulder, just before she slipped away indoors, she said, "Maybe we'll peel onions sometime."

Next afternoon he was lying in one of the beds reading the *Police Gazette* or, actually, looking at the pictures, when Stray appeared in the doorway, soft as a house-chime, looked to see if he was awake, nodded, came in, sat on the end of the bed.

"You . . . weren't looking for Reef?" he said.

"No."

"'Cause I think he's across the street, saw him . . . headin in the Double Jack, about an hour ago?"

"Frank," in the twilight through the dusty windowglass, her face just this side of some outburst he knew he would not be able to address, "if he wasn't your brother, just some customer the wind blew in, would you know what to do about him at all, would you even want to take the trouble . . . ?"

"Hard to say." Oh. Wrong again.

She gazed, impatient, a light tremor in arms and neck. "Damn all *this,* I can sure tell you that much."

He tried to make out, against the daylight flowing in off the plain, what he could of her face veiled in its own penumbra, afraid somehow of misreading it, the brow smoothed by the uncertain light to the clarity of a girl's, the eyes beneath free to claim as little acquaintance with the unchaste, he guessed, as she might need.

Actresses pray for light like this. The electric lamp-switch was near her hand, but she made no gesture toward it.

"You kind of see the story here. Is, it's all these Utahans in town hollerin at Sage to get married, some Mormon boy she can't hardly remember from back when she lived there, Cooper meantime wants her to ride off on that motor concern that never seems to get 'em more'n a mile 'fore he's down into the works with her passin him pry bars and things, so *she's* nobody to go looking to for advice of the heart, meantime your brother has it in his mind that I'm some li'l private health resort here for whenever he feels funny. What would you do? You was me. Which last time I checked, you wa'n't."

"Miss Estrella, he always has been a tough one to figure."

She waited for more, but that seemed to be it. "Oh well thank you, that really helps."

"Not like that he's square-dancin through his life," it seemed to occur to Frank. "Even if it don't *look* like hard work—"

"Oh how true, them faro boxes don't just rig themselves, do they? What kind of a future do you foresee for ol' Buck-the-Tiger there?"

"You mean how likely is he . . . to be . . . a good provider?"

Her laughter, accompanied by a slap at his foot, still had enough of a salt-water element back of it for even Frank to pick up. He lay there supine, wanting nothing right now but—say, was he serious?—to hold her, yes and rest his head against where that baby was and just listen, somehow remaining easy enough with that to allow her whenever she wanted to to stop whatever would happen, only it wouldn't begin, because here came loud intrusion from the street, Utahans in high frolic stomping up the stairs, singing pieces of what sounded like some very weird hymn tunes at each other. "Well now, *shit,*" declared Stray, looking quickly down to address her stomach—"You didt'n hear that—guess we'd better have one these lights on." In the electric light, they had a good long look at each other's face, and though he couldn't speak for her, Frank knew that in years to come, it likely could get him past many a hard mile to remember this couple-three seconds of soul-to-soul—baby or howsoever, the C chord in the day's melody he could always return to would be this serious young woman sitting down at the end of the bed, and the look those eyes seemed for a minute there to be giving him.

But then everything saddled up and proceeded down Mexico way.

At the Casino, back in the back rooms, with any number of telegraph receivers, both sounders and inkers, of occasionally non-store-bought design, each attached to a different set of wires from outside and chattering all day and night with news of horse races at every known track both sides of the border, prize-fights and other contests of wagering interest, quotations from financial and commodity markets in cities East and West, there was also a telephone instrument mounted on the wall, pretty constantly in use. But one day it rang while Reef happened to be right next to it, and he knew it was for him, and that it was bad news. This was part of the strangeness of telephones in those early days, before the traffic became quite such a routine affair. As if overdesigned to include all sorts of extra features like precognitive alarms.

It was Jimmy Drop on the other end, a longtime associate of Reef's, calling from Cortez. Even at this distance, with everything in between from hungry gophers to idle sharpshooters working against the signal, Reef could sense Jimmy's discomfort with the machinery he was hollering into. "Reef? That you? Where are you?"

"Jimmy, you're calling me."

"Well, yeah, yeah but—"

"How'd you know to call me here?"

"You told me Nochecita, before you left."

"Was I drunk?"

"Wouldn't say *not* drunk." A pause while a turbulent bath of noise that could have been fragments of speech or music surged along the lines. "Reef?"

Reef all at once wished he could just pretend they'd been cut off. He'd rather have skipped whatever Jimmy had to tell him right now. But he wouldn't.

"You know Deuce Kindred?"

"Works for the Owners Association in Telluride. Don't know how to behave at a poker table. That the one?"

"I'm sorry, Reef. It's your Pa."

"Pa—"

"They took him out of town at gunpoint. No word since."

"They."

"Him 'n' 'at Sloat Fresno, too, 's what I heard."

"One of Bob Meldrum's old-time pals. Number of notches to his credit, so I'm told."

"More'n there's states in the Union, Reef, I'd bring some U.S. Cavalry I was you."

"Well Jim you ain't."

Another pause. "I'll look in on your Ma, when I can."

"Know where they're headed?"

"Jeshimon."

Spoken as if Reef shouldn't have had the bad manners to make Jimmy say it out loud. And now there was nothing but his asshole between Reef and the force of gravity. Out here, even when you didn't pray much, you prayed not to hear that name too often. Didn't help that it was inside a day's ride from Nochecita.

Frank was sure a trooper for being so young, deciding to address the practicalities first and save any troubled feelings till later. "Train, or do we ride there?"

"Just me, Frank."

"Hell you say."

"I figured you'd go see to Ma and Lake."

"That's my part in all this, lookin after the women?"

"All what? Do you know what's goin on? I sure's hell don't."

They sat together on the outside steps, holding their hats and fooling with the brims. Clouds thickened overhead, now and then lightning pulsed out at the horizon. Wind inhabited and presently stirred the leaves of the cottonwoods. Behind windowpanes, through alkali dust, various young women would appear, observe them, shake their heads, and withdraw to go on with their own version of the day.

"Let's just see what's what. Just the one step at a time. That O.K.?"

And Webb's fate such an unknown in all this . . .

Another spell of dark, brimrolling silence. "And I wait around like some penny-ante remittance man, till you get killed, then the job passes to me, that it?"

"See how that mine school's educating you, you never used to be so quick."

But Reef was steadily growing calmer now, almost prayerful. As if, alongside what was avalanching down onto both brothers' understanding, a whole list of things had become far less important.

TELLING STRAY, THAT was another story. "Got no secrets from you, darlin'."

"You've 'got' to do this, I expect."

"By now, the thing is . . . If Pa's gone . . ."

"Oh, maybe not."

"Yeah, maybe not. . . ." He was looking not in her eyes but down there at the baby.

She did notice that. "It's his grandbaby. I'd hate if they were never to meet."

"It just has seemed for a while that somethin like this was bound to happen."

She was having a great entertaining interior conversation with herself it seemed. At length, "You be back?"

"Oh I will. Stray, I promise."

"Promise. My. Does the Pope know you said that, it's a certified miracle."

THE GIRLS WERE sorry to see them go, or said they were, but Cooper? you would have thought it was the end of the world. He came downstairs and followed Frank and Reef all the way to the depot, on foot, a stricken look on his face. "You O.K.?" Frank finally figured he should ask. "Hope you don't think like that we're runnin out, or . . ."

Cooper shook his head, downcast. "All 'is drygoods, it's really burdensome on a man, you know?"

"Just play 'em that 'Juanita' every once in a while," Reef advised, "they say it works wonders."

The brothers traveled together as far as Mortalidad, the stop nearest Jeshimon, then, because of who might or might not be looking, they said goodbye with little more than the nod you give somebody who's just lit your cigar for you. No gazing back out the window, no forehead creased with solemn thoughts, no out with the pocket flask or sudden descent into sleep. Nothing that would belong to the observable world.

It was well up into Utah. The country was so red that the sagebrush appeared to float above it as in a stereopticon view, almost colorless, pale as cloud, luminous day and night. Out as far as Reef could see, the desert floor was populated by pillars of rock, worn over centuries by the unrelenting winds to a kind of post-godhead, as if once long ago having possessed limbs that they could move, heads they could tilt and swivel to watch you ride past, faces so sensitive they reacted to each change of weather, each act of predation around them, however small, these once-watchful beings, now past face, past gesture, standing refined at last to simple vertical attendance.

"Don't mean they're not alive, o' course," opined somebody in a saloon on the way there.

"You think they're alive?"

"Been out there at night?

"Not if I could help it."

Not that he wasn't warned, but that didn't keep it from being the worst town Reef ever rode into. What was wrong with these people? For miles along the trail, coming and going, every telegraph pole had a corpse hanging from it, each body in a different stage of pickover and decay, all the way back to a number of sun-beaten skeletons of some considerable age. By local custom and usage, as the town clerk would presently explain, these strung-up wrongdoers had been denied any sort of decent burial, it being cheaper anyway just to leave them for the turkey vultures. When the townsfolk of Jeshimon ran out of telegraph poles back around 1893, trees being scarce out here, they turned to fashioning their arrangements out of adobe brick. Sophisticated world travelers visiting the area were quick to identify the rude structures with those known in Persia as "Towers of Silence"—no stairs or ladders, high and steep-sided enough to discourage mourners from climbing, no matter how athletic or bent on honoring their dead—living humans had no place up top. Some of the condemned were brought by wagon to the base of the tower, strung up by pulleys onto a boom that when it was all over with you could just keep hoisting the body on up, swing it around, and leave it to hang there by its one foot for the birds of death who then came down and landed hissing on perches molded for their convenience out of the red mud of the region.

So Reef passed beneath drifting enormous wing-shadows, down the grim colonnade, which, judging by the numbers, hadn't been that much of a deterrent. "No, quite the contrary," cheerfully admitted the Reverend Lube Carnal of the Second Lutheran (Missouri Synod) Church, "we attract evildoers from hundreds of miles around—not to mention clergy too o' course, like you wouldn't believe. You'll notice there's more churches here than saloons, making us unique in the Territory. Kind of professional challenge, get to their souls before the Governor gets to their necks."

"The what?"

"It's how he likes to be addressed. Thinks of this as his little state within a state. Whose main business you could say is the processing of souls."

"Well how about your bylaws, legal peculiarities, anythin a newcomer ought to know about?"

"None, sir, bylaws, blue laws, or in-laws, anything and everything goes here, otherwise the game wouldn't be honest. No deadlines in Jeshimon, pack anything anyplace you like, commit sins of your own choosing or even invention. Just, once the Gov takes notice, don't expect sanctuary in any of our churches, or for that matter anything much at all in the way of parsonical aid. Best we can do is knead you into shape for the ovens of the Next World."

Though Jeshimon was known as the place they brought the ones they didn't want found too soon, Reef learned from the Rev that, for a price, certain accommodations could be made. Because this was technically subornation, it counted, of course, as a sin and if you got caught at it, why you met an appropriate fate.

AT NIGHT from up in the hills, the first glimpse of Jeshimon was like a religious painting of hell used to scare kids with in Sunday school. In dense columns from different parts of the scene, something lurid and vaporous, like smoke, like dust, but not really either of these, was seen to rise, roll upward, collecting here and there in the sky in heaps as structured as cloud. When the moon went in behind one of these patches, its light was said to take on disturbing *colors,* colors which were to the preternaturally black skies here what the colors of a sunset are to an ordinary sky of daytime blue. Nothing any visitor wanted to contemplate for long—in fact, certain nights the view had been known to drive the more sensitive back over the ridgeline in search of other lodgings, no matter how advanced the hour.

In town an ambience of limitless iniquity reigned, a stifling warmth day and night, not an hour passing without someone discharging a firearm at someone else, or a public sexual act, often in a horse-trough among more than two parties, along with random horsewhippings, buffaloings, robberies at gunpoint, poker pots raked in without the hand being shown, pissing not only against walls but also upon passersby, sand in the sugar bowls, turpentine and sulfuric acid in the whiskey, brothels dedicated to a wide range of preferences, including arnophilia, or an unaccustomed interest in sheep, some of the ovine nymphs in these establishments being quite appealing indeed, even to folks who might not wholeheartedly share the taste, with fleeces dyed in a variety of fashionable colors, including the perennial favorites aquamarine and mauve, or wearing items of feminine—not to mention masculine—attire (hats for some reason, being popular) meant to enhance the animal's sexual appeal—"though some of the flock," as the Rev confessed, "given the level of duplicity prevailing here, do turn out to be mutton dressed as lamb or, on occasion, goat, for even these are regularly sought out by a small but reliable fraction of the pilgrims who daily make their way across the desert to this Lourdes of the licentious. . . . But let us not dwell further on such patently abominable behavior. Time for my rounds, come on along," invited the Rev, "and I'll show you the sights. Ah, here's the Scalped Indian Saloon. Shall we irrigate?" It was the first of many pauses in what would develop into a daylong exercise in transgression. "You know the principle in medicine where the cure grows right next to the cause. Swamp ague and willow bark, desert sunburn and aloe cactus, well, the same goes in Jeshimon for sin and redemption."

The music in the saloons tended toward choral part-singing, and there were more reed organs than parlor pianos, and as many turned-around collars among the customers as trail bandannas.

"We like to think of Jeshimon as being under God's wing," said the Reverend Lube Carnal.

"But wait a minute, God doesn't have wings—"

"The God you're thinking of, maybe not. But out here, the one who looks after us, is it's a kind of winged God, you see."

A troop of expressionless men on matched black Arabians appeared in the street. It was Wes Grimsford, the Marshal of Jeshimon, and his deputies.

"Notice anything in particular?" whispered the Rev. Reef didn't, which got him a look almost of pity. "It pays to be observant in this town. Observe the star Wes is wearing." Reef snuck a look. It was a five-pointed star, nickel-plated, like they tended to wear, except that it was on upside down. "With the two points up—that's the horns of the Devil, and signifies that Elderly Gent and his works."

"And it looked like such a godly town too," said Reef.

"Hope you don't meet the Governor. Keeps his hat on all the time, you can guess why, and is said to have a tail, too."

They all lived in fear of the Governor, forever to and fro in Jeshimon and apt to arrive anywhere in town without warning. What impressed a first-time viewer was not any natural charisma, for he had none, but rather a keen sense of something wrong in his appearance, something pre-human in the face, the sloping forehead and clean-shaven upper lip, which for any reason, or none, would start back into a simian grin which was suppressed immediately, producing a kind of dangerous smirk that often lingered for hours, and which, when combined with his glistening stare, was enough to unnerve the boldest of desperadoes. Though he believed that the power that God had allowed to find its way to him required a confident swagger, his gait was neither earned nor, despite years of practice, authentic, having progressed in fact little beyond an apelike trudge. The reason he styled himself Governor and not President or King was the matter of executive clemency. The absolute power of life and death enjoyed by a Governor within his territory had its appeal. He traveled always with his "clemency secretary," a cringing weasel named Flagg, whose job was to review each day's population of identified malefactors and point with his groomed little head at those to be summarily put to death, often by the Governor himself, though, being a notoriously bad shot, he preferred not to have a crowd around for that. "Clemency" was allowing some to wait a day or two before they were executed, the number of buzzards and amount of tower space being finite.

Webb wasn't quite gone when his killers brought him into town, and for that reason Reef got to Jeshimon in time to keep his father's carcass from the carrion birds, and then the big decision was whether to ride on after Deuce and Sloat or bring Webb back up to the San Miguel for a decent burial. He would question his own judgment in years to come, wonder in fact if he hadn't just been trying to avoid an encounter with the killers, whether he hadn't gotten cowardice mixed in with honoring his father and so forth, and by the time he could stop and think about it, there was nobody to talk it over with.

Maybe the worst of it was that he actually caught sight of them heading away toward the red-rock country, shadows in the near distance that were all but artifacts of the merciless daylight, the packhorse that had brought Webb wandering free and eventually stopping to browse. As if offended at the loose morality abroad in Jeshimon, Deuce and Sloat were disinclined to further gunplay. Though there was only one of Reef, they decided to run anyway. They galloped away giggling, as if this had been some high-spirited prank and Reef its grumpy old target.

The buzzards circled, stately and patient. The citizens of Jeshimon looked on with varying degrees of disengagement. Nobody offered to help, of course, until Reef found himself at the base of the tower in question, where a Mexican sidled up to him in the dusk and motioned him around a couple of corners to a roofless ruin crammed with all sorts of hardware gone to rust and dilapidation. *"Quieres un cloque,"* the man, scarcely older than a boy, kept saying. It didn't seem to be a question. Reef thought he was trying to say "clock," but then, peering into the shadows, saw at last what it was—a set of grappling hooks. How they got this far inland, what kind of ship they may have belonged to, sailing what sea, all without meaning here. The rope for it would cost extra. Reef shelled out the pesos without haggling, not too surprised at the existence of the silent market, for enough survivors must always want to scale the forbidden walls, unwilling to leave matters to the mercies of Jeshimon. Through dusk's reassembly of the broken day therefore, as the first star appeared, Reef found himself in growing desperation swinging iron hooks lariat style, trying not to be in the way when he missed the rim of the tower and they came falling back through the dark to clang in the beaten dust. His attempts soon gathered an audience, mostly of children, from whom ordinarily he would have drawn grace, but his amiability had deserted him. Many of these children kept buzzards for pets, gave them names, found them pleasant company, and might be betting, for all he knew, in their favor and against Reef.

At last the hooks dug in and held. By now he was tired, not in the best condition to begin climbing, but there was no choice. The Mexican who'd sold him the *cloque* was right there, growing impatient, as if Reef had rented his contraption by the hour. Maybe he had.

So he ascended, into night swelling like notes on a church organ. His bootsoles slipped repeatedly on the adobe surface—it was exactly not rough enough to allow him an easy climb. His arms were soon in agony, his leg muscles cramping as well.

About then he happened to sight Marshal Grimsford heading out here with a small party of deputized townsfolk, and Reef and Webb—that's how it felt anyway, like his father was still alive and this was their last adventure together—must flee without discussion. He shot a carrion bird, maybe two, among the great unhurried black ascent of the others slung the corpse across his shoulders, no time to think of the mystery of what had been Webb Traverse now a cargo of contraband to be run past authorities gunning for them. Rappelled down the dark, blood-red wall, stole a horse, found another outside of town to pack Webb on, hit the trail south with no sign of pursuit and only a dim idea of how he'd got there.

DURING THE RIDE back up to Telluride, among tablelands and cañons and red-rock debris, past the stone farmhouses and fruit orchards and Mormon spreads of the McElmo, below ruins haunted by an ancient people whose name no one knew, circular towers and cliffside towns abandoned centuries ago for reasons no one would speak of, Reef was able finally to think it through. If Webb had always been the Kieselguhr Kid, well, shouldn't somebody ought to carry on the family business—you might say, become the Kid?

It might've been the lack of sleep, the sheer relief of getting clear of Jeshimon, but Reef began to feel some new presence inside him, growing, inflating—gravid with what it seemed he must become, he found excuses to leave the trail now and then and set off a stick or two from the case of dynamite he had stolen from the stone powder-house at some mine. Each explosion was like the text of another sermon, preached in the voice of the thunder by some faceless but unrelenting desert prophesier who was coming more and more to ride herd on his thoughts. Now and then he creaked around in the saddle, as if seeking agreement or clarification from Webb's blank eyes or the rictus of what would soon be a skull's mouth. "Just getting cranked up," he told Webb. "Expressing myself." Back in Jeshimon he had thought that he could not bear this, but with each explosion, each night in his bedroll with the damaged and redolent corpse carefully unroped and laid on the ground beside him, he found it was easier, something he looked forward to all the alkaline day, more talk than he'd ever had with Webb alive, whistled over by the ghosts of Aztlán, entering a passage of austerity and discipline, as if undergoing down here in the world Webb's change of status wherever he was now. . . .

He had brought with him a dime novel, one of the Chums of Chance series, *The Chums of Chance at the Ends of the Earth,* and for a while each night he sat in the firelight and read to himself but soon found he was reading out loud to his father's corpse, like a bedtime story, something to ease Webb's passage into the dreamland of his death.

Reef had had the book for years. He'd come across it, already dog-eared, scribbled in, torn and stained from a number of sources, including blood, while languishing in the county lockup at Socorro, New Mexico, on a charge of running a game of chance without a license. The cover showed an athletic young man (it seemed to be the fearless Lindsay Noseworth) hanging off a ballast line of an ascending airship of futuristic design, trading shots with a bestially rendered gang of Eskimos below. Reef began to read, and soon, whatever "soon" meant, became aware that he was reading in the dark, lights-out having occurred sometime, near as he could tell, between the North Cape and Franz Josef Land. As soon as he noticed the absence of light, of course, he could no longer see to read and, reluctantly, having marked his place, turned in for the night without considering any of this too odd. For the next couple of days he enjoyed a sort of dual existence, both in Socorro and at the Pole. Cellmates came and went, the Sheriff looked in from time to time, perplexed.

At odd moments, now, he found himself looking at the sky, as if trying to locate somewhere in it the great airship. As if those boys might be agents of a kind of *extrahuman justice,* who could shepherd Webb through whatever waited for him, even pass on to Reef wise advice, though he might not always be able to make sense of it. And sometimes in the sky, when the light was funny enough, he thought he saw something familiar. Never lasting more than a couple of watch ticks, but persistent. "It's them, Pa," he nodded back over his shoulder. "They're watching us, all right. And tonight I'll read you some more of that story. You'll see."

Riding out of Cortez in the morning, he checked the high end of the Sleeping Ute and saw cloud on the peak. "Be rainin later in the day, Pa."

"Is that Reef? Where am I? Reef, I don't know where the hell I am—"

"Steady, Pa. We're outside of Cortez, headin up to Telluride, be there pretty soon—"

"No. That's not where this is. Everthin is unhitched. Nothin stays the same. Somethin has happened to my eyes. . . ."

"It's O.K."

"Hell it is."

THEY STOOD HUDDLED together in Lone Tree Cemetery, the miners' graveyard at the end of town, Mayva, Lake, Frank, and Reef, beneath the great peaks and behind them the long, descending trace of Bridal Veil Falls whispering raggedly into the cold sunlight. Webb's life and work had come to this.

Frank was up from Golden, just here overnight. He stayed close to Mayva, not saying much, figuring what he had to contribute was just, however temporarily, to be the living opposite of what lay all around them.

"I just wish I was with him," Mayva said, very low, almost without breath.

"But you're not," Frank pointed out, "and maybe there's a reason for that."

"Oh, children. I surely wouldn't want to be neither of them that did it. God will see it right, even if God is so awful slow sometimes. Takes his *goddamned* sweet time. And maybe if he's slow enough, somebody down here will have the chance before he gets around to it. . . ."

She was so quiet, not about to put on the kind of show you saw these Mexican widows going in for. What tears did come were so alarming in their suddenness and silence—just there all on Mayva's face, as if they were symptoms of a condition no doctor'd have the heart to name. If those hired triggers had been anyplace near, the force of her unvoiced rage could have fried them where they stood. Just greasy ashes by the trailside.

"Thought the Union would've sent flowers at least."

"Not them." It is just the meanest kind of disrespect, Reef thought, and fuck all these people. He happened at some point to look up the hillside and saw what he was pretty sure were elements of the Jimmy Drop gang up along the Tomboy Road with their hats off, maybe observing a moment of silence but knowing them more likely bickering about something considerably less important than life and death.

"Just as well, Ma, that it's only us and not about to be one of these funerals where half the town turns out for a parade and a picnic. . . . He's out of all 'at now. He'll be all right. And Frank and me will get the ones that did it." Reef wished he could have sounded different. More confident. His sister, who'd just seemed to be drifting through it smoothly as if she was on wheels, wheels on track set down in the nights by crews nobody ever saw, her face behind the veil just a marble mask, now flashed him her usual don't-believe-it-for-a-minute stare, and if it wasn't for Mayva being there, he sure would've felt like calling her on it. Seeing 's how little she'd cared for Webb when he was alive.

Which didn't mean she wasn't shaken, and shamed, by the force of her mother's grief. Lake was back from Silverton, and for good, even Reef could see that. She wore a shapely black dress that must have set many a Blair Street lowlife's pulses to throbbing but was now dedicated to memorializing her father. And he'd bet everything on the table that this would be the last time she was fixing to wear it. She saw him staring. "Least you two're wearing black hats," she said, "that's somethin."

"You can do the mourning," Reef said, "me and Frank will what Joe Hill calls organize. There's this other business to be done. Idea is to keep you and Kit clear of it, and the less you all know, the better."

"How about Mamma, and the less she knows?"

"Don't want her to be worrying."

"Thoughtful of you. Don't it occur to either of you she might want her children alive, instead of out looking for trouble?"

"We're alive."

"How long before she'll see you or Frank again? You're off into that old world o' family vengeance, it has its claim on you now, you're both out lost in country you don't know how to get back in from. What do you think it's like for her, that kind of 'business'? Might just as well be dead already, the both of you. Damn fools."

He didn't know yet what was behind that passionate speech, nobody did, not quite yet.

Back at the grimly daylit parlor of the house, "Here," Mayva said to Reef. "You better have this." It was Webb's old twelve-shot Confederate Colt.

"Don't feel right," Reef handing it on to Frank. "Yours if you want it, Francis."

"Well but I already have my .38 Special and all."

"But that's only five shots, and the way you shoot, half those are wasted, hell, you'll need at least twelve, Francis, just to get sighted in."

"Well if it's too heavy for you to handle, Reefer, I can sure understand, no shame in that."

"But I do know it always made you nervous," Reef said, taking it back.

This went on for a while. Mayva watched, puffing on her old pipe, her eyes switching back and forth between them as if in motherly despair. She knew they wanted her to squint at them through the smoke and shake her head the way she always had, *What am I supposed to do with these two?* When they heard the train coming up the valley, Frank took his hat and left the gun on the kitchen table. He and Reef had a fast, silent look, just long enough to make sure what they both knew, that it was really Mayva's and would stay with her. And sure enough, a couple of months later Lake heard shots from the town dump and had a look, and there was her mother, striking fear into the hearts of rats who'd left the mines after Repeal—at least making them wonder if life up here on the surface was worth it.

Back in Nochecita, back from burying Webb at Telluride, blowing up a few company outbuildings on the way back just for drill, equipment sheds reduced to sawdust, electric power junctions that filled the skies with green disaster, Reef found Stray in a peculiarly serene state. The Mormons and

Christers had all left town, the baby was imminent, Reef was sensible enough to understand that right now all he needed to do was keep silent and let whatever'd been under way without him just keep on like that.

When the baby was born, a boy, Jesse, Reef stood drinks all around at the Double Jack, and somebody said, "No more hellraisin for you, Reef, time to start bein careful," and he found himself turning back to that in the night watches that followed, wondering if it was strictly true.

Careful? Made sense up to a point. Maybe more sense down someplace like Denver than up here. You could step careful as a damn goat up here and they'd still gun you down, careful didn't buy you a minute extra on your time allotted. So as long as being in the Union you were good as dead anyway, there was the wider duty, out in the world at large, to attend to.

Webb was more than he'd ever seemed to be, had to've been or they wouldn't have had him killed. Reef might not be able to pull off successfully the guise of a respectable wife-and-kids working stiff the way Webb had. Meant he'd either have to level with Stray or pretend to be up to his old rounder ways so she'd think when he disappeared for days at a time that it was ramblin and gamblin and nothing serious.

One of those cases where you couldn't just fold. God, across the table of Fate, was picking His nose, scratching His ear, laying on tells with a prodigal hand, it had to mean something, and a faulty guess would be better than none. But Reef would find his way. One more or less clumsy step at a time as he always did, Reef would see his way slowly into it, why the life of his father was taken, why the owners could not allow it to go on, not up there, not in this country harrowed by crimes in the name of gold, swept over by unquiet spirits from the Coeur d'Alene and Cripple and Telluride who came in the rain and the blinding northers and lightning-glazed mountain faces, came forlornly to stare, all those used and imperiled and run into exile, Webb's dead, Webb's casualties, Webb's own losers he could never have abandoned. . . .

And Webb's ghost, meantime, Webb's busy ghost, went bustling to and fro doing what he could to keep things hopping.

"Home at last!" cried Neville, "home from innocent, all but oppressively wholesome America!"

"Back to the delights of Evil!" Nigel added, with every appearance of relief.

Lew had learned by now to keep a straight face around talk like this. In his work—his former job—he had managed a run-in or two with what you'd have to call Evil, in noonlit upper stories as likely as down some desperate arroyos at the end of day, and he was pretty certain neither of these boys had ever been close enough even to get goosebumps off of it, for all the time they spent, or if you like wasted, out looking for it. On the rare occasions they might actually find the article, he guessed, they would have little clue about what to do besides spin around and around, trying to see what it was that had sunk its pearly whites—or in Evil's case, mossy greens—into their more or less ambushed keesters.

The T.W.I.T., or True Worshippers of the Ineffable Tetractys, were headquartered in London at Chunxton Crescent, in that ambiguous stretch north of Hyde Park known then as Tyburnia, in a mansion attributed to Sir John Soane, which during its latest tenancy, dating roughly from the departure of Madam Blavatsky from the material plane, had become a resort for all manner of sandaled pilgrims, tweed-smocked visionaries, and devotees of the nut cutlet. At this most curious of moments in the history of spiritual inquiry, in keen competition with the Theosophical Society and its post-Blavatskian fragments, as well as the Society for Psychical Research, the Order of the Golden Dawn, and other arrangements for seekers of certitude, of whom there seemed an ever-increasing supply as the century had rushed to its end and through some unthinkable zero and on out the other side, the

T.W.I.T. had chosen to follow a secret neo-Pythagorean way of knowledge, based upon the sacred *Tetractys,*

1
2 3
4 5 6
7 8 9 10,

by which their ancient predecessors had sworn their deepest oath. The idea, as nearly as Neville and Nigel could explain it, was to look at the array of numbers as occupying not two dimensions but three, set in a regular tetrahedron—and then four dimensions, and so on, until you found yourself getting strange, which was taken to be a sign of impending enlightenment.

At the moment the boys, who planned to sponsor Lew for induction into the Order, were being kind enough as well to offer wardrobe advice.

"What's it matter," Lew wanted to know, "if everybody'll have on the same, what you call 'postulant' outfits anyhow?"

"Nevertheless," said Neville, "the cowboy boots are fatally inappropriate, Lewis—here at Chunxton Crescent it's barefoot or begone."

"What—not even socks?"

"Not even if that tartan were authentic," Nigel looking pointedly at what Lew at the moment had on his feet.

They had brought him tonight to the T.W.I.T. sanctuary, faced in Caen stone which at twilight somehow leached all color from the immediate surroundings, set back behind iron fencework in almost a miniature park, in which masses of shadow which might or might not have had counterparts in the animal kingdom moved with a sinister impatience. "Nice little hacienda," Lew nodded.

Inside, somebody was playing a duet on syrinx and lyre. Lew thought he knew the tune, but then it went off in some direction he couldn't follow. Englishfolk, not obviously exotic, were down on the carpeting in poses reminding Lew of contortionists at the ten-in-one. People strolled around in peculiar outfits or often next to nothing at all. Faces well known from the illustrated press went drifting by. Light was subject to strange modifications not all accounted for by the smoke in the air, as bright presences appeared from nowhere into full view and then as abruptly vanished from it. Humans reincarnated as cats, dogs, and mice crept about or slept by the fire. Stone pillars loomed in the further reaches of the place, with the impression of steps descending into subterranean mystery.

Lew was greeted by Nicholas Nookshaft, Grand Cohen of the London chapter of the T.W.I.T., a person in mystical robes appliquéd with astrological and alchemical symbols, and a bowl haircut with short fringes. "Neville and Nigel, allowing for some chemical exaggeration, tell us they saw you emerge out of an explosion. The question that arises is, where were you just before."

Lew squinted, perplexed. "Strolling down to the creek minding my business. Where else?"

"Couldn't have been the same world as the one you're in now."

"You seem pretty sure."

The Cohen elaborated. "Lateral world-sets, other parts of the Creation, lie all around us, each with its crossover points or gates of transfer from one to another, and they can be anywhere, really. . . . An unscheduled Explosion, introduced into the accustomed flow of the day, may easily open, now and then, passages to elsewhere. . . ."

"Sure, like death."

"A possibility, but not the only one."

"So when I went diving into that blast—"

Grand Cohen Nookshaft nodded gravely. "You found passage between the Worlds. Your mysterious assailants presented you with an unintended gift."

"Who asked them?" Lew grumbled.

"Yet mightn't they, and others like them, in providing such passage, be considered agencies of the angelic?"

"All respect, sir, I think not, they're more likely Anarchistic terrorists, for Pete's sake."

"Tsk. They are shamans, Mr. Basnight. The closest we in our fallen state may ever come to the uncivilized purity of the world as it was and shall never be again—not for the likes of us."

"Can't buy it, sorry."

"You must," insisted the Grand Cohen. "If you are who we are beginning to believe you might be."

Neville and Nigel, who had slipped away during this exchange, returned now in the company of a striking young woman, who regarded Lew out of eyes from which a suggestion of the Oriental might not have been altogether absent.

"Allow us," said Nigel, "to introduce Miss— Or actually, as she's a seventeenth-degree Adept, one ought properly to say 'Tzaddik,' except that obviously—"

"Well blimey, it's really only old Yashmeen, isn't it," added Neville.

"Well put Neville, and why don't you go reward yourself with a pie or something?"

"Perhaps Nigel you'd like one up your nose as well."

"Silence, driveling ones," snarled the girl. "Imagine how idiotic they'd be if they could talk."

The two gazed back with expressions in which hopelessly smitten erotic obsession could not really be ruled out, and Lew thought he heard Nigel sigh, "The Tetractys isn't the only thing round here that's ineffable."

"Children, children," admonished the Grand Cohen. Frankly as if she had not been standing a foot away, he began to acquaint Lew with the girl's history. She had been the ward of Lieutenant-Colonel G. Auberon Halfcourt, formerly a squadron commander in the Eighteenth Hussars, seconded some while ago to the Political Department in Simla for the odd extra-regimental chore, and currently believed operating somewhere out in Inner Asia. Yashmeen, sent back here a few years previously for a British education, had been placed under the protection of the T.W.I.T. "Unhappily, to more than one element active in Britain, her degree of bodily safety too readily suggests itself as a means of influencing the Colonel's behavior. Our custody hence extends rather beyond simple caution."

"I can look after myself," declared the girl, not, it seemed, for the first time.

Lew beamed in frank admiration. "A fellow can see that, surely enough."

"*You* are not soon to find out," she turned to advise him.

"Smartly taken at silly point!" cried Nigel and Neville together.

Later in the evening, the Grand Cohen took Lew aside and began to explain his personal concept of the Psychical Detective. "The hope being someday to transcend the gray, literalist world of hotel corridors and requisition vouchers, and enter *the further condition*—'To know, to dare, to will, to keep silent'—how difficult for most of us to observe these basic imperatives, particularly, you must have noticed, the one about keeping silent. *Have* I been talking too much, by the way? Frightfully awkward situation to be in, you appreciate."

"In the States, 'detective' doesn't mean—" Lew started to point out.

"Admittedly, ours is an odd sort of work. . . . There is but one 'case' which preoccupies us. Its 'suspects' are exactly twenty-two in number. These are precisely the cadre of operatives who, working in secret, cause—or at least allow—History upon this island to happen, and they correspond to the twenty-two Major Arcana of the Tarot deck." Going on to explain, as he had times past counting, that the twenty-two cards of the Major Arcana might be regarded as living agencies, positions to be filled with real people, down the generations, each attending to his own personally tailored portfolio of mischief deep or trivial, as the grim determinants appeared, assassinations, plagues, failures of fashion sense, losses of love, as, one by one, flesh-eating sheep sailed over the fence between dreams and the day. "There must always be a Tower. There must always be a High Priestess, Temperance, Fortune, so forth. Now and then, when vacancies occur, owing to death or other misadventure, new occupants will emerge, obliging us to locate and track them, and learn their histories as well. That they inhabit, without exception, a silence as daunting as their near invisibility only intensifies our challenge."

"And the crime, sir, if I'm not being too inquisitive, just what would be the nature of that?"

"Alas, nothing too clearly related to any statute on the books, nor likely to be . . . no, it is more of an ongoing Transgression, accumulating as the days pass, the invasion of Time into a timeless world. Revealed to us, slowly, one hopes not terribly, in a bleak convergence . . . History, if you like."

"So I can assume none of this will ever see a courtroom," said Lew.

"Suppose there were no such thing, after all, as Original Sin. Suppose the Serpent in the Garden of Eden was never symbolic, but a real being in a real history of intrusion from somewhere else. Say from 'behind the sky.' Say we were perfect. We were law-abiding and clean. Then one day *they* arrived."

"And . . . and this is how you explain villains and badmen among an otherwise moral population?" Not that Lew was looking for an argument. He was genuinely puzzled.

"You will see it in practice. I just wouldn't want it to be too rude a surprise."

AS IF INNOCENCE were some sort of humorous disease, transmitted, as in a stage farce, from one character to another, Lew soon found himself wondering if he had it, and if so who he'd caught it from. Not to mention how sick exactly it might be making him. The other way to ask the question being, who in this was playing him for a fish, and how deep was their game? If it was the T.W.I.T. itself using him for motives even more "occult" than they'd pretended to let him in on, then this was a serious manure pile, and he'd best find a way out of it, soon as he could.

There were mysteries enough. Windowless carriages were arriving at Chunxton Crescent in the middle of the night amid scientifically muffled hoofbeats, impressively sealed documents were shuffled aside whenever Lew approached the Grand Cohen's desk, less than professionally clandestine attempts were made to have a look in his own field-books. Was it by way of a friendly word of caution, or did somebody *want* him to be suspicious? maybe even trying to provoke him into doing himself some damage?

Miss Yashmeen Halfcourt seemed to him the most trustworthy of the bunch, both of them having been picked up, you might say, in more or less helpless condition, and brought here in under the protection of the T.W.I.T.

apparatus, for reasons that might not have been fully shared with them. How much this gave them in common, of course, was open to question.

"Is this what they call 'walking out'?"

"I hope not."

It was breezy today—Lew was packing the usual umbrella, slicker, dry socks, and miners' boots against the several kinds of weather to be expected during the average day in south England. Yashmeen was gathering appreciative looks from passersby male and female. No surprise, though she was turned out no more glamorously than anybody else.

Their route took them through the Park, generally toward Westminster. All around them, just behind a vegetational veil tenuous as the veil of *maya,* persisted the ancient London landscape of sacred high places, sacrificial stones, and mysterious barrows known to the Druids and whoever they had picked up their ways from.

"What do you know about Brother Nookshaft?" Lew was wondering. "What was he before he was a Cohen, for instance?"

"Anything," she supposed, "from a schoolmaster to a petty criminal. I don't see him as ex-military. Not enough of the indices there. Beginning with the haircut, actually. I mean it's not exactly Trumper's, is it."

"Think he might have only tumbled into all this? Some family business he's taken over?"

She shook her head, scowling. "These people— no, no, that's just the trouble, they're all so unanchored, no history, no responsibility, one day they just appear, don't they, each with his own secret designs. It might be politics, or even some scheme to defraud."

"You sound like a detective. What if they're sincere about who they say they are?"

An amused flash of her interesting eyes. "Oh then I've judged them ever so unfairly."

They walked in silence, Lew frowning as if trying to think something through.

"On this island," she went on, "as you will have begun to notice, no one ever speaks plainly. Whether it's Cockney rhyming codes or the crosswords in the newspapers—all English, spoken or written, is looked down on as no more than strings of text cleverly encrypted. Nothing beyond. Any who may come to feel betrayed by them, insulted, even hurt, even grievously, are simply 'taking it too seriously.' The English exercise their eyebrows and smile and tell you it's 'irony' or 'a bit of fun,' for it's only combinations of letters after all, isn't it."

It seemed she was about to go up to University, to Girton College, Cambridge, to study maths.

Lew must've been giving her a look, because she turned to him rather sharply. "Something wrong?"

He shrugged. "Next they'll be letting you folks vote."

"Not in your lifetime," she scowled.

"Only a bit of fun," Lew protested. It was dawning on him that Yashmeen might be more than what others were claiming on her behalf.

Evening drew on, the vast jangling thronged somehow monumental London evening, light falling seemingly without a destination across the wind-attended squares and haunted remnants of something older, and they went to eat at Molinari's in Old Compton Street, also known as the Hôtel d'Italie, reputed to be one of the haunts of Mr. Arthur Edward Waite, though tonight the place was only full of visitors from the suburbs.

AT FIRST A GREENHORN as to the true nature of the work, Lew depended on traditional readings of the Tarot deck, which in London in those days were pretty much referred to the designs provided by Miss Pamela ("Pixie") Colman Smith under the guidance of Mr. Waite. But Lew was soon disabused. "In the grammar of their iniquity," he was instructed, "the Icosadyad, or Company of Twenty-two, observe neither gender nor number. 'The Chariot' can turn out to be an entire fighting unit, not infrequently at regimental strength. Go calling on the Hierophant and the door could easily open on a woman, even in some way striking, whom you may in time come to desire."

"Man, oh man."

"Well, not necessarily you see."

As if testing a new policeman on the beat, the twenty-two lost little time in demonstrating to Lew this nomenclatural flexibility. Temperance (number XIV) proved to be an entire family, the Uckenfays, living in a disagreeable western suburb, each of whom specialized in a different pathological impulse he or she was unable to control, including litigiousness, chloral addiction, public masturbating, unexpected discharges of firearms, and, in the case of the baby, Des, scarcely a year old and already four stone, that form of gluttony known to students of the condition as *gaver du visage.* As of the latest information, The Hermit (IX) was the cordial proprietor of a cigar-divan where Lew soon became part of the regular clientele, The Wheel of Fortune (X) was a Chinese opium-den landlord, based in the Midlands, whose life of luxury was derived from "joints" all over London as well as Birmingham,

Manchester, and Liverpool, The Last Judgment (XX) was a streetwalker from Seven Dials, sometimes accompanied by her Pimp, and so forth. . . . Fine with Lew, who always liked to meet new and interesting people, and the chores they brought with them by way of self-introduction were easily disposed of. But then they started coming at him in twos.

Lew had been in England less than a week when one night a neophyte in the T.W.I.T. had come running in, face white as plaster, in his agitation forgetting to remove his hat, a mauve fedora. "Grand Cohen, Grand Cohen! forgive my interruption! they wanted me to make sure you got this personally." Handing over a scrap of pale blue notepaper.

"Quite so," nodded the G.C., "Madam Eskimoff's sitting tonight, wasn't it . . . let us have a look, then. . . . *Oh* dear." The paper fluttered in what suddenly resembled a nerveless hand. Lew, who'd been hoping for a quiet evening, looked over in an inquiring way. The Cohen was already shrugging off his ceremonial robes and looking for his shoes. Lew pulled his socks from a jacket pocket, grabbed his own shoes, and together they proceeded to the street and into a growler, and were off.

En route the Grand Cohen outlined the situation. "It likely has to do," he sighed, producing from an inner pocket a Tarot pack and flipping through it, "with . . . here, this one, number XV, The Devil"—in particular, the Cohen went on, with the two chained figures found at the bottom of the card, imagined by their artist Miss Colman Smith, perhaps after Dante, as simple naked man and woman, though in the earlier tradition these had been shown as a pair of demons, genders unspecified, whose fates were bound and who could not separate even if they wanted to. At present this unhappy position among the Major Arcana was occupied by a pair of rival University professors, Renfrew at Cambridge and Werfner at Göttingen, not only eminent in their academic settings but also would-be powers in the greater world. Years before, in the wake of the Berlin Conference of 1878, their shared interest in the Eastern Question had evolved from simple bickering-at-a-distance by way of the professional journals to true mutual loathing, implacable and obsessive, with a swiftness that surprised them both. Soon enough each had come to find himself regarded as a leading specialist, consulted by the Foreign Office and Intelligence Services of his respective country, not to mention others who preferred to remain unnamed. With the years their rivalry had continued to grow well beyond the Balkans, beyond the ever-shifting borders of the Ottoman Empire, to the single vast Eurasian landmass and that ongoing global engagement, with all its English, Russian, Turkish, German, Austrian, Chinese, Japanese—not to mention indigenous—components, styled by Mr.

Kipling, in a simpler day, "The Great Game." The professors' manœuvrings had at least the grace to avoid the mirrorlike—if symmetries arose now and then, it was written off to accident, "some predisposition to the echoic," as Werfner put it, "perhaps built into the nature of Time," added Renfrew. Howsoever, over their cloistering walls and into the map of the megacosm, the two professors continued to launch their cadres of spellbound familiars and enslaved disciples. Some of these found employment with the Foreign Services, others in international trade or as irregular adventurers assigned temporarily to their nations' armies and navies—all sworn to loyalties in whose service they were to pass through the greater world like spirit presences, unsensed by all but the adept.

"Perhaps you will find you can tolerate those two," said the Grand Cohen. "I can't, for very long. No one in the T.W.I.T. working that desk for more than a few days has been able to abide them. And, of course, of all the Icosadyad, they are the ones most capable of damage, who must be watched constantly."

"Thanks, Cohen."

They arrived at length at a dark, ancient block of flats south of the river, rising in a ragged arrangement of voids and unlighted windows to what in the daytime, Lew hoped, would not be as sinister as now.

Madame Natalia Eskimoff's rooms ran to mamluk lamps and draped fabrics in Indian prints, smoke rising from elaborate brass incense burners, furniture of carved figwood, and odd corners that seemed designed to warn off all but the most unfrivolous of seekers, and Lew was enchanted right away, for the lady herself was just a peach. Eyes huge and expressive as those you'd expect to see more in magazine illustrations than out in this troublesome world. Volumes of silver-streaked tresses that invited some reckless hand to unpin it all to see just how far down her form it would reach. Tonight she wore a black taffeta turnout that looked simple but not severe, and probably had set her back a bundle, as well as amber beads and a Lalique brooch. Other nights, depending on how swanky the function and fashionable the gown, there might also be observed, tattooed in exquisite symmetry below Madame Eskimoff's bared nape, the Kabbalist Tree of Life, with the names of the Sephiroth spelled out in Hebrew, which had brought her more than enough of that uniquely snot-nosed British anti-Semitism—"Eskimoff . . . I say what sort of name is that?"—though in fact she'd grown up in the Eastern Church and, to the disappointment of racial watchdogs throughout the island, what in fact she turned out to be, confoundingly, was a classical English Rose.

Looked into closely in her time both by Sir Oliver Lodge and Sir William Crookes, she had taken transatlantic liners to Boston to visit Mrs. Piper, traveled to Naples to sit with Eusapia Palladino (whom she was later to defend against charges of fraud at the infamous Cambridge experiments), could indeed be said to've attended some of the most celebrated séances of the day, the list of which was about to include one arranged by the ubiquitous and outspoken Mr. W. T. Stead, at which the medium Mrs. Burchell would witness in great detail the assassination of Alexander and Draga Obrenovich, the King and Queen of Serbia, three months before it even happened. She was known to the T.W.I.T. as an "ecstatica," a classification enjoying apparently somewhat more respect than a common medium.

"We don't go off into ordinary trances," Madame E. explained.

"More the ecstatic type," Lew supposed.

He was rewarded with a steady and speculative gaze. "I should be happy to demonstrate, perhaps on some night less exhausting than this."

It was something that had come out during the séance tonight, none of which Madame Eskimoff had any direct memory of, although like all T.W.I.T.-sanctioned sittings, it had been recorded by means of a Parsons-Short Auxetophone.

"We take electros of the original wax impressions immediately after every sitting. Part of the routine. I have listened to these tonight already several times, and even if details are here and there obscure, I felt it a grave enough development to summon you here."

It seemed that one Clive Crouchmas, a semi-governmental functionary who happened also to be a member of the T.W.I.T., though at a quite low beginner's level, had been trying to get in touch with one of his field-agents who had died in Constantinople unexpectedly, in the midst of particularly demanding negotiations over the so-called "Bagdad" railway concession. As the replies were expected to be in Turkish, Crouchmas had brought along an interpreter as well.

"He specializes in the Ottoman territories, which is where Renfrew and Werfner have often found their best opportunities for mischief, working as a consultant, in fact, with both of them, letting each imagine he's the only one who knows about the other and so forth. French farce. Being probably the only person in England who can stand the company of either one for more than a few minutes, old C.C.'s become quite useful to us as a channel between, though I must say I'm rather annoyed with him at the moment," grumbled the Grand Cohen. "He should know better than to be wasting your time, Madame, with this endless Turkish Pound-mongering."

Lew had a sketchy idea of the situation. The European powers had already invested years in the seduction and counterseduction necessary to obtain from the Ottomans the much-coveted railway concession, and if it finally were awarded to Germany, this would be a bitter development indeed for Great Britain, Berlin's chief rival in the region. Not least of the diplomatic anxieties set loose would be Turkey's clear sanction of a German line, to run across Anatolia, over the Taurus Mountains, along the Euphrates and the Tigris, through Baghdad all the way down to Basra and the Persian Gulf, which Britain up until now had believed lay firmly within her own sphere of influence, and thus open for Germany a so-called "shortcut to India" even more congenial to trade than the Suez Canal. The entire geopolitical matrix would acquire a new, and dangerously unverifiable, set of coefficients.

Madame Eskimoff placed the wax cylinder in the machine, started the air-pump, adjusted a series of rheostats, and they listened. The several voices were at first difficult to distinguish, and unaccountable whispers and whistling came and went in the background. One voice, seemingly Madame Eskimoff's, was much clearer, as if through some unexplained syntonic effect between wherever this spirit was speaking from and the recording machine. Later she explained that this was not entirely herself speaking but a "control," a spirit on the other side acting, for the departed soul one wished to contact, much in the same capacity as a medium on this side acts on behalf of the living. Madame Eskimoff's control, speaking through her, was a rifleman named Mahmoud who had died in Thrace back in the days of the Russo-Turkish War. He was responding as best he could to Clive Crouchmas's detailed inquiries as to per-kilometer guarantees for various branches and extensions of the Smyrna-Casaba line, and being translated into English by the third voice Crouchmas had hired for the séance, when without warning—

"Here," said Madame Eskimoff—"listen."

It was not exactly an explosion, though the mahogany sound-horn of the Auxetophone certainly became overloaded as if it were, shuddering, rattling in its mountings, quite unable to handle the mysterious event. Perhaps it was the form a violent release of energy in this world would appear to take to a disembodied reporter such as Mahmoud—the voice of an explosion, or at least the same abolition of coherence, the same rapid flying-apart. . . . And directly, before the last of it had quite racketed away, like a train over the next ridge, someone, a woman, could clearly be heard, singing in Turkish to one of the Eastern modes. *Amán, amán* . . . Have pity.

"Well. What do you make of it?" Madame Eskimoff inquired after a pause.

"From what one gathers," mused the Cohen, "though Crouchmas is not the voice of Allah in these matters, far from it, the Ottoman government's kilometric guarantees have lately become so attractive that, as if by miracle, phantom railways are beginning to blossom out in Asia Minor, among those treeless plateaus where not even panthers will venture, linking stations for towns which do not, strictly, exist—sometimes not even in name. Which is apparently where the person speaking by way of Mahmoud was located."

"But it doesn't happen that way usually," puzzled the comely ecstatica. "They like to haunt stationary places, houses, churchyards—but moving trains? notional rail lines? hardly ever. If at all."

"Something's afoot," groaned the Cohen, with an inflection almost of gastric distress.

"And did somebody just blow up a train line?" Lew feeling somewhat out of his depth here, "or . . ."

"Tried to," she said, "thought about it, dreamed it, or saw something—analogous to an explosion. Death is a region of metaphor, it often seems."

"Not always decipherable," added the Cohen, "but in this case Eastern-Questionable, beyond a doubt. More Renfrew and Werfner melodrama. Queer Street for the Tiresome Twins, I'd say. Not immediately clear which will murder the other, but the crime itself is as certain as the full moon."

"Whom do we have at Cambridge, keeping an eye on Renfrew?" inquired Madame E.

"Neville and Nigel, I believe. They're up at King's."

"Heaven preserve King's."

"Michaelmas term is upon us," said the Cohen, "and Miss Halfcourt begins her residence at Girton. That might provide us just the occasion to have a look in on the Professor. . . ."

Madame Eskimoff's tweeny had brought out tea and a gâteau, as well as a twelve-year-old Speyside malt and glasses. They sat in a sort of comfortable electrical dusk, and the Cohen, unable quite to let go of the topic, discoursed on Renfrew and Werfner.

"It is an unavoidable outcome of the Victorian Age itself. Of the character of its august eponym, in fact. Had the demented potboy Edward Oxford's pistol-shots found their mark sixty years ago at Constitution Hill, had the young Queen died then without issue, the insupportably loathsome Ernst August, Duke of Cumberland, would have become King of England, and Salic law being thus once more observed, the thrones of Hannover and Britain would have been reunited. . . .

"Let us imagine a lateral world, set only infinitesimally to the side of the one we think we know, in which just this has come to pass. The British people suffer beneath a Tory despotism of previously unimagined rigor and cruelty. Under military rule, Ireland has become a literal shambles—Catholics of any worth or ability are routinely identified when young, and imprisoned or assassinated forthwith. Orange Lodges are ubiquitous, and every neighborhood is administered from one. A sort of grim counter-Christmas runs from the first to the twelfth of July, anniversaries of the Boyne and Aughrim. France, southern Germany, Austria-Hungary, and Russia have combined in a protective League of Europe, intended to keep Britain an outcast from the community of nations. Her only ally is the U.S., which has become a sort of faithful sidekick, run basically by the Bank of England and the gold standard. India and the colonies are if possible worse off than they were.

"Now, we have also Victoria's unbending refusals to consider the passage of Time, for example her insistence for more than sixty years that the only postal image of her be that of the young girl on the first adhesive stamps of 1840, the year of dim young Oxford's assassination attempt. Her image, whether on medallions, statuary, or commemorative porcelain, is meant to be imperial as can possibly be, except that the young lady depicted is far too young for those trappings of empire. Add to this her inability to accept Albert's death, continuing to have his room kept as it was, fresh flowers every day, uniforms out to the cleaner's, and so forth. It is almost as if that fateful day on Constitution Hill, Oxford's shots had found their mark after all, and the Victoria we think we know and revere is really a sort of ghostly stand-in, for another who is impervious to the passage of Time in all its forms, especially the well-known Aging and Death. Though she may, technically speaking, have grown older like everybody else, grown into the powerful mother, internationally admired statesperson, and much-beloved though humorless dumpling of legend, suppose the 'real' Vic is elsewhere. Suppose the flowering young woman herself is being kept captive, immune to Time, by some ruler of some underworld, with periodic connubial visits from Albert allowed, neither of them aging, in love as passionately as in the last terrible moment ascending to the palace, the Princess Royal forever three and a half months in her womb, the lovely springtide of early pregnancy rushing through mother and child in a flow that Time will never touch. Suppose the whole run-together known now as 'the Victorian Age' has been nothing but a benevolent mask for the grim realities of the Ernest-Augustan Age we really live in. And that the administrators of this all-enveloping pantomime are precisely the twin professors Renfrew and Werfner, acting somehow as poles of temporal flow between England and Hannover."

Lew was dismayed. "Cohen, man, that's horrible."

The Grand Cohen shrugged. "Only a bit of fun. You Yanks are so serious."

"Those professors are no laughing matter," offered Madame Eskimoff, "and you are well advised, Mr. Basnight, to take the Icosadyad every bit as seriously as you do. I was among them, once, as the Fool—or 'Unwise One,' as

Éliphaz Lévi preferred—perhaps the most demanding of all the Trumps Major. Now I have a flock of suburban punters believing, poor souls, that I possess intelligence they will find helpful. Being unwise as ever, I cannot bring myself to disabuse them."

"You switched sides?" said Lew.

She smiled, it seemed to him a little condescendingly. "'Sides.' Well. No, not exactly. It had become an impediment to my calling, so I resigned and joined the T.W.I.T. instead, not without later occasion for regret. Hard enough being a woman, you see, but a Pythagorean into the bargain—well." It seemed that each British mystical order claiming Pythagorean descent had its own ideas about those taboos and bits of free advice known as *akousmata,* and Madame Eskimoff's favorite happened to be number twenty-four as listed by Iamblichus—never look into a mirror when there's a lamp next to you. "Meaning one must rearrange one's entire day, making sure one is finished dressing well before nightfall—not to mention hair and maquillage—all of which is sure to look different under gas or electric light anyway."

"Can't believe it'd run you much more than a minute or two," Lew said.

And there was that gaze again. "Hours can be consumed," she pretended to lament, "by hatpin issues alone."

As autumn deepened, Lew could be noticed hurrying from place to place, as if increasingly claimed by a higher argument—tensely vertical, favoring narrow black overcoats, slouch hats, and serviceable boots, a trimmed black mustache settled in along his upper lip. Despite the growing presence of electric street illumination, London in resolute municipal creep out of the Realm of Gas, he had begun to discover a structure to the darkness, dating from quite ancient times, perhaps well before there was any city here at all—in place all along, and little more than ratified by the extreme and unmerciful whiteness replacing the glare-free tones and composite shadows of the old illumination, with its multiplied chances for error. Even venturing out in the daylight, he found himself usually moving from one shadow to another, among quotidian frights which would only become unbearably visible with the passing of lamplighting-time into the lofty electric night.

This purposeful life did not keep him, for some while in fact, from trying to locate somewhere in Great Britain a source of Cyclomite, proceeding, desperately, from such opiated catarrh preparations as Collis Brown's Mixture on to cocainized brain tonics, cigarettes soaked in absinthe, xylene in unventilated rooms, and so on, each proving inadequate, often pathetically so, as a substitute for the reality-modifying explosive he had enjoyed back in his former or Stateside existence.

He had no shame about enlisting the aid of Neville and Nigel, always these days, it seemed, down from University. Each of them was reputed to have at least a thousand pounds a year, which it seemed they spent mostly on drugs and hats. "Here," Nigel greeted him, "do try a spot of 'pinky,' it's ever so much fun, really."

"Condy's fluid," explained Neville—"permanganate disinfectant, which one then mixes with methylated spirits—"

"Got the recipe from an Aussie we met whilst in the nick one Regatta weekend. Came to develop quite a taste for it after a while, though health aspects naturally did occur to us, so we're careful only to allow ourselves one bottle per year."

"Admire your restraint, boys."

"Yes, and *tonight's the night,* Lewis!" Abruptly producing a rather large bottle filled with liquid of a queer purple that Lew could swear was glowing.

"Oh, no, no, I—"

"What is it, the color you don't like? here, I'll adjust the gas," Neville helpfully, "there. Is that better?"

One morning they got Lew up early and bustled him into a cab before he was completely awake.

"Where we going?"

"It's a surprise. You'll see."

They rolled eastward and presently pulled up in front of a nondescript draper's shop in Cheapside that appeared not to have been open for some time.

"What's this?"

"The War Office!" cried Neville and Nigel, grinning mischievously at each other.

"Quit fooling, I know they just moved it, but not here."

"Some of their facilities would never dream of moving," said Neville. "Come along." Lew followed them through a narrow passageway next to the shop, leading back to a mews entirely invisible from the street, whose clamor back here had become abruptly inaudible, as if a heavy door had closed. They made their way along a sort of roofed alleyway to a short flight of steps, which took them on into regions somehow colder and remote from the morning light. Lew thought he heard water dripping, and utterances of wind, becoming gradually louder, until at last they stood before an entry scarred and dented all over as if by decades of assault.

Owing to a stubborn belief in Whitehall that the eccentric enjoy access to paranormal forces with nothing better to do than whisper suggestions for ever-more-improved weapons design, personnel offices throughout the Empire had been alert for at least a generation to the genteel stammer, the ungovernably darting eyeball, the haircut that no known pomade could subdue. Dr. Coombs De Bottle, actually, failed to meet these criteria. Suave, cosmopolitan, wearing a snow-white lab ensemble from Poole's of Savile Row in hand-loomed Russian duck, smoking black Egyptian cigarettes in an amber holder, not a hair on his face allowed anywhere it should not be, he seemed suited more to a calling of public ingratiation, the international arms trade, perhaps, or the clergy. But something, some actor's polish to his style of address, hinted at a nebulous past, and a grateful awareness of having, after all, found haven here. He greeted Neville and Nigel with a familiarity that Lew might have found suspect had there been less in the vast workshop they were now being ushered into to claim his attention and eventually, he supposed, trouble his dreams.

Electrical arcs stabbed through the violet dusk. Heated solutions groaned toward their boiling points. Bubbles rose helically through luminous green liquids. Miniature explosions occurred in distant corners of the facility, sending up showers of glass as nearby workers cowered beneath seaside umbrellas set up for just such protection. Gauge needles oscillated feverishly. Sensitive flames sang at different pitches. Amid a gleaming clutter of burners and spectroscopes, funnels and flasks, centrifugal and Soxhlet extractors, and distillation columns in both the Glynsky and Le Bel-Henninger formats, serious girls with their hair in snoods entered numbers into log-books, and pale gnomes, patient as lock-pickers, squinted through loupes, adjusting tremblers and timers with tiny screwdrivers and forceps. Best of all, somebody in here somewhere was making coffee.

Dr. De Bottle had led them back into a distant bay, where technicians were working at tables covered with homemade bombs in different stages of disassembly. "Our theory was to begin with devices confiscated from various failed bomb attempts and then kindly passed along to us, and, by careful analysis of each device, to return, step by step, to its original act of construction. Which proved usually to've been carried out in such appallingly primitive conditions that one began actually to feel sympathy for these wretches. They blow themselves up at a quite alarming rate you know, ignorance of proper solvent procedure alone accounting for dozens of Anarchist lives each year, just here in London. One must indeed suppress the missionary urge to go out among them . . . perhaps distributing inexpensive pamphlets, outlining for them even the simplest principles of lab safety . . . it would do ever so much good, don't you think?"

Lew, suppressing a reflexive lift of the brows, would have welcomed here any sort of smart remark from Neville or Nigel, but both had gone off apparently to inhale fumes of various sorts. "I'm not sure I follow the logic," Lew said—"saving bombers' lives, if each one you save could mean hundreds of innocent ones lost later down the line."

The Doc chuckled and inspected his shirt cuffs. "Innocent bourgeois lives. Well . . . 'innocent.' "

An assistant arrived with a wheeled cart bearing coffee in an Erlenmeyer flask, cups, and a plate of strange muffins. "You might not as an American appreciate this, but among the last surviving bits of evidence that a civilization once existed on this island is the game of cricket. For many of us, a cricket match is a sort of religious observance. Breathless hush in the close tonight sort of thing. 'Innocent' as it gets. And yet even here we have—" He gingerly held up a cricket ball, which all but glowed beneath the electric lighting. "For some time now, county pitches throughout England and Wales have been visited by a mysterious figure in white flannels, known around this shop as the Gentleman Bomber of Headingly, after the only known photograph of him with the usual cricketer's bag slung from one shoulder, inside which he carries a number of spherical hand-bombs disguised as cricket balls. This is one that we've managed to recover intact. Rubbing it against one's trousers will activate the arming device inside. You'll notice, perhaps, that it's far shinier and rather more tightly stitched than a British ball, rather like the Australian ball, or 'kookaburra.' And as the Ashes is currently in progress, and passions apt to be running high, Australians, with whom we are somewhat overrun at the moment, may be serving as an unwitting species of cover for the old G.B. of H., as well as easy targets of blame."

"He *throws bombs* during cricket games?"

"We try not to say 'bomb,' actually, it's more of a poison-gas grenade. And he does usually wait for tea."

"'Poison gas'?" A new one on Lew. But Dr. De Bottle had taken on a somber look.

"Phosgene." Something about the way he pronounced it. "More of a French term. *Phosgène.* We prefer to call it carbonyl chloride. Less . . . disquieting somehow. The trouble for the police is that, depending on the dispersal cloud, too often the victims aren't aware at all of having been gassed. And then suddenly, mysteriously as the newspapers say, forty-eight hours later, they're dead. Why are you looking at that muffin that way?"

"What? Oh. The color, I guess."

"Lovely shade of purple, isn't it, boiled logwood I believe, chef puts it in everything—go on, it won't poison you, bit of tannin, perhaps, if that."

"Well, and then these, um . . ." holding up a fragment of this muffin and pointing to a number of inclusions in some vivid, unmistakably turquoise shade.

"For pity's sake Lewis, don't eat them *all*!" cried Neville, followed closely by his co-adjutor, both of them traveling along in some curious exhilaration, inches above the floor.

"And see what we've found!" Nigel producing a sort of dinner pail with a quantity of beige substance in it which Lew recognized immediately.

"Happy Birthday!" they all but screamed in unison.

"Whose bright idea—"

"Come come Lewis, you are a Gemini, that's obvious, and as for the precise date, why, Madame Eskimoff knows all."

"Speaking of whom—"

At their last meeting Dr. De Bottle had asked Neville and Nigel plaintively when, if ever, Britain would get the Ashes back, and the boys had agreed to consult the ecstatica.

"Next year," Madame Eskimoff had replied, "but only if they've the sense to select this Middlesex spinner, young Bosanquet, who's been working on an absolutely fiendish ball, which looks as if it will be a leg-break but then goes the other way. Amazing physical dynamics, virtually uninvestigated. Said to be an Australian invention, but they'll be utterly confounded at finding a Pom who knows how to bowl it."

"I shall run to my bookmaker," Dr. De Bottle assured the boys graciously.

IT WAS DECIDED that Lew should go up to Cambridge with the Cohen to meet Professor Renfrew.

"Oh, I get it. You want me along for muscle."

"No, actually, here comes our protection now." A gent of average height and unthreatening appearance was approaching them with a watercress sandwich in a gloved hand. "Clive Crouchmas. You may recall his voice from Madame Eskimoff's séance the other night."

This person greeted the Cohen by raising his left hand, then spreading the fingers two and two away from the thumb so as to form the Hebrew letter *shin,* signifying the initial letter of one of the pre-Mosaic (that is, plural) names of God, which may never be spoken.

"Basically wishing long life and prosperity," explained the Cohen, answering with the same gesture.

Earlier in his career, Clive Crouchmas had been your bog-standard public official, unreflectively ambitious but not yet as greedy as he would soon find it possible to be. He worked at the Ottoman Public Debt Administration, an international body which the Turkish Sultan had authorized some years before to collect and distribute tax revenue, as a way of restructuring the debt of his overextended Empire. In theory the P.D.A. took the taxes on sales of fish, alcohol, tobacco, salt, silk, and stamps—the so-called "Six Indirect

Contributions"—and passed the money on to various bondholders in Britain, France, Austria-Hungary, Germany, Italy, and Holland. No one acquainted with the Second Law of Thermodynamics, however, would have expected a perfect transfer of funds—some of those Turkish pounds would always be lost in the process, creating opportunities it would have taken someone much farther along the ill-marked path to sainthood than Clive Crouchmas to pass up.

Ordinarily, Crouchmas had little to do with metaphysics, would not, indeed, recognize any appearance of the metaphysical even in the act of *morsus fundamento.* It was as alien to him as frivolity, of which there was plenty at these functions he seemed to be haunting these days. "Oh, Clivey!" three or four female voices at the edge of self-induced laughter would sing out in unison across the palm-abundant reaches of some hotel ballroom. Crouchmas was not even willing to say "What?" in reply. It would open doors allowing too many creatures of farce to commence running in and out.

But, oddly, he had been resisting material temptation. As the Eastern Question degenerated into an unseemly scramble for the vast wealth of the Ottoman Empire, expressed most vividly in the intrigues over which nation would end up getting the "Bagdad" Railway Concession, Clive was observed at Chunxton Crescent, silent, robed, for all the world like someone seeking a more spiritual path, though according to gossip—a secular force the T.W.I.T. would never transcend—he was there out of a mute fascination with Miss Halfcourt, welcoming any excuse to share her company, since he had mastered as yet few of the arts of moneyed lechery, being in that phase of his career where work still claimed priority over leisure pursuits.

For over a decade, the P.D.A. had also been collecting local tithes earmarked specifically for railway guarantees, to be paid yearly at so much per kilometer of track, to various European railway companies, before anyone else, even the Turkish government, got to see a piastre. This had not escaped the attention of a cabal within the P.D.A., which included Crouchmas. Pseudonymously and in carefully under-defined relation to the Imperial Ottoman Bank group of Paris, they had set up a small firm of their own designed to deal mainly with rogue bond issues, deemed by the Bank's advisory committees too unstable to get involved with, or indeed touch with a barge-pole.

"It's too good to pass up," he groaned aloud to Grand Cohen Nookshaft, his spiritual adviser. "Isn't it?"

"I'm thinking," said the Cohen, whose money had been in three-percent consols for longer than he could remember, or remember why, "I'm thinking."

"I've never understood," said Clive Crouchmas, "why, with all the precognitive talent around this place, no one has ever . . ." He paused, as if seeking a diplomatic way to go on.

"Some serious dissonance between psychical gifts and modern capitalism, I'd imagine," said the Cohen, somewhat shortly. "Mutually antagonistic, you'd have to say. We also do try not to become too mental, like some in your own shop, over this railway Concession."

"Were I not out here walking free amongst you all," declared Clive Crouchmas, "I should be Best Boy at Colney Hatch. The other night, for just half a second, I saw . . . I thought I saw . . ."

"It's all right, Crouchmas, one hears this sort of thing all the time."

"But . . ."

"Enlightenment is a dodgy proposition. It all depends how much you want to risk. Not money so much as personal safety, precious time, against a very remote long shot coming in. It happens, of course. Out of the dust, the clouds of sweat and breath, the drumming of hooves, the animal rises up behind the field, the last you'd've expected, tall, shining, inevitable, and passes through them all like a beam of morning sunlight through the spectral residue of a dream. But it's still a fool's bet and a mug's game, and you might not have the will or the patience."

"But suppose I did stick it out. I've been curious for some time—as members here move closer to enlightenment, is there any sort of discount on the dues we pay?"

It was raining when Lew arrived in Cambridge. Newspaper headlines announced—

ANOTHER ENCYCLICAL FROM PROF. MCTAGGART
VATICAN'S STRONGLY WORDED PROTEST
G. H. HARDY UNAVAILABLE FOR COMMENT
"*Multi et Unus*"—Complete Text Within

Chalked up on the ancient walls were graffiti such as CREATE MORE DUKES and EXPROPRIATE CHUCKERS.

After they had left Yashmeen at the Girton gatehouse, Lew and Clive Crouchmas proceeded to the Laplacian, a relatively remote mathematicians' pub beside a canal, where they were to meet with Professor Renfrew.

"Trinity people here, mostly," Crouchmas said. "No one's likely to recognize him."

"Why should that bother him?" Lew wondered aloud, but Crouchmas ignored the question, nodding out the door into the onset of evening.

Slowly, through the impure fen-light, the Professor's face became distinct, exhibiting a brightness . . . no, a denial of ordinary vision . . . a smile that would never break forth from any interior cordiality.

After three obligatory rounds of the dense, warm, unaerated product known on this island as beer, Crouchmas went off on mischief of his own, and Lew and the Professor made their way to Renfrew's rooms at one of the lesser quadrangles. When they had lit cigars and allowed a pulse of watchful silence to elapse, Renfrew spoke.

"You are acquainted with the ward of Auberon Halfcourt, I believe."

Lew guessed that Crouchmas in his fascination had been unable to keep from bringing her name up. He shrugged. "Routine chaperoning job, up and back, Mr. Crouchmas thought I should have a look in, was all, say howdy, so forth."

Which did not quite exempt him from a suspicious squint. "Poor Halfcourt. The man simply does not understand how things are done. Worse than Gordon at Khartoum. The desert has created in him fantasies of power which in Whitehall, mercifully, are felt to be impractical. And you have no idea how the girl's protectors at the T.W.I.T. have again and again blighted my life. One cannot make the slightest move, however innocent, without attracting their, I must say, zealous attention." It seemed to Lew that Renfrew's upper and lower jaws were moving independently, like those of a ventriloquist's figure. The voice at times did seem to come from somewhere else.

"They have one or two peculiar ways, I guess. But they pay good."

"Ah. You've worked with them before."

"Pickup and delivery—one or two, whatever you folks call them . . . muscle jobs."

"Do they have you under any sort of contract?"

"Nope. One chore at a time, and cash on the barrelhead. Better for everybody, see."

"Hmm. Then if, for example, *I* wished to engage you . . ."

"Would depend on the work, I guess."

"Young Crouchmas says you can be confided in. Come. Tell me what you think."

Pinned to a cork board on the wall Lew saw a photograph of a shadowy figure in white with a cricketer's bag, posed against one of those noteworthy arrays of cloud the Headingly ground was known for. The face was blurred, but Lew took a few steps back till it came more in focus.

"You recognize him?"

"No . . . thought for a minute I might."

"You recognize him." Slyly nodding as if to himself.

Lew had a gastrically dismal feeling but saw no reason to confirm the Professor's guess. Instead he sat through the same story he'd heard from Coombes De Bottle about the mystery gas-bomb thrower.

"You want me to find him? Collar him, hand him over to the police?"

"Not directly. Bring him to me first, if at all possible. It would be of the keenest importance that I speak with him, face-to-face."

"Suppose he was right in the middle of carrying out one of those phosgene attacks?"

"Oh, there would be a hazardous-duty bonus, I'm sure. *I* can't pay you that much, you see how reduced things are around here—it's as if my life had been subjected to its own sort of gas outrage—but others would be most generous, if you delivered him safely."

"So it's not what you'd call personal."

"Larking about at the seaside with Mrs. Renfrew sort of thing . . . so sorry, no . . . afraid not. . . ." The expression on his face was one Lew had noted from time to time among the British, a combination of smugness and self-pity, which he still couldn't explain but knew enough to exercise caution around. "No, a bit more, hm, general in scale. Which is why you might run into a spot of uproar with the police. They've been round more than once to tell me to keep out of it. Came all the way up from London, in fact, to inform me that the 'subject' is theirs alone to deal with."

"I can ask around at the Yard, see what that's all about." Then, unable to resist, "Your German colleague, what's his name, Werfner—is he as interested in this bird as you are?"

"No idea." Renfrew's reaction might have included as much as a blink, but too quickly for Lew to be sure, "though I really doubt Werfner knows a bosie from a beamer. Oh but haven't you met yet? I say what a treat you've in store!"

He motioned Lew to a smaller room, where a globe of the Earth hung gleaming, at slightly below eye-level, from a slender steel chain anchored overhead, surrounded by an æther of tobacco smoke, house-dust, ancient paper and book bindings, human breath. . . . Renfrew took up the orb in both hands like a brandy snifter, and rotated it with deliberation, as if weighing the argument he wished to make. Outside the windows, the luminous rain swept the grounds. "Here then—keeping the North Pole in the middle, imagining for purposes of demonstration the area roundabout to be solid, some unknown element one can not only walk on but even run heavy machinery across—Arctic ice, frozen tundra—you can see that it all makes one great mass, doesn't it? Eurasia, Africa, America. With Inner Asia at its heart. Control Inner Asia, therefore, and you control the planet."

"How about that other, well, actually, hemisphere?"

"Oh, this?" He flipped the globe over and gave it a contemptuous tap. "South America? Hardly more than an appendage of North America, is it. Or of the Bank of England, if you like. Australia? Kangaroos, one or two cricketers of perhaps discernible talent, what else?" His small features quivering in the dark afternoon light.

"Werfner, damn him, keen-witted but *unheimlich,* is obsessed with railway lines, history emerges from geography of course, but for him the primary geography of the planet is the rails, obeying their own necessity, interconnections, places chosen and bypassed, centers and radiations therefrom, grades possible and impossible, how linked by canals, crossed by tunnels and bridges either in place or someday to be, capital made material—and flows of power as well, expressed, for example, in massive troop movements, now and in the futurity—he styles himself the prophet of *Eisenbahntüchtigkeit,* or railworthiness, each and every accommodation to the matrix of meaningful points, each taken as a coefficient in the planet's unwritten equation. . . ." He was lecturing. Lew lit another cigar and settled back.

"ENJOYABLE VISIT?" the Cohen inquired a little too offhandedly, as if a practical joke were about to unfold.

"He offered me a job."

"Capital!"

Lew summarized the Gentleman Bomber of Headingly case, which the Cohen, like everybody in the British Isles except Lew, was intimately familiar with already. "Does this make me a double agent? Should I start wearing a fake nose or something?"

"Renfrew can be under no illusions about your relations with the T.W.I.T. By now he must have worked up a complete dossier on you."

"Then . . ."

"He thinks he'll be able to use you."

"The way you folks've been doing."

"Oh, but we're the pure of heart, you see."

It might have been the residual effects of Cyclomite abuse, but Lew swore he could hear an invisible roomful of laughter, and some applause as well.

Across the city noontide a field of bells emerged into flower, as the boys came swooping in over Murano, above wide-topped red-clay chimneys the size of smokestacks, known as *fumaioli,* according to the local pilot, Zanni. "*Very dangerous,* the sparks, they could blow up the balloon, *certo,*" drops of perspiration flying off his face at all angles, as if self-propelled. The comically anxious but good-hearted Italian had come aboard earlier in the day, after the boys had obtained the necessary clearances from the Piacenza branch of the Chums of Chance, known here in their native Italy as "Gli Amici dell'Azzardo." The *Inconvenience* having gone into dockyard facilities, the boys had been given temporary use of an Italian airship of the same class, the semi-rigid *Seccatura.*

From their stations the fellows now beheld the island-city of Venice below them, looking like some map of itself printed in an ancient sepia, presenting at this daylit distance an impression of ruin and sorrow, though closer at hand this would resolve into a million roof-tiles of a somewhat more optimistic red.

"Like some great rusted amulet," marveled Dr. Chick Counterfly, "fallen from the neck of a demigod, its spell enfolding the Adriatic—"

"Oh, then perhaps," grumbled Lindsay Noseworth, "we ought to set you down there right away, so that you can go rub it, or whatever amulet fanciers do."

"Here, Lindsay, rub this," suggested Darby Suckling, from his seat at the control panel. Next to him Miles Blundell gazed carefully at various dial-faces while reciting in a sort of torpid rapture, "The Italian number that looks like a zero, is the same as our own American 'zero.' The one that looks like a one, is 'one.' The one that looks like a two—"

"Enough, cretin!" snarled Darby, "we 'get the picture'!"

Miles turned to him beaming, his nostrils taking in the ambiguous smell of molten glass rising from the vomitoria beneath them, which only he among the crew found at all pleasant. "Listen." From somewhere in the light mist below could be heard the voice of a gondolier, singing of his love, not for any ringleted *ragazza* but for the coal-black gondola he was at this moment oaring trancefully along. "Hear that?" tears sliding down the convexities of Miles's face. "The way it goes along in a minor key, and then at each refrain switches off into the major? Those Picardy thirds!"

His shipmates glanced at Miles, then at one another, then, with a collective shrug, by now routine, returned to ship's business.

"There," said Randolph. "There's the Lido. Now, let's just have a glance at the chart. . . ."

Approaching the sand barrier which separated the Venetian lagoon from the open Adriatic, they descended to a few dozen feet of altitude (or *quota,* as the Italian instruments referred to it) and were soon scouting the so-called *Terre Perse,* or Lost Lands. Since ancient times numerous inhabited islands here had sunk beneath the waves, so as to form a considerable undersea community of churches, shops, taverns, and palazzi for the picked bones and incomprehensible pursuits of the generations of Venetian dead.

"Just to the east of Sant 'Ariano and— Ecco! Can you see it? if I'm not mistaken, gentlemen, Isola degli Specchi, or, the Isle of Mirrors itself!"

"Excuse me, Professor," Lindsay with a puzzled frown, "there's nothing down there but open water."

"Try looking *below* the surface," advised the veteran aeronaut. "I'll bet you Blundell can see it, can't you Blundell, yes."

"Something a little different today," sneered Darby Suckling. "A mirror-works under the water. How are we s'posed to carry this mission out?"

"With our accustomed grace," replied the skyship commander wearily. "Mr. Counterfly, stand by your lenses—we'll want as many plates of this little *stabilimento* as you can get us."

"Snapshots of the empty sea—whoo-whee!" the embittered mascotte twirling a finger beside his temple—"but ain't the old man just gone bugs at last!"

"I would for once feel compelled to agree with Suckling," gloomily added Lindsay Noseworth, as if to himself, "though perhaps in terms more narrowly clinical."

"Rays, boys, rays," chuckled Scientific Officer Counterfly, busy with his photographic calibrations, "the wonders of our age, and rest assured none of 'em strangers to the spectrum of this fabled Italian sunlight. Just wait till we're back in the developing room, and you shall see a thing or two then, by Garibaldi, that you shall."

"Ehi, sugo!" cried Zanni now from the helm, directing Randolph's attention to a trembling apparition in the distance, off to starboard.

Randolph seized binoculars from the chart table. "Confound it, boys, either that's the world's largest flying onion or it's the old *Bol'shaia Igra* once again, coming to town, planning to take in some Italian culture, no doubt."

Lindsay had a look. "Ah! that miserable Tsarist scow. What can they possibly want here?"

"Us," suggested Darby.

"But our orders were sealed."

"So? Somebody unsealed 'em. Don't tell me those Romanoffs can't afford a fellow, or even two, on the inside."

There was a moment of grim silence on deck, acknowledging that, quite beyond coincidence, everywhere they had gone lately, no matter what conditions of secrecy they might have taken to the sky under, the inexorable Padzhitnoff, sooner or later, had appeared on their horizon. Whatever mutual suspicions might have flowered among the lads themselves—by the simplest computation, twentyfold at least—their true apprehensions converged on those invisible levels "above," where orders, never signed or attributed, were written and cut.

Throughout the day the fellows found themselves unable to refrain from discussing the Russians' presence here, and how it might have come about. Though there was to be no encounter with the *Bol'shaia Igra* that day, the shadow of the bulbiform envelope, and the menacing twinkle of gunmetal beneath it, nonetheless would persist well into the later moments of ground-recreation.

"You cannot be implying that whoever issues Padzhitnoff's orders is intimate with whoever issues ours," Lindsay Noseworth was protesting.

"Long as we just keep on doing everything we're told," Darby scowled, "we'll never know. Wages of unquestioning obedience, ain't it?"

It was early evening. Having returned their borrowed airship to the A. dell'A. compound on the mainland, the team were gathered for dinner in the garden of an agreeable *osteria* in San Polo, beside a little-frequented canal, or, as the narrow waterway is known to the Venetians, *rio.* Wives leaned out onto small balconies to collect the clothes that had been drying all day. Somewhere an accordion was wrenching hearts. Shutters were beginning to close against the night. Shadows flickered in the narrow *calli.* Gondolas and less elegant delivery boats glided over water smooth as a dancing floor. Echoing in the chill dusk, through the wind-flues of *sotopòrteghi* and around so many occult corners that the sounds might have come from dreamers forever distant, one could hear the queerly desolate advisements of *gondolieri*—*"Sa stai, O! Lungo, ehi!"*—mingled with cries of children, greengrocers, sailors ashore, street-vendors no longer expecting reply yet urgent as if trying to call back the last of the daylight.

"What choice have we?" said Randolph. "No one would tell us who informed Padzhitnoff. Whom could we even ask, when they're all so invisible?"

"Unless we decided to disobey for once—then they'd show themselves quick enough," Darby declared.

"Sure," said Chick Counterfly, "just long enough to blast us out of the sky."

"So . . . then," Randolph holding his stomach as if it were a crystal ball and addressing it musingly, "it's only fear? Is that what we've become, a bunch of twitching rabbits in uniforms intended for men?"

"Cement of civilization, 'nauts," chirped Darby. "Ever thus."

The girls who worked here, recently down from the mountains or up from the South, glided about among the tables and in and out of the kitchen in a kind of compressed rapture, as if they couldn't believe their luck, out here, drifted like this into the pallid sea. Chick Counterfly, as the most worldly of the company, and thus spokesman by default in fair-sex encounters that might turn in any way ambiguous, beckoned to one of the comely *cameriere*. "Just between us, Giuseppina—a lovers' secret—what have you heard this week of other *pallonisti* around the Lagoons?"

"Lovers, eh. What kind of 'lover,'" wondered Giuseppina, pleasantly though audibly, "can think only of his rivals?"

"Rivals! You wish to say, that some other skyfarer—perhaps even more than one!—lays claim to your heart? *Ehi, macchè, Pina!*—what kind of 'beloved' is it who coldly tosses her admirers about, like leaves in a salad?"

"Maybe looking behind those leaves for a big *giadrul,*" suggested her Neapolitan colleague, Sandra.

"Captain Pa-zi-no!" Lucia singing from across the room. Giuseppina appeared to blush, though it might have been from residual sunset above the rooftops.

"Pazino . . ." Chick Counterfly suavely puzzled.

"It's Pa-djeet-noff," Giuseppina pronounced, while gazing at Chick with a formally wistful smile that might well, in this city of eternal negotiating, have meant, *Now, what may I expect in return?*

"Thundering toad-spit," exclaimed Darby Suckling, "with all the spaghetti-joints in this town to choose from, are you saying those dadblame Russians have come in *here*? how many of 'em were there?"

But she had tendered all she would, and deploying over one bared shoulder a gaze of mock reproach at the outspoken youth, was off to other tasks.

"Purple Thanksgiving," beamed Miles Blundell, who tonight had decided, by way of getting up to speed, to begin with the tacchino in pomegranate sauce, evidence of which already decorated the jumper of his liberty uniform.

"Not too promising a piece of news, Cap'n," Darby muttered, looking around the table for agreement—"maybe we should skip the eats and get the heck *out* of this place?"

"Not an option," declared Lindsay Noseworth, vehemently. "Whatever their intentions here—"

"Do, Noseworth, put a sock in it," sighed the Ship's Commander—"for, all here know but too well that as we have run away before, so may we again, and denying it shan't improve our odds against Sky-Brother Padzhitnoff. So while we may—*dum vivimus, bibamus*—that's if you'd do the honors, Lindsay," motioning with his wineglass toward the ice-filled bucket in the center of the table chilling the evening's wine. Sullenly, the second-in-command selected and opened two bottles, a Prosecco from a vineyard only a little north of here and a comparably effervescent Valpolicella from farther inland, proceeding then around the table, to pour into each glass equal amounts of the white and red vini frizzanti.

Randolph stood, raising his glass. "Red blood, pure mind," which the others repeated in more and less grudging unison.

The wineglasses were from a matched dozen, each having begun as a glowing parison at the end of some blowpipe over in Murano but days before. Tastefully ornamented in silver with the Chums of Chance heraldry and the motto SANGUIS RUBER, MENS PURA, the set had been that very day presented to the boys by current Shadow-Doge-in-Exile Domenico Sfinciuno, whose family in 1297, along with quite a few others among the Venetian rich and powerful of the day, had been disqualified from ever sitting on the Great Council—and hence made ineligible for the Dogedom of Venice—by then-sitting Doge Pietro Gradenigo, in his infamous decree known as the *Serrata del Maggior Consiglio.* But not even Napoleon's abolition of the office of Doge five hundred years later had any effect on the claim to what, by now, generations of Sfinciuni, in a curious inertia of resentment, had come to regard as theirs by right. Meanwhile they devoted themselves to trade with the East. In the wake of the Polos' return to Venice, the Sfinciuno joined with other upstart adventurers, likewise relegated by Gradenigo's lockout, whose money was newer than that of the Case Vecchie but quite sufficient to finance a first expedition, and headed east to make their fortune.

So there arose in Inner Asia a string of Venetian colonies, each based around some out-of-the-way oasis, and together forming a route, alternative to the Silk Road, to the markets of the East. Maps were guarded jealously, with death the not-infrequent price of divulgement to the unauthorized.

The Sfinciuno grew ever richer, and waited—they had learned how to wait. Domenico was no exception. Like his ancestors before him, he wore not only the classic Doge's hat with its upturned point on the back but also the traditional *cuffietta* or linen cap underneath, which usually only he knew he had on, unless of course he chose to show it publicly to favored guests, such as the Chums at the moment, in fact.

". . . and so," he told the assembly, "our dream is now closer than ever to being realized, as through the miracles of twentieth-century invention which these illustrious young American scientists have brought here to us, we may hope at last to recover the lost route to our Asian destiny usurped by the Polos and the accursed Gradenigo. Bless them! These *ragazzi* are not to be denied any form of respect, symbolic or practical, at the risk of our ducal displeasure, which is considerable."

"Why, it's like the Keys to the City!" exclaimed Lindsay.

"More like '*Attenzione al culo,*' " Chick muttered. "Try not to forget that this place is known for its mask industry." A vigorous advocate of inconspicuousness, Chick found ceremonies like today's both unnecessary and dangerous. Their mission in Venice, best performed without demands on time and visibility like the present one, was to locate the fabled Sfinciuno Itinerary, a map or chart of post-Polo routes into Asia, believed by many to lead to the hidden city of Shambhala itself.

"First," advised their cicerone in the matter, Professor Svegli of the University of Pisa, "try to forget the usual picture in two dimensions. That is not the kind of 'map' you are looking for. Try to put yourself back in the place of Domenico Sfinciuno or one of his caravan. What would you need, to determine where you are and where you must go? When the stars might not always be available, nor the peaks such as Khan-Tengri. . . . Not even Shiva's own paradise Mount Kailash, at certain times of day an all-but-blinding beacon from which to take one's range and bearing. . . . Because there are not only landmarks but also anti-landmarks—for every beacon, an episode of intentional blindness."

"Wait," Chick frowning as if puzzled. "Do I feel this conversation turning, how shall I say, abstract? Will this Sfinciuno Itinerary turn out to be not a geographical map at all but an account of some spiritual journey? Nothing but allegory and hidden symbolism—"

"And not one damn oasis you can get a real drink at," Darby put in bitterly. "Thanks a lot, Professor. We're in the religious-supply business now."

"The terrain is quite real, quite of this world—that, you may appreciate, is exactly the problem. Now, as in Sfinciuno's time, there are two distinct versions of 'Asia' out there, one an object of political struggle among the Powers of the Earth—the other a timeless faith by whose terms all such earthly struggle is illusion. Those whose enduring object is power in this world are only too happy to use without remorse the others, whose aim is of course to transcend all question of power. Each regards the other as a pack of deluded fools.

"The problem lies with the projection. The author of the Itinerary imagined the Earth not only as a three-dimensional sphere but, beyond that, as an *imaginary surface,* the optical arrangements for whose eventual projection onto the two-dimensional page proved to be very queer indeed.

"So we have a sort of anamorphoscope, more properly no doubt a *para*morphoscope because it reveals worlds which are set to the side of the one we have taken, until now, to be the only world given us." The classical anamorphoscopes, he went on to explain, were mirrors, cylindrical or conical, usually, which when placed on or otherwise near a deliberately distorted picture, and viewed from the appropriate direction, would make the image appear "normal" again. Fads for these came and went, beginning as early as the seventeenth century, and the artisans of Isola degli Specchi were not slow in learning how to supply this specialized market. To be sure, a certain percentage of them went mad and ended up in the asylum on San Servolo. Most of these unfortunates could not bear to look at any sort of mirror again, and were kept scrupulously away from reflective surfaces of any kind. But a few, choosing to venture deeper into the painful corridors of their affliction, found after a while that they could now grind and polish ever more exotic surfaces, hyperboloidal and even stranger, eventually including what we must term "imaginary" shapes, though some preferred Clifford's term, "invisible." These specialists remained at Isola degli Specchi under a sort of confinement within confinement so strict as to provide them, paradoxically, a freedom unknown in Europe and indeed anywhere, before or since.

"The Sfinciuno Itinerary," explained the Professor, "conflated from its original fourteenth- and fifteenth-century sources, was encrypted as one of these paramorphic distortions, meant to be redeemed from the invisible with the aid of one particular configuration of lenses and mirrors, whose exact specifications were known only to the cartographer and the otherwise hopelessly insane artisans who produced it, plus the inevitable heirs and assigns, whose identities are even today matters of lively debate. In theory each point of the fiendishly coded map had to be accounted for, though in practice, as this implied a degree of the infinite not even Dr. Cantor in our own time is certain of, the draftsman and the instrument-maker settled for about the fineness of detail provided by what were then the very latest compound microscopes, imported from the Low Countries, anticipating—and, it has been said, superior even then to—the plano-convex designs of Griendl von Ach himself."

Sometime before the first report of it in 1669, calcite or Iceland spar had arrived in Copenhagen. The double-refraction property having been noticed immediately, the ghostly mineral was soon in great demand among optical scientists across Europe. At length it was discovered that certain "invisible" lines and surfaces, analogous to conjugate points in two-dimensional space, became accessible through carefully shaped lenses, prisms, and mirrors of calcite, although the tolerances were if anything even finer than those encountered in working with glass, causing artisans by the dozens and eventually hundreds to join multitudes of their exiled brethren already wandering the far landscapes of madness.

"So," the Professor had gone on to explain, "if one accepts the idea that maps begin as dreams, pass through a finite life in the world, and resume as dreams again, we may say that these paramorphoscopes of Iceland spar, which cannot exist in great numbers if at all, reveal the architecture of dream, of all that escapes the net-work of ordinary latitude and longitude. . . ."

One day Miles Blundell, off on one of his accustomed fugues through Venice, pausing to gaze at ruined frescoes as if they were maps in which the parts worn away by time were the oceans, or to contemplate some expanse of Istrian stone and read in its naturally cursive markings commentaries on a forbidden coastline, stepped across into what later inquiry would suggest was the prophetic vision of St. Mark, *but in reverse.* That is, he returned to the Rialtine marshes and lagoon as they had been in the first century A.D., the dark cormorants in ungainly swoop, the cacophony of gulls, the smell of swamp, the huge fricative breathing, approaching speech, of the reeds beneath the scirocco that had blown his ship off course—where, ankle-deep in the ooze, it was Miles who appeared to some Being clearly not of the immediate region. Nearby, wading distance from the indistinct shoreline, lay a curious vessel which it seemed the Being had arrived in. Not the usual lateener, in fact appearing to have neither sails, masts, nor oars.

"Are you sure it wasn't just somebody wearing a mask or something? A-and what of that *winged lion*?" which Chick Counterfly, as Interrogations Officer, particularly wanted to hear about, "the Book, the page it was open to?"

"With its human face, yes, Carpaccio's ambivalent smile, the Porta della Carta, so forth, all artists' whim, I fear. . . . Unless you mean what the Being saw when it looked at me?"

"How would you know what it saw when it—"

"What was given to me to understand. To become as they'd say out here apoptotic, uninflected, unable, sometimes, to tell subject from object. While remaining myself, I was also the winged Lion—I felt the extra weight at my shoulder blades, the muscular obligations unforeseen. The Book, what of that? Somehow I knew the Book by heart, the Book of Promises, promises to savages, to galley oarsmen, to Doges, to Byzantine fugitives, to peoples living outside the known boundaries of the Earth, whose names are as little known—how important in its pages could 'my' promise be, a simple promise that 'here would thou our visitor's body rest,' here in some wet salt desert? While elsewhere in the Book waited matters far more important to be arranged, marriages and conceptions, dynasties and battles, exact convergences of winds, fleets, weather and market rates, comets, apparitions—what did a minor promise matter, even to the Evangelist? he was for Alexandria, wasn't he, he knew his fate lay there, that this was only an interruption, a perverse wind up from Africa, a false turn along the Pilgrimage he knew, by then, that he was on."

"Hey, Miles," jeered Darby, "there's an opening for Unit Chaplain if you're interested."

Miles, beaming good-humoredly, continued. "It wanted us to know that we, too, are here on a Pilgrimage. That our interest in the *itinerario sfinciunese* and the chain of oases set down in it is less for the benefit of those who have engaged us than for our own. When all the masks have been removed, it is really an inquiry into our own duty, our fate. Which is not to penetrate Asia in hopes of profit. Which is not to perish in the deserts of the world without reaching our objective. Which is not to rise in the hierarchies of power. Not to discover fragments of any True Cross however imagined. As the Franciscans developed the Stations of the Cross to allow any parishioner to journey to Jerusalem without leaving his church-grounds, so have we been brought up and down the paths and aisles of what we take to be the all-but-boundless world, but which in reality are only a circuit of humble images reflecting a glory greater than we can imagine—to save us from the blinding terror of having to make the real journey, from one episode to the next of the last day of Christ on Earth, and at last to the real, unbearable Jerusalem."

Chick Counterfly, whose allegiances were to be found in a world more tangible, nevertheless felt, as always, a stab of guilt at the passion with which Miles reported his visions. As their Venetian assignment went on, Chick had found himself attending less to shipboard matters and increasingly drawn to the *sotopòrteghi* of the city, and the chances for adventure offered by those tenebrous passages. Down in one of which, one blurry, wet dusk, a young woman named Renata, with a gesturing of her dark curls, beckoned him in with a cigarette-case of Russian silver and niello, which sprang open to reveal a collection of "smokes," Austrian, Egyptian, American, in varied shapes and sizes, some with gold-imprinted crests and writing in exotic alphabets such as the Glagolitic, old and new. "I pick them up, here and there, from friends. Hardly ever see two the same in one night." Chick selected a Gauloise, and they "lit up," she gently holding his wrist in the traditional way, pretending to examine his patent cigarette-lighter. "I've never seen one like this. How does it work?"

"There's a small prism of radioactive alloy inside, emitting certain *energetic rays,* which can be concentrated, by specially invented 'radio-lenses,' and focused at a point about where the tip of your cigarette is—*scusi,* was."

Renata was gazing at him thoughtfully from huge eyes of a curious verdigrised bronze color. "And it was you, Dottore, who invented these special lenses."

"Well, no. This hasn't *been* invented yet. I found it—it found me?—a fisherman in the fog, casting his lines again and again into the invisible river, the flow of Time, hoping to retrieve just such artifacts as this."

"*Affascinante, caro.* Does that mean, if I live long enough, I might get to see this on the Rialto someday for sale by the dozens?"

"Not necessarily. Your own future may never include it. Nor mine. It's not the way Time seems to work."

"Hmm. My *ragazzo*—well, more than that, business associate, too—is with the police. He wants to be a detective someday. He's always reading up on the latest criminal theories, and I know he'd be interested in—"

"Nonono, please, I am not one of Dr. Lombroso's *mattoidi,* only a simple contract balloonist."

"But not another Russian."

"'Another' . . . but can you be sure?" Stroking his whiskers roguishly.

"Maybe I've run into one or two and know the difference."

"And . . . ?"

"Would I remember?"

"*Prego,* professional curiosity, no more."

"Come, there's a *caffè* just past that next little bridge. You'll let me do the cards for you, at least, I hope."

"Your business associate—"

A shrug. "Down in Pozzuoli, up to no good."

They sat at a small veneered table, with room enough for their cups and the layout of miniature Tarocchi, or Tarot cards, Renata had produced a deck of from her handbag and shuffled, proceeding to put down a line of eight, above that a line of four, then two, then one, to form a rude cusp. "Allowing each of the upper cards to be influenced by the two just below it. The last card, as always, is the one that matters."

Which tonight proved to be number XVI, The Tower. She shuffled and repeated the layout twice more, and each time it converged to the Tower, causing her to grow still, to breathe less deeply. The only other Major Arcana dealt up seemed to be gentle suggestions about character reform, such as Temperance and Fortitude.

"In Protestant lands such as England," Chick observed, "those who read these cards believe that The Tower signifies the Church of Rome."

"An afterthought. The Tarocchi are much, much older. From long before Christ and the Gospels, let alone the papacy. Always very straightforward. This card, on this tabletop, for you, is a real tower, maybe even old Papà himself."

"The Campanile in the Piazza? It's going to be hit by lightning? Two parties are going to fall out of it?"

"Some kind of lightning. Some kind of fall."

AROUND DAWN, as if it had just occurred to her, "But—aren't you supposed to be with your unit?"

"As of midnight I was officially 'straggling,' and depending how early the boys are planning to get under way, why, I could be missing ship's movement, too."

"What will happen?"

"They could send a shore party after me, I guess. . . . See anybody suspicious out there?"

"Only the breakfast boat. Come on, I'll buy you something."

Two local fellows in a small boat had emerged from the luminous blur of the *sfumato,* which would not burn off till later in the morning—one rowing and the other tending a small charcoal stove whose glow was just about to be absorbed in the nacreous swell of daylight. Mussel-gatherers could now be seen out in the water, which came only up to their waists, moving about like harvesters in a field. Produce boats up from the Ponte di Paglia glided by, and small boats loaded with green crabs whose rattling struggles could be heard in the dawn.

Breakfast was ungraciously interrupted by Darby Suckling, who came abseiling down from some overhead purchase, sneering, "Gee, how *típico.* Let's go, Counterfly."

"*Pax tibi, Darbe.* Say hello to Renata."

"Arrivederci, sister."

"You used to be such a pleasant kid. What happened?"

"Eeeyynnhh, too many feebs to deal with over the years, I guess—oh *I'm* sorry, hope I'm not offending—"

"What if I *don't* come back to the ship?"

"Sure—first you, then one by one, like some damned *Farewell* Symphony, we blow out our candles, walk off, resign from the Sky. I don't think so."

"You'd never miss me, soon the winds'll be shifting, then it'll be winter routine—"

"The Sky's been good to you, Counterfly."

"It's the future I'm thinking of. I have some problems with the retirement plan." An old pleasantry in the business—there was no retirement plan, in fact no retirement. Chums of Chance were expected to die on the job. Or else live forever, there being two schools of thought, actually.

"Guess I could hit you with a sap and drag you back somehow," grumbled Darby. He had joined them at a small table outside for a breakfast of broiled fish, rolls, figs, and coffee.

"Lot of work," Chick said.

They strolled along the Riva, past a line of torpedo boats tied up there.

"Get a ground job?" Darby said, "sure thing, sucker. But what doing? not as if there's much call for our skills down below."

"We've aviated ourselves away from the clambake, that's certain," Chick said.

"Bet you Padzhitnoff doesn't feel that way."

"That's government work. According to my sources at the Italian War Ministry, he's based across the Adriatic, in Montenegro, doing photo reconnaissance of the Austrian installations in Dalmatia. The Ministry is keenly interested, not to mention Irredentist elements in both countries."

"Lot of this dang Irredentism going around lately," it seemed to Darby.

"Austria has no business down here in the Adriatic." Renata declared. "They were never a maritime nation and never shall be. Let them stay up in their mountains and ski, eat chocolate, molest Jews, whatever it is they do. We got Venice back, and so shall Trieste be ours again. The more they meddle here, the more certain and complete shall be their destruction."

· · ·

THE *INCONVENIENCE* WAS in a remote part of the Arsenale, out of drydock at last, shining and shipshape and somehow increased in size. Chick greeted his shipmates, who were a-thrum with excitement over reports that their Russian counterparts had been observed getting up buoyancy, carrying on board their ship a number of mysterious crates and casks, as if preparing for an engagement.

"Who with?" Darby shrugged. "Not us. How could it be us?"

"Any way of reaching Padzhitnoff?" Chick wondered.

Pugnax arrived in the company of Mostruccio, a small, ill-humored Venetian dog, with an ancestral resemblance to those observed in works of Carpaccio, Mansveto, and others, some of whom had had their own private gondolas to ride around in. Emerging from dreams in which, winged as any lion, he had soared in pursuit of pigeons above the roof-tiles and among the chimneys, Mostruccio was obliged to spend his waking hours back at ground level in embittered assaults upon the ankles of the unwary. . . . He had found in Pugnax a sympathetic soul, for, owing to often weeks of being cooped up in the gondola of the *Inconvenience,* Pugnax also dreamed of release, running, in the early morning, into a brisk wind, leaving behind whatever humans had accompanied him, along the wild beaches of Florida hard as pavement, or the frozen rivers of Siberia where Samoyeds raced alongside in a spirit of friendly competition. He approached Randolph, arranged his eyebrows in a format of petition, and inquired "Rrr Rr-rrururu rrf rr-rrff, rr rrff rrffr?" or "May Mostruccio come aboard as my guest?"

PEDESTRIANS BELOW were moving at their accustomed gaits, sitting at the tables in front of Florian and Quadri, if Francophile raising toasts to Bastille Day, feeding, photographing, or cursing the pigeons, who, aware of some baleful anomaly in their sky, stuttered wildly into the air, then, reconsidering, settled, only to sweep a moment later heavenward again, as if on the strength of a rumor.

Seen from the ground, the rival airships were more conjectural than literal—objects of fear and prophecy, reported to perform at speeds and with a manœuvrability quite unavailable to any official aircraft of the time—condensed or projected from dreams, estrangements, solitudes. In the moments just preceding those in which the Campanile came down, to whom was it given to see the fight in the sky but to certain *lasagnoni,* always to be found about the Piazza, recorded over the seasons by thousands of tourist-photographers and their images taken home in silent autumnal diaspora—blurry as bats at twilight, often scarcely visible as more than sepia gestures against the dreaming façade of the Basilica San Marco, or the more secular iterations of the Procuratie—because, it is said, of the long exposures necessary in the humid light of Venice, but in reality because of the aeronauts' dual citizenship in the realms of the quotidian and the ghostly, it was to the *lasagnoni* that the clarity of sight to witness the engagement was granted. To them alone. Dreamblown as the notorious pigeon population, contemplating the sky, they became aware that morning of something else about to emerge from the *sfumato,* some visitation . . . something that was to transcend both Chums and Tovarishchi, for all at once there was a great stunning hoarse cry from the invisibility, nearly a material thing, a lethal impedance in the air, as if something malevolent were making every exertion to take form and be released upon the world in long, dry, cracking percussions, as if jarring the fabric of four-space itself. At each salvo the two skycraft slid away at angles almost impossible to read correctly, so distorted had become the medium up here through which light must pass.

A giddiness of judgment seemed to have possessed both crews. The weapons-sighting situation oppressed them all, like a curse, with the little-understood enigmata of the simultaneous. By a few degrees or even minutes of arc, their gunners were abolishing Time—what they saw "now" in the sights was in fact what did not yet exist *but what would only be* a few seconds from "now," dependent on platform and target each maintaining course and speed—or idealizations of "course and speed," since winds were acting to modify both in not entirely predictable fashion.

The Campanile flowed hugely past on a severe diagonal, pigeon-stained, blotched both pale and dark, visibly out of plumb, leaning in as if about to confide a secret, haggard as the town drunk. . . .

In the next instant, Padzhitnoff saw the ancient structure separate cleanly into a multitude of four-brick groupings, each surrounded by a luminous contour, and hang an instant in space, as time slowed and each permutation of shapes appeared, to begin their gentle, undeadly descent, rotating and translating in all available modes, as if endeavoring to satisfy some demented group-theoretical analysis, until the rising dust-cloud they collapsed into obscured all such considerations in a great raw-umber smudge of uncertainty.

Among their weapons the lads had been packing their own unique model of *aerial torpedo,* invented by Dr. Chick Counterfly for the purpose not so much of annihilating or even damaging an opposing airship as of "reminding it of its innate susceptibility to gravitation." The normal complement was six projectiles—known to the Chums as "sky-fish," and listed in *Inconve-*

nience's armaments manifest as Contrabuoyancy Devices. The unspoken question, at the post-engagement critique held that day directly after midday mess, was whether it may have been one of these—fired at the *Bol'shaia Igra* without allowing for a number of critical factors, such as the humidity—that had toppled the Campanile.

"What stood for a thousand years," Randolph pronounced, "what neither tempest not earthquake, nor even the catastrophic Napoleon Bonaparte could touch, we have bumblingly brought down in an instant. What shall be the next target of our ineptitude? Notre Dame? the Pyramids?"

"It was an accident of war," Lindsay insisted. "And I am not so sure we did it anyway."

"Then you did actually see something, Noseworth?" inquired Chick Counterfly.

"I regret," sniffed Lindsay, "that seldom in the heat of engagement have I found sufficient leisure for *scientific observation,* though the well-known propensity of the other commander for attacking his targets with deciduous masonry would strongly if not inescapably suggest—"

"Yet being aloft, we were not at all in the path of the tower's collapse," pointed out Chick, patiently. "We had the weather-gauge. We were bearing down upon them."

"—coupled with their swift departure," Lindsay, oblivious, had continued, "as if in shame at what they had done—"

"Hey, Lindsay, you can still catch 'em if you hurry," taunted Darby.

"Or we might send in pursuit *your maternal relation,* Suckling, one glimpse of whom should prove more than sufficient fatally to compromise their morale, if not indeed *transform them all* into masonry—"

"Well, *your* mother," riposted the readily nettled youth, "is *so ugly*—"

"Gentlemen," implored Randolph, in whose voice it required little clairvoyance to detect a neuræsthenic prostration only with difficulty resisted, "we may have committed today a great wrong against History, beside which this petty squabbling shrinks to submicroscopic insignificance. Please be so kind as to save it for some more recreational moment."

They arranged to meet with Captain Padzhitnoff and his officers on an all-but-deserted stretch of Adriatic beach over on the Lido, toward Malamocco. The commanders embraced in a curious mixture of formality and sorrow.

"This is so terrible," said Randolph.

"Was not *Bol'shaia Igra.*"

"No. We didn't think so. It wasn't the *Inconvenience* either. Who then?"

The Russian aeronaut appeared to be struggling with an ethical question. "St. Cosmo. You are aware that something else is out there."

"Such as . . ."

"You have seen nothing? Detected nothing unusual?"

"Over the Piazza, you mean."

"Anywhere. Geography is irrelevant."

"I'm not sure—"

"They appear out of . . . some other condition, and they vanish back into it."

"And you believe it was they who knocked down the Campanile?" said Chick. "But how?"

"Vibrational rays, nearly as we can make out," said Chick's opposite number, Dr. Gerasimoff. "Adjustable to target's exact sympathetic frequency, thereupon inducing divergent oscillation."

"How convenient," muttered Lindsay darkly, "that one cannot analyze the rubble for evidence of the quadruple brickbats it is your delight to drop on anyone you take a dislike to."

The Russian, remembering his vision of the collapse, smiled wanly. "Tetraliths are only deployed in anger," he said. "A detail acquired from Japanese, who will never, unless they wish to offend, present you with four of anything—Japanese character for 'four' being same as that for 'death.'"

"You have been in Japan, Captain?" Randolph glaring meanwhile at Lindsay.

"These days, who in my line of work has not?"

"You wouldn't happen to know a Mr. Ryohei Uchida. . . ."

Nodding, eyes glittering with enthusiastic hatred, "Bastard we have been trying to assassinate for two years now. Nearly got him in Yokohama with nice, right-angled fragment, so close he was actually *standing inside angle,* but missed him by millimeters—*polny pizdets!* such luck, that man!"

"He seemed like quite a well-spoken gentleman when he interviewed us for the mission—"

Padzhitnoff squinted warily. "Mission?"

"Last year his people—an outfit called the Black Dragon Society?—wanted to hire us for some routine aerial surveillance."

"St. Cosmo, are you insane? Why are you telling me this? Don't you know who they are?"

Randolph shrugged. "A patriotic organization of some kind. I mean they may be Japanese, but they do take as much pride in their country as anyone."

"*Smirno,* balloon-boy! Here is political situation! Black Dragon's purpose is to subvert and destroy Russian presence in Manchuria. Manchuria has been Russian since 1860, but after war with China, Japanese now believe it belongs to them. Ignoring treaties, Chinese Eastern Railway, wishes of European Powers, even their own promise to respect Chinese borders, Japanese are gathering worst criminal classes in Manchuria, arming and training them as guerrilla forces to fight against us there. I respect you, St. Cosmo, and I cannot believe you would ever consider working for such people."

"Manchuria?" puzzled Randolph. "Why? It's a miserable swamp. Frozen half the year. Why would anyone take that much trouble over it?"

"Gold and opium," Padzhitnoff shrugged, as if everyone knew. Randolph didn't, though he could appreciate in theory that elements of the surface-world might go to war over gold—it was happening in South Africa at that very moment—the "gold standard" was even said to be a factor in the social unrest currently afflicting the United States. He knew also that sixty years ago there had been "Opium Wars" between China and Great Britain. But between the history and the ground-level emotions driving it, the fear of being poor, let's say, the blessedness of deliverance from pain, lay this strange interval forbidden to him to enter. He frowned. Both parties had lapsed into a perplexed silence.

Reviewing the conversation later, it seemed to Chick Counterfly that Padzhitnoff had taken a disingenuous line. "No reflections upon the Manchurian question can usefully neglect the Trans-Siberian Railroad," he pointed out. "From a high enough altitude, as we have often observed, indeed that great project appears almost like a living organism, one dares to say a conscious one, with needs and plans of its own. For our immediate purposes, in opening up huge regions of Inner Asia, it can only make more inevitable Russian, and to a degree, European access to Shambhala, wherever that may prove to lie."

"Then . . ."

"We have to assume they are here for the Sfinciuno Itinerary, the same as we."

Meanwhile, like a form of architectural prayer, civic plans had been set in motion to rebuild the Campanile *dov'era, com'era,* as if the dilapidations of time and entropy could be reversed. The texture of the choir of city bells had changed—without the deepest, La Marangona, to anchor them, the skyfarers felt that much closer to the pull of the sky and imminent departure. As if a significant polarity had been reversed and they were no longer held but summoned. Or as Miles put it one evening just at sunset, "Bells are the most ancient objects. They call to us out of eternity."

Deuce and Sloat were sharing quarters at Curly Dee's spread down the valley, where Curly and his woman ran a sort of road ranch for fugitives, ten-dayers, threats to society, and assorted cases of moral idiocy—a squalid, undersize bangtogether sagging between its posts, whose roof might as well have been made of window-screen, for all the good it did in a storm.

"What say we go into town, find us some pussy, bring 'em back here—"

"You don't bring women to a place like this, Sloat. They get distracted, all's they can see's the tobacco-juice, the rats, the meals from long ago, it wrecks their mood."

"You don't like this room?"

"Room, it ain't even a stall."

"Wouldn't want to think you 's going *domestic* or nothin."

"We'd best go into town. Big Billy's or Jew Fanny's or someplace."

They rode up into town. The electric lighting crept out to meet and saturate them, turn wrinkles in clothes and skin inside out. A seething of human and animal voices. Some in pain, some having a time, some doing business. Telluride. Creede, but with only the one way in and out.

"How about we go look in to the Cosmopolitan for a minute."

"Why? Th'only pussy in there chases mice."

"Pussy on the brain, Big S."

"Better'n opium smoke," dodging out of the way as Deuce playfully drew and brandished his .44. A sly reference to Deuce's on-and-off romance with Hsiang-Chiao, who worked in a laundry down the street. This was an old routine between the partners, and in fact each was to find his way that evening to his preferred recreation, reconnecting only hours later after a long spell of that glaring nightlessness Telluride was known for.

Close to dawn Deuce came lurching into the Nonpareil Eating House, Sloat walking shotgun right over his shoulder. The place was full of hungry drunks. Drovers with imperfectly developed social skills chased among the tables after saloon girls who were not too tired to move as fast as they had to. Place was full of lard smoke. Mayva was in and out of the kitchen cooking and working whatever tables Lake wasn't. Both women kept up a level of determined bustling, as if allowing the thousand details of the day to fill up what otherwise would've been some insupportable vacuum.

Deuce took this for "female restlessness," which he thought he understood. When Lake came over to inquire with a silent lift of the eyebrows and chin if they were there to eat or sit, he did not remark at the time how desirable she looked. What surprised him was the way she'd kept some fire in her eye, rare in a biscuit-shooter, that no long shift was about to put out. Later he would also become aware of a darkness just as indelible, that could not be, but maybe was, the stain of some undivulged sin.

"Don't be in a rush, boys, grocery wagon's due in before noon, bound to be something on it you can eat."

"Enjoying the scenery," said suave Deuce.

"Nothin like this down Cañon City, I expect."

"Oooh," lowed Sloat appreciatively.

"Coffee," Deuce shrugged.

"You're sure. Think it through now."

"Lake," Mayva called from the kitchen, just about the same time Sloat muttered, "Deuce." Steam and smoke curled out the kitchen window into cones of white electric light from bulbs installed high on stripped fir poles. Urgent Chinese conversation proceeded out in the street. Prolonged echoes of explosion rolled in from somewhere down the valley. Mine whistles went off up in the mountains. Morning came straining in through eyelashes and bootsoles, welcome as a marshal with a saddlebag full of warrants. Lake shrugged and got back to work.

Sloat sat nodding within some deep private smirk. "Civilians, now, my gosh. That gong's about to start kickin you back, li'l amigo."

"Don't much care who does or don't like it, Sloat."

Meanwhile in the kitchen, "Better watch 'at flirtin' of yours, Lake, he's dangerous goods, that little buckaroo."

"Mamma, I hardly caught his name."

"I saw what you were up to. Hundred men a day come through here, some of em regular celluloid-collar ads, too, and them, why you're all business, but in strolls some shifty-eyed little hardcase with trouble wrote all over him, and you're ready to—well I don't know what."

"I do."

"Lake . . ."

"Teasing you, Ma?"

WHAT WAS IT, exactly, that had started in to ringing so inside Lake, tolling, bone deep, invisible in the night . . . was it the way his face that morning, even with the smoke in the room, had slowly emerged into clarity? Like an old memory, older than herself, something that'd happened before, that she knew now she'd have to go through again. . . . And the way he was looking at her—a *knowing look,* worse than the most cocksure good-for-nothing that ever came her way, the assumptions being made, not just by him either, but by something *outside them.* Had to be the altitude.

As for Deuce, of course he "knew" who she was—she *had the man's face,* for Christ's sake. Deuce was an abbreviated customer, hardly much taller than she—in a fair fight she might've even taken him, but the fight was not fair. Would never be. His edge, so he believed, came from the poisoned halo of murder for hire, the pure badness of everything he did when he wasn't with her. Women could protest from now till piss flowed uphill, but the truth was, there wasn't one didn't secretly love a killer.

And it might turn out, to Lake's own surprise as much as anybody's, that she was one of these passionate young women who believed as the Mexican señoritas like to say that without love one cannot live. That any entrance of it into her life would be like unexpected laughter or finding religion, a gift from the beyond that she must not allow to just exit again and pretend it was gone forever. Unfortunately, "it" had now arrived in the form of Deuce Kindred, for whom her loathing would come to be inseparable from her passion.

Complicating matters but not keeping her awake nights was young Willis Turnstone, the doctor over at the Miner's Hospital she'd met when she was working there before they put her on steady at the eating house. Willis was pretty direct, and it didn't take more than one walk through the wildflowers before he'd declared his intentions.

"Can't say I love you, Willis," figuring she owed him just as direct of an answer. For she'd met Deuce by then, and it was just a simple case of the true article and its all-but-invisible shadow, and she didn't have to wait too many heartbeats to tell the difference.

"You are a mighty desirable length of calico, how come you're not married already?" was how Deuce got around to popping the question.

"Thought I'd take my time, I guess."

"Time is something you're given," he philosophized, "you don't take it."

It was not quite a reproof, and likewise short of a plea, but she must have caught something. "The way it is right now—nothin could make it better. But what about when we're old?"

"Unless we could beat it. Never get old."

She'd hadn't seen his eyes like this. "Hope that ain't Billy the Kid talk."

"No. Crazier." He was that close to just handing it all over to her. His soles ached, his fingers throbbed, his heartbeat was audible down the street and around a couple of corners, and she was gazing at him with no little alarm, trying to hang on to her own composure, expecting she didn't know what. They were both so easily ridden in on by these unannounced passions. Their eyes grew feral, neck muscles went out of control, they became indifferent to where they were, even who was around.

Deuce, in his unguarded state, could feel his heart melting and his penis blood-crazy for her, both at the same time. . . . Handicapped by his ignorance of human emotion, he would come to desire Lake beyond any limits he could have imagined. He would beg, actually beg, self-styled professional badman and all, beg her to marry him. Even respecting her wish that they not fuck until after the wedding.

"It didn't matter to me before. That's just it. Now it does. Lake? I'll change, I swear."

"I'm not saying start goin to church. Just think about who you hire on with. Don't have to be any 'better' than that." Some would've said she knew even then what he'd done. Could not have helped knowing, God sakes.

One day Mayva had swapped her shift with Oleander Prudge, who, though far too young to be acting as the conscience of Telluride, lost no time in going after Lake.

"They're saying Deuce Kindred's the one shot your father."

Not loud enough to stop conversation in the Nonpareil, but there it was at last. "Who's sayin that?" Maybe a pulse in her neck leapt into visibility, but she was not about to swoon.

"No secrets in this town, Lake, there's too much goin on, no time to cover up and not many who care, when you come right to it."

"Has my Mamma heard any of this talk?"

"Well let's hope not."

"It ain't true."

"Hmp. Ask your beau."

"Maybe I'll just do that." Lake slammed a plate down so hard that the stack of hotcakes on it, each glistening with bacon grease, went toppling, rudely surprising a single-jacker, who snatched his hand away screaming.

"Wasn't that hot, Arvin," Lake scowled, "but here, let me kiss it, make it better."

"You're dishonoring your father's memory," Oleander's snoot well in the air by now, "what you're doing."

Reassembling the stack on the plate, Lake gazed boldly back. "How I feel about Mister Kindred," trying for some schoolteacher's enunciation—"not that it's your concern, and how I felt about Webb Traverse are two different things."

"They can't be."

"You've had this happen to you? You even know what you're talking about?"

Was there close attention from up and down the counter? Thinking back, it would seem to Lake that everybody had been in on this from the minute the news reached town, with her and Mayva, poor geese, the last to know.

LATER THEY GLARED at each other, up insomniac in the new-sawn wood and paint smells of the room they shared.

"I don't want you seeing him no more. He comes in range of me, ever, I'll shoot him my damn self."

"Ma, it's this town, people like Oleander Prudge, don't care what they say, long as it hurts somebody."

"I can't show my face, Lake. You're making sorry fools out of all of us. This has got to stop."

"I can't."

"You better."

"He asked me to marry him, Ma."

Not news Mayva had been waiting to hear. "Well. Then you sure got your choice."

"'Cause I won't believe any of this spiteful talk? Ma?"

"You know better. I been crazy the way you're crazy now, hell, crazier, and it's over faster'n you can blow your nose, and someday you're gonna wake up, and then oh, you poor girl—"

"Oh. So that's what happened to you and Pa." She regretted it before it was even out of her mouth, but this was a wagon headed down a grade they could neither of them stop.

Mayva pulled her old green canvas club satchel out from under the bed and started putting things in it. Carefully, like any other chore. Her briar pipe and tobacco pouch, baby tintypes of all the kids, an extra shirtwaist, a shawl, a beat-up little Bible. Didn't take long. Her whole life, and no more than this to show. Well. She looked up at last, her face full of an incalculable sorrow. "Same as if you killed your father too. Not one Goddamned bit of difference."

"*What* did you say?"

Mayva took her bag and went to the door. "You'll reap what you sow."

"Where're you going?"

"You don't care."

"The train won't be in till tomorrow."

"Then I'll wait till it comes. I won't spend another night in this room with you. I'll sleep down there to the depot. And everbody can look. Look at the damn fool old woman."

And she was gone, and Lake sat there with her legs trembling but not a thought in her head, and didn't go after her, and though next day she heard the whistle and the racket when the train pulled in, and then later when it backed away down the valley, she didn't ever see her mother again.

"THIS . . . IS . . . DISGUSTING," Sloat shaking his head, "I mean I'm fixin to lose my damn lunch in a minute."

"Can't help it. You think I can help any of this?" Deuce risked throwing his runninmate a quick look, appealing for some understanding anyway.

No dice. "Got-damn fool. This is all your story that you're tellin yourself—listen, nobody gives a hair on a mine rat's ass if you marry her or not, but if you fuck up and do that deed, what's gonna happen once she learns the true facts of the case? if she don't know it already. How you fixin to find even a minute's sleep, her knowing it was you did her Daddy in?"

"Guess I live with that."

"Not for long you don't. You want to fuck her, fuck her, just *don't tell her nothin.*"

Sloat could not figure out what had happened to his partner. You'd've thought it was the first man he ever killed. Was it possible, even with those miners' lives as cheap as jug whiskey and as easily disappeared down the gullet of days, that Deuce was being haunted by what he did, and that marrying Lake looked like some chance at putting that one ghost to rest, some way, God help him, of *making it up* to her?

THE SNOWS LENGTHENED down the peaks, and soon the white-throated swift had taken wing, the shooting and headbreaking in town got worse, the military occupation began in November, and then deeper in the winter, in January, martial law was declared—the scabs came to work in relative peace, business was slow for a while in town but picked up, and Oleander Prudge made her debut as a nymph du pave, miners who thought they knew what was what coming away bewildered, shaking their heads. Despite her turnout, prim to the point of invisibility, her perpetual scowl, and her tendency to lecture her clients on points of personal grooming, somehow she quickly developed a following and before long was working out of a parlor house, from her own room, a corner room at that, with a lengthy view down the valley.

Lake and Deuce were married over on the other side of the mountains in a prairie church whose steeple was visible for miles, at first nearly the color of the gray sky in which it figured as little more than a geometric episode, till at closer range the straight lines began to break up, soon slipping every which way, like lines of a face seen too close, haggard from the assaults of more winters than anybody still living in the area remembered the full count of, weathered beyond sorrowful, smelling like generations of mummified rodents, built of Engelmann spruce and receptive to sound as the inside of a parlor piano. Though scarcely any music ever came this way, the stray mouthharpist or whistling drifter who did pass through the crooked doors found himself elevated into more grace than the acoustics of his way would have granted him so far.

The officiating presence, a Swede migrated west from the Dakota country, wore gray robes heavy with dust, face indistinct as if shadowed beneath a hood, not so much reciting the well-known words as singing them, in a harmonic-minor drone this congenial soundbox smoothed into dark psalm. The bride wore a simple dress of pale blue albatross cloth, fine as a nun's veil. Sloat was best man. At the big moment, he dropped the ring. Had to go on his knees in the dim light to look for where it might've rolled. "Well, how you doin down there?" Deuce called out after a while.

"Better not get too close," Sloat muttered.

When the deed was done, as his wife was bringing out a glass bowlful of wedding punch and some cups, the preacher produced an accordion and, as if unable not to, played them a thunderous country waltz from Österbybruk, where he and the missus both came from.

"What's in this?" Sloat was curious to know.

"Everclear alcohol," replied the preacher with an earnest face. "Hundred twenty proof? Some peach juice . . . certain Scandinavian ingredients."

"How's that?"

"Swedish aphrodisiac."

"Such as, um . . . ?"

"Its name? *Ja,* I could tell, you—but in Jämtland dialect it's almost the same as 'your moth-er's vagina,' so unless you say it exactly right, there's always the chance of a misunderstanding with any Swedish folks might be in earshot. Trying to save you trouble down the line, sure."

SHE WAS A virgin bride. At the moment of surrendering, she found herself wishing only to become the wind. To feel herself refined to an edge, an invisible edge of unknown length, to enter the realm of air forever in motion over the broken land. Child of the storm.

THEY WOKE UP in the middle of the night. She moved spooned in his embrace, feeling no need to turn to exchange a look, communicating by way of her unexpectedly articulate ass.

"Damn. We're really married, ain't we."

"There's married," she supposed, "and there's respectably married. Now we're on the subject, where'd that thing get to—oh, there we go. . . ."

"Damn, Lake."

INSIDE OF A week of the wedding night, Deuce and Sloat thought they'd go off on a brief tour of the region.

"You don't mind do you my dove?"

"What—"

"See some more that coffee," Sloat growled. Next thing she knew, they were out the door and across the ravine, and they weren't back by nightfall or in fact for another week, and when they did show up again it was in a storm of hoarse, high-pitched laughter she could hear from half a mile away that neither Deuce nor Sloat could control. They came in and sat there laughing, their eyes, dark from no sleep, drilling into her, not about to look elsewhere. She didn't feel frightened so much as sick.

When they quieted down enough, "You here for a while," she was able to ask, "or are you just back lookin to change your socks?" Which started them off again.

From then on, just about every day had its post-nuptial kick-up. Sloat had taken up residence, it seemed, and the question inexorably arose of his interest in the bride. "Go right on ahead pard," Deuce offered one night, "she's all yours. I could use a break about now."

"Oh now Deuce, only sidekicks get sloppy seconds, everbody knows that, and I ain't your damned sidekick."

"You turning this down, Sloat? maybe it ain't exactly Market Street material, but take a look here, it's still a nice package."

"She starts shiverin if I come closer'n ten foot of her. Is she afraid of me?"

"Ask her, why don't you?"

"You afraid of me, missus?"

"Yes."

"Well that's somethin I suppose."

Lake did not pick up right away that this was Sloat's notion of love-play. In fact, by the time she did figure it out, he'd be long gone.

But until then, oh how bad of a badgirl was she turning out to be here? Next thing she knew, she was naked and they were all on a bed upstairs in the Elk Hotel in Colorado Springs.

"Not since 'at Chinese one in Reno," Deuce was saying, "remember her?"

"Mmm! that sideways pussy!"

"Be serious," said Lake.

"Swear, had to get all into kind of a X shape, here, we'll show you—"

They kept her naked most of the time. Sometimes they put a pair of leather side hobbles on her to keep her attached to the bed, but enough chain so she could move. Not that they had to, she was always ready to oblige. After she had given in to the notion of being doubled up on, she found herself going out of her way looking for it, usually one in her mouth, the other from behind, sometimes in her ass, so she got quickly used to tasting her own fluids mixed with shit. "Guess this makes me really bad," she said in a quiet voice, looking up at Deuce.

Sloat grabbed a handful of her hair and forced her face back onto her lawfully wedded's cock. "That ain't what makes you really bad, fuckmouth whore, what makes you really bad is marryin my li'l compadre here."

"She got her a twofer," Deuce laughed. "Badgirl shit pays off."

She discovered in herself unsuspected talents for indirectness and flirtation, because she had to be careful never to make anything seem like a demand, around these two that could wreck a mood faster than monthly bleeding. Fact, Deuce and Sloat were the touchiest badmen she'd ever run across, anything could put them out of the mood. Streetcars in the street, one of them whistling the wrong tune. Only once had she been incautious enough to suggest, "Why don't you boys just leave me out of it and do each other for a change?" and the shock and outrage in the place, why you could feel it for days.

Sloat was partial to the color green. He kept showing up with these peculiar items, nearly always stolen from someplace, that he wanted her to wear, gauntlets, baby bonnets, men's bicycle hose, hats trimmed and plain, didn't matter long as it was some shade of green.

"Deuce, your partner is really crazy."

"Yehp, never could see green, bein a mauve man myself," producing a grease-blotched gingham apron checked in approximately that color. "You mind?"

They took her down to the Four Corners and put her so one of her knees was in Utah, one in Colorado, one elbow in Arizona and the other in New Mexico—with the point of insertion exactly above the mythical crosshairs itself. Then rotated her all four different ways. Her small features pressed into the dirt, the blood-red dirt.

For a while then, it settled into a three-party household of dubious coziness. The sidekicks appeared unwilling to break up their partnership just yet, and Lake was not about to let either of them ride off up the plateau any further than rifle range. Deuce snored, even when he was awake. Sloat did not think much of bathing, in fact he had a superstitious horror of the act, believing that if he so much as washed his hands, bad luck was sure to come his way. Lake sweet-talked him into it only once, and that night at the supper table something hit the roof with a huge bang, causing Sloat's soup to splash all over. "There! You see? You think I'm crazy now?"

"Goodness," said Lake, "it's a marmot."

"She's all right," Deuce confessed to his partner, "for bein such a pain in the ol' bunghole."

"It is your penance, *huevón,*" Sloat going into his comical Mexican accent.

"Catholic stuff. Nothin I can understand but thanks anyway."

"Don't matter what you understand, even what you think. *If* you think, *pinche cabrón*. You slay, you pay."

"Or get away." Deuce with a distant smile, as if pleased at his whole situation.

Sloat felt warning signs sure as a telegrapher getting word of a midnight train bearing down on the depot, full of dynamiters with mischief in mind.

One day in Telluride, Deuce was summoned to the offices of the same company rep who'd hired him to take care of Webb, what seemed now like years ago. "The dynamite outrages continue, Mr. Kindred."

Deuce didn't have to pretend to be puzzled. "Ol' Webb wa'n' the only anarchist in the San Juans, was he?"

"These all have the same modus, dynamite hooked up to a two-dollar Ingersoll, same hour, just before dawn . . . he even bombs by the moon, just like Traverse did."

Deuce shrugged. "Could be an apprentice of his."

"My principals feel they must ask you a question of some delicacy. Please don't take it the wrong way." Deuce saw it coming but stood easy, waiting. "Are you sure you got him, Mr. Kindred?"

"They put him in the miners' graveyard in Telluride, go dig him up and see."

"Proper identification might no longer be feasible."

"So you're sayin I just shot some ringer? first saloon bum I run into? Now the owners want their money back, that it?"

"Did I say that? Oh dear. We knew you'd be angry."

"Fuckin A John I'm angry, who the fuck do you think you are—"

Had to hand it to this corporate stooge, he didn't seem to care much about who he provoked. "There's also this matter of your personal relations with the subject's daughter—"

Deuce was in screaming mid-leap, feet off the floor and hands only inches from the rep's throat, when he was surprised by the appearance of a double-action .32 from some rig concealed beneath his target's store-bought suit, not to mention another weapon in the hands of a confederate whom the momentarily insane Deuce had failed even to notice. The rep skipped nimbly out of the way and Deuce crashed into a typewriter cabinet.

"We are not vengeful people ordinarily," murmured the rep. "The possibility of a copy-cat bomber had of course occurred to us. We will continue to give you the benefit of the doubt until our inquiries are done. Should it prove, however, that you've accepted payment for work not performed, well. Who knows then what form our resentment might take."

WELL, it could have been the cactus that mysteriously exploded next to his head one day down in Cortez, or maybe the ace of spades that arrived in the mail soon after that, but at some point Deuce had to gently start breaking it to Lake that there just might be some people after him.

She could still exhibit strange patches of innocence. She imagined it was money he owed, or something short-term like that, minor trouble, over before long.

"Who are they, Deuce? Is it something from back in Butte?"

He couldn't allow himself to go slack, especially when her eyes were guileless as this. "Not likely," he pretended to explain, "boys up there tend to be fairly thoughtful about takin' offense—too many insult opportunities, sufficient unto the day and so forth. No, if you can make it past the city limits, why all's forgiven in Butte."

"Then . . ."

"Listen, I'm pretty sure whoever it is, it's the owners up here, that they're workin for."

"But—" She frowned. She was trying to understand, wanted at least to look like she was, but it was beginning to feel like being in a skip that had just slipped its cable, heading for the center of the Earth. "Been doin somethin you shouldn't, Deuce?"

"Maybe. Nothin that wasn't done on their orders."

"A loyal trooper. Why would they send somebody after you, then?"

He looked at her steadily, widening his eyes as if asking, *Haven't you figured this out yet?* "Sometimes," he finally said, "they don't like to leave even the chance open that somebody might, later on, well say somethin'."

Soon word came in, unconfirmed but promissory as the first snow of autumn, that the owners had subbed the job out to Utahans, some really lethal ex-Danite posse riders who were finding their years of retirement not eventful enough. Old boys who liked to pack "Avenging Angels," which were typically Civil War-vintage Colts with the barrels sawed off short. Geezers on furlough from Hell. "Long-distance shooting ain't on their list of occupational skills, they don't mind some close-up work."

"You scared, Deuce?" Sloat inquired.

"Damn straight I am, if you had the brains you 's born with, you'd be too."

"What do we do? Run away?"

" 'We'?"

"I'm supposed to wait for them to show up? O.K. if I pack a shotgun or something? Couple of shells for it, maybe?"

"They're not looking for you, Sloat."

"Maybe they'll think I know where you went."

Deuce was too scared himself to take much account of what was there in Sloat's eyes staring him flat in the face. Later it was going to haunt him, for there would come a period where Deuce was visited by the darkest sorts of suspicions about his old runninmate. If that rep for example thought to meet with Deuce, why shouldn't he've done the same with Sloat, maybe with more fruitful results? Maybe Sloat, so afraid for his life, had made some kind of deal with the pursuers. "Sure," Deuce could hear him confessing, "I wanted to kill the old bastard right away, but Deuce—I don't want to go blamin now, but he might've lost his nerve some . . . don't know, somehow one morning, we woke up, over in the Dolores there, and Traverse was gone, and Deuce didn't look that upset, and we agreed to tell you folks the old man was dead. But he wasn't, understand what I'm saying?"

"I think we grasp your import, Mr. Fresno."

IN ANY CASE it was all getting too complicated to last, and the day finally did come when Sloat rode off up the trail headed vaguely south, the air unnaturally still that day, the dust he raised behind him refusing to settle, only growing thicker, until it seemed he had transmogrified into a creature of dust miles long, crawling away, Deuce leaning on the fence watching the dusty departure for the better part of an hour, silent for days after. . . .

With just the two of them now, Deuce went into a period of no sleep or too little. Kept waking up all through the night. Woke once one midnight with no sources of light in the sky, some malodorous evil heap of slag from the processing of moon-chaste silver their night's bed, to see close beside him a luminous face suspended above where her own would have to be, would have to, for this spectre floated high, too high, off the ground, or where the ground was supposed to be. Nor was it exactly her face, either. Because it did not reflect light, as from skies or hearthsides, but emitted its own, was marked by that clear sense of a resource being recklessly spent, with nothing gotten back—an expression, you'd say, of sacrifice. Deuce didn't like that, didn't want sacrifices, for they were never in his plans, nor in any cards he knew how to play.

After Webb was buried, and Reef had gone his way, Frank, fearing for his own safety, had glided back down to Golden on winds of inertia, considered asking around to see if anybody was looking for him but thought he knew the answer to that one. Being at the time young and unaware of how to proceed on anything but nerve, he stayed just long enough to gather up his gear and get on the electric down to Denver. Over the next year, he went through a number of disguises, including mustaches, beards, haircuts from some of the city's finest hotel barbers, but about all that stuck was a change of hat to something more narrow-brim and with the deepening color of passage down what seemed to him was becoming a long, embittered trail.

Soon he began to notice a pattern of approach—middle-ranking managers, urban in style with something also of the look of mine inspectors to them, offering to buy drinks, sliding into some vacant seat at a card table, eyeing Frank as if he was supposed to know what they meant. At first he thought it was about Reef, that these customers had been hired to track his brother down and wanted information. But that rapidly turned out not to be the case. One way or another, the conversation, when there was any, came around to matters of employment. Was he working, and who would that be for, and was he looking to change jobs and so forth. Slowly—not being much in the intuitive line, as at least a dozen women by then were happy to remind him—he figured out that these men were repping for the Vibe Corp. or its dependencies, and so his immediate response was invariably fuck this, though he was careful never to betray any annoyance. "All fairly jake as of right now," he learned to smile with every appearance of sincerity. "You have a business card? Soon as the need arises I'll sure be in touch."

Cautiously, he began to ask around about Webb's case. Not much luck. Not even much of a case anymore. Kept trying the Miners' Federation office for a while, but nobody would admit to knowing anything, and it hadn't taken Frank long to wear out his welcome.

Strange. You'd think they'd've been a little more forthcoming up on Arapahoe, but seemed like they had their important chores to run, time flowed along, new troubles every day, too many to keep up with, was how they saw it.

He was no detective, and had not spent much time investigating, but from keeping his ears open up and down the street, he could not escape a suggestion that Vibe Corp., who had spirited away his kid brother Kit, was also behind Webb Traverse's murder. This complicated for him any question of a serious future as a mine engineer, at least in the U.S. Maybe he'd have to think about going abroad. Every hiring office Frank walked into this side of the Rockies had heard of him, knew of Scarsdale Vibe's ample-spirited offers, and wondered why Frank wasn't at least a Vibe regional executive by now. How was Frank supposed to explain? The man might have had my father wiped away, carelessly as a wet ring on a bar top, and I am reluctant to accept his charity? Of course they thought they knew the whole story already, and were stunned at the Christian daring of Scarsdale's gesture to Frank, seeing that custom and usage in the mountains at this time would have been to see him drygulched as swiftly as possible, just in case of Anarchism in the blood or something like that. The New York industrialist was rising above these sordid matters of kinship and revenge—why couldn't Frank? Who could understand ingratitude like that? And what they could not understand, they were not about to hire any source of.

It sure soured him on silver and gold. He found himself after a while avoiding them altogether. He told himself he was just being practical. He'd seen too much misery from the ups and downs of both metals, especially after Repeal in '93. The table of elements was full of other possibilities, "the weeds of mineralogy," as one of his professors used to say, "just sitting there, part of the Creation, waiting for somebody to figure out how they can be made useful."

Which was how he began to work with less glamorous elements, such as zinc, and as a result spending more time in Lake County than he'd ever expected to.

Leadville was well past its glory days, into the post-Repeal era, no longer Haw Tabor's town, though the widow, already legend, still kept holed up at the Matchless workings with a firearm she had no hesitation in discharging at anybody who came too close, and there lingered some old numinous, center-of-the-world willingness to raise species of hell that hadn't been invented yet. Interest had shifted from silver over to zinc—there was a God-honest Zinc Rush on, in fact, the best-priced ore to be dug out of there at the moment, surpassing the value of gold and silver combined. Seems some bright engineer had invented a way to reprocess the waste heaps from those old pre-Repeal silver mines, so that some concentrating mills were realizing zinc content as high as 45 percent. The procedure up here with ordinary local zinc blende had been straightforward—first you got the sulfur to go off by roasting the blende to zinc oxide, and then you reduced the oxide to zinc metal. But the slag in Leadville, towering in black heaps all over town, not to mention covering the streets and alleyways, was an exotic and largely unknown mixture of drosses, scums, glances, pyrites, and other compounds of copper, arsenic, antimony, bismuth, and something the miners were calling "Molly-be-damned"—different elements came off at different temperatures, so there were matters of distillation to address. They loomed out there in black mystery above the bright interiors and the faro players and insatiably desired girls, and sometimes shadowy figures could be seen kneeling, reaching out to touch one of these slag piles, reverently as if, like some counter-Christian Eucharist, it represented the body of an otherworldly beloved.

"Little like alchemy," it seemed to Wren Provenance, a girl anthropologist a year out of Radcliffe College back east, with whom Frank had become unexpectedly entangled.

"Yeahp. Worthless sludge into foldin money."

"Centuries from now those heaps will still be there, and somebody will happen along and stare up at them and begin to wonder. Maybe take them for structures of some kind, government buildings, temples, maybe. Ancient mysteries."

"Pyramids of Egypt."

She nodded. "That shape is common to a lot of the old cultures. Secret wisdom—different details, but the structure underneath is always the same."

Frank and Wren had met up one Saturday night in Denver in a variety saloon. A Negro spoons-and-banjo act was racketing around up front. She was with some college acquaintances, including a couple of Harvard wisemen who wanted to go visit a Chinese saloon over in the Sons of Heaven section of town. To Frank's delight, Wren declined. "And don't forget to try some of that Bear Paw in Octopus Ink, fellas!" He stood waving till the cab disappeared around the corner.

When they were alone, "What I really need to see," Wren confided, "is the Denver Row, and a house of ill fame. Will you escort me?"

"A what? Oh." Frank recognizing in her hazel eyes a spark that he should know better by now than to be encouraging, and behind which was an inclination to shadow he could've even then been paying more attention to. "And . . . that's strictly for scientific reasons, o' course."

"Anthropological as can be."

Off they went to Market Street and Jennie Rogers's House of Mirrors. Wren was immediately surrounded by half a parlorful of girls and gently led upstairs. A little later he happened to look in a doorway, and there she was, not much on, what there was all black, tightly laced, stockings askew, standing in an open polyhedral of mirrors, examining herself from all the angles available. Transformed.

"Interesting turnout, Wren."

"All that riding and climbing and outdoor activities, my, it's a relief to be back in stays again."

The girls were amused.

"Look at this, you've got him going now."

"Mind if we borrow him for a while?"

"Oh," as he was dragged away, "but I thought *we* were fixin to—" unable to stop staring, or as he might have put it "gazing," at the intriguingly gussied-up Wren for as long as he could.

"Don't worry, Frankie, she'll be here when you get back," said Finesse.

"We'll take good care of her," Fame assured him with a wicked smile. Which got Wren to detach from her self-admiring long enough to turn and seek the girls' eyes, with one of those looks of insincere dismay you saw in erotic illustrations from time to time.

When she showed up again she was in yet another scandalous change of underlinen, holding a bourbon bottle by the neck and puffing on the stub of a Havana. A dress cavalry helmet with a gold eagle, braid, and tassels rested at some careless angle among her untended tresses.

"Havin' fun?"

Her upper lids would not take the trouble to allow much sparkling eyeball to flash his way. She spoke in a high drawl from which the effects of opium, he guessed, couldn't be ruled out altogether. "Fascinating material . . . volumes. . . . Some of these stockmen, my goodness." Then, seeming to recognize him, she smiled slowly. "Yes and your name came up."

"Uh-oh."

"They said you're far too sweet."

"Me? They just never see me in a bad mood, 's all. Some kind of red streaks on your stockings there."

"Lip rouge." If he was expecting a blush from her, he didn't get one. Instead she looked boldly back, eye to eye. He noticed the scarlet contours of her own lips were blurred and the kohl around her eyes had run down here and there, as if from tears.

Fame came sashaying in, in some incomprehensible though wicked peignoir, glided up behind, slipped an arm around Wren's waist, and the girls snuggled together in an undeniably charming tableau.

"Just can't stay away," Wren was whispering, ". . . you've simply ruined me for everyday bourgeois sexuality. Whatever am I to do?"

Having come west to search for Aztlán, the mythic ancestral home of the Mexican people, which she believed to be located somewhere around the Four Corners, Wren found more than she'd expected to. Maybe too much. She had the look of a trooper back off a long campaign in which more than once matters of life and death had arisen—her own, those of others, eventually a mingling of selves that had her insomniac and, to Frank at least, making no sense beyond occasionally scaring the shit out of him.

He had a passing acquaintance with the Mancos and McElmo country, but not much notion of its ancient past.

"Well, Frank, it's quite . . . unhappy is the best you could call it."

"You don't just mean Mormons, I guess."

"Hallucinatory country and cruel, not hard to understand that Mormons might have found it congenial enough to want to settle, but this is much older—thirteenth century anyway. There were perhaps tens of thousands of people back then, living all through that region, prosperous and creative, when suddenly, within one generation—overnight as these things go—they fled, in every appearance of panic terror, went up the steepest cliffsides they could find and built as securely as they knew how defenses against . . . well, something."

"There's some Ute stories," Frank recalled, "other tribes is how I always heard it."

She shrugged. "Incursion from the north—foragers at first, then all-out invasion forces who brought their stock and families with them. Maybe so. But this is something else, beyond that. Here." She had piles of photographs, Brownie snapshots most of them, taken up and down the canyons, including, carved into the rock, images of creatures unfamiliar to Frank.

"What in the . . . hay-ull?" Painted as well as carved here were people with wings . . . human-looking bodies with snake and lizard heads, above them unreadable apparitions, trailing what might have been fire in what might have been the sky.

"Yes." He looked over, and whatever it was there in her eyes now, he wished he'd seen it sooner.

"What?"

"We don't know. Some of us suspect, but it's too terrible. Not to mention . . ." She found, stared at, reluctantly handed over one of the plates.

"Old bones."

"Human bones. And if you look carefully, the longer ones have been deliberately broken . . . broken into. As if for the marrow inside."

"Cannibals, cannibal Indians?"

She shrugged, her face showing the onset of a sorrow he knew he couldn't help much with. "Nobody knows. Harvard professors, you'd expect more . . . but all they do is theorize and argue. The people who fled to the cliffs might even have done this to themselves. Out of fear. Something frightened them so much that this might've been the only way they knew to keep it from them."

"It wanted them to—"

"They may never have known what it . . . 'wanted.' Not really."

"And you—" It was all he could do not to reach for her, gather her into some kind of perimeter. But the moisture in her eyes was shining like steel, not dew, and nothing about her trembled.

"I was out there for a year. Too long. After a while it seeps into you. Somebody else now is writing up the report, career expectations will be a factor. I'm just one of the hired hands that dug in the dirt, climbed those red rocks and benches and carried the gear, got infected with the insanity of the place, and they know enough now not to pay any attention to hysterical girl graduates. It all has to be dated more closely than it is anyway. Whoever the people were, they only lasted a few years up in those cliffs. After that, nobody knows. Maybe they kept going. If they were the same ones who made the exodus southward from Aztlán and became the Aztecs, that might have something to do with those human sacrifices the Aztecs became famous for."

ONE NIGHT THEY WERE on Seventeenth Street again. Bartenders were busy with slings, sours, highballs, and fizzes. Republicans and Democrats got into political discussions which proceeded inevitably to fisticuffs. Wren was obliged to remove a real-estate agent's hand from her bosom with a steak fork.

At the Albany the bar mirror was legendary, 110 feet long, an animated mural of Denver's nighttime history. "Like readin the paper," said Booth Virbling, a crime reporter of Frank's acquaintance.

"Except for Booth here's stuff, which tends to be more back in the toilet area," Frank explained. "First time I seen you outside of Gahan's, what's up?"

"City politics the way it is, sure to be a flagrant atrocity any minute. Oh and somebody's been around looking for you."

"I owe em money?"

A cautionary glance at Wren.

"She knows everything, Booth, what is it?"

"One of Bulkley Wells's people."

"All the way down from Telluride just to visit?"

"You weren't fixin to go up there, I hope."

"Pretty dangerous town these days is it, Booth?"

"Your brother thought so."

"You've seen him?"

"Somebody did, out by Glenwood Springs. Reef was flush, but downhearted. All I heard." He spotted a principal witness in last year's notorious Ice Saw murder trial and went over to have a chat.

"What was that about?" Wren said.

Long habits of holding back information, especially from young women one was currently sparking, usually kicked in about this point. Once, out in the Uncompahgre Plateau, Frank, riding back from Gunnison or someplace, spotted a single storm cloud, dark and compact, miles away, and knew despite the prevailing sunlight and immensity of sky that no matter how he changed his direction now, he was going to cross paths with that cloud, and sure enough, less than an hour later it all grew dark as midnight, and there he was getting soaked and frozen and being momentarily deafened by lightning bolts that hit blasting all around, leaning along his horse's neck to reassure him that everything was just peachy, though being a range horse the critter had seen far worse and was presently trying to reassure Frank. Tonight in the Albany, Frank could see that Wren had arrived exactly here after unnumbered miles and Stations of the Cross—in the light off the great mirror her face was a queerly unshadowed celestial blue, that of a searcher, it seemed to Frank, who had come as far as she must to ask what he would be least willing to answer. He understood that there were such presences abroad in the world, and that although one may live an entire life without intersecting one, if it should happen, it became a solemn obligation to speak when spoken to.

He exhaled at length, looked her flat in the eye. "Wouldn't be my job customarily, see, it's for Reef to do, but there's been no word for a while, and well, Glenwood Springs, maybe he's been chased off of this and he's back to dealing faro someplace, showing hurdy girls the sagebrush in the moonlight, no argument, but there's just a point where it moves on to the next in line, and then if I don't do it either, then somebody'll have to go fetch Kit back out of that East Coast collegekid life he's all involved in, you'd know better'n me, but I'd really rather see Kit spared that trouble, for he's a good youngster but a bad shot, and in the real likely event they got him first, why, that'd be one more crime to square, see, and the job likely wouldn't ever get done."

She was gazing at him more directly than usual. "Where are they likely to be, then? Your gunmen."

"Best I've been able to learn is it's a pair of seminotorious gunnies named Deuce Kindred and Sloat Fresno, who likely hired on with the Mine Owners Association up in Telluride. And now according to old Booth, somebody from up there says they want to see me. Connection, you think?"

"Of course that's where you're headed."

"It's the last place I saw my Ma and my sister. Maybe they're still up there. I ought to have a look in anyway."

"It's a son and brother's job. Speaking anthropologically."

"How about you, were you fixin to go back down the McElmo?"

She frowned. "Not much future there. The place to be now, I'm told, is the South Pacific islands."

"Go specialize in cannibals, huh."

"That sounds funnier than it is."

Not really wanting to ask, "You want to come up to Telluride with me?"

Well, technically she was smiling, though it didn't quite get as far as her eyes. "I guess not, Frank."

He had the grace not to look too relieved. "I could've used the extra brain muscle was all I meant, for it's sure a two-faced town, deadfalls everyplace you step, ugliest and longest-runnin poker game in Creation, too much money changing hands too fast, and you never know who to trust."

"You weren't intending to go galloping in waving a pistol and demanding information, I hope."

"Why, how do you usually do it?"

"If it were I? Pretend I'm there on business, use a different name—the men you're after might have made enemies in town, maybe even among the people they were working for. If you kept your ears open, sooner or later you'd hear something."

"What you folks call 'research,' right? Hit all the saloons, cribs, card rooms, and parlor houses, hell, I couldn't keep that up more'n a week before somebody'd be on to me."

"Maybe you're a better actor than you think."

"Means staying sober for longer than I'd like."

"In that case we'd better get in some drinking, wouldn't you say?"

After passengers for Telluride had changed at Ridgway Junction, the little stub train climbed up over Dallas Divide and rolled down again to Placerville and the final haul up the valley of the San Miguel, through sunset and into the uncertainties of night. The high-country darkness, with little to break it but starlight off the flow of some creek or a fugitive lamp or hearth up in a miner's cabin, soon gave way to an unholy radiance ahead, in the east. It was the wrong color for a fire, and daybreak was out of the question, though the end of the world remained a possibility. It was in fact the famous electric street-lighting of Telluride, first city in the U.S. to be so lit, and Frank recalled that his kid brother, Kit, had worked for a while on the project of bringing the electricity for it up from Ilium Valley.

The great peaks first sighted yesterday across the Uncompahgre Plateau, snaggletoothing in a long line up over the southern horizon, now announced themselves at every hand, fearsomely backlit, rearing before the gazes of the passengers, who had begun to rubberneck out at the spreading radiance, chattering like a carful of tourists from back east.

Before long the trail up the valley beside the tracks was all bustling, like streets of a town—ore and supply wagons and strings of mules, the curses of the skinners riddling the evening, often in languages no one in the smoky little car recognized. Beside the tracks at one bend stood a local lunatic, who you could easily swear'd been there for years, screaming at the trains. "To-Hell-you-ride! Goin' to-Hell-you-ride! Beware, ladies and gents! Inform your conductor! Warn the engineer! ain't too late to turn back!" As meanwhile the luminosity ahead of them—whose sharp-edged beams now obscured many familiar stars—slowly grew brighter than the oil lamps inside the coach, and they came rolling into the simple narrowed grid of a town that seemed to've been shipped in all at the same time and squeezed onto the valley floor.

Frank got off and walked past a line of drovers who'd come into town just to stand there and wait to see the train, which now sat breathing and cooling, as brake and footplate men came and went with wrenches, crowbars, grease guns, and oilcans.

Ordinarily the most commonsensical of persons, now in this soulless incandescence he felt rushed in upon from every direction by omens of violence, all directed at him. Beards unknown for weeks to razor-steel, bared yellow eyeteeth, eyes rimmed in the hot flush of some unframable desire . . . Breaking into a sweat of apprehension, Frank understood that he was exactly where he should not be. He took a frantic look back toward the depot, but the train was already backing slowly away down the valley again. Like it or not, he had joined the company of those who follow their hunches directly to bottoms of barrels and ends of lines, up against this wall of thirteen- and fourteen-thousand-foot peaks and a level of hatred between the miners' union and the mine owners, dangerously high even for Colorado, that you could smell.

The other smell, which Frank found he had to light a cigar to cover up, was what the town got its name from, silver here being usually found along with telluride ore, and tellurium compounds, as Frank had learned at mine school, being among the most rotten-smelling in nature, worse than the worst boardinghouse fart ever let loose, that worked its way into your clothes, your skin, your spirit, believed here to rise by way of long-deserted drifts and stopes, from the everyday atmosphere of Hell itself.

THAT EVENING AT SUPPER in the hotel, through the window, he watched a troop of state Guardsmen on their way down Mainstreet heading down the valley west of town. Before them, on foot, stumbled a small collection of dirty men in ragged clothes. Even in the beaten dirt, there was a measured intention to the massed hoofbeats that made Frank wonder about local opportunities for refuge, though other diners were taking it pretty nonchalant. It seemed this was a vagging bee, in which the troopers went after any out-of-work miners unlucky enough to be visible and ran them in for "vagrancy."

"Sure enough military in town now."

"And with old Hair-Trigger Bob out there on the prowl, hell he's a one-man army already."

"Would that," Frank pretended to inquire, "be the famous gunfighter Bob Meldrum? here in Telluride?"

The men squinted at him, though in a friendly enough way, maybe because Frank's failure to shave that morning was just able to dispel any impression of excessive greenness.

"That's him, *joven.* Terrible times in these mountains, and nothing about to ease off neither, any day soon. Bob's just in his heaven, up here."

The others joined in. "He's pretty deaf, but you don't necessarily want to be yelling at him, nor try to guess which ear'd be better to aim for."

"Few things in life more dangerous than a deaf gunhand, 'cause he'll tend ever to err on the side of triggerplay, y'see, just in case he might've missed something specially provoking you might've said. . . ."

"Time he got Joe Lambert up at Tomboy in the stamp mill? Perfect Meldrum conditions, stamps all going like the hammers of Hell, nobody could hear nothing to begin with. 'Hands up'? Oh sure, thanks, Bob."

"Ask me, he hears just fine—only the way a snake does, through his skin."

"Hope you've brought something weightier than a pistol along, young fellow."

"All raggin' aside, son, I hope whatever your business, you at least know the man to see in Telluride."

"Ellmore Disco is the name I got," said Frank.

"That's him. You scheduled your appointment well ahead, I trust."

"Appointment . . ."

"Looky here, another one thought he'd waltz right in."

"Lot of people need to see Ellmore, son."

Some believed Ellmore Disco was Mexican, some said he'd come from even farther away, Finland or someplace like that. Not overall what you'd call a natty dresser, he concentrated his few dudish impulses on headgear, tending to fancy black beavers with snakeskin bands and a pencil roll to the brim, that you had to send to Denver for and then wait a few months. The only people he was ever documented to've shot at were those who, either by word or deed, disrespected one of his hats, and some of that behavior had certainly been provoking enough. Once at C. Hall & Co. up at Leadville, in the days when it was still Leadville, while Ellmore was out taking a short piss break from a hitherto friendly game of Seven-Toed Pete, a frolicsome shift boss had thought to fill his Stetson, trustingly left unattended, with jellied turtle consommé, never a favorite of Ellmore's to begin with. "Well, say!" he declared upon his return, "here's an awkward situation!" The miner must have sensed something ominous in this, for he began to creep toward the exit. Next thing anybody knew, both parties were out the door, and Chestnut Street had grown lively with detonation. The prankster escaped into open country at full express velocity, despite a flesh wound in the caboose and a couple of holes through the crown of his own hat, which seemed to've been a particular target of Ellmore's wrath.

Many having witnessed this tête-à-tête, at the next hat incident of course Ellmore was now obliged to behave the same way, if not a little worse. "Yet I'm basically a tranquil fellow," he continued to insist, though nobody paid that much heed. To strangers he was Ellmore the Evil, to friends an engaging enough customer despite these hat-related spells, whose unpredictability did nothing to harm his success in business. These days you'd find E. Disco & Sons to be the thrivingest enterprise between Grand Junction and the Sangre de Cristos. The store's secret seemed to be in its wide range of goods and prices, so that on any one day you were apt to observe managerial folk in lacquered silk hats milling on the floor with down-and-outers in ancient wool widebrims, all shiny with grease and battered from the day, looking for just about anything—bowlers and deerstalkers, mantillas, lorgnettes, walking sticks, ear trumpets, spats, driving-coats, watch-chain ornaments, chemisettes and combinations, Japanese parasols, electrical bathtubs, patent devices for thunderstorm-proof mayonnaise, cherry-pitting machines, drill bits and carbide lamps, ladies' bandoliers rigged out expressly for .22-caliber rounds, not to mention bolts of jaconet, pompadour sateen, tartalan, dimity, grenadine, crepe lissé, plain, striped, or in Oriental prints direct from Liberty's of London.

Frank arrived around midmorning and found a skylit interior surrounded by a mezzanine, the ironwork painted a light greenish gray. Ellmore's office was sort of cantilevered out over a main floor briskly echoing with shop-noise and giving off odors of fuller's earth, gun oil, and local citizenry, who were everywhere.

"The boss has been up to his ears in Texans all morning," he was informed. "See over back of Horse Supplies there? you'll find an entrance to the saloon next door, if time starts hanging heavy." Frank noticed how this clerk, mild enough in manner, was packing one of the more gigantic-size models of Colt pistol.

"Thanks, maybe I'll just sit and breathe and let the altitude do it for me cheap."

The office, when he finally got nodded in, was oversupplied with saloon furniture in the Grand Rapids style, bought for haul-away costs down in Cortez after that notorious night the old Palace got shot up by the Four Corners Boys. A studio photo said to be of Mrs. Disco directed a lidded smile at visitors.

Frank was gazing out the window over the busy main thoroughfare when Ellmore came barreling in.

"Caught me admiring your view."

"You're lucky to see it while it's boom times, for when these veins give out at last, there'll be nothing here to sell *but* the scenery, which means herds of visitors from places that don't have any—Texans, for example. That side the street you're lookin at's what we call the Sunny Side, you see those little miners' shacks over there? Too narrow for any but the undernourished to stand, let alone turn around, in—well someday each of those will be going for a million apiece U.S., maybe two, and up. Laugh if you like, everybody else does, one more Telluride jocularity, blame it on the altitude. But just wait. You heard it here first."

"Man of vision."

"Hell, Anarchists ain't the only ones with ideas about the future." Ellmore Disco did not appear to be of either Mexican or Finnish descent, at least not when, as now, he was smiling—more like music-hall Chinese, maybe, the way his eyes retreated into protective pouches, leaving the observer with a ruinous C major ("or as they say in this town, 'A miner'") octave on some abandoned upright, interrupted by a matched pair of winking gold canines that seemed longer and more saber-shaped than necessary, even for eating in mining-town steak houses.

He gestured now with a coffee cup that seemed a constant companion and, so rapidly it could've been spoken in a single breath, announced, "As to an interview with Cap'n Wells—I am in sympathy, sir, though far from being the Cap'n's social secretary, yet I know it's a common enough visitor's desire, for the fame of Bulkley Wells has reached around the globe, or damn near, this week for example a delegation in all the way from Tokyo, Japan, under orders from the Emperor himself, if ya don't meet with the Captain, boys, why don't bother coming back, basically, 'n' then o' course it's out with that wackyzacky they all pack for committin their hari-kari with, you can imagine how old Cal Rutan would enjoy an incident like 'at in *his* county. But it's how desperate some folks'll get, and not always foreigners neither, so what I must know from you now, is how unhappy are *you* likely to become, sir, if, heaven forfend, you should somehow fail to see the Cap'n this trip."

After making sure Ellmore was done, Frank said, "Busy gent, I expect."

"You'd be needing the good offices of brother Meldrum, not to mention assorted of *his* pardners to get past. . . . You mentioned mine work—what kind do you do, any blasting ever come into it for instance?"

"Some maybe."

They exchanged a cool, solid look then. Ellmore nodded, as if something had just occurred to him. "Nothing up on ground level though."

"First time I've been taken for a bomber."

"What's this here, indignation?"

"Not in particular. Kind of flattering, in its way."

"Engineer can't plead he don't know one end of a dynamite stick from the other, you can appreciate."

"Sets any number of dogs to barking. Sure. Should've just said pastry chef or something."

Ellmore spread his hands as if in innocence.

Frank swatted away an imaginary fly. "To be straight with you sir, gold's not much in my line, fact is I'm more of a zinc man, but—"

"Zinc, well that case, no offense but why ain't you up in Lake County, then?"

"Thanks, Leadville's a regular stop on my circuit ride, but this week, well what I've got's a new system for concentrating gold ore—"

"Only speaking for Tomboy and the Smuggler o' course, but they're content 'th what they got. Stamp it down to mush, run it over some quicksilver on a plate, they say it works good."

"Amalgamation process. Traditional, pays off nicely enough. Sure. But now this set-up of mine—"

"My guess is Cap'n Wells'll ask how much will it cost, and then say no anyway. But you go have a word with Bob, who's not that hard to find, though approachin' him can be fraught with danger, and no time of day sad to say's any better than another. . . . Oh look here, it's lunchtime now. Come down to Lupita's, where the menudo can't be beat, she soaks em tripes in tequila overnight, is her secret," pausing by a gigantic elk-antler hat rack with hats occupying every point, to select a gray sombrero with a band of silver medallions inlaid with lapis and jasper, Zuñi work by the look of it. "One of her secrets anyway. We'll pick up my boy Loomis on the way," who turned out to be the .44-packing clerk who had greeted Frank earlier.

They exited out the back, into Pacific Street, threading their way among ox and mule teams, piano-box buggies and three-spring phaetons, buckboards and big transfer wagons carrying loads between the train depot and the mines and shops, riders in dusters stiff and spectral with lowland alkali, Chinese pulling handcarts piled high with laundry—Ellmore waving, pointing his finger humorously pistol-like and occasionally grabbing hold of somebody to transact a moment's business. Seemed everybody knew him. Most were careful to compliment him on his choice of hat.

Lupita's was on a patch of hardpan tucked in between Pacific and the San Miguel River, up here more like Creek, with a collection of plank tables and long benches painted a sky blue not observed anywhere else in town, and set beneath a rusted shed roof held up by aspen poles. Cooking aromas began a half mile before you got there. Gigantic chicharrones were piled like hides at a trading post. *Ristras* of dangerously dark purple chilies hung all about. At night they were said to glow in the dark. Clerks and cashiers, birds of the night but newly risen, stockmen from down the valley, Mexican laborers streaked with brickdust, skinners waiting for the train sat alongside Negro newsboys and wives in their best hats, all indiscriminately filling the benches, grabbing and gobbling like miners in a mess hall, or standing waiting either for a seat or for one of the kids working in the kitchen to fill their lunch pails or paper sacks with chicken tortas, venison tamales, Lupita's widely-known brain tacos, bottles of home-brewed beer, sixty-degree wedges of peach pie, so forth, to take along with them.

Frank, expecting more of a motherly figure, was surprised at the arrival of the taquería's fair eponym, a miniature tornado of gold-accented black and white, whirling in out of nowhere, pausing long enough to bestow Ellmore a kiss on the brow, which he scarcely had time to lift his hat for, and, just before vanishing again into the unstable weather of the kitchen in the back, singing over her shoulder, it seemed mischievously, *"Por poco te faltó La Blanca."*

"Oh, hay-ull," Ellmore with the onset of a worried look, "there goes the rest of *my* day, what's going on I don't know about, Loomis, that'd bring *her* down into town?"

"La Blanca," it turned out, was a local name for "Hair-Trigger Bob" Meldrum's wife—folks agreed it should be "wife," given the dark history of Bob's displeasure—named for a white horse of supernatural demeanor she was always seen to ride, usually sticking to trails up in Savage Basin and the high passes more invisible than not and known best to such as the infamous Hole-in-the-Wall Gang, keeping scrupulously her distance, lips so bloodless in that windy transparency they seemed to disappear, leaving her black-fringed eyes the only feature you'd recall after she'd gone by. According to visitors, Texans and so forth, horses didn't even belong up on slopes like those, for the grades were too drastic, too sudden, too many thousand-foot chasms and the like, no way usually to switchback across what would often turn into plain damn faces of *cliffs,* obliging you to just get the deed done, straight down or straight up, praying for no ice patches, and a horse mountain-wise enough to judge the desperate declivity, Indian-pony blood being in such cases a clear preference. She inhabited this geometry of fear so effortlessly that Bob might almost've found her once upon a time in a story-kingdom of glass mountains every bit as peculiar as the San Juans, and trailside poets speculated that with all her solitary ranging—black cape billowing, hat down on her back, and the light of Heaven on her hair, flowered silk neckerchiefs Bob bought for her up in Montrose guttering like cold flames, in blizzards or spring-avalanche weather or the popcorn snows of August—she was riding out a homesickness too passionate for these realms of ordinary silver and gold to know much about, much less measure up to.

They lived up near the Tomboy mine, in a cabin uptrail from the mine tailings, but kept to themselves, not that too many even got to see them together, which no doubt encouraged a lot of romantic gas, even from those who hated Bob from hat to spurs but had seen her at least, fatally, once, out on some one or other of those destinationless rides. Bob these days, besides working as Buck Wells's representative on Earth, was also day guard at Tomboy, up before first light and out into the Basin, his eyes—some recalled them as "dark," while others said they changed to pale gray just before he intended to shoot his man—sharper than usual to make up for his allegedly bad hearing, sweeping ever to and fro, vanning everything down to pebble size and below, tuned for trouble of all kinds, which maybe unavoidably would have to include that La Blanca. Many reckless and basically thick-headed boys around town liked to imagine they knew what she was after, which in their dreams always took some form of relief from her deaf runt of a cabinmate, who didn't, besides, look all that tough, fourteen or whatever many notches it was supposed to be on his pistol. Hell, anybody can cut a notch, cheaper than cheap talk, ain't it?

"Say, but that Hair-Trigger Bob, now, he don't give too much of a hoot about who lives, who don't, nothing like 'at. . . ."

"Maybe what he don't understand is neither do I."

"Common saloon talk," Ellmore peering briefly at Frank as if he just might be another of these junior Romeos. "Listen, Loomis, now, this is getting me puzzled, I fear. Is Bob likely to approve of his missus all the way down the hill here? We need a handle on this fairly quick. You see that Loopy anyplace?"

Frank surfacing from his giant bowlful of fiery tripe, "This Mrs. Meldrum—she's troublesome?"

"*Joven,*" mumbled Ellmore through his food, "nobody can tell you much about her for certain. Now *trouble,* o' course . . . well there's always 'at Bob. . . ." His usually direct gaze was wandering out in the direction of Bear Creek, and his Oriental mask of a face could not have been tagged just then as undisturbed.

Lupita appeared with a florally painted bowl of cornmeal masa cradled in the crook of one elbow, swiftly taking from it and patting handfuls of dough one at a time into perfect paper-thin tortillas she then tossed spinning back into the little kitchen onto a sheet-metal *comal* salvaged after a memorable windstorm up by Lizard Head Pass to bake for a minute before being removed to a piece of apron held ready for the purpose, meantime informing Ellmore, "I don't think she was looking for you."

"You see her husband today?"

"I heard he had to go somewhere in a hurry. You don't look much like a man in love."

"In the soup, more like. How you say, *en la sopa*."

"Of course she's young," said Lupita. "It's the age when we all do those crazy things."

"Can't remember."

"*Pobrecito.*" Off she whirled again, singing just like a bird.

Frank became aware that Ellmore had been watching him with an interest deeper than sociability could account for. When he saw Frank looking back, he flashed a disingenuous gold eyetooth. "How's that menudo? See some of the old snot runnin' out there."

"Didn't notice," Frank passing a shirtsleeve beneath his nose.

"Lip's already gone too numb to feel it," advised Loomis. "Eat here for long, you'll need to grow a mustache, soak some of that up."

"You've noticed how the smaller a chili pepper gets, the hotter it usually is, right? First thing you learn. Well, these that Loopy's using are small. I mean *small, joven*."

"Well Ellmore, how . . . how small's that?"

"What about . . . invisible?"

"Nobody has ever . . . *seen* these chilies, but folks here still put them in Mexican recipes? How do they know how many to put?"

The company found the question stimulating. "You crazy?" hollered Ellmore. "*One's* enough to kill ya!"

"Plus everybody 'thin a hundred-yards radius!" added Loomis.

"'Cept for Bob, o' course, he eats em like peanuts. Says it calms him down."

BY THE TIME he came creaking back to his rooms at the Sheridan, after stopping down in the bar for a steak whose volume he estimated to run above half a cubic foot, Frank had contracted a case of the Rampaging Meldrumitis, having heard of little else all day. Captain Bulkley Wells stayed inaccessible as ever, pursuing his busy schedule—in London, perhaps, visiting his tailor, or off in the Argentine purchasing polo ponies, or touring, why not, on some other inhabited world altogether. And so far, as if they were words one did not use in front of the designated innocent, nothing even remotely to do with Deuce Kindred or Sloat Fresno.

Frank was able to keep his eyes open long enough to check his bed with a miner's gad and douse the electric lamp, but not quite to get both boots off, before drifting into his standard trailside slumber, less than five minutes of which had passed before his door was assaulted and the pleasures of oblivion postponed by some god-awful thumping and bellowing. "You gonna get your wife-grabbing, piss-yellow, slant-eyed ass out here, or am I gonna have to come in there?" inquired an unhappy voice.

"Sure thing," yawned Frank, in an amiable tone he hoped would not betray the briskness with which he was attending to the cylinder of his Smith & Wesson's.

"Well, which one is it? Speak up, I don't hear too good, and what I can't hear makes me very upset."

"I believe the door's open," Frank shouted. In the instant, it was. There stood a diminutive figure in a black hat, shirt, and gauntlets, Bob Meldrum unmistakably, with a mustache so wide Frank could swear its owner had to turn a little sideways to get through the doorway, and a halo of McBryan's which, like his fame, preceded him.

"Oh, say. What would that be, now, some li'l Ladies' Friend, I'll bet, oh? and nickel-plated too! My, but she's considerable pretty."

"Fact, it's a .38," said Frank. "Police model, though I have filed it down some, maybe a bit too much here and there, for it won't always stay cocked just as I'd like. Sure hope that won't be a problem?"

"You speak good English, for some got-damned opium-smoking son of a bitch don't even particularly look Jap."

"Just 'Frank' is O.K. Could be you've got the wrong room?"

"Could be you're fucking my wife in here and lying out of your ass?"

"Never been that crazy—maybe brother Disco's been misinforming you?"

"Oh, hell, you're the kid engineer," his eyes, to Frank's relief, beginning to grow less pale.

"Yes, and now, sir, I'll bet you would be . . . Mr. Meldrum, am I right?" Trying not too obviously to shout into either of his ears.

"True, God help me, too true," the darkly rigged-out gunslinger collapsing with an emotional sigh onto the settee. "You think it's easy being a hardcase in this town, with Butch Cassidy always coming up as a point of comparison? Hell, what'd he ever do, rode up the valley on some damned trick animal, pulled a gun, took the ten thousand dollars, rode out again, just like eatin a cherry pie, but years pass, legends o' th' West keep growing, folks mutter under their mustache when they think you can't hear, 'Well, he's mean but he sure ain't no Butch,' and how to hell you think that makes me feel? Nothing in here to drink neither, I'll bet."

"Suppose we go out anyplace you like, and you allow me to stand you a drink."

"Well *seguro,* but how's about you point that shined-up li'l 'sucker someplace else for a minute, my reputation and all?"

"Why, I'd almost forgotten. . . ." Feeling none too certain, Frank pocketed his revolver, expecting an immediate throwdown, but Bob seemed tranquil, for the moment anyway, going so far as to smile briefly, revealing a double array of gold dental crowns. Frank pretended to rare back as if bedazzled, shielding his eyes with a forearm. "Lot of bullion there."

"They were kind enough up at the mine to give me a price," Bob replied.

Bypassing the hotel's own genteel establishment, they headed for the Cosmopolitan Saloon and Gambling Club a short way down the street, where Bob was confident that people had the sense to leave him to drink in peace. "Now then," once they were set up with bottle and glasses, "had a nickel for every son of a bitch wanted to waste Cap'n Wells's time I'd be down in Denver highballing my way along Market Street, you take my meaning, and this whole godforsaken box canyon'd be all just a bad dream."

"Any chance of talking to him? Is he in town?"

Bob gave him a long, glitter-eyed once-over. "You just say what I think I heard? Wop anarchist sons of bitches rolling bombs at the man day in day out, stranger shows up askin' if he's 'in town'? why if I wa'n't so suspicious, I'd be laughing my ass off. Tell you what though, here's the very fella, Merle Rideout—he's amalgamator up at Little Hellkite, crazy as a bedbug 'th all them fumes and shit he breathes in all the time and twice on bullion day, but even so, why he might be willing to listen to some junior drummer try and talk him out of his job."

Merle Rideout was on his way down to one of the parlor houses but not at top speed. He allowed Frank to go into his pitch.

". . . And you no doubt heard of Mr. Edison's scheme down in Dolores using static electricity, though sad to say none too successfully—but now, my approach is different, uses *magnetism.* Back east in New Jersey, they've been pulling pyrites out of zinc blende with a Wetherill's magnet, supposed to be the strongest going—my rig's a variation on that, just a little sweetheart of a unit, and don't it have that Wetherill's all beat. And with the kind of electric current you can generate up in these parts—"

Merle was regarding Frank with a kindly enough expression, but one not inclined to be taken in. "Magnetic ore separation, yes indeed, fine for the less-critical mountainside audiences maybe, but having been around at least a magnet or two, I'm cautious is all. Tell you what though. Come on up the mine you get a chance, we'll talk. Tomorrow'd be good."

A silence abruptly fell, leaving for the moment only the electricity's hum. A group of men in enormous brand-new beaver sombreros had just entered the Cosmopolitan, chirping and singing in some foreign tongue. Each carried a pocket Kodak with its shutter ingeniously connected to a small magnesium flashlight, so as to synchronize the two. Shot-glasses halted halfway to mouths, the Negro shoeshine boy quit popping his rag, the Hieronymus wheel stopped short, and the ball took a bounce and then hung there in midair, just as if everything in the scene were trying its best to accommodate a photograph or two. Approaching Dieter the barkeep, the visitors, bowing one by one, began to gesture at various of the bottles stacked down at one end of the bar. Dieter, intimate with concoctions nobody'd even named yet, nodding in reply, reached, poured, and mixed, as conversation in the room resumed, folks having recognized the "Japanese trade delegation" Ellmore had mentioned to Frank earlier in the day, out now for a look at the nighttime sights of Telluride. Frank stopped staring just in time to observe Bob's eyes gone pale as summer sky above a ridgeline, and issuing from his ears twin jets of steam superheated enough to threaten the careful roll of his hatbrim. Unable to think of anything the irascible shootist might want to hear from him at the moment, Frank went to look instead into the possibilities of taking cover, noticing how others were doing the same.

"Well, Bob, which one of 'm d'you figure it is?" called out one of the regulars here, in an apparent belief that his advanced years would protect him from the wages of impertinence.

"Evenin Zack," screamed Bob, "frustratin as hell, ain't it, all these lookalikes, man hardly knows where to start shootin!"

"Say, and I sure don't see no Mizzus M. noplace, do you?" cried the heedless Zack, "maybe the one you're lookin for is *otherwise engaged—yeeeh*-heehheeh!"

"Course I could shoot you first, just to get sighted in," Bob supposed.

"Aw now, Bob—"

Fascinated, the Sons of Nippon had begun to gather about Bob in a semicircle, popping out to full length the bellows of their cameras, taking tentative aim, some even attempting to climb up on the billiard table to improve the angle of view, causing perplexity among those attempting to play on its surface. "Kid," neither of Bob's lips being seen to move, "that li'l *contraption* o' yours I was admiring earlier? d'you happen to have it handy, 'cause I may soon require your assistance, in a back-watching way, for this is making me begin to itch somewhat fierce, is the problem here?"

"I can talk a little of their lingo," Merle volunteered.

“Can you say, ‘I intend to kill all you sons of bitches one by one just so I don’t make no mistakes,’ something along those lines?”

“Let’s see, um . . . *Sumimasen,* folks, this here’s *Bobusan desu!*” Everybody bowed to Bob, who found himself hesitantly bowing back. *“Gonnusuringaa,”* Merle added, *“mottomo abunai desu!”*

“Aa!”

“Anna koto!”

All at once, magnesium flash-lights were exploding everywhere, each producing a column of thick white smoke whose orderly cylindrical ascent was immediately disarranged by attempts of customers, in some panic, to seek exit, the unexpected combination of brightness and opacity thus quickly spreading to fill every part of the saloon. Those who in their flight did not stumble over or into furniture soon collided with others, who felt obliged to collide back, and with interest. Peevishness grew general. Solid objects were soon moving through the fulgurescence invisibly and at high speed, with profanity being uttered at every hand, much of it in Japanese.

Frank decided to squat down by the end of the bar till the air cleared. He kept an ear out for Bob but in the uproar couldn’t be too sure of anybody’s voice. The loss of clarity and scale in the room was producing, for many, strange optical illusions, common among them that of a vast landscape swept by an unyielding fog. It became possible to believe one had been spirited, in the swift cascade of light-flashes, to some distant geography where creatures as yet unknown thrashed about, howling affrightedly, in the dark. Older customers in whose hearts the battles of the Rebellion yet persisted heard in these more temperate detonations of flashpowder the field-pieces of ancient campaigns better forgotten. Even Frank, who was usually immune to all degrees of the phantasmal, found that he could no longer orient himself with certainty.

When the smoke had finally thinned out enough to begin to see through, Frank noticed Merle Rideout in conversation with one of the Japanese trade delegation.

“Over here,” the visitor was saying, “the American West—it is a spiritual territory! in which we seek to study the secrets of your—national soul!”

“Ha! Ha!” Merle slapped his knee. “You fellows, I swear. What ‘national soul’? We don’t have any ‘national soul’! ’F you think any different, why you’re just packing out pyrites, brother.”

“An edge of steel—mathematically without width, deadlier than any katana, sheathed in the precision of the American face—where mercy is unknown, against which Heaven has sealed its borders! Do not—feign ignorance of this! It is not a—valid use of my time!" Glaring, he joined his companions and stalked out.

Frank nodded after him. "He seems upset. You don't think he'd do anything. . . ."

"Not likely," Merle said. "Looks like just some li'l laundry runner, don't he? Fact, he's sidekicks with famous international spy Baron Akashi, who's what they call a 'roving military attaché'—circuit-rides the different capital cities of Europe, keeping the Russian students over there all cranked up against the Tsar. Well, it turns out we got a anti-Tsarist crowd of our own, right up here in San Miguel County, and we call em the Finns. Is who's running their native Finland these days, is that same all-powerful Tsar of Russia. And make no mistake, they just hate his ass. Making them naturally of great professional interest to our pal there. Not that they don't also show more than average trade-delegation interest in the doings up at Little Hellkite, especially chemical, on or about bullion day."

"Maybe they're planning a hoist?"

"More like what folks call 'industrial spying.' What they *seem* to be looking for is my amalgamation process. But that could be just a cover story. Couldn't it." He took off his hat, slapped a dent into the top of it, replaced it. "Well. See you up at the mine tomorrow, then?" and was gone before Frank could say, "Sure."

Slowly, the disorder had begun to abate. Broken glass, splintered wood, and the contents of overturned cuspidors presented inconvenience everywhere as cardplayers crawled through the debris trying to reassemble full decks. Favoring their injuries, wiping their eyes, and blowing their noses on their sleeves, drinkers and gamblers went lurching out the doors and into the street, where rented horses had already been skillfully unhitching themselves and proceeding back to the corral, sighing now and then. Sportive ladies up from riverside cribs and parlor houses alike stood in twos and threes observing the scene, clucking like church wives. The Japanese visitors had vanished, and inside the Cosmopolitan, Dieter was back on duty behind the bar as if none of this had happened. Frank got warily to his feet and was just about to have a look into what bottles might've survived when Zack stepped nimbly up next to him, with an inquiring grimace.

"Why sure, old-timer, just name it. You haven't seen Bob around anyplace, have you?"

"My usual Squirrel and sarsaparilla, Dieter, and why yes young and I daresay short-timer, last I saw of your quarrelsome companion, he was heading off toward Bear Creek screamin something about going back to Baggs,

Wyoming and startin life anew, though I could have that part a little confused."

"No different from the rest of the evening," Frank guessed.

"Oh, hell," Zack reaching himself a towel to wipe off his lip, "just a little teacup social's all. Now, back in the summer of '89, the day Butch and his gang come riding in . . ."

At the Rodgers Brothers' livery stable next morning, more horseless riders than Frank had seen in one place outside of downtown Denver at lunchtime jostled after some advantage not clear to him right away, snarling at each other ominously and, wherever they could find room to, pacing about, puffing on cigars old and new. Boys kept arriving from the corral with horses saddled and bridled, producing copies of lengthy rental agreements to be signed, pocketing tips, policing what passed for a queue, and shrugging off abuse from the clerks, who were trying to keep track of it all from behind a long counter inside. The sun was well clear of the peaks by the time Frank obtained his mount, an Indian paint named Mescalero with mischief in his eye, and began his ascent to the Little Hellkite Mine by way of Fir Street, where he encountered Ellmore Disco, heading down to the store in a spiffed-up little trap perched on Timken springs.

"Gay times at the Cosmopolitan last night, I'm told?"

"I went in there with Bob Meldrum but lost him in all the confusion."

"Likely he's back up on the job by now. But"—Ellmore did not exactly say "fair warning," though that was the impression Frank got from his face—"if you see him riding anywhere in 'at Basin today, you might be mindful of the Sharps rifle he packs, specially its range, adding on, say, a mile or two extra?"

"He's angry at me for something?" puzzled Frank.

"Wouldn't be that personal, *joven*."

Off rolled Ellmore Disco, buggy hardware all going like a glockenspiel in a band. Frank ascended the Tomboy Road, the town below, revealed at the switchbacks through aspens in flickering leaf, each time a little more flattened out as it drew slowly away into heated woodsmoke haze, along with the sounds of framers' hammers and wagon traffic, before the oncoming silence of the Basin. The cicadas were in full racket. Hellkite Road—"Road" being likely a term of local endearment—peeled off to follow the rocky bed of a stream that came flowing down across the trail without the trouble of pipes or culverts.

The longer he stayed in this town, the less he was finding out. The point of diminishing returns was fast approaching. Yet now, as the trail ascended, as snowlines drew nearer and the wind became sovereign, he found himself waiting for some split-second flare out there at the edges of what he could see, a white horse borne against the sky, a black rush of hair streaming unruly as the smoke that marbles the flames of Perdition.

Even Frank, who was not what you'd call one of these spiritualists, could tell that it was haunted up here. Despite the day-and-night commercial bustling down below, the wide-open promise of desire unleashed, you only had to climb the hillside for less than an hour to find the brown, slumped skeletons of cabins nobody would occupy again, the abandoned bedsprings from miners' dormitories left out to rust two and a half miles up into the dark daytime sky . . . the presences that moved quickly as marmots at the edges of the visible. The cold that was not all a function of altitude.

Long before he sighted the Little Hellkite, Frank could smell it. The smell had come drifting by here and there since he'd arrived in town, but nowhere near as intense as this. He heard metal groaning overhead and looked up to see tram buckets loaded with ore headed down to the Pandora works at the edge of town for processing, the owners having found it too steep up here to put in expensive luxuries like stamp mills. He passed the junction house of the Telluride Power Company, a vivid red against pale mountainslopes logged off long ago, scarred with trail and bristling all over with stumps gone white as grave-markers, the hum of the voltage louder than the cicadas.

The little Basin swung into view. He trotted on in through the scatter of cabins and sheds, whose boards were all ragged lengths owing to having been dragged up here crossed over mules' backs, arriving ground down a foot or more shorter than when they'd left the yard in town and bleached in all the sunglare subsequent, till he found the assay office.

"He's down at Pandora, son."

"They told me he was up here."

"Then he's down one of these adits, talking to the tommyknockers, more'n likely."

"Uh-oh."

"Nahw, don't worry, old Merle goes a little crazy in the head sometimes, but come bullion day there's none can touch him."

Well, and who up here in this oxygen-short circus parade *wasn't* crazy in some way? Frank had a look down the nearest mine entrance, hearing in the gloom and chill which abruptly wrapped ears, temples, and nape the strike, the ring of mauls and picks from faraway passages, becoming less clear as to location the farther in he went, turning from the day, from all that could be safely illuminated, into the nocturnal counterpart behind his own eye-sockets, past any after-images of a lighted world.

At first he thought she was one of those supernatural mine creatures the Mexicans call *duendes* that you were always hearing stories about—though common sense right away suggested more of a girl powder monkey, being that on closer look she was calmly pouring what could only be nitro into holes drilled in these living mountain depths. "Course I didn't notice him," Dally snapped back a little later when Merle started in teasing her, "every-body busy just then trying to loosen that seam. Hired powder monkey don't mean hired fool. What's supposed to be important anyway? Halfway to hell, stared at by crazy Finns day in and day out as it is, grown men who the minute they get off-shift are headin straight down cliffsides on a couple of wood slats, am I gonna think twice about some Mine-Schooler with his head full of magnets?"

Dally's voice was hard to pin down to any one American place, more of a trail voice with turns and drops to it, reminders of towns you thought you'd forgotten or should never've rode into, or even promises of ones you might've heard about and were fixing to get to someday.

They were sitting in the amalgamator's shed, Merle having returned from chores down in the hole. He had his feet up on his desk and seemed in a cheerful mood.

"Oh I'll just walk out one morning," Dally assured them, "and that'll be the day I cut loose of—" indicating Merle with a shake of bright curls, "and sooner'd sure be better than later."

"And you can't imagine how I'm looking forward." Merle nodded. "Ain't about to take no bite out of *my* heart, hay-ull no—whatever your name is—Hey! you *still here,* little missy, you mean you ain't left yet? what's keeping you?"

"Must be the coffee up here." Reaching for the pot with town-wife grace across an iron stove nearly hot enough to break into a glow, just daring the 'sucker to touch her.

They had had this same exchange many times, father and daughter, in many forms. "I could be doing what I do anyplace," he might point out, "down in the safest town you can imagine, the front parlor of the world, in-stead of up in the damn San Juans like 'is. Now why do you suppose we're up here dodging bullets and avalanches and not down to Davenport Iowa or some such doily-draped venue as that?"

"You're trying to get me killed?"

"Guess again."

"Is . . . it's all for my own good?"

"There you go. This is school, Dally—fact it's damn college, a bar down the left-hand side of every classroom, the faculty packing shotguns and .44s, the student body either drunk all the time, sexually insane, or suicidally unsafe to be within a mile of, and the grades handed out are but two, survive or don't. O.K. so far or am I drifting too deep into metaphor here?"

"Tell me when you get to fractions."

She found a canvas miner's cap now, put it on, and headed for the door. "I'll be down to the company store, least till this shift gets off and everybody comes chargin' in, awfully nice meeting you Fred."

"Frank," said Frank.

"Sure, testing your memory's all."

She wasn't out the door half a minute before Merle, claiming, Frank guessed, some unwritten prerogative of the chemically deranged, looked him directly in the face and asked what he was up to, exactly, here in Telluride.

Frank considered. "Much easier if I knew how much I couldn't trust you."

"I knew your father, Mr. Traverse. He was a gentleman and a great card-player, knew dynamite inside out, saved my girl once or twice when a charge didn't go off just right, and sure's hell didn't deserve what they did to him."

Frank sat weaving on a folding camp chair that seemed about to collapse. "Well, Mr. Rideout."

"Merle would be better." He pushed across a matte-surface photograph of Webb Traverse, hat off, smoldering cigar in his teeth, regarding the lens with a sort of pugnacious glee, as if he'd just figured out exactly how he was going to destroy the camera.

"You're maybe not his spit," Merle gently, "but I do study faces, part of the business, and you're close."

"And who've you mentioned this to?"

"Nobody. No need to, looks like."

"What's this Sunday-morning voice?"

"Just wouldn't count on notching up Buck Wells, if that's what this is about. He's far too troubled of a soul. Might be he'll even do the deed on himself 'fore you ever get there."

"And good riddance too, but why should I want to wish the man harm?"

"Reports that you seem eager for a visit."

"Though standin direly in need, I'm sure, of having his Harvard-educated ass blown sky-high, Captain Wells is not right at the top of my list, fallin you see into a higher class of folk, for down here at saddle-tramp level he's of less interest than the actual trigger operatives hired to murder my Pa, heaven forfend a Harvard man should get his lilywhites soiled 'th that kind of work and all."

"Hope you're not thinkin' it was—"

"I know pretty much who. So does everybody in this close-knit li'l community, it seems. It's their whereabouts at present, is how Buck would come into this."

"Throw down on him, have him tell you what he knows."

"There you go, why didn't I think of that?"

"Whatever you do think of, best do it soon." Small Chinese children had also been known to look at Frank this way, though maybe not quite so troubled. "Word is around, Frank. Boys want you gone."

That was quick. He'd been hoping for another day or two at least. "What is it, somethin tattooed on my head? Is there anybody in this damn county I *am* fooling? *Damn.*"

"Easy now." From a drawer in a cabinet against the wall, Merle took more gelatin-silver prints. "Maybe these'll be some help." One showed a pair of what looked like drovers in town for the Fourth of July, one of them appearing to force the other to eat a giant firecracker, all lit and throwing bright sparks, flying, dying, filling the unmeasurable fragment of time the shutter was open, to the amusement of others in the background looking on from the porch of a saloon.

"You're not telling me—"

"Here, this one's a little clearer."

It was out in front of this exact same amalgamator's office. This time Deuce and Sloat were not smiling, and the light was more proper to autumn, you could see dark clouds in the sky overhead, and nothing was casting shadows. The two men were posed as if for some ceremonial purpose. For the gray day, the exposure was a little longer, and you'd expect one at least to have moved and blurred the image, but no, they had stood rigid, almost defiant, allowing the collodion mixture its due measure of light, to record the two killers with unrelenting fidelity, as if set in front of some slow emulsion of an earlier day, eyes, Frank, bending close, noticed now, rendered with that same curious crazed radiance which once was an artifact of having to blink a couple of hundred times during the exposure, but in this more modern form due to something authentically ghostly, for which these emulsions were acting as agents, revealing what no other record up till then could've.

"Who took these?"

"Kind of amateur hobby of mine," said Merle. "All this silver and gold around up here, acids and salts and so forth, and I just like to fool with the different possibilities."

"Mean little skunk, isn't he?"

"He was always after Bob Meldrum to take him on as a protégé. Even Bob, who keeps rattlesnakes for house pets, couldn't stand the kid more'n five minutes."

As if Bob's name was some password, Dally was in the door like a small explosion, her attention all focused onto Frank. "Boots on? Hair combed? Might be departure time for you, about now."

"What's up, Dahlia?" said Merle.

"Bob and Rudie, up by the shaft house, and the wrong one is smiling."

"They're after me? But last night that Bob, he seemed so friendly."

"Here you go—" Merle rolling his desk out of the way and opening a trapdoor which up to that point had been invisible. "Our own alternate means of egress. Some tunnelin' down there, ought to let you out by the ore station. If you get lucky, you can catch an empty bucket down to town."

"My horse."

"Rodgers's keeps a little barn over t' the Tomboy, just tie the reins over the saddlehorn, set him loose—they all find their way back. Might want these prints, I have negatives. Oh, and here."

"What's this?"

"What it looks like."

"Some kind of . . . meat sandwich. . . . What's it for?"

"Maybe you'll find out."

"Maybe I'll eat it."

"Maybe not. Dahlia, you better see him to town."

Down in the tunnel, Frank became aware of a curious swarming, half seen, half heard. Dally stopped and bent an ear. "Oboy. They're steamed." She called out in some peculiar, chimingly percussive language. From out of the dark tunnel, though Frank could oddly not tell the direction, came a reply. "You got that sandwich, Frank?"

They left it in the middle of the tunnel and took off running. "Why'd we—"

"Are you crazy? Don't you know who they are?"

They broke out into dusk almost balanced by electric light brighter than a full moon, circles of otherworld blindness up on tall poles along the road up to the ridgeline.

"Hurry, shift's almost changin, we're about to be stampeded over by that whole herd o' squareheads—" They climbed in an ore bucket, into iron shadows and an uncleansable telluric smell. "Worse'n a Texas shithouse in here, ain't it?" she said cheerfully. Frank muttered, about to pass out. A bell rang somewhere and the bucket shuddered into motion. Though they were keeping their heads low, Frank felt it the exact moment they cleared the edge and the valley dropped away, leaving them high above the lights of the town with nothing but the deep, invisible air below. Just then, back at the mine, the shift whistle began to shriek, sliding downward in pitch as they went hurtling away down into the dark gulf. The girl whooped back at it with delight. "To Hell you ride! Hey, Frank!"

Back down into town, actually, would not have been his first choice. He would much rather've kept on uphill, over the pass, down again to the Silverton road, maybe turned off for Durango and with luck picked up the train, or else just rode on till he was somehow into the Sangre de Cristos, where he knew he at least had a chance. Ride through the ghost bison, on into those big dunes, and let the spirits there protect him.

Soon they could hear the pounding of stamps, muffled at first like the percussion section of a distant marching band, fifes and cornets surely about to join in at any minute, practicing for some undeclared national holiday that didn't necessarily ever have to arrive, growing louder, sensed yet hidden, like so much else in these mountains. At some point the racket of the mill was overtaken by the racket from town, and then Frank remembered it was Saturday night.

Pandemonium did not begin to amount to a patch on what seemed to be approaching them instead of they it, swelling to surround them, a valley-wide symphony of gunshots, screaming, blaring on musical instruments, freight-wagon traffic, coloratura laughter from the pavement nymphs, glass breaking, Chinese gongs being bashed, horses, horse-hardware jingling, swinging-door hinges creaking as Frank and Dally presently arrived at the Gallows Frame Saloon, about halfway down Colorado Street.

"Are you sure they'll let you in here?" Frank as mildly as he could.

The girl laughed, once and not for long. "Look around you, Frank. Find me one face in here cares about who does what." She led him down the length of the bar lined with ten-dayers, fathom miners, and remittance men, through the tobacco smoke, amid card and dice tables a-bustle with challenge, insult, and imprecation. Somebody was playing on the piano some tune that would've been a march, except for some peculiar rhythmic hesitations that made Frank, who usually chose to avoid dancing, unexpectedly wish he knew how.

She noticed, of course. "That's 'ragtime.' You never heard rag? why even ask. Where were you from again? Never mind, I couldn't pr'nounce it."

She was holding her arms out in a certain way, and he guessed he was stuck, though it didn't turn out that bad, for Frank was a damn buck-and-wing artist next to some of the miners the girls in here were dancing with, especially the Finns. "Stomp around like they 's wearing skis," Dally said. After a while Frank noticed one or two that *were* wearing skis, and it wasn't even winter.

"Oh there's Charlie, stay right here, I'll be back." All right with Frank, who, having begun wondering when Bob and Rudie would make their appearance, needed to put in a little time next to some Circassian walnut. He was halfway through his first beer of the evening when Dally appeared again. "Talked to Charlie Fong Ding, who does all the laundry for the parlor house girls. There's a vacancy at the Silver Orchid, I know the place, it's safe, there's an escape tunnel—"

"You know the place?"

"Hah, lookit this, he's shocked. Charlie wanted to put money on it. Could've ate for a week bettin against your character."

"The Silver Orchid, Dally?"

"All my Pa's fault." At some point Merle had decided they must address the sensitive matter of sexual congress or, often as not, it being a mining town, sexual congregation. Through the good offices of California Peg, the *sous-maîtresse* of the Silver Orchid, where he had been a steady patron, Merle arranged for a program of study, brief and clandestine, "offering occasion to be sure," as Merle put it, "for Grundyesque screaming, but no worse when one thinks about it than giving a child a small glass of diluted wine at mealtimes so that she may grow up with some sense of the difference between wine with dinner and wine *for* dinner. You're old enough anyhow," he'd been telling her for years now, "and it sure 's heck beats hearing it from me, sooner or later you'll be hitching up with the perfect young gent, and knowing the story now'll save you both untold worlds of heartache—"

"Not to mention sparing *you* a lot of work," she pointed out.

"You'll see men at their best and worst, dear," Peg added, "and all in between, which is where you'll find most of them, but never, ever put money on the needs of men getting too complicated, least any more than, oh, say, the rules of blackjack."

So Dally, a girl of great good sense to begin with, came to pick up in and about Popcorn Alley a range of useful information. She discovered that lip-rouge for cracked lips made an interesting alternative to ear wax. For a month's wages from up at the mine, she acquired, from a hurdy girl at the Pick and Gad, a .22-caliber revolver, which she wore in plain sight mainly on account of she didn't own one dress or skirt to hide it under, but also for its simple presence, not as overwhelmingly obvious on her slight form as a full-size weapon would've been, yet leaving no one in doubt as to her ability to draw, aim, and fire it, which she practiced at devoutly whenever she got the chance, out in back of various spoil heaps, eventually able to win a little spare change from wagering with would-be crack shots among the miners. "Annie Oakley!" the Finns took to yelling when she came in sight, tossing small coins in the air in hopes she'd drill one for them, which now and then she was happy to do, providing many a future returnee to Finland with a lucky amulet to see him through the days of civil war and White Terror, sacking and massacre that lay beyond that—a promise that now and then odds might be beaten and the counterfactual manifest itself in that wintry world awaiting them.

Erotic refinement was not among the allurements of the Telluride row—for that, she gathered, you'd have to go down to Denver—but at least she came out of the elementary course at the Silver Orchid immune to, if not real comfortable with, the usual rude surprises which have blighted the marriage state for so many and, best of all, as Peg confided, without "Love," as defined by the heartsick and tumescent generations of cowpoke Casanovas out here, getting too mixed up in matters, which could easily have put her off of it altogether. "Love," whatever that turned out to be, would occupy a whole different piece of range.

"The sort of thing a girl should be talking over with her mother," she told Frank, "that's if her mother was handy and not hidden someplace among millions of folks in a city that might as well be on another planet. One more reason for me to be heading out of here to find her, sooner better than later, not to mention half the time Merle don't seem to want me around, and to tell the truth I'm gettin bored being around him, and miners are not the world's greatest beau material, and I sure need the change of scene. Let's see, there was somethin else, but I forgot."

"Hope you're not feeling like that you're responsible for him."

"Course I do. Sometimes he might as well be *my* kid."

Frank nodded. "Called gettin out of the house. Just one of those things everybody gets around to."

"Thanks, Fred."

"Frank."

"Deceived again! Now you've got to buy me a beer."

THE "VACANCY" at the Silver Orchid turned out to be a space between two walls, way in the back, reached through a false fireplace. There was room for

Frank and a cigarette, if he tore it in half. He was paid up at the Sheridan for another night but decided not to try and get his money back.

Clientele went crashing in and out. The girls laughed way too much, and without mirth. Glass broke frequently. The piano, even to Frank's tin ear, was seriously out of tune. Frank lay down between the walls with his coat rolled up for a pillow and drifted off to sleep. He was awakened about midnight by Merle Rideout hammering on the wall.

"Picked up your things at the hotel. Good thing you didn't. Bob Meldrum was in and out and making everybody nervous. Come along if you got a minute, want you to look at something." He led Frank outside under the chill, imponderable cone of an electric bulb high on a pole, and they walked amid the feral discourse of the cribs, while a gunshot occurred back down Pacific Street, somebody climbed to a rooftop and began to recite "The Shooting of Dan McGrew," and nearer at hand single-jackers climaxed and ruffled doves wailed, till they were down beside the river, where the Row had been squeezed to by more respectable forms of commerce, and it was possible to stand with the ungoverned electric town at your back, the untraveled night in front, with the San Miguel between, brand new out of the mountains throwing flashes of light like declarations of innocence.

"There is back in New York," said Merle, "a certain Dr. Stephen Emmens. Dismissed by many as a crackpot, but don't you be fooled, for he's the real article. What he does is, he'll take some silver, just the smallest trace of gold in it, and start to *pound on it,* at very low temperature, runnin' a bath of liquid carbonic to keep it cold, keep pounding onto it, pounding all day and night, till little by little the gold content, some strange and unknown way, *begins to increase.* At least up over point three hundred—sometimes even gone as high as nine ninety-seven."

"'Unknown way,' sure, this is how confidence operators talk."

"All right. Not 'unknown' to me, I just don't like to spook people if I don't have to. You've heard of transmutation?"

"Heard of."

"All it could be. The silver gets transmuted to gold, and spare me that face. Dr. Emmens calls the stuff 'argentaurum.'" Merle brought out an egg-size nugget. "This is the stuff itself, argentaurum, about a fifty-fifty mix. And this"—into the other hand sprang a blurry crystal about the size of a pocket Bible but thin as a nymph's mirror—"this is calcite, known in this particular format to some of the visiting labor as *Schieferspath,* a good pure specimen I happened to obtain one night back in Creede—yes, night does return now and then to Creede—off of a superstitious Scotchman holding a perfectly good nine of diamonds he couldn't bring himself to hang on to. Think of this piece of spar here as the kitchen window, and just take a look through."

"Well holy Toledo," said Frank after a while.

"Don't see much of that in mining school?"

Not only had the entire scene doubled and, even more peculiarly, *grown brighter,* but as for the two overlapping images of the nugget itself, one was as gold as the other was silver, no doubt at all. . . . At some point Merle was obliged to remove the wafer-thin rhomboid from Frank's grasp.

"It is that way with some," Merle remarked, "leaves em spoiled for anything but the one breed of ghost-light."

"Where's this from?" Frank's voice slow and stunned, as if he'd forgotten about the nugget altogether.

"This piece of spar? Not from around here, most likely Mexican, from down that Veta Madre someplace around Guanajuato, Guanajuato, where silver mines and spar go together like frijoles and rice, they say. For the other thing gets taken out of there, strangely enough, is the same silver for the Mexican silver dollars that Brother Emmens uses exclusively in that secret process of his. A mother lode south of the border there of pre-argentauric silver, with all that spar right in the neighborhood, see what I'm gettin at."

"Not really. Unless you're sayin that double refraction somehow is the *cause* of this—"

"Yes and how could something weak and weightless as light make solid metals transmute? does seem crazy, don't it—down here anyway, down at our own humble ground level and below, where it's all weight and opacity. But consider the higher regions, the light-carrying Æther, penetrating everyplace, as the medium where change like that is possible, where alchemy and modern electromagnetic science converge, consider double refraction, one ray for gold, one for silver, you could say."

"*You* could."

"Just saw it yourself."

"Far beyond anythin the folks at Golden must've wanted their mine engineers to know about, sorry. I'm only trusting you not to take too much advantage of my ignorance."

"Appreciate that," Merle twinkled back, "so I'll let you in on something. This Emmens process, even with what it costs—and the figure ten thousand dollars per run's been mentioned, but of course that's now, and it's bound to get cheaper—this stuff could *knock the Gold Standard right onto its glorified ass.* And what'll happen to metal prices then? Did the Silver Act, all the foofooraw went with that, get repealed for nothing? Will gold turn out to be worth no more than silver plus the cost of this process, and what'll there be then to crucify mankind on a cross of? Not to mention the Bank of England, and the British Empire, and Europe and all *those* empires, and everybody they lend money to—pretty soon it's the whole world, you see?"

"'And I'll sell you all the details of the Emmens process for just fifty cents'—that what you're leadin up to? My brain ain't quite made of pudding yet, Professor, and even if this is all on the straight, who'd be simple enough to want to buy any of that Argentina-whatever-it-is—"

"Bureau of the Mint, for one."

"Oh, boy."

"Don't take my word, ask around. Doc Emmens has been selling argentaurum ingots to the U.S. Mint since '97 or thereabouts, since the days of Lyman Gage, that old Gold Standard hand and bank president, you hadn't been so bughouse over zinc you might've heard what everybody else knows. Big chunk of our damn *U.S. economy* resting squarely onto it, how about that?"

"Merle. Why are you even showing me this?"

"Because maybe what you think you're looking for isn't really what you're looking for. Maybe it's something else."

Frank could not escape the strange impression that he had walked into a variety theater and some magician, Chinese for example, had summoned him up front to be the stooge in some long complicated trick with a line of patter Frank was too confused to appreciate fully. "Looking for . . ."

"Not this nugget. Not this little window of Iceland spar either. Fact," Merle's voice beginning to divide, like a kettle coming to the boil, into sharp little creaks of amusement, "there is a *whole catalogue* of things you're not looking for."

"Well tell me. What it is I'm really looking for. Besides a saloon, about now."

"Just guessin', but it's also what your father Webb was looking for, except he didn't know it any more than you do."

That damn Chinese feeling again.

"Go talk to Doc Turnstone. He might have an idea or two."

At the shift in the sound of Merle's voice, Frank felt a strange wave of internal disquiet. "Why?"

But Merle had retreated behind his professionally impassive magician's face. "You remember those tommyknockers you and Dahlia ran into up at the Hellkite?" Well, there had been a spell where Merle too was seeing *little people* down in the stopes, some done up quite peculiarly indeed, unusual hats, military uniforms not of the U.S. Army exactly, little pointed shoes and so forth, and one evening he was injudicious enough to mention this to his fellow man of science, whereupon Doc Turnstone confidently declared it to be the Charles Bonnet syndrome, mention of which he had lately run across in Puckpool's classic *Adventures in Neuropathy.* "Been attributed to any number of causes, including macular degeneration and disturbances of the temporal lobe."

"How about just some real *duendes*?" Merle said.

"That's not a rational explanation."

"All respect Doc, I can't agree, for they're down there, all right."

"You like to show me?"

Third shift, of course, best time for that sort of thing. In a spirit of scientific inquiry, the Doc had abstained from his usual evening laudanum, though this hadn't improved his mood, in fact to Merle he seemed quite jumpy as the two of them, wearing overalls and miners' waterproofs and packing electric torches, entered a hole in the moonlit hillside and made their way through ancient, dripping debris down a sharply inclined tunnel into an abandoned part of the workings.

"Having humans around causes 'em discomfort," Merle had explained up top. "So they tend to resort to places where the humans ain't."

Not only had the tommyknockers found this sector of the Little Hellkite congenial—in the years since its abandonment they had converted it into a regular damn full-scale Tommyknockers *Social Hall.* And abruptly there they all were, sure enough, a regular subterranean tableau. Those *duendes* were playing poker and pool here, drinking red whiskey and home-brewed beer, eating food stolen out of miners' lunch pails as well as the pantries of the unmarrieds' eating hall, getting into fights, telling tasteless jokes, just as you might find in any recreational club aboveground, any night of the week.

"Well, this one's easy," muttered the Doc as if to himself. "I've gone insane, is all."

"We couldn't both be having exactly the same kind of Charles Whatsisname trouble?" Merle supposed. "No. Wouldn't make sense."

"More sense than what I'm seeing."

So they became in a way conspirators against, if not the owners at least the everyday explanations owners and the like tended to favor. The belief, for instance, that tommyknockers are not little people in whimsical costumes but "only" pack rats. The thing that owners found comforting about pack rats was their habit of constantly stealing explosives. Every stick of dynamite a pack rat stole was one less in the hands of Anarchists or Union men. "Someplace," Dally declared, "there's at least one tommyknocker with a *hell* of a lot of dynamite stashed away. A dang dynamite El Dorado. Now what's he want with all that explosive?"

"Sure it's all the same critter?"

"I know it. I know his name. I speak their language."

"Don't," said the Doc, "don't bother telling me. Depends whether he's stealing detonator caps, too, I guess. How many of *them's* missing is what'd worry me a bit."

Frank found Doc Turnstone on the midnight-to-dawn shift at the Miners' Hospital. "Merle Rideout said I should look you up."

"Then you're Frank Traverse."

Were he and Merle in touch by direct wire, or what? Frank noticed the Doc staring at him. "Somethin?"

"Don't know if Merle mentioned it or not, your sister Lake and I kept company for a time."

Another one of Lake's admirers. "She's a beauty," friends and runninmates had always been quick to assure Frank, though he seldom ever could see it. He asked Kit once, who seemed to spend more time with her than anybody, but the kid only shrugged, "I trust her." As if that might be some help.

"Yehp but I mean are we going to have to go up someday against some damn reptile can't resist these charms of hers I'm always hearin about?"

"Think she can take care of herself. You've seen her shoot, she ain't bad."

"*That's* what a brother likes to hear."

"Fact is," Frank said now, "is we haven't seen much of each other lately."

Another, seemed like a minute, passed before the Doc shook himself like a dog emerging from a mountain stream and apologized. "Lake, she broke my, just damn broke my heart."

Well, well. "Had that happen," said Frank, though in fact he hadn't. "Cases like yours," kindly as he could, "what I usually tend to prescribe's Old Gideon, three-finger doses, for as long as it takes?"

The Doc beamed a little sheepishly. "Wasn't looking for sympathy. Not as if she swept through like an act of nature. Still, if you're buying . . ."

Back in 1899, not long after the terrible cyclone that year which devastated the town, young Willis Turnstone, freshly credentialed from the American School of Osteopathy, had set out westward from Kirksville Missouri, with a small grip holding a change of personal linen, an extra shirt, a note of encouragement from Dr. A. T. Still, and an antiquated Colt's in whose use he was far from practiced, arriving at length in Colorado, where one day, riding across the Uncompahgre Plateau, he was set upon by a small band of pistoleros. "Hold it right there, miss, let's have a look at what's in that attractive valise o' yours."

"Not much," Willis said.

"Hey, what's this? Packing some *iron* here! Well, well, never let it be said Jimmy Drop and his gang denied a tender soul a fair shake now, little lady, you just grab a hold of your great big pistol and we'll *get to it,* shall we?" The others had cleared a space which Willis and Jimmy now found themselves alone at either end of, in classic throwdown posture. "Go on ahead, don't be shy, I'll give you ten seconds gratis, 'fore I draw. Promise." Too dazed to share entirely the gang's spirit of innocent fun, Willis slowly and inexpertly raised his revolver, trying to aim it as straight as a shaking pair of hands would allow. After a fair count of ten, true to his word and fast as a snake, Jimmy went for his own weapon, had it halfway up to working level before abruptly coming to a dead stop, frozen into an ungainly crouch. "Oh, pshaw!" the badman screamed, or words to that effect.

"*¡Ay! ¡Jefe, jefe!*" cried his lieutenant Alfonsito, "tell us it ain' your back again."

"Damned idiot, o' course it's my back. Oh mother of all misfortune—and worse than last time too."

"I can fix that," offered Willis.

"Beg pardon, what in hell business of any got-damn punkinroller'd this be, again?"

"I know how to loosen that up for you. Trust me, I'm an osteopath."

"It's O.K., we're open-minded, couple boys in the outfit are Evangelicals, just watch where you're putting them lilywhites now—yaaagghh—I mean, huh?"

"Feel better?"

"Holy Toledo," straightening up, carefully but pain-free. "Why, it's a miracle."

"*¡Gracias a Dios!*" screamed the dutiful Alfonsito.

"Obliged," Jimmy guessed, sliding his pistol back in its holster.

"I'll settle for my life," proposed Willis. "Maybe buy you all a drink sometime?"

"Come on, right over that ridge there." They repaired to a nearby stockmen's saloon. "All this damned hard riding and other saddle activities," Jimmy explained presently, "the cowboy's curse in fact, show me a man's been any time at all on a horse, I'll show you a victim of the fulminatin lumbago. You've sure got the magic in your mitts, Doc, maybe you just discovered your promised land out here."

Willis, having already been stood an uncounted number of red whiskeys, put off semi-consciousness for a moment to consider this career assessment. "You mean I could hang out my shingle in one of these towns—"

"Well maybe not just any town, you'd want to check into prior claims, as some of these town croakers once they're set up don't want more competition. Known to get quite violent about it, in fact."

"Licensed physicians?" Willis astonished, "men of healing, violent?"

"And even if you didn't find a town right away, why, there'd always be work, I bet."

"How's that?"

"Circuit ridin' osteo-whatever-it-is, just keep moving spread to spread, like many a drover's learned to do, no dishonor in that."

Which is how life then took a turn for young Willis Turnstone. He had journeyed west having cherished, despite his heretical gifts, little beyond town-dweller dreams—of frequenting a not-too-earnest church, meeting and marrying a presentable girl with a college background, aging into the sort of local "Doc" no one would hesitate to play cards with, on a weekly low-stakes type of basis of course . . . yet one chance meeting with the notorious Jimmy Drop gang among the mind-poisoning vetches and creosote of a dusty high plain was all it took to steer him in a whole 'nother direction.

Not that the suburban imperative didn't continue to work its will. He found himself adding conventional medical skills onto his osteopathic ones, sending away back east for medical textbooks, learning to cultivate the local druggists in the towns he drifted through, finding that a couple Saturday nights of losing poker could be worth a semester in pharmacy school. By the time he blew into Telluride and started working at the Miners' Hospital alongside Dr. Edgar Hadley and Nurse Margaret Perril, he was as doctorly as they came in these parts, though long fallen into the habit of always diagnosing the rarest possible conditions to account for the symptoms his patients reported. Since they either died or got better on their own, and nobody kept count, there was no way to know how effective any of this was, and he was too busy himself ever to make a proper study.

He met Lake up at the Miners' Hospital, called in to treat a ten-dayer who'd been shot in the shoulder. The first suspect whose name crossed Willis's mind, Bob Meldrum, had been present but only, he swore, in a tutorial capacity, advising an apprentice regulator on how best to maintain order in the mines. "Use my initiative," said the eager lad. "Hell no," Bob replied, "use your .44. Here, like this—whoops." Too late, the gun had been fired and the miner's blood diverted from its return to the heart.

Lake was in simple gray and white, her hair covered and her demeanor professional, and the minute Willis saw her he was a goner, though it took him a couple of weeks to realize it in his mind.

They rode out to Trout Lake and picnicked. He showed up at her door with bunches of wildflowers. One night without thinking he told her he wanted them to get married. He met her mother, Mayva, and pounded on her back for a while. One day somebody mentioned that Lake had run off with Deuce Kindred.

Which so desolated the Doc that Jimmy Drop offered to go after the couple on his behalf. "'Sucker used to ride with us, not for long, nobody liked him, mean little brush snake. You want him out of the way, I'll see to it personal."

"Oh, Jim no I couldn't ask you to do that. . . ."

"No need to ask, Doc, forever in your debt."

"Forever's how long she would likely end up moping about it, and then where would I be?"

Jimmy's eyes narrowed uneasily. "They get like that, huh?"

"Just wouldn't want the possibility."

"Yehp . . . well yehp I can see that. . . ."

Course, the Doc would never get used to losing out. Lake was nowhere near the kind of girl he thought he was looking to settle down with, she was all his plans flying out the window, a chance to "choose wrong" early enough in life to do him some good. Now she'd gone off with a specimen too loathsome even for the Jimmy Drop gang. If she was not to be the great lost love of his life, she could've perhaps been the great unlistened-to commentator upon it.

"She what? Went off with who?" Maybe repeating himself a couple times, because the news had just sent him spinning.

"That's right," the Doc shaking his head slowly, "I still can't get a handle on it myself."

"This sure don't help," said Frank, "really. Who else knows?"

The keen squint he got was not so much pitying as scientifically curious.

Frank felt coming down over him, like an illness, the dry-skinned feverishness of shame. "No idea where they went to?"

"If I knew, would it be wise to tell you?"

"You have feelings for my sister and all, so don't take this the wrong way, but . . . when I find her, I will kill the bitch. O.K.? Him, goes without saying, but her—that *fucking*—I can't even say her name. How natural is it, that that could even *happen*, Doc?"

"Don't know. You mean, is it a well-known mental condition or something?" He looked around for his copy of Puckpool.

"Damn. Maybe I'll go out, kill somebody just for practice."

"You're going to have to calm down, Frank. Here," scribbling, ". . . you can take this over to the drugstore—"

"Thanks all the same. Maybe what I need to do is talk to Jimmy Drop."

"I know he and Kindred rode together briefly, long time back, but how likely is it they'd still be in touch?"

"Does not, make no, fuckin, sense." Frank staring deep into his hat, beginning to exhibit classic signs of melancholia and then some. "Sure they fought a lot, her and Pa, mostly when I was away at Golden, but this is like—Why didn't *she* just go ahead and shoot him down, she hated him that much? That would've made more sense."

The Doc poured himself another tridigital dose and sociably waved the bottle at Frank.

"Better not. Need to think."

"Unlike sound or light or one of them, news travels at queer velocities and not usually even in straight lines," offered the Doc.

Frank squinted up at the ceiling. "What . . . doesthat*mean*?"

Doc Turnstone shrugged. "Jimmy is usually down to the Busted Flush this time of the evening."

Though it was far too late for any of this old news to matter to anybody but Frank, it didn't keep him from skulking along through the insomniac town with his hat low on his eyebrows, convinced that everybody he saw was in on the story and smirking at him with contempt or, worse, pity—poor foolish Frank, last to know.

Jimmy Drop—very short Arapahoe Street haircut glossed down with bartender's hair wax, mustache trained in the Chinese style, trademark monocle effortlessly in place—was in the back room of the Busted Flush with some of his associates, playing a complicated game with an evil-looking packer's knife, whose point and blade-edge were to be brought into use whenever the matter of forfeits arose. Judging from the color of his shirt, Alfonsito appeared to be having the least luck tonight, much to the amusement of the others.

"Recognized you right off," Jimmy said when they were settled behind a labelless bottle of bourbon. "You and your brother got the same nose, except for Reef's was broke a couple times, o' course. I am proud to say I was there on both occasions."

"Wasn't you did it, I hope."

"No, no, just the usual professors, showing us poor ignoramuses the finer points of poker etiquette."

"Like don't play partners," Frank smiling quickly with one side of his mouth, aware of ways Jimmy might grow exercised but right now not caring much.

"Oh, he told you that one." The monocle twinkled. "Heard he went back east. Sounded like *all the way* back east."

"You'd know better'n me."

"Guess these days it'd be you that's lookin for Deuce. Wish I could help, but by now they might—he might be anyplace."

"You can say 'they.'"

"You know, I hate to gossip. Gossipin ought to be a felony, heavy penalties up to and includin the gallows for repeat offenders."

"But?"

"I only seen your sister but once, up by Leadville. Kind of a young lady by then, maybe ten or eleven? It was that one winter they built that big Ice Palace up there, up above Seventh Street."

"Remember it. Hard to believe it was really there." Three acres on a hilltop, arc-lights, towers of ice ninety feet high, biggest rink in Creation, replacement ice-blocks shipped in every day, ballroom, café, more popular than the Opera House while it lasted, but doomed to melt away when spring came.

"Reef was just out of the chute," Jimmy recalled, "but not really, I think we worked our first job together that spring. Your sister got hold of a pair of ice skates and was spending most of her time up at that Ice Palace. Like every other kid in Leadville. One day she was teachin the Dutch Waltz to some kid from town, management kid, not much older than she was, and Webb Traverse come in saw it and just pitched a fit. Ten years now, and I've known it noisier, but I still remember *that* go-round. Your Pa really wanted to kill somebody. It wasn't just that old hands-off-my-daughter business, we all know that one. This was home-for-the-insane carryin-on."

"I was down at work that day," Frank recalled, "some mucker's shift, and when I got back they were still at it. Heard the hollerin a mile away, thought it was Chinamen or somethin."

It was political, was the thing. If it had been a miner's son, even a saloon- or store-keeper's son, Webb might've grumbled some, but there it would have rested in peace. It was the notion of some little rich snot-nose never worked a day in his life creeping in grabbing the innocent daughter of a working man that got Webb all in a rage.

"It wasn't even about me personally," Lake wasn't too angry to point out later, she saw it clear enough, "it was your damned old Union again." Lucky for everybody there were cooler heads around, not to mention arms and legs that sort of came gliding in to form a social barrier and nudge Webb back off the ice, while Lake hung her head in the pearl-gray gloom, feeling mortified, and the boy skated off looking for another partner.

"As a Mex, maybe," figured Ellmore Disco. "You'd need the right hat o' course, and a mustache, though what with not shaving these last couple days, you've got a good start. We can consult with Loopy about the rest." They were in the Gallows Frame, and things were approaching that usual centrifugal Saturday-night run-up to the end of the world and a subsequent general drunken slumber.

"Ellmore, why are you helping me? I had you figured for the Mine Owners' Friend."

"The one thing no form of business can really do without," Ellmore instructed him, "is good old peace and quiet. Any disruptive behavior up here over and above the normal Saturday-night frolics will tend to discourage the banks down in Denver, not to mention the day-tripping into town of that pigeon population we've all of us come so much to depend on, next thing you know we're into a slack cycle and well, the less of that the better 's all. Now somebody like yourself, harmless-enough-lookin young fellow, barely steps into town he becomes a focus of attention for far too many bad actors, why then it's time, ain't it, for little E. Disco to start considering how best to help such a fellow make his exit."

Playing down the street at the Railbird Saloon just happened to be Gastón Villa and His Bughouse Bandoleros, a collection of itinerant musicians in white leather fringe jackets, spangled "chaps," and enormous face-hiding hats rimmed in *cholo* balls the colors of the spectrum running in order of wavelength. Gastón's father had once ridden the rodeo with some make-believe *charro* act—and when at last, one night over by Gunnison, he ran into an audience whose ideas of rejection proved fatal, his wife packed up all his old costumes and gear for Gastón, kissed him adios at the depot, and sent him off to become a saxophone player for the band of a Wild West show. Obliged more than once to leave his instruments in soak to pay hotel bills, bar tabs, and gambling debts, Gastón was to drift with the years into a variety of peculiar engagements, including the present one.

"Please, don't preoccupy yourself," he reassured Frank now—"here, you know what this is?" Bringing out a towering contraption of tarnished and beat-up brass covered with valves and keys, whose upper end flared open like something in a marching band.

"Sure. Where's the trigger on it again?"

"It is called the Galandronome—a military bassoon, once standard issue in French army bands—my uncle salvaged this one from the Battle of Puebla, you can see a couple of dents from Mexican bullets here, and here?"

"And the end you blow in," puzzled Frank, "wait a minute, now. . . ."

"You will learn."

"But till I do—"

"Caballero, you have been in these cantinas, the musical taste is not demanding. Nobody in this band was a musician when they joined up, but everybody was in some kind of trouble. Play *con entusiasmo,* as loudly as you can, and trust in the good will and bad ear of the gringo hellraiser."

Is how Frank became Pancho the Bassoon Player. Within a day or two, he was actually getting a sound out of the 'sucker, and before long most of "Juanita," too. With a couple of trumpets playing harmony, it wasn't that bad, he supposed. Affecting, sometimes.

Shortly before he left town, Frank entered a condition a little displaced from what he'd always thought of as his right mind. Having put it off as long as he could, he visited the miners' graveyard at the edge of town, found Webb's grave, stood there and waited. The place was full of presences, but no more than the valley and the hillsides around. Being a hardheaded sort, Frank had not been real intensely haunted by Webb's ghost. The other ghosts chided Webb about this. "Oh it's just Frank. When the moment comes he'll do the right thing, he's just always been a little overly practical, 's all. . . ."

"It's like we specialized, Pa. Reef is runnin on nerve, Kit's gonna figure it all out scientifically, I'm the one who just has to keep poundin at it day after day, like that fella back east trying to turn silver to gold."

"Deuce and Sloat ain't here in Telluride, son. And nobody here would tell you if they knew. Fact, they likely have split up by now."

"It's Deuce and Lake I want to find. Maybe he left her a while back, maybe she's another fallen woman now and he's ridin hard into what he calls his future. He could even be gone across 'at Río Bravo."

"He might want you to think so."

"He might not stay in the U.S. too long, for they'd be after him now, his old compadres, tough times, and any number of youthful hardcases who'll work cheaper, so he's yesterday's deadweight. Only place for him to go'd be south."

So ran Frank's reasoning. Webb, who knew everything now, saw no point in trying to convince him otherwise. All he said was, "D' you hear something?"

Some ghosts go *oo-oo-oo*. Webb had always expressed himself more by way of dynamite. Frank had a vision then, or whatever you call a vision when you hear instead of see it . . . not the comforting thunder of mine-blasting up in the mountains, but right down here in town, hammering up and down the valley, causing even the black-and-white dairy cows there to take a minute to look up before getting back to serious grazing . . . the bone-deep voice of retribution long in coming.

Faces he thought he knew turned out to be others, or not there at all. Saloon girls tried to engage him in metaphysical discussions, like did the dead walk, and so forth. Up on the Ophir road one night, Frank thought he saw his sister, heading down into the valley, keeping her face carefully averted, the way Lake was known to, as for some sorrow she would be forever unwilling to explain, if anybody should ask. He came to believe it must have been a wraith.

Frank came along with Merle to see Dally off at the station. "Like to ride with you, far as Denver anyway, but some of these boys have other ideas. So listen now—my brother Kit is back east going to college at Yale, which is in New Haven, Connecticut? not much further from New York than Montrose is from here, so you be sure and get in touch if you can, he's a nice kid, little dreamy till you get his attention, but the scrape ain't been invented he can't help you out of, just don't hesitate, hear me?"

"Thanks Frank, to be worryin about me, with all you've got to worry about yourself right now."

"Maybe 'cause you and Kit are two of a kind."

"Hell, that case I ain't going near him."

Along the platform Dally was getting looks from those accomplished in the parental arts, many indeed putting in with strenuous objection. "Allowing a child to journey without adult supervision across two-thirds of a continent to a nexus of known depravity such as New York City would surely bring prosecution in many if not most courtrooms of the land—"

"Let alone judgment in the dock of Christian Morality, certain and pitiless, by That Which all temporal powers, judges included, must one day bow to—"

"Lady," observed the impertinent snip under discussion, "if I can get through the average Saturday night in Telluride, there's nothing back east'll present much of a problem."

Merle beamed, as close as he ever got to fatherly pride. "You take care now, Dahlia." Everybody else was aboard, the train about to make its backward departure, as if it couldn't bear to lose sight of Telluride till the last minute.

"So long, Pa."

They had been in and out of each other's arms so often, she had no uneasiness with good-bye *abrazos*. Merle, who had a sense of the bets on the table here, knew he better not spook her now. Neither of them had ever had much interest in breaking each other's heart. In theory they both knew she had to move on, though all he wanted right now was to wait, even just another day. But he knew that feeling, and he guessed it would pass.

"Tengo que get *el* fuck out of *aquí,*" Kit reckoned. First thing up in the morning, last thing before climbing into bed at night, he found himself repeating it, like a prayer. Yale's charm had not only worn away at last but also was revealing now the toxic layers beneath, as Kit came to understand how little the place was about studying and learning, much less finding a transcendent world in imaginaries or vectors—though sometimes, to be sure, he'd caught hints of some Kabbalah or unverbalized knowledge being transferred as if mind to mind, not because of so much as in spite of Yale. To do with the invisible new waves especially, latent in the Maxwell Field Equations years before Hertz found them—Shunkichi Kimura, who had studied with Gibbs here, had returned to Japan, joined the Naval Staff college faculty, and co-developed wireless telegraphy in time for the war with Russia. Vectors and wireless telegraphy, a silent connection.

Gibbs had died at the end of April, and amid the general despondency in the math department, Kit realized it was the last straw, revealing Yale to be no more really than a sort of high-hat technical school for learning to be a Yale Man, if not indeed a factory for turning out Yale Men, gentlemen but no scholars except inadvertently, and that was about it.

'Fax was no help with this. Kit wouldn't have known how to begin to bring the subject up, even though 'Fax offered him more than enough openings.

"All the time you've been here, and you haven't joined any clubs."

"Too busy."

"Busy?" They looked at one another at some interplanetary range. "I say Kit, I mean you might as well be a Jew, you know."

This did not clarify anything. Jews at Yale at that time were an exotic species.

Early in his hitch at Yale, Kit had been at a track meet one day and seen a boy in his class being greeted by a party of older men dressed in what Kit recognized by now as very expensive town suits. They all stood and chatted, smiling and easy, paying no attention to the young athletes in plain sight all across the deep green field who ran, jumped, swiveled, and launched, entering unsuspected reaches of pain and body damage, striving toward the day's offers of simulated immortality. Kit thought, I will never look like this fellow, talk like that, be wanted in that way. At first it produced a terrible feeling of exclusion, a piercing conviction that because of where and to whom he had been born, some world of visible privilege would forever be denied him. There would arrive a point where, returned to his right mind again, he could ask, reasonably, why did I want *that* so much? though until then it had felt for months like his life had gone into eclipse.

He began to keep an eye out for this peculiar traffic, on the campus, in town, at ceremonies and socials, soon recognizing a purposeful two-step of college boys and older men whose story of success the boys wished to reenact. He supposed that was it.

In classes, Gibbs, before working through a problem, had been fond of saying, "We shall pretend to know nothing about this solution from Nature." Generations of students, Kit among them, had taken that to heart, in all its metaphysical promise. Though Vectorism offered a gateway into regions the operatives of Wall Street were unlikely ever to understand, let alone penetrate, there nonetheless, set closely every way Kit looked, were Vibe sentinels, eyes in leafy ambuscade, as if Kit were a species of investment, clues to whose future performance could be gathered only through minute-to-minute surveillance, shift an eyelid and they might miss out on something essential. Worse, as if the plan all along had been to drive him so far inside his head he'd lose the way back. Being the sort of mathematician he was, Kit found himself with contradictory allegiances, knowing that he must not turn by much from the mechanics of the given world, yet at the same time remaining aware that there was no role for his destiny as a Vectorist within any set of Vibe goals he could imagine, any more than the magnate could imagine Gibbs's grand system, or the higher promise.

"Because you can understand these airy-fairy scratch-marks," Scarsdale Vibe had scolded, when it became clear that Kit's reluctance to become a Vibe heir was not coyness merely for the sake of improving the deal, "do you imagine yourself better than us?"

"More a case of what it leads on to, I think," said Kit, not about to be badgered into a dispute with the gent paying the bills.

"While the rest of us, you mean, are left behind in this soiled Creation."

"Is that what I mean? Here—" still amiable, he drew toward them a block of paper quadrilled into quarter-inch squares.

"No, no, don't bother."

"It's nothing too spiritual."

"Young man, I am as spiritual a person as any you are liable to run into at the formerly proud institution you now attend." He stalked out, leaving a glowing trail of offended righteousness.

KIT DREAMED HE was with his father in a city that was Denver but not really Denver, in some kind of strange variety saloon full of the usual collection of lowlifes, though everybody was acting unnaturally well-behaved. Except for Webb, who was yelling. "The Æther! What'n the hell have I got here, a little damn Tesla on my hands? What do you care about the Æther?"

"I have to know if it exists."

"Nobody *has* to know that."

"Right now, Father, I do. I always believed that children came from Heaven. . . ."

He went silent, expecting Webb to complete the thought he was suddenly too sad to elaborate. Webb, as if with no idea what had brought on such intensity, couldn't answer. Everybody else, every boozehound, mule-skinner, opium smoker, and flimflam artist in the place, paid them no notice, preferring shoptalk, gossip, and chitchat about sports. He woke. The hand on his shoulder was that of his scout, Proximus. "That Professor Vanderjuice wants to see you up at the Sloane Lab."

"What time is it, Prox?"

"Don't ask me, I was asleep, too."

All the way out Prospect Street, past the cemetery, the feeling grew that something awful was about to happen. Kit doubted it was about Theories of Light, which he happened to be taking that semester with the Professor, who had studied it under Quincke in Berlin, back before Michelson and Morley, so there was kind of a distinct Ætheric residue there. Out of academic enclosure, south of the Green, splashing beer about the room, waving for emphasis a triangular slice from the Italian cheese-and-tomato pastries to be found everywhere in that neighborhood, the old bird thank goodness was quite another species entirely, recalling tales of the early electrical days that even the most beer-soaked of freshman attended to, wide-eyed.

At last he reached the rat's-nest office where Professor Vanderjuice was waiting with a solemn look. Rising, he handed Kit a letter, and Kit saw immediately that it brought news he was not ready for. The envelope was postmarked

Denver, but the date was illegible, and someone had already opened and read the letter inside.

Dear Kit,

Mamma asked me to write and tell you that Pa is gone. They say it happened over in the McElmo someplace. And not from "natural causes." Reef brought back his body and he is buried in the miners cemetery at Telluride. Reef says there is no need for you to come back right now, he and Frank will take care of all that must be done. Mamma is being strong, saying like she knew it would always happen, enemies wherever he went, borrowed time and so on.

I hope you are well and that someday we will see you again. Keep studying hard back there, don't quit and try not to worry much about this, for we are all able to do what we have to.

We miss you.

Your loving sister,

Lake

Kit gazed at the violated cover, so unraggedly slit open as to suggest a letter-knife from a desk-set of some quality. First things first. "Who opened this, sir?"

"I don't know," replied the Professor. "This is how they handed it to me."

"They."

"The provost's office."

"It's addressed to me."

"They have been keeping it there for a while. . . ." Pausing as if to consider the next part of the sentence.

"It's all right."

"My boy . . ."

"Your position. I understand. But if it means there was some doubt about passing it on to me at all . . ."

"We do our best around here not to be altogether bought and sold. . . ."

"Sir, there is still an implication here. Of conniving, at least. More, maybe, though that is so terrible . . ."

"Yes." The old fellow's eyes had begun to brim.

Kit nodded. "Thank you. I'll have to think about what to do." He felt inside himself the presence of a small, wounded girl who was trying to cry—not in pain, or to appease any who would harm her further, but as if in fear of being left to the hazards of a winter street in a city known to abandon its poor. He had not cried for a long time.

He wandered without any clear plan, wanting to be anonymous among the town mobility, wanting at the same time to be alone. He knew that nothing known to the alternate universe of vector analysis could bring him comfort or help him see a way out. Moriarty's wasn't open yet, Louis Lassen's lunch stand would have been good for a hamburger sandwich if Kit could've been sure he wouldn't choke on it. Canonical Eli venues were not the ticket today. He came to rest about a mile up the Quinnipiac on top of West Rock, lay on the ground, and let himself cry.

NOT A WORD then from any of the Vibes about his father, not even from Colfax—no condolences, inquiries as to Kit's current state of mind, nothing like that. Could be they believed Kit hadn't found out yet. Could be they were waiting for him to bring it up. Could be they didn't care. But there was the other possibility, growing more probable the longer the silence continued. That they knew all about it, because—but could he afford to pursue that line of thought? If his suspicions proved to have anything to them, what would that oblige him to do about it?

The academic year went two-stepping on toward summer, and the girls wondered why Kit had stopped showing up at dances. One day, gazing out across the Sound, he observed a peculiar dark geometrical presence where previously there'd been only the misted shores of Long Island. Day by day, when visibility permitted, he noticed whatever it was *increasing in height.* He borrowed a telescope from a classmate, took it up on top of East Rock, ignored the spooning couples and dedicated drinkers, and devoted what time he could to observing the structure's vertical progress. A trusswork tower, apparently eight-sided, was slowly rising over there. Whatever it was supposed to be, it was the talk of New Haven. Soon, at night, from that same general direction, came heavenwide multicolored flashes of light, which only the incurably complacent tried to explain away as heat lightning. Kit couldn't help recalling Colorado Springs and Fourth of July Eve 1899.

"It's Tesla," confirmed Professor Vanderjuice, "putting up another transmitter. I understand once you worked with him in Colorado."

"In a way it's how I got to Yale." Kit told him about meeting Foley Walker in Colorado Springs.

"That's odd," said the Professor. "The Vibe interests once hired me—" He looked around the office. "Do you mind taking a walk?"

They headed into the Italian neighborhood south of the Green. The Professor told Kit about the agreement he and Scarsdale Vibe had come to in Chicago ten years before. "I've never felt proud of it. There was always something vaguely criminal."

"Vibe was financing Tesla but wanted you to sabotage his work?"

"Morgan's had been doing much the same thing, but more effectively. Eventually Vibe saw there'd never be a practical system of wireless power transmission, that the economy had long before devised means to prevent it."

"But Tesla's building a transmitter now."

"It doesn't matter. If it ever gets to be too much of a threat to the existing power arrangements, they'll just have it dynamited."

"So they didn't really need your anti-transmitter."

"To tell the truth, I never worked all that diligently on it. One day, just around the time I was beginning to feel dishonest taking Vibe's money, the checks stopped arriving—not even a letter of dismissal. I know I should have quit sooner, but things worked out anyway."

"You were able to do the right thing," Kit said miserably, "but the longer this goes on, the more I owe them, the less likely it'll be I can ever turn it around. What can I do? How do I buy my way out?"

"You could first convince yourself that you owe them"—he would not say "him"—"nothing."

"Sure. In Colorado people get shot for that all the time. It's called poker."

The Professor breathed deeply, once or twice, as if preparing to lift an unaccustomed weight. "Allow for the possibility," he said as evenly as he could, "that forces unnamed for the moment are corrupting you. It is their inevitable policy. Those they may not at the moment harm, they corrupt. Usually all it takes is money, for they have so much that no one feels any moral hesitancy about taking it. Their targets become rich, and where's the harm in that?"

"And if money doesn't do the trick . . ."

"Then there must follow the slow and evil work they have made their specialty, conducted all in silence. Perhaps years of it, until one day, money having been traded off for time, the same soulless condition is brought about, with the money meanwhile having been put somewhere else and bringing a better rate of return."

They were passing the entrance of an "apizza" establishment. The aroma was distracting, you'd say compelling. "Come on," said the Professor, whose condition, over the preceding year, had progressed from a simple tropism to advanced pizzamania, "let's perhaps grab a slice, what do you say?"

As his relations with Scarsdale Vibe had dwindled to yearly tycoonical head-insertions into Sloane Lab and eventually, blessedly, to none at all, Heino Vanderjuice began to think that once or twice he'd detected, out at the far edges of his visual field, a glimmering winged object among the rusticated stonework and the rippling elms, and there grew upon him the curious notion that this might actually be his soul, whose exact whereabouts since 1893 had been in some doubt.

His conscience was also showing signs of feeling, as if recovering from frostbite. One day, chatting with young Traverse, he happened to pull an old copy of the British science journal *Nature* from a row of them on his bookshelf, and leaf through to one of the articles. "P. G. Tait on Quaternions. Regards their chief merit as being 'uniquely adapted to Euclidean space . . .' because—'lamp' this—'What have students of physics, as such, to do with more than three dimensions?' I invite your attention to 'as such.'"

"A physics student, as something else, *would* have need for more than three dimensions?" Kit puzzled.

"Well, Mr. Traverse, if you ever considered becoming that 'something else,' Germany would seem the logical place for you. Grassmann's *Ausdehnungslehre* can be extended to any number of dimensions you like. Dr. Hilbert at Göttingen is developing his 'Spectral Theory,' which requires a vector space of *infinite* dimensions. His co-adjutor Minkowski thinks that dimensions will eventually all just fade away into a *Kontinuum* of space and time. Minkowski and Hilbert, in fact, will be holding a joint seminar at Göttingen next year in the electrodynamics of moving bodies, not to mention Hilbert's recent work on Eigenheit theory—vectors right in the heart and soul of it all, mightn't it be, as you lads say, 'just the ticket'?"

Overflowing with an all-but-elated idea of how he might actually do someone some good, the old fellow produced as from empty space a ukulele of some dark exotic wood trimmed with tortoiseshell and, after strumming a peppy eight-bar intro, sang—

That Göttingen Rag

Get in-to, your trav'ling coat,
Leave Girl-y, a good-bye note,
Then hop-on, the very-next boat,
To Ger—manee—
Those craz-y, pro-fessors there,
They don't ev-er cut their hair,
But do they, have brains to spare—
You wait and see!
Out on that,
Ham-burg-A-merika Line, 'fore
You-know-it-you'll-be-chinnin-with
Fe-lix Klein—don't -cha pay-no-mind to
The rent or the house-key (say,

Howdy there, Hilbert! pleased to
meetcha, Minkowski!) Tell-ya,
Col-lege Joe,
You think there's nothin-that, you don't know,
You ain't seen nothing un-til you go—so!
Pack up that ba-a-ag—
Go east, young Yank, to where the
Sabers clank, a-and th'
Four-Color Problem's just a
Stu-dent prank, while they're
Frolicking, flirting 'n'
Doin' That Göttingen, Rag!

"Yes, a wonderful place, among my old stomping grounds, in fact. I keep in regular touch, and I could drop them a line if you like."

A plunge into advanced Vectorism. No looking over your shoulder. "Well, being busy is the thing I guess."

The Professor watched him carefully for a moment, as if judging the distance across a crevasse. "It works for some people," he said quietly. "But it's not a sure-fire cure. When human tragedies happen, it always seems as if scientists and mathematicians can meet the situation more calmly than others. But it's as likely to be a form of escaping reality, and sooner or later comes the payback."

Kit could not quite take the thought where it had to go. He wanted to trust the Professor, but he was alone in the matter. He replied, "Just trying to work through one problem-set at a time, sir, and not get too blind drunk on the weekends."

Likewise he wanted to trust 'Fax, who was a good skate all round, and yet strangers on and off campus with focused stares, too many to be coincidental, had made him wary. There had developed between him and 'Fax this exquisite stupor of assumption about who knew what, or didn't, branching and rebranching, none of it ever stated aloud, all pregnant eyebeaming and circumlocution. 'Fax in any case had never been the feckless character his father had assumed him to be. Out of the corner of his eye, out the corners of 'Fax's own, Kit had caught a whole unacknowledged range of activity going on.

It turned out 'Fax was mighty intrigued with the mysterious tower across the Sound. "We could sail over and take a look. You could introduce me to your pal Dr. Tesla."

For half an hour, they breezed down the harbor, among the beds of Fair Haven oysters staked to show the boundaries of each plantation. When they got out into the Sound, 'Fax began to cast anxious looks at water and sky. "Not happy about this wind," he kept saying. "And the tide's going out. Keep a sharp eye aft."

It was on them fast enough. One minute they were looking eastward at lightning flashes in black skies over Connecticut, the next they were all but careened and being borne toward the lee shore of Long Island and the looming face of Wardenclyffe. Sighting the tower, intermittently revealed through the torn mists, Kit might have imagined himself being storm-blown to some island as yet uncharted, in quite another ocean, had there been time for such reverie—but there was the little knockabout to be saved, the elements outwitted—bailing frantically, sailing loose-footed as they dared without even time to unship the boom—as the great skeletal tower drew steadily closer in the maritime uproar, a lone enigmatic witness to their desperate struggle.

THEY SAT IN a masonry transmitter "shack" designed by McKim, Mead, and White, gradually getting used to being alive and on dry land again. A workman's wife had brought them blankets and coffee Dr. Tesla had imported from Trieste. The rainlight came in through a series of high arched windows.

The thin young scientist with the hypnotic eyes and Wild West mustache had remembered Kit from Colorado. "The vectorist."

"Still at it I guess." Kit gestured across the Sound in the direction of Yale.

"I was sorry to hear of Professor Gibbs's passing. I greatly admired him."

"I hope he's in a better place," Kit said, more or less automatically, but understanding about a second and a half later that he had also meant *better than Yale,* and had maybe had Webb's departed soul in mind as well.

When Kit introduced 'Fax, Tesla kept a straight face. "A pleasure, Mr. Vibe, I have had dealings with your father only marginally more cordial than with Mr. Morgan, and yet the son is not guardian of the father's purse, as we used to say in Granitza . . . in fact, as we never said, for when, in daily life, was that likely to come up?"

Across the water and all around them the storm still raged. Kit, shivering, forgot Curls and Laplacians, likely debutantes, his own recent caress from the wings of Silence, and sat unblinkingly attentive as Tesla spoke.

"My native land is not a country but an artifact of Habsburg foreign policy, known as 'the Military Frontier,' and to us as Granitza. The town was very small, above the Adriatic coast in the Velebit range, where certain places were better than others for . . . what would you call them? Visual experiences that might prove useful."

"Visions."

"Yes, but you had to be in tip-top mental health, or they would prove only hallucinations of limited use."

"Back in the San Juans we always blamed it on the altitude."

"In the Velebit, rivers disappear, flow underground for miles, re-surface unexpectedly, descend to the sea. Underground, therefore, lies an entire unmapped region, a carrying into the Invisible of geography, and—one must ask—why not of other sciences as well? I was out in those mountains one day, the sky began to darken, the clouds to lower, I found a limestone cave, went in, waited. Darker and darker, like the end of the world—but no rain. I couldn't understand it. I sat and tried not to smoke too quickly the last of my cigarettes. Not until a great burst of lightning came from out of nowhere did heaven open, and the rain begin. I understood that something enormous had been poised to happen, requiring an electrical discharge of a certain size to trigger it. In that moment, all this"—he gestured upward into the present storm clouds, which all but obscured the giant toroidal terminal nearly two hundred feet above, whose open trusswork formed a steel cap of fungoid aspect—"was inevitable. As if time had been removed from all equations, the Magnifying Transmitter already existed in that moment, complete, perfected. . . . Everything since, all you have seen in the press, has been theatrical impersonation—the Inventor at Work. To the newspapers I can never speak of that time of simply waiting. I'm expected to be *consciously scientific,* to exhibit only virtues likely to appeal to rich sponsors—activity, speed, Edisonian sweat, defend one's claim, seize one's chance— If I told them how far from conscious the procedure really is, they would all drop me flat."

Suddenly apprehensive, Kit looked over at 'Fax. But his drowsing classmate showed no reaction—unless, like others of the Vibe persuasion, he was only pretending semiconsciousness.

"I have been around them long enough, Dr. Tesla. They have no idea what any of us are about." If he had waited an instant longer, this expression of solidarity would have been drowned out by a Parthian peal of thunder from somewhere over Patchogue Bay as the storm, having crossed the Island, withdrew to sea. Workmen came and went, the cook showed up with another urn full of coffee, the "shack" smelled like wet clothes and cigarette smoke, it could have been any Long Island workday, Neapolitans and Calabresi playing *morra* under the streaming eaves, wagons arriving with lumber and preshaped members of steel, welding torches spitting blue silent intensities through the rain.

There was plenty of room here, and the boys were invited to stay over. Tesla looked in later to say good night.

"Back in Colorado, by the way—those modifications to the transformer. You were right about all that, Mr. Traverse. I never had a chance to thank you."

"You have now. With interest. Anyway, it was pretty clear what you were up to. The curvatures had to be the right ones, and built exactly to shape."

"I wish I could offer you a job here, but—" gesturing with his head at 'Fax, who appeared to be asleep.

Kit with a sombre face nodded. "You might not believe it now, sir, but you are well out of that."

"If there is anything—"

"Let's hope there will be."

NEXT MORNING THE BOYS hitched a ride on a market wagon heading in to New York. Colfax seemed to be watching Kit more narrowly than usual. They rode swaying among sacks of potatoes and cabbages, cucumbers and turnips, along the dusty and clamorous North Hempstead Turnpike, stopping in from time to time at different crossroads saloons.

"There'll be search parties out by now," 'Fax supposed.

"Sure. If it was my kid, I'd have the whole damned Atlantic Fleet out."

"Not for me," 'Fax morosely insistent. "For you."

Abruptly Kit could see, as if arc-lit, his trail right out of this unpromising patch he was in. "Wouldn't've been too hard to get me out of the way, 'Fax. You could've just pulled one them 'North River jibes' of yours and forgot to say 'Duck,' let the boom do it for you. Must happen all the time out on that Sound."

"Not my style," 'Fax blushed, so taken aback that Kit calculated he'd got the seed planted, all right. "Maybe if you were more of a son of a bitch . . ."

"Then it'd be me putting *you* over the side, wouldn't it?"

"Well, one of us should be just a little meaner, 'stead of us both being unhappy like this."

"Who, me? I'm as happy as a Long Island steamer clam, what're you talking about?"

"You're not, Kit. *They know* you're not."

"Here I thought I was bein a real Sunny Jim."

'Fax waited, but not long, before looking him in the eye. "I've been keeping them posted, you see."

"About . . ."

"You. What you're up to, how you're feeling, they've been getting pretty regular reports, all along."

"From you."

"From me."

Neither surprised nor hurt but letting 'Fax think he might be, "Well . . . I thought we were pardners, 'Fax."

"Didn't say it was pleasant for me."

"Hmmm . . ."

"You're angry."

"No. No, I'm thinking. . . . Now, let's say you were to *tell them* I got lost in that storm yesterday—"

"They wouldn't believe it."

"They'd keep looking?"

"You'd have to hide darned well, Kit. The City, maybe it looks easy to you, but it isn't. Sooner or later you find you're trusting people you shouldn't, some who could even turn out to be on Father's payroll."

"What 'n hell do you suggest, then?"

"What I do. Pretend. You've been talking a lot about Germany lately, well, here's your chance. Pretend that our coming through that storm was a certified miracle. Go south of the Green someplace, go in a Catholic church, make a votive offering. Tell Father, who's a man of religion despite all appearances, that you vowed, if you survived the ordeal, to go study in Germany. Kind of, I don't know, math pilgrimage. Foley will be bending a much more skeptical ear, but it's possible to deceive him as well, and I can back you up on that."

"You'd really help?"

"Don't take this the wrong way, but . . . say, I've every reason to, wouldn't you think?"

"Guess so. Beats going over the side."

After a while Colfax said, "There're people who hate him, you know." He was looking sort of sidewise at Kit, almost resentfully.

"Hell you say."

"Look here, Kit, sarcasm aside, he is my father." Sounding so anxious for Kit to hear the truth that he was almost to be pitied for it. Almost.

IN THE BRIGHT LIGHT of day, the figures still looked sinister—not gargoyles, not that elaborate, but with something purposeful about the way in which, denying the official structure, they strained outward from the façade, erect, clenched, trying to escape the conditions of human shelter, seeking the outside, the storm, all that freezes, roars, goes lampless in the dark.

Kit took the elevator as far as it went and then climbed a spiral staircase of carved mahogany up to the executive offices, lit all the way to the top through windows showing in stained glass notable incidents in the history of the Vibe Corp. Cornering the Pickle Market. The Discovery of Neofungoline. Launching of the Steamer *Edwarda B. Vibe. . . .*

Should've taken some elective courses in the Drama Department, he thought. He knocked at the dark wood door.

Inside, Foley the dedicated substitute posed over by the window as if enthroned, against the marine daylight, a fine silver contour to his face as if it were familiar to the world as any on a postage stamp, as if proclaiming, *Yes, this is who we are, how it is, how it always is, this is what you may expect of us, impressive, isn't it? It better be.*

"This Germany business," said Scarsdale Vibe.

"Sir." Kit had expected he'd be quaking like the young aspen before the mountain winds, but some unaccustomed light, light under the aspect of distance, had crept round him instead, bringing if not quite immunity, at least clarity.

"Vital to your education."

"I believe I ought to go on to Göttingen."

"For mathematics."

"Advanced mathematics, yes."

"*Useful* advanced mathematics? Or—" He gestured in the air to suggest the formless, if not the unmanly.

"Sometimes the real world, the substantial world of affairs, possessing greater inertia, takes a while to catch up," Kit carefully pretended to instruct him. "The Maxwell Field Equations, for example—it was twenty years till Hertz discovered real electromagnetic waves, traveling at the speed of light, just as Maxwell had worked it out on paper."

"Twenty years," smiled Scarsdale Vibe, with the worn insolence of someone expecting to live forever. "I'm not sure I have that long."

"All sincerely trust that you do," replied Kit.

"Do you think you have twenty years, Kit?" In the short silence, as the slight but fatal emphasis on "you" reverberated, Scarsdale was aware immediately that he might have misplayed his hand, while for Kit things quietly fell into their rightful places, and he understood that he could not allow hesitation, any more than anger, to betray him. "Back in Colorado," trying not to speak too carefully, "what with avalanches and blue northers, desperate men, desperate and uncivilized, horses too, all apt to go unexpectedly loco from the altitude and so forth, you learn there's no telling what the future holds is all, even one minute to the next." And heard Foley over by the window grunt sharply, as if wakened from a snooze.

Scarsdale Vibe beamed with what Kit could recognize by now as an effort, by no means reliable, to contain some underdefined rage, the scale of whose potential for damage maybe not even Vibe himself suspected. "Your professors are unanimous in recommending you. You'll be happy to hear." He produced a steamship ticket and held it out to Kit, implacably cordial. "Forward of the stacks. Bon voyage, sir."

This might be all in code, but the shape of it was clear. Scarsdale Vibe at this pitch of things would feel just as comfortable as Kit would with an ocean between them, and willing to pay first-class rates if he had to, to put it there. So back in '63 had he paid not to have to go and fight—so had he continued to pay for the elimination from his life of many forms of inconvenience, including—what doubt could remain? ah, God—Webb Traverse. There it was, like a conjecture whose truth was obvious to all, though perhaps never to be proven with the furthest rigor.

No longer waiting, then, as the interview progressed, for any expression of condolence over Webb, understanding that the moment for it had passed forever, one of those negative results with resonance far beyond itself, Kit felt the way he had his first time on a bicycle, in a slow measured glide, knowing as long as he kept on moving just this way, he could not fall over. He might not even have to work too hard right now to conceal his thoughts, except for one pure and steady light he kept well within—the certainty that one day this would have to be put right—the moment his to choose, details such as how and where not as important as the equals sign going in in the right place. . . .

"Thank you, sir."

"Don't thank me. Become the next Edison." The man sat there smirking, secure in unquestioned might, unable to imagine how all he believed protecting him had just turned to glass—if not to be smashed to bits quite yet, then shaped for now into a lens that promised close and merciless scrutiny, or maybe someday, when held at the appropriate distance, death by focused light. And he should have said Tesla, not Edison.

Kit found himself at Track 14 in the Grand Central Station in time for the 3:55 back to New Haven, with no idea how he'd got there, having apparently by some buggy-horse reflex walked through the sulfurous city safe from all misadventure by streetcar-brake failure, armed assault, mad dogs, or unbribed coppers, straight to this poised and seething express. Some always had homes to return to, Kit had departure gates, piers, turnstiles, institutional doorways.

He still had no idea whether or not he'd got away with something, or whether he'd just put his life in danger. Back at Pearl Street, the two Vibes were sitting over brandy and cigars.

"A tough one to figure, that kid," Foley opined. "Sure hope we ain't got another Red in the root cellar like his old man."

"Our duty would be no less clear. There are hundreds of these abscesses suppurating in the body of our Republic," an oratorical throb creeping into Scarsdale's voice, "which must be removed, wherever they are found. No other option. The elder Traverse's sins are documented—once they were brought to light, he was as good as lost. Should there be moral reservations, in a class war, about targeting one's enemies? You have been in this game long enough to appreciate how mighty are the wings we shelter beneath. How immune we are kept to the efforts of these muckraking Reds to soil our names. Unless—Walker, have I missed something? you aren't developing a soft spot."

As Scarsdale's was not the only voice Foley had to attend to, he erred, as usual, on the side of mollification. He held out his glowing Havana. "If you can find a soft spot, use it to put this out on."

"What happened to us, Foley? We used to be such splendid fellows."

"Passage of Time, but what's a man to do?"

"Too easy. Doesn't account for this strange fury I feel in my heart, this desire to kill off every damned socialist and so on leftward, without any more mercy than I'd show a deadly microbe."

"Sounds reasonable to me. Not like that we haven't bloodied up our hands already here."

Scarsdale gazed out his window at a cityscape once fair but with the years grown more and more infested with shortcomings. "I wanted so to believe. Even knowing my own seed was cursed, I wanted the eugenics argument to be faulty somehow. At the same time I coveted the bloodline of my enemy, which I fancied uncontaminated, I wanted that promise, promise unlimited."

Foley pretended his narrowing of gaze was owing to cigar-smoke. "Mighty Christian attitude," he commented at last, in a tone as level as he could make it.

"Foley, I'm as impatient with religious talk as the next sinner. But what a burden it is to be told to love them, while knowing that they are the Antichrist itself, and that our only salvation is to deal with them as we ought."

It did not help Foley's present mood that he had awakened that morning from a recurring nightmare of the Civil War. The engagement was confined to an area no bigger than an athletic field, though uncountable thousands of men had somehow been concentrated there. All was brown, gray, smoky, dark. A lengthy exchange of artillery had begun, from emplacements far beyond the shadowy edges of the little field. He had felt oppressed by the imminence of doom, of some suicidal commitment of infantry which no one would escape. A pile of explosives nearby, a tall, rickety wood crib of shells and other ammunition began to smolder, about to catch fire and blow up at any moment, a clear target for the cannonballs of the other side, which continued to come in, humming terribly, without pause. . . .

"I didn't have my war then," Scarsdale had been saying. "Just as well. I was too young to appreciate what was at stake anyway. My civil war was yet to come. And here we are in it now, in the thick, no end in sight. The Invasion of Chicago, the battles of Homestead, the Coeur d'Alene, the San Juans. These communards speak a garble of foreign tongues, their armies are the damnable labor syndicates, their artillery is dynamite, they assassinate our great men and bomb our cities, and their aim is to despoil us of our hard-won goods, to divide and sub-divide among their hordes our lands and our houses, to pull us down, our lives, all we love, until they become as demeaned and soiled as their own. O Christ, Who hast told us to love them, what test of the spirit is this, what darkness hath been cast over our understanding, that we can no longer recognize the hand of the Evil One?

"I am so tired, Foley, I have struggled too long in these thankless waters, I am as an unconvoyed vessel alone in a tempest that will not, will never abate. The future belongs to the Asiatic masses, the pan-Slavic brutes, even, God help us, the black seething spawn of Africa interminable. We cannot hold. Before these tides we must go under. Where is our Christ, our Lamb? the Promise?"

Seeing his distress, Foley meant only to comfort. "In our prayers—"

"Foley, spare me that, what we need to do is start killing them in significant numbers, for nothing else has worked. All this pretending—'equality,' 'negotiation'—it's been such a cruel farce, cruel to both sides. When the Lord's people are in danger, you know what he requires."

"Smite."

"Smite early and often."

"Hope there's nobody listening in on this."

"God is listening. As to men, I have no shame about what must be done." A queer tension had come into his features, as if he were trying to suppress a cry of delight. "But you, Foley, you seem kind of—almost—nervous."

Foley considered briefly. "My nerves? Cast iron." He relit his cigar, the matchflame unshaking. "Ready for anything."

Aware of the Other Vibe's growing reluctance to trust reports from out in the field, Foley, who usually was out there and thought he had a good grasp on things, at first resentful and after a while alarmed, had come to see little point these days in speaking up. The headquarters in Pearl Street seemed more and more like a moated castle and Scarsdale a ruler isolated in self-resonant fantasy, a light to his eyes these days that was not the same as that old, straightforward acquisitive gleam. The gleam was gone, as if Scarsdale had accumulated all the money he cared to and was now moving on in his biography to other matters, to action in the great world he thought he understood but—even Foley could see—was failing, maybe fatally, even to ask the right questions about anymore. Who could Foley go to with this?

Who indeed? He had at least brought himself to reckon up what the worst outcome might be, and it came out the same every time. It was nothing to recoil from, though it did take some getting used to—maybe not massacre on the reckless, blood-happy scale of Bulgarians or Chinese, more, say, in the moderate American tradition of Massachusetts Bay or Utah, of righteous men who believed it was God they heard whispering in the most bitter patches of the night, and God help anybody who suggested otherwise. His own voices, which had never pretended to be other than whose they were, reminded Foley of his mission, to restrain the alternate Foley, doing business as Scarsdale Vibe, from escaping into the freedom of bloodletting unrestrained, the dark promise revealed to Americans during the Civil War, obeying since then its own terrible inertia, as the Republican victors kept after Plains Indians, strikers, Red immigrants, any who were not likely docile material for the mills of the newly empowered order.

"It is a fine edge here," the tycoon had hinted one day, "between killing just the one old Anarchist and taking out the whole cussèd family. I'm still not sure which I ought to do."

"There's thousands of em out there, and we've done away with our share," Foley puzzled. "Why even bother singling any of em out?"

"This boy Christopher, for one thing. He's different."

Foley was no innocent. He'd been down to Cooper Square and the Tenderloin, passed an evening, maybe two, in the resorts where men danced with each other or dolled up like Nellie Noonan or Anna Held and sang for the crowds of "fairies," as they called themselves, and it would have figured only as one more item of city depravity, except for the longing. Which wasn't just real, it was too real to ignore. Foley had at least got that far, learned not to disrespect another man's longing.

Surely bringing Kit back here from the hardrock misery of the San Juans had been an act of rescue, as much as bringing to the Christian faith the child of some murderous savage one had been obliged to slay. So reason, what was passing for it at Pearl Street, was brought into play, resulting eventually in a plan for the whole family. Mayva would receive a monthly stipend for herself and Lake. Frank would be offered a high-paying job when he graduated from the Colorado School of Mines. Reef—"Who, actually, hasn't been seen for a while. . . . Another itinerant gambler—he'll show up sooner or later and turn out to be cheapest of all, the sort who's content with a modest jackpot he never expected to win."

But a voice, unlike the others that spoke to Foley, had begun to speak and, once begun, persisted. "Some might call this *corrupting youth.* It wasn't enough to pay to have an enemy murdered, but he must corrupt the victim's children as well. You suffered through the Wilderness and at last, at Cold Harbor, lay between the lines three days, between the worlds, and this is what you were saved for? this mean, nervous, scheming servitude to an enfeebled conscience?"

On the train trip east, Dally kept pretty much to herself, there being nothing, as she quickly learned, quite like the rails these days for cowboy poets, who along with confidence men, R-girls, and purse-thieves, could be encountered on every train west of Chicago. They rode in the parlor cars marveling hour on hour at everything that passed, introducing themselves as "Raoul" or "Sebastian," chatting up young prairie wives traveling to or from husbands whose names seldom got mentioned. In the velvet-trimmed observation and dining cars everywhere, private and public, rolling and still, these birds smothered appetites and curdled stomachs. Coffee grew ice cold in the cup. Badmen out for mischief flinched, turned, and strode away, sleep crept like an irresistible gas, and those Wild West poets just went raving on.

Seeing Chicago again—not that anyone was asking, but if they had, she couldn't have described very clearly her feelings, and besides there wouldn't be much time between trains to see much. Somewhere in her head, she'd had this notion that because the White City had once existed beside the Lake, in Jackson Park, it would have acted somehow like yeast in bread and caused the entire city to bloom into some kind of grace. Rolling through the city, in to Union Station, she found herself stunned by the immensity, the conglomeration of architectural styles, quickening, ascending, to the sky-scrapers at the heart of it. Sort of reminding her of the Midway pavilions, that mixture of all the world's peoples. She looked out the windows, hoping for some glimpse of her White City, but saw only the darkened daytime one, and understood that some reverse process had gone on, not leavening but condensing to this stone gravity.

. . .

IN NEW YORK AT LAST she stood out of the traffic, watching shadows of birds move across sunlit walls. Just around the corner, on the great Avenue, two-horse carriages curvaceous and sumptuary as the beds of courtesans in a romance moved along, the horses stepping carefully in mirror-symmetry. The sidewalks were crowded with men in black suits and stark white high collars, in the tangible glare of noontide that came pushing uptown, striking tall highlights from shiny top hats, projecting shadows that looked almost solid. . . . The women by contrast were rigged out in lighter colors, ruffles, contrasting lapels, hats of velvet or straw full of artificial flowers and feathers and ribbons, broad angled brims throwing faces into girlish penumbras as becoming as paint and powder. A visitor from quite far away might almost have imagined two separate species having little to do, one with the other . . .

When lunchtime rolled around, her first day in the City, Dally went into a restaurant to eat. It was a cheery place, with sparkling white tile nearly everywhere, and silver plate ringing against thick crockery. The unmistakable church-supper smell of American home cooking. Clean napkins were rolled and waiting in the water glasses. By each long table stood a tall post with an electric fan spinning up on top, and a little cluster of electric bulbs, each in its glass shade, just below what she guessed to be the motor casing. No cuspidors she could see, nor cigar smokers—no tablecloths either, though the marble tops of the tables were kept scrupulously clean by girls in belted white dresses and little black bow ties, and their hair neatly pinned up, who moved about clearing dishes and setting new places.

"Looking for a job, dear? Mrs. Dragsaw over there's the one to see."

"Well, just my lunch today."

"You fetch your own, see that line yonder? You want me for anything, it's Katie."

"I'm Dahlia. You're from south Ohio, I'd guess."

"Why, Chillicothe. Not you, too?"

"No, but I've been through there a couple of times, pretty town, lot of duck hunters as I recall?"

"When it wasn't ducks, it was grouse. My Pa used to take us out all the time. Mostly waiting and freezing, but how I miss it. Everybody in here's a vegetarian, o' course."

"Oh, woe's me, had my mouth set for a nice *slab o' that bull meat*."

"The casseroles aren't too bad usually. . . . 've you got someplace to stay, Dahlia?"

"Managing, thanks."

"Thin ice in this town, 's all I meant. One step to the next."

"Katie!"

"Bug in *her* britches today. Well—you know where to find me." She withdrew into the hygienic brilliancy of the establishment.

Dally found a modest hotel for young ladies whose rent would not eat up her grubstake too fast, and set about hoofing the pavement looking for work. One day up in the theatre district after a job as an organ tuner's apprentice that didn't pan out, owing, as far as she could determine, to her lack of a penis, she happened to see Katie coming out of an alleyway with just as glum of a look on her face. "One more turndown," Katie muttered. "How do I get to be Maude Adams at this rate?"

"Oh I'm sorry. Same just happened to me."

"It's New York. Disrespect was invented here. But why do they have to go on about a girl's age?"

"So . . . you're an actress."

"Working days clearing tables at Schultz's Vegetarian Brauhaus, what else would I be?"

A couple days later, they were in a chop suey joint down on Pell Street, discussing the job situation.

"Artist's model," cried Dally, "really? that's so romantic, Katie! Why didn't you take it?"

"I know it's work and I should've jumped at it, but I always had my heart set on the stage." There were worse ways to make your living in this miserable town, worse than most folks could imagine, Katie assured her.

Apart from the chop suey, which was more of an uptown fad, the place smelled like serious cooking. Wood ceiling fans turned slowly, stirring the smoke from tobacco, peanut-oil and possibly opium, rippling the hanging strips of red paper which displayed the day's menu in Chinese lettering. There was sawdust on the floor and mother-of-pearl inlaid in the ebony furniture. Lanterns, silk banners, gold dragons, and bat images all around the room. Regulars sat eating shark fin, sea worm, and perfumed ham, and drinking pear wine, surrounded by dozens of white folks in their good clothes all gobbling away at giant plates of chop suey and calling, often rudely, for more.

In glided a squad of young Chinese men, all in step, silent, sporting dark American suits and pomaded haircuts with short to nonexistent sideburns, heading for the back of the establishment while the uptowners continued unbroken their heedless chattering.

"Mock Duck's boys," Katie whispered. "The real article. Not like the play-actors you'll be dealing with."

"If I get the job," Dally reminded her. "Sure you don't want it instead? Even if there is no stage?"

"Dear, *you're* exactly what they're looking for."

"Wish that sounded more reassuring, Kate. What'd you tell them?"

"Oh . . . I sort of suggested you had acting experience?"

"Ha. Sheriffs and bill collectors, maybe."

"Toughest house there is."

As the crowd was beginning to thin out, "Matinee starts in a couple o' minutes," said Katie. "Come on, we'll use the shortcut." She took Dally's arm and steered her toward the rear exit. Mock Duck's boys had gone all invisible. Outside, the girls proceeded through narrow streets among a scurry of Chinese tradesfolk and daytime errand-runners, guided presently by the helpful screams from up ahead of what proved to be a presentable young American blonde *en déshabillé*, struggling with two local toughs, who apparently wished to drag her down into a manhole. "That's Modestine. She has to take let's say a *short vacation,* and you'd be replacing her."

"But they're—"

"They're actors. White slavery as a real racket is recommended only for those who thrive on constant worry. Here. Say hello to Mr. Hop Fung."

Hop Fung, done up all in black, glowered at them and started to fuss in Chinese. "That's hello," Katie whispered. The enterprising Celestial had begun his career as an ordinary lobbygow or tour guide, but Chinatown was too close to the Bowery to insulate him for long from the allures of show business, and soon he was dreaming up—literally, for his office in those days was an opium "joint" off Pell Street—short melodramas that showed a sure instinct for what would catch the fancy of the Occidental rubbernecker. "Chop suey stories!" he informed Dally and Katie. "We give them plenty! Hot and spicy! O.K.? Start tomorrow!"

"No audition?" Dally wondered, and found Katie tugging on her sleeve.

"Little tip," she muttered, "if you're serious about being in the business—"

"Red hair! Freckles! Audition enough O.K.!"

Which is how Dally found her way into the white-slave simulation industry and the tunnels of Chinatown, began to learn some of the all-but-impenetrable signs and codes, a region of life withheld, a secret life of cities that those gypsy years with Merle had always denied her. . . . Every morning she commuted down on the Third Avenue El, had coffee at a wagon parked under the tracks, and strolled on to Hop Fung's office to review the schedule of comediettas, which tended to change from one day to the next, being careful near the corner of Mott and Canal to look up down and sideways, for here was the headquarters of Tom Lee's tong, the On Leong—and trying to keep clear altogether of Doyers Street, which was a kind of no-man's-land between the On Leong and their deadly rival tong the Hip Sing, who were based at the corner of Doyers and Pell. The two organizations had been fighting in earnest since around 1900, when rogue gunman Mock Duck arrived in town and threw in with the Hip Sing, presently burning down the On Leong dormitory at 18 Mott and taking over Pell Street. There was no telling when armed unpleasantness might flare up, or where, though Doyers seemed the preferred battleground, the bend halfway along being known as "the bloody angle."

By now she had moved in with Katie, who lived in a midtown Irish neighborhood between the Third and Sixth Avenue Els. Within a couple of weeks, she had uptown visitors gaping from their tour charabancs in amazement, ladies from out of town clutching their hats, as if pins might fail in the duty assigned them. Neighborhood pedestrians who might or might not be part of the show stood as in a *tableau vivant,* making no move to intervene. "O you fiends!" Dally cried, and "Spare me!" and "If your mothers but knew!" to all of which her abductors only grinned and cackled more hideously, dragging her toward the ineluctable iron hole in the street, making sure to pick up for later re-use any items of attire "torn" from her person, these being in fact lightly basted together before each performance, in order purposely to come away and add an element of "spice" to the show.

Word had gotten around. Show-business functionaries at all levels came down to observe Dally in performance, including restless impresario R. Wilshire Vibe, ever on the cruise for new talent, who had in fact been haunting Chinatown for weeks. Sometimes he showed up in disguise, his idea of a common workman involving spats and bespoke neckties from London, though presently he reverted to type, the not perhaps adequately subdued shine off his aquamarine morning-hat indeed causing Dally herself to fluff a line or two, not that anybody noticed. Afterward he introduced himself with an unaccustomed sheepishness while Chinese stagehands stood around impatiently waiting to set up for the next show.

"I'm thinking of putting something like this in my next project, *Shanghai Scampers,* and there might be a part for you."

"Uh, huh." She looked around to see who was handy if this customer proved to be the sort of pest it only took a girl a minute and a half in New York to tumble to.

"It's entirely legitimate," presenting her with his card. "Ask anybody in the business. Or just take a stroll up Broadway, you'll notice two or three of my little efforts playing to sold-out houses. Important question right now is, do you have a contract here?"

"I signed something. But it was in Chinese."

"Ah, when is it not. Indeed, the Chinese tongue is innocent simplicity next to a standard run-of-the-show contract in English. Not to worry my dear, we'll sort it out."

"Yes and here's my associate Mr. Hop Fung, and I must dash, so nice talking to you." She almost held out her hand as she imagined an actress might but was startled to hear this uptown smoothie slide into what sounded like real Chinese. Hop Fung, who hardly ever changed expression from his all-purpose scowl, broke into a smile so dazzling she wondered for a minute if it was him.

Shortly after, production money began to appear mysteriously in hefty amounts, usually delivered in the form of gold. The cast list was expanded and more fancy stage effects added on. All of a sudden, there were highbinders popping in and out of doorways and manholes faster than you could say chop suey, jabbering a mile a minute in that impenetrable lingo of theirs. Sinister young tong soldiers wearing chain-mail under their Western suits appeared to run dodging and blasting away with their .44s, the smoke soon bringing a picturesque imprecision to the scene. Horses, having been instructed to, reared and whinnied. A small band of police raced along Pell Street to the scene, while others, understood to be in the pay of the other tong, came charging up Mott waving their day clubs, both parties colliding at the corner, where, clubs in motion, they fell to arguing as to who had jurisdiction over the outrage, which of course was proceeding regardless. *Glans penis*–shaped helmets, dislodged, rolled in the gutters.

At this point a curious thing happened. As if all the expensive make-believe had somehow slopped over into "real life," the actual tong war in the neighborhood now heated up in earnest, gunfire was heard at night, Mock Duck himself appeared in the street down in his well-known spinning squat, firing two revolvers at a time in all directions as pushcart vegetables were destroyed and pedestrians went diving for cover, warnings were issued about what parts of Chinatown would be best avoided unless uptown tourists wished to suffer inconvenience, and Dally's white-slave engagement looked more and more precarious. Co-workers she had taken for the meanest and ugliest of highbinders turned out to be sensitive artistes in fear of their safety. Hop Fung was seen popping twenty-five-cent opium pills by the fistful. Doyers Street was occupied by little more than an eerie miasma of silence.

"Maybe I should be looking for another job, Katie, what do you think?"

"How about your old pal R. Wilshire Vibe?"

"Can't tell if he's 'the real thing.'"

"Oh, R.W.'s real as any of them," Katie assured her, "but it's a fast, not to mention godless, crowd, and I know personally more than one girl who's come to a sorrowful pass, including our own treasured Modestine."

"Her vacation—"

"Oh, child. There are farms upstate for such purposes, and sometimes these wealthy vermin find it cheaper than hiring a plug-ugly to introduce her to the river. Moddie got off lucky."

"Well thanks for getting *me* into this, Katie."

"I'm not talking about the Chinese, who are gentlemen first and last, their arrangements stay always within their race. But it was Moddie's choice to leave that genteel environment for the cruel jungles of the moneyed white."

"Well, guess I'll put on my pith helmet anyway and head across town."

"If you hear about *two* jobs . . ."

Dally found R. Wilshire at his offices on West Twenty-eighth Street. From open windows all up and down the street came the clangor of what sounded like a whole orchestra of saloon pianos. "Horrible, ain't it?" R. Wilshire greeted her cheerfully. "Night and day, and not one of those blessed instruments in tune. They call this Tin Pan Alley."

"Figured you more for the marble-halls type."

"Got to stay close to the sources of my inspiration."

"He means steal whatever he can," beamed a portly, white-haired gent in a plaid suit of acid magenta and saffron, who was carrying what appeared to be a sack of soup bones.

"He's out scouting unsigned dog acts," R.W. explained. "Con McVeety, say hello to Miss Rideout."

"I'm also looking for a card girl," Con said.

"A what?"

"I'm in vaudeville, see." Behind Con's back, R.W. was making frantic thumbs-down signals. "Don't mind him, it's simple envy. I need somebody presentable who doesn't drink and can hold up the printed signs that introduce the different acts. Right side up, if possible."

"McVeety," R.W. muttered. "Will you tell her, or shall I?"

Turned out that Con's fatality, a subject of wonder throughout the business, was for finding absolutely the worst acts in the city, acts that earned not only ejection but permanent banishment from even the least promising of Bowery Amateur Nights—at which Con in fact had long been in the practice of lurking backstage, waiting for the fateful Hook deployment, often able to sign artistes before that instrument ever made contact with their persons, booking them forthwith into such dubious venues as public toilets, patches of sidewalk in front of blind pigs, and, briefly, opium dens along Mott Street, till somebody pointed out to him that opium smokers provide their own entertainment.

"I take it the Chinatown situation grows more dangerous as we speak," said R.W. "But you'd have to be pretty desperate to work for this lowlife."

"These light-operatical tycoons have lost touch," Con pretended to confide. "For the Bowery is still the true heart of American show business."

"I wish I had something for you," R.W. shrugged. "Soon as the revenue picture improves, perhaps—"

"He means soon as he can find a bookie who's left the cash box unattended," Con chuckled. "I'll pay seven-fifty a week, cash in advance."

"What a rookie cop gets for a bribe," Dally said. "I thought we were talking about Art here."

The two other sets of eyebrows in the room went up and down, and there might have been a moment of silent discussion. In any case Con came back with "Ten?" and the deal was done.

AT THIS STAGE of his career, Con was just managing to come up every week with the rent on a failed dime museum he had purchased for a song, whose gaudy sign in front redesignated it MCVEETY'S THEATER. The former owners having been in some haste to absquatulate, random items of inventory had been left behind, the usual two-headed dogs in jars and pickled brains of notable figures in history, many from long before pickling as we know it was invented, the Baby from Mars, the scalp of General Custer, certified to be authentic, despite having passed from the Little Big Horn through an odyssey of secondary markets which included Mexico and the Lower East Side, a caged Australian Wild Cockroach the size of a sewer rat which nobody was willing to go near, and so forth. Con assembled these in a tasteful display he termed the Olio of Oddities and put them out in the foyer of his Theater. "Get em in the mood before the show starts, see."

Some kind of incentive, Dally soon realized with dismay, was sure needed. Her job as card girl being made difficult by audiences impatient, not to mention unfamiliar, with print, after a while Con allowed her to make brief speeches describing, as hopefully as she could, what they were in for. The nightly talent included Professor Bogoslaw Borowicz, who put on what he called "Floor Shows," which, due to his faulty grasp of the American idiom, turned out to be literal *displays of floors*—more usually fragments of them, detached and stolen from various locations around the city—Steeplechase Park, Grand Central station, McGurk's on the Bowery (". . . you will notice interesting textures of tobacco juice and sawdust . . ."), strange tilings from demolition jobs that raised advanced mathematical issues the Prof was then moved to go on about at stupefying length—as well as "trainers" of stuffed animals whose repertoire of "tricks" inclined to the rudimentary, narcoleptics who had mastered the difficult but narrowly appreciated knack of going to sleep while standing up, three minutes or less of which had audiences, even heavily opiated themselves, fighting to get out the exits, and crazy inventors with their inventions, levitating shoes, greenback duplicators, perpetual-motion machines which even the most distracted of audiences understood could never be demonstrated in any time frame short of eternity, and, strangely often, hats—notably The Phenomenal Dr. Ictibus and His Safe-Deflector Hat. This ingenious piece of headgear was invented to address the classic urban contingency of a heavy steel safe falling from a broken purchase at a high window onto the head of some unlucky pedestrian. "Bearing in mind that any concentrated mass is actually a local distortion of space itself, there happens to be exactly one surface, defined by a metric tensor or let us say equation, registered with the U.S. Patent Office, which, incorporated into a suitable hat design, will take the impact load of any known safe falling from any current altitude, transmitting to the wearer only the most trivial of resultant vectors, a brief tap on the head if that, while camming the safe itself harmlessly away toward the nearest curbside. Here's my assistant Odo, who will be happy to rig, hoist, and drop any safe you ladies and gents may care to designate, smack *on top of my head,* isn't that right Odo?"

"Unnhhrrhhh!" replied Odo, with an eagerness some might have taken as inappropriate, though offstage Dally found him to be a polite and well-spoken young man, who was trying to save up enough money to open his own dime museum, maybe a little farther uptown, and they fell into the habit of going for coffee after the last performance of the night.

From time to time, amid the unshaven faces and dicer-topped heads, she caught sight of R. Wilshire Vibe, always in the company of a different aspiring young actress, or, as R.W. preferred, *figurante.* "Just looking in," he greeted Dally, "haven't forgotten you, have you caught *African Antics* yet? Basically a coon revue, couple of boys who're going to be the next Williams and Walker. Here, take a couple of comps. *Shanghai Scampers,* say it's all but set, the score's written, job now is to get the pigeons all lined up on the window ledge, so to speak."

Meanwhile Con had decided to put on a Bowery version of William Shakespeare's *Julius Caesar,* to be called *Dagoes with Knives,* which Dally tried out for, landing, to her bewilderment, the part of Calpurnia, whom Con had decided to call Mrs. Caesar, Dally's competition for the part having been a blind-pig regular named One-Tooth Elsie and Liu Bing, a tong warrior's girlfriend looking for a different line of work, whose acquaintance with English, both Elizabethan and present-day, proved bothersomely remote. After he'd turned her down, however, Con had a visit from her beau and a few of his colleagues, all packing .44s and hatchets, which left Con with a sudden new perspective on the casting. "It was only a couple of lines," he apologized to Dally. "You're a much better choice, really, but this way I get to stay alive. I figure we can pretend she's talking Latin."

"Aw. I sort of liked that stuff about drizzling blood on the Capitol."

"Welcome to the business," Katie shrugged when Dally came back scowling. "*Courage,* Camille, it's only the first act."

"Meantime," loosening her stays, "this Vibe specimen is having a party Saturday night, and he says I can bring a friend along. You're probably not interested, rich folks's depravity and so forth—"

"Interested? Does Lillian Russell wear a hat? Completely different story, girl—let's see, Verbena owes me a favor, I know we can borrow her red ball gown—"

"Katie, for goodness' sake."

"No, not for you, you'd do better with your hair down, in something more, what they call 'ingenue'—"

They went uptown to look for ball dresses. Katie knew a seamstress who worked in a sub-basement of the I. J. & K. Smokefoot department store and had a line on returned or just-out-of-fashion numbers which could be picked up for a song. Smokefoot's was located along the Ladies' Mile, far enough north to avoid imputations of the unfashionable, yet not so far from others of its kind as to present inconvenience to any female client determined to shop the day through. All but clear of surface ornament, towering in gray modernity twelve stories high and engrossing an entire city block, it might've struck the visitor from out of town lucky enough to find an unjostled vantage point as more a monument for simple goggling at, than a real-life marketplace actually to be entered and engaged. Yet the size of the place was not due to whims of grandiosity but rather dictated by a need for enough floor-area to keep rigorously set a veil separating two distinct worlds—the artfully illusory spaces intended for the store's customers and the less-merciful topography in between the walls and below the bargain basement, populated by the silent and sizable regiment of cash-girls, furnace-stokers, parcel-wrappers, shipping clerks, needlewomen, feather-workers, liveried messengers, sweepers and dusters and runners of errands of all sorts who passed invisibly everywhere, like industrious spirits, separated often only by inches, by careful breaths, from the theatrical bustle of the bright, sussurant Floors.

As if two human figures in an architectural rendering had briefly come to life and begun exchanging pleasantries, oblivious to the lofty vision towering above them, the young women swept toward the Sixth Avenue entrance, to either side of which stood two doormen splendidly uniformed, living pillars before whose serene inertia one was either intimidated into moving along or not. Let the hair-oiled "bouncer" ply his trade in the Bowery, the electrical gates of Fifth Avenue mansions swing to or fro at the remote touch of a button—here at I. J. & K. Smokefoot's, without a word or indeed a physical movement, because of how and where the Pillars stood, a visitor might know in not too lengthy an instant how and where she stood as well.

"Jachin and Boaz," grinned Katie, indicating them with a head-toss. "Guardians of the Temple, First Kings someplace."

"But will these two let us in, do you think? and suppose they don't?"

Katie patted her shoulder. "Easier here than the employees' entrance, my girl. Give them the level gaze and the sketch of a smile, and as you pass, keep looking at them sideways, as if you were flirting."

"Me? I'm just a kid."

Inside was everything that outside was not—luminous, ornamental, beautifully swept, fragrant with perfumes and cut flowers, a-thrill with a concentrated *chic,* as if the crowds in the Avenues adjoining had been culled for particularly modish women and they'd all just this instant been herded in here. Dally stood breathing it in, till Katie took her arm. "Look at this bunch of old frumps, I declare."

"Huh? You think so?"

"Well, let's have a look around, as long as we're here."

They ascended by Otis escalator, a newly-introduced conveyance which Dally found miraculous, even after she'd figured out roughly how it had to work. Katie, who'd ridden them before, was no longer impressed. "Gawking is O.K., but not too much, please, it's New York. It all looks a lot more wonderful than it is."

"Sure is a long way from Chillicothe, though."

"All right, all right."

It being her first time in a department store, Dally put herself through the usual small humiliations, taking mannequins once or twice for real women, finding herself unable to locate price tags on anything, gazing in alarm at an approaching pair of young women, arm in arm, who looked exactly like her and Katie, both regarding Dally with such queer familiarity, closer and closer till Katie all but had to grab and shake her, muttering "Only hayseeds walk into mirrors, kid." By the time they got all the way upstairs, Dally had drifted into a kind of daze.

It was nothing, really, almost nothing, could have been another clothes dummy at this distance, sighted across the deep central courtyard that ran vertiginously up through all twelve floors, with only a filigreed ironwork railing between shoppers and a plunge to the main floor, past the tranquilly ascending diagonals of moving staircase and a scale replica of Yosemite Falls, down to where a tiny harpist in shadows thrown by palm trees seemed from up here part of the realm of the Hereafter. There on the other side of that hypnotic Deep and the arpeggiations ascending out of it stood a figure in lady-shopper's streetwear in a violet and gray check, the egret plume on her hat articulating sensitive as a hand, not looking at Dally in particular but somehow demanding her attention. Before the clarity of the apparition, Dally knew she had to get an immediate grip on herself, because if she didn't, the next thing she knew, she'd be running over there screaming, to embrace some woman who would of course turn out to be a stranger, and all the embarrassment, maybe even legal action, that was sure to go with that, and the word she'd be screaming would be "Mamma!"

The rest of the shopping tour floated by in nebulous incoherence. Dally seemed to remember tea with cucumber sandwiches, a horribly saccharine harp performance of "Her Mother Never Told Her," two smart young matrons scandalizing the tea-room by lighting up cigarettes—but none of it hung together, the details were like cards tossed on the table of the day that upon inspection could not be arranged into a playable hand.

On the way down to the basement, Dally made sure on every floor to look for her, but the woman, tall, fair, perhaps not real to begin with, had vanished. In addition, the harpist on the street floor turned out to be not an ethereal young woman in a long gown but a cigar-chewing bruiser, just released from a lengthy stay at the Tombs, named Chuck, who leered amiably at Katie and Dally as they passed.

In the basement Katie made inquiries, and her friend Verbena emerged from the scene behind the scene to lead them back and downward into an underlit chill where conversation did not exist either because it was forbidden or because there was too much work to be done, grimy pipes hanging from corroded brackets ran along the ceilings, the smell of cleaning and dyeing solvents and steam from pressers' irons pervaded all the space, workers slipped by silent as wraiths, shadowy doorways led to crowded rooms full of women at sewing machines who did not look up from their work except with apprehension when they felt the supervisor draw close.

· · ·

THEY TOOK the sixth Avenue El downtown and got off at Bleecker Street. There was some apricot-pink light left in the sky, and a southeast wind bringing up the aroma of roasting coffee from South Street, and they could hear river traffic. It was Saturday night in Kipperville. Bearded youths ran by, chasing girls in Turkey red print dresses. Jugglers on unicycles performed tricks along the sidewalk. Negroes accosted strollers, exhibiting small vials of white powder and hopefully inquiring faces. Street vendors sold corn on the cob and broiled squabs on toast. Children hollered behind the open windows of tenements. Uptown slummers bound for places like Maria's on MacDougal chatted brightly and asked one another, "Do you know where we're going?"

R. Wilshire Vibe lived in an Italianate town house whose builder had found himself helpless before the impulse to add Beaux-Arts detailing. It was on the north side of the street, with Ginkgo trees in front, a pergola, and a mews running behind.

A butler or two bowed them in the door, and they ascended into a ballroom dominated by a huge gas chandelier, blindingly bright, directly beneath which was placed a sort of circular couch in wine-colored plush skirted with gold tasseling and provided with satin cushions in matching shades, accommodating eight to sixteen non-dancers each facing radially outward, referred to not altogether in jocularity as an anti-wallflower device, for those willing to sit out dances here were obliged uncomfortably to occupy the great salon's dead center while the spectacle wheeled around them on a floor whose smoothness had been finely calibrated by repeated applications of cornmeal and pumice—the walls themselves, actually, being reserved for R.W.'s art collection, which required a tolerant eye and on occasion an educated stomach broadly indifferent to manifestations of the queasy.

Palm trees grew everywhere, arecas, palmettos, Chinese fan-palms, ranging from squat greenhouse specimens in wicker-covered pots to twelve-foot foyer varieties to stately coconut and date trees rooted somewhere far below and soaring to these ballroom altitudes through openings expressly made for them in the intervening floors and ceilings, creating a sort of jungle where exotic forms of life glided, stalked, and occasionally slithered, demimondaines with darkened eyelids, men with shoulder-length hair, circus artistes, soubrettes in drastically non-demure costumes offering trays of Perrier Jouët, society ladies with orange Tiffany orchid brooches vivid as flames at their bosoms, Wall-Street renegades who congregated near the gigantic bathrooms, where it was said R. Wilshire had installed ticker-tape machines in every water-closet.

A small orchestra on a stage at one end of the great room played selections from various R. Wilshire Vibe productions. Miss Oomie Vamplet sang "Oh, When You Talk That Talk," which she had made famous in her role as Kate Chase Sprague in *Roscoe Conkling*.

Having been deserted by Katie for somebody in a cheap suit representing himself as a talent agent who wouldn't have fooled your grandma, Dally wandered out through some French doors. From the roof garden, past soiled masses of gray and brown shadow, past the gaslit windows and streetlamps in unrecognized vigil below the elevated tracks, far uptown the illuminated city ascended against a deep indigo sky as if night up there had somehow neglected to fall, sparing it in its golden dream of lighted façades.

The young man was leaning on a parapet gazing at the city. She had noticed him the minute she came in, taller than the milling of partygoers around him, but nowhere near "grown," turned out almost too quietly, as if to advertise his inexperience. Maybe it was just all the smoke in the place, but his features seemed to her, even this close up, untouched—maybe never to be—by what she thought she knew already of the harshness of the world. Made her think of kids she had played with, an hour at a time, in towns passed through long ago, and the unforgiving innocence of newsboys among the evening throngs announcing grand thefts, fires, murders, and wars with voices pure as this customer's own had to be—no, not tough enough, not nearly, for what he would have to look in the face, sooner or later, rich kid or whatever, though she doubted this, she knew by now what these society boys were like, it was the Bowery Boy style with required changes of class detail, is all it was.

He turned now and smiled, a little preoccupied, maybe, and she became abruptly aware of this juvenile rag Katie had all but forced her into buying, with its high neckline and yards of stupid barn-dance flouncing . . . and in Congo violet! with plaid trimming! Aaahhh! What was she thinking? Or not thinking. It had been that near-supernatural moment in Smokefoot's, she guessed, that maternal spectre in violet and gray that had sent her judgment so out of kilter. She couldn't even remember now what the dress had cost.

He had opened a cigarette case and was offering her one. This had never happened before, and she had no idea what to do. "You don't mind if I . . ."

"I don't mind," she said, or something sophisticated like that.

From inside came a drumroll, cymbal tap, and short arrangement of "Funiculì, Funiculà," as the lights were now mysteriously dimmed to a cool interior dusk.

"Shall we, then?" gesturing for her to go in first. When she looked around, though, he'd disappeared.

Gee, that was fast.

Up by the bandstand, a good-looking older man in the usual magician's outfit, holding a glass of wine, tapped his wand against it, declaring, "It is difficult to drink semiprecious stone, but in a stone world, drinking anything else is an expensive luxury." He inverted the glass and out tumbled a handful of amethysts and garnets. When he turned the glass right side up again it had wine in it, which he proceeded to drink.

She felt an unaccustomed pressure against her leg and looked down. "Nice outfit," commented an oily voice which seemed to, and in fact did, proceed from the region of Dally's elbow, belonging to one Chinchito, a jumped-up circus midget currently appearing on the Bowery stage, whose value at these gatherings, according to Katie, had to do with a sexual appetite, not to mention organ, quite out of proportion to his stature. "How about getting lost," Dally suggested, although in tones not entirely free of fascination. Chinchito took this with a suavity earned over years of summary dismissal. "Don' know whatcher missin, Red," he winked, strolling away and soon obscured by the crowd.

Not the end of Dally's difficulties, however. She was next approached by a smooth gent with blindingly pomaded gray hair and a gigantic emerald ring on his pinky, who pressed upon her cup after cup of a strange incandescent liquid from a punch bowl until she was seeing nickelodeon shows in the wallpaper.

"I've watched you devotedly down in Chinatown. Try never to miss a performance. You make such an appealing captive," and before she knew it, he seemed to have taken one of her wrists and begun to slip onto it half of a pair of exquisite silver manacles.

"I think not," said a calm voice from somewhere, and Dally found herself being steered toward an elaborate box labeled CABINET OF MYSTERY by a tall figure in a cape who turned out to be the magician's assistant.

"Here, quickly. In here." Dally was not the swooning type but this would have done the job all right, because just before the door closed, the air seemed to grow clear and she recognized the very same woman she had seen in Smokefoot's store yesterday, now wearing dancer's tights and a velvet cape with spangles a-jitter all over it. And sneaking in by way of Dally's nose, something else, beyond time, before memory or her first baby words, the snoot-subverting fragrance of lilies of the valley.

She might've had time enough to mumble, "Well my, my, and whatever has become of my brain?" when, owing to some kind of a Mickey Finn in the punch—if Katie was right about this Vibe crowd, there had to've been—Dally did not so much pass out as experience a strange eclipse of time, at the far end of which she became aware of a door she ought to've seen all the time and yet only now was able to reach for and open. She stepped out into the Lower West Side, right in front of her rooming house in fact, and there sat Katie on the stoop in her scarlet turnout, smoking a Sweet Caporal. It was not long after dawn. The magicians who had rescued her were nowhere in sight, no more than their Cabinet of Mystery, which Dally thought to turn and look for but which had itself disappeared.

"You all right?" Katie yawning and stretching. "I won't ask if you had a good time, but I know I did."

"This is pretty strange, 'cause just a minute ago—"

"No need to explain, he was sure an appealing young specimen."

"Who?"

"I told you that gown would work magic. What do you mean 'who?' you don't have to be coy with me."

"Katie." She sat down next to her friend, in a great rustle of taffeta. "I can't remember a blessed thing."

"Not even the *name* of that magic act, I'll bet." With such an exceptional tone of regret that Dally, puzzled, reached to pat her shoulder before remembering her tall deliveress in the spangled cloak.

"You'll go away now," Katie puffing forlornly, "and maybe for good."

"Not a chance."

"Oh, Dahlia. You knew all along."

"It's peculiar. I did. But I didn't know I did. Not till she"—shaking her head in some wonder—"came for me?"

THE ZOMBINI RESIDENCE, which Dally recognized from her now-battered copy of *Dishforth's Illustrated Weekly,* was an extensive "French flat" in a recently-erected building on upper Broadway, which Luca had chosen for its resemblance to the Pitti Palace in Florence, Italy, and referred to as a *grattacielo* or skyscraper, rising as it did twelve high-ceilinged stories. The rooms seemed to run on for blocks, stuffed with automata human and animal assembled and in pieces, disappearing-cabinets, tables that would float in midair and other trick furniture, Davenport figures with dark-rimmed eyes in sinister faces, lengths of perfect black velvet and multicolored silk brocade a-riot with Oriental scenes, mirrors, crystals, pneumatic pumps and valves, electromagnets, speaking-trumpets, bottles that never ran empty and candles that lighted themselves, player pianos, Zoetropic projectors, knives, swords, revolvers and cannons, a coopful of white doves up on the roof . . .

"What you might call a magician's house," said Bria, who had been showing her around. Straight from some matinée, in her red spangled knifethrower's costume, she managed to look like a nun not above some mischief, as much of it in fact as a situation might require. She kept directing unsymmetrical grins in Dally's direction, which Dally took to mean something but couldn't decode.

In general, she found her newly-met stepbrothers and sisters a well-informed and considerate bunch of children, except when they were being horribly impossible to live with. The older ones worked onstage with their parents, went to school, had part-time jobs downtown, and were as apt to be down on the floor assaulting the carpet with one another's heads as sitting together peacefully on a Sunday morning, one in the lap of another, reading *Little Nemo* in the *Journal.* Among their more disgusting habits was drinking the water from the melted icebox ice. The really little ones, Dominic, Lucia, and Concetta, the baby, lived in a cheerful clutter of dolls and doll furniture, rolling chime toys, drums, cannons and picture blocks, cheerful majolica cuspidors, and empty Fletcher's Castoria bottles.

Dally wasn't in the house ten minutes before Nunzi and Cici accosted her.

"You need change for a quarter?" Cici said.

"Sure."

"Two dimes and a nickel O.K.?"

She saw Nunzi rolling his eyes, and when she looked in her hand, sure enough, Cici, the coin specialist in the family, had palmed and switched the dimes for three-cent pieces, adding to what was already a small fortune.

"Pretty good," said Dally, "but take a look at that quarter."

"Wait a minute, where is it? I just—"

"Heh, heh, heh," Dally rolling the coin side to side over the backs of her fingers, doing a couple-three passes, and producing it finally out of Cici's nose.

"Hey—how about the Indian Rope Trick," announced Nunzi, producing from his pocket a length of rope and a giant pair of scissors, while he and Cici hummed in harmony the familiar theme from *La Forza del Destino,* looping the rope in a complicated way, cutting it into several pieces, waving a silk cloth, and restoring the whole rope in one piece, good as new.

Recognizing this as a standard effect, "That's a pip, all right," said Dally, "but wait, I thought the Indian Rope Trick was where you climb straight up a long piece of free-standing rope till you disappear into thin air."

"No," said Cici, "that's the 'Indian Rope Trick,' this is the *Indian*-Rope trick, see, we bought the rope down the Bowery, off of a Indian guy? so it's a Indian Rope, see—"

"She gets it, *cretino,*" his brother slapping him across the head.

Concetta came crawling in, spotted Cici and looked up at him, her eyes hugely shining and expectant. "Ah, the lit-tle Concertina!" cried Cici, picking up his sister and pretending to play her like a squeeze box, singing one of his vast repertoire of Luigi Denza songs, the baby meantime squealing along and making no real effort to escape.

DALLY HAD IMAGINED once that if she ever found Erlys again, she'd just forget how to breathe or something. But having been gathered into the family chaos with little or no fuss, soon, like some amiable stranger, she was only looking for chances to scrutinize them both—Erlys when it didn't seem she was looking, and then herself in one of the mirrors that stood or hung everywhere in these rooms—for signs of similarity.

Even without theatrical shoes on, Erlys was taller than Luca Zombini, and kept her fair hair in a Psyche knot, out of which the less governable tresses continued, with the day, to escape. Dally, reckoning that the way a woman, in her continuum of Tidiness, deals with hair-irregularity can provide a clue to some other self she might be keeping less available, found, somewhat to her relief, that Erlys more often than not would go entire waking days without bother from the stray undulations, though she was known to blow away as needed the more persistent strands that got in her line of vision.

Erlys was everywhere, passing through the far-flung rooms, all but invisibly taking care of chores, smiling, speaking little, though the children seemed to know, and respect, her wishes more than their father's. Dahlia allowed herself to wonder if this wasn't one more "effect," with some reasonably twin assistant having long ago been switched for the real Erlys, who had earlier stepped over into the Cabinet of Ultimate Illusion, known also as New York City, and found there true disappearance, the kind the toughest audiences will believe in. In this curiously unbounded apartment, the only audience seemed to be Dahlia. Something, something like the silvering of a mirror, remained between them. If Dally wanted to throw herself into those arms in their carefully kept sleeves, she would not be pushed away, she was at least that sure, but past that, where all that ought to matter lay, she saw only a black-velvet absence of signs. Was she being played for a sucker? Were these people not related at all, but just some Bowery acting troupe between engagements pretending to be a family? Who'd be the best one around here to bring it up with?

Not Bria. Not even when she started working as Bria's knife-throwing dummy would Dally give that much trust away to her. She noted the girl's look of indifference when her father addressed her as "*bella,*" though that never kept him from saying it. He was clearly enraptured with all of his children, from the most obvious future criminal to the most radiant saint.

"Don't mistake me for one of these Neapolitan spaghetti-benders," Nunzi in a fair impression of his father, "I come from Friuli, in the north. We are an Alpine people."

"Goat-fuckers," clarified Cici. "They eat donkey salami up there, it's like Austria, with gestures."

Luca Zombini liked to explain the business, at various times, to those of his children he deluded himself were eager to learn, even someday carry on, the act. "Those who sneer at us, and sneer at themselves for paying to let us fool them, what they never see is the yearning. If it was religious, a yearning after God—no one would dream of disrespecting that. But because this is a yearning *only* after miracle, *only* to contradict the given world, they hold it in contempt.

"Remember, God didn't say, 'I'm gonna make light now,' he said, 'Let there be light.' His first act was to *allow light in* to what had been Nothing. Like God, you also have to always work with the light, make it do only what you want it to."

He unrolled an expanse of absolute fluid blackness. "Magician-grade velvet, perfect absorber of light. Imported from Italy. Very expensive. Dyed, sheared, and brushed by hand many, many times. Finished with a secret method of applying platinum black. Factory inspections are merciless. Same as mirrors, only opposite. The perfect mirror must *send back everything,* same amount of light, same colors exactly—but perfect velvet must *let nothing escape,* must hold on to every last little drop of light that falls on it. Because if the smallest amount of light you can think of bounces off one single thread, the whole act—*affondato, vero?* It's all about the light, you control the light, you control the effect, *capisci?*"

"Gotcha, Pop."

"Cici, a little respect here, someday I'm gonna make *you* disappear."

"Now!" cried two or three young Zombinis, jumping on the upholstery. "Right now!"

Luca had long been interested in modern science and the resources it made available to conjurors, among these the Nicol prism and the illusionary uses of double refraction. "Anybody can saw their assistant in half," he said. "It's one of the oldest effects in the business. The problem is, she always gets reassembled, there's always a happy ending."

"'Problem'? It should be an *unhappy* ending?" Bria puzzled. "Like those bloody horror shows they put on over there in Paris, France?"

"Not exactly. You already know about this stuff here." Bringing out a small, near-perfect crystal of Iceland spar. "Doubles the image, the two overlap, with the right sort of light, the right lenses, you can separate them in stages, a little further each time, step by step till in fact it becomes possible to saw somebody in half *optically,* and instead of two different pieces of one body, there are now two complete individuals walking around, who are identical in every way, *capisci?*"

"Not really. But . . ."

"What." Maybe a little defensive.

"Is it a happy ending. Do they go back to being one person again?"

He stared at his shoes, and Bria understood that she was maybe the only one in the house he could've counted on to ask this question.

"No, and that's been kind of a running problem here. Nobody can figure out—"

"Oh, Pop."

"—how to reverse it. I've been everywhere, asked everybody, college professors, people in the business, even Harry Houdini himself, no dice. Meanwhile . . ."

"Don't tell me."

"Yeah."

"Well, how many?"

"Maybe . . . two or three?"

"*Porca miseria,* so that's *four or six,* right? You realize you could get sued for that?"

"It was an optical problem, I thought it would be completely reversible. But according to Professor Vanderjuice up at Yale, I forgot the element of time, it didn't happen all at once, so there was this short couple of seconds where time went on, irreversible processes of one kind and another, this sort of gap opened up a little, and that was enough to make it impossible to get back to exactly where we'd been."

"And here I thought you were perfect. Imagine my disappointment. So these subjects of yours are out there leading double lives. They can't be too happy with that."

"Lawyers, heckling at shows, threats of violence. The usual."

"What do we do?"

"There's only one place in the world that makes these units. The Isle of Mirrors in that Lagoon over in Venice, might be only the name of some holding company by now, but they still do produce and market the finest conjuror's mirrors in the world. Somebody there is bound to have an idea."

"And we just happen to be booked in to the Teatro Malibran in Venice in a couple of weeks."

Yes, Luca Zombini had come home today with the surprising news that the act was booked to tour Europe, and the whole family, Dally included, were due to sail over on the liner S.S. *Stupendica,* only two weeks from now! As if a valve in a distant part of the basement had just been opened, the whole apartment was suddenly turbulent with preparation for the journey.

When Dally had a minute to speak to Erlys between chores, "Are you folks sure you need me along?"

"Dahlia." Stopped just dead in her tracks, a dustrag about to fall from her fingers.

"I mean walking in like I did—"

"No . . . no, we were, fact is, I guess, counting on you. Dally, sakes, you only just got here—and, well, what about the Chinese Gong Effect . . . ?"

"Oh, Bria can do that in her sleep."

"Don't know if you'd want to stay on here, we'll be subletting to those East Rumelian acrobats, it might not be ideal company for you."

"I'll manage, someplace. Katie, somebody."

"Dahlia, now look at me." Easier not to have to, but the girl obliged. "I know you never meant to stay on. It would've been too much to hope for. Either one of us."

A small shrug. "Never was that sure you'd even let me in."

"But you're in the door, and maybe you're, who knows, *supposed* to be with us? somehow . . . ?"

A silence, grave and unnatural, had crept over the lengthy apartment, as if to suggest, without a Zombini in earshot, that this would be the perfect moment to come out in a fierce and long-held whisper, "I was only a little baby—how could you just leave like that?"

A kind of smile, almost thankful. "Wondering when that'd come up."

"I'm not here lookin for anything."

"Of course not." Was that a New York snap creeping into her voice? "Well. How much did Merle tell you?"

"Nothing bad against you. Only that you left us."

"Bad enough, I'd say."

"He knew I had to come back here. He never stopped me."

"But no message for me. No 'the past is past,' nothing like that."

"If there was anything like that, I never heard about it. Maybe . . ." She looked up at Erlys, unsure.

"Maybe he thought you should hear the story from me."

"Well? It means he trusts you to tell me the truth."

Erlys remembered they were still standing at opposite corners of a bedsheet. Graceful as ballroom stepping, they moved toward each other, completed the fold, redoubled the sheet, glided apart. "I'm not sure how good a time this is to be getting into it all. . . ."

Dally shrugged. "When'll it be better?"

"All right." A last look around hoping for a smaller Zombini, any Zombini, to come in and delay this—"When Merle and I met, I was already pregnant with you. So . . ."

There. Dally found herself unexpectedly sitting on the davenport. Dust rose, cushions wheezed, and underskirts sighed around her. Two or three possibilities for snappy remarks drifted across her mind. "All right, then," her mouth unaccountably dry, "my real father—where is he?"

"Dahlia," nodding vigorously, as if not to relax into any easy distance, "he passed away. Just a little before you were born. Streetcar accident in Cleveland. Quick as that. His name was Bert Snidell. All that red hair of yours is from him. His family basically threw me out. Merle gave us a home. And your 'real' father, well that is Merle, more than the other would ever've been. That's any help."

Not much. "Do you think this is what I want to hear? A home? Some home. You sure skipped soon as *you* could, why not just leave me at the damn city dump on your way out of town?" Where'd that come from? Not exactly from nowhere, but from farther away than anything she'd felt up to now. . . .

But wouldn't you know it, before she could work up much more of a head of steam, the subgods of theatrical timing that seemed to rule this house decided about then to put into the situation after all, and here came Nunzi and Cici in matching white sharkskin suits, practicing Hindoo shuffles and French drops, cheerfully oblivious to the fury and consternation in the room, and full of the latest news about the sailing. And there Dally and Erlys would have to leave things for a while. In fact, the chore level being what it was, till they were on board the *Stupendica* and well out to sea.

The one time Mayva and Stray met, it was by pure accident, over in Durango.

"You two ain't married, by any chance?"

"Funny you should ask," Reef began, but Stray spoke right up.

"Not lately, M'z Traverse."

Mayva laughed and took her hand. "I'd like to tell you what a bargain you'd be gettin but I might need some time on that."

"Oh, I wouldn't blame much of it on you," said Stray, "good upbringin can only go so far."

"There was some Briggses in Ouray County, that wouldn't be your people, would it? Worked at the Camp Bird, maybe?"

"Think there might've been cousins on my Aunt Adelina's side over by Lake City for a while. . . ." And Reef turned around just in time to see the two of them disappear into some yardage place, jabbering away like a couple of birds on a rooftop.

Next day Reef and Stray were on the Denver & Rio Grande headed eventually for Arizona, together at first, soon to be separate. Her friend Archie Dipple had a plan, not as desperately insane as some, to go out and round up the camel herd imported years ago into Virginia City, Nevada, to pack out salt, later delivered into Arizona for the usual ore-related duties, eventually deemed unprofitable and set loose, by now reverted to the wild state, spread out over thousands of square miles of Sonoran Desert, where due to not-well-understood factors of Nature they were said to've reproduced with astonishing speed—"Even at let's say a half-dollar a head, it'll be enough to retire on and go live forever as far back east as you want—up in that Ritz Hotel, kids in cylindrical hats bringing you whatever you desire day or night—" Reef need act as no more than bunco-steerer, all the research chores and assumptions of risk to be borne by Archie as principal party, "thankless tasks, all of them, but no risk, no reward, ain't that how it goes?"

"Ever thus in the world of affairs," Reef agreed, trying to look just quizzical enough to suggest the perils of extravagance, yet not enough to offer provocation—these double-domes being in Reef's experience never quite as retiring as they looked, some of them damned touchy, as a matter of fact.

Whereas Reef's "friends," business and personal, were mostly no strangers to trouble, nor that complicated to understand, Stray's, apt to keep more to the shadows, tended to be practitioners of obliquity—as it quite often came down to, varieties of pimp. Advance men, middlemen, if you liked, and not all men, of course. These "friends" of hers, on the whole, kept getting Reef into way more trouble than any of his "friends" had so far got her. And heaven forfend it should ever've been as simple as pursuit by the law, or escape into a safer jurisdiction, no, these strange faces bobbing up out of her past were determined to *bring him in* as a partner on various schemes of enterprise, few of them hopeful.

During all the confabulating, she would usually be there watching, standing by the railing up in some gambling-saloon loft, or gazing in through the etched-glass paneling of an office door, as if only in girlish curiosity as to how these two separate figures in her life might be hitting it off, though she was ready enough to claim a commission, usually around 5 percent, on any of these deals that actually yielded a crop. Macking for a mack, so to speak.

That was how for years, all through that quarter of the continent, they had fought, fled, beckoned, resumed. . . . If you took a map and tried to follow them over it, zigzagging town to town, back and forth, it might not have been that easy to account for, even if you recalled how wild, how much better than "wild" it'd been not all that many years ago, out here, even with the workdays that had you longing for the comforts of territorial prison, yes hard as that, when whatever was going to become yours—your land, your stock, your family, your name, no matter, however much or little you had, you earned it, with never no second thoughts as to just killing somebody, if it even *looked* like they might want to take it. Maybe a dog catching their scent coming down the wind, or the way some trailhand might be wearing his waterproof, that could be enough—didn't matter, with everything brand new and the soldiering so hard, waking up each day never knowing how you'd end it, cashing 'em in being usually never too distant from your thoughts, when any ailment, or animal wild or broke, or a bullet from any direction might be enough to propel you into the beyond . . . why clearly every lick of work you could get in would have that same mortal fear invested into it—Karl Marx and them, well and good, but that's what folk had for Capital, back in early times out here—not tools on credit, nor seed money courtesy of some banker, just their own common fund of fear that came with no more than a look across the day arising. It put a shade onto things that parlor life would just never touch, so whenever she or Reef pulled up and got out, when it wasn't, mind, simple getting away in a hurry, it was that one of them had heard about a place, some place, one more next-to-last place, that hadn't been taken in yet, where you could go live for a time on the edge of that old day-to-day question, at least till the Saturday nights got quiet enough to hear the bell of the town clock ring you the hours before some Sunday it'd be too dreary to want to sober up for. . . . So in time you had this population of kind of roving ambassadors from places like that that were still free, who wherever they came to rest would be a little sovereign piece of that faraway territory, and they'd have sanctuary about the size of their shadow.

First thing Reef looked for in a new place was the sporting crowd. Though he said it gave him no pleasure to take what he called "sheep to the shed," Stray did see him maybe once or twice consent to anyway, usually around the time he or she'd be getting ready to leave town. "Give us enough for a couple of hours in the dining car," as he often put it, "don't we owe ourselves that at least?" Wherever they headed for had to be someplace where you didn't know from one card to the next who'd be likely to pull out a pistol or a dirk. Where you didn't yet keep such implements away in the drawer of some Chicago-built office desk, but always close to your person.

Did he ever say what? Say, "Please?" No, it was more like, "All the boys'll be up in Butte now"—big sigh—"drinking them Sean O'Farrells without me," or "Thought I'd go subdue the wild burro once more by the banks of Uncompahgre," with Stray always welcome to come along and so forth. But weren't there just as often reasons of her own not to? Times she just didn't want to go through that old walk to the depot to see him off, add them little few sniffles of hers to the weeping already on that platform, no thank you, no.

They had lived down in horse barns, army "A" tents with the old bloodstains onto them, city hotels with canopy beds, woke up in back rooms of deadfalls where the bars had toothmarks end to end. Sometimes it smelled like dust and animals, sometimes like machine oil getting overheated, not too much of the garden flowers or home cooking. But nowadays they were living in a nice little cabin up above the Uncompahgre. Jesse lay at ease among feather pillows and borrowed grandmothers' quilting in a dynamite crate—perfect for a baby because there were no nails to be sticking him, nails being known to attract electricity, of which there was plenty up on this stormy mountainside, so it was all wood pegs and glue holding the baby's box together. Watching Jesse, Stray had a look on her face, a smile more than ready for the stoveglow of the old partnership to pick up again, as if about to say, "Well, looks like here's where we stop riding the rails for a little," except that Reef would more than likely reply, "Why, sweetheart, you can see he's just itchin to get some wind in his face, ain't you Slick," picking the baby up and cowboy-dancing him facedown through the air fast enough for his fine hair to blow back off his brow, "He's a road baby, ain't you Jesse, just a road baby!" So his parents kept silent, even with this undeniable miracle in the room, each thinking their own miles-apart personal thoughts.

IT HAD NEVER BEEN Reef's intention to be part of any outlaw dynasty. "Thought I was entitled to a regular human life like everybody else," was how he put it. It gave him some difficult days, for he was never to forgive whatever it had been dealt him the hand he got. All set to do the one thing, and without warning it was taken away, and there was the other thing had to be done instead, whether he wanted to or didn't, there it was. . . .

Pretending to be out there with his rounder-type antics worked pretty good for a time, just enough to keep Stray annoyed, not enough to bring her out after him, or worse, try to hire somebody to do it for her.

But finally one day, less than a year into it, he tried something a little too close to home, and she came around a bend in the trail on her way to visit with her sister Willow, and there was Reef running some fuse—nothing major, a stick or two, just enough to blow a junction box belonging to a generating plant that supplied one of the workings up by Ophir—just a stupid grin, and his thumb up his ass. She sat there, with Jesse in a papoose rig peeking around from behind her, with her arms folded, waiting for something, which he figured out after a while was an explanation from him. And then, like it or not, he'd have to be straight with her.

"And when was it again you were gonna share this with me? When they've got the noose all around your neck?"

He pretended to lose his temper. "No damn business of yours, Stray."

"My dear, it's me."

"I know, that's the problem."

"This must be how a Kid talks to his Woman."

It wasn't only the pursuit, all the death-packing law, Pinkerton and public, at his back, plus the unknown and invisible others he hadn't found out about yet, none of those so much as the sworn opponent unreachably within, never to be appeased, believing unconditionally, poor fish, in the class war to come, commonwealth of toil that is to be, as the song went, "I smell it in the wind," he liked to mutter to himself, "I'm like a damn Christer and his deliverance with that. Brethren, the day is coming. Clear and no denying it."

Most of the time anyhow. Sometimes he was just after the explosion, it was like telling them in a voice too loud to ignore to fuck off. And sometimes it was so he wouldn't feel nagging at him the unfinished business with Deuce and Sloat, wherever they were these days. If Capital's own books showed a balance in clear favor of damnation, if these plutes were undeniably evil hombres, then how much more so were those who took care of their problems for them, in no matter what ignorance of why, not all of their faces on the wanted bills, in that darkly textured style that was more about the kind of remembering, the unholy longing going on out here, than of any real-life badman likeness. . . .

YES, well Stray and him, they could talk about it. Some. Say they could, and they couldn't.

It wasn't just Webb he had to look after anymore. The San Juan range was a battleground now, Union miners, scabs, militia, owners' hired guns, all shooting at each other and now and then hitting somebody for a one-way passage into that dark country where they all collected. They wanted his attention, them and the ones who'd died at the other places, the Coeur d'Alene, Cripple Creek, even back east at Homestead, points in between, all kept making themselves known. They were Reef's dead now, all right, and did they make a grand opera of coming around to remind him. Damn. He could no more run out on them than on some houseful of little orphan children put into his care unexpectedly. These dead, these white riders of the borderline, nervelessly at work already as agents on behalf of invisible forces over there, could still, like children, keep an innocence all their own—the innocence of the early afterlife, of tenderfeet needing protection from the insults of that unmarked otherworld trail so unforgiving. They trusted him so—as if he knew any better than they did—to see them along . . . trusted the bond between them, and he could no more subvert their faith than question his own. . . .

Sometimes he made the mistake of saying this out loud, in Stray's hearing. She would make a point of looking over at the baby, as if Reef had somehow just put him in danger, and then start in.

"This ain't puttin flowers on some grave, Reef."

"No? Thought everybody's dead was different. O' course, some do like the flowers, but then there's others's partial to blood, or didn't you know that."

"There's a Sheriff to take care of it."

No. It was something belonged to them, the ones across the Wall, nothing to do with the State or state law, nor especially with any damn Sheriff.

"My job is to prevent the sides from tangling," one of these Sheriffs tried once to instruct Reef.

"No, Burgess, your job is to see that they keep on killing Union people, without none of us ever getting to pay them back."

"Reef, now if they've broken the law—"

"Oh, eyewash. The law. You're just some li'l old saloon bum in their palace o' wealth, Burge. You think if somebody shoots you right here 'n' now, they're going to care? Send even flowers to Laureen and them *chavalitos*? Piece of paper back there goes in a pneumatic tube's all, next dumb animal comes blinkin out of the chute, pins on that star, and there ain't even a form to put your name down in, let alone any notices in the newspaper. Call that law, law enforcement if you like, o' course."

What he said to Stray was, "This is too precious to leave it to some office full of clowns."

"Precious. Jesus our Lord and Savior."

"Don't have to start crying, Stray."

"I'm not crying."

"Your face gets all red."

"You don't know what crying looks like."

"Darlin you must've had public execution on your mind for a while now, and I'm sorry, I know all 'at old calico recital, oh, Honey I don't want 'em hanging you, well I appreciate that, but now tell me, what else besides?"

"What else? You're feeling lively today, you really want to know what else? Listen to me, side o' beef—hangin you, I can understand, but they might decide to *hang me, too*. Is 'what else.'"

What he did not of course detect in this was the promise Stray knew straight enough she was making here, to stick by his side, even far as the gallows, if their luck should turn that way. But he didn't want to hear anything like that, hell no, and quickly pretended this was all about her safety. "Darlin, they're not gonna want to hang you. They're gonna want to fuck you."

"Course. *Then* hang me."

"No, 'cause by then you'll be casting that spell, and nobody'll want to do nothin but be down at them famous little feet."

"Oh. You are such a youngster."

"Don't be feeling sorry for me."

"I won't. Just grow up, Reef."

"What, and be like you all? Think not."

What a man gets for opening his heart and sharing his feelings. Reef knew his days in the family dynamite business were numbered now, though there had to be other ways to fight this fight apart from setting off explosions. About all he was sure of was that he had to keep on with it to make this thing right. But it was time, just about time, for Frank to be taking up some of the slack.

"I'm headin up to Denver, see if I can't just locate that old Frank."

She understood approximately what he was up to, and for once refrained from making with the remarks, just nodded him out the door, taking care to have Jesse in her arms when she did.

He rode out into the advent of winter, beneath the sheets and hoods of mountain-size night-riders, torn, swept, pausing only to build up a drift or congregate into an avalanche waiting to let go and wipe anything in its path from the Earth. Streams of runoff frozen onto the vertical rock walls looked like leafless groves of white aspen or birch. Sunsets tended to be purple firestorms, with blinding orange streaks running through. The other riders he met were friendly in the way of fellow troopers in the forces of those who would not descend to valleys, to southerly pastures, who would remain, as if there were something up here to be gotten through as a point of honor, some ongoing high-country misadventure, and it had to be here, among these white verticalities, for it would mean nothing anywhere else. Who would fasten their mean shacks to the mountain with steel cable and eyebolts and let the wind roar and be damned. And next morning be out in it picking up pieces of roof and stovepipes and what all hadn't been blown to Mexico yet.

When these altitudes passed over into the realm of the unearthly, the chances of life struggling through seemed too slim to consider. As the snows deepened in the towns, covering the street windows and then the upstairs, and the winds wheeled in from the north ever more fiercely, nothing here, no building or schemework of streets, seemed any more permanent than a night's bivouac—by spring all must be ghosts and sorrow, ruins of darkened wood and unheaped stones. Of course, some of that was just what a person's idea might be of what was possible—come up here from Texas or New Mexico or even Denver, and it looked like that nothing could survive and what were these people even thinking to settle up here.

Reef was riding a January colt named Borrasca, on the small side but quick and smart and trained like most horses up in this country—the terrain being what it was—to let you mount from whichever side, uphill or down, would let him keep his balance better. They passed along a valley lined on either side with avalanches waiting to happen.

Like mountains and creeks and other permanent features of the landscape, every slide in the San Juans had a name, no matter when it might have run last. Some liked to let go several times a day, some hardly ever, but they were all like reservoirs of pure potential energy, poised up there and waiting their moment. The one Reef was riding under just now had been named the Bridget McGonigal by a mine owner who'd since returned back east, after his wife, for her practice of likewise letting go at completely unpredictable moments.

Reef heard a blast high above, echoing slope to slope, and his bomber's ear could tell right away it wasn't dynamite, not nearly clean-edged enough—this concussion had more the ragged blur to it of black powder, so howitzer-happy National Guard amusements weren't out of the question, though usually the only reason for a powder charge was to move a large mass of snow instead of just bore holes into it, and why on such a gray and uninhabited day would there be any need for that, especially so far upslope, with the risks of triggering an avalanche . . .

Oh, well now, *shit?*

Here she came, the soul-smiting roar, quick as that, grown to fill the day, the bright cloud risen to the top of what sky he could still see in that direction, all down here suddenly gone into twilight, and him and Borrasca, dead in the path. Nothing anywhere close enough to get behind. Borrasca, being an animal of great common sense, let out with a hell-with-this type of whinny and began to move out of the area quick as he could. Figuring the colt would do better without a rider's weight, Reef kicked out of the stirrups and rolled off, slipped in the snow, fell, and got up again just in time to turn and face the great descending wall.

Later he would wonder why he didn't head downhill quick as he could and be planning how to try and swim his way up and out, if he stayed alive that long. Somehow he must have wanted to have a last look. And what he noticed right away was that the slide now, actually, was running in a slightly different direction, angling more to his left, and not as fast as he'd thought at first either. Afterward he calculated that what saved him was the weather, unusually mild that week, almost like spring, making the slide just wet and slow enough to've formed a snow-dam someplace in it, at some providential snag in the terrain, that steered the whole giant concern away from him by just enough. Known to happen. Everybody up here had an avalanche story, covered then uncovered again being a favorite among countless occasions of miracle. . . .

The great cloud, now a veil of mercy, hung between Reef and everything uphill, offering him a few minutes to get out of the sightlines from up there and hope whoever it was'd be fooled into thinking they'd got him. He took off at a run, or best he could in this wet snow, toward where the trail made its switchback, and first thing he saw when he got safely around the bend was Borrasca, unhurriedly stepping along, already down on the next stretch of road below, heading on back to the barn at Ouray. With no way of knowing how deep the snow was, and no history even as a kid of practicing any of the forms of squarehead insanity that went on in wintertime in these mountains, Reef unlatched his waterproof, folded it into a rough sort of sled, climbed onto it, grabbed hold of his hat, and trying hard not to scream, slid up and over the edge, down into the steep white unknown, with some dim thought of steering so as to cross paths below with Borrasca, praying as much as he ever did for no hidden rocks to be in the way. Approaching the trail below, he guessed he might be going a little too fast, and had to put out a foot, in fact two, finally roll off and over onto his side to brake himself, and as it was he nearly overshot the roadway and went off the *next* ledge, which was *really* steep, you might say vertical. But he managed to stop before the overhang and roll about six or eight feet down a little bank slip and onto the trail. He lay on his back for a minute looking up into the sky. Borrasca, coming along, was eyeing him curiously, but not that amazed to see him.

"Don't recall sayin I'd be back," Reef greeted him, "but nice seein you again howsoever, and let's go look at how far she ran out."

Jake with the colt, who stood there with his eyes rolling till Reef got aboard, and they resumed their journey.

They made it down to Ouray without running into any other riders, though somebody could always've been watching through field-glasses. Reef took the sunny view that as far as the Owners Association knew (who else could it've been?), he was now dead and gone, and therefore born again, "I say unto you born again," he murmured to the horse, who, if you went by his markedly human demeanor, may have known, in the Hindoo sense, something of what Reef meant.

"YOU'RE BACK in a hurry."

He told her what'd happened. "Only one thing to do."

"Uh-huh. That would be, you leave me here alone, with winter on the way, and the screaming baby."

He felt a familiar hollow vibrating of fear along his centerline, out to his palms and fingers. It was just the way she was looking at him. Nothing would help here. But he said, "We've always found the way back together. Ain't we?"

She just kept on with that look.

"What's different? Baby, sure, but what else?"

"Did I say anythin, Reef?" Damned if she would raise her voice. Ever. Ever fuckin again, and by then of course she was that much closer to letting it all run, and there he was just jabbering right along,

"Don't want you either one getting hurt, do I, for all I know these boys's up on that ridge right now, just waiting for this door here to open. You want to, please, forget the speech this time? Save it for when next we meet?"

She didn't want to, no, actually, "Willow can take little Jesse awhile, he'll be safe with her and Holt, but I don't know about you, you sorry lummox, you'll be needin somebody to cover your back. . . ." Well, this after years, just damn years, of swearing she would never come to it. Cowardly, this parlor-wife pleading. Knowing that he was already, the passing shade of him, slipped away over the doorsill, with that doomed carcass she loved beer belly and all only a detail now. Lord, how she, who never prayed, was praying that whoever it was hadn't got to the ridge yet, for she wanted at least that scrap of a chance he could go on being alive, someplace.

"First thunder from the east, darlin. That's when the Zuñis say winter's over, and that's when I'll be back. . . ."

Jesse was asleep, so Reef just kissed him real gently on his head before he went out the door.

WHICH WAS HOW Reef came to take on the guise of East Coast nerve case Thrapston Cheesely III, learning to look sicker than he was, to dress like a dude who couldn't sit a horse on a merry-go-round, sneaking into Denver to take dancing lessons from a certain Madame Aubergine, swearing her to secrecy under pain of an ancient Ute shaman's curse. He started using cologne and the same brand of hair pomade as Kaiser Wilhelm of Germany, and kept his dynamite, detonator caps, and miscellaneous exploder gear all in a matched and monogrammed set of alligator-hide luggage given him by the provocative and voracious Ruperta Chirpingdon-Groin, a touring Englishwoman fascinated by what she took to be contradictions in his character, and not exactly put off by what signals of danger did find their way through.

"Dear, *dear* Mizziz Chirpingdon-Groin, you mustn't be too upset with me though I admit I was *naughty* down in the kitchen there with 'at li'l Yup Toy and so forth, but you simply must forgive me, for what could one undeveloped lotus blossom mean to one who has spent even a moment in your own company, enchanting, *desirable* Mizziz Chirpingdon-Groin. . . ."

Yup Toy herself, waiting by a huge ice machine among a row of Oriental ice-girls in abbreviated sequined getups, her painted face a porcelain mask in the naphtha-light streaming from somewhere beneath, gazed, sucking at a scarlet fingernail, failing to look inscrutable to any but the habitually dismissive, such as Ruperta. To others more appreciative of her virtues, her mind was an open book, and many began to edge away, anticipating trouble up the tracks. Down in the unlighted depths of the great machine, a steam hammer relentlessly slammed away at blocks of raw ice, vapors rose and blew, a confusion of water in all its phases at once, through which the ice-girls, directed by a headwaiter with a pair of castanets, glided roller-skating among the tables, delivering galvanized buckets embossed with the name of this establishment brimming over with the low-temperature solid.

Reef joined Ruperta's loose salon of neuræsthenics traveling hot spring to spring in search of eternal youth or fleeing the deadweight of time, finding enough impulsive or inattentive cardplayers to keep him in Havanas and $3.50-a-quart Champagne, and Ruperta surprised enough now and then with silver and lapis Indian trinkets and the odd bushel of flowers to keep her guessing, she having figured him for a white savage masquerading as an exquisite. Which did not prevent them from going round and round on average once a week, memorable uproars that sent everybody running for the periphery, uncertain as to what distance was safe. In between these dustups, Reef had long, desultory conversations with his penis, to the effect that there wasn't much point missing Stray too much right now, was there, as it would only blunt the edge of desire, not only for Ruperta but whoever else, Yup Toy or whoever, might drift by over the course of their travels.

They finally parted company in New Orleans after a confused and repetitive headache of a night that began at the establishment of Monsieur Peychaud, where the Sazeracs, though said to've been invented there, were not a patch, it seemed to Reef, on those available at Bob Stockton's bar in Denver, though those Absinthe Frappés were another matter. After taking on fuel, the party moved out into the French Quarter hunting for modes of intoxication "more exotic," meaning, if you pushed it, some form of zombie powder. Ruperta tonight was in a narrow black bengaline costume with a Medici collar and cuffs of bastard chinchilla. Nothing on underneath except for stays and stockings, as Reef had had occasion to find out earlier, at their habitual late-afternoon rendezvous.

It had soon become apparent in this town that what you could see from the street was not only less than "the whole story" but in fact not even the picture on the cover. The real life of this place was secured deep inside the city blocks, behind ornate iron gates and up tiled passages that might as well've run for miles. You could hear faint strands of music, crazy stuff, banjos and bugling, trombone glissandi, pianos under the hands of whorehouse professors sounding like they came with keys between the keys. Voodoo? Voodoo was the least of it, Voodoo was just everywhere. Invisible sentinels were sure to let you know, the thickest of necks being susceptible here to monitory pricklings of the Invisible. The Forbidden. And meantime the smells of the local cuisine, cheurice sausages, gumbo, crawfish étouffé, and shrimp boiled in sassafras, proceeding from noplace you could ever see, went on scrambling what was left of your good sense. Negroes could be observed at every hand, rollicking in the street. The so-called Italian Troubles, stemming from the alleged Mafia assassination of the chief of police here being yet fresh in the civic memory, children were apt to accost strangers, Italian or not, with, "Who kill-a da chief?" not to mention "*Va fongool-a* your sister."

They ended up at Maman Tant Gras Hall, a concert saloon just off Perdido Street in the heart of the brothel district.

"Yes a no doubt charming *guignette*," cried Ruperta, "but my dears, the music!"

"Dope" Breedlove and his Merry Coons were the house band here, and everybody was having too good a time to let the likes of Ruperta get in the way. A few customers even came up and asked her to dance, which was enough to throw her into a peculiar smirking cataplexy, which sent them away with puzzled looks, whereupon she turned on Reef in high indignation, if not all-out panic. "Do you intend simply to sit there, while these grinning darkies humiliate us both?"

"How's that?" Reef genially enough. "Look—can you see what those people there are doing? It's called dancing. I know you dance, I've seen you."

"This music," Ruperta muttered, "is fit only for copulation of the most beastly sort."

He shrugged. "Seen you do that, too."

"My God you're vile. What can I have been thinking? For the first time, my eyes are open and you are truly revealed to me—you and your whole insane country, which actually tore itself apart for five years over this race of jungle throwbacks. Algernon, get us out of here, please, and quickly."

"See you back at the hotel?"

"Ah, unlikely, I think. Your traps, such as they are, will be somewhere down in the lobby." And easy as that, she was gone.

Reef lit a hemp-and-tobacco cigarette and reviewed his situation, while around him infectious melodies and rhythms went on refashioning the night. After a bit, shrugging, he approached a smiling young woman in an amazing plumed hat and asked her to dance. He could see the once-over she was giving him, but it was still more attention in a second and a half than he'd ever had from Ruperta.

When "Dope" and his crew took a break, Reef asked him, "What was that everybody at your table was drinking? Can I get you one?"

"Ramos gin fizz. Get yourself one, too."

The bartender shook them up at length in a long silver shaker, to some slow internal syncopation. When Reef brought the drinks back, the table was deep in a discussion of Anarchist theory.

"Your own Benjamin Tucker wrote of the Land League," a young man was saying in an unmistakably Irish voice, "in such glowing terms—the closest the world has ever come to perfect Anarchist organization."

"Were the phrase not self-contradictory," commented "Dope" Breedlove.

"Yet I've noticed the same thing when your band plays—the most amazing social coherence, as if you all shared the same brain."

"Sure," agreed "Dope," "but you can't call that organization."

"What do you call it?"

"Jass."

The Irishman introduced himself to Reef as Wolfe Tone O'Rooney, a traveling insurrectionist—though not, he was quick to add, a Fenian, an approach that was fine as far as it went, though, it seemed to him, coming as he did from a Land League family, his father and uncles on both sides having been founding members, not nearly far enough.

"The folks who invented boycotting," Reef seemed to recall.

"And a lovely technique it is, if you're out in the countryside, Sligo and Tipperary and whatnot. Drives the bloody Brits mental, besides now and then getting them to stop their hateful savagery. But in the cities, now . . ." After a short silence, Wolfe Tone appeared chirpily to rouse himself—"Thank heaven at any rate for this great and good U.S.A., and all her profusion of pennies, nickels, and dimes ever flowing, for without them we'd freeze and fail like the potato in a season of deep frost." He was just back from a tour of American cities to raise money for the League, having been especially impressed with the miners' struggle in Colorado.

"I was hoping while I was there I'd somehow get to meet the great Wild West bomb-chucker known as the Kieselguhr Kid, but sadly he'd not been heard from for some time."

Reef, not quite knowing how to reply but understanding that a shifty eye right now would be a bad idea, sat silently looking the Irishman in the face, where he thought for a moment he could detect the dawning of a certain light. Soon, however, Wolfe Tone appeared to sink back into his preferred state, a black broodfulness, which Reef eventually would come to recognize as a metaphorical device whose tenor always somewhere included lethal hardware in the dark of night.

"These white folks sure is moody," observed "Dope" Breedlove.

"And you fellows do smile a lot," Wolfe Tone shot back. "I can't believe anyone can stay that happy."

"Tonight," said "Dope," "it's because we just finished an engagement over on Rampart at the Red Onion," a brief eye-roll at this byword of peril throughout the musical brotherhood, "and we're all still alive to tell the tale. Besides not wishing to disappoint the many Caucasian music-lovers who come in here expecting that certain dental gleam. Oh yes suh, I *loves* them po'k chops!" he added in a louder voice, having sensed the owner, now in earshot, on the prowl trying to get the Merry Coons back to work.

When the band had resumed playing, "Took you at first for another damned English idiot like the crowd you came in here with," said Wolfe Tone O'Rooney.

"She's booted me out," Reef confided.

"Need someplace to stay? Maybe not as high-class as you're used to—"

"Neither was that Hotel St. Charles, come to think of it." Wolfe Tone was flopping at the Deux Espèces, a Louisiana-style road ranch deep in the red-light district, filled with desperados of one kind and another who were waiting, most of them, for ships to take them out of the country.

"This is Flaco, with whom you may find you share a passion."

"He means for chemistry," said Flaco, with a knowing scowl.

Reef flashed a look at the Irishman, who gestured at himself in wounded innocence.

"There's a kind of a community," said Flaco, "and all the boys get to know each other after a while."

"I'm more like an apprentice," Reef guessed.

"Right now everybody's talking about Europe. All the Powers are planning how best to move their troops around, and you'd naturally think the railroad, but there's these mountains everyplace, slowing everything down, so that means tunnels. Suddenly now all over Europe there's tunnels big and small got to be blasted. Ever do any tunnel work?"

"Some," said Reef. "Maybe."

"He's—" began Wolfe Tone.

"Yes, Brother O'Rooney. I'm . . . ?"

"Not political the way we are, Flaco."

"Don't know," said Reef. "Then again, neither do you. Have to think about that."

"All of us," said Wolfe Tone O'Rooney. With the same light in his eyes as last night, when the subject of the Kieselguhr Kid came up.

It was an old deception by now, natural as swallowing spit. Inside himself somewhere, he shrugged. Resisted thinking back to Stray and Jesse.

. . .

"We look at the world, at governments, across the spectrum, some with more freedom, some with less. And we observe that the more repressive the State is, the closer life under it resembles Death. If dying is deliverance into a condition of total non-freedom, then the State tends, in the limit, to Death. The only way to address the problem of the State is with counter-Death, also known as Chemistry," said Flaco.

He was a survivor of Anarchist struggles in a number of places both sides of the Atlantic, notably Barcelona in the '90's. Provoked by the bombing of the Teatro Lyceo during a performance of Rossini's opera *William Tell*, the police had rounded up not just Anarchists but anybody who might be in any way opposed to the regime, or even thinking about being. Thousands were arrested and sent "up the mountain" to the fortress of Montjuich which crouched thuglike over the city as if having just assaulted it, and when the dungeons there were full, prisoners were kept chained in warships converted to prison ships, lying at anchor down in the harbor.

"Fucking Spanish police," Flaco said. "In Cataluña they are an occupying army. Any of the prisoners of '93 who weren't Anarchists before going into Montjuich arrived rapidly at the heart of the matter. It was like finding an old religion again, one we'd almost forgotten. The State is evil, its divine right proceeds from Hell, Hell is where we all went. Some came out of Montjuich broken, dying, without working genitals, intimidated into silence. Whips and white-hot irons are certainly effective for that. But all of us, even those who had voted and paid our taxes like good bourgeoisie, came out hating the State. I include in that obscene word the Church, the latifundios, the banks and corporations, of course."

Everybody at the Deux Espèces was waiting for his own particular outlaw-friendly ship, of which there were several out on the sea-lanes at any given moment . . . as if there had once been a joyous mythical time of American Anarchism, now facing its last days after the Anarchist Czolgosz had assassinated McKinley—everywhere it was run, Anarchist, run, the nation allowing itself to lapse into another cycle of Red Scare delusion as it had done back in the '70s in reaction to the Paris Commune. But as if, too, there might exist a place of refuge, up in the fresh air, out over the sea, someplace all the Anarchists could escape to, now with the danger so overwhelming, a place readily found even on cheap maps of the World, some group of green volcanic islands, each with its own dialect, too far from the sea-lanes to be of use as a coaling station, lacking nitrate sources, fuel deposits, desirable ores either precious or practical, and so left forever immune to the bad luck and worse judgment infesting the politics of the Continents—a place promised them, not by God, which'd be asking too much of the average Anarchist, but by certain hidden geometries of History, which must include, somewhere, at least at a single point, a safe conjugate to all the spill of accursed meridians, passing daily, desolate, one upon the next.

Wolfe Tone O'Rooney was headed to Mexico, where he hoped to track down a consignment of "agricultural implements," seemingly vanished in transit, intended for League-connected elements he didn't describe too closely. Flaco was looking in the paper every morning for word of the tramp steamer *Despedida,* bound for the Mediterranean, where her ports of call likely would include Genoa, as good a place as any to start looking for tunnel work. He had convinced Reef to come along. They tended to congregate at a café down near Maman Tant Gras where "Dope" Breedlove and his fellow jass musicians came by in the early mornings after staying up all night playing in the smoke and river mists that came in the doors and windows. . . . They sat among the early market smells and ate beignets and drank chicory coffee and argued about Bakunin and Kropotkin, remaining for the most part, Reef noticed, easygoing no matter what disagreement might arise, because it was important not to draw attention. It was the U.S.A., after all, and fear was in the air.

One afternoon Reef walked in on Wolfe Tone O'Rooney slicing a potato in half and looking as guilty as if he were assembling a bomb. "Mysterious and multifold is the Way of the Potato," declared Wolfe Tone. He pressed the freshly exposed surface against a document that was on the table, and came away with a perfectly copied ink stamp, which he then transferred to a passport he seemed to be in the process of forging.

"Your ship's in," guessed Reef.

Wolfe flourished the document. "Eusebio Gómez, *a sus órdenes.*"

THE NIGHT BEFORE Wolfe sailed, he, Reef, and Flaco stood down by the river, drinking local beer out of bottles and watching the fall of night, "weightless as a widow's veil," observed the young Irishman, "and isn't it the curse of the drifter, this desolation of heart we feel each evening at sundown, with the slow loop of the river out there just for half a minute, catching the last light, pregnant with the city in all its density and wonder, the possibilities never to be counted, much less lived into, by the likes of us, don't you see, for we're only passing through, we're already ghosts."

Frank was to spend months that seemed like years traipsing to no purpose around an empty shadowmap, a dime novel of Old Mexico, featuring gringo evildoers in exile, sudden deaths, a government that had already fallen but did not yet know it, a revolution that would never begin though thousands were already dying and suffering in its name.

He met up with Ewball Oust one night in a saloon somewhere along the—one does not want to say accursed, exactly, but at least defectively blessed—circuit of engagements booked for Gastón Villa and His Bughouse Bandoleros. For the Bandoleros the border somehow was asymptotic—they might approach as closely as they wished, but never cross. As if his father's *charro* act had placed an interdiction on the bloodline, Gastón understood that to enter old Mexico would require of him something like a gift of grace for which he doubted his soul was eligible.

Ewball was a young fellow from Lake County, on the way down to the Veta Madre. The family, rolling in Leadville money, had agreed to remit him two hundred dollars a month, American not pesos, to stay down there and try to get by on his skills in mine engineering. If he survived the drinking water and the bandits, why, he might be allowed someday to return to the States, even to enjoy some marginal future in Business.

"More of a metallurgist that a mine engineer," Ewball confessed.

Frank had done some business in Leadville with a Toplady Oust, he believed.

"Uncle Top. Conceived in a choir loft during a rendition of 'Rock of Ages.' You're not that fellow with the magnets, are you?"

"I was. Lately obliged to seek a new line of work."

Ewball eyed the Galandronome, started to say something, thought better of it. "You know the Patio method?"

"Heard of it. Mexican silver process. What us gringos'd call heap amalgamation. Said to be a little on the slow side."

"Usually a hundred-percent recovery takes about a month. My family runs a couple of mines down in Guanajuato, they're sending me down to have a look, say they want to modernize, see if they can speed things up."

"Introduce em Mexes to the joys of the Washoe process, they going to go along with that?"

"They've been used to taking their time, Patio style's traditional around Guanajuato—quicksilver's cheap, ores tend to be free-milling, not much reason to change except for the time factor. So I figure what it is is, is that my folks just want me out of the country."

He sounded more bewildered than angry, but Frank reckoned that could change. "Maybe they want a faster return on investment," he said carefully. "It's understandable."

"You know the country down there?"

"No but it has been on my mind lately, and I'll tell you why, 'cause you'll appreciate the metallurgy." He started to tell Ewball about argentaurum, but Ewball was way ahead of him.

"Sounds to me like what you're really interested in is that Iceland spar," Ewball said.

Frank shrugged, as if it would be embarrassing to admit how much.

"*Espato* is what they call it down there. Sometimes you hear *espanto,* which is something either horrifying or amazing, depending."

"Like looking at somebody through a pure enough specimen and seeing not just the man but his ghost alongside him?"

Ewball regarded Frank with some curiosity. "Plenty occasions for goose bumps down in those drifts as it is. *Espantoso, hombre.*"

"I mean, calcite is an interesting mineral, but basically I could use some work."

"Sure, they're always hiring. Come on along."

"Hate to leave my instrument," taking up the Galandronome, "just when I learned— Here, listen to this." It was a Mexican-sounding tune, in some underlying march time but with those peculiar south-of-the-border hesitations and off beats to it. A couple of the Bandoleros wandered over with guitars and began strumming chords, and after a while Paco the trumpet player took over the solo from Frank.

Ewball was amused. "There's parts of Mexico they'd take you straight to the hoosegow for just whistlin that."

"'La Cucaracha'? It's somebody's girlfriend, likes to smoke that *grifa* stuff, what's wrong with that?"

"It's General Huerta," Ewball informed him, "brutal heart, bloody mind, and even if he prefers killing his own people you might not want to be crossing his path, 'cause he'll sure settle for a whistling gringo. You won't get the blindfold and you sure's hell won't get no free cigarette."

So, iron on iron and headlong as fate, Frank and Ewball were borne into the Bajío on the eve of a turn in history. They crossed the border at El Paso, came in to Guanajuato by train, Torreón, Zacatecas, León, and changing finally at Silao, by then sleepless, apprehensive, field-shirts stained as if ominously with the juice of local strawberries. All along the passage through the mesquite, beneath the soaring hawks of the Sierra Madre, arroyos, piles of ore tailings, cottonwoods, through black fields, where *tlachiqueros* brought sheepskins slung across their backs full of fresh maguey juice to be fermented, and campesinos in white lined the right-of-way, some packing weapons, some watching empty-handed the train's simple passage, "expressionless," as gringos liked to say, beneath their hatbrims, waiting, for a feast day to dawn, a decisive message to arrive from the Capital, or Christ to return, or depart, for good.

At the Guanajuato station, the northamericans, puffing on Vera Cruz puros, descended from the coach into an afternoon rainstorm, loping to shelter beneath an ungalvanized shed roof that was being so battered by the downpour that no one under it could hear or talk. Where the roof had rusted through, water descended almost wrathfully. "Couple pesos' worth of zinc could've squared this away, 's the thing," Frank commented, and Ewball, unable to hear him, shrugged.

They were approached by purveyors of chewing gum, sunglasses, straw hats, fire opals, and shockingly young women, by children offering to carry their gear and shine their boots, by hopefully loitering hotel trap-drivers with thoughts on where they should sleep tonight, all of whom they were able to refuse with a politely wagging finger.

The old stone city smelled of livestock, well-water, sewage, sulfur and other by-products of the mining and smelting of silver. . . . They could hear sounds from all invisible parts of the city—voices, ore mills, the bells of the churches striking the hours. Sounds echoed off the stone buildings, and the narrow streets amplified them.

Frank went to work at Empresas Oustianas, S.A., and caught on to the amalgamation work easy enough. He and Ewball had soon settled in to the cantina life, the only uncomfortable part being what Frank imagined were strange looks he would get every now and then, as if people thought they recognized him, though it could've been all the pulque or the absence of sleep. When he did sleep, he dreamed short, intense dreams nearly always about Deuce Kindred. "I ain't here," Deuce kept saying. "I am miles and miles away, you poor fool. No, don't go in that *callejón.* You won't find me. Don't go up that *subida,* no point to it. No point to your life, come to that. Mexico's the perfect place for you to be. Another fucked-up gringo." But as dream followed dream, here was the odd thing, it was the same intricate path, leading uphill, cobbled alleys at first, giving way to packed earth, twisting, now and then briefly acquiring roofs and becoming narrow passages—and stairways among dilapidated dwellings, many of them abandoned, small, gray, dusty, crumbled, stacked roof to doorsill up the steep mountainside. Frank woke each time convinced there was an actual counterpart somewhere in this daylit city.

Semana Santa rolled around, and nobody worked that week, so Frank and Ewball had a chance to wander the town in search of trouble they hadn't tried yet. Because the streets were narrow as alleyways and ran between high walls, most of the town was in some kind of shadow. Looking for sunlight, they headed uphill and soon, rounding a corner, Frank was gripped by the strangest feeling of having been there before. "I dreamed this," he said.

Ewball narrowed his eyes some. "What's up there?"

"Somethin to do with Deuce."

"He's here?"

"Hell, just a dream, Ewb. Come on."

They climbed up the red-brown mountainside, into sunlight and purple artemisia, where wild dogs wandered the roofless stones, till they were high enough to see, beneath the harsh radiance of the Good Friday sky, where cirrus clouds were blown to long, fine parallel streaks, the city below, spread east to west, stunned as if by mysterious rays to a silence even Frank and Ewball must honor—the passion of Christ, the windless hush . . . even the stamping mills were silent, even Silver itself taking its day of rest, as if to recognize the price Judas Iscariot received. Sunlight in the trees.

Just as it seemed some revelation would emerge from the tensely luminous sky, they were taken into custody by men in frayed, soiled, not even all that official-looking uniforms, each packing the same-model Mauser—unwilling to meet their eyes, as if not certain how protected they were by the opacities of their own.

"What—" Ewball started to ask, but the *rurales* were making lip-buttoning gestures, and Frank remembered it was a Catholic practice to stay dummied up on Good Friday between noon and three, these being the hours Christ had hung on the cross. In devout silence they took away Frank's revolver and Ewball's German self-loader, and conducted them amid impenetrable sanctity to the *juzgado,* just off Calle Juárez, where they were thrown together into a cell deep below ground level, hewn out of the primordial rock. Water dripped and rats took their time crossing open areas.

"*Mordida* problems," supposed Ewball.

"Don't figure your Company boys'll come get us out sooner or later?"

"Long odds. Being gringo hereabouts is not always the selling point you take it to be."

"Well but I'm th' one's telling you that all the time."

"Oh. And I'm the one that's just whistling cheerfully down the trail here, figuring nothing will ever happen."

"Least I know where the safety is on that Broomhandle, Ewb."

"'Was,' I think you mean. Those *pistoles* are long gone, in my opinion."

"Maybe these boys'll get confused with yours, too, just give up on it and let you have it back."

Sometime in the middle of the night, they were awakened and bustled down a series of corridors and eventually up some stairs to a street neither of them had noticed before. "Not too happy with this," Ewball muttered, walking funny because of a tremor in his knees.

Frank took his unhandcuffed hands out of his pockets and flashed him a thumbs-up. "No *esposas,* I think we're O.K."

They turned on to the widest street in town, which both northamericans knew led straight to the Panteón, or city cemetery. "You would call this O.K., huh," Ewball looking miserable.

"Hey, we could make a bet on it."

"Sure, great for you, you wouldn't have to pay off."

"Got no money anyway. Why I suggested it."

At the foot of the Cerro del Trozado, almost able to make out the cemetery walls at the top looming in the partial moonlight, they entered an opening in the hillside, nearly invisible behind a screen of cactus. "*¿Dónde estamos?*" Frank saw no harm in asking.

"*El Palacio de Cristal.*"

"I've heard of this place," Ewball said. "Whatever the charge against us is, it's political."

"Sure got the wrong cowboy here," said Frank, "I don't even vote."

"*La política,*" nodded one of the *rurales,* smiling.

"*Felicitaciones,*" his companion added.

The cell was a little roomier than the one in the *juzgado,* with a couple of corn-husk mattresses and a slop-bucket and a huge, unflattering cartoon of Don Porfirio Díaz charcoaled across the wall. "Seein 's they wouldn't shoot us till sunup," Frank said, "guess I'll go snuggle in with the *chinches* here for a while."

"How logical is that?" Ewball objected. "If we're going to be sleeping for eternity. I mean . . ." But Frank was already snoring.

Ewball was still awake an hour later when they were joined by another northamerican, who introduced himself as Dwayne Provecho, drunk but not very sleepy, who commenced a monologue, inviting Ewball's attention more than once to his knowledge of secret tunnels, there since the ancient silver-mining beneath Guanajuato, that were sure to lead them out of this place. "End of the world is coming soon, you see. This last time across, riding out of Tucson, you could hear it in the air, all the way to Nogales and over the *frontera,* it never quit. Kind of roar, beasts overhead, bigger than anything you ever ran into, wings moving against the moon like clouds, suddenly it all goes dark and you're not sure you want it to pass too quick, for when the light comes back, who knows what you'll see up yonder?"

"Real obliged," Frank opening one eye to assure him, "but maybe if we could all just get some sleep—"

"Oh—no no no, not a minute to waste, for it's the Lord on his return journey, you must see that, he started to go away, and then he slowed down, like he'd had a thought, and stopped, and turned, and now he's coming back for us, can't you see that light, can't you feel that heat radiating from him the closer he gets," and so forth.

Despite the presence of a larger-than-expected number of religious bores, as time passed, this Mexican hoosegow would turn out to be not nearly the hellhole of bordertown legend but a flexible and now and then even friendly arrangement, due in great measure to the money that Ewball's pockets were all at once mysteriously full of. "Where's this coming from? Ewb, it's starting to make me nervous, now. . . ."

"No say prayo-coopy, compadre!"

"Yeahp o' course, but somebody keeps bringin it over here all the time, *somebody you know.*"

"Regular as payday and safe as the Morgan Bank."

Ewball was trying to strike the carefree note, but Frank felt less chirpy. "Sure. And when'll they be wanting it back?"

"Someday, maybe, after we get out of here, but who's in any hurry for that?"

Tell the truth, neither one of them. This place was just a dream, so peaceful, compared to what they'd been brought here down out of, peaceful as the city above looked from great distances, but never, up close, managed to sound—no drunken miners or unannounced blasting, the beating of the stamp mills all night coming through the rock here muted, in polyrhythms as persuasive to sleep as the constant flow of sea to a crewman bunking below the waterline—at the edges of sleep's blessed vegetable patch. . . . Down here workaday anxieties were brushed away, while opportunities for recreation went ever unfolding, in a parade of subterranean attractions—a cantina complete with music and fandango girls, a small nickelodeon theater, or actually centavodeón, roulette and faro, *grifa* peddlers and opium joints staffed by elements of the Chinese community topside, suites of guest rooms luxurious as any in town, with the underground equivalent of a balcony from which one could view, it seemed for miles, the smoke-darkened walls and iron-riveted watchtowers and the brown corridors, often roofless, of this increasingly cozy captivity, with few of your usual knifers and drunks and mining-town riffraff—no, given the national politics at the moment unfolding, the other detainees here seemed more like, what would you call them, honest working stiffs with a dangerous light in their eyes. Outspoken professors, rogue *científicos* as well. Nor did certain hoosegow dynamics, such as those to do with one's rectal integrity, even seem to apply here, which did simplify the day for the two northamericans.

Another surprise came when the turnkey on the night shift proved to be a pleasant-looking young woman in an untypically squared-away uniform, named Amparo, or, as she preferred, Sergeant, Vásquez. A closely connected relation of somebody higher up, Frank imagined. She was seldom observed smiling, exactly, but then neither was she ever 100 percent jailhouse business. "Look out, now," muttered Frank, not entirely to himself.

"Oh, I don't know," said Ewball. "I think she likes us."

"Likes all 'em hidalgos you're throwing around, 's more likely."

"Damn. You're really consistent."

"Thanks. Or do I mean, 'How's that?'"

"Women. You ever run into one that no money changed hands?"

"Give me a month or two, I could probably come up with somethin' ran under a dollar somehow."

What the Sergeant made clear right away was that they could do anything they had the payback for, as long as they remembered to ask her about it first. Short of walk out, of course, though she daily brought down repeated promises of a speedy resolution to their case.

"Well, would you happen to know what it is we're in here for, 'cause nobody's exactly tellin us?"

"You look just a corker today by the way, your hair up in that silver concern and all."

"*Ay, lisonjeros.* They say it was something one of you did a long time ago, back on the Other Side."

"But then why run both of us in?"

"Yehp and which one of us is it?"

She only gazed back at them one at a time, boldly and not at all ill-disposed, the way women will tend to do in the Capital sometimes.

"Must be me they want," Frank guessed. "Can't be you, Ewball, you're too young to have any history with the law."

"Well I have been party to some bribery activities. . . ."

"You wouldn't be in here for that."

"Shouldn't you be looking more worried, then?"

Frank awoke very early in the morning from a dream of voyaging by air, high in the air, in a conveyance whose actual working principles were mysterious to him, to find the molten-eyed Sergeant Vásquez at the door, with a breakfast tray of chilled papayas and limes, already cut up to avoid any chance of knife-related mischief, bolillos freshly baked, sliced, and spread with beans and Chihuahua cheese and put in some oven till the cheese melted, a kitchen salsa featuring the energetic local chili known as El Chinganáriz, a pitcherful of mixed orange, mango, and strawberry juice, and Vera Cruz coffee with heated milk and chunks of unrefined sugar to go in it.

"You boys sure eat good," commented Dwayne Provecho, choosing that moment to pop his head in the door and exhibit a string of drool running off his chin and down his shirt.

"Sure Dwayne, you want to dig right in there." Frank noticed the Sarge giving him the eyeball heliograph from out in the corridor. "Be back. . . ."

"Maybe you don't want to get too friendly," she advised. "That one goes in the shadow of the *paredón.*"

"Why, what'd he do?"

She let it wait for a minute. "Running errands north of the border. Working for some . . . dangerous people. You know of"—lowering her voice and fixing him with a gaze beneath which self-delusion became impossible—"P.L.M.?"

Uh-oh. "Let's see, that's those Flores Magón brothers, *¿verdad?* . . . and that Camilo Arriaga too, local fellow if I'm not mistaken . . . ?"

"Camilo? he's a *potosino.* And el señor Provecho's employers—they might consider the Flores Magón a bit too . . . you say, *delicate*?"

"Well but look at him in there. Porkin away—ain't that pretty cheerful for a man's about to be lined up against the wall?"

"There are two schools of thought. Some would like to release him, follow him, keep a record, see what they can learn. Others only want to remove a troublesome element, the sooner the better."

"Well but there's people in here tons more of a threat than old Dwayne, *muñeca,* some in for fifty years so far, why's time all of a sudden so important? Something *big in the works,* maybe?"

"Your eyes," as she was in the habit of whispering when they were alone, "I never see eyes like this."

Oh well. "Sergeant now you tellin me you never had time to gaze in a gringo's eyes before?"

She kept silent, doing that thing with her own unreadable black-irised eyes that reliably set him to wondering. She had warned him today, that was the limit of her commission—and when finally Dwayne did get around to blurting all, Frank wasn't too surprised.

Dwayne smelled like tequila-and-beer *caldereros y sus macheteros* in unknown amounts, though Frank wasn't sure how much had actually got inside of him—there was too much clarity around his eyes, which had grown incandescent. "Here on a mission," was how he described it, "specifically to offer you some contract employment, it being widely believed, down here as back the other side, that you, sorry if I'm bein too direct, 're none other than that Kieselguhr Kid of Wild West legend."

"Heck of an assumption, Dwayne, seems like that you'd somehow know better, man been up and down the territory and so forth."

"You're . . . just a mine engineer and that's all."

"Yehp but there's plenty know their way around the dangerous substances 't's on your mind who'd be happy for the action, too, so when you get out of here, what you need to do's you pick out any mine in the Veta Madre, head for the first cantina downtrail of it, and you'll be up to your ears in qualified demolition folks before you figure out who's buying the next round."

"With half of 'm, brother, depending for their jobs on this ol' Porfiriato here keepin on forever, and all's I've got to do is guess wrong just once about that."

"Maybe you just did."

"Then I'm at your mercy, ain't I?"

"I wonder if you'd be this jocular with the real Kieselguhr Kid . . . wouldn't you be showin more respect, hell I don't know, some fear, even?"

"Kid, if I may so address you, I'm afraid all the time."

"What I meant was, there must be some room there in your mind for the chance you got the wrong fella?"

"Federales've got photos, I've seen 'm."

"Nobody ever looks like their 'mug,' you ought to know that by now."

"Also talked to Brother Disco up in Telluride. He predicted you'd be down here, and whose company you'd be in, too."

"Ellmore thinks I'm the Kid?"

"Ellmore says it's the only reason Bob Meldrum didn't just drill you the first time he laid eyes on you."

"I *frightened* Hair-Trigger Bob?"

"More like professional courtesy," opined Dwayne Provecho with a certain practiced avuncularity. "And just to show you all's on the up and up, tonight we break out of here."

"Just when I was gettin to like it. Why don't you go on ahead by yourself."

"Because everybody here thinks you're the Kieselguhr Kid and they're expectin a breakout."

"But I'm not."

"But someday some local bad-ass who thinks you are will be unable to resist plungin his *cuchillo* into your heart, just for the glory it'll bring him."

"Tactfully put," said Ewball, joining the conversation, "though it really is time we were on the trail, Frank."

"You too? Thought your people 's gonna buy our way out."

"So did I for a while."

"Uh-oh."

CARRYING DARK-LANTERNS, they entered a smooth-walled, vaulted corridor. Shadows bobbed, white shapes emerged ahead. "Oh boy," Ewball said.

"Ain't fixin' to be sick, are you?" asked thoughtful Dwayne. "Fellas, meet the *momias*."

There were about thirty of them, hanging on pegs, in two long rows it was going to be necessary to pass between. The bodies were concealed by sheets—only the heads were left uncovered, angled downward, faces in different states of mummification, some in the lanternlight without expression, others twisted in terrible agony. They all seemed to be waiting for something, with a supernatural patience, their feet a few inches above the floor, thin and distracted, keeping dignity and distance, serenely believing themselves in, but not inescapably of, Mexico.

"The Panteón is short on space," Dwayne was eager to explain, "so these boys get five years curing in the ground, then if the families don't pay the what they call grave tax, they get dug up again and hung there till somebody antes up."

"I thought it was something religious," Ewball said.

"You could call it that, it all gets turned to pesos and centavos, water to wine you might say, during the day they charge visitors to see it, we're gettin the three A.M. rate here, though from the looks on these faces we must've . . . *interrupted somethin.*"

"All right, Dwayne," Frank muttered. They reached spiral steps at one end of the crypt and ascended into moonlight.

Making their way down the canyon to the old Marfil station, they boarded the train there a little after sunup, and rode all day into the afternoon, Frank submerged in silence, refusing to drink, to buy drinks, to smoke, or even share the cigarillos he didn't smoke with his hoosegow buddies, who began to grow concerned.

"Hope you're not in love, *compinche.*"

"You're being haunted," Dwayne explained. "Every sign of it. Something in your notorious past, needs to be taken care of."

"You know, Brother Provecho, in jail this Kid refrain was one thing, but out here it's just tiresome, 's all. Sorry I'm not your man, actually Kid, and you're way better off right now needling somebody else might appreciate it more."

"Too late." Dwayne nodded out the window. "As I estimate maybe five more minutes for you to brush up on those legendary dynamite skills . . . Kid."

The train was braking to a stop, sure enough, and Frank began to hear commotion close by. He looked out the windows and saw, riding escort, a couple dozen men who looked to be under some oath of sobriety as to personal display—shaven upper lips, modest hatbrims no *charro*'d be caught dead in, cotton shirts and workers' trousers in a range of earth tones, no insignia, no evidence of any affiliation to anything.

"All for me, huh?" said Frank.

"I'm coming along," Ewball announced.

"Wouldn't have it otherwise." Someplace in the last few hours Dwayne had obtained a pistol it seemed.

After a few seconds, Ewball said, "Oh. Ransom money? 'S that it, that's what you're counting on, the legendary Oust fortune? Not a fruitful plan, *vaquero.*"

"Hell, they'll be happy 'th whatever they get. They're happy folks. What you see out there's so far just a small-time endeavor, one day to the next, no hostage too insignificant, long as it's bourgeoisie that can pay somethin."

"Ay, Jalisco," muttered Frank.

"Oh, and you'll want to meet El Ñato." An energetic presence had entered the carriage—officer's jacket from the defunct army of some country not too nearby, smoked lenses, steel practicalities where you might have expected silver ornaments, and perched up on one epaulette a very large tropical parrot, so out of scale in fact that to converse with its owner it had to lean down to scream into his ear.

"And this is Joaquín," El Ñato smiling up at the bird. "Tell them something about yourself, *m'hijo.*"

"I like to fuck the gringo pussy," confided the parrot.

"How's that?" Ewball blinking at the bird's theatrical-British accent, recalling somehow vaudeville Shakespeare and profligate nights.

A hideous laugh. "Got a problem with that, *pendejo*?"

El Ñato beamed fretfully. "There, there, Joaquín, we mustn't give our guests the wrong idea—it was only that one house-cat, one time, up in Corpus Christi, long, long ago."

"*Sin embargo, mi capitán,* the adventure has haunted me."

"Of course Joaquín and now gentlemen, if you wouldn't mind . . ."

There were horses saddled and waiting for Ewball and Frank, which it was now indicated they mount. "Not coming along, Dwayne?" Frank swinging up into a black leather saddle rig, built onto a military-style tree, he noticed, little unexpected this far out of town, free of carving or stamping or anything fancy except for the Mexican curb bits and "taps" over the stirrups. "Keep smart boys," Dwayne called back from the carriage doorway, "and maybe we'll be seeing you down 'em rails again someday." As the train began to move, El Ñato tossed him up a leather sack, small but with some heft to it, got his horse to rear dramatically, wheeled about, calling *"¡Vámonos!"* to his riders. The parrot flapped his wings as if signaling to a confederate in the distance. Surrounding the Americans, the *guerrilleros* moved off, alert, silent, picking up a trooping gait, until soon the train behind them seemed just one more chirring summer insect in the distant brush.

"RIDIN WITH ANARCHISTS NOW, got-damn never thought I'd be doin this. . . ."

"What's the matter," needled Ewball, "you'd feel more comfortable with just some everyday bandits?"

"Bandits may shoot, bandits may cut, but at least they ain't blowin things up every chance they get."

"We never blew nothín up!" protested El Ñato. "Nobody here knowss nothín about no explosives! Steal a li'l dynamite from the mines maybe, throw a stick here, stick there, but now all that's changed, now *you're* ridín with us, *¡el Famoso Chavalito del Quiselgúr!*—now we get respect!"

They rode till well after dark, ate, slept, struck camp, moved out hours before dawn. The escort were a humorless bunch, and any thoughts of even a companionable *copa* now and then were soon abandoned. Days went by like this, as they rode deeper into Mexico than Frank had ever believed anybody could without hitting a coastline, Ewball meantime acting less and less like a hostage and more like a long-lost brother who was trying to charm his way back into a family he thought was his own. Stranger than that, El Ñato and his lieutenants appeared to be falling for this routine, and soon even encouraging Ewball to join up and ride with their guerrilla unit. "You'll have to travel fast, keep up. But we don't always get to eat, or find a town to requisition, and the rule in the outfit being that first to find anything is first to enjoy it, *pues* . . . you'll keep up, I believe."

They rode down small-town boulevards lined with ancient palm trees, through precipitous canyons, the indigo mountains fanned like paper cutouts into the miles of haze. One day, looking down off a high ridge, Frank saw a rust-colored city spilling up and down the sides of a deep gulch. Piles of tailings loomed everywhere, which Frank recognized as spoil from silver mining. Rambling between the high uninflected walls of the town, alleyways were apt to turn to stairsteps.

They pitched camp outside of town, near a bridge over an arroyo. The wind funneling down the ravine never quit all the time they were there. Streetlights came on early in the dark brown afternoons and sometimes stayed on all the next day. Frank, seeming to enter a partial vacuum in the passage of time, found half a minute to ask himself if this was really where he ought to be. It was such an unexpected question that he decided to consult with Ewball, who was squatting next to a Maxim gun broken down into bits and pieces on a blanket and trying to remember how to get it back together.

"Old *compinche*— say, you look different somehow. Wait, don't tell me. The hat? maybe all those ammo belts there full of machine-gun bullets 't you're packing? The tattoo? Let me look— *¡Qué guapa, qué tetas fantásticas, ¿verdad?*"

"These folks knew it all along," said Ewball. "Just took me awhile to see it, was all."

"Hey! Tell you what. Don't be hasty. We, we'll switch. Yeah! Yeah, you can be the Kid, and I'll be the sidekick. O.K.? They never believe a thing I tell 'em, but maybe they will believe you."

"Who, me? Be the Kid? Aw, I don't know, Frank. . . ."

"Five minutes and I can teach you everything, Advanced Blasting course on the cheap, all the latest thinking— here, for instance, you ever wonder which end of these is the one you light?"

"Dammit now Frank now get that thing away from me—"

"Why it's this one here, see—"

"Ahhh!" Ewball was out the tentflap faster than the muzzle velocity of any known firearm. Frank placed the smoking cylinder, which on a closer look might've been no more than a giant Cuban claro in a Partidos wrapper, between his teeth and strolled out among the *tropa,* who, under the impression that he was actually smoking a stick of dynamite, scattered from his path muttering in admiration. The only one willing to engage him in conversation was the parrot Joaquín.

"Ever wonder why they call it Zacatecas, Zacatecas? Or why it's Guanajuato, Guanajuato?"

Frank, fallen by now into the doubtful habit of Conversation with a Parrot, shrugged in irritation. "One's a city, one's a state."

"*¡Pendejo!*" screamed the parrot. "Think! Double refraction! Your favorite optical property! Silver mines, full of *espato* double-refracting all the time, and not only light rays, naw, uh-uh! Cities, too! People! Parrots! You just keep floating along in that gringo smoke cloud, thinking there's only one of everything, *huevón,* you don't see those strange lights all around you. *Ay, Chihuahua.* In fact, *Ay, Chihuahua, Chihuahua.* Kid engineers! All alike. Closed minds. Always been your problem." Giving in at length to parrot hysteria, sinister in its prolonged indifference.

"Here's *your* problem," Frank approaching Joaquín with his hands out in strangling position.

The *comandante,* sensing psitticide in the air, came hurrying up.

"Apologies, Señor Chavalito, but with only a few more hours to go—"

"Few more hours, um, till what, Ñato?"

"*¡Caray!* Did I forget to tell you? sometimes I wonder why they even let me lead a unit. Why, your first commission, of course! We want you to blow up the Palacio del Gobierno tonight, ¿O.K.? Give it, you know, that special El Chavalito punch?"

"And you'll be on hand for that?"

El Ñato grew evasive, or, as he would have termed it, self-conscious. "To be honest, it isn't really the primary target."

"Then why?"

"Can you keep a secret?"

"Ñato—"

"All right, all right, it's the Mint. While you're creating a diversion—"

Later Frank couldn't remember if the word *loco* had come into the discussion, though its Mexican euphemism *lucas* might have. His point, simple enough, really, being that silver coinage in any quantity would weigh a great deal. At twenty-five grams to the peso, a good mule might carry five thousand pesos, a jack maybe thirty-five hundred, but the question was how far before the mule fell over and had to be replaced. Even with a string of mules long enough to make a Mint robbery worth the trouble, they would be sitting ducks for any federal posse.

"I knew that," said El Ñato. But Frank could tell his feelings were hurt.

It got no further, actually, than trying to steal the dynamite they would need from one of the silver mines on the slopes of Monte el Refugio, southeast of town. Before anybody could shout a warning, they found themselves in the middle of a fire-fight, maybe with mine guards, maybe *rurales,* hard to tell in the dark.

"Ain't like we blew into town all that quiet," Ewball muttered between squeezing off shots. "What's he expect?"

They got back to camp to find more shooting there, with El Ñato somewhere out on one flank, holding off what seemed to be a halfhearted assault. Nobody wanted to be shooting at night, though the clear suggestion was that daylight would be different and it might be wise to be gone by then.

"¡Ay, Chavalito!" screeched the parrot Joaquín, in some inaccessible dark frenzy from his cage, which was being loaded onto a pack mule, "we are in some *mierda, pendejo.*"

"Huertistas," said the comandante. "I can smell them." Frank must have had an inquisitive look, because Ñato glowered and added, "Like Indian blood. Like burned crops and stolen land. Like gringo money."

They moved out before dawn, angling away westward from the railroad and into a gullied and barren plateau, heading for Sombrérete and the Sierra beyond. Each time they went over a rise, the pointed ears of the horses in silhouette on the sky, everybody waited for rifle fire. Behind them after a while a dustcloud appeared.

There was discussion over whether to stop in Durango, Durango, but it seemed better to press on for the mountains. About noon the next day, Ewball rode up alongside Frank and directed his attention down into a little arroyo.

At first Frank took them for antelope, but they were running faster than he'd ever seen anything run. They disappeared into a cave in the base of a low cliffside, and Frank, Ewball, and El Ñato rode over to have a look. Three naked people crouched by the cave entrance, watching them, not in fear or expectancy, just watching.

"They're Tarahumares," El Ñato said. "They live in caves up north of the Sierra Madre—who knows what they're doing down here this far from home?"

"Huerta's folks ain't that far back. You think maybe that's who these people are running from?"

El Ñato shrugged. "Huerta usually goes after Yaquis or Mayas."

"Well they're goners if he catches them," Frank said.

"Rescuing Indians is the last thing I need right now. I have my own people to think of."

Ewball motioned to the three people to stay back in the cave and out of sight. "You all better keep moving, Ñato, I'll see what I can do, catch up with you in a little."

"Crazy gringo motherfucker," opined Joaquín the parrot.

Frank and Ewball proceeded up to a patch of rocks overlooking the valley. Inside of ten minutes, a line of soldiers appeared below, tightening, folding, stretching, repeating the motion, like a disembodied wing against an ashy sky attempting to remember the protocols of flight.

Ewball, humming "La Cucaracha," set about sighting in.

"Better save our rounds," it seemed to Frank, "ain't much we can do at this range."

"Watch."

After the crack, and a second of stillness, down on the valley floor a tiny mounted figure went lunging backward in the saddle, trying to grab the sombrero that had just forcefully departed from its head.

"Could've been a gust of wind."

"What do I have to do, start killing them, to get some respect here?"

"They get close enough, they'll sure try for us."

The detachment seemed to be in some confusion, riders going every which way, changing their minds every few seconds. "Ants in a anthill," chuckled Ewball. "Here, let's see if I can just shoot that rifle out of his hand now. . . ." He chambered another round and fired.

"Say, nice one. When'd you get so good? Mind if I—"

"Try a different angle, give 'em somethin' to think about."

Frank was able to get far enough around in the direction they'd been going to set up a nice crossfire, and eventually, leaving two or three Mausers behind them, the pursuers turned and made off for an evening at some fandango saloon in town, if they were lucky.

"Guess I'll go see to those Indians," said Frank. There was more. Ewball, obliging, waited. "Then I'm headin up north, back the Other Side. Adios Mexico for me. You interested? Or . . ."

Ewball smiled, snorted, indicated with his head the riders waiting for him, trying to make it look like he had no choice. *"Es mi destino, Pancho."* Ewball's horse, impatient, had already begun stepping away.

"Well," said Frank as if to himself, "*vaya con Dios.*"

"Hasta lueguito," said Ewball. They nodded, each touching his hatbrim, turned away.

Frank rode down to where he'd last seen the party of Indians, and found them in a shallow cave about a half mile farther up the valley. There were one man and two women, none of them wearing much in the way of clothing besides red bandannas around their heads.

"You saved our lives," said the man in Mexican Spanish.

"Me? no," Frank gesturing vaguely after the long-departed *anarquistas.* "But I wanted to make sure you're all right, and then I'm on my way."

"Somebody saved our lives," said the Indian.

"Yes, but they're gone now."

"But you're here."

"But—"

"You go north. We do, too. Let us go together for a while. With permission. You may find something you have been looking for."

He introduced himself as El Espinero. "Not my real name—it's a name the *shabótshi* gave me." He had demonstrated at an early age a skill for locating water by examining a random spill of cactus thorns, and he soon became a working *brujo,* gazing into scatterings of thorns and telling people what would happen to them in the near future, the grammatical tense that mattered most these days back up in the Sierra.

One of the women was his wife, and the other her younger sister, whose husband had been taken away and presumed murdered by the huertistas.

"Her *shabótshi* name is Estrella," said the shaman. He nodded, a smile beginning. "The name means something to you. She is searching for a new man now. You saved her life."

Frank took a look at her. This was a peculiar place to be reminded so abruptly of the other Estrella, Reef's sweetheart back in Nochecita, by now with any luck the mother of a walking, talking little one. This Tarahumare girl was very young, with a notable great fall of black hair, big expressive eyes, and a fiery way of using them. Dressed for the trail, meaning hardly at all, you couldn't say she was a chore to look at. But she was not Estrella Briggs either.

"I didn't save her life," Frank said, "the young fellow who really did that rode off a while ago, and I'm not sure we can find him now."

"Qué toza tienes allá," the girl remarked, pointing at Frank's penis, which did in fact at the moment resemble sort of a small—well, medium-size—log. This was the first time she'd mentioned him directly. Her sister and El Es-

pinero also examined the member, and then the three of them conferred for a while in their language, though the laughter was easy to translate.

After a day and a half's journey, El Espinero led Frank to a long-abandoned silver working, high over the plain, where nopales grew and lizards lay in the sun.

Frank understood that he had been waiting for the unreadable face of the one *duende* or Mexican tommyknocker who would lead him like this up some slope, higher than the last roofless wall, into a range of hawks and eagles, take him beyond his need for the light or wages of day, into some thorn-screened mouth, in beneath broken gallow-frames and shoring all askew, allowing himself at last to be swallowed by, rather than actively penetrating, the immemorial mystery of these mountains—and that now the moment of subduction had come, he would make no move to prevent it.

Frank had been looking at calcite crystals for a while now, through Nicol prisms of lab instruments whose names he'd forgotten, among the chats or zinc tailings of the Lake County mines, down here in the silver lodes of the Veta Madre and so forth, and he doubted anything like this piece of spar had ever been seen on Earth, maybe since the early days up in Iceland itself, yes quite a specimen all right, a twin crystal, pure, colorless, without a flaw, each identically mirrored half about the size of a human head and what Ewball would call "of scalenohedral habit." And there was this deep glow, though not enough ambient light in here to account for it—as if there were a soul harbored within.

"Be careful. Look into it, see things."

They were deep inside a cavern in the mountain, yet some queer luminescence in here allowed him to see as much—Frank couldn't avoid thinking—as much as he had to.

In the depths of the calcite now, without waiting too long at all, he saw, or later would say he thought he saw, Sloat Fresno, and exactly where Sloat had to be. No comparable message about Deuce, however. A couple years later, when he ran into Ewball again and told him about this, Ewball would frown, in a slightly mischievous way. "Shouldn't it've been a little, don't know, more *spiritual* than that? Deep wisdom, ancient truth, light from beyond, all that comes of it is one more cantina shooting? Pretty durn bleak for some magical crystal, ain't it?"

"What the Indian said was, 's that his and the women's lives got saved, no matter who it was did the savin—this case you, *compinche*—and that this wasn't a real piece of spar so much as the idea of two twin halves, of balancing out lives and deaths."

"So you still got two more deaths comin, one'd be Deuce, and if I could put in a word, the other *should* be old Huerta, 'cause that sumbitch is still out there makin ever'body's life miserable."

"HUNGRY?" said El Espinero.

Frank looked around and as usual saw nothing edible for a couple hundred miles' radius.

"See that rabbit?"

"No."

El Espinero took from his pack and hefted a sun-bleached stick with an elegant warp to it, peered into the distance, and threw it. "Now do you see it?"

"There it is. How'd you do that?"

"You have fallen into the habit of seeing dead things better than live ones. *Shabótshi* all do. You need practice in seeing."

After they ate, Frank passed around the last of his smokes. The women went off to smoke in private. El Espinero reached in his belongings and came out with some kind of vegetarian snack. "Eat this."

"What is it?"

"Hikuli."

It looked like what up north they called globe cactus. According to El Espinero, the plant was still alive. Frank couldn't recall ever eating something while it was alive.

"What's it for?"

"Medicine. Cure."

"For what?"

"For this," said El Espinero, with an economical slide of his hand indicating all the visible circumference of the cruel llano.

It didn't kick in for a while, but when it did, Frank was taken out of himself, not just out of his body by way of some spectacular vomiting but out of whatever else he thought he was, out of his mind, his country and family, out of his soul.

At some point he found himself in the air, hand in hand with young Estrella, flying quite swiftly, at low altitude, over the starlit country. Her hair streaming straight out behind her. Frank, who had never flown before, kept wanting to turn right or left and go explore arroyos filled with a liquid, quivering darkness, and tall cactuses and dramas of predatory pursuit and so forth that now and then seemed also to be glowing in these peculiar colors, but the girl, who had flown often, knew where they had to go, and he understood after a while that she was guiding him, so relaxed and flew along with her.

Later, on the ground, in fact, strangely, under it, he found himself wandering a stone labyrinth from one cave to another, oppressed by a growing sense of danger—each time he chose a branch, thinking it would lead him out to open air, it only took him deeper, and soon he was at the edge of panic. "Do not," said the girl, carefully, calming him somehow with an inexplicable clarity of touch, "do not be afraid. They want you to be afraid, but you do not have to give them what they want. You have the power not to be afraid. Find it, and when you do, try to remember where it is." While continuing to be the Tarahumare girl Estrella, she had also at the same time become Estrella Briggs.

They came to a cave in which it was raining, calmly but steadily. Inside this one cave, she explained, falling steadily for thousands of years, was all the rain that should have been falling on the southwestern desert—vaporous and gray, not from any spring within the mountain, or from clouds outside directly overhead, but as a result of the original sin, crime, or mistake that had produced the desert itself. . . .

"Think not," Frank objected. "The desert is something that has evolved over geological time. Not somebody's personal punishment."

"Back before the beginning of all that, when they were designing the world—"

"'They.'"

"'They.' The idea was that water should be everywhere, free to everybody. It was life. Then a few got greedy." She went on to tell Frank how the desert was made, to serve as their penance. And so to balance it, somewhere, hidden in the uncounted miles of wasteland, would be this one cave, dense with water forever falling. If any wanted to search for it, why, of course they were welcome, though the odds were they'd wander forever without finding it. Tales you heard of haunted silver and gold mines half the time were really about this one hidden cave of rainwater, precious beyond price, but the old desert madfolk believed they had to tell it in a kind of code, that others would be listening, that saying anything out loud would cause the place to grow that much more remote, dangerous to approach. . . .

At no point in this did Frank think he was dreaming, probably because he seldom remembered dreams, or paid attention to them even if he did. And though this all had the alert immediacy of daytime Mexico in its ongoing dispute with its history, it would someday be relegated as well to the register of experiences he had been unable to find any use for.

They returned to the desert camp among whirling colors including magenta, low-brilliancy turquoise, and a peculiarly pale, wriggling violet, appearing not only around contours but smudged and bleeding inside them as well, affording glimpses now and then of some solitary band of figures alone on the prairie toward sunset, the untouched depths of it windsweeping away for hundreds of miles, of air even of this purity beginning in this last light from its own glaciating thickness to blur the distant mountains toward a sketchwork suggestive of other worlds, mythic cities at the horizon. . . .

FRANK KNEW that El Espinero's wife was neither mute nor shy, having heard a number of animated conversations in, he guessed, the Tarahumare language among the three of them, but she never spoke a word to Frank, only looked at him with great sympathy and directness, as if there was something so obvious he ought to be seeing, which she wanted to tell him about but for some reason, some imperative of the spirit, could not. He was certain beyond words that she was the invisible beating heart of whatever had brought the family south into danger from the Mexican army, but none of them were about to share the reason with Frank.

They reached an almost invisible fork, and the Tarahumare party turned west, bound up into the Sierra Madre.

Frank smiled at Estrella. "Hope you find the right hombre."

"Just as happy it wasn't you," she said. "You are a good man, but kind of disgusting, with all that hair growing out of your face, and you always smell like coffee." When they parted, El Espinero gave him a necklace made out of sky-pale translucent seeds Frank recognized as Tears of Job. "Won't keep you safe, but you'll be healthier. Good for your breathing."

"Oh, by the way, that *hikuli*? got any more of that?"

El Espinero pointed, laughing, at a cactus near Frank's foot, and he and the women rode away laughing, for quite some time, actually, till they were over the ridgeline and out of earshot. Apologizing to the cactus as the *brujo* had instructed him, Frank removed it live from its home earth and stashed it in his saddlebag. In days to come, he would take it out for a nibble, or sometimes only to look at and wait for instructions. But he was never to have quite the same certitude again as he had felt flying with Estrella/Estrella over the teeming high desert or braving the stone grimness below it.

He worked his way north among the tall cactuses and greasewood, staying just out of sight of the railroad, until one day he became aware that the mountains had become geometrical impersonations of themselves, impossibly pointed and forbidding, no easier to accept than this out-of-scale plain he'd been riding through. What was there to do out here but run and pursue? What else made sense? Stand still, under this vast of a sky? Dry out, grow still as the brush, as a cactus, keep slowing down until entering some mineral condition. . . .

It came to pass that one day Frank rode in out of some irrigated cotton fields at the edge of the Bolsón de Mapimí, down the daylit single street of a little pueblo whose name he would soon forget, walked into a particular cantina as if he'd been a regular for years (adobe walls, perpetual 4:00 A.M. gloom, abiding fumes of pulque in the room, no Budweiser Little Big Horn panoramas here, no, instead some crumbling mural of the ancient Aztec foundation story of the eagle and the serpent, here perversely showing the snake coiled around the eagle and just about to dispatch it, and posed presentably among that old-time scenery, watching the struggle, a number of attractive señoritas with nineteenth-century hairdos and the painter's idea of Aztec outfits—the walls otherwise undecorated, missing paint in chips and scars from long-ago gunplay or thrown furniture), and found there right in front of him, sitting slouched and puffy-faced and as if waiting, the no-longer-elusive Sloat Fresno, quick as that, with his pistol already somehow in his hand, giving Frank time only to find his own and begin firing cold, no chance to rouse up any of those family emotions, none of that—old Sloat, who maybe never even recognized him, failing as it turned out even to get off his shot—blown over backward, one of the chair legs breaking under his already dead weight so he was sent into half a spin, throwing a dark slash of blood that trailed in the air and feathered in a crescent slap, unheard in the noise of the shots, across the ancient soiling of the *pulquería* floor. *Fín.* A prolonged and shallow-breathing stillness of burnt powder, smoke rising, ears humming, black Mexican eyeballs seemingly bent upon the newly inducted member of the dead, though everybody would recognize Frank if they saw him again, in case anybody came around to ask in the proper way.

Frank, whose thoughts had immediately turned to the possibility of Deuce Kindred close by and sighting him in, called out louder than necessary to nobody in particular, as if trying to see how jumpy folks might be, "*¿Y el otro?*"

"*Él se fué, jefe.*" A local elder, holding a clay *jarrito,* starting the day early.

"*¿Y cuándo vuelva?*"

More of a facial shrug than a smile. "*Nunca me dijo nada, mi jefe.*"

And no telling these days really who that *otro* might be, Deuce or whoever. As this did nothing to settle Frank's nerves, he remained in a state of coiled attention, reluctant to buy himself a drink or even to stash the damn pistol, which now seemed wired to his palm. From up and down the street, saloon bums were appearing, and discussing with onlookers what to do about

Sloat's remains, several parties having already shown interest in the contents of his pockets, though Frank, it was understood, got first pickings.

"Si el caballero quisiera algún recuerdo . . ."

Yeahp, if he wanted a souvenir of this—*pistoleros* of the region being known to take body parts, scalps, ears, penises sometimes, to advert to through the golden years of their retirement, bring out, inspect, show off.

Ah, shit.

This had been so quick, even, you could say, easy. You could. He would soon begin to understand how it all might turn, was already, well before he had the godforsaken little town at his back, turning, to regret.

In New York for a few weeks of ground-leave, the boys had set up camp in Central Park. From time to time, messages arrived from Hierarchy via the usual pigeons and spiritualists, rocks through windows, blindfolded couriers reciting from memory, undersea cable, overland telegraph wire, lately the syntonic wireless, and signed, when at all, only with a carefully cryptic number—that being as nigh as any of them had ever approached, or ever would, to whatever pyramid of offices might be towering in the mists above. With an obvious lack of desire to meet the boys in person, their employers remained unknown to them, and contracts which they didn't even get to sign were simply distributed, unannounced and often it seemed blindly, from on high. "Well we are their proletariat, ain't we," snarled Darby, "the fools that do their 'dirty work' for next to nothing? and if they're too good for our *work,* then they're sure's 'heck' too good for us."

One midnight, with the usual absence of ceremony, a street-Arab in a stiff hat and a variety of tattoos appeared and with an ingratiating leer handed over a grease-stained envelope. "Here you go, my good lad," Lindsay dropping a silver coin into the messenger's hand.

"'Ey! Whut's 'is? some koindt of a *sailboat* pitchuhv on it! whuh country's dis from, I eeask yiz?"

"Allow me to read it for you. It says, 'Columbian Exposition Chicago 1893.' And here, upon the obverse, you will be reassured to find, 'Columbian *Half-Dollar.*' In fact they first sold for a dollar apiece."

"So yiz paid double f' sumt'in's only good in Chicago ten yeeuhz ago. Swell. All I need's d' toime machine, I'm in business, ain't I?" The urchin, flipping the coin dexterously from hand to hand, shrugged and prepared to take his leave.

His remark, however, had produced an all-but-paralyzed silence among the Chums, quite out of proportion to what had seemed only an ungrateful quip, for reasons none of them, if pressed, could have articulated. He was halfway across a nearby ornamental bridge before Chick Counterfly recovered enough to call out. "I say, hold up a moment!"

"T'ings to do," the youth replied. "Make it snappy."

"You said 'time machine.' What did you mean by that?"

"Nuttin." But his feet told a different story.

"We must talk about this further. Where can we find you?"

"Evvrands to vrun vroight now. So I'll be back." Before Chick could protest, the impertinent nuncio had vanished into the sylvan surroundings.

"He was *passing a remark,* believe me, I know a remark when I hear one," glowered Darby Suckling, later during the plenary meeting that followed Evening Quarters. The contentious lad, having recently become Ship's Legal Officer, was eager these days to explore, and when possible to abuse, his prerogatives. "We should find a judge, get a writ, and make the kid spill everything he knows."

"More likely," guessed Lindsay, "Mr. H. G. Wells's speculative jeu d'esprit on the subject has been adulterated to profitable effect by the 'dime novels' of which our visitor, assuming he reads, is no doubt an habitué."

"Yet this," Randolph gesturing with the single sheet the youth had delivered, "was signed by the Chums of Chance Upper Command. About whom, in fact, there have persisted for years rumors of a highly secretive programme, related in some way to time-travel. This fellow may, for all we know, be a steady but perhaps not altogether, for his part, contented employee of theirs, and his curious remark thus some coded invitation to pursue the topic with him."

"If his preference in beverages proves as inexpensive as his reading habits," reckoned Lindsay, who was Unit Treasurer, "there might be enough in our purchase-of-information fund for one small glass of beer."

"Eehhnnyyhh, just draw another voucher on th' National Imprest," airily sneered Darby. "The Big Boys'll rubber-stamp it as usual, and maybe help us find out what they don't want us to know." He would recall these words in days to come with a certain bitterness, the little band by then having embarked on a journey of fateful discovery which each in his own way would come to wish he had not set out upon.

True to his word, the messenger, one "Plug" Loafsley, returned next day with lengthy and detailed instructions for getting to his personal headquarters, the Lollipop Lounge, which turned out to be a child bordello in the Tenderloin, one of several that Plug ran as part of a squalid empire also including newsboys' opium dens and Sunday-school numbers rackets. Lindsay Noseworth, hearing this, of course "hit the roof." "We must immediately terminate all connection with the little monster. No less than our moral survival is at risk here."

"In a spirit of scientific inquiry," proposed Chick Counterfly soothingly, "I have no objection myself—distasteful though it prove—to meeting with young Loafsley, in whatever iniquitous sty he may be pleased to call his office."

"And maybe I'd better tag along as a chaperon," suggested Darby Suckling. Were glances of complicity exchanged? Accounts vary. Howbeit, later that evening, the two shipmates, disguised in matching ensembles sportively checked in indigo and custard yellow, topped off with pearl-gray bowlers, were proceeding into the Tenderloin, following the directions young Loafsley had provided them, finding themselves, before long, deeper in that dark topography of Vice than either had suspected possible—until arriving, near midnight, in a thickening waterfront fog, before a corroded iron door, guarded by what would have been a small boy, except for his height of seven and a half feet, with a bodily aspect in proportion, if not indeed tending toward the stout. Something glandular, it would seem.

Rearranging a dicer the size of a washtub at a more authoritative angle, "Gents, dey calls me Tiny, wha' kin I do fuh yiz?"

"Try not to step on us," muttered Darby.

"Appointment with Plug," said Chick mollifyingly.

"Yaw dem Chumbs of Chantce!" cried the oversize "bouncer." "Hey, a real honuh to meet yiz, I reads all y' stuff, it's really swell—maybe all except fuh dat Nosewoit' kid, I ain't so sure about him."

"We'll tell him," said Darby.

The moment they stepped inside, they were hit by a strong polyaromatic gust, as if exhaled from the corrupted lungs of Depravity herself, which included alcohol fumes, tobacco and hemp-smoke, a spectrum of inexpensive scent in which opopanax and vervain figured prominently, with darker suggestions of bodily ejecta, overheated metal alloys, and recently-burnt gunpowder. A small house band, anchored by a contrabass saxophone and also including slide cornet, mandola, and "tin pan" piano, were tirelessly "ragging" someplace inside a protective manifold of smoke. Everywhere in the murk glided pre-pubescent houris, more and less lightly attired, dancing solo, or with customers, or with one another, drawing from Darby appreciative when not in fact hypnotized gazes.

A plump and energetic chanteuse of some ten summers, incandescently blond, now emerged from a back recess wearing a gown of artificial golden paillettes sewn, not to any underlying fabric but only—precariously—*to one another,* creating a louche aspect more eye-catching than even outright nakedness, and, accompanied by the tiny "jazz" orchestra, sang,

Dey high-hats us uptown,
Dey low-balls us downtown,
We're known all around town,
As Boids of d' Night—
Duh goilz of duh Bow-ry
Looks voi-gin and flow-ry
Alongside of how we-
'S regawded, awvright!
Siddown for a drink or
Jump up for a dance,
Dough ol' Missus Grundy, she
May look askance,
Yiz can bring da wife and kiddies,
Plus yuhv uncles and aunts,
(Dey'll love it) down in Hell's
Kitchen ta-night!

"You boys got da 'ying' for any o' dis in heeuh, hey, just name it, we'll see wha' we kin do," offered Plug.

"Actually—" began Darby, gazing at the underage "songbird," but he was interrupted by Chick Counterfly.

"Something you mentioned the other day—"

"Yeah, yeah? I'm just a kid, can't remember everyt'in, can I?"

"Something like, all you needed was a 'time machine.' . . ."

"So? Who wouldn't go fuh one o' dem?"

"Actually," Darby elaborated, "it was the way you said '*the* time machine.' Almost as if you knew of a *particular one,* someplace."

"Yiz woikin fuh duh coppiz, uh what?"

"There could be a nice steerer's fee in this one, Plug," mentioned Chick, casually.

"Yeeh? how noice?"

Chick produced an envelope stuffed with greenbacks, which the young tough refrained from touching but weighed with eyebeams sensitive as a laboratory balance. "Runnuh!" he called. Half a dozen small urchins materialized at the table. "You! Cheezy! Kin yiz foind d' Doctuhv in a huvvry?"

"Shaw t'ing, boss!"

"Giddoudahere den, tell 'm he's gonna have visiduhs!"

"You got it, boss!"

"Be witchiz in a minnit. Drink up, 's onna house. Uh, an' so's Angela Grace heeuh."

"Evening, boys." It was the very songstress in the spangled garment who, or perhaps which, had so compellingly claimed Darby's attention a moment before.

"We'uh movin offa duh Gophiz's toif inta Hudson Dustuhs tevritawvry now . . . leastways whut use ta be till all dese damn bushwahs stawhdit slickin up da place," Plug informed the boys as their party made its way westward and south, in the fog, which had now grown general. From far out in the Harbor came the dismal tolling of bell-buoys, the harsh fanfares of foghorns and steam sirens. "Can't see a damn t'ing," Plug complained. "Gotta use ah snoot. Yiz boids know what dat 'ozone' stuff smells like?"

Chick nodded. "I guess we're looking for an electrical generating station, then?"

"Blawngs tuh da Nint' Av'nya 'El,'" Plug said, "but the Doctuhv and dem, like, dey share it. Some deal wit' Mr. Mawgin. Da Machine, it uses a lotta 'juice,' see."

There was a dull, fog-muffled clank. "I think this may be your 'El,'" called Darby in an aggrieved tone. "I just walked into some dadblamed stanchion, here."

"Oh, poor baby!" cried Angela Grace, "let me kiss it?"

"If you can find it," muttered Darby.

"Now we just follas d' tvrain loine sout'," announced Plug, "till ah snoot tells us we're dere."

They approached a memorial arch, gray and time-corroded, seeming to date from some ancient catastrophe, far older than the city. The mists parted long enough for Chick to read a legend on an entablature, I AM THE WAY INTO THE DOLEFUL CITY—DANTE. Passing beneath the colossal arch, they continued to grope along over fog-slick cobblestones, among decaying animals, piles of refuse, and the smoldering fires of homeless denizens of the quarter, till at length, the pungent triatomic signature having become overwhelming, along with a harsh buzzing which filled the vicinity, they stood before a stone gateway dripping with moisture, the dwelling beyond largely invisible except for a scattering of bluish electric lights blooming in this vaporous midwatch, which neither aeronaut found himself able to read as to distance or elevation. Plug pushed a button on the gatepost, and a metallic voice from somewhere replied, "Later than you think, Mr. Loafsley." A solenoidal relay slammed into place, and the gate screeched open.

Inside, in a mews with a carriage house converted to a laboratory, they found an elfin figure, whom Plug introduced as Dr. Zoot, in workingman's fatigues, carpet-slippers, smoked goggles, and a peculiar helmet punctuated over its surface by not entirely familiar electrical fittings.

"So! Just in from the cows and chickens I'll bet, seeking some new *city fun* to tell the folks about back at those church socials! Well we might be able to fix something up for you. Thousands of satisfied customers, all of the best sort, for Mr. Loafsley has never disappointed me yet, ain't that right, lad?"

As if having glimpsed through the obscurity of Dr. Zoot's eyeglass lenses something unacceptably ominous, Plug, looking pale in the already harsh illumination of the laboratory, grasped Angela Grace firmly, and together they backed out through the door as if departing from the presence of royalty.

"Thanks, Plug," called the boys, "bye Angela Grace," but the two children of the depths had already vanished.

"Come along, then."

"We're not keeping you up, Doctor, I hope," Chick said.

"Later the better," said Dr. Zoot. "Not as many trains running this time of night, so the current is more dependable, though not a patch on German product, of course . . . but now, gents, voilà—and you tell me what you think."

The Machine's appearance struck neither lad as particularly advanced. Amid a hoarse droning, violent blue sparks leapt noisily between unwieldy electrodes that might not have seemed out of place in a dynamo of Grandmother's day. A once-unblemished exterior had become long pitted and stained with electrolytic wastes. What numerals were visible on the dust-covered dial-faces owed much to the design preferences of an earlier generation, as did the Breguet-style openwork of the indicator arrows. More alarmingly, even the casual eye could detect everywhere emergency weld-lines, careless shimming, unmatched fasteners, blotches of primer coat never painted over, and other evidences of the makeshift. The overwhelming impression was of revenue diverted from any but the simplest upkeep.

"This is it?" blinked Darby.

"Problem?"

"Can't speak for my partner," shrugged the acerbic juvenile, "but it's a little ramshackle for a time machine, ain't it?"

"Tell you what, how's about a sample ride, into the future, then and back, only charge you half price, and if you like it, we can try something more audacious."

With a gay panache somewhat compromised by the hideous shrieking of the hinges and a noticeable sag to the gutta-percha gasketry around the coaming, Dr. Zoot swung open the hatch of the passenger chamber and nodded them inside, where the boys found an odor of spilled—and to the instructed nose, suggestively cheap—whiskey. The passenger seating appeared to've been purchased at auction long ago, with unmatched upholstery as stained and worn as the wood finishes were scarred and cigar-burned.

"This will be fun," said Darby.

Through the single smeared quartz window of the chamber, the lads observed Dr. Zoot lurching frantically about the room, setting forward the hands of every timepiece he encountered, including those of his own pocketwatch. "Oh, please," groaned Darby, "ain't this kind of insulting? How do we undog this hatch and get the heck out of here?"

"We don't," replied Chick, indicating the absence of the necessary fixtures with an air more of scholarly curiosity than the panicked alarm one might, in the circumstances, have forgiven him—"no more than we are likely to find in here any means of controlling our 'journey.' We seem to be at the mercy of this Dr. Zoot person, and must now proceed in a faith that his character will prove not altogether diabolical."

"Swell. Something a little different for the Chums of Chance. One of these days, Counterfly, our luck's gonna run out—"

"Suckling, look—the window!"

"Don't see anything."

"That's just it!"

"Maybe he turned off the lights."

"No—no, there's light. Maybe not light as we know it, but . . ." The two boys squinted at where the quartz translucency had been, trying to make out what was happening. A kind of vibration, less from the physical chamber itself than from somewhere unsuspected within their own nervous organizations, now began to strengthen in intensity.

They seemed to be in the midst of some great storm in whose low illumination, presently, they could make out, in unremitting sweep across the field of vision, inclined at the same angle as the rain, if rain it was—some material descent, gray and wind-stressed—undoubted human identities, masses of souls, mounted, pillioned, on foot, ranging along together by the millions over the landscape accompanied by a comparably unmeasurable herd of horses. The multitude extended farther than they could see—a spectral cavalry, faces disquietingly wanting in detail, eyes little more than blurred sockets, the draping of garments constantly changing in an invisible flow which perhaps was only wind. Bright arrays of metallic points hung and drifted in three dimensions and perhaps more, like stars blown through by the shock-waves of the Creation. Were those voices out there crying in pain? sometimes it almost sounded like singing. Sometimes a word or two, in a language almost recognizable, came through. Thus, galloping in unceasing flow ever ahead, denied any further control over their fate, the disconsolate company were borne terribly over the edge of the visible world. . . .

The chamber shook, as in a hurricane. Ozone permeated its interior like the musk attending some mating-dance of automata, and the boys found themselves more and more disoriented. Soon even the cylindrical confines they had entered seemed to have fallen away, leaving them in a space unbounded in all directions. There became audible a continuous roar as of the ocean—but it was not the ocean—and soon cries as of beasts in open country, ferally purring stridencies passing overhead, sometimes too close for the lads to be altogether comfortable with—but they were not beasts. Everywhere rose the smell of excrement and dead tissue.

Each lad was looking intently through the darkness at the other, as if about to inquire when it would be considered proper to start screaming for help.

"If this is our host's idea of the future—" Chick began, but he was abruptly checked by the emergence, from the ominous sweep of shadow surrounding them, of a long pole with a great *metal hook* on the end, of the sort commonly used to remove objectionable performers from the variety stage, which, being latched firmly about Chick's neck, had in the next instant pulled him off into regions indecipherable. Before Darby had time to shout after, the Hook re-appeared to perform a similar extraction on him, and quick as that, both youngsters found themselves back in the laboratory of Dr. Zoot. The fiendish "time machine," still in one piece, quivered in its accustomed place, as if with merriment.

"Got a friend works at one of the Bowery theatres," the Doctor explained. "This hook here can come in mighty handy sometimes, specially when the visibility's not too good."

"What was that we just saw?" Chick as smoothly as he was able.

"It's different for everybody, but don't bother to tell me, I've heard too much, more than is good for a man, frankly, and it could easily do you some harm as well to even get into the subject."

"And you're sure that your . . . machine . . . is running up to its design specifications and so forth."

"Well . . ."

"I knew it!" Darby screamed, "you miserable psychopath, you nearly murdered us, for God's sake!"

"Look, fellows, I'll let you have the trip for free, all right? Truth is, the cussèd rig ain't even one of my designs, I picked it up for a pretty good price a couple of years ago, out in the Middle West at one of these, I guess you could call it a convention. . . . The owner, now I recall, did seem anxious to be rid of it. . . ."

"And you *bought it used*?" shrilled Darby.

"'Pre-owned' was how they put it."

"I don't suppose," Chick striving for his accustomed suavity of tone, "you obtained engineering drawings, operating and repair manuals, anything like that?"

"No, but my thinking was 's if I already know how to take apart the latest Oldsmobile, and put it back together again blindfolded, well how tough could this contraption be?"

"And your attorneys will agree with that, of course," snapped Darby.

"Aw, now, fellas . . ."

"Exactly where and from whom, Dr. Zoot," pressed Chick, "did you happen to purchase the unit?"

"Don't know if you've heard of Candlebrow U., institute of higher learning out there in the distant heart of the Republic—once a year, every summer, they hold a big get-together on the subject of time-travel—more cranks, double-domes, and bugbrains than you can scare off with any known weapon. I happened to be out there, just, you know, some drumming, nerve tonics and so forth, ran into this particular jasper at a saloon down by the river called the Ball in Hand, and the name he gave me then was Alonzo Meatman, though it could've changed since. Here, here it is on the bill of sale—though, if you're really gonna look him up . . . well I hope it won't be necessary to mention my name?"

"Why not?" Darby still in some agitation, "he's dangerous, you mean? you're sending us into another death trap, right?"

"Not him so much," Dr. Zoot fidgeting and unable to meet their gaze, "but his . . . associates, well, you just might want to keep an eye out."

"A criminal gang. Swell. Thanks."

"Say that I was just as glad to get back out again on the road soon as I could, and even then I didn't feel comfortable till I had the river between us."

"Oh, they don't like to cross running water," sneered Darby.

"You'll see, young fella. And you might wish you hadn't."

At Candlebrow U., the crew of the *Inconvenience* would find exactly the mixture of nostalgia and amnesia to provide them a reasonable counterfeit of the Timeless. Appropriately, perhaps, it would also be here that they would make the fatal discovery which would bring them, inexorable as the Zodiac's wheel, to their *Imum Cœli*. . . .

In recent years the University had expanded well beyond the memories of older alumni, who, returning, found Chicago-style ironwork and modern balloon-framing among—even in place of—the structures they remembered, earlier masonry homages to European models, executed often as not by immigrants from university or cathedral towns on the elder continent. The West Gate, intended to frame equinoctial sunsets, still retained two flanking towers of rusticated stone and Gothical aspect, quaintly dwarfed now by the looming and more boxlike dormitories just inside, and managing somehow, though itself not much older than a human generation, to present an aspect of terrible antiquity, evoking a remote age before the first European explorers, before the Plains Indians they had found here, before those whom the Indians remembered in their legends as giants and demigods.

The now-famous yearly Candlebrow Conferences, like the institution itself, were subsidized out of the vast fortune of Mr. Gideon Candlebrow of Grossdale, Illinois, who had made his bundle back during the great Lard Scandal of the '80s, in which, before Congress put an end to the practice, countless adulterated tons of that comestible were exported to Great Britain, compromising further an already debased national cuisine, giving rise throughout the island, for example, to a Christmas-pudding controversy over which to this day families remain divided, often violently so. In the consequent scramble to develop more legal sources of profit, one of Mr. Candlebrow's laboratory hands happened to invent "Smegmo," an artificial substitute for everything in the edible-fat category, including margarine, which many felt wasn't that real to begin with. An eminent Rabbi of world hog capital Cincinnati, Ohio, was moved to declare the product kosher, adding that "the Hebrew people have been waiting four thousand years for this. Smegmo is the Messiah of kitchen fats." With astonishing rapidity, Smegmo had come to account for the majority of Candlebrow Ventures' annual profits. The secret of its formula was guarded with a ruthlessness that would have embarrassed the Tsar of Russia, so at Candlebrow U., ubiquitous as the product was in the cuisine and among the table condiments of the Student Cafeteria, you kept hearing different stories about exactly what was in it.

Profits flowing from sales of Smegmo provided funding, on a scale almost describable as lavish, for the First International Conference on Time-Travel, a topic suddenly respectable owing to the success of Mr. H. G. Wells's novel *The Time Machine,* first published in 1895, a year often cited as a lower limit to the date of the first Conference, although no one had yet agreed on how to assign ordinal numbers to any of the gatherings, "because once time-travel *is* invented, you see," declared Professor Heino Vanderjuice, who the boys were delighted to discover was attending this year as a guest lecturer, "there's nothing to keep us from going as far back as we like, and holding the Conferences *then,* even back when this was all prehistoric around here, dinosaurs, giant ferns, flammivomous peaks everywhere sort of thing. . . ."

"All due respect to the Professor," protested Lindsay Noseworth at the nightly Unit meeting, "but is this what we have to look forward to around here, these sophomoric slogs through endless quagmires of the metaphysical? Frankly, I don't know how much of that I can tolerate."

"Lotta nice college 'nooky' around, though," commented Darby, leeringly.

"Another of your vulgarisms, Suckling, with which I must confess myself, no doubt mercifully, unfamiliar."

"An ignorance likely to continue," prophesied Miles Blundell, "until the year 1925 or thereabouts."

"You see!" Lindsay somewhat louder than necessary, "it's beginning! I imagined, naïvely it seems, that we had come here to discover, if we could, some purpose to these ever-more-dangerous expeditions out upon which we are ordered, our unreflective participation in which someday must surely, unless we begin to take steps to promote our safety, end in our dissolution."

"Assuming that this Dr. Zoot hasn't sent us here on a fool's errand," Randolph St. Cosmo reminded them, "from not entirely respectable motives of his own."

"Durn lunatic," Darby scowled.

Inside the campus athletic pavilion, a vast dormitory space had been created, aisled and numbered, accessible by way of complicated registering procedures and color-coded tickets of identification. . . . After lights-out, a space no longer entirely readable, forested with shadows, full of whispering, murmuring, glowing white lamp-mantles by bedsides, ukulelists playing and singing in the dark. . . . Soft-voiced pages recruited from among the children of the town circulated among the sleepers all through the night watches, with telegraphic messages from parents, sweethearts, time-travel societies in other towns. . . .

Meals were served throughout the day and night, according to a mysterious timetable and system of menu changes, in the dining-hall of the enormous student commons, reached not by way of the ceremonial entrance lobby and front desk but via semi-secret flights of stairs deep in the back regions, softly carpeted conduits which led ever downward to the serving line, where impatient mess staff allowed latecomers very little slack in following the correct sequence of doors and hallways, resulting at best in a stray flapjack or the dregs of a coffee urn and, as a penalty for arriving "too" late—a flexible concept around here—nothing at all.

The boys, having conscientiously mastered the intricacies of access and scheduling, proceeded now with their breakfast-laden trays into a cafeteria full of dark brown light, wood chairs and tables, glowingly waxed.

Miles, locating the patriotically colored Smegmo crock among the salt, pepper, ketchup, mustard, steak sauce, sugar, and molasses, opened and sniffed quizzically at the contents. "Say, what *is* this stuff?"

"Goes with everything!" advised a student at a nearby table. "Stir it in your soup, spread it on your bread, mash it into your turnips! My dorm-mates comb their hair with it! There's a *million* uses for Smegmo!"

"I have smelled something like this before," pondered Miles, "yet . . . not in this life. For . . . in the way that certain odors can instantly return us to earlier years . . ."

"Nasotemporal Transit," nodded the savvy youth. "There's a seminar on that tomorrow, over at Finney Hall. Or do I mean day before yesterday?"

"Well, sir, this Smegmo concoction here takes me back even *further* than childhood, in fact clear on back into a previous life, to *before I was even conceived*—"

"Miles, for goodness' sake," Lindsay, blushing and kicking his shipmate beneath the table, "T.A.L.P!" this being Chums of Chance code for "There Are Ladies Present." Indeed, a tableful of florescent "co-eds" nearby had been following the exchange with some interest.

"Oboy, oboy," Darby nudging Chick Counterfly, his long-standing partner in mischief. "Them sure ain't Gibson Girls, I betcha! Look at the hair-do on that blonde there! Whoo-wee!"

"Suckling," gritted Lindsay, "although, in a career which has tended increasingly to the squalid, further enormities without question await, none will prove to have been more objectionable, morally speaking, than these current manifestations of a diseased adolescence."

"You ever get around to having your own, let me know," Darby replied, in tones which suggested an intention to bite. "Maybe I can pass on a few tips."

"Why, you insufferable little—"

"Gentlemen," Randolph frowningly grasping his abdomen, "perhaps you will find it possible to put off this no doubt fascinating colloquy until a less-public occasion. And might I add, Mr. Noseworth, that these constant attempts to strangle Suckling do our public image little good."

Later that morning, together with Professor Vanderjuice, they piled into a motorcar to pay a visit to the municipal dump at the edge of town, gray with perpetual smoke, its limits undefined. "Walloping Wellesianism!" cried the Professor, "it's just a whole junkyard full!" Up and down the steeply-pitched sides of a ravine lay the picked-over hulks of failed time machines—Chronoclipses, Asimov Transeculars, Tempomorph Q-98s—broken, defective, scorched by catastrophic flares of misrouted energy, corroded often beyond recognition by unintended immersion in the terrible Flow over which they had been designed and built, so hopefully, to prevail. . . . A strewn field of conjecture, superstition, blind faith, and bad engineering, expressed in sheet-aluminum, vulcanite, Heusler's alloy, bonzoline, electrum, lignum vitae, platinoid, magnalium, and packfong silver, much of it stripped away by scavengers over the years. Where was the safe harbor in Time their pilots might have found, so allowing their craft to avoid such ignominious fates?

Though they took a careful inventory, neither Chick nor Darby was able to find, assembled or in pieces, the model of machine in which Dr. Zoot had dispatched them into that apocalyptic sweep of masses which still troubled their moments of reverie.

"We must find this Meatman person, whom the 'Doctor' mentioned," declared Chick. "A visit to his local tavern would seem in order."

"The Ball in Hand," recalled Darby—"and say, what are we waitin for?"

As the years had gone by, Earth making its automorphic way round the sun again and yet again, the Candlebrow Conferences themselves had converged to a form of Eternal Return. No one, for example, was ever seen to age. Those who, each intervening year, might have, in some technical sense, "died" outside the precincts of this enchanted campus, once having drifted back through the gates, were promptly "resurrected." Sometimes they brought their obituary clippings with them, to share chucklingly with colleagues. These were solid bodily returns, mind you, nothing figurative or plasmic about them. Even to suggest that possibility had been known to fetch more than one skeptic a "sock in the kisser" for its imputations of frailty and unmanliness. The advantages to this genial revenance were apparent to all, chief among them the pleasures of ignoring medical advice, indulging in strong drink and life-threateningly fatty foodstuffs, staying out after hours in the company of the louche and demonstrably criminal, gaming on a scale and at odds whose longitude might have produced apoplexy even in much younger and fitter specimens of time-scholar. And all of these diversions and more happened to be available in profusion down along the river, on lower Symmes Street and the alleyways adjoining, where the desperate men resorted, where heads were cracked routinely by the stiff-hatted security of the night, while only yards away flowed the river tidied as the inside of an office, the wooden traffic rocking at ease on its gaslit breast. . . . Some Candlebrow conferees had claimed to see in this a parable for that otherworldly flow, insulated from secular ills, which we know as the River of Time.

The boys found their way down to West Symmes Street and into the Ball in Hand, which proved to be a particularly low and disreputable haunt. Renegade carnival girls, some with Pygmy boyfriends escaped from the St. Louis Fair, danced, with a scandalous flourishing of petticoats, on the tabletops. A troupe of Polish comedians, each armed with his personal *giant kielbasa sausage,* ran about trading blows from these objects, principally to the head, with untiring vivacity. Negro quartets sang old favorites in seventh-chord harmonies. Faro and fantan were available in the back rooms.

A young person of neglected aspect, holding a bottle of some reddish liquid, accosted the boys. "You're the ones lookin fer Alonzo Meatman, I'll bet."

"Maybe," replied Darby, reaching for and grasping his regulation-issue "preserver." "Who wants to know?"

Their interlocutor began to shiver, to look around the room with increasingly violent jerks of the head.

"They . . . they . . ."

"Come, man, get a grip on yourself," admonished Lindsay. "Who are this 'they' to whom you refer?"

But the youngster was shaking violently now, his eyeballs, jittering in their orbits, gone wild with fright. Around the edges of his form, a strange magenta-and-green aura had begun to flicker, as if from a source somewhere behind him, growing more intense as he himself faded from view, until seconds later nothing was left but a kind of stain in the air where he had been, a warping of the light as through ancient window-glass. The bottle he had been holding, having remained behind, fell to the floor with a crash that seemed curiously prolonged.

"Rats," muttered Darby, watching its contents soak into the sawdust, "and here I was hankering after a 'slug' of that stuff."

No one besides the Chums, in the roomful of merrymakers, gave any sign of having noticed. Lindsay, queerly distracted, was groping in the empty space but recently occupied by the vanished youth, as if he had somehow chosen to become only invisible.

"I would suggest," Miles drifting toward the egress, "vacating these premises, before we meet a similar fate."

Outside, Chick, who had remained silent through the episode, approached Randolph. "Professor, be informed that I am now invoking the Scientific Officer's Discretionary, or S.O.D., Clause, as provided for in our Charter."

"Again, Mr. Counterfly? One assumes you have properly filled in your Finding of Unusual Circumstances Questionnaire?"

Chick handed over the elaborately engraved document. "All in order, I hope—"

"Look here, Chick, are you quite resolved in this? You remember the last time, over that Hawaiian volcano—"

"Which was mutiny pure and simple then," interjected Lindsay, "as it is now."

"Not in *my* legal opinion," chirped Darby, who had been scrutinizing the chit—"Chick's S.O.D. here's just as kosher as Smegmo."

"A somewhat hollow pronouncement, given the all-too-predictable thickness of association between you and Counterfly."

"You want thick?" snarled Darby, "here, try this."

"Our operating altitude," Chick endeavored to explain, "and the presence of unknown volcanic gases, may have affected my judgment then, it's true. But this time I mean to remain on the ground, with no dimensional issues."

"Except for the Fourth, of course," warned Miles Blundell, his voice solemn as if issuing from mortal distances. "Fifth, and so on."

His shipmates having departed, Chick entered the shadowy taproom once more, obtained a glass of beer, sat at a table with a view of the entrance, and waited, a technique learned years before in Japan, among the Zennist mystics of that country (see *The Chums of Chance and the Caged Women of Yokohama*), known as "just sitting." It was during the same trip, Chick recalled, that Pugnax had confounded a Zennist monastery, by answering the classic koan "Does a dog possess the Buddha-nature?" not with "Mu!" but with "Yes, obviously—was there anything else?"

Time did not so much elapse as grow less relevant. At length Chick saw the recently vanished "contact" reappear from vacant space, now bathed in hues of apricot and aquamarine.

"You again."

"Little trick of the trade. Had to see how serious you were," said Alonzo Meatman (for it was he).

"Maybe only lazier than my partners. They had a night of hell-raising to get on with, I just wanted to sit here and relax."

"Notice you haven't touched that beer, there."

"Would you?"

"Good point. Let me buy you something—Horst can make whatever you'd like, nobody's stumped him since the F.I.C.O.T.T., and then it was debatable."

"Since the . . . ?"

"First International Conference On Time Travel, and say, what a hootnanny that was." Everyone in the world of science and philosophy had shown up—Niels Bohr was there, Ernst Mach, young Einstein, Dr. Spengler, Mr. Wells himself. Professor J. M. E. McTaggart of Cambridge, England, dropped by, to give a brief address dismissing altogether the *existence* of Time as really too ridiculous to consider, regardless of its status as a believed-in phenomenon.

A brilliant gathering, you might say, a collaboration of the best minds upon the difficult, indeed paradoxical issue, sure to result in a working Time Machine (such was the Wellsian optimism of that era), before the century was out . . . except that this was not how the Proceedings proceeded. From initial bickering over what non-specialists would have to deem trivial matters, disputes had grown with astounding rapidity into all-out academic combat. Splinter groups proliferated. The celebrities in whom so much hope was invested soon departed by steam train and interurban electric, by horseback and by airship, usually muttering to themselves. Duels were proposed, shown up for, and resolved, for the most part, bloodlessly—except for the unfortunate affair of the McTaggartite, the neo-Augustinian, and the fatal steamed pudding. "Disputes as to the nature of reality whose outcomes depend in any way on wagering," as the County Coroner expressed it, "have seldom been known to conclude happily, especially here, in view of the vertical distance involved. . . ." For days, while the ill-fated encounter remained a topic for gossip, conferees were careful to find excuses not to walk too close to the Old Stearinery Bell Tower, inspired by the Campanile in the Piazza San Marco in

Venice, and at 322 feet the tallest structure visible in any direction out to the curve of the Earth, notorious locally for exerting a fascination upon minds healthy and disordered alike.

"YOU'VE BEEN WALKING, unaware, among them since you arrived," Alonzo Meatman was saying. "There's no discovering them unless they choose so."

"But for you they have chosen to—"

"Yes and 'do choose,' and 'will choose'—maybe even you, if you're lucky—what of it?"

Chick regarded young Meatman. Clearly, classically, what a homeopathist would call "the *lycopodium* type." Somehow the Chums organization attracted these in large numbers. Fear written in every cell. Fear of the night, of being haunted, of failure, of other matters that may not too routinely be named. First to get up into the rigging during a storm, not out of bravery but in desperation, as the only remedy they knew for the cowardice they feared ever crawling within. This Meatman specimen, it was clear, had climbed very high into the night, into a vulnerability to the perils of the storm that few could envy. "Stand easy, sky-brother," Chick replied, "I know only how much it is costing me tonight to seek you out—further than which, my bookkeeping does not extend."

Young Meatman seemed mollified. "You mustn't think of it, you know, as betrayal . . . or, *not only* betrayal."

"Oh? what more?"

He might have hesitated, but not quite long enough to sound unpracticed. "The most extraordinary offer of Deliverance to be tendered us since—that other Promise made so long ago. . . ."

Chick had a momentary vision of a ship's passageway somewhere, perhaps inside a giant airship of the future, crowded with resurrected bodies of all ages, dazed smiles and tangled bare limbs, a throng of visitors newly arrived from all periods of the past two millennia, who must somehow be fed, clothed, sheltered, and explained to, not to mention away—an administrative nightmare largely fallen to him to resolve. He had a kind of newfangled speaking trumpet in his hand. "Has it come to this?" His voice sounded unfamiliar to him. He could think of nothing further to say. They were all watching him, expecting something.

Now, at the Ball in Hand, he only shrugged. "Guess I'm game."

"Come along." Alonzo led Chick out of the tavern and up across the night campus, then through a looming Gothical gate, and downhill again into the northern purlieus of the University, a region of inexpensive student housing adjoined by an unlit sweep of aboriginal prairie, the streets into which they passed becoming narrower and lit by gas, rather than the electric lamps of the more "respectable" parts of town, which at each step were receding, it strangely seemed, disproportionately farther as the young men went on. At length they came to a street of ungainly row-houses, already halfway to self-demolition, the tattered millwork testifying to the spirit of haste and greed in which they had been erected but scant years before. Asphalt shingles lay fallen and broken. Fragments of window-glass sparkled in the dim light. Somewhere close, feeder lines to the interurban fretfully hummed and spat, while farther up the street, a pack of dogs swarmed into and out of the humid penumbræ of the streetlamps.

Alonzo seemed to expect a remark about the neighborhood. "We don't want that much attention, see, not just yet. When enough people find that they need us and start seeking us out, maybe then we'll move someplace bigger, closer to town. Meanwhile—"

"Discretion," Chick supposed.

The youth's face returned to its accustomed petulance. "Hardly necessary. They are not afraid of anything 'this' world may confront them with. You'll see."

Afterward Chick could not rid himself of an impression, lying deeper than he cared, or was able, to go, of having been psychically interfered with. In the event, somehow—as if *positive expressions* of silence and absence were being deployed against him—he could not escape the conclusion that, despite conventional signs of occupancy, these rooms were all, in fact, vacant. He found himself oppressed by a clearly visible veneer of disuse, not only of dust, which lay over everything, but also of a long stillness, perhaps of years, without a living voice, a strain of music, the not-quite-even percussion of human footfalls. The chill suspicion grew on him, further, that in here what seemed to be lamplight was not—that through some nonearthly means his optic sensorium was being locally addressed and systematically deluded, without disturbing the reign of an unresponsive darkness. Even more unsettling in its way was the change that had come over his companion the moment they stepped across the doorsill—a relaxation young Meatman did not bother to conceal, as if, having delivered Chick, he might now retreat unmolested into the quiescence of a tool returned at task's end to its crib, a state he seemed almost to prefer to the troublesome demands of the quotidian.

Abruptly, sweeping into the scene like an opera singer with an aria to unload, here came "Mr. Ace," as he called himself. Glossy black eyes, presented like weapons in a duel. The gently damaged, irrevocably educated eyes we associate with the visiting dead. When he smiled, or attempted to, it was not reassuring.

Dispensing with phatic chitchat, he began straightaway to tell the story of his "people."

"We are here among you as seekers of refuge from our present—your future—a time of worldwide famine, exhausted fuel supplies, terminal poverty—the end of the capitalistic experiment. Once we came to understand the simple thermodynamic truth that Earth's resources were limited, in fact soon to run out, the whole capitalist illusion fell to pieces. Those of us who spoke this truth aloud were denounced as heretics, as enemies of the prevailing economic faith. Like religious Dissenters of an earlier day, we were forced to migrate, with little choice but to set forth upon that dark fourth-dimensional Atlantic known as Time.

"Most who chose the Crossing made it through—some did not. The procedure is still hazardous. The levels of energy required to make that leap against the current, across the forbidden interval, are unavailable here at present, though certain of your great dynamos have begun to approach the necessary power-domain. We have learned to deal with that danger, we train for it. What we did not expect was your own determination to prevent our settlement here."

"First I've heard," Chick said at last, as sympathetically as he could.

"The Fraternity of the Venturesome—"

"Beg pardon?"

A strange electrical drone overtook and blurred Mr. Ace's voice for an instant. "The *nzzt* Chums-of-Chance? You are not aware that each of your mission assignments is intended to prevent some attempt of our own to enter your time-regime?"

"I assure you, that never—"

"You are sworn to obedience, of course." An intense, silent struggle as if not to laugh, as if laughter were an unfamiliar vice whose power to shake him apart Mr. Ace could not afford to risk.

"All this is sure news to me," said Chick. "And even if what you say's true, how could we be of any use to you?"

His great eyes seemed luminous with pity. "We might ask you to accept a commission from us now and then—though, regrettably, with no more detailed explanation than you currently receive from your own Hierarchy."

Chick must have been silent for a while.

"*ZZnrrt* compensation . . ."

"Oh. Sorry?"

"Mr. Meatman has not suggested the dimensions of our gratitude?"

"He wasn't clear. It sounded kind of religious."

"Excuse me?"

"Eternal life."

"Better. Eternal youth."

"Well, by ginger. Sure can't beat that."

Mr. Ace went on to explain—or, maybe not explain but certainly to allege—that scientists of his own time, in the course of their extensive research into time travel, had discovered, as an unintended windfall, how to transform the class of thermochemical reactions once known as "irreversible processes," notable among them human aging and death, so as actually *to reverse them.* "Once we acquired the *technique,* the whole problem became trivial."

"Easy for you to say, I guess."

"Now it is no more than a form of trade goods, like the beads and mirrors your own newcomers to the American shores once traded with the Indians. A gift of small worth, but tendered with great sincerity."

"So this is supposed to be like Squanto and the Pilgrims," Chick reported to the plenary session called hurriedly next morning. "We help them through their first winter, sort of thing."

"And suppose it isn't that," said Randolph. "Suppose they're not pilgrims but raiders, and there's some particular resource here, that they've run out of and want to seize from us, and take back with them?"

"Food," said Miles.

"Women," suggested Darby.

"Lower entropy," speculated Chick. "As a simple function of Time, their entropy level would be higher. Like rich folks taking mineral waters at some likely 'spa.' "

"It's our innocence," proclaimed Lindsay, in an unaccustomedly distraught voice. "They have descended on our shores to hunt us down, capture our innocence, and take it away with them into futurity."

"I was thinking of something a little more tangible," Randolph frowning in thought. "Negotiable."

"Yeeah a-and who says we're 'innocent'?" Darby piped up.

"But imagine *them,*" Lindsay in stricken tones, as if before some unbearable illumination, "so fallen, so corrupted, that we—even we—seem to them pure as lambs. And their own time so terrible that it's sent them desperately back—back to us. Back to whatever few pathetic years *we* still have left, before . . . whatever is to happen . . ."

"Say, Lindsay." It was Darby, for the first time in group memory concerned for his Puritanical shipmate.

After a moment's paralysis in the discussion, "There is always the possibility," Chick pointed out, "that they are only bunco artists, confederates of Dr. Zoot—or, even more underhandedly, that this is some theatrical exercise, a sort of Moral Drill, got up by Hierarchy to detect potential rebellion and suppress dissent. I wouldn't put it past them."

"So either way," said Darby, "we're totally—"

"Don't say it," Lindsay warned.

Understanding that he would not be allowed to learn any more from Mr. Ace than whatever story the sinister traveler chose to tell, Chick arrived at their next meeting with Miles, who alone among the crew possessed the clairvoyance the situation required. At his first sight of Mr. Ace, Miles began to cry, heedless and desolate, the tears of a high professional cleric after receiving a direct message from God. . . . Chick looked on in astonishment, for tears among this Unit were virtually unknown.

"I recognized him, Chick," said Miles forthrightly, when they had returned to the ship. "From somewhere else. I knew he was real and couldn't be wished away. He is not what he says he is. Assuredly he does not have our best interests in mind."

"Miles, you must tell me. Where have you seen him?"

"By way of these *visual conduits* that more and more seem to find me in the course of my day. For some time, it has been possible for me to look in on him and these other trespassers, as through 'windows' into their home space. I may have been invisible to them at first, but no longer—they've a way now to detect me whenever I observe them . . . and lately, whenever they know I'm watching, I see them *pointing something* back at me—not exactly a weapon—an enigmatic object . . .

"It is by way of these 'windows' that they cross over, for brief periods, to our own time and space. That is how this 'Mr. Ace' comes to us." Miles shivered. "Did you see how he looked at me? He knew. And he wanted me to feel guilt, out of proportion to the offense, which was after all only peeping. I think that ever since we arrived here at Candlebrow, some 'Agency' of theirs has been commissioned expressly to deal with us. Which must make any stranger in our midst, even—especially—the most innocent-looking, immediately suspect." At the deep alarm in Chick's face, Miles shook his head, reached out a steadying hand. "Not to worry—we are sound and straight as ever. If there were any 'double-crosser' in our midst, Pugnax would know, and soon be feasting on his entrails. As for immediate steps, I'd say make tracks, and the quicker the better."

· · ·

Soon the crew began to find evidence of Trespass everywhere, some invisible narrative occupying, where it did not in fact define, the passage of the day. And it was soon evident that at all levels, from local to international, a neuropathy had taken over the Chums of Chance organization. The Trespassers had studied their targets closely, knew of the Chums' unquestioning faith that none of them, barring misadventure, would ever simply grow old and die, a belief which over the years many had come to confuse with a guarantee. On learning that they might be no more exempt than any of the human supernumeraries they had been so carelessly aviating above all these years, some Chums of Chance turned in panic to the corrupt embrace of the Trespassers, ready to deal with Hell itself, to betray anything and anyone if only they could be sent back to when they were young, be allowed to regain the early boys'-book innocence they were so willing now to turn right around and violate on behalf of their insidious benefactors.

That there existed more than one such traitor soon became widely known, though not their identities. So, with anyone a likely candidate, there arose an unprecedented and widely destructive wave of slander, paranoia, and character assassination, which had continued unabated through the present day. Duels were fought, lawsuits brought, all for nought. The Trespassers went on undeterred with their dark confidence game, though some of their victims would seek, at last, out of conscience or contingency, to break free of the sinister contracts they'd been gulled into signing, even if the price be their immunity to death.

Other Units of the Chums of Chance meanwhile chose lateral solutions, sidestepping the crisis by passing into metaphorical identities, as law-enforcement squads, strolling theatrical companies, governments-in-exile of imaginary countries they could nonetheless describe in exhaustive, some would say obsessive, detail, including entire languages with rules for syntax and usage—or, in the case of the crew of *Inconvenience,* immersed at Candlebrow in the mysteries of Time, drift into the brief aberration in their history known as the Marching Academy Harmonica Band.

As if in a dream, they would come to recall attending Candlebrow U. not as visitors to a summer Conference but as full-time music students, waiting at a railway platform with their belongings and instruments piled nearby, for an interurban that would never come. What did finally glide to a stop beside them was a gleaming, spiffed-up Special with Harmonica Band Marching Academy insignia on it, filled with kids just their age in traveling uniforms of Chinese red and indigo.

"Sure, come on in, plenty of room."

"You'll take us?"

"Anybody. Room and board, long as you play harmonica."

So, without any fuss, they climbed aboard and before reaching Decatur had learned the rhythm parts to "El Capitán" and "Whistling Rufus," and rode on down the rails to join the student performers at the world-famous Marching Harmonica Band Academy, where soon they were fitted for uniforms, assigned quarters, and being reprimanded like everybody else for improvising during the more tightly arranged pieces like "My Country 'Tis of Thee."

The institution had its origins, like Candlebrow, in the intricacies of greed as then being practiced under global capitalism. German harmonica manufacturers, who led the world in production of the instrument, had for some years been dumping their surplus inventory on the American market, with the result that soon every community in the land had some kind of harmonica-based marching society, often numbering in the hundreds, who turned out for every national holiday parade as well as school graduation ceremonies, annual picnics, dedications of local improvements such as streetlighting or sewer lines. It was only a matter of time before this unforeseen outcome of the Law of Supply and Demand was consecrated as the Harmonica Marching Band Academy, a handsome set of Richardsonian Romanesque buildings located in "The Heart of the Mississippi Watershed," as the advertisements would put it. Each year youths from all over the Republic came to study here, emerging after four years as Master Harmonicists who more often than not would go on to eminence in the profession, some even founding schools of their own.

One evening early in their first spring semester, Randolph, Lindsay, Darby, Miles, and Chick were in the dormitory with some classmates, taking a break from studying for an examination in modal theory the next day.

"Never thought it'd be like this," declared one of the Third-Year Harpmen, eyeglass lenses reflecting the gaslight. "Rather be seeing some real action, get out there into the hullaballoo, just let the durn music go for a while, don't ya know."

A classmate, hands behind his head, lay puffing on an illicit cigarette whose fragrance, not to everyone's taste, filled the room. "Put in a chit, hoss, they'll be happy to have you."

"Dang perilous times, boys, got to forget about the soft duty, go where we can make ourselves useful—" interrupted by the precipitate entrance of young Mouthorganman Apprentice Bing Spooninger, the Band Mascotte, yelling, "Anybody seen that 'Zo Meatman? He's not in his rack, and it's after curfew and darn near lights-out!"

Uproar. Heads appearing over the edges of upper bunks. Jumping up and down, running around colliding with each other, looking under furniture, in closets, everywhere for the vanished harpman. The Chums by now understood that this was the "intro" to a musical number, as students broke out and started to play scales on every harmonica within reach, and heavens but there were, well, bell-metal bass harmonicas six feet long—great whopping *tubas* of harmonicas—ranging down to the tiniest possible two-hole silver and pearl Microharmonicas, with every note in the Universe in between, as at some all-but-imperceptible nod the fellows began sucking and singing—

That 'Zo Meat-man's gone A-WOL.
Yippy dippy dippy, doo!
Faster than you can say "Wall"—
What a nut-ty thing, to do!
[Comical bass]
Now, it ain't that I wouldn't, 'cause I can but I won't,
And I would if I wasn't, but I am so I don't!
[All] A-a-and,
That 'Zo Meatman's gone A-WOL.

[Bing as treble soloist] A . . . W . . . O . . . L . . . [Everybody looking on as if totally fascinated with the difficult vocal feat whose successful conclusion would allow them at last, chucklingly, to relax. Singin',]

Yippy dippy dippy,
Flippy zippy zippy,
Smippy gdippy gdippy, too!

segueing into a spirited cakewalk allowing opportunities for brief novelty effects, locomotive noises, barnyard animals—the mysteriously missing Alonzo Meatman, for example, having specialized in playing harmonica through his nose, typically getting mucus in number three and four holes and usually a "booger" substantial enough to block number two completely, presenting, and not for the first time either, a draw-note problem to anyone incautious enough to borrow the instrument, the resulting ill-will, in fact, contributing to Alonzo's long-seething resentment of and lowered tolerance for any *unorthodox behavior,* leading him more than once, at first furtively but then with growing confidence, to the office of the Harmonica Band Marching Academy Commandant.

The practice of boys informing on other boys, regarded with horror at more traditional institutions, had at the Marching Harmonica Band Academy come to command a curious respect even from those who were apt to suffer from it most. For a "squealer" such as young Meatman to go missing did not therefore immediately raise the suspicions of foul play it might have at another school. In fact, commonly the "squealer," being well paid for his spying efforts, enjoyed a considerable popularity with the other boys, especially on furlough weekends. With less pressure on him to create and maintain a *second or cover identity,* the little weasel had more energy to devote to normal Marching Harmonica Band activities. Exempt as well from the unannounced punishments it was the lot of the squealed-upon to undergo literally at any moment on the old Commandant's whim, squealers, suffering less anxiety, slept better and led generally healthier lives than their more vulnerable classmates.

Earlier that day Alonzo had paid his weekly visit to the "Old Man." Out the window breathed a spring afternoon, a sunny verdigris campus, dipping away to a windbreak of Lombardy poplars all at that distance in a green mist of budding, while before the window-frame bobbed the kindly seamed face of the Commandant, with its closely maintained white mustache and gold teeth which flashed when he smiled—to appearance the slow and amiable smile of the drug habitué, but in fact an all but nihilistic dismissal of whatever the world might present him—opiatedly explaining meanwhile to the young informant, as he had dozens of times previous, everything, everything—Chromatic Harp Safety, and the particular need to keep those nasal hairs closely trimmed lest one or two be caught between cover and plate and get pulled out, which beyond the pain and humiliation carried as well the risk of brain infection, and where and when the units slept and who stood the different kinds of watches such as Pitch Integrity Guard, protecting through the hours of darkness the famous D-Flat Reverberating Harmonica from the Phantom Filer, known to sneak in with a full set of professional harmonica-reed files to alter notes and create difficulties for soloists upon the instrument, obliging them at times to shift over to sucking the tonic chords and blowing the subdominant ones, producing a vaguely Negroid sound—though the intruder must take care to avoid as well the Provisional Anti-Urination Watch, set up against late-night visits to the latrine, peculiar, indeed pee-culiar, goings-on in there having been recently reported. . . . Out the window behind the Commandant on the Activity Fields could now and then be made out elements of the Harmonica Band engaged in "Physical Education," though not the usual Rugby Union or Lacrosse, no it was rather some horrible . . . nonregulation Combat-Inside-Ten-Meters, as the musicians, tiny figures in red sweatshirts bearing the golden crest of the Academy, attempted to strangle, kick, or, if suitable rocks happened to be to hand, beat each other, apparently, into unconsciousness if not further . . . bodies had begun, actually, to fall, and screams delayed by distance to float at last up from the green fields and through the Commandant's window to accompany his long recitation, punctuated with tuneful quotations on his personal gold-plated I.G. Mundharfwerke "Little Giant," from behind a desktop chaotically littered with books, papers, and (embarrassingly) outright refuse, such as orange peels, peach pits, and cigar stubs, drifted in places to depths of two feet and more, somewhat repelling Meatman, who had after all only come here to "rat" on his classmates, who would soon, bearing their playing-field casualties, come marching back between the magnolia trees, to the sprightly Offenbach air "Halls of Montezoo-HOO-ma!" the tranquil Old Man with syrup-slow ease continuing his digression, fading through the afternoon, into obsessively detailed allegations of odd latrine behavior, evoking in short flashes white porcelain fittings voluptuous of form, not necessarily toilets, though in some way vehicles for the mysterious but as yet unspecified "peeculiar goings-on," presently allowing the whole picture to be viewed, a rapid swoop down between the ranks of white fixtures, blurring moistly violet at the edges, into the Latrine itself, into dark proximities including—unavoidably—corruption and death, the rows of mirrors facing each other through a haze of secular use, the breath, atomized dentifrice and shaving preparations, ascents of tapwater vapor bearing traces of local minerals, each set of images chaining away for uncounted leagues, everything reflected, headed for the Point at Infinity along a great slow curve. . . .

After that meeting, curiously, Alonzo was heard from no more. The Commandant's A.D.C. signed him out, handed him his weekly voucher for services rendered, watched him saunter away between the symmetric lines of trees before turning back to his own desk-work. . . .

Meantime, now and then in the interstices of what was after all not a perpetual midwestern holiday, the former crew of the *Inconvenience* became aware of doubts creeping in. What if they *weren't* harmonica players? really? If it was all just some elaborate hoax they'd chosen to play on themselves, to keep distracted from a reality too frightening to receive the vast undiscriminating light of the Sky, perhaps the not-to-be-spoken-of betrayal now firmly installed at the heart of the . . . the Organization whose name curiously had begun to escape them . . . some secret deal, of an unspecified nature, with an ancient enemy . . . but they could find no entries in any of the daily Logs to help them remember. . . .

Had they gone, themselves, through some mutation into imperfect replicas of who they once were? meant to revisit the scenes of unresolved conflicts, the way ghosts are said to revisit places where destinies took a wrong turn, or revisit in dreams the dreaming body of one loved more than either might have known, as if whatever happened between them could in that way be put right again? Were they now but torn and trailing after-images of clandestine identities needed on some mission long ended, forgotten, but unwilling or unable to be released from it? Perhaps even surrogates recruited to stay behind on the ground, allowing the "real" Chums to take to the Sky and so escape some unbearable situation? None of them may really ever have been up in a skyship, ever walked the exotic streets or been charmed by the natives of any far-off duty station. They may only have once been readers of the Chums of Chance Series of boys' books, authorized somehow to serve as volunteer decoys. Once, long ago, from soft hills, from creekside towns, from libraries that let kids lie on the floor where it's cool and read the summer afternoons away, the Chums had needed them . . . they came.

> **WANTED** Boys for challenging assignments, must be fit, dutiful, ready, able to play the harmonica ("At a Georgia Camp Meeting" in all keys, modest fines for wrong notes), and be willing to put in long hours of rehearsal time on the Instrument . . . Adventure guaranteed!

So that when the "real" Chums flew away, the boys were left to the uncertain sanctuary of the Harmonica Marching Band Training Academy. . . . But life on the surface kept on taking its usual fees, year by year, while the other Chums remained merrily aloft, kiting off tax-free to assignments all over the world, perhaps not even remembering their "deps" that well anymore, for there was so much to occupy the adventurous spirit, and the others—"groundhogs" in Chums parlance—had known, surely, of the risks and the costs of their surrogacy. And some would drift away from here as once, already long ago, from their wholesome heartland towns, into the smoke and confusion of urban densities unimagined when they began, to join other ensembles playing music of the newer races, arrangements of Negro blues, Polish polkas, Jewish klezmer, though others, unable to find any clear route out of the past, would return again and again to the old performance sites, to Venice, Italy, and Paris, France, and the luxury resorts of old Mexico, to play the same medleys of cakewalks and rags and patriotic airs, to sit at the same café tables, haunt the same skeins of narrow streets, gaze unhappily on Saturday evenings at the local youngsters circulating and flirting through the little plazas, unsure whether their own youth was behind them or yet to come. Waiting as always for the "true" Chums to return, longing to hear, "You were splendid, fellows. We wish we could tell you about everything that's been going on, but it's not over yet, it's at such a critical stage, and the less said right now the better. But someday . . ."

"Are you going away again?"

"So soon?"

"We must. We're just so sorry. The reunion feast was delicious and much appreciated, the harmonica recital one we shall never forget, especially the 'coon' material. But now . . ."

So, once again, the familiar dwindling dot in the sky.

"Don't be blue, pal, it must've been important, they really wanted to stay this time, you could tell."

"What are we going to do with all this extra food?"

"And all the beer nobody drank!"

"Somehow I don't think *that*'ll be a problem."

But that was the beginning of a certain release from longing, as if they had been living in a remote valley, far from any highways, and one day noticed that just beyond one of the ridgelines all this time there'd been a road, and down this road, as they watched, came a wagon, then a couple of riders, then a coach and another wagon, in daylight which slowly lost its stark isotropy and was flowed into by clouds and chimney smoke and even episodes of weather, until presently there was a steady stream of traffic, audible day and night, with folks beginning to venture over into their valley to visit, and offering rides to towns nearby the boys hadn't even known existed, and next thing anybody knew, they were on the move again in a world scarcely different from the one they had left. And one day, at the edge of one of these towns, sky-ready, brightwork gleaming, newly painted and refitted and around the corner of a gigantic hangar, waiting for them, as if they had never been away, there was their ship the good old *Inconvenience.* And Pugnax with his paws up on the quarterdeck rail, tail going a mile a minute, barking with unrestrained joy.

Somewhere the Trespassers went on about their old toxic business, but by now the crew of the *Inconvenience,* more closely tuned to their presence and long disabused of any faith in their miracle-working abilities, were somehow better able to avoid them, to warn others of possible mischief, even now and then to take steps in opposition. Failed experimental casseroles from Miles's galley, dropped from altitudes moderate enough to maintain cohesion, seemed effective, as well as prank telephone calls to paving contractors ordering large volumes of cement to be delivered and poured at known Trespasser locations.

Needless to say, differences of opinion within the little band on how best to proceed were sharp, as was some of the language in their steering-committee meetings. The politics were not simplified by the unannounced reappearance of Harmonica Academy Marching Band squealer Alonzo Meatman, just strolling in one day whistling "After the Ball," in cakewalk rhythm as if among them no history had ever transpired.

He had brought with him, carefully and multiply sealed, a copy of the enigmatic map they had once journeyed to Venice in search of, thereby nearly meeting flaming destruction over the Piazza San Marco.

"We were there, too," said Meatman with a disagreeable smile, "only I guess you didn't see us."

"And now you're trying to sell this," Randolph supposed.

"Today, for you, it's free of charge."

"And what has given you the curious impression," inquired Lindsay, "that having once narrowly avoided dissolution by so injudiciously seeking this mischievous document, we might now exhibit toward it even the least vestige of interest?"

The treacherous Meatman shrugged. "Ask your Tesla machine."

And sure enough, as if having eavesdropped on this exchange as part of a detailed surveillance maintained over the Chums even from its deep bureaucratic distance, Higher Authority now chose once again to insert its own *weighty extremity* into their lives.

One night after Evening Quarters, the Tesla device came squawking to life, and the boys gathered around to listen. "Having taken delivery," announced a deep, reverberant voice, "from duly authorized agent Alonzo R. Meatman of the map informally known as the Sfinciuno Itinerary, signing all receipt forms properly, you are directed to set course immediately for Bukhara in Inner Asia, where you will report T.D.Y. to His Majesty's Subdesertine Frigate *Saksaul,* Captain Q. Zane Toadflax, Commander. It is assumed that the *Inconvenience* already has a complete allocation of current-model Hypopsammotic Survival Apparatus on board, as no further expenditure for that purpose will be approved."

The machine fell silent, the pointers of its dozen or so dials returning to their resting-pins. "What the heck are they talking about?" squinted Darby puzzledly.

"Professor Vanderjuice will know," Randolph said.

"Why, staggering sand-dunes!" exclaimed the Professor. "I happen to know just the fellow, Roswell Bounce, in fact he invented the Hypops apparatus, though the Vibe organization, which claims a monopoly, won't, I fear, be flexible about the price."

They found Roswell Bounce cheerfully leering at co-eds in the little plaza in front of the Student Union. As early as 1899, the Professor had informed them, Roswell had grasped the principles of what would become the standard-issue Hypopsammotic Survival Apparatus or "Hypops," revolutionizing desert travel by providing a practical way to submerge oneself beneath the sands and still be able to breathe, walk around, so forth.

"You control your molecular resonance frequencies, 's basically all it is," explained Roswell, "include a fine-adjustment feature onto it to compensate for parameter drift, so as to keep everything solid-looking but dispersed enough that you're still able to walk through it all 'th no more effort than swimming in a swimming hole. Sonofabitch Vibe Corp. stole it from me, and I feel no hesitation about beating their prices. How many were you looking for?"

They arranged for six units, one of which Roswell agreed readily to modify for Pugnax, all at a surprisingly reasonable club price, which included C.O.D. express delivery, with an additional discount for cash payment.

"A remarkable contraption," marveled Chick, who as Scientific Officer was especially intrigued.

"If we may move about these days beneath the sea wheresoever we will," opined Professor Vanderjuice, "the next obvious step is to proceed to that medium which is wavelike as the sea, yet also particulate."

"He means sand," said Roswell, "but it almost sounds like light, don't it."

"But setting aside the density, the inertia, the constant abrasion of working surfaces," Randolph wondered, "how can you travel underneath the sand and even see where you're going?"

"By redeploying energy on the order of what it would take to change the displaced sand into something transparent—quartz or glass, say. Obviously," the Professor explained, "one wouldn't want to be in the middle of that much heat, so one must arrange to translate oneself in Time, compensating for the speed of light in the transparent medium. As long as the sand has only been wind-deposited without local obstruction, we assume the familiar mechanics of water-waves generally to apply, and if we wished to move deeper, say in an under-sand vessel, new elements analogous to vortex-formation would enter the wave-history—in any case, expressible by some set of wave-functions."

"Which always include Time," said Chick, "so if you were looking for some way to reverse or invert those curves—wouldn't that imply some form of passage backward in Time?"

"Well that's just what I've been looking into here all summer," Roswell said. "They invited me to lead a seminar. Call me Professor if you want. You too,

Girlies!" he called out amiably to a group of presentable young women, some with their hats off and their hair down, who were picnicking on the grass nearby.

It took only a few days for the Hypops units to arrive at the express office in town, and the boys meanwhile prepared for departure with feelings of regret, unable to escape a suspicion that somewhere in the bustle of lectures, exhibits, picnics, and socials they had missed something essential, which might never be recovered, even by way of a working time machine.

"It was about flight," Miles, temporarily lapsing into English, theorized, "flight into the next dimension. We were always at the mercy of Time, as much as any civilian 'groundhog.' We went from two dimensions, infant's floor-space, out into town- and map-space, ever toddling our way into the third dimension, till as Chums recruits we could take the fateful leap skyward . . . and now, after these years of sky-roving, maybe some of us are ready to step 'sidewise' once more, into the next dimension—into Time—our fate, our lord, our destroyer."

"Thanks a lot, Bug-brains," Darby said. "What's for lunch?"

"Bug brains," replied Miles, with a kindly grin. "Fricaseed, I think."

The next Tesla transmission was to ascertain their exact moment of departure, but with no further details as to their mission. After weeks engaged with the mysteries of Time, the boys had run at last into the blank, featureless wall of its most literal expression, the timetable.

"Have a pleasant flight," the voice said. "There'll be further instructions when you arrive in Bukhara."

Darby tossed his sky-bag into his locker, seething with annoyance. "And how much longer," he yelled at the instrument, "are we supposed to put up with your damned disrespect?"

"Until mutiny is legalized," Lindsay warned primly.

"Can't say till *pigs fly,* can we?" Darby with a meaningful sneer at the X.O.

"Confound you, you insubordinate wiseacre—"

"They just can't abide anybody having too much fun, 's what it is," Darby was certain. "Anything they can't control is too much like skylarking for those autocratic bastards."

"Suckling!" Lindsay's face draining rapidly of its color. "It is as I have ever feared—"

"Oh compose yourself, Mrs. Grundy, I refer only to the Tsar-like, yet clearly illegitimate, aspects of their behavior."

"Oh. Oh, well . . ." Lindsay, taken somewhat aback, regarded blinkingly the newly legalistic Darby but did not pursue his reprimand.

"I'd be getting in the air," drawled the Tesla device, "if I were you fellows.

Mustn't jeopardize a perfect record of doing as you're told. Sheep can fly, too, after all. Can't they."

And presently, with Alonzo Meatman up in the ill-starred Bell Tower observing through binoculars, the *Inconvenience* rose over Candlebrow, with every appearance of sullenness, into a windless and humid day, and left the Mysteries of Time to those with enough of that commodity to devote to its proper study.

Three
Bilocations

While the *Inconvenience* was in New York, Lindsay had heard rumors of a "Turkish Corner" that really *was* supposed, in some not strictly metaphorical way, to provide an "escape nook to Asia." Like, "One minute you're in a horrible high-bourgeois New York parlor, the next out on the Asian desert, on top of a Bactrian camel, searching for a lost subterranean city."

"After a brief visit to Chinatown to inhale some fumes, you mean."

"Not exactly. Not as subjective as that."

"Not just mental transportation, you're saying, but actual, physical—"

"Translation of the body, sort of lateral resurrection, if you like."

"Say, who wouldn't? Where is this miraculous nook?"

"Where indeed . . . behind which of those heaped thousands on thousands of windows lighted and dark? A formidable quest, you'd have to say."

Well, the last week or so in its way had unfolded at least as suddenly.

Cameling along by night, Lindsay Noseworth found himself now actually enjoying his solitude, away from the constant chaos of a typical deck watch—visual field saturated in stars, four-space at its purest, more stars than he could ever remember seeing, though who'd had time for them, with so many small chores to keep his eyes bent to the quotidian? To tell the truth, he'd been growing doubtful about starlight in any practical way, having lately been studying historic world battles, attempting to learn what lighting conditions might have been like during the action, even coming to suspect that light might be a *secret determinant of history*—beyond how it had lit a battlefield or an opposing fleet, how might it have come warping through a particular window during a critical assembly of state, or looked as the sun was setting across some significant river, or struck in a particular way the hair, and thereby delayed the execution, of a politically dangerous wife one was determined to be rid of—

"Ahh . . ." D——n! There, there it was again, the fatal word! the word he had been forbidden, on doctor's orders, in fact, even to subvocalize . . .

The Chums of Chance C.A.C.A., or Comprehensive Annual Coverage Agreement, required quarterly health checkups at official Examining Stations, by insurance-company croakers. Last time Lindsay went in, back in Medicine Hat, Alberta, they had run some tests and caught signs of Incipient Gamomania, "That is, the abnormal desire to be married."

"Abnormal? What's abnormal in that? When have I ever kept it a secret that my governing desire in life is to be no longer one, but two, a two which is, moreover, one—that is, *denumerably* two, yet—"

"There. That's exactly the sort of thing we mean." Outside, it was summer, and in the last light, townsfolk were out bowling on the green. Laughter, calls of children, quiet bursts of applause, and something about it all made Lindsay, forever denied any such tranquil community, briefly fear for the structural integrity of his heart. Since then he had been receiving, with a somewhat alarming frequency, questionnaires printed on official forms, thinly disguised demands for samples of his bodily fluids, unannounced visits from bespectacled, bearded gentlemen speaking in a variety of European accents and actually *wearing white coats* who wished to examine him. Finally the *Inconvenience* had flown on without him, Chick Counterfly temporarily assuming X.O. duties, in order that Lindsay might enter the C. of C. Biometric Institute of Neuropathy, to undergo a "battery" of mental tests, upon release from which he was to proceed with all haste to a certain uncharted Inner Asian oasis serving as a base for the subdesertine craft in the region, for rendezvous with H.M.S.F. *Saksaul.*

Like Balaam's ass, it was the camel tonight who first detected something amiss, freezing in midstep, violently clenching every muscle in its body, and attempting un-camel-like cries it hoped its rider might at least become alarmed by the queerness of.

Presently, from just over the dune to his left, Lindsay heard someone calling his name.

"Yes do stop for a moment Lindsay," added a voice from the other side of the track, whose source was no more visible.

"We have messages for you," hissed an augmented choir of voices.

"All right now, old scout," Lindsay reassured the camel, "it's quite common out here, reported as long ago as Marco Polo, I've personally run into something like it in the Far North as well, yes plenty of times." More loudly, as if replying to the now-accelerating importunacy, "Simple Rapture of the Sands, absence of light, hearing grows sharper, energy reallocated across the sensorium—"

"LINDSAY*Lindsay*Lindsaylindsay . . ."

The camel looked around at him with a long eye-roll meant, mutatis mutandis, to convey skepticism.

"You must leave this track you were told never to step from, come to us, just over this dune—"

"I shall wait here," advised the aeronaut, as primly as the situation permitted. "If you will, come to me."

"Plenty of *wives* over here," the voices called. "Don't forget that this is the Desert. . . ."

"With its well-known demands upon the mind . . ."

". . . which so often may be resolved as *polygamy*."

"Heh, heh . . ."

"*Wives* in blossom, pan-spectral fields full of *wives* Lindsay, here is the Great Wife-Bazaar of the World-Island. . . ."

And not only the sibilant words but also liquid sounds, kisses, suction, mixed in with the unceasing friction of sand in its travels. An obscure local insult directed at himself? Or was it the camel they were trying to lure?

So star after star climbed to its meridian and then descended, and the camel took his way a step at a time, and all was saturated in expectancy. . . .

At dawn a brief wind arrived, from somewhere up ahead. Lindsay recognized the smell of wild "Euphrates" poplars coming into blossom. An oasis, a real one, had been waiting out there all night just past his reach, where now, among the redispositions of the morning, he rode in to find the rest of the crew, lying around experiencing the effects of the water here, which, somewhat odd-tasting but far from actually poisonous, was in fact much preferred, by the large population of travelers out here who knew of it, to either aryq or hasheesh, as a facilitator of passage between the worlds.

Lindsay shook his head at the tableau of chemical debauchery before him. For a terrible moment, he was certain, beyond reason, that none of these figures were his real fellow crewmen at all, but rather a *ghost-Unit,* from some Abode he wished never to visit, resolved on working him mischief, who had been painstakingly, intricately masked to *look like* Chums of Chance.

But then Darby Suckling caught sight of him, and the moment passed. "Eeyynnhh, will ya look at who's here. Hey, Nutso! When'd they let you out of that B.I.N.? I thought you'd be locked up for good."

Relieved, Lindsay limited his reply to a seventeen-syllable all-purpose threat of physical violence, failing even to mention Suckling's mother.

. . .

"NOW, SET THE Special Desert Detail. . . . Secure hatches fore and aft. . . . All hands prepare to submerge. . . ."

That excitement peculiar to under-sand travel could be felt as ship's personnel moved busily forward and aft in the dimly-lighted spaces of the subdesertine frigate *Saksaul*. Diamond-edged sand-augers cranked up to operating speed, beginning to bite all but frictionlessly into the sands of the Inner Asian desert, as steering-vanes smoothly came into play, increasing the angle of penetration. Any observer upon a nearby dune might have watched, perhaps in superstitious terror, as the craft, unhurriedly pursuing its dive into the lightless world, at last vanished beneath the sands, only a short-lived dust-devil remaining behind where the fantail had been.

Once having reached standard operating depth, the ship leveled off and was brought to cruising speed. Down in the engineering spaces, the Viscosity Gang began to throw one by one the switches that would couple to the ship's main engine their banks of so-called Eta/Nu Transformators, causing the observation windows up on the bridge to start trembling like drumheads, and a succession of colors to flow across the polished surfaces, as the view out the windows, pari passu, began to clear.

"Now light all cruising-lamps," ordered Captain Toadflax. As the searchlight filaments, fashioned of a secret alloy, became heated to the correct operating temperature and wave-length, the view beneath the dunes, blurry at first but soon adjusted, sprang vividly to life.

It as little resembled the upper-world view of the desert as the depths of an ocean do its own surface. Enormous schools of what might have been some beetle species swarmed, as if curious, iridescently in and out of the searchlight-beams, while, too far away to examine in any detail—in some cases, indeed, well past the smeared boundaries of the visible—darker shapes kept pace with the ship's progress, showing now and then a flash, bright as unsheathed steel. Presently, according to the charts, felt more than seen, there rose to port and starboard the jagged mountain ranges known to long-time Inner Asian sand-dogs as the Deep Blavatsky.

"Only way a man can hang on to his wits," as Captain Toadflax jovially informed his guests, "is to be stationed at an instrument he can't avoid tending to. These windows here are basically just for the entertainment of lubbers such as yourselves, no offense of course."

"None taken!" replied the Chums, as they had long learned to do, in cheery unison. Indeed, their demeanor today struck more than one observer as almost provokingly self-satisfied. Their mammoth airship was back at the oasis encampment, safely within a picket of Gurkhas fabled for their merciless dedication to perimeter defense. Miles Blundell, as Commissary, had put up a number of appetizing picnic luncheons, sizable enough to share with any members of the *Saksaul*'s crew whose delight in sand-duty cuisine might have begun, however tentatively, to ebb. And before them lay exactly the sort of adventure that was sure to appeal to their too-often ill-considered taste for the histrionic yet unprofitable.

"It is down here—" declared Captain Toadflax, "quite intact and, make no mistake, inhabited as well—that the true Shambhala will be found, just as real as anything. And those German professors," jerking an irascible thumb upward, "who keep waltzing out here by the wagonload, can dig till they're too blistered to dig anymore, and they still won't ever find it, not without the right equipment—the map you fellows brought, plus our ship's Paramorphoscope. And as any Tibetan lama will tell you, the right attitude."

"Then your mission—"

"As ever—to find the holy City ourselves, be there 'fustest with the mostest,' as your General Forrest used to say—no reason you shouldn't know that."

"Of course we don't mean to pry—"

"Oh, you lads are all right. I mean, if you aren't all right, then who is?"

"You shame us, sir. If truth were known, we are to be counted among the basest of the base."

"Hmm. Would've preferred someone a little more karmically advanced, but, howsoever—we do try aboard this vessel to ignore the rivalries going on above us whenever we may, and anyone that's after our results is more than welcome to them—they can read the whole story, right there in the papers, when we get back home at last, 'Heroes of the Sands Discover Lost City!' Ministerial speeches and archiepiscopal homilies, not to mention an opera girl on either arm, shaved ice by the ton, day or night at the touch of an annunciator, never-failing fountains of vintage Champagne, jewel-studded Victoria Crosses designed by Monsieur Fabergé himself—well . . . except that, of course, if anyone ever did actually discover a City sacred as that, he might not wish to wallow all that much among the secular pleasures, appealing though they be or, shall I say, as they are."

If any sinister meaning was hidden here, it either escaped the attention of the Chums or they had heard it just fine, and artfully concealed that recognition.

On the futuristic frigate glided, through the subarenaceous world, its exotically shaped steering-blades extended, its augers ever in finely-calibrated rotation clockwise and counterclockwise, among loomings of forbidding pinnacles and ominous grottoes never quite fully revealed by the searchlight beams.

Such to the dead might appear the world of the living—charged with information, with meaning, yet somehow always just, terribly, beyond that fateful limen where any lamp of comprehension might beam forth. The hum of the viscosity equipment rose and fell, in what had come to sound more and more like purposeful melody, reminding veterans of duty on the Himalayan station, of transmundane melody performed upon ancient horns fashioned from the thigh-bones of long-departed priests, in wind-beaten lamaseries miles above the level of a sea at this distance belonging more to legend than geography.

Randolph St. Cosmo, who had been gazing nearly mesmerized out the viewing windows, now gave a sort of stifled gasp—"There! isn't that a . . . watchtower of some sort? Have we been sighted?"

"Torriform Inclusion," chuckled Captain Toadflax soothingly, "easy to mistake. The whole trick down here's distinguishing man-made from God-made. That," he added, "and a head for the extra dimension. Urban terrain doesn't mean quite what it does up above—not if we can approach a town from below as easily as any other direction. Foundations, for example, become more like entry-ways. But I imagine you'll be eager to have a look at the map you've so kindly brought us. Least we can do in our all-but-boundless gratitude, you know."

Installed in the Navigation Room—a space so secret half the crew didn't even know it was there much less how to get to it—was one of the few Paramorphoscopes remaining in the world.

All paramorphoscopical activities aboard the *Saksaul* had been placed in charge of a civilian passenger, Stilton Gaspereaux, who proved to be a scholarly adventurer in the Inner Asian tradition of Sven Hedin and Aurel Stein, though beyond the Navigation Room chores his status on the ship was unclear. Unforthcoming about himself, he appeared more than willing to talk about Shambhala, and the Sfinciuno Itinerary.

"Among historians you'll find a theory that crusades begin as holy pilgrimages. One defines a destination, proceeds through a series of stations—diagrams of which were among the first known maps, as you see from this Sfinciuno document before you—and at last, after penitential acts and personal discomforts, you arrive, you perform there what your faith indicates you must, you go home again.

"But introduce to your sacred project the element of weaponry and everything changes. Now you need not only a destination but an enemy as well. The European Crusaders who went to the Holy Land to fight Saracens found themselves, when Saracens were not immediately available, fighting each other.

"We must therefore not exclude from this search for Shambhala an unavoidable military element. All the Powers have a lively interest. The stakes are too high."

The cryptic civilian had placed the Itinerary beneath an optically-perfect sheet of Iceland spar, deployed various lenses, and made some fine adjustments to the Nernst lamps. "Here it is, lads. Have a look."

The only one not flabbergasted, naturally, was Miles. He saw in the device immediately a skyship application as a range-finder and navigational aid. To look through it at the strangely-distorted and only partly-visible document the Chums had delivered to Captain Toadflax was like experiencing a low-level aerial swoop—indeed, engaging the proper controls on the viewing device could easily produce a long and fearful plunge straight down *into the map,* revealing the terrain at finer and finer scales, perhaps in some asymptotic way, as in dreams of falling, where the dreamer wakes just before impact.

"And this will take us straight to Shambhala," said Randolph.

"Well. . . ." Gaspereaux seemed embarrassed. "Yes I thought so too, at first. But there seem to be further complications."

"I knew it!" Darby exploded. "That 'Zo Meatman was setting us up for suckers all along!"

"It's strange, really. Distances, referred back to an origin point at Venice, are painstakingly accurate for the earth's surface and the various depths below. But somehow these three coördinates have not been enough. The farther we follow the Itinerary, the more . . . somehow . . . out of focus the details seem to drift, until at last," shaking his head in perplexity, "they actually become invisible. Almost as if there were some . . . additional level of encryption."

"Perhaps a fourth coördinate axis is needed," Chick suggested.

"I feel the difficulty may lie here," directing their attention to the center of the display, where, visible only at intervals, stood a mountain peak, blinding white, seeming lit from within, light pouring from it, bursting continually, illuminating transient clouds and even the empty sky. . . .

"Thought at first to be Mount Kailash in Tibet," said Gaspereaux, "a destination for Hindu pilgrims for whom it is the paradise of Shiva, their most holy spot, as well as the traditional starting point for seekers of Shambhala. But I've been out to Kailash and some of the others, and I'm not sure this one on the map is it. This one can also be seen at considerable distance, but not all the time. As if it were made of some variety of Iceland spar that can polarize light not only in space but in time as well.

"The ancient Manichæans out here worshipped light, loved it the way Crusaders claimed to love God, for its own sake, and in whose service no crime was too extreme. This was their counter-Crusade. No matter what transformations might occur—and they expected anything, travel backward or forward through Time, lateral jumps from one continuum to another, metamorphosis from one form of matter, living or otherwise, to another—the one fact to remain invariant under any of these must always be light, the light we see as well as the expanded sense of it prophesied by Maxwell, confirmed by Hertz. Along with that went a refusal of all forms of what they defined as 'darkness.'

"Everything you appreciate with your senses, all there is in the given world to hold dear, the faces of your children, sunsets, rain, fragrances of earth, a good laugh, the touch of a lover, the blood of an enemy, your mother's cooking, wine, music, athletic triumphs, desirable strangers, the body you feel at home in, a sea-breeze flowing over unclothed skin—all these for the devout Manichæan are evil, creations of an evil deity, phantoms and masks that have always belonged to time and excrement and darkness."

"But it's everything that matters," protested Chick Counterfly.

"And a true follower of this faith had to give all of it up. No sex, not even marriage, no children, no family ties. These being only tricks of the Darkness, there to distract us from seeking union with the Light."

"That's the choice? Light or pussy? What kind of a choice is that?"

"Suckling!"

"Sorry Lindsay, I meant 'vagina,' of course!"

"Sounds a little," Chick scratching his beard, "I don't know, puritanical somehow, doesn't it?"

"That's what they believed in."

"Then how'd they keep from dying out after the first generation?"

"Most of them went on about the business of what you'd call their normal lives, kept on having children, so forth, it depended what level of imperfection they could accept. The ones who kept strictly to the discipline were called 'Perfects.' The rest were welcome to study the Mysteries and try to join the small company of the Elect. But if they ever reached a point where they knew that's what they wanted, that's where they'd have to give everything up."

"And there are descendants living down here?"

"Oh, I expect you'll find it quite populated indeed."

Presently the optical-offset detectors of the *Saksaul* revealed in the near distance scattered but unmistakable ruins in the Græco-Buddhist and Italo-Islamic styles and, moving among these, other subdesertine vehicles, whose courses, upon being roughly plotted, appeared to converge with the *Saksaul*'s own, somewhere in the obscurities ahead. From above, below, and either side, structures more complex than geology could account for began gathering closer—domes and minarets, columned arches, statuary, finely filigreed balustrades, windowless towers, ruins written on by combat ancient and modern.

"We shall put in at Nuovo Rialto," the Captain announced. "Port and starboard liberty sections." This news was received ambiguously by the crew, "N.R." being a good liberty town for some needs but not others. The long-submerged port had been settled around 1300 on the ruins, by then already half swept below by the unappeasable sands, of a Manichæan city, which dated from the third century and according to tradition had been founded by Mani himself in his wanderings beyond the farther banks of the Oxus. There it remained and flourished for nearly a thousand years until Jenghiz Khan and his armies overran that part of Inner Asia, leaving as little as they could either standing or breathing. By the time the Venetians found it, little remained that had not succumbed to wind, gravity, and an excruciating departure of faith. In the brief time they occupied Nuovo Rialto, the Westerners managed to put in a network of cisterns to collect what rainwater came that way, run some pipe, even sink a few wells. Inexplicably, as if attending to ancient voices somehow preserved in the crystallography of the silica medium which was so mercilessly engulfing the town—as if secret knowledge had once been written that permanently into its very substance—they began to fall year by year under the influence of the old para-Christian doctrines. The first under-sand explorers here had identified Manichæan shrines dating from no earlier than the fourteenth century, clearly a thousand years more recent than they ought to have been.

The crew meanwhile were busy with the Passing of the Remarks traditional when entering a new liberty port.

" 'As above, so below,' ain't it."

"Never fails."

"Talk about battered caravanserais!"

"Lot of laundry to do, maybe I'll just stay on the ship. . . ."

"Place smells like Coney Island."

"What, the beach?"

"Naahh—Steeplechase Park, at the vaudeville show!"

"Now prepare for docking, starboard side to," the Captain announced. Nearby loomed a high, ruinous structure of great antiquity, of some red-brown color suggestive of blood spilled none too recently, whose supporting pillars were torch-bearing statues male and female, and whose pediment was inscribed in an alphabet invented, according to Gaspereaux, by Mani himself, and in which The Book of Secrets and other sacred Manichæan texts were also written.

It was here, evidently, that the sand-frigate planned to tie up. After evening "chow," enjoying a cigar on the fantail, Chick heard a high-pitched screaming, which seemed to him almost articulated into speech. He located a pair of under-sand goggles, slipped them on, and peered into the darkness beyond the settlement walls. Something large and heavy came thundering by, in high swooping hops, and Chick thought he recognized the smell of blood. "What in Creation was that?"

Gaspereaux had a look. "Oh. Local sand-fleas. Always coming round to see what's what whenever a new ship pulls in."

"What are you talking about? Whatever just went by was the size of a camel."

Gaspereaux shrugged. "Down here they are known as *chong pir,* big lice. Since the first Venetians arrived, these creatures, following a diet exclusively of human blood, have grown over the generations larger, more intelligent, one ventures to say more resourceful. Feeding upon the host is no longer a matter as simple as mandibular assault but has evolved into a conscious negotiation, if not indeed a virtual exchange of views—"

"People down here talk to giant fleas?" inquired Darby with his accustomed directness.

"Indeed. Usually in a dialect of ancient Uyghur, though, owing to the mouth structure unique to *Pulex,* one finds certain difficulties with phonology, notably the voiced interdental fricative—"

"Yes . . . oh, attendant? Over here? Time for the hose again?"

"Nonetheless, lad, a useful phrase or two might prove handy in the event of an encounter."

Darby patted the skeleton rig beneath his left lapel and moved his eyebrows up and down meaningfully.

"Afraid not," Gaspereaux objected, "that'd be pulicide. Covered down here by the same felony statutes that apply up there to homicide."

Nevertheless Darby kept his Browning close by him as, with mixed feelings of anticipation and terror, the boys buckled on their Hypops gear and set out on that evening's recreational visit to Nuovo Rialto. Moving through the sand took some getting used to, especially the lengths of time needed to perform even the simplest of motor tasks, but soon had resolved to a leisurely andante, with a sibilance, owing to the graininess of the medium, as much felt as heard.

Screaming came from different directions, and blood could be observed in jagged three-dimensional blobs, usually in the vicinity of taverns and other low resorts.

Had it not been for an overheard scrap of conversation, Chick would have been unaware of another motive, perhaps the frigate's real one, for which Shambhala might be serving only as a pretext. In the Sandman Saloon, he had fallen into conversation with Leonard and Lyle, a couple of oil prospectors headed for their next likely field of endeavor.

"Yehp we was into it over here well before the Swedes got in, been wildcattin' all over. . . ."

"Sodom and Gomorrah will just be a Sunday-school picnic in comparison to this place."

"How's that?"

"Oh, we're headed for the Holy Land."

"Or unholy, if you consider the Scriptures."

It seemed that one night in Baku, in a waterfront *teke* or hasheesh den, as if by supernatural direction, a drifter from the States with nothing to gamble but a pocket Bible had lost it to Lyle, in front of whose face the Good Book had fallen open to Genesis 14:10 and the phrase "the Vale of Siddim was full of slimepits."

"Dead Sea area, 'slimepit' being King James English for bituminous deposit," Leonard explained.

"It was like a light come on. Fact, we run to the door thinkin it was some kind of surprise gas burn-off outside. No, it was the Lord inviting our attention down to those onetime honkytonk cities of the plain which are fixin to be the next damn Spindletop, and you can bet the farm on that."

"Bigger'n that gusher up to Groznyi they couldn't figure how to cap," Leonard declared.

"So what are you doing here instead of there?" inquired the blunt Darby Suckling.

"Getting a stake together basically. Lots of quick cash to be had out here, no lengthy routines nor forms to fill out, if you get our drift."

"There's oil out here?" inquired Chick, though unable to prevent from creeping into his voice a faint note of disingenuousness.

The two wildcatters guffawed at length and bought the boys another round of the local aryq before Lyle replied, "Take a look down the hold of that frigate you come in on, tell us if you don't find some rods and tubing and calyx bits and all."

"Hell, we ought to know that prospector look by now, even with some of those boys's faces already familiar from Baku."

Darby found this amusing, one more bit of evidence proving how little adults could be trusted. "This whole Shambhala story of theirs is just a pretext, then."

"Oh the place is probably real," Leonard shrugged. "But I'd bet if your Captain sailed right into it, he might say *ässalamu äläykum* on his way through, but he'd have his eye more likely on that next anticline."

"This is distressing," Randolph muttered. "Once again we are being used to further someone's hidden plans."

Chick noticed the two oil gypsies exchanging a look. "What does occur to us all of a sudden," Lyle hitching his chair closer to the table and lowering his voice, "for somebody on that frigate is bound to be keeping logbooks of every bituminous possibility they come across out in these strata—locations, depths, estimated volumes—there's no telling what some folks'd be willing to pay for jealously guarded information like that."

"Dismiss the thought," protested Lindsay from a certain *equine altitude,* "for it would make us no better than common thieves."

"If the price was high enough, however," mused Randolph, "it would surely make us extraordinary thieves."

It had been a peculiar liberty weekend in Nuovo Rialto. The ship happened to have tied up at a quay belonging to an aryq shipper, along which many sailors were discovered each morning semi-paralyzed, having got no further in their pursuit of recreation, their Hypops units humming on in Dormant mode. A number of the crew reported being waylaid by sand-fleas, the queues at sick bay each morning running down passageways and ladders well into the Viscosity spaces. Some, apparently having enjoyed the accostments, didn't report them at all. The quarterdeck witnessed scenes of vituperation, smuggling attempts failed and successful, romantic melodrama as the more adventurous crew members discovered the complex allure of Veneto-Uyghur women, who were a byword of emotional volatility throughout the Subdesertine Service. When the time came at last to single up all lines, some 2 percent of the crew, about average as these things went, had announced plans to stay behind and get married. Captain Toadflax took this with the equanimity of a long-time trooper in the region, figuring he'd get most of them back when he came through town again at the end of the cruise. "Marriage or under-sand duty," shaking his head as at some cosmic sadness. "What a choice!"

As H.M.S.F. *Saksaul* merrily droned along beneath the desert, one paleo-Venetian oasis to the next—Marco Querini, Terrenascondite, Pozzo San Vito—her crew continued to pretend that prospecting for oil was the furthest thing from their thoughts. Randolph before long was obsessed, recklessly so, by the petro-geological logbooks Lyle and Leonard had mentioned, all closely held, as far as he knew, along with the detailed mission documents, inside Captain Toadflax's cabin safe. In his increasingly unbalanced state, Randolph sought Darby Suckling's advice.

"As Legal Officer," Darby said, "I'm not sure how much loyalty we owe them, especially when they're keeping so much from us. Myself, I'd favor the peterman option—ain't the safe built Counterfly can't blow, see him." Thus, although he was not, as later alleged, actually planning to steal, or even unauthorizedly scrutinize, the documents, it was an awkward moment when Q. Zane Toadflax entered his cabin one midwatch to find Randolph gazing at the safe, with a number of dynamite sticks and detonators on his person.

From then until the boys' departure, there were masters-at-arms posted outside Toadflax's cabin round the clock. When at last they surfaced near the compound where *Inconvenience* was moored, the farewells were notable for their economy.

The boys returned to the *Inconvenience* to find the pantries depleted, decks unattended to, and the Gurkhas all vanished—*Called away on a matter of some urgency,* according to the note left in Randolph's cabin—leaving the security of the vessel entirely to Pugnax. Though the sentiments of fawning gratitude exhibited now and then by specimens of his race had been seldom observed in Pugnax, today he was clearly overjoyed to see the boys again. "Rr rr-rff rf rrr rrf-ff rr rrff rr rrr rrff-rf rf!" he exclaimed, which the boys understood to mean "I haven't had two blessed hours' sleep since you fellows left!" Miles headed directly for the galley, and before he knew it, Pugnax was lying before a sumptuous "spread" which included Consommé Impérial, Timbales de Suprêmes de Volailles, Gigot Grillé à la Sauce Piquante, and aubergines à la Sauce Mousseline. The wine-cellar had been none-too-discreetly ransacked by the Gurkhas, but Miles was able to locate a '00 Pouilly-Fuissé and a '98 Graves which met Pugnax's approval, and he fell to and, presently, asleep.

THAT EVENING as the *Inconvenience* soared above the vast and silent desert, Chick and Darby strolled the weather decks, gazing down at circular wavefronts in the sand, revealed by the low angle of the setting sun, flowing away to the limits of this unknown world. Miles joined them and was soon off on one of his extra-temporal excursions.

"Whatever is to happen," he reported upon his return, "will begin out here, with an engagement of cavalry on a scale no one living has ever seen, and perhaps no one dead either, an inundation of horse, spanning these horizons, their flanks struck an unearthly green, stormlit, relentless, undwindling, arisen boiling from the very substance of desert and steppe. And all that incarnation and slaughter will transpire in silence, all across this great planetary killing-floor, absorbing wind, steel, hooves upon and against earth, massed clamor of horses, cries of men. Millions of souls will arrive and depart. Perhaps news of it will take years to reach anyone who might understand what it meant. . . ."

"I'm not so sure Darby and I haven't seen something like it already," mused Chick, recalling their brief though unpleasant experience in the "time-chamber" of Dr. Zoot. But its meaning, even as simple prophecy, was as obscure to them now as then.

Somewhere out past Oasis Benedetto Querini, H.M.S.F. *Saksaul* came to grief. Survivors were few, accounts sketchy and inconsistent. The first salvo came from nowhere, precisely aimed, ear-splitting, sending the bridge into a fearful cataplexy. Operators sat dumbstruck before their viewing screens, trying to re-scale the images before them, switching in every combination of enhancement and filtering circuitry they could think of in an effort to find their invisible attackers, who appeared to be using a frequency-shifting device of some power and sophistication, able to mask an entire under-sand fighting vessel from all known viewing equipment.

The copy of the Sfinciuno Itinerary which the Chums in their innocence had brought aboard had led H.M.S.F. *Saksaul* into ambush and disaster.

"Who are they?"

"German or Austrian, would be likely, though one mustn't rule out the Standard Oil, or the Nobel brothers. Gaspereaux, we are in a desperate state. The moment for which you came aboard has arrived. Get to the shaft-alley and put on the Hypops gear you find in the locker there along with a canteen of water, the oasis maps, and some meat lozenges. Make your way to the surface, get back to England at all cost. They must be told in Whitehall that the balloon is up."

"But you'll need all the men you can—"

"Go! find someone in the F.O. intelligence section. It is our only hope!"

"Under protest, Captain."

"Complain to the Admiralty. If I'm still alive, you can have me up on charges."

As days passed out here in this great ambiguity of Time and Space, it would not be long at all before Gaspereaux was back in London, endeavoring to reach the legendary Captain, now Inspector, Sands, soon to be known to Whitehall—as well as to readers of the *Daily Mail*—as "Sands of Inner Asia."

Meanwhile, for days, weeks in some places, the battles of the Taklamakan War were raging. The earth trembled. Now and then a subdesertine craft would suddenly break the surface with no warning, damaged mortally, its crew dead or dying . . . petroleum deposits far underground were attacked, lakes of the stuff would appear overnight and great pillars of fire would ascend to the sky. From Kashgar to Urumchi, the bazaars were full of weapons, breathing units, ship fittings, hardware nobody could identify, full of strange gauges and prisms and electrical wiring which later proved to be from Quaternion-ray weapons, which all the Powers had deployed. These now fell into the hands of goat-herders, falconers, shamans, to be taken out into the emptiness, disassembled, studied, converted to uses religious and practical, and eventually to change the history of the World-Island beyond even the most unsound projections of those Powers who imagined themselves somehow, at this late date, still competing for it.

Appearing these days in the infant science of counter-terrorism as an all-purpose code name, the bloke you sent out a discreet summons for to alert your own security staff to a crisis, the real "Inspector Sands," beleaguered, ever struggling to define and maintain a level of professional behavior, unaware of his drift into legend, soon enough aged beyond his years and sweated into a moodiness at home that could not but slop over onto the wife and kids, would find by midcareer no time even to take off his hat, hurrying as ever from one emergency to the next—"Ah, Sands, there you are, and high time, too. We've a suspect individual—just down there at the far wicket, can you see him?—no one can really place his accent, some think Irish, others Italian, not to mention that queerly-shaped bag he's brought with him—we're putting the 'stall' on him, of course, but if there's a *timed device* you see, well that won't do much good, will it?"

"In the shiny green suit, and sort of gondolier's hat, except for that . . . well it's not a ribbon, is it—"

"More of a feather, almost a plume, really—rather extreme wouldn't you say?"

"*Could* be Italian I suppose."

"Some sort of wog, obviously. The thing is, how shall one make out his short-term intentions? Not likely in here for a spot of Vic removal, is he?"

"The bag might be only for carrying his lunch."

"Typical of these people, who else would think of eating an explosive substance?"

"What I meant, actually, was . . . *instead* of explosives?"

"Quite so, I knew that, but it could be anything, then, couldn't it? His laundry for instance."

"Indeed. Though, what could you blow up with a bag of laundry, I wonder."

"*Oh,* bother, there now he's pulling something out of his pocket, I *knew it?*" Uniformed guards at once began to converge on the intruder, while outside in the street the metropolitan police were suddenly everywhere up and down St. Martin le Grand and over into Angel Street, swarming in and out of the horse-drawn and motor traffic, dropping suggestions into the ears of drivers best situated to create a general vehicular paralysis, should one prove useful. The clerk at the wicket having thrown himself sniveling beneath a nearby table, the subject quickly took up his bag and fled out the front exit and across the street toward the G.P.O. West, where all the telegraphic business was done. This was a vast and, to many, an intimidating space, in the center of which, sunk below floor level, four enormous steam engines labored to provide the pressures and vacuums that propelled to and fro about the City and Strand thousands of pneumatic dispatches per day, being tended by a sizable crew of stokers and monitored round the clock for entropy fluctuations, vacuum failures and so forth by staff engineers in gray drill suits and darkly gleaming dicers.

Cries of "There he goes!" and "Hold up, you bloody anarchist!" were absorbed in the relentless polyrhythms of the steam-machinery. Against the greased writhing of these dark iron structures, a brightwork of brass fittings and bindings, kept a-shine through the nights by a special corps of unseen chars, flashed like halos of industrious saints in complex periodic motion everywhere. Hundreds of telegraphers, ranked about the great floor attending each his set, scarcely looked up from their universe of clicks and rests—uniformed messenger boys came and went among the varnished hardwood labyrinth of desks and sorting-bureaux, and customers leaned or paced or puzzled over messages they had just received, or must send, as cheerless London daylight descended through the windows and rising steam produced an all-but-tropical humidity in this Northern Temple of Connexion. . . .

"'Ere then, Luigi, where're we off to in such a grea' rush?" as a constable, popping up out of the marblework unexpectedly, now attempted a sort of sliding football tackle upon the agile Mediterranean, who slowed down long enough to snarl,

"For God's sake, Bloggins, it's me, Gaspereaux, and if you'll be kind enough to—"

"Oh. Sorry, guv, didn't—"

"No, no, *don't touch your cap,* Bloggins I'm in *disguise,* can't you see, yes and what I actually need you to do, now, quickly as ever we can, is to *pretend* to put me under arrest—take me upstairs, without quite so much *friendly nudging* if possible—"

"(Got you, guv.) All right then, allegro vivatchy, my good man, we'll just-a put-a these-a lovely bracelets on shall we, as a formality only of course, oh this is my young Police Constable colleague who'll take charge of your interesting bag there as soon as he stops staring at it quite so fixedly, won't you Constable yes there's a good chap. . . ." Escorting the prisoner, for whom handcuffs did not noticeably interfere with his ethnic gesticulations, up a side staircase to a hallway milling with uniformed guards, and beneath an imposing archway into the offices of Internal Security.

"I say it's old Gaspereaux, what are you doing with that cheap grease-paint all over your face? Not to mention that beastly hat?"

"Only way I could find a moment to chat with you, Sands, eyes and ears everywhere sort of thing—" Across the room a cylinder of gutta-percha carrying a pneumatic message now arrived in its "D" box with a sort of jingling thud.

"Probably for me—" removing the form and scanning it. "Right. . . . Damned Suffragettes again I shouldn't wonder. Oh sorry, Gasper, you were saying?"

"Sands, you know me. The meaning of what I have seen, if I spoke of it, I would not understand, and if I understood it, I could not—"

"Speak, yesyes well of course then if you wouldn't mind sharing a hack down to Holborn—"

"Not at all, they'll be wanting this costume back in Saffron Hill anyway."

"Perhaps we might even find time for a pint somewhere."

"I know just the place."

Which turned out to be the Smoked Haddock, one of Gaspereaux's many locals, in each of which he would be known, Sands expected, by a different identity.

"Evening, Professor, all in order I trust?"

"Not if I can help it," Gaspereaux genially replied, in a tone higher, and with a coloring more suburban, than Sands had yet heard from him.

"Now then what is all this, my son, not a touch of the old occupational grandiosity I hope—"

"Sands, I most desperately need—"

"No prologues among us, Gasper, *tantum dic verbo* isn't it."

"Well then." He recited as dispassionately as he could what he had escaped, and what he feared had befallen H.M.S.F. *Saksaul.* "It is the old Shambhala business again. Someone, perhaps even one of ours, has found it at last."

"How's that?"

Gaspereaux repeated the fragments he'd heard. "And the place is . . . *intact.* Other sub-surface ruins out there are filled with sand, of course, but in Shambhala the sand is being *held away,* somehow, by some invisible sphere of force like a gigantic air bubble—"

"So anyone who knows where it is—"

“Can enter and occupy it, with no need for special equipment.”

“Well this is splendid news, Gasper.” But Gaspereaux was staring back with stricken eyes. “I meant, a—a shining moment for England, I should have thought—”

“We are not the only ones there, Sands. At this moment all the Powers present in the region are bringing in their forces. Frigate actions like the *Saksaul*’s are only the opening feints. Chances increase day by day for some sort of sustained conflict over possession of the city, in regimental strength if not larger.”

“But I’ve constant telephonic connection with Whitehall—why hasn’t anyone ever mentioned this?”

“Oh because I’m mad, I suppose, and it’s been all no more than a madman’s phantasy.”

“That’s just it, my boy, by now I know that your most deranged utterances are only conventional history prematurely blurted.” He produced a half-sovereign case in the shape of Mr. Campbell-Bannerman’s head. “Need to find a telephone box, I suppose. *Oh*dearohdearohdear.” Off he went. The dim blessed local, which when crossing the desert Gaspereaux had quite given up on ever seeing again, slowly, sympathetically, drew him into its cherished inability to imagine anything clearly beyond Dover.

The day Dally left for New York, Merle, pretending to himself he'd lost his spectacles, had gone rooting around through everything he could think of, opening boxes, looking under counterpanes and behind the framing of the wagon, till he caught sight of a stuffed old doll, Clarabella, the one who'd joined them, as Dally liked to put it, years back in Kansas City, just lying now in the housedust, and he was surprised to find himself with emotions somehow not his own, as if the forlornness were old Clarabella's there, all abandoned in the full light of day, with no more little girl to pick her up. One look at that face, and the way the paint was worn out, and it sure made a man's damn valves start in to dribbling, if not unseat completely.

He waited till after the next bullion day and then quit the amalgamator job at Little Hellkite, packed up developing chemicals and photographic plates and a few pictures he was content to hold on to after giving the rest away. A few of those he kept might have been of Dally. He found a couple of good horses and proceeded down the San Miguel and up over Dallas Divide and up through Gunnison and down the great long eastern slope to Pueblo, something at the back of his mind convinced that years ago on the way west to Colorado he had missed something essential, some town he hadn't seen, some particular piece of hardware that unless he found it again and put it to use, might even cross off a good part of the meaning of his life so far, is how important it was. Heading east, he was aware that Dally was someplace a thousand miles in front of him, but it wasn't as if he was planning on going all the way back east. Only as far as he had to.

One Saturday evening Merle rolled into Audacity, Iowa. It was just after suppertime, some light still in the sky, a few farm wagons heading back out of town into a haze that made the little oak trees look round and flat as lollipops, and he noticed a small crowd shifting and muttering and about to turn boisterous out in front of a flat-roofed clapboard building with multicolored gas lamps, already on before the streetlighting, spelling out against the fading day the name of the local moving-picture house, DREAMTIME MOVY. Merle parked the wagon and wandered over to join the crowd.

"Looks like some excitement." He noticed that, like a lot of these country theaters, this one had been converted from a church of some persuasion too small at last to support a minister. Made sense to Merle, who didn't see much difference between movie audiences and crowds at tent-meetings—it was the same readiness to be carried into some storyteller's spell.

"Third week in a row," he was promptly informed, "the blamed thing won't work, and we're waiting for Fisk to come out and give us the usual hooey."

"Worst possible place it could've happened, she's hangin on to this log in the river—"

"—bein swept down to this waterfall off this big cliff—"

"—current's too strong for her to swim, he just found out, ridin hard to get there in time—"

"And ever'thin just goes all discombobulated! Fisk don't know how close he is to bein run out of town."

"Here he is now, the miserable coot."

Merle moved over so as to put a little space between the woefully upset Fisk and the crowd. "How do, lens-brother, what's the problem, film break, carbons burn out?"

"Picture won't stay put. Sprocket and gear, near 's I can tell."

"I've run one or two of these rigs, mind if I have a look? What've you got, a Powers movement?"

"Just a regular Geneva." He led Merle to the back of the shadowy little ex-church and up some stairs to what had been the choir loft. "It's about all I can do to get it threaded in right, usually Wilt Flambo, who's the watchmaker in town, knows this rig inside out, I inherited the job when Wilt run off with that feed clerk's wife, and now he's off in Des Moines or someplace sending everybody picture postals about how much fun he's having."

Merle took a look. "Well this Geneva movement's fine, it's your sprocket tension's gone a little strange, is all, probably the shoe needs to be . . . there, O.K., light her off now, what're these, gas burners?"

"Acetylene." It worked fine now, and the two of them stood a minute and gazed at the screen as the lip of the perilous cascade drew ever closer. "Guess I'd better wind this back again to the beginnin of the reel. You sure saved my caboose, friend. You can have the honor of givin them all the good news."

"Frankly," Fisk admitted later over a friendly glass of beer, "it has always scared the hell out of me, too much energy loose in that little room, too much heat, nitro in the film, feel like it's all going to explode any minute, the stories you hear, if it was only the light it'd be one thing, but these other forces . . ."

They gave each other the sour, resentful tightlip smiles of professionals who have learned the dimensions of the payback for whatever magic is keeping the tip out front in their happy stupor—in this case the sheer physical labor of cranking the projector and the demonic energies a man was obliged to stand way too close to.

Merle got the job for a week or two while Fisk went back to tending his wagon-parts store and resting up. After a while, as he'd done before, Merle found himself withdrawing from the story on the screen, cranking the projector along and contemplating the strange relation these moving pictures had with Time, not strange maybe so much as tricky, for it all depended on fooling the eye, which was why, he imagined, you found so many stage-magicians going into the business. But if the idea was for still pictures to move, why there had to be a better way than this elaborate contraption of gear-trains and multiple lenses and matching up speeds and watchmaker's fancywork to get each frame to stop a split-second and all. There had to be something more direct, something you could do with light itself. . . .

ONE DAY UNDER A SKY of a certain almost-familiar shade of yellow, he came to the bank of a river on which young people were canoeing, not in high spirits or carefree flirtation but in some dark perplexity, as if they were here from deeper motives but couldn't just then remember what those were. He recognized the state of mind as if it were a feature of the landscape, like an explorer discovers a mountain or a lake, simple as coming up over a ridgeline—there it was, laid out neat as could be like a map of itself. He had found Candlebrow, or, if you like, it had found him—he drove in through the dilapidated portals of the campus, and recognized the place he'd been looking for, the one he'd missed first time around, streets lined with bookstores, places to sit and talk, or not talk, cafés, wood stairs, balconies, lofts, feasting outside at tables, striped awnings, crowds milling, night falling, a small movie show, lemon-white neon outside. . . .

The land here had a gentle roll to it. No voice, outside a playing field, was ever more than conversationally loud. Horses grazed in the Quadrangle. Field-scent percolated everywhere—purple clover, honeysuckle, queen-of-the-prairie. Picnickers brought with them horseshoes and ukuleles, baskets full of sandwiches, hard-boiled eggs, pickles, and bottled beer, down to the banks of Candlebrow's tranquil and famously canoeable river, the Sempitern. Every other afternoon thunderheads appeared to the westward and began to pile up, and the sky darkened to a biblically lurid yellow-gray by the time the first winds and raindrops arrived.

The conferees had gathered here from all around the world, Russian nihilists with peculiar notions about the laws of history and reversible processes, Indian swamis concerned with the effect of time travel on the laws of Karma, Sicilians with equal apprehensions for the principle of vendetta, American tinkers like Merle with specific electromechanical questions to clear up. Their spirits all one way or another invested in, invested by, the siegecraft of Time and its mysteries.

"Fact is, our system of so-called linear time is based on a circular or, if you like, periodic phenomenon—the Earth's own spin. Everything spins, up to and including, probably, the whole universe. So we can look to the prairie, the darkening sky, the birthing of a funnel-cloud to see in its vortex the fundamental structure of everything—"

"Um, Professor—"

"—'funnel' of course being a bit misleading, as the pressure in the vortex isn't distributed in anything so simple as a straight-sided cone—"

"Sir, excuse me, but—"

"—more of a quasi-hyperboloid of revolution which—say, where's everybody going?"

Those in attendance, some at quite high speed, had begun to disperse, the briefest of glances at the sky sufficing to explain why. As if the Professor had lectured it into being, there now swung from the swollen and light-pulsing clouds to the west a classic prairie "twister," lengthening to a point, about to touch down, approaching, it seemed all but consciously, the campus which lay in its direct path, at a speed not even the swiftest horse could hope to outrace.

"Hurry—this way!" Everyone was converging upon McTaggart Hall, the headquarters of the Metaphysics Department, whose storm-cellar was known throughout the region as the roomiest and best-appointed such refuge between Cleveland and Denver. The mathematicians and engineers lit gas-mantles and storm-lamps, and waited for the electric light to fail.

In the storm-cellar, over semiliquid coffee and farmhouse crullers left from the last twister, they got back to the topic of periodic functions, and their generalized form, automorphic functions.

"Eternal Return, just to begin with. If we may construct such functions in the abstract, then so must it be possible to construct more secular, more physical expressions."

"Build a time machine."

"Not the way I would have put it, but, if you like, fine."

Vectorists and Quaternionists in attendance reminded everybody of the function they had recently worked up known as the Lobatchevskian, abbreviated Lob, as in "Lob **a**," by which, almost as a by-product, ordinary Euclidean space is transformed to Lobatchevskian.

"We thus enter the whirlwind. It becomes the very essence of a refashioned life, providing the axes to which everything will be referred. Time no longer 'passes,' with a linear velocity, but 'returns,' with an angular one. All is ruled by the Automorphic Dispensation. We are returned to ourselves eternally, or, if you like, timelessly."

"Born again!" exclaimed a Christer in the gathering, as if suddenly enlightened.

Above, the devastation had begun. And now here one might have noted an odd thing about this tornado. It was not simply "a" tornado which descended upon Candlebrow with such distressing regularity but indisputably *always the same tornado.* It had been photographed repeatedly, measured for wind speed, circumference, angular momentum, and shapes assumed over time of passage, and from visit to visit these had all remained uncannily consistent. Before long the thing had been given a name, Thorvald, and propitiatory offerings to it had begun to appear heaped outside the University gates, usually items of sheet metal, which had been noted in particular as one of Thorvald's dietary preferences. Human food, while not so common, was represented by various farm animals live and slaughtered, though occasionally entire *thresher dinners* had also been known to've been laid out cooked and ready to eat, on long picnic tables, where it then required a level of indifference to fate quite beyond this carefree undergraduate body to risk actually stealing from, let alone inserting into one's face.

"Superstition!" screamed certain professors. "How are we supposed to maintain any scientific objectivity around here?"

"And yet suppose we did try to communicate with Thorvald—"

"Oh, it's 'Thorvald' now, my my quite chummy aren't we."

"Well, it is cyclic after all, so some kind of signaling might be possible using wave-modulation—"

There were in fact a couple different designs for a Thorvaldic Telegraph to be found for sale down on West Symmes, where Merle had begun to loiter for an hour or so a day. Here, each summer at Candlebrow, for miles up and down the riverside, a huge population of jobbers and operators appeared running pitches in a bazaar of Time, offering for sale pocket-watches and wall clocks, youth potions, false birth certificates duly notarized, systems of stock-market prediction, results of horse races at distant tracks well before post time, along with telegraphic facilities for placing actual wagers on the fates of these as-yet-unaccelerated animals, strangely gleaming electromechanical artifacts alleged to come from "the future"—"You say, now, the live chicken goes in this end here—" and above all instruction in the many forms of time-transcendence, timelessness, counter-time, escapes and emancipations from Time as practiced by peoples from all parts of the world, curiosity as to which was assumed to be the true unstated reason for attendance at these summer gatherings. Not surprisingly, a higher-than-average number of these more spiritual-type programs were being run by charlatans and swindlers, often wearing turbans, robes, shoes with elongated toes that concealed a "gaff" of some sort, as well as strangely modified hats serving the same purpose, and except for the out-and-out hopeless greed cases, Merle found most of them worth chatting with, especially those with business cards.

Soon enough, quicker than he would've thought, he became a fixture at the summer get-togethers. The rest of the year, it was like one day job after another just so for a month during the summer he could enter a realm of time-obsession and share it with others of the breed. It never occurred to him to question how this preoccupation had come about, whether by way of photography and its convergence of silver, time, and light or just with Dally out of the house finding Time so heavy on his hands that he was obliged to bring it a little closer to his face, squint at it from different angles, maybe try to see if it could be taken apart to figure how it might actually work. From here on, the alchemy, the tinkering, the photography would be relegated to day jobs of one kind or another. The nights, the flights and journeys proper to night, would be dedicated to the Mysteries of Time.

One evening about twilight, out of the corner of his eye, sailing past in the sky like one of the famous Giant Airships of 1896 and '7, Merle thought he saw the *Inconvenience,* and sure enough, a little later, down on West Symmes—

"Well, how are you, sir, I've thought of you often, and of course your lovely daughter, Miss Dahlia."

Merle had to squint his way past the mustache but recognized Chick Counterfly all right. "She's seeking a career in show business back east," Merle said, "thanks for asking. What are you boys up to these days? Last I read, you were over in Venice, Italy, knocking down their Campanile, which I should point out is the model for the one up on campus there, that's if you're still in the bell-tower demolition business?"

"These days trying to get fixed up with some Hypops equipment. Have you met Roswell Bounce, by the way? Father of the Hypops Apparatus himself?"

"That's me, get within ten foot of any of them units, start hearing 'ese little voices, 'Daddy, Daddy!' Why—it's 'at there Merle Rideout ain't it."

"Damn, Roswell, it's sure been a while since Cleveland," said Merle. "Followed that trial with great interest."

"Oh, I went to court, had to, but you can imagine the kind of lawyers I was able to afford, whereas that Vibe sonofabitch had his Wall Street flunkeys Somble, Strool, & Fleshway all lined up against me."

Bounce v. *Vibe* had proved reliable as a source of public entertainment and even made Roswell a sort of celebrity. Eccentric inventors were then enjoying in America a certain vogue as long-shot opponents of the mills of Capital. They were expected to lose, poignantly as possible, though now and then an educated side-bet on one winning might pay off big.

"Years go by, no satisfaction, I eventually develop litigious mania, 'paranoia querulans,' as the nerve croakers call it, even try to bring old Vibe to court over that, at least to recoup the mind-doctor fees, but as usual no dice."

"Well you're mighty cheerful," it seemed to Merle, "for somebody with chronic P.Q."

Roswell winked. "You know how there's some have found Jesus? Well, that happened to me, too, only my Savior turned out to be more of a classical demigod, namely," pretending to look furtively right and left, and lowering his voice, "Hercules."

Merle, recognizing the name of a popular brand of blasting agent, twinkled back discreetly. "Powerful fella. Twelve Labors instead of twelve Apostles, 's I recall. . . ."

"There you go," Roswell nodded. "So now it's more like 'paranoia detonans.' The man may've stolen my patents, but I still know how to build my own gear. Buckle on that Hypops, move around underground carefree as a gopher in a garden till one day I'll have the criminal bastard right overhead, and—well not to get too specific . . ."

"Kaboom, you might say."

"Oh, *you* might, I'm just another nutty inventor, harmless as your grandma."

Next afternoon the light took its deep yellowish turn, and here came that Thorvald again. Merle was rooting through the wagon looking through some of his old lightning-rod-salesman gear when Roswell showed up and stood gazing with interest. "You ain't one of these Anharmonic Pencil folks?"

"Beats me."

"What are you doin with that contraption?" indicating an arrangement of metal spikes, aimed upward in different directions, converging to a single common point at the bottom, fitted up with wires and connectors.

"Put this up on the barn roof, hook it on to your lightning rod—what in the trade we call an aigrette," said Merle.

"You mean lightning hits it—"

"Damndest thing. Gives off a glow. Lasts awhile. First time you think you're dreaming."

"Geometry professors call that a Pencil. If you ran a transversal plane of some kind across this, so as to cut these spikes into different lengths? Put in insulators, you'd have different currents in the different segments, whose ratios could be harmonic or anharmonic depending—"

"How you moved that plane around. Sure. You make it movable—"

"Tune it basically—" Off they went, forgetting about the imminent cyclone.

Thorvald hovered over them for a moment, as if trying to analyze how murderous it might be feeling today, then, briefly slowing and resuming speed, this being the Tornadic equivalent of a shrug, moved on to more promising prey.

"I want to know light," Roswell was confessing, "I want to reach inside light and find its heart, touch its soul, take some in my hands whatever it turns out to be, and bring it back, like the Gold Rush only more at stake, maybe, 'cause it's easier to go crazy from, there's danger in every direction, deadlier than snakes or fever or claim jumpers—"

"And what steps are you taking," Merle inquired, "to make sure you don't end up wandering around the badlands of our fair republic raving about lost mines and so forth?"

"I'm heading for California," replied Roswell.

"That ought to help some," said Merle.

"I'm serious. It's where the future of light is, in particular the moving pictures. The public loves those movies, can't get enough of 'em, maybe that's another disease of the mind, but as long as nobody finds a cure for it, the Sheriff will have to keep settling for traildust in my case."

"There sure is projectionist work everyplace you look," Merle said, "but the machinery itself, it's dangerous, and somehow, I'm not sure why, but—more complicated than it needs to be."

"Yes, it continues to puzzle me," Roswell agreed, "this irrational worship of the Geneva movement, and the whole idea of a movie projector being built like a clock—as if there could be no other way. Watches and clocks are fine, don't mistake my meaning, but they are a sort of acknowledgment of failure, they're there to glorify and celebrate one particular sort of time, the tickwise passage of time in one direction only and no going back. Only kind of movies we'd ever get to see on a machine like that'd be clock movies, elapsing from the beginning of the reel to the end, one frame at a time.

"One problem the early watchmakers had was that the weight of the moving parts would affect the way the watch ran. Time was vulnerable to the force of gravity. So Breguet came up with the tourbillon, which isolated the balance wheel and escapement off on a little platform of their own, geared to the third wheel, rotating about once a minute, assuming in the course of the day most positions in 3-D space relative to the gravity of the Earth, so the errors would cancel out and make time impervious to gravity. But now suppose you wanted to turn that around."

"Make gravity impervious to time? Why?"

Roswell shrugged. "It's that one-way business again. They're both forces that act in one direction only. Gravity pulls along the third dimension, up to down, time pulls along the fourth, birth to death."

"Rotate something through space-time so it assumes all positions relative to the one-way vector 'time.'"

"There you go."

"Wonder what you'd get."

Out came the patent pencils and, well, talk about being impervious to time—next thing they knew, they had wandered miles up the river and paused by an ancient sycamore. Above them its leaves all abruptly turned the other way, the tree brightening all over, as if another storm was about to break—as if it were a gesture of the tree itself, directed more to the sky and some sky-borne attention than necessarily intended for the diminutive figures beneath, who were now hopping up and down and shouting at each other in a curious technical patois. Anglers abandoned promising riffles to get up or downstream of the disturbance. College girls with their hair in Psyche knots and other swept-up arrangements and long floral dresses of zephyr gingham, lawn, and pongee paused in their strolling to gaze.

Usual thing. The day-by-day politics of this conference would've made an average recital of Balkan history seem straightforward as a joke told in a saloon. Over in the theoreticians' shop, nobody, however wise-looking, was able to avoid the combinations, coups, schisms, betrayals, dissolutions, misread intentions, lost messages, that writhed and crept below the cheery blandness of this midwestern campus. But the mechanicians understood each other. At the end of the summer, it would be these hardheaded tinkers with their lopsidedly-healed fractures, scars, and singed-off eyebrows, chronically short-tempered before the Creation's irreducible cussedness, who'd come out of these time-travelers' clambakes with any practical kind of momentum, and when the professors had all gone back to their bookshelves and protégés and intriguings after this or that Latinate token of prestige, it'd be the engineers who'd figured out how to keep in touch, what telegraphers and motor expressmen to trust, not to mention sheriffs who wouldn't ask too many questions, Italian fireworks artists who'd come in and cover for them when the townsfolk grew suspicious of night horizons, where to find the discontinued part, the exotic ore, the local utility somewhere on Earth able to generate them current with the exact phase or frequency or sometimes simple purity that would meet their increasingly inscrutable needs.

ONE DAY THERE WAS a flurry of rumors that the famous mathematician Hermann Minkowski was coming over from Germany to give a talk on Space and Time. Lecture halls for the event kept being announced and then switched to larger ones, as more and more people heard about it and decided to attend.

Minkowski was a young man with a pointed mustache and curly black hair brushed in a pompadour. He wore a black suit and high collar and pince-nez, and looked like a businessman out for some fun. He gave the lecture in German but wrote down enough equations so people could follow it more or less.

After everybody else had left the hall, Roswell and Merle sat looking at the blackboard Minkowski had used.

"Three times ten to the fifth kilometers," Roswell read, "equals the square root of minus one seconds. That's if you want that other expression over there to be symmetrical in all four dimensions."

"Don't look at me like that," Merle protested, "that's what *he* said, I've got no idea what it means."

"Well, it *looks* like we've got us a very large, say, astronomical distance there, set equal to an imaginary unit of time. I think he called the equation 'pregnant.'"

"Jake with me. He also said 'mystic.'"

They rolled cigarettes and smoked and gazed at the chalked symbols. A student loitered in the back of the room, tossing a wet slate-sponge from hand to hand, waiting to erase the board.

"Notice the way the speed of light kept coming into it?" Roswell said.

"Like being back in Cleveland, all those Æther folks. We were all probably on to somethin then, didn't know it."

"Way I figure, all's we need to do's translate this here into hardware, then solder it all up, and we're in business."

"Or in trouble."

"By the way, who's the practical one here and who's the crazy dreamer, again? I keep forgetting."

Frank came one day back over into west Texas, splashing up droplets out of the muddy river which transmuted briefly to sunlight he could no longer in his heart appreciate much.

He kept to the river up through New Mexico to San Gabriel, picking up the old Spanish Trail, drawn westward, visited each night now by a string of peculiarly clear-edged dreams about Estrella Briggs. Till one day there he was in the McElmo country, and it was almost like emerging from a stupor he had fallen into years back. He was headed for Nochecita, or the spur line of his destiny was. Where else? Like asking a damn avalanche to run uphill.

In Nochecita, maybe owing to the troubles south of the border, he found a hardcase element had moved in. Not dangerous, though definitely, a number of them, illegal—sociable enough, yet not about to suffer fools for any longer than they had to. New buildings had gone up near Stray's old place, so close sometimes that there remained only narrow slipways for the wind to pass, picking up speed, whereupon the pressure decreased, so much that as the unrelenting plateau wind passed through town, the flimsily braced older structure was actually being sucked to one side, then the other, all night long, rocking like a ship, ancient nails creaking, plaster apt to chip away if you looked at it for more than a second, walls of the rooms shedding soiled white flakes, a threat of collapse in some near future. The foundations had gone on crumbling back to pebbles and dust, and rain leaked in everywhere. Little or no heat in the place, floorboards not quite level. And yet the rent here, he heard people complain, kept getting higher each month, newer tenants continued to move in, earning more and eating better, as the place filled up with factory reps, real-estate salesmen, drummers of weaponry and medical supplies, linemen, water and road engineers, none of whom would ever quite meet Frank's eyes, respond when he spoke, or recognize him in any but the most muted and shifty ways. He wondered if he could be his own ghost, and haunting these rooms and corridors, as if the nearly negligible fraction of his life spent here had remained here, somehow still proceeding, just past visibility—Stray, Cooper and Sage, Linnet, Reef as the careless young rounder he'd been, all were just "over there," just like living in the world, changed from whoever they used to be, reluctantly allowing in more and more of the spirit-battering events of everyday, moved on, some of them, into colder places and harder times, bust, adrift, drawn west by those Pacific promises, victims of their own bad judgment . . . but Frank understood he was not to be any part of it.

Sometimes when he asked, one of the newcomers would try to tell him where Stray was, but he couldn't understand them, the words didn't fall into any kind of sense. The town abruptly became an unreadable map to him. Since Mexico he had been sorely conscious of borderlands and lines crossable and forbidden, and the day often as not seemed set to the side of what he thought was his real life.

He kept thinking he saw her, Stray with her hair down and her baby in her arms, out in town running chores or riding away, always away from him, toward the hills. Yet later, say three or four in the afternoon, when everybody but Stray and the little one, or their shadows, would have cleared out—when, alone, he could return to the empty rooms, he knew that before too long, from the other side of whatever it was separating them, he would begin to hear her "getting ready for supper." Frank stood at the flimsy kitchen door, with the papered-over glass, when the light came through, and listened, breathed, waited. He wondered if Stray, over on "her side," alone during the deepening sadness of these daytime hours, might've begun to hear in other parts of the house routine sounds of his own presence—footsteps, water running or draining—as if from some phantom rooms amputated from the rest of the building and occupied, like it or not, by the dead? . . .

Frank couldn't stand it for more than three nights, though by the time he left, it seemed like weeks. On the way out the street door, at the last minute, he ran into Linnet Dawes, who needed a minute or two to remember Frank. She was still a local belle, still teaching school, but had picked up a kind of glaze, as if part-timing now in more adult areas.

"Let me guess who you're looking for," Linnet said, coolly it seemed to Frank.

"Reef."

"Oh. Well your brother, he came by last year sometime, maybe the year before, to pick up Mrs. Traverse"—even Frank could detect some sarcasm—

"and little Jesse, but they didn't stay here more than another night. Thought I heard something about New Mexico, but neither of them was confiding in me, exactly."

"It's strange, I keep thinking I see Estrella here and there around town, just imaginin, I guess. . . ." Oh, was she flashing him a look here. "What? I pronounce somethin wrong?"

"That young lady," shaking her head, "created more damned drama around here. Who needed an opera house when *she* was performing? You start off thinking she's like one of these Oriental wise folks, far above all the pettiness and small potatoes, gazing down on the rest of us—instead, imagine our surprise to find out at last how large-scale of an egotist we've been dealing with, in fact so much of one that nobody ever took all of it in. Big mistake, poor suckers, all of us."

"So is that her I keep seein? Or ain't it—sorry, *isn't* it?"

"You are not that same 'cute mine-school boy I remember, looks like you've been through some educational activities, so maybe I don't have to be too tender about your feelings. Your brother left the country, more to the point he left his wife and child. Estrella's doing a good job with that little Jesse, credit where credit's due, didn't hurt any that her sister and her sister's husband were usually within a day or two's ride of her. It's a small ranch outside Fickle Creek, New Mexico. She's there sometimes."

"For somebody you don't like, you're sure keepin a close eye."

"Just professional reflexes. Your nephew is an engaging little customer, you'll see."

"If I'm down that way."

She nodded, one side of her smile higher than the other. "Sure. Say hello."

HE HIT THE PASS at the summit just about as Saturday night was settling in down in Fickle Creek, you could hear the gunshots and whoop-de-do from up here easy. From the toll station here, through ice-points falling, steeped in a cold, neutral green light far below, he could see a little city laid out around a plaza. Frank took a glass of red whiskey and bought a pocketful of cigars and started down.

He found a ramshackle old hotel a block square, the Hotel Noctámbulo, where insomnia prevailed. In each room, somebody was staying up working at some impossible midnight project—a mad inventor, a gambler with a system, a preacher with an only partly-communicable vision. Doors were left unlocked, strangers acted for the most part like neighbors, everybody free to roam each others' units. No matter how deep in the morning darkness,

Frank found he could always walk in in search of a smoke and conversation. Down in the courtyard, a festive crowd came and went all night. Everybody chiseled smokes.

Strange motorcycles, many of them homemade, went roaring raggedly into and out of town. Cowboy poets might allege how the noise "echoed off the steep mountainside" and on down the valley, but right on the spot, why it was too exotic a sound to carry much of any message, at least for no more than a few, though certain taverns on the way in, and even some going out, of town had already offered hospitality to the bands of riders.

Frank found he couldn't sleep, and headed down to the nearest saloon. Out in front, where once only horses had been tied, now stood Silent Gray Fellows and Indian V-twins, modified expressly for these mountains, with heavy-duty clutches, belts, chains, or gear-boxes. All up and down Main Street in these motor saloons mingled trick-riding artists up from the prairie carnival circuits for a little change of ventilation, and peach-fuzz desperados singing the harmony to Joe Hill's "Pie in the Sky" for ancient flat-out labor nihilists on whose palms the love lines, life lines, girdles of Venus and such had been years overmapped, into jagged white inscriptions no carnival Gypsy would dare to read, by wood fires, rock walls, barbwire unspooling too fast, bayonets in the bullpens of the Coeur d'Alene. . . . Motorized elements of the notorious Four Corners Gang, based up in Cortez, bought double shots of Taos Lightning for earnest hobbyists from as far away as Kansas, detached not all against their wills from some club tour or other, out and up through the night talking clutches and crankcases till the sun was in the window.

A pale individual in a black cape entered silently and sat down at the far end of the bar. As the barkeep set bottle and glass before him, crossing wrists in the usual way so as to put the bottle to the customer's right, this gent suddenly gave out with a blood-freezing scream, shielded his eyes with his cape, and rared back so violently he fell off of the barstool and lay on the floor, kicking up the sawdust.

"What 'n the world?"

"Oh, that's 'at there Zoltan, drives a Werner, climbed every hill over in his native Hungary and now he's off on a world tour lookin for fresh challenges. He's won trophies ain't been named yet, fears no mountain whatever its size, but show him anything looks like a letter *X*, why he goes all like he is there."

"Don't care much for saloon mirrors neither, 's why he sits all the way down to the end like that. . . ."

"Does this happen every time he comes in?" Frank wondered. "Why not just . . . put the bottle down first, then bring the glass, then—"

"Heard that suggestion a number of times, and real obliged, but it ain't exactly Denver here, not much the boys can depend upon for entertainment, and ol' Zolly's turned out to be a real addition. One night to the next, we make do."

Around the middle of the third shift, Frank went for some breakfast at the flapjack emporium up the street, where it didn't take him long to understand that Stray had been *right upstairs all along,* with some motor outlaw whose widely-recognized blue Excelsior was parked outside, and, well, the contentment in her face when she did step back down again into this pocket-size eating house, her bearing, her *hair,* for Lord sakes, was enough to divide a fellow into two, one saying, calmly, would you just look at her, how can any man begrudge and so forth, and the other wounded enough to soak a whole restaurant tablecloth with the snot and tears of it, never mind who was watching. As she glided on down, the attractively costumed waiter girls (more of them, really, than the size of the room and the time of night could quite account for) kept throwing her *certain glances.* . . .

Oh and look now here come lover boy himself, the regionally famous Vang Feeley, looking almost too legendary, it seemed to Frank, to have much of a carnal side left to him—his motoring outfit black, spare, undamageable. He walked without a word right past Frank, whose attitude was not much improved when he realized he'd been gazing, it seemed, for what must already be a long time, at the crotch of Vang's pants, well that general direction. . . . Whoa-oh. Such behavior might lie beneath the notice of Vang himself, but not of these pitiless, amused waitergals crowding the area, their remarks directed more and more, Frank couldn't help imagining, at himself, which by the time this eased off, why Vang had actually been outside for a while, consulting with Zoltan, who had recovered from his fit hours ago, over bike-hardware questions such as the silencer bypass situation, as, given the complexities in Vang's life right then, when the multiple outcomes of the night were apt to narrow to one in only clock-seconds, engine performance could mean everything.

Stray had lingered to finish half a cup of coffee, smiling around lazily at everybody, including Frank, whom she didn't recognize if she saw him at all, and when she was done, she reached to set her cup in with the dishes waiting to be got to, and with one hand loosely in a pocket of her duster, strolled admirably out the door to swing aboard behind and around damned old Vang, in the same motion bringing along and distributing duster and skirts in a routine as elaborate as any curtsey of Grandmother's day, lifting them, in fact, and to the delight of onlookers, high enough so as not to catch fire from the vehicle's exhaust. And joining the line of other well-wishers attentive as any string of train-watching cowboys down to the depot, Frank was out there too, to wave her adios.

When he got back to Denver, it was still Ed Chase's town, and Frank began to fall back into the old habits of squandering time and money, until one night, making his way along Arapahoe somewhere between Tortoni's and Bill Jones's, where he heard he'd been declared an honorary Negro, though this turned out to be somebody's idea of a practical joke, Frank ran into the Reverend Moss Gatlin driving a strange-looking horseless trolley car, with a miniature steeple and working church bells on the back end, and over the front window, where the destination sign usually was, the lighted-up words ANARCHIST HEAVEN. Moss was busy picking up every vagrant, ankle-biter, opium fiend, down-and-outer, brakebeam stiff, in fact any citizen looking even a little helpless—and loading them on board his A.H. Express. Frank must have qualified, because the Rev caught sight of him right away and tipped his hat. "Evenin, Frank," as if they'd only seen each other yesterday. He pulled on a lever and the conveyance slowed enough for Frank to swing aboard.

"Any faces you ever forgot?" Frank marveled.

"Couple wives maybe," said Moss Gatlin. "Now Frank, I never got to tell you how terrible that was about your Pa. You seen much of the subhuman pustules that done it?"

"Workin on it," said Frank, who since the half-second of otherworldliness down in Coahuila had found nobody really to talk to about it.

"Heard a story or two, though I wouldn't say word was around."

"Now you mention it, one or two of the newspaper gang lately have been flashing these funny looks, like they were about to say somethin?"

"Hope you ain't having too many of those second thoughts that stop a fellow just as dead as if it was him down in the sawdust."

"No thoughts," Frank shrugged, "second, third, whatever. It's done, ain't it."

"How'd your Ma take the news?"

"Well."

"Oh come on, you've got to tell Mrs. Webb Traverse. She's the one person on Earth has to hear that, and from you."

"I'm shamed to confess it Rev, but I don't even know where she is these days."

"She's been movin around some, but the latest I heard, she's living in Cripple. And as the Lord would have it, Frank, I'm headed up that direction, so if you want company . . ."

"You're not goin up there in this rig?"

"This? just borrowed it for the evening. Matter of fact—"

A white-haired individual in a buggy, hollering in some agitation, had been chasing them down the street for a while it seemed. "Hammers o' Hell," muttered the Rev, "I knew he'd take it the wrong way."

"That word 'Anarchist' up on the front," Frank now recalled, "did look like somebody'd hand-lettered it in, kind of crudely, hate to say."

"Jephthah runs this Christer road-ranch out on Cherry Creek, and this is how he gathers his flock. I thought he was off tonight, so I—It's all right Jeff!" Slowing down. "Don't shoot!"

"Those souls are mine, Moss."

"Who done all the work? I'll take fifty cents per head."

"De-frocked if I'll let you have any more'n twenty-five."

"Forty," said Moss Gatlin. The passengers gazed on with interest.

"Rev?" said Frank, "about my religious faith here—"

"Can we talk about it later?"

They rode the train up to Divide and changed to the narrow-gauge, and the Rev told stories about Webb, some of which Frank knew, some he'd guessed, a couple that were news to him.

"Sometimes," Frank admitted, "I feel funny about Sloat. It should've been the other one, 'cause Pa was nothin Sloat would've gone out and done on his own."

"Sloat was a traitor to his class, Frank, the worst kind of stoogin for the plutes, and you done us all a favor, maybe Sloat himself more than any. Case you're worryin about him. He won't get into Anarchist Heaven, but wherever he goes it'll be good for his soul."

"Plute Hell?"

"Wouldn't surprise me."

Hauling into Cripple Creek, Frank could see how forlorn and beaten down that recent battleground had become. The owners had sure won. The Union had gone invisible if it was there at all, though to Moss Gatlin it looked like they'd moved on and left a whole population of honorable fighters out of work and free to make what crawling arrangements they had to to get hired again, even for mucker work, or likely just leave for someplace else. Scabs were everyplace, wearing these peculiar South Slavic knitted caps. Camp guards stomping the streets they now owned, picking out foreigners they knew didn't speak English and rousting them, testing the general docility level in town.

"My ministry." He nodded to include somehow the whole off-shift population. "These Austrian boys that look so easy and obligin right now will come back as vengeful ghosts to haunt Colorado someday, because it is a law universal as the law of Gravity and as unforgiving that today's scab is tomorrow's striker. Nothin mystical. Just what happens. You watch and see."

"Where'll you be stayin, Rev?"

"Noplace that won't be different tomorrow night. Simplifies things. For you, now—that house there across the street is said to be pretty good. 'Less you want the National Hotel or something."

"Will I be seeing you?"

"When you need to. Rest of the time I'm invisible. Step careful now, Frank. Remember me to your Ma."

Frank got a room, wandered down to the Old Yellowstone Saloon, started drinking, brought a bottle back to the room, soon became drunk and miserable and fell into a stupor, from which he was roused sometime in the middle of the night by loud screams from the room adjoining.

"Everybody O.K. in here?"

A boy about fifteen years old crouched wide-eyed against the wall. "Sure—just fighting off some bedbugs." He worked his eyebrows energetically and pretended to brandish a horsewhip. "Back! Back, I say!"

Frank took out a tobacco pouch and rolling papers. "You smoke?"

"Havanas, mostly—but I guess I wouldn't mind one of those things you're making there."

They smoked awhile. Julius, which turned out to be the kid's name, was here from New York, part of a song, dance, and comedy act touring the country. When they'd got to Denver, the lead artiste had taken everybody's pay and skipped in the middle of the night. "Landlady down there is friends with Mr. Archer, and so here I am driving his grocery wagon."

"And I guess that team is giving you trouble, huh?"

"Only when I try to sleep." The boy pretended to look around wildly, eyes rolling a mile a minute. "It's the old show-business curse, see. You want work, whatever they ask you, you tell them yes. I was crazy enough to tell Mr. Archer I knew how to drive a wagon. I still don't know how to, and now I'm *really* crazy."

"Horses up here learn the trails pretty good. I bet yours could go over to Victor and back even with nobody driving."

"Swell, that'll save me a lot of work next run."

"Why not see if he'll let you do something else?"

"I need the money. Enough to get back to dear old East Ninety-third anyway."

"Long way from home."

"Far enough. You?"

"Lookin to find my Ma, latest I heard, she's here in Cripple, figured I'd have a look around tomorrow. Or do I mean today."

"What's her name?"

"Mrs. Traverse."

"Mayva? heck she's just a couple blocks from here, runs that ice-cream parlor, Cone Amor, over back of Myers."

"You foolin me? lady about yay high, real nice eyes, smokes a pipe sometimes?"

"Yeah! She comes in the store for rock salt, cooking chocolate, things like that. Best ice-cream sodas this side of the Rockies. Gee. That's your mom, huh? You must've had a great childhood."

"Well. She was always in the kitchen, known for cookin anything, don't surprise me she learned to make ice cream too. All long after my time, o' course."

"Then you got a treat coming, mister."

BEFORE HE EVEN KISSED her hello, she had him cranking the machine. "Cherry apricot, special of the day, sounds peculiar, but the truck shows up from Fruita every other day, and it's pretty much what comes along."

They stepped out a side door into an alleyway, and Mayva took out her corncob pipe and stuffed it with Prince Albert. "Still sayin your prayers, Frankie?"

"Not every night. Not always on my knees."

"Better'n I thought. Course I'm prayin for all of you, all the time."

Kit was over in Germany writing back regular letters. Reef was never much of a writer, but she thought he was over there in Europe too, someplace. Before Lake's name could come up, there was a jingle at the street door and in came a well-to-do matron with a couple of daughters around eight and ten. Mayva put the pipe someplace safe and went to tend to them.

"The children will have their cones, Mrs. Traverse."

"Comin right up, ma'am. Lois, that's a real pretty gingham dress, is that new?"

The girl took the ice-cream cone and devoted her gaze to it.

"And, Poutine, here's yours, special of the day, turns out to be my favorite, too."

The younger sister flashed a quick smile of apology and began to whisper, "We're not supposed to—"

"Poutine." Coins rang on the marble counter. The woman gathered her daughters and swept out, leaving a cloud of crabapple-blossom scent behind.

“ ’Fraid I’ll say some’n un-Republican, I guess.”

“You seein a lot of that, Ma?”

“Enough. Don’t get bent, I don’t.”

“What’s going on?”

“Nothin ’t’ll do you any good to know.”

Groping after the worst it could be, “The owners are paying you off. Widow’s compensation, a monthly check which will make everythin perfectly jake.”

“Been gettin one of those for a while, Frankie.”

“You’re letting those—”

“No lap o’ luxury here, case you missed that.” When she laughed, he saw how a couple of teeth were gone. “Hard times for everbody, you know, even them people too.”

He had a rough idea of the dimensions of insult she must have had to swallow from respectables like the one just out the door, of how many passed-by towns and back ends of mine booms moved indifferently elsewhere she might’ve had to get through, and how many embittered wives there must have been in them so without recourse that they’d had only Mayva to take it out on—

She was looking at him steadily, the old gaze, pure as smoke. “Heard you settled up with that Sloat Fresno.”

“Might’ve known you’d hear somethin. Durndest thing, Ma, the minute I wasn’t lookin for him, there he was.”

“Somethin steerin you, son. Them prayers you don’t always get around to.”

She might’ve been about to ask, “How ’bout the other one?” But disconnected her gaze, went darkly bustling after the cat who was about to fall into the eight-quart freezer again, and Frank guessed she was just as happy not talking about Lake. Any attempt, however gingerly, to bring up the topic would get him queer looks and a grief in Mayva’s face he couldn’t bear to see laid out all in detail.

The one time she did mention Lake was his last night in Cripple Creek. They’d been out at the National Hotel for supper, Mayva was wearing a flower and a hat newer than any Frank had seen on her, and they’d been talking about Webb. “Oh we both thought I was going to save him. I believed that for so long . . . that he wanted me to save him, for don’t women just love *that* eyewash. Chore-runnin angels, ’at’s us—never get tired of it. So the men end up convinced they can get away with anything, is why they ’s always pushin, just to see what it’ll finally take to get us to break. . . .”

“Maybe he really wanted to spare you that chore,” said Frank. “Savin him.”

“He was so damn angry,” Mayva said. “Always somethin.”

"So was everybody else up there," it seemed to Frank.

"You just saw the little stuff. He kept the other away from you kids and pretty much even from me, though we did have our war dances round and round the cookstove every now and then. Tryin to protect us, forgot to protect himself. I thought about it since, some days didn't do much else. He might've wanted to use that anger somehow, aim it where it'd do some good, but sometimes . . ."

"Do you think—"

"What, Frankie?"

They had themselves a good long silent look, not really uncomfortable, just itchy, as if it wouldn't take much to break apart—one of those rare moments when both of them knew they were close to thinking the same thing, that Webb all along really had been that legendary Phantom Dynamiter of the San Juans—that troops of fancy ladies and poker colleagues, invoked to explain his absences over the years, were all fiction, and had best pack up their bright bengalines and taffetas and satchels of cash and pile on the next train out to the Barbary Coast or beyond, for all it mattered. And that in each explosion, regardless of outcome, had spoken the voice Webb could not speak with in the daily world of all whom he wished—wished desperately, it now occurred to Frank—never to harm.

"Ma." He looked at the food on his plate and tried not to let his voice fade in and out too much. "If I keep on with this, if I try to find that Deuce Kindred and settle that up . . . way I did with Sloat . . ."

Mayva smiled grimly. "And what happens if she's there when you find him."

"I mean, it ain't like fixin the porch or somethin—"

"How over does it have to be that we can finally all sleep, well," patting his hand, "I sleep fine, Frankie. Sometimes a little lettuce opium just to get me into it, but don't feel like that you need to give me no happy endings here. Sloat was plenty and I'll always be proud of that."

"Just that when I first heard, I hated her so much—"

"She had at least the spirit to look me in the eye and say she was marryin that little horseapple. I had my chance right there but was too shook to take it I guess, and she was out the door, and now it's long over and done with."

"I'm having some more of this pie," Frank said. "You?"

"Sure thing. You boys were hard work, but that's only hard work. A daughter pretends to be so easy, a little lady, smilin, dancin, all the time she's waitin on that perfect moment that'll hurt the most. And mercy, did it." With a light in her eye now warning Frank it was all she had to say about it, at least to him.

. . .

FRANK TOOK THE NARROW-GAUGE out of Cripple, and it was some time before he noticed he was riding south. Something like a cloak of despair was settling down over his soul, useful, like a duster out on the trail. He still didn't understand how much harder and less inclined to mercy it was making him. He looked around the train car, as if the Rev, out circuit-riding, might be about to show up with some useful thoughts. But either Moss Gatlin wasn't there or he was choosing to stay invisible.

"I had this dream about running away with the carnival," Mayva had told Frank in the lamplight one evening, both just keeping easy company. "Since the summer I was twelve and went to one down in Olathe. They'd set up all their pitches beside the river, and I got to talking somehow to this one fellow who ran that horse-race game they called the Hippodrome, he must have sure had a case or something, kept asking me why didn't I come and work there, said he'd already been to the owner about me, and we could travel together all over the country, maybe the world, he understood my natural gifts and so forth. . . ."

"All the time we were growing up," Frank said, "you wanted to run away and join the carnival?"

"Yes, and there I was with all o' you, right *in* the carnival, and didn't even know it." And he hoped he'd always be able to recall the way she laughed then.

Down they journeyed, out of the mountains, seldom looking back, down through the prairie-smoke of eastern Colorado, onto a low-land that seemed to be awaiting reoccupation by ancient forces of mischief . . . in each face Deuce's criminal palps could sense an imminence almost painful, unremitting, agents of a secret infiltration proceeding before the event.

For a while it seemed the only towns they ever came to rest in were ones that had picked up a bad reputation among those obliged to visit regularly—vendors of farm machinery, saloon musicians, pharmacy drummers with giant sample valises full of nerve tonics and mange pills that would pass for hair restorers. "Oh, *that* place." Down the line and all across the land, you could find these towns it was better to keep clear of, unless you had grown long habituated to a despair that would someday be all defined by just its name, spoken among low-budget travelers in a certain way. There would be no laundries, bathing facilities, or cheap eats anywhere near the station. Well say, welcome to our li'l town, stranger, stayin long? In the train-station toilets, you could always find inscribed the last word in these matters—

Roses is red
Shit is brown
Nothing but assholes
Live in this town.

Each meandering river presented a distinction between the two sides, prosperity or want, upright or immoral, safe as Heaven or doomed as Sodom, sheathed in certainty or exposed in all helplessness to the sky and a tragic destiny.

When Deuce had left this part of the world, just a youth, geography had favored the vectorless. From any patch of these plains, there was more than enough compass for vanishing, roads of flight could just aim off along any heading, into terrain far from mapped even yet, Wild West or decadent East, north to the gold fields, down into Old Mexico, all angles between.

Former bank officers whose sleeping heads were pillowed on satchels of U.S. currency, fifteen-year-old gold prospectors who inside were already old and crazy, with growing into it just a bothersome detail, girls "in trouble" and boys who'd got them there, wives in love with clergymen, clergymen in love with clergymen, horse thieves and stackers of decks—and every last sinful absquatulator among them somebody's child, not so much gone as consciously committing absence, and folded that quick into family legend. "Then that one day they all just showed up again out of the blue, no more'n an hour on the road, he said, he'd met her in a drugstore, just over in Rockford, and before that weekend they were married—" "No, no, that was Crystal's cousin Oneida, string of little ones like elephant babies at the circus—" "No, now I'm sure that one was Myrna—"

The farther into it they moved, the deeper Deuce felt he was descending again into all he had ever wanted to rise above, to those unfairly walked out on as well as those he prayed he'd never see again. It was the light kept reminding him, yellow darkening to red to bitter blackness of the whirlwind brought among the sunlit, wildflowered meadows, thunder that began like the rumbling of sash-weights locked with old death-secrets of some ancient house back behind the sky's neatly carpentered casementing and soon rocking like artillery.

"And back down in slow dumb old 'Egypt,'" his sister Hope would tell Lake over a potato-salad recipe unvaried for generations, popovers and sweet corn and a chicken roasted straight from the yard, "we went on with our days, children of a captivity some escaped as Deuce did, while others of us never will. For there have to be our kind, too."

"Sure," said her husband Levi, as they were having a smoke out back, "but Deuce what'n the hell ever took you out that way?"

"Looked west, saw those mountains . . ."

"Not from no Decatur you didn't."

"Most times it was clouds, thunderclouds, so forth. . . . But sometimes when it was clear."

"Dipping into Mother Kindred's laudanum again, eh—"

"Leave her out of this if you wouldn't mind."

"No offense, just th't people with stories like that tend to end up in California, they're not careful."

"That could happen."

"Let us know."

And thanks and so forth, but they'd sleep in town. It would be impossible for him to sleep in that house, ever again. . . .

FOR A DAY OR TWO after they got married, Deuce had kept repeating to himself, I'm not alone anymore. It became a formula, something to touch to make sure, too hard for him otherwise to believe that she was here, inside the angle of his elbow, far down the line as anybody cared to look legal as you please. Course, there was that old Sloat, and he had to admit, well, maybe he hadn't been all that alone, really. . . . And then the activities among the three of them that followed, and after months more of domestic apprenticeship, the formula he found himself muttering, not always silently, had become, shit and when was I ever *not* alone?

But along with that, as time passed, he had also found himself engaged in pursuit of her forgiveness, as if it were a prize being held carefully as maidenhood—hungering after it the way some drover too long out in the brush might after the unspoiled object of his desire. Deuce, feeling this need, till recently unsuspected, slowly beginning to eat its way into his brain, would find occasion to blunder in small, stupid ways, breaking the Mexican flowerpot, forgetting to fix the roof before the next storm rode in, staying out at night pissing away the rent, just so there'd never be a shortage of things he could beg her forgiveness for.

What he didn't quite see was how little it mattered to her by now. If the marriage was coming more and more to resemble a kitchen-table poker game, why, she valued her forgiveness at not much more than some medium-size chip. She had allowed the immediacy of Webb's death—Webb's life—to pass like smoke into the steadily darkening air between them. From a thousand small tells he had remained too unschooled in deceit to know how to keep from letting slip, Lake in fact already knew, or suspected too much by now not to know. But it would have to be Deuce who turned all the cards face up. And the day, before they knew it, had accelerated upon them, avalanche style.

In her own way of knowing and not knowing, she would say something like, "Your father still kickin, Deuce?"

"Someplace back here. Last I knew." Waited for her to go on with it, but only got the careful face. "And my Ma, she died in that hard freeze in double-ought. Couldn't dig her a grave till spring."

"You miss her?"

"Guess so. Course."

"She ever cry on your account?"

"Cry, not when I was around."

"*Anybody* ever cry for you, Deuce?" Waited for him to shrug, then, "Well I hope you're not countin on much from me, I'm done 'th all my crying. Must've been that my Pa took the last of it, what d'you think? for my tears have all run and the drought has set in. Whatever happens to you, guess I won't be crying. That be all right with you?"

He was giving her this peculiar look.

"What," she said.

"Surprises me is all. Tears and so forth, thought you and him didn't get along."

"Did I tell you that?"

"Well no, not in so many words."

"So you got no idea how I felt and come to that still feel about him."

He understood by then that he'd do better to cut his losses and just dummy up, but he couldn't, something stronger than simple self-interest was pushing him, and he didn't know what it was but it frightened him because he couldn't control it. "You remember what it was like up there. Wasn't just the mountain trails where you 's only a step from the edge. Those Association boys, it ain't like once they hire you on that you have the choice. Wa'n' nothin special about me, just I was there. They would've hired anybody." There. That was way too much.

But how ready did she feel to say, "You could've stood up."

"What's that?"

"Could've been a man instead of crawling like a snake."

Then he might've taken in a short breath but no more. "Yeahp, that's what your Daddy tried, and look what they did to him."

"Excuse me, 'they,' what 'they' was that again, Deuce?"

"What are you tryin to say, Lake?"

"What are you trying not to?"

BEING AFRAID OF GHOSTS, Deuce had been waiting for Webb to find him. In dreams no different from his cursed youth, he left her in the night, went calling into the unmeasured shadows deep inside haunted barns, daring what was there to come out into the open country, which itself had grown malevolent. He waited up into the clockless nights for mountains miles high that only came out at night, waiting to drive an ownerless wagon straight uphill into autumnal graveyard terrain and be found by the man he had killed. Mosquitoes big as farm animals, with eyes as reincarnate and expressive as a dog's, and bodies warm and squeezable as a rabbit's, bumped slowly against him. . . .

Deuce sometimes felt like he had put his head into a very small room, one no bigger, in fact, than human head size, unechoing, close and still. "Well . . . maybe," he could hardly hear his own voice, "I could go out and kill a *whole lot* of other folks? and then I wouldn't feel nearly as bad about just the one. . . ."

As MUST HAPPEN to all badmen early and late, Deuce one day found himself putting on the deputy's star. Back in the mountains, right up till the day the Owners turned and came after him, he had felt not so much working on one side of the Law or the other as protected from the choice itself. Now, on the run, secure only in forward movement, he found the decision so easy that for a minute and a half one sleepless middle of the night he was sure he'd gone crazy.

One day, out in some haze-horizoned piece of grassland, Deuce and Lake noticed unexpectedly up ahead in the green circumference this narrow smoke-colored patch, and feeling peculiarly drawn, decided to have a look. As they rode closer, architectural details emerged from the bunchgrass and the dazzle of sky, and soon they were entering Wall o' Death, Missouri, built around the remains of a carnival, one of many inspired by the old Chicago Fair. The carnival after a while had moved on, leaving ruins to be converted to local uses, structural members from the Ferris wheel having for miles around been long incorporated into fence, bracing, and wagon hitches, chickens sleeping in the old bunkhouse, stars wheeling unread above the roofless fortune-teller's booth. The only structure not fallen all to pieces yet was the Wall of Death itself, a cylindrical wood shell, looking fragile but destined to be last to go, weathered to gray, with ticket booth, stairs winding around, chicken wire that once separated the breathless tip from the spectacle inside.

Visited by motorcycling pilgrims, as if it was a sacred ruin, scene of legendary daredevilry, when viewed from overhead reminding widely-traveled aeronauts of ancient Roman amphitheatres strewn across the old empire, empty ellipses at the hearts of ancient fortress towns, the onset of some suburban fatality in the dwellings presently appearing at human random around it, treeless perimeters becoming shaded boulevards astream with wheelfolk and picnickers, while around the dark corners, under the new viaducts, in the passages greased with night, the gray wall, the Wall of Death, persisted in the silence and forced enigma of structures in their vanishing. . . .

"Maybe there's an employee entrance around back somewhere," Lake offered. They eased their horses to a fence-riding gait.

And, well it was peculiar, but the folks inside did turn out to be expecting them, it seemed—they appeared bearing casseroles, pies, chickens plucked and otherwise, selected members of the Methodist choir lined up and sang "For It Is Thou, Lord," the Sheriff, Eugene Boilster, who'd been standing at the front sill of his office all morning scanning the grass-scape, likely the sky as well, stomped forward with both hands out in welcome.

"Glad you didn't get lost. The last two, or do I mean three, got lost."

Deuce and Lake understood inside of the next breath that they were being taken for some deputy peace officer and his missus supposed to be showing up today, who as it turned out never would, and maybe they exchanged a quick look. "Snug little community," Deuce said. "Forget to adjust for windage, you could miss her clean, never know it."

"Artillery fancier, eh?"

"Last resort if reason and persuasion don't work, of course, sir."

"You'll see."

BUT IT WAS NOT the minutiae of the day's offenses, the penises caught experimentally in laundry wringers, repeated thefts of the only automobile in town, willing victims of the formulations of Happy Jack La Foam, the local pharmacist, who'd have to be rescued from up telegraph poles and belfries, from temperance meetings or the unsympathetic weaponry of spouses in pursuit, not the fabric of the municipal day Deuce was really there to attend, he discovered, so much as to be on call around the clock for the more abstract emergency, the prophecy which loomed out beyond the sensible horizon of daybook fact, the unspoken-of thing they had hired him to deal with, which he came to fear could only be regarded—like you'd need a telescope to look at another planet—by way of the police ticker or printing telegraph in the back of the Sheriff's station. A specialist's apparatus, the next step on into the twentieth century from wanted men's faces on penny postals.

Out from under whose glass dome one day came ratcheting unwelcome news, from Mexico by way of Eagle Pass. Reporting officer C. Marín, responding to a report of firearms being discharged within town limits, found in the cantina Flor de Coahuila a northamerican male about twenty-five years of age, identified as (converging letter by letter as Deuce watched to the inescapable name) Sloat Eddie Fresno, dead of gunshot wounds inflicted according to witnesses by another northamerican male, no good description available, who then left the premises and had not been seen since.

Deuce's eyes were filling unexpectedly with salt water, some outrush of emotion trapped prickling just behind his nose, as he imagined himself on out to some picturesquely windswept grave, head bowed, hat off, "Big slow lummox, couldn't get out of your own way, they were bound to find you, shouldn't even been you, you were just along for the job, coverin your pardner's back, maybe deserving of hard labor but not to be shot down in some cantina surrounded by language you never learned much more of than *señorita chinga chinga* and *más cerveza* maybe, you old fool—damn, Sloat, what'd you think you were doing?" While creeping into him came the rectal message that somebody might be more than willing to do him up too, along with the quickening heartbeat of hatred, a co-conscious witness of all their past together violated and death's sovereign bobwire run straight through. Deuce needed to be the fuck out of this office, out the door saddled up and raising dust, finding and gut-shooting the sumbitch killed his runninmate, again and again, till there's more shit on the walls than blood. . . . Lake arrived in the middle of these reflections with a couple armloads of laundry full of sunlight and smelling like the first day of the world, the frail suggestion that none of this needed to come to pass. . . . "What is it now, my own guardian of the Law?"

"Old Sloat." He was shaking. "'Member him? my partner? Yours too 's I recall? Shot dead down the border. Maybe even by one of your got-damn brothers."

"Oh, Deuce, I'm sorry." Thought to put a hand on his shoulder, thought better. She knew she shouldn't but guessed she felt more happy than otherwise to hear the news. Against the unwavering serpent glare, she tried to be reasonable. "He had a way of trouble finding him, you know, it could be nothing at all to do with—"

"You just keep bein faithful to that Anarchist shithouse you grew up in," and that was it, he was out the door, no courtly kiss, touch of the hat, back-soon-my-darlin, only the surprisingly careful latchclick behind him.

The days would then proceed to drag their sorry carcasses down the trail of Time without word one from Deuce. Long as she didn't brood too much about what it was he thought he was out there doing, it was almost a relief to have him gone.

Later, alone, gliding into sleep, she was shocked awake by a familiar, keen, anal memory and swore for a minute, sitting bolt upright with her nightdress up around her hips, that Sloat had returned from the dead for the sole purpose of fucking her in his all-time favorite style. It was not the fondest way she might have remembered the passing of a loved—well, now and then desired—one, but again, it was Sloat who had come to her from out of the howling leagues of emptiness, that penis, as she had suspected for some time, harder when it wanted to be than the most obstructive barrier death could come up with.

Tace Boilster dropped over, mostly to sit and smoke cigarettes without having to go through a whole Bible lesson about it at home.

"I can guess where he's heading for," said Lake, "is Texas. Might not be where he is, of course."

"Somebody looking for him, Lake?"

"Wouldn't surprise me, but this time he thinks it's him out looking."

"Oh, my. Then I take it this time ain't the first?"

"He'll be back. Either way, he finds another offender to kill or doesn't, it's not fixing to be no church supper around this place."

"He better behave himself if I'm here," Tace said. But she had taken off her Sheriff's-wife face like a deputy might unpin a star. "Maybe you'd like to tell me a little what's goin on?"

"See one those readymades?"

"Sure thing. Have one with you."

"There's one already in your mouth, Tace."

"Uh-huh."

Lake lit up and told Tace the whole sad story. Not so comfortable with it that her voice didn't drop sometimes to a whisper and even a choked failure of voice altogether. Seeing at some point Tace's expression grow alerted and careful through the veils of smoke, "Guess somethin's really wrong with me, isn't it."

"What? you married somebody shot your Pa." She shrugged and opened her eyes wide, as if in puzzled inquiry.

"You see a lot of that around here?"

Tace allowed herself a short sigh through her nose. "One way or another I get to see it all. Young beaus, irate fathers, nothin new. You two maybe pushed a little further, 's all."

"That man kicked me out of the house. Just left me—I could have ended up in some crib in Mexico or dead, for all he cared. Should've been me that killed him."

"And it turned out to be Deuce. And then later on you two met up. Well? Ain't exactly like you planned it out together, is it?"

"Still bad enough. Pa's dead and gone and I haven't stopped hating him. What kind of unnatural daughter's that make me? A girl is supposed to love her father."

"Sure," said Tace, "in those Elsie Dinsmore stories or someplace. We all grew up on that stuff, and it poisoned our souls." She put her cigarette in her mouth and reached a hand gravely to rest on Lake's. "Tell me somethin. Did he ever try to . . ."

"What? Oh—"

"Have his way?"

"Webb? Webb could be mean as they come, but he wasn't stupid."

"Mine did."

"Your Pa? He—"

"Him, my brother Roy Mickey into the bargain." With a peculiar smile, squinting through the smoke, as if daring Lake to say something.

"Tace. Oh, my dear."

"Years ago, not the end of the world. And I was worried more for Ma, tell the truth. Didn't last long anyway, they all got to bickerin amongst themselves, before I knew it Eugene come along and I was clear of that house, praise the Lord, no worse for wear."

"Never would've happened in our family."

"Well don't sound so forlorn, you didn't miss much."

SHE DREAMED ABOUT MAYVA.

Squirrel on a fence post. "What are you looking at, bright eyes?" The squirrel, standing up straight, angled its head, didn't move. "Sure, easy for you, but wait 'll the weather turns." All the while getting the wash spread out on the fence, being careful not to dislodge the squirrel. "Crazy in the head, every one of you." That was always Mayva, who would get into these exchanges with animals, nearly conversations. A squirrel or a bird would sit for what seemed hours, while she talked to them, pausing now and then in case they had something to say in reply, which sometimes it appeared they did. Lake swore she'd heard creatures replying in their own languages and her mother nodding attentively, as if she understood.

"What'd that hawk have to say, Ma?"

"Range fire over by Salida. Some of her relations got scattered. She's just naturally concerned, 's all."

"And then later on," the girl's eyes as wide open as blue columbines in July, "somebody came in, said there really was a fire over there."

"Sure, Lake," the boys holding out their fingers Mexican style as if to say *atole con el dedo,* "but Ma could've heard that anywhere. She knows you believe everythin she says."

"No way she could've heard anything before the mail wagon came in." They'd go off laughing.

"She was only a dynamiter's daughter," Mayva was singing in this dream, "but caps went off, where'er she passed by. . . ."

"You do your best," she cried out at her mother, "to wreck us, and then you run away, out of reach, behind the wall of death."

"You want to come out after us, out there beside the old dark river, find us, read us off your list of complaints? Somebody sooner or later'll be happy enough to he'p you do that. Swear, Lake, you've gone sour in your old age."

Lake woke up, but so slowly it seemed for a while that Mayva was really there in the room.

"YOU COULD WAIT for him to come back," Tace advised. "It happens sometimes. What you might not want to count on is ever gettin back to that old domestic bliss."

"You mean put up with the son of a bitch again, maybe again and again, 'cause I don't have that much choice."

"And Eugene is gettin grumpy with all the extra chores."

"Oh that case I guess I better pray extra hard."

And then one day the wind was howling up in the telegraph wires and Deuce came riding back into Wall o' Death. Hadn't come close—no surprise—to finding out who got Sloat. Only out there a week or ten days, but it looked like a year's worth of weariness, head all hanging down, sort of a pale indoor look to him.

It didn't end anything, of course. Sloat would start coming in the window, off the empty night plain, going "Whoo-oo-oo, you little piss ant, how come you never saw it? Was I always supposed to be the one protectin you?" To which Deuce, if he was not by then too paralyzed in fear, would reply, "But, well but, I thought that was the deal, I mean you always said—" and so it would go back and forth till Lake struggled up into yet another day's first drift of unpromising light, muttering, "Person can't get *no* damned sleep around here. . . ."

"ALWAYS THOUGHT there was this great secret. The way they looked at each other when they said certain things in a certain way. . . . And now I'm being let in on it at last."

"Oh, child," said Tace Boilster. "You're sure of that, now."

Lake gazed at the Sheriff's wife. At their feet Boilster babies crawled and stumbled, dropped, picked up and threw things down again.

"Like that all you have to do," Tace went on, "is let go, let it bear you up and carry you, and everything's so clear because you're not fighting back anymore, the clouds of anger are out of your face, you see further and clearer than you ever thought you could. . . ."

"Yes."

"Inspect your shoes, Mrs. Kindred, it's gettin deep around here."

"He can change, Tace."

"And you're just the angel o' damn mercy's going to change him?"

"I know I can."

"Sure." She nodded, beaming, till she thought the girl was lulled, then snapped, "Into what?"

Lake only angled her head a little downward, pretending meekness though keeping her eyes onto Tace's.

"Let me guess. Into somebody *so much better*'n he is right now, that you won't have to think no more about what he did. Save yourself all that trouble."

"Why not?" Lake whispered. "Anythin wrong with wanting that?"

"Wanting? Well, wanting . . . if it was me, see, I'd be lookin to change him into somethin *worse.* Weaker, slower, bad enough judgment that I could just do the deed on him whenever I felt like?"

Lake shook her head. "Tsk. Law-enforcement wife, too. Well sure, don't think I haven't thought about it—just go find his pistol some night, put it down onto that snorin little head," clapping her hands once, "amen. Even with the blood and so forth to be cleaned up after and your Mr. B. to worry about, sure—but I don't, do I?"

Tace thought she might have caught a look, a shadow moving across the younger woman's face so fast, proceeding from some deeper source of sorrow that later she couldn't swear that she even saw it. And Lake meanwhile, perhaps after all a touch too cheerfully, was going on, "But supposing . . . what he did . . . was a kind of mistake, you know, just a mistake, Tace, didn't you ever make one of them?"

"Hires on to kill your Pa, some mistake."

Yes, one of the big questions, which just went on sitting there, and she wouldn't ask, and Deuce sure wouldn't bring it up—namely, how much did Deuce know before he went and did it? Had he signed up to just be their all-purpose gun? or to go after Webb in particular?

"You think he's so *good,*" Tace went on, "just a boy that's lost, that it? and you can bring him back, all you need to do's love him enough, love your enemy into some kind of redeemin grace for the both of you? Applesauce, young lady."

"Tace, you'd ever been up in those damn mountains you'd know, it was just so hard, never let up, you worked at all, that's who you worked for. Them—that was it. They'd tell you to trust their judgment, and what choice did you have? Even if it was something bad, folks took what they could. Deuce was all ready to do it, I wasn't there and neither were you, maybe he thought he saw Pa with somethin in his hand, those were desperate days, miners gettin shot all the time, if you were legally deputized, they tended to let you off."

Now, it's not as if this was a courtroom and Tace was the judge. No reason Lake should be trying this hard to convince anybody. Was Webb heeled that day? was it conceivable Webb went for Deuce first and Deuce only acted in self-defense?

Knowing Webb was gone was hard enough, but worse was this queer coldness, this lost trail back to what should have been unsoiled memories, to her whole childhood brought so brutally to an end, meantime having to live with somebody she had come to hate everything about, except when he put his hands onto her, and then. Oh, then.

And I can never leave him, she wrote in the little school copybook she used for a diary, no matter what he does to me, I have to stay, it's part of the deal. Can't run . . . sometimes like I'm trying to wake up and can't . . . and I already knew didn't I, long before we married, who he was, what it was he did, and yet I went ahead and married him. I didn't know, but I knew . . . maybe from the first time I caught him looking at me, there was that bright-eyed excuse for a smile, like we were well-known figures of public life and each of us was supposed to know who the other was, and not lift a finger, either one, even with all we knew. Some deal we made. With the empty spaces always in between how I ought to be feeling and what I was really up to, it was sneaking away to Silverton all over again, and nobody saw it, they thought it was just grieving for Pa or trying to keep busy, they told me time would pass and I'd get back to daily life . . . but I think I'm dreaming and can't wake up. . . .

Wish it could be Denver . . . be a saloon girl. . . . She crossed out the words, but went on daydreaming about it, whole dime novels full of lurid goings-on. Chandeliers and Champagne. Men whose faces were never too clear. Pain that felt just so good, imagined in detail. Girl intimates who lay around in fancy linen sharing laudanum on long slow winter nights. A loneliness nothing could touch. An embrace of distant, empty rooms, kept clean by the wind forever blowing through. A high-mountain sunlit spareness, a house framed in absolute rectilinear purity, dry, bleached, silent but for the wind. And her young face, remembered by a hundred no-goods all through the San Juans for its clean delicacy, unshielded before the days and what they were doing to it.

ONCE IT WAS CLEAR to him that she knew, and to her that he knew she knew and so forth, once they found themselves passed somehow through that fatal gate they'd both been so afraid of, opened as if by invisible guardians and shut again behind them, and she went on as always and didn't give any sign of fixing to shoot him or anything like that, Deuce must have felt easier about surrendering his hardcase ways in favor of helpless, unmanly pleading, couldn't stop offering his explanations, not that she was that interested, less so as time went on. "They told me he was a Union dynamiter. Was I supposed to ask him if they were right? They said they had proof, a whole secret life nobody ever saw. Course I believed it. Anarchist, no conscience at all. Women, children, innocent mine workers, didn't matter. They said—"

"I can't help you out, Deuce, I never knew that much of what he was up to. Talk to a lawyer, why don't you." Was this her own voice?

But even in her silences, he thought he heard something. "It was to save lives, that's how they saw it. I was only their instrument—"

"Oh—there's 'at whinin again."

"Lake . . . please forgive me. . . ." Down on his knees again with another display of the eyeball hydraulics, which was not as becoming in a man, she had discovered, as tales of romance in the ladies' magazines would lead you to think. Fact there were times it could be downright repellent.

"Maybe my mind was wandering those fateful moments, but I never heard that Swede say love honor and *forgive.* Get up, Deuce, it ain't working." She had chores to do anyhow—there was no way around that.

But the *really* strange thing was, that with all there was to send them off down forever separate tracks, he continued to desire her, as much—no, more than ever now—and she finally started paying attention as she felt it turning to power for her, flowing out of the invisible unknowability of men like bank interest into some account in her name she hadn't known was there, growing with the days—she learned how easily she could ignore his heated eyes across the room, slide away from his hands, choose her own moments and try not to smirk too much at how grateful he was, and not be assaulted for any of it, nor even screamed at. What was not so clear was if and when he'd wake from this obviously short-term opium dream, or how far it might be safe to push before he did wake up, maybe even too quickly for her to get to a safe distance away . . . skillful stepping, at least a sensitive touch, would be needed—she could not afford to relax, when any unguarded word, eye-movement, routine flash of jealousy, might trip the latch and send him back to good old Deuce, blind crazy out of the chute and looking for blood at long last.

AFTER WHAT HAD added up to years of dodging, false uttering, and hard riding to escape it, Deuce was relentlessly being delivered into his own life, and what a dismal prospect it was turning out to be.

Out there doing what each day demanded, he understood on one of them whose date he didn't record that the Furies were no longer in pursuit, Utahan or any other kind, that some statute of limitations had run and he was "free," though it felt like anything but.

Him and Lake, they had both wanted children, but as the days lengthened out, wheeled, the seasons repeated, and no little ones appeared, they came to fear that this was because of what lay poisonously between them, and that unless they could do something about it, no new life would ever be possible. They went out in the middle of the night to a distant riverfront hovel, Lake down on the dirt floor while a Sioux shaman with a look of incurable melancholy sang, shaking articles of feather and bone above her belly, Deuce forcing himself to sit clenched in a multiple humiliation—another man, an Indian, his own failure. They spent unreasonable sums on patent medicines that ranged from ineffective to dangerous, sending Lake more than once to Happy Jack La Foam for an antidote. They went to herbalists, homeopathists, and magnetists, most of whom ended up recommending prayer, which different sorts of Christer in the neighborhood were always happy to offer advice about the exact wording of. Their local reputation solidified, after a while the whispers stopped, and there was only small-town condescension to worry about.

"You can't let these other women get you down, child," said Tace. "You don't owe them one damn thing, sure 's hell not children. You live your life and hope they'll be busy enough with theirs not to be putting in so much with yours."

"But—"

"Oh, I know, sure—" she made a long arm and swept up little Chloe, who was just about to topple off the porch into the petunia patch. Held her up and pretended to inspect her, like a drummer with a sample. "They do have their appeal, can't deny that. And the Lord in his mysterious ways means for some of us to see them through at least till they can start in with families of their own, of course. But that's only for some of us, Lake. Others have other chores down here. Hell, I wanted to rob trains when I was a girl—more than wanted, I knew it was my destiny. Me and Phoebe Sloper, we'd go up back of that grade just over the river, put these big bandannas on our faces, and spend the day figuring how we'd do the deed. We had a sworn pact."

"What happened?"

"What do you think happened?"

So it started as no more than one of those basic little chats about the married universe that couples were known to get into when they found a minute, which was seldom, and the subject this one almost immediately converged to for Lake and Deuce was having—actually, not having—children. In the past they had blamed it on outside crises or stresses—a gang committing depredations in the next county, accusations of malfeasance from Kansas City–style reform groups—when it did get more personal, and pleasantries like your dick is too short or maybe you picked up some bug when you were out trampin around were exchanged, the conferences always adjourned in somebody's tears, with a resolution to keep on trying.

Tonight she was careless enough to ask why he was so desperate about the whole thing, and he was unwise enough to blurt, "I just feel like it's somethin maybe that we owe him."

For a second she couldn't believe he meant Webb. "My father."

"That if we—"

"A baby. *We* owe Webb Traverse, deceased, a baby. You think one'll be enough, or should *we* throw a couple-three more in the deal just to make sure?"

Deuce slowly grew wary. "I only meant—"

"Just marrying me didn't work, did it? Thought you'd give up that wonderful hired-killer freedom, and that would make all of it right. Now you've gone truly insane. You have drifted clear around that last bend of the river if you think having a child cancels out a murder. There's a price to pay for certain, but more likely it's no babies. Ever."

"Ain't just me." Something in his voice now warning her to step careful.

She didn't feel careful. "How's that, Deuce?"

"Them last days at the Torpedo, is all he talked about was you. He could've took all the rest leavin, but you, really, that was the last kick in the teeth. He was a dead carcass with a jackin hammer in his hand—the high-gradin, me and Sloat, just details, makin it official. You better think about that fore you start in on me."

She snorted, pretending to smile as if he was trying to embarrass her in public. "Easy story to tell, years later, no witnesses."

"He cried a lot, more'n you ever saw him do. Kept sayin 'Child of the Storm.' Guess it was somethin about you, you ever hear him say that? 'Child of the Storm.'" Not just the phrase but an uncanny impersonation of Webb's voice.

Deuce being a little customer and not expecting the blow, no time to brace for it, in fact she knocked him over with it. And seeing 's how that was so clean and easy, figured she ought to get in a few more before he could get up to start hitting her back. Deuce kept his guns at the office, and Lake, like most women who lived in town, was limited for purposes of self-defense to items available in the home, such as the rolling pin, soup ladle, stove-lid lifter, and of course the very popular frying pan, which had figured in more than one assault complaint in Wall o' Death County over the year preceding. Judges usually recognized a difference between a shorter spider type of handle and a longer fry-pan handle as indicating the degree of serious intent. Tonight Lake figured a twelve-inch Acme cast-iron fry pan would just do the trick, with both hands taking it off the hook on the kitchen wall and preparing to let Deuce have it. "Oh shit, Lake, no," his voice too slow for anything that might happen now. He had hit his head on something. He was a sitting duck.

She would wonder later if that was why she hesitated and looked around for some more merciful weapon. About the time Deuce was getting to his feet and looking over at the carving knife with some interest, Lake had about decided on the stove shovel. It worked pretty good, and it helped that by this time she had settled into a cooled and efficient rage. Back to horizontal went Deuce.

Tace and Eugene showed up at the door, the Sheriff still half asleep and preoccupied with his galluses, Tace grim-lidded and carrying a Greener shotgun, loaded and unbroken.

"This has got to stop," she began, then saw it was Deuce down bleeding all over the patterned oilcloth. "Oh, my." She lit up a cigarette and started smoking in front of her husband, who pretended not to notice.

Later, after the boys had gone off in search of medicinal whiskey, Lake remarked, "Well at least it wasn't fatal."

"Fatal? What's wrong with fatal? Only reason it wasn't is you girlied out with that tin shovel. Has the little bastard redeemed himself? When was that?"

Tace stalked back and forth.

"You could make a case," she said after a while, not at all reluctant but as if allowing herself a long-withheld treat, "that you are every bit as bad as your li'l wedded husband there. That you've both been all along in some unholy cahoots, your own job being to do what you have to to clean up after him and see he gets and stays clear of anybody's payback, including your own brothers."

Lake didn't answer, and after that nobody talked to anybody for a while unless they had to.

Yes well perhaps you did, but I saw the left one, didn't I," declared Neville.

"I'm sure you did," smirked Nigel. "Now, was that stage left or audience left?"

Nigel looked down. "This one." He pointed at one nipple. "Correct?"

The two youngsters were in the Great Court baths, discussing Miss Halfcourt, their desolate sighs merging into the hiss of the steam.

"Now it's rumored she's taken up with some sort of embryo Apostlet named Cyprian Latewood."

"As in Latewood's Patent Wallpapers? Surely not."

"The very feckless scion."

"These Mahommedan lasses do love a sod," Neville was of the opinion. "It's that harem mentality, being sweet on the eunuchs sort of thing. As long as it's always someone that impossible."

"But surely she's not . . . Mahommedan?" protested Nigel.

"Well some sort of Eastern wog Nigel."

"Excuse me?"

"Oh dear chap," Neville oozed, "you still can't be taking it personally."

"Better than taking it publicly, i'n't it." Referring to Neville's own extended period of tearful soliloquy at The German Sea as well as licensed premises further afield, after Yashmeen had returned a sub-Clerkenwell trinket in actually quite horrible taste, obtained by the temporarily deranged youngster at great effort and expense.

They lounged, steamed as puddings, each regarding the other's penis with lethargic annoyance. Their discussion of Miss Halfcourt's own nude person was owing to a stealthy excursion the night before. At the disconsolate hour when no one is awake but gyps and working mathematicians, there had arisen a tradition among the bolder girls of creeping to the river, up above Byron's Pool, the brighter the moon the bolder the company, to bathe. Word somehow always got to a group of lads, who were apt to show up as much from curiosity as from lust. And there in the moonglow would be Yashmeen, among her handmaidens. Eliciting a range of remarks, from catchphrases of the day such as "Div!" "Whizzo!" or "*That* is that of which *I* speak!" to all-night rhapsodizing in the rooms of friends, or sonnets written down later when the madness had receded enough to allow at least the grasping of a pen, or simply an abrupt passage into paralyzed dummyishness upon having spied her, or someone who might be she, in Cloisters Court.

In so much public attention, the two N's—ostensibly at King's reading philosophy and classics, now given the additional remit to keep an eye on Yashmeen, not only for the T.W.I.T. but for certain Desks in Queen Anne's Gate as well—found peculiar inconvenience. At Newnham and Girton, one expected Wrangleresses on the legendary order of Phillippa Fawcett, even romances with one's tutors à la Grace Chisholm and Will Young, which with luck might develop into some married collaboration—but certainly not this nautch-girl extravagance of looks and self-possession that Yashmeen presented. This was shocking the bourgeoisie, not to mention the mathematical persuasion, out of all known scale. And now there was this Latewood person, his family only a generation on from socio-acrobatic aggrandizement, himself assumed to be a sod and, less explicably, the object of Yashmeen's interest.

"Discovered the most frightfully promising recipe for *opium beer* the other day Nigel. One ferments opium with brewer's yeast, quite as if it were malt or barley or something. Adding enough sugar of course."

"I say. Sounds ever so degenerate, Neville."

"Actually it is, Nigel, having been invented by the duc de Richelieu himself."

"Not the Spanish-fly bloke."

"The same."

Which was enough to rouse them from their watery lassitude and return to the important educational task of obtaining enough drugs to get them through term.

"LINE AND STAFF," Cyprian Latewood recalled having heard his father instructing the children, "headquarters and field commands, and the enemy everywhere you can think of."

"Are we at war, Father?"

"Indeed."

"Are you a general?"

"More like a colonel. Yes, for the moment, at least, all quite regimental."

"Have you uniforms, you and your men?"

"Come down to the City someday, and you shall see our uniforms."

"And the enemy—"

"The enemy, sad to say, is too often found wearing the same uniform as we."

"So that you can't always tell—"

"You can't *ever* tell. One of many cruel aspects of a cruel world, but better you have it now, from me, than have to learn it through some possibly damaging experience."

"And you meekly accepted all that, of course," nodded an annoyed though sympathetic Reginald "Ratty" McHugh, fifteen years or so later.

"I did," supposed Cyprian, "and I didn't. What I was left with was the distinct sense of one more flag it was now possible to dishonor."

The boys were lounging about Ratty's rooms drinking ale, smoking Balkan Sobranies, and trying without notable success to mope themselves back into the lilies-and-lassitude humor of the '90s.

When, with the ineluctability of certain mathematical convergences, the topic of Yashmeen Halfcourt came up, everyone had something to say, until Cyprian blurted, "I think I'm in love with her."

"As gently as I can, Latewood . . . You. Sodding. *Idiot.* She, prefers, her, own, sex."

"Gosh, then I *know* I'm in love with her."

"How pathetically desperate, Cyps."

"When did I ever have a choice? There just have to be fellows like us, that's all, the old table d'hôte wouldn't be complete without us."

"Not an easy path, my son. 'Limited' scarcely begins to describe the degree of success one might expect with the type of woman—"

"Yes, well, 'the type,' that's just it, if it were only 'the type,' why, I'd be out there taking my chances, wouldn't I, be the pickings ever so slim. And feeling perhaps not quite as disgruntled as I do."

"So then it's old Yashmeen—"

"It's Miss Halfcourt, in particular."

"But Latewood, you're a sod. Aren't you. Unless you've been only pretending all this time, the way one must around this place?"

"Of course of course, but I'm also in . . . *in love,*" as if this were a foreign idiom he had to keep looking up in a phrase book, "with her. Do I contradict myself? Very well, I contradict myself."

"And all very jolly too, if one happens to be divine Walt, whom the world allows a bit more in the way of antinomy, I shouldn't wonder, than depressingly prosaic you. How exactly would you plan, let's say physically, to express your desire? Unless—oh, dear—you seek, somehow, to pass, perhaps, as one of her little Girtonian admirers, some swooning xanthocroid in a cricketing frock?"

"Confiding the deepest secrets of my heart to you, Capsheaf, and what do I get in return but a damned full-bore viva."

"Oh now see what we've done to him. You may use my handkerchief, if—"

"Perhaps not after what you've been using it for, Capsheaf, thanks."

"There's a good fellow, remember it could always be worse, you might have ended up like old Crayke, rather more fond than has proved wise, of, ehrm, that is . . ." Attempting to slide toward the egress.

"Fond of . . . ?"

"Well I'd assumed you knew, everyone else does. Here—spot of audit, perhaps—"

"Capsheaf?"

A sigh. "Shetland . . . I say how does one . . . well, actually, Shetland ponies. *D'accord?* now you're all up to date."

"Crayke and . . ."

"Oh, and female as well, so it seems."

"Hasn't the breed a certain . . . reputation for viciousness?"

"Yes well you'd be bitter too wouldn't you," put in Ratty McHugh. "Dreaming of attention from some Arab or Thoroughbred, and getting old Crayke instead? Really."

"He's still . . . here at Cambridge?"

"Retired up north, actually, he and his companion, to a quite pleasant little croft, been in the family apparently for centuries, up on Mainland, near Mavis Grind . . . both of them written up, with some regularity, in the orthopædic journals . . . spending hugely on solicitors of course—even assuming they could find a registrar who'd even think about legitimizing—well I mean, it wouldn't be cheap, would it."

"He—wants to . . . *marry* . . ."

"It might seem odd I suppose . . . unless of course one has actually met Dymphna, and understands how charming, at least most of the time, she can—"

"Excuse me, Capsheaf, but will this be at all typical of the sympathy I can expect around here?"

"Quite so. Listen to me, Cyps. In the brief time she's been here, this Halfcourt person has broken simply decks full of hearts. Your best course, in the brief time *you'll* be here, is to find a wholesome pursuit that will require all your attention, such as, oh, say, academic study? One might start by looking into Thucydides, actually."

"No use. Something in there is sure to remind me of Her."

Capsheaf threw up his hands and left the rooms, muttering, "And look here I say McHugh, why are you wearing that beastly shade of heliotrope?"

MEANWHILE . . .

"Ewh I say gehls, look it's *Peeng*-kyeah!"

"Halleewh, *Peeng*-kyeah!"

"See heah, we're off to an alfresceehwh in Honeys'ckle Walk, wewhn't you join us!"

"Yes, yes do, Peeng-kyeah!"

"Tell us, Peengkyeh—are you a nice mathematician?"

"Or a naughty one?"

Lorelei, Noellyn, and Faun—all blonde, of course, blondeness at Newnham and Girton having at that era grown beyond simple matters of pigment into a fully equipped *idéologie*. Hatlessness was likewise important, as was being photographed, as often as possible and by any and all processes that might offer themselves. "You are the girls of High Albedo," they were instructed, "the girls of silver darkness on the negative, golden brightness in the print. . . ."

The blondeness of this place was threatening to drive Yashmeen mental. An admirer of poetical inclination called her "the dark rock on our northern shore, against whose sleek indifference a turbulence of girls, blonde girls in their white veils, dash themselves without hope, again and again."

"Am I so—"

"Can't think of the word, Pinky? Try 'cruel.'"

"Try 'self-involved.'"

"Try '*sans merci.*'"

"Try everyone's patience," muttered Neville and Nigel, who, not exactly out spying, happened to overhear the exchange.

CYPRIAN WAS CAPTIVATED by eyes, but only by those that looked away, with either indifference or active distaste. It was not enough for her to return his gaze. She must then direct her own to other matters. It sent him into a swoon. It got him through that day and part of the next sometimes. Whatever she felt, it was not fascination, but presently they would find themselves chatting, usually while walking from one University obligation to another.

"I say, but really, Pinky—"

"Can't you even see how thoroughly I dislike that name? I shall begin to think you are another of these silly girls."

The look he turned his face to her with then might have been one of hopefulness too imperfectly concealed. She did not laugh, at least—though she could, it would seem to Cyprian later, have managed a smile less, somehow, bleak.

"You burn incense at the wrong altar," she whispered, aware of the effect her voice, when whispering, had on him. "Idiots, all of you."

He would not have believed that any girl's voice, a voice alone, saying anything, could produce an erection. Yet there it was, incontestably. "*Oh* dear . . ." But she had turned and vanished toward the Girton Gatehouse, and he was left with an inelastic embarrassment which showed little sign of resolving itself. Not even conjugating Greek verbs to himself in obscure gnomic tenses, effective in other circs, seemed to work.

"WHAT. HE DOESN'T DANCE?"

"Not a step."

"Dump him," advised Lorelei, Noellyn, and Faun in unison.

"I honestly can't imagine what Pinky sees in him," protested Faun, "can you, Lorelei?"

"'If she's content with a vegetable love . . .'" trilled Lorelei with a pretty shrug.

"It would depend upon which vegetable," supposed Noellyn, the thoughtful one.

"Oh, old Cyps is all right," demurred Yashmeen.

"For a pasty-faced sodomite with no control over his public impulses, you mean," frowned Faun.

"He carries a parasol," added Lorelei.

"And the unspeakable business with the Rugby blue in hall."

"But he makes me laugh."

"Yes they *are* good for that," conceded serious Noellyn, "though one does hear, more often than one would care to, this 'he makes me laugh' defense. There being laughter, that is, and laughter."

"And if laughing's what you fancy . . ." Lorelei held out one of the bottles of Mâconnais they had brought.

"And yet," said Yashmeen, "there isn't one of us, not even you, Noellyn, with that enchanting nose always in a book, who wouldn't go chasing after . . . I don't know, George Grossmith, if he tipped us the merest wink."

"Hmm. Junior or Senior?"

"And let's not forget that jolly Weedon," Lorelei pretended to sigh.

CYPRIAN MADE Professor Renfrew's acquaintance by way of Ratty McHugh. "Another of those envenomed lives," Ratty had concluded, "all the desire to work international mischief, and none of the resources, and therefore, within the ancient walls of this tiny place, dangerous to an alarming degree."

Renfrew in his all-seeing way understood immediately how it was with Cyprian and Yashmeen, and duly filed a summary in the running accumulation of dossiers he kept on everyone who had ever crossed his path, including waiters, window-cleaners, cricket umpires, up through F.O. eminences and even heads of state—though these mostly were represented by distracted handshakes on reception lines, nevertheless to be entered as "Reluctant to look directly at anyone in formal situations," or "Small hands, some evidence of early trauma, cp. Wilhelm II file." The data by now filled several rooms he was obliged to rent for the purpose, as well as odd cabinets, closets, and steamer trunks, and in private he called it his "Map of the World." Its blank spaces produced in him that refined horror any sensitive geographer might be forgiven, as well as hopes that enough intrepid young explorers would go out at his bidding and gather enough information to reduce the staring white patch of the Unrecorded to something he could tolerate.

Ratty, for some reason, was one of Renfrew's current favorites, and they even went now and then together to Newmarket during the racing season.

"And I thought I was obsessed," Cyprian would tease when Ratty was discovered, contrary to his louche reputation, burrowed in some weighty volume of government reports or, with the help of the eight volumes of Morse and Vassilev's Bulgarian-English Dictionary, attempting to master the intricacies of East Rumelian land-tenure since the Treaty of Berlin, particularly the impact of communal farming on the ancient *zadruga* tradition.

"Only because it's been part of a pattern," Ratty would begin to explain himself, "ever since the old Turkish *tchifliks* were broken up you know, and especially in view of the newly-emerging trend towards mobility in this system of *gradinarski druzhini*—" until noting the look on Cyprian's face, "nor do I find much problem in throwing this volume at you, Latewood, as, given your gossamer nature, it should cause no damage to either missile or target."

Palms up, all innocence, "I only wish sometimes *my* professors were that demanding, it would keep me out of no end of trouble."

"We are not all of us Renfrew's creatures, you know."

"Why does he look at Yashmeen like that?"

"Like what? Ordinary sexual interest, I expect, not everyone in this institution has to be a sod, excuse me, your feelings, I meant pouffe of course."

"No, no, it's something else."

Indeed it was. Ratty already knew in a general way about Renfrew's "Map of the World," but saw no point in sharing this with Latewood, who at this stage of things was hopelessly immune to the appeal of information and its uses. Ratty was keeping no running accounts on her himself, being more of an English Rose person, he supposed, but from what claptrap, street-sweepings, and failed canards came his way, Miss Halfcourt had *connections to the eastward,* a phrase Renfrew was habituated to and a guarantee that he would feel some hopeful curiosity.

THE TERMS WENT GLIDING, Lent and Easter, into the Long Vacation. Yashmeen returned to her tiny garret room at Chunxton Crescent and immediately noticed, if not exactly a divergence between the T.W.I.T. and herself, at least a growing impatience with what their "protection" by now had come to mean—an unrelenting surveillance, not limited to the Colonial Office and the Queen Anne's Gate brigade but including the less-visible attentions of the Okhrana, Ballhausplatz, and Wilhelmstraße, requiring periodic visits to Whitehall to enact the same weary and fruitless exercises before underlings often enough bedazzled but unable, sometimes, even to locate the proper dossier. Lew Basnight was about, but the doings of the Icosadyad made him unpredictable as a social companion, leaving little but lengthy, idiot-infested summer soirées. Against these, like a shoot in a garden, from some invisible bulb or seed far below, green, astonishing, emerged this all-but-erotic fascination with the thoughts of former Göttingen eminence G. F. B. Riemann. She secluded herself in the upper room with a number of mathematics texts and began, like so many of that era, a journey into the dodgy terrain of Riemann's Zeta function and his famous conjecture—almost casually thrown into an 1859 paper on the number of primes less than a given size—that all its nontrivial zeroes had a real part equal to one half.

Neville and Nigel spent the summer developing their own hypothesis that members of the Chinese race without exception could be depended upon for access to opium products. "Just wait for a Chinaman to show up," as Nigel explained, "and sooner or later he'll lead you to a 'joint,' and Bob's your uncle." They found themselves in Limehouse so often that eventually they took rooms there.

Cyprian was received warily back into the Knightsbridge domicile, if not the embrace, of his family. He had been introduced when a youth to sodomitical activities by an uncle with whom he journeyed to Paris to sell wallpaper, and to celebrate landing a major account one day with the Hôtel Alsace, over on the Left Bank between rue Jacob and the river, Uncle Griswold had brought the boy to an all-male house of ill-fame. "Like a duck to water," reported Griswold to Cyprian's father, whose disappointment was directed not at his brother but at Cyprian. "It was a test of character," he informed his son. "You failed. Perhaps Cambridge is the place for you after all."

Though Cyprian had a vague idea of Yashmeen's address, he did not call that summer. After a short while, to everyone's mutual relief, he took the boat-train for the Continent, ending up in Berlin for several weeks remarkable for their excess.

IN THE BRISKNESS of autumn again, everyone reconnected. New colors of clothing had become fashionable, notably Coronation Red. Privileged misses appeared with their hair cut in fringes like factory girls. The cricket talk was all of Ranji and C. B. Fry, and of course the Australian season lately under way. Engineering students met in New Court at high noon for mock duels to see who could draw and calculate fastest on the Tavernier-Gravet slide rules it was à la mode that season to pack around in leather scabbards that fastened to one's belt. New Court in those days was still a resort of the unruly, and interest in calculation soon deferred to drinking beer, as much of it and as quickly as possible.

Cyprian, while rejecting his family's High Church faith, strangely had begun—especially when the Mags and Nuncs and Matins responsories could be heard from services at Trinity or King's—to glimpse that, precisely because of its impossibilities, the disarray of self-important careerists and hierarchy-obsessed functionaries, the yawning and fidgeting town-lad choristers and narcotic sermonizing—it was possible to hope, not so much despite as paradoxically because of this very snarled web of human flaw, for the emergence of the incommensurable mystery, the dense, unknowable Christ, bearing the secret of how once on a hilltop that was not Zion, he had conquered death. Cyprian stood in the evenings, at the Compline hour, just outside the light cast from the chapel windows, and wondered what was happening to his skepticism, which was seldom being addressed these days except by such truly horrible specimens as the Te Deum in Commemoration of the Khaki Election by Filtham, which—although in the hymn-writing trade botching a Te Deum is thought to be next to impossible, the psalmodic formulæ being well established, even unto what notes to end on—nonetheless, from its stultifying length, in arguable violation of any number of child-labor statutes, as well as a relentless chromaticism that might have made even Richard Strauss uneasy, too "modern" to have retained any power to penetrate and sacredly stun, it was already known among schoolchild choristers from Staindrop to St. Paul's as "Filtham's Tedium."

Meanwhile Yashmeen was finding Girton increasingly tiresome, the epidemic idiocy, the impossible dress regulations, not to mention the food, unimproved by the saturated blonde light that descended into Hall through the high arch of overhead panes, bathing the nested tables and the linen and chattering girls. She took refuge more and more in the Zeta-function problem, to which she found herself adverting even as the classmate whose gaze during the day she had met and held came tiptoeing in after curfew, slipping naked into Yashmeen's own narrow bed, even in that rare and wordless moment, she was not quite able to ignore the question, almost as if he were whispering to her, of why Riemann had simply asserted the figure of one-half at the outset instead of deriving it later. . . . "One would of course like to have a rigorous proof of this," he wrote, "but I have put aside the search . . . after some fleeting vain attempts because it is not necessary for the immediate objective of my investigation."

But didn't that then imply . . . the tantalizing possibility was just out of reach . . .

. . . and suppose that at Göttingen, somewhere among his papers, in some as-yet-uncatalogued memorandum to himself, he had actually been unable *not* to go back to it, haunted as anyone since, back to the maddeningly simple series he had found in Gauss and expanded to take account of the whole "imaginary" mirror-world which even Ramanujan here at Trinity had ignored until Hardy pointed it out to him—revisited, in some way *relighted the scene,* making it possible to prove the conjecture as rigorously as anyone might wish . . .

"I say Pinks, you are *here* aren't you?"

"And where are you, saucy one, not down where you ought to be it seems, we must sort that out, mustn't we . . ." Taking the girl by her blonde hair, rather rudely, and in a single elegant movement lifting her own nightdress and straddling the impertinent little face. . . .

"So it's off to the land of lederhosen, is it," said Cyprian with as little peevishness as possible. Whatever was allowed between them by now did not include the display of hurt feelings.

"Shabby of me obviously, but I didn't really know myself until—"

"Good Lord, you're not apologizing. Are you quite well?"

"Cyprian, it's nothing I expected. We are sent here, most of us, aren't we really, to stay out of the way, not be a bother—the books, the tutoring, the learning, it's all incidental. For something to actually . . . light up, it's . . . no one would believe me, if I . . . oh, one or two boys in Hardy's classes, but certainly no one back at Chunxton Crescent. Hardy knows about zeroes of the ζ-function in a general way but isn't quite insane enough about it, whereas Hilbert thinks of nothing else, and he's at Göttingen, it's that obsessiveness I need, so Göttingen it is."

"Something . . . mathematical," he blinked. She began to glare but then saw what he was about. "I knew I'd regret it someday. Never able to do more than work out the cricket averages, you know. . . ."

"You think I'm a lunatic."

"Why should it matter to you anymore what . . . what I think?" Oh Cyprian, he immediately slapped himself mentally, no please, not now.

She was patient today. "What you think of me, Cyprian? It has been my stage-lighting—threatening sometimes to burn me away—illuminating me into some *beau-idéal*. . . . Who would not wish to become, even for a moment, that brighter creature . . . even if her fate be ashes?" She put her hand on his, and he felt just below his ears and down his neck a rapid fine shiver he could not control.

"Of course." He found a cigarette and lit up, belatedly offering her one, which she took and said she'd keep for later. "There's little future for you in simply hanging about here being adored. I know nothing about Riemann, but I do at least understand obsessiveness. Don't I." And for all that he still would not take his eyes from the long, compelling curve of her bared neck. She could not deny him this, it was unmistakably desire—though of rather a specialized sort, he shouldn't wonder.

IT WOULD HAVE BEEN too much to expect Professor Renfrew to stay clear of his propensity to meddle—the minute he learned of Yashmeen's impending departure for Göttingen, he began a campaign of inducement if not outright seduction—there were times she could not be sure.

"Not an assassination scheme," the Grand Cohen assured her on one of her many weekend recursions down the Great Eastern to Chunxton Crescent to consult. "That could mean his own destruction as well. More likely he wishes you to work some severe mischief upon the mental well-being of his opposite number, Werfner. This is a professorial fantasy dating back at least to the days of Weierstrass and Sofia Kovalevskaia, when it entered the folklore of academic endeavor. The years have not redeemed its root premise, which remains despicable as ever."

She frowned.

"Well you are presentable, there's no avoiding that. When you transmigrate into your next body, you might consider something a bit less eye-catching. Some member of the plant kingdom is often a safe bet."

"You want me to try and be reborn as a vegetable?"

"Nothing in Pythagorean doctrine that forbids it."

"You are a great comfort, Grand Cohen."

"I suppose I only mean, be cautious. Though desperately carnal themselves, those two, yet their allegiance is not to the given world."

"Of the flesh but not the world? How peculiar. How can that be? It sounds like maths, only more practical somehow."

"This came for you, by the way." He handed her a package which appeared to have undergone some wrathful treatment by the post office. She unknotted a length of string and tore away already tattered wrapping paper to reveal an inexpensively bound folio volume with a four-color chromolithograph on its cover of a young woman in the sort of provocative pose observed on postcards from the seaside, her finger held to her plump and shining lips.

"'Snazzbury's Silent Frock,'" Yashmeen read aloud. "'Operating on the principle of wave interference, sound cancelling sound, the act of walking being basically a *periodic phenomenon,* and the characteristic "rustling" of an ordinary frock an easily computed complication of the underlying *ambulational frequency*. . . . It was discovered only recently in the scientific laboratory of Dr. Snazzbury of Oxford University, that each individual toilette might be *tuned to itself* through certain structural adjustments in the tailoring—'"

"It materialized in the dining-hall," shrugged the Cohen, "or it was crudely made to appear as if it had. Renfrew's doing. Rancid mockery written all over it."

"There's a note. 'Every girl must have one. You never know when there'll be need. Your appointment has been arranged. Bring your charming friends.' An address and a date and time." She passed him the slip of paper.

"It could be dangerous."

But Yashmeen was interested in the general problem. "We assume the noiseless feature would only make sense indoors, but is it for stealth, meditation, means to an end, end in itself—under what circs should a woman wish to avoid the rustling of a dress? Why not simply wear trousers and a shirt?"

"When she must also appear plausibly feminine in public," supposed the Grand Cohen, "whilst engaged, in private, upon some clandestine assignment."

"Espionage."

"He must know you'll tell us everything."

"Will I?"

"Miss Halfcourt, are you attempting to flirt with me? Desist. Grand Cohens are flirt-proof. Part of the Oath. I admit I'm curious, as no doubt are you. My advice is to go in for a fitting and have a look round, if possible. Share what you wish."

IT WAS A BIT MORE SINISTER than that, actually. Those whose job it was to keep track of any recent invention with any weapons potential, however remote, and to find connections, if any, to military and political events in Europe, observed the traffic in Silent Frocks, which had picked up in recent days, with due alarm, drawing up lengthy reports, bringing in everything from Balkan troop movements to the price of diamonds in Belgium.

"Yes very nice indeed, we'll take a hundred of 'em."

Pause. "That would require a sum in advance. You gentlemen are . . . that is . . ." His gaze arrested by the enormous sheaf of banknotes the emissary had produced from a dark leather case embossed with an appropriate Seal.

"Will this be all right?"

And when the personages had quite left the premises,

"A hundred women on the move, all silent? For how long? Allow me to register a certain skepticism. Green, white, and mauve stripes, I expect."

"No, these aren't suffragettes. They want black crepon and a lining of Italian-cloth. We've no idea, we're only the agents in this."

Nonetheless, their voices did shake just perceptibly with gynecophobia, or the fear of women, of silent women, in these absolutely silent black gowns, advancing along corridors which seemed to recede behind them without limit, perhaps also fear of these unechoing corridors themselves, especially under certain conditions of low light . . . with no least fragment of music in the distance, without the comforts of commentary, their hands unoccupied with parasols or fans, lamps or weaponry . . . should one wait, withdraw, turn in panic and run? What clandestine purpose? More unsettling, how much official support?

YASHMEEN, LORELEI, NOELLYN, AND FAUN, down for a day's truancy in London with the Snazzbury fittings for an excuse, had been summoned to an atelier located in a dismal industrial building, closer perhaps to Charing Cross Road than to Regent Street, around a corner forever in the shadows of taller structures surrounding it. The sign, in modern lettering recalling the entrances to the Paris Métro, read L'ARIMEAUX ET QUEURLIS, TAILLEURS POUR DAMES.

"Here are the basic models. . . . Mademoiselles? If you please." Down a kind of helical ramp—the exact geometry was difficult to read in the artful framework of shadow it seemed to be part of—came gliding a line of young women in black, so silently that even their careful breathing might be heard, hatless, unrouged, hair swept up tightly and pinned so close to the head that they could be ambiguous boys, eyes enormous and enigmatic, lips set in what our University misses recognized as *cruel smiles* not without their element of the erotic.

"I say," murmured Lorelei, shivering a little, "I rather fancy that one."

"The costume or the girl?" inquired Noellyn.

"Can't say much for any of them," sniffed Faun.

"Oh Faun you are such a judgmental person. And that one, there coming along just behind, has been casting you ever such incendiary glances, hadn't you noticed?"

Yes and later in the fitting rooms—it turned out these haughty mannequins were employed also as fitters for the establishment. Yashmeen, Faun, Noellyn, and Lorelei, in their stays and stockings and underlinen, found themselves at the mercy of the Silent-Frocked corps, who crept up on them with measuring tapes and strange oversize calipers and commenced without preamble to take the most intimate sorts of measurements. Protests were useless. "Excuse me, I say I *do* know my measurements, and my hips are certainly not as enormous as what you're writing down there, even if it is in centimeters. . . ." "Oh please, why is it necessary to measure along the insides of my limbs, when surely the outsides would do as well . . . and, and now you're tickling, well not tickling perhaps but . . . hmm . . ." But their tormentrices carried on in determined silence, exchanging significant looks with one another and now and then finding eye-contact with the girls, which often provoked blushes and discomfiture, though it might be difficult for an accidental observer—or say a clandestine one—to judge the level of innocence in the room.

It seemed to Yashmeen that the secret of the Snazzbury frock lay *in the lining,* the precise, as one would say, microscopic fine-structure of the twilling, which after inspection seemed far from uniform in the way it skipped over threads, but rather varied, point to point, over the given surface—an extended matrix, each of its entries a coefficient describing what was being done upon the loom . . . these thoughts had come to preoccupy her so thoroughly that it was with a bewilderment comparable to awakening from sleep to find herself and her friends abruptly at the top of the enormous Earl's Court Wheel, three hundred feet above London, in a compartment the size of a metropolitan bus, packed in with thirty or forty other passengers, who appeared to be British holidaygoers, all busily eating sausage rolls, whelks, and pork pies by the hamperful.

"We're not moving," Faun muttered after a while.

"A full revolution takes twenty minutes," advised Yashmeen. "So that each car may have its pause at the top."

"Yes, but our car has already been here for five minutes at least—"

"It got stuck once for four hours," announced a person of distinctly suburban aspect. "For their inconvenience my uncle and aunt, who were courting at the time, each got a five-pound note, just like in the song—so, having between them a tidy fortune, they popped into the first magistrate they could find, and did the deed. Put the money into Chinese Turkestan railway shares and never looked back."

"Care for a nice bit of jellied eel?" one of the funseekers now wobbling a portion of the open-air snack favorite quite close to Noellyn's face.

"I think not," she said, about to add, "are you insane?" before recalling where they were, and how soon they were likely to be back on terra firma.

"Look, there's West Ham!"

"There's the Park, and Upton Lane!"

"There's a number of lads all in claret and blue!"

"Kicking something back and forth!"

The world, since the Chicago Fair of 1893, had undergone a sudden craze for vertical rotation on the grand scale. The cycle, Yashmeen, speculated, might only seem reversible, for once to the top and down again, one would be changed "forever." Wouldn't one. She drifted thence into issues of modular arithmetic, and its relation to the Riemann problem, and eventually to the beginnings of a roulette system which would someday see her past landlords and sommeliers and other kinds of lupine liminality, and become the wonder and despair of casino managers across the Continent.

THE GROUP THAT GATHERED at Liverpool Street Station to see her off included Cyprian, Lorelei, Noellyn, and Faun, a group of smitten young men, none of whom anyone seemed to know, and the toxically obtrusive Professor Renfrew, who presented her with a bouquet of hydrangeas. There were telegrams, including one from Hardy, whimsical to the point of unreadability, though when she was alone, she tucked it into a safe place among her luggage. The hydrangeas she threw over the side.

She would take the 8:40 boat-train, arriving at Parkeston Quay at Harwich around 10:10, and thence by steamer across the black and turbulent German Sea, waking at each great wavethump, intercepting in nameless oneiric crosstalk the fragmentary dreams of others, losing her own, forgetting all of it in the first merciless, cold striations of the dawn, as the boat raised the Hook of Holland.

"I say Cyprian you're looking a bit green!"

"Not to mention a number of *spots*."

"I believe I shall give him a squeeze just to see if he's sound," and a number of similar vegetable jokes, Cyprian thus providing Lorelei, Noellyn, and Faun a useful distraction from their own melancholy, otherwise likely, one gathered, to be insupportable. But in the score of departure, as if in obedience to some inflexible dynamic tradition, at some point a silence had to fall.

Cyprian waited then for the terrible onset, the intestinal certainty that he would never see her again. He would then hold off the woeful relapse long enough to get back to his rooms and surrender to tears, and this would go on indefinitely, if not forever, boring everyone within several miles' radius, squads of gyps wringing out mop after mop sort of thing—but though he waited, through that night, then the day (as her train crossed canals, passing wooded hillsides and the madhouse at Osnabrück, then at Hannover a change of trains for Göttingen), then another night and day—waited long after she had left Cambridge, in fact, but no such attack of sadness occurred, and presently he understood that some perverse variety of Fate, already familiar to him, which did not promise but rather withheld, was offering him the assurance that none of "this"—whatever it was supposed to be—was quite done with yet.

The tall black hull rose above them like a monument to the perils of the sea, no obvious connection to the waves of gaiety washing beneath it. Emptied hacks lined up four or five deep on the pier, the drivers in their shiny black plug hats waiting for the crowd to finish waving bon voyage and to turn one by one their faces inland once again, landward to the day they had taken this brief hour from.

"Only going on the road, Kate, back before you know it."

"The latest is that your old pal R. Wilshire Vibe was kind enough to set me up with an audition, and I went, and now I just had a callback, so maybe—"

"Don't say it! What horrible news!"

Katie flushed a little. "Well, that old R.W., he's not so bad. . . ."

"Katie McDivott. Shocking what's happenin to our youth ain't it—" But the ship's horn let loose with a bone-deep bellow that stopped all the pre-departure chatter on the pier.

KATIE STAYED until the liner had backed, turned, begun to dwindle into the complications of the harbor. She imagined hours among giant manned buoys, official boats, mid-river inspection stations. Her parents had sailed out of Cobh like everybody else, but she'd been born later, and had never been to sea. If they had been sailing into the future, toward some unknowable form of the afterlife, what was this journey of Dally's the other way? A kind of release from death and judgment back into childhood? She twirled her parasol in thought. A hack driver or two cast an appreciative eye her way.

. . .

IT WASN'T REALLY till Erlys and Dally got well out onto the ocean that either felt permitted, as if by the non-human vastness they had entered, either to speak or to listen. They walked together slowly round the promenade deck, arm in arm, nodding to passengers now and then whose plumed hats were agitated in the ocean breeze, avoiding stewards with laden trays. . . . The smokestacks leaned upward into the wind, the antenna wires sang. . . .

"I know it must've come as a shock."

"Well, yes and no. Maybe not so much."

"Merle is still the same person, you know."

"Yehp. Course that always was a mixed blessing."

"Now, Dahlia—"

"And you, you sound just like him."

Her mother was quiet for a moment. "You never know what's going to happen. Walking back down Euclid from the cemetery with a couple dollars to my name, here came that Merle in some crazy old wagon, asked if I wanted a ride. Like he'd been waiting up that particular side street just for me to come by."

"You're partial to women in mourning?" Erlys couldn't help wondering out loud then.

"It's almost dark and you're on foot. Was all I meant."

You could smell crude oil in the air. The first wheelfolk of summer, in bright sweaters and caps and striped socks, went whirring gaily in battalion strength along the great viaduct on tandem bicycles, which seemed to be a city craze that year. Bicycle bells going nonstop, the massed choruses of them, in all sorts of ragged harmonies, loud as church bells on Sunday though maybe with a finer texture. Roughnecks went in and out of saloon doors and sometimes windows. Elms cast deep shade over yards and streets, forests of elms back when there were still elms in Cleveland, making visible the flow of the breezes, iron railings surrounding the villas of the well-off, roadside ditches full of white clover, a sunset that began early and stayed late, growing to a splendor that had her and Merle gazing at it in disbelief, and then at each other.

"Will you just look at that!" She trailed a black crepe sleeve across the west. "Like those sunsets when I was a kid."

"I remember. Volcano blew up, out there in the East Indies someplace, dust and ashes stayed aloft, all the colors changed, went on for years."

"That Krakatoa," she nodded, as if it were some creature in a child's story.

"This ship's cook I run with briefly, Shorty, he was there—well, a couple hundred miles downwind, not that it mattered, said it was like the end of the world."

"I thought sunsets were just always supposed to look like that. Every kid I knew. We all believed it for a while till they started getting back to ordinary again, then we figured it was our fault, something to do with growing up, maybe everything else was supposed to fade down that way, too . . . by the time Bert asked me to marry him I wasn't all that surprised nor disappointed to find how little I cared one way or the other. Guess that's no way to be talking about the deceased, is it."

"But you're still just a kid."

"Better get some new 'specs' there, old-timer."

"Oh, feel as old as you like, o' course." The minute she'd settled into the seat next to him, her billowing widow's rig had got redisposed to reveal her neatly gravid waistline, at which, now, he nodded. "How soon is she due?"

"Around the first of the year maybe. Who said it's a girl?"

"Let's see your hand." She held out her hand, palm upward. "Yehp. Girl all right. Palm down, see, it's a boy."

"Gypsy talk. Should've known just from the looks of this wagon here."

"Oh, we'll see. Put a little money on it if you like."

"You planning to be around that long?"

Which is how it got arranged, faster than either of them really noticed at the time. He'd never asked her what she was doing alone on foot at so awkward an hour, but she got around to telling him all the same—the faro debts, the laudanum, the laudanum with whiskey chasers, bad loans and worse creditors, Bert's family the Snidells of Prospect Avenue, the sisters in particular, who hated the air she breathed, a list of small-town miseries magnified up to Cleveland scale that Merle must've run into once or twice in his rounds over the years but considerately sat and let her go over in detail, till she was calm enough not to take what he offered the wrong way.

"It ain't a Euclid Avenue mansion, you may've noticed that already, but it's warm and solid built, there's a leaf-spring suspension of my own design that you'd think you were riding on a cloud."

"Sure, well being an angel I'm used to that." But the brightest part of that luridly exploding childhood sky was now right behind her face, and some of her hair was loose, and she could detect in his gaze enough of what he must be seeing, and they both fell silent.

He was renting some space over on the West Side. He heated them up a kettle of soup on a little oil stove that burned overrun from down at the Standard kerosene works. After supper they sat and looked across the Flats and watched the river reflecting the lights of steamboat traffic and gas lamps and foundry fires for miles up the twists and bends of the Cuyahoga. "It's like looking down into the sky," she said, drowsy with the long day.

"Best you get some shut-eye," said Merle, "you and your friend there."

He was right about that wagon. She recalled later sleeping there better than she ever had before, maybe since. The weather was still merciful enough that Merle could sleep outside, in a bedroll under a waterproof up on sticks, though some nights he went into town to raise some species of hell she didn't inquire into, and he didn't come back till well after sunup . . . as fall started to creep in, they headed south, on down through Kentucky and into Tennessee, keeping ahead of the changing year, staying in towns she'd never heard of, always with somebody he knew, some brother craftsman to steer him to where there was work, which might be just about anything from running trolley cable to putting in a well, and soon as she got comfortable with the likelihood that even in hard times there would somehow be work, she could sit more quietly, just let her worries slide away somewhere else, pay full attention to this baby on the way, understanding one day so clearly, "That of course it would be not just 'a girl' but you, Dally, I dreamed about you, night after night, I dreamed your little face, your exact face, and when you were out in the world at last, I sure did know you, you were the baby of those dreams. . . ."

With exaggerated patience, after a moment of thought, "Yehp but then the next part is, first chance you get, you just—"

"No. No, Dally, I was going to come back and get you. I thought I'd have time, but it seemed like Merle didn't wait, just took off with you, no word of where to."

"All his fault, huh."

"No, Luca was dragging his feet too . . . kept saying, 'Yes, we could do that,' not 'We will' but—"

"Oh, so it was all *his* fault."

A narrow smile and headshake. "No mercy, no mercy, not this one."

The girl beamed at her falsely, but feeling no more malicious than that, allowing Erlys do the work of reckoning up what her child could still not forgive.

"I won't try to fool you. Luca Zombini when he came along was the first real passion of my life—how was I going to say no to that? With Merle, yes, moments of desire had ambushed us, even though he was, to be fair about it, what you'd call reluctant to press his case on a pregnant young widow, not so much out of courtliness as past experience—more or less bitter would be my guess."

"So you and Luca went wild the minute you laid eyes on each other."

"Still do, for that matter—"

"What. You two—"

"Hmmm, hmmm, hmmm," Erlys, with a disarming deep gaze, sang in a descending minor triad more or less.

"And little babies tend to put the kibosh on that sort of thing, I'll bet."

"Except that, as we began to find out all too soon, it didn't. And I was missing you more and more with the years slipping by one by one, those brothers and sisters you should've had all around you, and I was so frightened—"

"What of?"

"You, Dahlia. I couldn't have borne it if—"

"Please. What was I gonna do, pull out a pistol?"

"Oh, my baby." Dally was not ready for the choked-up treble she heard then, and what it seemed to betray—better late than never, Dally supposed—of self-reproach, maybe even sorrow. "You know you can have anything from me you want, I'm in no position—"

"I know. But Merle told me I couldn't take advantage. Is why I was never fixin to do more than drop in, say hello, be on my way again."

"Sure. Get me back for leaving you the way I did. Oh, Dally."

The girl shrugged, head angled downward, hair brushing forward along her cheeks. "Turned out to be all different anyhow."

"Worse than you thought."

"You know, I was expecting . . . some kind of a Svengali? customer in a cape, with you all sap-headed under his hypnotic spell and—"

"Luca?" Dally had known her mother to chuckle, but not to make a spectacle of herself. Passersby actually turned and promenaded backward for a while just to take it in. When Erlys could catch her breath, "Now I'm embarrassing you, Dally."

"All's I was gonna say is how strange it is how much he keeps reminding me of Pa. Of Merle."

"You can say 'Pa.'" Still a-blush and her eyes all lit up. "Maybe all I am's just some old Glamorous Assistant—you think?—always cursed to be drifting into the arms of one magician or another?"

It was drawing on to dinnertime. Detachments of dining-room staff came hurrying from the ship's greenhouse with bushels of carnations, tea roses, and cosmos. Stewards crept along the decks striking miniature gongs with velvet-padded hammers. Cooking odors began to find their way out the galley ventilators. Mother and daughter stood by the aft rail, arms round each other's waist. "Not a bad sunset there," Erlys said.

"Pretty fair. Maybe another volcano went off someplace."

Before dinner, as Dally was helping her with her hair, Erlys happened casually to inquire, "How about that young man who keeps looking at you in the dining salon?"

"When was that?"

"Miss Innocent Lamb."

"How would I know? You sure it isn't Bria he's gogglin at?"

"Don't you want to find out?"

"Why? A week on this scow, then it's all over."

"One way to figure, I suppose."

Dally pretended fascination with the steel edge of the horizon. Wouldn't you know it, of course her mother had tumbled right away. How could she have forgotten him? When was she supposed to start forgetting him? Trick questions, because she might as well've been back in R. Wilshire Vibe's ballroom and having that first momentous glance.

Erlys said, "He's a Yale man. Going over to Germany to study mathematics."

"Say, just my type."

"He thinks you're snooting him."

"Oh them Elis, they're fine ones to talk, they *invented* snooting—wait, wait, how do you know what he—Mamma? Have you been *discussing* me? With some . . ."

"Eli."

"Just starting to think I could trust you, too."

This had to be more than intent to tease. Didn't it? Erlys bent a beady eye upon the girl, wondering.

The first-class dining saloon was full of palm trees, ferns, flowering quince. Cut-glass chandeliers. A twenty-piece orchestra played operetta songs. Each water glass was carefully tuned to a 440 A, Champagne glasses an octave higher. The orchestra, when tuning up, by tradition encouraged guests to strike the edges of their empty glasses, so that just before mealtimes a pleasant glittery chiming filled the space and scattered out into the passageways.

FOURTH CLASS was separated from the weather decks by only the flimsiest of glass-and-sashwork partitions, a space long and narrow as a passenger coach in a train, rows and rows of bench seats and racks overhead for luggage. There were stewards just like in the other classes, who brought blankets with *Stupendica* insignia woven into them, Triestine coffee in mugs, newspapers in several languages, Viennese pastry, ice bags for hungover heads. A whole collection of American students bound for study in Europe were traveling in fourth class, gathering regularly in the saloon to smoke cigarettes and insult each other, and Kit found himself preferring the environment here over his palatial accommodations a couple-three decks up and forward of the stacks.

About the only other mathematician was Root Tubsmith, who was headed for the University of Berlin to study with Fuchs, Schwarz, and the legendary Frobenius, inventor of the formula for symmetric group characters which bore his name, and known for delivering the most perfect lectures in Germany. Root had decided to specialize in Four-Dimensional Geometry, having studied under Professor Manning at Brown. Unlike the Yale math department, the one at Brown taught Quaternions, but despite the language difference, Kit found Root a cheerful fellow, if a little too fond of the bottle, and planning, like Kit, to debark at Marseilles.

ROOT WAS HIS GUEST tonight in first class, and the minute they were seated and Root was engaged with the wine list, Kit found himself once again gazing across the saloon at a young woman with a striking head of red hair, who had just come in with a large party of performing Italians, the kids already beginning to juggle the silverware, somehow avoiding injury from the glittering edges and tines, others to spin plates on the ends of limber wands, East Indian fashion. Waiters, sommeliers and other mealtime functionaries, far from disapproving, were actually encouraging and presently applauding the various feats of skill, which it was soon clear were being executed to a high professional standard. Nothing spilled, dropped, or broken, flowers, birds, and silk scarves emerging from empty air. The Captain got up from his own table to go and sit with the family, whose patriarch genially reached behind his ear to produce a glass full of Champagne with the foam still on it, while the dinner orchestra struck up a species of tarantella. The young woman was at once there and somewhere else. Kit knew he'd seen her someplace. It itched at the corners of his memory. No, it was a little more supernatural than that. They knew each other, it's almost as if he had dreamed it once. . . .

After dinner, as the gentlemen were retiring to the Cigar Deck, Kit came sidling over through a screen of various-size Zombinis, and Erlys introduced him in a general way, which saved Dally from some chitchat. She was just as happy not to have to start in jabbering right away.

Unlike the usual Gibson Girl, who liked to avert her eyes, not to mention her nose, as if it were not a fellow's appearance so much as his odor she wished to appear indifferent to, Dally never knew how to stop looking, even at somebody she had zero interest in, though heaven knew that was not the case right now.

He was watching her with his eyes narrowed appealingly.

"Seen you before," she said, "at the R. Wilshire Vibe residence down in Greenwich Village if I'm not mistaken, one of those peculiar twilight socials of his?"

"I knew it was someplace like that. You were there with a girl in a red dress."

"Always nice to hear when you've made an impression. My friend's name was Katie, little late to be tellin you, though I suppose you *could* jump off the fantail, swim on back to New York, go look her up. . . ."

Kit stood swaying a little to the dance music and blinking politely.

"Yes and now as for that Yale University, if you don't mind me asking—any other Traverses in your class?"

"Think I was the only one."

"You wouldn't happen to have a brother back in southwest Colorado, I suppose. Frank?"

The look she got was not so much surprised as immediately on guard. "You're . . . from out there someplace?"

"Passin through, there a couple months, seemed like a couple years, don't miss it much, how about yourself?"

He shrugged. "It doesn't miss me." Neither was fooling the other. "How's that old Frank?"

"Last I saw of him, he 's headed out of Telluride, not sure if it was all his own idea."

An amiable snort. "Sounds about right."

"He said I should look you up."

Tipping an invisible hat, "Guess you did." Then fell into a silence which went on way too long.

Personable enough, when he wasn't so far inside his own head. "Um, Mr. Traverse? Sir? I could throw a fit or somethin, would that help any?"

Which belatedly drew the cowboy once-over she was at least used to, long enough for Dally to notice, along with everything else, what an agreeable shade of blue his eyes were. Damn old lobelias there.

He looked around. The Zombini family had long finished supper and left the table. The orchestra was back to Victor Herbert and Wolf-Ferrari, and dancers began to occupy the space. "Come on."

He led her out onto the promenade deck of the starlit *Stupendica,* enough moon to pick out the towering contours of clouds, couples all up and down the rail with nothing on their minds but spooning, the electric spill through the portholes dimming his face to a cryptic smudge of itself. Another young man, somewhere else and with different sorrows in his luggage, might've been working up to a declaration or at least a kiss. Dally felt like a seltzer bottle about to be deployed in some vaudeville interlude. Sure as hell couldn't be what they meant by Love at First Sight. Second.

"Listen. Did Frank tell you much of the family situation?"

"Some boys he was lookin for, him and your brother, the other one, the faro dealer, he'd already been in Telluride and gone, but nobody knew where, and Frank was worryin a lot 'cause somebody was looking for him."

"Well. Pretty talkative for Frank, guess he trusted you all right."

She smelled falsely. People in trouble were not usually her first choice of after-dinner companion, though come to think of it, what other kind of people did she know?

"I love those two knuckleheads," his whisper growing passionate, "they're my brothers, they think they're trying to protect me, but they don't know I'm deep in it, up to my ears, all this—" his gesture taking in the boat, the orchestra, the night, "the suit on my back, bought and paid for out of the same bank account that—"

"Should you be telling me this?" With the all-purpose wide-eyed gaze she had learned to use in New York, when trying to think of something to say.

"You're right. Maybe a touch too serious here for a youngster—"

"'Youngster'?" feigning polite interest. "How old are *you,* Reuben, to be calling anybody that? I'm surprised they even let you out of the yard."

"Oh, don't let the face fool you, I'm wise beyond my years."

"Wet behind 'em anyhow."

"Up till twenty minutes ago I guess I was just sailing along on Moonlight Bay here, on vacation from the whole thing. Then you show up, Frank and so forth, and if there's some danger, maybe I don't want to see you in it."

"You'd rather be all alone with it, sure. All-business hombre."

"You don't know, miss. One wrong step's all it would take." He touched an imaginary hatbrim and was gone quick as that.

"Might as well've been Luca waving his wand," she told Erlys. "Not exactly beau material, Mamma."

"Inclined to moodiness, you might say."

"I don't know what in blazes is going on with these people any more than I did in Colorado. Except that it's trouble, and fairly deep."

"Well. You sure can pick them."

"Me! you *threw* me at him—"

But Erlys was laughing and taking the girl's long hair and pushing it back from her face, a little at a time, over and over, a task to which there seemed no end, as if she loved the simple act, the feeling of Dally's hair beneath her fingers, the repetition, like knitting. . . . Dally sat in a kind of daze, listening, not listening, wanting it to go on forever, wanting to be someplace else. . . .

"You're always a revelation, Dally," she said after a while. "Guess I have to thank Merle for something anyway."

"How's that?"

"Seeing you this far." Slowly, reflectively, she surrounded the girl in an embrace.

"Reachin for the spigot again, are we?"

"Guess I could wait till later."

"Sacrifices o' motherhood. Heard about 'em someplace."

"WELL YOU SURE went gaga," Bria remarked.

"Thought I was covering it pretty well."

"Little young for college boys, don't you think?"

Dally looked at her knees, out the porthole, very quickly over at Bria's amused small face. "I don't know what's going on, Brì, I saw him just once at that party back in New York, you were there too's a matter of fact, throwin em knives around, and I couldn't get him out of my head then, and now here he is again. That has to mean something, doesn't it?"

"Sure. Means you've seen him twice now."

"Oh, Brì, it's hopeless."

"Listen to me. Find out about his friend, the sort of short blond guy who always drinks straight through dinnertime but never passes out?"

"Root Tubsmith, just got out of Brown."

"What was he in for?"

"Not the pen, it's a college, and he's another math whiz."

"Head for figures, good to have along on a shopping trip, see—just my kind of fella."

"Bria Zombini. Shame."

"Not lately. You gonna fix me up?"

"Ha. I get it. You're supposed to be chaperoning me."

"More like the other way around, I'd say."

IT HAD BEGUN to seem as if she and Kit were on separate vessels, distinct versions of the *Stupendica,* pulling away slowly on separate courses, each bound to a different destiny.

"You're high-hatting me again," Dally greeted him. Not "us Zombinis"—by now it was singular.

Kit regarded her a long while. "Daydreaming." There are many, perhaps most of us, for whom an ocean voyage, particularly on a first-class ticket, figures high on the list of human delights. Kit, however, landlocked all his life till arriving at New Haven and beholding the marvels of Long Island Sound, did not happen to share that regard for the aquatic. The enclosure, the repetition of daily faces, small annoyances anywhere else, here, intensified by the unavailability of dry land, achieved with little effort the feeling of malevolence, conspiracy, pursuit. . . . The farther out into the ocean they steamed, the more the horizon asserted itself, the less able or, come to that, willing was Kit to resist accepting the irreversible theft from his life, the great simple fact of Webb's absence.

He lapsed into silence, torpor, for scaleless moments seized by memories of desert plateau, mountain peaks, meadows full of Indian paintbrush and wild primrose, some unexpected river two steps off the trail—then released back into this twenty-knot push into the uncreated. He was not sure what it was he felt. If anyone had said desperation, he'd've shrugged and rolled a cigarette, shaking his head. Not it. Not it exactly.

Nor as it turned out was S.S. *Stupendica* all she seemed. She had another name, a secret name, which would be made known to the world at the proper hour, a secret identity, latent in her present conformation, though invisible to the average passenger. What she would turn out to be, in fact, was a participant in the future European war at sea which everyone was confident would come. Some liners, after 1914, would be converted to troop carriers, others to hospital ships. The *Stupendica*'s destiny was to reassume her latent identity as the battleship S.M.S. *Emperor Maximilian*—one of several 25,000-ton dreadnoughts contemplated by Austrian naval planning but, so far as official history goes, never built. The Slavonian steamship line that currently owned and operated her seemed mysteriously to have sprung, overnight, from nowhere. Even identifying its board of directors offered occasion for lively dispute in ministries throughout Europe. In shipping circles, nobody had heard of any of them. British naval intelligence was flummoxed. Though her boilers appeared to be of the Schultz-Thorneycroft design favored by Austria-Hungary, the engines were modified cousins of the same Parsons turbines to be found these days among the more sizable British men-o'-war, capable of twenty-five knots and more, should the occasion demand, for as long as the coal supply lasted.

Root Tubsmith had discovered this much this from nosing around in the lower spaces of the vessel, despite signs posted in all major tongues warning of the dire fate awaiting any who trespassed. He found shell-rooms-to-be and giant powder magazines fore and aft, not to mention, several decks up, located symmetrically about the ship, some very curious *circular cabins,* which seemed intended for gun-turrets—kept retracted to just below the main deck for the moment but ready, if needed, to be raised hydraulically to operating height, and their twelve-inch barrels, stored far below, brought up by hoist and fitted in a matter of minutes.

The shelter deck proved to be concealing a magazine full of torpedoes. Lighter decks topside were designed to fold upward and in other intricately hinged directions, to become armor-plating and casemates for the smaller-caliber guns. At the same time, the *Stupendica* was also able somehow to collapse, as she lost her upper decks, into classic battleship profile, till she was crouching upon the sea with no more freeboard than necessary, wide and low and looking for a fight. Deckhands were intensively drilled in the rapid rigging of stages, over the lifelines and onto which they were to leap, when ordered, nimbly as aerial artistes, and begin swiftly to paint the ship's sides in "dazzle" camouflage the colors of sea, sky, and storm cloud, in two-shaded false dihedrals to look like ships' prows, or running at angles close to the slopes of the waves, eventually to fade into and out of invisibility as the patterns tangled with and untangled from the clutter of whitecaps. "Something out there, Fangsley, I can *feel* it." "Can't make much out, sir. . . ." "Oh? Well what the bloody hell's that then?" "Ah. Appears to be a torpedo, actually, and headed straight for midships too." "I can see that, you idiot, I know what a torpedo looks like—" at which point the interesting exchange is abruptly curtailed.

As Kit and Root descended ladder by ladder into the engine spaces of the *Stupendica,* they found the ship deeper than they had imagined, and much less horizontally disposed. Faces turned to watch them. Eyes bright as the flames inside the furnaces blinked open and shut. The boys were sweating torrents before they got below the waterline. Down at the bottom of the ship, men worked skids full of coal across the deck to be dumped in piles in front of the boilers. Pulses of Hell-colored light lit up the blackened bodies of the stokers each time the firedoors were opened.

From what Root had been able to learn earlier, the passenger liner *Stupendica,* this peaceful expression of high-bourgeois luxury, had been constructed in Trieste, at the Austrian Lloyd Arsenale. At the same time, in parallel, also in Trieste at the neighboring Stabilimento Tecnico, the Austrian navy had apparently been building their dreadnought *Emperor Maximilian.* At some point in the construction schedule, the two projects . . . it was difficult for any of Root's sources to convey . . . *merged.* How? At whose behest? No one was quite sure of much, except that one day there was only the single ship. But in which shipyard? Different witnesses recalled different yards, others swore she was no longer "in" either, simply appearing unforeseen one morning off the Promontorio, fresh from some dead-of-night christening, not a soul visible on deck, silent, tall, surrounded by a haze of somehow defective light.

"This is beginning to sound like a sea story," opined an American stoker named O. I. C. Bodine, who lounged against a bulkhead drinking some horrible fermented potato mash as prelude to going off watch and into sleep. "Four shafts, see. Even the *Mauretania*'s happy with three. Not a civilian arrangement here. These are cruising turbines. Uh-oh, here comes Gerhardt—*Zu befehl, Herr Hauptheitzer!*"

The Chief Stoker exploded into a spectacular exhibition of cursing. "Easily upset," confided O.I.C. "Terrible mouth on the man. Just now thought he saw the telegraph look like it was about to move. Imagine what he's like when it *does* move. But we should always look for the good in everybody."

"So he's a decent sort at heart."

"Hell no, try pulling liberty with him. He's even worse ashore."

All of a sudden, it was like the entire Black Gang was having a violent paroxysm. The telegraph from the bridge started tolling like all the cathedrals of Hell on a particularly important feast day. Cruising turbines were lit off, oil and steam pressures began to rise, the Oberhauptheitzer, having produced from somewhere a Mannlicher eight-shot pistol, brandished it at the steam-pressure gauges in high irritation, as if to shoot them if they did not provide the correct readings. Cries of "*Dampf mehr!*" were heard from several directions. Kit looked around for the nearest ladder to the open air, but all had become many-tongued confusion. He found his head seized by a gigantic bituminous hand, which propelled him rapidly through the fierce spasms of light and the ungodly steel clangor toward the bunkers at the side of the ship, out of which men were loading coal on to skids to be dragged to the boiler furnaces.

"Sure," Kit muttered, "all you had to do was ask." For what seemed hours then, he made the same trip back and forth, gradually losing his shirt and singlet, being insulted in languages he did not speak but understood. Everything ached. He thought he might have lost part of his hearing.

All hell likewise had broken loose topside. As if syntonic wireless messages, traveling through the Æther, might be subject to influences we remain at present ignorant of, or perhaps, owing to the unnaturally shaky quality of present-day "reality," the receivers in the ship's Marconi room were picking up traffic from somewhere else not quite "in" the world, more like from a continuum lateral to it . . . around midafternoon the *Stupendica* had received a message in cipher, to the effect that British and German battle groups were engaged off the Moroccan coast, and that a state of general European war should be presumed in effect.

Anxious voices out of megaphones hitherto unnoticed began calling the crew to general quarters. Hydraulics engaged, as entire decks began ponderously to slide, fold, and rotate, and passengers found themselves, often lethally, in the way of this booming and shrieking steel metamorphosis. Bells, gongs, bos'n's pipes, steam sirens added to the cacophony. Stewards threw off their white livery to reveal dark blue Austro-Hungarian naval uniforms, and started shouting orders at the civilians who moments ago had been ordering them around, and who now mostly were wandering the passageways disoriented and increasingly fearful. "Right full rudder!" the Captain cried, and throughout the gigantic vessel, as the helm responded and the ship began to heel sharply over, approaching ever closer to her design maximum of nine degrees, hundreds of small inconveniences commenced, as bottles of perfume went sliding off the tops of vanity tables, wineglasses in the dining saloon tipped over and soaked the table linen, dance partners who would rather have kept an appropriate distance lurched into one another, causing foot injuries and couture damage, assorted objects in the crew's spaces fell from channel bars serving as shelves next to upper bunks in a shower of pipes, tobacco-pouches, playing-cards, pocket flasks, vulgar souvenirs of exotic ports of call, descending now and then onto officers' heads—"All ahead full!" as forgotten coffee cups reappeared only to shatter on the steel decks, forgotten sandwiches and pastries to which entropy had been typically unkind made themselves known amid multilingual expressions of distaste, clouds of dust and soot descended from overheads throughout the vessel, and the roach population, newborns, nymphs, and grizzled oldtimers alike, imagining some global calamity, ran where they might at the highest speeds available to them given the general uproar.

Dally was sent rolling out of her bunk and onto the deck, as, a second later, was Bria, landing right on top of her, exclaiming, "*Porca miseria!* What's this, then?"

Cici came running in. "It must be Pop, going crazy again!"

"Yeah, blame it on the magician," remarked the elder Zombini, draped in the doorway, "it's the old Liner-to-Battleship Effect. Everybody all right in here?"

Strangely, it was Kit Dally was worrying about.

After running madly round and round in the same tight circle at top speed a number of times, the vessel, as if getting a grip on itself, finally slowed down, easing back to vertical and steadying on to a new course southeast by east. From the giant magnetic compass mounted in the dining saloon for the entertainment of the passengers, the change of heading soon became generally known. "Where the heck are we going, then?" Pocket atlases came out of pockets. "Let's see, if we made that turn about here . . ." The nearest land ahead of them appeared to be Morocco.

In the engineering spaces, things slowly drifted back to normal, whatever that meant down here. The telegraph moderated its demands for speed, everybody was told at last to secure from general quarters, port and starboard shifts resumed. Peacetime again.

When the insults had migrated on to other targets and Kit had reached a sort of invisibility, "Well, this has all been mighty educational," he announced, "and I guess I'll be getting back up to my stateroom now, thanks for everything, and you especially, Chief Oberhauptheitzer, there. . . ."

"No, mister, no no—he does not understand—there are no staterooms, it is no longer the *Stupendica* up there. That admirable vessel has sailed on to its destiny. Abovedecks now you will find only His Majesty's dreadnought, *Emperor Maximilian.* It is true that for a while the two ships did share a common engine room. A 'deeper level' where dualities are resolved. A Chinese sort of situation, *nicht wahr?*"

Kit at first took this all for some sort of Black Gang jollification, and snuck up the ladders as soon as he could to have a look. Marine sentries with Mannlichers stood at the hatchway. "I'm a passenger," Kit protested. "I'm from America."

"I've heard of it. I'm from Graz myself. Get back below."

He tried other ladders, other hatches. He climbed ventilator shafts and concealed himself in the laundry, but none of it was good for more than five minutes in a grim, gray military world stripped of civilian amenities—no women, flower arrangements, dance orchestras, haute cuisine—though he was grateful for a lungful or two of fresh air. "No, no, bilge-crab, not for the likes of you. Back to the lower depths with you, now."

Kit was given a bunk in the crew's quarters, which were squeezed into the cusp of the bow, and O. I. C. Bodine came around to make sure he was getting along all right. He became the Phantom of the Lower Decks, learning where to hide when anybody appeared from topside, working regular stoker shifts otherwise.

For a Teutonic of executive rank, the Captain of this vessel appeared unusually indecisive, changing his mind every few minutes. For days S.M.S. *Emperor Maximilian* haunted the coast, running north, then south again, back and forth, increasingly desperate, as if trying to find the epic sea-battle the Captain continued to believe was in progress. . . . Although the first port of call had been advertised as Tangier—at the moment, according to scuttlebutt, under the control of local warlord Mulai Ahmed er-Raisuli—the Captain had decided instead to put in far to the south, at Agadir, Queen of the Iron Coast.

Kit discovered the reason for this when he noticed a stack of used plates and dishes from the first-class dining salon outside one of the empty coal bunkers. Curious, he stuck his head in and to his surprise discovered a group of hidden people who'd been living here all along, and most of whom spoke German. It seemed they were destined for plantation on the Atlantic coast of Morocco as "colonists" whose presence there would then justify German interest in the area. For reasons of diplomacy they were being kept sequestered down here in the engine spaces, and known only to the Captain, among whose orders had been encrypted a couple of clauses concerning their disposition as shadow-colonials on call, homesteading though the area was not promising for husbandry, the coast being as much at the mercy of the wind as its hinterland was at that of the tribesmen of Sus, who did not take kindly to Europeans in their midst. The coast was in fact closed to all foreign trade by edict of the young sultan Abdel Aziz, despite France, Spain, and England having made a deal allowing France the right of "peaceful penetration" elsewhere in Morocco.

Out there like a dream, out past the gray, unrelenting march of the rollers, the colonists would come to imagine they could see at the horizon, even smell on the wind, the fabled Canaries, which would soon embody their only hope of deliverance. Many would go crazy and set out in small boats or even swim west, never to be heard from again.

"What happened? We went to sleep in Lübeck and woke up here."

"I'm headed for Göttingen," Kit said, "if there's any message I can take for you, I'd be happy to."

"How good can your chances be of getting there if you're hiding down here like us?"

"Temporary setback," Kit mumbled.

TOWN-DWELLERS, Susi tradesfolk, Berbers from up the valley, merchants in with caravans from the mountains and the desert beyond left off the minutiae of day's business to stand along the beach and gaze, uncertain of their peril. Few here had ever seen a vessel bigger than a fishing boat, except for passing shapes farther out to sea, unreadable as to size. Tree-climbing goats up in the branches of argan trees paused in their browsing after the olivelike fruit to regard the metal visitation. Gnaoua musicians invoked the *mlouk gnaoui,* calling upon the doorkeeper of the Seigneurs Noirs to open the door of good and evil. Everyone agreed that the ship must have come from someplace very far away—to suppose it had originated with one of "The Great Powers" did little to clarify the question, as the phrase, here on this isolated coast, must embrace possibilities beyond secular geography.

The brilliant white walls of the town presented themselves to the tall predator drifting arrogant and unadorned in out of the daily uneventfulness, casting sharp-edged shadows through a haze of combustion from both its own stacks and fires set hastily ashore, whether in friendliness or fear was uncertain. . . .

And as if reincarnated from some intermediate or Bardo state, one night of no moon the civilian passengers, including Kit, slipped one by one from an opening in the side of the *Emperor Maximilian* originally intended for the launching of midget submarines and were rowed secretly ashore, after which the dreadnought put to sea again. Kit, not convinced he had a future in the Habsburg navy, had decided to debark here, and quickly found a room between the port and the Mogador road and begun hanging around a waterfront bar, the Tawil Balak.

"In town here we're pretty cosmopolitan," said Rahman the barkeep, "but you don't want to be going too far up the valley." One night some fisherman showed up off a steam trawler operating independently out of Ostend, the *Fomalhaut,* which a couple of crew members had jumped in Tangier. "We're shorthanded," the skipper told Kit. "You're hired."

The rest of the evening passed in a fog. Kit remembered getting into a discussion of the Two-*Stupendica* problem with Moïsés, a resident Jewish mystic. "Not unusual for these parts, actually. Jonah is the classic case. Recall that he was traveling to Tarshish, whose port, five hundred miles north of here, we call Cádiz today, one of whose alternate names is Agadir. But tradition in *this* Agadir is that Jonah came ashore just to the south of here, at Massa. There is a mosque commemorating the event."

"Two Agadirs," said Kit, puzzled. "He went out into the Atlantic? He landed both places at once, five hundred miles apart?"

"As if the Straits of Gibraltar acted as some metaphysical junction point between the worlds. In those days to pass through that narrow aperture into the vast, uncertain field of Ocean was to leave behind the known world, and perhaps its conventions about being in only one place at a time. . . . Once passed through, did the ship take two tacks at once? Did the wind blow two ways? Or was it the giant fish that possessed the power of bilocation? Two fishes, two Jonahs, two Agadirs?"

"This smoke in here I've been breathing," said Kit, "this wouldn't be . . . um, hasheesh?"

"Never heard of the substance," the holy person seeming offended.

It was dark in the establishment. As if there were less need for ordinary sources of light, a single lamp was burning evil-smelling sheep fat. Up in the Kashbah, people were singing themselves into trances. Somewhere out in the street, the Gnaoua musicians were playing lutes and keeping time with metal hand percussion, and they were invisible to all but those for whom they played.

THEY HAD LEFT the Bay of Agadir, rounding Ighir Ufrani as the sunlight was just touching the tops of the mountains, and set a course northeastward toward the English Channel, steaming just out of sight of the coast. Except for some local Moroccan fish, Mogador herring and *alimzah* and *tasargelt,* the catches as they moved north became bad to indifferent, which the rest of the crew blamed on Kit's presence, until suddenly one morning out in the Bay of Biscay the *Fomalhaut* blundered somehow into a giant school of fish of several kinds, so immoderately abundant as to put serious stress on the warps and winches. "It had to happen someday," the skipper supposed. "Bloody Jonah in reverse, is what it is. Look at this." Indeed several sorts of fish seemed to be present in the dynamic silver glittering that spilled into the pounds and prodigally across the deck and over the side again each time the cod-ends of the nets were untied. Kit was put to work sorting the catch, trusted at first only to tell edible fish from scruff, but soon developing a sense of nuance among turbot and brill, cod and hake, sole, plaice, and bream.

As soon as the starboard trawl was empty, they shot the port one again. There seemed no end to this continent-size school they had steamed into. Kit now found himself getting looks even stranger than before.

It went on for a day and a night until there was no more room on board, not even for a single sardine, and they came wallowing in to Ostend, into the Staketsel and down the channel, gunwales all but awash. There were fish in the lazarettes and rope lockers, fish spilled out the portholes and came flopping out of charts as they were unrolled on the chart table, hours later, crewmen were finding fish in their pockets, not to mention—"Ah, *pardon, mon chou,* that's not what you think it is—"

· · ·

MEANWHILE, leaving its military double to wander the mists, the *Stupendica* continued its civilian journey.

Bria tried to cheer Dally up. "Hey, you know what they say about shipboard romances."

"Is that what it was?"

"You'd know better'n me, you're the adventuress."

"How about his friend?"

"Ol' Rooty-Toot? I asked already, he said they got separated down in the engine room and nobody's seen Kit since."

How crazy did she have to get about this? Dally went searching all through the *Stupendica,* from moon deck to lower orlop, asking passengers, stewards, stokers, deck hands, officers if they'd seen Kit. No luck. At dinner she confronted the Captain.

"He may have debarked at Agadir, but I'll send a wireless message," the Captain promised.

Sure. All she hoped at this point was that the damn fickle Yalie hadn't gone over the side. She sought out the least populated spaces on the ship and lay in a deck chair glaring off at the waves, which helpfully turned dark, deliberate, steep-sided, whitecapped, while the sky clouded over and presently a storm swept upon them from off the starboard bow.

At Gibraltar the ship seemed to pause, as if waiting for clearance. She dreamed that passengers had been allowed to go ashore for a little while, and that she watched from some night eyrie, up in the stormy heights, directly above the merciless black "Atlantic." Where had that confounded Kit disappeared to? Briefly she had a clear image of him somewhere far below, at the base of the steep rock face, seeming to push a small, imperfect boat out into the gray magnitudes, about to embark on some impossible journey. . . .

The *Stupendica* moved along, keeping close to the Mediterranean coastline, passing port after port, houses and foliage spilling down pale cliffs, inhabitants busy with their lives in the steeply-pitched streets of each town, little lateen-riggers venturing out to circle like moths.

Erlys kept a considerate distance, not about to start in hammering on this romantic setback of Dally's, especially since neither seemed to have a very clear idea of how important it might be. Dally had expected Bria would be the first one to put her through this, except that somehow, quietly and with no effort her mother could see, Bria had gone cakewalking quite beyond any sound advice she might once have offered, playing not only Root Tubsmith but a good part of the fourth-class passenger list like fish in an ornamental pond.

As if she had exited her life briefly and been given the ability to travel on a parallel course, "close" enough to watch herself doing it, Dally discovered an alternate way to travel by land, port to port, faster than the ship was moving. . . . She sped, it seemed slightly above ground level, through the fragrant late-summer twilight, parallel to the course of the ship . . . perhaps, now and then, over a break in the dunes and scrub and low concrete walls, catching a glimpse of the *Stupendica,* under way, passing along the eternal coast, dogged and slow, all details, folds, and projections muted gray as a fly's body seen through its wings . . . as night came falling and the ship, outraced, crept on behind. . . . She would return to her deck chair out of breath, sweating, exhilarated for no reason, as if she had just escaped some organized threat to her safety.

They paused at Venice in the fog in the middle of the night to allow for some brief ghostly transaction. Dally woke, peered out the porthole and saw a flotilla of black gondolas, each with a single lantern, each bearing a single cloaked passenger, who all stood solidly gazing ahead into something only they seemed to understand. This is Venice? she remembered thinking, then went back to sleep. In the morning they put in at last to the *Stupendica*'s home port, Trieste. Crowds had turned out in the Piazza Grande to welcome her in. Ladies in enormous hats, on the arms of Austro-Hungarian army officers in blue, scarlet, and gold, promenaded along the Riva with all the certitude of dream. A military band played medleys of Verdi, Denza, and local favorite Antonio Smareglia.

Dally allowed herself to be swept gently ashore in the bustle of debarkation. It felt like she was standing still. She had never even heard of this place. Never mind Kit for the moment—where was she?

Followed by equivocal stares from the crew of the *Fomalhaut,* Kit collected his pay at Ostend and stepped wobbling onto the Fishermen's Quai, boarded the electric tram, and rode as far as the Continental, where for some reason he assumed there'd be a room reserved and waiting. But they had never heard of him. Almost taking it personally, he was about to invoke the Vibe name when he caught a glimpse of himself in one of the gold-framed lobby mirrors, and sanity intervened. Judas priest. He looked like debris washed up on the beach. Smelled that way too, come to think of it. Outside again, he caught another tram, which took him into town along the Boulevard van Iseghem before making a couple of left turns and heading back toward the Basins again. The crowds he saw were all far more street-plausible than he was. At the Quai de l'Empereur, almost where he started from, Kit got off with no better sense of what to do with himself, went in a little estaminet, and sat over in a corner with a twelve-centime glass of beer, reviewing the situation. He had enough money to put up someplace overnight at least, before figuring out how to get to Göttingen.

His ruminations were broken in upon by a violent dispute over in the corner, among an unkempt, indeed seedy, band of varying ages and nationalities, whose only common language Kit recognized presently as that of the Quaternions, though he couldn't recall ever seeing so many of that embattled persuasion gathered in one place before. Even stranger than that, he now grew aware that they seemed to *recognize him*—not that Masonic signs and countersigns were being exchanged, exactly, and yet—

"Here then, Kellner! a *demi* of Lambic for that bloke over there with the seaweed on his suit," called a cheerfully insane party in a battered skimmer that looked like he'd found it on the beach.

Kit made what he hoped was the universal sign for short funds by pulling out an imaginary pair of trouser pockets and shrugging in apology.

"Not to worry, this week it's all on the Trinity maths department, they're wizards at solving biquaternion equations, but show them an expense account and lucky for us their minds go blank." He introduced himself as Barry Nebulay, from the University of Dublin, space was made, and Kit joined the polyglot gang.

All last week and this, Quaternioneers had been converging on Ostend to hold one of their irregularly spaced World Conventions. In the wake of the transatlantic unpleasantness of the '90s known as the Quaternion Wars—in which Kit was aware that Yale, being the home of Gibbsian Vectors, had figured as a major belligerent—true Quaternionists, if not defeated outright then at best having come to feel irrelevant, could be found these days wandering the world, dispersed, under the yellow skies of Tasmania, out in the American desert, up in the Alpine wastes of Switzerland, gathering furtively in border-town hotels, at luncheons in rented parlors, in hotel lobbies whose surfaces, varying in splendor from French velvet to aboriginal masonry, raised ensembles of echoes—they were eyed suspiciously by waiters who brought in and ladled from oversize alloyed-steel kettles vegetables grown locally whose names did not readily come to mind, or animal parts concealed by opaque sauces—particularly, here in Belgium, forms of mayonnaise—whose color schemes ran to indigoes and aquas, often quite vivid actually . . . yes but what choices, if any, remained? Having been inseparable from the rise of the electromagnetic in human affairs, the Hamiltonian devotees had now, fallen from grace, come to embody, for the established scientific religion, a subversive, indeed heretical, faith for whom proscription and exile were too good.

The Grand Hôtel de la Nouvelle Digue was tucked well back of the Boulevard van Iseghem, far from the seawall it was named for, its appeal being chiefly to the cautious of purse, including the usual assortment of off-season tourists, fugitives, pensioners, abandoned lovers imagining they had found the anterooms of death. In fact, little was what it seemed. The rooms at the hotel were remorselessly appointed with objects of faux bamboo fashioned from pine, painted in exotic colors such as Chinese red, and featuring tabletops of cheap, perhaps synthetic, marble. In an attempt to grasp the propensities of Belgian Art Nouveau in its full modernity, woman/animal hybrid motifs were to be seen incorporated into basin and tub fittings, bed-coverings, drapes, and lampshades.

Kit looked around. "Pretty fancy."

"By this point," said Barry Nebulay, "no one is keeping very close tabs on who is or is not a registered guest. You would not be the only one dossing here free of charge." Kit, having decided to try to win enough at the Casino to get to Göttingen, presently found himself sleeping in a corner among piles of Quaternionist debris, along with a shifting population of refugees whose names, if he heard them at all, he quickly forgot.

Just down the corridor happened to be living a cell of Belgian nihilists—Eugénie, Fatou, Denis, and Policarpe, styling themselves "Young Congo"—persons of unfailing interest to the Garde Civique as well as to those French Second Bureau folks who visited Brussels on a regular basis. Whenever Kit ran into any of these youngsters—which seemed more often than chance would account for—there was always a moment of intense recognition, almost as if he'd once, somehow, actually *belonged to* the little *phalange,* until something had happened, something too terrible to remember, at least as momentous as the fate of the *Stupendica,* whereupon everything, along with memory, had gone falling dizzily away, not only downward but out along other axes of space-time as well. This had been happening a lot to him lately. While it was certainly a relief to have nothing weighing him down for the moment beyond his clothes—and though it was almost possible to convince himself he had escaped the Vibe curse and was now starting life afresh—the weightless condition he was going around in was peculiar enough to turn dangerous at any time. When he got a good look at the Digue, twenty-five feet high and lined with fancy hotels, and the sea just the other side of it, pounding away, higher than the town, he couldn't help imagining a conscious force, looking for a weak point, destined to overtop the promenade and sweep Ostend to destruction.

"So the black hordes of the Congo," meditated Policarpe. "Whom Belgians in their Low Country neuropathy imagine also in unremitting swell, silently rising, ever higher, behind some wall of force and death which no one knows how to make strong enough to keep them from overwhelming everything—"

"Their unmerited suffering," Denis suggested, "their moral superiority."

"Hardly. They are as savage and degenerate as Europeans. Nor is it a matter of simple numbers, for here in Belgium is the highest population density in the world, and no one can much be taken by surprise in that regard. No, we create this, I think—project it from the co-conscious, from out of the ooze of hallucination being mapped onto continually by the unremitting and unremittable hell of our dominion down there. Each time a member of the Force Publique strikes a rubber worker, or even speaks the simplest insult, the tidal forces intensify, the *digue* of self-contradiction grows ever weaker."

It was like being together back in *khâgne.* Everyone lay around in a sort of focused inertia, drinking, handing cigarettes back and forth, forgetting with whom, or whether, they were supposed to be romantically obsessed. Denis and Eugénie had studied geography with Reclus at the University of Brussels, Fatou and Policarpe were fleeing warrants issued in Paris, where even the intent to advocate Anarchism was a crime. "Like the Russian nihilists," Denis explained, "we are metaphysicians at heart. There is a danger of becoming too logical. At the end of the day one can only consult one's heart."

"Don't mind Denis, he's a Stirnerite."

"*Anarcho-individualiste,* though you are too much of an imbecile to appreciate this distinction."

Though there existed within the *phalange* a hundred opportunities to draw such distinctions, Africa remained the unspoken, the unpermitted term that kept them solid and resolute. That and the moral obligation, though some might have said obsession, with assassinating Leopold, King of the Belgians.

"Has anyone noticed," Denis ventured, "how many assorted figures of power in Europe—Kings, Queens, Grand Dukes, Ministers—have been going down lately beneath the implacable Juggernaut of History? corpses of the powerful toppling in every direction, with a frequency far higher than chance might suggest?"

"Are you authorized to speak for the gods of Chance?" inquired Eugénie. "Who can say what a 'normal' assassination rate is supposed to be?"

"Yes," Policarpe put in, "maybe it's not high *enough* yet. Considering how scientifically inevitable the act is."

The group had taken heart from the example of the fifteen-year-old Anarchist Sipido, who in solidarity with the Boers of South Africa had tried to assassinate the Prince and Princess of Wales in Brussels, at the Gare du Nord. Four shots at close range missed, Sipido and his gang were arrested and later acquitted, and the Prince was now King of England. "And the Brits," shrugged Policarpe, the realist in the group, "are still treating the Boers like dirt. Sipido should have paid more attention to the tools of our trade. One appreciates the need for concealment, but if one is out after Crown Prince, one needs caliber, not to mention a larger magazine."

"Let's say we placed a bomb, out at the Hippodrome," proposed Fatou, rouged, hatless, and wearing a skirt shorter than a circus girl's, though everybody but Kit was pretending not to notice this.

"Or in the Royal Bathing Hut," Policarpe said. "Anyone can hire that for twenty francs."

"Who's got twenty francs?"

"Something in the picric family might do nicely," Fatou went on, deploying maps and diagrams about the tiny room. "Brugère's powder, say."

"Always been a Designolle's man myself," murmured Denis.

"Or we *might* hire an American gunslinger," Eugénie gazing meaningfully at Kit.

"Heck, mademoiselle, you don't want to be lettin me near a gun, I'd need steel shoes just to protect my feet."

"Come, Kit, you can tell us. How many desperados have you . . . drilled daylight through?"

"Hard to say, we don't start countin till it's over a dozen."

At the cusp of the twilight, lamps were lit up and down the streets, against a hovering shadow of beleaguerment by forces semi-visible. . . . Beyond the Digue, waves thudded on the invisible strand. Policarpe had fetched absinthe, sugar, and paraphernalia. He was the phalanx dandy, sporting, after the style of Monsieur Santos-Dumont, a Panama hat to the precise dishevelment of whose brim he devoted the kind of time other young men might to grooming their mustaches. He and his friends were *absintheurs* and *absintheuses,* and spent a lot of time sitting around enacting elaborate drinking rituals. The Green Hour often stretched on till midnight.

"Or, as we like to say, *l'heure vertigineuse.*"

Around midnight a pair of voices arguing in Italian were heard outside the door, and the exchange continued for a while. Recently Young Congo had joined forces with a pair of Italian naval renegades, Rocco and Pino, who had stolen from the Whitehead works in Fiume the highly secret plans for a low-speed manned torpedo, which they intended to assemble here in Belgium and go after King Leopold's royal yacht, the *Alberta,* with. Rocco, never less than earnest, might only have lacked imagination—while Pino, seeming to express all that is immoderate in the southern Italian temperament, found himself driven regularly to distraction by the mental stolidity of his partner. In theory they made a perfect team for manned-torpedo work, Rocco's inability to imagine the non-regulation in any form promising—even now and then able—to deflect the exuberant though unprofitable fantasies of Pino.

The Siluro Dirigibile a Lenta Corsa represented a brief yet romantic chapter in torpedo history. With its targets limited to stationary objects such as ships at anchor, the mathematics of trajectory and aiming were enormously simplified, though the element of personal *virtù* came to assume signal importance, as the team must first bring their deadly craft undetected past too-often-unfamiliar harbor defenses until it actually *touched the hull* of its intended victim—whereupon, having initiated a timed fuzing sequence, they must then exfiltrate as fast and far as they could before the charge went off. Working uniform was usually a diver's suit of Vulcanized rubber for keeping warm during what might prove to be hours in frigid waters, the torpedo traveling mostly just below the surface, as perforce must Rocco and Pino.

"What a night!" exclaimed Pino. "Garde Civique all over the place."

"Top hats and green uniforms every time you turn around," added Rocco.

"Still, if you're not allergic to green quite yet," Policarpe offering the absinthe bottle.

"How many ships have you actually . . . blown up, Pino?" Fatou was presently cooing, while Rocco, throwing her fearful glances, was muttering in his partner's ear.

". . . just the kind of question an *Austrian spy* might ask—think, Pino, think."

"Pino, what's he saying?" Fatou tapping at one ear whose lobe had been left intriguingly naked of ornament. "Does Rocco think I'm a spy, really?"

"We have had dealings, you see, with one or two lady spies," purred Pino, attempting a look of chaste appreciation that fooled nobody, his efforts today toward the suave being further undone by a slept-on thicket of curls, a distressed Royal Italian Navy fatigue uniform stained with wine and motor lubricants, and an unfocused gaze that never came to rest anywhere, least of all upon anybody's face. "While I am able to take these episodes as part of life and move on, poor Rocco cannot forget. He has put into deep narcosis any number of gatherings, even Gypsies in a mood for all-night festivity, with his obsessions of *danger from lady spies*."

"*Macchè,* Pino! They . . . they interest me, that's all. As a category."

"Ehi, stu gazz', categoria."

"You are safe with me, Lieutenant," Fatou assured him. "Any government that hired me to spy would have to be hopeless idiots. . . ."

"My point exactly!" Rocco staring in righteous density.

She peered at him, at the just-arisen chance that, like the heedless *mezzogiornismo* of his companion Pino, this might be Rocco's way of slyly flirting with her.

"As usual," Eugénie had warned her, "you're too suspicious. You have to learn to listen more to your heart."

"My heart." Fatou shook her head. "My heart knew him for a rogue, long before he got close enough to hear it beating. Of course he's a *bad marriage risk,* but what's that got to do with anything?"

Eugénie demurely touching her friend's sleeve. "As it happens, actually, I may . . . hmm . . . fancy . . . Rocco?"

"Aahh!" Fatou collapsed on the bed, pounding it with her fists and feet.

Eugénie waited till she was quite done. "I'm serious."

"We can go out dancing together! Have dinner! The theater! Just like *boys and girls* would do! I know you're 'serious,' Génie—that's what has me worried!"

Both young women experienced some distress whenever the Italian duo were obliged to spend time in Bruges, the Venice of the Low Countries, just a short canal journey away, which since the Middle Ages had enjoyed a reputation for its pretty girls. This was not so important, Rocco and Pino both swore repeatedly, as the need to run frequent midnight exercises with the Torpedo, which was having its internal-combustion engine modified by the staff at Raoul's Atelier de la Vitesse, most of them Red mechanicians from Ghent. Once everyone was satisfied with the weapon's performance, Rocco and Pino planned to ride it through these nocturnal ghostways, invisibly, to the seaside and a certain *royal rendezvous*.

"They've put in a Daimler six-cylinder," explained Rocco, "with an Austrian military carburetor, still very hush-hush, and a redesigned exhaust manifold, which means we're already up to a hundred horsepower, and that's just cruising, *guaglion*."

"Why didn't you sell the plans to the English?" one of the Ghent machinists had thought to ask. "Why give them away to some stateless collection of Anarchists?"

Rocco was puzzled. "Steal from one government to sell it to another?" He and Pino looked at each other.

"Let's kill him," Pino suggested brightly. "I killed the last one, Rocco, so it's your turn."

"Why is he running away?" said Rocco.

"Come back, come back!" cried Pino. "Oh well. They're all so stolid up here."

HOTEL STAFF of a spruceness less rigorous than what they might've been held to in daylight hours were maintaining a fine balance between annoyance and bewilderment at the spectacle of these Quaternionist troupers, by now years in retreat from their great struggle for existence, still resolute and insomniac. Were this its afterlife, only some of those wearing the livery of the Grand Hôtel de la Nouvelle Digue could have been classified as ministering angels—the rest being closer to imps of ingenious discomfort.

"Is this a stag affair, or are there likely to be one or two lady Quaternionists?" Kit inquired, one would have to say plaintively.

"Rare birds," said Barry Nebulay, "though of course there is Miss Umeki Tsurigane, of the Imperial University of Japan, a former student of Professor Knott when he was there. Astonishing young woman. She's published as much as anyone in the faith—memoranda, monographs, books—Kimura has I believe translated some of them into English— Ah. And she's right over there," nodding at the bar.

"That one?"

"Yes. Presentable, wouldn't you say? You ought to hit it off, she was just in America. Come along, I'll introduce you."

Black trousers, drover's sombrero . . . black *leather* trousers, in fact *glove* leather, "Are you sure some other time wouldn't be more—"

"Too late. Miss Tsurigane, Mr. Traverse, of New Haven."

Around her slender neck, the beauteous Asian was also wearing a furoshiki printed in a woodland motif of peacock blue, taupe, and Chinese red, folded in a triangle so as to make a cowgirl bandanna, and knocking back boiler-makers and their helpers at an astonishing pace. A modest betting pool had already developed over how long she might keep it up before paralysis in some form set in.

"'Some Quaternionic Schemata for Representing the Anharmonic Pencil and Related Forms,'" Kit recalled. "I saw the abstract in *Comptes Rendus*."

"Not another Anharmonic Pencilist," she greeted him, calm and so far lucid. "There is by now quite a cult, I am told. Expecting all sorts of . . . strange things!"

"Uhm . . ."

"The Projective Geometry Symposium—you'll be speaking at it?"

"Uhm . . ."

"Will you be speaking at all? Anytime soon?"

"Here, let me buy you a couple more of those," offered Barry Nebulay, who then, like some angel of the alcoholic, was off to other good deeds.

"Yale—you studied there? Kimura-san, who is now at our Naval College—did you ever meet him?"

"A little before my time, but he is remembered with much respect."

"He and his American classmate, De Forest–san, have both gone on to contribute most materially to the field of syntonic wireless communication. Kimura-san's system—tonight, somewhere, it is on station with the Japanese navy, in service against the Russians. Both of those gentlemen studied Vectors with the eminent Gibbs Sensei. How much of a—coincidence, could that have been?"

"With the Maxwell Equations at the heart of the matter . . ."

"Exactly." She stood and looked up at him, more or less devastatingly, from under the brim of that cowgirl hat. "The festivities in there—would you mind escorting me?"

"Why, not at all, miss." The only hitch being that two steps into the Grand Salon, she had slipped away, or he had, and it would be days before they saw each other again. He had two choices, either leave and go sulk someplace or wander around and see what else might be up. Or, actually, only one choice.

Kit threaded his way out into the Grand Salon, wallpapered in aniline teal and a bright though sour orange, to appearances floral in theme, though few would insist on it, lit by hundreds of modern-looking sconces, each quarter-shade of Congo ivory scraped thin as paper to let its electric bulb shine through, roisteringly a-seethe tonight with Quaternionnaires from around the globe, all persuasions not to mention apostates therefrom, quasi-Gibbsites and pseudo-Heavisiders and full-bore Grassmanniacs, milling about, more than in the mood for a clambake, eccentrically attired, negligently when not defectively groomed, all, with perhaps no more than the usual quota of barking and drooling, gossiping breathlessly about vacant appointments, compulsive marriages, cretinous colleagues, and real estate both overpriced and otherwise, scribbling on one another's attire, performing with cigarettes and banknotes feats of vanishing and restoration right up in one another's faces, drinking Monopole de la Maison, dancing on tabletops, exhausting the patience of wives, vomiting into the pockets of strangers, getting into long, intensely hoarse disputes in fluent Esperanto and Idiom Neutral, the technical discussions being in large part impenetrable, the phatic or sociable chitchat tending to the only slightly less problematic.

". . . Heaviside's ham-fisted attempt to de-Quaternionize the Maxwell Field Equations—not even they have been safe from assault—"

"Face it. The *Kampf ums Dasein* is over, and we have lost."

"Does that mean we only imagine now that we exist?"

"Imaginary axes, imaginary existence."

"Ghosts. Ghosts."

"Yes, Q-Brother, yours is a particularly depressing case. From the mistakes in your last paper, your own struggle should be called a *Kampf* oops *Dasein.*"

"We are the Jews of mathematics, wandering out here in our diaspora—some destined for the past, others the future, even a few able to set out at unknown angles from the simple line of Time, upon journeys that no one can predict. . . ."

"Of course we lost. Anarchists always lose out, while the Gibbs-Heaviside Bolsheviks, their eyes ever upon the long-term, grimly pursued their aims, protected inside their belief that they are the inevitable future, the *xyz* people, the party of a single Established Coördinate System, present everywhere in the Universe, governing absolutely. We were only the *ijk* lot, drifters who set up their working tents for as long as the problem might demand, then struck camp again and moved on, always ad hoc and local, what do you expect?"

"Actually Quaternions failed because they perverted what the Vectorists thought they know of God's intention—that space be simple, three-dimensional, and real, and if there must be a fourth term, an imaginary, that it be assigned to Time. But Quaternions came in and turned that all end for end, defining the axes of space as imaginary and leaving Time to be the *real* term, and a scalar as well—simply inadmissible. Of course the Vectorists went to war. Nothing they knew of Time allowed it to be that simple, any more than they could allow space to be compromised by impossible numbers, earthly space they had fought over uncounted generations to penetrate, to occupy, to defend."

Accompanying these laments was some inappropriately chirpy music, which Kit had now come in earshot of. What appeared to be a music-hall contralto in a species of Poiret gown sat at a piano, accompanied by a small street-ensemble of accordion, glockenspiel, baritone saxophone, and drums, singing, in a bouncy 6/8,

O,
  the,
          Quizzical, queer Quater-nioneer,
That creature of i-j-k,
Why must he smile so cu-riously,
And creep-about quite that way? from
Wat-erloo out to Tim-buctoo, just as
Man-y as you please—
They're down, they say, in Tas-man-
I-ay, and they're
Up-there in-the trees!—and should you
Find one in your parlor at
The fullness of the moon,
You'll avoid a spot of awk-wardness,
If you sing this lit-tle tune . . . (-2-3-and)
Once I saw a Quater-nion chap, he was
Act-ing oh so queer—
There was some-thing *rather green and long* he was
Put-ting in his ear . . .
Yes it might have been a gherkin,
If it wasn't, dear oh dear! that
Quizzical queer Quater-nion-eer!

Which the captivated assembly had been tirelessly singing along with, over and over, since the chanteuse had come on shift, its time-signature working some ancient tarantellical magic as well, producing among the company an irresistible desire to dance with wild abandon, whatever that meant around here. Collisions were frequent, often forceful, Kit being able to avoid one only by having recognized, just before contact, a familiar deep voice. There sure enough in full barrel-rolling conviviality was Root Tubsmith.

"Thought you'd eloped with that redhead!" he greeted Kit.

"Got drafted into the navy," Kit said. "I think. Nothing's been rigorously what you'd call 'real' lately. Does seeing you in this condition mean that everything is normal again?"

"Of course," handing him a bottle of no-name wine, "next question."

"Wouldn't have a dinner jacket I could borrow?"

"Come on along." They found Root's quarters, which like Kit he seemed to be sharing with a dozen or so others of the Hamiltonian persuasion. Clothing in a wide selection of colors, sizes, and degrees of formality littered the available floor space. "Take your pick I guess. Closest we'll see to Anarchism in our lifetime."

Back down in the Salon, the noise and centrifugal jollification had picked up markedly.

"Maniacs," cried Root, "every one of us! Fifty years ago of course more than today, today the real maniacs have gone into foundations work, set theory, all abstract as possible, like it's a race to see who can venture out furthest into the borderlands of the nonexistent. Not strictly speaking 'mania,' not as we once knew it. The *good old days!* Grassmann was German and hence automatically among the possessed, Hamilton was burdened with early genius and in the grip of a first love he could never get beyond. Drinking a lot, though who am I to talk, didn't help. Heaviside was once termed 'the Walt Whitman of English Physics'—"

"What . . . excuse me . . . *does that mean?*"

"Open question. Some have found in Heaviside a level of passion or maybe just energy, beyond the truculence already prevailing among the different camps in those days."

"Well if Heaviside's the Whitman," remarked a British attendee nearby in a striking yellow ensemble, "who's the Tennyson, you see?"

"Clerk Maxwell, wouldn't you say?" suggested someone else, as others joined in.

"Making Hamilton I imagine the Swinburne."

"Yes and who'd be Wordsworth then?"

"Grassmann!"

"I say, what an amusing game. And Gibbs? The Longfellow?"

"Is there an Oscar Wilde, by any chance?"

"Let's all go to the Casino!" someone invisible screamed. Kit wondered how any of this crowd would get as far as the door, let alone inside it—though, as it turned out, the Quaternion folks all had members' privileges at the Kursaal, which included the Casino.

"Intriguing new field opening up," Root confided on the way in. "Quaternion Probability. Seems that, as a baccarat game proceeds, you can describe each *coup* as a set of, well you'd call 'em vectors—different lengths, pointing off in different directions—"

"Something like your hair, Root."

"But instead of finding a single resultant," Root continued, "we're working here with rates of change, rotations, partial differentials, Curls, Laplacians, in three dimensions and sometimes more—"

"Root, I got my fishing-boat pay, and that's about it."

"Stick around, my son, and you'll soon be wallowing in them francs."

"Sure. Think I'll just wander for a bit."

Being used to more of a saloon type of atmosphere, Kit found the European manners here oppressive, not a heck of a lot of bluffing, slandering, cheating, or getting into fistfights, it seemed. Where was the fun? Except for a scream now and then whose polarity was hard to read, high emotion had to wait either for later or maybe for some other offstage room set aside for pain, lost souls, and canceled futures, for everything that must not go on out here, for this was a temple of money, wasn't it, even if that did lead back to its own Unspoken, to figures like Fleetwood Vibe, to rubber and ivory and fever and black African misery whose awful depths were only beginning to appal public sentiment elsewhere in the civilized world.

Waiters on padded soles passed in and out carrying Champagne, cigars, opiated powders, intra-Casino correspondence sealed in small heavy envelopes. Maquillages became slowly blurred with perspiration and tears, beards disarranged, handkerchiefs soiled not infrequently with blood from bitten lips. Top hats brimmed with banknotes. Heads passing into slumber met baize surfaces in audible percussion. Staccato utterances from wheels, dealing-shoes, dancing-shoes, dice, filled the room and what might otherwise have been an intolerable silence. Electric lamplight kept the scene hard-focused and readable, all proceeding stepwise, by integers, little ambiguity allowed in the spaces between. And somewhere, that unanswerable wave-function the sea.

Oddly, Kit noticed, the room was also crawling with lopsided makeup jobs, and these weren't limited to women either—broken symmetries everywhere, as if each, at some forgetful or overconfident moment, had allowed into the mirror-frame something they oughtn't to see, and there went the whole concoction. When at length he did run into a symmetrical face, it was at a roulette table, and on a type known in these parts as a *sphinxe Khnopffienne.* The woman poised above the wheel was looking Kit directly in the face, right away ruling out all sorts of introductory chitchat, with a gaze animal, timeless, as if already onto whatever he thought he understood now—or even would come to understand later, should there not arise matters more immediately desperate to attend to—an indifference to most forms of terror, including those which Anarchists of the day were finding it often necessary to self-incorporate. The difficulty lay in the extraordinary pale amber of her irises—far too pale for safety, less a positive shade than a failure on the side of jaundice to achieve the titanium-white that surrounded them. Put another way, he supposed—if eyes as colorless as these were on a dog, you would quickly enough understand that it was no dog looking back at you.

This presentable enigma regarded him through the smoke of a slender cigar. "You are enjoying a moment's independence from the rest of that ring you came in here with?"

Kit grinned. "Suspicious-looking birds, ain't we? What happens to a man spends all his time sitting indoors and staring at numbers."

"You're those mathematics people out at the Nouvelle Digue? *Mon Dieu.*"

"And you must be staying at the Continental?"

She raised an eyebrow.

"Judging by that 'ice' you've got on, 's what I meant."

"This? It's paste. Of course if you did happen to know the difference—"

"Heck, I'd forgive you, whichever it was."

"Exactly how jewel thieves talk. Now I'm sure I cannot trust you."

"Not much point offering my services, then, I guess."

"You're American."

"Doesn't mean I ain't been up and down some boulevards," Kit declared. "In and out some hallway doors."

"One of these 'cute Yankees." She presented, as if from the air, a small ivory-colored rectangle bearing a line-drawing in violet of a shaft of daylight, falling through a few panes of glass roof to illuminate a piece of iron arcade girdering and, down in one corner, in a modern sans-serif face, the name Pléiade Lafrisée, with an address in Paris. "My business card."

"I won't ask what your business is, 'cause it's your business."

She shrugged. *"Conseilleuse."*

"I won! I won!" came a deep bellow from across the room.

"Come on," Kit motioning her with his head over to a chemin-de-fer table, "show you something. Congratulations, Root. Little excitement, hey?"

"Ahhh! but I forgot to keep any record of it," Root Tubsmith's eyeballs all but whirling in their sockets, chips spilling everywhere, one tucked absentmindedly behind each of his ears. "Card values, time of day, should've logged them, might as well have all been random luck." He pulled from his pocket a battered slip of paper, covered with formulæ full of upside-down triangles, capital *S*'s, and small *q*'s and frowned at it. "Think I'd better adjust some parameters here, room temperature, punter irrationality index, one or two coefficients in the retroversion matrix—"

"Ma foi."

"If you like, mademoiselle," Kit offered, "we could place a small bet on your behalf. . . ."

"Leave the details to you gentlemen, being the mathematicians and whatever."

"That's it."

Next thing Pléiade knew, she was ahead by about ten thousand francs.

"This is the point where the Casino detectives come over and make me give it all back."

"We're safe," Root assured her, "they're looking for the latest thing, Nicol prisms and stroboscopic monocles and wireless telegraph rigs in people's shoes. But our magic is more ancient, and the big advantage to being so outmoded is that nobody recognizes it when they see it."

"So I have—what do you call them? Quaternions to thank."

"That might present difficulty—but you can thank us, if you like."

"Come, then, I'll buy you all dinner."

The Gentleman's Code struggling briefly with the possibility of a free meal and losing, most of the party took her up on her offer, and they all headed for the restaurant next to the gaming room.

Whatever else this cupcake might be up to, she was no piker. For everything the Q's ordered, she added on more of the same. The wine had names and vintage dates on the labels. At some point after the soup, Pléiade inquired of no one in particular, "Yes but what is a Quaternion?"

Hilarity at the table was general and prolonged. "What '*is*' a Quaternion? Ha, hahahaha!" Heels drummed helplessly on the carpet, wine splashed, deep-fried potatoes were thrown to and fro.

"Cambridge personality Bertie ('Mad Dog') Russell observed," observed Barry Nebulay, "that most of Hegel's arguments come down to puns on the word 'is.' In that sense the thing about a Quaternion 'is' is that we're obliged to encounter it in more than one guise. As a vector quotient. As a way of plotting complex numbers along three axes instead of two. As a list of instructions for turning one vector into another."

"And considered subjectively," added Dr. V. Ganesh Rao of the Calcutta University, "as an act of becoming longer or shorter, while at the same time turning, among axes whose unit vector is not the familiar and comforting 'one' but the altogether disquieting *square root of minus one.* If *you* were a vector, mademoiselle, you would begin in the 'real' world, change your length, enter an 'imaginary' reference system, rotate up to three different ways, and return to 'reality' a new person. Or vector."

"Fascinating. But . . . human beings aren't vectors. Are they?"

"Arguable, young lady. As a matter of fact, in India, the Quaternions are now the basis of a modern school of Yoga, a discipline which has always relied on such operations as stretching and turning. Here in the traditional 'Triangle Asana,' for example"—he stood and demonstrated—"the geometry is fairly straightforward. But soon one moves on to more advanced forms, into the complex spaces of the Quaternions. . . ." He shifted a few dishes, climbed on the table, announced, "The 'Quadrantal Versor Asana,'" and commenced a routine which quickly became more contortionistic and now and then you'd say contrary-to-fact, drawing the attention of other diners and eventually the maître d', who came running over waving a vehement finger and was two steps away from the table when Dr. Rao abruptly vanished.

"*Uwe moer!*" The functionary stood fingering his boutonnière.

"Go it, Doc!" chuckled Root. Pléiade lit a cigar, Barry Nebulay was looking under the table for hidden compartments. Except for a couple of Dr. Rao's table partners who were now busily picking items of food off his plate, astonishment was general. Presently they heard the Doctor calling from the kitchen, "Out here, everyone—come, see!" and sure enough he had reappeared with his foot in a tub of mayonnaise, though, curiously, not quite the same person he had been before performing the Asana. Taller, for one thing.

"And blond now, as well," puzzled Pléiade. "Can you do it backwards and return to who you were?"

"I have still not learned how. Some master Yogis are said to know the technique, but for me it remains noncommutative—mostly, I just like to hop about. Each time I become somebody else. It is like reincarnation on a budget, without the element of karma to worry about."

Pléiade, whom Kit had decided he was better off not trusting, lingered through another bottle of wine before producing from her reticule a Vacheron & Constantin watch, flipping open the hunting-case, and executing a dazzling smile of social apology. "I must fly, do forgive me, gentlemen."

Some of that consulting, Kit supposed.

Root signaled the waiter, making broad gestures toward Pléiade. "She gets the check—*haar rekening, ja?*"

PLÉIADE'S RENDEZVOUS was with one Piet Woevre, formerly of the Force Publique, whose taste for brutality, refined in the Congo, had been found by security bureaux here at home useful beyond price. His targets in Belgium were not, as newspaper politics might suggest, German so much as "socialist," meaning Slavic and Jewish. The mere street profile of a frock coat worn longer and looser than any Gentile would present made him reach for his revolver. He himself appeared to be blond, although the rest of his coloring was not consistent with that shade. There were suggestions of a time-consuming daily toilette, including lip-rouge and a not unambiguous cologne. But Woevre was indifferent to most of the presumptions and passwords of everyday sexuality. He had left that sort of thing far behind. Back in the mapless forests. Let anyone think what they like—should it come to a need for corporal expression, he could maim or kill, had lost count of how often he had done this, without hesitation or fear of consequence.

He belonged to the unbroken realm and its simplicities—river-flow, light and no light, transactions in blood. In Europe there was too much to remember, an inexhaustible network of caution and contrivance. Down there he didn't even need a name.

At first glance, there might seem little to choose between the French Foreign Legion and the Belgian Force Publique. In both cases one ran away from one's troubles to soldier in Africa. But where the one outfit envisaged desert penance in a surfeit of light, in radiant absolution, the other sought, in the gloom of the fetid forest, to embrace the opposite of atonement—to proclaim that the sum of one's European sins, however disruptive, had been but facile apprenticeship to a brotherhood of the willfully lost. Whose faces, afterward, would prove as unrecallable as those of the natives.

One look at the Q's, ambling through town with tobacco crumbs on their shirts and small banknotes sticking out of their pockets, was enough for Woevre to become at once what passes, among deputies of evil, for smitten. That is, willing to drop the surveillance and shelve the files of all his other current assignments, to concentrate on this band of *rastaquouères* who had blown so problematically into town. Not to mention the presence of "Young Congo" at the same hotel.

"They could turn out to be only innocent mathematicians, I suppose," muttered Woevre's section officer, de Decker.

"'Only.'" Woevre was amused. "Someday you'll explain to me how that's possible. Seeing that, on the face of it, all mathematics leads, doesn't it, sooner or later, to some kind of human suffering."

"Why, your very own specialty, Woevre. Comrades in arms, one would think."

"Not when the suffering might easily be mine, let alone theirs. Because they do not distinguish."

De Decker, not himself a philosopher, feeling vague alarm whenever he encountered this tendency in field personnel, had appeared to shift his interest to some papers in front of him.

The man was a *bobbejaan*. Woevre felt a familiar itch in his knuckles, but the discussion was not quite over. "This wire traffic with Antwerp and Brussels." De Decker did not look up. "One particular group, 'MKIV/ODC,' which no one can quite identify, unless your people . . . ?"

"Yes it looks to our cryptos like some sort of weaponry—torpedo-related? who, at the moment, can say? 'Mark Four something or other.' Perhaps *you* might care to inquire into it. I know it's not part of your remit," as it appeared Woevre was about to protest, "yet another set of 'antennas' would be welcome."

"Graciously put. Consider me another loyal *gatkruiper*." Accelerated by an awareness of diminishing returns, Woevre was out the door.

"As if you hadn't enough to put up with," Pléiade Lafrisée remarked later.

"That's all the sympathy I get?"

"Oh . . . was there some stipulated amount? Did you sneak that into our agreement, too?"

"With invisible ink. What we'd like tonight, though, is a look through his room. Can you keep him occupied for an hour or so?"

Her hands had been busy with his person. She hesitated, thinking it over, until she sensed some brutal imminence, then continued. Later in her bath, she inspected a number of bruises, and decided they were all charming except for one on her wrist, which to a connoisseur might have suggested absence of imagination.

Woevre watched her leave the room. Women looked better from behind, but one saw them that way only when taking their leave after one was done with them, and what good was that? Why did this society insist on a woman entering a room face-first instead of ass-first? Another of the civilized complexities that made him miss intensely the forest life. Since returning to Belgium he had found only an increasing number of these, deployed around him like traps or mines. The need not to offend the King, to remain aware of rival bureaux and their own hidden schemes, to calibrate everything against the mortal mass of Germany, forever towering over the day.

Could it matter who spied for whom? The ruling families of Europe, related by blood and marriage, inhabited their single great incestuous pretense of power, bickering without end—the state bureaucracies, the armies, the Churches, the bourgeoisie, the workers, all were incarcerated within the game. . . . But if, like Woevre, one had seen into the fictitiousness of European power, there was no reason, in the terrible trans-horizontic light of what approached, not to work for as many masters, along as many axes, as one's memory could accommodate without confusion.

And what, furthermore, to make of this late rumor, drifting just below Woevre's ability to acquire the signal at all clearly—an unidentifiable noise in the night that sends a sleeper awake with heart pounding and entrails hollow—intelligence of a Quaternionic Weapon, a means to unloose upon the world energies hitherto unimagined—hidden, de Decker would surely say "innocently," inside the *w* term. A mathematical paper by the Englishman Edmund Whittaker which few here could make sense of was said to be pivotal. Woevre had noticed how the convention-goers kept giving one another these *looks*. As if parties to a secret whose terrible force was somehow, conveniently, set to one side—as if to be encountered only in a companion world they did not quite know how to enter or, once there, to exit. Here in this sub-sea-level patch of strategic ground, hostage to European ambitions on all sides, waiting, held sleepless without remission, for the blows to descend. What better place for the keepers of the seals and codes to convene?

NEXT EVENING KIT, having against his better judgment accompanied Pléiade to her suite, found himself in some perplexity, for at some point in the deep malediction of the hour she had mysteriously vanished. Only a moment before, it seemed to him, she'd been there at the seaward window, poised against the uncertain marine light, carefully mixing absinthe and Champagne to produce a strange foaming louche. Now, with no sensible passage of time, the rooms were resonant with absence. Next to the cheval-glass, Kit noticed a pale dressing-gown, of all-but-insubstantial chiffon, not draped over a chair but *standing erect,* now and then rippling from otherwise unsensed passages of air, as if someone were inside of it, perhaps stirred by invisible forces less nameable, its movements, disquietingly, not always matched by those of its tall image in the mirror.

Nothing now, not even the ocean, could be heard in the room, though the windows overlooked the long moon-stung waves. In the moonlight, against gravity, the thing poised there, faceless, armless, attending him, as if, in a moment, it would speak. In the curiously sealed quality of the silence in the room, they waited thus, the disquieted Vectorist and this wraith of Pléiade Lafrisée. Was it something he drank? Should he start conversing with a negligee?

To the distant pulse of the sea, among the tall-hatted monitory shadows, he made his way back to the hotel to find his bedroll gone through, though that couldn't have taken more than a minute, and his first thought was of Scarsdale Vibe, or a Vibe agent.

"We saw them," said Eugénie. "It was the political police. They think you are one of us. Thanks to us, you are now a nihilist outlaw."

"It's O.K.," said Kit, "it's something I was always planning to get around to anyway. Did any of them bother you folks?"

"We know each other," said Policarpe. "It's a peculiar game we all play. Against what looms in the twilight of the European future, it doesn't make much sense, this pretending to carry on with the day, you know, just waiting. Everyone waiting."

"In France," said Denis, "they speak of He Who Must Come. He is not the Messiah. He is not Christ or Napoleon returned. He was not General Boulanger. He is unnameable. Nevertheless one would have to be uncommonly isolated, either mentally or physically, not to feel His approach. And to know what He is bringing. What death and what transfiguration."

"We wait here, however, not, like the French, for some Napoleon, nothing that human, but kept hostage to the arrival of a certain military Hour, whenever the general staffs decide it has struck."

"Isn't Belgium supposed to be neutral?"

"*Zeker*"—a shrug—"there's even a Treaty, which makes it a *dead cert* we'll be invaded by at least one of the signatories, isn't that what Treaties of Neutrality are for? Each of the Powers has its plan for us. Von Schlieffen, for instance, wants to send in thirty-two German divisions against our own, let us say, six. Wilhelm has offered Leopold part of France, the ancient Duchy of Burgundy, if, when the mythical moment arrives, we will surrender all our famous shellproof forts and leave the railways intact—little Belgium once again busy at what she does best, tamely offering her battlefield-ready lowlands to boots, hooves, iron wheels, waiting to be first to go under before a future no one in Europe has the clairvoyance to imagine as anything more than an exercise for clerks.

"Think of Belgium as a pawn. It is no accident that so many international chess tournaments are held here in Ostende. If chess is war in miniature . . . perhaps Belgium is understood to be the first sacrifice in a general conflict . . . though perhaps not, as in a gambit, to provide a counterattack, for a gambit may be declined, and who would decline to take Belgium?"

"So . . . this is like Colorado, with changes of sign—it's negative altitude, this living below sea-level, something like that?"

Fatou stood close to him, looking up through her lashes. "It is the sorrow of anticipation, Kit."

THE NEXT TIME he saw Pléiade Lafrisée was at a café-restaurant off the Place d'Armes. It would not occur to him until much later to wonder if she had arranged the encounter. She was in pale violet peau de soie, and a hat so beguiling that Kit was only momentarily surprised to find himself with an erection. It was still early in the study of these matters, only a few brave pioneers like the Baron von Krafft-Ebing had dared peep into the strange and weirdly twilit country of hat-fetishism—not that Kit noticed stuff like that ordinarily, but it happened actually to be a gray toque of draped velvet, trimmed with antique guipure, and a tall ostrich plume dyed the same shade of violet as her dress. . . .

"This? One finds them in every other midinette's haunt, literally for sous."

"Oh. I must've been staring. What happened to you the other night?"

"Come. You can buy me a Lambic."

The place was like a museum of mayonnaise. This being just at the height of the *culte de la mayonnaise* then sweeping Belgium, oversize exhibits of the ovoöleaginous emulsion were to be encountered at every hand. Heaps of Mayonnaise Grenache, surrounded by plates of smoked turkey and tongue, glowed redly as if from within, while with less, if any, reference to actual food it might have been there to modify, mountains of Chantilly mayonnaise, swept upward in gravity-impervious peaks insubstantial as cloud, along with towering masses of green mayonnaise, basins of boiled mayonnaise, mayonnaise baked into soufflés, not to mention a number of not entirely successful mayonnaises, under some obscure attainder, or on occasion passing as something else, dominated every corner.

"How much do you know of La Mayonnaise?" she inquired.

He shrugged. "Maybe up to the part that goes *'Aux armes, citoyens'*—"

But she was frowning, earnest as he had seldom seen her. "La Mayonnaise," Pléiade explained, "has its origins in the moral squalor of the court of Louis XV—here in Belgium the affinity should not be too surprising. The courts of Leopold and Louis are not that different except in time, and what is time? Both monumentally deluded men, maintaining their power through oppression of the innocent. One might usefully compare Cléo de Mérode and the marquise de Pompadour. Neuropathists would recognize in both kings a desire to construct a self-consistent world to live inside, which allows them to continue the great damage they are inflicting on the world the rest of us must live in.

"The sauce was invented as a new sensation for jaded palates at court by the duc de Richelieu, at first known as *mahonnaise* after Mahon, the chief port of Minorca, the scene of the duc's dubious 'victory' in 1756 over the ill-fated Admiral Byng. Basically Louis's drug dealer and pimp, Richelieu, known for opium recipes to fit all occasions, is also credited with the introduction into France of the cantharides, or Spanish fly." She gazed pointedly at Kit's trousers. "What might this aphrodisiac have in common with the mayonnaise? That the beetles must be gathered and killed by exposing them to vinegar fumes suggests an emphasis on living or recently living creatures—the egg yolk perhaps regarded as a conscious entity—cooks will speak of whipping, beating, binding, penetration, submission, surrender. There is an undoubtedly Sadean aspect to the mayonnaise. No getting past that."

Kit was a little confused by now. "It always struck me as kind of, I don't know . . . bland?"

"Until you look within. Mustard, for example, mustard and cantharides, *n'est-ce pas?* Both arousing the blood. Blistering the skin. Mustard is the widely-known key to resurrecting a failed mayonnaise, as is the cantharides to reviving broken desire."

"You've been thinking about mayonnaise a lot, mademoiselle."

"Meet me tonight," a sudden fierce whisper, "out at the Mayonnaise Works, and you shall perhaps understand things it is given only to a few to know. There will be a carriage waiting." She pressed his hand and was gone in a mist of vetiver, abruptly as the other evening.

"Sounds too good to pass up," it seemed to Root Tubsmith. "She sure is a pip, that one. You need company?"

"I need protection. I don't trust her. But you know—"

"Oh ain't that the truth. She's trying to talk me into teaching her my Q.P. system. Well, maybe not 'talk,' exactly. I keep telling her she has to learn Quaternions first, and darn if she doesn't actually keep showing up for more lessons."

"She learning anything?"

"I know I am."

"I'll pray for your safety. Meantime if you never see me again—"

"Oh, be optimistic. She's a goodhearted working girl, is all."

THE USINE RÉGIONALE à la Mayonnaise or Regional Mayonnaise Works, where all the mayonnaise in West Flanders was manufactured and then sent out in a variety of forms to different restaurants, each of which presented it as a unique Speciality of the House, though quite extensive in area, was seldom, if ever, mentioned in guidebooks, receiving, in consequence, few visitors other than those employed there. Among the dunes west of town, next to a canal, visible by day for miles across the sands, rose dozens of modern steel tanks of olive, sesame, and cottonseed oils, which were delivered through a further maze of pipes and valves to the great Facilité de l'Assemblage, electrically grounded and insulated to allow production to continue uninterrupted by the disjunctive effects of thunderstorms.

After sunset, however, this cheerfully rational example of twentieth-century engineering dissolved into more precarious shadows. "Anybody here?" Kit called, wandering the corridors and catwalks in a borrowed lounge suit and some nifty razor-toed congress shoes. Somewhere invisible in the dark, steam dynamos hissed, and enormous batteries of Italian hens squawked, clucked, and laid eggs which rolled ceaselessly, day and night apparently, in a subdued rumbling, by way of an intricate arrangement of chutes cushioned in gutta-percha, to the Egg Collection Area.

Puzzling thing, though, shouldn't there've been a little more factory-floor activity around here? he couldn't see any shift-workers anyplace. This looked to be all going on without any human intervention—except now, suddenly, for whatever invisible hand had just pulled a switch to set everything into motion. Ordinarily Kit would have been fascinated by the technical details, as giant gas burners bloomed percussively alight, belts and pulleys lurched into motion, dripping-heads swiveled into place over the *cuves d'agitation,* oil pumps engaged, elegantly curved beaters began to gather speed.

But not a pair of eyes, nor the sound of a purposeful step, anyplace. Kit, who seldom panicked, felt close to it now, though this still might be all about nothing more than mayonnaise.

He didn't exactly start running, but his step might have quickened some. By the time he had reached the Clinique d'Urgence pour Sauvetage des Sauces, for the resurrection of potentially failed mayonnaise, at first all he noticed was the floor getting a little slippery—next thing he knew, he was on his back with his feet in the air, in less time than it took to figure out that he'd slipped. His hat had been knocked off and was sliding away on some pale semiliquid flow. He felt something heavy and wet in his hair. Mayonnaise! he seemed now actually to be sitting in the stuff, which was a good six inches, hell make that closer to *a foot deep.* And, and swiftly rising! Kit had blundered into flash-flooding arroyos slower than this. Looking around, he saw that the mayonnaise level had already climbed too high up the exit door for him even to pull it open, assuming he could even get that far. He was being engulfed in thick, slick, sour-smelling mayonnaise.

Trying to clear his eyes of the stuff, slipping repeatedly, he half swam, half staggered toward where he remembered having seen a window, and launched a blind desperate kick, which of course sent him flat on his ass again, but not before he'd felt a hopeful splintering of glass and sashwork, and before he could think of a way to reach the invisible opening to climb through, the mayonnaise-pressure itself, like a conscious beast seeking escape from its captivity, had borne him through the broken window, launching him out in a great vomitous arc which dropped him into the canal below.

He surfaced in time to hear somebody screaming *"Cazzo, cretino!"* above the rhythmic sputter of an engine of some sort. A blurry wet shadow approached. It was Rocco and Pino, in their dirigible torpedo.

"Over here!"

"È il cowboy!" The Italians, in their glossy Vulcanized working gear, slowed down to fish Kit out of the water. He noticed they were casting anxious looks back down the canal.

"Somebody after you?"

Rocco resumed speed, and Pino explained. "We just got her out of the shop and decided to have a look at the *Alberta,* thinking, how dangerous can it be, when there's no Belgian navy, *vero?* But it turns out there are Garde Civique, in boats! We forgot about that! All up and down the canals!"

"*You* forgot," muttered Rocco. "But it doesn't matter. With this engine we can outrace anything."

"Show him!" cried Pino. The boys got busy with choke controls, spark timers, and acceleration levers, and presently, sure enough, sending up a roostertail of water and black oil-smoke, they had the craft snarling along the canal at forty knots, maybe more. Whoever might be back there was probably breaking off the chase about now.

"We're going to stop in and surprise the girls," said Rocco.

"If they don't surprise us," Pino in what Kit recognized as romantic anxiety. *"Le bambole anarchiste, porca miseria."*

A mile or so past Oudenberg, they turned left onto the Bruges canal and crept in to Ostend, dropping Kit off at the Quai de l'Entrepôt before going off to look for a berth safe from the attentions of the Garde Civique. "Thanks, *ragazzi,* see you down the trail, I hope. . . ." And Kit tried not to stand there too long gazing after his deliverers from death by mayonnaise.

The crew of *Inconvenience* had been ordered to Brussels to pay their respects at a memorial service for General Boulanger, held each September 30 on the anniversary of his suicide, an observance not altogether free of political suggestion, there having remained within the Chums of Chance bureaucracy a defiant residue of Boulangism. Official correspondence from the French chapters, for example, could still be found bearing yellow-and-blue postage stamps, with the General's likeness printed in a sorrowful brown—to all appearances legitimate French issues, ranging from one centime to twenty francs, but in reality *timbres fictifs,* said to be of German origin, the work of an entrepreneur who hoped to sell them after a Boulangist coup, though sinister hints were also in the air of involvement by "IIIb," the intelligence bureau of the German general staff, reflecting a theory thereamong that Germany might stand a better military chance against a revanchist effort led by the somewhat discomposed General than any policy perhaps a bit more thought out.

The Brussels visit proved so melancholy that the boys had put in for, and to everyone's surprise been granted, ground leave at Ostend, the closest accredited liberty port. Here before long, seemingly by chance, they had become aware of the convention of Quaternionists-in-exile at the Grand Hôtel de la Nouvelle Digue.

"Haven't seen so many of those birds in one place since Candlebrow," declared Darby, looking through one of the remote viewers.

"For that embattled discipline," said Chick, "back in the days of the Quaternion Wars, Candlebrow was one of very few safe harbors."

"Bound to run into a few that we know."

"Sure, but will *they* know *us?*" It was just at that turn of the day when the wind was shifting direction from a land to a sea breeze. Below them crowds along the Digue streamed back to hotels, high teas, assignations, naps.

"Once," Randolph with a long-accustomed melancholy, "they would have all been stopped in their tracks, rubbernecking up at us in wonder. Nowadays we just grow more and more invisible."

"Eehhyyhh, I betcha I could even pull out my knockwurst here and wave it at 'em, and nobody'd even notice," cackled Darby.

"Suckling!" gasped Lindsay. "Even taking into account considerations of dimension, which in your case would require a modification of any salcician metaphor toward the diminutive, 'wiener' being perhaps more appropriate, nonetheless the activity you anticipate is prohibited by statute in most of the jurisdictions over which we venture, including in many instances the open sea, and can only be taken as symptomatic of an ever more criminally psychopathic disposition."

"Hey Noseworth," replied Darby, "it was big enough for ya the other night."

"Why, you little—and I do mean 'little'—"

"Gentlemen," their commander beseeched them.

However successfully it might have escaped the general view, the *Inconvenience* had come almost immediately to the attention of de Decker's shop, which maintained a primitive sort of electromagnetic monitoring station out in the dunes between Nieuport and Dunkirk, which lately had been logging mysterious transmissions at unprecedented levels of field strength. These were intended for *Inconvenience*'s Tesla rig, one of a number of compact power-receivers allocated to skyships around the globe for their auxiliary power needs. The locations of the Transmitters were kept as secret as possible, being vulnerable to assault from power companies threatened by any hint of competition. Unfamiliar with the Tesla system and alarmed by the strengths of the electric and magnetic fields, de Decker's people naturally conflated this with those recent rumors of a Quaternion weapon which had Piet Woevre so intrigued.

Woevre couldn't always see the skyship, but he knew it was there. When the wind was trained exactly across the dunes, he could hear the engines aloft, see the stars blotted out in large moving shapes of black against black. . . . He thought he had also glimpsed the crew up on the seawall, slouching along like a bunch of collegians in search of amusement, hands in pockets, taking in the sights.

It was October by now, the regular season was past and the breezes cool but not yet brisk enough to drive away pedestrians from the Digue, though Lindsay found it uncomfortable—"Far too desolate, one's face grows itchy with the salt, one feels like Lot's wife." In the sea-light and optical illusions out here, with all the demolition and new construction going on, the boys were often uncertain as to what a given mass at any distance might turn out to be—cloud, warship, breakwater, or, indeed, only the projection upon a perhaps too-receptive sky of some spiritual difficulty within. Hence, perhaps, the preference they had already noted in Ostend for interiors—casinos, hydropathics, hotel suites in a choice of disguises—hunting-lodge, Italian grotto, parlor of sin, whatever the lodger with the wherewithal might require for the night.

"And say, who are these strange civilians creeping around all of a sudden?" Darby wanted to know.

"The Authorities," shrugged Chick. "What of it?"

"'Authorities'! Surface jurisdiction only. Nothing to do with us."

"You are Legal Officer," Lindsay reminded him. "What is the problem?"

"'The' problem, Noseworth, is *your* problem, as Master-at-Arms—nothing is where it should be anymore. Almost as if persons unknown have been sneaking on board and rooting around."

"But one cannot imagine," pointed out Randolph St. Cosmo, "that much gets past Pugnax." Indeed, with the passing years Pugnax had been evolving from a simple watchdog to a sophisticated defensive system, with a highly-developed taste, moreover, for human blood. "Ever since that mission to the Carpathians," Randolph recalled, frowning a little. "And the way he drove off that squadron of Uhlans at Temesvár, almost as if he were hypnotizing their horses into unseating their riders. . . ."

"Some fiesta!" cackled Darby.

Still, their admiration for Pugnax's martial skills was not unmixed these days with apprehension. The faithful canine carried about a strange gleam in his eye, and the only member of the crew who communicated with him much anymore was Miles Blundell. The two had been known to sit together side by side back on the fantail, wordlessly deep into the hours of the mid-watch, as if in some sort of telepathic contact.

Since the mission to Inner Asia, Miles had been engaged ever more deeply with a project of the spirit which he found himself unable to share with the others in the crew, though it was plain to all that his present trajectory might take him perhaps further than he could find his way back from. Beneath the sands of the Taklamakan, while Chick and Darby had idled mindlessly at one liberty-port after the next, and Lindsay and Randolph had spent hours conferring with Captain Toadflax over how most effectively to carry on the search for Shambhala, Miles was being tormented by a prefiguration, almost insupportable in its clarity, of the holy City, separated by only a slice of Time, a thin screen extending everywhere across his attention, which grew ever more frail and transparent. . . . Unable to sleep or converse, he would often lose track of recipes, forget to stir the popover dough, wreck the sky-coffee, while the others continued calmly about the chores of the day. How could they not know of that immeasurable Approach? Thus he sought out Pugnax, in whose eyes the light of understanding was a beacon in what had without warning become dangerous skies.

For somehow, the earlier, the great, light had departed, the certitude become broken as ground-dwellers' promises—time regained its opacity, and one day the boys, translated here to Belgium, as if by evil agency, had begun to lapse earthward through a smell of coal smoke and flowers out of season, toward a beleaguered coast ambiguous as to the disposition of land and sea, down into seaside shadows stretching into the growing dark, shadows that could not always be correlated with actual standing architecture, folding and pleating ever inwardly upon themselves, an entire mapful of unlighted outer neighborhoods sprawled among the dunes and small villages. . . .

Miles, looking out at the humid distances from this height, at the hesitant darkness in which little could be read across a lowland fixed anciently under a destiny, if not quite a curse, contemplated the pallid vastness of twilight, in its suspense, its cryptic insinuation. What was about to emerge from the night just behind the curve of Earth? fog from the canals rose toward the ship. A smudged and isolated copse of willows emerged for a moment. . . . Low clouds in the distance bleared the sun, causing the light to break into suggestions of a city hidden behind what was visible here, sketched at in shadows of taupe and damaged rose . . . nothing so sacred or longingly sought as Shambhala, stained with a persistent component of black in all light that swept this lowland, flowing over dead cities, mirror-still canals . . . black shadows, tempest and visitation, prophecy, madness. . . .

"Blundell," Lindsay's voice missing today its usual aggravated edge, "the Commander has called Special Sky Detail. Please take your assigned station."

"Of course, Lindsay, I was distracted for a moment."

After securing the mess decks that evening, Miles sought out Chick Counterfly. "I have seen one of the Trespassers," he said. "Down there. Out on the Promenade."

"Did he recognize you?"

"Yes. We met and spoke. Ryder Thorn. He was at Candlebrow. At the ukulele workshop that summer. He lectured on the four-note chord in the context of timelessness, and described himself then as a Quaternionist. We had quickly discovered our common love of the instrument," Miles recalled, "and discussed the widespread contempt in which ukulele players are held—traceable, we concluded, to the uke's all-but-exclusive employment as a producer of chords—single, timeless events apprehended all at once instead of serially. Notes of a linear melody, up and down a staff, being a record of pitch versus time, to play a melody is to introduce the element of time, and hence of mortality. Our perceived reluctance to leave the timelessness of the struck chord has earned ukulele players our reputation as feckless, clownlike children who will not grow up."

"Never thought of it like that," said Chick, "all I know is, is it sure sounds better than when we sing a cappella."

"In any case Thorn and I found that we communicate as well as ever. It was almost like being at Candlebrow again, only maybe not as dangerous."

"You saved us then, Miles. You saw right into it. No telling what—"

"You fellows would have been saved by your own good sense," Miles declared. "Whether I'd been there or not."

But there was a sort of disconnection now in his voice that Chick had learned to recognize. "There's something else, isn't there."

"It may not be over." Miles was inspecting his Chums of Chance regulation-issue knuckle-duster.

"What are you planning, Miles?"

"We've arranged to meet."

"You might be in danger."

"We'll see."

So Miles, having duly submitted a special-request chit and received approval from Randolph, descended in civilian dress as a ground-party of one, to all appearances only another day-tripper among the seasonal throng creeping about the royal town below, ever hostage to the sea.

It was a bright day—at the horizon Miles could just make out the carbon smear of a liner. Ryder Thorn was waiting in the angle of the Digue by the Kursaal, with two bicycles.

"Brought your uke, I see."

"I have learned a 'snappy' new arrangement of a Chopin nocturne that might interest you."

They stopped at a patisserie for coffee and rolls and then pedaled south toward Diksmuide, the still air gradually accelerating into a breeze. The morning was alive with late summer. Harvest season was rolling to a close. Young tourists were everywhere in the lanes and by the canalsides, winding up their season of exemption from care, and were preparing to go back to schools and jobs.

The terrain was flat, easy cycling, allowing for speeds of up to twenty miles an hour. They overtook other cyclists, singly and in cheerfully uniformed touring groups, but didn't pause to chat.

Miles looked at the countryside, pretending to be less puzzled than he was. For the sunlight had to it the same interior darkness as the watery dusk last night—it was like passing through an all-surrounding photographic negative—the lowland nearly silent except for water-thrushes, the harvested fields, the smell of hops being dried in kilns, flax pulled up and piled in sheaves, in local practice not to be retted till the spring, shining canals, sluices, dikes and cart roads, dairy cattle under the trees, the edged and peaceful clouds. Tarnished silver. Somewhere up in this sky was Miles's home, and all he knew of human virtue, the ship, somewhere on station, perhaps watching over him at that moment.

"Our people know what will happen here," said Thorn, "and my assignment is to find out whether, and how much, yours know."

"I'm a mess cook for a ballooning club," said Miles. "I know a hundred different kinds of soup. I can look in the eyes of dead fish at the market and tell how fresh they're likely to be. I am a whiz with pudding in large quantities. But I don't foretell the future."

"Try to see my difficulty here. My principals think you do. What am I supposed to report back to them?"

Miles looked around. "It's nice country, but a little on the motionless side. I wouldn't say anything's going to happen here."

"Blundell, back at Candlebrow," Thorn said, "you were able to see what your companions could not. You spied on us regularly until you were discovered."

"Not really. No reason to."

"You have persistently refused to coöperate with our program."

"We may look like country boys, but when strangers show up out of nowhere with offers that sound too good to be true . . . well, common sense does sort of take over, is all. Can't blame us for that, and we're sure not going to feel guilty about it."

The calmer Miles got, the more worked up Thorn became. "You boys spend too much time up there. You lose sight of what is really going on in the world you think you understand. Do you know why we set up a permanent base at Candlebrow? Because all investigations of Time, however sophisticated or abstract, have at their true base the human fear of mortality. Because we have the answer for that. You think you drift above it all, immune to everything, immortal. Are you that foolish? Do you know where we are right now?"

"On the road between Ypres and Menin, according to the signs," said Miles.

"Ten years from now, for hundreds and thousands of miles around, but especially here—" He appeared to check himself, as if he had been about to blurt a secret.

Miles was curious, and knew by now where the needles went and which way to rotate them. "Don't tell me too much, now, I'm a spy, remember? I'll report this whole conversation to National H.Q."

"Damn you, Blundell, damn you all. You have no idea what you're heading into. This world you take to be 'the' world will die, and descend into Hell, and all history after that will belong properly to the history of Hell."

"Here," said Miles, looking up and down the tranquil Menin road.

"Flanders will be the mass grave of History."

"Well."

"And that is not the most perverse part of it. They will all embrace death. Passionately."

"The Flemish."

"The world. On a scale that has never yet been imagined. Not some religious painting in a cathedral, not Bosch, or Brueghel, but this, what you see, the great plain, turned over and harrowed, all that lies below brought to the surface—deliberately flooded, not the sea come to claim its due but the human counterpart to that same utter absence of mercy—for not a village wall will be left standing. League on league of filth, corpses by the uncounted thousands, the breath you took for granted become corrosive and death-giving."

"Sure sounds unpleasant," said Miles.

"You don't believe any of this. You should."

"Of course I believe you. You're from the future, aren't you? Who'd know better?"

"I think you know what I'm talking about."

"We haven't got the technical know-how," Miles said, pretending a massive patience. "Remember? We are only skyship-jockeys, we have trouble enough with three dimensions, what would we do with four?"

"Do you think we chose to come here, to this terrible place? Tourists of disaster, jump in some time machine, oh, how about Pompeii this weekend, Krakatoa perhaps, but then volcanoes are *so* boring really, eruptions, lava, over in a minute, let's try something really—"

"Thorn, you don't have to—"

"We have had no choice," fiercely, having abandoned the measured delivery Miles had come to associate with Trespassers. "No more than ghosts may choose what places they must haunt . . . you children drift in a dream, all is smooth, no interruptions, no discontinuities, but imagine the fabric of Time torn open, and yourselves swept through, with no way back, orphans and exiles who find you will do what you must, however shameful, to get from end to end of each corroded day."

Miles, taken by a desolate illumination, reached out his hand, and Thorn, seeing his intention, flinched and backed away, and in the instant Miles understood that there had been no miracle, no brilliant technical coup, in fact no "time travel" at all—that the presence in this world of Thorn and his people had been owing only to some chance blundering upon a shortcut through unknown topographies of Time, enabled somehow by whatever was to happen here, in this part of West Flanders where they stood, by whatever terrible singularity in the smooth flow of Time had opened to them.

"You are not here," he whispered in a speculative ecstasy. "Not fully manifest."

"I wish I were not here," cried Ryder Thorn. "I wish I had never seen these Halls of Night, that I were not cursed to return, and return. You have been so easy to fool—most of you anyway—you are such simpletons at the fair, gawking at your Wonders of Science, expecting as your entitlement all the Blessings of Progress, it is your faith, your pathetic balloon-boy faith."

Miles and Thorn directed their wheels back toward the sea. As evening descended, Thorn, who honored smaller promises at least, produced his ukulele and played the Chopin E-minor Nocturne, the tenuous notes, as light departed, acquiring substance and depth. They found an inn and ate supper companionably, and returned to Ostend in the owl-light.

"I could have passed my hand through him," reported Miles. "As if there'd been some failure of physical translation. . . ."

"What spiritualists might have called a 'plasmic hysteresis,'" nodded Chick.

"There is nothing immortal about them, Chick. They have lied to all of us, including those Chums of Chance in other units who may have been fool enough to work for them, in exchange for 'eternal youth.' They cannot provide that. They never could.

"You remember back at Candlebrow, after you brought me to meet 'Mr. Ace,' how disconsolate I was? I could not stop crying for hours, for I knew then—with no evidence, no reasoned proof, I simply knew, the minute I saw him, that it was all false, the promise was nothing but a cruel confidence game."

"You ought to have shared that," Chick said.

"Overcome as I was, Chick, I knew I would get through it. But you fellows—Lindsay is so frail, really, Darby pretends to be such a weathered old nihilist, but he's hardly out of boyhood. How could I have been that cruel to any of you? My brothers?"

"But now I have to tell them."

"I was hoping you could find a way."

Viktor Mulciber—bespoke suit, pomaded silver hair—though rich enough to afford to send a deputy, showed up at the Kursaal himself in a state of unconcealed eagerness, as if this mysterious Q-weapon were a common firearm and he hoping the seller would allow him a few courtesy shots.

"I am the one they send for when Basil Zaharoff is busy with a new redhead and can't be bothered," he introduced himself. "Everywhere one finds a spectrum of need, from bludgeons and machetes to submarines and poison gases—trains of history not fully run, Chinese tongs, Balkan *komitadji,* African vigilantes, each with its attendant population of widows-to-be, often in geographies barely sketched in pencil on the back of some envelope or waybill. One glance at any government budget anywhere in the world tells the story—the money is always in place, already allocated, the motive everywhere is fear, the more immediate the fear, the higher the multiples."

"Say, *I'm* in the wrong business!" Root exclaimed cheerfully.

The arms tycoon beamed as if from a distance. "No you're not."

Trying to get some kind of grasp on the working principles of the suddenly desirable weapon, the amiable death-merchant was conferring in an out-of-the-way estaminet with a handful of Quaternioneers, including Barry Nebulay, Dr. V. Ganesh Rao, today metamorphosed into an American Negro, and Umeki Tsurigane, along with whom Kit had tagged owing to his lately-intensifying fascination with the Nipponese peach.

"No one seems to know what these waves are," said Barry Nebulay. "They cannot strictly be termed Hertzian, for they engage the Æther in a different way—for one thing, they seem to be longitudinal as well as transverse. Quaternionists may have a chance someday of understanding them."

"And arms dealers, don't forget," smiled Mulciber. "It's said the inventor of this weapon has found a way to get inside the scalar part of a Quaternion, where invisible powers may be had for the taking."

"Of the four terms," nodded Nebulay, "the scalar, or *w* term, like the baritone in a barbershop quartet or the viola in a string quartet, has always been singled out as the eccentric one. If you considered the three vector terms as dimensions in space, and the scalar term as Time, then any energy encountered inside that term might be taken as due to Time, an intensified form of Time itself."

"Time," explained Dr. Rao, "is the Further Term, you see, transcending and conditioning **i, j,** and **k**—the dark visitor from the Exterior, the Destroyer, the fulfiller of the Trinity. It is the merciless clock-beat we all seek to escape, into the pulselessness of salvation. It is all this and more."

"A weapon based on Time . . ." mused Viktor Mulciber. "Well, why not? The one force no one knows how to defeat, resist, or reverse. It kills all forms of life sooner or later. With a Time-weapon you could become the most feared person in history."

"I'd rather be loved," said Root.

Mulciber shrugged. "You're young."

He wasn't the only arms rep in town. Somehow the rumor had found the others, in their train compartments, the beds of procurement ministers' wives, back in the brush up unexplored tributaries, spreading their blankets in any of a thousand desolate clearings on the baked and beaten red laterite where nothing would grow again, displaying to the lesioned and bereft their inventories of wonder—and one by one they made their excuses, and rescheduled their travels, and came to Ostend, as to some international chess tournament.

But they were too late, because Piet Woevre had had the jump on them all along, and so it happened that on a particular evening in autumn, among the teeming Inner Boulevards of Brussels, a hotbed of the illicit down toward the Gare du Midi, Woevre finally concluded the purchase with Edouard Gevaert, with whom he had done business in the past, though not of quite this nature. They met in a tavern frequented by receivers of stolen goods, had a formal glass of beer, and went out in back to close the deal. All around them the world was for sale or barter. Later Woevre learned that he could have got the article cheaper in Antwerp, but there were too many quarters of Antwerp, particularly around the docks, that he could no longer visit without more precaution than the object was likely to prove worth.

When he came into actual possession of it, Woevre, who hadn't been able to imagine it as anything but a weapon, was surprised and a little disappointed to find it so small. He'd been expecting something on the order of a Krupp field-piece, perhaps assembled from several parts, needing cargo wagons to bring it from place to place. Instead here was something in a sleek leather case, shaped exquisitely by northern Italian maskmakers to the exact facets of the shape within, a perfectly tailored black skin, a deployment of light among a careful clutter of angles, a hundred blurry highlights. . . .

"You're sure this is it."

"I hope I know better than to misrepresent anything to you, Woevre."

"But, the enormous energy . . . without a peripheral component, a power supply of some sort, how . . ." As Woevre stood turning the device this way and that in the uncertain light of dusk and streetlamps, Gevaert was unprepared for the yearning he saw in the operative's face. It was desire so immoderate . . . nothing this somewhat unworldly go-between had ever witnessed before, nothing many people in the world had, the desire for a single weapon able to annihilate the world.

WHENEVER KIT FOUND himself considering his plans, which he had once not long ago believed to include Göttingen, there was always the interesting question of why he should be lingering in this vaguely glandular shape on the map, beleaguered, paused at the edge of history, less a nation than a prophecy of a fate to be communally suffered, an all but sub-audible *ostinato* of fear. . . .

It had not occurred to him until lately that Umeki might be in any way an element in this. They had found excuses to fall more and more into each other's emotional field, until one fateful afternoon in her room, with rain in autumnal descent at the window, she appeared in a doorway, naked, blood beneath skin fine as silver leaf sonorously all but singing in its desire. Kit, who had imagined himself a fellow of some experience, was poleaxed by the understanding that there was no use in women looking any other way than this. He had the profound sense of having wasted most of the free time in his life up till now. It did not help in this assessment that she was wearing that cowgirl hat of hers. He knew as with the certainty of recalling a former life that he must be on his knees, adoring her flowery pussy with tongue and mouth until she was lost to silence, then, as if he did this every day, still holding her by each buttock exactly there, with her exquisite legs gripping his neck, getting to his feet and carrying her, weightless, clenched, silent, to the bed, and delivering what was left of his brain by then to this miracle, this sorceress from the East.

· · ·

KIT CONTINUED to catch sight of Pléiade Lafrisée now and then, out along the Digue, or across the gaming rooms, or up in the stands at the Wellington Hippodrome, usually attending to the whimsical schedule of some visiting sportsman. They all looked rich enough, these customers, but that could always be just flash. Howbeit, Umeki and so forth, it wasn't as if he was itching exactly to reconnect, he knew how limited was the use he'd been put to by her, and after the unfortunate business in the mayonnaise factory he was only hoping he'd seen her worst. But he did wonder what she was still doing in town.

One day Kit and Umeki were walking back from the café on the Estacade and ran into Pléiade, in animated conversation with Piet Woevre, coming the other way.

"Hello, Kit." She stared a moment through Miss Tsurigane. "Who's the *mousmée*?"

Kit with a reverse nod at Woevre, "Who's the *mouchard*?"

Woevre smiled back with a direct grim sensuality. Kit noticed he was heeled. Well. If anybody knew how to engineer death by mayonnaise, Kit bet it would be this ape. Pléiade had taken Woevre's arm and was trying to hurry him away.

"Old flame!" speculated Umeki.

"Ask Dr. Rao, I think they've been keeping company."

"Oh, she's *that* one."

Kit rolled his eyes. "The gossiping never stops with you Quaternion folks, do you all have to swear some oath to always lead an irregular life?"

"Monotony—it's something you Vectorists are proud of?"

October 16, the anniversary of Hamilton's 1843 discovery of the Quaternions (or, as a disciple might say, theirs of him), by tradition the climactic day of each World Convention, also happened to be the day after the bathing-season at Ostend officially ended. This time Dr. Rao gave the valedictory address. "The moment, of course, is timeless. No beginning, no end, no duration, the light in eternal descent, not the result of conscious thought but fallen onto Hamilton, if not from some Divine source then at least when the watchdogs of Victorian pessimism were sleeping too soundly to sense, much less frighten off, the watchful scavengers of Epiphany.

"We all know the story. It is a Monday morning in Dublin, Hamilton and his wife, Maria Bayley Hamilton, are walking by the canalside across from Trinity College, where Hamilton is to preside at a council meeting. Maria is chatting pleasantly, Hamilton is nodding now and then and murmuring 'Yes, dear,' when suddenly as they approach Brougham Bridge he cries out and pulls a knife from his pocket—Mrs. H. starts violently but regains her composure, it is only a penknife—as Hamilton runs over to the bridge and carves on the stone $i^2 = j^2 = k^2 = ijk = -1$," the assembly here murmuring along, as to a revered anthem, "and it is in this Pentecostal moment that the Quaternions descend, to take up their earthly residence among the thoughts of men."

IN THE FESTIVITIES attending departure, romance, intoxication, and folly were so in command, so many corridor doors opening and closing, so many guests wandering in and out of the wrong rooms, that de Decker's shop, declaring an official Mischief Opportunity, sent over to the hotel as many operatives as they could spare, among them Piet Woevre, who would rather have been working at night and toward some more sinister end. The minute he caught sight of Woevre, Kit, assuming he was a target of murderous intent, went running off into the hotel's labyrinth of back stairways and passages. Root Tubsmith, thinking that Kit was trying to avoid paying off a side-bet made several evenings ago in the Casino, gave chase. Umeki, who had understood that she and Kit would be spending the day and night together, immediately assumed there was another woman in the picture, no doubt that Parisian bitch again, and joined the pursuit. As Pino and Rocco, fearing for the security of their torpedo, ran off in panic, Policarpe, Denis, Eugénie, and Fatou, recognizing any number of familiar faces among the police operatives swarming everywhere, concluded that the long-awaited action against Young Congo had begun, and went jumping out of various low windows and into the shrubbery, then remembering absinthe spoons, cravats, illustrated magazines, and other items it was essential to salvage, crept back into the hotel, turned the wrong corner, opened the wrong door, screamed, ran back outside. This sort of thing went on till well after dark. In those days it was the everyday texture of people's lives. Stage productions which attempted to record this as truthfully as possible, like dramatic equivalents of genre paintings, became known as "four-door farce," and its period as the Golden Age.

Kit roved from one public place to another, riding trams, sitting at cafés, trying to keep to light and population. He saw no signs of citywide emergency, only the Garde Civique about their business well-mannered as ever, and the Quaternioneers he did happen to sight no more insane than usual—yet he couldn't shake some fearful certainty that he was the object of forces wishing his destruction. He was rescued at last from his compulsive promenade by Pino and Rocco, who accosted him around midnight down by the

Minque, or fish auction house. "We're going back to Bruges," said Rocco. "Maybe on to Ghent. Too many police around here."

"You need a ride?" Pino offered.

Which was how Kit found himself late at night, later than he ever thought it got, torpedoing away down the canal toward Bruges.

At some point in their cheerful velocity, the boys seemed to become aware that it was night, and that furthermore there were no navigational lights to be seen out here.

"I don't think anybody's chasing us," said Rocco.

"You want to slow down?" Pino said.

"Are we in a hurry to get to Bruges?"

"Something up ahead. Better throttle back just in case."

"Cazzo!"

Somehow they had taken a wrong turn and were no longer on the main canal, had wandered instead into a ghost-passage, fog-swept, all but stagnant with disuse, walled in masonry finely-set and windowless, crossed by footbridges that seemed to belong less to the Christian North than to some more exotic faith, some collateral notion of what it might mean to cross between the worlds. Out in the middle of the glaring night, somewhere disguised in echo and phase-interference, chimes had begun to sound, a harmonic-minor nocturne too desolately precise to be attributable to human timing and muscle-power, more likely one of the clockwork carillons peculiar to this part of Belgium, replacing a live carillonneur, whose art was said to be in decline. . . .

The town, once a thriving Hanseatic port, accessible from all corners of the Earth, strolled and swaggered through by beer-happy burghers and their opulently turned-out wives and daughters, grown rich from the wool business and trade with cities as far off as Venice, but since its channel to the sea silted up back in the 1400s, become like Damme and Sluis a place of silence and phantoms and watery daylight, nocturnal even at full noon, no watercraft to disturb the funereal calm of the canal surfaces. The odd thing was how swept and tidied the place looked. Not that sand, salt, and ghosts created much city grime. But somebody must be up and about, in the darkest hours, busily re-pointing the stone walls, hosing the narrow streets, replacing bolts in the under-bracing of the bridges. Creatures perhaps not entirely what we think of as human.

Drifting, as if permanently unmoored from the waking everyday, insomniacs had come out to stare, the orbits of their eyes struck to black when the fog parted to let in the all but unendurable moonlight. One shadow detached itself and approached, growing sharper and more solid as it came. Kit looked around. Rocco and Pino had vanished. "Now what 'n the hell?" The shadow was doing something with its hands.

Woevre. Here before him. Kit had been fleeing not away from but toward his own likely destruction.

A round went purring away, spattering his cheek with tiny stone fragments, the sound of the shot clattering among the ancient surfaces. He headed for the nearest cover, an archway under which anything could be waiting, calling out, "Shootin at the wrong fella!"

"No matter. You'll do." When the next shot came, Kit was crouched, his heart hammering, as far as he could tell behind cover. Maybe he was not the only target, or maybe Woevre was firing off rounds for the heck of it. The melancholy chiming continued.

Woevre stood unprotected in the nocturnal light, feeling an exaltation beyond anything he could remember, even from the days in Africa. He was no longer sure who it was he was shooting at, or how he had come here. It seemed somehow to be about the Italians in their manned torpedo, that was in the message which had come in to the office earlier in the day, but nothing like that stirred now in these bright empty canals. The activity of interest seemed to be in the sky.

Each time he risked a glance upward, it was there, directly above him, the thing he had been seeing for days, emerging now from the sky, from behind the sky, carrying the unidentified visitors he had seen walking along the Digue, as if they were in town on an organized mission.

He knew he must try to bring down the flying ship. He pocketed his Borchardt, and went fumbling for the weapon he had brought back from Brussels, with no idea even how to get the case open, much less use what was inside. He didn't know if it needed to be charged somehow with ammunition. But these were details. He was who he was, and trusted his intuitiveness with any weapon when the moment came.

But Woevre had not really seen it before, at least not out in the night like this, in the pitiless moonlight. He was overcome with certainty that the device was conscious, regarding him, not particularly happy to be in his possession. It felt warm, and he sensed a fine vibration. How could that be? Gevaert had mentioned nothing. Had he?

"Jou moerskont!" he cried. It did no good, whatever language the weapon could be screamed at in, it was not Afrikaans, its provenance was too far from those forests, from those slow, fatal rivers. . . . Something flashed, blinding him for a moment, leaving his field of vision a luminous green. The sound

accompanying was nothing he wanted to hear again, as if the voices of everyone he had ever put to death had been precisely, diabolically scored for some immense choir.

He looked up. He was somehow fallen, face upward on the pavement, struggling for breath, and the American was there, reaching down to help him to his feet.

"What happened old buddy, shoot yourself? Tricky piece of hardware there—"

"Take it. Take the fucking thing. I cannot bear it . . . this terrible light . . . *Voetsak, voetsak!*" He stumbled away, down the canal, across a bridge, into the neat walled intricacy of the dead town. Kit heard several more shots from that direction, and when the bells fell silent at last, and the cordite smoke had drifted all away, with the starers returned one by one to the fold of sleep, the moonlight grown oblique and metallic, Kit found himself alone with the enigmatic object, back inside its leather case. He slung it nonchalantly by its strap over one shoulder, meaning to have a look inside later.

KIT COULDN'T QUITE see the reason for all the fuss. But Umeki was soon spending hours with the instrument, her brow tensing and relaxing as if with sorrow and release from sorrow, as if gazing through the eyepiece at the unfolding of a prolonged, perhaps never-ending, dramatic performance from her own land. Whenever her eyes came away briefly from the instrument, they were unfocused, inflamed, as if subject to two sets of laws. Whenever Kit asked what was up, she answered at first in a low tobacco-stricken voice, at affecting length, in what he guessed must be Japanese.

Finally, "Right. First the mirrors—see, here, half-silvering, not on glass but on calcite, and this specimen—it's so pure! Any light-ray entering immediately becomes a pair of rays—one 'Ordinary,' the other 'Extraordinary.' Arriving at one of these half-silvered backings, each ray then is part-reflected and part-transmitted—so, four possibilities—both rays reflected, both transmitted, one of each, and the other way around. The fatal number four—to a Japanese mind, literally fatal. Same character as for death. Perhaps how I got drawn to the Quaternions. Let us say each of the four states is associated with one of the four 'dimensions' of Minkowskian space-time—or, in a more trivial sense to the four cusps of the surface reciprocal to that of the wave, what Quaternionists call the index-surface. Perhaps we are meant to ignore the optics altogether, as if the rays were no longer doubly refracted, but doubly *emitted,* from whatever object we may observe through this . . . as if in the co-

conscious there were some counterpart to the Extraordinary Ray, and we were seeing with the eye of that unexplored realm.

"And that's only the eyepiece." She removed an access panel, reached in, appeared to perform some swift, fancy translations and rotations, and came out again holding a crystal about the size of a human eyeball. Kit took it and scrutinized each face closely.

"All these faces are equilateral."

"Yes. This is a true icosahedron."

"The regular solid, not a 12 + 8 like you'd find in pyrites, but— This is impossible. There's no such—"

"Not impossible! To date, unidentified! And the sphere described through the twelve summits—"

"Wait. Don't tell me. No ordinary sphere, right?" The object shimmered at him, as if winking. "Something like . . . a Riemann sphere."

She beamed. "The realm of x + *iy*—we are in it! whether we want to be or not."

"An imaginary icosahedron. Swell." Trying to remember what he could of Felix Klein's magisterial *Vorlesungen über das Ikosaeder,* which had been required reading at Göttingen, but not having much luck.

"'Imaginary,'" she laughed, "not the best way to put it!" She took the crystal, with a certain reverence, it seemed to Kit, and replaced it in the device.

"What's this for?" A slender ebonite handle protruded from a brass-edged groove, which ran in a complicated curve. When Kit reached for it she slapped his hand away.

"Don't touch it! 'Ohmic Drift Compensator' regulates how much light is allowed to enter the silvering of the mirror! Special kind of refraction! Calibrated against imaginary index! Dangerous! Of the essence!"

"This unit is no bigger than a machine-pistol," Kit said. "How powerful could it be?"

"I'm speculating, but the speed of the Earth moving along in its orbit—consider it! eighteen miles per second!—take the square of that, multiply it by the mass of the planet—"

"Good bit of kinetic energy there."

"Recently Lorentz's paper in the *Proceedings* of the Amsterdam Academy—Fitzgerald and others—they have concluded that a solid body passing through the Æther at a very high speed can become slightly shorter along the axis of motion. And Lord Rayleigh, looking for second-order effects, wonders if such motion might not cause a crystalline body to become doubly-refracting. So far these experiments show negative results. But—that principle—if we turned it around, and *began* with a crystal in which double refraction is caused by a set of axes no longer uniform, with the units of space itself actually being altered, because of the Earth's motion—then already in such a crystal, implicit, embodied there, is that high planetary velocity, that immoderately vast energy, which someone has now come up with a way to couple in to. . . ."

"I really don't like thinking about that," Kit said, pretending to plug his ears.

In a dream early one morning, she stood before him holding the object. She was naked, and weeping. "Must I then take up the dreadful instrument, and flee to other shores?" Her voice, without its waking edge of cool sarcasm, defenseless, beckoned him into its sadness. This dream was about Umeki, but also one of those mathematicians' dreams that surface now and then in the folklore. He saw that if the Q-waves were in any way longitudinal, if they traveled through the Æther in any way like sound traveling through air, then among the set of further analogies to sound, somewhere in the regime, must be music—which, immediately, obligingly, he heard, or received. The message it seemed to convey being "Deep among the equations describing the behavior of light, field equations, Vector and Quaternion equations, lies a set of directions, an itinerary, a map to a hidden space. Double refraction appears again and again as a key element, permitting a view into a Creation set just to the side of this one, so close as to overlap, where the membrane between the worlds, in many places, has become too frail, too permeable, for safety. . . . Within the mirror, within the scalar term, within the daylit and obvious and taken-for-granted has always lain, as if in wait, the dark itinerary, the corrupted pilgrim's guide, the nameless Station before the first, in the lightless uncreated, where salvation does not yet exist."

He woke knowing for the first time in a long time what he had to do. It was like having a stuffed sinus go away. Everything was clear. This piece of hardware had turned out to be supremely dangerous, as apt to harm its user as its target. If military intelligence here in Belgium was getting it confused with a "Quaternion weapon," mythical or not, then the interest from other powers would be intense indeed. Introducing the vast population of the world's innocent to more trouble than its worth to any government. On the other hand, if it were with someone who understood and appreciated it . . .

Umeki turned deliberately, twisting the sheets, humming a tune of her own, and bit his nipple.

"*Konichiwa* to you too, my little plum blossom."

"I dreamed that you flew away on an airship."

"I don't ever have to leave. If—"

"You do. And I have to be without you." But with none of the sadness her voice had bowed so under the weight of in the dream.

Later they lay smoking, about to leave the room for the last time. "There's a new Puccini opera," she said. "An American betrays a Japanese woman. Butterfly. He ought to die of shame, but does not—Butterfly does. What are we to make of this? Is it that Japanese do die of shame and dishonor but Americans don't? Maybe *can't ever* die of shame because they lack the cultural equipment? As if, somehow, your country is just mechanically destined to move forward regardless of who is in the way or underfoot?"

As if just having remembered, he said, "Something I'd better give you."

She peered at him over the bight of a pillow. "It was never yours to give to anyone. It was mine before I knew it existed."

"I know that's just your way of saying thank you."

"I would be obliged to show this to Kimura-san, to see what he can make of it."

"Of course."

"The Japanese government—I'm not so certain about them."

"You're going home?"

She shrugged. "I don't know where that is. Do you?"

AT THE OSTENDE-VILLE STATION, Kit had a moment—soon dissipated in purposeful noise and coal-smoke, beer-drinking merriment, Root Tubsmith whanging away at a ukulele medley including Borel-Clerc's wildly popular "La Matchiche"—in which he glimpsed how Ostend really might not be simply another pleasure-resort for people with too much money, but the western anchor of a continental system that happened to include the Orient Express, the Trans-Siberian, the Berlin-to-Baghdad, and so on in steel proliferation across the World-Island. Not yet aware of how familiar, in the course of only a few more seasons, he was to become with the Imperium of Steam, and how, from Ostend, courtesy of the Compagnie Internationale des Wagons-Lits, one might, for comfortably less than two hundred francs, be hurled into the East, vertiginously and perhaps for good. He looked for Umeki among the crowds on the platform, even among subsets that would not possibly include her, wondering at the protocols of destiny, of being led, of turning away, of knowing where he did and didn't belong. She wasn't there, she wouldn't be. The more she wasn't there, the more she was. Kit supposed there was something in the theory of sets that covered this, but the train was moving, his brain was numb, his heart was incommunicado, the dunes slipped by, then the Bruges Canal and the larks swept upward from the stubble of the fields, gathering into a defensive front against the autumn.

Dally might have explained it if somebody had insisted—the Chicago Fair was a long time ago, but she had kept a memory or two of silent boats on canals, something began to stir as the vaporetto made its way from the train station down the Grand Canal, until, just at sunset, getting to the San Marco end, and there was the pure Venetian evening, the blue-green shadows, the lavenders, ultramarines, siennas, and umbers of the sky and the light-bearing air she was breathing, the astonishing momentum of the everyday twilight, gas-lanterns coming on in the Piazzetta, San Giorgio Maggiore across the water lit pale as angels, distant as heaven and yet seeming only a step, as if her breath, her yearning, could reach across to it and touch—she was certain for the first time in a life on the roll that whatever "home" had meant, this was older than memory, than the story she thought she knew. It was to gather into an upswelling of the heart she must struggle to contain, and might have begun to regret when a nearby tourist, in a vilely mucous specimen of British Accent, smirked to an effusive companion, "Oh, everyone says that, give it a day or two and you'll be screaming to get away," causing Dally to think about finding a gondola oar and hitting him with it, maybe more than once. But the evening itself, spreading mercifully its deep cloak, would see to this pest and his replicas in their thousands, they were like the gnats who rose in clouds here at nightfall, their purpose to infest the Venetian summer, to enhance its splendor with earthly annoyance, to pass quickly as they must, driven off, forgotten.

She, meanwhile, had just decided to live here forever.

The Zombinis' first engagement, at the Teatro Verdi in Trieste, had been a triumph. They got rhapsodically reviewed not only locally but in the Rome and Milan papers as well, and they were held over for an extra week, so by the time they got to Venice, the engagement here was already extended and the house sold out for weeks in advance.

"So this is the Malibran."

"Marco Polo's house is right around the corner."

"Hey, you think he'll come if we give him free tickets?"

"Here, Cici, think fast."

"Yaagghh!" Cici reminded himself that it only looked like a full-size elephant arcing through the air about to land on top of and squash him. He took a step to the side just in time, made a neat "pincette" pass, and slipped the animal into one of the profondes of his trick jacket, where it promptly vanished, though it is said today to be roaming comfortably the forests of its native Africa. Another Celebrated Tumbling Pachyderm Feat successfully negotiated.

From the wings, Vincenzo Miserere, the sales rep from the mirror factory on Isola degli Specchi, looked on in appreciation. Over the years he had seen acts come and go, and the high reputation of the Zombinis, whom he had taken the train to Trieste to see, was well deserved.

"I think once there were Zombinis around Venice," he told Luca. "Long time ago. Come on out to the factory while you're here, we've got a whole library full of old documents we're in the process of cataloguing. Professore Svegli from the U. of Pisa is giving us a hand with it. You might find something."

Bria had known about the Venetian Zombinis since she was a girl, when her father had motioned her one day into his study and dug from its sumptuous chaos an ancient volume, bound in shark leather, *The travels and adventures of Niccolò dei Zombini, Specchiere.* Back in the seventeenth century, Niccolò had been apprenticed by his family to the mirror-makers of the island, who like the glassmakers on Murano were fanatically protective about their trade secrets. Corporations today are gentle and caring compared to those early factory owners, whose secrecy and obsession just got meaner and meaner as the years and generations passed. They kept their workers confined to the one swampy little island, prisoners, forbidden to run away—the penalty for anyone who tried to was pursuit and death. But Niccolò made his escape anyway, and the book Luca was showing her began with his departure from the island. Luca got into the habit of reading the kids to sleep from it, one *guaglion* chasing another, place to place across the map of Europe and through the Renaissance, no telegraphs, no passports, no international spy networks, all you needed to stay ahead was better speed and some imagination. Niccolò managed to disappear into all the noise and confusion, which is what Europe was then.

"According to one version," said Luca, "he ended up sailing to America, where he got married, had kids, started a line of descendants, including us, though no more Zombinis ever went into the mirror business—we were everything else, stoneworkers, saloonkeepers, cowboys, gamblers, heck, down south before the Civil War? a couple of us were Negroes."

"Huh?"

"What, you never saw the family tree? Here, look, Elijah Zombini, master chef, first lasagna south of the Mason-Dixon, used grits instead of ricotta, you never heard of him?" And as had been happening since Bria was a baby, Luca went off into another one of his stories, and one by one the children fell asleep. . . .

Isola degli Specchi appeared on some maps and was absent from others. It had seemed to depend how high the water was in the Lagoon from day to day. Also, perhaps, on a species of faith, for there were otherwise-knowledgeable Venetians who denied its existence categorically. On the day Luca and Bria visited, it seemed like a normal enough island, reached by normal vaporetto, a normal mirror-works, casting rooms, batch crucibles, grinding workshops, the only peculiar element an entire wing that visitors were discouraged from entering, whose door read TERAPIA.

Professore Svegli was in the factory archives surrounded by documents written on ancient paper and parchment. "Your ancestor's records," he greeted them, "are as hard to track down as the man himself was."

"Surprised they just didn't destroy all the records they could find."

"It would not have occurred to them. Today we are used to thinking of identity as no more than the contents of one's dossier. Back then one man might have multiple identities, 'documents' might easily be forged or fictional. For Niccolò dei Zombini it was especially tricky, because at some point he also went crazy, a common occupational risk among these perfectionist mirror-makers. He should have ended up in the madhouse on San Servolo, but for some mysterious reason—was he pretending insanity as part of a plan to escape? did he have friends in the Palazzo Ducale?—he got away with behavior that would have had anyone else sent to the *manicomio,* and was allowed to keep on working. As things turned out, he might've been the only one who ever understood why."

The Professore carefully picked up a sheet of nearly-transparent vellum and laid it on a flat surface of white celluloid. "This is believed to be a master drawing of the so-called *paramorfico,* it's on uterine vellum, very rare and expensive, and not meant to see much of the light of day. There do appear also to have been working templates inked on cheaper grades of parchment, but most of those were ruined by use, as well as by the grinding materials, pitch, rouge, and so forth. Niccolò escaped from here apparently around 1660, taking a *paramorfico* with him, and neither was heard from again."

"What does it do?" Luca asked Vincenzo Miserere. "Does anybody still make them? Could I use one in my act?"

Miserere looked at him over the top of his pince-nez. "You ordered something like it last year," thumbing through a stack of invoice copies. "Glass, calcite, custom silvering. We call it La Doppiatrice."

"Right. Right. Now we're on the topic, I might need to talk to your field-support people." Proceeding to acquaint Miserere with the unaccountable malfunction that had produced a small population of optically sawed-in-half subjects walking around New York, while Bria tried not to roll her eyes too obviously.

The rep picked up a telephone on his desk, had a short conversation in Venetian dialect, and a few minutes later Ettore Sananzolo, who had in fact designed the apparatus, came in with a sheaf of engineering drawings under his arm.

"It's only a variation on the classic Maskelyne cabinet of forty years ago," he explained, "where you put a mirror edgewise into an empty cabinet at a forty-five-degree angle, so that it splits one of the back corners perfectly in half. With a good enough mirror and velvet lining, the audience thinks they're still looking straight back at the rear wall of an empty cabinet, when what they're really seeing is a reflection of one of the side walls. To disappear, the subject simply climbs into the cabinet and hides in the forty-five-degree angle behind the mirror.

"For the analogous trick in four-space, we had to go from a two-dimensional to a three-dimensional mirror, which is where the *paramorfico* comes in. Instead of the simple ninety-degree rotation when one plane represents another in three-space, we now have to replace one volume—the cabinet interior—with another one, in four-space. We pass from a system of three purely spatial axes to one with four—space plus time. In this way time enters the effect. The doubles you report having produced are actually the original subjects themselves, slightly displaced in time."

"More or less how Professor Vanderjuice of Yale sees the problem. So now, how do we fix it?"

"Unfortunately, you will first have to find each pair and somehow convince them to climb back into the cabinet again."

Over in the corner of his eye, he saw Bria grabbing herself by the head and trying not to comment, but Luca now curiously was feeling the first stirrings of hope. What Ettore asked was clearly impossible. By now these subjects had gone on for too long with their lives, no longer twinned so much as divergent, inevitably so in a city as gigantic as New York—they would have gone on to meet attractive strangers, court, marry, have babies, change jobs, move to other places, it would be like trying to put smoke back into a cigar even to find them anymore, let alone expect any pair of them to re-enter La Doppiatrice willingly. It was sort of like fathering a large number of real children, he supposed, twins, except that these came into the world already grown-ups, and chances were that none of them would ever visit. Not everybody would find this comforting, but Luca tried to.

Ettore pointed out on the drawings where adjustments would have to be made, as well as new parts installed, to prevent a recurrence of the problem.

"You've set my mind at rest," murmured Luca, "I don't know how to thank you."

"Money?" Ettore suggested. Vincenzo Miserere lit up one of those hard-as-a-rock black cigars and winked. Bria was peering at her father as if he had gone insane.

They went thumping back to Venice in a vaporetto, among the unquiet ghosts of all the crazy mirror-makers riding the *salso* in from the Lagoon and back out again, in and out of the city, attaching themselves to night-fishing boats, steamers, *sandoli,* out to the lost chance, the lost home . . . slipping beneath the surface to browse among the ancient workrooms and even sometimes terribly catch sight of themselves in some fragment of ancient mirror, for the silvering down here, surviving the corrosions of the sea and of time, had always been particularly tuned to the long-homeless dead. . . . Sometimes they were also visible at the edges of the screen in the movies that showed at the Malibran in between live stage acts. Back in New York the Zombini kids had been used to sneaking off downtown to watch the nickelodeon, they thought they were pretty wised up, but here somehow they found themselves grabbing each other so as not to fall into the collective dream and run screaming down the aisles away from trains pulling in to the Santa Lucia Station, or throw objects at especially monstrous villainies in the short melodramas, or make sure they were in their seats and not aboard a boat out in the Grand Canal.

That night at the theatre, after the show, Dally stayed behind in the abrupt swell of absence and echo to help stow props and equipment and set up some of the effects for the next night's performance. Erlys, who had lately been looking into thought-reading as a specialty and might have felt more than usually intuitive, kept throwing her these glances, each as thoughtfully directed as one of Bria's knives. At some point they were face-to-face across a cage of doves. "What is it," they both said at the same time. While Dally was figuring how to begin, Erlys added, "Never mind, I know what it is."

"I know I'm supposed to explain," Dally said. "Wish I could. You know how you'll pass through a place, after a long string of places you'd never want to stop in, let alone live, or could understand anybody else wanting to, and maybe it's the time of day, the weather, what you just ate, no way to tell, but you don't ride into it, it comes out to surround you, and you know it's where you belong. There's nothing else like this place anywhere, and I know it's where I belong."

Several dozen objections elbowed each other in Erlys's mind for precedence. She knew Dally had already examined and dismissed them all. She nodded, slowly, a couple of times. "Let me talk to Luca."

"So now I have to let her go," Erlys said. "I don't know how I can." They were in their hotel on the edge of San Polo, looking across the canal at Cannareggio, the sun behind them warping itself down into one of those melancholy mixtures of light and nebulosity that happened only here. "Finally, the payback for what I did. I find her, I lose her again."

"None of that was ever your fault," Luca said, "it was me. I was crazy."

"Didn't know any better myself, only a kid at the time, but that's no excuse, is it? I left her. I left her. Something I can never go back and change. Those Snidell sisters back in Cleveland, they had my number all the time. They still search me out in my dreams and tell me I don't deserve to live. How could I be that selfish?"

"Hey. Not like you abandoned her," he protested. "You knew the safest place you could've left her was with Merle, you knew she'd be warm, and loved, and never hungry."

She nodded, miserable. "I knew. Made it that much easier to leave."

"We tried to find them again. Couple years as I recall."

"Still not hard enough."

"We had to keep working too. Couldn't just stop everything to go chasing Merle all over the map. And he could've tried to find us, too, couldn't he?"

"He must've felt so betrayed. He didn't want to see me again, he didn't want me near her either."

"You don't know."

"Are we fighting?"

He reached to push some hair off her face. "I was afraid. I thought one day you'd just go off looking for her on your own, and I'd be left with the ordinary day again, without you. I got so desperate I thought about locks and chains, except you learned all those escapes."

"I was never about to go disappear on you Luca, it wasn't Merle I loved, it was you."

They sat side by side on the bed feeling thirty years older than they were. Light seeped out of the room. "I came back to the apartment that day," Luca said, "and here was this—I don't know, I thought she'd flown in from a star."

"It's how I felt when she was born."

He never carried handkerchiefs but knew how to produce from nowhere a silk scarf of any desired color. This one was violet. He handed it to her with a flourish. "Let me use it when you're through."

She touched her eyes with it and when she passed it back, the scarf had changed color to duck green. "Stronzo. You don't want her to go any more than I do."

"But we have no say anymore. Part of the deal."

"Can we just leave her in Venice? How do we know this time she'll be safe?"

"Listen, if she was helpless, foolish in the head, it'd be one thing, but this kid has walked through tong wars without a scratch. She's played the Bowery. We've both seen her in action, if she was able to handle New York before she even met us, she can do Venezia in her sleep. Maybe a couple francs in her name at the Banca Veneta wouldn't hurt, you know, just in case. And there's people here I can ask to discreetly keep an eye on her."

So that was how Dally got to be on her own in Venice. One day the vaporetto pulled away from the San Marco stop, and there were so many Zombinis at the rail calling good-bye that the boat was tilting. Later for some reason it would be Bria that Dally remembered, slim, steady, waving her hat at full arm's length, hair blown in a tangle, calling out, "Show's on, *ragazza. In bocc' al lupo!*"

SHE WAS EARNING a living before she knew it, putting to use the many light-handed and quick-fingered skills and the fast talk that went with them she had started learning from Merle before she learned to walk, and from the dealers and sharpers who'd come tumbleweeding through the different towns ever since her hands were big enough to palm bridge-size cards, and later learning from Luca Zombini to expand into juggling and magic tricks.

She was most comfortable performing in little *campielli* whose churches held only minor paintings, and which were scaled perfectly to gatherings of children and tourists on the way to better-known landmarks around town. Quite soon she had grown to hate tourists and what she saw them doing to Venice, changing it from a real city to a hollow and now and then outright-failed impersonation of itself, all the centuries of that irregular seethe of history reduced to a few simple ideas, and a seasonal human inundation just able to grasp them.

As summer went along, she settled in. She watched the American girls, breezing along the Riva without a care, so clean, starched, sunlit, and blithe, in their middy blouses and boating skirts and eyes luminous beneath the brims of straw hats, pretending to ignore the covetous gazes of naval officers, guides, and waiters, laughing and talking incessantly, and she wondered if she had ever stood a chance of becoming one of them. By now she was brown from the sun, lean and agile, hair cropped into a drift of curls short enough to fit under a red knit fisherman's cap which also served for her night's only pillow—she dressed these days as a boy and escaped all male attention but the sort directed at boys, though such birds of passage, usually in for the night or two, were quickly set straight.

It was not quite the Venice older folks remembered. The Campanile had collapsed a few years before and had not yet been rebuilt, and stories about its fall had multiplied. There were reports of an encounter in the sky, described by some as angelic. Street urchins and *lucciole* told of seeing, in a population of visitors not noted for its strangeness, young men in uniforms of no nation anybody could agree on, moving among the ancient water-mazes like ghosts of earlier times or, some speculated, times not yet upon us. "You've seen the old paintings. This has always been a town for seeing angels in. The battle in heaven didn't end when Lucifer was banished to Hell. It kept going, it's still going."

This according to an English painter type, maybe even the genuine article, named Hunter Penhallow, who had begun showing up every morning on her *fondamenta* with an easel and a kit full of paint-tubes and brushes, and while the daylight allowed, with breaks only for *ombreta* and coffee, worked at getting Venice "down," as he put it. "You have miles of streets and canals here, mister," she sought to instruct him, "tens of thousands of people, each one more interesting to look at than the last, why limit it to this one little corner of town?"

"The light's good here."

"But—"

"All right." A minute or two of pencil work. "It wouldn't matter. Imagine that inside this labyrinth you see is another one, but on a smaller scale, reserved only, say, for cats, dogs, and mice—and then, inside that, one for ants and flies, then microbes and the whole invisible world—down and down the scale, for once the labyrinthine principle is allowed, don't you see, why stop at any scale in particular? It's self-repeating. Exactly the spot where we are now is a microcosm of all Venice."

He spoke calmly, as if she would understand what all this meant, and in fact, because Merle used to talk like this, she wasn't totally puzzled, and was even able to refrain from rolling her eyes. Inhaling deeply on her cigarette stub, flicking it expressively into the *rio,* "That go for Venetians, too?"

Sure enough, it got her the once-over. "Take off that cap, let's have a look." When she shook out her ringlets, "You're a girl."

"More like young woman, but don't let's argue."

"And you've been passing—marvelously—as a rough little street-urchin."

"Simplifies life, up to a point anyway."

"You must pose for me."

"In England—signore—so it is said, a model can earn a shilling an hour."

He shrugged. "I can't pay that much."

"Half, then."

"That's twelve soldi. I'd be lucky to get as much as a franc for one painting."

Despite Hunter's young, almost adolescent face, what she could see of his hair was gray, nearly white, covered with a straw hat elegantly pinched and twisted out of its original shape Santos-Dumont style, suggesting at least some previous residence in Paris. How long had this jasper been in Venice, she wondered. She pretended to squint at his canvases in a professional way. "You're no Canaletto, but don't sell yourself short, I've seen stuff worse than this going for ten francs, on good tourist days maybe even more."

Finally he smiled, a fragile moment, like a patch of fog gliding past. "I *might* afford sixpence the hour, if . . . you'd act as my sales agent?"

"Sure. Ten percent?"

"What's your name?"

"Most folks call me Beppo."

They set up their pitch near the Bauer-Grünwald, in the narrow passage that ran between San Moise and the Piazza, because every visitor to the city sooner or later passed through here. Meantime at the *fondamenta,* he was sketching or painting her in a variety of poses, doing cartwheels down the canalside, eating a bleeding-red slice of watermelon, pretending to sleep in the sun with a cat in her lap, a scrawl of scarlet creeper on a bone-white wall behind her, sitting back in a doorway, face illuminated only from sunlight off the paving, dreaming among pink walls, redbrick walls, green waterways, gazing up at windows facing across *calli* so close you felt you could stretch and touch but didn't, flowers in front of it spilling over wrought-iron balconies, posing for him both as a boy and presently, in some borrowed costumes, as a girl. "You're not too uncomfortable in skirts, I hope."

"Getting used to it, thanks."

Hunter had somehow fetched up here, demobilized from a war that nobody knew about, obscurely damaged, seeking refuge from time, safety behind the cloaks and masks and thousand-named mists of Venezia.

"There was a war? Where?"

"Europe. Everywhere. But no one seems to know of it . . . here . . ." he hesitated, with a wary look—"yet."

"Why not? It's so far away the news hasn't reached here 'yet'?" She let a breath go by, then—"Or it hasn't *happened* 'yet'?"

He gazed back, not in distress so much as a queer forgiveness, as if reluctant to blame her for not knowing. How could any of them know?

"Then I guess you're a time-traveler from the future?" Not mocking, really, nor much surprised either.

"I don't know. I don't know how *that* could happen."

"Easy. Somebody in the future invents a time machine, O.K.? Every crazy promoter both sides of the Atlantic's been working on that, one of em's bound to succeed, and when they do, those contraptions'll just be common as cabs for hire. So . . . wherever you were, you must've hailed one. Hopped in, told the driver *when* you wanted to arrive at, and *ehi presto!* Here you are."

"I wish I could remember. Anything. Whatever the time-reversal of 'remembering' is. . . ."

"Well, looks like you escaped your war anyhow. You're here . . . you're safe." Meaning only to reassure him, but his dispirited look deepened now.

"'Safe' . . . safe." Whoever he was talking to now, it wasn't her. "Political space has its neutral ground. But does Time? is there such a thing as the *neutral hour*? one that goes neither forward nor back? is that too much to hope?"

Just then, not quite as if in answer, from one of the royal warships anchored off Castello, the Evening Gun sounded, a deep, songless chime of admonition pealing up and down the Riva.

It was about then that Dally started carrying his canvases, easel, and other gear for him, shooing away the local kids who were too importunate, in general taking care of what chores she could.

". . . OVERNIGHT, during a match, Dr. Grace appeared to me in a dream, ordered me to Charing Cross and onto the boat-train . . ."

"Yeah, yeah."

". . . it was so real, he was wearing whites and one of those antiquated caps, and knew my name, and began to instruct me in my duty, there was a . . . a war, he said, in 'Outer Europe,' was how he put it, queer sort of geography isn't it, even for a dream—and our country, our civilization, was somehow in peril. I felt no desire to join in, no passion, quite the opposite. I have been out on 'adventures,' I know that exhilaration, but it was simply not part of this . . . not available. You can see what I am, one more earnest village athlete, some amateur daubing, no depths to speak of. But there I was, surrendering to a most extraordinary call from the grave, the mass-grave-to-be of Europe, as if somewhere ahead lay an iron gateway, slightly ajar, leading to a low and sombre country, with an incalculable crowd on all sides *eager to pass into it,* and bearing me along. Whatever my own wishes . . ."

He was staying in a hotel room in Dorsoduro, with a restaurant downstairs. Morning glories wreathed among the ironwork. "Figured you'd be in a *pensione,* there's a couple of em just up that li'l Rio San Vio there."

"This turns out to be cheaper, actually—the *pensioni* include lunch, and if I stopped for that, I'd lose the best of the light, and if I didn't, I'd be paying for a meal I wasn't eating. But here at La Calcina, the kitchen's open to all hours, and I can pretty much eat when I want to. Besides, one has the company of eminent ghosts, Turner and Whistler, Ruskin, Browning sorts of chap."

"They died there? How good can the food be?"

"Oh, then call them 'traces of consciousness.' Psychical Research is beginning to open these matters up a bit. Ghosts can be . . . well, actually, look at them all." He waved an arm up and down the Zattere. "Every tourist you see here streaming by, everyone who plans to sleep tonight in a strange bed, is potentially *that kind* of ghost. Transient beds for some reason are able to catch and hold these subtle vibrational impulses of the soul. Haven't you noticed, in hotels, the way your dreams are often, alarmingly, not your own?"

"Not out where I'm sleeping."

"Well, it's true—especially in these smaller places, where the bedstead tends to be of iron or steel, enameled to keep away the *cimici.* Somehow the metal frame also acts as a receiving antenna, allowing dreamers to pick up traces of the dreams of whoever slept there just before them, as if, during sleep, we radiated in frequencies as yet undiscovered."

"Thanks, have to try that sometime." Beds and bedrooms, huh. She risked a quick lateral flick of the eyeballs. So far he had suggested nothing you'd've called improper, either to Dally or anyone else who'd come by in the course of the day. Not that she was interested in him romantically, of course, he wasn't her type, though there were days, she had to admit, when *anything* was her type, gnarled fishermen, dimpled gigolos, Austrians in short trousers, waiters, *gondolieri,* a hungering she must discreetly take care of all by herself, and preferably on late nights when moonlight was slim.

She wondered if this "War" of his was responsible in some way for removing bodily passion from his life. How long was he fixing to stay in Venice? When the bora blew down from the mountains, announcing the winter, would he ride it on out of town? Would she? In September, when the vino forte arrived from Brindisi, Squinzano, and Barletta, would he be gone in a couple of weeks as well?

One day, strolling in the Piazzetta, Hunter motioned her under the arcade and into the Library, and pointed up at Tintoretto's *Abduction of the Body of St. Mark.* She gazed for some time. "Well, if that ain't the spookiest damned thing," she whispered at last. "What's going on?" she gestured nervously into those old Alexandrian shadows, where ghostly witnesses, up far too late, forever fled indoors before an unholy offense.

"It's as if these Venetian painters saw things we can't see anymore," Hunter said. "A world of presences. Phantoms. History kept sweeping through, Napoleon, the Austrians, a hundred forms of bourgeois literalism, leading to its ultimate embodiment, the tourist—how beleaguered they must have felt. But stay in this town awhile, keep your senses open, reject nothing, and now and then you'll see them."

A few days later, at the Accademia, as if continuing the thought, he said, "The body, it's another way to get past the body."

"To the spirit behind it—"

"But not to deny the body—to reimagine it. Even"—nodding over at the Titian on the far wall—"if it's 'really' just different kinds of greased mud smeared on cloth—to reimagine it as light."

"More perfect."

"Not necessarily. Sometimes more terrible—mortal, in pain, misshapen, even taken apart, broken down into geometrical surfaces, but each time somehow, when the process is working, *gone beyond. . . .*"

Beyond her, she guessed. She was trying to keep up, but Hunter didn't make it easy. One day he told her a story she had actually already heard, as a sort of bedtime story, from Merle, who regarded this as a parable, maybe the first on record, about alchemy. It was from the Infancy Gospel of Thomas, one of many pieces of Scripture that early church politics had kept from being included in the New Testament.

"Jesus was sort of a hell-raiser as a kid," as Merle had told it, "the kind of wayward youth I'm always finding you keepin company with, in fact, not that I'm objecting," as she had sat up in bed and looked for something to assault him with, "used to go around town pulling these adolescent pranks, making little critters out of clay, bringing them to life, birds that could fly, rabbits that talked, and like that, driving his parents crazy, not to mention most of the local adults, who were always coming by to complain—'You better tell 'at Jesus to watch it.' One day he's out with some friends looking for trouble to get into, and they happen to go by the dyer's shop, where there's all these pots with different colors of dye and piles of clothes next to them, all sorted and each pile ready to be dyed a different color, Jesus says, 'Watch this,' and grabs up all the clothes in one big bundle, the dyer's yelling, 'Hey Jesus, what'd I tell you last time?' drops what he's doing and goes chasing after the kid, but Jesus is too fast for him, and before anybody can stop him he runs over to the biggest pot, the one with red dye in it, and dumps all the clothes in, and runs away laughing. The dyer is screaming bloody murder, tearing his beard, thrashing around on the ground, he sees his whole livelihood destroyed, even Jesus's low-life friends think this time he's gone a little too far, but here comes Jesus with his hand up in the air just like in the paintings, calm as anything—'Settle down, everybody,' and he starts pulling the clothes out of that pot again, and what do you know, each one comes out just the color it's supposed to be, not only that but the exact shade of that color, too, no more housewives hollerin 'hey I wanted lime green not Kelly green, you color-blind or something,' no this time each item is the perfect color it was meant to be."

"Not a heck of a lot different," it had always seemed to Dally, "in fact, from that Pentecost story in Acts of the Apostles, which did get in the Bible, not colors this time but languages, Apostles are meeting in a house in Jerusalem, you'll recall, Holy Ghost comes down like a mighty wind, tongues of fire and all, the fellas come out and start talking to the crowd outside, who've all been jabbering away in different tongues, there's Romans and Jews, Egyptians and Arabians, Mesopotamians and Cappadocians and folks from east Texas, all expecting to hear just the same old Galilean dialect—but instead this time each one is amazed to hear those Apostles speaking to him in his own language."

Hunter saw her point. "Yes, well it's redemption, isn't it, you expect chaos, you get order instead. Unmet expectations. Miracles."

ONE DAY HUNTER announced he was switching to nocturnes. Each twilight after that, he left his rooms and set out with his gear, to put in a full night's work. Dally switched her own day around to accommodate. "And this Venetian light you're always talkin about—"

"You'll see. It's nocturnal light, the kind you need to run a green-blue glaze for. The night moisture in the air, the blurs and beams and sky-scatter, the lamplight reflected in the *rii,* above all of course the moon. . . ."

She wondered sometimes what he would have made of American light. She had sat adrift in insomnia for hours watching fields of windows lit and lampless, vulnerable flames and filaments by the thousands borne billowing as by waves of the sea, the broken rolling surfaces of the great cities, allowing herself to imagine, almost surrendering to the impossibility of ever belonging, since childhood when she'd ridden with Merle past all those small, perfect towns, longed after the lights at creeksides and the lights defining the shapes of bridges over great rivers, through church windows or trees in summer, casting shining parabolas down pale brick walls or haloed in bugs, lanterns on farm rigs, candles at windowpanes, each attached to a life running before and continuing on, long after she and Merle and the wagon would have passed, and the mute land risen up once again to cancel the brief revelation, the offer never clearly stated, the hand never fully dealt. . . .

Here in this ancient town progressively settling into a mask of itself, she began to look for episodes of counter-light, canalside gates into dank gloom, *sotopòrteghi* whose exits could not be seen, absent faces, missing lamps at the ends of *calli.* So there was revealed to her, night by night in ever more depressing clarity, a secret and tenebrous city, down into whose rat-infested labyrinths she witnessed children her age and younger being drawn, infected, corrupted, and too often made to vanish, like a coin or a card—just that interchangeably held in contempt by those who profited from the limitless appetite for young bodies that seemed to concentrate here from all over Europe and beyond.

She was much more comfortable working nights and trying to find someplace to sleep during the day. Nights had been getting just too hazardous. She had of course been approached, and by some mighty unwholesome customers, too, carrying on their faces scars as certificates of their professional histories, and visible beneath black suit-jackets, Bodeo 10.4 mm pistols as evidence of their dedication to business. The night predators came around, they whispered, they flirted, brought flowers and cigarettes, respectfully keeping their distance, playing by a strict code, until the prey, trembling against the pavement, engaged. Then the weapon which had not been clearly seen, which had appeared only in tantalizing glimpses, came out into the legendary moonlight, and all doubts, and most hopes, vanished.

Dally made a point of being on her feet till they'd moved on, which so far they had, the weather being on their side, they only had to wait. One, Tonio, with a particular interest in Dally, an English suit, almost accentless English. "I know so many of you, American girls, out having fun every night, beautiful clothes, the Casino, the big hotels, the fancy-dress balls at the palazzi. What can you see in this? sleeping with the rats. Such a waste of a lovely girl."

All she had to do was start asking about the clothes, or what sort of room she'd be able to afford—she'd overheard these exchanges—and without quite knowing the moment the stakes of the game would've shifted to life and death, the hopeful young creature would be enfolded in the irreversible darkness of midnight beneath the *foschetta.*

It put her in a peculiar bind, her feelings for the city undiminished yet now with the element of fear that could not be wished aside, each night bringing new intelligence of evil waiting up the end of any little alleyway. Hunter argued that this was why so many people had come to love Venice, because of its "chiaroscuro."

"Thanks for the news, easy enough for you, I guess, but nights out here on the *masègni* are not quite as romantic as they are for tourists."

"You're calling me a tourist?"

"You'll leave someday. What would you call that?"

"Then, when I do, come with me."

The noon cannon went off. A boatful of cigarette smugglers hastily tied up at the canalside and began to unload their cargo. Bells began to peal across the city. "Oh, *patrone,*" she said at last, "Beppo, you know, she's-a not-a too sure. . . ." It did put a few new lines into his biography all right, but then time began to pass again as usual, and one day the bora came, and the first wine trains up from Puglia, and what do you know, he did not leave.

WINTER WAS COMING ON, and Dally needed someplace reliable to sleep during the day, the *fondamente* by now having been long out of the question. She was making do in courtyards, student hovels, back rooms of *osterie,* keeping on the go, but finally reluctantly, went to Hunter for advice. "Why didn't you ask?" he said.

"Why didn't I?"

His eyes shifted away. "Nothing simpler." And next thing she knew, he had fixed her up with a room in the palazzo of the seminotorious Principessa Spongiatosta, one of many acquaintances Dally hadn't known about till now.

She was expecting an older woman with ruinous features, a sort of human palazzo. Instead here was this bright-eyed dewdrop whom Time seemed not, or maybe, in Time's case, never, to have touched. There was a Prince, too, but he was seldom around. Off traveling, according to Hunter, but there was more he wasn't saying.

What intrigued Dally about the interior spaces at Ca' Spongiatosta as she took odd moments to drift around the corridors and anterooms were the rapid changes in scale, something like the almost theatrical expansion from comfortable, dark, human-size alleyways to the vast tracklessness and light of Piazza San Marco. Dark red tiles, a portico in Roman Composite Order, giant decorative urns, brown light, japonica, myrtle, geraniums, fountains, high walls, narrow waterways, and miniature bridges incorporated into the palazzo structure, too many servants for Dally to keep straight. There might in fact be more than one of the Princess—she seemed to be everywhere, and now and then Dally could swear her appearances were multiple and not consecutive, though what went on at the corners of Dally's eyes had always enjoyed with her about the same status as dreams. Mirror tricks? Luca would know. Wherever he was, and Erlys.

She had news soon enough. One day a servant brought her a note. Who had come blowing in to town with the bora but Bria Zombini. She was staying at a small hotel across the Iron Bridge in Dorsoduro. Dally showed up in a frock the Princess was kind enough to let her borrow. Bria was wearing high-heeled shoes, just balancing the inch or so Dally had grown over the past year, so they greeted each other eye to eye. Dally saw this very self-possessed young lady, her hair up underneath a wide-brim Parisian hat, flicking sweat off her upper lip and going *"Porca miseria!"* same as always.

They linked arms and strolled down the Zattere. "Been everyplace," Bria said. "Held over by popular demand, couple crowned heads, you know, the usual. They're all about to sail back now, I'm supposed to meet them in Le Havre, happened to be this side of the Alps and thought I'd look in."

"Oh, Bri, I miss you all somethin terrible, you know. . . ."

Bria narrowed her eyes a little, nodded. "But Venice has got you, and you think you want to stay over here now."

"Thought-reading, these days."

"Every letter you sent us—ain't that hard to see."

"How's our Mamma doing?"

Bria shrugged. "Guess she's a lot easier to miss when there's some distance in between."

"You two . . . you've been arguing?"

"Hah! *She's* not gonna be happy till I'm dead or out the door."

"What about Luca?"

"What about him? He's Italian, he's my pop. Thinks I'm some junior nun's got to be kept behind a gate with a lock. So it's two on one, swell situation, huh?"

Dally ducked her head and looked up through her eyelashes. "Boys . . ."

"Boys, men, what's the difference, I'm supposed to ignore all the attention, *ma via,* you know what they're like over here." Bria grinning so like the young rogue Dally remembered that she caught the smile too, and before they knew it their foreheads were together, stray hair wisps intermingling, third eyes touching, and they were laughing quietly together, for no good reason either could see.

"Well. What do I tell them, you gonna be a remittance girl?"

Dally's laugh faded. "Oh . . . think not."

"Why not? Papa thought you might want to stay. He says he can afford it."

"That's not it."

"Ahh? Some gentleman friend, I should've known. This Spongiatosta address."

"Not exactly."

"Nothing, uhm—" Wiggling both hands expressively.

"Ha. Fat chance."

"Eh, enjoy it while you can, you're still a kid."

"I wish I was. . . ."

Bria didn't think too long about opening her arms, and Dally was right there, sniffling. After a while, "Well, come on, you don't look a day over thirty."

"Need a cigarette's what it is, you happen to, uh . . ."

"Comin right up."

"Say, nice case there."

"Swiss insurance salesman. Wolf. No, Putzi."

"Yeah, Wolf'd be the one with the wife and kids."

"Thanks." They lit up.

ONE DAY HUNTER showed up in sunglasses, broad-brimmed straw hat, and fisherman's smock. "Feel like getting out on the water?"

"Let me borrow a hat and I'll be right there."

Some artist friends had a *topo* for the day. The water in the canals was an opaque green. At the point of the Dogana, where the Grand Canal and the Lagoon meet, the color became blue. "It never does that," said Hunter.

"Today it did," said a fierce young man sitting at the tiller.

His name was Andrea Tancredi. Hunter knew him, had run into him around town at the fringes of Anarchist gatherings, in cafés at exhibitions of experimental painting. After having been to Paris and seen the works of Seurat and Signac, Tancredi had converted to Divisionism. He sympathized with Marinetti and those around him who were beginning to describe themselves as "Futurists," but failed to share their attraction to the varieties of American brutalism. Americans, in fact, seemed greatly to annoy him, particularly the millionaires lately dedicated to coming over and looting Italian art. Dally decided not to mention where she was from.

They picnicked on Torcello in a deserted pomegranate orchard, drank primitivo, and Dally found herself looking at Andrea Tancredi more than she could account for, and when he happened to catch her looking, he stared back, not angry but not what she'd have called fascinated either. Coming back in the evening, sailing into the pealing of the bells, the swept green-and-lavender sky, the upside-down city just beneath the waves, her heart taken as always forever by this unexpected home, she was aware of Tancredi next to her, scowling at Venice.

"Look at it. Someday we'll tear the place down, and use the rubble to fill in those canals. Take apart the churches, salvage the gold, sell off what's left to collectors. The new religion will be public hygiene, whose temples will be waterworks and sewage-treatment plants. The deadly sins will be cholera and decadence." She would have said something, likely harsh, but he had rushed on. "All these islands will be linked by motorways. Electricity everywhere, anyone who still wants Venetian moonlight will have to visit a museum. Colossal gates out here, all around the Lagoon, for the wind, to keep out sirocco and bora alike."

"Oh I don't know." Hunter, who had seen Dally in a temper, had slid quietly between them. "I was always here for the ghosts, myself."

"The past," sneered Tancredi. "San Michele."

"Not exactly." Hunter found he could not explain.

Through God's blind mercy, as he told it to Dally a few days later, on their way over to Tancredi's studio in Cannareggio, after escapes from destruction and war in places he could no longer remember clearly, he had found asylum in Venice, only to happen one day upon these visions of Tancredi's, and recognize the futuristic vehicle which had borne him to safety from the devastated City so long ago, and the subterranean counter-City it took him through, and the chill, comfortless faith in science and rationality that had kept all his fellow refugees then so steady in their flight, and his own desolate certainty of having failed in his remit, one of those mascottes who had brought only bad luck to those who trusted him, destined to end up in cheap rooms down at the ends of suburban streets, eventually indifferent to their own fates, legends of balefulness, banned from accompanying all but the most disreputable and suicidal of voyagers. But lately—was it Venice? was it Dahlia?—he was beginning to feel less comfortable as one of the lost.

So Dally thought she ought to have a look.

TANCREDI'S PAINTINGS WERE like explosions. He favored the palette of fire and explosion. He worked quickly. *Preliminary Studies Toward an Infernal Machine.*

"It would actually work?" Dally wanted to know.

"Of course," Tancredi a bit impatiently.

"He's a sort of infernal-machine specialist," Hunter pointed out. But Tancredi showed a curious reluctance to speak of what the design might actually do. What chain of events could lead to the "effect."

"The term 'infernal' is not applied lightly or even metaphorically. One must begin by accepting Hell—by understanding that Hell is real and that there move through this tidy surface world a silent army of operatives who have sworn allegiance to it as to a beloved homeland."

Dally nodded. "Christers talk like this."

"Oh, the born-again. Always with us. But what of the died-again who have gone to Hell from a condition of ordinary death, imagining that the worst has happened and that nothing can now terrify them?"

"You're talking about an explosive device, *vero?*"

"Not in Venice, never. Fire here would be suicidal insanity. I would not bring fire. But I would bring Hell in a small bounded space."

"And . . . that would be . . ."

Tancredi laughed grimly. "You're American, you think you have to know everything. Others would prefer not to know. Some define Hell as the absence of God, and that is the least we may expect of the infernal machine—that the bourgeoisie be deprived of what most sustains them, their personal problem-solver sitting at his celestial bureau, correcting defects in the everyday world below. . . . But the finite space would rapidly expand. To reveal the Future, we must get around the inertia of paint. Paint wishes to remain as it is. We desire transformation. So this is not so much a painting as a dialectical argument."

"Do you understand what he's talking about?" she asked Hunter.

He raised his eyebrows, angled his head as if in thought. "Sometimes."

It came to remind her in a way of Merle, and his brotherhood of crazy inventors whose collegial mysteries-of-science discussions had escorted her to the doors of sleep in lieu of lullabies.

"Of course it's to do with Time," Tancredi frowning and intense, aroused despite himself at the possibility that she might really have been thinking about the subject, "everything that we imagine is real, living and still, thought and hallucinated, is all on the way from being one thing to being another, from past to Future, the challenge to us is to show as much of the passage as we can, given the *damnable stillness* of paint. This is why—" Using his thumb against a brushful of orpiment yellow, he aimed a controlled spatter of paint at his canvas, followed by another brushful of scarlet vermilion and a third of Nürnberg violet—the target patch seemed to light up like a birthday cake, and before any of it could dry he was at it with an impossibly narrow brush, no more than a bristle or two, stabbing tiny dots among larger ones. "The energies of motion, the grammatical tyrannies of becoming, in *divisionismo* we discover how to break them apart into their component frequencies . . . we define a smallest picture element, a dot of color which becomes the basic unit of reality. . . ."

"It isn't Seurat," it seemed to Hunter, "none of that cool static calm, somehow you've got these dots behaving dynamically, violent ensembles of energy-states, Brownian movement. . . ."

And in fact the next time she visited Tancredi, Dally thought she could see emerging from the glowing field of particles, like towers from the *foschetta,* a city, a contra-Venezia, the almost previsual reality behind what everyone else was agreeing to define as "Venice."

"Not like Marinetti and his circle," Tancredi confessed. "I really love the old dump. Here." He led her to a stack of canvases in a corner she hadn't noticed before. They were all nocturnes, saturated with fog.

"In Venice we have a couple of thousand words for fog—*nebbia, nebbietta, foschia, caligo, sfumato*—and the speed of sound being a function of the density is different in each. In Venice, space and time, being more dependent on hearing than sight, are actually modulated by fog. So this is a related sequence here. *La Velocità del Suono.* What are you thinking?"

It was her first visit here without Hunter. What she was thinking was that Tancredi had better kiss her, and soon.

Smells like a tannery," it seemed to Kit.

"Perhaps . . . because Göttingen a tannery *is.*" Gottlob pointed out.

"*Particularly* the mathematics department," added Humfried. "Remember, they have preserved Gauss's brain here. What, after all, is the cortex of anyone's brain but one more piece of animal hide? *Ja?* at Göttingen they will pickle yours for you, stain it, process it into some altogether different form, impervious to the wind, to carnal decay, to minor insults, both physical and social. A cloak of immortality . . . a future pursued in the present tense—" He stopped and gaped at the doorway. *"Heiliger Bimbam!"*

"Say Humfried, you're about to drop your monocle there."

"It is she, she!"

"Well, *'à la mode'* maybe, with that tortoise-shell rim onto it, but—"

"Not 'chichi,' idiot," said Gottlob. "He refers to our 'Göttingen Kovalevskaia,' who has just now, however improbably, found this *degenerate swamp* of ours. If you would ever sit facing the door, you would miss far fewer of these wonderful events."

"Look at that, serene as a swan."

"Something, huh?"

"Even in Russia this never occurs."

"She's Russian?"

"That is the rumor."

"Those eyes—"

"Those legs."

"How can one know that?"

"Roentgen-ray spectacles, *natürlich.*"

"Those curves are everywhere continuous but nowhere differentiable," sighed Humfried. "*Noli me tangere,* don't you know. Held to stronger criteria, like a function of a complex variable."

"She's complex, all right," said Gottlob.

"And variable."

The lads collapsed into laughter, before whose loudness and puerility any young woman of the day might have been excused at least a dip in confidence. But not the self-possessed beauty who now approached. No, though being openly stared at—more in wonder, mind you, than indignation—Yashmeen Halfcourt continued to glide, through the Turkish smoke and beer-fumes, directly toward them, in her bearing a suggestion that she might, with or without a partner, begin to dance a polka. And that hat! Draped velvet toques had always been Kit's undoing.

"Swell that you're all on such close terms with her—so! who'll introduce me?"

Amid a great creak and scrape of beer-house furniture, Kit's companions had swiftly vanished.

"Converging to zero," he mumbled, "what a surprise. . . . Good evening, miss, were you looking for one of those boys that suddenly ain't here anymore?"

She sat down, took a look at him. The Eastern eyes, the tension of whose lower lids had found a perfect balance between heat and appraisal, certainly were promissory of heartbreak.

"You are not English." Her voice unexpectedly just a little screechy.

"American."

"And is that a revolver you're carrying?"

"This? No, no this is the, what they call the *Hausknochen*? Get in off the street and up the staircase with." He produced a gigantic key whose transgression of scale, beyond all parameters of the tasteful, had in its time provoked unease even in the most collected of spirits. "Everybody around here packs one of these."

"Not everybody. All they've given me is this." She held up and jingled at him a silvery ring with a little pair of latchkeys. "Feminine, yes? This, plus of course a set of signs and countersigns before I'm even allowed to use them, as I am chaperoned without mercy. How is a person expected to prove Riemann's Hypothesis when half her time is taken up getting in and out of rooms?"

"Another one of them Zetamaniacs, eh? Sure are a lot of you folks pouring in to town, is it's like a silver camp in Colorado here, eternal renown in em hills, so forth."

Yashmeen lit up an Austrian cigarette, held it between her teeth, grinned. "Where have you been? This has been going on everywhere, since Hadamard—or Poussin, if you like—proved the Prime Number Theorem. The first nugget out of the ground, as you'd say. Is it the problem that offends you, or those of us trying to solve it?"

"Neither one, it's an honorable pursuit, just kind of obvious, is all."

"Don't patronize me." She waited for a protest, but he only smiled. " 'Obvious'?"

Kit shrugged. "I could show you."

"Oh please do. While we're at it, you can also show me how your *Hausknochen* works. . . ."

He guessed he was hearing things, but before long, having translated themselves without inconvenience out the door, down the street and up the stairs, here they were, actually up in his room with two bottles of beer he'd located in the patent *Kühlbox.* He sat just taking in her image for a bit, presently venturing,

"They tell me you're kind of famous?"

"Women at Göttingen form a somewhat beleaguered subset." She looked around. "And what is it you do here again?"

"Drink beer, work on my sleep allowance, the usual."

"I took you for a mathematician."

"Well . . . maybe not *your* kind. . . ."

"Yes? Come, don't be too clever."

"All right, then." He squared his shoulders, brushed imaginary beer foam off his almost-matured mustache, and, expecting her to disappear just as quick as beer-foam, winced in apology. "I'm a sort of, hm . . . Vectorist?"

Despite the shadow of an intent to flinch, she surprised him instead with a smile which, for all its resemblance to the smiles one gives the afflicted, was still able to turn Kit's extremities to stone. That is, is it was *some smile.* "They teach vectors in America? I'm amazed."

"Nothing like what they offer here."

"Isn't England where you ought to be now?" as to a naughty child one expected to become, in a short while, naughtier.

"Nothing but Quaternions over there."

"*Oh* dear, not the Quaternion Wars again. That is *so* all rather fading into history now, not to mention folklore. . . . Why should any of you keep at it this way?"

"They believe—the Quaternionists do—that Hamilton didn't so much figure the system out as receive it from somewhere beyond? Sort of like Mormons only different?"

She couldn't tell how serious he was being, but after a decent interval she stepped closer. "Excuse me? It's a vectorial system, Mr. Traverse, it's something for engineers, to help the poor prats visualize what they obviously can't grasp as *real maths.*"

"Such as your Riemann problem."

"Die Nullstellen der ζ-Funktion," saying it the way some other girl might say "Paris" or "Richard Harding Davis," but with a note as well warning that though she might possess an active sense of humor, it did not extend to Riemann. Kit had seldom, if ever, in those years up and down the New York–New Haven Trail, from debutantes to nymphs of the Tenderloin, run into anything as passionate as this stretching of spine-top and untilting of face. Her neck so uncommonly slender and long.

"Hate to tell you, but it's not all that hard to prove."

"Oh, a *Vectorist* proof, no doubt. And only excessive modesty has kept you from publishing."

Rummaging through the domestic clutter for a piece of paper with some blank space still on it, "Actually, I've been looking for a way, not to solve the Riemann problem so much as to apply the ζ-function to vector-type situations, for instance taking a certain set of vectorial possibilities as if it was mappable into the set of complex numbers, and investigating properties and so forth, beginning with vector systems in the prime-numbered dimensions—the well-known two and three of course, but then five, seven, eleven, so forth, as well."

"Only primes. Skipping the fourth dimension, then."

"Skipping four, sorry. Hard to imagine a less-interesting number."

"Unless you're—"

"What?"

"Sorry. I was only thinking out loud."

"Aw." Was this amazing girl flirting? How come he couldn't tell?

"Death to reveal, I'm afraid."

"Really?"

"Well . . ."

Which is how Kit first heard about the T.W.I.T. back in London, and of the ghostly neo-Pythagorean cult of tetralatry or worship of the number four, currently the rage in certain European circles, "not to mention ellipses and hyperbolæ,"—loosely allied, in fact, as a sort of correspondent group, with the T.W.I.T. These days, among those inclined to studies of the mystical, the fourth dimension, owing to the works of Mr. C. Howard Hinton, Professor Johann K. F. Zöllner, and others, was enjoying a certain vogue, "or should I say 'vague'?" remarked Yashmeen.

"O.K. Here's the Riemann proof—" He wrote down, without pausing, no more than a dozen lines. "Leaving out all the obvious transitions, of course. . . ."

"Of course. How eccentric-looking. What were these upside-down triangles again?"

All at once there came a horrible metallic banging and rattling from down at the street entry, accompanied, from beneath the window, by some tone-deaf beer-society in vulgar song. She stared at Kit, lips compressed, head nodding emphatically. "So—it's all been a trick. Hasn't it, yes. A squalid trick."

"What?"

"Arranging for your little beer-mates to show up just as I was about to find the screamingly obvious fallacy in this . . . 'proof' of yours—"

"It's only Humfried and some pals, trying to get a *Hausknochen* in the lock. If you want to hide someplace, I'd suggest that closet, there."

"They . . . live here?"

"Not here, but none of them more than a couple-three blocks' distance. Or do you Riemann folks say 'metric interval'?"

"But why should your friend use *his* key—"

"Um actually, as it turns out, every *Hausknochen* fits pretty much every lock around here."

"Therefore—"

"Social life is unpredictable."

Shaking her head, eyes on the floor, "*Auf wiedersehen,* Herr Professor Traverse." By mistake the door she chose to exit by was not the back door, though it looked—and from its swing, weighed—about the same, indeed seemed to be located in the same part of Kit's rooms, *as* the back door, and yet, strangely, was *not* the back door. How could this be? Actually, it was not even a door to begin with, but something designed to allow the human brain to *interpret* it as a door, because it served a similar function.

On the other side of it, she found herself out on the corner of Prinzenstraße and Weenderstraße, known to mathematicians here as the origin of the city of Göttingen's coördinate system. "Return to zero," she muttered to herself. "Begin again." She didn't find this sort of excursion especially out of the ordinary—it had happened before, and once she had learned that no harm was likely to come of it, she had been able to shrug and get on with her day. It was no more upsetting than waking from a lucid dream.

Back in quotidian space, Kit, having observed Yashmeen apparently walk through a solid wall, had scarcely time to register puzzlement before up the stairs and into the room came thumping Humfried and his creature, Gottlob. They were indeed seldom noted apart, being driven by a common fascination with the details of others' lives, no matter how trivial. "All right, where is she?"

"Where's who, and speaking of *where,* Gottlob, *where's* 'at twenty marks you owe me?"

"Ach, der Pistolenheld!" screamed Gottlob, attempting to hide behind Humfried, who as usual was looking for food.

"No, no, Gottlob, control yourself, he will not shoot at you, here, see, this interesting sausage—" Eating half of it immediately and offering the rest to Gottlob, who shook his head vigorously no.

Humfried had been obsessed for a while now with a connection he thought he saw between automorphic functions and the Anharmonic Pencil or, as he preferred, *das Nichtharmonischestrahlenbündel,* though he had decided to write all his papers in Latin, which no one had done since Euler.

Gottlob, on the other hand, had come to Göttingen from Berlin to study with Felix Klein, on the strength of Klein's magisterial *Mathematical Theory of the Top* (1897), approached by way of functions of a complex variable, and also to get away from the sinister influence of the late Leopold Kronecker, keepers of whose flame regarded the complex domain with suspicion if not outright abhorrence—only to find at Göttingen a dwarf variety of the same monumental quarrel between Kronecker and Cantor then raging in the capital, not to mention the world. Fundamentalist Kroneckerites had been known to descend on Göttingen in periodic raids, from which not all of them returned.

"Ach, der Kronecker!" cried Gottlob, "he needed only to step out into the street, and mad dogs ran away or, knowing what was good for them, at once regained their sanity. Only five feet tall, but he enjoyed the abnormal strength of the possessed. Each time he appeared, one could count on weeks of panic."

"But . . . folks say he was very sociable and outgoing," said Kit.

"Perhaps, for an insane zealot who believed 'the positive integers were created by God, and all else is the work of man.' Of course, it is a religious war. Kronecker did not believe in pi, or the square root of minus one—"

"He did not even believe in the square root of *plus two,*" said Humfried.

"Against this, Cantor with his *Kontinuum,* professing an equally strong belief in just those regions, infinitely divisible, which lie *between* the whole numbers so demanding of all Kronecker's devotion."

"And that's what has kept driving Cantor back into the *Nervenklinik,"* added Humfried, "and he was only worrying about line-segments. But out here in the four-dimensional space-and-time of Dr. Minkowski, inside the tiniest 'interval,' as small as you care to make it, within each tiny hypervolume of *Kontinuum*—there likewise must be always hidden an infinite number of other points—and if we define a 'world' as a very large and finite set of points, then there must be worlds. Universes!"

In fact, a mystical Cantorian cult of the very, indeed vanishingly, negligible, ever seeking escape into a boundless epsilonic world, was rumored to be meeting weekly at Der Finsterzwerg, a beer-hall just outside the old ramparts of the town, near the train station. "A sort of Geographical Society for the unlimited exploration of regions neighboring the Zero. . . ."

As Kit had rapidly discovered, this sort of eccentricity abounded at Göttingen. Discussion ran far into the night, insomnia was the rule, though if one did wish to sleep for some reason, there was always chloral hydrate, which had its own circle of devotees. He saw Yashmeen now and then, usually across the smoke-clouded depths of some disreputable *Kneipe* by the river, but seldom to talk to. One evening he happened to be walking along the promenade on top of the old fortifications, and near the statue of Gauss passing to Weber a remark forever among the pages of silence, noticed her gazing out over the red-tile roofs of the town, and the lights just coming on.

"How's 'at old Zeta function?"

"Something amuses you, Kit?"

"Every time I see one them Zetas, it makes me think of a snake up on its tail being charmed by a snake-charmer, ever notice that?"

"These are the reflections that occupy your time?"

"Let me put it a different way. Whenever I see one, it reminds me of you. The 'charmer' part anyway."

"Aaah! Even more trivial. Do none of you ever think beyond these walls? There is a crisis out there." She scowled into the stained orange glow of the just-vanished sun, the smoke rising from hundreds of chimneys. "And Göttingen is no more exempt than it was in Riemann's day, in the war with Prussia. The political crisis in Europe maps into the crisis in mathematics. Weierstrass functions, Cantor's continuum, Russell's equally inexhaustible capacity for mischief—once, among nations, as in chess, suicide was illegal. Once, among mathematicians, 'the infinite' was all but a conjuror's convenience. The connections lie there, Kit—hidden and poisonous. Those of us who must creep among them do so at our peril."

"Come on," Kit said, "let a trivial fellow buy you a beer."

· · ·

THAT WINTER, IN St. Petersburg, troops at the Winter Palace fired on thousands of unarmed strikers who had marched there in respectfulnesss and innocence. Hundreds were killed and wounded. In Moscow the Grand Duke Sergei was assassinated. More strikes and fighting followed, along with peasant and military insurrections, on into the summer. The Navy mutinied at Kronstadt and Sebastopol. There was street-fighting in Moscow. The Black Hundreds carried out pogroms against Jews. The Japanese won the war in the East, obliterating the entire Baltic Fleet, which had just sailed halfway around the world to try to lift the siege of Port Arthur. A general strike in the autumn cut the country off for weeks from the rest of the world and, as people came slowly to realize, stopped history. In December the Army beat down another major uprising. In the East there was fighting all up and down the railroad lines, banditry, eventually a Muslim rebellion in Inner Asia. If God had not forgotten Russia, He had turned His attention elsewhere.

For the rest of Europe, the year that followed was to be remembered as the year of Russians everywhere, fleeing into mass exile, as the Revolution went collapsing at their heels—the Peter and Paul Fortress and sooner or later death if they stayed. Who would have thought the Tsar had so many enemies?

Kit had begun to notice Russians in the Weenderstraße. Yashmeen was convinced they were in town to spy on her. They were trying to blend in, but certain telltale nuances—fur hats, huge unkempt beards, a tendency in the street to drop and begin dancing the kazatsky to music only they could hear—kept giving them away.

"Say, Yash, what's with all those Russians?"

"I'm trying not to take it personally. My parents were Russian. When we lived on the frontier, my family and I one day were taken in a raid and sold as slaves. Some time later, Major Halfcourt found me in a bazaar in Waziristan and became my second father."

Not feeling as surprised as he might've been, "And he's still out there someplace?"

"Whatever he's been up to, it is of enough political weight that someone thinks they can use me somehow."

"Are you in touch?"

"We have our own means, which neither distance nor time can affect."

"Telepathy or something."

She frowned. "Perhaps you think I am a girl with Æther between her ears, easily influenced by the beliefs of the T.W.I.T."

"Dang, Yash, you sure *read my mind* there," with what he hoped was enough of a twinkle that she wouldn't take offense, for her unannounced ferocities, however playful, continued to cause him some dismay.

She was fooling with her as-ever transcendentally interesting hair, always a sign of trouble down the line. "Even with the Revolution, news comes back. Thousands of miles, multitudes of tongues, unreliable witnesses, deliberate misinformation and all, it finds its way back to the T.W.I.T. people at Chunxton Crescent, and what comes out of their shop can surprisingly often be trusted—even the War Office admits it's better 'gen' on the whole than their own."

"Anything I can do, just fire away."

She gave him a look. "To the world here, I enjoy a reputation as 'my own person' . . . yet I am also, ever . . . *his.* My other family have gone on to destinies I cannot imagine. Only in dreams do I catch glimpses of them, moments so fugitive, so slight, that afterward there is the sensible ache here, in my breast, of cruel incompletion. My true memories do not begin until the moment *he* first saw me in the market—I was a soul impaled, exactly upon the cusp between girl and young woman, a cusp I could literally feel as it penetrated me, as if to bisect me— I do hope that is not a blush, Kit."

Well, sort of, but more from perplexity than desire. Today she wore an ancient coin, pierced and simply suspended from a fine silver chain around that ever-fascinating neck. . . . "It's an Afghani dirhan, from the early days of the Ghaznivid Empire. He gave it to me, for luck." Over its nine or ten centuries of circulation, thieves had nipped and shaved silver from around the outer border, but the inner circle survived, crowded with ancient writing. It was the outward emblem of a hidden history of assault and persistence, the true history of its region and perhaps of this young woman, through this life and who knew how many previous. "Thank you for the offer, Kit. If anything arises, I shall certainly seek your advice. I am ever so grateful," with eyes a-dance in the luxury of believing little beyond the assumption that he would allow her to get away with this, yet expect no favors in return. He ate it all up like a fairground ice-cream cone, even if he had to pretend indifference. You sure never got this in New Haven. They didn't know how to flirt like this even in New York. This is the world, Kit reflected, and a couple nights later, around three A.M., as an extra smack of the bamboo stick, *She* is the world.

Meanwhile Yashmeen, a fine one to scold the trivial, had taken up with a wealthy coffee scion named Günther von Quassel. On their first date, Günther, a devotee of the less than universally respected Ludwig Boltzmann, had tried to explain to her the Riemann problem by means of statistical mechanics.

"Here. Tell me please, as *n* grows infinitely large, what the *n*th prime is?"

Sighing, though not with desire, "Its value—as any Gymnasium child at all acquainted with the Prime Number Theorem knows—approaches *n* log *n*."

"So. Looking at the entropy of a system—"

"Some sort of . . . steam-engine word, isn't it? Am I a boiler engineer, Günni?"

"Except for the usual constants," writing as he spoke, "one may express the entropy as . . . the summation, of $p(E_k)$, times log $p(E_k)$. All in order so far?"

"Of course, but this is only statistics. When do we get to the mathematics?"

"*Ach, die Zetamanie* . . . your Prime Number Theorem is *not* statistical?"

But she was looking at what he'd scribbled down, the two something-log-somethings. "This E_k . . . ?"

"The energy of a given system, you use the *k* to index if there is more than one, and there usually is."

"And is there insanity in your family, Günther?"

"You do not find it odd that the *N*th prime for very large *N* may be expressed as one measure of the chaos in a physical system?"

None of which kept Yashmeen from pursuing the attachment.

"As a crime," Humfried pointed out, "often of the gravest sort, committed in a detective story, may often be only a pretext for the posing and solution of some narrative puzzle, so romance in this town is often pursued as little beyond a pretext for running in and out of doors, not to mention up and down stairs, while talking nonstop and, on auspicious days, screaming."

Yashmeen one day overheard Günther confessing to his intimate Heinrich, "There is only one girl in this town I have ever wanted to kiss." It was doctoral-candidate talk, of course, though Yashmeen in her Riemannian obsession appeared to be unaware of the Göttingen tradition that required successful Ph.D.'s in mathematics to kiss the statue of the little goose-girl in the fountain of the Rathaus square, getting soaked and with luck delirious in the process.

Yashmeen grew exercised. "Who is this person?" she demanded of Heinrich, who assumed she was teasing.

"All I know is, he says that she waits every day near the Rathaus."

"For whom? Not for Günther?"

Heinrich shrugged. "Geese were mentioned?"

"Real geese, or University students?" as she went storming out into the Platz, where she began to loiter menacingly. For days. Günther happened by, or did not happen by, but never in the company of any imaginable rival. Naturally she failed to pay much attention to the fountain nearby, or the little statue. One day she did hear him singing—

Her idea of banter
Likely isn't Cantor,
Nor is she apt to murmur low
Axioms of Zermelo,
She's been kissed by geniuses,
Amateur Frobeniuses,
One by one in swank array,
Bright as any Poincaré,
And . . . though she
May not care for Cauchy,
Any more than Riemann,
We'll just have to dream on . . .
Let
    it occur in spots in
Whittaker and Watson—
Unforeseen converging,
Miracles emerging,
Epsilonic dances,
Small but finite chances,
For love . . .

Concerned for her mental stability, everybody felt obliged to put in their two pfennigs, including Kit. "Yash, you want to forget this customer, he's not for you. I mean, what if he is tall, muscular, even in some strange German way some'd think presentable—"

"You forgot brilliant, amusing, romantic—"

"But you are being used by your racial memory here," declared Humfried indignantly, "you are out looking for some Hun."

"Are you saying I want to be overrun and conquered, Humfried?"

"Did I say that?"

"Well . . . suppose I do, is that, one, any business of either of you, two, anything I feel that I must apologize for, two point one—"

"Yash, you are flat correct," Kit nodded, "we're all just night-riders here miles up a posted trail, making pests of ourselves. Ought to be shot, well, shot at, anyway."

"Günther may be all you say and worse, but until you experience emotions the way we women do, you will find in your relations with us much struggle and little success."

"I could manage some sniffling maybe, would that help?"

She was already halfway out the door, scowling over her shoulder in reproof, when who should come bounding athletically up the stairway but the very Adonis under discussion, yes Günther von Quassel himself, brandishing a *Hausknochen* in menacing fashion, approaching, as the stairs brought him to their upper limit, a comparable level of brute rage. "Now Günni," she greeted him, "you mustn't murder Kit, must you?"

"What here is he *doing*?"

"I live here, you oversize bratwurst."

"Oh. *Ja*. This is true." He considered. "But Fräulein Yashmeen . . . she does *not* live here."

"Say, Günther, that's really interesting."

Günther gazed at him, for what any but the erotically smitten would have considered far too long. Yashmeen, meanwhile, playful as Kit seldom saw her, kept snatching away Günther's dueling-society cap and pretending to throw it down the stairs. Each time he would respond to the prank only after several seconds had gone by, though with as much alacrity *as if it had just happened.* In fact, according to Humfried, a disciple of Professor Minkowski, it ought to be obvious to all that Günther inhabited his own idiomatic "frame of reference," in which time-discrepancies like this one were highly important, if not essential, features. "He is not 'here,'" Humfried explained, "not completely. He is slightly . . . somewhere else. Enough so, to present some inconvenience to any who value his company."

"Yeah, but how many of those could there be?"

"Oh you're all so horrid," Yashmeen said.

Günther meanwhile insisted that Yashmeen's presence here amounted to an affair of honor. "Obviously, we must now a duel fight."

"How's that?"

"You have insulted me, you have insulted my fiancée—"

"Oh, Günni?"

"Ja, Liebchen?"

"I'm not your fiancée, remember? we talked about this?"

"*Egal was, meine Schatze!*— meanwhile, Mr. Traverse, as challenged party you shall have the choice of weapons—how lucky to have provoked your quarrel here, in the dueling capital of Germany. At my disposal, and yours, are matched pairs of the *Schläger,* the Krummsäbel, the Korbrapier, even, if it should be your vice, the épée—a weapon which, though not up to German standards, is I am told quite all the rage now in England—"

"In fact," said Kit, "I was thinking more along the lines of, maybe, pistols? I happen to have a couple of Colt six-shooters we can use—though as for 'matched,' well . . ."

"Pistols! Oh, no, no, impulsive, violent Mr. Traverse—here we do not duel to *kill,* no! though of course wishing to maintain the honor of the *Verbindung,* one's deeper intent is, upon the face of the other, *to inscribe one's mark,* so that a man may then bear for all to see evidence of his personal bravery."

"Is that what that is on your face, looks like a Mexican tilde?"

"Unusual, no? Later we worked out the probable frequency the blade must have been vibrating at, given the restoring moment, elastic constants, all in the most gentlemanly way, which I am sure your American gunslinger has no concept of. Oh it is true, *ja,* there do creep among us certain *desperate maniacs,* who have come away from their affairs carrying actual *bullet scars* on their faces, but this takes a degree of indifference to mortality that few of us are blessed with."

"Are you saying pistols'd be too dangerous for you, Günni? Where I'm from, when it's about Honor? why a man's pretty much obliged to use a pistol. Blades, that'd be just too—I don't know—quiet? mean? . . . sneaky, even?"

Günther's ears quivered. "Am I to understand, sir, that you mean thus to classify the German as a subspecies of some *less valiant race,* is this correct?"

"Wait—I've insulted you again? you're . . . calling me out, twice now? Well! That sure ups the ante, don't it? say, if you're going to get offended at every little thing, maybe we'd better have all our chambers full, six shots apiece, what do you think?"

"This *cowboy,*" Günther in plaintive appeal, "seems unaware that civilized beings are repelled by the stench of powder."

"Listen, Porkbarrel, what's this really about? I told you it wasn't going to converge, and it never will."

"There. Again. Three times, now."

"Just the same, about halfway through, you skipped a step. Not to mention in one of your series you grouped some terms together wrong, reversed sign a couple times, even went and *divided by zero,* yeah you did, Günni, look, right here, you're lucky somebody took the time to read it that close—basic stupid mistakes—"

"Four!"

"—and instead of all this carving on folks, why not consider if this is really the best field of study for you, if all you want's your face on a souvenir postcard."

"You insult Geheimrat Hilbert now!"

"At least he's got the right hat."

After repeated consultations with the Prussian dueling bible, a small brown volume known as the *Ehrenkodex,* Kit, Günther and their seconds met down by the river, as soon as there was light to see by. It was one of those profoundly agreeable spring mornings, which more rational souls might choose to celebrate in some less lethal way. The tanneries had not quite cranked up to operating speed, and the air still smelled like the countryside it had passed over. Willows swayed alluringly. Farther off, ruinous watchtowers emerged from the mists. Early bathers came blinking by, wraithlike and curious. Students in dressing-gowns, Tyrolean hats, colored spectacles, carpet slippers, and exotic pajamas with Oriental prints on them, sleepily queued up to stake demented wagers with the bookmakers found haunting such affairs. Now and then someone, edging into consciousness, remembered he was still wearing his *Schnurrbartbinde,* or nighttime mustache-keeper. Those principally involved stood around bowing back and forth for a while. A vendor appeared with a cart carrying a steaming tub brimful of boiled sausages, and beer arrived as well, both in barrels and in bottles. A photographer set up his tripod and Zeiss "Palmos Panoram" for any who might wish visual mementoes of the encounter.

"Very well, I did divide by zero—once only, mea maxima culpa, no effect on the result. I did not omit any step where you said I did. You, rather, incapable appear, of following my argument."

"Hogwash Günther, look, between steps, here to here, this function of time, you assume it's commutative, just glide on past it, when in fact—"

"So?"

"You just can't make that assumption."

"I may do as I wish."

"Not when this needs a minus sign here. . . ." Thus, despite the restlessness of the crowd, who had been chanting *"Auf die Mensur!"* for quite some time actually, the young men found themselves in yet another mathematical exchange, which soon bored everyone into wandering away, including Yashmeen, who had in fact left much earlier, on the eager arm of a graduate anthropologist visiting from Berlin, who hoped to define here among the dueling clubs of Göttingen a "control-group" for examining the deeper meanings of facial inscription, especially as practiced among northern tribes of the Andaman Islands—departing, in fact, to shouts of "Stephanie du Motel!" and rude whistling, as the community, being fully up to date on the details of the romance, had found itself divided as to Yashmeen, some regarding her as a brave and modern young woman, like Kovalevskaia, others as a faithless harlot whose mission in life was to lure promising mathematicians into premature demise by duel, as the infamous Mademoiselle du Motel had done to group-theory godfather Evariste Galois back in 1832.

. . .

AMONG THE RUSSIAN VISITORS to Göttingen were some of decidedly mystical inclination. Yashmeen recognized them right away, having met, and on occasion eluded, several at Chunxton Crescent, but here, farther east, there was no avoiding the momentous events unfolding close by. By 1906 there were Russians everywhere, flown and fleeing westward, and many brought copies of young Ouspensky's book *The Fourth Dimension.*

An unkempt individual with a single name, vaguely Eastern, was observed hanging around with Humfried and Gottlob. "He's all right. He's a Theosophoid, Chong is. That's like a Theosophist, only not entirely. He's here to learn about the Fourth Dimension."

"The what?"

"And the others, of course."

"The other . . . ?"

"Dimensions. You know, Fifth, Sixth, so on?"

"He believes Humfried to've been his teacher in a previous life," added Gottlob, helpfully.

"How odd. There are educators among the invertebrates?"

"But look here!" cried Yashmeen, "that's no Chinese Bolshevik—it's old Sidney, well blimey if it isn't old Kensington Sid, with some vegetable dye—I say Sid! it's I! old Yashmeen! Cambridge! Professor Renfrew! Remember?"

The Eastern personage gazed uninformatively back at her—then, seeming to reach a decision, began to speak with some intensity in a tongue no one could identify, not even by its language-family. More cognizant listeners understood this as an attempt to distract.

Dr. Werfner of course had spotted him right away and assumed he'd been sent out as one of Renfrew's operatives, as did Yashmeen, who assumed he was there to spy on her, for he did seem to show an uncommon interest in the Russians who passed through town. Whenever they sought out Yashmeen to discuss the transtriadic dimensions, Chong was sure to be there.

"Four is the first step beyond the space we know," said Yashmeen. "Dr. Minkowski suggests a continuum among three dimensions of space and one of time. We can look at the 'fourth dimension' as if it *were* time, but is really something of its own, and 'Time' is only our least imperfect approximation."

"But beyond the third," persisted one of their Russian visitors, "do dimensions exist as something more than algebraists' whimsy? Can we be given access to them in some more than mental way?"

"Spiritual," declared Gottlob. As far as anyone could recall, it was the first time he had ever used the word.

"The soul?" Humfried said. "The angels? The invisible world? The after-life? God?" By the end of this list, he had acquired a smirk. "At Göttingen?"

Kit meanwhile had begun to frequent the Applied Mechanics Institute. Since Prandtl's recent discovery of the boundary layer, things over there had been hopping, with intense inquiry into matters of lift and drag, powered flight poised like a new-feathered bird at the edge of history. Kit had not thought much about aerodynamics since his brainless sojourn in the Vibe embrace, when in the course of golfing parties out on Long Island he had become acquainted with the brambled guttie, a gutta-percha ball systematically roughened away from the perfectly spherical by molding little knobs all over the surface area. What he could not help noticing then, even though he was not all that crazy for the game, so inordinately populated by the likes of Scarsdale Vibe, was a particular mystery of flight—the undeniable lift of heart in seeing a struck ball—a tee shot especially—suddenly go into a steep ascent, an exhilarated denial of gravity you didn't have to be a golfer to appreciate. There being enough otherworldliness out on the links already. Finding himself more and more drawn to the microcosm on the other side of the Bürgerstraße, Kit soon understood that the brambling of the golf-ball surface had been a way to keep the boundary layer from detaching and falling apart into turbulence which would tend to drag the ball down, denying it its destiny in the sky. When he mentioned this in conversations at the saloons along the Brauweg frequented by engineering and physics students, some immediately suggested implications for the Earth, a brambled spheroid on the grand scale, in its passage through the Æther, being lifted not in the third dimension but on a euphoric world-line through Minkowski's "four-dimensional physics."

"What happened to vectorism?" Yashmeen teased.

"There are vectors," Kit replied, "and vectors. Over in Dr. Prandtl's shop, they're all straightforward lift and drift, velocity and so forth. You can draw pictures, of good old three-dimensional space if you like, or on the Complex plane, if Zhukovsky's Transformation is your glass of tea. Flights of arrows, teardrops. In Geheimrat Klein's shop, we were more used to expressing vectors without pictures, purely as an array of coefficients, no relation to anything physical, not even space itself, and writing them in any number of dimensions—according to Spectral Theory, up to infinity."

"And beyond," added Günther, nodding earnestly.

. . .

IN HILBERT'S CLASS one day, she raised her hand. He twinkled at her to go ahead. *"Herr Geheimrat—"*

"'Herr Professor' is good enough."

"The nontrivial zeroes of the ζ-function . . ."

"Ah."

She was trembling. She had not had much sleep. Hilbert had seen this sort of thing before, and rather a good deal of it since the turn of the century—since his own much-noted talk at the Sorbonne, he supposed, in which he had listed the outstanding problems in mathematics which would be addressed in the coming century, among them that of the zeroes of the ζ-function.

"Might they be correlated with eigenvalues of some Hermitian operator yet to be determined?"

The twinkle, as some reported later, modulated to a steady pulsation. "An intriguing suggestion, Fräulein Halfcourt." Usually he addressed her as "my child." "Let us consider why this should be so." He peered, as if she were an apparition he was trying to see more clearly. "Apart from eigenvalues, by their nature, being zeroes of *some* equation," he prompted gently.

"There is also this . . . spine of reality." Afterward she would remember she actually said *"Rückgrat von Wirklichkeit."* "Though the members of a Hermitian may be complex, the eigenvalues are real. The entries on the main diagonal are real. The ζ-function zeroes which lie along Real part = ½, are symmetrical about the real axis, and so . . ." She hesitated. She had *seen it,* for the moment, so clearly.

"Let us apply some thought," said Hilbert. "We will talk about this further." But she was to leave Göttingen shortly after this, and they would never have the chance to confer. As years passed, she would grow dim for Hilbert, her words those of an inner sprite too playful to frame a formal proposition, or to qualify as a fully habilitated Muse. And the idea itself would evolve into the celebrated Hilbert-Pólya Conjecture.

One morning Lew walked into the breakfast parlor at Chunxton Crescent to find Police Inspector Vance Aychrome, angelically revealed in early sunbeams through the stained-glass dome overhead, relentlessly despoiling a Full English Breakfast modified for the Pythagorean dietary here, including imitation sausages, kippers and bloaters, omelettes, fried potatoes, fried tomatoes, porridge, buns, baps, scones, and loaves in various formats. Robed acolytes crept timidly between the tables and the great kitchen with caddies, tureens, and trays. Some wore mystical facial expressions as well. Late risers, sandals twinkling, sought to avoid the Inspector, preferring to fast rather than compete with his all-but-entitled insatiability.

"One fancies a wee fry-up at this hour," Aychrome somehow between huge mouthfuls greeted Lew, who, smiling grimly, went looking for some coffee, a fool's errand around here on the best of mornings, which this already wasn't. These English were a people of many mysteries, none more peculiar than their indifference to coffee.

"All right," he called out, "who's taken the bloody Spong machine again," not that it mattered—coffee around here was apt to taste like anything but coffee, owing to folks's tendencies to use the only grinder in the house to prepare curry powder, incense, even pigments for indecipherable works of art, so he ended up, as usual, with a chipped mug full of pale, uneventful tea, and took a seat across from Aychrome, gazing in some fascination. Assuming he was not here only to deliver another gentle suggestion from Scotland Yard to back off of the Gentleman Bomber case, Lew took from an inner pocket a Tarot deck thinned to the twenty-two Major Arcana and dealt them one by one onto the table, between the remains of a vegetarian haggis and a platterful of pea fritters, until Aychrome began to nod frantically and wave about a finger dripping with what Lew hoped was only treacle. "Ggbbmm-hhgghhkkhh!"

Indeed. The card was not Renfrew/Werfner's number XV after all, but XII, The Hanged Man, whose deeply veiled secret meanings always seemed to place it in a particularly critical area of investigation. Lew had got to thinking of it as his own personal card, because it had been the first "future" card that Neville and Nigel had turned over for him. Last time he'd checked, its position in the Icosadyad was occupied by one Lamont Replevin, of Elflock Villa, Stuffed Edge, Herts.

When at last Aychrome's mouth seemed relatively unengaged, "So, Inspector," as chirpily as possible given the hour, "nothing too political I hope."

"Hmm," as if to himself, "bit of this . . . kedgeree, I think . . . yes lovely . . . and where was that marmalade pot . . . ah very nice indeed." Lew was thinking about leaving the man to his appetite when Aychrome, as if just bitten by an insect, fixed him with a pop-eyed stare, wiped his mustaches, and barked, "Political! well I should say so, but then it's all political, isn't it."

"According to the dossier, this Replevin is an antiques dealer."

"Oh beyond a doubt, except that there's a sheet on the subject half a mile long. The Lombro work alone is most suggestive, yes, most suggestive indeed."

Lew was aware that Inspector Aychrome was a zealous disciple of the criminological theories of Dr. Cesare Lombroso, notably the popular one that deficiencies of moral intelligence were accompanied by an absence of corresponding tissue in the brain, and a consequently warped cranial development which could be observed, by the trained eye, in a subject's facial structure.

"Some faces are criminal faces, is the long and short of it," declared the Metropolitan veteran, "and woe unto them that ignore it or can't interpret it properly. This one," handing across a "mug" photo, "as you can see, has International Mischief written all over his map."

Lew shrugged. "Seems like a wholesome enough fellow."

"We've had men watching the place, you see."

"Why?"

Aychrome gave the room a quick melodramatic once-over and lowered his voice. "Germans."

"Beg pardon?"

"The subject Replevin runs a shop in Kensington, dealing, according to his file, in 'Trans-Oxanian and Græco-Buddhist antiquities,' whatever those may be when they're at home, which is visited by a constant stream of suspect characters, some of whom we already know, bad hats just from their facial types alone, forgers and counterfeiters, fences and collectors . . . but our main worry at the Yard is the high proportion of German traffic between here and Inner Asia that always seems to find its way through Replevin's establishment. Most of the archaeology out there is being done by German teams, you see, a perfect excuse for these visitors to keep entering the country with dozens of their huge heavy crates labeled, helpfully, 'Antiquities.' And then Sands calls in about the Inner Asian show—this Shambhala state of affairs—and as if that wasn't enough, the Gas Office are on the doorstep stark mental with what *they're* overhearing."

"'Gas Office.'"

Gripping a knife and fork expressively in either fist, the Inspector was happy to explain. Lamont Replevin, it seemed, was a practicing devotee of communication by means of coal-gas—that is, gas-mains city and suburban figured, in his map of London, as networks of communication, every bit as much as pneumatic or telephone lines. The population who communicated by Gas, who indeed were unwilling to communicate in any other way, appeared pretty substantial and, according to Aychrome, was growing daily, as *secret interconnections* continued to be made among urban and local or village gas-mains, and the system expanded, net-wise, as if destined soon to cover all Britain. For those blessed with youth, money, and idle time, it amounted to little more than a faddish embrace of the Latest Thing, though many corresponded by gas for emotional reasons, including those so vehemently discontented with the post office that they might have been out seeking to chuck bombs into post-boxes, were it not for the many Suffragettes queued up ahead of them. Scotland Yard, taking the lively interest one might expect, had set up a department to monitor Gas traffic.

"As to Replevin, we're frankly of mixed opinion at the Yard. Some feel he's only in it for, as they say, the æsthetics of the thing. I'm not much for modern poetry, but I know codes when I see them, and our Lamont seems to be using a particularly fiendish one. The cryptos have been on it around the clock, but so far they haven't cracked it."

"Is any of it being sent in clear? English? German?"

"Oh, aye, not to mention Russian, Turkish, Persian, Pashto, spot of Mountain Tadjik as well. Something going on out there, all right. We're not allowed, of course, to visit the premises officially, but we wondered if, in light of all this Shambhala to-do, it being up your street here at the T.W.I.T., and you personally enjoying a freedom from legal constraint we can only dream about . . . well, you see."

"If it was me? I'd just break open a crate and see what's inside."

"And find it full of precious Chinese rubbish, and next thing I'm down in Seven Dials on the graveyard watch poking me torch into dustbins. Perhaps not." He regarded the ruinous aftermath of his breakfast. "Don't suppose there'd be anything like a nice dish of baked beans on these premises? There never do seem to be any."

"Something religious, I think." Lew waved his thumb at a sign over the entrance to the kitchen which read κυάμων 'απέχου, "Avoid beans"—according to Neville and Nigel a direct quote from Pythagoras himself.

"Well. I'd better finish up this spotted dick, then, hadn't I."

That wasn't all that was on the Inspector's mind, but it took a Yarmouth bloater and several currant buns for him to get to it. "I'm supposed to reiterate once again how little enthusiasm there is around the Yard for your continued interest in the so-called Headingly bomb subject."

"Closing in on him at last, are you?"

"We've several very promising leads, and the investigation just now's at a particularly sensitive stage."

"Sounds familiar."

"Yes, and who's to say we mightn't've had him by now, too, if not for these unauthorized dilettantes all pottering about and queering the pitch."

"You don't say. How many of us are there?"

"One. It only *seems* like a dozen of you."

"But he knows I'm after him. Thought you Yard folks would've appreciated having some kind of sacrificial goat out there, to draw him in, maybe force him into a mistake."

"Full of yourself today."

"Ordinarily I'd be full of my breakfast, but it don't look like there's much left."

"Yes well if you don't mind I believe I shall take a bit of this 'shape' here, unusual color I must say, what's it made of I wonder mgghhmmbg. . . ."

"Maybe you don't want to know."

At that moment an acolyte came in with a message for Lew to report with all dispatch to Grand Cohen Nookshaft's office. Inspector Aychrome industriously wiped his face, sighed tragically, and prepared to withdraw to the Embankment again, and his chill home-element of grimy brickwork, blue lamps, and the smell of horses.

The Grand Cohen received Lew in official regalia with an emphasis on lamé surfaces and faux ermine trimming. On his head, in some vivid shade of magenta, with gold Hebrew lettering embroidered on the front, perched what would have been a yarmulke except for its high crown, dented Trilby style fore and aft. "Any last-minute toadying, lad, better get it in while you can, coz me term's almost up, yes it'll be back to Associate Cohen for little Nick Nookshaft, a truly blessed release, and the turn of the next poor 'sap' to enjoy this thankless groveling before the contempt of a High Directorate who only go on reducing one's budgets year after year, while like missionaries sent onto hostile shores, we are left to God's whim, and back beyond the sea, amid the pleasures of Home, those who signed our edicts of exile roar and frolic."

"Sure sounds like somethin's cooking around here," said Lew.

"Ever so frightfully sorry," eyes downcast. "You reproach me."

"Naw, Cohen, I'd never—"

"Oh yes, yes, nor would you be the first. . . . You see what a state I'm in. . . . Brother Basnight, we would not have wished to drag you into this Shambhala business, but with hostilities imminent, perhaps by now under way, we shall need everyone on station. Inspector Aychrome has briefed you on Lamont Replevin, but there are aspects of this the Met cannot appreciate, and so it falls to me to add that Replevin has come into possession of a map of Shambhala."

Lew whistled. "Which everybody's after."

"But makes no sense unless observed through a device called a Paramorphoscope."

"Want me to do a hoist?"

"If Replevin knows what he has, then he's already moved it to safety. But he may be operating from an entirely different set of premises."

"Guess that means I'll have to go have a gander. Can you give me an idea what I'm looking for?"

"We do have a similar map of Bukhara, thought to be from the same period." He produced a sheet on which had been reproduced a design that Lew could make no sense of at all.

After a quick consultation in *Kelly's Suburban Dictionary,* Lew found his hat and was out the door. By the time he got to the railway station, evening was already gathering, along with a proper winter fog, which went on thickening, drops of water condensing on everyone's hat, producing a shine that to certain nervous constitutions approached the sinister. The first pale husbands of the evening stood waiting for suburban trains never meant to arrive at any destination on the rail map—as if, to be brought to any shelter this night, one would first have to step across into some region of grace hitherto undefined. Lew entered a compartment, slouched in a seat, pulled his hatbrim over his eyes, the wheels were ponderously cranked and he was off for the remote and horrible town of Stuffed Edge.

THE SUBURBS OUT this way tended to be corrupted versions of the Mother City, Wenlets combining the worst of village eccentricity and big-city melancholia. Descending to the platform at Stuffed Edge, Lew found a prospect bleak and hushed, all but unmodified by vegetation . . . a scent of daylight oil hung over the scene, as if phantom motor vehicles operated on some other plane of existence, close but just invisible. Streetlamps had been lit up, he guessed, for hours. Far away, down by the police station, a dog was howling at a moon no one could see, perhaps imagining that, summoned repeatedly enough, it would appear with food of some kind.

Elflock Villa turned out to be a semi-detached residence of singular monstrosity, painted a vivid yellowish green which had refused to dim at the same rate as the day. Even before he got inside, Lew could smell the coal-gas—"the smell," as he had put it in more than one field report, "of Trouble." If any of the neighbors had noticed, none were in evidence—indeed, strangely for this suburban hour, very few windows hereabouts seemed to be lighted at all.

Having inserted a Vontz's Universal Pick, before which the door bolt, as if having read his mind, smoothly withdrew, Lew stepped into the overwhelming smell of alchemized coke and a suite of equivocal shadows, whose walls were covered with Lincrusta-Walton embossed in Asian motifs, not all of them considered respectable. Stationed everywhere, not only in the niches intended for them but also, like obtrusive guests, in the dining-room, the kitchen, even (perhaps especially) the lavatories, life-size sculpture groups exhibited the more disreputable of classical and biblical themes, among which bondage and torture seemed particularly to recur, the bodies of the subjects athletically perfect, materials not limited to white marble, drapery arranged to reveal and arouse. No degree of the allegorical avoided an excuse to present an impudently hipshot youth, or a captive maiden in some appealing form of restraint, naked and charmingly disheveled, in her face an awareness dawning of the delights awaiting her in the as-yet-unilluminated deeps of her torment and so forth.

As silently as possible, Lew crossed an expanse of black floor-tiles, each surrounded by silvery grouting, some composite with that soft a shine to it. The tiles, a combination of scalene polygons of different shapes and sizes, had a radiant blackness which likewise failed to be onyx or jet. Visitors of a mathematical bent had purported to see repeating patterns. Others, doubting its solidity, were often afraid to walk upon the silvery web . . . as if *Something* had built it . . . *Something that waited* . . . that would know exactly when to cause it to give way beneath the unwary visitor. . . .

Lew descended to the kitchen, the businesslike beam of his Apotheosis Sparkless Torch sweeping the gloom until it revealed a human form, hanging from the ceiling by one foot beside the ominously hissing stove, just like the figure in the Tarot card, except that its head rested halfway in the open oven door, where remnants of an exploded pork pie, almost certainly owing to a failure to include steam-vents in its crust, horribly coated the oven's interior. The hanging man's face was partly covered by a hinged mask of magnalium, connected to the oven by gutta-percha hoses. In the process of shutting off the gas and opening windows, Lew discovered that the "corpse" was breathing after all. "I say, would you mind letting me down?" it groaned, gesturing toward the ceiling, where Lew saw a block-and-tackle arrangement whose hoisting line ran over to a cleat on the wall. Lew undid the line and carefully lowered Lamont Replevin (for it was he) to the smart linoleum flooring. Removing the metal device from his face, Replevin crawled over to a nearby tank of pressurized oxygen, also equipped with a breathing mask, and administered himself a volume of the useful element.

Upon tactful inquiry, Lew learned that, far from desiring any premature exit, Replevin was enjoying a regular daily broadcast of the ongoing drama *The Slow and the Stupefied,* currently a great rage among the gas-head community.

"You hear it? See it, smell it?"

"All of those and more. Via the medium of Gas a carefully modulated set of waves travels from the emissions facility to us, the audience, through the appropriate hoses to the receiving-mask you have seen, which one must of course wear over ears, nose, and mouth."

"Have you ever considered," the question emerging not as gently as Lew had intended, "eh, that is . . . gas-poisoning? some kind of . . . hallucination . . ."

Seeming only now to notice Lew, Replevin stared, a chill glint in his eye. "Who are you, by the way? What are you doing here?"

"Smelled gas, thought there might be some danger."

"Yes yes but that wasn't the question was it?"

"Oh. Sorry." Out with one of several phony business cards he always kept handy, "Pike's Peak Life and Casualty. I'm Gus Swallowfield, Senior Underwriter."

"I'm quite satisfied with my coverage at the moment."

"For fire, I'm sure, with all this gas around—but now how about burglary."

"Burglary insurance? how odd, I must say."

"At the moment most theft policies are written in the U.S., but there's a great future here in Great Britain. You saw how easily I strolled in here—and I got a pretty good idea of your household effects on the way in. In less than half an hour, that could all be inside a pantechnicon and rolling away to be resold at any of a dozen markets, well before tomorrow's dawn. You know the business, sir—a legitimate bill of sale and no one can be charged with receiving."

"Hmm. Well, come along. . . ." Replevin conducted Lew upstairs, across the shimmering web of the foyer flooring, into a private suite of offices, dominated by a lurid sculpture executed in a purplish stone streaked with several colors of the red family.

"Pavonazzetto," Replevin said, "also known as Phrygian marble, once believed to take its coloring from the blood of the Phrygian youth Atys, the one you see right there, in fact—driven mad through the jealousy of the demigod Agdistis, he is shown in the act of castrating himself, thus to be presently conflated with Osiris, not to mention Orpheus and Dionysus, and become a cult figure among the ancient Phrygians."

"Sure took things seriously back then, didn't they?"

"This one? all too contemporary I fear, *The Mutilation of Atys,* by Arturo Naunt, Chelsea's own, shocking the bourgeoisie since 1889. If you'd like to see some genuine Phrygian pieces, there are plenty of those about."

Among bridle hardware, fragments of silk from Chinese Turkestan, seals both ceramic and carved in jade—"Here for example—a Scythian koumiss vessel, third century B.C. You can clearly see the Greek influence, especially in the friezework. And almost certainly an image of Dionysus."

"Worth a few what you call quid."

"You're not a collector, I take it."

"I can appreciate it's old. How do you find stuff like this?"

"Thieves, grave-robbers, museum officials both here and abroad. Do I sense moral disapproval?"

"Way out of my line, but I could frown a little, if you'd like."

"It's a gold rush out there now," Replevin said. "The Germans in particular are everywhere. Shipping things out by the caravan-load. Naturally now and then something will fall off a camel."

"What's this?" Lew nodded at a scroll on the desk opened to a specific couple of feet, as if someone had been consulting it. Replevin immediately grew shifty, which Lew pretended not to notice. "Late Uyghur. Found its way to Bukhara, like so many of these pieces. I fancied the design, interesting complexity, a series of wrathful deities from Tantric Buddhism would be my guess, though depending on the angle you hold it at, sometimes it doesn't look like anything at all."

He might as well have been screaming "Be suspicious!" To Lew it looked like symbols, words, numbers, maybe a map, maybe even the map of Shambhala they wanted so much to see back at Chunxton Crescent. He beamed vaguely and pretended to shift his attention to a statuette of a bronze horse and rider. "Would you look at that! Mighty handsome critter, ain't it?"

"They were horsemen above all," said Replevin. "Your American cowboys would have felt entirely at home."

"You wouldn't mind if . . ." Lew producing a tiny German hand camera and removing the lens cover.

"Please do," after hesitating just long enough for Lew to understand that he had been appraised for harmless idiocy and pronounced genuine.

"O.K. if we turn up the gaslight?"

Replevin shrugged. "It's only raw light, isn't it."

Lew brought over a few electric lamps as well, and began taking snapshots, making sure that any he took of the scroll included other pieces, just for cover. He moved out of the offices to shoot some more, keeping up a professional patter, for misdirection's sake.

"Hope you don't take this the wrong way, but hanging upside down with your head in the oven and the gas on? taken strictly from a risk point of view, I wouldn't be doing my job if I didn't inquire how you were fixed for life insurance."

Replevin was not reluctant to bend Lew's ear on the topic of Gasophilia, which could be said to date from Schwärmer's epochal discovery that gas-pressure, analogous to voltage in an electromagnetic system, might be modulated to convey information.

"Waves in a timeless stream of Gas unceasing, illuminating-gas in particular, though including as well waves of sound, which might, as in that mainstay of Victorian science, the Sensitive Flame, modulate waves of light. To the cognizant nose in particular, the olfactory sector—or smell, as it is known, can be a medium for the most exquisite poetry."

"Sounds almost religious, sir."

"Well, out in south India, if you go into a particular sort of temple, for instance the one at Chidambaram, into the Hall of a Thousand Pillars, asking to see their god Shiva, what they'll show you is an *empty space,* except that it's not really what *we* mean when we say 'empty,' of course it *is* empty, but in another way, one that's not at all the same as nothing *being* there, if you follow me—"

"Sure."

"They worship it, this empty space, it's their highest form of worship. This volume, or I suppose nonvolume, of pure *Akaša*—being the Sanskrit for what we'd call the Æther, the element closest to the all-pervading Atman, from which everything else has arisen—which in Greek obviously then becomes *'Chaos,'* and so down to van Helmont in his alchemist's workshop, who being Dutch writes the opening fricative as a *G* instead of a *Chi,* giving us *Gas,* our own modern *Chaos,* our bearer of sound and light, the *Akaša* flowing from *our* sacred spring, the local Gasworks. Do you wonder that for some the Gas Oven is worshipped at, as a sort of shrine?"

"I don't. But then I never *didn't* wonder either."

"Am I annoying you, Mr. Swallowfield?"

In Lew's experience of English English, this usually meant he was about to overstay his welcome. "All done here. I'll bring these back to the office, we'll write you up a sample policy, feel free to make any changes you like, or to say hell no altogether." And he withdrew again out into the empty suburban lamplight, the stridently unpopulated evening.

One day, the day he would be some time coming to terms with his idiocy in not seeing the obvious approach of, Kit was summoned to the local branch of the Bank of Prussia in the Weenderstraße and beckoned into its back regions by Herr Spielmacher, the International Manager, hitherto friendly enough but today, how would you put it, a little distant. He held a thin sheaf of papers.

"We have a communication from New York. Your *Kreditbrief* is . . ." he gazed for a long time at an interesting photograph of the Kaiser on an adjoining desk.

So. "No longer in force," Kit suggested.

Brightening, the banker risked a fast look at Kit's face. "You have heard from them?"

Had been all along, Kit realized—just wasn't listening.

"I am authorized to pay you the balance of the funds as yet undrawn this period." He had the sum ready in a small pile of mostly fifty-mark notes.

"Herr Bankdirektor," Kit held his hand out. "Nice doing business with you. I'm happy we can part company without any embarrassing shows of sentiment."

He slipped outside, doubled down a few back alleys, and entered the Bank of Hannover, where on his arrival in Göttingen, perhaps with some hidden talent for precognition, he had set up a small account with his winnings from the tables at Ostend, and insulated, he hoped, from any Vibe arrangements.

"You seem disturbed," noted Humfried that evening. "Usually you are so typically American, without a thought in your head."

It wasn't till later, on the way to meet Yashmeen, that Kit was able to let the situation catch up with him some. It seemed now that Scarsdale Vibe had been far too eager to agree to Kit's plan to attend Göttingen. Whatever the long-term plan had been, here apparently was the payoff. Kit could not see this quite as clearly as he'd have liked, but he had felt it in the bright gazes directed at him in the bank.

He found Yashmeen up on the third floor of the Auditorienhaus as usual, in the reading room, a chaos of open books converging at her radiantly attentive face. He recognized a bound copy of Riemann's *Habilitationsschrift* of 1854 on the foundations of geometry but didn't see the 1859 paper on primes.

"What, no ζ-function?"

She looked up, not at all distracted, as if having known the moment he came in. He wished. "This has been scriptural for me," she said. "I see now the conjecture was there only as an enticement to bring me 'in' a certain distance, to get me ready for the real revelation—his astounding re-imagination of space—more than the usual *Achphänomen* . . . an angel, too bright to look at directly, lighting one by one the pages I must read. It has made me a very difficult person."

"I'll say."

They left the Auditorienhaus and walked through the evening. "Had a piece of news today," Kit began, when out from behind a bush jumped a demented young man, screaming *"Tchetvyortoye Izmereniye! Tchetvyortoye Izmereniye!"*

"Yob tvoyu mat'," sighed Yashmeen in some exasperation, evading his grasp before Kit could move in. The young man ran off down the street. "I should start carrying a weapon," she said.

"What's that he was hollering?"

" 'Fourth Dimension!' " she said. " 'Fourth Dimension!' "

"Oh. Well, guess he came to the right place. Minkowski would sure be the one to see."

"They're all over the place lately. They call themselves 'Otzovists.' God-builders. A new subset of heretics, this time against Lenin and his Bolshevists—said to be anti-Materialist, devout readers of Mach and Ouspensky, immoderately focused on something *they* call 'the fourth dimension.' Whether Dr. Minkowski, or in fact any algebraist in the street, would recognize it as such is another matter. But they have been able with little effort to drive the Materialists in Geneva quite mental with it. Lenin himself is said to be writing a gigantic book now, attempting to *refute* the 'fourth dimension,' his position being, from what I can gather, that the Tsar can only be overthrown in three."

"Intriguing thought. . . . But what do these folks want with you?"

"It's been going on for a while. They don't say much, usually only stand there looking at me with these haunted stares."

"Wait, let me guess. They think you know how to travel in the fourth dimension."

She made a sour face. "I knew you'd understand. But it gets worse. The T.W.I.T., it seems, have also come to town. They want me out of Göttingen and back under their wing again. Whether I want to leave or not."

"Saw them, wondered who they might be. Your Pythagorean friends."

" 'Friends.' "

"Well, Yash."

"At dinner yesterday evening, Madame Eskimoff—perhaps you'll meet her—said that when spirits walk, beings living in four-dimensional space pass through our own three, and the strange presences that flicker then at the edges of awareness *are* those very moments of intersection. When we enter, even in ordinary daylight, upon a chain of events we are certain we have lived through before, in every detail, it is possible that we have stepped outside of Time as it commonly passes here, above this galley-slave repetition of days, and have had a glimpse of future, past, and present"—she made a compressive gesture—"all together."

"Which would be to interpret the fourth dimension as Time," said Kit.

"They call it 'the already seen.' "

"That's what they're here for? That's what they think they can use you for?" He thought he saw a connection. "Riemann."

"At the heart of it. But, Kit." She performed that strange preening stretch of the neck that had first captured his attention. "You see, it happens to be true."

He reminded himself that the night they first met he had witnessed her disappearance into a solid wall. "All right. Is it something you can control? go in and out of when you want to?"

"Not always. It started harmlessly enough, when I was much younger, thinking about complex functions for the first time, really. Staring at the wallpaper. One night, at some god-awful hour, I understood that I couldn't get away with only one plane, I'd need two, one for the argument, one for the function, each with a real axis and an imaginary one, meaning *four axes,* all perpendicular to one another at the same point of origin, and the more I tried to *see* that, the crazier ordinary space became, until what you might call *i, j,* and *k,* the unit vectors of our given space, had each rotated an unknown number of degrees, about that unimaginable fourth axis, and I thought I had brain fever. I didn't sleep. I slept too much."

"The mathematician's curse."

"Then you . . ."

"Oh . . ." Kit shrugged. "I think about it, sure, everybody does, but no more than I have to."

"I knew you were an idiot."

"*My* curse. Maybe we could swap?"

"You don't want mine, Kit."

He considered lecturing her on what her real curse was, but thought better of it.

"The first time I was in your rooms—something like it happened then. I thought I'd found some kind of *Schnitte*—one of those 'cuts' connecting the sheets of Riemann's multiply-connected spaces—something that would allow access to a different . . . I don't know, 'set of conditions'? 'vector space'? Unreal, but not compellingly so—I was back in ordinary space-time before I knew it, and after a while the memory faded. That's when it *really* happened. Up at Rohns Garten, I was sitting at a table with classmates, eating some kind of strange German soup, no forewarning, *Batz!* here was the room, the view out the window, but as they *really were,* a three-dimensional section through a space of higher dimensionality, perhaps four, perhaps more. . . . I hope you aren't about to ask how many. . . ."

They went in a café where they were unlikely to be interrupted.

"Teach me how to disappear, Yash."

Something in his voice. She narrowed her gaze.

"They've cut off my letters of credit."

"Oh, Kit. And here I've been banging on—" She reached a hand and placed it on one of his. "I can lend you—"

"No, *nichevo,* right now money's not what I'm worried about so much as staying alive. My Pa always used to say, if it doesn't work with gold, the next step will be lead. Somehow I've gotten to be a threat to them. Maybe they finally made an educated guess about how much I really know. Maybe something's happened back in the States, we got lucky and nailed one of them, or they got another one of us. . . ." He held his head briefly. "Just too much I don't know. Except they don't have to be nice anymore. And I'm crossed off. Delivered into exile."

"I may be in that same predicament, and soon. With trivial changes of sign, of course. No one is saying anything clearly. It's this damned English practice of talking in code, so everything has to be deciphered. I am guessing that since the revolution in Russia my father's position has become precarious. And so, perforce, my own. There is also the Anglo-Russian Entente, and the fourth-dimension business, which is after all the current rage in psychical research. Take your pick." There was more—something she feared. Even Kit, who wasn't very sensitive, could see that—but she was keeping her own troubled counsel.

Her eyes were wide again, speculative, and she took a slow breath or two. "Well, *you're* free, then."

"I'm what?"

"I thought Americans knew that word."

"Believe the word you're groping for is 'poor.'"

"Your arrangements with the Vibe people are canceled?"

"Null and void."

"And you owe them nothing."

"Well, they might not agree."

"But if another offer were presented . . ."

"You mean from your T.W.I.T. people?"

She shrugged prettily, more with her hair than her shoulders. "I could ask."

"I'll bet."

"Shall I, then?"

"It would depend on the pay, I guess."

She laughed, and he thought of the carefree girl so long ago sashaying in through the smoke of that *Bierstube*. "Oh, you'll see how they pay!"

KIT LOOKED, looked away, looked again. Except for the absence of a mustache, there, right in the middle of Göttingen, was the spit of Foley Walker. Hat and all. Kit felt like somebody had just taken a shot at him. Life in Göttingen appeared to proceed on its blade-twinkling way, wheelfolks on brand-new bikes crashing into each other or careering out of control and scattering pedestrians, beer-drinkers quarreling and bowing, preoccupied Zetamaniacs forever on the verge of walking off the edge of the Promenade being rescued by companions, a town he had never loved all at once become a place, now he was obliged, it seemed, to leave it, whose most quotidian detail shone with a clarity almost painful, already a place of exile's memory and no returning, and here just to make that official was the angel, if not of death at least of deep shit, and nobody else seemed to notice, despite Foley's telltale fatality for the garish, exhibited here in an outfit no description of whose tastelessness can be comfortably set upon one's page. . . . Well, actually, it was a three-piece sporting ensemble popular some years back, woven so as to present different colors depending on the angle it was viewed from, these including but not limited to brownish pink, saturated grape, and a certain necrotic yellow.

Next time Kit looked back, of course there was no Foley now, if that's what the apparition had been. The fourth dimension, no doubt. Despite Yashmeen's helpful citation of the Pythagorean *akousmaton* that goes, "When away from home, never look back, because the Furies are in pursuit" (Iamblichus 14), Kit soon found himself paying close attention to the street and what went on in it, not to mention double-checking doors and windows before he tried to get even an hour or two of sleep, which was becoming a problematical chore. Why hadn't Foley stepped around, he wondered, just to say hello? Did he think Kit hadn't seen him?

But Foley, as if possessed of the master *Hausknochen* for all Göttingen, was keeping his acts of visitation for the night, and so it came about that with no transition at all, soles and palms aching and pulse thudding, Kit was sitting up staring into the dark at this eidolon, inelegantly turned out contrary to a whole raft of public-decency statutes, which had come monitory and breathing in to violate Kit's insomnia. "Let me tell you about the minié ball in my head," Foley began. "And how over the long comfortless years it has changed, I guess a chemical person would say transmuted, not to gold, that would be too much to expect, but to one of these rare metals that are said to be sensitive to electromagnetic waves of one sort and another. Zirconium, silver-bearing galena, one of them. Vibe Corp. digs it out of veins all over the world, including your own native Colorado. That's how it happened I could hear those voices—through that precisely warped little sphere of metal, because they were all out there, where hardly any of us ever hear them, those waves from far away, traveling forever, through the Æther, the cold and dark. Without enough of the right mineral concentrated there in your brain, you can live your whole life and never hear them. . . ."

"Don't mean to interrupt, but how'd you get in here?"

"You haven't been listening, Kit—please—now—this is for your own good."

"Like stopping my money was."

"'Your' money? Since when?"

"We had a deal. Don't you people honor deals?"

"Don't know nothing about honor, I'll spare you that lecture, but I can tell you about being bought, and sold, and the obligations that come with that."

"You'd know."

"See, it's what we thought *you* knew. Figuring you for a smart kid. We assumed too much."

"If Vibe went back on his word, then something changed. What was it, Foley?"

"You weren't honest. You knew things, but you didn't tell us."

"*I* wasn't honest?" This was getting close to the edge, and Kit felt less than surefooted. He reached for a cigarette and lit up. "What do you want to know? Ask me anything."

"Too late. Trouble you for one of them?"

Kit pushed the pack over. "You come all the way here just to threaten me, Foley?"

"Mr. Vibe is currently on a tour of Europe, and wanted me to look in."

"What for? He cut me out of his life, that would sort of limit any further socializing."

"It's the boss's scientific curiosity, see, how a subject might react to philanthropy in reverse, where the charity gets taken away, instead of handed out? Would he get angry? sad? desperate? give in to suicidal thoughts?"

"Tell him I'm happier'n a fly on shit."

"Ain't sure he'll want to hear that."

"Make something up, then. Anything else?"

"Yeah. What's a man do for entertainment in this town?"

When he was sure Foley had gone, Kit found a bottle of beer, opened it, and raised it to his tenebrous face reflected in the window glass. " 'Away from Göttingen, there is no life,' " he quoted the motto on the Rathskeller wall, and a few minutes later his family's own. " 'Well. Reckon *yo tengo que* get *el* fuck out of *aquí.*' "

IT DIDN'T SEEM like the weekend had arrived, it didn't seem like there was much of a calendar in force at all anymore. Nonetheless, as dusk gathered over the town, Kit was rushed upon and seized by a small group of classmates.

"Zum Mickifest! Komm, komm!"

Among students of mathematics here, chloral hydrate was the preferred drug. Sooner or later, whatever the problem being struggled with, having obsessed themselves into nightly insomnia, they would start taking knockout drops to get to sleep—Geheimrat Klein himself was a great advocate of the stuff—and next thing they knew, they were habitués, recognizing one another by the side-effects, notably eruptions of red pimples, known as "the dueling scars of chloralomania." On Saturday nights in Göttingen, there was always sure to be at least one chloral party, or *Mickifest.*

It was a peculiar gathering, only intermittently, as you'd say, brisk. People were either talking wildly, often to themselves and without seeming to pause for breath, or lounging draped in pleasurable paralysis across the furniture or, as the evening went along, flat on the floor in deep narcosis.

"You have the *K.O.-Tropfen* in the U.S.?" inquired a sweet young thing name of Lottchen.

"Sure," said Kit, "they show up in drinks a lot, usually with criminal intent."

"And keep in mind," Gottlob announced, with lengthy pauses between words, "that the English word 'pun,' upside down, is . . . 'und.'"

Kit squinted, waiting for him to pursue the thought. Finally, "I'm . . . not real sure I actually . . ."

"Group-theoretical implications," Gottlob slowly explained, "to begin with—"

Somebody started screaming. Very slowly everyone looked around, and then began making their way into the kitchen to see what had happened.

"He's dead."

"What do you mean, dead?"

"Dead. Look at him."

"No no no," Günther shaking his head in annoyance, "he does this all the time. Humfried!" screaming in the horizontal mathematician's ear. "You have poisoned yourself again!" Humfried emitted an alarming rhonchus. "First we shall have to wake him up." Günther looked around for their host. *"Gottlob! Wo ist deine Spritze?"* While Gottlob went looking for the syringe which seemed to be a standard accessory at these gatherings, Günther went in the kitchen and found a pot of coffee left to cool against just such a contingency. Humfried had begun to mutter, though not in German—in fact in no language anybody in the room recognized.

Gottlob brought over a gigantic syringe of some dented and tarnished gray alloy, stamped "Property of the Berlin Zoo" and *"Streng reserviert für den Elefanten!"* and attached to it a long ebony nozzle.

"Ah, thank you, Gottlob, now somebody help me roll him over—"

"This is the part where I leave," said Lottchen.

Humfried, his eyes fluttering open wide enough to register the syringe, screamed and attempted to crawl away.

"Now now, sleepyhead," chided Günther playfully, "what you need is some nice black coffee to perk you up, but we don't want you trying to *drink* it do we, dribbling it all over your shirt, no, so just to make sure it all gets where it's going—"

Those who were still awake began to gather around to watch, which Kit knew was also a regular part of these *Mickifesten.* The intensity of Humfried's monologue picked up, as if he were aware of his audience and his obligations as an entertainer. By now Gottlob and Günther had pulled his trousers down and were attempting to insert the huge nozzle into his rectum, bickering over points of technique. Someone else was in the kitchen concocting an emetic from mustard and raw eggs.

Anyone expecting a chance to look into the mysteries of death and return would be disappointed tonight.

"Only the vomiting? You will not administer strychnine?"

"Strychnine is for French schoolchildren, not as good an antidote for chloral as chloral is for strychnine."

"Noncommutative, so?"

"Asymmetric, at any rate."

Günther gave Humfried a professional once-over. "I am afraid he will have to go to the hospital."

"Let me do that," Kit said, feeling less obliging than anxious for no reason he could think of, until about a block from the hospital, there, huge and in no one's control, least of all his own, came Foley, running at him with something in his hand. "Traverse! Come here, goddamn you." He might have been drunk, but Kit did not delude himself that it gave him any kind of an edge on Foley.

"A friend of yours," said Gottlob, who was holding Humfried up from the other side.

"I owe him money. Any way we could lose him?"

"This part of town is my second home," Gottlob began, when there was the sound, dishearteningly distinct, of a gunshot. *"Verfluchte cowboy!"* screamed Gottlob, and ran off.

The chloral-addled Humfried, by now able to walk, grabbed Kit by the arm and steered him quickly into the nearest hospital entrance. "Trust me," he mumbled. "*Achtung, Schwester!* Here another dope-fiend is!"

Next thing Kit knew he was surrounded by orderlies and being bustled down a corridor.

"Wait a minute, folks, where's that fellow I brought in?" But Humfried had vanished completely.

"Imaginary-companion syndrome, quite typical," murmured an interne.

"But I'm the sober one here."

"Of course you are, and here is a *special souvenir* we give to all visitors as a reward for being so sober," dexterously jabbing him with a hypodermic. Kit dropped like a stone. And so it was off to the *Klapsmühle.*

Foley, in one of his canonical outfits, was seen leaving town the next morning, with what was described as a grumpy expression on his face.

KIT WOKE TO SEE looming over him the face of a Dr. Willi Dingkopf, framed by a haircut in violation of more than one law of physics, and a vivid necktie in fuchsia, heliotrope, and duck green, a gift from one of the patients, as the Doc presently explained in a voice hoarse from too much cigarette-smoking, "Hand-painted, as therapy, to express, though regrettably not control, certain recurring impulses of a homicidal nature." Kit gazed at, or perhaps into, the tie's ultra-modern design, in which its disturbed artist had failed to include much of anything encountered in the natural world—yet, who knew? maybe if you studied it long enough, familiar shapes *might* begin to emerge, some in fact what you might call, what was the word, entertaining—

"Hey! what are you— You just *hit* me with, with that *stick*?"

"An ancient technique, borrowed from the Zennists of Japan. Why were you staring so at my necktie?"

"Was I? I didn't—"

"Hmm . . ." writing in a note-book, "and have there been any . . . voices? seeming to arise in the classical three-space but, if we perhaps would take one more, conceptually all-but-trivial . . . *step*? into a further, as you would say . . . dimension?"

"Voices, Doc? from another dimension?"

"Good! reasoning powers, you see? you're getting saner already! You must not feel alone in this, Herr Traverse. No! You have merely undergone a small perturbation of the Co-conscious aggravated by chloral abuse, which, once out of your acute phase and among these wholesome surroundings, tends to pass quickly."

"But I didn't say I heard any voices. Did I?"

"Mm, some memory loss as well . . . and, and 'Traverse,' what sort of name . . . you are not *also Hebraic,* by any chance?"

"What? I don't know. . . . Next time I talk with God, I'll ask."

"*Ja*—well, now and then one finds an *Hebraic indication,* accompanied by feelings of being not sufficiently Gentile, this is quite common, with corollary anxieties about being *too Jewish* . . . ?"

"You sound anxious yourself, Doc."

"Oh, more than anxious—alarmed, as I observe, strangely, you are not. By the millions now into your own country they are *streaming*—how naïve do Americans have to be, *not* to see the danger?"

"Jews are dangerous?"

"Jews are smart. The Jew Marx, driven by his unnatural *smartness* to strike at the social order . . . the Jew Freud, pretending to heal souls—it is my livelihood, of course, I take exception—the Jew Cantor, the *Beast of Halle,* who seeks to demolish the very foundations of mathematics, bringing these Göttingen people paranoid and screaming to my door, where naturally I am expected to deal with it—"

"Wait, excuse me, Herr Doktor," somebody piped up the next time

Dingkopf delivered this speech, which happened to be during a group-therapy session, "Cantor is a practicing Lutheran."

"With a name like that? Please."

"And far from ruination, what he may have led us to is a paradise, as Dr. Hilbert has famously described it."

"Dr. . . . *David* Hilbert, you will note."

"He's not Jewish either."

"How well informed everyone is today."

The *Kolonie* proved to be a well-ventilated complex of glazed yellow brick buildings, solidly constructed on the principles of Invisibilism, a school of modern architecture which believed that the more "rationally" a structure was designed, the *less visible* would it appear, in extreme examples converging to its so-called Penultimate Term—the step just before deliverance into the Invisible, or as some preferred to say, "into its own meta-structure," minimally attached to the physical world.

"Until one day one is left with only traces in the world, a few tangles of barbed wire defining the plan-view of something no longer quite able to be seen . . . perhaps certain *odors* as well, seeping in, late at night, from somewhere upwind, a wind which itself possesses now the same index of refraction as the departed Structure. . . ."

This was being explained earnestly to Kit by someone in a guard's uniform, whom Kit, in his innocence, assumed was a guard. On the shoulder of the uniform was displayed a patch showing a stylized human brain with some sort of *Teutonic ax-blade* sunk halfway into it, which Kit took for *Kolonie* insignia. The weapon was black and silver, the brain a cheerful aniline magenta. The motto above read *"So Gut Wie Neu,"* or "Good As New."

They were out on the "Dirigible Field," a notional sort of plane surface where *Klapsmühle* activities included earth displacement, rock excavation, and surface dressing, under the supervision of a platoon of "engineers" with real-looking surveyors' instruments and so forth, who did not appear to be inmates of the *Kolonie,* though around here one so seldom could tell.

There was great excitement in the *Kolonie* today, for at any moment, a real Dirigible was actually expected to come and land at the Dirigible Field! Most of the residents had never seen a Dirigible, but there were a few with no shyness about describing it to the others. "It will come to deliver us from this place, all are welcome, it is the express flight to Doofland, the ancestral home of the mental inmate, it will descend, a gigantic triumph of bohemian décor, luminescent in every color of the spectrum, and the Ship's Band will be playing old favorites such as 'O Tempora, O Mores,' and 'The Black Whale of Askalon,' as we happily troop on board, into the streamlined gondola suspended exactly at the Point of Infinity, for the Dirigible's secret Name is the Riemann Ellipsoid," and so forth.

A football, booted from very far away, now came sailing overhead, and some mistook it momentarily for the Dirigible, whose arrival, it was hoped, would not conflict with any of the football games that seemed to be in constant progress on the Dirigible Field all day long and particularly in the dark, which was actually the preferred condition, though it made for a different style of game.

"This ball has about as much bounce as *the head of Jochanaan,*" somebody cried out, a reference to a recent therapeutic excursion the inmates had made to Berlin to see a performance of Richard Strauss's opera *Salome,* from which Dr. Dingkopf had come away muttering about "a severe neuropathic crisis of spirit abroad in present-day Germany," although the group themselves—not unreasonably, given Strauss's own description of the work as a scherzo with a fatal conclusion—had kept breaking into insane laughter, which soon spread from the one-and-a-half-mark seats to the "normal" folks in the rest of the theatre. Since this trip, *Kolonie* attendants had been obliged to put up with the new catchphrase, whether on the football field or in the dining-hall ("What are we eating?" "Looks like *the head of Jochanaan*"), or to listen to the religious bickering of the Five Jews, which somehow was the only part of the opera that everyone, it seemed, had memorized, note for note, perhaps to annoy Dr. Dingkopf, who did begin to show the strain after a while, being reported wandering about the grounds at odd hours singing *"Judeamus igitur, Judenes dum su-hu-mus . . ."* in a distracted tenor.

"Ich bin ein Berliner!"

"Excuse me?" The patient seemed anxious to speak with Kit.

"He will not harm you," Dr. Dingkopf assured him as attendants adroitly steered the patient away. "He has come to believe that he is a certain well-known pastry of Berlin—similar to your own American, as you would say, *Jelly-doughnut.*"

"How long's he been in here?"

Shrug. "A difficult case. The *Jelly-doughnut* being such a powerful metaphor for body and spirit, to find one's way back to sanity merely through reason becomes quite problematic—so we must resort to Phenomenology, and accept the literal truth of his delusion—bringing him into Göttingen, to a certain *Konditerei* where he is all over powdered with *Puderzucker* and allowed to sit, or actually recline, up on a shelf ordinarily reserved for the pastries.

When he starts in with his *'Ich bin ein Berliner,'* most customers try only to correct his diction, as if he is from Berlin and has meant to say *'Ich bin Berliner'*—though sometimes he is *actually purchased*—'Did you want a bag for that, madame?' 'Oh, no, no thank you, I'll eat it right here if I may.'"

"Well—if *that* doesn't bring him back to reality . . ."

"*Ach,* but no, he only remains inert, even when they attempt to . . . *bite into*—"

SEVERAL HOURS LATER, Kit became aware of a huge, soft, indistinct mass in the gloom of the dormitory, giving off the unmistakable scent of freshly-baked pastry.

"Shh—don't react, please."

"It's O.K., I was only lying here, observing the wallpaper in the dark."

"Oh? Really? Is it—what is it saying to you?"

"It's already led me to certain unexpected conclusions about the automorphic functions. How's everything with you?"

"Well first, allow me to point out—*I'm not really a jelly doughnut.*"

"Got to say, the resemblance is, well, amazing, and you can talk, and everything?"

"It was the only way one knew of to contact you. Your friend Miss Halfcourt sent me."

Kit had a look. Another victim of enchantment—all Yashmeen had had to do, he reckoned, was give this customer a kiss.

"It's like invisibility," the apparition continued, "only different? Most people can't admit they see me. So in effect they don't see me. And then the cannibalism issue of course."

"The . . . I don't exactly . . ."

"Well. Puts them in a bind, doesn't it. I mean, if I'm human, and they're considering me for breakfast, that makes *them* cannibals—but if I *really am* a jelly doughnut, then, being cannibals, they *all* have to be jelly doughnuts as well, don't you see?" He began to laugh merrily.

Kit glanced up at the radium dial of the clock on the wall. It was half past three in the morning.

"Let's be on our way, shall we?" The oversize pastry item led him down a corridor, around a few corners, out through an equipment room into the moonlight. "I'd like to escort you all the way out, but it'll be breakfast time soon and . . . well, you understand."

They found Kit sleeping by the fence. Dr. Dingkopf was waiting back at his office with a great bundle of release papers to be signed. "Your British friends have interceded on your behalf. What does my own professional judgment matter, twenty years of clinical experience, next to this sinister tribal conspiracy . . . even in England . . . not the pure-blooded nation it once was . . . Halfcourt . . . Halfcourt? what kind of a name is that?"

YASHMEEN CAUGHT UP with him at the café they'd been in the other evening. He hadn't exactly got back to sleep nor seen much point in shaving. "Come. Let us walk Der Wall." It was a peaceful morning, a breeze ruffled the leaves of the lindens.

"How much do you know of Shambhala, Kit?"

He turned his head, peered at her out of one eye. Wasn't everybody being a little too damned businesslike this morning? "May have heard the place mentioned once or twice."

"An ancient metropolis of the spiritual, some say inhabited by the living, others say empty, in ruins, buried someplace beneath the desert sands of Inner Asia. And of course there are always those who'll tell you that the true Shambhala lies within."

"And? Which is it?"

She frowned quickly. "I suppose it is a real place on the globe, in the sense that the Point at Infinity is a place 'on' the Riemann sphere. The money invested to date by the Powers in expeditions to 'discover' the place is certainly real enough. The political forces being deployed . . . political and military as well . . ."

"But not specially your mug of beer."

"My—" She allowed a dotted quarter-rest. "Colonel Halfcourt is involved. If I'm deciphering this properly."

"In trouble?"

"No one is sure." Not for the first time, he had the dispirited feeling that she was expecting something from him he couldn't even name, let alone provide. "There are a hundred reasons why I should be out there with him. . . ."

"And just one that you shouldn't." Was he supposed to try and guess?

They stared at each other over what might have been Ætheric distances. "At your level of intuition, Kit," with a troubled smile at last, "we might be here for hours."

"Who could object to hours spent in charming company?"

"I think that's supposed to be 'in *such* charming company.'"

"Whoops."

"We spoke last time of employment with the T.W.I.T."

"That's who got me out of the *Klapsmühle*?"

"Lionel Swome. You're about to meet him. What were you doing in there?"

“Hiding, I guess.” He told her about Foley’s night visit.

“It sounds like you dreamed it.”

“Makes no difference. The message he was delivering was the thing. Sooner I’m out of here the better.”

“Let’s stroll up the Hainberg for a bit, shall we.” Both of them scanning ahead and behind, she brought him presently to a restaurant on a hillside, with a view of the walls of the tranquil town, where sat T.W.I.T. travel coördinator Lionel Swome at a table under an umbrella for the afternoon light, with a bottle of Rheinpfalz from last autumn, and two glasses. After introductions, Yashmeen flourished her parasol and was off down the mountain again.

“Right,” said Swome. “You’re about to do a bunk, I’m told.”

“Amazing! I only just decided a couple minutes ago, on the way up here—but you people with your mental telepathy, I keep forgetting.”

“And you’ve no restrictions as to where you go.”

Kit shrugged. “Further away the better, doesn’t matter to me—why? does it to you?”

“Inner Asia?”

“Just fine.”

Swome studied his wineglass, not drinking. “There are those who prefer other Deidesheimers—Herrgottsackers and such—to those of the Hofstück. But year for year, if one takes the time to—”

“Mr. Swome.”

A shrug, as if having come to an understanding with himself. “Very well—Miss Halfcourt being in a comparable situation, you two are about to solve your mutual difficulties—by eloping together to Switzerland.”

Kit tugged an invisible hatbrim down over his face. “Sure. Everybody’s going to believe that.”

“Maybe nobody you know. But those we seek to deceive just might, especially when we provide abundant evidence—travel permits, hotel reservations, bank correspondence, and so on. Up to a point you and the young lady will carry on in as obviously newlywed a manner as possible—Mr. Traverse? you are with me here? good—and the next moment, presto—you shall each have disappeared in a different direction, in your own case, eastward.”

Kit waited for him to go on. Finally, “And . . . ?”

“The ex-bride-to-be? Hmm, no idea. Someone else’s desk really. Meanwhile, as you’ll be out there, perhaps there is one small errand you wouldn’t mind having a bash at for us.”

“And . . . that would be to do with um, what’s its name again . . .”

“Shambhala. Yes, in a way.”

"I'm not a Theosophist or even much of a world traveler, I hope somebody's mentioned that to you. Maybe you'll want at least a little field experience here."

"Your chief virtue, precisely. No one out there knows a blessed thing about you. We've any number of old Inner Asia hands on the lurk at the usual oases and bazaars, but everyone there knows everyone else's story, it's all a stalemate, best thing now is to inject some element of the unknown."

"Me."

"And you come well recommended by Sidney Reilly."

"Um . . ."

"No doubt you'll recall him as 'Chong.'"

"That guy? went around in that turban all the time? Well I'm sure a hoosier, I thought he was the real thing."

"Oh, Sidney's that, all right. You may run into him again while you're out in the 'Stans, as he's forever to and fro, but you probably won't recognize him then either."

"So if I should get in trouble—"

"He wouldn't be the one to see about that." A keen gaze. "You don't suffer from 'nerves,' I hope."

"Do I seem a little jumpy right now? must be these folks that are after me, no telling what they're fixing to do and so forth. But out there? Inner Asia, million miles from nowhere? hell I'll be just dandy."

"Here's what we'd like you to do for us, then." The T.W.I.T. functionary, nodding, produced a map from a note-case and spread it on the table. "We have our long-standing arrangements—Colonial Office, One Savile Row, other less official tie-ins. We can clear you"—tracing out with his fingertip a tentative route—"at least to Kashgar."

"That's where Miss Halfcourt's father is stationed."

"Now and then. He leads a peripatetic life. But as you'll be out his way . . ."

"Wait a minute." Kit reached to take one of Swome's cigarettes from his case on the table. "They don't have any idea where he is, do they."

"The lines have been down, in a way. Temporary but bothersome. There's never been a revolution in Russia on quite that scale, you see, and it's followed the railroads out into Asia as well, and the consequences are still unrolling. Auberon Halfcourt has been out there trooping since the Afghan difficulties, there's no predicament he can't get himself out of. We're not worried so much about his safety . . ." pausing, as if Kit was supposed to finish the thought. Kit did not oblige him. ". . . as about getting hold of his report on whatever just happened at Shambhala—apparently all the Powers were in on it—inconceivable that he should have missed it. And time being of the essence, obviously—we don't want the others, Germany or Austria in particular, jumping in with their version of events, we need to keep some control over the history. . . ."

"I've noticed a lot of Russians in town," Kit said, expecting to be told to mind his own business, but Swome had been brooding about Otzovists, it seemed.

"These anti-Leninist Bolshies, I suppose you mean. Dear oh dear yes. In their single-minded concentration on Miss Halfcourt and her four-dimensional skills, they seem willing to ignore all secular risks, especially to the recent Anglo-Russian Entente. A degree of deception has accordingly become necessary, though the T.W.I.T. in theory are supposed to be above international politics.

"One must be ever so careful. They're not always what they appear, these seekers. Too often they prove far less metaphysical than you'd hope, in fact so sworn to the solid world that *you* begin to feel like a mystic, just by default. Madam Blavatsky herself, recall, was working for the Tsarist secret service, known back then as Third Section, before it became the Okhrana. . . . And what's it matter really, materialist or spiritualist, they're all bloody bomb-chuckers aren't they. Easy enough to deal with of course, one more benefit of the Entente, a word dropped in the right ear and it's run Bolshie run."

"Will I have trouble with them, seeing 's how I'm headed out that way, 's what I was getting at."

"To me they seem a bit too European for Kashgar, not quite up to it, more comfortable really here or Switzerland. Kashgar is the spiritual capital of Inner Asia, as 'interior' as one can get, and not only geographically. As for what lies beneath those sands, you've your choice—either Shambhala, as close to the Heavenly City as Earth has known, or Baku and Johannesburg all over again, unexplored reserves of gold, oil, Plutonian wealth, and the prospect of creating yet another subhuman class of workers to extract it. One vision, if you like, spiritual, and the other, capitalist. Incommensurable, of course."

"So the job—"

"Is to find Auberon Halfcourt, see what he has to report, get it back to us in as much detail and as soon as possible."

"In person?"

"Isn't necessary. We appreciate your need to lie doggo for a bit. We'll give you a list of runners between there and here, reliables every one. . . . Oh, and if you do have to come out quickly yourself, we'd suggest making it via Constantinople, because our lines through there are a bit more secure."

"Why would I have to come out quickly?"

"Any number of reasons, take your pick. Another revolution, tribal uprisings, natural disasters, good heavens man, if we had to cover every contingency we might as well be writing espionage novels."

Yashmeen was waiting at the edge of town.

"So"—Kit with what he hoped was a cheerful tone—"we're running off together."

"You're not angry, I hope. Kit?"

"Oh don't worry, Yash—we'll see it through."

"It's how their minds work."

"It'll be fun."

Her quick glance was only with difficulty to be distinguished from alarm. "'Fun.'"

HAVING A DAY FREE, Kit, Yashmeen, and Günther decided to make a farewell visit to the little-known but rewarding Museum der Monstrositäten, a sort of nocturnal equivalent of Professor Klein's huge collection of mathematical models on the third floor of the Auditorienhaus. They traveled in a motor-diligence out toward the Brocken. The brushland grew hilly and witchlike, clouds came from directions indeterminate and covered the sun. "An older sort of Germany," commented Günther, with a less-than-reassuring smile. "Deeper."

It was not so much a conventional museum as a strange underground temple, or counter-temple, dedicated to the current "Crisis" in European mathematics . . . whether intended for exhibition, worship, study, or initiation could not be read from any exterior, because there was none, beyond an entranceway framing a flight of coal-black steps sloping downward in a fathomless tunnel to crypts unknown. As if to express the "imaginary" (or, as Clifford had termed it, "invisible") realm of numbers, the black substance from which it was constructed seemed not so much a known mineral as the residue of a nameless one, after light, through some undisclosed process, had been removed. Now and then a load-bearing statue was visible in the form of an angel, wings, faces, and garments streamlined almost to pure geometry, and brandishing weapons somehow *not yet decipherable,* featuring electrodes and cooling fins and so forth.

They found the inside strangely deserted, lit only by a few whispering gas-sconces which receded down the corridors leading away from the shadows of the entrance-hall. Yet there was the smell of German tidiness constantly exercised, of Sapoleum and floor-wax, of massive applications of formalin gas still pungently lingering. The corridors seemed swept by generations of sighing, which occasionally had reached wind force—a sadness, a wild exclusion from the primly orthogonal floor-plans of academic endeavor. . . .

"Somebody must be in here, at work?" it seemed to Kit. "Guards, staff?"

"Perhaps they hide from visitors they do not know," Günther shrugged. "How could anyone's nerves here remain unafflicted?"

From time to time, where there was light, it was possible to make out spacious murals, almost photographically precise, their colors unmodified by the daily interior purifications, depicting events in the recent history of mathematics, such as Knipfel's *Discovery of the Weierstrass Functions* and the recently installed *Professor Frege at Jena upon Receiving Russell's Letter Concerning the Set of All Sets That Are Not Members of Themselves* of von Imbiss, which exhibited *parallax effects* as one walked past, with such background figures as Sofia Kovalevskaia or a mischievously hydrophobic Bertrand Russell actually entering and departing the scene, depending on the viewer's position and velocity. "Poor Frege," said Günther, "just about to publish his book on arithmetic, and this happens—here he is basically saying *'Kot!'* which is German for 'How much will it cost me to revise these pages?' You see the way he appears to be striking himself on the forehead, which the artist has cleverly indicated with the little radiating streaks of green and magenta. . . ."

Signs directed them down into a corridor vaulted with iron trusses, which led to a series of panoramas of quite stupefying clarity known to convince even the most skeptical of visitors, who might find themselves surrounded 360 degrees by a view of ancient Crotona in Magna Grecia, beneath the precipitously darkening sky of an approaching storm, with robed and barefoot Pythagorean disciples, in some spiritual transport whose illumination was mimicked here by the fluorescence of gas-mantles soaked in certain radioactive salts . . . or seeming to have entered the very lecture hall at the Sorbonne where Hilbert on that historic August morning in 1900 was presenting the International Congress with his list of the celebrated "Paris problems" he hoped to see solved in the new century—yes, here was Hilbert beyond a doubt, Panama hat on his head, somehow optically presented as three-dimensional and even more lifelike than a figure in a wax museum, even to the thousands of drops of sweat running down everybody's face. . . .

According to the design philosophy of the day, between the observer at the center of a panorama and the cylindrical wall on which the scene was projected, lay a *zone of dual nature,* wherein must be correctly arranged a number of "real objects" appropriate to the setting—chairs and desks, Doric columns whole and damaged—though these could not strictly be termed *entirely* real, rather part "real" and part "pictorial," or let us say "fictional," this assortment of hybrid objects being designed to "gradually blend in" with distance until the curving wall and a final condition of pure image. "So," Günther declared, "one is thrust into the Cantorian paradise of the *Mengenlehre,* with one rather sizable set of points in space being continuously replaced by another, smoothly losing their 'reality' as a function of radius. The observer curious enough to cross this space—were it not, it appears, forbidden—would be slowly removed from his four-dimensional environs and taken out into a timeless region. . . ."

"You will want to go that way, Kit," Yashmeen said, indicating a sign that read ZU DEN QUATERNIONEN.

Of course, of course, no business of Kit's, they obviously needed some time together, departure in the air, things to say. . . . Released, Kit descended dark stairways uncomfortably steep even for the moderately fit—as if modeled after some ancient gathering-place, such as the Colosseum in Rome, stained with Imperial intention, promises of struggle, punishment, blood sacrifice—and stood at last before a rubber curtain, waiting, until it was mysteriously drawn aside and he found himself injected into overamplified Nernst light at the verge of white explosion, and there he was, undeniably at the canalside in Dublin sixty years ago as Hamilton received the Quaternions from an extrapersonal source nearly embodied in this very light, the Brougham Bridge receding away in perfect perspective, the figure of Mrs. Hamilton gazing on in gentle consternation, Hamilton himself in the act of carving into the bridge his renowned formulæ with a pocket-knife part real and part imaginary, a "complex" knife one might say, though a "real" reproduction of it was on view in a nearby gallery dedicated to famous "props" in the general mathematical drama, pieces of chalk, half-finished cups of coffee, even a *thoroughly crumpled handkerchief,* said to have belonged to Sofia Kovalevskaia and dating from Weierstrass's time in Berlin, an example of Lebesgue's notorious "surface devoid of tangent planes," an eccentric distant cousin of the family of functions, everywhere continuous and nowhere differentiable, with which Weierstrass, in 1872, had inaugurated the great Crisis that continued to preoccupy mathematics even to the present—there in its own free-standing display case, under a hemisphere of glass, illuminated from somewhere below, preserved in a constantly renewed atmosphere of pure nitrogen. How did this handkerchief get into its tangentless condition? Repeatedly wadded up in a tightened fist? Opened, cried and noseblown into, squeezed again back into a tight ball? Was it a record, a chemical memoir, of some extraordinary passage between the kindly professor and the student with the eloquent eyes? From wherever she had been, Yashmeen had reappeared to take Kit's arm and gaze for a while at the forlorn relic.

"She was always my inspiration, you know."

"All jake with you and the Teutonic god there?"

"He's very sad. He said he will miss you. He wants to tell you himself, I think." She wandered off as Günther, his eyes gleaming in the shadow of his hatbrim, approached Kit with a look of deep, though not fathomless, discontent. He was enroute to Mexico to manage one of the family coffee plantations. His father had been adamant, his uncles were looking forward to his arrival.

"Practically my neck of the woods," Kit said. "If you get up to Denver—"

"It is our strange German vertigo, everything in motion, like water draining down the sink, this unacknowledged tropism of the German spirit toward all manifestations of the Mexican, wherever they may occur. The Kaiser now seeks in Mexico the same opportunities for mischief toward the U.S. as Napoleon III before him . . . no doubt I have some blind pathetic little part to play."

"Günni, you seem kind of, I don't know, short on that old self-confidence today—"

"You were right, you know. That day of our duel. I have been only another *Rosinenkacker* on holiday, lost in his banal illusions. I must now bid farewell to the life I might have had, and take up again the stony road, a pilgrim on a penitential journey. No more mathematics for von Quassel. It is a world-line I shall, after all, never travel."

"Günni, I was a little harsh, I think."

"You will be kind to her." With a, you might say, Germanic emphasis on "will" that Kit didn't know how seriously to take.

"I'm her road partner for a week or so, that's really all it is. Then, so they tell me, other forces come into play."

"*Ach, das Schicksal.* From chloral to coffee," Günther brooded. "The antipodal journey from one end of human consciousness to its opposite."

"Fate is trying to tell you something," Kit speculated.

"Fate does not speak. She carries a Mauser and from time to time indicates our proper path."

They moved along in regret and reluctance, feeling through the ponderous stone envelope the afternoon as it deepened. Back in town waited another evening in its coercive penultimacy, and yet none could quite suggest detaching from these corridors commemorative of the persons they had once imagined themselves to be . . . who, each of them, had chosen to submit to the possibility of reaching that terrible ecstasy known to result from unmediated observation of the beautiful. Were their impending departures not only from programs of mathematical study but indeed from further hope of finding someday that headlong embrace?

"Children." The voice could not be located, it was everywhere in the corridors. "The Museum is closing now. The next time you visit, it might not be exactly where it stands today."

"Why not?" Yashmeen could not refrain from asking, though she knew.

"Because the cornerstone of the building is not a cube but its four-dimensional analogy, a tesseract. Certain of these corridors lead to other times, times, moreover, you might wish too strongly to reclaim, and become lost in the perplexity of the attempt."

"How do you know?" said Günther. "Who are you?"

"You know who I am."

Frank had sworn that once he was out of Mexico he was out, that his unfinished business in northamerica would have first claim on him. Mexican politics was not his business, even if he could keep the forces and matériel straight in his mind, which was seldom. So of course here he was, right back in the ol' caldo tlalpeño.

He was working out of Tampico, not far outside of which began a zone running all the way to the U.S. frontier, where runners of contraband operated freely. He had met up again with Ewball Oust, who had shifted his interests from rural Anarchism to arms procurement, and soon he and Frank were moving modest consignments of war matériel, mostly on a cash-and-carry basis.

One night eating supper down on Calle Rivera near the market, they fell into conversation with a German traveler, a coffee grower with an estate in Chiapas and a dueling scar on his right cheek, shaped like a tilde. In Mexico he had become known as "El Atildado," also used to describe a man of flawless personal toilette, a gift Günther von Quassel had also been blessed with. When they exchanged business cards and he saw Frank's name, his eyebrows went up. "I knew a Kit Traverse at Göttingen."

"My baby brother, I'll bet."

"We nearly fought a duel once."

"Kit give you that?" nodding at Günther's cheek.

"It did not get that far. We settled it peaceably. Your brother actually frightened me too much."

"You're sure this was Kit."

Günther told Frank how Scarsdale Vibe and his deputies had obliged Kit to leave Göttingen.

"Well maybe that's a blessing," Frank too morose to believe it, really. "Those damn people."

"He is a resourceful young man. He will prevail." Günther had with him a patent Thermos flask full of hot coffee. "If you would do me the honor," offering some. "A new variety. Gigantic *Bohnen.* We call it Maragogype."

"Thanks. Course, I've always been an Arbuckle's man myself," Frank noting the closest thing yet to a flinch cross the *cafetalero*'s face.

"But—they put waxes," Günther taking an aggrieved tone. "Resins from, from *trees,* I believe."

"Grew up on it, the frontier wife's friend, why, since I was a tiny one it's always been Arbuckle's for me."

"*Ach,* how you have degraded your sense of taste. But you seem young, still. Perhaps there is time to correct this disorder."

"All kiddin aside," Frank sipping, "it's mighty good coffee. You know your business."

Günther snorted. "Not my business. I am here at my father's demand. I do my duty to the family firm."

"Been down that road," said Ewball. "Plantation life not what you expected?"

Young Von Quassel allowed himself a chilly smile. "It is exactly what I expected."

EWBALL HAD A FATALITY for running across old acquaintances from *el otro lado* and an earlier day, in the years between grown older and meaner, and sometimes into a notoriety neither could have imagined back in those times of sensation and carelessness. There was for instance "Steve," nowadays suggesting folks address him as "Ramón," a fugitive from some bucket-shop catastrophe up north, keeping ever on the move, still not able to stop flimming as loud and fast as he could, who showed up one day downtown in the middle of a brief sandstorm, in the same little courtyard where Ewball, Frank, and Günther and a couple dozen blackbirds happened to be sheltering. The *norte* howled as if at some invisible moon. Sand whistled and rang through the fancy wrought-ironwork, and "Ramón" entertained them with tales of cascading debt. "Tell you, I'm sure getting desperate. If you hear about anything you think's too crazy or dangerous for you, why, pass it along. There's this stock-margin situation up north. Right now I'd fuck an alligator at high noon in the Plaza de Toros if there was a peso to be had out of it." Before slouching away into the yellow opacity, he invited them all up to a wingding at his villa that evening.

"Come have a look at it while it's still ours, meet the new wife. Little *reunión,* hundred folks maybe, go on all week if we wanted it to."

"Sounds good," Ewball said.

Günther, off to do some business with the extensive German colony here in Tampico, shook hands with Frank and Ewball. "You will go to this fiesta tonight?"

"We're staying at the Imperial," Frank said, "down in the basement, way in back. Drop by, we'll go up there together."

Away to the west and the Sierra, in grand residences faintly visible through the mists that rose from the malarial lowlands, the gringo population cringed on top of their breezy river-bluffs, waiting for the native uprising they all believed imminent, as they lay supine in their bedrooms night after night, beset, in the few hours of sleep they did find, by nearly identical nightmares of desert flight, pitiless skies, faces in which not only the irises but the entire surfaces of eyes were black, glistening in the sockets, implacable, reflecting columns of flame as wells blazed and exploded, nothing ahead but exile, loss, disgrace, no future anyplace north of the Río Bravo, voices invisible out in the oil-reek, from out of the diseased canals, accusing, arraigning, promising retribution for offenses unremembered. . . .

FRANK AND EWBALL moseyed into Steve/Ramón's party to find a ballroom murmurous with tiled fountains, where uncaged parrots glided from one ornamental palm to another. A dance band played. Couples danced tropical versions of the bolero and the fandango. Guests were drinking Ramos gin fizzes and chewing coca fresh from the jungles of Tehuantepec. Laughter was more or less constant in the room, but somewhat louder and more anxious than in, say, the average Saturday-night cantina. Out in the front hall, concealed by giant pots full of orchids, was an array of steamer trunks, packed and ready to roll. The same could be seen in most of the villas rented by gringos in Ramón's set, each a reminder of the pit waiting in the shadows of near futurity, for how could this last, this unnatural boom, this overextended violation of reality?

"It's Baku with skeeters," old oilpatch hands assured Frank.

"Time to get out of the country," revelers were heard to say more than once, "for we're all just hostages here down below the border line, up north they're borrowing like it's the end of the world, half of it with stocks for collateral, anything goes wrong up there with the trusts and it won't matter how much oil's in the ground, it'll be adios *chingamadre,* so to speak."

Günther had shown up with a tall blonde beauty named Gretchen, who spoke no English or Spanish and only a few words in her native German, such as *"cocktail"* and *"zigarette."* As it turned out, she showed a propensity, strange in such an eye-catching young lady, for disappearing, and Frank noticed Günther had a worried expression.

"I'm supposed to be looking after her for an associate," he said. "She has a history of impulsiveness. If it were not for—" he hesitated, as if about to ask for Frank's intercession.

"If I can help . . ."

"Your name actually came up today, in a context I have myself lately only begun to investigate."

"I've had some dealings with the German colony. In Tampico it's hard not to."

"This had to do with a certain delivery in Tampico for transshipment to Chiapas."

"Coffee-picking machinery," Frank suggested.

"Quite so." Gretchen reappeared drifting by the French windows along a colonnade, a glazed look in her eyes even at this distance. "When you have a moment . . . as soon as I . . ." Distracted, he sped off after the restless Valkyrie.

The shipment at issue proved to be a quantity of Mondragón semiautomatics from Germany, intended for the Mexican Army.

"Nice little unit," Frank said. "Started off as a Mexican design twenty years ago, Germans have been refining it since. The bolt gets blown back, ejects the old case, chambers a new round, you don't have to touch a thing. Weighs about as much as a Springfield, all's you got to do's keep squeezin 'em off till the magazine's empty, that's ten rounds, unless you can find some of those thirty-round Schnecken rigs they make for the German airplanes 'ese days."

"I'll ask," said Günther.

The crates of rifles could be re-manifested as "silver-mining machinery"—one of the principal cargoes railroads here and up north had been built to carry in the first place—thus finding safe-passage tuned to the duplicities of an economic order they might someday destroy. There would be no problem on this end getting help from the stevedores' union, who were by nature anti-Porfiristas.

"You might also want to have a word with Eusebio Gómez, who's acting as a subagent," Günther said.

Frank found him down at the docks on the Pánuco, the rough iron flank of a steamer ascending behind him. "I'm taking my commission in merchandise instead of cash," Eusebio explained, "on the theory that Mondragóns will get you through times of no money better than the other way around, as anyone who's tried to shoot anything with a hidalgo can tell you."

"Got to say you speak some mighty fine English, there, Eusebio," nodded Frank.

"In Tampico everybody speaks northamerican, it's why we call it 'Gringolandia' here."

"I bet you see a lot of Irish around too, huh? those *irlandeses?*"

"Señor?"

"Oh they're easy to spot—red-nose drunk all the time, jabbering, dirt-ignorant, idiot politics—"

"And what the bloody fuckall would you know about it—*este . . . perdón,* señor, what I meant to say, of course—"

"Ah-*ah* . . . ?" Frank grinning and waving his finger.

Eusebio's fists and eyebrows begin to unclench. "Well, you got me, sure. Wolfe Tone O'Rooney, sir, and here's hoping you don't work for the bloody Brits, or I'd be obliged to deal with that somehow."

"Frank Traverse."

"Not Reef Traverse's brother." Which was the first word Frank had had of Reef since Telluride.

They found a little cantina and got a couple of bottles of beer. "He wanted to finish the obligation himself," Wolfe Tone said. "He felt it was wrong to shift the burden over to you."

Frank told him about the Flor de Coahuila and the end of Sloat Fresno.

"So it's over?"

"Far's I'm concerned it is."

"But the other one."

"Deuce Kindred."

"He's still out there?"

"Maybe. I ain't the only one lookin for him. Somebody'll get him if they haven't already. If that bitch is still in the picture, could even be her, wouldn't surprise me much."

"Your . . . sister."

Causing Frank to squint inquiringly through the smoke of his cigarette. "She's got the best position on the pool table right now."

"Doesn't mean she'd do it?"

"Sure would be a funny one though, wouldn't it? If all this time she was just playin the long game, you know, gettin married to him, pretendin that whole li'l wifey business, waitin for the right moment, and then, well, kapow."

"A man might almost think you miss her a little."

"Hell. Only way I'd miss her's if my sights was off."

Wolfe Tone O'Rooney was after weapons for the Irish cause, primarily, but found himself drawn more and more, the longer he stayed in Mexico, into the gathering revolution here. He and Ewball hit it off right away, and soon the three of them had become regular passengers on the trolley out to Doña Cecilia, eventually blending in with dockworkers, roughnecks, and families on the way to the beach.

Their preferred place of business in Doña Cecilia was a cantina and gambling den known as La Fotinga Huasteca. The house band consisted of gigantic guitars, fiddles, trumpets, and accordion, with rhythms provided by a *batería* including timbales, guiros, and congas. Everybody here knew the words to everything, so the whole place sang along.

Into this tropical paradise one day who should come strolling but their old jailmate Dwayne Provecho, acting like he owned the place. Ewball's ears went back, and he set about repositioning his feet, but Frank felt only dull vexation, something like chronic dyspepsia, at this latest addition to an already worrisome list.

"Well, lookit this," Ewball snarled in greeting, "figured you'd be in Hell by now, bed-buddyin 'th that dirty li'l back-shootin Bob Ford."

"Still packin 'em old *resentimientos,*" Dwayne shaking his head, "gonn' affect your range and accuracy someday, podner."

"Careful who you call that."

"Have a warm beer," Frank suggested without bothering to keep the weariness out of his voice.

"Why Kid, how Christian of you," pulling over a chair and sitting down.

Frank's eyebrows descended briefly from the shadow of his hatbrim. "You stayed on my good side there maybe eight seconds, Dwayne, ever think of ridin the rodeo? Say, Mañuela, this prosperous-lookin gent would like to buy us cervezas Bohemias all around, with maybe some Cuervo Extra to go with that, doubles if you wouldn't mind."

"Sounds good," Dwayne bringing out a flashroll of American you could've wallpapered the place with, and peeling off a sawbuck. "Business is just bountiful. How's it with you fellas?"

"Thought they paid you off in rat cheese," muttered Ewball.

"About to put you fellows in the way of a whole new career, this is the thanks I get?"

"You're just our guardian angel," Frank reaching for his tequila glass.

"With what's rollin down the rails here," Dwayne said, "it ain't just money, it's history. And the next stop could be up north, 'cause anybody needs a revolution, it's sure us gringos."

"Then why ain't you up there?" Frank pretended to ask.

"He'd rather be down here soldiering on the cheap," Ewball explained, "ain't that it, Dwayne, all these greasers whose lives don't mean all that much to you?"

"Why, I feel like that these are my people," replied Dwayne with an air of dismissive sanctity. What he did not seem to be taking in was how much Ewball had changed since last they'd met. Maybe still figuring he was dealing with the same boomtown remittance man.

"There he goes, insultin the whole country. Fact of the matter," Ewball growing gleeful with aggravation, "these folks down here at least still have a chance—one that the *norteamericanos* lost long ago. For you-all, it's way too late anymore. You've delivered yourselves into the hands of capitalists and Christers, and anybody wants to change any of that steps across 'at *frontera,* they're drygulched on the spot—though I'm sure you'd know how to avoid that, Dwayne."

Which should have sent Dwayne into some fit of offended dignity, but instead, as Frank expected, turned him oily as the Pánuco River on a busy day.

"Now, boys," he said, "let's not sour what could be a happy reunion—for it seems I'm so snowed under at the moment that it'd be almost a mercy if you could take some of this business off of my hands. Especially seein how well connected you boys seem to be around Tampico—"

"Damn," Ewball as if he'd just figured it out, "that's why we haven't seen him around here before—Dwayne! ol' Dwayne, why, you just hit town today, didt'n you?"

"Let me prove my good faith here," Dwayne said, "how's a nice big consignment of them Krag-Jørgensens sound to you-all?"

"Blam! Blam!" Ewball supposed. "Kachunk, blam!"

"Come on, now, everbody likes a Krag. That handy trapdoor magazine? been a great favorite for years now with riflemen of many nations, includin the one we currently find ourselves in here."

"Who do we get sold to this time?" Ewball inquired mildly.

When Dwayne had gone off to the next segment of his important day, Frank said, "Well, things *are* kind of slow."

"Up to you. I'm staying as far out of that poisonous little bastard's way as I can without swearing off alcohol."

"He says the folks to see are in Juárez. One day up and back."

"Unless it's another of Dwayne's special little surprises, o' course. Go on ahead, I'll mind the shop, but you get bushwhacked on this don't come cryin and I'll try not to say I told you so."

"Jake with me."

"Vaya con Dios, pendejo."

Just what kind of a weapons jobber would pick a place like this to meet in? It appeared to be another of these damned ladies' gathering spots, just off the lobby of a reputable hotel near the Union Depot, tables surrounding a patio, clean as a whistle, plaster on the walls white as new, a stepping-off place for gringos making their first trip south, friendly señoritas in charming native outfits bringing afternoon tea in matching crockery and so on. Not a patch on the old El Paso—meaning three or four years ago, before the Law and Order League got into the act. What'd happened to all those very small back rooms down in the Chamizal, cigar smoke, self-destructive behavior, windows you could always jump out of? Since the good citizens had forced everything interesting out of town and across the river to Juárez, these damned little tearooms were showing up on every block. He looked again at the business card Dwayne's contact in Juárez had given him—E. B. Soltera, Regeneration Equipment.

Though not entirely tuned to female emanations, Frank noticed now a sudden dip in the chitchat level as tables full of respectable wives and mothers, bundled in unstained white dresses, first turned and then inclined their heads one to another to pass behind the brims of their pure white hats remarks on the apparition gliding toward Frank across the room. All he could think of was to sort of fan himself with the little card and keep pointing at it with his eyebrows up.

"Business name. Hello, Frank."

It was Stray, all right. Days and nights must have gone by when he'd been too claimed by trail business to imagine them ever meeting up again, but she did manage to cross his mind, once a week, maybe, cross it and often as not smile back over her shoulder. And now would you just look. Not exactly trail-beat, more rosy and plump in a city way, though some of that could have been the turnout and the rouge and all. . . . "Sure didn't expect . . ." On his feet, shaking his head slowly. "Well, I wouldn't've bet."

"Oh, all you got to do here in E.P.T.'s just sit still, sooner or later everbody you ever knew shows up, your whole life, everthin hoppin like Mexican jumpin beans 'ese days."

He was about to go through the gentlemanly routine, but she took her own seat without fuss, so Frank sat down again, still a little discombobulated. "Place to be, eh?"

"For some kinds of business. Guess you finally got tired of that little old Smith," sighting down her parasol at one of the matronly starers, who quickly looked away. "These Krag-Jørgensens'll be U.S. Army issue, which th' Army as you know's been replacing 'em with a newer Mauser type of model, so there's a lot of Krags out on the market right now, if you know where to look. Not that I ever get my hands on too much of the merchandise, of course."

"Go-between."

"Yeahp, percentage on a percentage, same old tale o' woe. Business with the Army sure ain't like it was, no more them two-three day binges with your good compadre supply sergeants, now it's all timing, quick in, quick out, for gosh sakes they're always on the telephone, Frank, they've even got the *wireless telegraph.* So even if I shouldn't be sayin so—buyer beware."

"I'll make a note, but you'll probably get your price, other side the river they're gettin crazier as the days go by, and the money this side's comin from some unexpected pockets."

"Best not tell me, I hear too much as it is."

For a full minute then, they sat face-to-face, as if waiting for time to slow down. Then they both spoke at once.

"Bet you're thinkin about—" Frank blurted.

"This used to be—" she began. He smiled sourly and nodded her to go on ahead. "It was your brother's old stomping grounds here, El Paso. One of 'em. He drifted around the sanatoriums posing as a rich-kid lung case from back east, workin 'em dayrooms like ridin a circuit. Though he never did get the accent right. When he could find a nurse who'd keep still for it, he'd get her to check him in, maybe even split the proceeds, which'd often as not turn out considerable. I used to come in, pretend to be his sister, got some funny looks from some nurses. Take notice of a few poker hands now and then, pass along the news, nothing nobody ever thought through. Then off we went. Or maybe just me, I forget."

"Good old days."

"Why, hell no."

Frank scrutinized his hatband. "Oh, but," slowly, "you never know with that Reefer, do you, one these days he'll just come breezin in—"

"No."

"You sound pretty sure."

"Not with me anymore."

"Come on, Stray. Bet you an ice-cream cone." He told her about running into Wolfe Tone O'Rooney, and how Wolfe had seen Reef in New Orleans. "So we know he got that far anyhow."

"Sakes. Three years, doesn't mean he's still alive, does it?"

"I feel like that he is, don't you?"

"Oh, 'feel'—listen, last I knew they were trying to kill him, hell I saw them, Frank. Come down off that mountain like they's chasin old Geronimo or somethin. Too many to count. Could've had it out, I suppose, found a little Derringer for the baby, showed him real quick how to sight the bastards in, but they just rode on through, me and Jesse wa'n' worth *their* time, 'fore the dust settled they're over the next ridge and it might as well been the edge of the world, 'cause they never showed again. But there we waited. Don't know—every day Jesse woke up thinkin he'd see his Pop, you could tell that plain enough, and then the day, and the days, went on, and there was all these other things to do. We still kept waitin, both of us. There's 'ese women like to wait, you know, *love* to even, I've run into a few. They get it confused with good works or somethin. More likely enjoyin the peace and quiet. It sure ain't for me."

"Well. What's 'at young Jesse *up to* these days?"

"Walkin, talkin, fears no man whatever his size, be drivin a rig next time I turn around. Willow and Holt, they have this little place up in northern New Mexico, he's pretty much in there with them when I'm on the road." Watching his eyes, as if for the shape his disapproval would take.

But Frank was too busy beaming like an uncle. "Be nice to see him before he gets too fast for me anyhow."

"Too late for that. Already playin with the dynamite, too." Adding, before Frank could, "Yeahp, just like his daddy."

LATER, OUTSIDE, back from a stroll by the dusty green river, Frank saw, coming quickly behind them along the sidewalk, almost like a mirage in the blaring of heat and light, two local reps out from some metropolis of the bad, faces or at least gaits he might have run across before. "If these are friends of yours . . ."

"Oh, my. That'd be old Hatch, and his saddle pal of the day." She didn't turn around to look, but had reached casually beneath her duster and come out with a little over-and-under. Twirling the parasol for, he guessed, distraction. "Well," Frank checking his own outfit, "I was hoping for more caliber there, but happy to see you're heeled, and say—let's figure on one apiece, how's that? They don't look *too* professional."

"Nice to see you out in public again, Miss Estrella. This here your beau?"

"This yours, Hatch?"

"Wasn't looking for no round and round," advised the other one, "just being neighborly."

"Six hundred long empty miles to Austin," Hatch added, "sometimes good neighbors is all you can count on." Nobody packing anything Frank could see, but this was town.

"Well, neighbors," her voice maintaining a smooth contralto, "you're a long way from the old neighborhood, hate to see you come all this distance for nothin."

"Be easy to fix that, I would guess."

"Sure, if it was anythin but simple damn thievery."

"Oh? Somebody around here's a *damn thief*?" inquired Hatch in what he must have been told was a menacing voice. Frank, who'd been watching the men's feet, took a short off-angle step so as to have speedier access to his Police Special. Coat buttons meantime were being undone, hatbrims realigned for the angle of the sun, amid a noticeable drop-off in pedestrian traffic around the little group.

Though having been obliged not long ago to gun Sloat Fresno into the Beyond, and not yet given up on the hope of doing the same for his partner, Frank still harbored too many doubts about triggerplay to be out looking to repeat it with just anybody—still, there was no denying he'd lost a whole ensemble of hesitancies back down the trail, and Hatch here, though enjoying perhaps even less acquaintance with the homicidal, might have detected this edge, raising the interesting question of how eager he might be to back up his sidekick.

For really it was the sidekick who presented the problem. Restless type. Fair hair, hat back on his head so the big brim sort of haloed his face, shiny eyes and low-set, pointed ears like an elf's. Frank understood this was to be his playfellow—Stray meantime having slowly drifted into a pose that only the more heedless of their safety would've read as demure. The daylight had somehow thickened, as before a tempest on the prairie. Nobody was saying much, so Frank figured the verbal part of this was done, and the practical matter nearly upon them. The elfin sidekick was whistling softly through his teeth the popular favorite "Daisy, Daisy," which since Doc Holliday's celebrated rejoinder to Frank McLaury at the O.K. Corral had been sort of telegraphic code among gun-handlers for Boot Hill. Frank gazed brightly, all but sympathetically, into the eyes of his target, waiting for a fateful tell.

Out of nowhere, "Well, hi everbody," a cheerful voice broke in, "whatchy'all doin?" It was Ewball Oust, pretending not to be a cold, bleak-eyed Anarchist who'd left all operational doubt miles back in the romantic mists of youth, whenever that was.

"Damn," breathed the pointy-eared gent, in a long, unrequited sigh. Everybody at their own pace went about relocating their everyday selves.

"So nice runnin into you again," Hatch as if preparing to kiss Stray's hand, "and don't you be a stranger, now."

"Next time," nodded the sidekick with a poignant smile at Ewball. "Maybe in church. What church y'all go to?" he seemed to want to know, in an oily voice.

"Me?" Ewball laughed, far exceeding the humor of the moment. "I'm Mexican Orthodox. How about you? Amigo?"

Whereupon the sidekick was observed to take a hesitant step or two backward. Stray and Hatch over his hat crown exchanging a look.

"Sorry I'm late," said Ewball.

"You're right on time," said Frank.

"My keeper," Frank introduced Ewball to Stray. They had given up looking for a decent saloon in El Paso and were sitting in a cantina across the river. "Worries about me all the time."

"You part of this deal?" her eyes more sparkling, it seemed to Frank, than business talk quite required.

Ewball shifted his eyes a couple-three times back and forth between her and Frank before shrugging. "Pretty much Frank's." Waiting a second before adding, "This time around. I just happened to be in town for a teetotalers' convention."

"She's got the goods, Ewb," said Frank, "and we're figurin out a rendezvous point. Seems like that that Dwayne was straight-shootin on this one after all."

"Be lookin for the imminent return of the baby Jesus any day now." Ewball finished his glass of tequila, took Frank's beer to chase it with, rose and took Stray's hand. "Been a pleasure, Miss Briggs. You children behave, now. Eyes of Texas are upon you."

"Where you fixin to be later?" Frank said.

"Usually, midnight will find me in Rosie's Cantina."

"South side of town, as I recall," said Stray, "just outside the city limits."

"Happy they're still in business, gay little establishment, used to be at least one presentable dancin girl?"

"That's the place. The L.&O.L. makes noises, but not so much since 'em seventeen mounted cowboys started runnin their patrol."

After Ewball left, she just sat looking at Frank for a while.

"Expectin you to be more, don't know, froze up by now. Way men will get sometimes?"

"Me? Same warm, easy fellow here."

"Heard that you found that Sloat Fresno."

"Luck."

"And that didn't—"

"Estrella, maybe there's kids out there one notch makes 'em a hardcase, but us older gentlemen are not always that eager for a career in firearms activity."

"You looked more'n ready to do Hatch's friend back there."

"Oh, but they wa'n that serious. Sloat was somethin somebody would've had to do."

She might have hesitated. "Had to. 'Cause . . . what, 'cause Reef didn't do it?"

"Reef is somewhere doin what he's doin, 's all, I just happened that time to walk in onto Sloat. And no luck with Deuce anyplace, so old Sloat may end up bein my one and only."

"You've been on this awhile now, Frank."

He shrugged. "My Pa is still dead."

In fact, Frank, who by day you wouldn't think got too carried away by his imagination, was plagued at night by variations on one recurring dream about Webb. He stands before a door that will not open—wood sometimes, iron, but always the same door, set into a wall, maybe in the anonymous middle of some city block, unattended, no one in control of who enters and who can't, a blank door hardly different from the wall it is set into, silent, inert, no handle or knob, no lock or keyhole, fitting so tightly into its wall that not even a knifeblade can be slipped between them. . . . He could wait across the street, keep vigil all night and day and night again, praying though not in the usual way, exactly, for the unmarked hour when at last the quality of shadow at the edges of the door might slowly begin to change, the geometry deepen and shift, and unasked-for as that, the route to some so-far-undreamable interior lie open, a way in whose way back out lies too far ahead in the dream to worry about. The sky is always bleak and cloudless, with late-afternoon light draining away. Through the clairvoyance of dreams, Frank is certain—can actually see—his father, just the other side of the closed door, refusing to acknowledge Frank's increasingly desperate pounding. Pleading, even, by the end, crying. "Pa, did you ever think I was good for anything? don't you want me with you? On your side?" Understanding that "side" also means the side of the wall Webb is on, and hoping that this double sense will be enough, smart or powerful enough, like a password in an old tale, to gain him entrance. But though he tries to stop it, his crying at some point will steepen from sorrow into hoarse rage, heedless assault on the dumb solidity before him. Reef and Kit are usually around someplace, too, though how close depends on how much silence lies among them all. And Lake, she's never there. Frank wants to ask where she is, but because his motives are recognizably impure, whenever he tries to, or it even looks like he's about to ask, his brothers turn away, and that more often than not is what he would wake from, into the borderlands of the early night, having by now come to understand that it had been prelude and étude to whatever waited deeper in.

IT HAD RAINED in the night, and some of the ocotillo fences had sprouted some green. Stray had just got word that the Krags were delivered safely and en route to their invisible destiny.

"Time to get back to what we were doin I guess," she said.

"I'm back and forth a lot," Frank said. "Ain't out of the question is it we'll maybe do this again. Like you say, sit still long enough in El Paso."

"You know when I saw you in that little tearoom I thought it was Reef for a second. Sorrowful, ain't it? All this time."

"Stranger things," Frank with a small lopsided smile. "Have faith."

"I always figured me for the one that wouldn't stick." They looked out across the river. In the early light, Juárez was all pink and red. "Every time he stood by me, that one big night down in Cortez, Leadville all the time, o' course, Rock Springs when they come after us with those repeating shotguns . . . him always there like that, between me and them, making sure I got out—I wouldn't deny none of it, couldn't, but is it too forward of a gal to in fact mention returning the favor once or twice, and not with some little Ladies' Friend neither? Creede? whoo-ee. . . . For a while there, we were unbeatable. . . .

"By the time Jesse showed up, though, maybe it was beginnin to soak in, we're too old for it, no mess that getting out of it meant any hope of getting out for good anymore—at best just for some breathin time till the next one jumped us, maybe. And meantime the inches, it's always inches ain't it, kept gettin shorter, all narrowin down, sometimes had to schedule a week ahead just to pick m'nose."

Frank was gazing at her, the face men got in dance halls sometimes, almost a smile.

"Not like that I was ever some lady," she tentatively dropped a hook, "got used to certain comforts I didn't want to give up—where'd I ever see any of that? hell I was twenty before I owned a mirror I could sit and look into. *There* was a mistake, I give the thing right away, went back to saloon mirrors and shop windows, where there was still some mercy to the light."

"Oh, make up another one, I saw you when you were twenty." If she hadn't known better she might have taken his gaze for resentful. Finally, "Stray, the first time I saw you, I knew I'd never see anybody that beautiful again, and I never did, until you walked in that li'l doily joint the other day."

"What I get for fishin."

"That mean the deal's off?"

"Frank—"

"Hey. I love him too."

It hadn't been all fishing, of course. She got sometimes to feeling too close to an edge, a due date, the fear of living on borrowed time. Because for all her winters got through and returns to valley and creekside in the spring, for all the day-and-night hard riding through the artemisia setting off sage grouse like thunderclaps to right and left, with the once-perfect rhythms of the horse beneath her gone faltering and mortal, yet she couldn't see her luck as other than purchased in the worn unlucky coin of all those girls who hadn't kept coming back, who'd gone down before their time, Dixies and Fans and Mignonettes, too fair to be alone, too crazy for town, ending their days too soon in barrelhouses, in shelters dug not quite deep enough into the unyielding freeze of the hillside, for the sake of boys too stupefied with their own love of exploding into the dark, with girl-size hands clasped, too tight to pry loose, around a locket, holding a picture of a mother, of a child, left back the other side of a watershed, birth names lost as well behind aliases taken for reasons of commerce or plain safety, out in some blighted corner too far from God's notice to matter much what she had done or would have to do to outride those onto whose list of chores the right to judge had found its way it seemed . . . Stray was here, and they were gone, and Reef was God knew where—Frank's wishful family look-alike, Jesse's father and Webb's uncertain avenger and her own sad story, her dream, recurring, bad, broken, never come true.

What with card games in the changing rooms and the platoons of ladies who gathered each shift's end at the tunnel entrances in their respective countries, it wasn't like either Reef or Flaco was squirreling much away, though there was no shortage of work. "It's a seller's market," they kept hearing as they went gypsying from one European tunnel to the next, "you boys can write your own ticket." The Austrian Alps in particular were just hopping. Everybody expected war between Austria and Italy to break out any minute, over old territorial claims Reef wasn't sure he'd ever understand, and even if the countries remained at peace, Austria still wanted to be able to move massive forces south whenever it took a mind to. Within the period 1901–6, on the new Karawankenbahn alone, forty-seven tunnels were driven through the mountains, with similar blasting opportunities in the Tauern and Wochein ranges.

At the Simplon a massive tunnel project had been under way since 1898 to connect train lines between Brigue in Switzerland and Domodossola in Italy, replacing a nine-hour trip by horse-drawn diligence. Reef and Flaco arrived in time for some epic difficulties. On the Swiss side, hot springs had driven everybody out and stopped work—an iron door was keeping in a great reservoir of very hot water three hundred yards long. All effort was redirected to the approach being made at the same time from the Italian side, where the hot-water springs were only slightly less bothersome. Since two parallel galleries were being driven through the mountain, it was often necessary to cross over from one to the other and work back for short stretches in the opposite direction. It did not help to be one of those folks who became nervous in tight places.

Two-foot drills got worn down to three inches faster than poolchalk and needed changing dozens of times a day. The noise was hellish, the air wet and hot and stifling when it wasn't full of stone dust, which the new Brandt drills, mounted on tripods like Hotchkiss machine guns, being faster, were supposed to be cutting down on. But there weren't enough of them for everybody, and Reef usually found himself single-jacking or augering with a breastplate rig holding the butt end of the drill against his body.

Old-timers on the crew—Nikos, Fulvio, Gerhardt, the opera singer, the Albanian—when they first penetrated the mountain, prepared to fight frozen rock, had found instead a passionate heart, a teeming interiority, mineral water at about 120 to 130 degrees, and a struggle some days to simply get out alive by shift's end, although some never did. . . .

"We are fucking crazy," Nikos informed Reef several times each day, shouting over the racket of the drilling. "Nobody but crazy people would be in here."

Some of the boys on the shift were part-time Anarchists interested in furthering their chemical education. Most did all they could to keep their faces hidden from a daily parade of visitors, few of whom found it necessary to identify themselves. Engineers, inspectors, company officials, idly curious in-laws, government police from every jurisdiction in Europe were known to show up unexpectedly with briefcases, magnesium flash cameras, and questions ranging from the keenly intrusive to the stupidly repetitive.

"Any of them you'd like put out of the way," Ramiz, the Albanian, offered, "I give you a good price, flat fee, no extras. Nothing to lose, because I can't go back." He was on the run from a long-standing blood vendetta back home. The ancient code of the region, known as Kanuni Lekë Dukagjinit, allowed any wronged family one consequence-free rifle shot, but if the offender was still alive after twenty-four hours, they couldn't take any further revenge for as long as he stayed on his own property. "So nearly every village has a family like mine, sometimes two, locked up in their houses."

Reef felt a personal interest. "Well how do folks eat?"

"The women and children are allowed to come and go."

"Was it you who . . . ?"

"Not me, I was a baby at the time. It was my grandfather, he shot a guest of the other family, who was staying with them one night—something to do with the League of Prizren and the fighting that was going on back then. Later on, nobody said they could remember much, not even the man's name after a while. But in the Kanuni, the rules are the same for guests as for family."

By the time Ramiz hit adolescence and became a legitimate target himself, being cooped up did not hold the same appeal it might have for a more mature individual. One night, "Maybe I went crazy, I can't remember," he slipped out a window, up a gulch, across the hills, and down to the sea, where he found a boat. "Turks. They knew what was going on all right, but they lived by a different code."

"So . . . your grandfather, your father? Still at home?"

He shrugged. "I hope so. I'll never see them again. *Jetokam, jetokam!* Strange how I am alive! Is this how revenge is taken in America?"

Reef told a version of his own story. In it, Deuce Kindred and Sloat Fresno became more like critters of pure evil than guns for hire, and of course there were no rules about sanctuary on your own property—in fact, it had taken him this long to catch on, nothing like Ramiz's Kanuni at all, though everybody liked to talk about the Code of the West as if it really existed and you could borrow a copy from the local library when you needed to check on details.

"Avenging your family is still allowed I guess, though lately as civilization comes creepin out from back east, authorities tend to frown more and more on it. They tell you, 'Don't take the law into your own hands.'"

"In whose hands, then?"

"Marshal . . . sheriff."

"The police? But that . . . is to remain a child."

Reef, who'd been feeling calm enough till then, found that his voice had dried up. He sat there with a hand-rolled cigarette stuck smoldering to his lip, and couldn't meet the other man's eyes.

"*Më fal.* I meant no—"

"It's O.K. That isn't why I left."

"You killed them."

Reef gave it some thought. "They had powerful friends."

Among the many superstitions inside this mountain was a belief that the tunnel was "neutral ground," exempt not only from political jurisdictions but from Time itself. The Anarchists and Socialists on the shift had their own mixed feelings about history. They suffered from it, and it was also to be their liberator, if they could somehow survive to see the day. In the shower-baths at the end of the shift, the suffering could be read on each body, as a document written in insults to flesh and bone—scars, crookedness, missing parts. They knew each other as more comfortable men, in the steam-rooms of hydropathics, for instance, would not. Amateur bullet removals and bone settings, cauterizations and brandings, some souvenirs were public and could be compared, others were private and less likely to be talked about.

One day Reef happened to notice on Fulvio what looked like a railroad map executed in scar tissue. "What was that from, you walk in between a couple of bobcats fucking?"

"An encounter with a Tatzelwurm," said Fulvio. "Dramatic, *non è vero?*"

"New one on me," said Reef.

"It's a snake with paws," said Gerhardt.

"Four legs and three toes on each paw, and a big mouth full of very sharp teeth."

"Hibernates here, inside the mountain."

"Tries to. But anybody who wakes it up, God help them."

Men had been known to quit work here, claiming that the Tatzelwurms were becoming enraged by all the drilling and explosions.

Reef figured it for some kind of routine they put the newcomers through, this being the first tunnel job he'd run into it on. Sort of Alpine tommy-knockers, he figured, till he began to notice long, flowing shapes in unexpected places.

Tunnelers brought pistols in to work and took shots whenever they thought they saw a Tatzelwurm. Some lit dynamite sticks and threw them. The creatures only became bolder, or maybe more indifferent to their fate.

"Ain't exactly mine rats there."

"In Europe," speculated Philippe, "the mountains are much older than in America. Whatever lives in them has had more time to evolve toward a more lethal, perhaps less amiable, sort of creature."

"It is also a good argument for Hell," added Gerhardt, "for some primordial plasm of hate and punishment at the center of the Earth which takes on different forms, the closer it can be projected to the surface. Here under the Alps, it happens to become visible as the Tatzelwurm."

"It is comforting to imagine this as an outward and visible manifestation of something else," chuckled one of the Austrians, puffing on a cigar stub. "But sometimes a Tatzelwurm is only a Tatzelwurm."

"The really disturbing thing," Fulvio with a shiver, "is when you see one and it looks up and sees that you are watching it. Sometimes it will run, but if it doesn't, then prepare to be attacked. It helps if you don't look at its face too long. Even in the dark, you will know where it is, because it will be screaming—a high whistling scream that like the winter cold will creep in to occupy your bones."

"Once you have had the encounter," Gerhardt agreed, "it is with you forever. This is why I believe they are sent to us, to some of us in particular, for a purpose."

"What's that?" Reef said.

"To tell us that we shouldn't be doing this."

"Tunneling?"

"Putting railroads."

"But we're not," Reef pointed out. "The people who are paying us are. Do *they* ever see the Tatzelwurm?"

"It visits them in their dreams."

"And it looks like us," added Flaco.

REEF SHOULD HAVE KNOWN what was coming when the favogn blew in. All of a sudden, case-hardened veterans of hot-water inundations, explosions, and gallery collapses became languorous and feeble under the assault of this warm, dry and unrelenting wind, barely able to lift a tin cup, let alone a drill. The favogn was supposed to come from the Sahara Desert, like the scirocco, though there were endless debates over this. The wind was alive. Talk of dynamic compression and adiabatic gradients didn't carry as much weight as the certainty of its conscious intent.

For years now, the tunnel-in-progress here had been a regular stop for leisured balneomaniacs of the era, traveling spa to spa, all over Europe and beyond, habitués of mineral waters, seekers after compounds of elements not even discovered yet, some of them rumored to provide therapeutic rays not yet assigned letters of any alphabet, though known and discussed among spa cognoscenti from Baden-Baden to Wagga Wagga.

One day a party of these visitors showed up, about half a dozen of them, having groped their way through Moazagotl clouds and so forth. All more or less lethargic from the wind. Except—"Oh, come look at these funny little men with their big mustaches, running about in their underwear setting off dynamite, it's simply too amusing!"

Reef was dismayed to recognize the voice of Ruperta Chirpingdon-Groin. Judas Priest and how far and fast did he have to run before he was looking up his own ass again and reliving the same mistakes, no doubt deed for deed? Edging closer, a familiar old feeling vibrating from penis to brain, he carefully had a look.

Oh, boy. Desirable as ever, maybe more so, and as for income level, well that ice twinkling in the subterranean dusk looked real enough, and he'd bet her turnout there was straight from Paris, too. A couple of the other drillers stood gaping, unable to shut their mouths, stroking themselves without shame. This gallantry had been claiming her attention for a while, when she happened to look over at last and recognize Reef.

"Wot, you again. Why haven't you yours out as well, or have I grown so unattractive?"

"Must've forgot what to do with it," Reef beamed, "waitin for you to remind me."

"I'm not sure after New Orleans that I should even be speaking with you."

A young Italian gentleman of university age, wearing what appeared to be a hunting suit modified for mountain activities, crept forward. "*Macchè, gioia mia*—is some difficulty with this *troglodita*?"

"*Càlmati,* Rodolfo." Ruperta adjusted her grip on the modish ebony alpenstock she was carrying, just impatiently enough for her companion to notice and be warned. "*Tutto va bene. Un amico di pochi anni fa.*" The youth, directing a short and vicious glare at Reef, stepped back and pretended to resume an interest in hydraulic drilling.

"Good to see you maintainin 'em standards," Reef nodded. "Wouldn't do to get déclassé or nothin."

"We're in Domodossola for a night or two. The Hôtel de la Ville et Poste, I'm sure you know it."

She had been amusing herself by waiting for Rodolfo to fall asleep and then getting decked out in scarlet lustra-cellulose, draping on some Ambroid jewelry, and joining the girls who loitered by the end of the tunnel, often finding herself late at night on hands and knees up on Calvary Hill being penetrated by a small queue of tunnel hands, often two at a time, who cursed her in unknown tongues—as she seemed eager to let Reef know about the first chance she got. "Large, work-roughened hands," she murmured, "bruising me, scratching me, and I do try to keep my skin ever so soft and smooth, here, feel here . . . remember . . ." Reef, who always knew what she was up to—Ruperta after all was not very complicated when it came to fucking, one of her major advantages if you really wanted to know—obliged by seizing her with careful brutality, pushing her face among some pillows, and tearing some rather high-priced underlinen, and despite the presence of young Rodolfo in a nearby room, they then double-jacked their way to a mutual explosion memorable only till the next time it happened, which was to be presently.

The watershed moment, however, came in the course of one of the long postcoital monologues Ruperta somehow found necessary and which Reef had come to find sort of relaxing. He was almost ready to fall asleep when the name of Scarsdale Vibe entered the stream of idle chatter, and he reached for another cigarette.

"Familiar name."

"I should think so. One of your American demigods."

"And he's over here now?"

"*Tesoro,* sooner or later everyone is. This Vibe person has been buying up Renaissance art in what even for an American is indecent haste. His next target according to the gossip is Venice. Perhaps he'll buy *it* as well. Is he a friend of yours? I can't quite imagine that, but we shall be in Venice soon, and then perhaps you'll introduce us."

"Didn't know I was invited along."

She gave him a look and, possibly by way of formal invitation, reached for his penis.

Philippe was an alumnus of the infamous children's prison in Paris known as the Petite Roquette, and had gained an early appreciation of institutional spaces. He had become especially partial to cathedrals, and liked to think of this mountain as such a transcendent structure, with the tunnel as its apse. "In a cathedral what looks solid never is. Walls are hollow inside. Columns contain winding staircases. This apparently solid mountain is really a collection of hot springs, caves, fissures, passageways, one hiding-place within another—and the Tatzelwurms know it all intimately. They are the priesthood of their own dark religion—" He was interrupted by a scream.

"Ndih'më!" It was coming from a little side gallery. *"Nxito!"*

Reef ran into the smell of new-milled pine shoring and saw the Tatzelwurm, much bigger than he'd been led to expect, standing over Ramiz. The critter was depending on its looks to intimidate its victims, hypnotize them into some kind of compliance with their fate, and it seemed to be working on the Albanian. "Hey, Ace!" Reef yelled. The Tatzelwurm whipped its head around and stared him full in the eyes. *Now I have seen you,* was the message, *now you are next on my list.* Reef looked for something to hit it with. Drill bit in his hand was worn too short, nearest picks and shovels weren't near enough, looked like his only bet was close quarters with the jacking hammer. By the time he'd figured this out, something had gone funny with the light, shadows had appeared where they shouldn't have been, and the Tatzelwurm had disappeared.

Ramiz had been working in his underwear and had a long gash on his leg that was bleeding pretty good. "Better get back to the *spital,*" Reef said, "get that seen to. Can you walk on it?"

"I think so."

Philippe and a couple of others had shown up. "Be right with you all," Reef said, "just want to make sure it's gone."

"Here." Philippe tossed him a Mannlicher eight-shot, which Reef could tell by the balance had a full magazine. He carefully stepped into the shadows.

"Hello, Reef." It seemed to leap out of the rock-face, condensed in a kinetic blur of lethal muscle and claw, screaming as it came.

"Holy shit." With the Tatzelwurm about a foot away, Reef had just time to squeeze off a shot, whereupon the critter exploded in a great green foul-smelling cloud of blood and tissue. He fired again just on general principles.

"Green blood?" said Reef later, after a long shower.

"Did we forget to mention that?" said Philippe.

"It spoke my name."

"Ah, *bien sûr.*"

"I heard it, Philippe."

"You have saved my life," declared Ramiz, "and though we would both much prefer to forget the whole matter, I am now obliged, someday, somehow, to repay you. An Albanian never forgets."

"Thought that was an elephant."

He worked through to the end of the shift, showered again, unlocked his private pulley-rope, lowered his clothes from the overhead, hung his wet working gear on the hook, raised it again and padlocked the rope, got dressed, just like any other day. But this time he went in the office and collected his pay, and trudged down into Domodossola and didn't look back. They had been good friends, that crew. It was a busy period of history. He might get to see some of them again.

IT WAS SAID that great tunnels like the Simplon or St.-Gotthard were haunted, that when the train entered and the light of the world, day or night, had to be abandoned for the time of passage however brief, and the mineral roar made conversation impossible, then certain spirits who once had chosen to surrender into the fierce intestinal darkness of the mountain would reappear among the paying passengers, take empty seats, drink negligibly from the engraved glassware in the dining cars, assume themselves into the rising shapes of tobacco smoke, whisper a propaganda of memory and redemption to salesmen, tourists, the resolutely idle, the uncleansably rich, and other practitioners of forgetfulness, who could not sense the visitors with anything like the clarity of fugitives, exiles, mourners, and spies—all those, that is, who had reached agreement, even occasions of intimacy, with Time.

Some of them, rarely but never quite by accident, were known to engage a passenger in conversation. Reef was alone in the smoking car, some nameless black hour, when a not entirely opaque presence appeared in the plush seat opposite.

"What could you have been thinking?" he inquired. It was a voice Reef had not heard before but recognized nonetheless.

"About what?"

"You have a wife and child to look after and a father to avenge, and here you are in some damn lounge suit you didn't pay for, smoking Havanas you wouldn't ordinarily even know how to find, much less afford, in the company of a woman who has never had a thought that didn't originate down there between her legs."

"Pretty direct."

"What happened to you? You were a promising young dynamiter, your father's son, sworn to alter the social terrain, and now you're hardly much better than the people you used to want to blow up. Look at them. Too much money and idle time, too little fucking compassion, Reef."

"I earned this. I put in my time."

"But you'll never earn these folks's respect or even any credibility. It's never going to get much better than contempt. Clear all the happy horseshit out of your mind, try to remember what Webb looked like, at least. Then turn your thoughts to the man who had him murdered. Scarsdale Vibe is in easy reach right now. Scarsdale how-about-you-all-go-live-in-shit-and-die-young-so's-I-can-stay-in-big-hotels-and-spend-millions-on-fine-art Vibe. Look him up when you're down there in Venice, Italy. Better yet, sight him in. You can still stop all this idle fuckfuck, turn around, and get back to yourself again."

"Assuming for the sake of argument—"

"We're coming out of the tunnel. I have to be someplace else."

Kit and Yashmeen walked up from the little hotel in Intra, along the shore of the lake, to the churchyard at Biganzano, where Riemann's grave was. Saloon steamers, private launches, and sailboats could be seen through the trees, out on the lake. Carriages and cargo wagons passed along the road. The tramontana blew her hair back from her face. Kit couldn't keep from looking at her every step or two, though he'd rather've been staring into the sun.

They had made the same journey as Riemann, who had arrived here in June of 1866 on his third and last visit, for which Göttingen professors Wilhelm Weber and Baron von Waltershausen had obtained some money from the government. Riemann knew he was dying. If he thought he was fleeing anything, it could not have been the hungry mouth of death, for this was in the middle of what would be known as the Seven Weeks' War, and death was all around. Cassel and Hannover had fallen to the Prussians, the Hannoverian army under von Arentschildt, twenty thousand strong, had concentrated at Göttingen and begun to march south trying to escape the Prussian columns converging on them but were stopped by von Flies at Langensalza, and surrendered on June 29.

Not that Riemann would find Italy any more tranquil. A bit to the east of Lago Maggiore, the final battle for the Veneto, between Austria and Italy, was shaping up. He had passed from the rationalized hell of the struggle for Germany into Sunny Italy and the summer of Custozza, and nine thousand dead, and five thousand missing, and soon down into his own casualty-list of one.

Forty years later on, their own plunge through Deep Germany, into the folk-dream behind the Black Forest, where there was said to be room for a hundred thousand troops and ten times as many elves, Kit and Yashmeen had found themselves trying to spend as much time in the train as possible. At Göttingen there had been at least the sense that one was still connected, however tenuously, to the rest of Europe. But as they moved southward and consonants began to grow blurry, presently there was much less to engage the rational mind—instead, everywhere, elf-grottoes, castles, set dramatically on pinnacles, to which there was no visible access, country people in dirndls and peculiar green hats, Gothic churches, Gothic breweries, shadows with undulating tails and moving wings passing across the valley floors. "Maybe I need a drink," said Kit. "Schnapps, something. How about you, my turtledove?"

"Call me that one more time in public," she advised serenely, "and I shall strike you with a piece of furniture."

Other passengers were enchanted. "Aren't they sweet," wives observed, and husbands blessed them with pipesmoke.

At the Haupt-Bahnhof in Frankfurt, the largest railway station in Germany, known locally as "the Wonderstructure at the Gallows-field," the station restaurant seemed to breathe hesitantly, as if still not quite recovered from the Wagnerian moment five or six years earlier when the brakes failed on an Orient Express engine and it jumped the tracks and came crashing into the restaurant among the marble pillars and chandeliers and chattering diners, another incursion into the bourgeois calm to join the collapses of the Campanile in Venice and of the roof at the Charing Cross Station in London only a year before, nonlethal equivalents of an Anarchist bomb, though some believed equally laden with intent.

To Kit and Yashmeen, it seemed more like the revenge of Deep Germany on the modern age of steam. They bought sandwiches in the buffets and kept close to the train, clinging with increasing desperation to the machinery of transport against the onset of a lassitude thick as grease, a creeping surrender to the shameless German primitivism all around them. Switzerland arrived just in time, rising before them like a lime sorbet after a steady diet of roasted ducks and assorted goose products.

AT RIEMANN'S GRAVE she swept off her hat and stood with her head bowed, allowing the mountain wind to do as it wished with her hair. "No," as if answering a voice which had just suggested it, "I think I should not cry." Kit waited with his hands in his pockets and a respect for whatever it was that had her so in its grasp.

"In Russia, when I was a small child," Yashmeen continued after a while, "I should not remember it now, but I do, wanderers, wild-looking men, came to our doors seeking shelter as if they were entitled to it. They were the *stranniki*—once, they had led everyday lives like other men, had their families and work, houses filled with furniture, children's toys, pots and pans, clothes, all the tack of domestic life. Then one day they simply turned—walked out through the door and away from that, from all of it—whatever had held them there, history, love, betrayals forgiven or not, property, nothing mattered now, they were no longer responsible to the world, let alone the Tsar—only God could claim them, their only allegiance was to God. In my little town, and it was said all over Russia, families had dug secret rooms beneath their houses, where these men could rest on their journeys. The Government feared them more than it feared Social Democrats, more than bomb-throwers, 'Very dangerous,' Papa assured us—we knew he didn't mean dangerous to us—we also understood it was our duty to help them in their passage. Their holy mission. Even with them down under the house, we slept as peacefully as we ever did. Perhaps more so. We told each other stories about them, ambassadors from some mysterious country very far away, unable to return to that homeland because the way back was hidden. They had to keep wandering the world whose deceptions and melodramas, blood and desire, we had begun to sense, perhaps not seeking anything with a name, perhaps only wandering. People called them *podpol'niki,* underground men. Floors that had once been solid and simple became veils over another world. It was not the day we knew that provided the *stranniki* their light."

Kit had one of those moments of extralogical grasp more appropriate to mathematical work. "Then leaving Göttingen . . ."

"Leaving Göttingen. No. It was never my choice," as if trying to explain it to Riemann, to the fraction of him that had lingered here forty years as if waiting for the one graveside confession he must not miss, "not for any trivial reason. Not when it means exile into . . ." she did not quite include Kit in her gesture—"this. Whatever hopes I may have had for the ζ-function, for the new geometry, for transcendence by way of any of that, must be left behind, souvenirs of a girl's credulity, a girl I scarcely know anymore. At Göttingen I had no visitation, no prophecy, no plan, I was only safe . . . safe in my studies, comfortably in and out the doorways of the daily farces and flirtations, the quiet Sunday walks up on the wall around the old town. Now I am expelled from the garden. Now in a smooth enough World-Line comes this terrible discontinuity. And on the far side of it, I find that now I am also *strannik.*" Her extraordinary eyes remained directed at the grave. "There are teachers. Teachers who have us for a while, allow us to see particular things, and then send us on, without regard to how we may have come to feel about them. We depart, wondering if now, perhaps, we will not be in a state of departure forever. We go off to dwell night by night beneath the floors of Europe, on another sort of journey into another sort of soul, in which we must discard everything, not only the objects we possess but everything we have taken to be 'real,' all we have learned, all the work we have put in, the theorems, the proofs, the questioning, the breath-taken trembling before the beauty of an intractable problem, all of which was perhaps illusion."

It did seem to him she might be putting it a little dramatically. "Letting all of that go." He wanted to light up a cigarette but held himself there, tense. "Big step, Yashmeen."

She gazed for a while through the wind back at Monte Rosso, and the lighted Swiss peaks beyond. "It was so easy to forget this other world out here, with its enemies and intrigues and pestilent secrets. . . . I knew it must claim me again, I had no choice, but, Kit, you . . . perhaps no one after all has the right to ask. . . ."

"Just an innocent American cowpoke don't know what he stumbled into. Why do you say 'no choice'? You want to tell me what's going on?"

"No. Not really."

YASHMEEN HAD ARRANGED to re-connect with elements of the T.W.I.T. at the fabled Sanatorium Böpfli-Spazzoletta, on the Swiss side of Lago Maggiore. Kit, not sure if he'd be welcome, tagged along anyway. The place was gigantic, offering enough of a range in levels of taste to please everyone, from the most god-awful kitsch to austere anterooms of death befitting the consumptive chic then so enchanting Europe. They had to wander around for twenty minutes before they could even figure out how to ask directions. From somewhere came sounds of a dance orchestra, though it was still pretty early in the day.

"Act normal, Kit. And don't say my name."

It would've taken Kit a minute anyway to recognize Reef—who this had to be—seeing that his brother had undergone some redesign, the hat being a high-crowned black Borsalino whose brim was Reef-modified to keep the rain off at least, the suit definitely not of American cut, his hair longer and strangely greased, his mustache gone. Kit would have taken him for a tourist from someplace out in Deep Europe, except for the voice, and the old amiable lopsidedness to his face so long beaten at by realities difficult to mistake for other than American—personable as it needed to be, but only when it needed to be, the rest of the time wary and remote.

"Long way from 'em San Juans," Kit mumbled. "Just where'n the hell did you blow in from?" feeling this stealthy onset of emotion. But Reef was being cautious.

"Tunnelin for the railroads," gesturing outside with his head, "Alps and so forth." They sat there nodding and beaming a while. "Little cardplay in the hydropathics maybe. How come you're not back in the U.S., hobnobbin with that summer set at Newport, Rhode Island, playin polo, whatever."

"Guess you'd say I'm on the run." While Reef slowly shook his head and pretended to snicker, Kit gave him the abridged version, up to spotting Foley in Göttingen. "Really all went sour the minute it started, I should've got off before Glenwood Springs, turned around, come back, but . . ." But couldn't figure how to say more. Somewhere not far below these social niceties was a moment that waited, something to do with their father and some terrible calculating, with brothers seeing each other again, with re-connection of paths and promises and so forth, and Kit would just as soon it all took its time arriving.

Reef watched him fret for a while. "Some night we'll stay up all night and swap should-ofs, meantime be content that you held on longer'n me at least."

"Just stupid. Just slow. Can't believe how long it took me to see." Kit sat there watching the floor as if it might drop away, nodding as if listening to himself. A waiter came by and Reef asked him something in some dialect that got him a quizzical over-the-shoulder second look.

"Like the man never heard tunnel Italian before."

Ruperta Chirpingdon-Groin and her party had descended by way of the St.-Gotthard Tunnel from league after league of peaks like ocean waves frozen in place, fading into merciless light, tending to eternity—a circuit of Alpine hotels and hydropathics so remote the hotels had to print up their own postal stamps just to get mail as far as a regular Swiss post office, full of giggling nitwits, quite a number of them British actually, running about the corridors, jumping off balconies into the snowdrifts, hiding in serving-pantries and falling down dumbwaiter shafts. They had detrained at Bellinzona, where the motor-diligence from the Sanatorium was waiting for them, and so up to the famed institution overlooking the Swiss shores of Lago Maggiore. Goats grazing by the roadside turned their heads to watch them pass, as if long familiar with Böpfli-Spazzoletta clientele. From somewhere came a repeated figure being played on an alpenhorn.

Though he was not ready to share it with his brother, not even Reef had been exempt from the folly up there. "What kind of a dog's that?" he asked Ruperta at one point.

"Mouffette? She's a papillon . . . a sort of French ladies' lapdog."

"A— You say," gears in his mind beginning to crank, "'lap'—*French . . . lap-dog?*" Somehow gathering that Ruperta had trained her toy spaniel to provide intimate "French" caresses of the tongue for the pleasure of its mistress. "Well! you two are . . . pretty close then, I guess?"

"I *wuv* my ickle woofwoof, ess I doo!" Squeezing the animal tightly, one would think painfully, except for the apparent enjoyment with which Mouffette was fluttering her eyelids.

"Hmm," said Reef.

"And today I must go across the lake, and the mean old people there won't allow my ickle pwecious to come with Mummy, and we were both wondering if her good Uncle Reef would look after her for the day, see that she gets her chopped filet and her boiled pheasant, as she's *so* particular."

"Sure, you bet!" His thoughts taking wing. The day alone with a French "lap" dog! who might be more than happy to do for Reef what she was obviously already doing for old 'Pert here! who in fact, m-maybe all this time's been just droolin' for one-them penises for a change, and will turn out to know *plenty of tricks!* A-and—

It took a while for Ruperta to get her toilette perfect and her bustle out the door. Reef found himself pacing and smoking, and whenever he took a look over at Mouffette could've sworn she was fidgeting too. The dog, it seemed to Reef, was giving him sidewise looks which if they'd come from a woman you would have had to call flirtatious. Finally after an extended farewell notable for its amount of saliva exchange, Mouffette slowly padded over to the divan where Reef was sitting and jumped up to sit next to him. Jumping on the furniture was something Ruperta seldom allowed her to do, and her gaze at Reef clearly assumed that he would not get upset. Far from it, what he actually got was an erection. Mouffette looked it over, looked away, looked back, and suddenly jumped up on his lap.

"Oboy, oboy." He stroked the diminutive spaniel for a while until, with no warning, she jumped off the couch and slowly went into the bedroom, looking back now and then over her shoulder. Reef followed, taking out his penis, breathing heavily through his mouth. "Here, Mouffie, nice *big dog bone* for you right here, lookit this, yeah, seen many of these lately? *come* on, smells good don't it, mmm, yum!" and so forth, Mouffette meantime angling her head, edging closer, sniffing with curiosity. "That's right, now, o-o-open up . . . *good* girl, good Mouffette now let's just put this—*yaahhgghh!*"

Reader, she bit him. After which, as if surprised at the vehemence of his reaction, Mouffette jumped off the bed and while Reef went looking for an ice bucket, ran off somehow into the vast hotel. Reef chased her for a while but found it was getting him funny looks from the staff.

In the days that followed, Mouffette took every occasion to jump up in Reef's lap and gaze into his eyes—sarcastically, it seemed to Reef—opening her mouth suggestively, sometimes even drooling. Each time Reef tried not to flinch. Each time Ruperta, exasperated, would cry, "Honestly, it isn't as if she means to *bite* you."

"REEF, allow me to present Miss Yashmeen Halfcourt. Yash, this strange-lookin old skeezicks is my brother Reef."

"A pleasure, Miss Halfcourt."

"Mr. Traverse." For a minute she had thought she was seeing Kit and his own somehow aged or gravely assaulted double. "I see you move in smart society," shifting her eyes to the Chirpingdon-Groin party.

"Luck of the rails, miss," a roguish readjustment Kit had seen too often beginning to creep among his brother's features. "It seems one day they needed a fourth player for this game they call 'auction' bridge, all the go now in the London clubs, I'm told, scores much higher than the regular bridge game, you see, so if one is playing for so much a point, why . . ." The old wistful shrug, as if to say, *Easy me, what can I do? It's my curse, just a mark who can't resist a big payoff.* Kit with an effort refrained from gazing heavenward.

"Yes. It's very like a Russian game we call *vint.*"

"Heard of that one. Never could catch on to the scoring, though. Maybe you'll teach it to me sometime."

Across the vast reception hall, Ruperta's ears, emerging from her coiffure, were observed to grow rapidly incandescent.

"Well," as she put it later, "your brother's little wog seems to've taken quite a fancy to *you.* He's rather a fresh face himself, perhaps we might arrange a swap, what do you think?"

"Strictly business, 'Pert."

"Obviously. You couldn't call her nobility—the shallowest sort of *avantyuristka,* I can't believe they even let persons like that in the door here, I believe I shall have a word in fact with Marcello."

"Now, 'Pert, try to think back, it wa'n't 'at long ago you were playin pretty much the same hand."

"You hateful beast."

Meantime, Kit and Yashmeen sat eating dinner at a table with a view of the darkening lake and an evening storm sweeping up from the south.

"Reef was always the reckless one," he recalled, "what folks call 'wild,' and Frank was the reasonable one, may've gone crazy now and then for a minute and a half, but I was never around to see it."

"And what about you, Kit?"

"Oh, I was just the baby."

"I think you were the religious one." Hard to tell just then if she was teasing. "Look at what you got into. Sectarian vector wars, trafficking with the unseen, priesthoods and heresies . . ."

"Guess it was always pretty practical for me." It wasn't, but he'd have to wait for some three o'clock mathematician's insomnia to work any of that through.

She was looking at him meanwhile in a way he knew he should be smart enough to decipher. "In the world. Of the world. No," shaking her head, "vows of abstinence, or . . ."

It did not help his abrupt discombobulancy that Yashmeen had showed up looking exceptionally radiant, her black hair pouring all the way down to her waist, where it whispered against the bow at the back of a frock that seemed made only to flirt in, her mouth carefully rouged in a shadowy cerise into the first derivative of a kiss of unknown duration. . . . Just damned impossibly nifty, is what he supposed he meant.

"No money in Vectors," he blurted, "that's a whole range of luxury items right there. Abstinence takes care of itself, pretty much."

"But there was no end to the distraction. Did you expect quite so much? I didn't. There always seemed to be something." She glanced his way, experimentally. "Someone."

"Oh," his pulse growing percussive, "helps to be easy on the eyeballs, no doubt."

She was smiling, but with her eyes narrowed. Seemed to be waiting for him to pursue the thought, though he had no idea where. "Well," cursing himself in the instant, "I wonder what that old Günni's been up to. Must be in Mexico by now."

Her eyes drifted away, as if into some private realm of annoyance. "Would you really have fought a duel over me, Kit?"

"You mean Günni and me both, or just me?" What was wrong with his brain here?

"You, Kit."

It called for at least a moment of speculative gazing, but Kit only bounced back, "Why sure, who wouldn't?" She waited an extra heartbeat, then put down her glass and looked around for her reticule. "I say something?"

"You *didn't* say something." She was on her feet and extending a gloved hand. *"Ite, Missa est."*

Lionel Swome had no objection to Kit dossing at the Sanatorium, and Reef found him in his room opening the free bottle of Champagne that had come with it.

"Just got here in time."

"I was fixing to drink it all, but I could let you have a couple cc's maybe."

"Hey! cheer up there, runt o' the litter. Guess what?"

"Do I have to?"

"Maybe this time we've caught us a good hand for a change."

Kit blasted the cork across the room, knocking askew a sepia photographic portrait of Böpfli and Spazzoletta, posed beside a hydropathic pump. He drank the overflow and handed the bottle over. "Your idea of a good hand."

"It's your ol' benefactor Scarsdale Vibe."

Kit was instantly on rectal alert. His hands ached and he began to sweat. "Seems he's over here in Europe," Reef went on, "lookin to buy some of that Fine Art, all up and down the continent doin what the millionaires do. And at the moment, in fact, he's right in the neighborhood, headin for Venice Italy—"

"Foley mentioned it already. Wasn't good news then, ain't now."

"Depends, don't it. Fate is handin this one right to us, Kit, there might never be a better time."

"For . . ."

Reef peered at his kid brother, as if into a shadowy room. "Still too early to fold. Hand ain't been called yet."

Kit went over to the window and looked at weather racing up the lake to collide with the mountains. His policy of juvenile optimism no matter what was beginning to annoy even him, besides not working anymore anyway. "And who," in sudden great weariness, "'s running with Vibe these days? Besides Foley, that is."

"Could be one or two other Pinks in the brush, we'd sure have to keep an eye out."

"So we're going to find him and kill him, is that the plan?"

Reef pretended to squint upward at his brother through an imaginary telescope. "Well *you* sure are a bloodthirsty customer for being so short 'n' all."

"Then—we don't kill him? Reefer? What *do* we do?" Since the last time he'd been face-to-face with Scarsdale Vibe, at the Pearl Street offices, Kit had little trouble imagining himself aiming and firing with a steady hand and a composed spirit. It had come to this anyway. This far.

Reef on the other hand looked to be all passion and no plan. "Rifle at long range, sure, but face-to-face'd be better, say we took more of a, don't know, Italian approach? How are you with a dirk? I can back you up—glue on some false mustachios—pretend to be a waiter or something, maybe, maybe bring him a glass of *poison Champagne*—"

"Reef, we, um, better think this one through?" Was Reef figuring somehow on Kit, the scientific one, to come up with a plan?

"Too bad we can't talk to Pa."

"According to some of Yashmeen's friends—"

"Oh not you too, I got to listen to this stuff day and night from 'Pert and that bunch, little of it goes a long way, brother."

"They do séances?" Kit reached for the packet of smokes on the table between them and lit one up. "And you never tried to contact Pa? Just curious."

"Nothin but some fad thing for them. They do rope me in time to time, don't mind, 'specially if it's next to some interestin young lady, never can tell what hand-holdin in the dark can lead to—but I don't talk about Pa, or us, or Colorado, none of that. They think I'm from your part of the country, Harvard and so forth."

"Yale."

"You bet, but, now, you're worryin me here a little, Kit, supposed to be this hardcased man of science?"

Kit shrugged inside an envelope of smoke. "Don't know how scientific it is, but lately there's this 'Psychical Research'—laboratories, experiments and so forth."

"And ain't it just the bunk."

"So were wireless waves, and not all that long ago. Roentgen rays, whatever rays are coming next. Seems every day somebody's discovering another new piece of the spectrum, out there beyond visible light, or a new extension of the mind beyond conscious thought, and maybe someplace far away the two domains are even connected up."

Reef shook his head as if embarrassed. "They build a wireless telephone that we can talk to Pa on it, you'll let me know, won't you."

As it turned out, that evening, as dusk crept over the rooms and suites, something like this very piece of equipment was about to materialize on their earthly plane, in the person of Madame Natalia Eskimoff. The kindly ecstatica, luminous from hiking up in the mountains, grasped right away their melancholy, if not their longer-term plans for revenge. She leaned against the walnut hotel bar still in her excursion suit, sipping at some ancient Scotch from a heavy tumbler of Bohemian crystal engraved with unreadable Böpfli-Spazzoletta heraldry, regarding the brothers amiably but with her own parameters for patience. "I do hope you're not after mumbo jumbo in the dark," she said, "glowing giant amœbas that leave sticky residues. White-faced children in nightclothes who glide room to room, whose feet don't touch the floor."

In P.R. circles Madame Eskimoff's séances were known, you'd say notorious, for their impertinence. "As if the presences one encounters are so fragile they will get offended, or sulk, if the question is too direct. *Bozhe moi!* these people are dead! How much more rude does it get?"

They found a room, closed the drapes against the insupportable night, the waxing gibbous moon and the mountain heights almost as bright, inaccessible as the country of death, stars revealed now and then through snow blown in long veils off the peaks, miles of continental wreckage sweeping, frozen, neutral ground, uninhabited, uninhabitable, forever. Madame Eskimoff turned down the lights. The sitters included Kit, Reef, Yashmeen, and Ruperta, there to supervise the politics of who sat next to whom.

"I'm going upcountry, going to be harder to keep in touch, other things to do, further away though when you all get here we'll be together again, hope you're takin care of all them chores I used to seein's it's less important to me now, less and less, and there never was much I could do to help anyway. . . ."

The voice emerging from the darkly painted lips of Madame Eskimoff, slurred, effortful, as if brought upward against the paralysis of dream, spoke Webb's words but bore little resemblance to what either brother could remember of Webb's voice. They listened for the stogie-smoker's hoarseness, the ridgerunner's twang, but what they heard was European, more like the cross-border inflections that reps and drummers and spies on that continent pick up after years there out in the field. The concluding silence, when it came, was sharp as a cry. Color returned to Madame Eskimoff's face, tears collected in her eyes. But when she surfaced, she had no memory of sorrow, or indeed any emotion.

"It wasn't even Pa's voice," Reef in an angry whisper. "I tell you, Kit, it's just a con game."

"That was the voice of her control," Yashmeen pointed out. "Also a go-between, but working from the other side. We use mediums, mediums use controls."

"No disrespect," Reef murmured, "but speakin as a old bunco man myself, that's just the kind of dodge I'd use if I didn't know what the deceased sounded like but wanted folks to think it was him talkin. . . ." He was surprised to see Madame Eskimoff nodding and smiling, as if in gratitude.

"Fraud is the element in which we all fly, isn't it," she said, "it bears us aloft, there isn't one of us hasn't been up on fraud, one time or another, before some damned beak of the materialistic—'Ha! I saw that, what's that going on with the toe of your shoe there?' Insufferably smug guardians of the daylit world, no idea of how easy it is to detect that sort of mischief, usually from mediums who cannot manage a trance. Some never will. It requires great capacity for surrender, and a willingness to forgo any memory of what went on during it."

"Well, and that's mighty convenient too, don't you think?"

"I do indeed, and when I hear doubts like yours, what I usually suggest is that the doubter try it for himself."

"What you just did? Thanks but I'm not a very supernatural type of fella—"

"You can never be sure, the gift shows up in the strangest people." She gently took Reef's wrist and led him back to the table.

"It ain't so much going into it," he was trying to explain, "it's 'at comin out again."

"You'll do fine."

"I mean I'd hate to get, uh . . ."

"Stuck."

"There you go." Yashmeen and a flâneur of Ruperta's acquaintance named Algie arranged a quick foursome, as if it was going to be a bridge game. No sooner had the sitters joined hands than Reef was under, like that, off in some sub-ecstasy. Next thing anybody knew, he was singing, operatically, in the tenor register and the Italian language, though Kit knew for a fact that Reef was tone-deaf, couldn't get through "For He's a Jolly Good Fellow" without changing key. After a while whoever the control was arrived at a high C and held it long enough to send Sanatorium staff running off to find medical assistance.

"I seen others who died in bed," Webb began to speak, really Webb this time, "in easy reach of all they built and loved, surrounded at the end by the children, the grandchildren, friends, folks from town that nobody knew their names, but that wasn't in the cards for me, not in that flat-broke world it was given us to work and suffer in, those were just not the choices.

"No point makin excuses. I could've done 'er different. Not driven you all away. Figured how to honor those who labor down under the earth, strangers to the sun, and still keep us all together. Somebody must've been smart enough to manage that one. I could've worked it out. Not as if I was alone, there was help, there even was money.

"But I sold my anger too cheap, didn't understand how precious it was, how I was wasting it, letting it leak away, yelling at the wrong people, May, the kids, swore each time I wouldn't, never cared to pray but started praying for that, knew I had to keep it under some lid, save it at least for the damned owners, but then Lake sneaks off into town, lies about it, one of the boys throws me a look, some days that's all it needs is a look, and I'm screamin again, and they're that much further away, and I don't know how to call back any of it. . . ."

It could have been a heart-to-heart in some friendly saloon. But the one thing his sons wanted, they wouldn't get tonight. They wanted to hear Webb say, with the omnidirectional confidence of the dead, that seeing Scarsdale Vibe had hired his killers, the least the brothers could do at this point was to go find him and ventilate the son of a bitch.

Afterward, as expected, Reef couldn't remember a thing. Madame Eskimoff and Yashmeen went off to the Turkish baths, and Algie headed for the billiard room. Kit sat down at the table and looked across it at his brother. "I didn't do anything real embarrassin, did I?" Reef wanted to know.

"It was him, Reef. His voice, hell you even *looked* like him."

"Could've been the light."

"I sure don't know what to believe."

"Take a picture next time. Whenever that is." Reef oddly unsure of himself. He gazed resentfully at his hat. "Look at me. This hat. What am I doing here with these people? I thought I made my choice back in New Orleans. Thought it was Anarchism from here on in all the way till they couldn't afford to have me around 'cause it's the type of persuasion only has one outcome don't it. Kit." It almost sounded like a call for help. "I don't even know who I fuckin am anymore."

IN THE DREAM they are all together at a social of some kind, it is unnamed but familiar high country, spruce and aspens, water running everywhere, creeks, ponds, fountains, more food than a church supper, cooks in those tall cooks' hats carving and dishing it out, barbecued ribs and baked beans, ice-cream cones and sweet-potato pies, presentable girls, many of them distant relatives, each face all but unbearably distinct, familiar though never met before, fiddles and guitars and an accordion and people dancing, and off at the edge of it Kit sees his father alone at a wood picnic table with a pack of cards, playing poker solitaire. He notices at the time the cards are not only marked with numbers, they somehow *are* numbers, some real, some imaginary, some complex and even transcendent, Webb setting them each time in a five-by-five matrix whose eigenvalue situation is not so straightforward, but in parallel to this Kit is still about six years old, and goes running over to Webb. "You all right, Papa?"

"Real dandy, Christopher. Everthin all right with you?"

"I thought you looked, looked like you were feeling lonely?"

"Just 'cause I'm sittin here alone? Sakes, alone ain't lonely. Ain't the same thing at all. They didn't teach you that yet in school? Here." The boy comes in close and stands awhile in Webb's one-arm embrace, while Webb continues to lay down the cards, making remarks—"Well look at this," or "Now what do I do here?" and Kit's trying to identify characteristic polynomials, at the same time nestling close to his father as he can get. "There's worse than being lonely, son," Webb tells him after a while. "And you don't die of it, and sometimes you even need it." But just as Kit's about to ask what you need it for, something out in the great never-sleeping hydropathic, a sneeze, a dropped omelette pan, a swamper whistling, woke him up.

Kit coalesced slowly into the dark institutional hour when guests deferred to all day lay shelved, numbered, irrelevant. Confused for a moment, thinking he was somehow in jail, that the sounds of the place going about its slow digestive life were all voices and flows and mechanical repetitions he was forbidden to hear in daytime, he stared mouth-upward at nothing, hope, or maybe only the *vis inertiæ* which had kept him till now in motion, draining away—approaching a terrible certainty he couldn't immediately name but which he knew he had to live under the weight of now.

He must have wanted all along to be the one son Webb could believe in—no matter what kind of trouble Reef might be rambling around out there looking to get into, or how pro- or anti-Union Frank's engineering ambitions might turn out to be, Kit had always thought he would be there for his father no matter what, if only because there was nothing in the way of it, nothing he could see. But then just like that there he was, out of the house and down in the meanest part of the U.S., and before he could even remember who he was, Webb was gone. If he could only've been surer of Kit, maybe when the awful hour came to claim him, he could have fought back by just enough extra will to survive after all. Restricted now to séances and dreams, he could no longer say this to Kit in so many words but must use the stripped and dismal metonymies of the dead.

Just because Webb hadn't denounced him tonight didn't mean Kit was off the hook. He had betrayed his father, that wouldn't change—collaborated with his father's murderers, lived the rich-kid life they were paying him to live, and now that that was over, he understood that whatever he might want to use for an excuse, it couldn't be his youth anymore, or what might be left of his compromised innocence. He had turned against Webb the night he got back from Colorado Springs with Foley's proposition, and had made no effort to make it right, till it was too late to do anything right.

He lay there, sick and hollow with shame. How had this happened? What used to be home was five thousand miles away now and another couple-three straight up and down, and the only one back there who mattered anymore was Mayva, the dwindling, resolute figure at the depot, in the wind and the immense sunlight, the weight of all the shining metal under the earth balanced against her and what she wanted, which God knows had always been little enough. "Your Pa spent most of his life down there. . . . All he gave them, for what he got back . . . their bought-and-sold vermin, and there's still traces of his blood all up and down this country, still crying out, that's if blood was known to cry out, o' course—"

It might have been comforting to think of himself as one of Yashmeen's holy wanderers, but he knew the closest he'd ever got to a religion was Vectors, and that too was already receding down a widening interval of space-time, and he didn't know how to get back to it any more than Colorado. Vectorism, in which Kit once thought he had glimpsed transcendence, a coexisting world of imaginaries, the "spirit realm" that Yale legend Lee De Forest once imagined he was journeying through, had not shown Kit, after all, a way to escape the world governed by real numbers. His father had been murdered by men whose allegiance, loudly and often as they might invoke Jesus Christ and his kingdom, was to that real axis and nothing beyond it. Kit had sold himself a bill of goods, come to believe that Göttingen would be another step onward in some journey into a purer condition, conveniently forgetting that it was still all on the Vibe ticket, paid for out of the very account whose ledger he most wished to close and void, the spineless ledger of a life once unmarked but over such a short time broken, so broken up into debits and credits and too many details left unwritten. And Göttingen, open to trespass by all manner of enemies, was no longer a refuge, nor would Vectors ever have been Kit's salvation.

Someplace out ahead in the fog of futurity, between here and Venice, was Scarsdale Vibe. The convergence Kit had avoided even defining still waited its hour. The man had been allowed to go on with his dishonorable work too long without a payback. All Kit had anymore. All there was to hold on to. All he had.

As light began to seep in around the edges of the window blinds, Kit fell asleep again and dreamed of a bullet en route to the heart of an enemy, traveling for many years and many miles, hitting something now and then and ricocheting off at a different angle but continuing its journey as if conscious of where it must go, and he understood that this zigzagging around through four-dimensional space-time might be expressed as a vector in five dimensions. Whatever the number of n dimensions it inhabited, an observer would need one extra, $n + 1$, to see it and connect the end points to make a single resultant.

While Kit struggled through the cheerless and unproductive time of night known to Chinese of his acquaintance as the Hour of the Rat, and Reef was off being entertained in some steamy hydropathic swimming tank with an undetermined number of erotomaniac tourist ladies, Ruperta Chirpingdon-Groin was wrapping up an all-night frolic with Yashmeen, most of which regrettably had been passed in negotiation—there was to be no question of sweet equality or even symmetry. As this process of counter-feinting, flirtation, and deception carried its own low-intensity erotic energy, it did not apparently collapse into the bothersome chore it too often becomes for men and women, so the long evening wasn't a total loss. Yashmeen had been granted ten minutes' reprieve from worrying about her uncertain future, and Ruperta's jealousy, a beast with an exotic dietary, had been fed. The women were in fact surprised to find a sky full of morning light outside the curtains, the sun about to clear the peaks, a sailboat or two already out on the lake.

All the world in love with love, except it seemed for Kit, whose desires were consulted by no one, least of all himself. When he and Yashmeen met in the Kursaal later in the day, both were disoriented from lack of sleep, and his announcement of a detour to Venice for purposes of vendetta might have exhibited a certain bluntness.

"Can I square this with Brother Swome? He says I need to pick up the train to Constantza, and according to the schedule he gave me, there's some extra time to get there. How much of a hurry do you reckon he's in?"

"I think getting me out of Göttingen was the main point for them. You were a convenient element, you did your job. You needn't feel obligated to them any further."

"But this . . . other thing, we need to see about it while the chance is open. And as long as Reef thinks he needs me to watch his back, I can't walk away from it. And whatever happens, it'll move fast."

She watched him, her brow troubled. "Good job your ticket's to Kashgar, then, isn't it."

"Maybe nothing'll happen."

"Or maybe they'll kill you."

"Yashmeen, the son of a bitch has destroyed my family. What am I—"

"Only envy. You are lucky to have any recourse. A name, someone who can be held to account. Too many of us have to sit foolishly by while something comes out of the dark, strikes, returns to wherever it came from, as if we are too fragile for a world of happy families, whose untroubled destinies require that the rest of us be sacrificed."

"But if it was you, and you had the chance—"

"Of course I would. Kit." A hand on his arm for only as long as it had to be. "My plans are no longer mine to make, these T.W.I.T. people believe that I owe them my continuing survival, and someone has decided now is the moment to collect the debt."

"So they're taking you back to London?"

"First we go to Vienna, and then Buda-Pesth. Some mysterious burst of Psychical Research activity. I gather I am to be an experimental subject, but when I ask for details, they say it would compromise the integrity of the study for me to know too much."

"Is it worth writing you care of the T.W.I.T., or will they open and read your mail?"

"I wish I knew."

"Who can we trust, then?"

She nodded. "Noellyn Fanshawe. We were at Girton together. Here is her address, but don't expect quick replies."

"And your father—"

She handed over a sealed Sanatorium envelope, embossed with the usual grandiose coat of arms.

"What's this? Thought you two only used telepathy." He slipped it into an inside coat-pocket.

Her smile was thin, formal. "Telepathy, marvelous as it is, would not be—you say, 'a patch'?—a patch on the moment you actually put this into his hands."

She'd said more flattering things, he supposed, but none so trusting. He had a quick third-party glimpse of them, renegades keeping up a level of professionalism even if the profession had more or less done with them.

He saw her off from a little quay where a lake steamer waited. T.W.I.T. personages milled around, repeatedly throwing her looks of impatience and, it almost seemed, of reproof. The sky was dark with rushing rain clouds. She wore a simple waist and skirt, and a waterproof with a hood, and no hat. He would not know how to manage cow-eyed pleading even if they gave lessons. He took her hand and shook it formally but didn't let it go right away. "Do you think—"

"We would ever have run away together in real life? no. I find it hard imagining anyone stupid enough to believe we would."

The boat backed into the lake, turned, and she was swept away, not bothering to look back. Kit found Reef nearby, smoking cigarettes, pretending not to notice.

Kit allowed himself for a minute to wonder how many more of these tearless adieux he was supposed to go through before the one he really didn't need, the one that'd finally be one too many.

And here came Neville and Nigel again, drinking opiated highballs of British cough syrup and aerated water from a portable seltzogene they had also been discharging at passersby, causing a spot of grumbling among the T.W.I.T. membership. At the moment the two were on their way to see the comic operetta *Waltzing in Whitechapel, or, A Ripping Romance,* based loosely, and according to some reviews tastelessly, on the Whitechapel murders of the late '80s.

"Aahh!" Neville was peering at his reflection in the mirror. "Bags! *Piggott's* should have such 'bags'!"

"Do come along Lewis," said Nigel, "we've an extra ticket."

"Yes, and by the way," said Neville, "here's something else," but Lew easily dodged the stream of seltzer, which hit Nigel instead.

That evening the Strand, as if by some consensus, was exhibiting that sinister British craving for the dark and shiny so well known to experts in erotic neuropathy, not to mention students of the chimpanzee—crowds in mackintoshes, patent boots, and top hats, the soiled allure of marcasite brooches and earrings, pomaded temples struck to chill glitter in the public lighting . . . even the pavement, slick with rain and oily exudations, contributing its own queasy albedo. The streetlighting carried, for those, such as Neville and Nigel, who could hear it, the luminous equivalent of a steady, afflicted shriek.

Up and down the street, buskers pranced and spun before the theatre queues—conjurors produced small animals from nowhere, tumbling routines featured skull-and-pavement clearances running typically in the millimeter range, while just in front of the Duke of Cumberland's Theatre a ukulele quartet were playing and singing a medley of tunes from *Waltzing in*

Whitechapel, including one intended to be sung Gilbert and Sullivan style by a chorus of constables to a matching number of streetwalkers—

You know, it's . . .
Only copper propa-
gaaaan-da, that
Policemen never woo, woo, woo!
—You
Know I'd be just as cud-dly as a
Paaaan-da,
If only-I-knew,
You wan-ted-to-cud-dle-me too! E-
-ven in Ken-ya, Tangan-yi-ka and U-
gaaaan-da,
It's not that unheard of . . .
Coz it's a
Proper crop o' propa-
gaaaanda, that
A flat-tie can't fall in love!

In the theatre, Lew dropped a shilling into the box on the back of the seat in front of him, took out a pair of opera-glasses, and began scanning the crowd. The moving field came to rest at length on whom but the co-tenant of Tarot card XV, Professor P. Jotham Renfrew, apparently down from Cambridge taking in a show, his face flattened into a lurid two-dimensional chromo of itself, sitting in a box with somebody in a foreign uniform, whom it took Lew only a moment more to recognize as his former fellow Archduke-minder, the Trabant Captain, now regular K. & K. Landwehr Colonel, Max Khäutsch, hardly changed from the Chicago days, unless perhaps grown slightly more mineral, toward the condition of a statue in a park frequented by the irregular of spirit.

Lew had little time to dwell on the past, however, for with a great crash of cymbals the orchestra began to play the overture.

Waltzing in Whitechapel turned out to be one of those modern works in which a group of players are struggling to put on a musical comedy *about* Jack the Ripper, "Rather than letting old Jack just go carving about under his own steam," as Nigel began to complain during the applause for the first number.

"But honestly Nigel, it would be an actor up there in any case, wouldn't it," objected Neville.

"Well that may be so Neville," furtively removing from his coat a silver flask of Morphotuss cough preparation and taking a belt or two, "but as it's an actor playing an actor playing Jack, why that's so artificial don't you agree?"

"Yes but it's all artificial Nigel, including the blood everyone's come for, and one must simply get over that mustn't one."

"If you'd prefer real blood," advised a quiet voice from a seat behind them, "I'm sure something could be arranged."

"I say," Neville shifting in his seat as if to look back.

"For pity's sake, Neville," hissed Nigel, crazed eyeballs flickering to and fro, "don't turn round, it could be *Him.*"

At intermission, Lew headed for the bar and found Colonel Khäutsch already working on a brandy and soda. If he was surprised to see Lew, he had grown professionally weary enough over the years not to show it.

"Business, eternal business. One would prefer two weeks' furlough in Berlin, but *K. und K.* matters often oblige one to postpone one's entertainments. . . ." Khäutsch shrugged with his eyebrows at different heights. "There I am, complaining again. *Sowieso*. . . . How is your life progressing, Lewis? You are not still working as a 'spotter'?"

"Not lately, more like a hired goon. You're not still riding herd on that Franz Ferdinand, are you?"

A sour smile and shake of the head. "The feckless idiot who once drove us mad is exactly the same as he was—how much can these people change, after all? But the Imperium have since found, mercifully, other ways for me to serve them— Ah, but here is someone you may wish to meet." Making his way toward them through the crowd came Professor Renfrew.

Well, not exactly. Lew didn't technically jump, but a number of muscle groups did seem poised to. He resisted the urge to seize himself by the head and perform some violent though as yet dimly imagined readjustment.

"Allow me to present my German colleague, the Professor-Doktor Joachim Werfner."

The German professor sure did look a hell of a lot like Renfrew, though maybe a little more informally turned out, frayed cuffs, uncombed hair, eyeglasses tinted a strange bruised green.

Careful not to seem too impressed by the resemblance, Lew reached to shake hands. "You're visiting London, Professor? How're you enjoying it?"

"Mostly business, though Max has been so kind as to acquaint me with Piccadilly Circus, where one can actually find a species of Munich beer."

"I can sure sympathize, we probably share the same opinion of English beer, it's like drinking your evening dinner."

For a while they discussed what the penny press had been calling the "Ripperetta."

"It is curious," said Khäutsch, "that these Whitechapel murders occurred not that long before the tragedy at Mayerling, which to some of us in Austria has always suggested a common origin."

"Not this again," Werfner pretended to groan.

"One of those strong impressions from youth," explained Khäutsch. "I was in those days a lieutenant who fancied himself a detective, and believed I could solve it."

"Austrian Crown Prince and his girlfriend had a suicide pact or something," Lew tried to recall. "So we ended up with old F.F. instead."

"The world was given a *Liebestod* for romantic fools. The harsher truth is that Rudolf was put out of the way."

Lew looked around. "Should we be . . . ?"

Khäutsch shrugged. "Only a little harmless *Fachsimpelei.* Violent death in high places is of professional interest to us all, not so? The case was closed long ago, and anyway the 'truth' was never as important as what lessons Rudolf's successor, Franz Ferdinand, might draw from it."

"You're saying that somebody at the top—"

Khäutsch nodded solemnly. "Elements who could never have tolerated Rudolf on the throne. He found so little in Austria to admire, and his beliefs were simply too dangerous—he ranted incessantly about our corruption, our worship of the military, especially the German military—he feared the Triple Alliance, saw evidence of the anti-Semitic everywhere, in general he hated the whole Habsburg idea, and was unwise enough actually to publish these opinions, naturally in the Jewish newspapers."

"And the girlfriend—"

"*Ach, die Vetsera.* Dumpy little thing, no one's idea of a grand passion, but just the sort of story to divert an otherwise-fatal public curiosity, *cherchons la femme,* always useful in politics."

"Then who do you think did it?"

"For a while my favorite suspect was the Emperor's chamberlain, Count Montenuovo—but then one day I had my illumination from above, and knew that it must really have been Jack the Ripper"—general muttering—"himself, working under contract. Considering that he disappeared from London around November of '88, and Mayerling was at the end of January '89—time enough for Jack to get to Austria and become familiar with his target, yes?"

"They were shot, Max," protested Werfner with exaggerated gentleness, "not butchered. Jack was not a firearms person, the only similarity is that the list of suspects in the 'Ripper' case is also long enough to populate a small city, each more plausible than the one before, the stories, one by one, convince us utterly, that here, at last, must surely be the true Ripper, inconceivable that anyone else *could* have done it—until the *next* fanatic steps forward to make his or her case. Hundreds, by now thousands, of narratives, all equally valid—what can this mean?"

"Multiple worlds," blurted Nigel, who had floated in from elsewhere.

"Precisely!" cried the Professor. "The Ripper's 'Whitechapel' was a sort of momentary antechamber in space-time . . . one might imagine a giant *railway-depot,* with thousands of gates disposed radially in all dimensions, leading to tracks of departure to all manner of alternate Histories. . . ."

Chinese gongs, vigorously bashed, announced that the second act was about to begin. They all arranged to meet afterward at a reception in one of the gigantic hotels off Trafalgar Square and, when they arrived, found it seething with a cosmopolitan throng whose elements could not always be easily identified, among bushels of cut flowers, thoughtfully turned-out young women, valets on tiptoes and Champagne on ice, deep carpeting, and electric chandeliers. A small dance orchestra played, while couples experimented with the "Boston." People in turbans and fezzes were observed. Neville and Nigel after a quick survey chose the most lethal drink at the bar, currently the rage in London, a horrible combination of porter and Champagne known as a "Velvet."

Being good sports, they did put in with chitchat from time to time until, all but invisible to the others, a certain Oriental Presence was detected going out the door. "I say," said one to the other, exchanging a meaningful look as, humming together, in "Chinese" harmony, the widely-known pentatonic theme

Tngtngtngtng tong-tong
Tng-tng tong . . . ,

the two hopheads drifted off, mindless as sailors. Soon after that a seraphic youth in a lounge suit came gliding by, his nearer eyeball seeming to roll a fraction of a degree in Colonel Khäutsch's direction, and Khäutsch, likewise excusing himself, disappeared into his own labyrinth of desire.

The Professor-Doktor put in his monocle and had a squint at Lew, which rapidly became a sort of *confidential twinkle.* "You and Max actually looked after the Crown Prince at one time?"

"Oh, Chicago—back when the Prince was a pup. I was in it only a week and a half, Colonel Khäutsch did all the work."

"You would be surprised, perhaps appalled, at what has become of Franz Ferdinand. In somewhat indecent eagerness to ascend the throne when

Franz Josef dies, he has set up his own shadow-state at the Belvedere, the great palace once built for Prince Eugene of Savoy. His circle are difficult people to admire, their motives do not always coincide perfectly with those of the Ballhausplatz, the Crown Prince himself entertaining most unwholesome fantasies, for example about Bosnia, which Max fears will land us all in great trouble one day—and Max is never mistaken, his grasp of the Balkan situation is unequaled in Europe."

"He says the same about you."

Werfner shrugged. "My market value tends to fluctuate. At the moment it is up, because of the Anglo-Russian Entente. Germany spent years trying to keep the two countries apart, and must now sit and watch all that careful work come unraveled. So to anyone with a thought on the subject, the Wilhelmstraße, perhaps ten minutes longer than customary, might be paying attention."

Lew listened guardedly to this impersonation of a *gemütlicher alter Junge*. According to most of the Werfner stories he'd heard, lives by the trainload were said to hang on his every pause for breath. The mystery of why Werfner should be in town at all, so far out of his ground, so close to his British adversary, would not go away. There persisted the classic nightmare scene of the man who is standing *where he should not be*. Despite both professors' frequent and strenuous denials of twinship, some symmetry was being broken. Violated. It was enough to drive Lew back to his pernicious habit of Cyclomite-nibbling. He went looking for a W.C. in which to do this, though he supposed he could surreptitiously spread the stuff on a biscuit and administer it that way.

"WERFNER'S IN LONDON," Lew told the Cohen next day.

"So the two N's have reported." It seemed to Lew that the Cohen was looking at him strangely. More than strangely, and how strange was that? "Things are becoming odd. We've other ops on station, of course, but I think that from here on you'll be authorized—trusted—to take any initiative you see fit. Should an opportunity arise."

Lew heard a somber note. "Cohen, could you get specific?"

"Metaphorical will have to do. Think of those two professors as 'sidewinders' out on the trail. Sometimes a man has the luck to avoid them. Sometimes he must take other steps."

"You're not suggesting . . ."

"I'm not suggesting anything. It would be better to have everyone prepared, that's all." Little Nick Nookshaft's eyes held oh, so wide, lips in a small circle.

It did not descend all at once upon Lew's understanding what this meant—much less what it was they'd been playing him for all this time—but it didn't take that long either. Somehow, having managed to get through a nice stretch over here in England free of gunplay, unexpected knife deployment, blows from saps, fists, or handy items of furniture, he had grown foolishly to expect that throwdowns and death maybe were not going to figure quite as prominently in case-resolution as they once had, back there in the old days in the U.S. How civilized, how English he thought he'd become, while the T.W.I.T., it was now growing clear to him, had just gone on, with it mattering nary a bedbug's ass if he wore a cowboy hat or a City bowler, or what English vowel sounds or hidden social codings he might've learned, for when the hole cards were all turned up at last, here he was, nothing more than their hired gunslinger from the States, on ice, held ready for some terrible hour.

But one thing about London, hurt pride didn't hurt for long, because there was always another insult just around the corner waiting to be launched. Much more intriguing right now was the Cohen's utter lack of surprise about the news that Werfner was in town. It could have been some deep talent of the Cohen's for putting on a poker face, but then again, suppose . . .

Lew sought out the two N's, who had been eating raspberries marinated in ether, and now, giggling, found themselves unable to keep from singing, and repeating da capo, a tune from the third act of *Waltzing in Whitechapel,* which Nigel accompanied with ukulele chords, thus—

Oh, Sing-
-ing Bird,
Of Spital-fields—
How lonely i'-all-feels,
Wiv-out your mel-
o-dee! When shall my
Brick Lane bunt-ing
Chirp-again,
To my throbbing-brain,
Her dear refrain,
Soft-leee? Al-
though it's spring
In Stepney, so-we're-told,
Here in my
Heart-it's-cold
As any-win-

try sea—until my
Singing Bird of
Spit-alfields,
Perched on her lit-tle heels,
Comes trip-ping back,
To meee!
—(My dar-ling),
[D.C.]

During a pause for breath, Lew ventured, "You boys have studied with Professor Renfrew, right?"

"Yes, at Kings," Neville said.

"And Professor Werfner, whom we ran into at the theatre last night—wasn't he just a dead ringer for Renfrew?"

"His hair was different," Nigel mused.

"Clothing a bit more distressed as well, I thought," added Neville.

"But Neville, you're the one that said, 'Oh I say Nigel, whyever is Professor Renfrew talking in that droll German accent?' And you said, 'But Neville it can't be old Renfrew you know, not with those frightful shoes,' and you—"

But Lew just then was seeing something extraordinary, something he would never have dreamed possible with these two—they were exchanging signals, not exactly warnings but cues of hand and eye, the way actors in a vaudeville skit might—they were *impersonating British idiots.* And in that luminous and tarnished instant, he also understood, far too late in the ball game, that Renfrew and Werfner were one and the same person, had been all along, that this person somehow had the paranormal power to be in *at least* two places at the same time, maintaining day-to-day lives at two different universities—and that everybody at the T.W.I.T. had known all about this, known forever, most likely—everybody except for Lew. Why hadn't anybody told him? What *else* could they be using him for, that required keeping him that blindly in the dark? He should have felt more riled about it but guessed it was no more disrespect than normal, for London.

Once he was willing to accept the two professors as a single person, Lew felt curiously released, as if from a servitude he had never fully understood the terms of anyway. Well. Take his money and call him Knucklehead. So it was simple as that.

He spent the rest of the day upstairs among the T.W.I.T. library stacks, trying to reduce his ignorance some. There turned out to be several shelves of books and manuscripts, some in languages he didn't even recognize, let alone read, on the strange and useful talent of being two places or more at once, known in the Psychical field for about fifty years as "bilocation." North Asian shamans in particular seemed to be noted for it. The practice had begun to filter into ancient Greece around the seventh century B.C., and become a feature of Orphic, and presently Pythagorean, religions. It was not a matter of possession by spirits, demons, or in fact any outside forces, but rather a journey the shaman took from within—observing a structure, from what Lew could gather, much like dreaming, in which one version of you remains behind, all but paralyzed except for basic activities like snoring and farting and rolling over, while another goes calmly off to worlds unexpected, to fulfill obligations proper to each of them, using daytime motor skills often extended into such areas as flying, passing through walls, performing athletic miracles of speed and strength. . . . And this traveling double was no weightless spook—others could see it solid and plain enough, in fact too plain, many reporting how figure and ground were kept separate by an edge, overdefined and glimmering, between two distinct *kinds of light*. . . .

At some point Dr. Otto Ghloix, a visiting alienist from Switzerland whom Lew recognized from the T.W.I.T. mess-hall, stuck his head around a corner, and they fell into conversation.

"This person Renfrew/Werfner appears afflicted," it presently seemed to Dr. Ghloix, "by a deep and fatal contradiction—deeper than consciously he can appreciate, and as a result the conflict has no other place to go but outward, ejected into the outside world, there to be carried out as what technically we call *Schicksal*—Destiny—with the world around him now obliged to suffer the disjunction in himself which he cannot, must not, admit . . . so pretending to be two 'rivals' representing the interests of two 'separate nations' which are much more likely secular expressions of a rupture within a single damaged soul.

"And after all, who better than a fallen geographer to be acting this out, to occupy Number XV, The Devil—someone who might have answered the higher calling, learned the secret geographies of the *beyul,* or hidden lands, and brought the rest of us in our raggedness and dust, our folly and ignorance, to far Shambhala, and rebirth in the Pure Land? What crime more reprehensible than to betray that sacred obligation for the shoddy rewards to be had from Whitehall or the Wilhelmstraße?"

"I guess what's bothering me right at the moment," said Lew, "is how much coöperation he's had—I guess I say 'he'—from folks here at the T.W.I.T."

"Because no one told you what they knew."

"Well wouldn't you take it a little, I don't know, personally?"

"You may not need to, it is after all quite common in these occult orders to find laity and priesthood, hierarchies of acquaintance with the Mysteries, secret initiation at each step, the assumption that one learns what one has to only when it is time to. No one decides this, it is simply the dynamic imperative operating from within the Knowledge itself."

"Oh." Lew was able to keep a straight face, nod, and silently roll himself a cigarette, which he lit up in the deepening dusk from the coal of Dr. Ghloix's Corona. "Simplifies things, in a way," he supposed, through an exhalation of Turkish smoke. "Considering the time I might have gone on wasting with detective stuff. Trying to get their two stories to jibe—eyewitness accounts, ticket stubs, surveillance reports, hell, if any of it ever came to court, well there'd go the whole concept of an alibi, wouldn't it?"

After the Doc had taken his leave, and dark had fallen, and Lew had lit a small Welsbach unit on the table, and the dinner gong, hushed by distance, had sounded, who should appear but the Grand, soon to be Associate, Cohen, bringing a tray with a tall glass of parsnip juice and some vegetarian analogue of the Melton Mowbray Pork Pie cooling on a china plate. "We missed you at supper."

"Guess I lost track of the time. Thanks."

"There's to be a poetry reading in here tonight, Indian bloke, mystical stuff, quite a smash with the sisters, perhaps you'd help me light off the old P.L." by which he meant the *Plafond Lumineux,* a modern mixed arrangement of gas-mantles and electric incandescent bulbs arching across the entire library ceiling and covered by a pale translucent canopy of some proprietary celluloid which smoothed these sources, when at last they had all been lit, into a depthless dome of light somehow much brighter than their sum.

The Cohen glanced at the table where Lew had been reading and taking notes. "Bilocation, eh? Fascinating topic. Rather up your street I imagine, stepping back and forth over thresholds sort of thing."

"Maybe I'll go in the shaman business, find some nice li'l igloo, hang out my shingle."

Cohen Nookshaft's expression was not unsympathetic. "You'd have to get cracking, learn a systematic approach. Years of study—if it was what you wanted."

"If it was what I wanted."

They stood and watched the ceiling, its smooth and steady radiance. "Quite pleasant, isn't it," said the Cohen. "Of course it helps to have some allegiance to light."

"How's that?"

As if imparting a secret Lew could not help thinking he had somehow, without knowing how, become ready to hear, the Cohen said, "We are light, you see, all of light—we are the light offered the batsmen at the end of the day, the shining eyes of the beloved, the flare of the safety-match at the high city window, the stars and nebulæ in full midnight glory, the rising moon through the tram wires, the naphtha lamp glimmering on the costermonger's barrow. . . . When we lost our æthereal being and became embodied, we slowed, thickened, congealed to"—grabbing each side of his face and wobbling it back and forth—"this. The soul itself is a memory we carry of having once moved at the speed and density of light. The first step in our Discipline here is learning how to re-acquire that rarefaction, that condition of light, to become once more able to pass where we will, through lantern-horn, through window-glass, eventually, though we risk being divided in two, through Iceland spar, which is an expression in crystal form of Earth's velocity as it rushes through the Æther, altering dimensions, and creating double refraction. . . ." He paused at the door. "Atonement, in any case, comes much later in the journey. Do have something to eat, there's a good chap."

ONLY THING TO do really was to try and take Renfrew by surprise. On the way up to Cambridge once again, English country, green and misty, booming past, brick courses inside the little tunnels spinning by in helical purity, the smell of fens, the distant reach of water-sky reflecting the German Sea, for the first time in a good while Lew felt the desolate stomach-spasms of exile, and found himself longing for Chicago, and an early evening in autumn, with or without an appointment to be kept later in the evening, just about to walk into Kinsley's at suppertime, where there'd be a steak waiting with his name on it.

And then he was running back over the years since Troth had left him, and wondering how much had really happened to him and how much to some other version of Lew Basnight, bilocated off somewhere he could gain no clear sense of. He drifted into one of those minute-and-a-half-long mid-afternoon dozes, whose subject seemed to be the little vest-pocket .25-caliber FN Browning he was packing, nice unit, strictly for self-defense, not the kind of piece you'd go out gunning for anybody with. . . . He woke as a voice, maybe his own, whispered, "Not to mention a good suicide weapon . . ."

Whoa there now, Detective Basnight. It was routine to have these, what were known in the business as Grumpy Thoughts now and then, and he guessed he'd known socially or worked alongside of more than enough Pinks and finks who'd ended up clocking out before shift's end, and who's to say how far Lew might have taken his own contrition at working as long as he had on the wrong side, for the wrong people—though at least he had tumbled early, almost from the start, to how little he really wanted the rewards his colleagues were in it for, the motorcars, lakefront galas, introductions to desirable women or useful statesmen, in an era where "detective" was universally understood code for anti-Union thug . . . somewhere else was the bilocational version of himself, the other, Sherlock Holmes type of sleuth, fighting criminal masterminds hardly distinct from the sorts of tycoons who hired "detectives" to rat on Union activities.

Could be all those Catholics he'd run into in this line of work, Irish and Polish in Chicago, Mexicans in Colorado and so forth, had it right all along, and there was nothing in the day's echoing cycle but penance, even if you'd never committed a sin, to live in the world was to do penance—actually, as his teacher Drave had pointed out back during that winter in Chicago, another argument for reincarnation—"Being unable to remember sins from a previous life won't excuse you from doing penance in this one. To believe in the reality of penance is almost to have proof of rebirth."

He found Renfrew in a hectic mood, as close to desperation as Lew could recall. The Professor's shoes did not match, he seemed to be drinking cold tea out of a flower vase, and his hair was at least as neglected as Werfner's the other night. Lew thought about passing a few pointed Jack the Ripper remarks, just to get the fellow going, but reckoned that Renfrew by now either knew Lew was onto the real story or he was more likely past caring, and in any case it would be a distraction from the business at hand, which Lew had yet to get any inkling of. Renfrew had meantime pulled down a gigantic ten-miles-to-the-inch wall map of the Balkans, in several rarely encountered colors which just failed to be rose, amethyst, orpiment, and cerulean.

"Best procedure when considering the Balkans," instructed Renfrew, "is not to look at components singly—one begins to run about the room screaming after a while—but all together, everything in a single timeless snapshot, the way master chess players are said to regard the board.

"The railroads seem to be the key. If one keeps looking at the map while walking slowly backward across the room, at a certain precise distance the structural principle leaps into visibility—how the different lines connect, how they do not, where varying interests may want them to connect, all of this defining patterns of flow, not only actual but also invisible, potential, and such rates of change as how quickly one's relevant masses can be moved to a given frontier . . . and beyond that the teleology at work, as the rail system grows toward a certain shape, a destiny— My God I'm starting to sound like Werfner.

"Poor fellow. This time he has taken a long walk down Queer Street I fear, far beyond the last stop of any known rail line which can bring him back. He has been working on his own long-range solution to the Macedonian Question, kept secret among the secrets of the Wilhelmstraße but brought only recently to my attention. His plan," one hand poised as if holding an invisible fescue, "is—insanely—to install all across the Peninsula, from a little east of Sofia, here, roughly along the Balkan Range and the Sredna Gora, coincident with the upper border of the former Eastern Roumelia, and continuing on, at last to the Black Sea—*das Interdikt,* as he calls it, two hundred miles long, invisible, waiting for certain unconsidered footfalls and, once triggered, irreversible—pitiless. . . ." He fell silent, as if some agency had been attending and as silently instructed him to go no further.

"And this *Interdikt* concern again, what was it, exactly?" Lew had the sudden certitude that right now in Göttingen some bilocational Lew was asking Werfner the same question, whose answer neither of him wanted to hear but were helpless not to ask. And that in both places both Lew Basnights would be getting the same offended narrow stare.

His recent lack of sleep evident, Renfrew sighed pointedly. "It's long been under study at Charlottenburg, I can assure you of that."

"Thanks, Professor, that clears it up. Well! If there's nothing more, I guess I'll go find a pub and do some deep analysis on this. Care to join me?"

"It's to do with our Gentleman Bomber," blurted Renfrew, "oh, the Gentleman B. is indeed very much in this now, which makes his immediate detection and apprehension that much more necessary you see."

Lew, who didn't see, paused at the door, one eyebrow up encouragingly.

"He has been reported in the Cambridge vicinity," said Renfrew, almost importunate. "On the lurk round Fenner's, as if he were reconnoitering."

"And when's the next cricket match there?"

"Tomorrow, with I.Z."

"All right, say he's fixing to toss one of those suffocation specials of his—what's that got to do with this *Interdikt* scheme of your"—he might have hesitated—"colleague, Dr. Werfner?"

No reply, only weaving now a bit insomniac facing his multicolored map, having moved so close to it that his nose was only an inch—ten miles—above the terrain.

"Poison gas? Werfner plans to use it somehow as part of this *Interdikt*?"

"I'm not at liberty, actually." Whispering.

"But the Gentleman Bomber might be more forthcoming, if somebody could just detain him long enough to ask, is that it? Well. I'll see if I can't round up some more crew for tomorrow, and maybe we'll just get lucky with this galoot."

Lew went over to Fenner's cricket ground, through the owl-light, some rain threatening, just to have a look. There was always the possibility, frankly attractive, that Renfrew had gone off his head at last, owing to the stress of international events. It would certainly make Lew's life easier. But wait now—who was this, standing on the cinder path, in the corruption of late-afternoon light, the world all at once evacuated, as if in response to a civic warning everyone but Lew had heard?

He watched the figure's hands and feet, waiting for the appearance, in the ever-thickening gloom, of a sphere of a certain size. He unbuttoned his suit jacket, and the weight of the little Browning swung itself easily within his reach. The figure might have noted this, for he began to move away. "Say, haven't we met?" called Lew in the most American tones he could locate given the cloudiness and uncertainty of the hour. The reply was a laugh, unexpectedly blithe, and an acceleration off into the evening and the approaching rain. By the time a light drizzle had begun, the stranger had vanished, making no appearance next day, at the match, which I Zingari, beginning on a rather damp pitch, eventually won by eight wickets.

BACK IN LONDON, Lew went out again to Cheapside to consult Dr. Coombs De Bottle, who seemed a bit more tattered and fretful than last time.

"You're the tenth, or perhaps hundredth, person to ask me about carbonyl chloride this week. Somewhere in that order of magnitude. The last time the hierarchy all got this curious, it was just after the Jameson Raid. Now they're driving us mental again. Whatever do you imagine could be afoot?"

"Hoping you could tell me. Just got a fast look at our old pal the Gentleman Bomber, up at Cambridge, but it was too dark to get in a shot at him. What you folks call bad light."

"The Metropolitans have fallen curiously silent about him. I'd rather hoped he'd left the country, like Jack the Ripper or something."

"This phosgene story I heard—it's a different modus, more like a trip-lever concern that just sits there till a target comes along, and all on a much bigger scale than a single bomb-thrower."

"Sounds like a combination of gas projector and land mine," in a tone of mild astonishment, as if this were an altogether new one on him.

"About all I can tell you. Kind of sketchy, I guess."

"Phosgene vaporizes at forty-six degrees Fahrenheit, so it would have to be stored in pressure tanks of some sort. The trip-lever would then, through suitable linkage, simply open a valve. The pressure in the tank could be higher or lower depending on how forcefully one wished to project the gas.

The theory as I understand it is to direct the agent along a line, say against a line of troops advancing. One reckons in weight deployed per unit length of line, say pounds per yard, per hour."

"Try tons per mile."

"Good God. How extensive is this?"

"War Office boys must already know all about it, but the figure I have is two hundred miles. You could talk to them."

THE COHEN WAS INCLINED to a philosophic view. "Suppose the Gentleman B. is not a simple terrorist but an angel, in the early sense of 'messenger,' and in the fateful cloud he brings, despite the insupportable smell, the corrosive suffocation, lies a message?" According to Coombs De Bottle, some did survive the attacks. Even in fatal cases there could be a delay of up to forty-eight hours. Successful treatment was known to require four or five hours of absolute rest. "So phosgene is not a guarantee of certain death," said the Cohen. "And perhaps victims are not meant after all to die, perhaps the Messenger's intention is actually benevolent, a way of enforcing stillness, survival depending as it does upon a state of quiescence in which his message could be contemplated, possibly, later, acted upon . . . ?"

THEN ONE MORNING Lew stumbled down to the breakfast salon to find that everyone had left town. If this had been Colorado, it might have suggested an imminent visit by a sizable party, heeled no doubt and in the mood for triggerplay—in which case leaving town would've been no more than a prudent step. But no one in particular showed up at Chunxton Crescent. Lew waited, but somehow the place only went along, breathing silently, the corridors empty, the wall surfaces inside and out sending back echoes that arrived at each ear a tiny fraction of a second apart, producing an illusion of spirit-presences repeating the words of the living. Acolytes and servants crept about as always, without much to say. Cohen Nookshaft and Madame Eskimoff had vanished, Neville and Nigel as well, no one seemed to be in charge. Deliveries of coal, ice, milk, bread, butter, eggs, and cheese continued to arrive.

It rained. The rain ran down the statuary in the garden. Dripped off the noses of satyrs and nymphs. Lew contemplated a photograph of Yashmeen, in the gray light through the garden windows. He'd had a postal from her a week ago, bearing regular Swiss stamps as well as the bright red private hotel stamp of the Sanatorium Böpfli-Spazzoletta, saying she was off to Buda-

Pesth, no reason given. An impersonation of carefree youth out touring the Continent, it seemed to Lew. Except that the same red stamps were showing everywhere among the daily post at Chunxton Crescent like drops of blood in the snow. Postal cards, envelopes of different sizes, not likely all sent by Yashmeen. Was that where everybody had gone, Switzerland? Without telling Lew, of course. Hired gunhand and so forth, no need, was there.

He surveyed his options. No one here that he could talk to, really, even Otto Ghloix had disappeared, no doubt back to his native Switzerland with everybody else. Lew should have felt more abandoned than he did, but strangely, what it really felt like was a release from a bad contract. Whatever was making them all so distraught, it hadn't occurred to any of them that Lew might've turned out to be of some use. Fine, then. There'd be enough detective work elsewhere in this town to keep the bill-collectors happy, and it was long past time Lew set up on his own anyway. The T.W.I.T. could just go hire another gorilla.

"But it's your destiny!" the Cohen would plead.

"Yes Lewis, here, take a puff of this and think it over."

"Sorry boys, I don't think I'm chasing Tarot cards anymore, no, from here on it's anxious husbands and missing necklaces and exotic poisons for me, thanks."

And if that wasn't exactly who he was either—if, not having wanted much for a while, this wasn't even exactly what he "wanted"—he was determined at least never to have to go back, never to end up again down some gopher-riddled trail through the scabland, howling at the unexplained and unresponsive moon.

Four
Against the Day

Cyprian's first post was at Trieste, monitoring the docks and the emigrant traffic to America, with side trips over to Fiume and newcomer's rounds at the Whitehead torpedo factory and the petroleum harbor, as well as down the coast to Zengg, headquarters of the increasingly energetic New Uskok movement, named after the sixteenth-century exile community who at one time had controlled this end of the Adriatic, then as much a threat to Venice at sea as to the Turks back in the mountains, and even today a dedicated cadre for whom the threat of Turkish inundation, immediate and without mercy, remained living and verifiable. Who continued to wait, all along the Military Frontier, night and day, for the fateful breach—manning the ancient watchtowers and recording on military maps of the region every least spark appearing in the terrestrial night, its compass-bearing and magnitude, keeping ready the dry tinder and paraffin for the alarm beacons, never allowing themselves more than half a minute before deliverance into light. Obvious implications for the Macedonian Question. Heaven knew what esoteric bureaux Cyprian's Neo-Uskok reports found their way in among.

Trieste and Fiume, on either side of the Istrian Peninsula, had both become points of convergence for those in Austria-Hungary seeking to embark for passage west. Most, in the daily streaming of souls, were legitimate, though enough were traveling in disguise that Cyprian must loiter all day at dockside, and keep detailed logs of who was going to America, who was coming back, who was here for the first time. Out and In—like debits and credits, entered on facing pages in his operative's notebook. After a few years of false uttering in a number of hands, allowing a lurid carnival of identities to enter his writing—he had returned to his schoolboy's script, to distant Evensongs, to the wolving of the ancient chapel organ as the last light is extinguished and the door latched for the long night.

At sunset he could be found still lingering down by the docks, looking out to sea. Work did not hold him—sunsets had precedence. The promise of the evening—a density of possibility here that was decidedly absent in places like Zengg. Sailors, it went without saying, sea-creatures everywhere. A sky of milk-blue flesh descending to vermilion at the sea, the theatrically colored light thrown back to stain every west-facing surface . . .

CYPRIAN'S DESCENT into the secret world had begun only the year before in Vienna, in the course of another evening of mindless trolling about the Prater. Without thinking, he had drifted into conversation with a pair of Russians, whom he took, in his state of innocence at the time, to be tourists.

"But you live here in Vienna, we do not understand, what is it that you do?"

"As little as possible, one hopes."

"He means, what is your work?" said the other one.

"Being agreeable. And yours?"

"At this moment? Only a small favor to a friend."

"Of . . . excuse me, a friend of both of you? All quite friendly are we?"

"A pity that one must not quarrel with sodomites. The insolence in his voice, Misha, his face—something ought to be done about it."

"By this friend, perhaps," replied saucy Cyprian. "Who doesn't much care for insolence either, I expect."

"On the contrary, he welcomes it."

"As something he must patiently put up with." Holding his head a little averted, Cyprian kept sneaking glances at them, up and sidewise, through restless lashes.

The other man laughed. "As an opportunity to correct a perverse habit he does not approve of."

"And is he also Russian, like yourselves? knout-fancier, that sort of thing perhaps?"

Not even a pause. "He much prefers his companions unmarked. Nonetheless, you might at least think before using your interesting mouth, while it remains yours to use."

Cyprian nodded, as if chastened. The exquisite reflex of rectal fear passing through him then could have been simple cringing before a threat, or a betrayal of desire he was trying, but failing, to control.

"Another Capuziner?" offered the other man.

The price they settled on was not so high as to provoke more than ordinary curiosity, though of course the topic of discretion did arise. "There are wife, children, public connections—usual impedimenta we imagine you have learned by now to deal with. Our friend is very clear on this point—his reputation is of absolute importance to him. Any mention of him to anyone, no matter how trivial, will get back to him. He commands resources that allow him to learn everything people say. Everyone. Even you, cuddled down in your frail nest with some manly visitor you believe really wants to 'keep' you, or bragging to another forlorn butterfly, 'Oh, he gave me this, he bought me that'—every living moment, you must *attend to what you say,* for sooner or later your exact words are recovered, and if they are wrong words, then, little miss, you will find you must go fluttering for your life."

"And don't imagine 'home' as a very safe place to be," his companion added, "for we are not without resources in England. Our eye is ever upon you, wherever those little wings should take you."

It had not occurred to Cyprian that this city might, by now, have anything more to reveal to him beyond the promise of unreflective obedience, day into night, to the leash-pulls of desire. Certainly, outside the Prater, and its role as a reservoir of Continental good looks, to find Vienna exhibiting behavior even a little more complex, especially with (it seemed here impossible not to gather) a political dimension as well, predictably sent his boredom coefficients swooning off the scale, and any number of alarm-devices into alluring cry. Perhaps the pair of go-betweens had already detected in him this shallowness of expectation. He was handed a card with an address printed on it—in Leopoldstadt, the Jewish quarter north of the Prater, across the railroad tracks.

"So. A Jewish friend, it seems. . . ."

"Perhaps one day a detailed chat on Hebraic issues could bring you some profit, financial as well as educational. Meanwhile let us proceed in orderly steps."

For a moment a wing of desolate absence swept down across the garden tables here at Eisvogel's, eclipsing any describable future. From somewhere in the direction of the Giant-Wheel came the infernal lilt of yet another twittering waltz.

The Russians, self-designated Misha and Grisha, having obtained one of his addresses, a coffeehouse in the IX Bezirk, were soon leaving messages for Cyprian there about once a week, scheduling appointments at unfrequented corners all about the city. As he grew more aware of their surveillance, as perhaps he was meant to, he spent less time in the Prater and more in cafés reading newspapers. He also began taking day-trips, prolonging them, sometimes through the night, to see what radius of freedom the watchers would allow him.

With no chance to prepare, he was summoned at last one night to the address in Leopoldstadt. The servant who opened the door was tall, cruel, and silent, and almost before Cyprian could step across the threshold, he was manacled and blindfolded, then roughly propelled down a corridor and up some stairs to a room with a peculiar absence of echo, where he was unbound only long enough to be stripped and then re-secured.

The Colonel himself removed the blindfold. He wore steel-rimmed eyeglasses, the bone-structure beneath a rigorously shaven scalp betraying to the keen student of ethnophysiognomy, even in the room's exhausted light, his non-Prussian, indeed crypto-Oriental, blood. He selected a rattan cane and without speaking proceeded to use it on Cyprian's unprotected naked body. Being chained tightly, Cyprian was unable to put up much resistance, and his unfaltering erection would in any case have made any protests unpersuasive.

So these assignations began, once a week, always conducted in silence. Cyprian experimented with costume, maquillage, and hairstyles in an attempt to provoke some comment, but the Colonel was far more interested in whipping him—wordlessly and often, employing a strange delicacy of touch, to climax.

One evening, near the Volksgarten, Cyprian was out in the street just drifting, when from somewhere not immediately clear he heard a chorus of male voices hoarse from hours of repetition singing "Ritter Georg Hoch!" the old Pan-German anthem, and here in Vienna, these days, anti-Semitic as well. Understanding immediately that it would be better not to have to encounter this lot, he slipped into the first wine cellar he saw, where whom should he run into but old Ratty McHugh, from school. At the sight of a face from a past all at once too measurably more innocent, he began to sniffle, not enough to embarrass anyone but so surprising them both that old Ratty was moved to inquire.

Though Cyprian had developed by now a clearer idea of the consequences if he spoke of his arrangements with the Colonel—death certainly not being out of the question, torture certainly, not the pleasurable sort he expected of his mysterious client but the real article, nonetheless he was tempted, almost sexually so, to tell all to Ratty in a great heedless rush, and see how much would in fact get back to the Colonel, and what would happen then. He had intuitively kept shy of any guessing as to whom his old school chum might be working for these days, and in particular from which Desk. With the sense of taking a step into some narcotically-perfumed and lightless room, calibrating the seductiveness of his tone, he whispered, "Do you think you could get me out of Vienna?"

"What kind of trouble are you in?" Ratty of course wanted to know. "Exactly."

"'Exactly' . . ."

"I am in regular contact with people who might help. Though I mayn't speak for them, my impression is that the more detailed your account, the further they'd be prepared to extend themselves." The old Ratty had never spoken with quite so much care.

"Look here," Cyprian imagined he could explain, "it isn't 's if one starts off *intending* to live this way . . . 'Oh yes planning, you know, to seek a career in sodomy.' But—perhaps less at Trinity than at King's—if one wanted anything like a social life, it was simply the mask one put on. Inescapable, really. Every expectation, most of us, of leaving it all behind after the final May Week ball, and no harm done. Who could have foreseen, any more than the actress who falls in love with her leading man, that the fiction might prove after all more desirable—strangely, more durable—than anything the civilian world had to offer. . . ."

Ratty, bless him, didn't blink any more than he usually did. "My alternatives were a bit less colorful. Whitehall, Blackpool. But it's only fair to warn you, you might have to absorb a bit of character assessment."

"From your lot. Rather harsh, are they."

"Manly as they come, little or no patience with anything else."

"Crikey, my very type of chap. Are you still as fond of booking insane bets as you were in your Newmarket period? At the right odds, I'll wager I could seduce any of that manly brigade you'd care to choose. Take no more than one evening."

WITHIN THE WEEK Ratty had set him up an appointment with Derrick Theign, a tall and careworn functionary, from his accent stationed out here, perhaps, actually, for a while now. "I suppose I do enjoy it here, more than one ought, so I've been told. Though with field reports up to one's ears, where one possibly finds time, for any of . . . well, the other, that's if one fancied that sort of thing, which of course one doesn't, much."

"'Much.' Oh, dear."

"But I must say I *am* ever so frightfully keen on these chocolate and raspberry articles—would you mind if we obtained . . . perhaps several of them actually, not to take *along,* you see, but to *eat here,* even if it's rather *more quickly* than may be considered—"

"Derrick, if I may so address you—I'm not giving you 'nerves'? Little nondescript, unthreatening me? Hadn't we better—"

"No, not at all, it's just the . . . hmm. Dash it all. Then again . . ."

"Yes do go on, please—'the' what?"

"The maquillage, you know. I'm finding it—"

"Oh I say, did I get my eyes wrong again? I'm always doing that. Which side is it tonight?"

"No, no, they're fine, in fact it all looks . . . well, smashing actually."

"Why, Derrick."

"I mean, do you do it yourself? or does someone else?"

"You must have heard of Zsuzsa, no? well, I spent most of this afternoon in her salon, she's really the only one to see when—you know how you get those little premonitions that you're about to meet someone it won't be lost on—"

"Good—that's the smile I want, exactly, now hold it just like that and don't be alarmed, but we are not, at the moment, unobserved."

"Where?"

"Just passing by . . . there."

"Ah."

"They've been back and forth now more than once—unless I'm mistaken, they're out of Misha and Grisha's atelier. You have got in with a colorful crowd, Latewood. Now . . . in a moment they'll turn and start back, by which point I'd better have my hand on your leg—will that be any sort of problem for you?"

"Well . . . which leg were you thinking of, Derrick?"

"Yes . . . here they are again."

"Hmm . . ."

"Presently, and as naturally as possible, we shall get up and leave together, allowing them to follow us. Do you know the Hotel Neue Mutzenbacher, near the Imperial Stables?"

"Know *of* it. Rather a museum of bad taste, wouldn't dream of going *in* there, personally."

"Really. Always seemed a jolly enough place to me."

" 'Always,' Derrick? You are . . . an habitué of . . . of the Mutzi, then?"

"Its décor is more than made up for by its most useful A.M.E., or Alternate Means of Egress, that's if you don't mind some sewage."

"One develops a tolerance . . . though look here, if your own lot use it, mightn't it be known to old M. and G. as well?"

"Still, they'd have to wait outside for a bit, wouldn't they, to make sure, before they went crashing in."

"Make sure of—"

"My own authenticity in this."

"And that would take how long?"

"Dunno. Long enough, one hopes. How long do your rendezvous last on average, Cyprian?"

"Hours and hours sometimes. Depending on how infatuated he is, of course."

"Yes though as many must become quickly bored— ah jolly good and there's the Stiftskaserne, not much farther now. . . ."

THE *FIAKER* TOOK THEM southward toward the reddened fraction of moon, lights of the city converging behind them, the driver humming to himself appropriate *Fiakerlieder* but refraining from bursting into full song.

"This isn't the way to the station."

"To the Süd-Bahnhof, it is."

"But that's for Trieste, not for home. Derrick? I don't want to go to Trieste . . . I was supposed to be going quite the other direction, wasn't I, toward Ostend, toward . . ." He could not quite repeat "home."

"With luck they will also assume we want the Ostend Express—so perhaps they will have pulled their people over to the Staatsbahn. Classic misdirectional exercise, sit back, not to worry, eventually we'll have you headed the right way. If that's what you really want. Here are your tickets, transit documents, letter of credit, spot of the ready—"

"A thousand Kreuzer? That isn't even ten quid."

"Dear, dear. What was your customary fee again?"

Cyprian stared back boldly. "The least one can get by on in Vienna is thirty K. per day."

"Out where you'll be, I imagine you'll find life less expensive. As to 'home' "—passing electric lamplight flaring at intervals, like a prison searchlight, off his eyeglass-lenses—"you might take some time to consider how congruent with 'England' that word can be for you these days. Curiously, it may actually be safer for you in Trieste . . . or even *further east.*"

His eyes were difficult to make out, but from the set of his shoulders and the modulations of his lips, Cyprian could gather some of what he wasn't saying. After a moment's psychorectal entertainment, "Among the Turks, I suppose you mean."

"Almost a charming reflex, Latewood, were it not so predictable among your lot. Yes—to retreat, not for the first time, from the dangerous polyphonies I must deal with daily to these single-note brothel tunes—it's the Turks I mean, with all their fabled equipment and so forth. Exactly."

"Hmm." Cyprian gazed at the shadow-steeped operative. "You're *entangled,* aren't you, or for the moment anyhow. It's all right, I'm not surprised, you are attractive in a battered sort of way."

"Indeed. It's why all the sodomitic case-files end up on my desk. Oh, but"—

shaking his head vigorously, as if out of a trance—"was I complaining again? Frightfully sorry, sometimes it just comes as you'd say *spurting out* like that—"

THE RUSSIANS PRESENTED little problem. "You've your choice of simple or qualified *Kuppelei*, Misha—"

"I'm Grisha."

"Whatever, it's the only choice you'll be offered. Six months or five years. If you insist on being difficult, we will produce documents showing that poor little Cyprian was your legal ward at the time you led him, under false pretenses, into an immoral life—and that can fetch you up to five years in a Habsburg prison, most likely confined in a cell Belgian style, a pound and a half of bread a day, meat and soup on occasion I'm told, better than being an average free man in your native Russia, yet presenting perhaps a bleak lookout for an epicure of the rank you have come to occupy. . . ."

At some point it was decided that Cyprian could safely be told that his whereabouts and medium-term plans, almost before they'd been worked out in any detail, had all but routinely been passed on to the Colonel, who, Cyprian had learned, by now specialized in south Slavic politics as well as sex-practices, which were widely believed to include irregularities of gender.

"Croatia-Slavonia! But it's his—"

"Yes?"

"His garden of delights. Sooner or later he's apt to visit, and then he'll kill me, or one of those Russians will, oh *thanks* Theign, just *ever* so much."

"I shouldn't worry about them. You're not on their list anymore."

"Since when? And why not?"

"Disappointed? Since your Colonel was arrested"—elaborately lifting out and consulting a Swiss calendar watch in gunmetal and black porcelain—"actually, on Thursday last. I say, did we forget to tell you? ever so sorry. No, he's no longer in play. That chapter is over. We have moved on. Though in the business, it is never too fanciful to envision a reunion someday, especially as it seems he may, one must admit inexplicably, have taken a fancy to you."

"Not even if England expects it, Theign."

"Oh," shrugging, "yes I am given to understand that a spot of chastisement might come into it, fairly pro forma, but little beyond that—"

"Not *these* people, for God's sake, even the silliest cretin on their list knows that if you turn, you die. Chastisement. What bloody remote planet is it you're from again?"

"We know 'these people,' Latewood."

Cyprian grew thoughtful. "All important news, undoubtedly, but why tell me? Why not keep me ignorant and afraid, as usual?"

"Say that we were beginning to trust you."

"He chortles. Bitterly."

"Say it was even something you needed to know—"

"—for what you're about to ask me to do."

IN TRIESTE he could at least imagine himself growing to some sort of manhood, perhaps even into an Old Upper Adriatic Hand—a dangerous reverie, for he had soon grown fairly sensible of how little he had to say in the matter of where he was to be posted from then on. Yet what end to the drama could he've expected? Foreign Section were using him as unquestionably as any of his former clients had. The same *now say this, now wear this, do this.* If it was his destiny, all along, to be an object of someone's administration, why not just join the Navy, some navy, and be done with it?

Derrick Theign, whose code name out here was "Good Shepherd," managed to come out every few months or so, always an evening arrival and the same suite at the Métropole, held for him since the days when it was also itself known as the Buon Pastore—never for more than a night, and then he'd be off again, to Semlin, over to Zagreb usually, and points east whose names were never spoken aloud, less out of caution than fear. The meetings with Cyprian were never about anything of moment, unless one included certain charged silences which often would stretch uncomfortably as they sat drinking together among the red plush and ormolu. Cyprian began to wonder if Theign weren't actually finding excuses to repeat this cycle of arriving, falling silent, getting what he must imagine as some *grip on himself,* packing up abruptly the next day, and leaving. It was an index of how far Cyprian's insouciance had lapsed that he never thought of simply asking his field supervisor what was afoot. When the matter of Venice arose, he was taken by surprise.

"Venice."

"Not an unreasonable place for a listening post. It has occupied a fateful geopolitical cusp ever since it lay at the ancient intersection of Western and Eastern empires—as it still does in our day, though the empires have mutated around it, the Prophet's own still waiting their terrible moment, the protection of Christ's own falling now to Vienna and St. Petersburg, and the newer empires far less pertinent to God, Prussia worshipping little beyond military splendor, and Britain its own mythic reflection, readjusted day to day in mirrors of faraway conquest."

"Was I asking?"

They were soon cozily, all but domestically, established in a *pensione* in Santa Croce, within easy dash of the train station and the Mestre bridge, gathered at the moment at a kitchen table with a bottle of grappa and a tin of peculiar biscuits. Some sort of strange sheep's-milk cheese from Crotona. Steam-whistles sounded outside.

Cyprian had learned that Theign held a commission in the Navy as a senior lieutenant, reporting to the Naval Intelligence Department at the Admiralty. His remit here in Venice, at least officially, was to look into a reported theft of secret engineering drawings from inside the menacing walls of the Arsenale itself—so catastrophically had the Italian maritime fate been compromised that he was finding it next to impossible even to learn what the drawings were *of*. "I can't imagine what they're all so mysterious about. Cruisers, frigates, all the usual, submarines and submarine destroyers, torpedoes, torpedo boats, torpedo-boat chasers, miniature submarines that can be carried inside battleships and launched from the bow as if they themselves were torpedoes."

"I thought all that undersea business went on over in Spezia, at the San Bartolomeo works," Cyprian said.

"Quite the swot," Theign glared. It was a sore point. Time and again he had been referred to offices at La Spezia set up for the express purpose of misleading foreigners, especially ones like Theign, who might as well have worn sandwich-boards fore and aft reading SPY. "The boats everyone knows about," he muttered, "*Glauco* class and its successors, of course. But these others are somewhat specialized. . . ."

We of the futurity know that the unit in question was the sinister Siluro Dirigibile a Lenta Corsa or Low-Speed Steerable Torpedo. "What makes it particularly malevolent," Theign confided, perhaps indiscreet with pride when at last, after exceptional effort, he did manage to acquire the elusive gen, "is that it does not require of its crew any bravery at all, only that facility for creeping about which one associates with the Italian character."

"Oh that's just such a big myth," Cyprian looking for an argument today, it seemed. "They are as direct as children."

"Indeed. Most of the children of *your* acquaintance being, at best, corrupted, how 'direct' is that, exactly?"

"Get about more and you'll see."

"One thing that didn't occur to the Royal Italian Navy," Theign continued, "was observation from overhead. We know the Russians have had a program—Voznab, or *vozdushnyi nablyudenie,* aerial surveillance—for years, their aerostats and airships have been equipped with some advanced sort of masking device that mimics open sky, so that one often can't see them even when one knows they're up there. They keep forward bases in Serbia, which puts them less than an hour from here, perhaps two from Spezia. Some of the photographic plates actually show up on the Rialto from time to time."

·

One day Theign came in looking preoccupied. "Your friends Misha and Grisha have gone to ground. . . ."

"And might I have any idea where. Actually no, not a clue, so sorry. . . ."

"Let's think for a moment shall we. Beginning with Vienna—would they have stayed on there?"

"Yes—and also, as you'd imagine, no. Misha loved the place, Grisha hated it. If they had a kick-up, one of them could easily have gotten on a train."

"Grisha, you mean."

"Misha was hardly a stranger to the joys of the unpremeditated gesture. . . . But I say Derrick, you people *have* been watching the trains, haven't you?"

"Except for one small though bothersome gap in our . . . ehrm, earlier information."

"*Oh* dear."

"Cyprian, they may want you for a bit back at the Metternichgasse."

Through his eyelashes Cyprian bestowed a sidewise gaze known to produce reflexes of desire up to and including, on at least one admittedly singular occasion in Ashby-de-la-Zouch, Leics, a proposal of marriage. "And where do you want me, Derrick?"

It proved at last to be the one silly question that Derrick Theign would find insupportable. What he intended then as a humorous tap on the cheek became first, unmistakably, a caress, and then, provoked by Cyprian's venturesome laughter, a rather sharp slap. The next either of them knew, Theign had taken him painfully by his hair and they were kissing, not at all the way Englishmen would be expected to—if they must—but like foreigners, heedlessly. Enough saliva to soak into Cyprian's shirt collar. Erect penises all round. The spell of Venice in those days, it was said.

"I wouldn't have preferred *this* scenario," Theign muttered not long after, while tending to various abrasions.

"Too late for that now, isn't it?"

"It does put you in rather a different cubbyhole."

Cyprian already skeptical, "Oh of *course* I wouldn't be the only one."

"One does try to avoid it, you see, whenever possible."

"'It.' Oh, Derrick . . ." All but tearful.

"Don't go sodomitical on me now, when you'll be needing your wits about you, if *that's* not asking too much."

As the petals of unreflective desire, those narcotic days on the Lagoon, began to curl up, lose aroma, and drop one by one to the unadorned tabletop of daily business, Theign half-invented a local operative, "Zanni," to resolve whose fictional crises he then found brief but always welcome opportunities to get out of the house, even if it must be into the swarming *calli* of Venice. Somehow immersion in the Italian mobility comforted him, clarified his mind like a well-timed Partagas. His Naval Intelligence job, in this city of masks, actually concealed a deeper project. "Zanni" was one of many code names for his contact with a small bicycle factory over on the *Terraferma* that had just gone into designing and building motorcycles. When forces did begin at last in Europe to move in appreciable numbers, there would have to be a way to maintain the flow of information. Telegraph and cable lines could be cut. Wireless was too vulnerable to Ætheric influences. The only secure method, it seemed to Theign, was a small international crew of motorcyclists, fast and nimble enough to stay ahead of the game. "They'll be designated R.U.S.H., that's Rapid Unit for Shadowing and Harassment."

"'Shadowing.'" Cyprian, somewhat embarrassed, had not heard the term before.

"Following a subject, keeping as close as his own shadow," Theign explained.

"Obliged almost to be someone's . . . projection."

"If you like."

"So close in fact as to begin *to lose oneself*. . . ."

"Just what you people fancy isn't it, surrender of the ego sort of thing."

"Derrick, I can't even ride a horse."

"Don't you understand that we're trying to save your life? This way, whatever happens, wherever you're assigned, you'll be only hours from neutral ground."

"Given fuel enough, who isn't?"

"Depots are in place. You'll have maps. What do you imagine it is I do out here?"

"Wouldn't think of prying—though one has of course noticed, when you're about, the *naphthal fragrance*—have you considered wearing something a bit less odor-retentive than Scottish tweed? for instance this new Italian 'sharkskin,' from which everything slips away smoothly as a satin gown."

"I keep forgetting the reason I don't have you transferred—it's the fashion advice! Of course! Well. You'll be interested in this—here's one of the night-uniforms, prototype model, more leather here than *your sort* may be used to, but it does keep the wind out."

"Hmm . . . I do rather fancy these metal studs—each with a purpose of its own I'm sure—though don't they seem rather . . . conspicuous?"

"You'll be moving too fast for it to matter."

"All right if I just . . . slip into . . ."

"Not at all and mind you, these are only the fatigues, wait till you see the dress uniform."

"Derrick, you do like me a little, I think. . . ."

Later that evening Theign summoned Cyprian into his office. "See here, Latewood, in all the time we've known each other, we've never yet had a serious talk about death."

"Probably a good reason for that," Cyprian looking around the room nervously.

"I assume it's the usual sodomite sensibility?"

"How's that?"

"All you people with your repertoire of avoidance techniques—denying the passage of time, seeking out ever-younger company, constructing your little airtight environments stuffed with art undying . . . there isn't one of you with anything real to say on the subject. Yet in our business it's everywhere. We must tithe a certain number of lives yearly to the goddess Kali in return for a European history more or less free of violence and safe for investment, and very few are the wiser. Certainly not the homo brigade."

"Yes, well, was there anything else Derrick? And why won't this door open?"

"No, no, we simply *must chat.* A jolly little chat. Won't take long, I promise."

It seemed Theign wanted to talk about field skills. Not until later would Cyprian understand that this was a periodic exercise—Theign's way of evaluating the current negotiability of those under his command he might wish one day to shop. But it struck Cyprian at the time only as a theoretical conversation about predators and prey, with Cyprian explaining the advantages of being the hunted.

"So you end up smarter, sneakier, nastier than the competition," Theign summarized. "Useful among professional pouffes, I shouldn't wonder, but these engagements out here are a bit more than simple sodomitic rivalries. The consequences are rather more serious."

"Are they."

"We are talking about the fates of nations. The welfare, often the sheer survival, of millions. The axial loads of History. How can you compare—"

"And how, *vecchio fazool,* can you fail to see the connection?"

Theign had of course mastered in his first year at Naval Intelligence that blank and slightly openmouthed expression so useful to His Majesty's agents abroad. It produced in Cyprian not the false sense of superiority intended but a queasy despair. He had never cared before, particularly, about being understood by an object of fascination. But somehow when it became obvious that Theign didn't *want* to understand, Cyprian became guardedly terrified.

"I've heard from Vienna, by the way. They have you scheduled in for next week. Here are your tickets."

"Second class."

"Mm. Yes."

Though ordinarily he enjoyed doing as he was told, and especially the contempt that went with that, Cyprian found himself puzzled now at Theign's assumption that of course he would take the train back to Vienna unescorted, unsupervised, unquestioning, into the embrace of what he had assumed was the known enemy, instead of running for cover, as prey was expected to do.

"We are coöperating fully with the Austrians in this matter," Theign waited to let him know till Cyprian was boarding the train at the Santa Lucia Station, in a note delivered by an Italian urchin, who then disappeared into the swarm. "So in your conversations I would suggest sticking to English, as the German appropriate to your chosen métier may soon become exhausted."

The passage, especially from Venice to Graz, was not without moments of jollification, though it helped for one to have developed, if not an active taste for, at least the gift of concealing any revulsion from, local sausages, small pets, not always of the indoor sort, concertina music, and the peculiar whining accent of the region. Young Austrian cavalry Aspirants in that fatally alluring shade of aniline blue kept coming through from amusements elsewhere in the train and launching at him, as he imagined, glances of heated inquiry. As luck would have it, desire was off to parts undisclosed, on a species of budget holiday—with any number of sexual possibilities aboard, considered in both a professional and a recreational way, for some strange and he hoped not medical reason Cyprian spent the journey scowling, slouching, and brooding unstirred and, likely for that same reason, unapproached. It might have had something to do with Misha and Grisha, for it could not be easily imagined that the inconvenienced duo had simply shrugged off his defection, nor that an unknown number of part-time contract workers across this continent and the next would not be seeking to restore the balance-sheets on their behalf—while queued up behind the Russians waited the Evidenzbüro, who had not wished compromised their own surveillance of the Colonel, the British Secret Service, obliged at least to keep an eye on those employees abroad who consort with known intelligence operatives from elsewhere in Europe, plus Turkish, Serbian, French, and Italian nonce-operatives, as the politics of the day might demand, all regarding Cyprian as a likely candidate for deception, assault, and elimination. In terrible fact, he was now running for his life.

Cyprian Latewood's return to Vienna was accompanied either in or outside of his head by the Adagio from the Mozart Piano Concerto in A Major, K. 488. It might have been prophetic, had he been listening. This was a period in the history of human emotion when "romance" had slipped into an inexpensive subfusc of self-awareness, unnaturally heightening the effect of the outmoded pastels peeping from beneath, as if in some stylistic acknowledgment of the great trembling that showed through, now and then, to some more than others, of a hateful future nearly at hand and inescapable. But many were as likely to misinterpret the deep signals as physical symptoms, or another case of "nerves," or, like the earlier, dimmer Cyprian, some kind of "romance" in the offing, however little prepared he might have been for that.

The Vienna interviews went pleasantly enough. The Hotel Klomser, only a few blocks from the War Ministry, served apparently as a traditional spot for discussions like this. Colonel Khäutsch was mentioned only in euphemisms and circumlocutions, some of them, given Cyprian's imperfect grasp of the idiom, nearly impenetrable. Local baked goods were kept within his easy reach in piles far exceeding normal angles of repose. The coffee here, internationally respected as an aid to loquacity, had been roasted with fanatical precision on ultramodern machines whose heating-times, chamber temperatures, and humidities could be read to hundredths of a unit, suggestive of either a local *Feinschmeckerei* evolved far beyond that of the rest of the world, or just the usual compulsive application of any engineering improvement, however trivial.

"That is, if we may regard the history of civilization as distinguished by the asymptotic approach of industrial production tolerances, with time, to some mythical, never-attained Zero. What do you think, Mr. Latewood?"

"Wehggnh ucchh uh gweh-ungghh nyuk aikh annkh ngkh hnnh ikhgghhlnghawh," replied Cyprian, his speech losing, into a congested volume of Sachertorte mit Schlag, much of whatever acceleration it was picking up from the coffee, though the interrogators were able to recognize this as, "There was a question just like that on my little-go."

Theign had warned him about the interviewing techniques. "Don't be too clever with them. 'Mit Schlag' could easily take on another meaning."

Cyprian was surprised to learn how well known Theign was in this town, and how many people were eager to be remembered to him. Over his years on the Vienna station Theign had apparently put together his own prætorian apparatus, more or less by intuition, and in the strangely crowded daytime corridors of the Hotel Klomser, Cyprian was introduced to some of them.

He recalled having run into Miskolci around the Prater, had in fact narrowly avoided once or twice doing business with him. Miskolci was not exactly a vampire, but in obedience to phases of the moon had been known to go about randomly waylaying and rudely biting the odd civilian. Back in the late '90s, when vampirism became fashionable owing to the international popularity of the novel *Dracula,* granting biters of all sorts license to obey their impulses in public, Miskolci discovered that, far from being alone with a depraved taste, he was part of a quite-extensive community. A subcircuit of the Buda-Pesth telephone exchange had apparently been reserved for the use of hæmatophages, as they were then known, so one of Miskolci's most valuable assets, for Theign, had been this red haze of connective threadwork, already in being, which surrounded him. His own specialized gift had lain secret until one week at the height of the first Moroccan crisis, when it became desperately essential to know the mobilization schedule of a certain army corps. Theign's shop had the right prima donna, but she had become somehow reluctant to sing. "Perhaps I can help," offered Miskolci. "Lock us in, come back in an hour." An eventful hour—Theign could hear the screaming through the soundproofing and around a couple of turns in the corridor. When next seen, the subject appeared superficially unharmed but upon scrutiny carrying in his eyes an expression that gave some of Theign's colleagues unsettling dreams for years afterward—as if written there was an introduction to ancient mysteries better left mysterious.

Theign had met Dvindler in the baths, which at the time, he was finding convenient for fact-gathering—though he had learned after no more than a single visit to avoid the Zentralbad, where one found nothing beyond a literalism of the hydropathic. For the more poetic list of features he sought, Theign must spend time looking in the outer districts. Eventually the Astarte-Bad, far out on one of the "K" or river-quay lines, proved to be the ticket—Viennese Orientalism taken to newly questionable frontiers of taste, lurid mosaics showing pre-biblical orgies sort of thing. A non-Teutonics-only hiring policy. The sexes, perhaps by design, imperfectly segregated, so that one might at any clouded turn of a corridor stumble into the partner of one's dreams, though in practice one seldom did. The new construction always going on somewhere in acoustical contact suggested relatively low property values out here, which, far from distracting, was by many interpreted as erotic.

"For constipation," Dvindler announced by way of self-introduction, "rely upon it, F.I.P., or Faradically Induced Peristalsis, is quite the best thing."

"Excuse me," Theign said, "do I take that to mean you actually intend to run an electrical current, how shall I put this delicately—"

"There is no way to put it delicately," Dvindler said. "*Komm,* I'll show you."

Theign looked around. "Shouldn't there be a physician or something in attendance?"

"It takes five minutes to learn how. It is not brain surgery!" Dvindler chortled. "Now, *where is* that rectal electrode? Someone always— Ah!" producing a long cylinder with a knob of a certain size on one end and a wire coming out the other, which led to an interruptor device, whose primary coil was connected to what seemed to Theign an alarming number of Leclanché cells, hooked up in series. "Hand me that jar of Cosmoline, if you would be so kind."

Theign, expecting to be repelled, found himself looking on in fascination. Apparently the trick was to coördinate two electrodes, one inserted in the rectum and the other to be rolled about on the abdominal surface, enabling the current flowing between to simulate a peristaltic wave. If the application was successful, one excused oneself and headed rapidly for some nearby toilet. If not, well, besides being part of a general program of intestinal health, the procedure was valued by some, such as Dvindler, on its own merits.

"Electricity! the force of the future—for everything, you know, including the élan vital itself, will soon be proven electrical in nature."

The interruptor on the secondary coil made a not disagreeable buzzing sound, which after a while seemed to blend in with the liquid echoes of the larger establishment. Dvindler was singing quite cheerfully to himself, a tune of the city which Theign slowly recognized as Beda Chanson's "Ausgerechnet Bananen." On the way out, he borrowed five K. from Theign for the battery fee.

And as for Yzhitza, well, Theign must have been having an especially bad couple of weeks, because she mistook him for a German businessman desperately in need of recreation, addressing him in what she imagined to be his native tongue, so that for a few minutes he was less than clear about what was going on. But somehow, despite his low energy state and an attitude toward women that never got more comfortable than ambivalent, he was surprised to find his sexual interest kindled, indeed commanded, by this actually quite ordinary-looking professional. At times, he had to admit, enjoying himself inordinately. "*Liebling,* you were never even a challenge," she confessed later, after rolling up for him a record of success at what the Kundschaftsstelle liked to call "*Honigfalle* work" that only one or two rogue historians might disagree had changed the course of European history. By then Theign had moved on into much colder operational country, and could nod impassively, taking it at face value.

On weekday evenings Cyprian, appearing each time measurably fatter, even to the casual surveillant, came lurching out of the same back exit of the Klomser and made his way—his thoughts interrupted only by an occasional high C from Leo Slezak over at the Opera House—sometimes by *Fiaker,* sometimes on the Verbindungsbahn if he saw a train coming, to his old sanctuary of desire the Prater, though nothing much was then ever observed to take place. The declining sun was a chilled and violent orange, throwing opaque indigo shadows full of foreboding—owls patrolled the vast park, marionettes occupied tiny volumes of light in a general dusk, the music was as horrible as ever.

It was nostalgia for its own sake, really. The more he found himself addressed—even *called out to*—as *"Dickwanst"* and *"Fettarsch,"* the more his Prater-longings began to ebb, and he turned to quarters of the city he would not, as recently as months ago, even fleetingly have considered, such as Favoriten, where he went to move among the crowds of Bohemian workmen when the factory shifts changed, not so much seeking exotic flirtation as to be absorbed somehow into a mobility, a bath of language he did not speak, as he had once sought in carnal submission an escape route from what it seemed of the world he was being asked to bear. . . .

He kept blundering into huge Socialist demonstrations. Traffic came to an astonished halt as tens of thousands of working-class men and women moved in silence down the Ringstraße. "Well!" Cyprian heard an onlooker remark, "talk about the slow return of the repressed!" The police were out in large numbers, with head-assault high on their list of activities. Cyprian caught a couple of good whacks and found upon hitting the pavement that his recent weight gain was an unforeseen asset.

Out on his perambulations one day, he heard from an open upstairs window a piano student, forever to remain invisible, playing exercises from Carl Czerny's *School of Velocity,* op. 299. Cyprian had paused to listen to those moments of passionate emergence among the mechanical fingerwork, and at that moment Yashmeen Halfcourt came around the corner. If he had not stopped for the music, he would have been around another corner by the time she reached the spot where he was standing.

For a moment they stared, both seeming to recognize an act of mutual salvation. "In four dimensions," she said later, as they sat in a coffeehouse in Mariahilf at the sharp intersection of two busy streets, at the vertex of two long narrow rooms, able to see down the length of both, "it wouldn't have mattered."

She had a job at a dressmaker/milliner's nearby, owing, she thought, to the hidden intercession of the T.W.I.T., because one day on the racks there had appeared a version of the Snazzbury's Silent Frock she once had been measured for in London.

"What I really need is a cloak of invisibility to go with it," she supposed.

"Surveillance."

"Since you put it that way."

"One of those conclusions I find I jump to more and more these days. Do you know who it is?"

"I think they're local. But some Russians as well."

The schoolgirl confidence he remembered was no longer there—something significant had shaken her. He was surprised at how far he thought he could see into her present difficulties, farther than she would have known how to give him credit for, farther than he could have himself imagined a year and a half ago. He patted her gloved hands, he hoped not as awkwardly as it felt. "If it's only the Okhrana, that'll be easy—there isn't one who can't be bought, and they work for kopecks. The Austrians might prove a bit more problematic, especially if it's the Kundschaftsstelle."

"The city police I could understand, but . . ." With such unstudied bewilderment in her voice that he had to step away, pretending to brush his hat, so as not to lunge into the obvious and counterproductive embrace this might, to another smitten youth, have called for in the circs.

"If you are willing to wait a few days—no more than a week, say—there might be a way I can help."

Having no doubt heard this sort of thing, with required changes of emphasis, from other men in less-perilous times, she narrowed her eyes, yet waited another half-moment, as if allowing some further point to become clear. "You have had dealings with them before. Both offices."

"The Okhrana are playing on a somewhat unpredictable pitch just now. Doings in the East—the Japanese war, rebellions up and down the rail lines. It's a good time to redeem one's tickets . . . so I'm told. As for the Austrians . . . they may require a bit more intensive labor."

"Cyprian, I cannot—"

Resisting what was almost the need to place a gloved finger across her lips, "The question will not arise. Let us see what will happen." Perversely, he was pleased—though less pleased with himself for feeling so—at the way she hesitated now, as if unwilling to lie because she could no longer gauge how successfully he might catch her out.

He tried to stay off the subject of what he'd been up to himself, assuming she'd think whatever she thought. When Venice came up, she only said, "Oh, Cyprian, how lovely. I've never been there."

"In a strange way, neither have I. As a matter of fact—do you have a moment?"

They were in the Volks-Prater, and there happened to be nearby a popular facsimile of Venice known as Venedig in Wien. "I know it's frightfully decadent of me, but I've come to think of this as the real Venice, the one I never get to see. These gondolas are real, actually, and so are the *gondolieri.*"

Cyprian and Yashmeen bought tickets and boarded one of the gondolas, and lay back together and watched the foreign sky stream past. Every now and then, a replica of some Venetian landmark—the Doge's Palace, or the Ca' d'Oro—would come looming up. "First time I rode in one of these," Cyprian said, "was here. If I hadn't come to Vienna, I probably never would have."

"I doubt I ever shall."

Her voice brought him a twinge. He couldn't remember seeing her ever quite this miserable. He would have done anything, for that instant, to see her somehow restored to her old impossible ways. Except perhaps blurt, "I'll take you. I promise." Instead he thought he'd better go in to speak with Ratty McHugh.

"So!" cried Ratty with a certain forced joviality, "here we all are again. Yashmeen still in the picture, I see." He seemed to Cyprian not so much puzzled as curious in a professional way.

"Not quite as she was."

"She always made me think of Hypatia. Before the Christian mobs of course."

"More of a sibyl these days. Deeper than maths, but that's as far as I can see. Perhaps because of some rogue psychic gift, perhaps only the secular gravity of whatever her father is up to out in Inner Asia, she's being bedeviled by two or three Powers at once, England as you must know something of already, Russia, of which she is officially still a citizen, and Austria, with of course Germany towering in the shadows backstage, whispering cues."

"The Shambhalan Question no doubt. Yes and it hasn't half been playing havoc with the old rota, putting blokes into Colney Hatch at quite an unprecedented rate. If it were my department I'd have had Auberon Halfcourt pulled back years ago. No one even knows where the bloody place is, for pity's sake."

"Perhaps if we—"

"Oh of course we should meet, I'm only complaining in a recreational way, or do I mean therapeutic? Let's make it the Dobner shall we, that's the look we'll need, a simple reunion of English co-alumni."

So amid the click of billiard balls and exquisite whores with tiny waists and huge darkened eyelids and lashes and sumptuously plumed hats, Yashmeen and Ratty shook hands across the moderate distance produced by a few years out of University, though Cyprian was pleased to see him semi-smitten and then embarrassed because of it. Not that Yash hadn't gone out of her way today with an ensemble of beaded crêpe lisse in some æthereal shade of violet, and a terribly smart hat whose plumage sent enchanting shadows across her face. After a spell of appropriate theatre, they went off carefully, separately, to rendezvous at a nondescript apartment nearby, behind the Getreidemarkt, one of several maintained by Ratty's shop for purposes just such as these.

By the unwritten rules of these transitory dwellings, the cupboards yielded a sketchy culinary history of those who had passed through—bottles of Szekszárdi Vörös, Gewürztraminer and apricot brandy, chocolates, coffee, biscuits, tinned sausages, wine, boxes of dried noodles of various shapes and sizes, a white cloth bag of tarhonya from the previous century.

"Are these the same Russians you remember from Göttingen?"

She raised her brows and turned up her palms.

"For or against the Tsar I mean, it does make a difference. Obviously there's the Anglo-Russian Entente, but the other lot, though technically Russians I suppose, are also the most evil sort of bomb-chucking Socialistic dregs aren't they, more than happy to see all Romanoffs obliterated, and no hesitation to make deals with anyone, including Germany, that might hasten the day."

"Why, Ratty," said Cyprian, mild as could be. "Some would say they're the only hope Russia has."

"Oh don't let's . . . please. Was there anyone else?"

"People who said they were from Berlin. They would appear without warning. Wishing to meet. Sometimes we did. Usually in the rooms of a Dr. Werfner."

"The one Renfrew was always on about," Ratty nodded, writing rapidly. "His so-called conjugate. And . . . this was something political?"

"Ha!"

"Ever so sorry, delete that—"

"It sounded disingenuous," she smiled. "What isn't political? Where have you been since we were children at Cambridge?"

"The suburbs of Hell," said Cyprian.

"Bringing you from Göttingen to Vienna—might it have been merely some loco parentis tactic of the T.W.I.T. to separate you from this Otzovist lot? Aren't Chunxton Crescent aware of how simply teeming with Bolshies Vienna is these days?"

"It may not be the whole story," she admitted, ". . . there seemed also to be an . . . Hungarian element."

Ratty took hold of his head and held on to it firmly. "Explain. Please."

"We did spend a week or two in Buda-Pesth. Took the steamer down the Danube, met with some rather peculiar people in smocks. . . ."

"How's that."

"This sort of anti-fraud uniform everyone has to wear when they're doing research into what they call down there the 'parapsychical.' No pockets, all but transparent, rather short hemline . . ."

"I say. You didn't, ehrm, happen to bring one back with you, or . . . ?"

"Why, Cyprian."

"Yes actually Cyps, if we could stay on the topic for just a moment longer—what I suppose we are most interested in knowing, Miss Halfcourt, is why they all left Vienna as suddenly as they did."

"I must be very clear with you, that this aptitude of mine, if it exists, has little to do with 'predicting the future.' Some of those who were with me here and in Buda-Pesth believe that *they* can. But—"

"Perhaps somebody 'saw' something? Compelling enough to leave town because of? If it's anything we can verify . . . please, do go on. Since Mrs. Burchell's astoundingly prophetic account of the Serbian outrage, my principals have been quite receptive to the less-orthodox sources."

"They were terrified. Not a matter of whether but of how soon, something—some event, or set of events—would happen. The Russians above all—far beyond the usual *nervnost'*, which since the revolution has been the national malady."

"Was anyone specific?"

"Not with me. I would come into a room, they would literally have their heads together, and when they saw me, they'd stop talking and pretend everything was normal."

"And it hadn't to do with a certain . . ." pretending himself to finger a dossier, "Monsieur Azeff, notorious for blowing up Romanoffs whilst shopping his comrades, in on whom the Socialist Revolutionary hounds are said now to be closing at last—"

"Oh, Yevno, that clown. Not particularly, no. Though of course his name has been coming up for years. But not enough to cause this degree of fear. As if what towered above them out there in the dark, across the lines, were not exactly a new and terrible weapon but the spiritual equivalent of one. A desire in the mass co-conscious for death and destruction."

"I say, how jolly. And so you woke up one morning and found—"

"They didn't all vanish at once. After a bit one began to notice this ominous vacuum. But I saw no point in asking. Having twigged that no one intended to tell me."

"Was that to spare you information that might've upset you? Or did they imagine that you were involved somehow?"

"Whatever they had expected of me in Buda-Pesth, I had failed them. But that might have been separate from this other matter of the departures. Could I borrow a cigarette from somebody?"

FRESH FLOWERS IN THE ROOM, silver coffeepots and cream jugs, surrounding a darázsfészek, a somewhat oversize Dobos torte, a Rigó Jancsi, rain at the windows, a single opening in the dark sky allowing a shaft of sunlight far down Váci út to illuminate the dismal slum of Angel's Field.

Madame Eskimoff looked pale and grim. Lajos Halász, one of the local sensitives, had fallen asleep in the bathtub, remaining that way for the next three days. Lionel Swome was seldom observed away from the telephone, either murmuring with apprehensive glances at the others or listening attentively to the schedule of telephonic transmissions—which the hotel subscribed to and were available to all guests—listening for a stock-exchange report, a sports result, an operatic aria, an unnameable item of intelligence. . . . "Why not just have the bloody thing surgically sewn to your ear!" screamed the Cohen. "Here's another idea," Swome replied, at this point actually attempting, in a somewhat more than halfhearted way, to insert the instrument into the Cohen's anus, the presence of trousers notwithstanding.

Everyone had lost patience, bickering even when silent—

"As if by telepathy," Ratty suggested brightly.

"No. They were all talking out loud. Telepathy under those conditions would've been impossible."

AFTER THE INTERVIEW with old Ratty, Yashmeen seemed to regain her spirit. "Lovely to see you back to your old self," said Cyprian.

"And who would that be?"

They were out strolling in the evening and had wandered into Spittelberggaße, where Viennese of both sexes, in the limitless civic passion for window-shopping, were inspecting a variety of women intriguingly displayed in lighted show-windows up and down the street. Yashmeen and Cyprian paused before one of these, through which a lady in a black corset and matching aigrette, with a certain air of command about her, gazed back.

Yashmeen nodded at his visibly erect penis. "You seem interested." She had suspected in men—particular men, now and then—a desire for self-surrender, having noted it in Cyprian as long ago as Cambridge. All but pulling him through the streets, she approached and inspected a number of cafés before arriving at one in Josephstadt. "This looks all right. Come along."

"A bit elegant. Are we celebrating something?"

"You'll see."

When they were left alone, she said, "Now, about this frightfully irregular sexual life of yours, Cyprian—whatever are we to do?"

Aware of exceeding even the most indulgent of limits to self-pity, "I should mention I've been a catamite these last few years. Someone whose pleasure has never really mattered. Least of all to me."

"Imagine that it does now." Beneath the virginal tablecloth, she had lifted her foot, her shapely foot in its closely laced wine-cordovan boot, the tip of whose toe she now placed unambiguously against his penis. To his bewilderment, that hitherto disrespected member grew swiftly attentive. "Now," beginning rhythmically to press and release, "tell me how this feels." But he could not trust himself to speak, only smile reluctantly and shake his head—yet in another moment he had "spent," almost painfully, in his trousers, rattling the coffee service and the pastry plates and soaking the tablecloth extensively with coffee in his efforts to avoid notice. Around them the restaurant went its imperturbable way. "There now."

"Yashmeen—"

"Your first time with a woman, if I'm not mistaken."

"I—hm? what are you—we . . . didn't . . ."

"Didn't we."

"I meant that if we ever really—"

"'If'? 'Really'? Cyprian, I can smell what happened."

SUMMONED TO VENICE AT LAST, Cyprian, with time on the train to think, kept reminding himself that it had not, after all, been the sort of thing one ought to be taking too romantically, indeed how fatal a mistake it would be to do so. As it turned out, however, this was too much to expect of Derrick Theign, who, ordinarily a bit more taciturn, now flew without warning into high-tessitura dismay, the moment Cyprian arrived at the *pensione* in Santa Croce loudly ejecting what would soon amount to gallons of mucus and saliva, smearing and setting askew his spectacles, chucking about household objects, some of them fragile and even expensive, destroying items of Murano glass, slamming doors, windows, shutters, briefcases, pot-lids, whatever was slammable and handy. Later in the day, as if having in all this percussion belatedly heard its cue, the bora arrived, bringing from every dismal pocket of ill-fortune and mental distress upwind of here its imperatives of mortal flaccidity and blue surrender. The neighbors, who didn't usually complain, being not above a spot of drama themselves from time to time, did complain now, and some quite aggrievedly, too. The wind racketed through every loose tile and unsecured shutter.

"A sweetheart. A bloody *sweetheart* for *God's* sake, I could vomit. I *shall* vomit. Haven't you a cherished photograph of the beloved, which I might perhaps vomit *on?* Have you any idea of how sodding *completely* you have just destroyed *years* of work, you ignorant, fat, ill-dressed—"

"One way to look at it, of course, Derrick, but objectively one can't say she's really a 'sweetheart'—"

"Nance! Pouffe! Sod!"

Yet Theign, for all his apparent loss of impulse-control, was careful to refrain from bodily violence, which Cyprian in any case now, curiously, found himself not as eager for as he once might have been.

Signor Giambolognese from downstairs had his head in the door. *"Ma signori, um po' di moderazione, per piacere. . . ."*

"Moderation! You're Italian! What do you people bloody know about moderation?"

Later, when Theign was calmer, or maybe only too tired to scream, the discussion resumed. "'Help her.' You've the sheer sodomitical *side* to ask that of me."

"Strictly a business arrangement, of course."

"That might take some thought." Theign threw his eyebrows into engagement, usually not a hopeful sign. "What can you pay me with? What perverse coin? The bloom's been off your rosebud for quite some time—*if* I still wanted it, which I'm not at all sure I do, why, I'd just take it, wouldn't I. The price of rescuing your maiden from these Austrian beasts one would think you'd have learned something about by now might be higher than you want to pay—it could even mean being sent someplace that would make the Gobi seem like Earl's Court on a Bank Holiday—oh yes we've rooms full of files on all these mapless horrors—which chiefly exist, in fact, to send you miserable lot out into, in the sure and certain hope we'll never have to set eyes on you again. Are you quite resolved that's what you want? What do you imagine you'd be 'saving' her for anyway? beyond the next willy down the queue, or willies, Turkish more than likely, she'd welcome the change in size I'm sure."

"Derrick. You want me to assault you."

"How intuitive. Enough to know better than to try, one hopes."

"Well. If this isn't just as manly as it gets."

When Foley Walker returned from Göttingen, he and Scarsdale Vibe met at an outdoor restaurant in the foothills of the Dolomites near a river in clamorous descent, the surroundings filled with an innocent light reflected not from Alpine snows but from man-made structures of some antiquity.

Scarsdale and Foley had agreed to delude themselves that in this sun-spattered atrium they had found temporary refuge from the murderous fields of capitalist endeavor, no artifact within miles of here younger than a thousand years, marble hands in flowing gestures conversing among themselves as if having only just emerged from their realm of calcium gravity into this trellised repose. . . . The table between them offering fontina, risotto with white truffles, veal and mushroom stew . . . bottles of Prosecco waiting in beds of chipped ice packed down from the Alps. Girls in striped head-scarves and flowing skirts hovered thoughtfully just offstage. Other customers had been discreetly seated out of earshot.

"All humming along in Germany, I take it."

"The Traverse kid did a skip."

Scarsdale stared at a truffle as if he were about to chastise it. "Where to?"

"Still looking into that."

"Nobody disappears unless he knows something. What does he know, Foley?"

"Likely that you paid to have his Pappy put out of the way."

"Of course, but what happened to 'we,' Foley? You are still the 'other' Scarsdale Vibe, are you not?"

"I must've meant that technically it was your money."

"You are a full partner, Foley. You see the same set of books I do. The mixing of funds is a mystery deep as death, and if you like we can observe a minute of silence to contemplate that, but don't be disingenuous with me."

Foley took out a huge jackknife, opened it and began to pick his teeth, Arkansas style, as he had learned to in the war.

"How long do you think he's known?" Scarsdale kept on.

"Well . . ." Foley pretended to think about it and finally shrugged. "Would that matter?"

"If he took *our* money, all the time knowing what he knew?"

"You mean he'd owe us the money?"

"Did he catch sight of you when you were there, at Göttingen?"

"Mmmnh . . . I'm not sure."

"*Damn,* Foley." Serving-girls withdrew into the pale archways, solemnly waiting for a better moment to approach.

"What?"

"He saw you—he knows we're onto him."

"By now he's likely slipped into the depths, wherever lost souls go, so what's it matter?"

"Your personal guarantee. Could I have it in writing?"

Up here in north Italy, as in France one might buy ordinary village wine hoping to find a few cases of overrun from a great vineyard nearby, Vibe's theory was to buy all the school-of-Squarciones he could put his hands on in the hopes that someplace in there might be an unattributed Mantegna somebody had overlooked. It was the current fashion to disrespect the painting skills of the famed Paduan collector and impresario himself, so any actual Squarciones kicking around, including embroideries and tapestries (for he had begun his working life as a tailor), would be going for a song. In fact, Scarsdale had already picked up a minor angel just by singing "On the Banks of the Wabash, Far Away" to a sacristan who might have been insane. Well, actually, he had Foley sing it. "But I can't carry a tune in a bucket," Foley pointed out, "and I don't know the words."

"Candlelight, sycamores, you'll pick it up."

Scarsdale had never been reluctant to hand out tasks to Foley that were embarrassing at best and often competitive with some of Foley's old Civil War nightmares. Though they betrayed some mysterious flaw in the industrialist's self-regard which someday could prove worrisome, these exercises in personal tyranny happened on average no more than once or twice a year, and

Foley had been able so far to live with them. But on this European excursion, the humiliation rate seemed to have picked up a notch—in fact not a day went by that Foley didn't find himself carrying out some chore better left to a performing monkey, and it was beginning to irritate him some.

At the moment they were out in the Lagoon among the Lost Lands, Scarsdale underwater and Foley up in a little steam *caorlina* fitted for diving. The millionaire, rigged out in rubber hoses and brass helmet, was down inspecting a mural, preserved for centuries beneath the waves by a varnishing technique now lost to history, attributed (dubiously) to Marco Zoppo, and known informally as *The Sack of Rome*. Seen through the brilliant noontide illumination, approached with the dreamy smoothness of a marine predator, the depiction seemed almost three-dimensional, as with Mantegna at his most persuasive. It was of course not just Rome, it was the World, and the World's end. Haruspices dressed like Renaissance clergy cowered beneath and shook fists at a sky turbulent with storm, faces agonized through the steam rising from vivid red entrails. Merchants were strung by one foot upside down from the masts of their ships, horses of fleeing and terrified nobility turned their heads calmly on necks supple as serpents to bite their riders. Peasants could be seen urinating on their superiors. Enormous embattled hosts, armor highlighted a millionfold, were struck by a radiance from beyond the scene's upper edge, from a breach in the night sky, venting light, light with weight, in percussive descent precisely upon each member of all these armies of the known world, the ranks flowing beyond exhaustion of sight, into shadow. The hills of the ancient metropolis steepened and ascended until they were desolate as Alps. Scarsdale was no æsthete, the Cassily Adam rendition of Little Big Horn was fine enough art for him, but he could see right away without the help of hired expertise that this was what you'd call a true masterpiece, and he'd be very surprised indeed if somebody hadn't already sold reproductions of it to some Italian beer company to use in local saloons over here.

Up above in the boat, beneath a Stetson long in service, in the shade of whose brim his face could not be quickly read, Foley supervised the Italians working the air pump. Through the blue-green water he could see the gleam off the helmets and breastplates of the divers. Now and then, fitfully, his hands would begin to approach the nozzles of the plenum chamber from which the air-supply hoses led below. Before touching the apparatus, however, the hands were taken back, often directly into Foley's pockets, where they remained for a time before beginning their next stealthy approach. Foley did not seem to notice that this was happening, and if questioned about it would probably have expressed genuine puzzlement.

He also did not notice that he was being observed from the shore by the Traverse brothers through Reef's new pair of twenty-four-line marine glasses finished in claret-colored Morocco, a gift from 'Pert Chirpingdon-Groin. They had been putting in an hour or two a day tracking Scarsdale around town, just to see if there was going to be any such thing as a clear shot.

In a distressed light over the Grand Canal, autumnal and hazy, the last of the summer tourists were drifting away, rents had become cheaper, and Reef and Kit had found a room in Cannareggio, where everybody seemed to be poor. Bead-stringers sat in the little open spaces and uncheerful *lucciole* appeared at dusk. *Squadri* of young *rio*-rats burst out of alleyways screaming *"Soldi, soldi!"* The brothers walked around the canalsides all night, up and across and down the little bridges, among the fluent breezes of the nocturnal city, scents of late vegetation, broken bars of song, calls upward to shuttered windows, small unseen liquid gestures now and then out in the misty waterways, the creak of a gondola oar against a *forcheta,* the glare of the paraffin lamps at the late-night fruit markets reflecting off the shiny skins of melons, pomegranates, grapes and plums. . . .

"So how we going to do the Hottentot on this bird?"

"The what?"

"French—it means assassination." Reef had guessed that tracking his target and outwitting tycoonical security would not be the only obstacles to getting the deed done. "Got to be sure, Professor—I can count on you in this, can't I?"

"You keep asking."

"Since that *spiritual confab* we had up north there with Pa, seems like that there's something else on your mind now, and settling this score ain't it exactly."

"Reefer, anytime it's a matter of your back, you know I'm there."

"Never disputed that. But look here, it's wartime, ain't it. Not like Antietam maybe, big armies all out in the light of day that you can see, but the bullets are still flyin, brave men go down, treacherous ones do their work in the night, take their earthly rewards, and then the shitheads live forever."

"And what is it they're fighting about again?"

"'They,' I wish it was 'they,' but it's not, it's us. Damn, Kit, you're in this. Ain't you?"

"Well Reefer, that sounds like Anarchist talk."

Reef shifted into what Kit had to assume was a calculated silence. "Worked with a number of that persuasion over the last few years," he said, finding in a shirt pocket the hard black stub of a local cigar and lighting up. Then, twinkling malevolently, "Guess there can't be too many of 'em in the mathematics line."

If Kit had been feeling touchy he might have shot back with something about Ruperta Chirpingdon-Groin, but decided only to nod at Reef's turnout. "Nice suit."

"All right." Chuckling into a cloud of evil smoke.

They stumbled, exhausted, on into the imminent daybreak in search of strong drink. On the San Polo side of the Rialto bridge they found a bar open and went in.

Early one morning the previous April, Dally Rideout had woken up knowing without being told that the new peas, the word in her thoughts being *bisi,* were in at the Rialto market. It had seemed like an occasion. She had already forgotten—having nightwalked into the dialect the way we can pass gently from dream out into the less fluid terms of waking—exactly when conversations in the street had turned less opaque, but one day the bobwire was down, and she had been reckoning for a while in etti and soldi and no longer steering *campo* to *campo* looking up to uncommiserating walls for names of alleyways and bridges, serenely alert to saline winds and currents and the messages of bells. . . . She looked in mirrors to see what might have happened, but found only the same American mask with the same American eyes looking through—the change must lie elsewhere.

And months later here she was at the same market, early as usual, a nice sharp wind raising a steel-gray nap on the water in the Grand Canal, looking for something to bring back to the kitchen of Ca' Spongiatosta, where they were finally allowing her to do some cooking, after she had showed Assunta and Patrizia one of Merle's old soup recipes. Today there were topinambur from Friuli, the Treviso radicchio was in, the verza looked good, and just to make the morning complete, well what do you know, who should come sauntering out of this little dive by the fish market but Mr. Go-away-you're-too-young-for-shipboard-romance himself, yehp that Kit Traverse all right, same hat, same worried look, same potentially fateful baby blues.

"Well, Eli Yale. Ain't this peculiar." Over his shoulder appeared a face you couldn't miss the family resemblance in, which she figured must belong to the third Traverse brother, the faro dealer.

"Well bless me, Dahlia. Thought you'd be back in the States by now."

"Oh, I'm never goin back. What happened to you, you get to Germany O.K.?"

"For a while. Right now me and Reef here," Reef smiling and tipping his hat, "have got some business in town, and then we're off again."

Well *auguri, ragazzi,* and damn if this was about to ruin her day. More of these birds that come flying in, was all—look around, gather in flocks like the pigeons in the Piazza, fly off again. No, as Merle used to say, *apiarian by-product* of hers. Despite which, "You fellows staying around here?"

After a warning look sideways at Kit, "Just some little pennsilvoney," Reef insincerely twinkled, "forget just what part of town."

"Forthcomin as ever I see, family trait, well it's all been mighty nice and I have to get to work now." She moved off.

"But say," Kit began, but she kept moving.

Later the same morning, walking with Hunter past the Britannia, once known as the Palazzo Zucchelli, damned if there wasn't Reef Traverse again, accompanied this time by a slender blonde woman in one of those slanted feathery hats, and a beefy individual whose eyes were made more complex than they perhaps were by gray sun-goggles, bustling out of the hotel and heading apparently for a day on the Lagoon.

"Good God—Penhallow, I say, it isn't you? Well I mean of course it's you, but dash it all, how can that be, don't you see! Though I suppose you could be some sort of *twin* or something—"

"Do stop driveling, Algernon," advised his companion, "it's far too early in the day," though in fact the *sfumato* had burned off an hour ago.

Reef widened his eyes slightly in Dally's general direction, which she read as, *Don't let's get into it just now.*

"Hullo, 'Pert," Hunter taking her hand it seemed emotionally, "lovely to see you, and where else could it've been but here?"

"Yes and whatever have you been up to," Algernon went on, "one moment you're quite splendidly eighty-seven not out, they offer old Barkie the light, and next day not only you, but the entire side as well, are all"—he shrugged—"gone." A species of giggle.

In the slightly baffled pause that followed, their owners taking notice of Dally for the first time, eyebrows came into play, fingertips investigated ear-orifices. Reef, though in full sunlight, had found some way to keep inside his own shadow. The blonde woman put forth her hand and introduced herself as Ruperta Chirpingdon-Groin. "And these are—I don't know, some collection of idiots I've fallen in with."

Briefly taking the hand, "What pleasure, signorina. I am Beppo, Mr. Penhallow's beesiness associat-eh."

"You speak most frightfully good English," the Chirpingdon-Groin woman examining the white kidskin of her glove, a bit puzzled. "And your hands are far too clean for an Italian's. Who are you, exactly?"

Dally shrugged. "Eleanora Duse, I'm, eh, researching a role. Who are you?"

“Oh, dear,” Ruperta’s face growing even less distinct behind her blue sun-veil.

“Here,” Hunter producing his sketchbook and opening it to a charcoal rendering of Dally, as a girl, lounging pensively beneath a *sotopòrtego,* “here’s who she is. Exactly.”

They gathered round, as if this were one more Venetian sight they must take in, and all started twittering, except for Reef, who, patting his pockets as if having forgotten something, touched his hatbrim and disappeared back into the hotel. Ruperta seemed to take it personally. “Damned cowboy,” she muttered, “can’t wait till I’m gone.”

“How long are you in town?” Hunter more anxious than Dally had seen him lately.

Ruperta rearranged her scowl and began to recite a complicated itinerary.

“If you’re free tonight, then,” Hunter suggested, “we might meet at Florian’s.”

Dally congratulated herself for not smirking—she knew it was a place Hunter had ordinarily little patience with, though she had found its tables and chairs a productive field for scavenging cigarettes, coins, uneaten bread, not to mention on lucky days a forgotten billfold or camera, walking-stick, *qualsiasi,* that could be turned for a few francs. And that evening, sure enough, long after the King’s Band had left off playing, there they were, together out in front of Florian’s, Hunter’s eyes exclusively engaged with those of the Englishwoman. Romantic Venice. Dally snorted and lit up half an Egyptian cigarette. Next evening Hunter was out with his tack as usual, bright-eyed and bushy-tailed, painting through the night, unapproached by any of yesterday’s party, seeming no more melancholy than usual. Whatever this cookie might be to him, Dally was sure not about to put her nose in.

AT FIRST she had wondered briefly at the readiness with which the Principessa Spongiatosta had taken her in, attributing it to some kind of a history between her and Hunter. After a while she wasn’t so sure. She had pretty much moved into Ca’ Spongiatosta by now, the life of the *fondamente* not so easygoing these days, better left to younger *rio*-rats. . . . “But just ’cause you’re off the pavement,” she was soon reminding herself, “don’t mean you’re any safer.”

The Principessa’s daily life was an incomprehensible plexus of secrets, lovers male and female, young and old, a relation not so much to the Prince as to his absence, though she had been known to scowl at and occasionally curse any who by so much as a gesture might have taken her for only another depraved young wife. The Prince's absence was more than an unclaimed half of the Principessa's bed—there was business afoot, sometimes as it seemed far from Venice, and she appeared quite often to be acting as some sort of necessary link, when not actually in his place—closeted for hours in remote shuttered rooms, never talking louder than a murmur with a dapper English individual named Derrick Theign who dropped by at least once a week with a gray morning hat in his hand, leaving his card when the Princess wasn't in. The *camerieri,* ordinarily amused at the goings-on here, seem to shy away whenever he came in sight—covered their eyes, spat, crossed themselves. "What thing goes on?" Dally asked, but nobody would say. It did not appear to be romantic, whatever it was. Sometimes Theign showed up when the Prince was away, but more often it seemed to be the Prince—who, like the *levante,* could blow into town at any season—that Theign was eager to see.

It hadn't taken Dally long to learn what this Princess could be like, and sometimes she found herself just wanting to give the woman a kick. "Your friend sure knows how to bring on the blues," she told Hunter.

"For a long time I imagined her quite deep indeed," said Hunter. "Then I saw that I was mistaking confusion for depth. Like a canvas that gives the illusion of an extra dimension, yet each layer taken by itself is almost transparently shallow. You see what sorts of visitor come by. You see how long she can concentrate on anything. She's living on borrowed time."

"Some hothead with a stiletto," Dally trying to keep from sounding too hopeful.

"Oh, perhaps not. But the risks she takes, not necessarily the romantic sort—well . . ."

"It's all right, Hunter, I'd rather not know."

"You're in no danger over there as long as you keep a sharp lookout."

And something there did always seem to be lurking, though Dally wasn't sure what it was. Sometimes the Princess was seen conferring spiritedly with Spongiatosta security details posted about the streets nearby, whose livery bore the ancient family arms, a sponge couchant on a field chequy with flames at the foot. She lingered in secluded alcoves with tidied young women whose skills lay officially in the secretarial line, who never visited the palazzo more than twice, not that Dally was counting, exactly. Who on departing cast back quizzical but not quite sorrowful gazes at the Principessa's bedroom windows. Hunter remained constant among her other visitors, and if it was in any way to keep an eye on Dally, he was a gentleman and stayed inconspicuous about it.

. . .

SOMEPLACE OUT ON the Atlantic between New York and Göttingen, Kit had half come to hope that someday, in some dreamed future, when his silence had grown plausible to Pearl Street, then would have been his moment to return, agent at last for Webb's vengeful ghost, return to daylit America, its practical affairs, its steadfast denial of night. Where acts such as the one he contemplated were given no name but "Terror," because the language of that place—he might no longer say "home"—possessed no others. But here was the hour, imminent, in a town he was having trouble even making sense of. Sitting out in the Piazza with a couple hundred others, drinking tiny cups of the bitter burned sludge these folks called coffee, while pigeons sought jointly or severally the pearl gray of the maritime sky, Kit wondered how more or less real Inner Asia was likely to turn out than what he was looking at now. The town was supposed to've been built on trade, but the Basilica San Marco was too insanely everything that trade, in its strenuous irrelevance to dream, could never admit. The numbers of commerce were "rational"—ratios of profit to loss, rates of exchange—but among the set of real numbers, those that remained in the spaces between—the "irrationals"—outnumbered those simple quotients overwhelmingly. Something like that was going on here—it even showed up in this strange, patternless subset of Venetian address numbers, which had already got him lost more than once. He felt like a person familiar with only real numbers watching a complex variable converge. . . .

"What, you again? Alone with your thoughts, don't let me interrupt, just out gatherin my lunch." Her hair like a gong, redirecting his attention.

"Sorry about this morning, Dahlia. Didn't mean for you to go stomping off that way."

"Me? I never stomp. Grew out of my cowgirl boots a long time ago."

"Listen, sit down, I'll buy you somethin. Actually, here's Reef, let him buy you somethin."

She looked around the field of little tables quickly, as if she didn't want to be recognized. "Does it have to be Quadri?"

"Just headed for the first empty seat."

"This place has been tainted for fifty years, ever since the Austrians all started comin here, back when they were occupying the city. Nothin in this town's ever done with. Try Lavena there sometime, coffee's better."

"Say, Dahlia, thanks for the D. and D. today there with 'Pert." Reef, puffing on a Cavour, on the way someplace else, joined them for a minute. "She tends to get a little insecure when they look like you do, and it can go on for weeks."

"Happy to help. I think." A silence fell. "Well," Dally piped after a while, "you boys are up to *something illegal,* I'll bet! why, anybody can tell, just looking at you."

"Oh," Reef a little nervous it seemed, "we usually are."

"You're already sittin at the wrong caffè, which leads an observer, and there's enough of those, to calculate you're both strangers in town, maybe even short on resources."

"We're really O.K.," Reef muttered.

"I might be able to help some."

"Not for this," Kit said.

"See, it's really dangerous," Reef explained, as if that would be enough to send her away.

"In which case you probably shouldn't be calling attention to yourself every time you move, or open your mouth—me, on the other hand, I know how to go around unseen, unheard, more important I know people here, who if they ain't the exact ones you need, they'll know people that might be. But please, keep on like this on your own if it's what you want."

Reef started in on his hatbrim, never a good omen. "Tellin you straight out, we don't have much money to throw around."

"I ain't looking for your money, Mr. Traverse—though I can't speak for others in this town, 'cause it's the usual story, once upon a time people used to do favors for free, but not lately."

"Not even when it's in the public interest?" said Kit, getting him another of those cautionary looks from his brother.

"Illegal, yet in the public interest. My. Now what could that be? Let me think a minute."

"Where'd you run into this one," Reef squinting at them both. "One of your old college 'flames'?"

"Ha!" exclaimed Kit and Dally, more or less together.

"She's on the square, Reefer."

"You already told me."

Oh? Not having blushed for a while, Dally figured this was not the moment either. Reef was looking at her carefully. "Miss Rideout, it's not my practice to force situations onto people."

"Especially li'l bitty American girls look like they ain't got a brain in their head, right?"

"Oh, now." Reef put his hat back on and stood. "Got to go run some 'Pert-connected chores, maybe we'll talk later. Areeferdirtcheap, kiddies."

"What'd he say?"

"Rounder Italian, I think."

Kit and Dally began to walk, Dally putting her head into a tobacconist's from time to time to light another cigarette at the shop's lamp. It was not, presently, their pace that accelerated so much as a certain concentration between them, brought on in no small measure by the city itself. She found them a secluded table in a garden in back of a tiny *osteria* between the Rialto and Cannareggio. They ate a polenta with squid in squid ink, and a zuppa di peoci that couldn't be beat. Once she would have thought, Our first "date"—now she was wondering only, what in hell kind of trouble's this boy got himself into now?

"Here it is then." Kit throwing down a glassful of grappa.

She waited, her eyes wide open.

"This is what we come here to do. You breathe a word and we're all dead, right?"

"Deaf and dumb," she assured him.

"I'm gonna tell you what it is. You ready?"

"Kit—"

"O.K., you know who Scarsdale Vibe is."

"Sure. Carnegie, Morgan, all them princes of capital."

"Vibe is the one who . . ." he paused, nodded to himself, "who hired those boys to kill my Pa."

She put her hand on his hand and left it there. "Kit, I guessed it all the way back on the boat, but thanks for trustin me with it. Now you and your brother're fixin to go get Vibe for it, is what this is about, I guess."

"So when you offered to help us, you already had some idea."

She kept her eyes lowered.

"Well you can get out of that if you want," he said in a kind of low voice. "Real easy." They sat there for a while. She didn't dare move her hand. It was modern times, and ungloved hands did not touch deliberately unless it meant something.

As to what that might be, of course . . .

For his part, Kit had got as far as noticing her eyes, which even allowing for this Venetian light seemed strangely silver-green. Green eyes in a redhead, nothing too unusual in that—but irises set in a ground somehow lambent as unpolished silver, to which all other shades of color were referred, how could that be? Photographs of themselves. And why should he be paying so much attention to her eyes?

"It gets worse, I'm afraid. Something must have happened back in the States, because now Vibe's people are after me. Is why I'm not in Germany anymore."

"Sure that you're not just . . ."

"Crazy? That I wouldn't mind."

"And you two are really . . ." She couldn't bring herself to say it, because she couldn't tell how serious any of this was.

"'Planning to do the deed,'" Kit suggested.

"And get out of town ahead of the carabinieri. Where are you headed, if it's not too forward of a gal to ask?"

"Reef, ask him. Me, Inner Asia is the plan right now."

"Oh sure, just down the road there from Outer Asia. No chance you'd ever be stickin around here for a while, always did have that whole other life, now you'll be a fugitive from justice and who knows what all besides."

She had an idea how miserable she looked, and pulled her hand away. Kit reached for it again. "Listen, don't think it's—"

She smacked his hand and smiled grimly. "Don't bother with that. You and whoever, your business."

"Me and— What's that mean?"

A level gaze he couldn't read. Sunlight came into the little place and abruptly her hair went incandescent. They lingered then in one of those paralyses where anything anybody said would be wrong.

"Look," Kit exasperated, "you want my word on it? give you my word. Solemn word. Right back here—same spot exactly, that jake with you? Let me write down the name and address, o' course a firm date could be a different matter—"

"Save it." She wasn't glaring exactly, but it was no sunny smile either. "Someday maybe you will promise me somethin. And then, look out, mister."

Wasn't as if they'd ever had the time to get creatively lost in this maze of *calli,* was it, or go out sailing on the Lagoon in some little *topo* with one-them orange sails, or wander church to church rhapsodizing over the great paintings, let alone pause up on the Iron Bridge at sunset to kiss while lanterned boat traffic passed beneath them and accordions choired their newfound love. None of that Venetian stuff was about to happen, not this damn lifetime.

What did she want? Wasn't this just Merle all over again? That alchemy, the magic crystals, the obsessive assaults on the Mysteries of Time, she'd really believed once that she had to get away from that before it drove her as crazy as her Pa, and now, would you just look, here she was getting it back, here was another lunatic, somebody this time leaving her, to go search for an invisible city over the edge of the world. *Cazzo, cazzo . . .*

"Forget about him," advised the Principessa. "Tomorrow night at Palazzo Angulozor there will be a wonderful ball. Come, please. I've a hundred gowns just hanging here with nothing to do, and you and I, we are the same size."

"I'm too sad," Dally demurred.

"Because he is leaving," sniffed the Principessa, who had heard the story in general but none of the details, though heaven knew that had never kept her from dispensing advice. "Might be gone for a year, maybe more, maybe forever, *vero?* Like a young soldier, going off to serve. And you think you'll wait for him."

"Do I. Who the hell are you," Dally flared, "to be making fun of my feelings? You're the one's always pissing and moaning about 'one cannot live without love.'"

Whatever basis they were on by now allowed for this sort of impertinence. The Principessa shrugged, amused. "That's what this is?"

"Maybe not up to your standards, Princess."

"And the young man? What are his feelings?"

"Don't know and I ain't about to ask."

"Eh! *Appunto!* It is all a romance tale *you* have made up."

"We'll see."

"And when? While you are *waiting,* I know a dozen young men, very rich, who would love to make your acquaintance."

"I don't know."

"Come. Indulge me. Let us look at a few things. I am thinking of one old *straccio* in particular, green 'meteore,' perfect with your eyes, trimmed in Venetian guipure, which might just do the trick."

THEY WERE ALL out on the roof of the place in Cannareggio. Ruperta had left on the noon train, headed for Marienbad, inconsolably eyeing every fellow traveler in range. Her egotism being so monstrous that she could see no further than her next romantic adventure, she had been a perfect companion for Hunter, who had decided to go along as far as Salzburg. Love in the air? Say, did Dally give a rip?

"So I'm in on this Hottentot o' yours?"

Reef shrugged. "Forty mule, I guess."

"What's that."

"French, it means for lack of anything better. There'll have to be somebody to keep us from making too many wrong turns."

"Thanks. That's it? a cicerone, nothin a little more, I don't know, physical? I pick pockets and snatch hangers off of tourist ladies. I throw knives with good accuracy up to twenty meters. I've fired guns with names and calibers you never heard of."

"We were fixin to handle that part of it ourselves, actually."

“You don’t see me in a markswoman role here, fine. More in the line of what then, nurse? cook? Wait! what have we here, why it’s one-them *cordite elephant guns* if I ain’t mistaken.”

“You ain’t. Rigby Nitro Express, point 450 caliber, shoots a nickel-plated hollow-point.”

“Which expands on impact,” the girl nodded, “and is sure not your average sporting bullet. Maybe that Vibe oughta change his name to Jumbo. Mind if I—”

“Please.” Reef handed it over and she made a point of hefting it for balance, opening and closing the breech, taking a stance, sighting in on various bell towers around town. After a while she murmured, “Sweet weapon,” and handed it back.

“ ’Pert’s idea of a good-bye gift,” Reef said.

“She knows about this that you’re fixin to do?”

“She’s a city girl, she thinks I’ll be usin it for pheasants or somethin.”

“Trying to kill somebody like Vibe,” it seemed to Dally, “best take your lesson from the famous attempt fifteen years ago on Henry Clay Frick, the Butcher of Homestead, which is never go for a head shot. Aiming for Frick’s head was Brother Berkmann’s big mistake, classic Anarchist mistake of assumin that all heads contain brains you see, when in fact there wa’n’t nothin inside damned Frick’s bean worth wastin a bullet on. People like ’at, you always want to go for the gut. Because of all the fat that’s built up there over the years at the expense of poorer folk. Death may not be too immediate—but in the course of probin around in that mountain of lard lookin for the bullet, a doctor, especially one that treats the upper classes, bein more used to liver ailments and ladies’ discontents, is sure to produce, through pure incompetence, a painful and lingering death.”

“She’s right,” Reef agreed after a short period of wordless stupor, gazing as at some Indian guru of the violent, “and drygulchin’d be out of the question too, way too many people around, can’t be hittin any of ’em by mistake. A fella’d have to walk right up to old Scarsdale, face-to-face. Is where I guess you’d come in, Kit.”

“Maybe not,” Kit said.

“Oh, he stopped your money, hell that’s society-page gossip, not hot lead from ambush.”

“Breeze in, howdy, Mr. Vibe how you been keepin and what a surprise seeing you here in Venice Italy—sure, Reef, you know what’ll happen.”

“What’ll happen?”

“Man wants me out of the way, I’m tellin you.”

Dally growled in some impatience with all this dawdling. "Listen now, you two do understand don't you, there's others lined up waiting for a shot at this buzzard, and you ain't exactly next."

Reef, as if this was news to him, "You don't say. Why, you mean there's actually other people hate him as much as we do?"

"You're in Anarchist country, buckaroo. Sooner or later over here, they're bound to run out of royalty to shoot at and start lookin around for more of the riffraff—politicians, captains of industry, so forth. And that's a list Scarsdale Vibe has been on for some time."

"You know any Anarchists?"

"In town here, plenty."

"Reef thinks he's one," noted Kit.

"You really think they might have somethin in the works already?" Reef said.

"Most of it's talk. You want to go have a look?"

They got off at the San Marcuola stop and walked over a couple of bridges and under a *sotopòrtego* and into alleyways so narrow they had to walk single file till Dally said, "Here." It was a caffè called Laguna Morte. Inside were Andrea Tancredi and some artist friends, and as it happened the topic under discussion was Scarsdale Vibe, as the latest in a series of American millionaires who had come here with designs against Venetian art.

"The newspapers like to call it 'spoils of war,'" declared Tancredi, "as if it is only some metaphorical struggle, with large dollar sums replacing casualty figures . . . but out of everyone's sight and hearing, the same people carry on a campaign of extermination against art itself." Even with Kit's Italian on the sketchy side, he recognized this as passion, and not the usual coffeehouse eyewash.

"What's wrong with Americans spending money on art?" objected a piratically bearded youth named Mascaregna, "*macché,* Tancredi. This town was built on buying and selling. Every one of those Great Italian Paintings sooner or later has had a price tag. The grand Mr. Vibe isn't stealing anything, he's paying a price both sides have agreed on."

"It's not the price tag," Tancredi cried, "it's what comes after—investment, reselling, killing something born in the living delirium of paint meeting canvas, turning it into a dead object, to be traded, on and on, for whatever the market will bear. A market whose forces are always exerted against creation, in the direction of death."

"*Cazzo,* let them have whatever they can take away," shrugged his friend Pugliese. "Clear some room on these crumbling old walls for us."

"The American's sins are far greater than art theft, in any case," Mascaregna said. "We must not forget the vast unmapped city of unprotected souls he has brought to the edge of the abyss. Too many even for God to forgive."

"What Mr. Vibe needs," said Tancredi, "is trouble he cannot pray himself out of."

"La macchina infernale," Dally ventured.

"Appunto!" Tancredi, known as reluctant to touch anyone, gave her an appreciative squeeze. Kit, noticing this, swung her a look. She let her eyes go as wide as possible and twirled an invisible parasol.

The boy shook hands shyly with Kit and Reef. He did not, this particular afternoon, seem like one driven to any desperate pass. "This Vibe, eh?"

It would have been as good an opening as any. The brothers exchanged a look, but somehow let it pass.

Later they would remember his eyes.

"HOW SERIOUS you think this kid is?" Reef wanted to know.

"Lately," Dally said, "he's been talking a lot about Bresci, Luccheni, and some other famous Anarchist gunhands, enough to make folks nervous anyway."

"This was supposed to be easy," Reef said. "Just plug the son of a bitch and be done with it. Now all 'f a sudden we're lookin to hand the job over to somebody else?"

"Who's to say," Kit carefully, "we couldn't get it done quicker by just standing back, letting the forces of History roll on over him?"

"That Harvard talk?"

"Yale," Kit and Dally said together.

Reef blinked at them for a minute. "'Who's to say'? Well, to begin with . . ."

THE PRINCIPESSA HAD finally talked Dally into going to the ball that night, and had also let drop the interesting piece of news that one of the guests would be Scarsdale Vibe. Sheltering indoors from an unusually insanity-inducing bora, Kit, Reef, and Dally sat playing poker and discussed this development, drinking grappa, Reef filling the air with malodorous smoke from his cheap Italian cigars. Everybody waiting for something, a good hand, a cheerful thought, the carabinieri at the door, beneath a strange heavy feeling of bad news rolling up the rails.

"Ever seen one of these?"

"Whoa, where'd that come from?"

"Torino, Italy."

"No I meant—"

"Simple sleight o' hand, Venice is a colorful town but there's too many blind corners. They call this the Lampo, cute, ain't it? Repeater, fires a Gaulois 8 mm, this li'l finger ring here's your trigger, middle finger fits right in there"—she demonstrated—"muzzle just peeks out of your fist, push out and the bolt goes back, squeezin your hand again chambers a round—*bam*."

"Well hell, you could go right up to him with this."

"Could, I guess."

"But you wouldn't."

"Boys . . ."

"He's teasin you," said Kit.

"Guess I was," Reef sighed dramatically.

"Liven up the evening anyway," Dally supposed.

"Hey! Maybe you'll meet some Italian prince, fall in love, at least git outside of some good eats." Reef, laughing at his brother's annoyance, started coughing out clouds of cigar smoke.

"Strangle on 'at thing while you're at it, why don't you?"

"Too bad I never went in for jewel-thief activities, Dahlia, you'd be the perfect accomplice."

"Jeez, Kit, your brother is so charming."

"He smells good too," muttered Kit.

"You go on ahead, Dahlia," Reef said, "a party's a party, never turn one down, raise all the hell you want, anything useful comes your way just let us know, we'll be outside doing some reconnaissance. Somehow there'll be a way to get him."

Outside, citizens were being blown horizontal, hanging on to whatever they could, shoes flown off their feet sailing away out over the stormy Lagoon. Roof tiles were picked away one by one, gondolas bounced booming end over end down the Riva, leaving spalled-off chips of lacquer to eddy behind in tiny black tornadoes, as overhead, shed feathers counter-whirling in a pale silvery turbulence, tutelary Venetian angels sought shelter among untended bells, wind-beaten, signaling now hours canonical only to storm, calling celebrants to invisible masses for the souls of the wrecked and sea-taken, as below the grounded pigeons and waterbirds were fleeing the Lagoon shivering into sotopòrteghi, into courtyards within courtyards, denying sky, pretending citizenship in the labyrinths of earth, gone glitter-eyed and shifty as rats in corners. Venetians pulled on rubber boots and waded through the high water. Visitors, taken by surprise, went teetering along elevated duckboards, negotiating rights-of-way as they might. Hastily fashioned signs with painted arrows appeared at corners to indicate drier routes to take. Water heaved crazily out in the canals, gunmetal gray, smelling like the sea, some sea somewhere. Piazza San Marco was a great ornamental basin, belonging to the sea, dark as the sky it was reflecting, a ground for oblongs of orange light from the windows of the caffès and shops under the Procuratie, images scattered and re-scattered by the wind.

"Now but what about that old Dahlia," said Reef later, when she'd gone back to Ca' Spongiatosta, "time comes to get out of town in a hurry, how you fixin to handle that?"

"Don't think she'll miss me all that much."

Reef smiled back with the patented tightlip look which had served him faithfully across so many gaming tables. The burden of which was "Oh, go on ahead 'th whatever you had in mind, just don't blame me later on," being useful for throwing other players into paralyses of doubt, as well as making him look like a compassionate opponent who worried that he might win too much of the others' rent or baby-food money.

Grasping invisible reins and making get-on-with-it motions, Kit finally said, "What?"

"I'll tell you a story someday. Maybe."

In the unrelenting drizzle, some five or six carabinieri were arranged strategically along the *fondamenta,* preventing people from crossing the bridge to the Palazzo. Greatcoat collars turned up against the chill. No telling how long they would have to be posted here. Under the aspect of a painting not hanging on any recognized wall, titled *Failure.* Kit and Reef slunk by, trying to be part of the *imprimatura.* Along the pavement opposite, figures in black, bent as if against some wind of fatality, moved in a viscid streaming, beneath black umbrellas in fitful undulation, each step a struggle, all traffic fragmented into private missions of desire. . . . Isolated from consequences as the middle of the night.

Electric lights in the windows, torches carried to and fro by servants, the flames continually beaten at by the wind. A heavy interior susurrance, inflected by ancient stone, issuing out onto the *rio* along with a small string orchestra playing arrangements of Strauss Jr., Luigi Denza, and hometown luminary Ermanno Wolf-Ferrari.

Kit caught sight of Dally in the Principessa's borrowed gown and a dark silk paletot, her incendiary hair done up in an ostrich-plume aigrette dyed indigo, sweeping in the gate and up the marble steps to the *piano nobile,* and for a heartbeat and a half just forgot where he was and what he was supposed to be doing here.

Scarsdale Vibe arrived in a private gondola and mirrored by Foley Walker stepped on to the *fondamenta.* There was the unmistakable snap of a gunshot.

Sudden as a storm out on the Lagoon, bodyguards in black were rising up from everywhere, long-annealed *teppisti* newly arrived in town from strike-breaking duties in Rome and the factories of the North, armed, silent, masked, and on the move.

"Christ, it's an army," Reef muttered. "Where'd they come from?"

And here right in the middle of it came this skinny kid in a borrowed suit, shirt-collar too big, immediately read as out of place and therefore in disguise and therefore a threat. "It's that Tancredi kid, what'n the hell's he doing here?"

"Oh no," Kit said. "This ain't good."

There was no way to get to him, he was inside the black funeral train, already rolling, of his terrible intention.

"Via, via!" they were kind enough to warn him off, but he kept approaching. He was doing the one thing authority cannot abide, will never allow to pass, he was refusing to do as he was told. What was the object he held in his hand, carefully, as if it might explode at the slightest jar? "His hands were empty," Pugliese said later, "nobody found a weapon."

Mascaregna shook his head, disconsolate. "He said he had an infernal machine, which would bring down Vibe and, some distant day, the order Vibe expresses most completely and hatefully. This was his precious instrument of destruction. It gave off a light and heat Tancredi alone could sense, it blinded him, it burned fiercely in his hands, like the glowing coal in the Buddhist parable, he could not let it go. If Vibe was an acquirer of art, then here was Tancredi's creation, his offering, the masterwork he thought would change any who beheld it, even this corrupted American millionaire, blind him to the life he had been inhabiting, bring him to a different kind of seeing. No one gave him a chance to say, "Here it is, here is a bounded and finite volume of God's absence, here is all you need to stand before and truly see, and you will know Hell."

Flame stabbed out of the muzzles of brand-new Glisentis, shots echoed off the water and the stone walls, tremendous, ripping apart the silence. Tancredi's limbs had flown open, as if he were preparing to embrace as much as he could of what the world had just been reduced to—the first rounds contracted him to a remnant, bowing down as if before some perverse nobility, around and behind him rising the ancient splendor of the Palazzo, as he slipped and fell in his own blood and passed into a void in the day where bells were silent, the city he both loved and resented taken away, no longer his to transfigure.

At first it seemed they might only be prodding at the remains with their boot-tips—to be expected of professionals, after all, just making sure the subject didn't suddenly come to life again. But this grew less tentative, and soon the *assassini* were delivering brutal kicks, as forcefully as they could, shouting insults till the *fondamenta* sounded like a jailyard, while Scarsdale Vibe all but danced up and down in delighted approval, loudly offering procedural advice.

"Make sure you damage the face, fellows. *Batti! batti la faccia,* yes? Destroy it. Give the little shitass's Mamma something to cry about." When his voice was too hoarse to go on, he approached and looked down for a while on the torn corpse in its bath of public light, feeling blessed at having witnessed firsthand this victory over Anarchist terror. Foley, for whom it had once been the vernacular of daily life in a Union regiment, stood by and didn't comment.

Rising fog had begun to mix with the slow dissipation of gunsmoke. A party of rats, having taken immediate interest, had emerged from the canal. Out of consideration for any late-arriving guests, one of the gunmen, using the boy's hat, was trying to sluice away some of the blood from the pavement with hatfuls of canal water.

Vibe stood at the highest point of the little bridge without speaking, back turned, a solid black silhouette, head and cloak, held waiting in an unmistakable tension seeming not to grow in size so much as, oddly, to take on mass, to become rectified into an iron impregnability. For an instant, before he made his deliberate way back into the shelter of the lighted and melodious palazzo, he turned and stared straight at Kit, leaving no doubt that he recognized him, and even with the falling night, the *foschia* and the guttering torchlight, Kit could see enough of the triumphant smirk on the man's face. *You pathetic little pikers,* he might have been chuckling, *who—what—did you think you were up against?*

"ACCORDING TO THE POLICE, Anarchists specialize, Foley, did you know that? The Italian ones usually go after royalty. Empress Elisabeth, King Umberto, so forth."

"Guess that makes you American royalty," quipped Foley.

"King Scarsdale. Yes. Has a lilt to it."

They were up in the grand dining room at the Bauer-Grünwald eating roast tenderloin of lamb and guzzling Pommery. The room was busy with eaters whose supply of cash far exceeded any degree of hunger they could remember or imagine. Waiters conversed in undertones which only just managed to be polite, in which the word *cazzo* occurred often. Chandeliers, whose crystalline arrangements were set to exquisitely fine clearances, shivered and chimed as if able to sense each negligible settling of the building into the primeval Venetian ooze beneath.

Later Scarsdale was astonished to see Foley out carousing on the embankment, whirling round and round with not one but three young women, accompanied by some local maniac with an accordion. From time to time, firecrackers went off as well.

"Foley, what in heaven's name?"

"Dancin that tarantella," Foley replied, out of breath.

"Why?"

"Celebrating. Just happy that *they* didn't get you."

If Scarsdale heard an emphasis on "they" he gave no indication.

"WHERE'N THE HELL'D all 'em pistoleros come from?" Reef had been repeating, like a sort of prayer in time of defeat.

"They were hired for the evening," Dally said. "And there'd have been no way to buy them off, not with what your Mr. Vibe was paying them."

"Why didn't somebody say something?" Reef more annoyed than plaintive.

"I did—you just didn't want to hear about it. Everybody else in these *calli* knew."

"We figured there'd be extra hands," Kit said, "just not so many. Dumb luck we got away, we could look at it like that."

"That kid sure didn't get anyplace," Reef scowling at his brother. "Sorry, Dahlia."

She was shaken, more than she was willing to let on. It seemed years she'd been dropping by to see Tancredi and his paintings. She was aware in almost a neural way of all the creation that would not happen now, the regret and horror at what she had almost been a part of, and worst of all the shameful, shameful relief at still being alive. They might never have become lovers, but shouldn't they have been allowed some time to find out? He was a virtuous kid, like all these fucking artists, too much so for the world, even the seen world they were trying to redeem one little rectangle of canvas at a time.

"I should've seen it coming," Dally said. "Somebody shopped him. This miserable town, a thousand years of ratting to the law."

"I could at least have said be careful," Kit mumbled.

"Listen, children," Reef throwing things in a valise, "when they invent the time machine, we'll buy tickets, hop in, come back to last night, and all shall be made jake. Meantime the old sidewinder has took his charmed life someplace else, and no telling when we'll get another shot. If ever. I sure don't know how the hell long we're supposed to keep doin this." He went out the door, and they heard him on the stairs.

"Well I'm just as glad it didn't happen," she said quietly. "One dead is one too many." Looked up at Kit and the silent term was clear in her face—one dead, one about to head off into exile.

Kit paused in his efforts at disguise, mostly to do with combing shoe polish into his hair. "I do keep my promises, Dahlia."

She nodded, kept nodding, figured there was plenty of time later to get around to crying.

"You know if there was any way I could stay—"

"There isn't. You don't need my permission."

"Vibe saw me there, at the scene. If he didn't already figure it out, he has now, and there's none of them who'll just let it be anymore."

"That case you'd best get going, don't end up the same way."

Though Kit had never made much sense of Venice, it almost seemed normal compared to what he was headed into. Dally recognized the condition. "Here they say *bagonghi,* the way it feels when you go staggering around all over the place like a circus clown." He went to sleep and woke with the single operatic image of Vibe turning to stare him mercilessly in the face, having known all along exactly where he'd been stationed across the little canal, while all around them day-wage assassins revealed themselves, as if Time's own prætorians had risen up to defend it. The rose-dyed smile, the smile of a pope in a painting, framed in a face that didn't customarily smile, one you'd prefer never to see, for it meant trouble on the tracks.

It was probably also the undeniable moment, if one had to be singled out, of Kit's exclusion from what had been spoken of at Yale as a "future"—from any routes to success or even bourgeois comfort that were Scarsdale Vibe's to control. Kit was not sure how much he'd ever wanted that, but now there wasn't even the choice. Yashmeen's *stranniki* had delivered themselves entirely into the service of God and the Mysterious Death, but as far as Kit could see, this journey ahead of him was not for God, not for Yashmeen, who was the love of somebody's life no doubt, just not Kit's, nor any longer even for the cause of Vectorism—maybe nothing more than the simple preservation through flight of his increasingly worthless ass.

THEY MIGHT HAVE imagined some effortless departure into a golden fog, but as it turned out, the brothers did not part on what you'd call affectionate terms. As if the gunplay at the Palazzo had been catching up with Reef or something, he'd now cranked himself into a grim mood.

"You don't have to come wave good-bye at the depot, fact it's better you don't, 'cause I won't be wavin back anyway."

"Something on your mind Reef?"

Reef shrugged. "You never wanted in on that deal. You dragged your feet all the way. Well it's over now and so long, kid."

"You're blaming me for what happened?"

"You sure wa'n' no help."

Kit's fingers began to ache, and he peered back at his brother, hoping he'd heard wrong.

"Your fairy godfather's still out there drinkin Champagne and pissin on Pa's memory. And there's nothin you can say anymore, 'cause you don't know nothin." Reef turned and went glaring away, shoulders hunched, up onto the Ponte degli Scalzi, soon absorbed into a mobility of hundreds of separate futures, whose destiny could not be told in any but a statistical way. And that was that.

OFF ON THE night steamer for Trieste, the lights through the fog apt to slide off into spectral effects, billowing like cloaks flourished by sleepless masqueraders, Giudecca invisible . . . likewise the shrouded *Stromboli* and the other Italian warships at anchor . . . the calls of the gondolieri taking on in the *foschia* a queer anxiety, the leather sides of trunks and valises wet and shining in the electric glare . . . Dally kept disappearing, with Kit each time expecting her not to be there when the view cleared again. Lighters and *traghetti,* carrying travelers, baggage, and cargo, crowded the little fetch, each vessel a waterborne stage for high-intensity theatricals, passionate practical advice from all directions, trunks handed up in the vaporous scurry, always just about to topple comically, with their owners, into the canal. Musicians in twos and threes were playing all along the Zattere, some from the King's Band, picking up a few extra soldi. Everything in minor modality.

Nobody would have come to see Kit off, his brother was on the rails again, already miles out of town, and now Dally thought of it, what in blazes was she doing here saying good-bye—nothing better to do? What could sentimental embraces at the water's edge mean to this jasper anyway?

Around them travelers drank wine out of cheap Murano souvenirs, clapped shoulders, brushed away leaf and petal debris from last-minute bouquets, argued over who had failed to pack what. . . . Dally was supposed to be past the melancholy of departure, no longer held by its gravity, yet, as if she could see the entire darkened reach of what lay ahead, she wanted now to step close, embrace him, this boy, for as long as it took to establish some twofold self, renounce the somber fate he seemed so sure of. He was gazing at her as if having just glimpsed the simple longitude of what he was about to do, as if desiring to come into some shelter, though maybe not her idea of it . . . so, like terms on each side canceling, they only stood there, curtains of Venetian mist between them, among the steam-sirens and clamoring boatmen, and both young people understood a profound opening of distinction between those who would be here, exactly here day after tomorrow to witness the next gathering before passage, and those stepping off the night precipice of this journey, who would never be here, never exactly here, again.

Dearest Father,

I write in uncertainty as to whether you shall ever read this—so, paradoxically, in a kind of faith, now made perhaps more urgent by doubts which have arisen concerning those to whose care you entrusted me, so long ago.

I believe that the T.W.I.T. no longer act in my interest—that my continued safety is now of little consequence to them, if not indeed a positive obstacle to plans of their own kept entirely hidden from me. We are at present in Switzerland, and due to entrain in a day or two for Buda-Pesth, where, unless my "gifts of prophecy" have deserted me, danger and perhaps sorrow await.

The unexpressed term, as ever, remains Shambhala—though you, who have long and honourably served within its sphere of influence, may find it easy to dismiss the anxieties of one who knows it only at second (let us say, third) hand. Yet, like those religious charlatans who claim direct intercourse with God, there are an increasing number at the T.W.I.T. who presume a similar intimacy with the Hidden City, and who, more disturbingly, cannot separate it from the secular politics of present-day Europe.

History has flowed in to surround us all, and I am left adrift without certainty, only conjectures. At Göttingen, for a while, after the revolution in Russia, I was perceived as useful by at least one group of heretical Bolshevist refugees. The recent understanding between England and Russia has seemingly enhanced my value to the British War and Foreign Offices. As for what use I still may be to the T.W.I.T., only they can say—but will not. It is as if I possessed, without my knowledge, some key to an encrypted message of great moment, which others are locked in struggle to come into control of.

Those in whose company I travel but among whom, I fear, I am no longer counted, once presented themselves as seekers after a kind of transcendence. . . . I believed, for many years—too many—that I might someday learn the way. Now that they have forfeited my trust, I must look elsewhere. . . . For what mission have I here, in this perilous segment of space-time, if not somehow to transcend it, and the tragic hour into which it is passing?

Mathematics once seemed the way—the internal life of numbers came as a revelation to me, perhaps as it might have to a Pythagorean apprentice long ago in Crotona—a reflection of some less-accessible reality, through close study of which one might perhaps learn to pass beyond the difficult given world.

Professor McTaggart, at Cambridge, took what one must call the cheerful view, and I confess that for a while I shared his vision of a community of spirits in perfect concord, the old histories of blood and destruction evolved at last into an era of enlightenment and peace, which he compared to a senior combination-room without a master. I am today perhaps more of a Nietzschean, returned to thoughts of the dark future of slavery and danger from which you sought to rescue me. But one's rescue is surely, at the end of the day, one's own responsibility.

I had the obvious thought once that all this wandering about must have an object—a natural convergence to you, and that you and I need only be reunited for all to come clear at last. But more and more lately, I find I cannot set aside your profession, the masters you serve, the interests which all this time out there in Inner Asia, however unconsciously, you have been furthering. These are matters upon which you always observed the strictest vow of Silence, and I expect no argument I advance, even now as a competent adult, could induce you to break it. Though I cannot with certainty say when or even if I may see you again, I was haunted by the possibility that, if we ever did meet at last, we might both, against our wills, stumble into a serious, perhaps a fatal, row.

But you came to me last night in a dream. You said, "I am not at all as you have imagined me." You took my hand. We ascended, or rather, we were taken aloft, as if in mechanical rapture, to a great skyborne town and a small band of serious young people, dedicated to resisting death and tyranny, whom I understood at once to be the Compassionate. Their faces were strangely *specific,* faces which could easily appear in the waking day here below, men and women I should recognize in the moment for who they were. . . .

They used to visit all the time, coming in swiftly out of the empty desert, lighted from within. I did not dream this, Father. Each time when they went away again, it was to return to "The Work of the World"—always that same phrase—a formula, a prayer. Theirs was the highest of callings. If there was any point to our living in that terrible wilderness, it was to persist in the hope of being brought in among them someday, to learn the Work, to transcend the World.

Why have they remained silent, for so long? Silent and invisible. Have I lost the ability to recognize them? the privilege? I must find them again. It must not be too late for me. I imagine sometimes that you have led an expedition to Shambhala, troops of horsemen in red jackets, and are there now, safe, among the Compassionate. Please. If you know anything, please. I can go on wandering, but I cannot remain at this stage of things—I must ascend, for down here I am so blind and vulnerable, and it torments my heart—

Do you know of the sixteenth-century Tibetan scholar-prince Rinpungpa? Mourning the recent passing of his father, which has made him the last of his dynasty, his new reign beset with enemies, Rinpungpa believes he can look for advice only toward Shambhala, where his father has been reborn and now dwells. So the prince writes him a letter, though he knows of no way to deliver it. But then, in a vision, a Yogi appears to him, who is also himself, the man of clarity and strength he knows he must become, now that his father has gone to Shambhala—and Rinpungpa also understands that it is this Yogi who will be his messenger.

Mr. Kit Traverse, who brings you this letter, like myself, journeys at the mercy of Forces whose deployment and strength he has but an imperfect grasp of, which may well cause him damage. He must continue, as must I, an intensive schooling in modes of evasion and escape, even, with luck, now and then, counter-attack. He is not my "other self," yet in some way I feel that he is my brother.

Father, I have long known of a strange doubleness to my life—a child rescued from slavery yet continuing her journey along the same ancient road of abasement. Somewhere another version of me is at Shambhala with you. This version of me which has stayed behind, like Prince Rinpungpa, must be content with writing a letter. If you receive it, please find a way to answer.

My love.

Insh'allah.

. . .

AFTERWARD PEOPLE WOULD ASK Kit why he hadn't brought along a hand camera. By then he was noticing how many Europeans had begun to define themselves by where they'd been able to afford to travel, part of the process being to bore interminably anybody who'd sit still for it with these ill-framed, out-of-focus snaps.

He kept some of the ticket stubs, so he knew in a general way that his route had taken him via Bucharest, to Constantza, where he boarded a small, bedraggled steamer, sailed along the Black Sea coast to Batumi, where you could smell the lemon groves before you saw them, got on a train there and crossed the Caucasus where Russians stood out in front of dukhans to watch them go by, raising their vodka glasses amiably. Fields of rhododendrons spilled down the mountainsides, and giant walnut logs came floating steeply downstream, destined for saloon bars like those in Colorado that Kit had once lounged against as a boy. Last stop on the line was Baku on the Caspian Sea, where he had the impression, though not the photographic evidence, of a very remote sandswept oil port, night in the daytime, skies of hell, boiling red and black, *shades of black,* no escape from the smell, streets that led nowhere, never more than a step from some drugged stupor or rugrider's blade, with life not only cheap but sometimes of negative value—according to Western field reps more than happy to bend his ear on the topic, nobody to depend on, too much money to be made, too easy to lose it . . . the only relief from it being the parties held aboard corporate yachts moored among oil tankers down at the quays, portholes sealed against the sand and the smell of oil. The futures of these visitors, actuarially speaking, did not to Kit seem bright, and he left Baku regarding in some horror from the weather decks the port receding under black skies, among pillars of fire, wellsprings of natural gas burning since the days of the ancient fire-worshippers, scrawls of oil towers and loading piers against the blurred light off the water.

So he crossed the Caspian Sea, among Bnito oil tankers and sturgeon fleets, boarding at Krasnovodsk the Trans-Caspian Railroad, which took him along the edge of the Qara Qum opening vastly, incomprehensibly to the left, while to the right, like a parable, irrigation ditches and cotton fields spread up toward the mountains, with folks selling melons at the water stops. What he found memorable as he proceeded was less the scenery than a sort of railroad-metaphysics, as he stood between carriages, out in the wind, facing first one side, then the other, two radically different pieces of country. Plains flowed by right to left, mountains left to right, two opposite flows, each borne by the unimaginable mass of the entire visible world, each flowing at the speed of the train, an ongoing collision in silence, the vectorial nature of whose currents was clear enough, though not the roles of time and his own observing consciousness with its left- and right-handedness. The effect of rotating ninety degrees from a moving timeline, as expected, was delivery into a space containing imaginary axes—the journey seemed to be unfolding in three dimensions, but there were the added elements. Time could not, somehow, be taken for granted. It sped up and slowed down, like a variable that was dependent on something else, something so far, at least, undetectable.

At Merv the tracks swung leftward into the desert, open as weatherless sky, herds of gazelles darting like flocks of birds across it. The structure out here was revealed immediately—desert punctuated by oases in a geography of cruelty, barkhans or traveling sand-dunes a hundred feet high, which might or might not possess consciousness, cloaked and hooded, not earthly projections of the angel of death, exactly, for species here had gained a reputation for their ability to hold on even under the worst conditions—the predators tended to be skyborne, the prey to live beneath the surface, with the surface itself, defining them one to another, a region of blankness, a field within which the deadly transactions were to be performed. Oases, or distant smoky blurs of saksaul trees, appeared like moments of remission in lives of misfortune—rumored, hallucinated, prayed for, not always where they were supposed to be.

From his briefing by Lionel Swome, Kit gathered that the Trans-Caspian, as well as the Trans-Siberian and other lines, had been of the essence of the 1905 revolution, and there was still plenty of post-revolutionary evidence as they rolled along—sheds burned to charcoal crosshatching, abandoned freight cars, groups of riders in the distance moving too swiftly and coherently to be camel caravans.

"Last year it was worth your life to spend much time out here. You had to be armed and travel in numbers. Banditry pure and simple."

Kit had fallen into conversation with a footplate man who was deadheading back out to Samarkand, where he lived with his wife and children.

"But since Namaz Premulkoff broke out of prison last year in Samarkand, that has begun to change. Namaz is a great hero in these parts. He brought fifty men out of jail with him, and in no time at all they had become a bit more than mortal. The exploits were remarkable enough, but practically speaking Namaz also brought a discipline to the great anger and discontent out here and, most importantly, revealed the Russians to be the true enemy." He nodded out the window at a purposeful dustcloud in the distance. "These are no longer bands of peasants uprooted from their land—they are now organized units of resistance, their target is the Russian occupation, and the people support them widely and absolutely."

"And Namaz still leads them?"

"The Russians say they killed him back in June, but no one believes it." He fell silent, till he noticed Kit's inquiring look. "Namaz is not dead. How many of the people have ever seen him in person? He is everywhere. Physically present or not—they believe. Let the Russians try to kill that."

The principal crossing from world to world was over the wood bridge at Charjui across the wide yellow Amu-Darya, known in ancient times as the Oxus.

They stopped not at Bukhara but ten miles outside it, because the Mahommedan community there believed the railroad to be an instrument of Satan. So here instead was the new city of Kagan, with its smokestacks and mills and local dignitaries grown suddenly rich on real-estate chicanery—the waste expelled from holy Bukhara, which lay out there ten miles away as if under a magical proscription, invisible but felt.

Stops at Samarkand, Khokand, at last to the end of the line at Andizhan, from which Kit had to proceed by dirt roads to Osh, and finally over the mountains to behold at last the huge fertile market-oasis of Kashgar, unbelievably green as a garden in a vision, and beyond it the appalling emptiness of the Taklamakan.

"LIKE DAMNED STANLEY AND LIVINGSTONE all over again," Kit was heard to mutter more than once in the next few days. "The man is not lost, and there was never any question of 'rescue.'" Somebody had been telling Yashmeen stories, likely to scare her, it seemed to Kit, into venturing outside the T.W.I.T. sphere of safety. Which would account for why they had spirited her away from Göttingen.

Indeed, far from "lost" or "in danger," Auberon Halfcourt was quite comfortably settled into a high-European mode of residence at the palatial Hotel Tarim, Indian cigars ready for the cutter each morning with his newspaper, fresh flowers in his sitting-room, a sinful profligacy of fountains and dripping deep foliage just past the French doors, concerts at the hour for tea, gazelle-eyed young women arriving and departing on a variety of errands, often done up in actual *houri outfits* of fabrics woven by a workshopful of European craftsfolk, originally brought out here as slaves, who had chosen, over their generations, to remain, far from their homes, under some dark system of indenture, passing on the secrets of how to rig the looms for these imponderable yarns of infinitesimal diameter, producing not so much lengths of cloth as surfaces of shadow, to be dyed in infusions of herbs native only to, and gathered, generally at great risk, from the all-but-inaccessible stretches of the waste country beyond this oasis.

Except for a detail or two, comparable luxuries were being enjoyed just across the courtyard by his Russian opposite number, Colonel Yevgeny Prokladka. The hired musicians—rabab, hand drums, and *ghärawnay,* or Chinese flute—had learned "Kalinka" and "Ochi Chorniya," the girls, though having, many of them, some idea of what animal fur was, had never actually worn it until now, much less taken advantage of the claims it appeared to have on the Colonel's attention—while the cuisine was resolutely Russian, based on the huge classic cookbook *A Gift to Young Housewives,* by E. N. Molokhovets, which the Colonel had had installed in its own cabinet in the hotel kitchen on his arrival. When he wished to make a public impression, he rode a splendid gray Orloff, which besides towering over most other horses in the streets, had an inclination to the adventuresome, which the Colonel suspected was only bad judgment but was taken usually by the locals here for bravery.

At the moment, voices from the British side of the courtyard, raised in dispute, could be heard all over the establishment—one of the routine weekly rows between Halfcourt and Mushtaq, his colleague of many years, whose ferocity in combat was by now legendary, at least among those who, misled by the abbreviation of his stature, had dared and somehow survived its effects. "Nonsense Mushtaq, here, you need to *relax, man,* better have a drink, oh so sorry your religion, devoutly dry aren't you people, slipped my mind of course—"

"Spare your long-suffering and far better informed coadjutor this staff-college twaddle, sir. Time, as it seems I must again point out, grows short. Having broken off its idle mischief in the foothills of the Tian Shan, the *Bol'shaia Igra* is now reported over the west Taklamakan, where its mission is obvious to the lowest camel-thief."

"Oh do let's bring the Gatling out then! yes, and hope that *evil balloon* happens to sail just overhead! perhaps we shall get off a lucky shot or two! Unless of course you'd recommend wiring down to Simla for a regiment or two? Our options Mushtaq are dashedly few and not one of them practicable—but I say, your teeth—didn't used to be that color, did they?"

"Events of late have forced me to resume the use of betel, sir. Far more beneficial to one's health, may I add, than alcohol."

"It's the spitting part I could never quite get the hang of."

"Much like vomiting, actually, though perhaps more discreet." The two glared at each other, while from Colonel Prokladka's establishment could be heard the sound of massed local instruments, and a laughter whose loudness and constancy did not quite make up for an all-but-complete absence of merriment.

The Russian colonel had surrounded himself with a cadre of disreputables, each with a tale of abrupt dismissal from duties west of the Urals and reassignment out here, and who by now, among them, controlled every imaginable form of vice in the town, as well as some not yet available anywhere else—his own A.D.C. or *lichnyi adiutant,* Klopski, for example having imported from Shanghai and installed a number of *peculiar machines,* steam-driven and lit by naphtha lamps brighter and more modern than any to be found in Europe, which projected, so as entirely to surround an operator seated at the control panel, in varied though not strictly natural colors, a panorama presenting a series of so-called Chinese Enigmata, so compelling in its mimickry of alternate worlds that any impulses toward innocent play had become soon enough degraded into uncontrollable habit, with souls uncounted now as willingly in bondage to these contraptions as any opium-smoker to his pipe. "Where is the harm?" shrugged Klopski. "One miserable kopeck per go—it isn't gambling, at least not as gambling has been known up till now."

"But your kiosks," protested Zipyagin. "Especially the ones in the bazaar—"

"Ever the village scold, Grigori Nikolaevitch. It isn't doing *your* sector any harm, not from what your girls tell me."

"The ones *you* visit? *Yob tvoyu mat',* I wouldn't believe too much of what *they* say." Social grimaces resembling smiles passed among them. They were gathered in seedy *zastolye* for this nightly moral exercise at a highly illegal drinking-room out past the edge of town, almost monopolizing the place except for a handful of furtively boozing local folk.

"Nor any slackening in the opium trade, none at all. Everyone profits from these 'Chinese' units of yours, Klopski, including imams without number."

"They're entitled to a percentage, I should think."

"They'll convert you, it's so certain nobody will bet on it anymore."

"Actually I did experiment with Islam briefly. . . ."

"Vanya, I thought we all knew each other. When was this? Did you go out into the desert and *begin to spin*? your mind proceeding to flee in all directions at once?"

"It was just after Feodora's letter. And then that cavalry rogue Putyanin who said he'd had her in St. Petersburg just before we shipped out—"

"So as I recall you went after him with a hand-grenade—

"He had drawn his pistol."

"It was aimed at his own head, Vanya."

"*Poshol ty na khuy,* how would you know? You were the first one out the door."

THE CHIEF ITEM of concern in this paradise of the dishonorable was a prophet known locally as "the Doosra," operating somewhere north of here, who had been driven—according to those, naturally, with the feeblest grasp of the concept—"mad" by the desert. As often happened out here, he had changed into a living fragment of the desert, cruel, chaste, unstained by reflection. It was uncertain how this had come about—hereditary madness, operatives from over one of the horizons, shamanic influence closer to home—one day, somehow, though never having ventured out of the Taklamakan, he announced, as if having been conducted to a height nowhere on earth obtainable, a sharply detailed vision of north Eurasia, a flood of light sweeping in a single mighty arc from Manchuria west to Hungary, an immensity which must all be redeemed—from Islam, from Buddhism, from Social-Democracy and Christianity—and brought together under a single Shamanist ruler—not himself but "One who comes."

The Doosra's discovery of the Mark IV Maxim gun, as Lieutenant-Colonel Halfcourt duly wired Whitehall (in clear, much to its annoyance), was "hardly among the more promising developments vis-à-vis Pan-Turanian hopes." Remote lamaseries, caravans on the move, telegraph stations at significant wells, began to fall before the implacable shock-wave of a revelation which few to date, if any, had shared, and many simply blamed on the Doosra's known enthusiasms for opium, ganja, and any number of local fusel oils, singly or combined, named and nameless. The interests of England, Russia, Japan, and China out here, not to mention those of Germany and Islam, were already, for many, woven too intricately to keep track of. Now with yet another player joining the Great Game—All-Turkic, for pity's sake—the level of complication, for many of the old Inner Asia hands, grew far too harrowing, mental damage within Colonel Prokladka's shop being perhaps the most spectacular, with its midnight explosions, mysterious cases of hallucination, actual invisibility, and unannounced howling exits out through mud archways and into the wind-ruled wastes forever.

"They think they go to join some sacred band," Chingiz, the Colonel's *denshchik,* confided to Mushtaq at one of their daily get-togethers in the marketplace. "What they cannot see yet is that he is not another Madali or even Namaz, this is not another holy war, he does not seek an army to follow him, he despises people, all people, sends away all who would be disciples, that is both his fascination and the force of his destiny. What is to come will not occur in ordinary space. The Europeans will find great difficulty in drawing maps of this."

"Rejected disciples have too often become dangerous."

"It is but one of many ways he invites his dissolution. He gives loaded revolvers as personal gifts. Publicly humiliates those who profess to love him most deeply. Comes drunk into the mosque during prayers and behaves most sinfully. None of it matters, for in any case he is but a precursor, who sometime must give way to the True One. How he does this is not as important as the timing."

"You visit the shaman often, Chingiz?"

"He is thy shaman too, Mushtaq."

"Alas, I am too old for these adventures."

"Mushtaq, you're thirty. Besides, he keeps a supply of wild mushrooms, sought at his behest by prospectors who are guided by their guardian spirits, in parts of Siberia not even the Germans know about. It would do thee far more good than the poisonous nutmeat of the south."

"That of course would be a different matter."

ONE DAY THE NOTED UYGHUR troublemaker Al Mar-Fuad showed up in English hunting tweeds and a deerstalker cap turned sidewise, with a sort of ultimatum in which one might just detect that difficulty with the prevocalic *r* typical of the British upper class. "Gweetings, gentlemen, on this Glowious Twelfth!"

"By God he's right Mushtaq, we've lost track of the time again. Bit oddly turned out, wouldn't you say, for a tribal chieftain in these parts?"

"I am here to deliver a message fwom my master, the Dooswa," declared the Uyghur fiercely, flourishing an ancient Greening shotgun whose brasswork carried holy inscriptions in Arabic. "Then I am going out after some gwouse."

"Fond of the English, are you sir."

"I love Gweat Bwitain! Lord Salisbuwy is my *wole model*!"

This is the only place on earth, Auberon Halfcourt reflected, where lethargy of the soul can arrive in spasms. Summoning up what he hoped was a pleased smile, "On behalf of H.M. Government, we declare ourselves at your service, sir."

"Weally? You mean it?"

"Anything in our power."

"Then you must suwwender the city to the Dooswa."

"Ehrm—that is, I'm not sure it's mine to surrender, is the thing, you see. . . ."

"Come, come, you can't fool an old camel-twader."

"Have you spoken to any of the Russians yet? the Chinese?"

"The Chinese are no pwoblem. My Pwinciple's intewests lie quite in the other diwection."

Perhaps because he had been eavesdropping, Colonel Prokladka showed up about then. A glance, controllable by neither, pulsed between him and the Uyghur. "Wwetched son of a camel-dwiver," Al Mar-Fuad was heard to whisper as he rode out of town.

"I SHALL NEVER understand them," Halfcourt plaintively confessed to Prokladka. "Their strangeness—in language, faith, history—the family interweavings alone—they can turn invisible at will, simply by withdrawing into that limitless terrain of queerness, mapless as the Himalaya or the Tian Shan. The future out here simply belongs to the Prophet. It might have gone differently. This madman in the Taklamakan might actually have founded his pan-shamanic empire. The Japanese, let us say at German solicitation, might have attended in greater numbers, so as to draw off the odd Russian division in the event of a European war. We should have the bazaars full of yakitori pitches and geishas in bamboo cages. I've been out here twenty-five years, ever since old Cavi ate the sausage at Kabul, and all the meddling of the Powers has only made a convergence to the Mahommedan that much more certain."

"We are neither of us mountain fighters," Prokladka brimming with collegial tears, "Russians prefer steppes, as your people prefer Low Countries, or better yet oceans, to fight in."

"We could share what we know," offered Halfcourt, with seemingly emotional abruptness.

The *Polkovnik* gazed back, pop-eyed and bloodshot, as if actually considering this, before giving in to a laughter pitched so high and so uncertain in its dynamics as to bring into doubt his ability to control it. *"Polny pizdets,"* he muttered, shaking his head.

Halfcourt reached to pat his arm. "There there, Yevgeny Alexandrovitch, it's all right, I was ragging you of course, inscrutable British sense of humor sort of lapse, and I do apologize—"

"Oh, Halfcourt, these profitless wastes . . ."

"Do I not dream, with little respite, of Simla, and Peliti's veranda at the height of the season? And the wanton eyes of those who pass, it seems endlessly without me, over the Combermere Bridge?"

· · ·

Beyond Kashgar, the Silk Road split into northern and southern branches, so as to avoid the vast desert immediately to the east of the city, the Taklamakan, which in Chinese was said to translate as "Go In and You Don't Come Out," though in Uyghur it was supposed to mean "Home Country of the Past."

"Well. It's the same thing, isn't it, sir?"

"Go into the past and never come out?"

"Something like that."

"Are you talking your rubbish again, Mushtaq? what of the reverse? Remain in the exile of the present tense and never get back in, to reclaim what was?"

Mushtaq shrugged. "When one has heard enough of these complaints, lamentable though they may be . . ."

"Apologies, you are right of course Mushtaq. The choice was made too long ago, too deep in that no-longer-accessible homeland, to matter now whether I chose, or others chose for me, and who can draw boundaries between the remembrancer and the remembered?"

His argument here could not be termed altogether ingenuous, there having been at least, notably, one Remembered whose contours had remained for him all too defined. "All too damnably clear." Unable not to whisper this aloud, later, when Mushtaq had returned to sleep and Halfcourt had lit up another transnoctial cheroot, unwilling to forgo the flaccid swoon of yielding to memory . . . her form, already womanly, held at wary attention that ill-omened day among the negotiable flesh, hair covered and mouth veiled, eyes belonging entirely to herself, though they were to find him, unerring as an Afghani sharpshooter, the moment he rode in under the gate of sun-baked mud, he and Mushtaq, disguised as Punjabi traders, pretending to be in the market for some of the highly esteemed donkeys of the Waziri. He knew full well what this was, this gathering of girls, he was an old trouper by then at the costume theatricals they were forever at out here, and watched the other visitors who came by, the sweat and saliva and where it flowed, and where it flew. His intent toward the child, he would protest, had never been to dishonor but to rescue. Rescue, however, had many names, and the rope up which a maiden climbed to safety might then be used to bind her most cruelly. In that instant he had become, awkwardly, two creatures resident within the same life—one conveyed without qualification into the haunted spaces of desire, the other walled in by work-demands in which desire was never better than annoying and too often debilitating—the two selves sharing thenceforth this miserable psychic leasehold, co-conscious, each at once respectful and contemptuous of the other's imperatives.

Colleagues he knew of it happening to had struggled, grown insomniac and worn, cultivating destructive habits, inflicting on themselves wounds ranging from minor to mortal. Auberon Halfcourt saw the danger and at first, day to day, somehow kept avoiding it, though with scant assistance from Mushtaq, who, the instant Yashmeen arrived, discovered the advantages of absence. "I have been barefoot over these particular coals more than once, Your Aggravation, expect nothing, my cousin Sharma will take over the laundry, the cigar merchant is anxious for his last two payments, I believe that is all, ta-ta, until our reunion in less vexatious times," and he had simply vanished, in so brief a twinkling that Halfcourt suspected some exercise of local magic.

Intentionally or not, this posed the question, from the time she stepped across his doorsill, no longer of whether but of when Yashmeen must go. Her pale eyes from time to time narrowing in conjecture he would never learn to read, her naked limbs flickering against the green-shadowed tiles of the baths and fountains, her silences often sweet as heard singing, her odors, fugitive, various, a soon-inseparable part of the interior climate, borne from any corner of the wind-rose, somehow overcoming even cigar-smoke, her hair compared by one of the local balladeers to those mystical waterfalls that hide the Hidden Worlds of the Tibetan lamas. Previous to Yashmeen, of course—which made it especially awkward now—he had never been so much as fascinated, let alone enamored. One did not, however much in widely-known fact some did, undergo such passionate attachment to a child. One suffered, was ruined, raved intoxicated through the market spaces, abasing oneself before the wog's contempt, seeking at length the consolations of the Browning, the rafter, the long hike into the desert with an empty canteen. Self-slaughter, as Hamlet always says, was certainly in the cards, unless one had been out here long enough to have contemplated the will of God, observed the stochastic whimsy of the day, learned when and when not to whisper *"Insh'allah,"* and understood how, as one perhaps might never have in England, to await, to depend upon, the ineluctable departure of what was most dear.

Colonel Prokladka and his shopmates, for whom there were no secrets in Kashgar, at least no secular ones, looked on in sorrowful amusement. Had there been a way to turn it to political use, they would of course have undertaken some program of mischief—but as if the girl had somehow charmed even that iniquitous fraternity, none ventured beyond a rough courtliness that sometimes could even be mistaken for good manners. There was an

Anglo-Russian Entente, after all. Yashmeen visited regularly with the girls of the *Polkovnik*'s harem, and everyone male in the vicinity had the sense not to interfere, though a subaltern or two had been reported for unauthorized peeping.

As always they were more preoccupied with ways to turn a dishonest ruble—hasheesh, real estate, or their colleague Volodya's latest scheme, insane even by the standards prevailing here, to steal the great jade monolith at the Guri Amir mausoleum in Samarkand, either by breaking it up into smaller blocks or by engaging the semi-mythical aeronaut Padzhitnoff to spirit away the whole chunk using some technology as yet undeveloped in the world at large. Volodya was obsessed by jade, the way others are by gold, diamonds, hasheesh. It was he who kept slyly reminding Auberon Halfcourt that out here the local word for jade is *yashm.* He had been sent east in 1895 for his part in an illicit jade deal at the time of the construction of Alexander III's tomb. Now, at Kashgar, he wasted everyone's time planning to raid the tomb of Tamerlane, despite a long-standing and universally believed-in curse that would release upon the world, in the event of such desecration, calamities not even the great Mongol conqueror had thought of.

Lieutenant Dwight Prance had shown up one night unannounced, like a sandstorm. Halfcourt remembered him from when he first came out here, a scholar of geography and languages at Cambridge, one of Professor Renfrew's. Well-meaning, went without saying, none of them knew how not to be. Now he could scarcely be recognized—the man was filthy, sun-beaten, got up in some tattered wreck of a turnout intended, he supposed, to be read as Chinese.

"I gather that something's afoot to the east of here . . . ?"

The distracted operative, with one of Halfcourt's Craven A's already burning, lit another, then forgot to smoke it as well. "Yes and how far 'east' being almost beside the point, when one has been engaged for the past—my God! it's been a year . . . more than a year. . . ."

"Some . . . Chinese involvement," prompted Halfcourt.

"Oh, as if boundary-lines mattered anymore . . . if only . . . no, we're well past that—now we must think of the entire north Eurasian land-mass, from Manchuria to Buda-Pesth, all, in the eyes of those we must eventually face, territory unredeemed—all the object of a single merciless dream."

"I say, Eurasia Irredenta," Halfcourt beaming through the smoke of his cigar, as if pleased with the coinage. "Well."

"They prefer 'Turania.'"

"Oh, that!" Waving the cigar, almost one would say dismissively.

"Known to your shop, is it."

"What, old Pan-Turania? Japanese mischief," as if identifying some item of porcelain.

"Yes. The usual Turkish and German meddling as well. . . . But for *this* performance, the familiar Powers have been cast in subordinate roles, removed into the shadows at the margins of the stage . . . while up in the glare, poised between the worlds, stands a visitor—say, a famous touring actor from far away, who will perform not in English but in a strange tongue unknown to his audience, yet who for all that keeps each of them transfixed, mesmerized, unable to remove his gaze even to glance sidewise at his neighbor."

"So that none of them can . . . quite think straight?"

"So that by the end of the piece, sir, each, imprisoned in his own fear, is praying that it all be only theater."

Halfcourt was giving him a long appraising stare. Finally, "Has this Asiatic Beerbohm Tree of yours got a name?"

"Not yet . . . the general feeling out there is that by the time his name is revealed, all will be so irreversibly on the move that, for any step we might conceive, here or in Whitehall, it will be far too late."

ONE EVENING shortly after his arrival, Kit was sitting out in the courtyard with the Lieutenant-Colonel. Each had by him a traditional twilight arrack-and-soda. Pastry vendors called from the street. Invisible birds, collecting against the night, sang boisterously. Across the way came the smell of somebody cooking cabbages and onions. The evening call to prayer broke over the city like a victim's cry.

"We are each in some relationship," Halfcourt was saying, "largely undiscussed, with the same young woman. I cannot speak as to another's feelings, but one's own are so . . . automatically suspect really, that one hesitates to admit them, even to one's counterpart in hopelessness."

"Well, you have my silence," said Kit, "for what that's worth."

"I imagine—how shall I refrain from imagining?—that she is grown by now quite beautiful."

"She is a peach, sir."

They sat among the choiring clepsydras of the evening garden, time elapsing in a dozen ways, allowing their cigars to go out, keeping a companionable silence.

At last Kit felt he could venture, "Pretty forlorn lookout for me. I don't know that I'd've come all the way out here if she hadn't set it up, so you can guess how easy I can be made a sap of."

A lucifer flared. "At least you've a likelihood of seeing her again?"

"No chance you'll get back there anytime soon?"

"My postings are not of my own choice, I'm afraid." He squinted at Kit for a while, as if trying to read a contractual clause. Then, nodding briefly, "She must have asked you to look after me. . . ."

"No offense, sir . . . I can guarantee that Yashmeen has you very much on her mind, in, in her heart, I'd say. . . ." Some articulation of smoke across the twilight advised him of how little further he could take this.

Auberon Halfcourt was by now too annoyed to be feeling much pity for this boy. Young Mr. Traverse clearly had no idea of what to do with himself. Thought he was out on a nature hike. Years before taking flannel, Halfcourt, his secret commission in a tin box in the safe of a P&O steamer, sailed out into the preternaturally blue Med, in a deck chair with his assumed name stenciled onto it, through the Suez Canal, pausing midway to take a dip in the Great Bitter Lake, proceeding then across the Red and Arabian seas to Karachi. There at Kiamari he boarded the Northwestern Railway, which was to carry him by causeway over to the salt delta of the Indus, on through radiant clouds of ibis and flamingo, mangrove giving way to acacias and poplars, into the plains of Sind, up along the river clamoring down from the mountains, toward the frontier, switching to narrow-gauge at Nowshera, on to Durghal station and the Malakand Pass where raptors soared, into native disguise and eastward through the mountains, shot at and formally cursed, over the great Karakoram Pass at last, into East Turkestan and the high road to Kashgar. Nowadays, of course, it might as well all be on a Cook's tour.

By the Edwardian standards of rationally-arrived-at code of values and stable career, young Traverse here was an obviously drifting wreck without much hope of ever being straightened out. What on earth sort of family produced wastrels like this? As long as he was this far from the orbit of an ordinary life, he might as well be pressed into service for a mission the Lieutenant-Colonel had had in mind since Prance had brought his news. Without an unambiguous go-ahead from home, Halfcourt had decided to resurrect a long-shelved plan to project a mission eastward to establish relations with the Tungus living east of the Yenisei.

"Of course you're free to refuse, I've no authority, really."

They went in to the library, and Halfcourt took down some maps.

"A journey from the Taklamakan to Siberia, over fifteen hundred miles as the *bergut* flies, northeast across the Tian Shan, across the southern Altai, to

Irkutsk and the Angara, and on into shamanic Asia. Islam does not flourish there. Few if any Christian explorers will journey there—they prefer polar wastes, African forest, to this wilderness without issue or promise. If they must be among the Tungus, say for reasons of anthropology, then they will approach from the sea, against the river."

For his own part, Kit supposed he was game, imagining that the journey here so far had been too easy, that *stranniki* do not depend upon railway travel, that this must be the next stage in a mission beyond Kashgar, that Yashmeen and Swome had perhaps known nothing of.

He was to be accompanied on his journey by Lieutenant Prance. They looked over the maps in Halfcourt's library. "We must begin here," Prance pointing. "This great Archway known as the Tushuk Tash. Which means 'a rock with a hole in it.'"

"This area all around it, the Kara Tagh? looks like it hasn't been mapped very well. Why bother with it, why not skirt it completely? Be a lot more direct."

"Because this Arch is the Gateway," declared Prance—"unless we enter by way of it, we shall always be on the wrong journey. Everything between here and the Tunguska country belongs to the Northern Prophet. We may follow the same route there as ordinary travelers, but if we do not pass first beneath the Great Arch, we shall arrive somewhere else. And when we try to return . . ."

"'We may not be able to,'" said Kit. "Yes, and some would call that metaphysical hogwash, Lieutenant."

"We will be disguised as Buriat pilgrims, at least as far as Lake Baikal. If you are lucky enough to grow into your role, perhaps, somewhere on the journey north, all will become clearer to you."

Fine one to talk, given his own, one could say, regionally inappropriate appearance—pale, redheaded, eyes perhaps a bit too far apart, more reasonable-looking in a top hat and frock coat, and some setting a bit more urban. His attempts at disguise would not, Kit feared, suggest the Buriat pilgrim so much as the British idiot.

Early next morning Halfcourt was in Kit's room, shaking him awake and puffing cigar-smoke like a steam engine. "Bright eyes, everyone, heave out and trice up, for you've an audience in half an hour with the Doosra himself."

"Shouldn't it be you, you're the ranking English speaker around here."

Halfcourt waved his cigar impatiently. "Far too well known. What's needed is an unknown quantity to everybody out here, but marginally less so to me, it being at the margins, you see, that I do most of my business."

· · ·

THE DOOSRA WAS YOUNGER than Kit had imagined and lacked gravitas. Plumper than the general run of desert ascetic, he was packing a new Japanese "38th Year" Arisaka rifle—basically a .26-caliber Mauser whose eponymous Colonel had improved some on the bolt design—captured in a raid whose bloodiest details the young visionary had no reluctance to share with Kit, in fluent English, though his plausibility was not helped by a pronounced University-nitwit accent. Kit had arrived on one of the small shaggy local horses, more like a pony, with his stirrups almost touching the ground, whereas Al-Doosra was mounted on his legendary Marwari, and some horse it was, a horse of great bravery and endurance, all but deathless, finely quivering with some huge internal energy, as if poised to ascend and fly at any moment. Many in fact were the people out here who swore they'd seen the horse, whose name was Ogdai, soaring against the stars.

"I am only a servant in this matter," said the Doosra. "My own master will be found in the north, at his work. If you wish to seek him for yourself, he will receive you. He will satisfy all your questions about this world, and the Other. You can then come back and tell the English and Russian officers in Kashgar all they wish to know. Will you assure me that you have their trust?"

"I don't know. How will I find him, the one you prepare the way for?"

"I will send with you my loyal lieutenant Hassan, who will help you through the fearful Gates and past those who guard them."

"The . . ."

"It isn't only the difficult terrain, the vipers and sandstorms and raiding parties. The *journey itself* is a kind of conscious Being, a living deity who does not wish to engage with the foolish or the weak, and hence will try to dissuade you. It insists on the furthest degree of respect."

AROUND MIDNIGHT Mushtaq looked in. Halfcourt had been reading Yashmeen's letter again, the one the American had brought. His cigar, ordinarily a cheery coal in the dimness of the room, had in this sorrowful atmosphere gone out.

"I am contaminated beyond hope, Mushtaq."

"Find her again, sir. Even if you must ascend the highest tower in the cruelest city in the world, do what you must to find her. At least write back to her."

"Look at me." An elderly man in a shabby uniform. "Look at what I have done with my life. I must never so much as speak to her again."

That said, one day he creaked up onto one of the tough, low-set Kirghiz horses and went riding out alone, perhaps in search of the Compassionate, perhaps of whatever, by now, had become of Shambhala. Mushtaq had refused to go with him. Prokladka, convinced that the Englishman had lost his mind at last, went on with his devious activities in Kashgar.

Some weeks later Auberon Halfcourt appeared at a book-dealer's in Bukhara, clean, trimmed, and pressed—respectably turned out, in fact, except for the insane light in his eyes. He was no surprise to Tariq Hashim, who had seen at least a generation of these searchers pass through—most of them, lately, German. He led Halfcourt into a back room, poured cups of mint tea from a battered brass pot, and from a lacquered cabinet inlaid with ivory and mother-of-pearl produced, reverently, it seemed to the Englishman, a box containing a loose stack of long narrow pages, seven lines to the page, printed from wood blocks. "Early seventeenth century—translated from Sanskrit into Tibetan by the scholar Taranatha. Included in the part of the Tibetan Canon known as the Tengyur."

Since he had left Kashgar, Halfcourt had been dreaming persistently of Yashmeen, always the same frustrating narrative—she was trying to get another message to him, he was never where he should have been to receive it. He tried now to summon the benevolence of dream.

"I have also heard of a letter, in the form of a poem," he said carefully, "from a Tibetan scholar-prince to his father, who has died and been reborn in Shambhala. . . ."

The bookseller nodded. "That is the *Rigpa Dzinpai Phonya,* or Knowledge-Bearing Messenger, by Rimpung Ngawang Jigdag, 1557. Directions for journeying to Shambhala are addressed by the author to a Yogi, who is a sort of fictional character, though at the same time real—a figure in a vision, and also Rinpungpa himself. I do know of a variant currently for sale, which contains lines that do not appear in other versions. Notably, 'Even if you forget everything else,' Rinpungpa instructs the Yogi, 'remember one thing—when you come to a fork in the road, take it.' Easy for him to say, of course, being two people at once. I could put you in touch with the seller, if you were serious."

"I'm serious," Halfcourt said. "But I don't read Tibetan."

Tariq shrugged in sympathy. "Translations of these guides to Shambhala are usually into German—Grünwedel's *Shambhalai Lamyig,* of course . . . most recently, three pages from Laufer's volume of Uyghur Buddhist literature, author unknown, supposedly thirteenth century, which all the Germans who come through here seem to be carrying in their rucksacks."

"I suppose what I'm asking," Halfcourt struggling not to give in to a strange premonitory sense of exhilaration and sorrow he had been feeling for days, of something gathering, "is, how practical are any of them, as directions to finding a real place."

The bookseller nodded perhaps for longer than he had to. "It helps to be a Buddhist, I'm told. And to have a general idea of the geography out here. It is all but certain, for example, that one should be looking north of the Taklamakan. Which does not narrow anything down much. But it is all I know anyone to be agreed upon.

"I am myself submissive to the way of the Prophet, very conventionally so I'm afraid. But Shambhala—though it is all very interesting, I'm sure—"

By now the city outside was saturated in shadow, the women gliding away in loose robes and horsehair veils, the domes and minarets silent and unassailable against unwished-for depths of blue, the markets wind-ruled and deserted, every insane desert vision ever experienced out here, for just a moment, plausible.

There are places we fear, places we dream, places whose exiles we became and never learned it until, sometimes, too late.

Kit had always thought he would return somehow to the San Juans. It had never entered his mind that his fate might be here, that here in Inner Asia would be his bold fourteeners and desert snows, aboriginal horsemen, trailside saloons and altogether-incomprehensible women, somehow most desirable whenever there was other business, often deadly in nature, at hand.

It was not until he finally saw Lake Baikal that he understood why it had been necessary to journey here, and why, in the process of reaching it, penance, madness, and misdirection were inescapable.

Prance had stayed back in Irkutsk, pleading exhaustion, but Hassan was insistent that for a devout Buriat the object of pilgrimage must be the great stone at the mouth of the Angara, where the river flowed out of the lake.

"But that was only a cover story," Kit reminded him. "We aren't Buriats, either of us."

Hassan's gaze was open but unreadable. "We have nearly completed the journey."

"And the Prophet? The Doosra's master? Shall I speak to him?"

"You spoke to him," said Hassan.

"When—" Kit began, and in the instant, there was Baikal.

He had gazed into pure, small mountain lakes in Colorado, unsoiled by mine tailings or town waste, and was not surprised by the perfect clarity which had more than once taken him to the verge of losing himself, to the dizzying possibility of falling into another order of things. But this was like looking into the heart of the Earth itself as it was before there were eyes of any kind to look at it.

It was a mile deep, so he'd been told by Auberon Halfcourt, and sheltered critters unknown elsewhere in Creation. Trying to sail on it was dangerous and unpredictable—winds rose in seconds, waves became small mountains. A journey to it was not a holiday excursion. In some way he was certain of but had not quite worked through, it was another of those locations like Mount Kailash, or Tengri Khan, parts of a superterrestrial order included provisionally in this lower, broken one. He felt swept now by a violent certitude. He had after all taken the wrong path, allowed the day's trivialities to engage him—simply not worked hard enough to deserve to see this. His first thought was that he must turn and go back to Kashgar, all the way back to the great Gateway, and begin again. He looked around to tell Hassan, who he was sure had already seen into his own thoughts. Hassan was of course no longer there.

BACK AT THE BEGINNING of their journey, though it lay only a short distance from Kashgar, near the village of Mingyol, and could sometimes be seen from odd angles looming in the distance, the great stone Arch known as the Tushuk Tash was considered impossible actually to get to even by the local folks. A maze of slot canyons lay in the way, too many of them ever to have been counted. All maps were useless. Cartographers of different empires, notably the Russian, had been driven to nervous collapse trying to record the country around the Tushuk Tash. Some settled for embittered fantasy, others more conscientious left it blank.

When Hassan had heard that Kit and Prance must begin their journey by first passing beneath the great pierced rock, he had excused himself and gone off to pray, aloof and morosely silent, as if the Doosra had sent him to accompany them as some kind of punishment.

Some spoke of the colossal gate as a precipice, a bridge, an earthen dam, a passage between high rock walls . . . for others it was not a feature of the landscape but something more abstract, a religious examination, a cryptographic puzzle. . . . Hassan had always known it as "the Prophet's Gate," bearing not only the title but also the sanction of a Prophet who was understood to be not only the Prophet Mahommed but another as well, dwelling far to the north, for whom Hassan's master the Doosra was the forerunner.

It had taken them all day. They went into a gray region of deep ravines and rock towers. Hassan led them without error through the maze of canyons.

What earthly process could have produced them was a mystery. With the sun at this angle, the Kara Tagh looked like a stone city, broken into gray crystalline repetitions of city blocks and buildings windowless as if inhabited by that which was past sight, past light, past all need for distinguishing outside from in. Kit found he could not look at this country directly for more than a minute or so—as if its ruling spirits might properly demand obliquity of gaze as a condition of passage.

When they came at last to stand before the Gate, it did not seem like a natural formation but a structure of masonry, shaped stones fitted together without mortar, like the Pyramids, long before recorded history would have begun. In the distance, its peaks shimmering white, rose the Altai range, which their route would take them past. Kit looked up—it was a perhaps fatal risk, but he had to.

In the still-luminous sky, the thing was immense—a thousand, maybe fifteen hundred feet high, at least, flat across the top, and beneath that a great sharply pointed Gothic arch of empty space. Huge, dark, unstable, always in disintegration, shedding pieces of itself from so high up that by the time they hit the ground they'd be invisible, followed by the whizzing sound of their descent, for they fell faster than the local speed of sound. . . . At any moment a loose rock fragment might fall too fast for Kit to hear before it slashed into him. Down here everything was dark, but up there the gray conglomerate was being struck by the final light of day to an unanswerable brilliance.

Hovering, so high and stationary that at first she could have been mistaken for a flaw in his field of vision, a golden eagle caught the rays and seemed to emit light of her own. Among the Kirghiz these eagles were used for hunting, and needed two men to handle them, being known to bring back the carcasses of antelopes and even wolves. The longer she hung above him at her majestic altitude, the more certain Kit became that this was a messenger.

The Chinese remind us that the journey of a thousand miles begins with a single step, yet they keep curiously silent about the step itself, which too often must be taken, as now, from inaccessible ground, if not indeed straight down into an unmeasured abyss.

The moment he passed through the Gate, Kit was not so much deafened as blinded by a mighty release of sound—a great choral bellowing over the desert, bringing, like a brief interruption of darkness in the daytime, a distinct view now, in this dusk, of sunlit terrain, descending in a long gradient directly ahead to a city whose name, though at the moment denied him, was known the world over, vivid in these distances, bright yellow and orange, though soon enough it would be absorbed into the same gray confusion of exitless ravines and wind-shaped rock ascensions through which they had labored to get here and must again to regain the Silk Road. Then the vision had faded, embers of a trail-fire in the measureless twilight.

Turning to Hassan, "Did you see . . ."

"I saw nothing, sir." In Hassan's face sympathy and a plea for silence.

"Heard nothing?"

"It will be night soon, sir."

THROUGHOUT THE JOURNEY, then, Kit had dreamed of the moment he had stepped through the Gate. Often the dream came just before dawn, after a lucid flight, high, æthereal, blue, arriving at a set of ropes or steel cables suspended, bridgelike, over a deep chasm. The only way to cross is face-skyward beneath the cables, hand over hand using legs and feet as well, with the sheer and unmeasurable drop at his back. The sunset is red, violent, complex, the sun itself the permanent core of an explosion as yet unimagined. Somehow in this dream the Arch has been replaced by Kit himself, a struggle he feels on waking in muscles and joints to become the bridge, the arch, the crossing-over. The last time he had the dream was just before rolling in to Irkutsk on the Trans-Siberian. A voice he knew he should recognize whispered, "You are released." He began to fall into the great chasm, and woke into the wine-colored light of the railroad carriage, lamps swaying, samovars at either end gasping and puffing like miniature steam engines. The train was just pulling into the station.

AFTER PASSING THROUGH the Prophet's Gate, they had proceeded along the southern foothills of the Tian Shan, one Silk Road oasis to the next—Ak-su, Kucha, Korla, Kara-shahr, guiding on the otherworldly white pyramid of Khan Tengri, Lord of the Sky, from which light poured, burst continually, illuminating even the empty sky and transient clouds, past nephrite quarries where dust-covered spectres moved chained together on their own effortful pilgrimage toward a cup of water and a few hours' sleep, through evening hailstorms that left the desert blindingly snow-covered in the morning, pockets of green garnet sand queerly aglow in the twilight, and sandstorms making it all but impossible to breathe, turning the day black—for some of those it overtook, black forever. By the time they arrived wayworn at the oasis of Turfan, beneath the Flaming Mountains, redder than the Sangre de Cristos, Kit had begun to understand that this space the Gate had opened to them was less geographic than to be measured along axes of sorrow and loss.

"This is terrible," he said. "Look at this. These people have nothing."

"Which hasn't kept the Germans from picking it over," Prance said. Up until about 800 or 900 A.D., he went on to explain, this had been the metropolis of the ancient kingdom of Khocho. Some scholars, in fact, believed this to be the historical Shambhala. For four hundred years, Turfan had been the most civilized place in Central Asia, a convergence of gardens, silks, music—fertile, tolerant, and compassionate. No one went hungry, all shared in the blessings of an oasis that would never run dry. Imperial Chinese journeyed thousands of hard miles here to see what real sophistication looked like. "Then the Mahommedans swept in," said Prance, "and next came Genghis Khan, and after him the desert."

At Turfan they turned north, away from the Taklamakan, toward Urumchi and the pass just beyond, which cut through the Tian Shan and led down into the lowlands of Dzungaria, looking to head north by northwest, skirt the Altai, and, depending which river by that time was clear of ice, find a steamer to take them down to pick up the Trans-Siberian Railway east to Irkutsk.

They made root soup, shot and barbecued wild sheep, but let the wild pigs go their way in deference to Hassan, who had moved quite beyond dietary prohibitions but saw no use in telling the English about it.

Other foreign parties were out and about, many of them German archaeological scavengers, though sometimes Prance, held by the gravity of memory, lay peering attentively through his field-glasses for what seemed hours before announcing, "They're Russian. Notice how low their tents are pitched."

"Should we—"

"Good reasons for and against. They're probably more interested in Germans and Chinese. With the Entente, the Great Game is supposedly ended out here, but old suspicions linger, and some of these Russian troopers would as soon shoot as look at us."

In higher country one day, they blundered into a stampede of about fifty *kiangs,* wild red Asian asses, each with a dark stripe down its back, rolling their eyes and moving fast, likely spooked by the approach of humans. "Holy Toledo," said Kit, "that's sure some wild ass stampede." They took refuge in a grove of flowering hemp which they had first begun to smell about midday, long before it came in sight. The plants were about twelve feet high, the fragrance alone enough to stun a traveler into waking dream. Hassan for the first time seemed encouraged, as if this were a message from a realm with which he had done business. He went about like an Englishman in a rose-garden, carefully inhaling aromas, peering at and selecting flowering and fruiting heads of ganja, until he had picked a good-size bale. For days then the fragrant tops hung upside down in the sun, tied to the cargo lashings on the camels, swaying as they stepped along. Whenever Prance attempted to remove a bud, Hassan appeared from nowhere and slapped his hand away. "Not cured yet. Not ready to smoke."

"And when it is . . ."

"I must reflect. It is not really for English, but perhaps we may strike a bargain."

The wind, which was alive, conscious, and not kindly disposed to travelers, had a practice of coming up in the middle of the night. The camels smelled it first, then slowly everyone else in the party began to hear it, its unstoppable crescendo, giving them too little time to devise shelter, and to which often the only resort was to submit, pressed against the earth flat as any stalk of grass, and try not to be taken away into the sky.

Wolves gathered and watched all night, it was uncertain whether to look after them or take what was left when the wind was done with them. Prance seemed to live on little else but a local stomach remedy the Uyghurs called *gül kän,* made from fermented rose petals, which he carried an enormous canteen of and was reluctant, indeed surly, about sharing with anybody else. Hassan retaliated by keeping a wary eye on his supply of ganja, which he was using, it turned out, as a sort of trade goods, endearing the party to everyone on the route from Finnish Tatars hunting in the Altai to Cossack ice-fishers at Lake Zaisan. The Irtysh by then was still frozen, so they pressed on to Barnaul on the Ob in time for the great boom and rip of the spring thaw, waking everybody just before dawn, echoing back up into the mountains, and presently caught a steamer there, filled with miners, traders, and Tsarist functionaries, and they all went bouncing like a toboggan 120 miles down to the tiny railroad workers' settlement of Novosibirsk, to wait beside the wide-gauge tracks for the train to Irkutsk.

"So this is Irkutsk."

"The Paris of Siberia."

More like Saturday night in the San Juans all over again, as it turned out. All day, all night. The town was a peculiar combination of rip-roaring and respectable. Gold miners drank vodka, played *vint,* argued politics, and shot at each other in a spirit of fatalistic play. The *kupechestvo* stayed in their substantial homes over in Glaskovsk, keeping to parts of town relevant to business, pretending to ignore the lowlife element, which well within living memory had included themselves.

"Some pilgrimage," Kit looking around through a pall of tobacco and hemp smoke at the spectacle inside the Club Golomyanka, where he and Prance had stopped in to celebrate, or at least commemorate, their arrival.

"Out here pilgrimage is a matter of kind and wrathful deities. Timing. Guidance."

"What's that mean?"

"Ask Hassan."

"Hassan disappeared the minute we got to the Lake."

"Exactly."

Their instructions were to report to a Mr. Swithin Poundstock, a British national active in the business of importing and exporting, "And it won't do," Auberon Halfcourt had been most emphatic, "to press him for further details." They found him down at the port of Irkutsk, in his warehouse going about with an inkpot and brush stenciling on a number of heavy crates the somehow unconvincing term NAUSHNIKI. "Earmuffs," Prance muttered. "I think not, not in this life." Despite the air of general bustle in the great dim space, a number of employees seemed to be chiefly engaged in observing Kit and Prance with ill-disguised unfriendliness.

"How's Halfcourt?" the merchant greeted them. "Barking mad of course, but what else?"

"He sends—" Prance began.

"And listen, what about Hassan?"

Prance frowned in perplexity. "The native guide? I don't know, he disappeared."

"*Before* he disappeared," with perhaps a touch of impatience, "did he leave anything for me?"

"Oh." From a Gladstone bag, Prance handed over a small package wrapped in oilcloth, through which Kit could detect the distinctive nasal signature of wild hemp. With an effort he refrained from comment, which was just as well, for Poundstock was not quite done. He led them toward the back of the facility, where, slowly growing louder, a rhythmical and metallic percussion could be heard. They arrived at a steel door, before which stood two large, thuggish personalities each packing an 1895 model Nagant revolver. "What," muttered one of them, "you again?"

Inside, a large coining press of a certain vintage was stamping out what looked like British gold sovereigns. Except that they weren't gold, more a coppery silver, as Poundstock explained. "Old Chinese coins, basically. What they call 'cash.' Silver, bronze, the content varies depending what comes in that day. We melt it down, cast ingots, roll fillets, cut blanks, strike the design, and electroplate with a very thin layer of gold. Can't tell them from the real thing."

"But they're all—"

"Don't say it. Thanks to friends at Tower Hill, the dies we use are perfectly genuine. It really is young Vic here on every one of these. And that's what matters, isn't it."

"I don't know. Can they be spent? Legally?"

"Interesting concept, especially out here. We'll start you off with a thousand, how's that? You be the judge. Two? Not as heavy as you'd think, really." With a stove shovel, he filled a sturdy brass-trimmed box with pseudo-sovereigns. "All yours. One last thing, the standard sermon, and you can be off to your adventures." He ushered them into an adjoining office, dominated by a map of eastern Siberia.

"Here is where you'll be operating—the three great river basins east of the Yenisei—Upper Tunguska, Stony Tunguska, Lower Tunguska. For years the Tungus clans who occupy each of these river valleys have been at war, in particular the Ilimpiya, who live along the Lower Tunguska, and the Shanyagir, who occupy the Stony Tunguska. The key figure in this, perhaps even the one your Doosra reports to, is a shaman of great regional fame named Magyakan, who has been active on behalf of the Ilimpiya."

"And which representatives of the great Powers are we likely to meet?"

"You've probably already met," Poundstock shrugged. "Bon voyage, gents."

And they were on the move once again, aboard a river steamer down the Angara, as it was known at this end—its name would change farther along to Upper Tunguska—past the city, beneath the great flying bridge, borne by the current flowing out of Lake Baikal, north into the beating heart of shamanic Asia.

The other passengers were *siberyaki,* prospectors, gamblers, Cossack enterprisers, fugitives from the wide, well-lit streets and whatever these might have required as appropriate behavior. They passed alder swamps and bamboo groves and pale green reindeer moss. Bears foraging for cowberries paused to watch them. Baby Siberian cranes learning to fly rose briefly against the sky.

At Bratsk there was a deep gorge with pine forests and violent rapids, which everybody had to get out and go around by land, through a vast swarm of mosquitoes so thick it darkened the sun, to where another boat waited to continue the journey.

They got off a couple of days later at Yeniseisk, and found Kirghiz horses and brush supplies, and Kit was surprised to hear Prance talking the lingo a mile a minute. "Tungus, Buriatic, Mongol, question of accent, really, a certain attitude of the vocal apparatus, embouchure, breathing. . . ."

They picked up their luggage at the dock, including the box full of Poundstock's gold-plated sovereigns. Prance's instructions were to hand them out to any natives likely to be useful, filling them in when possible on the topic of the Queen whose image appeared on the obverse. "I tell them she's alive," he admitted, with little embarrassment. "That she is our greatest shaman. She has conquered time. She never ages. Sort of thing."

"What about all the Germans out in these woods telling them otherwise? They're gonna find out she's dead, Prance."

"I tell them she is the ruler of Shambhala."

"They must know that's horseshit, too."

"It worked for Dorzhieff in Tibet. He told the Dalai Lama that the Tsar was the king of Shambhala—though that wouldn't do out here, the Tungus hate any Tsar no matter who it is, just on principle. We're supposed to find the local shaman and see if he can't put in a good word, anything to help along the old Entente, don't you know."

"So, see if I have this straight, the Tsar is King of Shambhala, Victoria is Queen of Shambhala, that makes it a Shambhala-Shambhala alliance—sort of, I don't know, quadratic isn't it? and aren't they related somehow?"

"By marriage," with a look Kit was used to by now, a mixture of impatience, disapproval, and fear that there was some joke he wasn't getting.

KEEPING MAINLY TO RIVERBANKS, they made their way among wildcat coal-mining works, thickets of willow and wild cherry, meadows full of wildflowers that seemed to Kit enormous, violets as big as your hand, yellow lilies and blue veronica you could shelter from the rain under, looking for word of the shaman Magyakan, if not the man in person. Like the taiga, he was everywhere, and mysterious—a heroic being with unearthly gifts. They heard tales of how he had been shot once with a rifle, by a Russian soldier, and had calmly reached into his body and pulled out the bullet, over an inch long, shining and bloodless. Presented it to the sky. Living witnesses had beheld this. He had power over the iron creatures of Agdy, Lord of the Thunder, and knew how to call them down at will, their eyes flashing, their fury inexorable. "You see what happens out here," Prance instructed Kit, "you get these conflations, 'Agdy' is the Hindu fire-god Agni, of course, but almost certainly also Ogdai Khan, son of Jenghiz Khan, who succeeded to the Mongol Empire and extended his father's conquests east and west, from China to Hungary."

"What if it's just the name of whoever sends these iron things down at those Shanyagir folks?" Kit inquired, for whatever annoyance value there might be in that.

"There are no iron things, there are no iron things, that's the point," screamed Lieutenant Prance. "These bloody shamans tell the people anything, no matter how insane, and the people believe them, it's like Americans, only different."

"Think this Magyakan is the one the Doosra was talking about?"

Prance had no idea, and moreover, as he was quite happy to let Kit know, he didn't care.

"Strange attitude for a divinity scholar to be taking, isn't it?"

"Traverse, for God's sake." Prance had been smoking all day and developed an impatient growl. "There is light, and there is darkness."

"Let me guess. The Church of England is light, and everything else—"

"Not quite how it sorts out. Differences among the world religions are in fact rather trivial when compared to the common enemy, the ancient and abiding darkness which all hate, fear, and struggle against without cease"—he made a broad gesture to indicate the limitless taiga all around them—"Shamanism. There isn't a primitive people anywhere on Earth that can't be found practicing some form of it. Every state religion, including your own, considers it irrational and pernicious, and has taken steps to eradicate it."

"What? there's no 'state religion' in the U.S.A., pardner, we've got freedom of worship, it's guaranteed in the Constitution—keeps church and state separate, just so's we don't turn into something like England and keep marching off into the brush with bagpipes and Gatling guns, looking for more infidels to wipe out. Nothing personal o' course."

"The Cherokee," replied Prance, "the Apache, the massacre of the Sioux Ghost Dancers at Wounded Knee, every native Red Indian you've found, you people have either tried to convert to Christianity or you've simply killed."

"That was about land," said Kit.

"I suggest it was about the fear of medicine men and strange practices, dancing and drug-taking, that allow humans to be in touch with the powerful gods hiding in the landscape, with no need of any official church to mediate it for them. The only drug you've ever been comfortable with is alcohol, so you went in and poisoned the tribes with that. Your whole history in America has been one long religious war, secret crusades, disguised under false names. You tried to exterminate African shamanism by kidnapping half the continent into slavery, giving them Christian names, and shoving your peculiar versions of the Bible down their throats, and look what happened."

"The Civil War? That was economics. Politics."

"That was the gods you tried to destroy, waiting their hour, taking their revenge. You people really just believe everything you're taught, don't you?"

"Guess I'll have go to Cambridge and get smart," Kit not really taking offense. Possibilities for amusement being limited out here in the taiga, why a man had to take what came along in the way of recreational squabbling. "What got you into the divinity racket anyhow?"

"I was a religious youth," replied Dwight Prance. "It might easily have taken other forms, choir-singing, sandal-wearing, sermonizing on street corners, it just happened to be the one choice certain to cancel itself out."

"That's what you wanted?"

"It's what happened. As I spent more time studying religions, particularly Islam and Christianity, and began to notice the many close connections to secular power, I grew more . . . hmm, contemptuous, you'd say, of the whole enterprise."

"Church and state."

Prance shrugged. "Quite natural to find Cæsar setting up these cozy arrangements with God whenever possible, as they're both after the same thing, aren't they."

"And you've gotten more interested—"

"In the arrangements. Yes. Did you imagine I was praying every night?"

"Then if you're not out here soldiering for Christ—who for, exactly?"

"A handful of men in Whitehall you've never heard of, whose faces no one recognizes."

"And the money's good?"

Prance's laughter held little of the sacred, and seemed to go on for an unnaturally long time. "You'd have to speak to them about that, I expect."

From time to time, Kit recalled the purity, the fierce, shining purity of Lake Baikal, and how he had felt standing in the wind Hassan had disappeared into, and wondered now how his certainty then had failed to keep him from falling now into this bickering numbness of spirit. In view of what was nearly upon them, however—as he would understand later—the shelter of the trivial would prove a blessing and a step toward salvation.

A heavenwide blast of light.

As of 7:17 a.m. local time on 30 June 1908, Padzhitnoff had been working for nearly a year as a contract employee of the Okhrana, receiving five hundred rubles a month, a sum which hovered at the exorbitant end of spy-budget outlays for those years. Accordingly the great ship was riding a bit lower in the sky, its captain and crew having put on collectively at least thirty extra poods, roughly half a ton, and that didn't include the weight of the masonry Padzhitnoff planned to drop on designated targets, which it was necessary to bring along as ballast, since most structures out here in Siberia seemed to be made of wood and brush, a difficulty which, though challenging the *ekipazh* in a military way, failed to contribute much to their spiritual ease until they first sighted Irkutsk from the air and were amazed by the stately brick-and-masonry homes of the nouveau riche fur traders and gold magnates, crying *"Právil'no!"* and embracing. When extra lift was needed, however, Russian design philosophy had ever been just to add on as much buoyancy and engine power as you had to, and so as the *Bol'shaia Igra* evolved through the years, weight control was never the serious engineering issue it often proved to be in the aeronautics of other lands.

These days there was little but nervousness among the cringers and climbers at all levels of Razvedka. Since the naval defeat at Tsushima and the massive demonstrations in the cities, the pogroms and terror and blood, the unthinkable possibility had been dawning that God had abandoned Russia. What had been certain and mandated by Heaven was now as loaded with uncertainty as any peasant's struggle with the day, and all, regardless of wealth or position, must stumble blindly.

"I AM A WARRIOR, not a scientist," protested Ofitser Nauchny Gerasimoff. "You should be sending in professors."

"That can wait," Padzhitnoff said. "Okhrana believe this Event could have been man-made, and they want to know weapons implications."

Gennady, the *umnik* of the crew, gestured casually at the dead ranks of barkless virgin timber passing below. "Man-made? This? God didn't do this?"

"General Sukhomlinoff is more inclined to suspect the Chinese, though he does not rule out the Germans."

"He probably has another real-estate scheme in mind, seeing the land's already been cleared free of charge." Gennady pretended to look down in amazement. "In fact, who're all those people in suits, riding on camels down there? *Zi!* wait! It's real-estate agents, out on caravan!"

"The General is eager to know how this was done," Padzhitnoff said. "He keeps saying, 'Remember who invented gunpowder.'"

Pavel Sergeievitch, the intelligence officer, gazed at the horizonless disaster. "No sign of fire there. No crater, not even a shallow one. It wasn't munitions—none we know of."

"What do the people who live down there say?"

"That it was Agdy, their God of Thunder."

"That's what they heard? thunder?"

"Sound-pressure of some kind. . . . Even so, it appears the energy only moved laterally."

"But not quite radially," Padzhitnoff said. "Helm, take us up three hundred meters. I want all of you to see something curious."

They ascended into a sky from which color had drained absolutely, as if in the same terrible moment that these millions of trunks had gone white, and, having reached the desired altitude, still in the air, looking down like icons of saints painted on the inside of a church dome.

"It looks like a butterfly," remarked Gerasimoff.

"An angel," said Pavel.

"It is symmetrical, but not the ellipse of destruction one would expect."

PADZHITNOFF CONVENED A MEETING of the officers, which, as it turned out, would not be adjourned for weeks. They gathered in the wardroom and worried together, in shifts. The crew welcomed the slack and fell into a sort of holiday routine. Some played chess, others drank. Everybody smoked, some failed to sleep. Those who did sleep dreamed about playing chess and woke worrying about what kind of mental trouble they might be in.

Meanwhile the *zastolye* in the wardroom had grown philosophical.

"Were it not for the electromagnetic readings, I should say it was a meteorite that exploded about five miles up. But why should the area remain actively radiant like this?"

"Because what exploded was brought by a conveyance, from somewhere else, out in Cosmic Exterior."

"Because there is an important time term hidden somewhere in the expression. With such an enormous discharge of sound, light, and heat—why no crater?"

"If the object exploded too high above the ground to do more than blow trees over—"

"—or the local distortion of other variables was so intense that the crater somehow actually got displaced *along the time axis.*"

"Perhaps moved elsewhere in space as well."

"Khuy," summarized Bezumyoff, the know-it-all or *vseznaĭka* of the crew, "in that case we're fucked, aren't we—there is now potentially a hole in the Earth no one can see, waiting to materialize with no warning at all, in fact it may appear *at any moment,* directly beneath St. Petersburg, for example—"

This may just do the trick, thought Captain Padzhitnoff, the nervous collapse which no feat of Japanese naval ordnance, no Russian winter, no mystical intrigue at Tsarskoe Selo had been able to provoke, might only have been waiting for this spectacle of a crew he believed he had come to understand attempting to deal with the Event of 30 June. It had not escaped his notice that eyewitnesses living below had unanimously reported stones falling from the sky, at least suggesting the *Bol'shaia Igra*'s own traditional specialty. The possibility had to be entertained—had they field-tested some new munitions device, for example, over an "uninhabited" piece of Siberia, and had the result proven so terrible that now they'd all developed a collective amnesia about it, perhaps as a way of protecting their mental apparati?

"Believe if you like in some extraterrestrial origin for this thing—but suppose instead it were extra*temporal*—a four-, perhaps five-dimensional surface intersecting with 'our' continuum."

"Ouspenskian!"

"Bolshevik!"

"It certainly resembles a capacitance effect, though on a planetary scale—a slow, incremental investment of energy, followed by a sudden catastrophic payback."

"Exactly what I'm saying. Time-travel isn't free, it takes energy. This was an artifact of repeated visits from the future."

"*Nichevo.* Something that wasn't supposed to be where it was. Maybe deliberate, but maybe not. It's all we can say."

MEANTIME, in another part of the taiga, Kit and Prance were going round and round as usual, on the interesting topic of which one was less constitutionally able to clean up after himself, when with no announcement, everything, faces, sky, trees, the distant turn of river, went red. Sound itself, the wind, what wind there was, all gone red as a living heart. Before they could regain their voices, as the color faded to a blood orange, the explosion arrived, the voice of a world announcing that it would never go back to what it had been. Both Kit and Prance remembered the great roaring as they passed through the Prophet's Gate.

"It's up by Vanavara," Kit said when the day had resumed. "We ought to go up there and see if there's anything we can do."

"You go if you want. I was not sent here for this." Prance was hugging himself as if for warmth, though it was summer.

"Because . . . ?"

"My remit was political. This is not political."

"Maybe it is. Maybe it's war."

"Out here? Over what, Traverse? Logging rights?"

TWO SMALL BLACK BIRDS who had not been there now emerged out of the light as it faded to everyday green and blue again. Kit understood for a moment that forms of life were a connected set—critters he was destined never to see existing so that those he did see would be just where they were, when he saw them. Somewhere on the other side of the world, an exotic beetle stood at a precise distance and compass bearing from an unclassified shrub so that here, in this clearing, these two black birds might appear to Kit, precisely as they were. He had entered a state of total attention to no object he could see or sense, or eventually even imagine in any interior way, while Prance was all but hysterical.

"Our mortal curse to be out here in the way of whatever force decides to come in out of that unlimited darkness and wipe us from the Creation," Prance delivered into religious mania. "As if something in the Transfinitum had chosen to reenter the finite world, to reaffirm allegiance to its limits, including mortality . . . to become recognizably numerical again . . . a *presence come to Earth. . . .*"

AND SOON THE DRUMS BEGAN. The *dungur,* rising to them out of the taiga inscrutable and vast. Through the long twilight into the pale evening. One drum would have been soul-rattling enough, but there were at least a dozen. Deep and far-reaching. Kit stood nearly paralyzed. It went on for days. After a while he thought he heard something familiar in it. He had begun to mistake it for thunder. Not ordinary thunder but whatever it was Agdy had brought down on the day of the Event. Were they trying to commemorate it? summon it back? Or provide homeopathic echoes to protect them from its return?

"I WAS SHOT AT TODAY," Prance announced. "Again."

"Was it as much fun as last time, what'd you call it, 'exhilarating'?"

It had become disagreeably evident that young Prance was widely taken now for a Japanese spy, allowing Kit only so much slack to try and convince the Englishman's many ill-wishers otherwise.

"If only you didn't ask so many questions all the time. Scholarly curiosity's one thing, but you just don't know when to quit. And you don't look too local either."

"Well I certainly don't look Japanese." Then into Kit's silence, "Do I?"

"How many Japanese does anybody out here ever get to see? Prance ol' buddy, let's face it, out in these parts—you're Japanese."

"But I say look here, I'm *not* Japanese. I mean am I walking about in sandals? gesturing with fans, speaking in unsolvable riddles, any of that?"

Kit raised his eyebrows and angled his head. "Deny it all you like, but what about me, I go on coverin your back long enough, folks here start thinkin I'm Japanese, too, where are we then?"

Among Siberians one school of thought placed the origins of the mysterious visitation in Japan. Not good news for Prance, actually.

"But it was sighted coming in from quite the other direction—from the south*west,*" he protested. "China."

"Maybe they're what you'd call a little 'dis-Oriented'? If it was a projectile, or perhaps a ray of some kind, it might not even have been dispatched through what we think of as ordinary space."

"And . . . what do we 'think of as ordinary space' again, one does keep forgetting."

"Up and down," Kit patiently, "left and right, to and fro, the three axes we know from our everyday lives. But *someone* may have command of Quaternion space—three imaginary axes plus a fourth scalar term containing energies few of us can imagine."

He had been thinking, with deep anxiety, about the Quaternion weapon he'd turned over to Umeki Tsurigane in Ostend. For the likes of Piet Woevre, the instrument had promised an advanced level of destructiveness, a chance to introduce large populations to the embrace of death and death's companion, Time, which the *w* term might easily be taken to mean. Might the Tunguska Event have been caused by the discharge, planned or inadvertent, of a Q-weapon? It wouldn't have been Umeki-san, but perhaps someone she had trusted. Who had perhaps betrayed her. And if someone had betrayed her, how fatally? And what did that make Kit?

FOR A WHILE after the Event, crazed Raskol'niki ran around in the woods, flagellating themselves and occasional onlookers who got too close, raving about Tchernobyl, the destroying star known as Wormwood in the book of Revelation. Reindeer discovered again their ancient powers of flight, which had lapsed over the centuries since humans began invading the North. Some were stimulated by the accompanying radiation into an epidermal luminescence at the red end of the spectrum, particularly around the nasal area. Mosquitoes lost their taste for blood, acquiring one instead for vodka, and were observed congregating in large swarms at local taverns. Clocks and watches ran backward. Although it was summer, there were brief snowfalls in the devastated taiga, and heat in general tended to flow unpredictably for a while. Siberian wolves walked into churches in the middle of services, quoted passages from the Scriptures in fluent Old Slavonic, and walked peaceably out again. They were reported to be especially fond of Matthew 7:15, "Beware of false prophets, which come to you in sheep's clothing, but inwardly they are ravening wolves." Aspects of the landscape of Tierra del Fuego, directly opposite the Stony Tunguska on the globe, began to show up in Siberia—sea ernes, gulls, terns, and petrels landing in the branches of fir trees, swooping to grab fish out of the streams, taking a bite, screaming with distaste, and throwing them back. Granite cliffs rose sheer and unexpected out of the forest. Oceangoing ships unmanned by visible crews, attempting to navigate the shallow rivers and creeks, ran aground. Entire villages came to the conclusion that they were not where they ought to be, and without much advance planning simply packed up what they had, left behind what they couldn't carry, and headed off together into the brush, where presently they set up villages no one else could see. Or not very clearly.

And from everywhere in the taiga, all up and down the basins of the Yenisei, came reports of a figure walking through the aftermath, not exactly an angel but moving like one, deliberately, unhurried, a consoler. Accounts differed as to whether the outsize figure was man or woman, but all reported having to look steeply upward when trying to make out its face, and a deep feeling of fearless calm once it had passed.

Some thought it might be some transfigured version of the shaman Magyakan, whose whereabouts had been puzzling folks along the Stony T. No one had seen him since the Event, his *izba* was empty, and the magical force that had kept it from sinking, like everyone else's dwelling in Siberia, into the summer-thawed earth, had abated, so that the cabin now tilted at a thirty-degree angle, like a ship at sea about to slide beneath the waves.

None of the strange effects lasted long, and as the Event receded in memory, arguments arose as to whether this or that had even happened at all. Soon the forest was back to normal, green underbrush beginning to appear among the dead-white trunks, the animals fallen speechless again, tree-shadows again pointing in their accustomed directions, and Kit and Prance continued to make their way through it with no idea what this meant for their mission out here.

KIT HAD ALMOST gotten used to riding Kirghiz horses, or more often their shaggier pony-size cousins, his feet all but dragging along the ground, when one day he and Prance came across a band of reindeer herders, moving the herd to new pasture, and he immediately caught sight of one reindeer, pure white, who seemed to be looking back at him pretty intently, before disengaging himself from the herd and trotting over.

"As if he knew me," as Kit explained it later.

"Of course, Traverse," Prance blithely demented, "and what did he *say* to you?"

"Told me his name. Ssagan."

Prance stared. "That's a Buriat pronunciation of *tsagan,* which is Mongol for 'white.'" He went over to the critter and began talking Buriat, now and then pausing as if to listen.

It didn't seem that odd to Kit, talking with reindeer. Folk out here were said to do it all the time. Since the visitation at the Stony Tunguska, he had noticed that the angle of his vision was wider and the narrow track of his life branching now and then into unsuspected side trails.

The herders were reluctant at first, believing Ssagan to be the reincarnation of a great Buriat teacher. They consulted with him for days, shamans came and went, wives put in with useful advice. Finally, from what Prance could learn, Ssagan convinced them that Kit was a pilgrim who could not proceed farther without Ssagan to pilot him through confusions in the terrain.

THEY HAD ENTERED a strangely tranquil part of Siberia, on the Mongolian border between the Sayan and Tannu-Ola ranges, which Prance had been briefly through and said was known as Tuva. Kit reckoned if a fellow was going to come riding in anywhere on a white reindeer, he could do a lot worse than here. After Kit dismounted and took his saddlebags, Ssagan, as if having discharged a duty, turned abruptly and went off the way they had come, to rejoin his herd, wherever they'd got to by now, without looking back.

"He says he's done all he can," said Prance. "His job was to bring us here."

They slept that night in a bark hut with a pointed top, and woke into the dawn to an unearthly guttural singing. Some Tuvans were tending a herd of sheep. The man singing was standing alone, but after a while Kit heard a flute accompanying him. He looked around, but there was no flute-player, no other musicians of any kind, in fact. He looked at the singer more closely and could see lip movements that matched up with the sound of the flute. It was all coming from the one voice.

"They call it *borbanngadyr,*" Prance explained. "Perhaps shamans are not the only ones who know how to be in two states at once. On the other hand, perhaps there really is a flute-player but he's invisible, or a ghost. It all needs to be looked into more closely, which is why I think I'll stay here for a while if you don't mind."

There was something else. Prance seemed almost embarrassed. "This is the heart of Earth," he whispered.

"Funny," said Kit, "all's I see's a bunch of sheep."

"Exactly. Traverse, I know we've had our differences—"

"Still broodin about that time back in the woods there, I knew it—but I wasn't really *aiming* at you, Dwight."

"Not that. I believe . . . all the signs are here, you must have seen them . . . these high peaks surrounding us, the Tuvan script that resembles Tibetan characters—and these are the only known Buddhists in the world who speak Old Uyghur or any sort of Turkic language, for that matter. Everywhere one sees images of the Wheel of Life. . . . A Tibetan Buddhist enclave in the middle of a prevailing Islamism. What does that suggest to you?"

Kit nodded. "Ordinarily it would have been the reason for our trip out here, and somebody would write it up and report it back to Lieutenant-Colonel Halfcourt. But the problem for me these days is—"

"I know. There may not be a 'mission' anymore. What happened up on the Stony Tunguska—we don't know how they reacted back in Kashgar, Shambhala may have vanished in that instant from their list of priorities. We don't even know what it's done to us out here. Far too soon to say. As to our purpose now—no one has the wisdom or the authority to tell us anything."

"We're on our own," Kit said.

"And separately, too, I fear."

"Nothing personal."

"Not anymore, is it?"

As Kit rode away over a patch of open steppe, the wind came up, and presently he heard the peculiar, bass throat-singing again. A sheepherder was standing angled, Kit could tell, precisely to the wind, and the wind was blowing across his moving lips, and after a while it would have been impossible to say which, the man or the wind, was doing the singing.

AFTER A BIT, Lieutenant Prance thought he'd begun to detect a presence overhead, which was neither eagle nor cloud, and which slowly drew closer until he could make out a vast airship, from which a crew of animated youngsters were regarding him with great curiosity. Lieutenant Prance greeted them in a high voice with a sort of tremolo to it. "Are you kind deities? or wrathful deities?"

"We endeavor to be kind," supposed Randolph St. Cosmo.

"Me, I'm wrathful," snarled Darby Suckling, "what's it to you, Bo Peep?"

"I only meant that whenever they appear," said Prance, "these guardian deities, one must show them compassion, regardless of their level of threat to one personally."

"Never work," muttered Darby. "They'll squash you like bugs. But thanks anyway. For nothing."

"According to the classical Tibetan sources, the relevant parts of the Tengyur, to begin with—"

"Kid . . ." Darby looking around in some distraction, as if for a firearm.

"Perhaps we could discuss this over a '99 Château Lafite," suggested Randolph.

So was Dwight Prance taken aloft and on to an uncertain fate.

. . .

KIT MEANTIME HAD fallen in with a band of *brodyagi*, former hard-labor convicts who had been sentenced years before to internal exile in Siberia, and settled in Siberian villages. Unable to live with the misery and poverty of the life, they chose mobility, each for his own reason but all for the same reason. Around 1900 the practice of internal exile was officially abandoned, but by then they were long gone, wanting only to get back to Russia. Easiest way would have been to pick up the dilapidated, brush-covered road known as the Trakt that ran clear across Eurasia, and head west. "But things interrupt, detours happen," explained their leader, a Siberian short-ax genius known only as "Topor," who with a single ax could do every job from tree-felling to the most finely detailed bone scrimshaw, including milling lumber of any size and cross-section, trimming taiga deadfall for the fire, dressing out game, mincing herbs, chopping vegetables, threatening government officials, and so forth—"some of us have been out here for years, found local girls, got married, had children, abandoned them again, allegiances to the past and the former Russian life fading, like reincarnation, only different, and still some inertia of escape bears us on, west. . . ."

Once Kit would have said, "A vector." But the word now did not occur to him. At first he thought of the holy wanderers that Yashmeen had told him about. But these *brodyagi* tended to be not so much God-possessed as violently insane. They drank incessantly, whatever they could get their hands on, some of it pretty horrible. They had devised a steam-distillery with which they could turn everything they found with any discernible sugar content into a species of vodka. Fusel oils made up one of the major nutritional groups in their diet. They came back to camp with sacks full of strange mottled red mushrooms that sent them off on internal journeys out to Siberias of the soul. There was apparently a two-part structure to the narrative, part one being pleasant, visually entertaining, spiritually enlightening, and part two filled with unspeakable horror. The fungomaniacs did not seem put out at any of this, regarding one as the price of the other. To enhance the effect, they drank one another's urine, in which alchemized forms of the original hallucinatory agent were present.

One day Kit heard shouting in the taiga. Following the sound, he came upon cleared right-of-way and no track, and later in the day track running between the trees, with clearances of only inches. At night he heard steam whistles, mysterious passages, invisible weight hurtling through the forest, and next day somewhere among the trees the voices of section hands, surveyors, work crews, not always calling in local languages, in fact sometimes Kit swore he was hearing phrases in English, and from putting them together he understood that this railway line was supposed to provide a link between the Trans-Siberian and the Taklamakan.

KIT PROCEEDED THROUGH the dark forests as if there were no doubt as to his way. At first light he found himself in a clearing above a meandering river, where, far below through the humid breathing of the taiga, a plume of steam from a riverboat was just visible. . . .

He had left the *brodyagi* miles back among the trees. Finally, just at nightfall, he came upon the camp of a small exploring party—high-pitched tents, pack horses, a fire. Unaware of how he looked, Kit strolled into the firelight and was surprised when everybody grabbed for a weapon.

"Wait. I know him." It turned out to be Fleetwood Vibe, in a broad-brim hat with a hatband of Siberian tiger skin.

Kit declined food but did chisel a few smokes. Unable to help asking, "How about your father, what do you hear from him?"

Fleetwood fed pieces of deadfall to the fire. "He is no longer of sound mind. Apparently something happened in Italy while he was there. He is beginning to see things. The directors are muttering about a coup d'état. The trust funds are still in effect, but none of us will ever see a penny of his fortune. It's all going to some Christian propaganda mill down south. He's disowned all of us."

"And 'Fax, how's he handling that?"

"It set him free. He's pitching professionally, under another name, out in the Pacific Coast League. Pretty good career so far, earned-run average just under two, a no-hitter last season. . . . He's married to a barmaid from Oakland."

"Houseful of kids, another on the way, never been happier."

Fleetwood shrugged. "Some are meant for that. Others can only keep moving." This time he was seeking not a waterfall or the source of a river, not to map in a stubborn gap in the known terrain but a railroad—a hidden railroad existing so far only as shadowy rumor, the legendary and famous "Tuva-to-Taklamakan."

"That must have been the one I've been hearing."

"Show me." He brought out a map, of sorts, mostly in pencil, smudged and beginning to be split at the creases, decorated with cooking grease and cigarette-burns.

"Unless you're bound for the Stony Tunguska," Kit said. He angled his head up at the pale sky. "As close as possible to where *that* happened."

Fleetwood looked stricken, as if someone had seen into his history and detected at the heart of it the impossibility of any redemption. "It's only the first step," he said, "only what brought me out here. Do you remember once, years ago, we talked of cities, unmapped, sacramental places . . ."

"Shambhala," Kit nodded. "I may have just been there. If you're still interested, it's Tannu Tuva. Or I left somebody there at the edge of madness who was making a good argument that's where it is."

"I wish . . ." Through the fear and guilt, a kind of perverse shyness. "I wish it could be Shambhala that I seek. But I no longer have the right. I have since learned of other cities, out here, secret cities, secular counterparts to the Buddhist hidden lands, more indelibly contaminated by Time, deep in the taiga, only guessed at from indirect evidence—unmanifested cargoes, power consumption—ancient before the Cossacks settled, before the Kirghiz or the Tatars. I almost sense these places, Traverse, so close now, as if at any moment, just behind my shoulder, beneath the next unconsidered footfall, their gates could open . . . dense with industry, unsleeping, dedicated to designs no one speaks of aloud, as one hesitates to speak the name of the wilderness Creature that feeds on all other creatures. . . .

"As nearly as I've been able to triangulate, they lie in a cluster, located quite close to the event of 30 June . . . for practical purposes their rail depot is Krasnoyarsk. Though there's no official acknowledgement of that, no records kept, anyone booking passage there on the Trans-Sib is automatically a subject of interest to the Okhrana." He had tried the previous winter to approach the secret cities. In the unhopeful light of evening arival, from the bruise-colored shadows of Krasnoyarsk, invisible functionaries in fur hats and heavy greatcoats had watched the platforms, escorting those with approved business to unmarked ice-vessels moored by the frozen Yenisei, turning back the others like Fleetwood whose motives seemed little more than idle tourism. "But now, given the Event, it may be possible to enter . . . perhaps somehow terms have been renegotiated.

"Whatever goes on in there, whatever unspeakable compact with sin and death, it is what I am destined for—the goal of this long pilgrimage, whose penance is my life."

Kit looked around. The dark miles were empty of witnesses. He could kill this self-pitying loudmouth so easily. He said, "You know, you're like every other so-called explorer out here, a remittance man with too much sense of privilege, no idea of what to do with it."

There was just enough light from the fire to see the despair in Fleetwood's face, despair like a corrupt form of hope, that here at last might be his great crisis—the unappeasable tribesmen, the unforeseen tempest, the solid terrain gone to quicksand, the beast stalking him for miles and years. Otherwise what life could he expect as one more murderer with his money in Rand shares, destined for golf courses, restaurants with horrible food and worse music, the aging faces of his kind?

The two of them might have been sitting right at the heart of the Pure Land, with neither able to see it, sentenced to blind passage, Kit for too little desire, Fleetwood for too much, and of the opposite sign.

Neither got much sleep that night. Both were troubled by unpleasant dreams in which one, not always literally, was murdering the other. They woke into a midnight storm that had already taken one or two tents. The bearers were running in all directions, screaming in one or more dialects. Prevented by the inertia of dream from entering the present tense, Fleetwood's first thoughts were of his duty to the past. In the light from the fallen star of 30 June, in its pallid nightlessness, he had dreamed insomniac the possibility of another fallen thing like the one he had once helped the Vormance people so terribly bring to its victims. Would young Traverse, would someone, for God's sake, bring this to an end? He looked over, through the wind-beaten confusion, at where Kit's bedroll should have been. But Kit had left sometime in the night, as if taken by the wind.

Having journeyed eastward through the day, the *Inconvenience* had set down beneath the bleak sunset with the menacing flank of a sandstorm not far off. At first glance no one appeared to live here. From the air it had seemed a single giant roof of baked mud, as if you could walk across the entire city without descending to the invisible streets. Beneath the unpenetrated surface, the world, scarcely comprehensible, went about its business, the cosmetics artists in hidden rooms who knew how to conceal white patches appearing on the skin, which, leprosy or not, found on anyone outside the lepers' quarter meant summary execution . . . the *rishta*-doctors patiently removing guinea-worms, making an incision, trapping the three-foot-long creature's head in a cleft at the end of a stick, and then slowly winding it out of the incision, around the stick, cautiously, so as not to break the *rishta* and cause an infection . . . the secret drinkers and merchants' wives insatiably drawn to caravan drivers who would be gone long before morning.

Nobody aboard *Inconvenience* slept soundly that night. Darby had the 4:00 to 8:00 A.M. watch, and Miles was rattling around the galley preparing breakfast, and Pugnax was on the bridge, looking east, still as stone, when the Event in the sky occurred, the early daylight deepening past orange, too general in space or memory to know where to look till the sound arrived, ripping apart the firmament over western China—by which time the terrible pulse had already begun to fade to a counter-stain of aquamarine, and a mutter of drumfire at the horizon. They were all gathered at the quarterdeck by now. A sudden hot wind enveloped them, gone nearly before they could think of how to get in out of it. Randolph ordered the special sky detail set, and they ascended to have a look at whatever it was.

In the pale blue aftermath, the first thing they noticed was that the city below was not the same as the one they had arrived at the night before. The streets were all visible now. Fountains sparkled everywhere. Each dwelling had its own garden inside. Markets seethed in cheerful commotion, caravans came and went through the city gates, tiled and gilded domes shone in the sun, towers soared like song, the desert was renounced.

"Shambhala," cried Miles, and there was no need to ask how he knew—they all knew. For centuries the sacred City had lain invisible, cloaked in everyday light, sun-, star-, and moonlight, the campfires and electric torches of desert explorers, until the Event over the Stony Tunguska, as if those precise light-frequencies which would allow human eyes to see the City had finally been released. What it would take the boys longer to understand was that the great burst of light had also torn the veil separating their own space from that of the everyday world, and that for the brief moment they had also met the same fate as Shambhala, their protection lost, and no longer able to count on their invisibility before the earthbound day.

They proceeded rapidly eastward, high above the taiga. Evidence of disaster somewhere ahead began to appear. They arrived over the scene of devastation shortly after the *Bol'shaia Igra.*

"It was the Trespassers," Lindsay declared.

"We do know they are far more advanced than we in the applied sciences," Randolph said. "Their will to act is pure and uninflected. Would a catastrophe of this size be beyond their means? Technically? morally?"

"At least we cannot say this time that we were *sent here,*" added Lindsay, meaningfully glaring at Darby Suckling.

"That hardly establishes anybody's innocence," opined the Legal Officer, but before they could get into a dispute, the Tesla device wheezed into active status. Miles began throwing appropriate switches, and Randolph took the speaking-horn.

It proved to be Professor Vanderjuice, transmitting from Tierra del Fuego, where he had been measuring variations in the Earth's gravity. "Discombobulated dynamos!" he cried, "apparently we happened to be at the point on Earth directly opposite this Event. Everything here just went chaotic—magnetic storms, all communication interrupted, the wiring in the power supplies melted . . . as for the gravity readings, it is difficult even this soon after to quite believe, but . . . gravity itself for a moment simply vanished. Motor launches, tents, cookstoves, all went flying up into the sky, perhaps never to land again on Earth. Bless me, if I hadn't been down by the water fishing, why, I might have been taken anywhere.

"Now that Gibbs is gone, I've no one back at Yale to consult with about this," said the distraught academician. "It is still possible to contact Kimura, I suppose, and Dr. Tesla. Unless the terrible rumors about him are true."

According to Professor Vanderjuice, the story was abroad that Tesla, seeking to communicate with the explorer Peary, then in the Arctic, projecting unspecified rays from his tower at Wardenclyffe in a direction slightly west of due north, had mistaken his aim by a small but fatal angle, causing the beam to miss Peary's base at Ellsmere Island, cross the Polar region over into Siberia, and hit the Stony Tunguska instead.

"Here is what puzzles me about the story. Did Tesla want to send Peary a message, or beam him a quantity of electric power, or for some undisclosed reason blast him off the map? Tesla may not even have been involved, for it is unclear just who is at Wardenclyffe anymore—Tesla seems to have abandoned the place after Morgan's abandoned him. That is all I can find out at this antipodal remove."

"It sounds like capitalistic propaganda," said Darby. "Dr. Tesla has always had his enemies in New York. The place is a nightmare of backbiting, tort lawyers, and patent disputes. It is the fate of anyone who does serious science. Look at Edison. Look particularly at our colleague, Brother Tom Swift. He spends more time these days in court than in the laboratory."

"The last time I saw Tom, he looked older than I do," the Professor said. "Nothing like perpetual litigation to age a man before his time."

THEY ARRANGED a sky-rendezvous with the *Bol'shaia Igra,* over Semipalatinsk. Seen from the ground, the two airships together accounted for a quarter of the visible sky. The boys wore matching sable hats and wolfskin cloaks, purchased at the great February market in Irbit.

"Why didn't you tell us about Trespassers sooner?" Padzhitnoff struggling to be amiable. "We've known since Venice, and we might have been able to help."

"Why should you have believed anything we told you?"

"Officially, of course not. Must always be 'some American trick.' You can imagine emotions up at staff level—very delicate balance of interests out here, who needs Americans to come blundering in, like galloping cowboys, disrupting all known quantities?"

"But unofficially . . . *you,* as a sky-brother, *might* have believed us?"

"I? since Tunguskan *obstanovka,* I believe everything. Back in St. Petersburg"—a shared look of not so much disdain as sympathetic resignation to the ways of the surface-world—"they want to believe it was a Japanese weapon. Russian military intelligence wants us to confirm it was Japanese—or at least Chinese."

"But . . . ?"

"American government? What do they think?"

"We don't work for them anymore."

"*Zdorovo!* You are working for whom now? Large American corporation?"

"Ourselves."

Padzhitnoff narrowed his gaze, which remained friendly. "You—balloon-boys—*are* large American corporation?"

Randolph shrugged. "I guess not quite yet. Though with what's been coming in on investments, we may have to incorporate soon. We're looking into Switzerland, Neutral Moresnet, a couple of remote island territories—"

"What do you think of Rand shares? Will bubble burst? Most of our money is there, and in armaments."

"We have been gradually reducing our exposure in South Africa," Lindsay said, "but what's looking very promising lately are Chinese Turkestan railway bonds."

"Some *tchudak* in bar in Kiakhta told me same thing. He was blind drunk, of course."

In a clicking and whistling cascade of electrical noises, the Russian wireless receiver now came to life. Padzhitnoff picked up and was soon chatting away a mile a minute, consulting maps and charts, sketching, calculating. When he was done, he noticed Chick Counterfly looking at him strangely. "What."

"You just had that whole conversation in clear?"

"Clear? What is 'clear'?"

"Not encrypted," clarified Miles Blundell.

"No need! Nobody else is listening! This is 'wireless'! New invention! Better than telephone!"

"All the same, I'd be looking into some kind of encryption system."

"Much work for nothing! Not even Russian Army does that! Balloon-boys, balloon-boys! Too careful, like old people!"

Returning from the taiga, the crew of *Inconvenience* found the Earth they thought they knew changed now in unpredictable ways, as if whatever had come to visit above Tunguska had jolted the axes of Creation, perhaps for good. Below, across the leagues of formerly unmarked Siberian forest and prairie, they saw a considerable webwork of rail, steel within cleared rights-of-way below shining as river-courses once had. Industrial smoke, in unhealthy shades of yellow and reddish brown and acid green climbed the sky to lick at the underside of the gondola. Birds they were used to sharing the sky with, migratory European species, had vanished, leaving the region to the eagles and hawks that had formerly hunted them. Huge modern cities of multiple domes, towers of open girderwork, smokestacks, and treeless plazas sprawled beneath, without a living creature in sight.

By dusk they had approached the fringes of a great aerial flotilla. Below them the taiga was falling silent, as if beginning to yield to the hours of darkness and sleep. Of the light seeping from the day, enough remained to reveal a sky crowded everywhere with cargo balloons, immense and crewless, hung at all altitudes upon the sky, the sunset illuminating finely-etched load-rings and rigging, cargo nets and laded pallets swaying in the rising winds of the evening, each borne by a different envelope, some perfectly spherical, others shaped like watermelons, Polish sausages, or prize cigars, or streamlined like ocean-cruising fish, or square or pointed or sewn together tightly into stellated polyhedra or Chinese dragons, solid, striped, or streaked, yellow or scarlet, turquoise or purple, a few of the newer craft equipped with low-horsepower engines, which now and then emitted brilliant gasps of steam, just enough to keep station. Each was tethered by steel cable to a different piece of rolling-stock somewhere below, moving invisibly on its own track, guiding its buoyed cargo to a different destination, all across the map of Eurasia—as the boys watched, the highest envelopes of the fleet were taken by the arc of Earth's shadow advancing, flowing then in swift descent among the lacquered-silk flanks of the others, sweeping down onto the countryside at last, to release it from quotidian light. Soon all that could be seen were an earthbound constellation of red and green running-lights.

"As above," remarked Miles Blundell, "so below."

SLOWLY AS GOD'S JUSTICE, reports began arriving out of the East, from what seemed incomprehensibly eastward, as if the countless tiny engagements of an unacknowledged war had at last been expressed as a single explosion, in an almost-musical crescendo of a majesty usually encountered only in dreams. Photographs would in due course begin to emerge, as if from a developing-bath, and be circulated . . . then copies of copies, after a while degraded nearly to the most current of abstract art, but no less shocking—virgin forest—every single trunk stripped white, blown the unthinkable ninety degrees—flattened for miles. Reactions in the West were uniformly hushed and perplexed, even among those known as chattering fools. No one could dare to say which was worse—that it had never happened before, *or that it had,* and that all the agencies of history had conspired never to record it and then, displaying a sense of honor hitherto unnoted, to maintain their silence.

Whatever had happened out there provided its own annunciation, beginning upriver from Vanavara and booming westward at six hundred miles per hour, all through that darkless night, one seismograph station to the next, across Europe to the Atlantic, via posts, pendulums, universal joints, slender glass threads writing on smoked paper rolls driven clockwork-slow beneath, via needles of light on coatings of bromide of silver, there was the evidence . . . in distant cities to the west, "sensitive flames," some of them human, dipped, curtseyed, feebly quivered at all-but-erotic edges of extinction. Questions arose as to the timing, the "simultaneousness" of it. New converts to Special Relativity took a fascinated look. Given the inertia of writing-points and mirrors, the transit times at focusing lenses, the small variations in the speed at which the bromide paper might have been driven, the error of the seismograph recordings more than embraced the "instant" in which a hitherto-unimagined quantity of energy had entered the equations of history.

"Power being equal to the area under the curve," as it seemed to Professor Heino Vanderjuice, "the shorter the 'instant,' the greater the amplitude—it begins to look like a singularity."

Others were less restrained. Was it Tchernobyl, the star of Revelation? An unprecedented harrowing of the steppe by cavalry in untold millions, flooding westward in a simultaneous advance? German artillery of a secret design more powerful by orders of magnitude than any military intelligence office had ever suspected? Or something which had not quite happened yet, so overflowing the tidy frames of reference available to Europe that it had only seemed to occur in the present, though really originating in the future? Was it, to be blunt, the general war which Europe this summer and autumn would stand at the threshold of, collapsed into a single event?

DALLY RIDEOUT, still moping around about Kit, not that she expected any word from him, had gone on maturing into an even more desirable young package, negotiable on the Venetian market as a Circassian slave in old Araby, pale redhead's coloring, bruisable skin inviting violent attention, hair gone beyond the untamed spill she had hit town with, now a blazing announcement of desire about which no one was ready to be convinced otherwise. That same summer day, she had been approached scarcely steps from Ca' Spongiatosta by a disagreeable gent with the usual 1894 Bodeo tucked into his belt, no longer willing to cut her any slack. "Tonight, the minute it gets dark, understand? I'm coming for you. Better be wearing something pretty." She went through the rest of the day in dread of nightfall, with *teppisti* following everywhere and making little secret of it.

Who was there to talk to about this? Hunter Penhallow was not really the best choice, more than ever preoccupied with his own ghosts, failing to retrieve memories which avoided him as if wishing consciously to be cruel. The Princess was off on one of her daytime adventures and would not be back till evening, by which point Dally herself, she reckoned, had best be well hidden.

But that night it would not get dark, there would be light in the sky all night. Hunter walked out into quite a different sort of "nocturnal light," to pass these unnaturally skylit hours working in a cold frenzy, while all up and down the little waterways, on bridges, in *campielli* and on rooftops, out on the Riva, over on the Lido while the moneyed guests in the new hotels stared down at the beach, wondering if this had been arranged just for them and how much extra it would cost, all manner of Venetian artists had likewise come out, with watercolor gear, chalk, pastels, oils, all trying to "acquire" tonight's light as if it were something they must negotiate for—or even with—throwing desperate looks heavenward from time to time as if at a common subject up there posing, as if to make sure it had not moved or disappeared, this gift from far away, perhaps another Krakatoa, no one knew, perhaps the deep announcement of a change in the Creation, with nothing now ever to be the same, or of some more sinister advent incomprehensible as that of any Christ fixed in paint on the ceilings, canvases, plaster walls of Venice. . . .

Cocks crowed at intervals, as if being reminded haphazardly of their duty. Dogs wandered bemused, or lay peacefully next to cats with whom they ordinarily didn't get along, each appearing to take turns guarding the sleep of the other, which in any case was brief. The night was too strange. Skippers of vaporetti were detained wherever they pulled in by insomniac Venetians out lining the landings who imagined them privy to the doings of some wider world. When the morning newspapers finally arrived, they were sold out in a few minutes, though none had any explanation for the cold and gentle light.

Somewhere in the unsketched regions of Ca' Spongiatosta, "You are a step," the Princess warned, "the turn of an eye, the whisper of a skirt, from the *mala vita.* I can protect you, but can you protect yourself?" The two young women sat in an upper room of the great Palazzo, in muted shadow, as reflected water-glare flickered across the ceiling. The Princess was holding Dally's face, lightly but imperiously, between exquisitely-gloved palms, as if the price of inattention would be a sound slap, though an uninformed observer could not have said which, if either, was in command. The Princess still wore an afternoon dress of dark gray satin, while the girl was all but naked, her small breasts visible through the *brides picotées* of her newly-purchased lace chemise, the nipples darker than usual and more defined, as if recently and purposefully bitten. In this fractional light, her freckles seemed darker, too, like a reverse glittering across her flesh. She would not reply.

Back on the Trieste station, no longer entirely welcome in Venice, in a warren partially below street level, seething with tobacco smoke, most of it Balkan in origin, Cyprian Latewood conferred with a newly-arrived cryptographer named Bevis Moistleigh. Gaslight, which remained on through the long day, revealed aboriginal limestone forming parts of certain walls, and produced ambiguous highlights off the ebonite valve-handles and chromium plating of communal coffee urns of quite ancient Italian design, not to mention those individual *macchinette* not secreted in file drawers. The place ran on coffee.

"What is this? I can't read it—all these little circles. . . ."

"It's the Glagolitic alphabet," explained Bevis. "Old Slavonic. Orthodox Church texts and so forth. You've been out here awhile, I'm surprised you haven't learned it."

"Little occasion to go into any Orthodox churches."

"Not yet. The time comes, however."

Cyprian found he could neither pronounce nor make sense of the strings of characters the young crypto wizard was showing him, straight or transliterated.

"Of course not, it's in code, isn't it," said Bevis. "Fiendish code, I might add. Right off I noticed it uses both Old and New Style alphabets—quite pleased with myself until twigging that each letter in this alphabet also has its own *numerical value,* what was known among ancient Jewish students of the Torah as 'gematria.' So, as if there wasn't quite enough threat to the old mental balance already, the message must now be taken also as *a series of digits,* wherewith readers may discover in the text at hand certain *hidden messages* by adding together the number-values of the letters in a group, substituting other groups of the same value, so generating another, covert message. Furthermore, this particular gematria doesn't stop at simple addition."

"*Oh,* dear. What else?"

"Raising to powers, calculating logarithms, converting strings of characters to terms of a series and finding the limits they converge to, and— I say Latewood, if you could see the look on your face. . . ."

"Feel free, please. As there's little enough hysterical giggling out here, why we must snatch it wheree'er we find it, mustn't we."

"Not to mention field-coefficients, eigenvalues, metric tensors—"

"I say, it could take forever, couldn't it. How many working here in your shop?"

Bevis indicated himself, with a single finger, held like a pistol to his head. "You can imagine how quickly it all rushes along. So far I've been able to decipher one word, *fatkeqësi,* which is Albanian for 'disaster.' First word of a message intercepted months ago, and I still don't know what to have looked out for back then, or even who sent it. The event, whatever it was, is long over with, the lives lost, the mourning frocks handed along to the widows next in line. The Eastern-Question brigade, having done their worst, pass along to promotions, gongs, landed ease, and whatever, leaving us ash-cats of the Balkans among their miserable debris, with all the tidying-up to do. Irredentism? Don't make me laugh. Nothing out here is ever redeemed, or for that matter even redeemable—"

"All quite chummy then?" Derrick Theign with his head in the door, an inspection visit no doubt, "excellent, boys, do carry on. . . ."

"That person gives me the chills," confided Bevis.

"Step carefully, then."

"Bevis," Theign was in the habit of pronouncing each time he looked into young Moistleigh's cubbyhole—*"the Story of a Boy."* Before the cryptographer could even look up in annoyance, Theign had passed along the corridor to perplex someone else.

"And another peculiar thing," Bevis regarding with suspicion Theign's form receding into the smoky establishment, "he has me working on Italian ciphers. They are supposed to be our allies, are they not? Yet day after day, all this naval material finds its way onto my morning pile. They have this practice in the Royal Italian N. of encrypting long articles from the daily papers, so one can practically break the code in one's sleep as long as one is willing to read a good deal of rubbish every day, then endless typing, translation into both English and German, a tremendous drain on one's time don't you know—"

"German?" no more than idle curiosity, really, "Bevis, where are these deciphered messages being routed, exactly?"

"Dunno—one of Theign's people takes care of that. Oh I say, German, I never thought of that, they're *not* supposed to be allies, are they?"

"Another of his elaborate games no doubt."

They turned back to the intractable blocks of Glagolitic code. By now enough caffeine had found its way to the brain centers which took care of such matters for Bevis that he felt comfortable moving to greater questions. "And further—suppose the messages could be inscribed somehow into 'the world,' into a self-consistent collection, analogous to a mathematical 'group.'

The physical engine would have to be designed and built of course, perhaps something along the lines of Mr. Tesla's Magnifying Transformer. And because the 'great world' is no more than the distribution, dense without practical limit, of just these symbols, written in just this code, any errors in the original inscription, however minor, could in time prove immense—even if not obvious immediately, one day someone will notice an inevitable blur, a cascade of false identity, a disintegration into massive absence. As if some great departure that no one can quite make out were under way, an emigration of reason itself."

"Something on a scale—" Cyprian imagined.

"Hitherto unprovided for in the future tense of any language. No matter what alphabet it's written in. As we like to say, 'High susceptibility to primordial variables.' "

"A departure—"

"An emigration."

"To . . . ?"

"Or worse—some sort of Crusade."

When they stepped outside at last and went to supper, Cyprian happened to notice the sky. "Something's wrong with the light, Moistleigh," as if it were physics he hadn't studied, some form of reverse eclipse that a cryptanalyst could explain, and possibly even repair. But Moistleigh was standing stricken, like the crowds in the Piazza Grande and along the *Rive,* glancing nervously upward from time to time though not gazing steadily, for who knew what sort of counterattention that might invite?

AFTER LEAVING VENICE, Reef had caught up with Ruperta at Marienbad, and for a while the old sad routine recommenced. He won more at the table than he lost, but on the other side of the ledger, Ruperta kept finding occasions, some describable as desperate, to claim his attention. Neither of their hearts must have been in it any longer, however, because one day she just took off without telling him. An empty bedroom, no information at the front desk, fresh vasefuls of flowers waiting for the next happy couple. The lapdog Mouffette, whom Reef had always suspected of being a cat in disguise, had vomited in his Borsalino.

Taking care to look woeful, while secretly feeling like he'd just walked out the gates of the pokey, Reef went back to touring the hydropathics, pretending different sorts of neuræsthenia, most successfully Railway Brain, the idea being to claim he'd been in a traumatic train accident in the recent past—and preferably in some nearby country whose records of the event would not be that easy to come by—with no immediate symptoms till the day before he appeared at the gate to check himself in, whereupon he could choose to suffer from a range of conditions, all carefully researched during his time at other establishments in the company of other hydro cases. The beauty of Railway Brain lay in its mental nature. The spa doctors knew that none of the ailments presented were real, but pretended to go about curing whatever it happened to be—the business office downstairs was happy, the croakers thought they were putting one over, the obscenely rich cardplayers got to lose enough money week by week to absolve them of their sins against the laboring classes, not to mention allow Reef to afford imported Havanas and tip widely.

On the night of 30 June, all the neuræsthenics of Europe, emerging from electric bathtubs and playing-rooms out onto what ought to've been dark terraces and pavement, glowing all over with radioactive mud-bath slime, electrodes dangling off their heads, syringes forgetfully poised inches from veins, came out of their establishments to marvel at what was going on in the sky. Reef, recently among them, happened to be in Mentone in and out of the hazardous bed of one Magdika, the blonde wife of a Hungarian cavalry officer noted as much for his readiness to take offense as his skill with dueling weapons. Since his arrival Reef had become intimate with the rooftiles and laundry chutes of the Splendide, and was indeed at the moment stuck like a fly to the façade of that establishment, inching along a perilous window-ledge as the exercised voice of the unexpectedly-arrived husband slowly faded, to be replaced by one more cosmically annoyed, and seeming to proceed, how peculiar, *from the sky,* which now Reef noticed—risking, at the most precarious step of his passage, a look upward and freezing and breathless at what he saw—was an evening sky which had refused the dusk, chosen a nacreous glow instead, an equivalent in light of the invitation to attend that Reef was now receiving from the overhead voice—"Really Traverse you know you must abandon this farcical existence, rededicate yourself to real-world issues such as family vendetta, which though frowned upon by the truly virtuous represents even so a more productive use of your own precious time on Earth than the aimless quest to get one's ashes hauled, more likely in your case to result in death by irate Hungarian than anything of more lasting value . . ." and so forth, by which time Reef was on the ground, running in the queer illumination down the boulevard Carnolès, he understood, for his life, or anyhow the resumption of it.

YASHMEEN WAS IN VIENNA, working in a dress shop in Mariahilf which had been gathering some celebrity for designs not yet quite discovered by the midinettes of Paris and so not yet dispersed into the greater market of the World. One day as she was writing up a request for overdue payment, she became aware of a fragrant presence close by.

"Oh! I didn't hear you—"

"Hullo, Pinky." Uttered in a note so low and somehow austere that Yashmeen did not immediately recognize her old Girton schoolmate Noellyn Fanshawe, grown less æthereal than the scholarly beauty of old, still hatless, her hair now drastically cropped, brushed back from her face, every bit of the charming little skull it had once been such delightful play to go searching for among all those blonde curls now brutally available, unequivocal as a blow or a gunshot. Her eyes, accordingly, enormous and somehow smudged away from the declarative light of the shopgirl's day in which it was Yashmeen's current fate to dwell.

"Noellyn! I had no idea you were in town."

"Here on a whim."

"You came in so quietly . . . ?"

"It's this Silent Frock I imagine."

"You know we're even stocking them here now—it's quite caught on."

"And you re-calibrate them as well, I'm told."

"Is it this one you're wearing?" Yashmeen cupped her hand behind one ear and leaned toward the dress. "Twirl about." The girl complied. "Can't hear a thing."

"It's daytime. Traffic. But at night, when I particularly need it, it's been acting up."

"I'll just fetch the *Facharbeiter*." She took a flexible brass-and-ebonite speaking-tube from its cradle. "Gabika, come out here."

Noellyn allowed herself a brief grin. "I've stopped saying 'please' to them, too."

"You'll see."

The technician who presented himself from the back room was young and slender, with very long eyelashes. "A house-pet," Noellyn said. "I wish I were interested enough, I'd borrow him for the evening."

"Let's go back to the fitting-salon. Gabika, we shall need this immediately."

"He reminds me a bit of Cyprian Latewood. Did you ever see that old vegetable again, by the way?"

But Yashmeen felt somehow willing to share only the most general sort of news. She had grown, she supposed, overcautious, yet the possibility remained that Noellyn was here at the behest of the T.W.I.T. Or someone even more determined.

Yashmeen helped her friend out of the ingenious garment, which Gabika bore away respectfully to his work-table. She poured them coffee from an elaborate urn, and they sat a moment appraising one another. "I can't get used to that boy's crop on you. Lovely as it is."

"I had no choice. You don't know her, we met last year in London, before I knew it, there I was all bewitched. She took me late one night to a hairdresser's in Maida Vale, I didn't notice the little straps and buckles on the chair till too late, and in less than a minute they had me quite sorted out. There were all these horrible machines in the place, and at first I thought I was in for one of those new 'permanent wave' things, but my friend had a different idea. 'You are to be my captive boy for a while, perhaps I shall let you grow it back in, depending how quickly I grow bored with the look.' The woman with the shears was charming but merciless, quite took her time about it, while my friend sat there with her skirts up, tossing herself off shamelessly through the whole thing. After a while I wished for the freedom of my hands so I could do the same."

"But she didn't let you."

"And I did beg ever so sweetly."

"Poor Noellyn." She took the other girl's chin lightly between thumb and finger. "Cross those pretty wrists behind your back for just a moment, there's a good girl."

"Oh but Yashmeen, I didn't come here to—"

"Do it."

"Yes, Yashmeen."

Gabika returned with the recalibrated Silent Frock to find them flushed and murmuring, with their clothing in some disarray and a decided musk note in the room, mingling with the background atmosphere of brewing coffee. He was used to these tableaux by now, had in fact quite come to look forward to them, perhaps explaining why he'd been on the job now for nearly two years without asking for a raise in salary.

Finding that perhaps against expectation they were actually delighted to see one another again, the two young women passed a pleasant evening together, going to early dinner at Hopfner's and then returning to Yashmeen's rooms in Mariahilf. By the time it had occurred to either to look out the window, it was, or should have been, well after dark. "What time is it, Yashmeen, it can't be this early still."

"Perhaps time has slowed down, as they say in Zürich. This watch reads eleven."

"But look at the sky." It was certainly odd. The stars had not appeared, the sky was queerly luminescent, with the occluded light of a stormy day.

· · ·

IT WENT ON for a month. Those who had taken it for a cosmic sign cringed beneath the sky each nightfall, imagining ever more extravagant disasters. Others, for whom orange did not seem an appropriately apocalyptic shade, sat outdoors on public benches, reading calmly, growing used to the curious pallor. As nights went on and nothing happened and the phenomenon slowly faded to the accustomed deeper violets again, most had difficulty remembering the earlier rise of heart, the sense of overture and possibility, and went back once again to seeking only orgasm, hallucination, stupor, sleep, to fetch them through the night and prepare them against the day.

Toward the end of October, all hell broke loose over the Austrian announcement that they were intending to annex Bosnia. Theign looked in, more haggard than usual.

"We need someone on the spot," he told Cyprian. "We may have to pull some people out."

"And you thought of me straightaway."

"Not my first choice, but there's really no one else. You can have young Moistleigh along if you feel you need a bodyguard."

Bevis was happy enough to be out of the subterranean funk of his crypto facility. "Yes do me good to get out of the old coconut-shy for a bit."

There was an open bottle of šljivovica on Theign's desk, but he didn't offer either of them any.

"What's this?" Cyprian said.

"Map of Austria-Hungary."

"Oh. Do I get a magnifying lens with it?"

"What's the scale here?" muttered Bevis.

Theign squinted at the legend. "Seems to be one to fifty million, if I've counted the naughts correctly."

"A bit too naughty for me," Cyprian muttered.

"Not at all, perfect for the traveler, last thing one would want I'd imagine, to be out in the open somewhere struggling in a fierce mountain wind with some gigantic volume of mile-to-the-inch sheets."

"But this thing is too small to be of any use to anyone. It's a toy."

"Well. I mean it's good enough for the F.O., isn't it. This happens to be the very map they use. Decisions of the utmost gravity, fates of empires including our own, all on the basis of this edition before you, Major B. F. Vumb, Royal Engineers, 1901."

"It would certainly explain a good deal about the F.O.," Cyprian staring at the map bleakly. "Look at Vienna and Sarajevo, they're not even half an inch apart, there isn't even room here to spell out their names, all it says is 'V' and 'S.'"

"Exactly. Puts the whole thing literally in a *different perspective,* doesn't it . . . almost godlike as you'd say."

The tone of voice, the expression on Theign's face, made Bevis anxious.

"Usual Theign," Cyprian assured him later.

"No, no, he doesn't care, can't you see that, none of the details matter to him, not only the map, he knows we won't live long enough to use it. . . ."

Yashmeen arrived one morning at the shop in the Mariahilfe Straße to find the door locked, in fact chained shut, a municipal notice of confiscation plastered across those windows that weren't broken. Back at her flat, the landlady, whose eyes would not meet hers, asked for her identity papers, claiming not to know who she was.

"Frau Keuler, what's going on?"

"I do not know how you have obtained the keys to this flat, but you will give them to me now."

"I got these from you—we see each other every day, I've always paid the rent on time, please, what's wrong?"

"If those are your belongings, I want you to pack them and be out of here as soon as possible."

"But—"

"Must I call the police? *Judensau.* You are all alike."

Jewish pig? For a minute she was too bewildered to see it. Vienna had been anti-Semitic forever, of course, from end to end, the inner city, the Ring, the Vienna Woods for that matter, even, since 1897, officially so, under the party of "Christian Socialists" headed by Jew-hating perennial Burgomeister Dr. Karl Lueger. In the national elections last year, the party had also tripled its membership in the Reichsrath. She had had no reason to pay attention till now—it was the air people breathed in this place, reaching a level of abstraction where actual blood was no longer the point. *"Wer Jude ist, bestimme ich,"* as *der schöne* Karl liked to say—"Who is a Jew, I determine." Hatred of the Jew was sometimes almost beside the point. Modern anti-Semitism really went far beyond feelings, had become a source of energy, tremendous dark energy that could be tapped in to like an electric main for specific purposes, a way to a political career, a factor in parliamentary bargaining over budgets, taxes, armaments, any issue at all, a weapon for prevailing over a business rival in a deal. Or in Yashmeen's case a simple method of chasing somebody out of town.

Cyprian didn't take it quite so casually. "Well. It's dangerous here for you now. Has been for a while actually. Dangerous people in power."

"Who? Not that kind old gentleman."

"Not Habsburgs, exactly. Prussophiles, I suppose is what I mean. Lovers of might. They want to preside over the end of the world. But now you really must come to Trieste."

She laughed. "Appropriate. Here they call it a Jewish city."

"Oh in Vienna," Cyprian replied, "they think *Shanghai* is a Jewish city."

"Well, actually . . ." she began.

THE ANNEXATION CRISIS had everybody in motion, and even Ratty McHugh, his life like everyone else's these days run more and more by train schedules, was dislodged from Vienna far enough to meet Cyprian in Graz, in the garden of the Elefant Hotel.

"Sorry there's only so much I can do at the moment, this Bosnian pickle and so forth."

"Theign making trouble at your shop as well, I shouldn't wonder."

They were both smoking, and the resulting haze between them produced somehow an impression of sympathy each was ready to accept without misgivings. "There are those among my shopmates," Ratty admitted, "who'd as soon see him in a different line of work. Far too matey with the Ballhausplatz, for one thing. Well, common Anglo-Habsburg interests, foremost being Macedonia, one keeps telling oneself, by now a bit wistfully. But he's got resources, he's dangerous, and it's even money at this point whether or not he can be contained."

"One couldn't just have him shot, I suppose."

"Oh, dear."

"Only lighthearted banter, Ratty. Not easy for you, I quite appreciate, these never-ending crises."

They had left the garden and were strolling across the bridge toward the Murgasse, where there was an automatic restaurant.

"The Balkan Peninsula is the boardinghouse dining-room of Europe," Ratty grumbled, "dangerously crowded, eternally hungry, toxic with mutual antagonism. A paradise for arms dealers, and the despair of bureaucrats. I wish I were on the Chinese desk. But you're itching to be filled in, I can see that.

"Well. Turkey has been in Bosnia for nearly five hundred years. It is a Mahommedan country, in fact a Turkish province. It was a staging area for the Turks on their way to the Siege of Vienna, and of course Vienna never forgot *that.* Thirty years ago Austria finally had its revenge. The infamous Article 25 of the Treaty of Berlin took Bosnia away from Turkey and put it under Austrian 'protection.' As well as allowing Austrian troops to garrison Novi Pazar, which had been the furthest thrust of Turkey west and northward into Europe. The understanding was that one day Austria would leave, and Turkey would re-establish herself, though neither régime was ever in much hurry for this. All seemed secure. But suddenly in Constantinople here came the Young Turks with their revolution, and who knew? they might wish to see the agreement actually honored! So Franz Josef, at the urging of the vile Aerenthal, pre-emptively issues his rescript 'annexing' Bosnia to the Dual Monarchy. Serbia is unlikely to let that sort of thing pass, and Russia must support Serbia, just as Germany must honor its promises to Austria, and so on, and so on, in three-quarter time, into a general European war."

"But," Cyprian blinking politely, "can they really be that obtuse in Vienna? I had always found them so up-to-the-minute, don't you know, clear-headed, rather a, well, a grasp on things."

"Oh dear." Ratty gazed at Cyprian in some concern. "It certainly *seems* as if both the Emperor and the Sultan were recognizing in Russia a common enemy. Neither gentleman talks to me, so how would I know. Austria have agreed to pay reparations to Turkey for taking away Bosnia—and further, quite unaccountably, to withdraw their troops from Novi Pazar, thus effectively handing it back to the Turks and giving up their own long-cherished dream of a railroad link from Sarajevo to Mitrovitsa, and thus to the Ægean Sea. But whatever that 'really' means, some Austrian idea of a sop or whatever, they have still annexed Bosnia. That fatal act, and the steps Germany has taken in its support, mark the end of things as they were. Isvolsky and Grey want a conference. The Dardanelles have come into play, and we must assume Bulgaria as well. . . . The Treaty of Berlin is perhaps not dead, but alive only conditionally, clearly a sort of zombie, stalking the corridors of Europe doing its masters' bidding. Wagers, many of them substantial, are being booked throughout the diplomatic community. There are European Apocalypse Pools among the workers at the bureaux concerned, as to the date of a general mobilization. This year, next year, soon. It is now inescapably on its way."

Ratty was watching him now with almost a pleading expression, like a convert to some outer domain of faith who is not sure his friends will understand. "They never tell you, really. How could they—Professor Renfrew might have entertained suspicions. In theory. Passed on what he thought he knew. But once we're out here, Cyps, well in the soup—one must find one's own way through—or not, as the case may be. It's like having the lights brought up for a bit, long enough to see how fearfully much is in play . . . the dimensions of possibility out here. . . ."

Cyprian narrowed his eyes. "Ratty?"

"I've heard where they're sending you, and what your orders are. I would intervene, if I could."

Cyprian shrugged. "Of course I'm a crucially important fellow, but my real concern is who'll look after Yashmeen. Her friends, as nearly as I can tell, are not her friends. I rather wondered if one of your lot—"

"Of course. But, Cyps, you, out there—it's going to be dangerous." Ratty was in full gaze now, a gaze full of rain in the quadrangles, pipe-smoking along the river, dawns inflecting the roof slates out the window, pints and bottles, horse races won and lost, moments of splendid understanding, nearly in reach, withdrawn across the night.

"It's dangerous *here*. Look at these people," flicking his gloved hand at the array of Austrian townsfolk visible at the moment. Frowning, shaking his head. "Or was it something in particular."

"Theign, I suppose."

"Yes. Care in motion, as the horoscopes always say. I thought actually that I might bring Yashmeen to Trieste."

"We've one or two very good people there. And there's your own op, the neo-Uskok chap, Vlado Clissan, as well."

"We've already been in contact. Vlado can be counted on."

"He does hate Theign."

"The very phrase I was groping for."

Ratty put his hand briefly on Cyprian's sleeve. "I always gave you more trouble than I ought, whenever her name came up. I hope you understand it was only a youthful idea of ragging."

Tilting his head, "And my youthful ideas about being in love. I don't imagine that I am now, Ratty, but I do need to be sure she's safe. I know what a nuisance you must think me—it isn't what you lot are really about—and I am grateful."

"In quieter times—"

"We wouldn't have the Blutwurst Special," nodding at a plate behind the pure lead-glass and chrome-steel compartments of the Automatik. "An obvious response to deep crisis."

"Hmnh. Always been more of a toad-in-the-hole man myself."

· · ·

Leaving the Südbahn, she gazed backward at iron convergences and receding signal-lamps. Outward and visible metaphor, she thought, for the complete ensemble of "free choices" that define the course of a human life. A new switching point every few seconds, sometimes seen, sometimes traveled over invisibly and irrevocably. From on board the train one can stand and look back, and watch it all flowing away, shining, as if always meant to be.

Stations one by one entered the past. The Semmering tunnel, the Mur Valley, ruined castles, the sudden traveling company of hydropathic addicts, the beastly shades of resort fashion, the inevitability of Graz. Then due south across the Slavonian plain, and up into the hills again, and the tunnels there, and Ljubljana, and across the moorland, up into the Karst, first glimpse of the sea, down at last through Općina to the South Station in Trieste. Eleven and a half hours express, a journey between worlds.

Cyprian had arranged for her to stay at a *pensione* in the Old City, back behind the Piazza Grande. It was close enough to the Piazza Cavana for her to be mistaken now and then for one of the nightwalking ladies who worked in the area. Soon she had become close friends with some of these industrious fireflies. Cyprian observed a neuropathic level of caution going to and from their meetings. Theign himself had largely abandoned Venice for Vienna these days, but certain of his creatures were sure to be about.

And as for any assistance from Theign's shop with her predicament, Yashmeen would not, after all, be able to count on much. "No, no Latewood my dear chap it won't do," choosing a moment close enough to Cyprian's departure for the Balkans not to mask the clarity of the insult, Theign's drawl growing more insufferable as he proceeded, "you see. Yes your little friend it seems is a person of interest to the Okhrana, and just at this moment it is the Okhrana toward whom most particularly one must endeavor to show consideration, with the Anglo-Russian understanding still so new, so fearfully sensitive, we must all support F.O. in this, set aside our unimportant little personal dreams and wishes mustn't we."

It did not take Cyprian altogether by surprise. "We had an agreement," he pointed out calmly enough, "and you might as well be an Austrian double, you contemptible pile of shit." Theign launched one of his virile slaps, Cyprian dodged out of the way—rather than be defied, Theign chose to look ridiculous pursuing Cyprian through the rooms and presently into the street screaming threats of bodily insult, but Cyprian was determined today not to be struck, and at length Theign gave up the chase. It was not a valid use of his time.

"I suppose," Theign called at last, "you want to be released from your part of the agreement."

"No." Wanting of course to abandon the whole corrupted project, which was sure now to be more dangerous than he knew how to measure or anticipate. He must go on with it—but God help him, why? Discussing it later in Vienna with Max Khäutsch, Theign too would find himself unable to keep from shrugging in contempt, a repeating bodily tic, out of his control—"The boy always was a fool. Either he knows what's waiting for him out there or he hasn't a clue, and in either event he's going through with it."

"Perhaps," Khäutsch would speculate in the peculiar whisper he reserved for shop talk, "he is tired, and wishes for an end. Cannot quite manage it himself, wants us to do it for him."

Cyprian and Theign had remained poised at opposite ends of the Venice flat. "Suit yourself!" shrieked Theign at last, off without further formalities for the train that would again take him to Vienna, where lately, it was an open secret, he had been spending more and more time. In ordinary circs this news alone might've been enough to draw Cyprian's soul, frail as a Fortuny gown, through a bright, small-radius ring of panic. But as his own train headed across the Mestre bridge, bound for Trieste, all he could consider with any clarity was Yashmeen, dreading what he was now obliged to tell her, wondering what recourse there could still be left for the likes of them against the storm gathering, so generally that this time not even Theign might be able to escape.

"HARDLY THE MOST hopeful news I could bring you."

She shrugged. In stays and a dark-plumed hat today, she seemed to stand a foot taller, and spoke in measured cadences which ran counter to the accelerated coffee-rhythms of Trieste. He remembered how little she needed protecting. How far they were from Cloisters Court, and the twilit chapel at King's. "And how likely am I to run into this Theign person?"

"I haven't told him you're here. That doesn't mean he hasn't found out, of course."

"Do you think—"

She stopped herself, but he had heard the silent part of the question. "Your trouble in Vienna? I wouldn't put it past him."

She was giving him a peculiar look. "You two were intimate once. But—"

"Is he the love of my life? Yashmeen . . . *You* are the love of my life." What had he just said?

She appeared to ignore it. "Yes but you continue to do whatever he tells you to. Now you're going out there on his orders."

"'And England's far,'" he quoted, not exactly in reply, "'and honour a name.'"

"And what does that mean? *his* game isn't cricket. You're forever, all of you, banging on so about honour. Is it from having a penis or something?"

"I shouldn't wonder." But he had thrown her quickly a look she knew she must not respond to.

"And if he's sending you into a trap?"

"Too elaborate for Theign. He'd simply use a hired stiletto."

"What shall I do here in Trieste then? In this Jewish city? While I wait for my man to return?"

Once he would have snarled back at her, and the phrase "thankless task" would almost certainly have to be deployed by one of them. But lately he was finding a perverse fascination in Patience, not so much as a virtue but more as a hobby requiring discipline, like chess or mountain-climbing. He smiled as blandly as he knew how. "What do they recommend back at Chunxton Crescent?"

"They have been curiously silent."

For a moment it was like watching each other from opposite sides of a deep opening in the earth. He marveled at the ease with which she could let hope glide away.

"I'll put you in touch with Vlado Clissan. He should be able to keep away the usual sorts of pest anyway."

"When will you be back from wherever it is?"

"It's all fairly straightforward, Yashmeen, just pop over the mountains and back, shouldn't be long. . . . What are you doing for money?"

"I'm an adventuress, money's never a problem, even when I don't have it. And what is that look? *This* cannot be about 'honour.'"

THEY MET AT the Caffè degli Specchi and she was all, it seemed defiantly, in white, from kid boots he must make an effort to keep from gazing at to her draped velvet hat and the white egret plume on it, though the year was darkening and taking on a chill, and the modish ladies in the Piazza Grande were giving her looks. "I won't thank you for anything," she warned him.

"I hope not." He glanced about at the overcast day, the indifference of commerce going on all around with or without them. Electric trams came racketing across the Piazza, bound for the train station or one of the *Rive.* Delivery cartmen rolled barrels of coffee down plank inclines and along the cobbles of the streets. The city smelled overwhelmingly like coffee. Most of the pedestrian traffic seemed kitted out for some formal, if not ceremonial, purpose. Boat whistles sounded in the bay. Lateeners and steam vessels glided in and out. Military personnel of all ranks rambled, ogled, preened, and glared.

They lit cigarettes and sat in front of small cups of coffee. "I've delivered you to this," gesturing at the scene with his head. "I deserve your curse, not your thanks."

"It's lovely. And where else should I be? If I turned back now, to England again, what would await me there? At Chunxton Crescent I'm regarded as having, in some way dark to me, failed. I shall never understand the motives of the T.W.I.T., their policies change day to day, they will help me, or not help, and may have even chosen, as we speak, to work me some serious mischief."

"But it's Limbo here. Well, Limbus actually, *in Limbo* being the ablative—"

She pretended to run him through with her parasol. "If Limbo is a sort of suburbs of Hell, then it is perhaps exactly the place for me. Between fire and outer darkness, enjoying the equipoise. Until I receive another omen anyway."

"That's what happened in Vienna? An omen?" He sat blinking. He had not cried since one drunken evening in Vienna after discovering Derrick Theign in the embrace of a miserable little five-kroner *Strichmädchen* that Theign had kept insisting was one of his colleagues. He had resolved in fact to give up tears as an unproductive indulgence. But now, faced with this attempt at sophisticated cheer, he was in danger of reverting. He found and clapped on a pair of blue-lensed sport spectacles.

"I'll be all right," she assured him. "You be as well, understand? or risk my displeasure."

A sailor from the Lloyd Austriaco, and quite presentable, too, Cyprian had to admit, now appeared, working his way round the caffès in the Piazza, holding a ship's bell and striking it with a small hammer and a not untheatrical flourish. Passengers gathered their impedimenta and began making their way toward the Molo San Carlo. There was this damnable stricture in Cyprian's throat. "You don't have to see me over the horizon," he croaked.

A tight-lipped smile. "I have a light schedule today."

The military band did not make things easier. Having detected a larger than usual turnout of British travelers, and waiting with some infernal clairvoyance until Cyprian thought he had a grip on himself, just as he turned to bid Yashmeen a breezy *arrivederci,* they began to play an arrangement for brass of "Nimrod"—what else?—from Elgar's *Enigma Variations.* Teutonic bluntness notwithstanding, at the first major-seventh chord, an uncertainty of pitch among the trumpets contributing its touch of unsought innocence, Cyprian felt the tap opening decisively. It was difficult to tell what Yashmeen was thinking as she offered her lips. He was concentrating on not getting her vestee wet. The music took them for an instant in its autumnal envelope, shutting out the tourist chatter, the steam horns and quayside traffic, in as honest an expression of friendship and farewell as the Victorian heart had ever managed to come up with, until finally, the band moved mercifully on to "La Gazza Ladra." It wasn't till Yashmeen nodded and released him that Cyprian realized they had been holding each other. "Well, I never saw what the big mystery was," she shrugged, "it's only 'The Volga Boatmen,' isn't it."

"No. No, I always thought it was 'Auld Lang Syne.'"

"Oh but do let's not quarrel Gonzalo."

"But of course not, Millicent," he chirped back, flashed his teeth, and started up the brow.

"Drop me a postal, now don't forget!"

"As soon as ever I can!" Adding, for some reason, under his breath, "My life."

AFTER HE HAD disappeared behind the breakwater, Yashmeen strolled down the Riva Carciotti, found a spot, lit up a cigarette and lounged awhile, beaming mindlessly upon the shifting scene. A cat followed her back to her room and would not leave. She named her Cyprienne, and before long they were close friends.

One day Yashmeen, out in the bora, just for a still-bracing Δt, had a relapse into her old Zetamania. She remembered that Littlewood, after struggling with a reluctant lemma one winter at Davos, through weeks of föhn—the bora's opposite, a wind so dry and warm that in some parts of the Swiss Alps it is called a "scirocco"—had reported that when that wind dropped for a day, the solution, as if by magic, was there. And no doubt because the bora, known in these parts as the "wind of the dead," descending out of the Karst, blowing uninterrupted for long enough, will also—with required changes of sign—have its effect upon the mathematical mind, as the brain lobes for this sort of thing began to relax, and strange and even counterintuitive thoughts to arrive from somewhere else co-conscious with the everyday, something similar happened now to Yashmeen. Just for the instant, the matter was illuminated, unequivocally, something as obvious as Ramanujan's Formula—no, something of which Ramanujan's Formula *was a special case*—revealed why Riemann should have hypothesized *one-half* as the real part of every $\zeta(0)$, why he had needed to, at just that point in his thinking . . . she was released into her past, haunting her old self, almost close enough to touch—and then of course it was gone again and she was more immediately concerned with the loss of her hat, flying away to join hundreds of others in migration to some more southerly climate, some tropical resort of hats where they could find weeks of hat *dolce far niente* to grow new feathers, allow their color to return or find new shades, lie and dream about heads that Fate had meant them to adorn. . . . Not to mention the need to keep her manteau from becoming a sort of *anti-parachute* which sought to lift her free of the pavement. She stood disbelieving, hair progressively loosening and flaring into a wet dark aurora, a grin less puzzled than aggravated turned against the incoming Adriatic norther, which for a moment, with that rogue conjecture, had delivered her into shadowy abduction wherever it might have led, and she could imagine, after all, visiting this coast for its wind, as a different sort of tourist might a hydropathic, for some miraculous spring, some return to youth.

And of course it was just in that instant that she met up with Vlado Clissan, who was staggering for shelter into the same doorway. The bora, as if collaborating, lifted her skirts and underskirts without warning over her face, as if a classical goddess were about to arrive in a cloud of crêpe lisse, and in the moment one of his hands had seized her, down between her bared legs, which opened further almost by reflex, one leg lifting, sliding up alongside his hip to clasp him tightly while she tried in the infernal wind to stay balanced on her other foot. Her hair, all undone now, lashed his face, his penis was somehow out in the rain and uproar, this could not be happening, she only had glimpses of his face, his smile fierce as the storm, he was tearing the fine batiste of her drawers, she felt every divided second of his entry and penetration, her clitoris was being addressed in an unfamiliar way, not rudely, actually quite considerately, perhaps it was the angle . . . but how could she be thinking of geometry . . . but if she didn't keep some attachment to that, where *would* they be taken? Out to sea. Up above the town and into the immemorial Karst. Up into the Karst, to a vineyard gate and an *osmizza* just inside that served meals and wine, the lights of Trieste far below, a wine ancient before Illyria, nameless, wind-finished, ethereal in its absence of color. And because here on this coast wine had never simply been wine, any more than politics was simply politics—there lay as-yet-undiscovered notes of redemption, time-reversal, unexpected agency.

"I was down there looking for you. Latewood gave me your address."

"He said you . . ." Her conversational resources faltered. Had she ever wanted so much to keep looking into a man's eyes? What was this? Vlado was not, she must be clear with herself, in no way was he a substitute for Cyprian, some desperate bounce she had taken because Cyprian had left, despite her best efforts to persuade him to stay. . . .

IT WASN'T EXACTLY the Hôtel de Ville, nor was she sleeping too frightfully well. The place seemed surrounded with tram lines, and the noise was, well, not really unremitting, there were quiet spaces between trams, unpredictable, even, she imagined, mathematically so. But it was the coffee metropolis of the Austrian Empire here, if not of the world, and she was never farther than half a block from the counter-soporific fluid, so she was able to get through most days without falling into slumber inconveniently, say in the middle of an attempt to avoid what she imagined, in her sleepless and paranoiac state, to be pursuit.

Vlado, who was unpredictably in and out of town, showed up at the door it seemed only when he desired her, which turned out to be often. How could a girl not be flattered? Obviously it could not be, could it, as simple as desire, but it was not the careful protocol of courting that required appointments in advance either. She had learned to recognize his step on the carpetless stairway—among the bull-elephant thundering of sailors, the imperious creep of philandering merchants, the march-tempo of Austrian military, each insisting on his primacy, there was no mistaking Vlado, the sensitive crescendo of his no less fervid approach.

By now she had heard enough through the walls to know that when one is having an orgasm in Croatian, the thing to scream is *"Svr šavam!"* though she didn't always remember to, memory having been, in the event, often disengaged.

Vlado kept an address in Venice, a couple of rooms in Cannareggio, in the old ghetto, multiply-nested among Jews pushed heavenward floor above floor . . . and nearly impossible to locate. And somehow that's where she found herself more and more. I'm turning Jewish, she thought, all that Viennese anti-Semitism is conjuring up what it most hates, how odd. . . ."I don't know. I was expecting horses, abduction up into the Velebit, wolves at night."

He pretended to think about this. "You wouldn't mind if I did a little business while we're down here. And take in the city sights of Venice of course, a gondola ride, Florian's, that sort of thing. Wolves, we can arrange wolves I'm sure."

. . .

ONE DAY THEY took the train to Fiume and boarded the mail steamer for Zengg, with a dozen German tourists and a small herd of goats. "I have to show you this," he said. He meant, "This is who I am," but she didn't understand until it was too late to matter. Eventually the narrow passage between the island of Veglia and the mainland opened out into the Morlacca Canal, and within two hours they stood off Zengg, facing a fierce bora which came barreling down through a gap in the Velebit. It was as if the sea would not allow them to enter. The sea here, Vlado said, the currents and wind, were a composite being with intentions of its own. It had a name which was never spoken. Coastal sailors here told of individual waves with faces, and voices, which persisted from day to day, instead of blending back into the general swell.

"Stationary waves," she speculated.

"Sentries," replied Vlado.

"How are we going to get into port then?"

"The captain is one of the Novlians, an old Uskok family. It is in his blood. He knows how to do business with them."

She watched the hillside town, pastel houses, bell-towers, a ruined castle at the top. The bells now all began to ring at once. The bora carried the sound out to the steamer. "Each campanile in Zengg is tuned to a different ecclesiastical mode," said Vlado. "Listen to the dissonances." Yashmeen heard them move through the field of metal tones like slow wingbeats . . . and at the base of it the sea's outlaw pulse.

Ashore it seemed that all the Uskok hinterland, not only in geographical space but also a backcountry of time, had come piling into town as if for a fair or market. The old rivalries between Turkey and Austria, even Venice enigmatically hovering as always, were still alive, because the Peninsula was still the mixture of faiths and languages it had always been, the Adriatic was still the fertile field wherein merchant shipping must be prey to the wolves of piracy who lurked among the maze of islands that so confounded the Argonauts even before history began.

"Until the early sixteenth century, we lived on the other side of the mountains. Then the Turks invaded, and forced us off our land. We came over the Velebit range and down to the sea, and kept fighting them all the way. We were guerrillas. The Austrian Emperor Ferdinand I gave us an annual subsidy. Our great fortress was just inland from Split, at Clissa, which is where my name comes from. We fought the Turks on land and kept them on the other side of the Velebit, but we also learned to fight them at sea. Our boats were better, more nimble, they could go where vessels of deeper draft could not, and if we had to land, we could beach and hide them by sinking them, do our business, come back, raise them again and sail away. For generations we defended Christendom even when Venice could not. And it was Venice who sold us out. They made a deal with the Turks, guaranteeing their safety in the Adriatic. So we did what anybody would have done. We kept attacking ships, only now Venetian ships as well as Turkish. Many of these carried unexpectedly rich cargoes."

"You were pirates," she said.

Vlado made a face. "We try to avoid that word. You know the play by Shakespeare, *The Merchant of Venice*? Very popular with us, of course from the Uskok point of view, we keep hoping till the end for Antonio to come to grief."

"You ate people's hearts," she said, "so the stories go."

"Myself, personally? no. Raw heart is an acquired taste, and by that time, 'Uskok' had come to embrace the *mala vita* of all Europe, including a number of quite notorious British Uskoks, several of whom were hanged in Venice in 1618, some of them nobility."

"There are English people who'd be impressed by that," Yash supposed, "while others might attribute it to hereditary idiocy."

They had climbed to the ruin of the ancient fortress. "The Venetians did this. They hanged Uskoks, sank our ships, destroyed our fortresses. Dispersed the rest of us, completing what the Turks had begun. Since then, four hundred years, we have been exiles in our own land. No reason to love Venice, and yet we continue to dream of her, as Germans are said to dream of Paris. Venice is the bride of the sea, whom we wish to abduct, to worship, to hope in vain someday to be loved by. But of course she will never love us. We are pirates, aren't we, brutal and simple, too attached to the outsides of things, always amazed when blood flows from the wound of our enemy. We cannot conceive of any interior that might be its source, yet we obey its demands, arriving by surprise from some Beyond we cannot imagine, as if from one of the underground rivers of the Velebit, down in that labyrinth of streams, lakes, coves, and cataracts, each with its narrative, sometimes even older than the Argonauts' expedition—before history, or even the possibility of connected chronology—before maps, for what is a map in that lightless underworld, what pilgrimage can it mark out the stations of?"

"A list of obstacles to be braved," she said. "What other sort of journey is there?"

They stayed overnight at the Zagreb Hotel. Shortly after sunrise Vlado disappeared upcountry on one of his political errands. She had coffee and a palačinka and drifted through the narrow streets of the town, at midday, on an impulse too hidden from her to account for, entering a little church, kneeling and praying for his safety.

At dusk she was at a table outside a café, and knew from the way he came strolling through the little piazza that there had been a recreational element in his day he would not tell her about. The moment they were in the room, he had seized her, turned her around, forced her onto her face and knees, lifted her dress, and entered her savagely from behind. Her eyes filled with tears, and a great erotic despair filled her like an unending breath. She came with the intensity she had grown to expect with Vlado, trying this time to do so in silence, to keep at least this for herself, but with no success.

"You have eaten my heart," she cried.

Cyprian, embarking from the Molo San Carlo on the Austrian Lloyd express steamer *John of Asia,* found the decks aswarm with butterfly-hunters, bird-watchers, widows and divorcées, photographers, school-girls and their guardians, all of whom, without undue exercise of the organs of fantasy, might be supposed foreign spies, it being clearly in the interests of Italy, Serbia, Turkey, Russia, and Great Britain to know what was afoot at the Austrian installations at Pola and the Bocche di Cattaro and the coastline approaching infinite length which lay in between.

Yashmeen's white tall figure, parasol over her shoulder, already a ghost in full sunlight, went fading into the crowds flowing in and out through the trees between the quay and the Piazza Grande. A young birch in a sombre forest. But he still could see her pale phantom long after it ought to have vanished behind the lighthouse and the breakwaters.

If there is an inevitability to arrival by water, he reflected, as we watch the possibilities on shore being progressively narrowed at last to the destined quay or slip, there is no doubt a mirror-symmetry about departure, a *denial* of inevitability, an opening out from the point of embarkation, beginning the moment all lines are singled up, an unloosening of fate as the unknown and perhaps the uncreated begins to make its appearance ahead and astern, port and starboard, everywhere an expanding of possibility, even for ship's company who may've made this run hundreds of times. . . .

The plan was to pick up Bevis Moistleigh at Pola, the Austrian naval base five hours down the coast at the tip of the Istrian Peninsula. Bevis had been down there pretending to be a neuræsthenic on a budget, staying at a modest hotel off the Via Arsenale.

They passed smoothly along the red-and-green Istrian coast, and as they neared Pola, a ship's officer went up and down the weather decks advising tourists with cameras that for military reasons photographs were now prohibited. Cyprian noticed a sprightly young creature scampering all round the ship in a translucent sailor-girl's outfit of white lawn and lace, hatless, charming everybody in her path, including Cyprian, he supposed. He learned with little effort that her name was Jacintha Drulov, that her mother was English and her father Croatian, both aristocrats, who had both unfortunately passed away in her infancy in the course of separate golfing accidents, and that she was now under the protection of her mother's cousin Lady Quethlock, with whom she had recently spent a brief holiday in Venice before returning to school at the Zhenski Tzrnogorski Institut in Cetinje. As soon as Cyprian observed guardian and ward together, certain nuances of touching, intentions to touch, withholdings of touch, as well as publicly inflicted torments of a refinement he recognized, suggested strongly that he was in the presence of a Lady Spy and her apprentice. This was confirmed by the mutterings of a pair Cyprian had already spotted as senior desk agents, of the sort who consider the employment of nubile children as field "ops" quite inexcusable.

"What can the damned fool woman have in mind?"

"Lucky bitch, actually. I know what *I'd* have in mind."

When Bevis Moistleigh came aboard at Pola and caught sight of Jacintha, he was instantly and publicly smitten. Cyprian felt frightfully happy for him of course, there being little enough passion in the world isn't there, yes—but decided to keep his suspicions about the devious dewdrop to himself for the moment, partly to see how much Bevis could find out on his own.

THE *JOHN OF ASIA* had begun to pass among island cities, variations on the theme of Venice, domes, villas, and shrines arpeggiated along the irregular Croatian coastline, white campanili and towers less explicable, older, grayer, put up against some ancient approach no longer definable, and all-but-uncharted *strange miniature islets* holding antique structures too small for worship, sentry duty or imprisonment. Fish known locally as "sea swallows" darted among the wave-tops. From the saloon, where two-headed eagles adorned the furniture, the drapes, and for that matter anyplace else one looked, Cyprian gazed out at the flowing scenery, as Bevis reeled out a line of patter no girl, however desperate for company, would ever have sat still for, except that Jacintha here appeared to be listening with a most peculiar eagerness.

"As many have demonstrated, notably I suppose Baden-Powell, one cannot overestimate the value of appearing to dwell in a state of idiocy. In fact Jacintha did you know that there is now an *entire branch* of spy-craft known as Applied Idiotics—yes, including my own school, a sort of training facility run by the Secret Service, near Chipping Sodbury actually, the Modern Imperial Institute for Intensive Instruction In Idiotics—or M.6I., as it's commonly known."

"How ever so much more exciting Bevis, than the dull little girls' academy I must attend, so relentlessly normal, don't you know."

"But I say Jacintha at M.6I. no aspect of school life was exempt really, even the *food* was idiotic—in hall for example the chip-shop approach was actually extended to deep-frying such queer items as chocolate bonbons and fairy cakes—"

"What, no fish Bevis."

"Dear me no Jacintha, that would be 'brain food,' wouldn't it—and the school uniform featured these ever so excruciatingly tight *pointed hats,* which one must wear even—indeed, especially—while one slept, and unspeakably awful neckties of the sort that, out in the civilian world, frankly, only, well, idiots would ever be found wearing . . . one's physical training began each dawn with a set of exercises in eye-crossing, lip relaxation, irregular gaits of as many varieties as there are dance-steps. . . ."

"That many? Really?" Jacintha flourishing her lashes.

"Let me show you." He motioned to the band. "I say, do you chaps know 'The Idiotic'?"

"Sure!" replied the accordionist, "we play 'Idiotic'! You give us money!"

The little orchestra struck up the lively two-step currently sweeping civilized Europe, and Bevis, seizing Jacintha, began to stagger quite uncoördinatedly about the pocket-size saloon, while the game lass did her best to follow his lead, both of them singing,

Out on the floor, used
To be such a bore,
Till we discov-ered
What thrills were in store, with
That step ex-otic, known as
'The Idiotic' . . .
Head like a pin? drool down your chin?
Could qualify-you
To give it a spin, tho'
It sounds neurotic,

It's just 'The Idiotic'!
Take all those

Waltzes and polkas,
Stuff 'em all-down-a-hole, 'coz
There's a scat-terbrained rhyth-m to-day . . .
It's the new 'Idiot-ic,'
And it's kinda hypnotic,
In its own imbecil-ical way!
(Say),

Try, it once-and-you'll-find
You've, gone out-of-your-mind
For—the craze of the mo-ment,
That's one-of-a-kind,
And it's just-so narcot-ic, that
I ven-ture to say . . . you'll
Be doing 'The
Id-iotic,' till they
Gotta-come take you a-way!

"And I must say Jacintha the girls at the dances we were obliged to attend were not *nearly* as jolly as yourself. Quite serious you know, obsessed by ever such dark thoughts. Actually, well, institutionalized, many of them. . . ."

"*Oh,* dear," chirped Jacintha, "how dreadful for you Bevis, obviously you escaped, but however did you manage to?"

"Ah. Certain arrangements. Always possible among gentlemen and no hard feelings."

"Then you are still with the same . . ." the lightly foreign shading she put on vowels producing its inviting effect, "gentlemanly apparatus?"

Now, Bevis's having been tipped for Idiotics instruction had been no random decision. No, no—indeed, crypto genius and all, in other areas of life idiocy came as naturally to him as a gift for leg-spin delivery might to another youth. A girl aboard an Austrian vessel, attending a Tsarist school and accompanied by English nobility, could of course be working for any number of shops—and Entente or not, in the present climate of annexation and crisis, Cyprian supposed due diligence called for a spot of intrusion about now.

But young Jacintha was ahead of him it seemed. She had approached him and, standing quite close, begun pulling at his necktie with some insistence. "Come Cyprian, you simply must dance with me."

No one could remember ever seeing Cyprian dance. "Sorry . . . under a court injunction, actually. . . ." Jacintha, her head set at a sweetly enticing angle, begged as if her heart would be broken forever if he did not immediately jump up and make a fool of himself all up and down the saloon. "Besides," she whispered, "however bad you think you are, you *must* be better than your friend Bevis."

"Oh, must I. Those charming feet are to be adored, not assaulted."

"We shall have to see about that too, then, shan't we," with a steady gaze experience would no doubt improve to a point where men would offer to pay her to speak just these words—for now Cyprian could not avoid thinking of Yashmeen in a similar exchange, though loyalty, if that's what it was, did little to moderate the erection he seemed to have been visited by, here. Jacintha regarded it with an all but predatory little smile.

Meanwhile, out on deck, Lady Quethlock was engaged in conversation with two other spies pretending to be idiots.

"No, no," she was saying, "not gold, not gems, not oil or ancient artifacts, but the source of the world's most enigmatic river."

"What, the Nile? But—"

"Eridanus, actually."

"But that's the old Po, isn't it?"

"If you believe Virgil, who's fairly late in the game—but the geography, regrettably, doesn't bear it out. If one goes back to the Argo, in Apollonius of Rhodes's account of that strange transpeninsular passage from Euxine to Cronian Seas—the forces of Colchis both in pursuit and waiting in ambush, the personal complexities of Medea to be dealt with and so forth, the Argonauts sailing into the mouth of the Danube and upstream, and somehow, nervously one imagines, emerging into the Adriatic—cannot be credited unless at some point they go by underground river, most likely the Timavo, a river to the sea at whose mouth according to Apollonius lie so many islets that the Argo can scarcely thread her way among them. The Po Delta has few if any such islands, but over on this side of the Adriatic, just over there in fact off our port beam as we speak, it's a different story, isn't it."

"But Virgil—"

"Is confusing Padus with Timavus, I expect."

"So these," a gesture out to the passing shore, "are the Amber Islands of legend."

"May be. I am hoping to resolve the question."

"Ah, the lovely Jacintha."

"Have you a moment Aunt? I do need some advice."

"You are perspiring, girl. What have you been up to?"

Jacintha had her hands behind her back and her head bowed, a proper little captive. Through her translucent dress the company could see every fine movement of her limbs, and were duly entertained.

THOUGH CYPRIAN AND BEVIS had decided to go in by way of the Herzegovina, Metković having for a few seasons now been implausible as a tourist destination because of the fever, they continued down to Kotor before debarking, Jacintha's company being a useful pretext for not getting off earlier at Ragusa. Cyprian, with no more than a vague code about honoring the idiocy of others, blinked rapidly but went along with the change in plan.

After a farewell whose poignancy if any, was lost on Cyprian, he and a signally glum Bevis Moistleigh ate at a waterfront restaurant that served a local brodet full of skarpina, eels, and prawns, then proceeded to the quay and engaged a boat which took them along the south shore of the Gulf of Cattaro, beneath all manner of fjord scenery, through a narrow canal known locally as "the Chains" and into the Bay of Teodo, all under the gaze of lenses, multiplied beyond counting, stationed at every vantage, though the specular highlights that twinkled at them from shore were not due only to optical devices. At Zelenika they sat drinking sage-flavored grappa before boarding the train for Sarajevo, which took them all the way back along the coast, through Hum and fever-ridden Metković, where they turned inland and began to climb into the Herzegovina toward Mostar, six hours away, then six more to Sarajevo.

IN SARAJEVO pale minarets rose above the trees. Swallows traced fading black trails across the afternoon-light, beneath which the river through town appeared red. At the Café Marienhof across the street from the tobacco factory, down at the Turkish bath, in dozens of chance meetings in the Bazaar, immediately, unable to help it, someone would be remarking on the Austrian outrage.

"Vienna must no longer be content with drifting along 'occupying' us as it has since 1878, bringing us the blessings of Austrian progress—railroads, prostitution, horrible furniture—"

"Jesuit operatives everywhere trying to turn us all Catholic."

"—yet till now it was all delusion, a sort of gentle madness, for we remained a part of Turkey, as we have always been."

"And now Austria's harmless phantasy has become acute suicidal mania. This 'annexation' is a Habsburg death-warrant."

"Perhaps one for Europe as well. . . ."

And so on. Silence, however welcome, would have betrayed the unspoken Law of the Café, which was that jabbering, regardless of topic, never pause. Voices enough, this autumnal crescendo of danger, were blowing along the river valleys, following the trains and mountain diligences, hounding, begging, unquiet—breezing in to remind native and tourist alike of how quaint, excitable, and precipitous was the national character . . . calling out, beware, beware the lover up all night with a girl he desires, and who will not yield to him. Beware the Black Hand and the Macedonian hotheads, beware even the Tarot cards the Gypsies set out for money or idle divertissement, beware the shadowed recesses at the Militär-Kasino, and the whispers therewithin.

And presently, from somewhere in the city, perhaps up on one of the hillsides, where the Mahommedans lived, or from around windings of the river, there would come an explosion. Never too close—almost exotic, almost an utterance in a language one never had to bother to learn till now. . . .

Though wearing a Turkish fez whenever the situation demanded—in Bosnia the fez was like the veil, an emblem of submission, and wearing it one of the costs of doing business—Danilo Ashkil was descended from Sephardic Jews who had fled the Spanish Inquisition three and a half centuries earlier, eventually settling in Salonica, which even then, despite being Turkish, was already recognized as a welcoming environment for Jews on the run. Danilo had grown up in a fairly respectable Ma'min household but was soon down by the waterfront hanging around with "dervishes," gamblers, and hasheesh smokers, getting into the usual trouble but finally proving too much of a social liability for his parents, who sent him here to Sarajevo to live with a Bosniak branch of the family, some of whose devotion to work and piety they hoped might rub off. True to his destiny, however, he was soon out on the street, having learned early in childhood to mock the confusion of tongues he was obliged by the day to move among, having come, in this way, by adolescence, not only to master Italian, Turkish, Bulgarian, Greek, Armenian, Arabic, Serbo-Croatian, and Romany as well as the peculiar Jewish Spanish known as Judezmo, but also when necessary to be taken for a native speaker of one or another tongue without in every case wishing to correct the impression. Well before the Austrian annexation, his skill with languages and gifts of permeability among all elements of the population had brought him to the attention of the Evidenzbüro. For traveling operatives of all the Powers, he had become the one indispensable man in the Balkans to drop by and visit. But now he was in danger, and it had fallen to Cyprian and Bevis to see him to safety.

Danilo, having arranged to meet Cyprian at a café just below the Castle, found a pale and sybaritic youth, the clogged certainties of whose university

English bore overlays of Vienna and the Adriatic coasts. He also noted a defective sense of history, common among field operatives, given their need to be immersed in the moment. So it was history—Time's pathology—that he must first address.

"I know it is difficult for an Englishman, but try for a moment to imagine that, except in the most limited and trivial ways, history does not take place north of the forty-fifth parallel. What North Europe thinks of as its history is actually quite provincial and of limited interest. Different sorts of Christian killing each other, and that's about it. The Northern powers are more like administrators, who manipulate other people's history but produce none of their own. They are the stock-jobbers of history, lives are their units of exchange. Lives as they are lived, deaths as they are died, all that is made of flesh, blood, semen, bone, fire, pain, shit, madness, intoxication, visions, everything that has been passing down here forever, is real history.

"Now, imagine a history referred not to London, Paris, Berlin or St. Petersburg but to Constantinople. The war between Turkey and Russia becomes the crucial war of the nineteenth century. It produces the Treaty of Berlin, which leads to this present crisis and who knows what deeper tragedies awaiting us. Ever since that war, Austria has dreamed of how it would be if the Turks were their friends. Germans come down here on tours and marvel at how *Oriental* everything is. 'Look! Serbs and Croats, wearing fezzes over their blond hair! Blue eyes, regarding us from behind the Muslim veil! Amazing!' But as you have probably seen by now, the Ballhausplatz are desperately afraid. They come to town, these men so practical and full of daylit certainties, and all the while you can look at them and see how they have spent the night, they have felt something stir in the darkness, shapes and masses, as ancient nightmares resume, and once again the Muslim hordes move westward, unappeasable, to gather, again, before the gates of Vienna—never mind that it's been unfortified for centuries, the old glacis built over with public offices and bourgeois housing, the suburbs penetrated easily as any Austrian whore—it cannot be true, God would not permit—but here is their hour at hand, and in their panic, what is the first thing they think to do? they turn and swallow Bosnia. Yes, that will fix everything! Leaving us all now to wait, here in the winter twilight, for the first thunder of spring."

Cyprian listened patiently. Bevis arrived, threw himself into a chair, and sat brooding, no doubt about his Anglo-Slavic ingenue. When Danilo paused to drink his raki, Cyprian nodded and said, "We're supposed to bring you out."

"And Vienna . . ."

"They won't know right away."

"Soon enough."

"By then we'll be out."

"Or dead."

"We'll take the narrow-gauge to Bosna-Brod, change there, return by way of Zagreb to Trieste."

"Rather obvious crossing-point, isn't it?"

"Just so. The last one they'll expect."

"And . . . how many of these deliverances have you achieved?"

"Thousands," Bevis assured him. Cyprian with difficulty did not flash him quite the look he wished to—smiled instead at Danilo with one side of his mouth, rolling his eyes briefly Bevis's way and back again.

"I shall need a weapon," Danilo said, in a tone which suggested that next he would be discussing money.

"The Black Hand are the people to see," abruptly advised Bevis Moistleigh, with a shrug of the brow meant to be read as, *Isn't that obvious?* The silence this released upon them was almost felt, like a drumbeat. What was a lower-level crypto like Bevis expected even to know about that widely-feared Serbian organization? It occurred to Cyprian not exactly for the first time that Bevis might have been set to spy on him, perhaps by Derrick Theign, perhaps by one of the many elements spying in turn on Theign.

IT WAS A COMMONPLACE among Balkan hands that if one was keeping an eye on liberation movements, and looking for members to turn double-agent and betray their own, the South Slavic population would provide slim pickings, if any at all. Nationalists and revolutionaries here actually believed in what they were doing. "Only now and then might there be a Bulgarian, or a Russian pretending to be a local person. A Russian will shop his mother for a glass of vodka."

And wouldn't you know it, who should Cyprian run into that evening, acting just about that desperate, but his onetime antagonists Misha and Grisha. It was across the river near the Careva Ulica, in Der Lila Stern, a former Austrian military brothel converted to more equivocal uses. Cyprian and Bevis drank Žilavka with seltzer water. A small cabaret band played behind a striking young vocalist and dancer in harem-inspired costume, though the veils were meant more to be seen through than to protect. "I say," Bevis remarked, "she's smashing!"

"Yes," said Cyprian, "and do you see those two Russians heading for our table, I think they may want to settle an old score with me, so if you wouldn't mind pretending to be a sort of armed bodyguard, perhaps a bit on the impulsive side, there's a good chap . . ." nervously fingering the Webley in his inside jacket pocket.

"Kiprskni!" they cried, "imagined you were dead!" and other pleasantries. Far from bitter over the Colonel Khäutsch business, the two, as if delighted to see an old familiar face, were not slow to inform him that they'd left their Prater ways far behind.

"Shoot you?" cried Misha. "No! Why should we want to? Who would pay money for that?"

"Even if somebody did, it wouldn't be worth our while," added Grisha. "True, you have lost some weight, but *tchistka* would still take too long."

"Your Colonel is somewhere out here now," Misha mentioned casually. "There was quite a scene in Vienna."

Cyprian had heard the story, which had entered the folklore of the business. When time had run out for the Colonel at last, his fellow officers had left him alone in an office at the War Ministry with a loaded pistol, expecting a well-behaved, traditional suicide. Instead Khäutsch seized the Borchardt-Luger and began shooting at everyone in range, shot his way out of the Ministry, into the Platz am Hof—next door at the Kredit-Anstalt they thought it was a robbery, so they started shooting too, the Hofburg briefly became Dodge City, and then Khäutsch was gone—according to legend, on board the Orient Express, headed east. Never seen after that. "Never officially," said Misha.

"Blackmail doesn't work anymore," Grisha all but in tears. "Preferring your own sex? What is that? If anything, these days, is path to career advancement."

"They're not yet that enlightened in H.M. Secret Service, I fear," said Cyprian.

"Turkey was a paradise," repined Misha, "those boys with eyes black as figs."

"Not anymore, of course. Constantinople is wasteland. Nothing young about Young Turks, who are in fact gang of puritanical old busybodies."

"Though I must say," Cyprian said, "they've shown admirable restraint about putting the Ottoman lot through the usual bloodbath, except for unregenerate cases like Fehim Pasha, the old head of espionage. . . ."

"Yes, that Brusa job," beamed Grisha. "Quite stylish, wouldn't you say?"

Cyprian squinted. "You two weren't . . . in some way . . . *factors* in that operation?"

Misha and Grisha looked at each other and giggled. Somewhat horribly. Cyprian felt an intense longing to be somewhere else.

"About the only thing English and Germans have agreed on lately," said Misha.

"Poor Fehim," said Grisha, at which point his companion, who was facing the street entrance, began acting oddly.

Cyprian, ungifted in the clairvoyant arts, nevertheless understood who had just walked in. After a bit he risked a tentative look over his shoulder. Khäutsch wore a monocle that many on first glance mistook for an artificial eye, and though he gave Cyprian a swift once-over, he did not seem to recognize him—though that could have been part of whatever his current game was.

"I say but Latewood," muttered Bevis, tugging urgently at Cyprian's arm.

"Not now, Moistleigh, I am succumbing to nostalgia."

All through the descent of darkness, the muezzins had been crying out calls to prayer from their hundred towers, before sunset, after sunset, and again deep in the last turn of the day. In here music of similar modality accompanied the *tsifté-télli* as if, like praying, it required of the body conveyance beyond the day's simplicities.

A great many young men in town seemed to know the Colonel, though as many made a point of steering shy as they came up to greet him. Out of curiosity, Cyprian drifted over and joined the group loosely gathered around the Colonel's table. At closer range he noticed a fatal unevenness in the length of Khäutsch's mustache, fraying at coat and trouser cuffs, cigarette burns and the depredations of moths as well as more earthbound pests. The Colonel was discoursing on the virtues of the Fifteenth Military District, otherwise known as Bosnia. "In Vienna the general staff always included some Prussian component, which made a life of human pleasure difficult if not impossible. Officers' honor . . . suicide . . . that sort of thing." An embarrassed silence had begun to descend. "But out here one finds a more balanced approach to life, and the Prussophiles do less harm." He plunged in a heavy-drinker sort of way into his own history, a detailed inventory of complaint. Ears did not exactly perk up. It coldly dawned on Cyprian, however, that Khäutsch wasn't that drunk. The eyes remained purposeful as a serpent's, recalling unavoidably chastisements Cyprian had undergone at the hands of this droning, seedy pub bore, some of which he had actually found, at the time, erotic. Was the whining recital supposed to be a seduction?

"It's important!" It was Bevis again, pulling him back to their table.

"Ever so sorry, Moistleigh, what was it then?"

"That belly dancer." He nodded in her direction, forehead corrugated earnestly.

"Lovely girl, yes, what about her."

"She's a bloke!"

Cyprian squinted. "I suppose so. Do wish I had hair like that." When he looked back at the other table, the Colonel, curiously, had vanished.

Somehow they got back to their pension, and next day Cyprian went from one hotel to another, learning eventually that Khäutsch, booked into the Europe under another name, had already checked out, having invoked a standing arrangement, involving either cash or threats of death, that his next address not be divulged.

DANILO, who knew everything, showed up at Cyprian's room with a warning. "I hesitated to disturb you with this news, Latewood, for you seemed another of these neuræsthenic youths one finds everywhere lately. But you must be told. You have come to Sarajevo on a dummy assignment. All to lure you out here to Bosnia, where it is easier for the Austrians to take you. Your English employers have shopped you to them as a 'Serbian agent,' so that neither they nor, in the current climate, even Russians will feel especially inclined to spare you. It seems you owe England nothing anymore. I advise you to go. Save your life."

"And Colonel Khäutsch's part in this?"

Danilo's eyebrows went up, his head to a doubtful angle. "He has too many precautions of his own to take. But you might feel more comfortable out of town."

"I take it you never meant to come out, then."

"I assumed by now they'd have resolved the political question." He looked away, and back. "Even so . . ."

"Do go on, it's only disposable me."

"For reasons you may not need to know, I find it more of a problem now to stay."

"The Crisis deepens, or something."

Danilo shrugged. "Here. You'd better wear these." He handed Bevis and Cyprian each a fez. Cyprian's was so small it had to be forced onto the back of his head with a sort of screwing motion, while Bevis's kept falling over his eyes and ears. "Wait, then, we'll switch fezzes." Most strangely, this did not resolve the difficulty.

"Makes no sense," Bevis muttered.

"It happens sometimes," Danilo darkly, "but more in the old tales than in our present day. The head of an infidel betrays him by *rejecting the fez*. Perhaps you are both quite devout Christians?"

"Not especially," Cyprian and Bevis protested at the same time.

"The fez knows," said Danilo. "You cannot fool the fez."

. . .

TWO WEEKS LATER things had desperately deteriorated. Cyprian and Danilo were adrift and mapless in a region of mountains and forest and unexpected deep wooded ravines, into some of which, actually, they had just missed falling. Equally distressing, they had lost Bevis. On the way up to Bosna-Brod, he had simply and unaccountably vanished from the train.

They searched through carriages full of Jewish families traveling to the mineral springs at Kiseljak, engineers from the manganese mine at Cevljanovic, coal and iron miners, wives and children and faithful sweethearts (a category which caused Cyprian vague discomfort), on the way to visit inmates at the prison in Zenica, all with no success. Fearing mischief, Cyprian, wanting only to go on, had felt obliged to get off and look for Bevis.

Danilo seemed afraid now for his life. "Forget about him."

"We're both supposed to bring you out."

"He can take care of himself, he is no longer your concern."

"Oh? Did Theign shop him, too?" Cyprian sensed a familiar melancholy oozing ever closer.

"English. You are fools."

"Nevertheless—" Cyprian reached for the emergency cord, and in the heated discussion with guards and conductors that followed, Cyprian pretended to fall into a sort of hystëria he had often found useful, Danilo looking on as if it were a performance in a park, as remote from his day as puppets hitting one another with clubs.

The last time either of them remembered seeing Bevis aboard was a little before Lašva, the junction for Travnik and Jajce. "There was a connection waiting," the conductor shrugged. "Your friend might have changed trains and gone up to Jajce." He agreed to wire the Bosna Line office back in Sarajevo, Cyprian and Danilo got off, and the train went on. They backtracked, searching defiles and streamsides till they lost the daylight, asking fishermen, crossing-guards, peasantry, wanderers, but none had seen a young Englishman in a seaweed-green suit. Not until well after dark did they get to Lašva, where they found an inn and tried to sleep till first light, before catching the morning train up to Jajce. Cyprian gazed out the windows, first one side, then the other. Danilo just as resolutely did not.

"It might even have been his own idea," he said after a while.

"You'll be next, I imagine," Cyprian was afraid he rather snapped back.

"Some choice—the fucking Austrians out there or your dubious protection. Either way, I'm dead." In Jajce there was a hundred-foot waterfall, with most of the town up on an egg-shaped hill, and an ancient fortress. They decided to walk from the station out, to the Grand-Hôtel, on the theory that if Bevis were in the neighborhood, he'd likely be there. The place looked like it had been transported in, by some dark art, direct from the Austrian Alps. Cyprian cupped an ear. "Is that yodeling I hear? Will the staff be wearing those, those *hats*? lederhosen? Actually, lederhosen in the present circs . . ." he lapsed into a moment's heated reverie.

Nobody at the reception desk had seen Bevis. "But those gentlemen over there have been waiting for you, I believe."

Cyprian was down into a spinning crouch and trying to remember where he'd put his pistol. Danilo waited with a caustic smile, shaking his head slowly side to side as the two visitors, creating around themselves a zone of avoidance, approached.

Black Hand, Danilo was sure. "As long as they think we are Serbian agents, they will be sympathetic—*Zdravo, gospodini.*"

Wasting no time on pleasantries, Batko, the larger of the two, nodded them toward the restaurant bar. Cyprian had an impression of dark wood and antlered heads. Batko ordered šljivovica all round. His companion, Senta, took out a pocket notebook, studied it briefly, and said, "Here it is, then—you must keep clear of all trains."

"Ne razumen," puzzled Danilo.

"Austrians are trying to make sure you two never get to the Croatian border. They have sent in motor vehicles, and at least a dozen well-armed men."

"For little us?" said Cyprian.

"We of the—" Batko, pretending to pout, left a pulse of silence where it was advisable not to insert "Black Hand"—"will always protect our own. But you are guests in Bosnia, and tradition says that guests are last to die. And considering who it is that wants to kill you . . ." He shrugged.

"Your choices from here on are few." Senta produced a small, damaged map, apparently removed from a guidebook. "You can go on foot, up the river, here, two days, to Banjaluka, and if you feel by then that you must risk the train again, try for Zagreb. Or you can go back the way you came, back through Vakuf, to Bugojno, where you can pick up the diligence route, through the mountains, down to the coast, and find a boat out of Split. There are of course a thousand footpaths, and it's easy to get lost, it is nearly winter, there are wolves, so the carriage road might be best for you, as long as you stay alert."

"Once we got over the crestline," Cyprian said, "I'd feel comfortable enough in the Velebit, and I know people there. But I don't suppose we could hire a guide for this side," which provoked some merriment.

"These are busy times for everyone," explained Batko. "If you really needed help, you could try shouting 'Union or Death,' but there'd be no guarantee. . . ."

The discussion proved academic, soon enough.

CYPRIAN AND DANILO made their way along a valley, leaves on the steep hillsides changing color, willows down by the water gone leafless and broodful, small waterfalls loud in the autumnal withdrawal of humans and livestock, the air cool and still, and no sign of unwelcome attention since they had left Batko and Senta, faces furrowed in sad farewell, by the chlorine works outside of town.

That evening they bought a trout and some cooked crayfish in a bag and had just entered an olive grove where they were thinking of settling for the night, when with no warning the air was filled with the high-speed purring of 9 mm Parabellum ammunition striking, for the moment, surfaces other than human and bouncing mercifully elsewhere, though it was now of the essence to find one's way inside the moment, with death invisible and everywhere, "like God," it occurred to Danilo afterward. Plaster was spalled off the stone walls by the road. Patches of white dust were kicked up into the air. They went running through the olive grove, leaves of the trees twitching in the invisible storm, nearly ripened fruit falling. Geese somewhere woke up and began to clamor, as if this sort of thing was supposed to go on only in the daytime.

"Do you have your pistol?"

Danilo waved a little Portuguese army .32 Savage. "It doesn't matter, I've only two clips for it."

They ran half blind for higher ground. The dark saved them. So they were chased off, uphill, among rock pinnacles, into the forest and the mountains and progressively wilder terrain, and all question of alloyed steel, geometric purity of gauge, railways and timetables and the greater network, not to mention European time as it usually passed, ceased to be any part of their day, and they were swept back into the previous century. Autumn kept rolling in, the colors darkening, the black that rests at the heart of all color reasserting itself. The mountains were draped in banners of cloud torn as if from distant battles already begun, projections of the Crisis. . . . Sheep that had mingled with the shadows of clouds across the valley floors were presently gone to shelter against the winter nearly upon this country, the limestone mountains seemed to climb the sky, to grow more proud, as temperatures fell, and the first snow appeared on the heights. Chimney smoke from lignite fires collected in the valleys. The light in these mountains toward dusk grew solemn and awful. The fugitives longed to be in out of it, and yet knew their only chances for deliverance here lay outdoors, away from refuge-huts, hunting lodges and hydropathics. They must be where the stone martens glided like ghosts from shadow to shadow, and cave entrances offered not security but fear.

All converged to black, black unmitigated by candleflames or woodsmoke. Each night a drama commenced, in languages even Danilo could not always understand. Outside of the little upland basins called *poljes,* where were the village folk who had so carefully avoided them in the light—where, among these limestone wastes, were there even villages? Not a soul remained outdoors after dark to gather, kindle, cook, or husband—all community withdrew to dens, tunneling, the dorsal indifference of the beast. The still surfaces of mountain ponds reflected starlight of white gold, now and then obscured by whatever was abroad in this mineral desert.

One evening, just before sunset, they looked up at the wall of mountains, and all the way to the ridgeline there were these strange patches of light, everywhere, too bright for snow yet not orange or red enough for fire, as great sheets of glowing vapor swept the valley beneath, and against the reflection in the river of this incandescent passage, erect on an ancient bridge, above its pure arch in silhouette, stood a figure, cloaked, solitary, unmoving, not waiting, not beckoning, not even regarding the spectacle up on the mountainside, yet containing in its severe contours a huge compressed quantity of attention, directed at something Cyprian and Danilo couldn't see, though presently they understood that they ought to have.

THEY WERE CAUGHT one night on a nameless black mountainside, by a storm that had descended from the north and a premonitory silence. Danilo, a city-dweller all his life, looked around, as if expecting an umbrella-vendor to appear.

"*Djavola!* this weather!"

"Unless you're British," Cyprian pointed out, "then it's almost like home, yes quite cozy actually. . . . Do you think we've lost them by now?"

"They've lost us. Driven us up here, where the mountain can do the work for them. Saves them bullets, too."

They had come to a fearful halt, pressed against the ice-slick rock risen uncounted ages ago as if just for this hour. . . . There was no light from anywhere. They knew the terrain opened everywhere into ravines whose walls dropped straight down. Neither knew the way down off this fierce black precipice.

When he tripped and fell, Cyprian for the first time was delivered into an embrace that did not desire him, as he became only another part of the mechanical realm, the ensouled body he had believed in until now suddenly of far less account than mass and velocity and cold gravity, here before him, after him, despite him. As the storm roared all around, he slowly struggled to his knees and, finding no pain beyond the expected, to his feet. Danilo had vanished. Cyprian called, but the storm was too loud. He didn't know which direction to start looking in. He stood in rain just at the edge of sleet and considered praying.

"Latewood."

Not far. Carefully, night and storm-blind, Cyprian moved toward the voice. He came upon a drenched and broken animal presence he could not see.

"Don't touch anything. I think my leg is broken."

"Can you—"

"I can't stand on it—just tried." Long ago, in rented rooms, shadows of colonnades, public gardens, bourgeois amenities of a world at peace, Cyprian had come to imagine himself gifted at hearing the residues of truth behind the lies everyone tells in the dark. Here, now, in this less compromised blackness, what he heard from Danilo was too plain. "You must bring me out," the barely covert voice said—without the possibility of another meaning. "We must use this." It was an ancient Mauser they had found in an empty house back down the mountainside.

"But we'll need it for—"

Patiently, Danilo explained. Cyprian took off his coat, which was nearly blown from his grasp, and then his shirt, the cold hitting him like a street-brute indifferent to anything he might have appealed with, tore the shirt into strips and attempted with fingers rapidly losing all sensation to tie the rifle to Danilo's broken leg for a splint. "Can you straighten it?" Ice-points were now being driven horizontally at their faces.

"I can, but I'm not sure I want to." Even through his numb hands, Cyprian could feel the wrongness. Hands tuned to the musculature of limbs, the refined appreciation of bodily perfection, now found themselves failing before the need to put right this insult. "Do it," Danilo shouted angrily against the wind. There was no reason out here not to cry as loudly as he must for the pain. *"En tu kulo Dio!"*

With the rifle butt under his armpit, Danilo found he could hobble short distances, at least at first. But the going was too slow, it hurt too much, and before long Cyprian found himself supporting Danilo's weight again. He knew they had to follow divides till they came to a major ravine and then descend to the streambed and keep heading downhill till they found human habitation. Before they froze to death. That was the theory anyway. But shelter, any pocket of calm air in which a flame might last long enough to take hold, a ledge wide enough for five minutes of sleep, none of these domestic pleasantries were about to appear. There was frostbite to consider, at every step, every change in the wind. If they even stopped moving, they would freeze. Moving was the key, arrival at a place of safety was for now a luxury too remote to think about. Wolves called to one another, as if keeping track of an evening menu considerately delivered among them. Occasionally, when the storm had passed, there would be moonlight to pick up and set aglow a pair of interested eyes. Only long enough for the creature to turn its head to a different angle, as if not wishing to reveal its gaze for too long. By now Danilo was running a fever. His weight slowly grew toward the absolute inertia of a corpse. Sometimes, unaccountably, he would no longer be there.

"Where are you?" Cyprian could feel the wind taking his voice away into its vast indifference.

"Where are you?" he cried. He wished, terribly, for no answer.

THE RAIN BLEW down the valley, at the verge of snow, stinging, thin, a white European rover with vicious intentions.

"I'd been expecting, I don't know, a weekend in the country sort of thing," Cyprian said. "'Snow? not to worry, mean temperature in Sarajevo is fifty degrees Fahrenheit, a light ulster should do the trick.' Fucking Theign, thanks ever so much."

They had found a very small village, an accretion of stonework hanging from the side of a mountain, and had been allowed to winter there. One passed from one chamber to another, some of them roofed, some not, by way of rough stairs and archways, snow-pierced tunnels, muddy courtyards, whose construction, beginning long ago with a single farm shed, had extended over centuries. Bitter-cold sleet and snow, wind-borne, raced among the ravines, wailed among the tiles of the roofs. The other side of the valley was often invisible, clouds descended in salients sharply run like the defenses of a walled town, all color disappeared, the summer was a country of wistful legend, no longer real or recoverable. Wet dogs, descended from ancestors who had lived here during the Dark Ages, recalling sunned walls in whose shade they had once lain, now sought the uncertainties of indoor life. There were lignite workings across the valley, Cyprian could smell it when the wind was right, and now and then it was possible to cross over with a donkey and scavenge some, an all-day task in the best of weather and usually extending over a night or two—but what preoccupied the residents most was the location of firewood caches—these were more like hoarded treasure as the season deepened, and village opinion held it legitimate to kill, at least aim and shoot at, anyone who took wood not his own. The smell of woodsmoke anywhere among the stone baffle-work was an outward sign of some family event kept otherwise inside shutters of silence. "She thinks she's cold again," they nodded, or, "Snežana is boiling more potatoes. There can't be too many left by now."

At first from fever, then in long calm descents to sleep, as he slowly began to mend, Danilo began to talk about Salonica, the city of his youth, the women by the fountains in the mornings, his mother's pastel de kwezo, parades in the streets of wrestlers and Gypsy musicians, the all-night cafés. "At first I tried to get back there as often as I could, but responsibilities in Sarajevo piled up, and one day I woke to find I'd become a Bosniak. I wish I could show it to you someday, Latewood, Salonica is all the world in a single city, and you must meet my cousin Vesna, she sings in a hasheesh joint down in the Bara, you'll love her as I do. . . ."

Cyprian blinked politely. No questions of desire, either between themselves or for third parties, had ever arisen—it might have been the general exhaustion the young men both had to fight moment by moment, or their simple discovery that neither was the other's sort, or, strangest of all, that in some scarcely acknowledged way, Cyprian had become Danilo's mother. He was surprised to find emerging in his character previously unsuspected gifts, notably one for soup, as well as an often-absurd willingness to sacrifice all comfort until he was satisfied that Danilo would be safe for another spell, however brief.

This first encounter with release from desire brought Cyprian the unexpected delight of a first orgasm. He was sitting up in a black and thickly clouded night, tending to Danilo's sleep, as if he must be prepared in an instant to intervene if needed, to walk the other man's painscapes of dream or delirium. All at once, no not all at once, more like the way one wakes sometimes very slowly to the awareness there is light in the room, he found that for some undefined time now he had not even been imagining desire, its arousal, its fulfillment, any occasion for it. The imbalance he was used to experiencing as a numb space in the sensorium of the day, as if time were provided with sexual nerves, a patch of which had been waiting unaddressed, was, somewhat mysteriously, no longer there—it was occupied by something else, a clarity, a general freshening of temperature. . . .

Of course it passed, the way a pulse of desire itself will, but the odd thing was that he found himself always unexpectedly trying to locate it again, as if it were something at least as desirable as desire.

Danilo was getting about quite well on a stick with the head of a wolf for a handle, carved over the winter from mountain ash for him by his friend Zaim. He came in one day to find Cyprian cutting up potatoes, winter carrots and onions to put into a soup, and for the first time they talked about their passage through the mountains.

"It was luck," Cyprian shrugged. "We were lucky."

"It was the will of God," Danilo said.

"Which of your several Gods would that be, again?"

"There is only God."

Cyprian was nowhere near as certain. But seeing the usefulness of remaining attached to the day, he only nodded and went on chopping up vegetables.

WHEN THEY GOT BACK again to steel and parallel tracks, they found the lines nervous with an all but mortal appetency, bands of irregulars carrying ancient long rifles whose brass fittings were incised with holy verses from the Quran, Bosnian Catholic units with Mannlichers furnished by their Austrian masters, Turkish guerrillas heading for Constantinople and the revolution at home, Austrian regular army swarming at the frontiers, stopping everyone, with no indulgence shown English tourists, which was what Cyprian had been hoping to pass for, or even German ones, who were there in numbers, as if to witness some godless spectacle, a passion play without a Christ.

It is in the nature of prey, Cyprian was later to reflect, that at times, instead of submitting to the demands of some predator, they will insist upon being difficult. Running for their lives. Putting on disguises. Disappearing into clouds of ink, miles of bush, holes in the earth. Even, strange to tell, fighting back. Social Darwinists of the day were forever on about the joys of bloody teeth and claws, but they were curiously uncelebratory of speed and deception, poison and surprise.

The important thing in considering disguises, Cyprian supposed, was not to look Russian. It wasn't that the skills he needed came to him suddenly by any special providence—there was little this time out he had not done before. At Bosna-Brod he was obliged, from within a toilette whose relation to any sort of taste was better left unexplored, to play the part of a civil-service wife, contemptuous of all that was not English, demanding in a shrill tessitura to be allowed through to reunite with a husband for whom, though fictional, Cyprian was carefully able to suggest less than complete adoration, while carrying on a tirade against all things Bosnian, the accommodations, the food—"Whose idea was this mutton-and-spinach horror?" "Is kapama, is good, eh?"—even, as if forgetting how risky it might prove, the men—"What possible maiden's prayer can you be thinking yourselves the answer to, with those ridiculous baggy trousers and headscarves . . ." the odd thing being that these particular irregulars were as handsome and muscular as once upon a time anyone could have desired . . . but it was more important to locate all the firearms, visible and otherwise, likely to be hostile, a matter of minutes, and to choose—almost, by now, automatically, more than one likely avenue of escape . . . at times he invoked the opposite of disguise and withdrew into a fatalistic submissiveness so complete that after he and Danilo had passed by, no one even remembered seeing them, though by then Danilo's injury had reasserted itself, along with his despair. There were hours in their passage Cyprian wanted to cry for the other man's suffering but knew with the absence of mercy peculiar above all to prey that survival, in cases like theirs, did not lie in the direction of sentiment.

At Belgrade they found both rivers under interdiction. It made Cyprian that much more angrily determined to get out. In late-winter fog, among domes and spires of rusted iron and stone, oversize angels, broken, defaced, but still standing in hilltop isolation, their faces strangely, carefully specific, Danilo and Cyprian moved south through Serbia but learned presently that all roads over the mountains to the coast would be snowed in for weeks yet.

IN PLJEVLJE THEY STOPPED for a day just to get their bearings. There was snow on the brown heights. It was a small pretty town with four minarets and one campanile and the Pasha's *konak* sprawling across the foothills. Austrian garrisons were in the process of pulling out, as they were all through the *Sanjak* of Novi Pazar, as part of a bargain with Turkey over the annexation—blue masses fragmented by snow falling intermittently, lines passing radially one by one, as if some great apocalyptic wheel had begun at last to turn . . . clutch-plates slamming into engagement, chattering drafts of youngsters in ill-fitted uniforms marched off into general dusk.

"If we could find a way to get to Kossovska Mitrovitsa," Danilo reckoned, "eighty, maybe a hundred miles, we could catch a train south to Salonica."

"Your childhood home," Cyprian recalled. "Your cousin Vesna and whatnot."

"Years. Until now it has not felt like exile."

Back in January, Austria's reptilian foreign minister Aerenthal had finally got a concession from the Sultan to build a line from the Bosnian border, through the *Sanjak,* to the Turkish railhead at Kossovska Mitrovitsa. Now it lay there, this notional railway not yet built, invisible across the snow and passes and valleys, an element of diplomacy waiting to enter material existence.

Cyprian and Danilo followed it as best they could. They rode with sutlers and camp followers, the phantom rolling-stock of military and farm wagons, mostly their own damaged feet, till one day they saw minarets, and Turkish barracks on a hill rising behind an unremarkable town, and that was Kossovska Mitrovitsa.

They boarded a physical or material train and rattled south, shivering with the winter damp, creaking and toppling in and out of sleep, as if drugged, indifferent to food, smoke, alcohol. . . . All the way down through Macedonia, past stations of pilgrimage, finding shrines and sacred places deserted, the wind blowing through, the station platforms desolate, Cyprian was gazed at now and then, though not in any predictable way, from crossing or trackside, in depot archways, as if by comrades-in-arms who had shared an obscurely shameful reverse upon the field of honor—not an outright defeat, but an incentive to withdraw from some engagement offered. Destiny having advanced a pawn, the gambit had been declined, and the despondency of the unsought went moaning in the wires down all the rights-of-way, beneath the Black Mountain of Skoplje, through the city itself, past Mount Vodno, along the valley of the Vardar, through the wine country of the Tikveš Plain, through Demir Kapija, the Iron Gate, and all the way down to the Ægean, to the end of the line, Salonica—where, out of the nicotine and hasheesh mists of the Mavri Gata or Black Cat seamen's tavern, unaccountably came running a thin young woman with fair hair, who leapt on Danilo, embracing him not only with arms but legs as well, screaming his name over and over.

"This is my cousin," Danilo mentioned at last, when he had stopped sobbing enough to talk. "Vesna."

Once, in another life, Cyprian would have replied in his most withering tones, "Of course, charmed I'm sure," but now he found himself possessed, mouth, eyes and sinuses between, by a smile he could not control. He took her hand. "Your cousin told me his family were here. I'm as happy as he is to see you. Possibly more so." The relief he felt was enough to make him start crying, too. Nobody noticed.

CYPRIAN AND DANILO had arrived at Salonica to find the city still reverberating like a struck gong from the events of the preceding spring and summer, when the Turkish sultan had been obliged to restore the constitution, and the insurgents known as the Young Turks had come to power in their country. Since then Salonica had been running on nerve. The city seethed with rudely awakened legions of transient riflemen, as if this ancient scented spill of red roofs, domes, minarets, and cypresses down steep dark hillsides were the flophouse of Europe. Everyone had assumed as written fate that Salonica would fall under Austrian influence—for Vienna dreamed of the Aegean the way Germans dreamed of Paris—when in fact it was the chaste young revolutionaries of Turkey who had already set about re-imagining the place—"Enjoy the skyline while you may," Danilo all but tearful, "the mosqueless idea of a city is nearly upon us, dull, modern, orthogonal, altogether lacking God's mystery. You Northern people will feel right at home."

Down at the port, between the train station and the gas works, in the beer halls and hasheesh bars of the Bara district, the girls were venal and intermittently (but then strikingly) beautiful, the men dressed in flashy white or pearl-colored turnouts and matching shoes whose spotlessness Cyprian understood it would literally be worth his life to compromise or even to comment on aloud.

At the Mavri Gata there was enough hasheesh smoke to confound an elephant. At the end of the room, as if behind an iconostasis of song, oud, baglamas, and a kind of hammered dulcimer called a santouri were being played without a break. The music was feral, Eastern in scale, flatted seconds and sixths, and a kind of fretless portamento between, instantly familiar though the words were in some slurred jailhouse Greek that Danilo confessed to picking up only about one word in ten of. In these nocturnal modalities, "roads," as the musicians called them, Cyprian heard anthems not of defined homelands but of release into lifelong exile. Roads awaiting the worn sole, the ironbound wheel, and promises of misery on a scale the military staff colleges were only beginning to contemplate.

Vesna was a flame, a brilliant focus of cognizance known in this town as a *meraklоú*. "*Tha spáso koúpes,*" she sang, "I will smash all the glasses and go out and get drunk because of how you spoke to me. . . ." Knives and pistols appeared from time to time, though some were only for sale. Eligible customers were introduced to sleeping-drafts in their beer and robbed of everything including their socks. Sailors deserted their men-o'-war for street-sparrows who vowed to defy pimp or husband no matter how fatal the consequences. Tough customers in from Constantinople on business sat at tables in the back, smoking out of *argilés,* counting to themselves without moving their lips, scanning every face that came and went. Their presence (Cyprian was aware by way of Danilo) was not inseparable from the activities of the Young Turkey Party and its Committee of Union and Progress, headquartered here in Salonica. There were things these young idealists needed in the way of matériel, parts of town that must be gone in and out of without molestation, that only "dervish boys" knew how to help with. There were also the Germans, ubiquitously conferring with Committee operatives, too saturated in entitlement to bother with altered identities, simply being German, as if the value of emulation were too obvious to require comment. Albanian children with heaps of koulouria on trays balanced firmly atop perfectly flattened heads came running in and out. Glass broke, cymbals were bashed repeatedly, *kombolói* clicked in dozens of rhythms, feet stamped along with the music. Women danced the *karsilamás* together.

"*Amán,*" Vesna cried, she ululated, "*amáaáaáan,* have pity, I love you so. . . ."

She sang of longing so deep that humiliation, pain, and danger ceased to matter. Cyprian had left so much emotion behind that it took him all of eight bars to understand that this was his own voice, his life, his slight victory over time, returned to fair limbs and spring sunrises and a heart beating too fiercely for reflection driving him toward what he knew he needed, could not live without. *Stin ipochí,* as the song, too many of the songs, went—back in that day . . . what had happened? Where was desire, and where was he, who had been almost entirely fashioned of nothing but desire? He regarded the dawn outside the street door, the cyclic fate of one more room-size Creation assembled from scratch through the dark hours one mean blow, petty extortion, faithless step at a time, a little world in which a city's worth of lives witlessly, gleefully, in its entire force, had been invested, as it would be, night after night. It was the absence of all hesitation here that impressed Cyprian, setting aside the ouzo and hasheesh whose molecular products, occupying by now every brain-cell, discouraged careful analysis. It was a world entirely possible to withdraw from angelwise and soar high enough to see more, consider exits from, but nobody here in the smoke and breaking waves of desire wanted exit, the little world would certainly do, perhaps in the way that for some, as one of Vesna's songs suggested, children, though also small, though comparably doomed, are forever more than enough.

NEWS HAD FILTERED through at last on the status of the annexation crisis and the doings of the great. The German ambassador had met with the Tsar, bringing a personal note from the Kaiser, and shortly after that the Tsar announced that on second thought the annexation of Bosnia would be fine with him after all. The continent relaxed. The Tsar's decision might have had to do with the recently mobilized German divisions poised at the frontier of Poland, though this was speculation, like everything else at this bottom dead center of the European Question, this bad daydream toward which all had been converging, murderous as a locomotive running without lights or signals, unsettling as points thrown at the last minute, awakened from because of some noise out in the larger world, some doorbell or discontented animal, that might remain forever unidentified.

If Cyprian thought however briefly that now he might be entitled to some relaxation, he was swiftly disabused. One night at the Mavri Gata, Danilo showed up with a noodle-thin and mournful Bulgarian whose name people were either unable to pronounce or remember, or unwilling to utter aloud for fear of certain Greek elements in town. Among the *dervisidhes,* because of his appearance, he went by the name of Gabrovo Slim.

"It is not the best time to be Bulgarian in Salonica," he explained to Cyprian. "The Greeks—not these *rembetes* in here but the politicals who work out of the Greek embassy—want to exterminate us all. They preach in the Greek schools that Bulgaria is the Antichrist. Greek agents work with the Turkish police to make death lists of Bulgarians, and there is a secret society here called 'The Organization' whose purpose is to carry out these assassinations."

"It is about Macedonia, of course." Cyprian said.

An ancient dispute. Bulgarians had always thought Macedonia was part of Bulgaria, and after the war with Russia so it became at last—for about four months in 1878, till the Treaty of Berlin handed it back to Turkey. The Greeks meanwhile believed it was part of Greece, invoking Alexander the Great, and so forth. Russia, Austria, and Serbia were seeking to extend their influence in the Balkans, and using the Macedonian Question as an excuse. And strangest of all, there were those dominant figures in the Internal Macedonian Revolutionary Organization—the I.M.R.O.—like Gotse Deltchev, who actually believed that Macedonia belonged to the Macedonians themselves, and deserved to be independent of all the powers. "Unfortunately," Gabrovo Slim said, "I.M.R.O. is split between the Deltchev people and others who are nostalgic for that short-lived 'Big Bulgaria' as it was before the Treaty of Berlin."

"And your own thoughts on the matter?" Cyprian was already chuckling to himself.

"Ha!" They laughed bitterly together for a while till the Bulgarian stopped abruptly. "The Greeks think I'm I.M.R.O., is the problem."

"*Oh* dear. And are you?"

"This close." Gabrovo Slim held forefinger and thumb about a centimeter apart, next to his right ear. "Last night. There have been other attempts, but not quite like that."

"I told him how we got out of Bosnia," said Danilo helpfully.

"Oh, I'm the Scarlet Pimpernel, now, is that it?"

"It is your destiny," declared Vesna, who had been listening.

"*Tsoupra mou,* you are my destiny."

"Here is the plan," said Cyprian next evening, at the Café Mazlum down by the Quay, where it seemed the whole town had turned out to hear the great Karakas Effendi sing. "You may have been following the news out of Constantinople, political ferment and whatnot, and noticed that many of our Turkish brothers here in Salonica have begun returning to their capital in anticipation of some effort of larger scale to talk sense to the Sultan. What you'll do therefore is put on a fez—"

"No. No. I'm an Exarch."

"Danilo, explain to him."

"You'll put on a fez," explained Danilo, "and, unnoticed in all the Turkish excitability, board a train to The City, and once you get there," he wrote on a piece of paper and handed it over, "follow your nose to the spice bazaar in Eminönü, just beyond that is the Stamboul quay—you'll find this slip number and ask to talk to Khalil. There are always Black Sea coasters going to Varna."

"If I can even get out of Salonica, with all these Organization people watching."

"We will make sure I.M.R.O. are watching them."

"Meanwhile," Cyprian said, "you and I must exchange hats and coats. When I leave here, they'll think I'm you. Although I must say your garments are not nearly as stylish as what you're getting in exchange. In case you think there's not enough sacrifice or something."

So it was that Cyprian, pretending to be Gabrovo Slim, shifted quarters up the street to a *teké* called the Pearl of the Bara, and immediately noted an improvement in his weekly budget, owing to a reduced outlay on "black stuff," as hasheesh was known among the dervish boys, since all he had to do was stand for a minute or two out in the corridor and breathe until Oriental-rug patterns began to writhe across his field of vision in luminous orange and celestial blue.

Though Vesna was deeply involved with a gangster from Smyrna named Dhimitris, she and Cyprian said good-bye as if each were a part of the other. He had no idea why. Danilo looked on with the fatalistic respect of the matchmaker for the laws of chance he must forever struggle with. The boat's steam-horn blasted out its final admonition.

"You did a good thing," said Danilo.

"The Bulgarian? I worry about that one, I wonder if he'll even get that fez on his head."

"I don't think he'll ever forget."

"The important thing for him," Cyprian said, "is to be home again, among his people."

They embraced, but that was the formal version, for their embrace had happened long before.

ON THE WAY BACK TO TRIESTE, Cyprian, having had quite enough of railways for a while, took Aegean, Ionian, and Adriatic coasters and mail-steamers, spending as much time as he could chatting, smoking and drinking with the other passengers, as if alone he might be jumped by something unwelcome. As if the linear and the quotidian, adhered to faithfully enough, could save him, save everyone. At Kotor again, for no reason he knew of, he debarked, having decided to pop up and have a quick look at Montenegro. On the road up to Cetinje, he paused at a switchback to look back down at Kotor, and understood how much he had wanted to be exactly here, beholding exactly this lovely innocence of town and harbor betrayed to the interests of war-making, this compassionate denial of the vast cruelty of the late Balkan winter, the sunlight beginning to return each day for a little more than the five hours the mountains and the season had allowed it.

Only to find out that, good God, after a winter of so much hardship and misdirection, Bevis Moistleigh had been holed up in Cetinje with Jacintha Drulov all this time, that the lovestruck young imbecile had actually made his way, in that season of acute European-war hysteria, across an inhospitable terrain disjointed according to ancient tribal hatreds he would never clearly understand, driven by something he thought was love. "Spot of Bosnophobia as well, I shouldn't wonder," as Bevis explained airily.

Plum and pomegranate trees were coming into flower, incandescently white and red. The last patches of snow had nearly departed the indigo shadows of north-facing stone walls, and sows and piglets ran oinking cheerfully in the muddy streets. Newly parental swallows were assaulting humans they considered intrusive. At a café off Katunska Ulica near the marketplace, Cyprian, sitting across a table from the cooing couple (whose chief distinction from pigeons, he reflected, must be that pigeons were more direct about shitting on one), at great personal effort keeping his expression free of annoyance, was visited by a Cosmic Revelation, dropping from the sky like pigeon shit, namely that Love, which people like Bevis and Jacintha no doubt imagined as a single Force at large in the world, was in fact more like the 333,000 or however many different forms of Brahma worshipped by the Hindu—the summation, at any given moment, of all the varied subgods of love that mortal millions of lovers, in limitless dance, happened to be devoting themselves to. Yes and ever so much luck to them all.

He felt a strange sober joy at the ability, which he seemed to have picked up only recently, to observe himself being annoyed. How odd.

"I say do look at Cyprian, he seems rather stunned."

"Yes are you quite all right, Cyprian?"

"Eh? of course. Why shouldn't I be."

"Have we offended you, Cyprian?" Jacintha carelessly radiant.

"Look at her," crooned Bevis, "she's her own Ultraviolet Catastrophe."

"I am offended only by certain sorts of wallpaper," Cyprian smiled tightly.

"We always assumed you'd be about looking for us," Bevis said.

Cyprian stared back, he trusted not too rudely. "Because . . ."

"Well because you're not one of these bloody Theign people. Are you. If you were one of his, you'd be safely back on some neutral station by now, Geneva, New York or whatever."

"Oh, Moistleigh. I was in the neighborhood, that's all. Lovely to see you both." There had been a time, and not too long ago, when this sort of thing would have promised a good week of queasiness and resentment. Instead he felt, against the face his soul would have if souls had faces, a brisk vernal equipoise, as if he were aloft, maintaining an angle of attack into the advance edges of a storm none would have seen to the end of. It surprised him, and did not surprise him.

After picking up a modest sum at the tables, Reef drifted around Nice for a while, sitting in cafés drinking no-name wine, or in hotel bars drinking pineapple Marquises with *trois-six* chasers. But he couldn't see himself pursuing the life of a flâneur forever. What he really needed to do was to go out and blow something up. Clear his mind. No sooner had this thought occurred to him than who should appear but his old Simplon Tunnel *compañero* Flaco, even more anarchistic and dynamite-crazy than before, which was going some.

"Flaco! What are you doin down this neck of the woods?"

"Was back in Mexico for a while, almost got done for a oil-refinery job, had to spend some money, get out fast. But you know who I ran into in Tampico? your brother Frank! or Pancho, is what they call him there. And he said to tell you he 'got one of them.' Said you would know what that means."

"Well, old Frank. Well damn. He didn't mention which one?"

"No, that was it. He had three wagonloads of go-devil squibs he wanted to sell, you know, these little oil-well torpedos, hold about a quart of nitro each? Beautiful. We were in the market for some of them, he gave us a fair price. *Buen hombre,* your brother."

"I'll say. See him again, tell him he better be watching his ass down there."

"Oh I'll see him again. Hey! everybody in Mexico will be seein everybody again, know why? 'Cause everythin there is all ready to explode! Match is lit. I'm goin back soon's I can."

"Real thing, this time?"

"*¡Seguro, ése!* lot of fun, too. Fun for all. You want to come along?"

"Don't know. Think I should?"

"You should come. What the hell's there to do over here?"

Well, first thing come to mind'd be the old sorry unfinished saga, so miserably aborted in Venice, of Scarsdale Vibe, whom Reef ought to be shadowing right now in fact, looking for that big moment to present itself. But since Ruperta's exit, Reef had been working without much information, and Vibe might not even be this side the ocean anymore. And since the chilly parting with Kit, his heart hadn't been that much in it either, tell the truth. . . .

"I'm staying in the old town here," Flaco said, "down near Limpia, ship's sailing day after tomorrow, you know that bar, L'Espagnol Clignant, you can leave a message with Gennaro."

"It would surely be nice, *mi hijo,*" said Reef. "Like some old days I can almost remember."

Flaco peered at him closely. "You working a job here, is that it?"

No reason he shouldn't confide, given what he recalled of Flaco's inflexible hatred of all the figures of consequence yet to be assassinated, both sides of the Atlantic.

They sat outside a café in back of the Square Garibaldi. "I try to avoid places like this," Flaco muttered. "Just the kind of bourgeois target anarchists love to bomb."

"We could find someplace else."

"Hell, let's trust in professional courtesy," Flaco said, "and the laws of probability."

"One thing to try and keep to an honorable deal with your dead," it seemed to Reef, "another to just go spreading death any way you can. Don't tell me I'm infected with bourgeois values. I've got to where I like these cafés, all this to-and-fro of the city life—rather be out here enjoying it than worried all the time about some bomb going off—" which is of course exactly when it happened, so unexpected and so loud that for many days afterward those who survived would not be certain it had really occurred, any more than believe someone had actually desired to send such long-evolved and dearly-bought civility into this great blossoming of disintegration—a dense, prolonged shower of glass fragments, green and clear and amber and black, from windows, mirrors and drinking glasses, carafes and bottles of absinthe, wine, fruit syrups, whiskey of many ages and origins, human blood everywhere, blood arterial, venous and capillary, fragments of bone and cartilage and soft tissue, wood splinters of all sizes from the furniture, shrapnel of tin, zinc and brass, from torn ragged sheets down to the tiny nails in picture frames, nitrous fumes, fluid unfurlings of smoke too black to see through—a huge, glittering passage skyward and back again, outward and across the street and down the block, passing through the rays of a completely indifferent noontide sun, like a long heliograph message sent too fast for any but angels of destruction to read.

Leaving these so abruptly wounded bourgeoisie, crying like children, children again, with no obligation but to look helpless and pitiable enough to move those who had the means to defend them, protectors with modern weapons and unbreakable discipline, and what was taking them so long? As they cried, they found they were able to look into one another's eyes, as if set free from most of their needs to pretend adulthood, needs in force up until what was still only a few seconds ago.

"Flaco, *damn* that wa'n' one of you crazy sumbitches was it?" Reef looking with interest at the blood that seemed to be all over him. He managed to crawl out from under what was left of the table and grab Flaco by the shirt. "Still got your head on, all that?"

"Worse than bein back in that tunnel," Flaco with a big stupid grin about to start crowing like a rooster with surprise at still being alive.

"Let's have a look, see if . . ." But it was not very damn hopeful. There weren't many dead, but enough. Flaco and Reef lifted away wreckage, beat out a couple of small fires, found people wounded whose bleeding could be stopped with tourniquets, one or two who'd passed into shock and had to be covered with burned and blood-smeared tablecloths for warmth, and figuring, about the time the police and a few wild dogs began to show up, that they'd done what they could, they left. An early *gregaou* had swept upon the coast, and when the smoke had cleared some from his head, Reef thought he could smell snow in the air.

"Some of these *bandoleros,*" Flaco still grinning, "they don't care who the hell they do this to."

Reef almost said, "Why?" but was suddenly dizzy and had to sit down. Everything hurt.

"You look like shit, *pendejo,*" Flaco advised him.

"That arm of yours ain't about to win no prizes either."

"I don't think I broke it?" Flaco having a look—*"¡Caray!"*

"Let's go see the knife fella," Reef suggested. This was Professeur Pivoine, who was a sort of neighborhood couturier of flesh wounds from the frequent street encounters in the Quartier Riquier. He could take out bullets too but admitted he was less of an artist at that.

They found the instruments sharp and sterile and the Professeur in the mood for medical knifeplay. Afterward Reef passed into one of those twilit states where it seemed his brother Kit was there, hovering a foot or two in the air and glowing in a peculiar way.

"I'm sorry," Reef tried to say, his voice paralyzed as if in a nightmare when the light goes away and we hear a footfall and want to say "Who's there?" but can't.

"It's all right," Kit said, "you didn't do anything wrong. Nothing I wouldn't've done."

What the fuck are you talking about? he struggled to say, I did everything wrong. I ran away from my baby son and the woman I loved. Reef knew he was crying. All he could have cried for, and he was crying over this. It was like one of those orgasms early in life, a timeless event whose power can't be measured. He shook with it. He felt tears and snot all on his face. Kit just floated around up there by the ceiling, going "Easy, easy" and other reassuring phrases, and then after a while he began to fade.

THOUGH THE OUTLOOK for Anarchists in a shooting revolution is never too promising, Flaco was determined to go back to Mexico. Just before he sailed, he and Reef came limping into L'Espagnol Clignant for a bon voyage drink. They had sticking-plaster and surgical stitching and black patches of dried blood all over them that caused Gennaro the bartender at least a half hour's merriment.

"So you just gonna stay out on that old track, try to get you a capitalist with that elephant gun," Flaco said.

"Ought to be you folks's beef too, after that kid Tancredi they went and mowed down."

Flaco shrugged. "Maybe he should've known better."

"Pretty cold, Flaquito. Kid's in his grave, how do you just let that go?"

"Maybe I'm losing faith in assassinating the great and powerful anymore, maybe all it is, is just another dream they like to tease us with. Maybe all I'm lookin for these days is a nice normal shootin war with peons like me I can shoot back at. Your brother Frank at least had the sense to go after the hired guns that did the real work."

"But that don't mean Vibe and them don't deserve it."

"Course. But that's retribution. Personal. Not a tactic in the bigger fight."

"Beyond me," said Reef. "But I've still got to go after that murdering bastard."

"Well good luck, *mi hijo.* I'll say hello to Pancho when I see him."

SHOULD I KNOW BETTER? she wondered.

After weeks of torches streaming by the window, thunderstorms in the mountains, visits from the police, as if in an eternally descending current, the roar louder than crying, or speech, blood finding its voice, neither attempting to rescue the other but reaching back each one, again and again, to pull the other deeper, away from safety. Before they went down to Zengg to embark again for Venice, Vlado, as if having seen some lethal obstacle ahead, entrusted to Yashmeen a green schoolboy's copybook manufactured in some Austrian part of the empire, with *Zeugnisbüchlein* printed on its front cover, which he called *The Book of the Masked.* Whose pages were filled with encrypted field-notes and occult scientific passages of a dangerousness one could at least appreciate, though more perhaps for what it promised than for what it presented in such impenetrable code, its sketch of a mindscape whose layers emerged one on another as from a mist, a distant country of painful complexity, an all but unmappable flow of letters and numbers that passed into and out of the guise of the other, not to mention images, from faint and spidery sketches to a full spectrum of inks and pastels, of what Vlado had been visited by under the assaults of his home wind, of what could not be paraphrased even into the strange holiness of Old Slavonic script, visions of the unsuspected, breaches in the Creation where something else had had a chance to be luminously glimpsed. Ways in which God chose to hide within the light of day, not a full list, for the list was probably endless, but chance encounters with details of God's unseen world. Its chapters headed "To Listen to the Voices of the Dead." "To Pass Through the Impenetrable Earth." "To Find the Invisible Gateways." "To Recognize the Faces of Those with the Knowledge."

Well, secret lore he'd been sworn never to reveal, she'd have expected that. She knew by now that in those mountains, with centuries of blood as security, such ferocious undertakings were never questioned. "But this is written down," she couldn't quite keep herself from objecting. "I thought it was supposed to be spoken, passed on face-to-face."

"Maybe it's a fake, then," Vlado laughed. "A forgery. For all you know we have workshops full of calligraphers and illustrators, busy as dwarves in a cavern, for even back up there in the mountains we know there are comfortable profits to be realized from the gullibility of American millionaires and their agents, who are everywhere these days with their famous satchels full of greenbacks, buying up everything they see, oil paintings, antique crockery, fragments of castles, not to mention marriage prospects and racehorses. Why not then this quaint native artifact, with its colorful yet indecipherable visions?"

She took it anyway. Telling herself she was attracted to its humility, its ease of concealment.

· · ·

In their visits to Venice, they had gotten in the habit of going to the movies. They went to the Teatri Minerva and Rossini, but their favorite was the Malibran next to the Corte del Milion, traditionally said to be the site of Marco Polo's house. They sat in the dark and watched the film shot here not long ago from a gondola by Albert Promio and his crew from Lumière of Paris. At some point the image had entered the Arsenale, in dreaming glide, down uncountable brown canalsides, among the labyrinths, the basins and gondola workshops, rope-walks, the ancient stagnant pools. She felt a tremor pass through Vlado's body. He had leaned forward to stare, at a pitch of apprehension she had never seen, not even at invisible horsemen and gunshots in the night.

Reef was back in Venice before he knew why. Here was where everything had gone off the rails, though coming back to it was likely to be no more useful than haunting is to a ghost. He was feeling a little desperate. The bomb at the café in Nice had lit up a whole high range like lightning at night, showing him the country ahead under a sombre and unreadable aspect. He was not sure he could prepare for everything its shadows might hold.

He had been over on the Lido doing some practice shooting with his .450 cordite express rifle. He needed to get his eye back, to concentrate on distant targets and failing light and treacherous crosswinds. No one was there to raise the objection that he did not at this point even know where his target might be. He had found no one in Venice with any line on Scarsdale Vibe. He wandered around various *fondamente* at different hours of day looking for Dally Rideout, but she had disappeared. When he visited Ca' Spongiatosta, he was turned away rather rudely by the Principessa herself and given the bum's rush by two liveried *pistolieri.*

Now, all at once, rearing out of the water in a great smoking splash of Italian profanity, came a species of Adriatic sea-monster from which two creatures in rubber suits dismounted and came trudging up the sand. Having passed by semimiraculous routes known to inland sailors since Argonauts threaded their way through the European continent, not always aboveground, Pino and Rocco were back in town with their manned torpedo, by now grown somewhat in size—returned at last to Venice, their journey eased by never in their hearts having left to begin with. On recent nights they had been observed in bars of San Marco hotels, drinking local gin fizzes known as Casanovas and arguing about association football, and after the bars closed, deep in the predawn hours, their deadly vehicle had been heard howling like a high-speed ghost up and down the canals and *rii.* . . . This evening they had decided to make a run over to the Lido, where next thing they knew they were hearing these enormous blasts from shore, which with the elaborate caution of the pursued they had assumed to be directed at themselves.

Reef carefully slung the rifle on his shoulder and nodded. "Boys. Nice-lookin rig you got there."

"That is an elephant gun," said Pino.

"I heard this was elephant country. You mean it ain't?"

"We were going up to the hotel," Rocco pointing at the lampless mass of the Excelsior, "and get a drink."

"I didn't think they'd open till it got warmer," said Reef.

Rocco and Pino looked at each other. "They have stayed open all winter," Rocco said, "they only pretended to close."

"There is," Pino indicating the sand wastes around them, under the chill and failing sunset, "a certain clientele."

Sure enough, inside the new luxury hotel the lights were blazing, corridors echoing with the undeparted, desire coalescing briefly into glimpsed figures then dissipating again, carried as if helpless before some indoor wind, across dancing floors and terraces, along shadowy colonnades, where from someplace music echoed, though the orchestra stand was unoccupied. White-coated barmen were busy mixing drinks, though nobody was at the bar.

"There's a storm on the way," Rafaello greeted them. He had a purple orchid in his lapel, and knew Rocco and Pino. "You made it in here just in time."

Slowly the room was filling up with ragged refugees, shivering and staring. By later in the evening, it became clear that business depended now as much on the storms of winter and spring as it would in summer on warmth and clear sky.

"And after a while," Pino was saying, "we got attached. Gave it a name. *Il Squalaccio.*" Once it had a name, it seemed impossible they could ever blow it up. They took it back into the shop, rethought the design, built extensions fore and aft, new compartments, installed a bigger engine, pretty soon they had a dwarf variety of submarine.

"Mr. Traverse?" Reef looked in the mirror and recognized Kit's friend Yashmeen, whom he'd last seen up at Lago Maggiore in the old Chirpingdon-Groin era.

"Hello once again." She was there with a tall, good-looking galoot from someplace across the Adriatic. They'd been on their way back to Trieste when the storm hit and cast them upon the lee shore of Lido, though their main worry now seemed to be a motor launch they'd spotted behind them.

"They followed us all the way from the Bacino, kept their running lights off, and if the storm hadn't blown up, they'd have probably sunk us by now."

"*Attenzione,*" murmured Pino.

A party of men had come in all together, some remaining by the door, others beginning to work slowly through the room, peering at faces. She turned toward Reef. "Pretend to be fascinated."

"Sure. Where'd your partner get to?"

"Vlado must have seen them before I did."

Rocco came over. "*Austriaci.* They must be looking for Pino and me."

"It's me and Vlado," she said.

"We can offer you a lift," Pino purred, as usual failing to disguise his lecherous intentions. "*Il Squalaccio* will sleep four comfortably."

Reef picked up his elephant gun and headed outside. "I'll cover you folks. Make a run for it when you can." On the beach he found an abandoned bathing-machine and set up a position, took a wood match, held it in the rain long enough to soften the head of it, then smeared the wet phosphorus over the sights front and rear till they were glowing enough to see.

Presently Yashmeen was crouching next to him, hatless, breathing deliberately, and rounds had begun to hum about the vicinity. Reef pulled her close, steadied the rifle on her shoulder, and fired off a couple of his own. Back at the giant hotel, they could see the darkly-clad Austrians hit the wet sand.

The wind took the sounds of the gunfight over the dark beaches as far as Malamocco. Survivors of a winter in the open, despised, evicted, willingly lost, shivered in pockets of rude shelter gathered around driftwood fires and wondered aloud what it might be.

The knot of gunmen moved past, making for the jetty, where a low, dark mass waited, visible mostly from the wreathing of motor exhaust which surrounded it. "Oh," she groaned, and Reef could feel her muscles growing tight. She had seen Vlado among them, bleeding, taken, and knew she must not call out to him.

"Where's your boat?" She was silent and did not move. "Miss Halfcourt." She nodded, arose as the snarl and sputter and the shriek of bad bearings rose to a maximum and then slowly withdrew.

She and Vlado had run aground on the Lagoon side. The little vessel was not quite dismasted, but Reef saw no way for them to get across to Venice in it, short of rowing.

"Would you like a tow?" Rocco and Pino and *Il Squalaccio.*

Out on the water, squinting through the rain for the lights of San Marco, Reef said, "Here I thought *I* was livin the high life. Your friends back there—did I hear 'Austrians'?"

"Likely an Englishman too, named Theign."

"I don't keep good track of the politics, but last I heard, now, England and Austria, ain't that different sides?"

"It's not what you'd call really official."

"And they're after you? are you not official either?"

She laughed, or maybe that's not what it was. "I think they were after Vlado." Her hair was all snarled, her frock was torn. She bore distant resemblance to a lady in need of protection, but Reef was cautious.

"Where you been stayin?"

"Trieste. Not sure I should go there anymore."

By the time they reached Venice the storm had blown on over the *terraferma* and the moon was out in high spooky shine. They moved cautiously into the skein of little canals, the engine throttled back to a muffled grumble, everything in the night queerly lit, just about to ascend into some glow less bearable. At last they stepped onto a narrow *fondamenta.* "We'll hide this for you in a little *squero* we use," Rocco said. "It will be safe."

"Buy you boys a gin fizz next time I see you," Reef touching his hat.

"If God wishes," said Pino. The midget submarine moved off, the boat in tow at a lopsided angle.

They climbed a couple flights of stairs, first marble, then wood. Reef let them in to a room full of moonlight.

"Your place?"

"Some boys from down the Amalfi coast, we've done business together, they keep it handy for whoever. Good for a couple-three days maybe."

He found a bottle of grappa, but she waved it away and collapsed on the divan, allowing herself only one utterance of Vlado's name, her whisper as close to defeated as anyone, including herself, had heard it.

"He could have got away in all that confusion—tell you what, I'll go out, ask around a little. There's a bathtub in there, soap and so forth, you take her easy, I'll be back soon."

"This needn't be—"

"It ain't. Figure like that I'm trying to accommodate a friend of my brother's is all."

On the way back down the stairs he allowed himself the couple minutes of descent to calculate that Kit was likely out someplace on a camel right now fighting off half an army of screaming Chinese and probably had more on his mind than what this very strange young lady might be up to. Which didn't excuse how Reef had turned his back and walked away. Just a shitheel way of proceeding, and he couldn't even remember why anymore.

He found an all-night bar off the Campo Santa Margherita that had always been good for up-to-the-minute gossip till the Rialto cranked back up to speed in the morning, stood drinks, kept his ears open, once in a while asking a stupid-cowboy question or two. Everybody had heard about the shootout over on the Lido, and agreed that the only thing preventing war with Austria was that no Italians had been directly involved. The *mavrovlaco* was well known and a sort of outlaw hero in these parts, being, like his people for generations before him, an enemy of Austria and her ambitions in the Adriatic. Every time he left his mountain stronghold, they tried to follow and capture him, and this time the sea had betrayed him, for no one human ever would.

Reef got back to find Yashmeen fallen asleep on the divan, having spread her wet hair out behind her on a towel to dry. The celebrated Venetian moonlight came in the window, everything looked sketched in chalk. He stood over by the window with his back to the considerably haunted city and smoked and watched her sleep.

She was wearing a white batiste shift of some kind, transparent to moonlight, and in her sleep it had drifted above her hips. One hand rested between her legs, which were slightly apart. Reef somehow found himself with this erection.

Fine thing. On the run, her beau in some very deep trouble indeed, and what dishonorable thoughts was he entertaining here? She chose that moment to shift in her sleep, turning so that he was now gazing at her, you'd say, admirable ass, and though what he ought to be doing now was taking a walk over to that Piazza or something, instead, true to his idiot nature, he'd unbuttoned his trousers and begun stroking his penis, unable not to gaze at the pale buttocks and dark cleft, the black spill of hair and naked neck, just a step or two away. As he was hitting the run-up to his grand finale, she rolled over and regarded him with shining, enormous eyes, which had been open for some time it seemed, her hands pretty much occupied the same way as his. He let go of his penis long enough to shrug, smile and turn his glistening palms up and outward, in an appeal, charming so he'd been told, for forbearance.

"Are you committed to this disgusting activity," she inquired, her attempt at a Girtonian drawl undone by a tremor she could not suppress, "or might the vagina hold some interest for you, beyond the merely notional?"

Before he understood this was not a request for information, he had taken the two or three paces that mattered and was quickly on the divan and inside her, and not a moment too soon, as it turned out. She fastened her teeth, hard and unapologetically, between his neck and shoulder and let out thus muffled a long cry that was at least half a growl. He grabbed a handful of her hair, which he'd been wanting to do since he came in the room, brought her face around to his, and surprising himself, for he was not that much of a kisser, kissed Yashmeen until she started biting his lips and tongue and then maybe half a minute more, just to make sure of what was going on.

She pulled away long enough to hiss, "You unprincipled swine," and they were kissing again.

He was expecting reproaches, but she was more interested in his Egyptian cigarettes. He located his match-safe and lit one for her. After a minute she said, "Did you find out anything?"

"Not much."

"You'd better tell me. I am not some frail American wildflower."

"They took him inside the Arsenale."

She nodded gravely, and in the lamplight he could see the color leaving her face.

"We could get in," he said.

"Oh? Then what? be shot at again." When he didn't answer, "And what else?"

He flicked ash into his trouser cuff. "How serious are you about the way you look right now?"

She peered into the cheval-glass. "You don't approve? We have it off once, and you're my fashion adviser?"

He blew a smoke ring, on the chance it would get her attention. It rotated, expanded slowly into the moonlight, becoming a keen ghost-white. "Those were Mannlichers tonight over on that Lido, so I calculate them Austrian amigos of yours were not just out for a day of trapshootin. They were surely lookin for your friend Vlado, but if they also have a description on you now—"

She took a lock of her hair and examined it in the mirror. "Then I shall need a disguise, and some of this will have to go." She waited, as if for him to reply. "Well. When a girl needs a marcel wave in a hurry, there's only one man in this town to see." Reef had already fallen into snoring oblivion.

By the time she got down to his insufferably fashionable corner of San Marco, just behind the Bauer-Grünwald, Signor Fabrizio was just opening for business.

"And our Ciprianuccio, he is safe and well?"

"Traveling on business," she said, not it seemed calmly enough to keep the *parruchiere* from crossing himself fretfully. His mood did not improve when he learned what she wanted. Of the many men and women who had worshipped her hair, Fabrizio was the extremist with the zealous roll to his eyeballs that one tried not to arouse unnecessarily.

“I can’t cut it off. *Macchè,* Yashmeen. How could I cut it off?”

“But it will belong to you, then. You can do whatever you want with it.”

“If you put it that way . . .”

She followed his gaze. They were now both looking at his penis. “No. You wouldn’t.”

He shrugged.

“It gets worse. I want to be blonde. Dark blonde at least. A Cadorina.”

“Mother of God.”

“And if anyone can do this thing . . .”

The penis pleasantry was only Fabrizio’s little joke, of course. Yashmeen’s hair was to have a peculiar and not altogether dishonorable fate. It was to be bleached gently, re-curled, and fashioned into an elaborate wig in the eighteenth-century Venetian style, appropriate for a Carnevale costume, as part of which in fact it was to appear in the near future, at a fateful masked ball.

When the Campanile in the Piazza San Marco collapsed, certain politically sensitive Venetian souls felt a strange relocation of power. Somehow, they believed, the campanile of San Francesco della Vigna, a little north of the Arsenale, where the angel visited St. Mark on the turbulent night recorded by Tintoretto, a close double of the one that fell, had come to replace it as a focus of power, as if by a sort of coup in which the Arsenale, and the bleak certainties of military science, had replaced the Palazzo Ducale and its less confident human struggles toward republican virtue.

Like the cemetery island of San Michele visible across the water, the Arsenale also presented to the civic view a Mystery surrounded by a wall, high pale brickwork, blank except here and there for a decorative iron tension-rod retainer or a tile rainspout, and topped by crenellations in a two-bladed halberd shape. All around the forbidden perimeter, the people of Castello went on with day-to-day lives, dogs shit on the paving-stones, church bells were heard, vaporetti put in and departed, pedestrians walked in the shadow of the Mystery as if it were not there, as if it were there but could not be seen. The ancient maps showed that what was visible from the entrances amounted only to a fraction of the entire works. To those forbidden to enter, the maps were like visions of prophets, in a sort of code, outward and visible notation for what lay within.

Vlado Clissan, aware of a region of silence behind him, risked a glance back at the walls of the Arsenale, obstructing the salt wind, ascending, blank and functional, to take up half the sky. A veil of masonry. Mysteries there. He knew that before long a door, somewhere in the wall, usually kept invisible, would open. He would pass with his captors inside, and the next world would commence.

In a long-abandoned corner of one of the ancient foundries he had had fitted out as an office, Derrick Theign was sitting on a folding chair, eyes quiescent and pale in a white face he was able somehow to relax into a mask never contemplated in Venice, which everyone, and particularly those in Vlado's position, ought nonetheless to recognize. It had been known to frighten subjects into blurting information they didn't actually have, confessing to acts they had never thought of committing.

"Your people are trading in naval secrets. Uskok piracy brought up to date, I suppose—no point in seizing physical ships, when one can traffic in their souls."

Vlado laughed. "If I were a pirate, I would prefer a physical ship carrying a physical cargo worth physical money. And I would get to deal with a better class of middleman."

Theign might have been hoping for a more intellectual discussion, though it remained a given that, in the process now under way, *a moment would arrive.* Chats like this, delaying things, giving the subject any reason to hope, however transitory, would provide a much more effective blow to the spirit when the Webley finally did make its appearance—that drop into stillness useful to executioners, a paralysis of Will, or whatever it is analogous to Will that kept these people so perversely resisting to the end.

"I saw you with someone, didn't I, over on the Lido? Only a glimpse in all the confusion, but she seemed quite appealing. Actually."

"To you?" Careful not to seem too puzzled and provoke anything too soon.

Theign shrugged. "More to the point, how appealing to you? And how deeply of your persuasion? Or would she've been there more in a decorative role?"

"Are you asking, what would I consider trading her for?"

"Of course that does happen now and then. But I did not wish to insult either of you."

"I don't know where she is. Even if I did, she'd be of little use. . . ."

Theign watched Vlado's face until the unpleasant thought had fully surfaced there, then nodded, one grown man to another. "Right. Unless our plans for both of you were the same. In which case, if you told me, it wouldn't matter so much."

"Where she is."

"That's if you knew, of course."

This was not the same as being in a tavern where an enemy puts a pistol in your face and says, "Make your arrangements with God, for you are about to be a dead man." In a tavern, always, somewhere, close enough to hand, there would be a second pistol, a third, a chance. In this sober and unsociable vacancy, no such hope was evident. Any bet made in here would be for the highest possible stakes.

LATER, at Cimiez, with the northeast wind driving the seasonal visitors indoors, when Yashmeen began to hear reports of a shootout near the Arsenale, between what might've been Austrian mercenaries and what might've been Dalmatian revolutionists, she put her faith, like a good Emotional Anarchist, in the Law of Deterministic Insufficiency.

"What's that?" said Reef.

"Like a card comes up that you could never have predicted."

"Oh but hell darlin, if you've been counting 'em careful enough—"

"That may be true for only fifty-two cards. But when the deck is orders of magnitude larger, perhaps approaching infinity, other possibilities begin to emerge. . . ." Her own way of saying, *Vlado is immortal. Able to take care of himself, impossible to worry about. . . .*

Reef studied her, backing into a baffled smile he'd found more and more occupying his face. At first when she talked like this, he had put it down to some kind of belief without proof—religious, or superstitious anyway. But then wheels all up and down the Riviera, at Nice, Cimiez, Monte Carlo, Mentone, through the winter season and into the spring, like village gossips, had begun to chatter a different story. Pockets began to go out at the seams from all the winnings being stuffed into them.

The system had its origins in a ride she'd taken with Lorelei, Noellyn, and Faun on the Earl's Court Wheel, centuries ago in her girlhood. "Thirty-seven numbers on the wheel," she instructed him. "The zero belongs to the house. Of the other thirty-six, twelve—if you include one and two—are primes. Going clockwise, taking three numbers at a time, in each set of three you will find exactly one prime."

"So they're spread out pretty even."

"But the wheel makes more than one revolution. The numbers repeat again and again, like a very fast clock with thirty-seven hours. We say thirty-seven is the 'modulus' of the wheel, as twelve is the modulus of an ordinary clock. So the number that a roulette ball comes to rest at is actually that number 'modulo thirty-seven'—the remainder, after dividing by thirty-seven, of the total of moving compartments the ball has had a chance to fall into.

"Now, by Wilson's theorem, the product $(p-1)$ factorial, when taken modulo any prime p, is always equal to minus one. On the roulette wheel, $p-1$ is thirty-six, and thirty-six factorial also happens to be the number of all possible permutations of thirty-six numbers. It is thus obvious from the foregoing that—"

She was interrupted by the thud of Reef's head on the table, where it remained.

"I don't think he's been following this," she muttered. But continued to whisper the lesson to him, as if choosing to believe he had only fallen into a light hypnosis. Apparently it worked, because in the coming days he began to win at roulette far outside the expectations of chance. If she continued to whisper further educational advice at appropriate moments, neither would discuss the matter.

Why Reef should be finding her this irresistible, when the rule as he had come to learn it was that desire always fades, was not a question he lost much recreational time over. Her irresistibility filled the day, leaving little time for thought. No sooner would one of them be over the doorsill than she was lifting her skirts, or reaching for his penis, or simply lying back, eyes steely and wet, holding his gaze in a grip he knew no way out of, while she caressed herself, until, without needing to decide, he came to her. Always him to her, he noted to himself, that was the pattern, best to keep that in mind.

ONE DAY she remembered the schoolbook Vlado had given her, stuffed into her luggage and forgotten. She began to read in it, a little of it every day, like a devout person with a religious text. She read not in hope but in terror, not in certitude but a terrible broken anxiety over Vlado's fate. She found she could make out some of the symbols, vector and Quaternion notation she remembered Kit showing her back in Göttingen. It appeared to be a mathematical argument of the classic sort, one even Riemann might have made, except that everywhere terms containing time stood like infiltrators at a masked ball, prepared at some unannounced pulse of the clock to throw back their capes and reveal their true identities and mission. There were moments in the text when she felt herself about to grasp an intelligence so grand and fatal that she deliberately retreated, willed herself to forget whatever gift for mathematical linkage or analogy might allow her to go on, into certain madness. What she could not make herself forget was Vlado, the living hand that had made these marks across this paper, the hand she still so hopelessly wished to feel buried in her hair, resting against her lips.

Cyprian came churning back at last in to a winter mirage of Venice, no sleep to speak of for weeks, bedraggled, squinting at the tarnished city through the rain on the Lagoon, shivering in the wind's raking assault, eyes scratchy, hair all jagged and drastically in need of attention from Signor Fabrizio—he longed for some time in a steaming tub with a cold bottle of anything alcoholic with bubbles. Pity the *galleggianti* wouldn't be open till May. At the moment he must settle for lighting up another Sobranie, coughing repellently, and ranging the wet deck trying to stay on his feet. Filthy weather. What had he ever seen in this place, that had brought him back? Who cared anymore where he was or if he'd ever return? Yashmeen, of course, was the answer he hoped for, but after his turn on the Peninsula, he found it would not serve to be thinking ahead in too chirpy a fashion.

She was no longer in Trieste. He had spent a week there looking for her, everywhere he could think of, and learned only, from Vlado Clissan's associates, who had vowed to take revenge, of Vlado's melancholy fate at the hands of Derrick Theign. "He has gone mad," said Vlado's cousin Zlatko Ottician. "He is dangerous now to everyone."

"I'll have a look round Venice." Even if Vienna was now the more likely place to find Theign. Cyprian was moving in a stunned vacuum his skin could not successfully define. It did not improve his mood to reflect that he might be as much to blame as anyone—Vlado had been his one dependable operative, as much as possible in this game his friend, and it was difficult to see Theign's behavior as anything but a sort of murderous housecleaning.

"Must . . . stay on feet. . . ." There! at that exact moment, he spotted the treacherous bastard himself in a *traghetto,* emerging from the mists, standing up in his usual pose, as ever too self-absorbed to pass for Venetian, gliding past oblivious to the little steamer and Cyprian at its rail taken by an unexpected rage. The apparition faded again into the rain. "No, no," Cyprian muttered, "won't do. . . ." Some reap the whirlwind, he was left to glean the undelineated fog—penance, he supposed, for never having learned to think analytically. Now when he most needed a clever plan, his mind was become all staring Arctic vacancy. The far more resourceful Bevis Moistleigh, whose interests just then were if anything more precarious than Cyprian's, would be off with his charming Jacintha someplace annoying, larking among the early daffodils or whatever. Expecting gratitude was of course a mug's game, one paid back obligations in timely fashion at the going price, and gratitude figured in hardly at all . . . but, well, really.

Cyprian's only comfort at the moment was the loaded Webley-Fosbery service revolver in his kit. If worse came to worst, which it must, failed expectation being the rule of this business, why he could always produce the firearm, couldn't he, and use it against some target to be designated when the moment arrived. Theign preferably, but not ruling out himself. *Cazzo, cazzo . . .*

He found the old *pensione* in Santa Croce occupied by a party of British tourists who took him for a local cicerone seeking employment. The bora howled among the chimneys, as if amused. Nobody there knew anything about previous tenants, but Signora Giambolognese downstairs recalled their many evenings of high drama, screaming and thumping about, and greeted Cyprian with one of those wary smiles, as if he were about to tell a joke. "He lives in the Arsenale, your friend."

"*Macchè,* nell '*Arsenale—*"

She turned up both palms, shrugged. "*Inglesi.*"

Outside again, on a sudden whim he turned into the *calle* of the *traghetto* to the Santa Lucia Station and saw, just coming out of the British consulate, who but Ratty McHugh, assuming Cyprian to be a street-beggar and twitching his gaze away. But then back again—"Oh I say. Latewood?"

"Hmmn."

"We've got to talk." They went back inside to a remote courtyard-within-a-courtyard where Ratty had an office. "First of all, we're deeply sorry about what happened at the Arsenale. Clissan was a good man, among the best, which you must have known better than anyone."

It turned out that Theign was not really *domiciled* inside the Arsenale but maintaining offices there to be used for a pied-à-terre when he was in town. "Not to mention damned convenient for gathering any naval intelligence one might wish to pass on to one's Austrian masters."

"And the Italian Navy don't especially mind?"

"Oh, it's the usual. They think he'll lead them to some greater apparatus, he's content to let them go on dreaming. Bit like marriage, I suppose."

Cyprian then noticed a pale gold wedding ring. "Gorblimey. I say congratulations old man, major step in life, can't imagine how I missed it in the Bosnian papers, who is she and so forth Ratty?"

"Oh it's old Jenny Invert, you remember her, we all used to go to Newmarket together."

Cyprian squinted. "That girl from Nether Wallop, Hants, three feet taller than you 's I recall, wizard trapshooter, president of the Inanimate Bird Association chapter down there—"

"The very lass. She believes I'm some sort of junior diplomat, so if you two ever do meet again, though I shall try my best to see it never happens, you won't suddenly start, well, reminiscing about any of . . . this—"

"Silent as the grave old man. Though she could be ever so useful at the moment with our problematical acquaintance couldn't she, dead shot and all."

"Yes the last time you joked about that Cyprian, in Graz wasn't it, I may've acted a bit shirty, though I've since been thinking it over and, well . . ."

"No need to apologize Ratty, as long as you've come to your senses on the subject's the main thing isn't it."

"He's being very careful. Never out of doors without at least two great simians looking after his flanks. Itineraries subject to change without notice, always in code in any case, which no one really can break, as the key also changes day to day."

"If I could locate Bevis Moistleigh, I'd put him to work on it. But, like you, the only chords on *his* ukulele these days are for 'I Love You Truly.'"

"Ah yes wait that's F major, C seventh, G-minor seventh—"

"Oca ti jebem," a Montenegrin pleasantry Cyprian had found himself using with some frequency lately.

Ratty threw an inquiring stare. "And your own, ehrm . . ."

"Don't."

"We know she's not in Trieste anymore. Stopped here for a bit, left in the company of some American, parts unknown, I'm afraid. I did promise to keep an eye on her, but—"

"Shame, Ratty, special circle of Hell for that sort of thing."

"Knew you'd understand. See here, I'm back to London tomorrow, but in case a clear angle of fire should open up—" He took a mallet and began to strike vigorously at a nearby Chinese gong. A person in a checked suit put his head in the door and raised his eyebrows. "This is my colleague Giles Piprake, no known problem he can't sort out."

"Your bride's never complained," muttered Piprake.

"Cyprian here needs to go speak with the Principe Spongiatosta," said Ratty.

"I do?" puzzled Cyprian.

"Exactly how Ratty expressed it to the vicar, and look what happened," said Piprake. "I gather this is about Derrick 'Rogue Elephant' Theign."

"Prince who again?" inquired Cyprian in some dismay. "Surely not, umpire?"

"Among the very best of our reliables," Ratty informed him.

"He and Theign were regular associates. If not partners in the deepest sorts of evil enterprise. In fact—" looking nervously over at Piprake.

"Theign once arranged an assignation for you with the Prince, yes, we know. How did it go, I always meant to ask."

"Aaaahh!" screamed Cyprian, attempting to hide beneath an open dossier on Ratty's desk.

"Sensitive," Ratty said, "hasn't been in the business long—Latewood, do pull yourself together, there's a good chap."

"I must remember not to wear yellow," Cyprian as if making a note to himself. Piprake, eyebrows oscillating, withdrew to telephone the Prince.

"You'll keep us apprised," said Ratty. Cyprian rose and put on his hat with one of those music-hall flourishes.

"Indeed. Well Ratty ta-ta, and best to your wife."

"Don't go near her I'm warning you, she'll have you married to some horribly unsuitable friend of hers before you can remember the word 'no.'"

The Princess was nowhere to be seen at Ca' Spongiatosta, but the Prince was in the entry before the *valletto* could even take Cyprian's hat, cheerful and splendid in some shade of heliotrope hitherto unobserved upon the planet.

"Facciam' il porco," the Prince greeted him, eagerly yet one hoped in jest.

Angling his head in regret, *"Il mio ragazzo è molto geloso."*

The Prince beamed. "Exactly what you said last time, and in that same phrasebook accent. *Qualsiasi, Ciprianino.* Captain Piprake tells me that we may share an interest in neutralizing the plans of a former mutual acquaintance who has since chosen a most dangerous path of vice and betrayal." They ascended to the *piano nobile* and passed through a gallery hung with the Prince's collection of modern Symbolists, including some oils by Hunter Penhallow, notably his meditation on the fate of Europe, *The Iron Gateway,* in which shadowy multitudes trooped toward a vanishing line over which broke a hellish radiance.

The Prince gestured him into a room notable for its Carlo Zen furniture and vases by Galileo Chini. In the corner was a pale cream writing-desk accented with copper and parchment painted in spidery designs.

"Bugatti, isn't it?" Cyprian said.

"My wife's taste," the Prince nodded. "I tend toward the more ancestral myself."

Servants brought cold prosecco and glasses on a silver antique tray, and Alexandrian cigarettes in a Byzantine box at least seven hundred years old.

"That he should have pursued his schemes from Venice," the Prince said, "this clouded realm of pedestrian mazes and municipal stillness, suggests an allegiance to forces already long in motion. But that is only the mask he has chosen. Other nations, Americans notoriously, style themselves 'republican' and think they understand republics, but what was fashioned here over corroded centuries of doges' cruelty lies forever beyond their understanding. Each Doge in his turn became more and more a sacrificial animal, his own freedoms taken, his life brought under an impossibly stringent code of conduct, taking comfort, while he wore the *corno,* in a resentful brutality, waiting each day for the fateful escort of thugs, the sealed gondola, the final bridge. His best hope, pathetically slender, might be for some remote monastery and a decline into ever-deeper penitence.

"The doges are gone, the curse remains. Some today, often in positions to do great harm, will never come to understand how 'power'—*lo stato*—could have been an expression of communal will, invisibly exercised in the dark that surrounds each soul, in which penance must be a necessary term. Unless one has performed in his life penance equal to what he has exacted from others, there is an imbalance in Nature."

"Which must be—"

A princely hand ascended into the tobacco smoke. "I was speaking of Venetian history. Today that antique machinery of choice and limitation is available no longer. Today . . . suppose there were a foreign Crown Prince, for example, who passionately hated Italy, who upon succession to the throne of his empire would, certain as the sunrise, go to war with Italy to take back territory he believes to be his family's . . . and further, suppose there were living and working in Italy agents of this emperor-to-be, particularly active in Venice, men whose lives had become dedicated only to promoting the interests of the enemy—if no other life, no number of lives mattered, no loyalties, no code of honor, no ancient tradition, only these agents' pure wicked need that their Principal prevail at all cost. . . ."

"Whom could one trust then to defend the interests of the Nation? The Royal Army? the Navy?"

"In theory. But an enemy with Imperial resources can buy anyone."

"If there is no one who cannot be bought . . ."

"We must fall back on probabilities and ask who is *likely to remain unbought.*"

They sat and smoked until the room had taken on a three-dimensional patina, as if from years of fine corrosion. "Not a straightforward problem, you see," said the Prince at last.

"There are friendships," it seemed to occur to Cyprian, with a narrowing of the eyes translatable as, *Of course we have not been discussing anyone in particular.*

"Yet may not friends, too, defect, often for reasons less predictable than a cash arrangement? Unless . . ."

"I have recently returned," said Cyprian carefully, "from a place where it is much more difficult, at least for the great Powers, to subvert personal honor. A place less developed no doubt than the sophisticated cultures of the West, still naïve, if not quite innocent."

"Despised, disrespected, beneath suspicion," suggested the Prince.

"They do not require vast sums, nor advanced weapons. They possess what all the treasuries of Europe cannot buy."

"Passion," nodded the Prince.

"May I make some inquiries?"

He saw a look of sympathy come over the Prince's face. "I am sorry about your friend."

"Yes. Well. He had many friends. Among whom—"

But the Prince was making another of those princely gestures, and before he knew it, Cyprian was back out on the *salizzada.*

ONE DAY, on the Riva, in front of the Metropole, Cyprian came unexpectedly face-to-face with Yashmeen Halfcourt, on the arm of a battered and rangy individual from whom, having been for some time in a state of unsatisfied desire, Cyprian found himself struggling to keep his eyes averted, not to mention a minute and a half's worth of disorientation at seeing Yashmeen again. Her hair was shorter and lighter, and she was expensively turned out in aubergine taffeta trimmed with silver brocade, elbow-length sleeves with three or four lace ruffles, capeskin gloves in a dark claret, lovely kid boots in the same shade, a hat with plumes also dyed to match and its brim raked to one side, one or two curls swinging roguishly as if disarranged in passion. Cyprian, while making this inventory, realized with dismay how far from even presentable he must look.

"You're alive," she greeted him, difficult to say with how much enthusiasm. She had been smiling, but now her demeanor was oddly grave. She introduced Reef, who had been scrutinizing him in the direct way he'd come to associate with Americans.

"I heard about Vlado," Cyprian said, hoping she would at least not play at salon sociability.

She nodded, folded her parasol and tightened her grip on Reef's arm. "It was a near thing that night, they might have got me too, and if Reef hadn't been there. . . ."

"Really." Deciding to give her cowboy the once-over after all.

"Just happened to show up," Reef nodded.

"But too late for Vlado."

"Sorry there."

"Oh," detaching his gaze, "it's being taken care of. The story isn't over. Not by a long chalk." Presently he sidled off down the Riva.

For the next week or so, Cyprian managed to go a little crazy, resuming, though not on a full-time basis, his old trade of compensated sodomy. In this city there was no shortage of pale men with tastes he understood, and he would need money, a pile of a certain height of it, to go after Theign properly. When his lapse into squalor had earned him enough, he went down to Fabrizio's to have his curls abbreviated into a more combative look, and then caught the evening train to Trieste.

Heading once more over the Mestre bridge, into the smoky orange sunset, Cyprian felt the sadness peculiar to the contemplation of recent time unrecapturable. Anything earlier, childhood, adolescence, they were done with, he could get by without any of that—what he wanted back was last week, the week before. He refused, though not altogether successfully, to think about Yashmeen.

In Trieste the neo-Uskok membership, now being led by Vlado's cousin Zlatko Ottician, greeted him warmly, having heard some exaggerated accounts, already half folkloric, of his adventures on the Peninsula.

They sat eating gibanica and sardines and drinking some herbal grappa called kadulja. Everybody was talking a dialect part coastal Čakavština, part seventeenth-century Uskok maritime slang. Opaque to Cyprian, but more important, to Vienna.

How to proceed? There was a good deal of discussion, in the caffès and taverns, out walking the Rive, of ways and means. No argument that Theign must be killed. Some favored a quick end, unnamed assassins in the dark, while others wanted him to suffer and understand. Poetic justice would be to shop him to some instrumentality famous for torture. Qualified as they were, none of the Great Powers would really serve this purpose, because Theign had done regular business with them all, likely thinking that would be enough to keep him protected. So his reckoning must come from a less exalted direction, the lower parts of the compass rose, the faceless, the despised, the Mavrovlachi of Croatia. Vlado's own.

"As many guns as you need," Zlatko promised.

"You chase him into our sights, we'll do the rest," said his brother Vastroslav.

ON LOOKING INTO Theign's Austrian connections, Cyprian was fascinated to discover how intimate he had grown with the military Chancellery of Crown Prince Franz Ferdinand, who from the Belvedere in Vienna directed a web of intrigue aimed at refashioning the map of Europe, by way of protégés such as the current foreign minister Aerenthal, architect of the annexation of Bosnia.

"Which does suggest," murmured Cyprian to himself, "that Theign must have known about the annexation long, long before the step itself was taken, yet he pretended to be as surprised as any of us. Effectively, it was the first phase of their damned general European war, and he sent me into the thickest of it, where I could take no action that would not lead to my destruction. I say, I must kill this evil bastard immediately, really I must."

As long as it remained in the interests of both England and Austria-Hungary that Russia be kept from acquiring too much power in the Balkans, Theign had been able apparently to justify any degree of coöperation with the Ballhausplatz by pleading the Macedonian Question, remaining thereby safe from any suspicions of treason.

In addition, through 1906 and '07, not yet accounted-for amounts of time and money had been spent, not to mention discomfort inflicted, up to and including anonymous death in unfrequented corners of the cities of Europe, to see that no Anglo-Russian understanding ever came about. It having been of the essence to Germany that England and Russia be enemies forever, the operatives most active in this must have been German or their creatures the Austrians, without doubt including Theign's handpicked prætorians. But with the Entente in force, Theign must have been waiting, with his usual predator's gift of patience, for reassignment. It would probably be best to move quickly.

As Cyprian's field skills, held to the whetstone of European crisis, had sharpened, so Theign's, from overindulgence in various luxuries, including Viennese cuisine, had deteriorated. Cyprian would never become a Venetian, but he had learned a useful thing or two, among these that whatever rumors were worth in other towns, here in Venice they could be trusted as scientific fact. He went out to Castello, and sat at caffès and *bàcari* and waited, and presently there was Theign, accompanied by his brace of plug-uglies. Cyprian recited the appropriate formulæ and became invisible. Before long, in the intricate though mismatched dance which then began, he had learned every minute of Theign's daily timetable, and managed to hover unobserved within mischief-making distance, hiring pickpockets to make off with notecases, arranging at the fish-market for Theign to be assaulted with a dubious haddock, taking to the rooftops of Venice himself to launch the odd furtive tile at Theign's head.

One night he happened to shadow Theign to a palazzo in San Marco, near the Rio di San Zulian. It was the Austro-Hungarian consulate, for pity's sake. How much more blatant did the man imagine he could be? Cyprian decided to materialize.

He had the Webley ready, calibrating exquisitely his placement half in, half out of the fog. Theign, secure in some cloak of exemption, did not appear to be surprised. "Well, it's Latewood. We thought you were dead."

"So I am, Theign, I'm haunting you."

"Reports to the Belvedere on your mission have been simply glowing, the Crown Prince himself—"

"Spare us both, Theign, and make your arrangements."

Theign lurched defensively, but Cyprian had vanished. "You do move quickly for a lazy sod!" Theign cried into the empty courtyard. Once Cyprian might have felt some remorseful twinge at this appeal to their past.

As the crisis approached, he found himself less able to tolerate the everyday. He wasn't sleeping. When he drank to get to sleep, he found himself awake again after less than a fitful hour of dreams in which Yashmeen betrayed him, again and again, to some apparatus known, for the purposes of dream, as "Austria." But even in the dream he knew it could not be that. He woke imagining that the true name had been revealed, but that the shock of waking had dislodged it from his mind.

"It will be tonight, then, if all goes well," the Prince said, with a smile whose bleakness had more to do with inconvenience than regret. He and Cyprian had arranged to meet, furtive as an assignation, in the late afternoon at Giacomuzzi. "You have every right to be present."

"I know. But with the Ottician brothers in town, it is best now to step out of the way and allow them their repayment."

The Prince peered back doubtfully. "There was more you wished?"

"Only to thank you for your efforts in this matter, *Altezza*."

The Prince had always possessed the princely gift of knowing when and how to conceal his contempt. This was necessary in the world not only because truly murderous people could be overly sensitive to insult, but also, incredible as he would once have imagined it, he himself was wrong now and then. A man who does not know how much to ask for is of course contemptible—but sometimes, not often, he will simply want nothing for himself, and that must be respected, if only for its rarity.

"You will come out to the island next week for our annual ball?"

"I've nothing to wear."

He smiled, allowing Cyprian to think it was nostalgia. "The Principessa will find something for you."

"She has exquisite judgment."

The Prince squinted at the sky through his glass of Montepulciano. "In some things, most likely."

THE MOMENT HE EMERGED from the station and set foot on the Ponte degli Scalzi, Theign understood that he ought to have remained in Vienna. Protected, if not safe. At the moment his prætorians were all elsewhere, on assignment at various borders of his domain, but if necessary Vienna itself would have enfolded and defended him. He tried to imagine that he had not come to Venice, perhaps for the last time, in any way because of Cyprian Latewood. Those fires certainly had been banked for ages. He was unwilling, however, to let the pale little sod have the last move in this. Latewood had been merely, inexcusably lucky, but had not been at the game long enough to deserve his luck.

At first Theign was more annoyed than alarmed at the absence of Vincenzo and Pasquale. It had always been their custom to meet him at the platform, and this time he had given them ample notice. As he ascended the bridge, he likewise rose into the cold light of a suspicion that he might have sent them word too soon, allowing the message to be intercepted and unwelcome forces to mobilize.

"Signor Theign, I believe you have forgotten something back on the *terraferma.*"

Unknowns, standing at the peak of the bridge. Night was falling. He could not make out either of their faces clearly enough.

They brought him to an abandoned factory at the edge of Mestre. Associates surrounded the place, keeping to the shadows. "Ghosts," Vastroslav said. "Industrial ghosts. Your world refuses them, so they haunt it, they walk, they chant, when needed they wake it from its slumbers."

Rusted pulleys and driveshafts with broken leather belts drooping from them ran everywhere overhead. The floor was stained black from campfires built by transient visitors. On a metal shelf were various instruments, including a gimlet, a butcher's saw, and Zlatko's 11 mm Montenegrin Gasser, should a quick end become necessary.

"To save everyone trouble," Vastroslav said, "there is nothing you can tell us. Nothing you can pay us. You have stepped into a long history of blood and penance, and the coin of these transactions is struck not from metal but from Time."

"Do let's get on with it then, shall we?" said Theign.

They took his right eye with a woodworker's gouge. They showed him the eye before tossing it to the rats who waited in the shadows.

"One eye was missing from Vlado's corpse," Zlatko said. "We shall take both of yours."

"Two eyes for an eye," Zlatko smiling grimly, "this is Uskok practice—for we are savages, you see, or in a moment," approaching with the gouge, "you *don't* see."

"Whenever you people torture, you try merely to cripple," Vastroslav said. "To leave some mark of imbalance. We prefer a symmetry of insult—to confer a state of grace. To mark the soul."

Soon the pain had driven Theign past words into articulated screaming, as if toward some rhapsodic formula that might deliver him. Zlatko stood by the shelf of tools, impatient with his brother's philosophical approach. He would have used the pistol straight off, and spent the rest of the evening in a bar.

ONE DAY CYPRIAN HAD A MESSAGE from Yashmeen, which began "I must see you." The rest of it he wouldn't remember. She had been apparently to visit Ratty, who had passed on Cyprian's whereabouts.

She and the American, who today was not in evidence, were staying at a *pensione* near San Stae. She greeted Cyprian in a pale shirtwaist and skirt that looked simple but must have cost at least two hundred lire. Her hair bobbed to about shoulder length. Her eyes fatal as ever.

"So old Ratty's back in town. You certainly must have charmed him, either that or he's growing careless."

"I was happy to see him again."

"Been a while, has it?"

"Since Vlado and I left Trieste, I suppose. I can't remember."

"No. Why should you?"

"Cyprian—"

"And Vlado looked after you all right, did he."

Her eyes grew larger and somehow darker. "I owed him my life, more than once."

"In that case I suppose I must rescue you sometime as well, and see what happens."

"He wanted you to have this." She was holding out to him some sort of school copybook, ragged, faded by the elements. *The Book of the Masked.*

After hesitating, Cyprian took it from her. "Did he actually say it was for me? Or do you only want it off your hands?"

"Cyprian, what am I to do with you? you're acting like a perfect bitch."

"Yes." Suddenly reluctant to breathe. "It's . . . everything just lately. Nothing. Haven't slept." Nodding at the bed. "Appears you haven't either."

"Ah." Her expression changed. "Of course Reef and I have been fucking, we fuck whenever we can find a moment, we are lovers, Cyprian, in all the ways you were never permitted. What of it."

He was rectally possessed by fear, desire, least resistibly hope. He had seldom seen her this cruel. "But I would have done—"

"I already know that."

"—anything you commanded. . . ."

"'Commanded.' Oh and shall you, then?" She stepped closer, took his trembling chin between gloved finger and thumb. "Perhaps then if you behave, someday, some exquisite night, we shall allow you to admire us from afar. Restrained appropriately, I expect, poor Cyprian. Quite helpless."

He was silent, met her eyes, looked away as if before a danger he could not bear to see.

She laughed as if she had just detected, by clairvoyant means, a question. "Yes. He knows all about you. But he's not as easy as I am. Much as you might desire him." He kept his gaze down and did not speak. "Tell me I am mistaken." He risked another quick glance. Her eyes were implacable. She held his head still with one hand and with the other struck him in the face, surprising them both, then again, repeatedly, the scent of glove-leather flooding him, a smile slowly possessing her own face, until he whispered what she wanted to hear.

"Hmmn. You shall not so much as look at him without my permission."

"What of his own—"

"His own what? He's an American. A cowboy. His idea of romance begins and ends with me on my back. You are a curiosity to him. It may be years before he gets around to you. It may be never. And meanwhile you shall have to suffer, I suppose."

"What about 'Welcome back, Cyprian, so lovely to see you alive,' and so forth?"

"That too I imagine."

"I mean I no more than step across the street for a packet of cigarettes and you're—" He gestured with his head at the eloquent bedsheets, his eyes desolate. Desolate enough, he hoped.

"You went out *there,*" she said, "when you didn't have to. How was I supposed to feel?"

"But we had agreed, I thought—"

"Had we."

And then one of those silences fell, and a curious thing had happened to time, for although they were the same people they had been when he had stepped on board the S.S. *John of Asia* last year, at the same time they were two entirely different people who had no business being in the same city together let alone the same room, and yet whatever it was between them was deeper now, the stakes were higher, the danger of how much there was to lose terribly, incontrovertibly clear.

IN THE SCALES of the average working day, Cyprian's self-regard, almost uniquely among gentleman ops of the day, had seldom accounted for much more than a newborn gnat's eyelash. Colleagues had been routinely astonished to discover that he avoided the higher social circles, indeed owned no formal attire. Though more than happy to remark upon the appearance of others in regard to dress and grooming, Cyprian himself often went days without shaving or changing his collar or dittoes, on the assumption that he was all but invisible before the public gaze. At first Derrick Theign, among other handlers, had assumed it was a pose—"'Who, little C.L.?' Come off it Latewood, even tattered as you are, you're not exactly a drug on the market of desire quite yet, princes of world industry might be sniveling at your shoetops if you'd only do something about your hair for example."

"Wrong sod, I'm afraid," Cyprian would only mumble, with what might, in a person more vain, pass for self-deprecation. Most who met him found it difficult to reconcile his appetite for sexual abasement—its specific carnality—with what had to be termed a religious surrender of the self. Then Yashmeen entered the picture, had a look, and understood in a pulsebeat, in the simple elegant turn of a wrist, what she was looking at.

The hope it ignited was unexpected—almost, in her life at the moment, unaffordable. But hadn't she just been out in the Riviera casinos willing to risk far more against longer odds? Laboring through a world every day more stultified, which expected salvation in codes and governments, ever more willing to settle for suburban narratives and diminished payoffs—what were the chances of finding anyone else seeking to transcend that, and not even particularly aware of it? And Cyprian, of all people. Dear Cyprian.

Then something also began to happen that was very odd indeed. For years Yashmeen had been the one obliged to put up with passions directed at her by others, settling for moments of amusement, preferring like a spectator at a conjuring performance not to know too much about how it worked. Heaven knew she had tried to be a good sport. But sooner or later she would run out of patience. A certain exasperated sigh and another broken-hearted amateur was left to flounder in the erotic swamp. But now, for the first time, with Cyprian's return, something was different, as if with his miraculous resurrection something had also been restored to her, though she resisted naming it.

Men had never provided much challenge—all her memorable successes were with women. Having learned how, with little difficulty, to command the desires of London shopgirl and haughty Girtonian alike, Yashmeen was agreeably surprised now to find the same approach working with Cyprian, only more so. The gentle make-believe of princesses and maidservants and so forth was deepened, extended into realms of real power, real pain. He seemed not held back by the caveats she had come to sense ever in effect, retarding the souls of British womanhood—willing to transgress perhaps any limit she might devise. It was more than the usual history of flogging one expected from British schoolboys of all ages. It was almost an indifference to self, in which desire was directed at passing beyond the conditions of the self—at first she thought, as other women on the face of it might, well then it's only self-hatred isn't it, perhaps a class thing—but no, that *wasn't* it. Cyprian took altogether too much pleasure in what she obliged him to do. "'Hate'? no—I don't know what this is," he protested, peering in dismay at his naked form in her mirror, "except that it's yours. . . ." With such smoothly presentable curves, this could have been narcissism—but that wasn't quite it either. His gaze was not for the mirror, but for her. At first she thought to cover the mirror when they were together, and learned that it made no difference. His eyes remained adoringly lifted to Yashmeen alone, except for the times when she commanded him to direct them elsewhere.

"No," he whispered.

"Are you saying no to me? I shall give you such a thrashing—"

"I shan't let you do that," in the same whisper.

She adjusted the line of her shoulders, a gesture she had learned particularly aroused him. "Right. I believe I shall have that defiant bottom. Now, Cyprian."

"No," even as his small sleekly-gloved hands moved languorously to the fastenings of his trousers, and he turned and slowly undid them, and lowered them for her, looking back over his shoulder.

He thought he knew being aflame. But this was sustained explosion, reaching now and then a quite unendurable *brisance.* Yet he endured it, not so much because it was her will as, unbelievably, what had become her need. How could he disappoint her need? It seemed too ridiculous, though the evidence lay everywhere. She was behaving like a love-smitten girl. She brought Cyprian armloads of flowers and extravagant underlinen. She praised him outside his hearing, at what some might have found excessive length. He had only to be minutes late for a rendezvous to find her anxiously trembling, moments away from tears. No formal cruelties she might then devise for his penance would quite cancel his memory of her undissembled need, as if he really had surprised her in a vulnerable moment.

"I have lived under this curse so long," he confessed to her, in the breathless, nearly tearful tone he soon found himself slipping into, the equivalent in discourse of sinking to her feet, in a quest for certainty beneath them, "who'd've imagined anyone would see into it, to meet its terms so exactly . . . so honorably . . . Colonel Khäutsch was cruel, at least for as long as he was erect, Theign was content to have power and be obeyed, those were desires I could understand, but, but . . ."

"Before this is done with," she informed him, "if it ever is, you will no longer imagine, you will believe." Amused at the melodrama in her own voice but herself half believing what she'd said, her great eyes shining so. Cruelly, but that was the least of it. Except for a holidaygoer at Wigan once, whose words might have been partially obscured by a strange fried-potato sandwich, it was probably the most romantic declaration anyone had yet made him.

He kept on trying to understand. One could look out over London, from the top of the Earl's Court Wheel at twilight, one by one as the lights came on and the drapes were drawn. It was going on behind every other window one could see, common as stars in the sky, the reversals of power, wives over husbands, pupils over masters, troopers over generals, wogs over whites, the old expected order of things all on its head, a revolution in the terms of desire, and yet, at Yashmeen's feet, that seemed only the outskirts—the obvious or sacramental form of the thing. . . .

"Don't get too spiritual about this," she cautioned, though it was meant perhaps more for herself, and her own outlandish hopes on the subject. "You know it's your body that loves this," stroking him untenderly, "not only parts of your body traditional to such matters but slowly, as your education proceeds, you may be certain, with every square inch of it, every hair, whether left in place or painfully removed, every starved nerve. . . .

"This again." She flicked at it with a scarlet fingernail, and he drew a sharp breath not altogether in pain. "You are thinking about a man. Tell me."

"Yes." He would not insist on "love"—but what else could one feel just at this moment? "Men, actually."

"Yes. Not *one particular* man?"

He was silent for a while. "No. A generic shadow—with a substantial physique I suppose. . . . That doesn't mean—" he turned to her, borne on a wave of undisguised tenderness.

"Don't for a moment imagine that I shall crop my hair and put on a dildo for you, Cyprian."

"I wouldn't dream of asking. Of begging." As if he could not quite resist, he added, "Of course if there were any changes *I* might make, hair, you know, wardrobe, maquillage sort of thing that *you'd* find more appealing—"

She laughed, pretending to examine him by the candlelight. "'Of course.' You're nearly my height, your bones are fine and your features delicate enough, but the brain behind them is filled with little, I fear, beyond the usual boy's delusions about the charms of womankind. As you are, you cannot rival the least *clairvoyante* of my friends."

"And as I might be?"

"Am I your tutoress? Come here, then."

LATE AT NIGHT they would lie together watching lights, moving and still, reflected in the canals.

"What was there for you to doubt?" she whispered. "I have loved women, as you have loved men—"

"Perhaps not 'loved'—"

"—and what of it? We can do whatever we can imagine. Are we not the world to come? Rules of proper conduct are for the dying, not for us."

"Not for you, anyway. You're much braver than I."

"We will be as brave as we must."

IT WAS MID-APRIL, Carnevale had been over for weeks, and Lent was coming to a close, skies too drawn and pallid to weep for the fate of the cyclic Christ, the city having slowly regained a maskless condition, with a strange dull shine on the paving of the Piazza, less a reflection of the sky than a soft glow from regions below. But the silent communion of masks was not quite done here.

On one of the outer islands in the Lagoon, which had belonged to the Spongiatosta family for centuries, over an hour away even by motor craft, stood a slowly drowning palazzo. Here at midnight between Holy Saturday and Easter Sunday began the secret counter-Carnevale known as Carnesalve, not a farewell but an enthusiastic welcome to flesh in all its promise. As object of desire, as food, as temple, as gateway to conditions beyond immediate knowledge.

With no interference from authority, church or civic, all this bounded world here succumbed to a masked imperative, all hold on verbatim identities loosening until lost altogether in the delirium. Eventually, after a day or two, there would emerge the certainty that there had always existed separately a world in which masks were the real, everyday faces, faces with their own rules of expression, which knew and understand one another—a secret life of Masks. It was not quite the same as during Carnevale, when civilians were allowed to pretend to be members of the Mask-world, to borrow some of that hieratic distance, that deeper intimacy with the unexpressed dreams of Masks. At Carnevale, masks had suggested a privileged indifference to the world of flesh, which one was after all bidding farewell to. But here at Carnesalve, as in espionage, or some revolutionary project, the Mask's desire was to be invisible, unthreatening, transparent yet mercilessly deceptive, as beneath its dark authority danger ruled and all was transgressed.

Cyprian rode over with the Prince and Princess in their steam launch, embarking in the twilight from the landing at Ca' Spongiatosta. For half an hour or so, as the moon rose and took over the sky, Cyprian had the disoriented sense that they had ascended, high above the Lagoon, the sky a smudged wilderness of illuminated smoke, colors everywhere more brilliant than expected, and from the perilous altitude he thought he saw far below merchant ships getting up steam, produce-boats on the way back out to Torcello and Malamocco, vaporetti and gondolas. . . .

They could hear the gathering for miles across the water. "It must have been like this a hundred years ago," the Prince observed, "off San Servolo, with all the lunatics screaming." The light ahead was a soiled electrical yellow, glaring off the water, intensifying as they approached. They pulled up to an ancient stone quay, the doomed palazzo swaying above them. Servants with torches, dressed in black tonight as Doge Gradengio's cutthroat squad the Signori di Notte, escorted them inside.

· · ·

NEAR MIDNIGHT, Cyprian, all decked out in a black taffeta ball toilette borrowed from the Principessa, an abbreviated mask of black leather over his eyes, his waist drawn in to an impossibly slender circumference, his small painted face framed by Signor Fabrizio's re-imagining of Yashmeen's hair, curled, powdered, sculpted, woven with seed pearls and Parma violets, was making a devastating high-heeled entrance down marble stairs and into the sea of masks and flesh below. Reef, up in one of the loggie, just about to light up a cheroot, stood gaping instead, not sure at first who it was, finding himself with an erection which now threatened to demolish the trousers of the Pierrot costume Yashmeen had insisted he wear. With some idea of getting a closer look, he wandered down into the general commotion, through which a small dance orchestra was just audible.

"Well howdy there, cowpoke." It was Cyprian all right, his voice soft and amused, sent upward into a register suitable for dalliance, standing so close that Reef could smell his perfume, something floral, elusive, night-blooming. . . . Without delay the youth, out for mischief tonight, had reached his tiny gloved hand boldly to stroke first Reef's nipples, also by now grown painfully rigid, and then, no this could not be happening, Reef's penis, which, far from shrinking from the brazen assault, now continued to exhibit a mind of its own, Cyprian, his eyes hypnotically fixed on Reef's, was about to say more when his playful hand was suddenly grasped and pulled away.

"Cyprian, I have spoken and spoken to you about this, and still you disobey me," whispered Yashmeen, in satin domino, speaking from behind a lace veil that covered her face from hairline to just below her chin, "have you no shame? You know you shall have to suffer the consequences now. Come along, both of you." She took Cyprian firmly by the elbow and steered him through the crowd, some of whom took the opportunity to caress the misbehaving creature as he tried to pass. Cyprian could scarcely breathe, not only from the constriction of his corset, and Yashmeen's intentions toward his body, but mostly from Reef's presence, the dark energy just behind him, almost touching. They had never been all together quite like this till now, the proceedings had been limited to the two heterosexual legs of the triangle. What could she possibly have in mind? Would he be obliged to kneel and watch them coupling? Would she abuse him as she was used to, but openly in front of Reef, and would he be able to bear that humiliation? He did not quite dare to hope.

They found an upper room, full of gilt furniture and dark heavy velvet hangings. Pale *amoretti,* who over the generations had seen it all, lounged about the ceiling, nudging, smirking, grooming the feathers of one another's little wings, passing world-weary remarks at the unfolding spectacle below, which would not in fact depart unduly from the erotic vernacular of these islands.

Yashmeen reclined among the cushions of a red velvet divan, allowing the already precarious hem of her costume to slide upward and reveal her much-commented-upon legs in black silk hosiery, which she now pretended to inspect and adjust. Reef took a step forward, maybe two, to improve his view. "No, stay where you are. Just there . . . good, don't move. Cyprian, *tesoro,* you know where *you* must be." Bowing his head, gracefully lifting his skirts as if to curtsy, Cyprian sank to his knees in a great rustling of silk taffeta. As Yashmeen had arranged them, he could not help noticing, his face was now level with and quite close to Reef's penis, which Reef, at Yashmeen's suggestion, was removing from his trousers.

It did not take nearly as long as Cyprian would have wished. He had grown fond over the years of preliminaries but now was able to get in no more than a few trailing tongue-kisses, a quick electrifying blink or two from his long eyelashes to the underside of the heated organ before hearing Yashmeen's command, "Quickly now. Into his mouth Reef in one stroke, no more, and then you must be perfectly still and allow this wicked little *fellatrice* to do all the work. And you, Cyprian, when he spends you must not swallow any of it, you must keep it all in your mouth, is that understood?" By now she could barely maintain the tone of command, having aroused herself with kid-gloved fingers busy at clitoral bud and parted labia now sleekly framed among the foam of lace around her hips. "You are both my . . . my . . ." She could not quite pursue her thought, as Reef, having lost all control, came bursting in a great pungent flood, which Cyprian did his best to accommodate as he had been ordered to.

"Now come here, Cyprian, crawl to me, and heaven help you if you try to swallow, or let a drop fall, bring me that impudent little face, put your mouth here, yes just here," as her strong thighs closed pitilessly on his head, his scented wig askew, her own adored hair, and her hands at the back of his neck keeping him where he was. "Now use your tongue, your lips, whatever you must, but I want all of it, out of your mouth and inside me, yes for you are nothing here but a little go-between, you see, you shall never, never, enjoy the privilege of having anything but your wicked mouth where it is now, and I do hope Cyprian you are not touching yourself without my permission, because I shall be ever so angry if you . . . yes, dear creature . . . exactly. . . ." She was wordless for a while, and Cyprian lost track of the time, surrendering altogether to her scent, her taste, Reef's taste, the muscular enclosure of her thighs, until she parted them briefly and he thought he heard footfalls on the carpet behind him, and then large lawbreaking hands were lifting his gown. Without being told he arched his back and felt Reef, ready to roll once again, pull down the exquisite drawers Yashmeen's seamstress had stitched together all of Venetian lace from Melville & Ziffer, praying that nothing would tear, and then the hard hands on his bared hindquarters as Reef laughed and slapped him there. "Well if *this* ain't just the sweetest thing." In one painful, well, not really painful slow lunge, Reef entered him. . . . But here let us reluctantly leave them, for biomechanics is one thing but intimacy quite another, isn't it, yes and by now Reef and Yashmeen were smiling too directly at one another, with Cyprian feeling too absurdly grateful here held between them so securely as to make the vigorous seeing-to he was now receiving seem almost—though only almost—incidental.

From then till Ascension Day, the day Venice got remarried each year to the sea, as the two young men, one who had never imagined the other, one who had gone beyond imagining and now only hoped that nothing would turn out to be too "real," made firm the third connection in their triad, both wondered how close to "love" any of this might be venturing.

"It's only gratitude, really," Cyprian shrugged. "She was in a predicament once, it happened that I knew where one of the exits was, of course it all looks like a miracle to her, but I know better, and you should too, I suppose."

"I've seen 'em swept up," Reef argued. "This is the article, all right."

Assuming it was no more than the kind of flirtatious dialogue he'd long grown used to, "You have developed a clinical eye for . . . this condition?"

"Love, ol' buddy. Word make you nervous?"

"More like impatient."

"O.K. We'll see. Don't suppose you're a betting man . . . ?"

"A traveler on a budget right at the moment, I'm afraid."

Reef was chuckling, apparently to himself. "Don't worry, buckaroo, your money's safe from me. Just, when you finally do get that face powder all out of your eyes, don't come asking me for no free advice, 'cause I sure won't know what to say."

"And . . . the two of you . . ." managing to raise both eyebrows in what he hoped Reef would read as sympathy.

"Better ask her," Reef with at least two expressions struggling for space on his face. "I'm just here on the extended tour, you might call it."

"Reef is in the nature of a holiday," she had admitted to Cyprian, "from all you complexos, so fascinating when encountered in the salons of the swank, yet in private able to grow tiresome with such remarkable speed."

One day Cyprian had just emerged from about an hour of smoking and soaking in the tub when Reef strolled in. "She's not here," Cyprian said. "She's off shopping."

"Ain't her I'm lookin for." Cyprian had scarcely taken note of Reef's expressively erect penis, before Reef had seized his hair and was pushing him to his bare knees.

"We mustn't, you know . . . she'll be ever so angry. . . ."

"What about it? lettin a woman ramrod you around like 'at all the time, hell if you'd just once talk back to her . . . They *want* to be told what's what, ain't you figured that one out?"

Once Cyprian would have snapped back, "Oh? Have you been ordering her around on a regular basis, I must've failed to notice that." But now, kneeling demurely, he was content to take Reef's penis into his mouth and gaze upward through his lashes at Reef's distant face, slightly hazed by tears of desire.

Before long Reef was off on one of his rodeo rides and Cyprian was screaming into a lace pillow, as usual, and the air was vivid with smells of lilacs and shit and frangipani. Sunlight off the canal glimmered into the windows. Yashmeen was gone all afternoon.

"Our little secret, I imagine."

"Don't it ever—"

"What?"

"Guess I'm just curious. How a man can let somebody do that to him, without even—"

"Maybe you're not just somebody, Reef."

"Never mind that, now. I'm sayin if it was me, I'd want to kill anybody tried that on me. Hell, I'd *have* to kill 'em."

"Well don't worry, I'm not about to harm you. Dangerous as I am."

"You don't feel like that you've been . . . I mean don't it hurt?"

"It hurts, and it doesn't hurt."

"Japanese talk. Thanks. Knew a certain Nip mystic, back in San Francisco, used to talk like 'at all the time."

"The only way to find out if, and how much, and all that, Reef, is to try it, but you'd probably take offense if I even suggested that." Once he would have been flirting all out, but now— "So I shan't."

Reef squinted. "You're not talkin about"—he made circling gestures with his fingers, "you doin me, nothin like that." Cyprian shrugged. "Not exactly no whanger you got there."

"That much less to be afraid of. Isn't it?"

"Afraid? Son, it ain't the pain, hell, livin is pain. But a man's honor— When it's your honor, it's life and death. You don't have that, where you're from? England?"

"Perhaps I've only failed to see a connection between honor and desire, Reef."

Disingenuous as always—for Cyprian had in fact begun to appreciate that out "in the field" it was precisely his strong desire to be taken that offered him a practical edge, released him from wasting time and energy over questions of rectal integrity, or who in a given encounter would be dominant—that whatever "honor" meant, it no longer had much to do with these outmoded sexual protocols. Let others, if they wished, keep floundering along in the old swamps—Cyprian worked better on firmer ground.

On the other hand, it encouraged people who didn't know him well to confuse submissiveness with sympathy, especially those with the curious belief that sodomites, having few troubles of their own, could never become bored listening to the difficulties of others.

In many respects a product of his home island, not given to nasal intrusion, Cyprian, bewildered as always by the American willingness to confess anything to any stranger at any length, now found himself more and more an audience for Reef's confidences.

"And there was the days when I used to see em on the trains, sometimes be sittin right next to em, these young fellas who were out riding county to county, crossin em state lines, supposed to be looking for work but really just crazy to get away from the whole thing. Ain't that they hate the kids. They'll show you tintypes of the kids more often than not, hell, they love em *chavalitos.* Maybe they even love the wife, they'll show you her picture, too, sometimes there in a pose, or got something on, or not on, that the authorities might call 'calculated to arouse,' and it's clear as a drugstore's front window, 'Not bad, right? and if you as a normal enough fellow think she looks even a little wicked, well, odds have just improved there'll be somebody else too, back there, with the same opinion, just as normal as you, who, maybe even right this minute, this complete stranger, is doin me a favor and he don't even know it.'

"If they only could be a little calmer in their mind, they sure wouldn't get into no discussion about their wife's pussy. But they 's always too wrapped up, so desperate to talk that it didn't matter what I thought, they expected *me* to understand, it must have looked to them like that I did. Each time something would keep me from passin remarks. Maybe I was havin one of those psychic predictions about the day when I'd be joinin them.

"They always looked so worried. Some of em you couldn't buy a smile. Sat there under their hatbrims, reachin down, drinkin up one longneck after another from the case we'd all chipped in on and brought aboard at the last trackside saloon we managed to stop at. Or two. Sometimes it'd be almost a kind of party, a convention, Grand Army of the Matrimonial Republic, tellin each other war stories of the lines they'd had to fall back from, sometimes slow enough, sometimes in a blind panic they'd pretend was somethin else, 'Guess I went a little crazy there,' or 'Can't remember much of that week,' or 'I stayed pretty fucked up for a while.'

"Well and now here we are, not all that many years later, and it's my turn in the other seat, to bend the ear of the feller sitting next to the window, the one who got on back at the last station, namely, you."

"My turn to just sit and listen."

"No choice, pardner."

Cyprian reached, probably meaning no more than to squeeze Reef's shoulder, but Reef frowned and ducked away. "Done some shitty things, Cyprian, but that's the one there's no forgivin. Way my little boy looked at me, that last time . . . ain't like he knew anythin was different. That was it. Just a baby. Always went to sleep never once thinking I wouldn't be there when he woke up. But that one morning I wasn't." He and Cyprian had a look, too stressful for either of them to hold for too long. "I don't even know why I did it anymore. But that's too easy, ain't it."

"How much of this have you told Yashmeen?"

"No more'n she tells me about her younger days. Why? You fixin to go run and rat on me now?"

"Not I, but perhaps you should. Sometime."

"Easy for you to say."

"HAPPENS IN JAIL SOMETIMES," Reef theorized. "Seems like that if you're looking at much time inside, things just slide into that old triangle of two parents and a kid, without much plannin it out."

"But we are not in jail. Are we?"

"Course not. Don't even know why I said that."

"You're free to leave anytime," Yashmeen said. "We all are. That was always the point."

"I might've felt free to leave once," Reef said. But he wasn't about to look anybody in the eye.

"He doesn't know why he said that either," Cyprian put in. Yashmeen's face, poised between anger and amusement, was not a text either of the young men was willing just then to read.

What fascinated Cyprian lately about her face was what happened to it when she and Reef were fucking. True to her promise, she had allowed him to watch them now and then. As if Reef had arrived as some agent of transfiguring—not so much because of as *against* his dogged re-penetrations—her face, which Cyprian had once kept, like a photograph folded securely in everyday memory, as a charm against Balkan misfortune, now, veiled with sweat, grew in passion fiercely exquisite, revealing to him, as if by rays newly discovered, the face of another unsuspected woman. Not possessed so much as evicted, for some unstated use, by forces which had never seen reason to declare themselves.

Far away in the back-country of his spirit, perhaps in the co-conscious one heard them on about these days in fashionable circles, he felt something begin to shift.

NOW, AFTER YEARS OF AVOIDANCE, it was Reef's turn to dream about his father. Something about the situation he was in with Yash and Cyprian must have loosened up a seam, and the dream came and found him. He had thought once that being the Kieselguhr Kid in Webb's place would take care of all his mortal illusions, and now look at this that he'd come stepping into. Webb, even on the trail back from Jeshimon so long ago, that luminous and strident hallucination—would Webb recognize him now, recognize his politics anymore, his compulsions? In the dream they were no longer in the ghostly canyons of the McElmo but in a city, not Venice but noplace American either, with an unmappable operational endlessless to its streets, the same ancient, disquieting pictures engraved on its walls as back in the McElmo, spelling out a story whose pitiless truth couldn't be admitted officially by the authorities here because of the danger to the public sanity. . . . It was darker out here than he had any idea of. In the distance Reef caught sight of a procession of miners in their long rubber coats, only one of them, about halfway along, with the candle stub in his hat lit. Like postulants in habits, they proceeded single file down a narrow street like a humid drift lit back or front by the yellow lamp. As Reef came closer he saw that the bearer of the light was Webb.

"Small victories," Webb greeted him. "Just to come away with one or two. To praise and to honor the small victories where and however they happen."

"Hasn't been too many of them lately, Pa," Reef tried to say.

"Not talking about yours, you numbskull."

Understanding that this was Webb's attempt to pass on another message, like up at the séance in the Alps, Reef saw just for one lucid instant that this was the precise intelligence he needed to get him back to where he had wandered off the trail, so long ago. And then he was awake and trying to remember why it was important.

THEIR PLAN HAD BEEN to flee up into the Garfagnana and live among their kind, among the wolves, Anarchists, and road agents. Live on bean-and-farro soup and mushrooms and chestnuts simmered in the harsh red wine of the region. Steal chickens, poach a cow now and then. But they got no farther up the valley of the Serchio than Bagni di Lucca, birthplace of European roulette as we have come to know it, gamblers' instincts prevailed, and all at once everybody was reverting to type. Soon, as if despite their best intentions, they were rolling in francs. Sometimes they could be seen out sauntering under the trees, Reef in sparest black, Borsalino brim shadowing his eyes, lean and attentive, Cyprian billowing in whites and pastels and extravagantly checked hunting caps, Yashmeen between them in a casino toilette of summer-weight crêpe in palest lilac, and packing a parasol which she seemed to be using as an organ of discourse. Sometimes the clouds came piling over the mountains, thickening the light to dark gray, draping sheets of rain across the hillsides. Swallows lined up under eaves and along telegraph wires to wait it out. Then the three remained indoors, fucking, gambling, pretending to lose just enough to stay plausible, bickering, seldom venturing into questions of whatever should become of them.

What they would find difficult were not so much the grander elements—they had discovered that they all three tended politically to be Anarchists, their view of human destiny was pessimistic with excursions into humor only jail occupants and rodeo riders might recognize—what really made the day-to-day so laborious and apt at any turn to come apart in disaster were rather the small annoyances, which, through some homeopathic principle of the irksome, acted more powerfully the more trivial they were. Cyprian had the habit, of long standing, though until now no one had noticed it really, of commenting ironically on nothing in particular by singing, as if to himself, to the tune of the *William Tell* Overture,

Very nice, very nice, very *nice-in-deed,*
Very nice, very nice, very *nice-in-deed,*
Very nice, very nice, very *nice-in-deed,* very
Ni-i-i-ce, very *nice-in-deed!*

Reef imagined that adversity had taught him the art of assembling exquisite gourmet meals from whatever ingredients the day put in his path, though the other two were seldom known to share this belief, preferring on more than one occasion to go hungry rather than choke down more than a mouthful of whatever horror of Reef's might be on the menu. All Reef could offer was consistency. "Say surly topple!" he would scream and there it would be, another evening's culinary ordeal. "French. Means it's on the table." The pasta asciutta was always overdone, the soup always had too much salt. He would never learn to make drinkable coffee. It did not help when Cyprian's response to the worst of these efforts was to sing,

Yes! yes! it'sveryniceindeed, it's
Ver-y, ver-y, nice in-(deedle-eedle-eedle-eedle),
Nice! nice! yes
Ver-y nice indeed, yes,
Ver-y, ver-y, ver-y, *nice-in-deed!*

"Cyprian, better watch 'at shit." There would then be a silence, prolonged until Yashmeen, in her accustomed role of soother and mediatrix, assuming Cyprian was done singing, began, "Well, Reef, this meal, actually, ehrm—"

Which was Cyprian's cue to continue,

Very nice very nice very nice-nice-nice, it's
Ver-y, ver-y nice indeed, very
Nice very—

At which point Reef would seize a dishful of pasta fazool or overdone tagliatelle and throw it all violently across the table at Cyprian in a great slithering shower. "Startin to goldang annoy me, here?"

"Look at this, you got it all over my—"

"Oh, you're both so childish."

"Don't holler at me, tell the canary there."

"Cyprian . . ."

"Just leave me alone," Cyprian pouted, removing pasta from his hair, "you're not my mother, are you."

"Luckily for you. I should long ago have given in to impulse, and you would be enjoying a much different state of health."

"Go git him, Yash."

"And as for you—"

"You might explain *al dente* to him, at least."

"Missed one right by your ear there."

ONE DAY IN MONTE CARLO, who should show up but Reef's old New Orleans Anarchist bunkmate Wolfe Tone O'Rooney, on his way to Barcelona, which was all about to explode, as it had been doing periodically, with Anarchist unruliness.

"Just give me a minute to find my elephant gun and a change of socks, and I'll be right along."

"Class-brother," Wolfe Tone declared, "we need you safe and well. Your fate is not to be in the *línea del fuego*."

"Hey, I'm as good a shot as any of you stumblebums."

Wolfe Tone explained then that, terrible as it might turn out to be for the Anarchist cause, Barcelona was only a sideshow. "Governments are about to fuck things up for everybody, make life more unlivable than Brother Bakunin ever imagined. Something truly terrible is in the works."

"Out there." But Reef didn't argue. Which should've surprised him more than it did.

THEY ACCOMPANIED the Irish Anarchist as far as the French border with Spain, and took an end-of-the-season pass around the French casinos. But along with the mysteries of Desire, Cyprian was now feeling a shift in its terms, an apprehension that something was coming to an end. . . . The sources of Desire were as unknowable as those of the Styx. But no more accountable was *absence* of desire—why one might choose *not to embrace* what the world judges, it often seemed unanimously, to lie clearly in one's interest.

"You are not the same person," Yashmeen told him. "Something happened out in Bosnia. I feel . . . that somehow I am coming slowly not to matter as much to you as something else, something unspoken." She glided away, as if it had cost her strength to say it.

"But I adore you," Cyprian whispered, "that can never change."

"Once I would have wondered how far you would go to prove it."

"As far as you say, Yashmeen."

"Once that would have been exactly your answer." Though she was smiling, her pale brow was inflected with some premonition, some soon-to-be-desolate awakening. "Now I may no longer ask. I may no longer even wonder."

It was not the usual lovers' oh-but-do-you-really? routine. She was struggling with some deep uncertainty. He was on his knees, as always. She had two gloved fingers carefully beneath his chin, obliging him to look directly into her face till she slapped his own away. The classic tableau had not changed. But in the stillness of both now might be detected a tonic readiness to rise or turn away, abandon the scene, as if roles in a drama had been reassigned.

Reef came into the room in a cloud of cigar smoke, glanced their way, proceeded into a farther chamber. Once he would have taken their tableau as an invitation, and once it would have been.

One day at Biarritz, drifting in the streets, she heard accordion music from an open doorway. A curious certainty took hold of her, and she looked in. It was a *bal musette,* nearly empty at that time of day, except for one or two dedicated wine-drinkers and the accordionist, who was playing a sweetly minor-key street waltz. Light came in at some extremely oblique angle to reveal Reef and Cyprian formally in each other's arms, stepping in rhythm to the music. Reef was teaching Cyprian to dance. Yashmeen thought about making herself known but immediately decided against it. She stood and gazed at the two determined young men, and wished that Noellyn could see it. "If anyone can get that slothful mope out on the floor, Pinky," she'd remarked more than once, "it's you."

It was around this same time that Yashmeen discovered she was pregnant with Reef's child—and, as Cyprian would be pleased to imagine, in some auxiliary sense, in ambiguous lamplight and masked fantasy, his own.

She dreamed, the night she knew for certain, of a hunter arrived at last, a trainer of desert eagles, to unmask against her soul the predatory descent that would seize her, fetch her away, fetch her back, held fast in talons of communion, blood, destiny, to be plucked up off the defective Riemann sphere she had been taking for everything that was, and borne in some nearly vertical angle of ascent into realms of eternal wind, to hover at an altitude that made the Eurasian continent a map of itself, above the glimmering of the rivers, the peaks of snow, the Tian Shan and Lake Baikal and the great inextinguishable taiga.

Hunter and Dally showed up one day in London, having come by express from Venice, where accostment by Bodeo-packing *coglioni* was showing no signs of dropping off, the Principessa Spongiatosta seemed eager to pimp Dally to some doubtful parasitic creeper upon the tree of the Italian nobility, and Dally had concluded that Kit Traverse wasn't coming back from Asia anytime soon, if ever. But before they were through the Alps, she already missed Venice like a refugee.

Ruperta Chirpingdon-Groin was kind enough to help her find a pleasant small bed-sit in Bloomsbury, while Hunter returned to the starched bosom of collateral relations someplace west of Regents Park. Though never especially having wanted Hunter for herself, Ruperta in general could not abide seeing anybody else even pretending to be content. Once satisfied, however, that nothing too passionate was going on between her and Hunter, Ruperta promoted Dally to the status of Minor Annoyance, which was as close to admiration as she ever got, though Dally would never trust 'Pert farther than she could throw a grand piano. Since Venice, and that first finicky handshake outside the Britannia, the two had observed a truce whose purpose seemed to be to maintain Hunter's fragile peace of mind.

"But she likes you," Hunter insisted. "You really ought to let her show you round a bit. She knows everyone."

"Little too nervous about you and me," it seemed to Dally. "Thinks we're sweethearts or something."

"Who, 'Pert? Why she's the most naïvely trusting person I know."

"The woman gets jealous of oatmeal, Hunter." Dally had recently walked in on Ruperta with her face inches from a bowl of steaming porridge, addressing it in a low, vicious snarl—"Oh, yes, you think she wants you now, but wait till you cool a bit, start to congeal, see how keen she'll be then—" while her four-year-old niece Clothilda sat patiently nearby with a spoon and a milk jug. Neither seemed in the least embarrassed, not even when Ruperta angled her ear toward the porridge bowl as if it were attempting to explain itself.

"Well . . . I imagine they were only playing. Some sort of breakfast-table game or something."

"DO COME ALONG DARLING," Ruperta one day appearing out of nowhere as usual, "today your life changes, for you've ever such a treat in store."

Dahlia was immediately on guard, as who wouldn't be. Ruperta, keeping up a London patter largely unintelligible, witched them into a taximeter cab and next thing Dally knew they were in a sinister sort of tea-room in Chelsea across the table from a voluptuous person in a Fedora and a velvet suit. Dally recognized the overgrown thumbnails of a sculptor.

"Miss Rideout, this creature is Arturo Naunt."

"This one shall be my next angel," Arturo declared, gazing at Dally with a brightness of eye she thought she had left behind in Italy. "Tell me, my dear, what is it you do."

Dally had noticed that these English asked questions the way others made statements, with a drop at the end instead of a lift. "I'm an exile."

"From America."

"From Venice."

"A Venetian angel! *Perfetto!*"

Not exactly the sort of angel Dally imagined, however. 'Pert excused herself with the usual depraved smirk, while Dally and Arturo after a moment of mindless exchanges proceeded to Victoria Station. Dally had her trusty Lampo in her reticule, expecting at any moment to have to deal with a chloroformed handkerchief, but the journey to Peckham Rye was uneventful, even, thanks to Arturo's comprehensive grasp of scandals current in Greater London, entertaining.

From the station they found their way uphill to a cemetery dedicated to soldiers fallen in colonial engagements of the nineteenth and what had elapsed of the twentieth centuries, none of the monuments ever quite plumb, a crazy, blown-about field of mineral stumps. Quotations from Henry Newbolt's cricket masterpiece "Vitaï Lampada" seemed to occur on every other slab, though what Arturo had come for was something rather different.

"Here." They had paused before a sentimental sort of military pietà, in which a life-size infantryman with a nearly unbearable sweetness to his face lay dying with his head in the lap of a hooded young woman, rendered in black marble, a pair of predators' wings emerging from her back, who gently consoled him, one hand touching his face, the other raised in a curious half-beckoning, half-commanding gesture. "One of my better A.O.D.'s," commented Arturo.

By which it seemed he meant "Angel of Death." Dally came close, peered beneath the hood. She saw a face you could encounter at any time, turning a city corner or boarding the omnibus, and then it'd be Katie bar the door, wouldn't it—the face of a girl this dying boy had dreamed about, the girl who tended the hearth in a home grown impossibly distant, who promised unvoiceably carnal delights, at the same time that she prepared to conduct his spirit to shores unvoiceably far beyond the sunset.

"Fiona Plush," said Arturo, "lovely girl. Became fascinated regrettably with a variety artist who fancied them curvaceous. Was presently observed bringing her lunch to work in a Pegamoid traveler's satchel with a faux alligator grain. The more she ate the more she wanted to eat. Drapery issues arose. If you look closely in there at the eyeball treatment you'll see I've caught the hunger there—rather nicely, I think—that false compassion which is of the essence in the A.O.D. trade, if you can keep a secret."

"And now—let me just jump ahead here—you're in the market for a new model."

"Perhaps a new approach as well. You must have noticed how people admire your hair."

"Guess you're fixing to do away with the hood."

"Well. Tradition has been to hide the face, I mean, it's Death isn't it. The best you 'd expect is a skull, and depending how nightmare-prone you are, it only gets worse from there."

"But this Angel here is—"

"True, but that's old Fiona, not her fault she's presentable, though I finally did have to slim her down a bit."

In the days following, they were to visit other graveyards, and the more of Naunt's A.O.D.'s Dally had a look at, the stranger matters became. There were perverse intentions at work here, procreative as much as mortal. In the complicated drapery of the A.O.D.'s garment, at certain times of day, beneath the duress of the prevailing light, one saw clearly in the shadows of the gown the shape of an infant, or sometimes more than one, clinging to what might have been an indifferent body. When the clouds thickened, drifted or passed, or the day drew to evening, these figures disappeared, or sometimes modulated to something else that likewise did not invite close inspection.

Dally had put in a little time as a sculptor's model. Back in New York, in one of the capitalist temples downtown, among the allegorical statues lining a particular marble corridor, she could still be found as *The Spirit of Bimetallism,* face correct as a face on a ceremonial urn, garlanded, chiseled onto each iris a wedge of radiant attention aimed at her right hand, which held suspended a symbolic sun and moon as Justice holds her scales . . . like the other models, little chance, in the expression she had assumed, of wistful regret for what she'd come to. What had they been like as girls, Supply, Demand, Surplus Value, Diminishing Returns? Had any of them sat on a porch at the edge of some prairie, riding a store-bought rocker through the pearl afternoon, into the evening, imagining her family gone off without her, the house a shell, taken over by these slow, wood rhythms? Was she from even farther west, say up in the mining country, freezing through her days and nights in some shack above the snowline, was that how she'd come to be a child of gold and silver? Noticed by a mine owner, or an owner's lieutenant, brought to the city, some city, introduced to some sculptor fellow, some smoothie who'd been to France, veteran of artists-and-models shenanigans, knew his way around the salons down in Kipperville. . . .

Unlike others in the modeling line, she had taken the actress's approach and actually *read up on* the abstractions she was instructed to embody, as a way of "getting inside the character." What was the point in trying to incarnate Bimetallism unless you could learn everything you could about It? So with Arturo Naunt and his A.O.D.'s. This job of riding herd on military souls—Dally couldn't help seeing it from the Angel's point of view. Maybe the hood had been there not to conceal but to protect, the way the shawl of a classic *semeuse* was sometimes drawn over her head for the sun—against something from above, potent yet deflectable, some radiance or unsuspected form of energy . . . God's grace?— Why should the Angel of Death, acting as agent for God, need to be screened from grace? What other, unsuspected dark energy, then? What anti-grace?

There was friction from the beginning. Arturo wanted repose, stillness—what Dally gave him was a dynamic athlete, surrendered to a wind only she could feel, mindlessly orgasmic from its velocity. "Well. I'm not Charlie Sykes, am I," he was often heard to mutter. Like the face of Fiona Plush before her, Dally's was too specific for prolonged viewing. We have seen these faces, at the changes of daylight, against the long, featureless walls of suburban warehouses, on days of fog or of distant fires whose ash drops unseen, steadily, accumulating white as frost . . . their faces seem to require this derangement in the light, and perhaps a willingness to see them, however anxiously denied by those of us who do.

· · ·

MEANTIME 'PERT, who had been busy trying, with little success, to plant doubts about the girl in Hunter's mind, had also learned through elements of the T.W.I.T. something of his earlier adventures and the frailties resulting, and appointed herself a sort of anti-muse, hoping out of meanness to provoke Hunter at least into work unlikely to endear him to the British public. Her history was soon to undergo a certain adjustment, however. In September, Hunter would invite her to accompany him to Gloucester Cathedral, where as part of that year's Three Choirs Festival, a new work by Ralph Vaughan Williams would be having its first performance. Ruperta, who despised church music, must have seen some irresistible opening for idle mischief, because she went along wearing a sportive toilette more appropriate to Brighton, with a hat she had always found particularly loathsome but kept handy for occasions just such as this. The composer was conducting two string orchestras set like cantores and decani facing each other across the chancel, with a string quartet between them. The moment Vaughan Williams raised his baton, even before the first notes, something happened to Ruperta. As Phrygian resonances swept the great nave, doubled strings sang back and forth, and nine-part harmonies occupied the bones and blood vessels of those in attendance, very slowly Ruperta began to levitate, nothing vulgar, simply a tactful and stately ascent about halfway to the vaulting, where, tears running without interruption down her face, she floated in the autumnal light above the heads of the audience for the duration of the piece. At the last long diminuendo, she returned calmly to earth and reoccupied herself, never again to pursue her old career of determined pest. She and Hunter, who was vaguely aware that something momentous had befallen her, walked in silence out along the Severn, and it was hours before she could trust herself to speak. "You must never, never forgive me, Hunter," she whispered. "I can never claim forgiveness from anyone. Somehow, I alone, for every single wrong act in my life, must find a right one to balance it. I may not have that much time left."

Ordinarily he would have humorously disputed her theory of moral bookkeeping. But later he would swear he had seen her surrounded then by a queer luminous aura he knew he could not banter away. Possessing one of those English ears on which flatted-seventh sonorities are never lost, Hunter had of course immediately fallen for the *Tallis* Fantasia, would always love it, but the change of heart he himself needed would have to proceed from some other source. The time was rising like a river in a season of storm to rush in waves and whitecaps through the alleyways and plazas of his soul, and he did not know if he could climb high enough to escape it.

When his paintings had started to get peculiar, Dally noticed immediately. In the compositions appeared deliberate vacancies—a figure would be over on one side of the canvas looking at, or gesturing toward, the other side as if there were someone there—but there was no one there. Or two subjects would be likewise engaged, crowded together on one side while nearby, close enough to touch, opened this somehow blazingly luminescent space, as if an essential term had been left out. Sometimes in the empty part of the composition, even the background would be missing, and it would be the raw imprimatura which assumed the quality of a presence, demanding to be observed. . . .

"What is it?" Dally wanted to whisper, afraid for him. "What is it you don't show?"

He usually referred questioners in this vein to the immoderate light-space appearing in Turner's *Dido Building Carthage,* then hanging in the National Gallery. "If one must steal, it's always advisable to steal from the best."

"Not buying that one, Hunter, sorry."

"Or perhaps having a solid background now in Angel of Death work, you might want to come round and pose for one of these empty spaces, should things over at Arturo's shop ever grow tiresome."

"A little creepier than that, actually." She told him about the latest episode at the Chelsea atelier. Naunt the other day had requested her to dispense with the usual A.O.D. drapery and wear instead only a pair of military jackboots. Then, from a back room, emerged what was known in the business as a Well Set-Up Young Man, likewise unclothed except for a dark blue line-infantry helmet. "You know the position, Karl," instructed Naunt. Karl without comment got on all fours and presented his—Dally couldn't help noticing—presentable bottom. "Now Dahlia, if you'd just get behind him, gripping him by the hips in rather a firm, no-nonsense way—"

"You said she'd be wearing a dildo," Karl reminded him somewhat breathlessly.

"What's going on, Arturo," Dally inquired, "if you don't mind sharing your thoughts here?"

"Maternal tenderness," Naunt explained, "is certainly one of the A.O.D.'s attributes, but hardly the only one. Anal assault, not unknown in the military imagination, is an equally valid expression of her power, and the submission she expects, as well as a source of comfort, indeed at times provides pleasure, to the object of her attentions."

"So then I'm supposed to . . ."

"Don't worry about the penis element, I can put that in later."

"I should hope so," muttered Karl.

"These artistic types," Hunter sighed, when she told him. "So. Did you two, ehrm . . ."

"Must be my puritanical American upbringing," she said. "Sodomizing idiots has never been my cup of tea."

As destiny would have it, whom did she run into out on the town that very evening but her old admirer the American impresario R. Wilshire Vibe, for whose product in recent years the West End had been proving more congenial than Broadway.

"Well, Je-hosaphat, saw that hair all the way from Shaftesbury Avenue, thought the place was on fire. You may be in a position to do me *such a mitzvah,* young lady." It turned out that he'd been looking for a "typical Irish lass" to decorate his latest effort, *Wogs Begin at Wigan,* and nobody who had showed up at casting calls so far had quite filled the bill. Even better, the part was a first-act walk-on, and one of the *figurantes* in the big third-act number in *Roguish Redheads* just a few doors down was leaving, so if Dally could sprint along the Strand fast enough to get into costume and makeup in time, why she'd be a perfect replacement.

"What you call a twofer," she said.

"There you go. You aren't committed elsewhere or anything, are you?"

"Oh, a sort of amateur religious pageant, but I think I can get out of it."

From doing walk-ons, she soon had a couple of lines, then eight bars of a duet with a character juvenile whose vocal range was half an octave, well inside Dally's own, and before she quite knew what was going on, she found herself celebrated as one of the wonders of the world as defined by Shaftesbury Avenue, the Strand, Haymarket, and Kings Way, though recognized as well by suburban audiences from Camberwell Green to Notting Hill Gate, often by quite peculiar people who were not above calling out to her in the street, offering Scotch eggs and digestives, snapping photos, asking her to sign theatre programs, bits of chip-shop newspaper, husbands' cheerfully inclined heads. Understanding that none of this could last much beyond one season, almost in innocence amazed that she could watch so calmly the ardor of others as if from inside some glacial and lucid space, Dally was invited to weekends at some of the more sizable manor houses of the British countryside, required to do nothing but look the way she looked—as if her appearance possessed a consciousness, and must be allowed to obey its impulses—attended by domestic staff, puzzled by extravagant acts of abasement from young men whose names she did not always hear, let alone remember. They begged for items of her intimate apparel to sew into their hats. Her toes became objects of adoration, not always in private, requiring her to change soaked or laddered stockings sometimes three or four times in the course of an evening. Men were not her only admirers. Grown women, mad poetesses, beauties of photogravuredom, offered to abandon husbands, ponying up fistfuls of currency which even on a per-hour basis Dally couldn't make sense of. She was given jewelry which had reposed in the vaults of distinguished families for centuries, as well as rare orchids, stock-market advice, Lalique creations in opal and sapphire, invitations to far-off sheikhdoms and principalities. Always, not exactly lurking, but obstinately staring from behind some Himalayan rhododendron or swiftly melting ice sculpture, never out of his habitual uniform of tropical white dittoes and Panama hat, persisted the figure of her newest faithful suitor Clive Crouchmas, into whose gravitational field Ruperta had been able to steer the girl with no more than a twitch of her cigarette.

From Turkish railway intrigues, Crouchmas had by now grown into one of the world authorities in the dark arts of what was becoming known as "borrowing in quasi-perpetuity." He was the one the various Powers preferred to consult—when they could get an appointment. Government spending being not altogether disconnected from arms procurement, he was in communication as well, if not especially intimate, with the likes of noted death merchant Basil Zaharoff. Indeed it was the fabled arms magnate's reported desire for Dahlia Rideout, because of her hair color, to which Zaharoff was notoriously susceptible, that had got Clive himself interested in the first place.

"Yes I suppose that's so," Ruperta had shrugged, "even if one doesn't care for the type."

"And she isn't . . ."

"Spoken for? Whatever that might mean in her case, you could always make arrangements. These girls. Always another. It's like a florist's inventory, isn't it, cheaper toward the end of the day."

Clive sat there, among the pure white napery, the perfectly shining silver and spotless glassware, his mouth slightly open. Once, when they were small children, Ruperta had offered him a pound for one of his lead soldiers, and upon his handing it over she had picked up a nearby cricket bat and begun, rather solemnly, to pound him with it. He should have been crying but later recalled feeling only admiration, while perhaps making a note to try this on someone else. A *horrible* little girl whom, over time, he came to regard as the expediter of his less-confidable dreams.

. . .

WELL, IT WAS that Principessa all over again, it seemed to Dally. Were procuresses the only sorts of women Hunter knew? As it turned out, being a kept crumpet was not nearly the sordid horror she might have imagined. Crouchmas himself was just a breeze. Mostly he liked to watch her masturbating—so sweet, really. Nothing to go to the police about, was it. He played as fair as he could, respected her feelings, didn't try to set her up in some dismal little bed-sit in Finsbury or someplace, nor, when they did rendezvous, was it in shabby hotel rooms but in actually quite swell surroundings, right out on Northumberland Avenue, in the full dazzle of the great city and all it offered—the Métropole, the Victoria sorts of place, always fresh flowers, vintage Champagne—the soiled opacity of his daily business, its hundreds of small weaselly arrangements with go-betweens who did not always remember which name they were supposed to be using, transmuted to clarity and grace and herself in expensive *déshabillé* and a warm fog of self-pleasure, while he sat at his safe distance, watching.

DALLY HAPPENED TO MEET Lew Basnight at a weekend party at Bananas, the sumptuous Oxfordshire manor of Lord and Lady Overlunch. She was wearing a gown made of printer's muslin, enjoying just then a great chic among the bohemian of spirit. The pressmen in Fleet Street used it to clean the type after each day's run—you fetched it out of the bins and took it to a Clever Seamstress in Regent Street you knew, and showed up at your function looking like the day's *Globe* or *Standard,* and spent the entire evening deciding whether people were admiring your toilette or only trying to read it.

There were T.W.I.T. in attendance tonight, for these days there were T.W.I.T. everywhere, as if something fateful were in progress that made their attendance indispensable. Dally had recently had a Tarot reading done, Earl's Court, nothing fancy, nothing swell, the same reading a shopgirl might pay sixpence for, so when Lew explained what kind of detective he was, she at least knew her way around the twenty-two Major Arcana.

"You're one of these T.W.I.T. folks?"

"Used to be, opened my own practice, more like a consultant on retainer now if that Icosadyad decides to really start acting up. Always something new, though over the years," he calculated, "I've been out in search of them all—simplest turned out to be the hardest, Moon, Sun, and so forth, tried to avoid them whenever I could."

Today in fact he'd been lying beneath the Sun, hat down over his eyes, half snoozing or as some would have it meditating, from sunrise till hard overhead noon. The Sun was trying to tell him something—"Beyond the usual, 'Say, it's me. It's me,' o' course, which is more or less standard by now."

Later on, tonight at the Overlunch manor, it was the Moon which had found him, among these tailcoated and Vionnet-gowned guests drifting the pavilioned gardens, reflected in the obsidian smoothness of the ornamental lake, calling down from the sky, again, "It's me. . . . It's me . . ." as the giant crayfish clattered slowly out of the bathing-pool, and the dog began to bay from some distant part of the grounds, and here came the strong and beaming Moon herself, just above a bared and passing shoulder, beaming down on these privileged at play, with their circus-striped tents, their lamps radiantly lensed from within fantastic grottoes of ice, their Oriental knife corps with clever white accents at toques and teeth.

Then at last, pure and unmistakable, The Star. "It's me. . . ."

In ordinary divination practice, The Star, number XVII, which at first glance signified hope, was just as apt to portend loss. It showed a presentable young woman, unclad, down on one knee, pouring out water from two vases, her nakedness meant to suggest that even when deprived of everything, one may still hope. A. E. Waite, following Éliphaz Lévi, believed that in its more occult meaning the card had to do with the immortality of the soul. Lew in his earlier days, perhaps understandably, was more interested in that naked woman part, though various T.W.I.T. advisers tried to talk him past it. He seemed convinced, so compelling was the vision of deck-designer "Pixie" Colman Smith, that one evening he would turn a bend in the landscape and there would be the same exact conjunction of earth and water, the tree on the knoll, the bird on the tree, and there for the moment oblivious to his presence, with the sweep of foothills and mountains behind her, this glorious naked blonde. Old Tarot hands had seen this condition of point-missing before, and even had a word for it—"Pixielated." "The present occupant of that Arcanum might not even be female," he was warned repeatedly, to little effect.

Dally had been staring, her expression more and more radiant. He narrowed one eye quizzically. "What?"

"That was the last card she turned up for me," Dally said. "At Earl's Court. The Star."

"Well," Lew angled his thumb aloft and eastward, where sure enough a very bright, luminous object had been slowly on the rise all evening, "it's a good one to get, all right." It was the Dog Star Sirius, which ruled this part of the summer, and whose blessings, tradition held, were far from unmixed.

"Tell me, then," she asked, as if it was an affliction they shared, "who was it? When you finally tracked them down. Who turned out to be The Star?"

His usual practice at this point was to say, "Well, now, I might've been exaggerating about that one, I never did find out, exactly." But, much as Lew would rather go off to the terrace down beside the dark little lake and smoke a cigar by himself, he had some business with this young lady.

"Can you spare a minute, Miss Rideout?"

She had been having a fairly pleasant time up till now, but these parties did tend to have their payback arrangements, and she guessed this was tonight's. She put down her Champagne glass, took a deep breath, and said, "Sure." A pulse of silence swept the terrace, leaving a stray half bar of dance-orchestra music, unexpectedly dissonant, to stain the evening, before it resumed, playing now in 3/4, too fast to be called a waltz or for any but the determinedly athletic or the insane to keep up with, and as a result couples were dancing at a number of different speeds, trying to arrive someplace recognizable at the end of each four bars, everybody crashing into furniture, walls, each other, staggering away from these collisions at unpredictable angles, giggling incessantly.

"The fellow you came here with."

"Mr. Crouchmas."

"Known him long?"

"Who wants to know?"

"I'm only the go-between," Lew said.

"For who? The T.W.I.T.?"

"It's not them, but I can't say any more."

"Clive and I are ever such good friends," Dally said, as if Crouchmas were any of who knows how many West End juveniles.

"Some folks who take a lively interest in his business dealings," said Lew, "would pay handsomely for certain information."

"That's if I knew what it looked like, which I wouldn't, being's I don't exactly read the financial pages, can't even understand the headlines, if you want the truth."

"How about German?"

"Not a word."

"Know it when you see it?"

"Guess so."

Out in the dark grounds, a peacock suddenly made a loud gargled "Ooohkh(?)" then cried "HAI!" in almost a human voice.

"Brother Crouchmas has picked up a few German connections over the years," said Lew. "Started back with Turkish railway guarantees—he'd rake in the money for a year or two, then he'd either resell the lines outright, or the operating licenses for them, mostly to respectable German firms through the Deutsche Bank, where in fact he's kept a personal account, right up to the present day, by now in the fairly well-off range. When asked how patriotic or even loyal can that be, he'll tell you the King is the Kaiser's uncle, and if that isn't a connection, he'd like to know what is."

"Man has a point. But now, just for argument's sake, how 'handsomely' are we talking here?"

"Oh, a nice retainer fee." He wrote a number on a business card and handed it to her, aware that eyes were directed their way. "How come I don't see waterworks, nose elevation, none of that usual how-dare-you routine? Most young ladies by now—"

"I'm only Clive's little tart, ain't I. What wouldn't a girl like that do for a sum like this?"

SHE OUGHT TO HAVE felt worse about her espionage expeditions, at least that she was "betraying" him, but somehow she couldn't get that deep about it. Time and again it was emphasized to her, by way of Lew Basnight, that this wasn't personally directed against Crouchmas, it was more in the nature of gathering information, as much of it as possible, given the rapid changes in Turkish politics. Even if she'd read any of the documents, which she hadn't, there would've been no way for her to tell how much, or even if, he could be hurt by them.

"Someone is clearly fascinated," it seemed dismally to Hunter, "with Crouchmas's simultaneous attachments to England and Germany. As if just having discovered a level of 'reality' at which nations, like money in the bank, are merged and indistinguishable—the obvious example here being the immense population of the dead, military and civilian, due to the Great War everyone expects imminently to sweep over us. One hears mathematicians of both countries speak of 'changes of sign' when wishing to distinguish England from Germany—but in the realm of pain and destruction, what can polarity matter?"

IT WAS A TALL BUILDING, taller than any in London, taller than St. Paul's, and yet no one had ever been able to make it out with enough clarity for it to qualify as a "sight" tourists might be impressed by—more a prism of shadow of a certain solidity, looming forever beyond the farthest street one knew how to get to. The exact way to enter, let alone visit, remained a matter of obscurity, indeed was known only to adepts who could prove they had business within. The rest of the town looked up, and up, past a slate confusion of rooftops, and of course it was there, massively blocking the sky and whatever city features might lie behind it, a blackness nearly obsidian, hovering, all but breathing, descent built into its structure, not only the shedding of rain and snow but more meaningfully within, the downward transfer of an undiscussed product from the upper levels to hidden cargo docks below, by chute, by lift, by valves and conduits—though the commodity was not exactly a fluid, the equations governing its movement were said to be hydrodynamic in nature.

All day it had been raining. Up here the dark glass facings captured shapes of storm clouds rushing by, as if camouflaging, in its own illusion of movement, a warship of Industry sailing the storm-flows above the city. Inclined windows passed the smoky and violent light down into deserted passageways. Dally could search here, room after room, for days—open drawers and cabinets and find strange, official-looking documents concerning foreign arrangements never made public. . . . A royal charter, signed by King Ernest Augustus, granting some affiliate of Crouchmas's shadowy firm the right to build a tunnel across the North Channel of the Irish Sea, between Galloway and Ulster, intended for the transport of military forces and a pipeline for illuminating gas. A railroad right-of-way, straight across the Balkan Peninsula, conceded in Cyrillic and Arabic script all woven in and out of the loveliest green guilloche by the no-longer quite-unabsorbed entity of East Roumelia. A deed for a huge tract of British soil, in Buckinghamshire a bit east of Wolverton and north of Bletchley, leased in apparent perpetuity to sovereign Obock, no typist's copy but the original deed, an impressive document heavy as lead-foil and edged with an elaborate steel-engraved cartouche, glowing all but tropically in the misted greens, yellows, and oranges of some color process too proprietary even to have a name, depicting in fine detail palms, dhows, natives collecting salt or loading coconuts onto merchant vessels, historic moments such as the 1889 occupation of the fort at Sagallo by the Cossack adventurer Atchinoff and the archimandrite Païsi (faces too direct in their gazes to be merely fanciful), which ended in a shelling by French warships and seven innocent dead. Smooth-sliding wood drawer after drawer, stuffed with these territorial mysteries. No one seeming to care who opened them, who looked in—she had encountered no guards, no demands for identification, not even locks. Where there had once been locks were now open cylinders, corroded, occupied by nothing but shadowy exemption from the unrelenting rainlight she worked in now, breathing carefully, waiting to be walked in on in the act of reading forbidden data. But no one walked, up here.

Outside, the wind was pouring fiercely over figures she herself might have posed for not that long ago, reproduced now by hundreds in some modern variation on Portland stone which seemed to ring faintly in the long gusts, ring down the afternoon, with no one to listen. Frieze creatures, upper-floor caryatid faces, mineral loneliness. Where were any human eyes, let alone the blank lunes that served as eyes for others of their kind, to be met across these perilous chasms? They must be content to register the shadows that raced among the versatile diffractions of soot ascending to the summits of these towers daily scrubbed nacreous by the winds, so polished as to reflect the shapes of the clouds as they soared distant above the dark, the golden city-top, clouds edged like faces, cleanly contoured as handclaps, chasing beyond city limits across the vistas of bleared glacial grassland this day of storm, above this wet misfortune of country spaces. . . .

The lift bore her smoothly to the street floor. It felt like ascent. Invisible within her celebrated beauty, she glided through the lobby and back out into the clamorous city.

"Is that the young lady, sir?"

"Oh, God . . ." Clive Crouchmas in a stricken voice. "God help me. . . ."

"Sir, we'll just need this signed then, as proof we've delivered the service we were engaged for."

Dally hailed a cab and was driven away, the detectives touched their hats and slid around the corner, the rain started up again, Crouchmas continued to huddle in the grand false-Egyptian entryway. Those with business there came and went, casting glances. Night fell in a long hum, resonating across the bases of lowering clouds with a great frictional gathering of electromotive force, while beneath crept a solemnity of omnibuses, arriving or leaving every few minutes. Crouchmas had forgotten his umbrella. He made his way through the rain to a dingy establishment near the docks where soddenness was not remarked upon and drank for a while, ending up at the one place in London he was still able to think of as home, the establishment of Madame Entrevue, where, though requests for certain activities—mutilation of the poor, ritual sacrifice—more easily come by out in the economy at large, might be reason to turn a client away, for most needs they had to let one in the door. Cigar smoke scented the rooms. Telephones rang faintly down corridors not always visible.

As he had often noticed them doing lately, his thoughts now flew southward, as if by magic carpet, to Constantinople. "I'll shop the bitch to a harem, is what I'll do." That this was no longer an option in the New Turkey did not at the moment occur to him.

Madame was her usual sympathetic self. "But did you think all this time it was about your looks? Your inexhaustible virility? Consult the mirror, Clive, and come to terms. You have a solid reputation for hardheadedness, why go sentimental now?"

"But she was not one of the usual, I was actually—"

"Don't say it—we don't use language like that in here."

Later in the evening he happened to run into old "Doggo" Spokeshave.

"Well if you've Constantinople in your plans, Crouchmas, it happens that old Baz Zaharoff's Wagon-Lits arrangement ought to be free for a bit."

"You have the disposition of that, do you Spokeshave."

"I shouldn't think he'd mind, no, Crouchmas."

"And where's B.Z. off to then?"

"Japan, so the rumor goes. If not himself, then his people certainly. All very queer in his shop at the moment, Crouchmas, I must say."

"But I say Spokeshave, shouldn't the Nip have a rather complete weapons inventory by now?"

"Yes but it's *they* who want to sell *him* something, you see. Everyone's being ever so dark about it. The item doesn't even have a name anyone agrees on, except for a *Q* in it somewhere I think. Something they came into possession of a few years ago and now have up for sale on most attractive terms, almost as if . . ."

"As if they don't really need it, Spokeshave?"

"As if they're afraid of it."

"*Oh* dear. Who's old Baz think he'll sell it to then?"

"Oh, there are always climbers in the game, aren't there, why Crouchmas just look at your own territory."

"What? The rugriders."

"Any number of Balkan interests as well, I shouldn't wonder. Especially if Baz could price it cheaply enough, don't you know."

"Well I shall certainly have a look into it when I'm out there. Might take you up on Compartment Seven as well. Never hurts to be seen as an intimate of old Baz, does it?"

"I should know, shouldn't I."

"I MAY HAVE TO GO to Constantinople for a while," he said smoothly. "It's those old Ottoman railway guarantees again. Ghosts—they never go away. Even with the new régime figuring them in as budget expenses at so much per mile, there are still tidy sums to be obtained, if one can find one's way through the Young Turkish labyrinth. But the thing must be done in person. I don't suppose you'd be able to pop down for a few days, join me."

"The new show won't go into rehearsal for a while," she said. "Let me see if it's possible."

Lew after making a brief telephone call gave her the go-ahead. "They say anything you can find out down there will be of 'inestimable value.' "

"That's it? No 'Good luck Dally, of course we'll pay per diem,' nothing like that?"

"No, but on a personal note—"

"Why, Detective Basnight."

"Watch your back. Please. I hear things about this Crouchmas fellow. Nobody trusts him."

"There's some would say he's a sweet old duck, and I'm a mercenary minx."

"Oh hell, now you're just flirting."

To make sure he thought so, she lightly touched his sleeve. "I will be careful, Lew, don't worry."

He'd found himself wondering lately if it was Dally who might have turned out to be The Star. Some announcement of Lew's final release from his obligations, if any still existed, to the T.W.I.T. Would the light of her innocence—minx or whatever—even be enough to show him decisively that the "Major Arcana" he had dogged for so long had never necessarily been criminals or even in a condition of sin? And that the T.W.I.T. had judged them so out of a profound and irreparable condition of error?

He felt it within his remit to accompany her to Charing Cross. The platforms smelled of sulfurous coal-smoke and steam. The engine trembled, muscular, Prussian blue under the electric lamps. One or two grinning devotees asked her to sign their shirt cuffs. "Don't forget to bring me back some Turkish Delight."

"About the only kind I'm likely to see—it's just a working holiday for ol' D.R." When he handed her her valise, she leaned up and kissed his cheek. "Well," adjusting her hat and turning to ascend the iron steps, "here I come, Constantinople."

The idea in Clive Crouchmas's mind of shopping Dally into a harem had been fine as far as it went, but revenge for some is not as sweet as profit, and it had soon occurred to him that she might more constructively serve as a bribe to somebody useful. Besides, the puritans now in power in what some were beginning to call Istanbul were resolved to do away with all vestiges of the sultanic, and actually Clive was obliged to put up with some rather disrespectful treatment in the very offices of the Ottoman Debt Agency in Cağaloğlu where he had once engineered some of his more, he supposed, Byzantine schemes. Even worse, others—German, to no one's surprise—had been there before him, and pickings were slim. With the prospect of returning to England more or less empty-handed, Clive, blaming Dally for the whole contretemps, had an episode of insanity in which it seemed the only way to come out of this ahead would be to sell her into white slavery someplace else, by way of unreconstructed elements of the Old Turkey, and their Habsburg co-adjutors in what finally turned out to be Hungary.

Somehow, because his description of Dally had included her celebrated red hair—a feature widely associated with the traveling companions of Basil Zaharoff—her would-be abductors Imi and Ernö had fallen under the impression, as they boarded the Orient Express at Szeged and made their way, stealthy as operetta pirates, both wearing peculiar black Central European Trilby hats, toward Dally's compartment, that this was to be the kidnapping of a *Zaharoff girl,* for whom the international arms tycoon would pay a tidy sum in ransom money.

Kit Traverse, meanwhile, was sitting in a Wagons-Lits train headed the other way, toward Paris, which according to schedule should've been rolling into Buda-Pesth about now, except for a slow start owing to mysterious revolutionary activities on the line, so that both his train and Dally's happened to arrive at the same time in Szeged. Kit looked out the window and observed across the tracks in the train opposite a presentable redhead in some kind of trouble. There might still be five or ten minutes to just stroll over there and see what was what.

"ZAHAROFF GIRL!"

"No—who, me?"

"Zaharoff girl! Red hair! Look!"

"Suggest you get them meathooks out of my hair," said Dally.

The two looked at each other as if they might have to consider some remote possibility of error. A moment of thought processes ensued.

"Zaharoff girl!" they started screaming again.

"Fellas," Kit Traverse in the doorway beaming, "think you may have the wrong compartment here?"

"That can't be you out there," said Dally.

Kit made out a young woman in a smart traveling ensemble, sunlight streaming in the train window behind her, lighting up her hatless hair. He focused in till he was sure of who he was seeing. "Well."

The 7.62 mm Nagant tucked in his belt had not escaped the attention of either Imi or Ernö, who began quickly to adjust their demeanor to suggest mental soundness.

"This is Compartment Number Seven, yes?"

"So far so good."

"Always reserved for Zaharoff *úr,* and his esteemed lovely Zaharoff girls. You are coming from Vienna?"

"No," said Dally.

"Zaharoff girls always board at Vienna."

"Well now see that's just it—"

"Imi, Crouchmas *úr* did say 'Zaharoff girl,' didn't he?"

"That's what he said."

"You," Imi turning to Kit, "are Mr. Zaharoff? Crouchmas *úr* told us you would be somewhere else."

"Clive Crouchmas sent you two? Why that miserable toad," declared Dally.

"Now then, *Fönök,*" Ernö in a confidential voice, pretending to draw Kit to one side, "say that we wanted to buy a submarine . . ."

Quick as that Imi had a little FN Browning in his hand. *"Bocsánat."*

"First of all I am not Basil Zaharoff the well-known merchant of death, and this is not a Zaharoff girl but in fact my wife Euphorbia, yes and we are planning to spend our honeymoon in Constantinople, the British War Office were kind enough to make available to us this accommodation, which is vacant this week owing to Mr. Z. as you already pointed out being elsewhere—"

The *chef de brigade* stuck his head in about then, and all weapons abruptly vanished. "Madame . . . messieurs? We shall be pulling out shortly." He saluted, allowing himself a quizzical stare at everybody.

"You gentlemen'll excuse me for a moment I'm sure," Dally herding them all like chickens out into the corridor.

"We'll be playing a little *kalabriás* in the smoking salon," advised Ernö. "We'd like to resolve this before we reach Porta Orientalis."

"You've got the wrong folks," sang Kit wearily. "Ask around—the chief, the conductors, ask anybody."

"If you have bribed them," Imi pointed out, "we can always pay more than you."

"Not if I'm really Basil Zaharoff," Kit, resisting the urge to wink, ducked away down the corridor. As a logical puzzle, it might not have passed muster at Göttingen, but here it might buy him five minutes, and that was all he needed.

He jumped off Dally's train in time to see his own disappearing down the tracks in the general direction of Paris, France, so it seemed he would be here in—what was the name of this place?—Szeged, for a while.

Years later they would be unable to agree on how they found themselves on the Széchenyi-Tér tramline, fleeing into the heart of the city. Kit knew that this was the sort of story grandfathers told to grandchildren, usually so that there could then be a grandmother's version, more practical and less inclined to grant slack. . . . Which is to say that what Kit recalled was running a perilous evasive action while squads of homicidal Hungarians, notable for their stature and eagerness for gunplay, kept appearing at unexpected moments during the escape—while Dally remembered only shifting quickly into a sturdier pair of boots and packing a few necessities in a satchel, which she threw down to Kit and jumped after onto the tracks with the train already rolling out of the station, and took his hand, and off they went. It wouldn't be till Kiskúnfélegyháza an hour down the line that Imi and Ernö would notice that the young couple were missing.

As they ran across the tracks, their hearts were pounding. They both agreed on that.

Kit as a matter of fact was already on the run. He had been living in Constantinople, tending bar at the Hôtel des Deux Continents, off the Grande Rue over on the European or honkytonk side of the Golden Horn in Pera, long enough almost to've come to believe his life had found its equilibrium at last. Folks out here talked about fate, but for Kit it was a matter of stillness.

It had taken him a while, from Kazakh Upland to Kirghiz Steppe to Caspian Depression, short hops in little steamers along the Anatolian coast, the invisible City ahead of him gripping him ever more surely in its field, as he felt the weight of reverence, of history, the nervous bright edge of revolution, around the final cape and into the Bosphorus, the palaces and small harbors and mosques and ship traffic, beneath the Galata Tower, docking at last at Eminönü.

PERA WAS A CONSUMMATE BORDER TOWN, a little state, a microcosm of the two continents, Greeks, Jews, Syrians, Armenians, Bulgarians, Persians, Germans up to their mischief. Since the dramatic march of the "Army of Freedom" from Salonica to Constantinople to put down the Sultan's threatened counterrevolution, things had been hopping, both at the Pera Palace bar and, on a less exalted level, at the Deux Continents. Though the Committee of Union and Progress had declared itself no longer a secret organization, the intriguing, hasheesh conspiracies and back-alley beatings and murders went on as always.

Ottomanists, nationalists, and pan-Islamics within the C.U.P. struggled for power, and outside it strikers, *komitadji*, socialists, and dozens of other factions each pursued its claim to a piece of the New Turkey. All showed up at the Deux Continents sooner or later.

It being too much to expect arms dealers to ignore this sort of thing, who should Kit find himself concocting a Champagne cocktail for one evening but the distinguished Viktor Mulciber, last seen in an estaminet in Ostend five or six years ago. He was using a different pomade on his hair, one even less subtle, if possible, than before, filling incalculable cubic feet of otherwise-tolerable space with its chemically floral miasma. It became clear that Viktor remembered Kit more as an engineer than a mathematician. "What is it that keeps you here? You like the city? Is it a girl? A Greek bathhouse boy? The local hasheesh?"

"Keep going," Kit shrugged.

"Right now, for engineers, it seems to be a seller's market. Aviation in particular. You have any background in that?"

"Göttingen. Hung around some at Dr. Prandtl's shop at the Applied Mechanics Institute. All pretty theoretical."

"Any aircraft concern in the world would simply hand you a blank check, get down on its knees, and beg in the most humiliating way possible that you name your price."

Well, the man was a drummer, though what he was trying to sell Kit was unclear. "Anybody in particular?"

"Since the air show in Brescia last year, Italy seems to be the place. Pilots like Calderara and Cobianchi are designing their own machines, auto factories and bicycle-makers are getting into the business." He wrote an address on the back of one of his cards. "This is in Turin, a good place to start."

"Mighty kind of you, sir."

"No need to grovel, lad, there's a finder's fee, and it's good for business."

Kit would ordinarily have pocketed and lost the card, and gone on with his life in the City, in oscillation between Europe and Asia, comfortable as a slow flap of wings, except for what happened a few nights later. Headed home after his shift at the Deux Continents, he was passing a *meyhane,* a roomful of drunks and a Gypsy band audible from inside, when suddenly in a burst of resinous smoke a young man came flying through the doorway into Kit's path, nearly knocking him over. After him came three others, two with drawn pistols, one large enough not to need one. Kit had no idea who was who, but by some ancient reflex to do with the odds, which didn't appeal to him much, he drew his Nagant, distracting the trio long enough to allow their target to slip away down a narrow vaulted passage. The two pistol-packers went chasing off after him—the third stood gazing. "We know where you work," he said at last in English. "You have stepped into the wrong argument. Be very careful now."

Next evening somebody picked his pocket. Seriously deranged street apes took to leaping out at him from unsuspected angles. *Politissas* who used to roll their eyes his way found excuses to look elsewhere. One night Jusuf the manager took him aside.

"The man whose life you thought you saved the other night," he said, and made an eloquent gesture of finality. "He was an enemy of the C.U.P. Now you are, too." He handed Kit a wad of Turkish pounds and a train ticket as far as Buda-Pesth. "Best I can do. Would you mind leaving your recipe for the cocktail you invented?"

"'Love in the Shadows of Pera,'" Kit said. "It's just Creme de Menthe and beer." Next thing he knew here he was in Szeged up to the same hollow heroics. Except for Dally, of course.

Not sure who was after them or, in Kit's case, why, they kept on the move till they had found their way past the city limits, along a little irrigation canal, lined with willows and into a paprika field.

"Where were you headed for anyway?" she got around to asking. "Paris? England?"

"Italy," Kit said. "Venice."

In the instant she remembered the promise she'd more or less inveigled him into making year before last sometime, but she didn't quite dare to bring it up now. Seeing how she hadn't exactly waited for him. What'd she been thinking of, leaving Venice? she must've been crazy. He was looking at her as if to say—and then, what do you know, he did say, "You don't remember, I bet."

She pretended to gaze at the paprika fields ripening to a red no match for her hair—or lips, for that matter (it was occurring now to Kit)—and tried to think back to the last time she'd felt so wobbly on her feet. "Course I remember."

They were already too close not to turn and slide into an embrace smooth as the solution to a puzzle. There in the silence before the clamoring weeks of harvest would take over the fields, with the pepper pods stirring audibly in the hot lowland breezes, they found to no one's surprise but their own how far ahead of them their bodies had been, how impatient with the minds that had been keeping them apart.

"If this is a bad idea, I mean, your dress in all this dirt—"

"Oh, it's terrific dirt," she informed him between kisses, "feels good, smells good . . . look at all these peppers here, they love it . . . it'll wash out, why are you even . . . oh, Kit . . ."

Who by now, his pants down and his shoes still on, had entered, and reentered, and so forth, and the cycle, now exclusively theirs, wet, high, and headlong, whirled away from time as other less-urgent lovers might have known it, until presently, calm for the moment, refusing ever to uncouple, they lay in warm semirefuge from the midday sun, in the light and shade between the rows of low plants and the smell of the earth.

When she remembered how to talk, "Where've you been, Siberia or someplace?"

"As a matter of fact . . ."

"Tell me later."

They got as far as a little grove of acacias before they had to start kissing, and presently fucking, again. "Must be all this paprika," Kit speculated.

Then somehow they were back in Szeged and booking into a three-and-a-half-kroner room at the Grand-Hôtel Tisza.

"For young English *újházaspár,*" loudly announced Miklós the desk clerk, ignoring all the agricultural smudges and handing over a pair of tickets, "compliments of this Hotel! Wonderful show tonight at the Varosi Színház! The incomparable Béla Blaskó, our famous actor from Lugos, singing and dancing in a new operetta straight from Vienna! If only you had been here last week to see Béla as Romeo"—producing a local newspaper and opening it to the theater review—"look, they said 'fiery . . . passionately loving . . .' but—no need to tell you two, eh?"

"Well," Kit demurred.

"Oh, c'mon," Dally said mischievously, "it'll be fun."

As it turned out, it was a pretty good show, though they didn't quite catch the whole thing. They did make sure to have an early supper beforehand, just up the riverside promenade from the Színház at the Café-Restaurant Otthon. Instead of a menu, a telepathic waiter named Pityu brought them wine and bread and bowls filled with some miraculous combination of fish, paprika, and green peppers.

"This can't just be soup," she said, "what on earth is it?"

"Halászlé," said Pityu, "only here in Szeged, three kinds of fish, all just pulled out of the river there."

"And you knew—"

"I know everything," he laughed, "or maybe it is nothing, my English gets strange sometimes. But your friends Imi and Ernö have gone back to Buda-Pesth, so you don't have to worry about them at least."

"Then you must know I'm not a Zaharoff girl either," said Dally, exercising her eyelashes.

"My mother, who still lives in Temesvár, would say your destiny is much more demanding than that."

THE OPERETTA, all the rage in Vienna at the moment, was called *The Burgher King,* in which the ruler of a fictional country in Central Europe, feeling disconnected from his people, decides to go out among them disguised as a member of the urban middle class.

"Why not as a peasant, Your Highness? a Gypsy, maybe a laborer?"

"One requires a certain level of comfort, Schleppingsdorff. If one spent one's whole day working and sleeping, there would be no time for observation, let alone thought . . . would there."

Notable among the jolly drinking songs and sentimental love ballads was the rousing waltz which had rapidly become an anthem for Viennese window-shoppers—

Machen wir ein-en Schaufen-sterbum-mel,
Ü-berwerfen sie irgendwas Fum-mel, auf
Straßen und Gassen, lass uns nur lauf-en
Al-les anstarren, aber nichts kauf-en. . . .

On one of these merry show-window strolls, the camouflaged monarch meets and falls in love with a horrible little bourgeoise, Heidi, who of course happens to be married. Royal advisers fly into a panic in the form of a trio, sung *molto agitato.* One of them, Schleppingsdorff, decides to disguise *him*self as well and pretend to romance the soubrette, the H.L.B.'s best friend, Mitzi. Unfortunately, it is Heidi with whom Schleppingsdorff is immediately fascinated, while Mitzi, already obsessed with the Burgher King, goes through the motions of returning Schleppingsdorff's attentions, just so she can be close to the B.K. and pounce at the first sign of trouble, which she tries to bring about by encouraging Schleppingsdorff in his pursuit of Heidi. Meanwhile the comic basso, the husband, Ditters, runs to and fro trying to figure out what his wife is up to, quite soon becoming insane from the effort. It is all great fun.

The first act closed with young Béla Blaskó, playing the Burgher King, wearing a silk hat at a rakish angle and twirling a cane, in front of a corps of dancers and singers performing the peppy

No need for feel-ing so down,
Just spend a night-on-the-town,
That-Dan-ube won't, look-so blue—
not if you do, like I do—
Just get on out-to-the *ucca,*
Take a stroll up—the a-ve-nue,
You'll find that ci-ty beat puts-a
—Synco-pation in-your shoe,
Find-one-of-those
Austro-Hun-gar-i-an ladies,
So super-ficially deep,
Down where the gi-golos creep,
Too full of rhyth-m to sleep,
All-you-need's-a
Good-time girl from the K and K,
Who can't tell you if it's night or day,
And slip away on a cruise, from
Those Austro-Hungarian blues!

Which by the first-act curtain had Dally mesmerized into some peculiar wide-eyed state.

"Ain't like I never saw a charming leading man before, seen 'em come and go, but this lad is the goods, I tell you—and Hungarian, too!"

Kit guessed so. "But what's with that piece of business where he bites old Heidi's neck, what was that all about?"

"Something they do in these parts? You're the one with the college education." Her look just short of what you'd call innocent.

Kit peered back, trying to resist the nitwit smile that was about to take over his face. "Well, hard to say, you know, my Hungarian being a little rusty and all, but . . . didn't it look to you like that she was, sort of . . . going for it?"

"What. Having her neck bitten." Slipping she was sure she didn't know why into her country-weekend mode of English accent.

"Well here, let's just—"

"Kit now what'n 'e hell are you—" But sweeping her hair somehow out of the way and lengthening her bare neck for him. At some point they became aware that the show had resumed, the Burgher King and his associates up to the usual tuneful intrigue.

Kit and Dally were sitting in a box, and nobody seemed to be watching them. She slipped to her knees and began getting rouge and saliva all over his trousers. His fingers were deep in her hair. Their pulsebeats were hammering louder than the music. "This is crazy," whispered Kit.

"Come on," she agreed. They got back to the room with no more than a bellhop's presentation of a bushel of gladioli and the usual garment fastenings to slow them down. For the first time it seemed Kit had a minute to admire her in her full rangy nakedness and glow. But only a minute, because she had run at him, borne him to the bed, straddled and begun to ride him in an extended episode of heat, laughing, cursing, hollering in some language of her own that Kit was too carried away to translate. Presently she had collapsed forward into a long kiss, her undone hair surrounding them in a fiery nimbus.

"Are those freckles? Why are they glowing like that?"

"Paprika flashback," she murmured, and shortly was asleep all naked and wet in his arms.

BEST BET, it seemed to them, was to stay clear of the Szeged station, go up the river by steamer instead as far as Szolnok, catch the local there to Buda-Pesth, and from there take the Wagons-Lits via Lake Balaton to Pragerhof, where they would pick up the Graz-Trieste train and ride second class to Venezia.

That seemed devious enough. But Lake Balaton looked too good to pass up. They detrained at Siófok and were soon reclining in the water, along with hundreds of families on vacation.

"Some headlong escape, here."

"We really ought to be moving faster than this."

"Trainloads of screaming Turks headin up the line."

"Wavin 'em swords and Mausers and so forth." By now they were looking into each other's eyes. Again. There seemed no limit to how long this would go on. The sun set, the little gaff-riggers put in to their home piers, other bathers departed, the *fogások* swam in close to see what was up, and this confounded gazing would just not stop. Somewhere on a terrace, a dance band started playing. Lights came on in the restaurants facing the water, in gardens and hotel rooms, and there Kit and Dally remained until the first star, when, as if reminded of all there was to be wishing for, they found their way back to the ceiling of their room, which is where, in this exuberant elopement, they were tending to spend most of their time.

"SOMEBODY'LL BE OUT LOOKING for you, won't they?" Kit said.

"Not sure. Some would feel a lot easier in their minds if I wasn't ever found, I guess." The sun through the window lit her from behind, as she paced the little room, observing him carefully. Having had too much attention from peculiar quarters, she had learned to be careful about what she told men, while more and less nervously waiting for Kit to start inquiring into her colorful past. He didn't seem to be looking for a fight, but men were like storms in the sea, on you before you saw them coming, and there you'd be, swamped and confounded. She decided to let him in on what she could. Who else had she ever confided in? You trusted people until they betrayed you, but the alternative, trusting nobody ever, turned you into one more Clive Crouchmas, and the world had enough of them already. "Kit, how much do you want to know about what I've been up to?" Had she really just said that?

"How much of it would I understand?"

"A lot of it'd be international high finance."

"Oh. No, uh, functions of a complex variable, nothing like that, I suppose."

"Mostly adding and subtracting, but it does get kind of—"

"You're right, o' course, I'd just get lost. . . ."

"No, listen—" Mentally she held her nose and flexed her toes, and cannonballed straight down into her history with Clive Crouchmas. Kit listened attentively and did not noticeably fly into a jealous frenzy. "I was spying on him for some people," she concluded, "and he found out."

"He's dangerous, then? Your old beau."

"Maybe. I could go back to London, I'm supposed to have a small part in a new show, but right now I'm not sure if I should. Maybe it's better to lay low for a while."

"Thing that's really been on my mind—"

She stopped in her tracks, smooth muscles poised, microscopic golden hairs all along her bare legs alert in the sunlight.

"—is, is what do we do for money till I find some work up in Italy?"

"Oh. We're all right for money. Don't even worry that darlin brain." But fair being fair, she did give him maybe a minute and a half to say something unpleasant like "*His* money," or "What did you have to do for it?" before tiptoeing purposefully over to where he sat, and taking him by two handfuls of his hair, and bringing his mercifully silent face to the fragrance of her pussy.

The light didn't come in exactly the way it was supposed to in churches—not mediated by sacred images of stained glass but by new leafage on trees outside, holes broken in the adobe by federal artillery, accidentally passing shadows of birds and clouds. It was Holy Week in the Sierra, still freezing at night but tolerable during the day. Sometimes a breeze off the mountain came through. This part of Chihuahua was safe for the time being. Though the federales had driven off Madero's force at Casas Grandes, they had no appetite for fighting in the open and remained for the moment in their garrisons.

Nearly every day somebody from the recent battle died here. Wounded lay in ragged rows on the ancient tile floor, the priest and the doctor passed among them once a day, women from town came when they could—when there was not a child to see to, a *novio* to be with or bid good-bye, a family death to mourn—and tried to clean wounds and change bandages, though sterile dressings on this side of the border were luxury items.

One day Frank woke from a dream of running, running without effort or pain at a speed not even horses got up to, not pursued or in pursuit, just running for the hell of it, the heaven of how it felt, he guessed. As long as he kept moving forward this way, easy, weightless, he knew somehow he could never be in trouble of any kind. Ahead of him there seemed to lie a concentration of light, something like a city after dark, and he wondered what it might be. At the rate he was running, he ought to be there before long. But all at once he was back on the floor of the cold, broken church, immobilized and hungry, among the smells of casualty and dying, with a face he was about to recognize bending close, in its mouth, being lit, then held out to Frank, a store-bought Mexican cigarette.

"I saw them bring you in." It was the Indian shaman El Espinero, who had once showed him how to fly.

"Well *¿qué tal, amigo?*" Frank took the cigarette and inhaled on it as deep as he could given the situation with his ribs, at least one of which had to be cracked.

The *brujo* nodded and lit one up for himself. "You think you are dreaming, *¿verdad?* No, as it happens, my village is just up there," he motioned with his eyes back up at the mountains. "I was in Durango for a little while, but now I am here, scouting for Don José de la Luz Blanco." He took a quick inventory of Frank's damage. "You were with him and Madero at the fighting."

"Yes. I should've been someplace else."

"But you will recover. Only one bullet."

"One more than I needed. The rest was falling off the horse, and underneath the other horse, and so on."

"The Chihuahua horses are the best in the world, but they know it well, and a man on the ground means little to them, unless he is Tarahumare. They respect us because we can run faster."

"This horse was kind enough to drag me as far as an irrigation ditch anyhow. . . ." Frank exhaled smoke into a momentary sunbeam, and the *brujo* watched it vanish with patient interest.

"Somebody is looking for you."

"Should I be jumping up and getting the hell out of here?"

El Espinero laughed. "Yes, I think so. It is your other Estrella."

"She's here?"

Yeahp and on the arm of some impossibly good-looking Mexican dude. No surprise. Frank wished he could go back to sleep.

"This is Rodrigo."

"Mucho gusto," Frank nodded. Well she wasn't about to be traveling alone all her life was she, besides being, have mercy, even more beautiful now than, what would it be, two years ago, closer to three, sun in her face and hair, a confidence in how she carried herself, no more little dainty .22 beneath some ladylike frock but a serviceable Colt strapped to one of a pair of, he could not help noticing, interesting legs in britches of trail-grade whipcord.

Old Rodrigo here was looking down at Frank with a certain disdain, perhaps that of a Mexican of the land-owning class for a gringo saddle-tramp who has allowed himself to be stepped on by one or more horses, so the situation was not what you'd call uncompetitive. Not that Frank could blame him, much.

"Pretty becoming rig you're in there, Estrella, but where'd all that high fashion get to?"

"Oh it and me we got to a fork in the trail, it's all that straight silhouette these days, wisdom of the seamstress trade, sad but true, can't put no ol' cowgirl into nothin that narrow, she starts trying to take what she thinks is normal-size steps, and just wrecks the stitches somebody spent all night puttin in."

"And how's business been?"

"I'm more of a diplomat these days," gesturing lazily with her head at Rodrigo. "Madero's people seem to have mistook this one for his look-alike, some federal big shot. Truth is he just wandered up the wrong piece of trail. So now we're all dickering."

"Prisoner exchange. How does 'at pay, good?"

"Sometimes." Making an effort, he noticed, not to let Rodrigo catch her eye. Did she think Frank would mind if it wasn't all strictly business? And how much, and so forth.

"What're you smoking these days?"

"Store-boughts. Here, keep the pack."

Frank drifted off and when he drifted back, everybody had left including El Espinero. Stray had put the cigarettes under the rolled-up shirt he was using for a pillow to keep them safe, which seemed such a tender thought he wished he'd been awake for it.

NEXT DAY SHE SHOWED UP AGAIN, and it took Frank about a minute to identify her new companion, owing to a beard and a growth of hair his sombrero was having trouble staying on top of. "This raggedy excuse for an Anarchistic troublemaker says he knows you."

"By God it's 'at there Ewball Oust ain't it," said Frank. "Don't tell me you—"

"Yeahp, swapped him for Rodrigo, who's now on his way back to the family mansion in Texas. Another one out of my reach. *Adiós, mi guapo—*" She shrugged and pretended to look sad. "Frank, tell me I got a bargain here."

"Well, give me a minute."

"Thought you was wounded or someth'n *compinche,* this don't look much worse'n foot blisters." Ewball had somehow managed to keep a tin canteen of tequila away from federal attention, and cheerfully poured *copas* for everybody.

Stray regarded Ewball, shaking her head and pretending to sigh in dismay. "Maybe I'll get back into arms dealin after all."

"Footsoldiers like me are a dime a dozen," Ewball agreed cheerfully. "But for matériel you're sure in the right part of the world, here. Artillery, just for openers. *Federales* are hitting us with howitzers, machine guns, time shrapnel, best we can do is throw dynamite sticks and trust in the Lord."

"I could look around. How big of a piece are we talkin?"

"Caliber wouldn't be as important as mobility, we need something's easy to break down and pack around on mules, like you heard of that Krupp mountain gun, somethin along those lines'd be nice."

She was taking notes. "Uh-huh, what else?"

"Disinfectant," Frank put in, a little feverish today, "as many tank cars of that as you can find. Plus pain medicine, any kind, laudanum, paregoric, hell, anythin's got opium in it, damn country's in way too much pain."

"Tobacco," Ewball added.

After a while they got into a discussion about Anarchists and their reputation for rude behavior, such as rolling bombs at people they haven't been introduced to.

"There's plenty of folks who deserve being blown up, to be sure," opined Ewball, "but they've got to be gone after in a professional way, anything else is being just like them, slaughterin the innocent, when what we need is more slaughterin of the guilty. Who gave the orders, who carried 'em out, exact names and whereabouts—and then go get 'em. That'd be just honest soldiering."

"Don't they call that nihilism?" Stray objected.

"'Cute, ain't it? when all the real nihilists are working for the owners, 'cause it's them that don't believe in shit, our dead to them are nothin but dead, just one more Bloody Shirt to wave at us, keep us doin what they want, but our dead never stopped belongin to us, they haunt us every day, don't you see, and we got to stay true, they wouldn't forgive us if we wandered off of the trail."

Frank hadn't seen Ewball like this, it was more than drunk tearfulness, Ewb had been out in this, maybe longer than he thought he'd stay alive for, and over the years had gathered up, Frank guessed, a considerable number of dead he now felt were his. Not quite the same as Frank's two-second interlude with Sloat Fresno back down the Bolsón de Mapimí five, no, six years ago. How much had Frank advanced since then? Deuce Kindred was still out there, maybe still with Lake, maybe, by now, not.

Next evening Frank woke up into some long dissertation Ewball was handing Stray about Anarcho-syndicalist theory and praxis to feel a strangely familiar melancholy in the twilight that he couldn't for a minute locate, till down the aisle between the wounded, her small face warmly illuminated by a cigarette in her mouth, came his favorite back-east girl anthropologist, Wren Provenance.

"Knew I should've went easy on the laudanum tonight," he greeted her.

Wren was wearing trooper's boots, campesino trousers, a man's shirt a few sizes too large with some buttons missing, and nothing in the way of underlinen to veil from the casual onlooker's gaze her flawless little breasts, though Ewball and Frank, attempting to be gentlemen about it, were trying not to stare, or at least not for too long at any one time.

She had been up at Casas Grandes, the archæological site just down the road from the recent battle of the same name, under semi-official Harvard auspices, studying the mysterious ruins thought to have been built by refugees fleeing from their mythical homeland of Aztlán up north.

"Thought you were headed for the South Seas," Frank said.

"Just not romantic enough there, I guess."

When Madero and his small army had arrived here, one by one all her male co-workers, some apologizing over their shoulders, had fled to avoid being shot.

Stray had been looking her over, with some interest. "Why didn't you leave?" she wondered.

"Oh, too busy probably. Loud noises, flashes of light, no worse than bad weather, one more field condition to work under—and work's the thing really."

"Really. But what are you doing for a social life, if I'm not being too curious?"

"As the day may provide," Wren shrugged, "or not provide. Right now, actually, sleep has emerged as the most important issue."

"Known to do that, I guess, 'emerge.' Nice Indian bracelet there."

"Jasper and turquoise. One of the classic Zuñi designs."

"Hmm. How much'd you pay?"

"It was a gift."

"Travelin man."

"What makes you think so?"

"Indians at every train depot west of Denver sell these."

"Why that two-timing double-crossing snake. He made me feel like it was so— I don't know, special."

"They're all like 'at, darlin. Even ol' Frank here."

"Frank, shame on you too, then."

The ladies were having a swell time. After a while Frank found himself chain-smoking Stray's Buen Tonos and trying not to cringe too noticeably. His ribs were throbbing and he figured he better not laugh too much either, though the way things were drifting, this was not fixing to be a problem.

In came a campesino with a message for Stray. She stood, took her field portfolio and slung it by a strap over her shoulder. "Dealin never stops. Ewball, you better not go too far, Don Porfirio's boys might want you back after all."

When he thought she was out of earshot, Ewball said, "I think she likes me."

"Well you're a handsome devil but you sure ain't no Rodrigo," it seemed to Frank.

"You don't mind do you compadre, I mean seein's how it is with you and ol' Wren here—"

"You may have things a little backwards," Wren through a fixed smile, eyes aglitter. "But thanks all the same, Ewball, it is just ever such a boost to a maiden's self-esteem to find that she is keeping apart two people who ought to be together, for whom indeed, by every anthropological principle we know to be valid, it is an unnatural violation of scientific reality *not* to be together. Tell me, Frank, are you stupid, or blind?"

"That's the choice, huh. . . . Let me think."

Ewball waved a beer bottle at Wren. "Answer is 'stupid.' Always has been. Care for another cerveza, there, *tetas de muñeca?*"

"Why yes, that would be so thoughtful of you, there, *pinga de títere.*"

"Uh-oh," said Ewball and Frank in unison.

"SAY, REMEMBER those little cactuses?"

El Espinero had been sitting there in the dark for some time, beaming at Frank, eyeballs somehow reflecting more light than was available. "I apologize for waiting until you ask. But the *hikuli* is not for everyone."

Had he brought any along? Does the Easter Rabbit bring colored eggs? Before too long, Frank found himself in a strange yet familiar City, an outer arc of low warehouses up at the ridgeline, dropping down to a grid of wide boulevards and canals and open plaza spaces, down one of which now comes strolling, among the folks on pilgrimage here streaming in and out of town, an apprentice practitioner who seems to be Frank himself, as he used to be, before the Broken Days came upon the land and the people, bearing a small leather pouch containing the sacred Scrolls entrusted to him the day he left the pigs snuffling in the dust, his mother whispering, as she handed the bag to him, before he turned and went away down the path, looking back once, perhaps again, as his sisters at early chores dwindled among the green hillsides, soon hearing someone playing a reed instrument whose wood simplicity touches his heart, finding a mule train headed up here to the City, the line of beasts beginning slowly to switchback up the range in the yellow sun, which warms and releases the keen smell of bruised cilantro in bales, and strings of chilies destined for clay pots to be set out on long common tables in the basements of the City's Temples, beneath low, rough-joisted ceilings, shadowed in dark brown, smelling of musk-scented hay tracked in from the lavish pens of the Sacred Peccaries—the string of mules on this uphill journey bearing also maguey stems just harvested by the *tlachiqueros,* and glossy swamp-beaver hides flashing darkly from beneath canvas tie-downs, to be traded for velvet, gold and silver brocades, giant feathers from very yellow, red, and green parrots, enormous parrots whose wingspreads darken the sun, each feather of but a single color, plucked far away at great personal risk, in a precariousness of stone and windy space, from beneath the birds' wings as they soar past deploying claws the size of ceremonial lances, in fact the same feathers as those gathered for the glory of that inner circle of the priesthood known as the Hallucinati, who enjoy strolling out in groups in the evenings to impress visitors from the outer districts, or like "Frank" here, up from the lowlands and beyond, who come flocking in to town just to gaze upon the promenading hierarchy and their female attendants who have spent hours on eye adornment, parrot-patterning their orbits in bright yellow with red stripes and green crescents, with their hair drawn back from sweetly convex child-brows, sacred girls, some of them beauties celebrated enough to provoke discussion during mule-train coca breaks, for coffee is not the only stimulant found among these caravans, where everyone moves and talks at high speed and, like the mysterious Capital they are bound for, avoids sleeping or even catnapping—they look forward to some *paseo* time after the factors have taken delivery, to going out at any hour they like and finding it impossible to know if it's even day or night, the City itself being entirely indoors and nobody but the most senior Astrologers even being allowed to view the sky. Cafés are open on every street corner, ceremonial maidens gathered between shifts, dozens to a table, temple gongs and bells contributing their timbres and rhythms to the urban bustle. "Frank" wanders through it all, enchanted with everything, stalls selling mangoes and star fruit, agave fermenting in terra-cotta bowls, *ristras* of dark purple chilies strung to dry, pearly green aromatic seeds being crushed in heavy stone mortars, death's-heads and skeletons of raw sugar which children come running up to buy with obsidian coins bearing likenesses of notable Hallucinati, and run off crunching the sweet splintery bones which the dim light in here passes through as through amber, stalls hung all over with brightly-colored pamphlets, illustrated, in no inferable arrangement, with narrative caricatures erotic and murderous, hand-tinted heliographs in luminescent violets and saffrons and coal blacks, veined with rust and damp green. . . . He begins to read, or no not exactly read one of these stories. . . . It is the tale of The Journey from Aztlán, and presently he is not so much reading as engaged in a confab with one of the high priests, finding out this is a city not yet come fully into being, but right now really just a pausing point of monochrome adobe, for this gaudy, bright city they hope to find someday, Frank sees, is being collectively dreamed by the community in their flight, at their backs a terror not of the earth they thought they knew and respected, ahead of them, somewhere, a sign to tell them they have truly escaped, have found their better destiny, in which the eagle would conquer the serpent, the trespassers, content with what they had seized and occupied of Aztlán, would give up the pursuit and continue with their own metamorphosis into winged extraterrestrials or evil demigods or gringos, while the fugitive people would be spared the dark necessity of buying safety by tearing out the hearts of sacrificial virgins on top of pyramids and so forth.

At some point he performed a manœuvre like a bird circling and landing, except in mental space. Standing there against the light seemed to be Wren, offering him the exact same periodical. "Brought a little light reading for you." The text was in no alphabet he'd ever seen, and he ended up looking at the pictures, erotic and murderous as ever, illustrating the adventures of a young woman who was called upon repeatedly to defend her people against misshapen invaders who preferred to fight from the shadows, and were never clearly shown.

Soon over his shoulder he noticed El Espinero following along attentively. Finally, "Here, you take it."

"No, it's meant for you. So you don't forget where you were just now."

"Since you mention it—" but a sort of temporal stupor intervened and the *brujo* had vanished. The "magazine" was now a Mexico City newspaper in black and white from a few days ago, and there was nothing in it about Casas Grandes, or the battle there.

Stray had grown increasingly fascinated with Ewball, even though, as she reminded him every chance she got, he wasn't really her type. Having been successfully swapped for Rodrigo, whose family in gratitude had been more than generous about Stray's fee, there was no real reason for Ewball to be hanging around here with important Anarchist business, she was sure, to claim him elsewhere. "Oh I don't know," he mumbled, "sort of vacation I guess. The Revolution's doing fine on its own, anyway."

One day they both disappeared, and come to find out damn if they hadn't taken off together on the Juárez train amid public displays of affection. And who had chosen to linger here instead but Wren Provenance, who, like a mother with a small baby, got to see Frank stand on his feet and take his first steps, who went with him for walks that took them farther and farther from the wrecked church, till one day what was clear to everybody else came to pass and they found themselves down some little arroyo under the willows and cottonwoods enthusiastically fucking, while a variety of wildlife looked on with interest. "Like this," slipping out of her trousers and straddling him, "Don't look so shocked, it's me, remember?" hands in each other's hair, hands everywhere, come to that, kisses, and when had they kissed so hungrily before? bites, nails, heedless words maybe, neither could remember.

"Well how'd that happen?"

She gave him a look. Her impulse was to say, "Don't ask me, it never happens to me, fact I tend to forget about it for long stretches . . ." which of course is how the monologue would go hours later, alone with her thoughts. But at the moment she refrained from sharing any of this with Frank.

"Well," a minute or two away from broodful, "long as it don't get filed under good works or somethin like that."

"Frank." She had been lying with her face against his chest but now pushed upright again, as if to have a good look at him. And she could not, would not keep from smiling. "I'm beginning to think that that Ewball was right about you. Haven't been taking your daily stupidity pills, have you."

"All right." Pulled her back down where she'd been. "All right."

THE HARSH HUM filled the valley. Everybody looked up. The biplane slowly became visible, as if emerging from the resolute blankness of history. "Now what in 'e hell's that?" Frank wondered. Though this was the first time it had come up this way, the Tarahumares appeared to know what it was. It might be bringing anything, to a degree of unpleasantness unknown so far in modern warfare, which was already unpleasant enough. Townsfolk would reckon events for years to come as occurring before or after the airplane came.

EL ESPINERO BROUGHT FRANK a cane shaped from a nice piece of oak from farther up in the Sierra, "A gringo might call it a 'walking stick,' but the Tarahumare use these as *running-sticks,* when our legs get sore and we can't run any faster than a galloping horse." As usual Frank couldn't tell how serious he ought to take that. But there must've been some sorcery in the stick, all right, because the more Frank used it, the less he had to use it.

"What does that mean?" said Wren.

"Native magic makes you nervous, huh? Some anthropologist you turn out to be."

When she was sure he was able to sit a horse again, she took hold of him by his shirt front and said, "Look, I'm going to have to go back to work."

"Back at Casas Grandes."

"Think I've spotted one or two of the old crew back in the vicinity."

"Mind if I ride along?"

"Didn't know you were interested."

The site still bore the signs of abrupt departure, though as Wren had suggested, one or two Harvard halfwits were to be observed nosing around the perimeter. Seeing the spectacle of mud dilapidation, sliding toward abandonment since long before the first Spaniards showed up, Frank understood immediately that this was where the *hikuli* had taken him the other night, what El Espinero had wanted him to see—what, in his morose and case-hardened immunity to anything extraliteral, he had to begin to see, and remember he saw, if he was to have even an outside chance of saving his soul.

They approached a huge remnant, clearly put together as right-angled as anybody could ask for. "This was the main building," she said.

"Well. *Casas grandes,* for sure. I'd say about four and a half acres here, just by eye."

"And at least three stories high when it was new. Some of the others ran five or six."

"And these were the same folks—"

"You can see how thick the walls are. They were not about to be caught twice."

"But if it was them ended up in the Valley of Mexico, then this was a stopover and didn't last either."

"Nobody knows. And at the moment I'm also very curious about these Mormon settlements suddenly appearing all over this part of the Sierra Madre."

"Just like back at the McElmo," Frank said.

"A professorial person," she supposed, "would ask at least why the Mormon odyssey and the Aztec flight should have so many points in common." She did not appear pleased at the thought.

"Maybe I'll talk to El Espinero. What about those pictures—have you found any of them here?"

She knew which pictures. "Pottery, stone tools, corn grinders, no sign of the creatures they drew on the rock walls up north—so absent in fact that it's suspicious. As if it's deliberate. As if they're almost desperate to deny what's pursuing them by not making any images of it at all. So it ends up being everywhere, but invisible."

He understood for a moment, as if in the breeze from an undefined wing passing his face, that the history of all this terrible continent, clear to the Pacific Ocean and the Arctic ice, was this same history of exile and migration, the white man moving in on the Indian, the eastern corporations moving in on the white man, and their incursions with drills and dynamite into the deep seams of the sacred mountains, the sacred land.

WREN HAD A LITTLE HOUSE at the edge of town with a vegetable patch and scarlet madreselva climbing up the walls and a nice view off the ridge, with the Casas Grandes ruins an easy mile or so down the road. Frank spent the days out and about doing odd jobs, some carpentering and plastering, repair work from the fighting mostly, and the nights in bed with Wren, as honorably as he knew how to inhabit the joys of domestic fucking. Sometimes he searched her sleeping face, so obliged to sorrows older than itself, wishing he knew what it would take for him to set up a perimeter she might at least dream quietly inside of, because she sure was making a lot of noise at night. All he'd ever known how to do really, like Webb and Mayva before him, was move from one disappointment to another, dealing with each as best he could. Wren was on her own trail, and he was afraid that at some point she would scout too far forward, through a canyon or across a stream invisible to everybody else, and pass into the cruel country of the invaders, the people with wings, the serpents who spoke, the poisonous lizards who never lost a fight. Where she would come to no supernally-lighted city but instead into a merciless occupation, lives of slavery only barely, contemptuously disguised, which eventually would gather in her own as well. He knew that in her unspoken story of long pilgrimage and struggle he only happened to be on the same piece of trail for the moment. Understanding that she wished to protect him against whatever lay at its grim destination, he felt a queer twinge of gratitude.

These apprehensions, fugitive and as hard to recover as dreams, were confirmed by El Espinero, with whom Frank would visit now and then up at Temósachic, where the *brujo* took him out to gather herbs whose names he forgot as soon as he heard them, as if they were protecting themselves against future gringo mischief, and when the season turned, the husband of Estrella taught him to stalk antelope Tarahumare fashion, while rigged out in an antelope skin, and whenever they came in eyeball range of each other, Estrella looked through, past and around him as if he were invisible, which after a while he understood he was.

"Except," advised El Espinero, "not to the young lady Wren. She will see you no matter what."

"Even if we—"

"You will not be together for long. You know that already. But she will always see you. I have read the thorns, that is what they say." They watched a couple of giant woodpeckers systematically eating a tree.

"The professors she works for return in September to the other side," Frank said, "and soon after that the work is finished for the year. I can't see ahead anymore. I should be warning her about something, keeping her safe from it, but—"

El Espinero smiled. "She is your child?"

"How can I just—"

"I looked also at the thorns of your life, Panchito. You walk very different paths. Yours is not as strange as hers, maybe." Frank knew that whenever the *brujo* spoke to a white person of "paths," he was thinking not too kindly of the railway, which like most of his people he hated for its destruction of the land, and what had once grown and lived there. Frank respected this—who at some point hadn't come to hate the railroad? It penetrated, it broke apart cities and wild herds and watersheds, it created economic panics and armies of jobless men and women, and generations of hard, bleak city-dwellers with no principles who ruled with unchecked power, it took away everything indiscriminately, to be sold, to be slaughtered, to be led beyond the reach of love.

Wren got on the Juárez train one day in late October. Frank had thought of riding with her at least as far as San Pedro Junction anyway, but when the moment came he found he couldn't.

"I'll say hello to the girls on Market Street," she said, and though their kiss went on for what could have been hours, so little did it have to do with clock time, she was already miles away down those rails before their lips even touched.

Reef, Yashmeen, and Cyprian, having passed a few profitable weeks at Biarritz and Pau before the seasonal lull as English tourists gave way to those from the Continent, returning now eastward to the casinos of the Riviera, wandered across the Anarchist spa of Yz-les-Bains, hidden near the foothills of the Pyrenees, among steep hillsides covered with late-ripening vines, whose shoots were kept away from the early frosts by supports that looked like garlanded crucifixes. White columns and shadowed archways emerged from the mists of a cheerfully noisy *gave* a short distance up the valley, beyond which lay the trail-head of a secret and secure route into and out of Spain. Veterans of the Cataluñan struggle, former residents of Montjuich, hasheesh devotees enroute to Tangier, refugees from as far away as the U.S. and Russia, all could find lodging at this venerable oasis without charge, though in practice even those against the commoditizing of human shelter were often able to come up with modest sums in a dozen currencies, and leave them with Lucien the concierge.

In town, in an elliptical plaza, opening out unexpectedly, into afternoon sun and long shadows, dozens of small groups had set up camp, like bathers at the seaside, with coffee messes, cooking fires, bedrolls, flowers in flowerpots, awnings and tents. It might have reminded Reef of a mining camp early in the history of a silver strike, except that these solemn young folks carried with them an austerity, a penultimacy before some unstated future, a Single Idea, whose power everything else ran off of. Here it was not silver or gold but something else. Reef could not quite see what it was.

Grouped near one of the foci of the ellipse, a choir was practicing a sort of counter–Te Deum, more *desperamus* than *laudamus,* bringing news of coming dark and cold. Reef thought he recognized faces from the tunnels, as did

Yashmeen from the Chunxton Crescent days, and Cyprian, after a moment of blankness, was amazed to discover who but old Ratty McHugh, with a beard, apparently his own, sandals, and a local goat-herder's cap.

"Ratty?"

"Around here I'm 'Reg.'" What Cyprian remarked more than any change of turnout was the radiance of an awakened spirit which Ratty, free unarguably now from the rigid mask of his old office self, was still learning how to keep contained. "I'm not in disguise, no, no this is who I really am—the government career, all that's over for me, your fault, Cyprian really. The way you dealt with Theign was an inspiration to so many of us—sudden personnel vacuums all over Whitehall, amounting in some shops to mass desertion. Unless you have worked there you can have no idea of the joy in being released from it at last. I felt as though I were on ice skates, simply glided in one morning, through the Director's door which queerly I don't even recall opening first, broke into a meeting, said my ta-tas, kissed the typewriter lass on my way out, and damned if she didn't kiss me back, put down what she was doing, and come along with me. Just let it all go. Sophrosyne Hawkes, lovely girl—there she is, over there."

"And that young woman with the familiar face she's talking to, isn't that—"

Ratty beamed. "It is indeed Mrs. McHugh, the old dutch herself, who will be delighted to see you again. Do you need any help meanwhile getting your eyebrows down out of your hat?"

"Yes really Cyprian," said Yashmeen, "you of all people."

"I wasn't—"

"Bit of luck really," Ratty said, "nothing I arranged or even deserved. Came home that night with old Sophrosyne, expecting a bloodbath, and the two of them just hit it right off. Mysteries of womanhood. We were up all night telling our deepest—well, deep*er* secrets, and it turned out that all along, since before we married, actually, Jenny had been at work as a sort of crypto-suffragette—whenever she went out to 'visit her mother,' the two of them were actually at rallies or loudly insulting government ministers or smashing up shop windows or something."

"Why didn't you tell me earlier?" Ratty had asked.

"Your post, dear Reginald. It wouldn't have done, really, I mean every so often we do attack Whitehall, don't we?"

"All moot now isn't it, my pickled onion. You may go and hammer away at your pleasure, though one might suggest some treacle-and-brown-paper arrangement such as burglars use, to avoid injury from broken glass don't you know. . . ."

"And you wouldn't mind if I went to prison as well, oh just for a little bit?"

"Of course I should mind, ever so frightfully my own plasmon biscuit, but I shall try somehow to bear it," and so on at quite nauseating length.

By the time Jenny was out of Holloway and sporting the brooch of honor designed by Sylvia Pankhurst for veterans of residence in that dismal place, Ratty, having tracked rumors and attended to messages he previously would have either ignored or dismissed as supernatural claptrap, had found his way to a secret path which would eventually lead the cheerful ménage here to the hidden lands of Yz-les-Bains and beyond.

"So these days you're working for . . . ?"

Ratty shrugged. "You see us. We work for one another, I suppose. No ranks, no titles, chain of command . . . no structure, really."

"How do you plan things?" Yashmeen was curious to know, "assign duties? Coördinate your efforts, that sort of thing?"

"By knowing what has to be done. Which is usually obvious common sense."

"Sounds like John McTaggart Ellis McTaggart all over again," she muttered.

"The senior combination-room of a college without a master," Ratty recalled. "Hmm. Well perhaps not exactly *that.*"

"And when you folks are out on the job—what do you pack generally?" is what Reef wanted to know.

"Catch as catch can," supposed Ratty, "anything from a little antique pinfire pistol to the very latest Hotchkiss. Talk to Jenny, actually, she's more militant than I've ever been, and an even better shot now than she was as a girl."

"And sometimes," the hopefulness in Reef's voice obvious to all, "you'll also . . . blow something up?"

"Not often. We've chosen more of a coevolutionary role, helping along what's already in progress."

"Which is what, again?"

"The replacement of governments by other, more practical arrangements," Ratty replied, "some in existence, others beginning to emerge, when possible working across national boundaries."

"Like the I.W.W.," Reef recalled vaguely from some argument back down the trail.

"And the T.W.I.T. I suppose," said Yashmeen.

"Feelings differ as to the T.W.I.T.," said Jennifer Invert McHugh, who had joined them. "So many of these mystical fellowships end up as creatures of their host governments."

"All the while preaching nonattachment," Yashmeen agreed.

"Then you have been . . ."

"In it but not of it. I hope."

"Surprising how many ex-T.W.I.T. one keeps running into."

"The high rate of personal betrayal," Yashmeen imagined.

"Oh dear."

"One recovers. But thank you for your concern."

"A legacy, one finds, of these ancient all-male structures. Blighted the hopes of Anarchism for years, I can tell you—as long as women were not welcome, it never had a chance. In some communities, often quite famous examples, what appeared to be unguided and perfect consensus, some miracle of social telepathy, was in fact the result of a single male authority behind the scenes giving out orders, and a membership willing to comply—all agreeing to work in silence and invisibility to preserve their Anarchist fiction. Only after the passage of years, the death of the leader, would the truth come out."

"And therefore . . . ?"

"It did not exist. Could not, not with that sort of patriarchal rubbish."

"But with women in the equation . . ." Yashmeen prompted.

"It depends. If a woman's only there under the romantic spell of some bearded good-for-nothing then it might as well be croquettes in the kitchen as bombs in the basement."

"But—"

"But if she's able to think critically," Sophrosyne said, "keep men busy where they'll do the most good, even if men don't know half the time where that is. Then there's a chance."

"As long as men can let go of that old we-know-what's-best illusion," Ratty said, "just leave it out there for the dustman."

"Dustwoman," said Jenny, Sophrosyne and Yashmeen more or less at the same time.

THE NEXT DAY Reef, Cyprian, and Ratty were out on the Anarchists' golf course, during a round of Anarchists' Golf, a craze currently sweeping the civilized world, in which there was no fixed sequence—in fact, no fixed *number*—of holes, with distances flexible as well, some holes being only putter-distance apart, others uncounted hundreds of yards and requiring a map and compass to locate. Many players had been known to come there at night and dig new ones. Parties were likely to ask, "Do you mind if we *don't* play through?" then just go and whack balls at any time and in any direction they liked. Folks were constantly being beaned by approach shots barreling in from unexpected quarters. "This is kind of fun," Reef said, as an ancient brambled guttie went whizzing by, centimeters from his ear.

"It's like this," Ratty had been trying to explain, "we've recently obtained a map that's causing us all a good deal of concern."

"'Obtained,'" Cyprian wondered.

"From some people in Tangier, who would probably feel I've already told you too much—"

"Were it not . . ." Cyprian suggested.

Ratty found his ball, well in the rough. "Oh, they're still alive. Somewhere. We hope so, anyway." He addressed and readdressed the ball from several directions. "Bit like snooker, isn't it? I believe I'll try for that one over there," waving at a distant flag. "You don't mind the stroll, do you?"

"Well what's it a map of?" Reef squinting at the scorecard, which he had innocently volunteered to keep, but had lost all sense of how to fill in, three, or possibly that was six, holes ago.

"Purportedly? the 'Belgian Congo,'" Ratty observing his ball slicing away toward quite another green from the one he'd chosen. "But it's in code, it's really the Balkan Peninsula, you see, we've learned the transform that far at least—one references this dossier of two-dimensional map-shapes, which are invariant, and wordlessly familiar as a human face. They are also common in dreams, as you may have noticed."

"So . . . given a shape broader in the north, tapering to the south . . ."

"Right."

"It could be Bosnia," said Cyprian.

"South Texas," said Reef.

"Then beyond the simple geography, there's the quite intolerable tyranny over people to whom the land really belongs, land which, generation after generation, has been absorbing their labor, accepting the corpses this labor produces, along with obscene profits, which it is left to other and usually whiter men to gather."

"Austrians," Cyprian said.

"Most likely. The rail lines come into it as well, it's all like reading ancient Tibetan or something. . . ."

Later in the evening, owls known here as "hooting cats" went calling up and down the little valley. Toward midnight, the waterfall grew louder. Windows one by one went dark all over Yz-les-Bains. In Coombs De Bottle's rooms the air grew opaque with tobacco smoke.

Coombs had known since quite early on the job that his days with the War Office were numbered and few. The moment he became aware of the statistics on self-inflicted Anarchist bomb casualties, and began to contemplate an effort to reach out to the community of bombers and instruct them in Bomb-Building Safety, a certain conflict of interest became obvious to everyone at the War Office lab except for Coombs himself.

"But these are British Anarchists," he tried to argue, "not as if they were Italian, or Spanish, is it."

"Clever appeal to British racialism," Coombs said now, "but it didn't work, that's how determined they were to sack me."

If this was a map, it was like none Cyprian had ever seen. Instead of place-names there were hundreds of what looked like short messages. Everything reproduced in just one color, violet, but cross-hatched differently for different areas. Small pictures, almost newspaper-cartoon drawings, of intricate situations Cyprian felt it was important to understand but couldn't. There were no landmarks or roads he knew, either.

Coombs De Bottle turned up the lamp and held the map at a different angle to the light. "You'll note a bold horizontal line, along which certain disagreeable events, attributed to 'Germany,' are scheduled to occur, unless someone can prevent them. And here, you see these short darkened segments—"

"Land mines," said Reef.

"Probably. Good. How could you tell?"

"All these little lopsided circles," Reef gesturing with his cigar ash. "Like what the artillery boys call their 'ellipse of uncertainty.' Might be like that each one of these is showing direction and range on what damage they expect."

"That's why we think it may refer to poison gas."

Reef whistled. "So these'd likely be pointing downwind."

"Where did this map come from?" asked Yashmeen.

"Ultimately, from Renfrew," said Ratty, "by way of another former student, who'd received it from another, and so on. One more of these trans-national plexuses—by now Renfrew's web extends around the planet, and other planets as well, shouldn't wonder."

"The difficulty with these gas schemes," said Coombs, "is that one sows these sinister fields and then, oddly often, forgets. An advance turns into a retreat, and in the course of falling back one then may be quite classically hoist by one's own petard. This one is also somewhat vague as to operational mode. Remotely operated? Electrical? triggered by the weight of a tank or a human foot? launched into the altitudes like skyrockets, where they then burst in silent invisible clouds?"

Cyprian had been closely scanning the map with a Coddington lens. "Here then, the line-segment of interest seems to be labeled 'Critical Line'—Yashmeen, isn't that Riemann talk?"

She looked. "Except that this one's horizontal, and drawn on a grid of latitude and longitude, instead of real against imaginary values—where Riemann said that all the zeroes of the ζ-function will be found."

Cyprian happened then to be watching her face just as she said not "would" but "will," and noted the innocent expression of faith—there was no other word for it, was there?—eyes for the rare moment as unnarrowed as they would ever be, lips vulnerably apart, that saint-in-a-painting look he usually saw only while she was being seen to by Reef. The Zeta function might be inaccessible to her now as a former lover. He would never understand the blessed thing, yet it had had the extraordinary capacity to claim her mind, her energies, a good part of her life. She saw him looking, and her eyes tightened again. But the deed had been done on his heart, and for the hour he did not see how he could ever live without her.

He turned back to his scrutiny of the map. After a bit, "Here's another odd sort of note, in very small italic print. 'Having failed to learn the lessons of that now mythical time—that pleasures would have to be paid for in later years again and again, by confronting situations like the present one, by negotiating in damaged coin bearing imperial faces too worn to be expressive of any fineness of emotion—thus has the Belgian Congo descended into its destiny.'"

"What," Reef asked pleasantly, "doesthat*mean?*"

"Remember, everything on this map stands for something else," Coombs De Bottle said. "'Katanga,' here, could be Greece. 'Germans' could as well be the Austrians. And here," pointing into the middle of the map, "our current focus of concern, this relatively small area, undefined in previous communications—"

"'. . . having recently undergone a change of administrative status,'" Cyprian read through the magnifying device.

"Novi Pazar?" Ratty speculated.

"How's that, Reg?"

Ratty, who found he still liked to talk shop, shrugged in a diffident way. "Persistent long-standing nightmare I suppose. Unpleasantness develops with Turkey, say over Macedonia, Turkish forces have to be taken out of Novi Pazar for deployment southward, and we know that at least three Serbian divisions are poised to march in and occupy the Sanjak. Which would not be kindly regarded by Austria, who would in fact be all too eager to intervene in an armed sort of way, obliging the usual assortment of Powers then to come piling on—"

"General European war."

"The very phrase."

"Well?" Yashmeen said, "why not let them have their war? Why would any self-respecting Anarchist care about any of these governments, with their miserable incestuous stew of kings and Cæsars?"

"Self-interest," said Ratty. "Anarchists would be the biggest losers, wouldn't they. Industrial corporations, armies, navies, governments, all would go on as before, if not more powerful. But in a general war among nations, every small victory Anarchism has struggled to win so far would simply turn to dust. Today even the dimmest of capitalists can see that the centralized nation-state, so promising an idea a generation ago, has lost all credibility with the population. Anarchism now is the idea that has seized hearts everywhere, some form of it will come to envelop every centrally governed society—unless government has already become irrelevant through, say, family arrangements like the Balkan *zadruga.* If a nation wants to preserve itself, what other steps can it take, but mobilize and go to war? Central governments were never designed for peace. Their structure is line and staff, the same as an army. The *national idea* depends on war. A general European war, with every striking worker a traitor, flags threatened, the sacred soils of homelands defiled, would be just the ticket to wipe Anarchism off the political map. The national idea would be reborn. One trembles at the pestilent forms that would rise up afterward, from the swamp of the ruined Europe.

"I wonder if this isn't Renfrew and Werfner's '*Interdikt*' field again, running across the Peninsula, waiting to be triggered."

"Then," Reef figured, "somebody'd need to go out and disarm it."

"Phosgene decomposes violently if it's exposed to water. That might be the simplest way, though failing that, one might set it off before it could do any harm, which might prove a bit stickier. . . ."

"How could it be set off and not do harm?" Yashmeen protested. "According to the map, unless the map is a bad dream, it runs straight across the heart of Thrace. This thing is terrible. Terrible." Jenny and Sophrosyne looked over attentively, possibly recognizing behind her voice the silent interior conversation she had been engaged upon since they had all met. Ratty and Reef stood in a corner puffing on cigars, gazing politely. Cyprian, however, had detected the same note as the women, having kept since Yashmeen's first announcement of her pregnancy a running log of every gram of weight gain and distribution, changes in her face, the flow of her hair when she moved and how it gave back the light, how she slept and what she ate or didn't eat, her lapses into vagueness and episodes of temper, as well as variables so personal he entered them in code. He was in no doubt as to why she wanted to go on this mission, and whom she thought she would be saving.

Close observation and silent concern being one thing, and free advice quite another, the time came nonetheless when Cyprian felt he really ought to say something to her. "Are you crazy?" was how he approached the topic. "You can't seriously mean to have a baby out there. It's primitive. It might as well be the jungle. You'll need to be near competent medical help. . . ."

She wasn't angry, she rather beamed as if wondering what had taken him so long. "You're still living in the last century, Cyprian. All the nomadic people of the world know how to have babies on the go. The world that is to be. We are out here, in it. Look around, old Cyprian."

"Oh, I see, now I'm somehow to get all swotted up on modern midwifery, is that it?"

"Well it wouldn't do you any harm, really, would it." He looked so perplexed, not to mention crestfallen, that she laughed and took his little chin in the old commanding way. "Now, we're not to have any difficulties over this, I hope."

Just after his return from Bosnia, Cyprian had sworn to himself that he would never go back to the Balkan Peninsula. When he allowed himself to imagine inducements—sexual, financial, honorific—that might get him to change his mind, he was puzzled to find there was nothing the world could plausibly offer that he wanted enough. He tried to explain to Ratty. "If the Earth were alive, with a planet-shaped consciousness, then the 'Balkan Peninsula' might easily map on to whatever in this consciousness most darkly wishes for its own destruction."

"Like phrenology," Ratty supposed.

"Only some form of madness would take anyone east, right now, into the jaws of what's almost certainly on the move out there. I don't suppose you people would have any assignments available to a fair-sized city, such as, oh, Paris, where the less bourgeois choices are easier to make and certainly not as hazardous to pursue?"

"Now then," Ratty perhaps recognizing a rhetorical component, "you know you're the closest thing we have to an Old Balkan Hand."

Since the moment in Salonica at the Mavri Gata when he discovered that Danilo's cousin Vesna, far from a figure of despair and self-delusion, had been altogether real, and that anything was therefore possible again including, and why not, marching off to Constantinople and creating a new world, Cyprian had begun to "relax into his fate," as he put it. Once he would have been reckoning up, anxiously, how much remained to him of youth, looks, desirability, and whether it would get him at least to the next station of the pilgrimage, but that—he knew now, knew as if with some inner certitude—was no longer quite the point, and in any case would take care of itself. The young and desirable must carry on as they always had, but without little C.L., it seemed.

Yet anti–Balkan Peninsula vows taken in some heat might after all, it seemed, be modified. "How would we go in?" Cyprian asked, as if interested only in a technical way.

Ratty nodded and beckoned over a cheerful individual who had been eating bouillabaisse as if he had just received word of some looming fish shortage. "Say hello to Professor Sleepcoat, who will now play you an interesting piece on the piano."

The Professor went over to the Pleyel by the window and quickly ran an octave scale on the white keys from F to F. "Recognize that?"

"Catchy tune," Cyprian said, "but it's not quite right, is it." The Professor started to play it again. "There!"

"Exactly—it's this B natural," banging on it two or three times. "Should be flatted. Once it was actually a forbidden note, you know. You'd get your knuckles rapped for playing it. Worse than that, if it happened to be during the Middle Ages."

"So it's one of the old church modes."

"Lydian. In the folk songs and dances of the Balkan villages, as it happens, although the other mediæval modes are well represented, there is this strange and drastic absence of Lydian material—in our own project, to date, we've found none at all. Bit of a mystery for us. As if it were still forbidden, perhaps even feared. The interval which our awkwardly unflatted B makes with F was known to the ancients as 'the devil in the music.' And whenever we play it for anyone out there, even whistle it, it seems they either run away screaming or assault us physically. What could it be they're hearing, that's so unacceptable?"

"Your plan," Cyprian guessed, "is to go out there and find the answer to that."

"Also to look into some rumors recently of a neo-Pythagorean cult who regard the Lydian with particular horror. Not surprisingly, they tend to favor the so-called Phrygian mode, quite common through the region." He addressed the keyboard again. "E to E on the white keys. Notice the difference. It happens to coincide with a lyre tuning that some attribute to Pythagoras, and may be traceable all the way back to Orpheus himself, who was a native of Thrace, after all, and was eventually worshipped there as a god."

"In view," added Yashmeen, "of the similarity, if not identity, between Pythagorean and Orphic teachings."

The Professor's eyebrows went up. Yashmeen felt it only fair to mention her former connection with the T.W.I.T.

"It *would* be ever so jolly," pouring a bistro glass brimful of local Jurançon white, "to have an ex-neo-Pythagorean along on this jaunt of ours. Insights as to what the T.W.I.T.'s Balkan counterparts might be thinking and so forth."

"If they exist."

"Oh, but I believe they do." Touching her sleeve briefly.

"Fascination alert," muttered Cyprian. He and Reef were long familiar with the scenario that developed among those meeting Yashmeen for the first time. Surely as sociable hours rotate and contract to the wee variety, initial fascination, as the evening progressed, would turn gradually to intimidation and bafflement.

"I'll be in the bar," said Reef. Yz-les-Bains was in fact one of the few places on the continent of Europe where a sober Anarchist could find a decent Crocodile—equal amounts of rum, absinthe, and the grape spirits known as *trois-six*—a traditional Anarchist favorite, which Loïc the bartender, a veteran of the Paris Commune, claimed to have been present at the invention of.

So the idea—"whose" idea was a meaningless question around here—was for them to be deployed into Thrace among a party of less than worldly song-gatherers, out late in the European twilight, far from safety, accosting local peasantry and urging them to sing or play something their grandparents had sung or played to them. Though Professor Sleepcoat seemed unconnected to the politics of the day, it had filtered in to him at least that since about 1900, searches for musical material were being undertaken in nations all over Europe, and one certainly could note in his manner an edge of impatience, as if time were running out. "Bartók and Kodály in Hungary, Canteloube in the Auvergne, Vaughan Williams in England, Eugénie Lineff in Russia, Hjalmar Thuren in the Farøe Islands, on it goes, sometimes of course simply because it's possible, given the recent improvements in portable sound recording." But there was also an urgency abroad which no one in the field would speak of, as if somehow the work had to be done quickly, before each people's heritage of song was somehow lost for good.

"I'll be the outrider I guess," Reef said, "though it wouldn't hurt you two to be checked out on some kind of personal hardware, just for back-covering purposes—and Cyprian, you'll be doing the navigating, and Yash, why I expect there's some kinda chores we could find for you. . . ."

Before becoming familiar with Reef's ideas of affectionate teasing, Yashmeen once would have reliably flown into full wet-hen indignation at talk like this. Now she only smiled formally and said, "Actually I happen to be the true beating heart of this mission." Which was so. Reef was running as always on what, except for its lack of analysis, would've been class hostility, but usually had more to do with how some suit-wearing bastard happened to've looked at him that day. Cyprian was absolutely without political faith—if it couldn't be turned into a quip, it wasn't worth considering. Yashmeen certainly was the one who shared most deeply the Anarchist beliefs around here. She had no illusions about bourgeois innocence, and yet held on to a limitless faith that History could be helped to keep its promises, including someday, a commonwealth of the oppressed.

It was her old need for some kind of transcendence—the fourth dimension, the Riemann problem, complex analysis, all had presented themselves as routes of escape from a world whose terms she could not accept, where she had preferred that even erotic desire have no consequences, at least none as weighty as the desires for a husband and children and so forth seemed to be for other young women of the day.

But lovers could not in general be counted as transcendent influences, and history had gone on with its own relentless timetable. Now at Yz-les-Bains, though, Yashmeen wondered if she hadn't found some late reprieve, some hope of passing beyond political forms to "planetary oneness," as Jenny liked to put it. "This is our own age of exploration," she declared, "into that unmapped country waiting beyond the frontiers and seas of Time. We make our journeys out there in the low light of the future, and return to the bourgeois day and its mass delusion of safety, to report on what we've seen. What are any of these 'utopian dreams' of ours but defective forms of time-travel?"

After a send-off party that went on all night, to be remembered for an innocence in which everything was still untouched by cause and effect, they came out into a stormy dawn and walked together arm in arm the slick cobbles of the little streets, under pedestrian bridges and up and down sets of steps in the wet light to their rooms to try and catch a few hours' sleep before departure for the Peninsula.

Then they were on the train as the points were thrown one by one, like a magician forcing a card on spectators not sure how much they wanted to be fooled, for this time down the tracks none of them was finding any way to enjoy the usual tourist's suspension of disbelief before a variety performance, it was no longer "travel," really, but three kinds of necessity.

And it was not the sights out the windows of wintry speeding Europe so much as the fucking that went on when the sleeping-carriage shades were drawn. The old Orient Express fantasy available on any given night in Europe at a music-hall somewhere.

Outside Zagreb, as if she could sense something wheeling to a close, Yashmeen, her beautiful ass elevated for Reef, who had just entered her, beckoned Cyprian over and without preliminaries, for the first time, took his penis, already achingly erect, into her mouth.

"Oh I say Yashmeen, really that isn't—"

She paused, disengaging her mouth for a moment, and glared at him affectionately. "Pregnancy makes a woman do strange things," she explained. "Indulge me," and recommenced sucking and, to his great delight, biting too, at first gently but then with increasing severity, so that it was not long before Cyprian was climaxing awed through this artfully calibrated pain, with Reef, aroused by the sight, not far behind, hollering "Whoopee!" as he was known to do. "Yes I should imagine," Cyprian added, nearly breathless.

"The rule," she reminded him when it seemed he was about to bring up the matter of roles and "places" later approaching Beograd, "is that there are no rules." At about which point, by accident, of course, Cyprian happened to catch Reef's eye.

"Don't get any 'cute ideas," Reef said, immediately brusque.

"Well you do have an appealing bottom," Cyprian mused, "in an abbreviated, muscular sort of way. . . ."

"Damn," Reef shaking his head, "there goes *my* appetite. You two figure somethin out, I'm going down that smokin salon, grab me a cheroot."

"There's ever such a nice panatela right here," Cyprian couldn't help remarking, "all ready for you."

"That? why, that ain't even a Craven A." And Reef stalked out, not nearly as annoyed as he was pretending to be. For Yash was right, of course. No rules. They were who they were, was all. For a while now, anytime he and Yash happened to be fucking face-to-face, she would manage to reach around and get a finger, hell, maybe even two sometimes, up in there, and he guessed it wasn't always that bad. And to be honest he did wonder now and then how it might be if Cyprian fucked him for a change. Sure. Not that it had to happen, but then again . . . it was shooting pool, he supposed, you had the straight shots, and cuts and English that went with that, but around these two you also had to expect caroms, and massés, and surprise balls out the corner of your eye coming back at you to collide at unforeseen angles, off of cushions sometimes you hadn't even thought about, heading for pockets you'd never've called. . . .

And the fact was that Reef, for all the chattering and silly ways, had grown really fond of the kid. He had ridden with men, no-foolin-around 100-percent *machos* that were a hell of a lot more trouble to get along with. Touchy, sentimental about the damndest things, cantina music, animal stories, badmen pimping their wives with tears in their eyes as they took the money, spend any time at all in company like this and either you develop a vast patience or become violent.

What surprised him about the three of them together—what he couldn't understand really—was that he kept waiting to feel jealous about something, having a personal history himself of purely mean sumbitch ways when it came to these third-party situations, he couldn't tell you how many nights a lamp going out behind a window curtain or some glimpse of two heads together in a buggy half a mile away had sent him into some homicidal seizure. Waking up in some barrelhouse with vomit all in his hair and not always his own vomit, either. But among the three of them something was different, jealousy hadn't ever figured into it, in some way never could. Once he would've thought, well of course, how could a man ever get jealous of a creampuff like Cyprian? But as he got to know him better, Reef saw how Cyprian could handle himself when he had to, and it wasn't all to do with that Webley Reef knew he was packing. Once or twice, unexpectedly, he'd seen Cyprian drop the pose of theatrical hysteria he used to get through the working day on, and emerge into a region of cool self-control—you could see him straighten up and begin to breathe deliberately, as professional lurkers in the shadows outside casinos, waiting for the incautious and self-satisfied, faded away muttering, or flâneurs commenting in dialect had fallen silent, lost their grins, believing that Cyprian had understood every word, and not looking forward to how personally he might want to take it.

IN BEOGRAD THEY JOINED UP with Professor Sleepcoat and his party, which included the technician Enrico, the student volunteers Dora and Germain, and an accountant named Gruntling who was there at the University's insistence owing to budget overruns on the last trip out here, most of them in a column titled "Miscellaneous" whose details Professor Sleepcoat could somehow not recall.

At Sofia they all descended to the platform of the Tsentralna Gara to find a city re-imagined in the thirty-odd years since the Turks had been driven out, winding alleyways, mosques, and hovels replaced with a grid of neat wide streets and Europeanized public works on the grand scale. As they rode into town, Cyprian stared in dismay at the Boulevard Knyaginya Mariya Luiza, which seemed to be full of stray dogs and serious drinkers in different stages of alcohol poisoning.

"It used to be much worse," the Professor assured him. "Arthur Symons called it the most horrible street in Europe, but that was ages ago, and we all know how sensitive Arthur is."

"Kind of like Omaha," it seemed to Reef.

The next day Gruntling went to the bank and stayed till closing time, and then the party headed north, up into the hills.

Each morning the accountant took a sack of silver Bulgarian leva and counted out twenty-five of them. "This is only a quid," objected the Professor. "All right," said Gruntling, handing him the coins, "then that makes this a 'quo.' Try not to spend it all in one place."

"It's five dollars," Reef said, "I don't know what he's complaining about." Most of the outlays were in smaller coins, nickel and bronze stotinki, for meals usually on the run—kebabcheta, banichka, palachinki, beer—and someplace to doss in the evenings. For a few stotinki, one could also find a child eager to turn the crank that ran the recording device by way of reduction gears and a flywheel that smoothed out variations in pitch. "Like pumping the bellows of a church organ back in the last century," it seemed to Professor Sleepcoat. "Without all those anonymous urchins we wouldn't have had Bach." Which got him a look from Yashmeen, who in other circs might've inquired sweetly how much of Western culture throughout history did he think might actually have depended on that sort of shamefully underpaid labor. But it was not a discussion anybody had the leisure to get into any longer.

One nightfall the Professor was out working late, when from up the valley he heard someone singing in a young tenor voice, which at first he took for a typical Transylvanian swineherd's *kanástánc* that had found its way here somehow seeping over ridgelines and fanning down watersheds. But presently another young voice in a higher range, a girl's, answered, and for the duration of the twilight the two voices sang back and forth across the little valley, sometimes antiphonal, sometimes together in harmony. They were goatherds, and the words were in Shop dialect sung to a Phrygian melody he had never heard before, and knew he would never hear again, not this way, unmediated and immune to Time. Because what he could make out were words only the young had any right to sing, he was unavoidably reminded of the passing of his own youth, gone before he'd had a chance to take note of it, and thus was able to hear lying just beneath an intense awareness of loss, as if the division between the singers were more than the width of a valley, something to be crossed only through an undertaking at least as metaphysical as song, as if Orpheus might once have sung it to Eurydice in Hell, calling downward through intoxicant fumes, across helically thundering watercourses, echoing among limestone fantastically sculptured over unnumbered generations by Time personified as a demiurge and servant of Death— And the recording equipment, of course, and Enrico, were back at the inn. Not that any recording was necessary, really, for the two singers had repeated the song often enough, well into the onset of the night, for it to enter into the grooves of Professor Sleepcoat's memory, right next to the ones dedicated to regrets and sorrows and so forth.

Later the Professor seemed to have Orpheus on the brain. "He couldn't quite bring himself to believe in her desire to come back with him to live in the upper world again. He had to turn around and look, just to make sure she was coming."

"Typical male insecurity," Yashmeen sniffed.

"Typical female lust for wealth wins out in the end, is the way I always read that one," commented Gruntling.

"Oh he's the Lord of Death, for goodness' sake, there's no money over there."

"Young woman, there is money everywhere."

THE MAIN TASK for Reef, Cyprian, and Yashmeen right now was locating the *Interdikt* line, and disabling it. The countryside was full of hints, deliberate misdirections—any mirage of something unnaturally straight, shimmering across the terrain, could send them off on fools' errands to waste the precious hours. Townspeople were friendly enough until Cyprian brought out the map—then they shifted their eyes away and even began to tremble, conferring in dialects suddenly gone opaque. The use of such terms as "fortification" and "gas" was hardly productive, even with those untroubled enough to stop and chat. "You don't look for them," they were often warned—"if they want to, they find you. Better if they don't find you." At the fringes of these discussions, the good folk were averting their faces, repeatedly and compulsively crossing themselves, and making other hand-gestures less familiar, some indeed quite complicated, as if overlain, since ancient days, with manual commentary.

Finally one day their luck took a turn. They were at Veliko Târnovo, where the Professor had gone to look into a variant of the *ruchenitsa* wedding dance, rumored to exhibit syncopations hitherto unrecorded on the underlying 7/8. It was mid-February, St. Tryphon's Day, coinciding with a ritual pruning of vines. Everybody was drinking homemade Dimyat and Misket out of casks and dancing to a small local band made up of tuba, accordion, violin, and clarinet.

Reef, who never missed a chance to kick up his heels, was out there with a variety of appealing partners, who seemed actually to have formed a queue. Yashmeen, somewhere past the middle of her term, was content to sit under an awning and watch the goings-on. Cyprian was looking and not looking at young townsfolk he'd once have termed desirable, when all at once he was approached by a thin, sunburned individual all togged out for the wedding.

"I know you," said Cyprian.

"Salonica. Year before last. You saved my life."

"Why, it's 'Gabrovo Slim.' But as I recall, about all I did was try to find you a fez that would fit properly."

"Thought you'd be dead by now."

"Doing my best. Was that you that just got married?"

"My wife's little sister. With luck she'll be able to work through harvest before they have their first." His eyes had kept sliding away to look at Yashmeen. "She is your wife?"

"Not that lucky." He introduced them.

Slim beamed in the direction of Yash's belly. "When is baby?"

"May, I think."

"Come be with us when baby comes. Better for you, for baby, for father especially."

"Here's the very bloke," said Cyprian with every appearance of gaiety.

Reef got congratulated and re-invited to stay with Slim and his family, who as it turned out had a small rose farm near Kazanlâk, in the heart of the Rozovata Dolina, or Valley of the Roses. Cyprian, who had been inhabiting a one-to-one-scale map of the Peninsula since arriving, immediately grew alert. The Valley ran east-west, between the Balkan range and the Sredna Gora, and certainly was as likely a place as any to be looking for the *Interdikt.*

He waited till he and Slim had a moment to chat before bringing the topic up. "Have you noticed anything peculiar going on out there?"

With perhaps some general idea already of Cyprian's profession, "Interesting you should ask. People have been seen who should not be there. Germans, we think." He paused before looking directly at Cyprian. "Bringing machinery."

"Not farm machinery."

"Some of it looks electrical. Military also. Dynamos, long black cables they bury in ground. Nobody wants to dig them up to see what they are, though there were rumors that some local *mutri* thought they'd go steal what they could, and bring it down to Petrich, on Macedonian border, where you can sell nearly anything. Someplace between Plovdiv and Petrich, they disappeared, along with whatever they got. Never seen since. In Bulgarian crime world, these things ordinarily are looked into, and appropriate action taken, but by next day everything was dropped. First time anyone has seen those people afraid of anything."

"How difficult would it be, do you think, to have a look round, without anyone knowing?"

"I can show you."

"You're not afraid?"

"You will see if it is something to be afraid of."

DESPITE HAVING KNOWN that it would happen at some point in the journey, when they announced that the time had come for them to take off on their own, Professor Sleepcoat was devastated. "I should have known better than to come out this time," he groaned. "It's like musical chairs. Except that the music stopped two years ago."

"We'll keep our ears tuned for Lydian material," Yashmeen promised.

"Maybe there is none anymore. Maybe it's gone forever. Maybe that gap in the musical continuum, that silence, is a first announcement of something terrible, of which this structural silence is only an inoffensive metaphor."

"You'll let them know back at Yz-les-Bain that we—?"

"Part of my remit. I shall miss you, however."

EVEN TO THE INDIGENOUS, used to twittering fools from the north and west in tourist attire, the three seemed gravely passionate, as if behaving not as they wished but as they must, in answer to unheard voices of duty. Who could know, finding them in any of these hill towns, climbing, descending, never a step in front of another you'd call level, thinking only when they must about the next meal, their faces shadowed by hatbrims of woven straw, taken from the flanks or beneath by sunlight off the ancient paving-stones or sun-battered earth too often into areas of angelic implication—what were they doing out here this late in history? when everyone else had long turned, withdrawn, re-entered the harsh certainties of homelands farther west, were preparing or prepared. . . .

Slim's farm, from what Reef could tell after a quick appraisal that by now was second nature to him, enjoyed a good strategic position, in a little valley of its own, the creek running down out of the Sredna Gora bordered by other small farms, each with its murderous dog, alongside it a road that unfolded in slow curves, now and then a shade tree, geese up and down the roadside or running from ambush hissing and honking, traffic along the road easily seen for miles, most of it farm carts and horsemen uniformed and irregular, all carrying at least one rifle, all known locally, and called out to, by their diminutives.

The farmhouse was teeming with children, though when Cyprian actually counted, there were never more than two. Their mother, Zhivka, turned out to have a way with roses, and kept a private patch out in back of the house where she carried on hybrid experiments, having begun years ago by crossing *R. damascena* with *R. alba* and gone on from there. She had names for each one, she talked to them, and after a while, when the moon and the wind were right, Cyprian heard them talking back. "In Bulgarian, of course, so I didn't catch it all."

"Anything you'd like to share?" muttered Yash, big as a barge and having an uncomfortable day.

"They were discussing you and the baby, actually. Apparently it will be a girl."

"Yes here's a nice heavy flowerpot, just a moment now, stand quite still. . . ."

As her time approached, the women in the neighborhood drew closer around Yashmeen, Reef went out to raise whatever hell was available in these parts, and Cyprian was left to churches, fields of rosebushes six or seven feet high, extended sunsets, steel-blue night. Men avoided him. Cyprian wondered if, in a trance he could no longer remember, he had not offended someone here, perhaps mortally. It was not—in this he was certain, perhaps it was the only thing he could be certain of—the severity in the faces turned to him was not that of desire. This was one delusion he was not allowed the comfort of in what it sometimes seemed might be his ultimate hours, and did it matter two pins, really? He wasn't looking for erotic company any longer. Something else, perhaps, but fucking strangers was scarcely by now of much concern.

THE BABY WAS BORN during the rose harvest, in the early morning with the women already back from the fields, born into a fragrance untampered with by the heat of the sun. From the very first moment her eyes were enormously given to all the world around her. What Cyprian had imagined as terrifying, at best disgusting, proved instead to be irresistible, he and Reef to either side of the ancient bed, each holding one of Yashmeen's hands as she rose to meet the waves of pain, despite the muttering women who plainly wanted the two men elsewhere. Hell, preferably.

The afterbirth went into the ground beneath a young rosebush. Yashmeen named the baby Ljubica. Later in the day, she held her daughter out to the men. "Here. Take her for a while. She'll sleep." Reef held the newborn carefully, as he remembered holding Jesse the first time, stood shifting foot to foot, then began to move carefully around the little room, ducking his head for the slant of the roof, presently handing her over to Cyprian, who took her warily, her lightness fitting so easily after all into his hands, nearly tugging him off the floor—but more than that, the familiarity, as if this had already happened countless times before. He wouldn't dare say it out loud. But somehow, here was a brief moment of certitude, brought back from an exterior darkness, as if to fill a space he could not have defined before this, before she was really here, tiny sleeping Ljubica.

His nipples were all at once peculiarly sensitive, and he found himself almost desperate with an unexpected flow of feeling, a desire for her to feed at his breast. He breathed in deeply. "I have this—" he whispered, "this . . ." It was certain. "I knew her once—previously—perhaps in that other life it was she who took care of me—and now here is the balance being restored—"

"Oh, you're overthinking it all," Yashmeen said, "as usual."

For much of that summer, Reef and Cyprian were out in search of the elusive "Austrian minefield." They made their way among tobacco patches and fields of sunflowers, wild lilacs in bloom, geese honking up and down the village streets. Shaggy dogs came running out of sheep pasture barking homicidally. Sometimes Yashmeen came along but more and more she stayed at the farm, helping with chores, being with Ljubica.

When the roses were in and Gabrovo Slim found himself with some time, true to his word he took Reef and Cyprian out to a promontory, wind-scoured and overlooking a treeless plain. Beside a small outbuilding rose a hundred-foot tower supporting a toroidal black iron antenna. "That wasn't here before," Slim said.

"I think it's one of those Tesla rigs," Reef said. "My brother used to work on them."

Inside the transmission shack were one or two operators with their ears all but attached to speaker-horns, listening attentively to what seemed mostly at first to be atmospheric static. The longer the visitors listened, though, the more possible it became that now and then they were hearing spoken words, in a number of languages including English. Cyprian shook his head, smiling if not in disbelief at least in a polite attempt not to offend.

"It's all right," said one of the operators. "Many in the field believe that these are voices of the dead. Edison and Marconi both feel that the syntonic wireless can be developed as a way to communicate with departed spirits."

Reef immediately thought of Webb, and the séance back there in Switzerland, and his jocular remarks to Kit about telephoning the dead.

From outside now came a massed mechanical uproar. "Motorcycles," Cyprian said, "judging by the throb. I'll just go have a look, shall I."

Six or seven cyclists in leather fatigues that time and terrain had only made more stylish, riding stripped-down four-cylinder touring bikes—he identified them immediately as Derrick Theign's elite "shadowing" unit, R.U.S.H., whom he hadn't seen since the Trieste station.

"Is that you, Latewood?" Behind a pair of smoked goggles Cyprian recognized Mihály Vámos, a former hill-climbing champion on the Hungarian circuit. They had put in some time together in Venice—enough, one hoped—drinking late at night, helping each other out of the odd canal, standing around on small bridges in the moonlight smoking, trying to figure out what to do about Theign.

"Szia, haver," Cyprian nodded. "Handsome machines you're riding these days."

Vámos grinned. "Not like those little Puchs they had us on at first. Some Habsburg jobber friend of Theign's, attractive terms, all they did was keep breaking down. These new ones are FNs, experimental models—light, rugged, fast. Much better."

"The Belgian arms factory?"

"Oh, these are weapons, all right." He had a look at Cyprian. "Happy to see you're still out getting in trouble. We certainly owe you our thanks."

"For . . . ?"

Vámos laughed. "We didn't hear in bloody detail about Theign. Messages from the Venice station stopped arriving one day, and since then we've operated independently. But it appears you did us all a service."

Cyprian offered him a local cigarette, and they lit up. "But you're still on station out here? What if fighting were to start? how would you be expected on your own, to . . ."

Vámos gestured up at the Tesla transmitter. "The War Office maintains receiving facilities on the Sussex coast, and cable links to London. We thought that's where you'd be by now, back in England happy and secure, drinking tea in a garden someplace. Who in his right mind would want to be out here?"

There seemed no point in not bringing up the *Interdikt.* Without going into names or dates, Cyprian gave Vámos a quick summary of what he'd been up to.

"Oh. That." Vámos took off his goggles and wiped them on his shirt while pretending to look carefully at the sky. "Around here they call it the *Zabraneno.* Whoever installed it, it no longer belongs to anyone—the Germans and Austrians pretend they never heard of it, the local people are terrified, the Turks send their probes every month or so, believing it is like the Great Wall of China, there to keep *them* from invading. The British as always are of two minds as to its usefulness. None of us know how to dismantle the thing, so the best we can do is wait, ride patrol, east to west, west to east, see that no one triggers it by accident."

"And has it ever . . . ?"

Vámos had an unaccustomedly solemn look. "It behaves as if it's alive. Knows when someone's coming and takes steps to protect itself. Anyone who passes within a certain radius. We have learned the way in, for all the good that does us. I suppose now you'll want to see it."

Gabrovo Slim remembered an appointment with an attar-factory rep from Philipopolis, and left apologizing. Cyprian and Reef each climbed on behind one of the R.U.S.H. cyclists and were taken snarling across the foothills of the Sredna Gora, past trees grown over with ivy, a sinister topiary of green creatures stooped and hooded that almost looked like familiar animals but were deformed past comfortable recognition, that seemed to watch the riders as they passed, only a breath of wind away from having faces revealed from inside their dark green hoods. . . .

And creeping at the edges . . . or actually by now industriously in and out like a loom shuttle all through the structure of the field of vision, mapped onto the crossed invisible threads on which all that is is deployed, Cyprian, out in the ungentle wind, acquiring a variety of interdental insect life, was witnessing distortions, displacements, rotations . . . something else was there, just about to appear, something he understood had always been there, but that he had not been receptive to. . . .

"Here is where we must dismount," said Mihály Vámos, "and walk carefully." In single file, walking a zigzag pattern, as if counting paces, they approached a long structure of weathered concrete, strangely dark in this unaccustomed summer cold, a repetition of elements all grimly turned the same way, as toward intruders unknown but equally undeserving of mercy.

Vámos led them into a sort of enlarged casemate, built not long ago but already begun to corrode. Inside, in the afternoon-ochre shadows, flaking communiqué forms that once had screamed with emergency were still pinned to a framed ancient announcement-board, though many had fallen off and blown in drifts into the corners. Tunnels led off into stone darkness, toward adjoining structures unindicated miles away in what so clearly announced itself as a great barrier fortification.

In a storeroom they found hundreds of canisters, brand new, dust-free, each labeled PHOSGÈNE.

"They're real enough." Vámos said. "Phosgene isn't especially exotic anymore, there are production plants everywhere, it's only chlorine and carbon monoxide. With access to enough electric current, it's easy to produce chlorine from salt water, and carbon monoxide can be collected from nearly any combustion process. Expose them together to light and you get phosgene."

"Born of light," said Cyprian, as if about to understand something.

"It seems this isn't a gas weapon, after all," said the *motoros*. "'Phosgene' is really code for light. We learned it is light here which is really the destructive agent. Beyond that the creators of the *Zabraneno* have proceeded in the deepest secrecy, though the small amount of published theoretical work seems to be German, dating back to the early studies of city illumination—they were devoting great attention to the Æther then, using as their model the shock wave that passes through air in a conventional explosion, looking for similar methods to intensify the light-pressure locally in the Æther. . . . From military experience with searchlights, it was widely known how effectively light at that candle-power could produce helplessness and fear. The next step was to find a way to project it as a stream of destructive energy."

"Fear in lethal form," said Cyprian. "And if all these units, all along this line, went off at once—"

"A great cascade of blindness and terror ripping straight across the heart of the Balkan Peninsula. Like nothing that has ever happened. Photometry is still too primitive for anyone to say how much light would be deployed, or how intense—somewhere far up in the millions of candles per square inch, but there are only guesses—expressions of military panic, really."

"God," said Reef.

"Maybe not."

Slim had mentioned black cables. "But I don't see any light sources here."

The look he got from Vámos was not one Cyprian would remember with any sort of comfort, "Yes. Odd, isn't it?"

As they were leaving, Vámos said, "Is this what your people sent you to find?"

"They said nothing about code," Cyprian quietly furious. "More damned code."

The riders left them at a crossroads near Shipka. "*Sok szerencsét,* Latewood," nodded Vámos. By the protocol of these things, particularly perhaps in

Thrace, one did not turn and look back. Soon the engine sounds had faded and the hawk-bearing wind resumed.

"What do we tell Yash?" Reef wondered.

"That we couldn't find it. We'll pretend to keep looking for a while, but in the wrong directions. We must keep her and the baby well away from this, Reef. At some point declare the mission a failure and get back to . . ."

"Lose your train of thought there, podner?" Reef inquired after a while.

"I'm wondering what to tell Ratty's people. They're under such a deeply mistaken impression, aren't they."

"That's if those motorcycle boys were givin us the 'straight dope.'"

"They're the guardians of the thing now. Of this whole sad, unreadable Balkan dog's dinner, come to that. They don't want the job, but they've got it. I don't want to believe them, but I do."

From then on, in moments when his time was less closely claimed, Cyprian would find himself waiting for a vast roar of light, toxic and pitiless, turning the sky blank of all detail, from which not even his dreams would be exempt.

When they got moving again, Reef was delighted at how easily this baby took to being out on the road. Ljubica cried for the reasons any baby would, but no more, as if she knew her trooper's destiny and saw no point in delaying her embrace of it. Any object she learned to hold, she would next start throwing around. Though Reef did and didn't need it just then, she reminded him of his son Jesse back in Colorado.

"You're acting like she's your second chance," Yashmeen said.

"Anythin wrong with that?"

"There is if you think you're entitled to one."

"Who says I ain't?" he almost said, but thought better of it.

They were heading east toward the Black Sea, with some half-thought-out idea of setting up in Varna, resuming the old resort life, raising a few leva with some low-intensity gambling and so forth, baby to the contrary notwithstanding, whatever.

"Somebody said the King's summer palace is there."

"And . . ."

"It's still summer, ain't it? When the King's in town, there's suckers around, you never heard that? ancient proverb."

The topic of the *Interdikt* had not arisen again. Ljubica's birth had taken the question, for Yashmeen, to a far lower priority. That neither young man was bringing it up suggested to her that they might all somehow be of the same mind. Even an amateur neuropathist observing them at this time would have diagnosed a postpartum *folie à trois.* The rest of the world were heading for cover, the dreams of bourgeois and laborer alike were turned rattling with terrible shapes, all the prophesiers agreed there was heavy weather ahead—what were these people thinking? and with an infant to look after, too. Irresponsible if not outright hebephrenic, really.

There was a perfectly good road to the sea, but somehow they could not stay on it. They kept turning uphill, into the Balkan Range, even backtracking westward again, as if blindly obeying a compass fatally sensitive to anomaly.

At certain hours of midday, pine branches with dark streaks of shadow between reached trembling toward them like the arms of the numberless dead, not pleading so much as demanding, almost threatening. Birds here had not sung for generations, no one alive in fact could remember a time when they had sung, and these skies belonged now to raptors. The country was well prepared for what was soon to break over it.

Up above the red tile roofs of Sliven, having climbed through clouds of butterflies inquisitive as to Ljubica's status, which she was doing her best to explain to them, they came upon a strange rock archway twenty or thirty feet high, and the minute she caught sight of it, Ljubica went a little crazy, waving arms and legs and commenting in her own language.

"Sure," Reef said, "let's go have a look." He cradled her in one arm and together with Yashmeen they made their way over to the formation, Ljubica gazing up as they passed under it and out the other side. They returned to find Cyprian talking and smoking with a couple of boys who'd been lounging around. "That arch you just walked under? They call it the *Halkata.* The Ring."

She thought she knew his voice by now. "Oh, another local curse. Just what we need." But he was gazing at her, unwilling to speak, his eyes agleam. "Cyprian—"

"If you walk under it with someone, you will both—you will all, it seems—be in love forever. Perhaps it's your idea of a curse. Not mine."

"Then go ahead, it's your turn."

His smile just managed not to be wistful. "And anyone who passes through it alone, according to my informants here, turns into the opposite sex. I'm not sure where that would leave me, Yashmeen. Perhaps I don't need the confusion. The last time I was out here," he continued later that evening, down in Sliven, in a room they had taken for the night in an old house off Ulitsa Rakovsky, "I had to put my impulses away for the duration, Balkan gender expectations being a bit as you'd say emphatic. Details one had simply ignored at Cambridge or Vienna demanded the most urgent attention here, and I had to adapt quickly. Imagine my further surprise when I discovered that women, who appear to be without power, in reality run the show. What did that mean then, for one's allegiance to both sexes at once?"

"*Oh* dear." And Ljubica was laughing too. Reef was off in some local *krâchma.* Yashmeen and Cyprian watched one another with some of the old—already, "old"—speculative trembling.

UP IN THE BALKAN RANGE one day for the first time, defying the predators above, they heard birdsong, some kind of Bulgarian thrush, singing in modal scales, attentive to pitch, often for minutes at a time. Ljubica listened intently, as if hearing a message. All at once she leaned out of the crocheted shawl Cyprian was carrying her in and stared up past them. They followed her gaze to where an old structure of some kind, destroyed and rebuilt more than once over the centuries, hung above a deep canyon, seemingly impossible to get to past the rapids in the river and the steep walls of bare rock. At first they weren't even sure what it was they were seeing, because of shifting curtains of mist thrown upward by the roaring collision of water and rock.

"We need to go back," it seemed to Reef, "climb up top, try to get to it by coming downhill."

"I think I see a way," said Cyprian. He led them up into a skein of goat paths. Here and there steps had been cut into the rock. Soon, audible above the boiling uproar below them, came choral voices, and they had reached a path, kept clear of brush and fallen rock debris, ascending in the long departure of light to a dark mossed arch above them, underneath which stood a figure in a monk's robe, with its hands held out, palms upward, as if presenting an invisible offering.

Reef had pulled out a pack of Byal Sredets and offered them to the monk, who held up a finger and then, inquiring with his eyebrows, another, and took two cigarettes, beaming.

"Zdrave," Cyprian greeted him, *"kakvo ima?"*

He got a long stare of appraisal. At length the man spoke, in University-accented English. "Welcome home."

THE CONVENT BELONGED to a sect descended from ancient Bogomils who did not embrace the Roman Church in 1650 with most of the other *Pavlikeni* but chose instead to go underground. To their particular faith, over the centuries, had become attached older, more nocturnal elements, going back, it was claimed, to the Thracian demigod Orpheus, and his dismemberment not far from here, on the banks of the Hebrus River, nowadays known as the Maritza. The Manichæan aspect had grown ever stronger—the obligation of those who took refuge here to be haunted by the unyielding doubleness of everything. Part of the discipline for a postulant was to remain acutely conscious, at every moment of the day, of the nearly unbearable conditions of cosmic struggle between darkness and light proceeding, inescapably, behind the presented world.

Yashmeen at dinner that evening, with a discreet scream of recognition, took note of the convent's prohibition against beans, a Pythagorean dietary rule she remembered being also observed by the T.W.I.T. Before long she was able to discover more of the Pythagorean *akousmata*—arguing strongly, she felt, for a common origin. She could also not help noticing that the hegumen, Father Ponko, had the Tetractys tattooed on his head.

He was more than willing to talk about the Order. "At some point Orpheus, never comfortable in any kind of history that could not be sung, changed identities, or slowly blended with another demigod, Zalmoxis, who some in Thrace believed was the only true God. According to Herodotus, who heard it from Greeks living around the Black Sea, Zalmoxis had once been a slave of Pythagoras himself, who upon receiving his freedom went on to pile up a good-size fortune, returned here to Thrace, and became a great teacher of Pythagorean doctrine."

There was an icon of Zalmoxis in the church, where Yashmeen and Reef found Cyprian after the evening service kneeling on the stone floor, before the carved iconostasis, gazing into it as if into a cinema screen where pictures moved and stories unfolded which he must attend to. Shadowless faces of Zalmoxis and the saints. And depending on a kind of second sight, a knowledge beyond light of what lay within the wood itself, of what it was one's duty to set free. . . .

Yashmeen knelt beside him. Reef stood close by, holding and slowly rocking Ljubica. After a bit Cyprian seemed to return to ordinary candlelight.

"How devoted you look," he smiled.

"Oh, you are ragging me."

He shrugged. "Only surprised."

"To find me in a sacred place. Trivial, housewifely me. Have you forgotten the church up on Krâstova Gora, where I first learned not only that my baby would be a girl but exactly what her face would look like? I knelt and received that, Cyprian, and I pray you may arrive at a moment of knowledge remotely like it."

They rose, and walked out of the narthex, the three of them and Ljubica, out into the scent of myrtle in the deepening dusk. "When you leave here," Cyprian said quietly, "I shan't be coming with you."

At first she didn't hear the quietness of it, and thought he was angry, and was about to ask what she'd done, when he added, "I must stay here, you see."

Though she could not trust herself then to speak, Yashmeen already knew. She had begun to feel him leaving as long ago as their tour of the French casinos, as if he had discovered a way back, not a reversion to any known type, more a reoccupying of a life he might have forgotten or never noticed there all the time waiting, and she had come slowly to understand she could not go with him wherever he was bound, watching helplessly as each day the distance opened a bit more. Despite their bravest hopes. If he had been desperately ill, she would at least have recognized and carried out her duty to him, but that slow departure, as if into the marshes of Time, miasmata rising, reeking, odors that went directly to the most ancient part of the brain, summoning memories older than her present incarnation, had begun, even long before Ljubica, to overwhelm her.

"It may be," Cyprian said as gently as he thought he had to, "that God doesn't always require us to wander about. It may be that sometimes there is a—would you say a 'convergence' to a kind of stillness, not merely in space but in Time as well?"

Gentle or not, Yashmeen took it personally anyway. The extent of her statelessness had unfolded for her like the progress of a sky from dawn into its shadowless day, a wandering in which she would count as home only the web of sympathetic spirits who had dug spaces beneath their own precarious dwellings to harbor her for a night or two at a time. Who might not always be there when she needed them to be.

Reef on the other hand thought Cyprian had only come up with some new way to be difficult, and would soon be on to something else. "So you're fixin to be a nun. And . . . they ain't supposed to chop nothin off, nothin like 'at. . . ."

"They are taking me in as exactly the person I am," Cyprian said. "No more of these tiresome gender questions."

"You're free," Yashmeen speculated.

Cyprian was apologetic. "I know you were counting on me. Even if it was only for body mass, another tree in the windbreak. I feel that I just fell over and left you all exposed. . . ."

"You know, you're so damn clever all the time," Reef said, "it's hard to trust anything you say."

"Another British vice. I'm sorry for that, too."

"Well, you can't stay here. Hell, be Bernadette o' Lourdes if you want, just not out here. I know it's your particular patch and all, but Pete's sake, take a look around. One thing I'm never wrong about is knowin when there's a fight on the way. Nothin telepathic, just professional. Too damn many Mannlichers all over the place."

"Oh, there won't be any war."

How could either of them say, "But you see how impossible it would be to defend this place, no clear lines of retreat, no escape." Cyprian must have known by now what happened to convents in wartime. Especially out here, where it'd been nothing but massacre and reprisal for centuries. But that was Balkan politics. In here other matters were more important.

"They have adapted the *σχημα*," Cyprian explained, "the Orthodox initiation rite, to their own much older beliefs. In the Orphic story of the world's beginning, Night preceded the creation of the Universe, she was the daughter of Chaos, the Greeks called her *Νυξ*, and the old Thracians worshipped her as a deity. For a postulant in this order, Night is one's betrothed, one's beloved, one seeks to become not a bride at all really, but a kind of sacrifice, an offering, to Night."

"And shall we"—Yashmeen pausing as if to allow the term "ex-beloved" to occur in silence—"be allowed there? At your ceremony?"

"It could be months, even years away. In the Eastern rite, they cut off the novice's hair, which she must then weave into a kind of girdle, and wear it under her habit, round her waist, forever. Which means that before they'll even consider me as a candidate, I must first grow my hair long enough—and given my current waist measurement, that could be quite some time."

"Listen to yourself," said Reef.

"Yes Cyprian, how vain, really, you're supposed to be renouncing all that."

He grabbed two handfuls of the roll of fat in question and regarded them doubtfully. "Father Ponko admits that the hair-length rule is nothing to do with consecration, really—it's to give us time to think about the step we plan to take, as it's not for everyone."

"Having your hair cut off is nothing," the hegumen announced one day to the assembled postulants, "compared to the Vow of Silence. Talking, for women, is a form of breathing. To renounce it is the greatest sacrifice a woman can make. Soon you will enter a country none of you have known and few can imagine—the realm of silence. Before crossing that fateful frontier, each of you is to be allowed one question, one only. Think closely, my children, and do not waste this opportunity."

When it was Cyprian's turn, he knelt and whispered, "What is it that is born of light?"

Father Ponko was watching him with a look of unaccustomed sorrow, as if there were an answer he must on no account give, lest it call down the fulfillment of some awful prophecy. "In the fourteenth century," he said carefully, "our great enemies were the Hesychasts, contemplatives who might as well have been Japanese Buddhists—they sat in their cells literally gazing at their navels, waiting to be enfolded in a glorious light they believed was the same light Peter, James, and John had witnessed at the Transfiguration of Christ on Mount Tabor. Perhaps they asked themselves forms of your question as well, as a sort of koan. What is it that was born of *that* light? Oddly, if one reads the Gospel accounts, the emphasis in all three is not on an excess of light but a deficiency—the Transfiguration occurred at best under a peculiar sort of half-light. 'There came a cloud and overshadowed them,' as Luke puts it. Those *omphalopsychoi* may have seen a holy light, but its link with the Transfiguration is doubtful.

"Now I must ask you in turn—when something is born of light, what does that light enable us to see?"

It turned out, as Yashmeen was quick to grasp, that Father Ponko was approaching the Transfiguration story from the direction of the Old Testament. He seemed under no illusions about her religiosity but was always willing to chat with the unbelieving. "You are familiar with the idea of the Shekhinah—That which dwells?"

Yashmeen nodded, her years with the T.W.I.T. having provided her a broad though shallow footing in British Kabbalism. "It is the feminine aspect of God." Eyes brightening, she told him of the transcendent status enjoyed at Chunxton Crescent by card number II in the Major Arcana of the Tarot, known as The High Priestess, and of the Mayfair debutantes who showed up there on Saturday nights in veils and peculiar headgear and with very little idea of what any of it might mean—"Some thought it had to do with the Suffragette movement, and they spoke vaguely of 'empowerment' . . . some, men chiefly, were in it for the erotic implications of a Judaeo-Christian goddess, and expected orgies, flogging, shiny black accoutrements and so forth, so naturally for them the whole point got lost in a masturbational sort of haze."

"Always that risk," agreed Father Ponko. "When God hides his face, it is paraphrased as 'taking away' his Shekhinah. Because it is she who reflects his light, Moon to his Sun. Nobody can withstand pure light, let alone see it. Without her to reflect, God is invisible. She is absolutely of the essence if he is to be at all operative in the world."

From the chapel came voices singing what the hegumen had identified as a *canone* of Cosmas of Jerusalem, dating from the eighth century. Yashmeen stood very still in the courtyard, as if waiting for some vertigo to pass, despite having already understood that vertigo was somehow designed into the place, a condition of residence. She recognized here what the T.W.I.T. had always pretended to be but was never more than a frail theatrical sketch of. "Talk about reflection," she found herself muttering.

The present tense seemed less accessible to her each day, as postulants circled Cyprian, and he was carried farther from her, as by a wave passing through some invisible, imponderable medium. . . . And Ljubica, who gazed at the daily life of the convent as if she knew exactly what was going on, who uncounted times had fallen asleep with her small fist around one of Cyprian's fingers, now must seek other ways to return accurately to what she remembered of the realms of the not-yet-created.

The hegumen seemed to recognize her from a previous metempsychosis. "The mooned planet," said the hegumen, "the planetary electron. If self-similarity proves to be a built-in property of the universe, then perhaps sleep is, after all, a form of death—repeated at a daily frequency instead of a generational one. And we go back and forth, as Pythagoreans suspected, in and out of death as we do dreams, but much more slowly. . . ."

WITH NO RESOURCES to express his feelings to Cyprian, Reef settled for practical planning. "Figure on heading west, through the mountains, to the Adriatic coast. Any hot springs, hotel de luxes up that way you could recommend?"

"It depends how far north you're planning to go. I never got south of Montenegro. Oh, but you might want this."

It was the Webley-Fosbery .38 that had seen him through Bosnia and the years since.

Reef pretended to look it over. "Nice little iron. Sure you wouldn't like to hang on to this?"

"What for? Brides of Night don't carry service revolvers in their kit."

"I could think of one or two developments. . . ."

"But, Reef." A hand on his shoulder. "That's what you mustn't do." The two men looked in each other's eyes, for longer than either could remember doing.

CYPRIAN CAME WITH THEM as far as the river. Above them cloud had begun to enfold the convent and the church, as if denying them second thoughts. The morning seemed to be darkening toward some Balkan equivalent of Transfiguration.

She handed Ljubica to Cyprian, and he held her ceremonially, and kissed her loudly on her stomach as always, and as always she squealed. "Don't remember me," he advised her. "I'll see to all the remembering." Back in Yash's arms, she beamed at him calmly, and he knew he had only minutes before regret would force him into a mistake of some kind. "Go safely. Try to stay out of Albania."

As if seized by something ancient, Yashmeen cried, "Please—don't look back."

"I wasn't planning to."

"I'm serious. You mustn't. I beg you, Cyprian."

"Or he'll take you below, you mean. Down to America."

"Always makin with em jokes," Reef in a hollow chuckle.

And none of them looked back, not even Ljubica.

And Cyprian was taken behind a great echoless door.

FOR DAYS Reef and Yashmeen each latched into a separate sorrow, couldn't even talk about it. Reef gave up his restless scouting of likely honky-tonks, and when evening came and the gray light fell like fine ash, he only sat heartbroken, indoors preferably, by a window, holding the baby sometimes. Being in her own partial vacuum, Yashmeen knew of no way to chirp him out of it.

"I didn't see it coming," Reef said finally, "but I guess you did."

"It wasn't us," she said. "Nothing we did. Nothing we should have done."

"Don't say 'he must've loved God more'n us,' is all."

"No because I don't think that's true." She was all ready to start crying then.

"I mean God don't normally run up and bite people on the ass, but if he *did,* see—"

"Reef. Cyprian loved us. He still does."

Somehow neither saw much further point in going to the Black Sea coast. They turned and headed west. One evening Reef came in to find Yashmeen sitting distraught by a pile of Cyprian's discarded clothing, picking up item after item. "I could pretend to be him for you," she cried, not loud enough to wake Ljubica, the hopefulness in her voice more than he knew how to respond to, "I could wear his shirts, his trousers, you could tear them off, and take my arse and fuck my mouth, and imagine that he's . . ."

"Darlin . . . please. . . . That ain't goin to do it. . . ." Too damn close to tears himself if you really wanted to know.

He had begun to hold her with a tenderness she had seen before this only when he held Ljubica. I am not his child, she protested, but to herself, even as she settled further into his embrace.

· · ·

THEY MADE THEIR WAY up off the Plain of Thrace, into the Rhodopes and then the Pirin range, over toward Macedonia. Some days the light was pitiless. Light so saturated with color, brought hovering to such tension, that it could not be borne for long, as if it were dangerous to be out in country filled with light like this, as if anyone beneath it were just about to be taken by it, if not over into death then some transformation at least as severe. Light like this must be received with judgment—too much, too constantly, would exhaust the soul. To move through it would be to struggle against time, the flow of the day, the arbitrarily assigned moment of darkness. Sometimes Reef wondered if maybe somebody hadn't triggered that *Interdikt* after all, and this was the residue from it. . . .

In mid-October, after declaring war against Turkey, divisions of the Serbian, Greek, and Bulgarian armies invaded Macedonia, and by the twenty-second, fighting between Serbians and Turks was heavy around Kumanovo, in the north. Meanwhile Bulgarian forces were pressing south toward the Turkish border and Adrianople just beyond.

Each day then would show Reef, Yash, and Ljubica only a further narrowing of choices, as they were pressed by the movements of forces toward the west and south. Rumors were everywhere, a storm of fearful hearsay from gatherings at street-corners and well-heads. . . . "It's what we were sent out here to stop," Yashmeen said. "This must mean that we failed, and the assignment is over."

"The job now's just to get out of here," Reef figured. He began to spend time each morning at whatever *mehana,* crossroads, or other gathering place might be handy, trying to pick up what news he could and figure the safest direction to be heading in. "Is they're comin in from all directions, is the problem here, Serbs from the north, Greeks from the south, Bulgarians from the east. Turks on the run everyplace, shouldn't last long, but what a commotion."

"So we keep heading west."

"Only choice. Try and scoot between the armies. Then, if we get that far, worry about that Albania."

THE FIGHTING had been moving obliquely away from them, from Philippopolis, toward the Turkish border and Adrianople. They crept south, in the partial vacuum, behind Ivanoff's Second Army, which was on the right of the general advance.

They crossed over into Macedonia. Even the crows were silent now. Heading west through Strumica and Valandovo, they found the pomegranate orchards full of refugees, and they kept on into the valley of the Vardar beyond, and the Tikveš wine country, where the harvest had just been brought in.

According to rumor the Serbians had defeated the Turks at Kumanovo, but had been slow in following up their advantage. The countryside was filled with Turkish soldiers either cut off from their units or in flight, all looking deeply unhappy, many wounded, some about to die. Monastir was said to be a Serbian objective now, which meant there would be fighting to the westward as well.

Reef took to scavenging weapons wherever he could, field-issue and hunting pieces, Mausers and Mannlichers as well as more ancient firearms, some with Arabic inscriptions or trimmed with elk-horn or boar-tusk ivory, ammunition of all calibers from 6.5 to 11 mm, sometimes discovered in abandoned encampments, more and more often taken from the dead, who had begun to appear in increasing numbers, like immigrants into a country where they were feared, disliked, pitilessly exploited.

As the landscape turned increasingly chaotic and murderous, the streams of refugees swelled. Another headlong, fearful escape of the kind that in collective dreams, in legends, would be misremembered and reimagined into pilgrimage or crusade . . . the dark terror behind transmuted to a bright hope ahead, the bright hope becoming a popular, perhaps someday a national, delusion. Embedded invisibly in it would remain the ancient darkness, too awful to face, thriving, emerging in disguise, vigorous, evil, destructive, inextricable.

"There's fighting out ahead of us now, so best we step careful," Reef reported. Each day brought them closer to the horizon of the unimaginable. All Europe could be at war by now. Nobody knew.

When Ljubica heard her first explosions from up in the mountains to the northwest, between Veles and Prilep, though she hadn't been sleeping, she seemed to wake from wakefulness, her eyes widening, and let out a laugh, "Which from an older child," her mother trying not to be too offended, "one must describe as *uproarious*."

"Gets it from her grandpa," Reef nodded, "dynamite baby. In the blood."

"Glad to see you both enjoying yourselves. Could we try not to get caught in any of this?"

A major battle was shaping up, and Reef, Yash, and Ljubica happened to be heading into its rear areas. They joined processions across the plains, between stagnant ditches, farm carts pushed and pulled by younger sons, piled with furniture that would end up being burned for warmth as the days grew colder and the terrain higher, dogs in unending negotiation over what was guarded and what fair targets, forming temporary packs to gang likely sheep, scattering at the arrival of the flock's own sheepdog. Krupp guns thumping in the distance, village crones wandering the hillsides, the constant birds of prey patrolling the sky.

After being defeated at Kumanovo, three Turkish army corps had fled south, toward the fortified city of Monastir, one of the last Turkish bastions in Europe, pursued by the Serbian First Army, whose orders were to finish them off. While the Sixth Corps went directly to Monastir, the Fifth and Seventh deployed in the mountains just to the north to engage and try to slow the Serbian forces coming down by way of Kičevo and Prilep. A stretch of mountain fighting followed, notably at the Babuna Pass above Prilep.

One morning at first light they awoke into a firefight the likes of which few out here had ever encountered and would never have expected in this antiquated world of bolt-action weaponry. Among the frantic popping of Mauser against Mauser, something new on Earth. Machine guns, the future of warfare. Russian Madsen guns and a few Montenegrin Rexers. It was the devastation and final descent of the Ottoman project, the centuries of Turkey in Europe, the last garrisons falling one by one. . . .

"What is it?" she whispered, holding the baby tightly to her.

"Oh just some bees, darlin," Reef affecting the roguish smile that apparently would never fail him. "Serbian bumblebees, just be sure and keep your heads down."

"Oh," going along with it, not that there was much choice at the moment, "that's all." Ljubica was trembling but quiet, as if determined not to cry.

"You got that Webley someplace handy, am I right?" trying not to holler too loud. Only if they get close enough, he had said, when he gave it to her. Otherwise we're fine. Was it going to be close enough this time?

Troops were running by screaming, whether in panic terror or battle cry, whether Serbian or Turk, nobody was about to look out there and see.

Howitzer shells started dropping nearby. Not a sustained barrage, but it would only take one.

"Once they get their line and length," she said, "we may have to vacate the premises."

"I think," said Reef, "you mean 'range and bearing,' darlin."

"A cricketing term," she explained. "I once played briefly at Girton a million years ago. My secret dream was always to play for a team of nomads like I Zingari. . . ."

It had become their practice to adopt this style of chitchat during moments of danger. Whether it fooled Ljubica for a minute was debatable, but it kept Reef and Yash occupied. Like the terrible footfalls of an invisible angel, the blasts were coming closer. Presently the shells were visible, rising and falling slowly and steeply out in the monochrome autumn, each time descending with a harsh, buzzing shriek. Finally one landed so close that all the lethal noise of that day was gathered and concentrated into its one split second, and Ljubica changed her mind and began to cry, disengaging from her mother's shelter and facing out into whatever it was, screaming, not in fear but in anger. In numb fascination her parents gazed at her. It was a minute before they understood that the machine-gun fire had stopped. There was some more ordnance, but much farther away now.

"Full of surprises ain't you," Reef taking Ljubica and with calibrated softness kissing her streaming eyes. "No more bumblebees, kid." When it was quiet again, he thought of something. "Be back in a minute." He went off in the direction the machine-gun fire had been coming from. Ljubica wrinkled her forehead and waved an arm and made an inquisitive sort of "Ah?"

"Your father's needs are simple," Yashmeen explained, "and so it wouldn't surprise me if—why yes, look, just what I thought. See what Papa has brought home."

"A miracle," Reef said. "It's all in one piece." He held up a peculiar-looking rifle whose barrel seemed much wider than usual, though this turned out to be a perforated casing for air-cooling the weapon. "Folks, meet the Madsen machine rifle. Been hearing about these for a while now. Every Russian cavalry division used to carry some, but they decided to get rid of 'em awhile back and a lot came on the market out here, especially up in Montenegro, where they're known as Rexers. Lookit this. Five hundred rounds a minute on auto, and when the barrel gets too hot—" He produced a duplicate barrel, twisted off the first, and replaced it. He had also managed to scavenge a number of quarter-circular magazines holding forty rounds each.

"I'm happy for you, of course," said Yashmeen.

"Oh and here." Somewhere in this ashen field among the corpses and blood and the seep of cordite smoke and fragments of steel he had found a patch of wildflowers, and now he handed them each a small bouquet. Ljubica immediately began to eat hers, and Yash just gazed at Reef until her eyes were too wet, and then she wiped them with her sleeve.

"Thanks. We should be moving."

Now and then in the weeks that followed they would find themselves wondering—though they could never find the time to just sit and talk it through—if the permission they had felt when Cyprian was with them, the freedom to act extraordinarily, had come from residence in a world about to embrace its end—closer to the freedom of the suicide than that of the ungoverned spirit.

THE WINTER COMING DOWN. The war unpredictably everywhere. They sheltered often in the temporary thatch huts of Sarakatsàni, for it was these people of no country, no native town, no fixed abode, the nomads of the Peninsula, who would see them to safety, who shared their own food, tobacco, and sleeping space. Yashmeen gave them jars of rose preserve that Zhivka had put up for them, brought this far miraculously unbroken, and they gave her a wooden baby-carrying rig to strap to her back, which she and Reef, who had started calling Ljubica "the papoose," took turns with. Ljubica rode along perched up like a lookout, inviting her parents' attention to horsemen, sheepdogs and sheep, drops of rain . . . the obstinate accompaniment of horse and field artillery, flanking, pursuing. At last they came over the Bukovo Pass and down into Ohrid, beside its pale wind-rippled lake, in among red roofs, acacias and alleyways, its town clamor, which did not include guns, welcome as silence. Turkish deserters slept on the beach, haunted the mosques, traded weapons for cigarettes.

There had been forty thousand Turks at Monastir, German-trained under the legendary Liman von Sanders, whose plans included sending his murderous creatures into the Ukraine when the time arrived for war with Russia. An intimidating claim, to've been schooled in the arts of mass death by Germans. But now the Serbs knew they could beat them.

THEY LOOKED ACROSS THE LAKE, up at the black peaks, already with some snow on them. A chasm had opened in the clouds, which light poured down through, a vertical torrent of light, cleaving through all the imaginable shades of gray which inhabited the sky, as if presenting the day with choices it seldom if ever saw.

"It's Albania," she said. Cyprian had told them to stay out of Albania. Everybody had. Not that the folks there weren't warm and hospitable as ever, but there was some kind of revolution going on up north, against the Turks, the Greeks had invaded and occupied the south, and much of the fighting was informal, by way of long-range rifles. "There may be one paved road somewhere, but it's bound to take us right into the worst of the fighting."

"Let's see. Winter in the mountains, no map, everybody shootin at everybody else."

"That's about it."

"Hell, let's do it."

BEFORE SETTING OFF down the shore of the lake, as if they were only out here on holiday, they bought postal cards illustrated with scenes of the War, and stamps each printed in two or three languages, not to mention Turkish and Cyrillic alphabets, with provisional overprints in these as well as Roman face. Some of the photographs showed terrible scenes of slaughter and mutilation, reproduced not in simple black and white but varying shades of green, a quite fluorescent green as a matter of fact—shell craters, limbless men at field hospitals, gigantic cannons, aeroplanes flying in formation. . . . They posted them, in the sure and certain hope of none arriving, to Yz-les-Bains, Chunxton Crescent, Gabrovo Slim and Zhivka, Frank and Mayva in the U.S.A., Kit Traverse and Auberon Halfcourt, Hotel Tarim, Kashgar, Chinese Turkestan.

At the south end of the lake, they went down the footpath to Sveti Naum and crossed into Albania. Traffic was unremitting both ways, Mahommedan refugees driven from their homes in Albania by the Greek invaders, and Turkish remnants from the defeat at Monastir fleeing south trying to find their way to the fortress at Yanina, the last residue of the Ottoman Empire in Europe and the only safety left to them here in Epirus. The guards at the gate, when they paid attention at all, shrugged everybody through. They were no longer sure, for one thing, whom they were reporting to.

Reef, Yash, and Ljubica had entered a theatre of war where everybody shot at everybody, not always for reasons the targets could appreciate in detail, though pissed off enough seemed to provide all the motive folks needed.

They were ambushed outside Pogradeci, on the road to Korça, by a band of irregulars, not more than half a dozen, Reef estimated, though the distinction between guerrillas and road agents had become for the moment meaningless.

"Stop up 'at little baby's ears a minute would you darlin, got to have us some recreational skeet here," Reef snapping a magazine into the Madsen gun and, after settling everybody in behind some rocks by the roadside, murmuring something like, "At long last," started off in semiautomatic mode but soon, as the assailants began to curse and scatter, the appeal of the change lever in front of the trigger-guard grew irresistible, and Reef entered the domain of five hundred rounds per minute, and before he could holler anything too gleeful the magazine was used up and the barrel not even warm, and whoever they'd been, they didn't seem to be there anymore.

"What he does best, of course," Yashmeen murmured as if to Ljubica.

A little farther down the road they ran into a Greek army detachment coming to investigate the rapid fire they thought they'd heard. Since the war began there'd been Greek troops everywhere in the south of Albania, which they thought of as Epirus, belonging to some idea of Greece more abstract than anyplace their own homes and families might've happened to be. Reef, with the Madsen stashed well out of sight, shrugged and made vague gestures in the direction the bushwhackers had gone off in, and he had soon obtained a pack of cigarettes and a ride in a supply wagon as far as Korça, nowadays under Greek occupation.

After shivering under a shredded tent all night, they were up early and out again into the freezing predawn, and on the road. Past Erseka they began to climb up into the Gramoz Range, the beech trees leafless in the rising winds, winter peaks above shining desolate as Alps, on the other side of which, where they were known as the Pindus, lay Greece.

As the sun was going down they found a farm outbuilding that seemed deserted, until Reef came in from scavenging for firewood and found Ljubica sitting next to one of the savage and ill-disposed sheepdogs known in Macedonia as a *šarplaninec.*

Dogs out here were famous for biting before they barked—Cyprian had been pretty repetitious on that point—but here was Ljubica, all sociability, talking away in her personal language, and the critter, looking something like a shaggy brown-and-blond bear with a kindly enough face, was listening to her with great interest. When Reef approached, they both turned their heads to stare, politely but unmistakably in warning, the dog raising her eyebrows and clicking her tongue, which somebody back in the tunnel days had once told Reef was Albanian for "No."

"O.K., O.K." Reef slowly backed out through the doorway again.

It would be many years before he learned that this dog's name was Ksenija, and that she was the intimate companion of Pugnax, whose human associates the Chums of Chance had been invisibly but attentively keeping an eye on the progress of Reef's family exfiltration from the Balkan Peninsula. Her task at this juncture was to steer everyone to safety without appearing to.

Accordingly, the next day Reef was out doing some forward scouting, Yash and Ljubica dug in back up the valley, when from someplace he smelled woodsmoke and heard donkeys, and next thing he knew, there were these three Albanians who had the drop on him. "Well *tungjatjeta,* fellas," Reef trying to recall some tunnel Albanian and flashing his all-purpose charming smile.

The Albanians were also smiling. "I fuck your mother," the first one greeted him.

"I fuck you, then I fuck your mother," said the second.

"First I kill you and your mother, then I fuck you both," said the third.

"You folks are usually so . . . friendly," Reef said. "What's up?" He had an enormous 11 mm Montenegrin Gasser in his belt, but this, he sensed, was not the time to be reaching for it. The men were packing older-type Mannlicher rifles and one Gras, likely all taken from dead Greeks. Some small argument had developed, which Reef dimly understood was about who would get to shoot him, though nobody seemed that eager, ammo he guessed being in short supply, especially for the Gras, 11 mm like his pistol, which might be all they were after. So it would be between the Mannlichers. They were now looking around in the mud for suitable pieces of straw to draw. The nearest cover was a ditch with a berm ten yards to his right, but then Reef caught the gleam off a rifle barrel there, and then a couple more. "Oh, oh," he said, "looks like I'm a dead duck here. How do you folks say it, *një rosë vdekuri,* right?"

Buying him a minute and a half of grace, which turned out to be just enough, because a voice somewhere began calling his name, and presently a wiry figure came ambling out from behind a stone wall.

"Ramiz?"

"*Vëlla!* Brother!" He ran to Reef and embraced him. "This is the American who saved my life back in the Swiss tunnel!"

The three riflemen seemed disappointed. "Does that mean we don't get to shoot him?"

"Thought you'd be in America by now," Reef said.

"My family. How could I leave?" As it turned out, this village was inhabited by refugees from all over the country, north and south, targets of blood-feud revenge who had found it possible no longer to remain each a prisoner in his own home, and decided that setting up a village-size compound all together would be the best way to have a little more room to move around in while still honoring the Kanun of Lekë Dukagjin. A community founded on vengeance suspended.

"You were lucky," Ramiz said, "strangers don't get this close, usually."

"Just looking for a safe couple of nights," Reef said, and gave him a rundown on Yash and Ljubica.

"You are crazy to be out here, too many Greeks loose in these hills." He poured rakia. "*Gëzuar!* Bring them both here! Plenty of room!"

Reef got back to the village with Yash and Ljubica just as it began to snow, and for the next few days they were snowed in. By the time they were able to journey on, he'd picked up a little more Tosk dialect and learned to play "Jim Along Jo" on a clarinet, which everybody here seemed to own at least one of, some of the men getting together nights after supper with their instruments and playing in three- or four-part harmony and drinking rakia.

Reef and Yashmeen were to find themselves standing against the snow descending, in a comradely persistence too unquestioned for either to have thought of as honorable, their backs often as not to the wind, tall, silent, bowed over their own hearts, over the small life it had become their duty, unimposed, emerged simply from the turns of their fate, to protect—not only it seemed from the storm, because later, sheltered for a moment, in Përmeti or Gjirokastra, both remembered feeling the presence of a conscious and searching force which was not the storm, nor the winter nor the promise of more of the same for who knew how long . . . but something else, something malevolent and much older than the terrain or any race that might have passed in unthinking pilgrimage across it, something which swallowed whole and shit into oblivion whatever came in range of its hunger.

Reef had once been notorious all over Colorado as the most luckless fisherman west of the Great Divide, but this trip he'd brought along a fishhook all the way from Yz-les-Bains, which he began now to drop and somehow, contrary to all expectation, manage every other day or so to pull out some kind of trout from one of the rivers. The snow came and went, but when it went, it became mostly rain, cold and miserable. On a rare day of sunshine, up near a town in the Vjosa Valley, he and Yash allowed themselves a moment of slack just to stand and gaze.

"I'd stay here forever."

"Don't sound too nomadic to me."

"But look at it." Pretty scenic, Reef guessed, a dozen minarets brightly ascending among the trees, a little river you could see the bottom of rushing through the town, the yellow light of a café in the dusk that could become their local, the smells and the murmuring and the ancient certainty that life, however reduced now and then to the arts of being intelligent prey, was preferable to the plague of eagles beginning to take over the land.

"That's the worst of it," Yashmeen said. "It's so beautiful."

"Wait till you see Colorado."

She looked over at him and after a heartbeat or two he looked back. Ljubica happened to be in Reef's arms, and she pressed her cheek against his chest and watched her mother the way she did when she knew Yash was just about to start crying.

Once through Gjirokastra, they began the long switchback out of the mountains and down to the Adriatic Sea—mingling part of the way with Turks still headed south. There was a cease-fire in effect now among all parties except for Greece, still trying to take Yanina, the last Turkish stronghold in the south. Half the Turkish army by now were dead, wounded, or taken prisoner, and the rest were heading in desperation for Yanina. Reef gave them the rest of his cigarettes. It was all he had. Kept one or two, maybe.

At last they came over the Muzina Pass, and there presently was the sea, and the whitewashed houses ascending from the deep curve of the little harbor of Agli Saranta.

Down in town, a winter rainstorm outside, which back up in the mountains they knew would be snow, Ljubica sleeping bundled in a wolfskin, they felt as if they were still moving, borne on some invisible conveyance, following some crooked, complicated path, now and then interrupted by sojourns in semipublic gathering places like this one, filled with layers of stale tobacco smoke, political arguments over obscure issues—a fluorescent blue sense of enclosure, the only view outside through a window at the harbor, and beyond it the furious sea.

They found a fishing captain who agreed to take them over to Corfu his next time out, and drop them at the town. With a winter norther coming down off the mountains, roughening the strait with whitecaps besides an already perilous swell, they headed south down the channel, the wind on their port quarter. Reef, no sailor, spent the time vomiting, often into the wind, either because he didn't care or couldn't wait. Once they were in the lee of Pantokratoras, the wind dropped, and within the hour they had come to safety at last in the town of Corfu, where the first thing they did was go to the Church of St. Spiridion, patron saint of the island, and light candles and offer thanks.

They would stay the rest of the winter and into the spring and the radiant sunshine, and out on the main esplanade a cricket game with a visiting XI from Lefkas, everyone in white, and nothing imaginable of darkness or blood, for the duration of the game in its blessedness . . . Ljubica exclaiming in road-baby demotic every time the bat and ball made contact. At the end of the game, little of which, including who'd won, Reef was able to figure out, the Lefkas side presented their opposite numbers each with one of the hot-pepper salamis for which the island was famous.

Persisting behind the world's every material utterance, the Compassionate now took steps to re-establish contact with Yashmeen. As if the Balkan assignment had never been about secret Austrian minefields at all, but about Cyprian becoming a bride of Night, and Ljubica being born during the rose harvest, and Reef and Yashmeen getting her safely to Corfu—thereby successfully carrying out the "real" mission, for which the other, mines and all, was what the Compassionate liked to call a metaphor—one day as she and Ljubica were sitting at a café out on the Esplanade, there was Auberon Halfcourt, holding a bottle of ginger beer, trotting up in a fiacre as if he were keeping an appointment. . . . It would be his granddaughter who spotted him first, having recognized the horse, who like the other horses here wore a straw hat with holes for his ears to poke through.

After formal kisses all round, Halfcourt took a seat.

"But what are you doing in Corfu?" Yashmeen in beaming bewilderment.

"Waiting for you." He pushed across to her a battered piece of greenish pasteboard.

"My postal. You actually got it?"

"One of the Russians who'd routinely been reading all my mail since the day I arrived at Kashgar deemed this more important than anything H.M. Government might have had to say. Cabled me instantaneously." She had written, "We hope to reach the Adriatic."

"Meaning it would be either here or Durazzo, but Durazzo lately having become rather a casus belli, one went into a trance and summoned the old intuitive powers don't you know, and Corfu it was."

"Oh and this"—gesturing around at the Parisian arcades, the leafy, well-watered paradise—"had nothing to do with it."

They sat and drank ouzo in the twilight. Up at the old Venetian fort the evening gun went off. Breezes stirred the cypresses and olive trees. Corfiots strolled to and fro.

"Seeing you again," he said, "once I thought it would be one of those moments of surrender to fate, with an unpleasant outcome guaranteed. It did not prevent me from wanting to, however." They had not seen each other since before 1900. Whatever his feelings might prove to be, her own were not so much in conflict now as expanded. Her love for Ljubica being impenetrable and indivisible as a prime number, other loves must be accordingly re-evaluated. As for Halfcourt, "I am not who I was," he said. "Out there I was the servant of greed and force. A butler. A pastry-cook. All the while believing myself a military professional. The only love they permitted me was indistinguishable from commerce. They were destroying me and I didn't know it."

"Have you resigned your commission?"

"Better than that. I have deserted."

"Father!"

"Better than *that,*" he went on in a sort of cheerfully serene momentum, "they think I'm dead. Through my Russian colleague Volodya, I am also comfortably set, thanks to a transaction in jade—your namesake mineral, my dear—destined one day to be considered legendary. You may think of me as the man who broke the bank at Monte Carlo. And—"

"Oh, I knew there would be more." She was visited by the certainty that he was deep in some intrigue with a woman.

As if having read his daughter's mind, the old renegade exclaimed, "And by heaven here she comes, even as we speak!"

Yashmeen turned to see approaching up the esplanade, dwarfed by her shadow from the sunset, a tiny Asian woman all in white, who was waving at them.

"That American chap who brought your letter out to Kashgar is the one actually who introduced us. Ran into him last year in Constantinople, tending bar. And there was Umeki. Ah yes, my little Japanese eggplant."

Indeed it was Umeki Tsurigane, who had been posted to the Japanese embassy at Constantinople as a "mathematical attaché," on some mysterious mission on behalf of the technical establishment of her country when she happened to stroll one early evening into the bar at the Deux Continents, and there was Kit Traverse in front of a room-long mirror agitating the contents of a silver cocktail shaker.

"You were supposed to die of shame."

"Doing my best," Kit setting a shot glass and a beer glass in front of her. "Your usual boilermaker, mademoiselle?"

"No! Champagne cocktail! Tonight that might be more appropriate!"

"I'll have one with you."

He might have meant to ask about the Q-weapon and the Tunguska Event and so on, and for about one drink and a sip or two from another it looked like the reawakening of old times, except that Auberon Halfcourt showed up around then on his clandestine way out of Russia, and "I don't know what happened," she told Yashmeen, "I was fascinated!" And her life took one of those turns.

"An old rogue's dream," added Halfcourt fondly. But Yashmeen was observing how the young woman gazed at her father, and diagnosed it as a case of true erotic mania. What Halfcourt felt, exactly, was, as it had always been, something of a mystery to her.

THEY FOUND REEF in a taverna, down by the harbor in Garitsa. Ljubica, now pushing the age of one and newly up on her feet, held on to a barstool and with a lopsided smile that suggested this was nothing new, regarded her father drinking ouzo and acquainting Corfiots with the intricacies of Leadville Fan-Tan.

Yash introduced Umeki with eyebrows raised and a private hand-signal curiously suggestive of a meat-cleaver cutting off a penis, Reef merely beaming back as he always did at any presentable young woman in flirting range.

"Your brother," Umeki smiled, "he is—a bartender—and a matchmaker!"

"I knew all that math stuff'd be good for somethin. Here, let me just dishonestly relieve these folks of a couple more leptas and maybe there'll be enough for supper."

They all sat at a long table and ate tsingarelli and polenta and yaprakia and a chicken stoufado with fennel and quince and pancetta in it that Nikos the owner and cook said was an ancient Venetian recipe from back in the centuries when the island had belonged to Venice, and Reef snuck his baby daughter tiny sips of Mavrodaphne, which did not put her to sleep but made her quite rowdy as a matter of fact, pulling the tail of Hrisoula, the ordinarily imperturbable taverna cat, until she actually meowed in protest. A small *rembetika* band arrived with a singer, and presently Yash and Ljubica were up dancing a species of *karsilamás* together.

Later in the evening, Halfcourt took Yashmeen aside. "Before you ask about Shambhala . . ."

"Perhaps I wasn't going to." Her eyes were shining.

"For me, Shambhala, you see, turned out to be not a goal but an absence. Not the discovery of a place but the act of leaving the futureless place where I was. And in the process I arrived at Constantinople."

"And your world-line crossed that of Miss Tsurigane. And so."

"And so."

By the time they agreed to part, Stray and Ewball had forgotten why they ran off together in the first place. Stray recalled it had something to do with her early notions of the Anarchist life and its promise of a *greater invisibility,* extending for all she knew clear around the world. By the time of the coalfield troubles in southern Colorado, she had assembled her own network of sources for medical supplies, begun in the days of the Madero revolution and expanded one local doctor, one union hospital, one friendly pharmacist at a time. She had always had the gift for knowing whom to trust and how far, finding herself now using her deal-making skills to get food and medicine where they were needed in these less clearly defined campaigns of the revolution north of the border, and the possibility of a vast unseen commonwealth of support certainly had its practical appeal.

It wasn't exactly a religious experience, but somehow, a little at a time, she had found herself surrendering to her old need to take care of people. Not for compensation, certainly not for thanks. Her first rule became "Don't thank me." Her second was "Don't take the credit for anything that turns out well." One day she woke up understanding clear as the air that as long as a person was willing to forgo credit, there were very few limits on the good it became possible to do.

Stray had been accustomed to search out the real interests that lay behind spoken ones, and think of ways to reconcile them. Though the interests at war in the coal country were clear enough, she had some trouble deciphering Ewball's own in wanting to head down there. Profit and power for Ewball were not objects of desire, though she would never come to believe that he didn't want to be leader of something, or have access to resources of one sort or another. But it was invisible, whatever that was, his Anarchist remit. It never occurred to her he might just love getting into trouble.

To her not particularly bitter disappointment, it became rapidly evident that Ewball also took the Anarchist view of love, marriage, childrearing and so forth. "Think of me as an educational resource," he told her. "Jeez Ewball, I don't know, it's basically your dick," she replied.

Nevertheless, due to feelings of mental ambivalence which were just beginning at that time to be understood, it had one day occurred to Ewball, after an absence measurable in years, to drop in on his family in Denver, having got it into his head that Stray might want to meet his parents, which she didn't, all that much. One fleece-clouded weekday, with about half an hour's warning over the telephone, they showed up at his family home.

The Oust residence was still fairly new, big and cross-gabled, with a round tower and a lot of spindlework and shingling, and large enough to accommodate an indeterminate number of Ousts and Oust in-laws at any given time.

Ewball's mother, Moline Velma Oust, answered the door in person. "Ewball *Junior*? Well convey your fundament in to the parlor!"

"This is my mother. Ma, Miss Estrella Briggs."

"You are welcome to our home, Miss Briggs." The Ousts had been living down in Denver for some while now, Leadville having fallen on dismal times, lots and houses for sale everywhere you looked, and no takers. "Remember that one across the street? Their For Sale sign went up, we took a stopwatch, less than five minutes on the market, gone for ten thousand. These days you couldn't pay somebody to live in it." Moline would have taken as her exemplar the Lake County legend Baby Doe Tabor, seeing herself dressed in stylish mourning up at some shafthouse with a rifle across her knees, defending family property, and by extension the glory days of some legendary town, to the bitter end. But so far her husband, Ewball Sr., had shown little interest in being Haw Tabor, that is, dead.

"I see you admiring our new Steinway piano, Miss Briggs. Do you play, by any chance?"

"Not much, song accompaniments mostly."

"I'm such a devotee of the Schubert lieder myself. . . . Oh, do play us something, won't you!"

Stray got maybe four bars into a one-step of the day called "I'm Going to Get Myself a Black Salome," when Moline remembered she had to see to the majolica, which was being dusted today. "Mexican refugees, you know, it's so difficult sometimes—oh dear, no offense, I hope you're not one of Ewball's—that is—"

Having run into this sort of thing once or twice, Stray tried to steer her through it. "'Ewball is a dear,'" she prompted, "'but he brings home the most peculiar girls sometimes'?"

Moline, seeming visibly to relax, favored her with a squint and a one-sided smile. "Guess you know the general outline, then. He's got no sense of money, and there are young ladies of the syndicalist persuasion who just have an instinct for that."

"Mrs. Oust," Stray said calmly, "I'm not after anybody's money, got enough of my own, thanks, fact it's been me picking up all the saloon tabs lately, and I sure wouldn't mind you havin a word 'th old Ewb about that, 'cause I figure it must be his upbringing?"

"*Well.*" Off to that majolica after all. But either she was the kind of good-natured soul who can't stay upset for long, or she found Stray a refreshing enough change, or she just had the attention span of a chipmunk, because in a couple of minutes she was back with lemonade in a cut-glass pitcher and matching glasses, waving off one of the girls, *"'Tá bien, no te preocupes, m'hija."*

"*You.*" A man of middle age in galluses, holding a fistful of U.S. mail, stood in the doorway red-faced, shaking, and just about to explode.

"Howdy, Pa."

Introducing Stray did not deflect the elder Oust from his furious intention. "Ewball, what the hell," waving the wad of correspondence.

"Now Father," appealed Moline, "how many sons write home as regularly as our own here?"

"That's just it. Pinhead!" he spat. As a stamp collector of average obsessiveness, his unhappiness with his son had grown from bewilderment into an all but homicidal rage. It seemed that young Ewball had been using postage stamps from the 1901 Pan-American Issue, commemorating the Exposition of that name in Buffalo, New York, where the Anarchist Czolgosz had assassinated President McKinley. These stamps bore engraved vignettes of the latest in modern transportation, trains, boats, and so forth, and by mistake, some of the one-cent, two-cent, and four-cent denominations had been printed with these center designs upside down. One thousand Fast Lake Navigation, 158 Fast Express, and 206 Automobile inverts had been sold before the errors were caught, and before stamp-collector demand had driven their prices quite through the roof, Ewball, sensitive to the Anarchistic symbolism, had bought up and hoarded as many as he could find to mail his letters with.

"Even right side up," shouted Ewball Senior, "any nincompoop knows enough to keep stamps in mint condition—uncanceled, original gum intact! for chrissakes—otherwise the secondary-market value goes all to hell. Every time you mailed one of these letters here you wasted hundreds, maybe thousands of dollars."

"Exactly my point, sir. Inversion symbolizes undoing. Here are three machines, false idols of the capitalist faith, literally overthrown—along with an indirect reference of course to the gunning down of Mark Hanna's miserable stooge, that resolute enemy of human progress—"

"I voted for McKinley, damn it!"

"As long as you are truly penitent, the people in their wisdom will forgive you."

"Rrrrr!" Oust Senior threw the letters in the air, dropped to all fours and charged screaming at Ewball, into whose ankle he unhesitatingly sank his teeth. Ewball, in considerable pain, sought with his other foot to step repeatedly on his father's head, the two men filling the air of the parlor meanwhile with language unfit for the sensitive reader, let alone those ladies present, who gathering their skirts and moving cautiously, were attempting to pull the disputants apart, when all at once the curious Œdipal spectacle was interrupted by a loud gunshot.

A woman in a simple dress of dark gray henrietta, calm and solid, holding a Remington target pistol, had entered the room. Gunsmoke rose toward the ceiling, from which still descended the last of a fine shower of plaster, lighted by the window behind to surround her briefly in a bright cloud. Stray, looking upward, noticed there were several patches of damaged ceiling along with the one just created. The Ousts, father and son, had abandoned their struggle and risen to their feet, somewhat apologetic, less to each other than to this matronly referee who had just called a halt to their recreation.

"Thought I'd look in." She slid the ten-inch barrel of the weapon beneath the band of the white muslin apron she was wearing.

"As always, Mrs. Traverse," said Ma Oust, "we are in your debt. Please don't worry about the ceiling, we were planning to have it redone anyway."

"Ran out of the B.B. caps, had to use a .22 short."

"Quite unobjectionable, I'm sure. And as you're here, perhaps you wouldn't mind seeing to our house-guest, Miss Briggs. She might rather enjoy the Chinese Room, don't you think? Estrella, dear, anything you need, Mrs. Traverse is a miracle-working saint, and this house would be simply chaos without her."

When they were alone, Mayva said, "We only met but that once in Durango."

"Reef and I always meant to come see you in Telluride soon as the baby was born, but one thing and another . . ."

"I sure heard enough about you over the years, Estrella. Always figured

Reef's future'd be with one of them girlies that tread a bit closer to the Abyss . . . but here you are, a young lady showin nothin but class."

"Guess you must miss him."

"Yeahp but you never know who'll show up. How's my grandbaby?"

"Here, look." Stray had snaps of Jesse she always carried in her purse.

"Oh the little heartbreaker. If he don't just favor Webb."

"You can keep these—"

"Oh, no, that's—"

"I always have extras."

"Well I'm obliged. But how can he be this grown-up already?"

"Don't remind me."

They were in the Chinese Room by now, fussing with drapes, coverlets, and dresser scarves in various "Chinese" motifs. "Ewball and Frank, they've rode together off and on, I take it."

"We were all down in Mexico a while back. Frank got a little banged up but nothin serious."

Mayva looked up awkwardly, hopeful. "I know that's where he was when he took care of that one killer the owners hired. Do you know if he might've found the other one down there too?"

"Not so far's I know. This was more like a battle we got mixed up in. Frank fell off a horse. Took some time to mend."

She nodded. "He's the patient one in the family." She looked Stray in the eyes. "I know it's all any of us can do."

Stray put her hand on Mayva's. "Somebody'll get that Deuce Kindred someday, and Mr. Vibe too, it wouldn't surprise me. People that bad have a way of bringin it to themselves sooner or later."

Mayva took Stray's arm and they went down to the kitchen. "You can imagine how happy I was havin to go to work here, in a millionaire's mansion. Ran into 'em all on the train when they 's movin down from Leadville. Started playin with the little ones. Forgot how much I missed that. Next thing I knew, there 's old Moline pourin her heart out. Everthin about Denver had her worryin, big-city vices, schools for the children, low-altitude cookin, and she somehow got it into her head I was jake with all that. Turns out she's good people, good enough, just a little flighty now and then. He's all right too, I suppose, for a plute."

Too fast almost to register, the years had taken Mayva from a high-strung girl with foreign-looking eyes to this calm dumpling of a housekeeper in a prosperous home that might as well be halfway back east, set upwind from the sparks and soot of the trains, where she kept portraits and knickknacks dusted, knew how much everything cost, what time to the minute each of the

Oust kids would wake (all but the one maybe, the one with the destiny), and where each of the family was likely to've gone when they weren't in the house . . . her once spellbinding eyes brought back, as field-creatures are re-enfolded at the end of day, into orbits grown pillow-soft, on watch within, guarding a thousand secrets of these old Territories never set down, and of how inevitable, right from the minute the first easterners showed up, would be the betrayal of everyday life out here, so hard-won, into the suburban penance the newcomers had long acceded to. The children in her care never saw past the kind and forever bustling old gal, never imagined her back in Leadville raising all those species of hell. . . .

"We lived up in a cabin above the snowline, brought home a little piñon that Christmas for a tree, shot a ptarmigan for a turkey. Storm outside, baby blue electricity running down the stovepipe. Little Reef loved 'em thunder-gusts, waving his arms, hollering 'Ah! Ah!' every time one came booming down. Later on with blasting in the mines, he'd get this little frown, like, 'Where's the lightning, where's the rain?' Just the dearest thing."

Mayva brought out the baby tintypes, Reef in a christening dress, maybe a sailor hat, all that usual decking-out, for he was a sweet baby, his mother said, though by the time he was three or four, Stray couldn't help noticing, he was already halfway to the face he was always going to have, that lopsided hammered-on look, like he'd already made up his mind to it, even as a kid.

"Do you think he'll be back?" Mayva said.

The kitchen was dim and cool. The afternoon was quiet for a minute, no father and son going round and round, midday chores all seen to, Moline taking a nap someplace. Stray gathered the older woman into her arms, and Mayva with a great dry-eyed sigh rested her forehead on Stray's shoulder. They kept like that, silent, till somewhere in the house there was a series of thumps and some bellowing and the day started up again.

Despite warnings from the U.S. State Department to all gringos to get their backsides across the border immediately, Frank stayed in Chihuahua. While his bones were knitting and he'd been attending to his romantic and, it could be argued, spiritual life, the Madero Revolution had moved on, specifically south to the Capital, where it lost no time in lapsing into some urban professionals' fantasy of liberal democracy. Old allies were ignored when not disowned, denounced, or thrown in the hoosegow. In Chihuahua especially there was a good deal of grumbling—actually more like rage—among the people who knew what it had cost them to put Francisco Madero in the Presidential Palace, who now saw the dreams they had come down out of the Sierra Madre to fight for being disregarded and flat-out betrayed. Soon there were large groups of armed folks gathering in the towns with banners and signs, some reading LAND AND JUSTICE, some LAND AND LIBERTY, some just LAND, but always the word someplace—*¡TIERRA!* Little rebellions began, ex-Maderistas picking up their old Mausers again, and soon there were almost too many to keep track of. Many were rebelling in the name of disaffected ex-minister Emilio Vázquez, so after a while any new uprisings got automatically labeled "Vazquista," though Vázquez himself had fled to Texas and by now was more of a figurehead.

Here in Chihuahua the collection of drifters, road agents, mountain fighters and bitter-end Magonistas that Frank had been running with at the time of the Casas Grandes battle were still around, most of them. Madero was far away now, bewitched by his new power into a more genteel version of Porfirio Díaz. Sooner or later that would have to be dealt with. *La revolución efectiva* was yet to come. Toward the end of the year word came north from

Morelos that Emiliano Zapata had raised an army down there and begun a serious insurrection against the government. Some of Frank's old compadres immediately headed for Morelos, but anybody who liked shooting at *federales* could still find plenty of that right here in Chihuahua.

Before long Frank found himself down in Jiménez in southern Chihuahua, attached to an irregular unit fighting on behalf of Pascual Orozco, once a major force in the Madero Revolution in Chihuahua, nowadays also in open revolt against the government. Frank had joined up in Casas Grandes, where a former Magonista named José Inés Salazar was raising a small army. In February they combined with troops led by the former lieutenant governor of the state, Braulio Hernández, who had just taken the silver-mining town of Santa Eulalia. By early March the combined forces controlled Ciudad Juárez and were threatening the city of Chihuahua. The governor panicked and fled—Pancho Villa, still loyal to the Madero government, tried to attack the city but was beaten back by Pascual Orozco, who'd finally made his move after months of indecision. Salazar and Hernández recognized Orozco as commander in chief of what was now a two-thousand-man army, and Orozco declared himself governor of the state.

Within weeks this army had quadrupled, and new insurgencies, now calling themselves Orozquista, were reported from all around the country. A march on Mexico City seemed imminent. Madero's war minister, former fencing coach José González Salas, was put in command of the campaign against Orozco. By the middle of March, he was in Torreón with six thousand troops, about 150 miles down the Mexican Central line from the rebel headquarters at Jiménez, and the skirmishing had begun.

FRANK NOTICED how immoderately, and at what length, El Espinero had laughed when he'd heard Frank was headed down to Jiménez. Frank was used to this and had learned to wait to see what it meant. It turned out that the country around Jiménez had been famous since the days of Cortés for its meteorites, including those found at San Gregorio and La Concepción, and a gigantic one known as the Chupaderos, whose fragments, weighing in all perhaps fifty tons, had been taken away to the Capital in 1893. Meteorite hunters combed this area all the time, and kept finding new ones. It was like there was a god of meteorites who had singled out Jiménez for special attention. Frank found he was using his own off-duty time to ride out into the Bolsón de Mapimí and have a look around. He remembered the giant crystal of Iceland spar El Espinero had showed him years before, which had led him to

Sloat Fresno. It could have been out here that he saw it, maybe even someplace close by, Frank had never made a map and couldn't remember now.

He found and picked up the strangest-looking damn rock he'd seen in a while, black and pitted all over, smooth in some places and rough in others. Small enough to keep in a saddlebag. He was not supposed to be sensitive to such things, but every time he touched the thing, even lightly, he began to hear a sort of voice.

"What are you doing here?" it seemed it was saying.

"You're sure a long way from home to be askin that."

ONE PRONG of the government attack was headed straight up the Mexican Central Railway. "Perfect conditions for the *máquina loca,*" it seemed to General Salazar, this being the technical term for a locomotive loaded with dynamite and deployed at high speed against the enemy. "Find that gringo." Frank, often sought out for his engineering skills, was summoned to the General's tent. "Doctor Pancho, if you wouldn't mind reporting to Don Emilio Campas, he'll be taking some people south, and we may need your advice."

"*A sus órdenes.*" Frank went looking for an appropriate steam locomotive to modify and found a switching engine just done making up a freight train for the Parral line, and brought it to a siding where his crew were already waiting—a couple of old-timers from Casas Grandes who shared the Magonista faith in politics through chemistry and who knew where to put the bundled sticks and run the fuzing for the best effect, and the basic work was done in half an hour.

They moved out ahead of another train carrying soldiers and accompanied by some cavalry, eight hundred troops in all, headed south, toward the Durango border. The sun hammered the barren badlands. About thirty miles down the line, between Corralitos and Rellano, they ran into an armored train full of *federales,* heading north. The train behind Frank braked to a stop, the riflemen got off, the cavalry deployed to left and right. Frank allowed his own locomotive to slow a little while he looked back and saw Salazar raise his sword and then bring it down in a great flash of white-gold desert light that could almost be heard. "*Ándale, muchachos,*" Frank hollered, pulling out some matches and commencing to light fuses. After throwing in the last of the coal and firewood, and checking the gauges, the rest of the crew jumped off.

"You're coming, Doctor Pancho?"

"Be right with you," said Frank. He opened the throttle all the way and the engine began to pick up speed. He swung down onto the step and was just about to jump when a peculiar thought occurred to him. Was this the "path" El Espinero had had in mind, this specific half mile of track, where suddenly the day had become extradimensional, the country shifted, was no longer the desert abstraction of a map but was speed, air rushing, the smell of smoke and steam, time whose substance grew more condensed as each tick came faster and faster, all perfectly inseparable from Frank's certainty that jumping or not jumping was no longer the point, he belonged to what was happening, to the shriek from ahead as the engineer in the federal train leaned on his steam horn and Frank automatically responded with his own, the two combining in a single great chord that gathered in the entire moment, the brown-uniformed *federales* scattering from their train, the insane little engine shuddering in its frenzy, the governor valve no longer able to regulate anything, and from someplace a bug came in out of the blind velocity and went up Frank's right nostril and brought him back to the day. "Shit," he whispered, and let go, dropped, hit the ground, rolled with a desperate speed not his own, praying that he wouldn't break his leg again.

The explosion was terrific, shrapnel and parts of men and animals flew everywhere, superheated steam blasting through a million irregular flueways among the moving fragments, a huge ragged hemisphere of gray dust, gone pink with blood, rose and spread, and survivors staggered around in it blinded and coughing miserably. Some were shooting at nothing, others had forgotten where, or what, bolt-handles and triggers were. Later it was estimated that sixty *federales* had been killed instantly and the rest were at least demoralized. Even the vultures for days were too scared to approach. The Twentieth Battalion mutinied and shot two of their officers, retreat was sounded, and everybody hightailed it any way they could back to Torreón. General González, wounded and dishonored, committed suicide.

Frank found a horse wandering in the Bolsón in only slightly better shape than he was, and came tottering back sometime in the middle of the night to find everybody at the Orozquista camp drunk, or asleep, or occupying some dream of victory that even Frank in his exhaustion could see was just loco. A couple of weeks later, three thousand of Orozco's rebels went down to Pancho Villa's headquarters at Parral to finish off the last of the Maderista loyalists in the region. Villa, greatly outnumbered, quite sensibly lit out of town before anybody got there, but this did not prevent them from sacking Parral, dynamiting homes, looting, killing. Frank missed out on the festivities, having found an empty freight car down at the yards and gone to sleep, half hoping that when he woke he'd be in some fresh part of the Republic, far from all of this.

When news came that Madero, despite deep misgivings, had chosen Victoriano Huerta to lead the new effort against the Orozquistas, Frank, who was not often subject to feelings of dread, began to grow a little nervous, remembering his brief run-in with some of Huerta's badmen in uniform seven or eight years before. Even with the life expectancy of a military bandit down here being comparable with a field rodent's, this Huerta somehow kept showing up, as if enjoying the favor of some particularly cruel junta of ancient gods. When Huerta's forces reached and occupied Torreón, Frank knew that Orozco's insurgency was pretty much doomed. As the *federales* lingered on in Torreón, some in Jiménez began to grow hopeful again, but Torreón was the key to any advance south against the Capital, and without it there would be no rebel victory. Huerta had cannon, and Orozco did not.

And sure enough, in the weeks ahead, as Huerta slowly moved north from Torreón, the Orozquista fortunes would begin to turn. Each time the rebels engaged, they would be defeated, desertions would increase, until finally at Bachimba the *máquina loca* tactic would fail, and with it all Orozco's hopes. Huerta would return to the Capital triumphant.

Long before this, if only Frank had been sane, he would have reckoned enough was enough, and gone back north and tried to leave Mexico to its fate. Nothing he could think of was keeping him here—Wren, whom the day did not provide nearly enough asskicking activities to allow him to forget entirely, was on the Other Side, as if beyond a frontier less political than created out of the unforgiving canyon cut by Time in its flow. Pascual Orozco, though Frank wished him well, including the Mexican miracle of somehow staying alive, was not a politician to whom Frank could pledge his life. But what was it worth, then, his life? Who or what could he see himself pledging it to?

He had been spending more and more time down at the trainyard outside Jiménez, like some mindless drover, watching the trains, watching the empty tracks. One day he bought a one-way ticket to the Capital, got on the train and headed south. No cries of *adios compañero,* good luck Frank, nothing like that. Couple handfuls of beans per day for somebody else was all it came to.

In the Capital, at a dark, out-of-the-way restaurant near the train station, Frank ran into Günther von Quassel, whom he hadn't seen since Tampico. Günther was drinking imported German beer in a stein. Frank ordered a bottle of the local Orizaba product.

"Well, Günni, what in 'e hell you doin all the way up here, thought you 's in Chiapas growing coffee and so forth."

"Here on business, now I can't get back. Whenever there is trouble in Oaxaca, and lately that is fairly constant, the rail lines to Chiapas are cut. My overnight stay becomes unexpectedly prolonged. So I haunt the train stations hoping to slip through a loophole in the laws of chance."

Frank mumbled something about having been up north.

"Ah. Lively times, I expect."

"Not lately. Just another unemployed Orozquista these days."

"There is a job open on the estate, if you're interested. If we could ever get back there. We would pay you handsomely."

"Some kind of a plantation foreman, keepin 'em unruly native Indians in line? I get to carry a whip and so forth? Think not, Günni."

Günther laughed and waved his stein to and fro, splashing foam on Frank's hat. "Of course, as a northamerican you must be *nostalgic for the days of slavery,* but in the highly competitive market which coffee has become, we cannot afford to linger in the past." Günther explained that before a harvest left the *cafetal,* the coffee "cherries" had to have their pulpy red outer coatings removed, as well as a parchment layer under that, and finally what was called the "silver skin," leaving at last the exportable seed. Once all done by hand, these jobs were nowadays more efficiently performed by various sorts of machine. The von Quassel plantation was in the process of being mechanized, and the machinery, including stationary engines, electrical generators, hydraulic pumps, and a small but growing fleet of motor vehicles, would all require regular maintenance.

"Lot of work for one beat-up *guerrillero,*" it seemed to Frank.

"You would train your own crew, *natürlich.* The more they learn, the less you work, everyone benefits."

"How about Zapatistas, any of them in the picture?"

"Not exactly."

"Approximately? Maybe you better tell me."

Considering the number of insurgencies against the Madero régime currently in progress all over the country, Chiapas so far, according to Günther, was quiet, violence there taking the more usual form of either family vendettas or what some called "banditry" and others "redistribution," depending on which was doer and which done-to. Since late last year, however, there had been a serious rebellion going on close by in Oaxaca, growing out of a dispute between Che Gómez, the mayor and *jefe político* of Juchitán, about two hundred miles or so west of Günther's plantation, and Benito Juárez Maza, the governor of Oaxaca, who last year had tried to replace Gómez by sending federal troops to Juchitán. The *jefe* resisted—in the fighting that followed, a federal relief detachment was wiped out, and finally it took federal cavalry and artillery to gain control of the town. Meantime the chegomista army controlled the rest of the region. Madero, who wasn't that fond himself of the governor, had invited Gómez up to Mexico City, under a federal safe-conduct, to talk it over. But Gómez had got no more than a few miles up the railway across the Tehuantepec Isthmus before he was intercepted by Juárez Maza's people, arrested, and shot to death.

"This did not end the rebellion by any means. The *federales* are bottled up now in Juchitán and a couple of other towns, while several thousand unreconstructed chegomistas own the countryside, including, when they wish, the railway. Which is why at the moment Chiapas is cut off from the rest of the country."

THEY ATE IN A DINING-ROOM lit from above through an ancient skylight of wrought-iron trusswork and weathered panes. Older city hands, reporters and such, had gathered at smaller tables in alcoves and smoked cigarettes and drank madrileños. The light, initially golden, steadily darkened. Rain arrived about the same time as the soup, and dashed at the skylight.

"I hesitate to ask favors unless things get desperate," said Günther, "but the harvest is under way, my foreman, I am convinced, is a crypto-Zapatista, and I make myself insane every night imagining what everyone is up to."

"Is there a back way in?"

"There is somebody I can talk to." After coffee and cigars, when the rain had stopped, they walked through the wet streets, among crazed motorists racing up and down the avenues, mud-colored omnibuses and ten-centavo jitneys, armed irregulars in private carriages, troops of cadets on horseback, poulterers in from the Valley of Mexico driving flocks of turkeys with willow wands in and out of the traffic—entering at last the spiffy new Hotel Tezcatlipoca, where Günther's acquaintance Adolfo "El Reparador" Ibargüengoitia—one of a population of newly-emerged entrepreneurs, working between the bullets, as they liked to put it, to solve problems created by revolution and re-revolution—kept a penthouse suite with a view out over Chapultepec Park and beyond. Anxious men in dark suits, apparently, like Günther, there in need of a repairman, wandered around in a fog of tobacco smoke. Ibargüengoitia by contrast wore a white tailor-made suit and crocodile shoes to match. Crying, "*Wie geht's, mein alter Kumpel!*" he embraced Günther and waved him and Frank on in. A young woman got up vaguely as a parlormaid brought Champagne in an ice bucket, and Günther and Ibargüengoitia went off behind a mahogany door to confer.

At one of the windows, Frank noticed a telescope on a tripod aimed, as it happened, west at the new Monument to National Independence, a tall granite pillar towering above Reforma, with a winged and gilded figure on top—supposedly Victory, though everybody called it "The Angel"—twenty-some feet high and at about the same level as Frank was at the moment. Frank went to squint through the eyepiece and found the field entirely occupied by the face of the Angel—looking directly at Frank, a face of beaten gold, taken into a realm proper more to ceremonial masks than specific human faces, and yet it was *a face he recognized.* With his other eye, Frank could see The Angel standing in the declining sunlight, vertiginous in its weight of bronze and gold, as if poised to fly unannounced and without mercy straight at him, while behind it a tall peak of cumulus drifted slowly upward. Frank felt as if he were being warned to prepare for something. The blank gold face looked into his, deeply, and though its lips didn't move, he heard it speak in urgent Spanish ringing and distorted by tons of metal, the only words he could recognize being "*máquina loca,*" "*muerte*" and "*tú.*"

"Señor?" When his eyes refocused, whoever had spoken had moved on. He had apparently been hunkered in a corner away from the window, breathing cigarette smoke and aware of little else. He stood up and saw Günther across the room in a farewell *abrazo* with the Repairman. "No guarantees some gang of local *sinvergüencistas* won't decide to rob your stage, of course," Ibargüengoitia was saying, "but . . . unpredictable times, *¿verdad?*"

In the elevator going down, Günther regarded Frank with something like amusement. "You have been watching that Angel," he said finally. "Unwise policy, I have found."

As it turned out, Ibargüengoitia had arranged to slip them into Chiapas by way of a coaster out of Vera Cruz, down to Frontera, Tabasco, from there by *diligencia* to Villahermosa, Tuxtla Gutiérrez, and across the Sierra to the Pacific coast. They arrived at the *cafetal* a week later, on horseback, around midday, the foreman all but dragging Günther down out of the saddle going into a long list of crises, and Frank, before he knew it, was looking at a weirdly designed pulping machine whose operating manual was in German, and a couple of local folks in charge of it who did not seem to register that Frank had absolutely no idea what was even wrong, much less how to fix it.

The stationary engine was just fine, the shafts, pulleys, belts, and clutches were worn but serviceable, the pipes from the tank where the coffee cherries were soaking in water were clear and the pump working, so it had to be either the confounded unit itself or the way somebody had connected it up. After a frustrating hour of disassembly and reassembly, Frank leaned close to the machine and whispered "*Tu madre chingada puta,*" looked around once or twice, and gave the 'sucker a theatrically furtive kick. As if abruptly coming to its senses, it shuddered, engaged, and the grater-cylinder at issue began to rotate. One of the Indians opened the valve from the tank and cherries began to flow through in a red stream about the texture of cook-tent beans, coming out as pulp mixed with seeds still in their so-called parchment, ready for the next stages of washing and stirring.

There were of course separate difficulties with the machines that did the stirring, drying, rolling, rubbing, and winnowing, but over the next couple of weeks Frank systematically worked his way through the cams, gearing, and set-screw adjustments of this Machine-Age nightmare that Günther kept calling "the future of coffee," even picking up a word or two of technical German. Somehow that year's coffee crop was all brought in without incident, processed into burlap sacks and ready for the factors' agents.

Outside, the political storm raged along, and occasionally blew in through a window. Many of the migrant workers here on the estate were Juchitecos who drew inspiration from Zapata as well as the martyred Che Gómez. Late in the autumn, Chamula Indians fighting for San Cristóbal in its ill-fated rebellion against Tuxtla had begun showing up with their ears missing, the penalty exacted for losing the recent Battle of Chiapa de Corzo. Frank found a couple of these who actually enjoyed learning the work, and pretty soon they were running most of the technical chores, leaving Frank more time to go into town and relax, though he was never sure what happened when he wasn't actually looking at them in the light, because peculiar as the Tarahumare had been, some of these Chiapas tribes made them look as humdrum as metallurgy professors. There were midgets and giants down here, and *brujos* who took the shapes of wildcats or raccoons or themselves multiplied by dozens. Frank had observed this, or thought he had.

For this particular stretch of Pacific slope, Tapachula was town—you wanted to relax or raise hell or both at the same time, you went in to Tapachula. Frank tended to spend time at a cantina called El Quetzal Dormido, drinking either maguey brandy from Comitán or the at first horrible but after a while sort of interesting local moonshine known as *pox,* and dancing with or lighting panatelas for a girl named Melpómene who'd drifted down from the ruins and fireflies of Palenque, first to Tuxtla Gutiérrez and then, with that boomtown certitude some young folks possess of knowing where the money is being spent least reflectively at any given season, to Tapachula, where there were cacao, coffee, rubber, and banana plantations all within an easy radius, so the town was always jumping with pickers, tree-shakers, nurserymen, bean-polishers, *guayuleros,* and centrifuge operators, none in a mood for moderation of any kind.

Melpómene told Frank about the giant luminous beetles known as *cucuji.* Each night in the country around Palenque, illuminating the miles of ruins hidden among the jungle trees, you could see them by the millions, shining all over their bodies, so brightly that by the light of even one of them you could read the newspaper, and six would light up a city block. "Or so a *tinterillo* told me once," grinning through the smoke of a Sin Rival. "I never learned to read, but I have a tree full of *cucuji* in my yard. Come on," and she led him out the back and down a cobbled alley and into a dirt lane. All at once, ahead of them, above the tops of the trees, shone a greenish yellow light, pulsing off and on. "They feel me coming," she said. They rounded a corner and there was a fig tree, with near as Frank could tell thousands of these big luminous beetles, flashing brightly and then going dark, over and over, all in perfect unison. He found if he stared too long into the tree, he tended to lose his sense of scale and it became almost like looking into a vast city, like Denver or the Mexican capital, at night. Shadows, depths . . .

Melpómene told him how the Indian women of Palenque captured the beetles and tamed them, giving them names which they *learned to answer to,* putting them into little cages to carry like lamps at night, or wearing them in their hair beneath transparent veils. Nights were populated by light-bearing women, who found their way through the forest as if it were day.

"Do all these critters here have names?"

"Most of them," giving him a look of warning not to make fun of this. "Even one named after you, if you'd like to meet him. Pancho!"

One of the fragments of light detached itself from the tree and flew down and landed on the girl's wrist, like a falcon. When the tree went dark, so did Pancho. *"Bueno,"* she whispered to it, "pay no attention to the others. I want you to light up only when I tell you. Now." The bug, obligingly, lit up. *"Ahora, apágate,"* and again Pancho complied.

Frank looked at Pancho. Pancho looked back at Frank, though what he was seeing was anybody's guess.

He couldn't say when exactly, but at some point Frank came to understand that this bearer of light was his soul, and that all the fireflies in the tree were the souls of everyone who had ever passed through his life, even at a distance, even for a heartbeat and a half, that there existed such a tree for each person in Chiapas, and though this suggested that the same soul must live on a number of trees, they all went to make up a single soul, really, in the same way that light was indivisible. "In the same way," amplified Günther, "that our Savior could inform his disciples with a straight face that bread and wine were indistinguishable from his body and blood. Light, in any case, among these Indians of Chiapas, occupies an analogous position to flesh among Christian peoples. It is *living tissue.* As the brain is the outward and visible expression of the Mind."

"Too German for me," Frank mumbled.

"Consider—how is it that they all go off and on at once?"

"Good eyesight, fast reflexes?"

"Always possible. But recall that there are also tribes up in these mountains who are known to send messages routinely across hundreds of miles, *instantaneously.* Not at the finite speed of light, you understand, but with a time interval of *zero.*"

"Thought that was impossible," said Frank. "Even wireless telegraph takes a little time."

"Special Relativity has little meaning in Chiapas. Perhaps after all telepathy exists."

Perhaps after all. Frank meant to bring it up with Melpómene next time he was in the Quetzal Dormido, but she beat him to it.

"There'll be a little disturbance tonight," she said.

"*Caray,* your *novio*'s back in town!"

She flicked cigar ashes at him. "It's those Mazatecos again. A gang of them are getting together right now to march over here. They should arrive a little after midnight."

"Mazatán, that's fifteen miles away. How do you know what's going on there 'right now'?"

She smiled and tapped herself lightly on the center of her forehead.

Around midnight there was some hollering and explosions and a number of gunshots, moving into town from the west. "*¿Qué el* fuck*?*" Frank, a little sleepy by now, inquired—"Oh, beg pardon, *querida,* meant *¿Qué el chingar?* of course."

Melpómene shrugged. Frank looked out the window. Mazatecos without a doubt, disposed to mischief.

Political experts tended to label the resentments expressed regularly by Mazatán against Tapachula as another "Vazquista" rebellion, though people down here understood it more as one of those town-against-town exercises that had been simmering in Chiapas since long before the Spaniards showed up. Lately, perhaps further aroused by the climate of national rebellion, elements in Mazatán had clearly been spending idle days and nights preoccupied with plans to attack Tapachula, clean out the contents of both banks in town, and kill the local *jefe.* But their planning somehow always failed to include Tapachula's volunteer self-defense force, who were there waiting for them every time, now and then chasing them all the way back down to Mazatán, and occupying the town to add to the humiliation. "Almost as if they knew in advance," Frank puzzled. "But who warns them? you? Who tells you?"

Which got him an enigmatic smile and little more. But Günther had been giving it all some thought.

"It is like the telephone exchange," he declared. "Not even 'like'—it *is* the telephone exchange. A network of Indians in telepathic communication. It does not seem to be sensitive to distance. No matter how far any of them may wander, the single greater organism remains intact, coherent, connected."

Winter arrived on the calendar, though not in the *tierra caliente.* But something like a shortening of days, a defection of sunlight, was occurring in the spirits of everybody at the *cafetal.* Something was on the way. Indians began casting strange looks at one another and avoiding everybody else's eyes.

One evening Frank was sitting near Melpómene's fig tree, watching the *cucuji* put on their show, and at some point, the way you drift into sleep, he fell into a trance and without *hikuli* this time he found himself back again in the same version of ancient Tenochtitlán that El Espinero's cactus had once taken him to.

His mission was a matter of life and death, but its details were somehow withheld from him. He did know that he must find his way to a part of the city hidden from most of its inhabitants. The first step was to pass beneath a ceremonial arch—which he understood would one day be obliterated, as the Spaniards had once obliterated all the Aztec structures of Tenochtitlán. The Arch was of pale limestone, with a triumphal sculpture on top, a sinister figure, all curves, tresses, wings, drapery, standing in a chariot. He recognized the gold face of the Angel of the Fourth Glorieta on Reforma, but understood this was a different Angel. As a gateway the structure seemed to define two different parts of the City as incommensurate as life and death. As "Frank" passed beneath it, it was seen to take on a ghostly light and to grow taller and more substantial.

He found himself in a part of the City where savagery prevailed and mercy was unknown. Robed figures passing by stared at him with a searching sort of hatred. Artillery fire and gunshots were audible, both close and more distant. Blood was splashed against the walls. There was a smell in the air of corpses and gasoline and burning flesh. He desperately wanted a cigarette but was out of smokes. He looked behind him for the gateway, but it had vanished. Now and then a pedestrian would look fearfully at the sky, cry out or run for cover, but when Frank looked up, he could see nothing beyond a shadow which approached from the north, like a storm, covering more and more of the field of stars. He knew what it was but could not find its name in his memory.

He arrived at the edge of a great plaza, which stretched away into the lightless midwatch, all but empty of pedestrian life, lying between two official but unnamed structures, faced with local volcanic *tezontle* and *tepetate*—both these monuments, despite modest height and emotional illegibility, as intimidating, perhaps as cruelly intended, as more ancient pyramids of this valley. There was gunfire now, more or less unremitting, and Frank could not see how to proceed. Neither of the two enigmatic structures provided any safety. He saw before him the mortal expanse of dark hours he must pass here, until the roosters started in and the sky slowly retained more and more light, perhaps revealing in silhouette, on the jagged rooftops, human figures who might have been there all along, attending to the hostilities.

When Frank returned to the indicative world, there was Melpómene with news from the Capital of the Huerta coup, and it slowly became clear to him that the two mysterious buildings in his vision had been the Presidential Palace, where Madero had taken refuge among forces loyal to him, and the arsenal known as the Ciudadela, a mile and a half to the west, where rebels headed by Félix Díaz, the nephew of Porfirio Díaz, were dug in. Between was the center of the Capital, a place of warfare and thousands dead left where they fell, under the open sky, which would go on for ten days that February and become known as the Decena Trágica. The shadow overhead, all these centuries in pursuit of the Aztecs and their generations, southward in their long flight, came at last to hang in the sky over the Valley of Mexico, over the Capital, moving eastward from the Zócalo to gather itself above the penitentiary called "*el palacio blanco,*" and condense at last one by one into the .38-caliber rounds that killed Madero and Pino Suárez and put Huerta into power, and despite the long and terrible struggle, and the people's faith so misplaced, had after all allowed the serpent to prevail.

Deciding not to stick around to see what kind of a price if any the new régime might have put on his head, Frank left Mexico aboard a coffee boat out of Vera Cruz, concealed in the hold beneath several sacks of cargo. By the time he got to Corpus Christi, he was so cranked up from breathing coffee dust that he was ready to run all the way to Denver on foot. "Stay in Texas," pleaded a fandango girl named Chiquita as he was speeding through San Antonio.

"Darlin ordinarily I'd love nothin better on account of how Mexico once my other land *mi otra tierra* as we say down there has made me more than usually aware of San Antonio home of the Alamo cradle of Texas independence and so forth without getting into the details of who stole what from who

I'm sure you can understand that sooner or later somebody in some saloon'll bring the matter up maybe no more'n a slide of the eyeballs in the mirror back there yet a promise of business to be transacted in the near future that could range anywhere from the price of a beer to one of us's life you see . . ." by which time in any case he was out the door again and halfway to San Angelo.

Soon as he got to Denver, he went to the bank to see if any of the money he'd been sending back had actually made it out of Mexico, and to his amazement found a nice piece of change in the account. Besides the salary from Günther and one or two heavy-machinery commissions, there was the ten dollars a day in gold that Madero's people had been paying him back in 1911 in Chihuahua, which seemed to include a falling-off-your-horse bonus added in there as well. It was the first time he was aware of getting paid for being stupid. Could there be a future in this?

FRANK WAS IN A BAR on Seventeenth Street one night when who should he run into but Dr. Willis Turnstone, onetime disappointed beau of Frank's sister Lake, just off his night shift at the hospital nearby.

"Notice you're favoring that leg, there," the Doc said after a while.

Frank told him the tale. "Somethin you can do for that?"

"If I can't, my partner sure can. Chinese fellow, cures everything by sticking you full of gold needles. Lay there looking like a porcupine, next thing you're up doing the fox trot all night long."

"Needles. Have to give that some thought."

"Here's our card. I'm just around the corner, come on by sometime and we'll have a look."

After a few sociable rounds, the Doc said, "You notice I didn't once ask about your sister."

"Appreciate that. Guess you're over it. Wish I could say I was."

"Over it and how. I am engaged to marry the most perfect of angels. I can't begin to describe her. Oh Frank she is adorable in every way. Mother, muse, and mistress, all in one, can you imagine? Of course you can't. Say, you seem a little peakèd, all of a sudden."

"Lookin for a spittoon to throw up in?"

"Can't here, there's a house rule."

DOC TURNSTONE'S OFFICE was a block and a half from Mercy Hospital, and three flights up. "Weeds out the malingerers!" chuckled his partner Dr.

Zhao. "Let's see your tongue. Aha." He took both Frank's wrists and attended for a while to various pulses. "How long have you been pregnant?"

"How's that?"

"Making jokes!"

The door opened, and a young woman in one of those dark velvet chapeaux that were showing up all over town put her head in. "Hi Honey, are you— Aaahh! You!"

"Not me," chirped Dr. Zhao. "And your fiancé had to go make a house call. Oh! You must mean this patient here!"

"Howdy Wren. Mind if I don't get up right away?" All these needles must've been doing something to Frank. Ordinarily a man would be heartbroken if not totally crushed to meet an old flame again calling another man "Honey," and a doctor, too. But what was kicking in instead was some strange town-busybody reflex that set Frank to going, well, well, Wren and the Doc, wonder how that'll turn out, so forth.

"Frank, I hope you're not . . ."

He had always appreciated this bluestocking awkwardness about her . . . as if jealousy were something that only characters in books knew how to deal with, and when one met with it out in the world, why, one was quite at a loss. . . . "Tell me," he said somewhat drowsily, "how'd you two lovebirds meet?"

"Got to go brew up some Chinese herbs," muttered Dr. Zhao. "I'm leaving this door open. Better behave!"

"I got back to the States," Wren said, "reported in to the hospital for some insurance checkup that Harvard was insisting on, Willis happened to be on duty, we were about to pass in the corridor, took one look at each other, and . . ."

"*¡Epa!*" Frank suggested. He'd heard about the phenomenon but never observed it in action.

Wren shrugged, exactly like a helpless feminine victim of Fate. "Willis is good," she said. "A good man. You'll see. He knows your friend Estrella, too. They're involved in some mysterious project down in the coalfields."

All right, now she was talking. The plutes it seemed, curse their souls if they had any, were at it again, this time in southern Colorado, where it was coal and not gold that men went down underground to risk their lives and health for, and the miners tended to come from Austria-Hungary and the Balkans more than Cornwall and Finland. Since last September the mine workers' union had been out on strike against Rockefeller's Colorado Fuel and Iron Company—since November the Trinidad field had been under a state of martial law. Both sides had plenty of rifles, and the state National Guard also had machine guns. The shooting and skirmishing had been nearly constant, when weather permitted—storms that winter had been fierce and deadly, even for Colorado. Families evicted from company housing had been living all winter in tent colonies outside Ludlow and Walsenburg. Stray had gone down there at the beginning of the strike and moved into one of the tents around December, against the advice of everybody who cared about her.

"Which is a sizable number of folks," said Doc Turnstone.

"You mind tellin me what she's doin down there?"

"There's a sort of informal plexus of people working as best they can to help the strikers out. Food, medicine, ammunition, doctoring. Everything's voluntary. Nobody makes a profit or gets paid, not even credit or thank-yous."

"Sounds like Mexico all over again."

"You've had enough of that for a while, I guess."

"Hell no. Now you boys've got this leg workin so good."

"There does just happen to be a small convoy heading over to Walsenburg, and they're shorthanded."

"I'm on the way."

"Old associate of yours will be there too. Ewball Oust?"

"Well. Sure is my week, ain't it?"

THEY MET UP, as arranged, in Pagosa Springs. "How's 'at leg doin?" said Ewball.

"Still kicks up when there's a norther headin in." Frank nodded vaguely in the direction of Ewball's penis. "How's 'at third leg, or shouldn't I be askin."

If Ewball had been hoping the subject of Stray wouldn't arise, he gave no sign. "Oh," pretending to inspect a barrel hitch on one of the loads, "one more big mistake on my ticket I guess. Just never should've interfered the way I did."

"'Seemed like a good idea at the time.'"

"There you go. But now she's all yours, pardner." Ewball gave it a hoofstep or two, then added, "She always was."

"News to me, Ewb." But who, outside of Stray herself, would know any better than Ewb here? it started Frank thinking, anyway.

Keeping a wary eye out for mine guards, Ku Kluxers, company detectives, and other assorted vermin, they took the little convoy, mules and wagons, up over Wolf Creek Pass, down into the San Luis Valley. Nights were generally sleepless, for there were sure to be riders out scouting for them, though moonlight was on the wane.

"Another thing you should know," Ewball thoughtfully stirring the grounds in the coffeepot with his stolen Signal Corps thermometer he liked to use to get the temperature just right.

Frank snorted. "Never, gol, durn, ends."

"Your mother. She's in Denver, and working for mine—"

"Well if 'at don't take the cake." The usual reply would've been more like, "Thought your mother worked on the Denver Row," but this was well beyond trailside pleasantries.

"—and her and Stray had a nice long confabulation, too, seemed like."

"You took Estrella home to meet your folks."

"She didn't even want to, I should've known better."

"Should've been watchin your back Ewb, it's that Bourgeois Fever creepin up on you."

"All in the past now. Yes quite, quite ended. And another thing about Stray— Did I ever tell you—"

"Ewb."

And with no time intervening, the sun was up again and the coffee in the pot frozen from the long night.

It was a nervous passage across the San Luis Basin. In the distance, riders whose hats, dusters, and mounts blended with the terrain would now and then appear, proceeding at top speed across the treeless plain, each headed in a slightly different direction, the less thoughtful wearing dark clothes that stood out against the ashen country, for anybody at even a little elevation sooner or later would find it just too hard to resist considering these riders as rifle targets. As would the more adventuresome among the horsemen themselves, willing to gamble on the wind, the accuracy of the rifleman's sights and size of the load, or just that the high ground was too far away—against the payoff of that well-known lift of spirit when you're shot at and missed.

You didn't see as much idle ranging out here as in days of old, there was too much afoot now. Where the telegraph couldn't be trusted, messages still had to go through. Winchesters, Remingtons, and Savages had to be put into the right hands. Figures of consequence seeking to avoid the Pinkerton-infested Denver & Rio Grande had to be escorted instead over these shelterless trails.

It was a relief to be through Fort Garland, out of the flatland and climbing again into broken country. They took their string up the Sangre de Cristos over North La Veta Pass, in a descent of steel light, yellow intensities among the purple towers of cloud—the Spanish Peaks rising ahead of them across the valley, and the snowy thirteeners of the Culebra Range chaining away to the south. And below them, presently, at a turn of the trail, the first rooftops of Walsenburg, sod giving way to shakes, beyond which, embattled and forlorn, lay the coalfields.

Scarsdale Vibe was addressing the Las Animas–Huerfano Delegation of the Industrial Defense Alliance (L.A.H.D.I.D.A.) gathered in the casino of an exclusive hot-springs resort up near the Continental Divide. Enormous windows revealed and framed mountain scenery like picture postcards hand-tinted by a crew brought in from across the sea and all slightly color-blind. The clientele looked to be mostly U.S. white folks, pretty well-off in a flash sort of way—vacationers from back east and beyond, though an observer might be forgiven if he thought he recognized faces from the big hotel bars in Denver, with a few that might've fit in on upper Arapahoe as well.

The evening was advanced, the ladies had long since retired, and with them any need for euphemism.

"So of course we use them," Scarsdale well into what by now was his customary stem-winder, "we harness and sodomize them, photograph their degradation, send them up onto the high iron and down into mines and sewers and killing floors, we set them beneath inhuman loads, we harvest from them their muscle and eyesight and health, leaving them in our kindness a few miserable years of broken gleanings. Of course we do. Why not? They are good for little else. How likely are they to grow to their full manhood, become educated, engender families, further the culture or the race? We take what we can while we may. Look at them—they carry the mark of their absurd fate in plain sight. Their foolish music is about to stop, and it is they who will be caught out, awkwardly, most of them tone-deaf and never to be fully aware, few if any with the sense to leave the game early and seek refuge before it is too late. Perhaps there will not, even by then, *be* refuge.

"We will buy it all up," making the expected arm gesture, "all this country.

Money speaks, the land listens, where the Anarchist skulked, where the horse-thief plied his trade, we fishers of Americans will cast our nets of perfect ten-acre mesh, leveled and varmint-proofed, ready to build on. Where alien muckers and jackers went creeping after their miserable communistic dreams, the good lowland townsfolk will come up by the netful into these hills, clean, industrious, Christian, while we, gazing out over their little vacation bungalows, will dwell in top-dollar palazzos befitting our station, which their mortgage money will be paying to build for us. When the scars of these battles have long faded, and the tailings are covered in bunchgrass and wildflowers, and the coming of the snows is no longer the year's curse but its promise, awaited eagerly for its influx of moneyed seekers after wintertime recreation, when the shining strands of telpherage have subdued every mountainside, and all is festival and wholesome sport and eugenically-chosen stock, who will be left anymore to remember the jabbering Union scum, the frozen corpses whose names, false in any case, have gone forever unrecorded? who will care that once men fought as if an eight-hour day, a few coins more at the end of the week, were everything, were worth the merciless wind beneath the shabby roof, the tears freezing on a woman's face worn to dark Indian stupor before its time, the whining of children whose maws were never satisfied, whose future, those who survived, was always to toil for us, to fetch and feed and nurse, to ride the far fences of our properties, to stand watch between us and those who would intrude or question?" He might usefully have taken a look at Foley, attentive back in the shadows. But Scarsdale did not seek out the eyes of his old faithful sidekick. He seldom did anymore. "Anarchism will pass, its race will degenerate into silence, but money will beget money, grow like the bluebells in the meadow, spread and brighten and gather force, and bring low all before it. It is simple. It is inevitable. It has begun."

The next day Scarsdale, in his private train The Juggernaut, descended the grades, from the realms of theory to the hard winter realities of Trinidad, to see what was what on the ground, and look the anticapitalist monster in the face. He thought of himself as a man of practice, not theory, and he had never flinched from "the real world," as he liked to call it.

Somewhere en route to the Trinidad field, strolling through the cars, Scarsdale opened a door at the end of one carriage and there in the vestibule stood— It was a being, much taller than he was, its face appallingly corroded as if burned around the edges, its features not exactly where they should be. The sort of malignant presence that had brought him before to levels of fear he knew he could not emerge from with his will undamaged. But this time he felt only curiosity. Scarsdale caught the figure's eye, raised a finger as if to speak, as it moved past him and continued down the aisle of the train car. "Wait," Scarsdale puzzled, "I wanted to talk to you, smoke a cigar, socialize a little."

"Not now, I've got something else to do." The accent was not American, but Scarsdale couldn't place it. And then the apparition was gone, leaving the tycoon bemused at his own lack of terror, and unable to imagine that this had not been in some way aimed at him, intending, as always, his destruction. Who else could it possibly have been after by this point, at the stage things had come to?

Foley came blinking in, awakened by something only he heard.

"Somebody was here on The Juggernaut that wasn't supposed to be," Scarsdale greeted him.

"Been through the place a dozen times," Foley said.

"It doesn't matter, Foley, it's all in the hands of Jesus isn't it. Could happen anytime in fact and to tell you the truth, I look forward to being one of the malevolent dead."

Foley knew exactly what that meant. On battlefields after the engagement, with cannonballs on the ground everywhere, he had kept company with ghosts by the thousands, all filled with resentments, drifting, or stationed by cemetery gates and abandoned farmhouses where half-mad survivors would be most likely to see them, or not sure, some of them, which side of the barely-visible line they walked. . . . Not the companionship he would have chosen. At first he put Scarsdale's desire to be among them down to civilian ignorance. Didn't take him long, however, to see that Scarsdale understood them better than he did.

After dropping the shipment off at Walsenburg, Frank and Ewball rode down to Trinidad for a look. There were militiamen all over the place, unhappy-looking young men in stained and ragged uniforms, unshaven, insomniac, finding excuses to roust the strikers, who were Greeks and Bulgarians, Serbs and Croats, Montenegrins and Italians. "Over in Europe," Ewball explained, "all busy killin each other over some snarled-up politics way beyond any easy understanding. But the minute they get over here, before you can say 'Howdy,' they just drop all those ancient hatreds, drop 'em flat, and become brothers-in-arms, 'cause they recognize *this* right away for just what it is."

Somehow they kept coming west to these coalfields, and the owners put out stories about sharpshooters from the Balkan War and such, and Greek mountain fighters, Serbs with an appetite for cruelty, Bulgars with a reputation for unspeakable sex, all these alien races coming over here and making miserable the lives of the poor innocent plutes, who were only trying to get by like everybody else. Even if some of these immigrant miners had seen military action over there, why come here, to these godforsaken canyons? It wasn't for three dollars a day, there was more to be made in the cities, it sure wasn't to go down into explosions, cave-ins, and lung disease and choose to shorten their lives digging coal so some owner could live high and mighty—so then why come here of all places? The only explanation that made sense to Ewball, who had been acting more and more strangely the closer he got to Trinidad, was that some of them had to be already dead, casualties of the fighting in the Balkans.

"For the unquiet dead, see, geography ain't the point, it's all unfinished business, it's wherever there's accounts to be balanced, 'cause the whole history of those Balkan peoples is revenge, back and forth, families against families, and it never ends, so you have this population of Balkan ghosts, shot dead, I don't know, up some mountain in Bulgaria or someplace, got no idea where they are, where they're going, all they feel is *that unbalance*—that something's wrong and needs to be made right again. And if distance means nothing, then they surface wherever there's a fight with the same shape to it, same history of back-and-forth killing, and it might be someplace in China we never get to hear about, and again it might be right here a city block away, right down in the depths of the U.S.A."

"Ewball, man, that is some bughouse talk."

IN TRINIDAD Frank noticed a figure out on the porch of the Columbian Hotel, big, unsmiling, sun-darkened and slouched against the siding watching the traffic in the street with a look of unreachable contempt.

"Not an hombre I would care to tangle assholes with there," Frank remarked.

"Sure about that?"

"Uh-oh. Ewb, what's 'at look on your face?"

"The gentleman happens to be Foley Walker, the devoted sidekick of your old family friend Mr. Scarsdale Vibe."

"Well, there's somethin to think about." Frank pulled his hatbrim lower and thought about it. "That mean Vibe's in town, too?"

"Somebody has to be out ridin that Champagne-and-pheasant circuit, make sure the plutes don't lose their nerve. Rockefeller couldn't make it, but old Vibe's just as happy to as a fly on shit."

They found a saloon up the street and went in. Ewball seemed in a state of almost juvenile impatience. "So?" he said finally, "so? you gonna make it two notches or what?"

"It might have to be three if there's 'at Foley to get past. Is he really as bad as he looks?"

"Worse. They say Foley's a born-again Christer, so he can act as bad as he wants because Jesus is coming and nothin a human can do so bad Jesus won't forgive it."

"But you'd be someplace coverin my back, right?"

"Why Frank, how thoughtful of you to ask."

They checked in at the Toltec Hotel. Frank understood he would eventually be heading up to Ludlow to find Stray, but right now the chance that Vibe might present a clear enough target seemed to take precedence. They decided to track the magnate's comings and goings.

Out reconnoitering, they thought once they'd caught a quick glimpse of Mother Jones herself, being hustled on board a train out of town, a comical exercise at the time because she would then turn around and come right back, having friends among the railroad workers all up and down the line, who'd put her aboard or leave her off wherever she liked. What Frank noticed about this white-haired lady was her hell-with-it attitude, a love of mischief she must have kept safe and protected from the years, from the plutes and what their hired apologists called "life," as if they ever knew what that was—protected like a child, the child she had been. . . .

A small pack of dogs came whirling down Main Street, as if carried by a miniature tornado. Lately there had been more dogs in town than anybody could remember. As if somebody saw an urgent need to get them out of the canyons, where there was trouble on the way that they really didn't need to be around for.

THERE WERE ALWAYS ROOMS in these shootout resorts, small and spare, side rooms, anterooms for their mortal business, where members of the troupe might go to get ready—greenrooms without lines to remember, chapels without God. . . .

After any number of careful observations, Ewball had determined the best time to go for Scarsdale would be right after lunch. "He eats at the hotel, then him and Foley take a short walk down to the C.F.I. office, where they spend the afternoon seein what new kind of evil they'll cook up. There's a foot or two between buildings I can wait back in."

"You?"

So arising the delicate question of who would get to shoot whom. "Well he is yours by all the laws of vengeance, sure," Ewball said, "that's if you want him."

"Why shouldn't I?"

Disingenuousness having begun to ooze from and presently saturate Ewball, "Don't know. Just that Vibe's likely to be pretty much a sitting duck—the dangerous target'd be Foley. Dependin how much work you're eager to do."

"You want to go after Vibe? and me take Foley? well you have my blessin Ewb, and no hard feelins, no matter what people say afterwards."

"How's that, Frank?"

"Oh, you know, psychological talk and that." Frank noticed that Ewball's smile was no longer what you'd call amiable. "A way of gettin back at your Pa, and so forth. Back-east thoughts, horseshit of course."

Ewball considered for a minute. "Here," finding a silver quarter. "We'll flip for it, how's that."

TWO FACING ROWS of storefronts receded steeply down the packed-earth street. Where the buildings ended, nothing could be seen above the surface of the street, no horizon, no countryside, no winter sky, only an intense radiance filling the gap, a halo or glory out of which anything might emerge, into which anything might be taken, a portal of silver transfiguration, as if being displayed from the viewpoint of (let us imagine) a fallen gunfighter.

Frank decided to borrow a .44 Peacemaker from Ewball instead of depending on his Smith & Wesson, which needed a new extractor spring. All those years ago, when he and Reef had let Mayva keep Webb's old Confederate Colt, Frank had thought to take with him the cartridges that were still in it. They had rattled around in and out of saddlebags, duster pockets, satchels, and cartridge belts, and Frank never used them, not even for Sloat Fresno, telling himself they were really only to remember Webb by. Not that he was fooling himself—they were for Deuce someday, of course. But unless the little reptile returned to the scene of the crime, how likely was it that Frank would ever get to use them?

Scarsdale Vibe would have to do—second choice, but no point trying to explain that to Ewb, who had these strange theoretical branches of Anarchist principle he was very reluctant to climb down off of. Frank stood in the tight little alleyway, between a photographer's and a feed-and-seed, with Ewball across the street, and waited for the imperial tycoon who'd turned thumbs down on Webb Traverse ten years ago.

They passed the mouth of the alley so quick Frank almost missed them. He stepped out behind them and said, "Vibe." The two men turned, Foley bringing out what Frank needed a minute to recognize as one of those German Parabellums, and being given that minute was enough to tip Frank that something was up. Ewball was sauntering across the street, using a passing wagon for cover part of the way, Ewb's left hand almost prayerfully supporting the barrel of his own weapon.

Even in a town full of murderous Anarchists who hated him worse than Rockefeller, Scarsdale had seen no need to walk around these streets heeled. In his accustomed tone of command, at exactly the moment he should not have adopted it, he now barked, "Well you see them as clearly as I do, Foley. Take care of it." In reply, smoothly as if it were another long-practiced personal chore, Foley stepped away swiveling, lined up the Luger's muzzle with his employer's heart, and chambered the first round. Scarsdale Vibe peered back, as if only curious. "Lord, Foley . . ."

"Jesus is Lord," cried Foley, and pulled the trigger, proceeding to empty all eight rounds into what, after the first, was a signed deal. As if come to his ancestral home after long and restless journeying, what had been Scarsdale Vibe settled facedown into the dirtied snow and ice of the street, into the smell of horses and horse droppings, to rest.

Foley stood looking awhile at the corpse, as citizens went running, some for the marshal, some for safety. "Oh and another thing," he pretended to address it, his demeanor oddly gay.

Frank, having counted off the full clip, nodded. "Well, sir."

"Hope you fellows don't mind, but it's payday today, and I've been in line years ahead of you."

There was a squad of militia coming up the street, and Frank and Ewball, having re-concealed their revolvers under their coats, found little trouble in blending in with the nervous townsfolk of Trinidad. Foley waited, in patient good humor, watching Scarsdale's blood, nearly black in this midwinter light, slowly flow out into a liquid frame around him.

"Just too embarrassing," muttered Ewball. "How am I gonna hold my damn head up?"

"You wanted to be the one," Frank guessed.

"It's worse than 'at." He gazed deeply at Frank, as if hoping this late in their history for Frank to show some mind-reading skills. "It wasn't just bringin over a supply wagon," he said softly.

"It's been more'n enough for me," Frank said, not wanting too many details.

. . .

Stray had been in Trinidad for a while before she'd heard about the tent colony at Ludlow. It had been there since late last September, when the strike began. Little by little, flooring got put in, latrines were dug, a phone line was run to the Union office in Trinidad. After some shooting in early October between mine guards and the people in the tents, both sides had begun to store up guns and ammunition. Winter was coming. The shooting went on.

"You're sure you wouldn't rather be in town," said Sister Clementia.

"Let me run up there with a wagon," Stray said, "and I'll just take a look." Only look. But she knew already it was where she had to be. About the time she moved into one of the tents, the governor declared martial law, and soon nearly a thousand troops, infantry, cavalry, and support, under the command of a Colorado Fuel and Iron stooge named John Chase, who styled himself "General," had set up base camps outside Trinidad and Walsenburg.

Stray found the Colony had maybe 150 tents and nine hundred people living in them, mostly families, except for bachelor neighborhoods like the Greeks, who tended to keep to themselves, and their own language. A family had just moved out, so Stray moved in. Before nightfall she was sitting at the bedside of a feverish, crusty-nosed Montenegrin girl about three, trying to feed her a little soup.

In the morning she and her neighbor Sabine were out taking some bedding over to a tent across the way. Stray looked off at the higher ground and saw gun emplacements every direction.

"Not happy with this," she muttered. "Wide-open damn field of fire here."

"Hasn't anybody shot at us yet," commented Sabine, which was about when somebody did.

It wasn't that Stray ever got to thinking of herself as charmed. Whenever she was out in good light, rounds buzzing by but none connecting, she got used to the dirt kicking up in little bursts around her, the fading hum of spent ammo bouncing away. At first she was so jittery she dropped what she was carrying and ran for cover. As the winter went on she got to where she could crisscross the whole patch with her arms full of snow shovels, blankets, live chickens, maybe a gallon and a half of hot coffee in a tin coffeepot balanced on her head, and not spill anything. Sometimes she was almost sure the marksmen who had the high ground were playing with her. She got to know the flirters from the bad shots. When she got back one day from one of these trips, guess who'd turned up.

"Hi, Ma."

"How the hell'd you get here?"

"Colorado and Southern. Don't worry, it didn't cost me a cent. Nice to see you too, Ma."

"Jesse, this is crazy. You don't need to be here. Willow and Holt need you back there."

"Ain't that much to do. All the big chores me and Holt, and Pascoe and Paloverde, got done way before it even snowed."

"It's dangerous here."

"More reason for somebody to be watchin your back, then."

"Just like your father. Damn snake-oil salesmen. Never could talk either of you into anything." She gazed into his face, something she'd found herself doing more and more of as he grew, and when she had the chance. "Don't get me wrong, it's not that you're the spit of him or nothin, least not all the time, but every so often . . ."

Company searchlights set up on towers began sweeping the tents all night long.

"Ma, this is drivin me crazy. It's keepin me awake."

"You used to hate the dark."

"I was a little kid."

The Colorado militia were in fact giving light a bad name. Military wisdom had it that putting searchlights on the enemy allowed you to see them, while blinding them to you, giving you an inestimable edge both tactical and psychological. In the tents, darkness in that awful winter was sought like warmth or quiet. It came for many to seem like a form of compassion.

Finally one night Jesse took his repeater and went out exploring. "Just havin a look," is what he told his mother, who heaven knew had used that line often enough. Sometime after midnight, Stray, who had learned to sleep through all sorts of noise, dreamed she heard the distant crack of a single rifle shot, and woke, into blessed darkness. A little later Jesse tiptoed in and carefully snuggled in next to her, both of them pretending she was asleep. She had taught him never to claim credit for anything if he could help it, which didn't keep him going around next day with a shiteating grin all over his face that reminded her of Reef when he thought he was getting away with something.

It was the winter everybody ate rabbit stew. The strike relief rolls numbered about twenty thousand men, women, and children. The wind occupied and owned the Trinidad field, and the cold grew more bitter. The storms of early December were the worst anybody could remember. Snow drifted four feet deep in places. Tents collapsed under it. Around the middle of the month, strikebreakers began to show up, shipped in cattle cars from as far away as Pittsburgh, Pa., though many of them were from Mexico, escorted by Guardsmen all the way from the border, promised everything, told nothing.

"Like Cripple Creek all over again," those who remembered pointed out. Back then, ten years ago, the scabs had been Slavs and Italians, some of whom had stayed on and joined the Union, and this time around they'd become the ones who were on strike.

"And while of course it behooves a man to break the head of any Mexican kept in blind ignorance who's been shipped in to steal your job," preached the Reverend Moss Gatlin, who, never one to forgo a good fight, had been here since the strike was called, "we must also understand how eminently practical in the long term is Christian forbearance, if by it we may thus further the dumb scab's education, just as your own insulted heads at Cripple and the San Juans once got beaten into them the lesson that a job however obtained is sacred, even a scab's job, for it carries the ironclad obligation to resist from then on the forces of ownership and the mills of evil, with whatever means are available unto you all." Older these days, using a cane, still limping lopsidedly forward into the battle, he held regular Sunday services out at the tents as well as delivering midnight sermons in friendly saloons.

Through January the mood among the militiamen grew sharply uglier, as if somebody knew what was on the way. Women were raped, kids teasing soldiers were grabbed and beaten. Any miner caught in the open was fair game for vagging, arrest, assault, and worse. In Trinidad, cavalry of the state militia charged a band of women who were marching in support of the strike. Several, some only girls, were slashed with sabers. Some went to jail. Through God's mercy, or dumb luck, none were killed.

One day Jesse came back to the tent cloaked in a strange distant elation, nothing that made his mother happy, for it reminded her of too many crazy gun artists out of her past when they thought they'd found that final throwdown. "I saw the Death Special, Ma." This was a rumored and widely feared armored motorcar, with two Colt machine guns on it, mounted fore and aft, that the Baldwin-Felts "detective" agency had come up with for penetrating, controlling, and thinning down the size of ill-disposed crowds. It had already been through here, sweeping the colony with machine-gun fire, slashing up the canvas tents and killing some strikers.

Jesse and his friend Dunn, out exploring, found a couple of Guardsmen in a galvanized shed, working on the Death Special's engine. They were big, blond, and forthright and acted friendly enough, but could not conceal a contempt for the people this vehicle was designed to shoot down. Dunn thought he knew how to hustle grown-ups, and had a pocket usually full of coins to prove it. But Jesse could see they thought they knew all about Dunn and him and where they'd come from—one look at these red faces and bulging eyes and he understood that if it should come down to it, he would not be able to save his life, or his mother's or Dunn's, by appealing to anything these grownups might feel for kids, even kids of their own. . . . Pretending to have a friendly chat with potential targets of their Death Special was a level of evil neither boy had quite suspected in adults till now.

As it turned out, there was a whole fleet of Death Specials, improved versions of the original model, which had been little more than an open touring car with steel plate on the sides. As for this one here, the two mechanics wouldn't get to see any action in it, that'd be for officers, but now and then, for functional checkout purposes, they were allowed to drive a couple-three miles into open country and blow apart a mesquite bush.

"With a rifle it's too personal," one of the Guardsmen said, "when you're sightin 'em in one by one, gives you a minute to get to know them 'fore you do your deed, but this 'sucker—time it takes to get your finger off of the trigger it's already fired ten or twenty rounds, so there's no question of careful aiming, you just pick out what they call a zone you want to tear up, even shut your eyes if you want, don't matter, it's all done for you."

Though they couldn't help bragging about the machinery they were working on, it seemed peculiar to the boys how they also kept talking about the Death Special as if it were a poor little victim at the mercy of some vast and dangerous mob. "Even if they surrounded it, shot out the tires, we could hold out inside till help showed up."

"Or plow a path right through 'em and out the other side," added the other one, "and escape that way."

"You with those tent people, son?" his friend asked abruptly.

Men had been calling Jesse "son" all his life, and it was more or less always insulting. Only one man had the right to call him that, but where the hell was he? Jesse would have to be real careful here about showing how much he didn't like it. "Nah," he said, easy enough, before Dunn could put in anything. "Town."

The militiaman looked around at the bleak, spoil-scarred country that ran on way too long. "Town? Which town would that be, son? Trinidad?"

"Pueblo. Come down on the train, me and my pardner," indicating Dunn, who had still not closed his mouth all the way.

"That so," the other one said. "I lived in Pueblo awhile. Where do you all go to school?"

"Central, where else?"

"You boys're playin some serious hooky, ain't you?"

"I won't tell nobody if you don't," Jesse shrugged.

Before he left, he stole two .30-caliber machine-gun rounds, one for him and one for his Ma, believing that as long as these particular ones couldn't be fired, he and Stray would be safe from harm.

FRANK WAS IN AGUILAR, on the rail line between Walsenburg and Trinidad, in the 29 Luglio Saloon—named for the date back in 1900 when an Anarchist named Bresci assassinated King Umberto of Italy—to see about a perhaps imaginary machine gun, said to be an air-cooled Benet-Mercier, still in its shipping case, fallen somehow off a supply wagon in Pueblo. Most of the customers in here were Italian, and everybody at the moment was drinking grappa and beer, discussing the situation just up the canyon at the Empire mine, which like everywhere else in this frozen and strikebound countryside was fairly miserable, not to mention dangerous. Across the room a drunken Calabrese timber man lay unconscious in the lap of a drably turned out yet appealing, in fact familiar young woman, in a tableau which suggested to several in the room, though not to Frank, the famous sculpture the *Pietà,* by Michelangelo. Noticing Frank's prolonged stare, the barroom Madonna called out, "Sorry, Frank, you'll have to wait in line, but hell, the evening's young."

"Heard you were here in the zone, Stray, just didn't recognize you in that rig."

"Not too handy in the saddle, but around these parts it helps to look like a Sister of Charity."

"You mean they're not as likely—"

"Oh hell they'll shoot soon as look at you. But this gray color here blends in better, so you're less of a target."

"I came over here with that Ewball, but he took off again." Frank figured he might as well bring up.

She gently slid out from under the Italian on her lap. "Buy me one of whatever that is in your fist and I'll tell you the whole sordid tale."

"Ewb did mention somethin about . . ." he took some time wondering how to put it.

"Damn, I knew it," she said finally. "I broke his heart, didn't I? Keep tellin myself, 'Stray, you got to watch 'at shit,' then I go ahead and do it anyway." She nodded and hoisted her glass.

"He struck me as kind of confused. Broken heart, I wouldn't know."

"Never happened to you Frank?"

"Oh, all the time."

"How's 'at professor lady o' yours?"

Frank, without meaning to, went into a long recitation about Wren and Doc Turnstone. Stray lit a cigarette and squinted at Frank though the smoke. "Now, you're sure she didn't break . . . your heart or nothin." For a long time, she'd had Frank figured for Reef without the loco streak, till she saw he wasn't quite as easy to read after all—going after Sloat Fresno had been a surprise, as had been his involvement with the Madero revolution. And now here he was in the coalfields, which were about to explode. "You plannin to stay here or go back to Denver?" she said.

"Any reason I shouldn't stay here awhile?"

"You mean aside from war breakin out any minute."

They sat watching each other till she shook her head. "No business back in Denver, I guess."

"Reminds me, how's my Ma, heard you saw her up there a while back."

"I really love Mayva, Frank. For somebody I see once every ten years anyway. You should write to her sometime."

"I should?"

"Never met Jesse either, did you."

"Bad uncle too," Frank angling his head.

"Ain't what I meant, Frank." She took a breath, as if plunging into a room on fire. "We're livin over at the tents 'ese days if you take it in mind to visit."

Frank tried to sit still for what went throbbing through him in a wave or two. Keeping his face composed, "Well maybe if you're still there . . ."

"Why shouldn't—?" she stopped then, the answer being clear enough.

"Figured you knew. They're fixin to do away with all 'em tents, and before the week's out, 's what I heard."

"Guess you better visit us soon, then."

Which is how he found himself creeping alongside her nun's shadow in the acid-yellow assault of searchlight beams, through melting and refreezing snow, having thought to salvage from his saddlebags only a pack of storeboughts and a can of tobacco and as many cartridges as he could stash about his person for the Krag and the Police Special with its new spring.

Jesse wasn't there when they got to the tent, but Stray wasn't worried. "Likely out with these Balkan folks he's friends with. It's their Easter or somethin. They've taught him to handle himself at night pretty good. He's safe enough. You can sleep over there by the stove. If he comes in he's usually pretty quiet." Frank had had a vague general plan to stay awake long enough to see how Stray looked underneath that hospital nun's rig, but somehow he must've been tireder than he thought. He slept till somebody's rooster cut loose and the harsh daylight commenced.

He'd just stepped outside to piss when who should he catch sight of but a face out of the past, a humorless customer trotting down the hillside in militia uniform, narrow-brim hat, leggings and campaign shirt, with a high forehead, lidless long eyes and mouth in a slit, a lizard's face. Not a nickel's worth of mercy.

Frank pointed with his head and asked Kosta, who was across the trench pissing, "Who is that sumbitch? I've seen him someplace."

"Is fucking Linderfelt. When they attack tonight, it'll be him out front, yelling Charge. Linderfelt is the devil."

Frank remembered now. "He was in Juárez, headin up some mercenaries called themselves 'the American Legion,' jumped the gun, tried to attack the city before Madero did and later on had a warrant put out on him for looting. Had to jump back across the border real quick. Thought he'd've been some buzzard's lunch long ago."

"He's a lieutenant in the National Guard now."

"Figures."

"Buzzards have more sense 'n that anyway."

The shooting had begun at first light, and soon grew general, and went on in spasms all day.

The militia were up on Water Tank Hill with a couple of machine guns. Their riflemen were set in a line along a ridge up there. There were some strikers in a railroad cut to the east that had the Guardsmen sort of enfiladed, but the militia were also higher, and on through the daylight it was a standoff. Thoughts turned to the night ahead. "Don't know how gentlemanly they're gonna be after the sun goes down," Frank said.

"They turn into somethin else," she said.

Jesse came squirming in under the edge of the tent with a Winchester repeater, all out of breath. "Tried to get down that railroad cut. Mostly on my belly. Ran out of bullets. Who's this?"

"This is Frank Traverse. He's your Pa's brother. Just come in town for some of the clambake activities." The boy headed for a canteen of water and drank for a while.

"She's sure been givin me an earful about you, Jesse," Frank said.

Jesse shrugged, a touch elaborately. "What is that, looks like an old Krag."

"One of several crates full," Stray recalled, "if I'm not mistaken, that I sold him years ago."

"Sometimes you'll get attached," Frank said quietly. "Nice thing about a Krag, see, is the trapdoor, a real handy feature when there's a lot goin on, you just open it up like this, anytime, throw in your rounds loose, and they all get lined up inside and pushed one by one through here, feed on up the other side each time you work the bolt. Here, try it."

"He wants to sell you one," Stray said.

"I'm happy with my Winchester thanks," Jesse said. "But sure, long as I'm not wasting anybody's ammo." He took the Krag and aimed out the tentflap at a distant group of horsemen, maybe uniformed cavalry but no uniform Frank knew of, sighting in, breathing carefully, pretending to squeeze off a round—"Bam!" and chamber a new one. Not much Frank could teach him.

Later Frank was tending to the firearms and Stray was kneeling next to him. "I wanted to say," Frank said.

"Oh you been sayin it, don't worry."

He gave her a closer look, just to make sure of her face. "Fine time to be gettin around to this."

"Somethin goin on over there I should know about?" Jesse called across the tent.

"The minute it's dark enough," said Frank, "just before all the lights come on, that's when we move. Head north, get to that wide draw that's up there."

"Run away?" Jesse glared.

"Damn straight," Frank said.

"Cowards run away."

"Some do. Sometimes they're just not brave enough to run. You been out there. How many cowards about to go runn' into that?"

"You think—"

"I think we can make it to that arroyo. Then it's just keepin ahead of Linderfelt."

"You want to just check outside that flap for us?" said Stray.

The boy took a careful look outside. "Reckon two minutes before them lights'll be on."

"Now'd be a real good time," Frank said. "Nothin much else to do here."

"Dunn," Jesse remembered.

"Where'd he get to?" Stray gathering up a pistol and some ammunition, looking around for her hat.

"Right here," said Dunn, from behind the stove.

They all went out under the sides of the tent. A small band of horsemen was galloping past, a forward propulsion of muscle and hide, and hooves like massed weapons. The bunch might've been state militia, Baldwins, sheriff's posse, Ku Klux Klan or any of the volunteer ranger groups. It was getting too dark out to tell. They were carrying torches. Rising with the flame was thick black smoke. As if the purpose was not to cast light but blackness.

The gunfire was unremitting now. Rifle smoke from the Guardsmen's positions rose in the cold air. It didn't help much to know where they were, because soon enough they would be here, in one of their pitiless charges, which came only in the dark, and when they were sure of their victims.

Jesse ran and was nearly to safety when a ragged shape rose up in his path and a hand gripped his arm and the cold metal snout of a service .45 was pressed to his head. "Where we going so fast, li'l dago?"

"Let go my arm," Jesse said.

"You're the tent kid used to come around the shop." The gun muzzle stayed where it was. Jesse tried to think of ways he could come out of this with only pain, maybe something cut or broken that would only cost him some time for it to heal.

"You been shootin at us today, ain't you son?"

"You been shootin at me," said Jesse.

He got a long red-eyed look. The gun came away, and Jesse tensed up for what he was afraid was coming next. "I'm really fuckin tired. I'm hungry. Ain't none of us been paid since we come down this miserable place."

"Sure know how that feels."

They stood as if listening to the shooting all around the junction.

"Get your anarchist ass out of here," the trooper said at last, "and if you people pray, pray I don't see it in the daylight."

"Thank you, sir," Jesse saw no harm in replying.

"Name's Brice." But by that time Jesse was running too fast to answer with his own.

THEY TOOK SHELTER with hundreds of others, at least for a few minutes, in the wide arroyo north of town, waiting for some letup in the shooting to get someplace safe. But the militia were trying to take the steel bridge over the arroyo, which would cut off any more escape to the westward. The searchlights swept in and out of the draw, throwing black shadows you could feel, like a breeze, as they went by. Now and then one of the kids went climbing up to see what was going on back at the tents, and had to be yelled at.

Frank felt a hand at his shoulder and thought at first it was Stray's. But when he looked, he could only just make her out, through the blowing needles of spring snow, sheltering Jesse with her body. No one else was near him. Just as likely to've been the hand of some dead striker, reaching back through the mortal curtain to try and find something of Earth to touch, anything, and that happened to be Frank. Maybe even Webb's own hand. Webb and all that he had tried to make of his life, and all that had been taken, and all the paths his children had gone off on. . . . Frank woke after a few seconds, found he'd been drooling down his shirt. This would not do.

Stray and the boy were both about the same height, Frank noticed for the first time. Jesse was asleep on his feet. Half a mile away, the tents were all being set on fire, one by one, by the heroes of Linderfelt's Company B. An impure reddish light leapt and shifted in the sky and the troopers made sounds of animal triumph. Shots kept ripping across the perilous night. Sometimes they connected, and strikers, and children and their mothers, and even troopers and camp guards, took bullets or fought flames, and fell in battle. But it happened, each casualty, one by one, in light that history would be blind to. The only accounts would be the militia's.

Stray opened her eyes and saw Frank looking at her. She looked back, and they were both too tired to pretend it wasn't desire, even here in the middle of hell.

"When we get a minute," she began, then seemed to lose the thought.

Frank sensed the bright awful chance they really might never even get to touch again. Last thing he needed to consider right now. "Just get you and him back to your sister's place safe, O.K.?" he said finally. "It's the one thing you got to worry about right now, all the rest can wait."

"I'm goin with you, Frank," Jesse's voice slurred with exhaustion.

"You need to go with your Ma, make sure she gets out of here in one piece."

"But the fightin ain't over."

"No, it ain't. But you already put in a long day of good fightin, Jesse, and these ladies here, babies and so forth, they need a trusty rifle shot who'll cover 'em till they can get over to that little ranch past the tracks. There'll be plenty more fightin to do, everbody'll get their share."

He knew the pale smudge of the boy's face was turned to him, and Frank was just as glad not to have to see the expression on it. "Now that I know how to get to your Uncle Holt and Aunt Willow's place, 'cause you drew me that map and all, I'll come down there quick as we can get this wrapped up."

They both heard that "we," not the one they'd hoped for but this other collective of shadows, dead on their feet, not half a dozen words of English among them, rifle butts dragging in the dirt, filing away east up the wagon road into the Black Hills now, trying to stay together.

"We'll be up there," moving his head toward the Hills, "supposed to be a mobilization camp someplace. Jesse you take care now—" and the boy ran to embrace him with such unexpected fierceness, as if he could hold everything, the night about to end, the shelter of the arroyo, hold it all still, unchanging, and Frank could feel him trying not to cry, and then making himself unclasp, step away, get on with this terrible onset of morning. Stray was there just behind him.

"O.K., Estrella." Their embrace might not have been so close or desperate, but no kiss he could remember had ever been quite this honest, nor this weighted with sorrow.

"There's trains heading south all the time," she said, "we'll be fine."

"Soon as I can—"

"Never mind that, Frank. Jesse, you want to carry this here?" And they were gone, and he wasn't even sure what it cost them not to look back.

That summer had been memorable for its high temperatures. All Europe sweltered. Wine grapes turned on the vine to raisins overnight. Piles of hay cut and gathered early as June burst spontaneously into flame. Wildfires traveled the Continent, crossing borders, leaping ridgelines and rivers with impunity. Naturist cults were overcome with a terrible fear that the luminary they worshipped had betrayed them and now consciously planned Earth's destruction.

Reports had reached *Inconvenience* of an updraft over the deserts of Northern Africa unprecedented in size and intensity. To feed the great thermal ascent, air masses were being drawn down from the Alps and the Mountains of the Moon and the Balkan heights, and a sky-craft, even one the size of *Inconvenience,* had only to approach the flow and Saharan anti-gravity would take care of the rest. All that was really needed was to let go.

There was discussion, of course, about the financing. These days the boys were pretty much on their own. The National Office had finally become so cheap with budget allocations that the crew of *Inconvenience,* after a meeting which lasted five minutes including the time it took to brew the coffee, had voted, finally, to disaffiliate. Nor were they alone in this decision. For some time, in fact, worldwide, the organization had been drifting into a loose collection of independent operators, with only the "Chums of Chance" name and insignia in common. There were no repercussions from above. It was as if the National had vacated its premises, wherever they'd been to begin with, and left no forwarding address. The boys were all free to define their own missions and negotiate their own fees, whose entire amount they would now get to keep, rather than tithing half and even more back to the National.

This greatly improved flow of revenue, along with recent advances in lightweight engines of higher horsepower, had allowed *Inconvenience* to expand to considerable size, with the mess hall alone occupying more space than the entire gondola of the previous version of the ship, and the kitchen grown nearly as enormous. Miles, as commissary, had installed patent refrigerators and hydrogen-burning stoves of the latest design, and hired a top-notch cooking staff, including a former sous-chef at the well-known Tour d'Argent in Paris.

Tonight's meeting was about whether or not to take the *Inconvenience* into the great updraft over the Sahara without somebody paying for it in advance. Miles called the session to order by bashing upon a Chinese gong acquired years before from an assassination cult active in that country, during the boys' unheralded but decisive activities in the Boxer Rebellion (see *The Chums of Chance and the Wrath of the Yellow Fang*), and wheeled around a refrigerated Champagne cart, refilling everyone's glass from a Balthazar of '03 Verzenay.

"Not 'on spec,' sky-brothers," protested Darby, whose appreciation for the field of contract law had by now grown perhaps to the fringes of unhealthy obsessiveness. "We're not in this racket for free. No client, no cruise."

"Don't you boys just have adventures anymore?" piped up Pugnax's companion Ksenija, though she barked it in Macedonian. Not long before, Pugnax had met up with the fiercely beautiful *šarplaninec* sheep-dog, and convinced her to come aboard *Inconvenience.* Sometimes he thought he'd been waiting for her all his life, that she had always been down there, moving somewhere just visible, among the landscapes rolling beneath the ship, deep among the details of tiny fenced or hedged fields, thatched or red-tiled rooftops, smoke from hundreds of human fires, the steep shadowed mountains, pursuing by day the ancient minuet with the flocks. . . .

The vote was unanimous—they would venture into the updraft, and pick up the costs out of overhead. Darby had apparently voted against his own legal principles.

Because no one had yet measured the forces likely to be in play, ordinarily no skyfarer with his wits about him would have ventured within a hundred miles of the desert phenomenon, yet hardly had the boys secured the Special Sky Detail than they began to feel tremors in the hull, which presently became leaps of metal exhilaration, almost a breaking into some unimagined freedom, as the ship was seized and borne downslope off the Balkan Peninsula, faster and faster southwestward across the Mediterranean and the coast of Libya, directly toward the huge vertical departure somewhere ahead.

Those not actually on watch stood at the windows of the Grand Saloon and stared as the strangely red cylindrical cloud slowly rose, like a sinister luminary, up over the horizon—sands eternally ascending, bright and calamitous off their starboard bow and closing, empty and silent and forever rushing skyward, pure aerodynamic lift, anti-paradise. . . .

And as they entered and were taken, Chick Counterfly thought back to his first days aboard the *Inconvenience,* and Randolph's dark admonition that going up would be like going north, and his own surmise that one could climb high enough to descend to the surface of another planet. Or, as the commander had put it then, "Another 'surface,' but an earthly one . . . all too earthly."

The corollary, Chick had worked out long ago, being that each star and planet we can see in the Sky is but the reflection of our single Earth along a different Minkowskian space-time track. Travel to other worlds is therefore travel to alternate versions of the same Earth. And if going up is like going north, with the common variable being cold, the analogous direction in Time, by the Second Law of Thermodynamics, ought to be from past to future, in the direction of increasing entropy.

Now, out in the suffocating heat of the sandstorm, Chick stood on the flying bridge, in protective desert gear, and took thermometer readings, measuring altitude meanwhile with an antique but reliable sympiezometer, salvaged from the wreck of the first *Inconvenience* after the little-known Battle of Desconocido, in California.

With the visibility only marginally improved, Chick was dismayed to note that the column of mercury in the instrument now stood higher, indicating an increase of atmospheric pressure and hence a lower altitude! Though the ship was still being carried by a rising air-current, as Chick reported with some urgency to Randolph, yet somehow it was *also making its descent* to a surface none could see. The skyship commander chewed and swallowed half a bottle of soda-mint tablets and paced the bridge. "Recommendations?"

"We still have our Hypops gear from the old Inner Asia assignment," it occurred to Chick. "It might enable us at least to see through some of this." He quickly rigged himself and the Commander into the strange futuristic arrangements of helmets, lenses, air-tanks and electrical power-supplies, allowing both aeronauts to ascertain that the ship was indeed about to crash into a range of mountains which appeared to be masses of black obsidian, glittering with red highlights, the razor-sharp crestlines stretching for miles before vanishing into a vaporous twilight. "Lighten ship!" cried Randolph, and Miles and Darby hurried to comply, the ominous red lights flaring after them, like molten lava at a time of geologic upheaval.

After the danger was averted with the usual "inches to spare," Randolph and Lindsay repaired to the chartroom to see if they could find any maps to match the terrain, so far unfamiliar to any of them, above which the ship now cruised.

After a comprehensive review that extended through the night, the two-lad Navigational Committee determined that the ship had most likely come upon the Pythagorean or Counter-Earth once postulated by Philolaus of Tarentum in order to make the number of celestial bodies add up to ten, which was the perfect Pythagorean number. "Philolaus believed that only one side of our Earth was inhabited," explained Chick, "and it happened to be the side turned away from the Other Earth he called Antichthon, which was why nobody ever saw it. We know now that the real reason was the planet's orbit, the same as our own except one hundred eighty degrees out, so that the Sun is always between us."

"We just flew through the Sun?" inquired Darby, in a tone his shipmates recognized as prelude to a quarter-hour of remarks about the Commander's judgment, if not sanity.

"Maybe not," Chick said. "Maybe more like seeing through the Sun with a telescope of very high resolution so clearly that we're no longer aware of anything but the Æther between us."

"Oh, like X-ray Spex," sniggered Darby, "only different."

"Antichthon," announced Miles, like a streetcar conductor. "The other Earth. Watch your step, everyone."

IT WAS LIKE their Harmonica Marching Band days all over again. They were on the Counter-Earth, on it and of it, yet at the same time also on the Earth they had never, it seemed, left.

As if all maps and charts had suddenly become unreadable, the little company came to understand that in some way not exhausted by the geographical, they were lost. Deposited by the great Saharan updraft on a planet from which they remained uncertain as to the chances of return, the boys could almost believe some days that they were safely back home on Earth—on others they found an American Republic whose welfare they believed they were sworn to advance passed so irrevocably into the control of the evil and moronic that it seemed they could not, after all, have escaped the gravity of the Counter-Earth. Sworn by their Foundational Memorandum never to interfere in the affairs of the "groundhogs," they looked on in helplessness and a depression of spirit new to them.

Their contractual operations began to bring in less revenue than sources unrelated to the sky—rent on surface properties, interest from business loans, returns on investments of many years standing—and the boys had begun to wonder if their days of global adventure might not be behind them, when one night in the early autumn of 1914, they were visited by a shadowy Russian agent going by the name of Baklashchan ("An alias," he assured them—"the more threatening ones were all spoken for"), who brought news of the mysterious disappearance of their old friendly nemesis Captain Igor Padzhitnoff.

"He's been missing since the summer," Baklashchan said, "and our own operatives have exhausted all clues. We wondered if someone in the same line of work might not have a better chance of finding him. Especially given the current world situation."

"World situation?" frowned Randolph. The boys looked at one another puzzledly.

"You are . . . unaware . . ." Baklashchan began, then hesitated, as if remembering a clause in his instructions forbidding him to share certain information. He smiled in apology, and handed over a dossier containing the most recently observed movements of Padzhitnoff's ship.

Despite the "Eleventh Commandment" prevailing among free-lance adventurers of the time, the boys agreed unhesitatingly to take the case. Initial payment was in gold, which Baklashchan had packed in on a Bactrian camel, which stood patiently beneath the shadow of the *Inconvenience* cast by a nearly full moon.

"And please do convey our regards to the Tsar and his family," Randolph reminded the emissary. "We cherish our memories of their hospitality at the Winter Palace."

"We should be seeing them quite soon," said Baklashchan.

In the protracted journey which was to follow, covering eventually most of the World-Island, it would not escape the boys' attention that something very peculiar indeed was going on down on the Surface. More and more often, detours became necessary. Entire blocks of sky were posted as off-limits. Now and then there would arrive, from nowhere immediately visible, great explosions of a deep and unprecedented intensity which caused structural members of the skycraft to groan and tremble. Miles began to encounter unexpected shortages when making commissary purchases. One day his most reliable wine purveyor brought alarming news. "Shipments of Champagne have been suspended indefinitely. All through the growing region now, the countryside is torn up with trenches."

"Trenches," Miles said, as if it were a foreign technical term.

The merchant gazed back at length, and may have gone on speaking, though he could no longer be heard clearly. Miles was aware in some dim way that this, as so much else, had to do with the terms of the long unspoken contract between the boys and their fate—as if, long ago, having learned to fly, in soaring free from enfoldment by the indicative world below, they had paid with a waiver of allegiance to it and all that would occur down on the Surface. He switched his order to still wine from Spain, and the *Inconvenience* flew on, dodging from place to place across the great counter-planet, so strange and yet so familiar, the elusive Padzhitnoff always just a step or two ahead.

"And another odd thing," announced Chick one evening at their regular weekly review of progress on the case. "The travels of Captain Padzhitnoff," tapping a pointer across the map that covered the entire forward bulkhead of *Inconvenience*'s wardroom, "over the years, have pretty closely matched our own. No surprises there. But looking only at the months just before he disappeared, everyplace we'd been that year," tapping one by one—"the Riviera, Rome, St. Petersburg, Lwów, the High Tatra—old Padzhy's gone as well. Where we haven't been yet, he seems to have left no trace."

"Swell!" Darby ejaculated. "We're chasing ourselves now."

"We always knew he was haunting us," shrugged Lindsay. "Likely this is only more of the same."

"Not this time," declared Miles, retreating into his customary silence, and only resuming the thought some months later, one night off the coast of Cyrenaica, as he and Chick were on the fantail sharing a smoke and regarding the luminosity of the sea. "Are ghosts dreadful because they bring toward us from the future some component—in the vectorial sense—of our own deaths? Are they partially, defectively, our own dead selves, thrust back, in recoil from the mirrorface at the end, to haunt us?"

Chick, who regarded the metaphysical as outside his remit, settled as usual for nodding and puffing politely.

Not until some additional months later, in the baleful mists above West Flanders, would Miles abruptly recall his sunlit bicycle excursion long ago with Ryder Thorn, who had been possessed that day by such a tragic air of prophecy. "Thorn knew we'd come back here. That there would be something down there we ought to pay attention to." He gazed, as if desire were all it would take, down through the gray rainlight, at terrain revealed now and then through the clouds, like a poisoned sea brought still.

"Those poor innocents," he exclaimed in a stricken whisper, as if some blindness had abruptly healed itself, allowing him at last to see the horror transpiring on the ground. "Back at the beginning of this . . . they must have been boys, so much like us. . . . They knew they were standing before a great chasm none could see to the bottom of. But they launched themselves into it anyway. Cheering and laughing. It was their own grand 'Adventure.' They were juvenile heroes of a World-Narrative—unreflective and free, they went on hurling themselves into those depths by tens of thousands until one day they awoke, those who were still alive, and instead of finding themselves posed nobly against some dramatic moral geography, they were down cringing in a mud trench swarming with rats and smelling of shit and death."

"Miles," said Randolph in some concern. "What is it? What do you see down there?"

Not many days after that, somewhere over France, Miles happened to be on watch in the Tesla shack when a red smear appeared without warning in the vaporous sky ahead of them, and slowly grew larger. Seizing the voice-cone of the apparatus, Miles began calling into it, *"Neizvestnyi Vozdushnyi Korabl! neizvestnyi vozdushnyi korabl!"* which was Russian for "Unknown airship! unknown airship!" Not "unknown," by then, to Miles, of course.

A familiar voice replied, "Looking for us, balloon-boys?"

It was the old *Bolshai'a Igra,* all right, grown by now to dozens of times its former size. The Romanoff crest had vanished from its envelope, which instead was now all a single chaste expanse of saturated red, and the ship's name had been changed to *Pomne o Golodayushchiki.*

"Remember the Starving," explained Captain Padzhitnoff, whose former athletic glow seemed now to have grown phosphorescent, as if arising from a source less material than blood.

"Igor!" Randolph beamed, *"Dobro pozhalovat,"* as somewhere on the Russian vessel a bell, a scale model of the famous Tsar-Bell of Moscow, given the crew by Nicholas II himself, began to clamor.

"Means 'Come and get it!'" said the Captain. "We would be honored to have you all join us for midday meal."

There was beet and cabbage soup, buckwheat cooked like oatmeal, and black bread, from which a strange sort of cranberry-flavored beer had also been fermented, and in the middle of the table, where the boys usually had a lemonade pitcher, an enormous jug full of vodka from the ship's distillery.

The connection with the Okhrana having been long severed, Padzhitnoff related, these days his ship and crew flew everywhere across Europe and Inner Asia, no longer dropping brickwork but sending food, clothing and—since a great influenza epidemic the boys had not till now been aware of—medical supplies, gently down by parachute to whatever populations below were in need of them.

"Someone hired us to find you," Randolph told him forthrightly. "Our instructions were to notify them as soon as we did. But we have not yet reported in. Should we?"

"If you tell them you can't find us, do you owe them money?"

"Nahh, we had 'em strike all the penalty clauses," said Legal Officer Suckling.

"If it's who we think it is," Pavel Sergeievitch, the ship's intelligence officer, chuckled professionally, "they'd rather send out assassination teams anyway. Revenge is better than rubles."

"Baklashchan is unfamiliar by name, but not his type," said Padzhitnoff. "He is another *podlets*—a cringer. Thousands of them have denounced us, thousands more will. Under Tsar, with Okhrana, our status was always in question. . . . These days, I think we are fugitives, declared enemies of whatever is in power now."

"Where is your base of operations, then?" Chick inquired.

"Like good bandits, we have hideout in mountains. *Shtab* is in Switzerland, though we are not Red Cross, being far less saintlike, in fact funded from profiteering in coffee and chocolate, big business in Geneva till 1916 when everybody but us got arrested and deported. We are on our way back there now, if you're interested. We'll show you our private Alp. Looks like solid mountain, but it's all hollowed out inside, full of contraband. You like chocolate? We give you good price."

Back aboard *Inconvenience* the boys met in the wardroom to discuss their course of action.

"We've signed a contract," Lindsay reminded everybody. "It continues in force. We must either turn Captain Padzhitnoff over to the authorities of his country or escort him to safety, and become fugitives from justice ourselves."

"Maybe Russia's not his country anymore," Darby pointed out. "Maybe it ain't 'justice' he's fleeing from. *You* don't know, dimwit."

"Not perhaps to the degree of certitude prevailing among the general public as to your mother's preference for the genitalia of the larger and less discriminating zoo animals," Lindsay replied. "Nevertheless—"

"Oooh," murmured the other boys.

From a bookshelf nearby Darby had already produced a legal volume and begun to thumb through it. "Yes. I quote from the English Slander of Women Act of 1891—"

"Gentlemen," Randolph pleaded. He gestured out the windows, where long-range artillery shells, till quite recently objects of mystery, glittering with the colors of late afternoon, could be seen just reaching the tops of their trajectories and pausing in the air for an instant before the deadly plunge back to Earth. Among distant sounds of repeated explosion could also be heard the strident massed buzzing of military aircraft. Below, across the embattled countryside, the first searchlights of evening were coming on.

"We signed nothing that included any of this," Randolph reminded everyone.

THE TWO AIRSHIPS reached Geneva in convoy. The great silent ghost of Mont Blanc stood sentinel behind the city. Padzhitnoff's crew were quartered south of the river in the older part of town, where some of them had lived as University students in the years before the Revolution. The boys settled in eventually on an entire floor of adjoining suites, with a view over the lake, at the former Helvetia Royale, one of the great Swiss tourist hotels which once, before the war, had swarmed with visitors from Europe and America.

Despite the influenza and shortages, the town was lively with all sorts of business. Each city block held multiple chances for accostment by someone with a deal in coal, or milk, or rationing cards. Spies, speculators, and confidence men mingled with refugees and invalid internees from all the belligerent powers. Since 1916 there had been agreements in effect among Britain, Germany and France allowing severely wounded prisoners of war to be exchanged and returned to their home countries by way of Switzerland, while those less seriously disabled could be interned under Swiss custody. Transport trains had begun to appear after dark, hurtling through the country often at express speed, bearing the consumptive, the shellshocked and imbecile. Village children crept from bed, taverns emptied out so the customers could stand by trackside and watch the carriages drum darkly through town. Whenever the trains paused to bring aboard a new draft of passengers, or to stand beneath dark green trusswork holding up strangely pointed spherical tanks to take on water, citizens appeared from nowhere with flowers for the ailing prisoners whose names they would never learn, bottles of homemade schnapps, chocolates hoarded for years. Suspecting that their country was the scene of a great experiment in the possibilities of compassion in the depths of war, they may have felt some need simply to be there and contribute what they could.

Out in Europe, the great Tragedy went rushing on, lit by phosphorus flares and shell-bursts, scored for the deep *ostinati* of artillery against the staccato chorales of machine-gun fire, faint suggestions of which found their way backstage from time to time along with smells of cordite and poison gas and rotting bodies. But here in everyday Switzerland it was the other side of the tapestry—a ragged, practical version of the grander spectacle out there. One could imagine the drama, have terrible dreams, infer from those who came off after their turns what they must have been doing out there. But here backstage the business was of a different nature.

Pomne o Golodayushchiki had more than enough work, and Captain Padzhitnoff was happy to pass on the overflow to the *Inconvenience.* At first most of this involved cargo jobs—flying in goods it was no longer easy for the Swiss to import, such as sugar, cooking fat, pasta. . . . The boys spent a lot of time mostly waiting in border towns like Blotzheim, though there were also plenty of flights inside the country, redistributing hay during hay famines and cheese during cheese shortages, which in the later years of the war grew chronic here. After a while the missions expanded across the borders, running in oranges from Spain or wheat across the sea from Argentina. One day Padzhitnoff appeared, looking as authoritative as he ever did, and announced, "Time for promotion, balloon-boys! No more cargo handling—from here on, you are moving personnel!"

Now and then, the Captain explained, there arose *osobaia obstanovka*—"special situation," his favorite military term—in which an exchange of internees by train would be inadvisable. "Some person of particular interest, who cannot be repatriated without certain awkwardness. You understand."

Faces remained blank, except for Miles, who was nodding gravely. "If we lacked the necessary maps and charts," he said, "you could lend them to us."

"Konechno. We regret that our ship is no longer built for speed demanded by *special situation.*"

They soon found themselves hovering in the dead of night over prisoner-of-war camps in the Balkans. They revisited Siberia for the first time since the Tunguska Event to negotiate for captured members of the Japanese-American expeditionary force, and were also instrumental in the relocation of Admiral Kolchak's government from Omsk. They were shot at by everything from hundred-mile guns to dueling pistols, without result, sometimes on impulse, not always by someone with a clear idea of what they were shooting at. It was a new experience for the boys, and after a while they learned not to take it any more personally than bad weather or faulty maps. It had not occurred to any of them, until Miles pointed it out, that their involvement in the European war had really not begun until they took refuge on neutral ground.

One morning in Geneva, out in the street, Padzhitnoff, after a long night in the taverns down by the riverside quays, and Randolph, a resolutely early riser in search of a brioche and cup of coffee, happened to cross paths. The city was washed in a strangely circumspect light. Birds had long been up and about, but discreetly so. Lake steamers refrained from blowing their sirens. Tram cars seemed to ride on pneumatic wheels. A supernatural hush hung over the steeples, the mountains, the known world. "What is it?" Padzhitnoff wondered.

"Today? nothing special." Randolph took from his pocket a booklet-size ecclesiastical calendar he used for writing himself notes in. "Martinmas, I think."

Toward noon the bell of the Cathedral of Saint Pierre known as La Clémence began to ring. Soon all the bells in the city had joined in. Back in Europe something called an armistice had taken effect.

ONCE HOSTILITIES WERE OVER, contract offers, which had previously so eluded the boys, began to pour in. The *Inconvenience* continued to fly in and out of Switzerland on the same kinds of relief and repatriation jobs that had occupied it before, but now there were also civilian assignments, more in the tradition of the boys' earlier adventures. Spies and sales representatives in particular could be found lurking at all hours in the lobby of the Helvetia Royale with fists full of francs and propositions of a grandiosity unknown to the world before 1914.

One lunchtime just as Darby was preparing to scream, "Not fondue again!" Pugnax came strolling in to the mess decks with a mysterious light in his eyes, and in his mouth a large embossed envelope, sealed with wax and bearing a gilt crest.

"What's this? wondered Randolph.

"Rff rff rr RR-rff!" commented Pugnax, which the boys understood to mean, "Looks like some money!"

Randolph scanned the letter thoughtfully. "A job offer, back in the States," he said at last. "Sunny California, no less. The lawyers who sent this are withholding the names of their principals, nor does it seem clear what we're to do exactly, beyond wait for instructions once we're there."

"And, eeyynnhh . . . how much were they offering?" Darby inquired.

Randolph held the sheet up so that all could see. The sum, clearly visible, represented about twice the combined net worth of everyone on board.

"Something criminal, one presumes," warned Lindsay.

"This offer must obviously be subjected to the most exhaustive moral and legal scrutiny," Darby declared, pretending to eyeball the sum once again. "OK, everything looks fine to me."

The prospect of well-remunerated work in California—which up till then had figured for the boys as a remote and mythical locale—soon overcame scruples even as unresponsive as Lindsay's, though as self-selected conscience of the crew, he could not resist asking, "Who will tell Captain Padzhitnoff?"

Everybody looked at Randolph. Randolph looked at his bulbous reflection in the silver tea-service for a while, and finally said, "Rats."

Padzhitnoff's shrug and smile were notable for an absence of bitterness. "You don't need my authorization," he said. "You've always been free to go."

"But it feels like we're deserting you, Igor. Deserting—" he waved his hand a little desperately, as if to include all the waiting populations of unconnected souls adrift, orphans and cripples, unsheltered, sick, starving, incarcerated, insane, who must yet be helped to safety.

"War is not over. May never be. Consequences may never end. My crew have had four years, a University education, in learning to manage famine, disease, broken cities, all that now must follow what has happened. Horror, pointlessness—but we did get educated. You may have been differently educated. Your own obligations may be to different consequences."

"American consequences."

"Nebo-tovarishch"—a hand on his shoulder—"I cannot—would rather not—imagine."

So it came about, one evening, just as the first stars appeared, that the *Inconvenience* rose from the shores of Lake Geneva and set her course west-southwest.

"We should pick up prevailing westerlies off the coast of Senegal," reckoned Lindsay, who was Weather Officer.

"Remember when we had to go where the wind took us?" Randolph said. "Now we can just light off the engines and let 'er rip."

"Our clients," Lindsay reminded everyone, "are insistent that we be on the Pacific coast as soon as possible, travel costs being covered contractually only up to a certain sum, above which we become responsible."

"Eehhnnyyhh, what idiot put a clause like that in there?" sneered Darby.

"You did," chuckled Lindsay.

Crossing the Rockies, they found aloft an invisible repetition of the material terrain beneath them. Three-dimensional flows of cold air followed the flow of rivers far below. Air currents ascended sunny sides of mountains at the same steep angles as colder air drained down the shady sides. Sometimes they would be caught in this cycling, and hung over the ridgeline repeating great vertical circles until Randolph ordered the engines engaged.

It proved a struggle after that, for the wind desired them to go south, and numberless standard cubic feet of engine propellant were wasted against the northerly imperative before Randolph, calculating that they had exceeded their energy allotment, gave up the ship's immediate future to the wind, and they drifted thus over the Río Bravo, and into the skies of Old Mexico. So they were borne onward, before winds of obscure sorrow, their clarity of will fitful as the nightly heat-lightning at their horizon.

It was just at that moment of spiritual perplexity that they would be rescued, with no advance annunciation, here, "South of the Border," by the Sodality of Ætheronauts.

How could they have ever crossed trajectories? Afterward none of the boys could remember where it happened, during which toxic ascent, amid what clamor of bickering by now grown routine, they had blundered into this flying-formation of girls, dressed like religious novices in tones of dusk, sent whirling, scattering before the airship's star-blotting mass, their metallic wings earnestly rhythmic, buffeting, some passing close enough for the boys to count the bolts on gear-housings, hear the rotary whining of nitronaphthol auxiliary power-units, grow rigidly attentive to glimpses of bared athletic girl-flesh. Not that these wings, with their thousands of perfectly-machined elliptical "feathers," even in this failing, grime-filtered light, could ever have been mistaken for angels' wings. The serious girls, each harnessed in black kidskin and nickel-plating beneath the inescapable burdens of flight, each bearing on her brow a tiny electric lamp to view her control panel by, regrouped and wheeled away into the coming night. Were glances, even then, cast back at the lumbering, engine-driven skycraft? frowns, coquetries, indistinct foreknowledge that it was to be among themselves, these sombre young women, that the Chums were destined after all to seek wives, to marry and have children and become grandparents—precisely among this wandering sisterhood, who by the terms of their dark indenture must never descend to Earth, each nightfall nesting together on city rooftops like a flock of February chaffinch, having learned to find, in all that roofs keep out, a domesticity of escape and rejection, beneath storm, assaults of moonlight, some darker vertical predation, never entirely dreamed, from other worlds.

Their names were Heartsease and Primula, Glee, Blaze, and Viridian, each had found her way to this Ætherist sorority through the mysteries of inconvenience—a train arriving late, a love-letter mistimed, a hallucinating police witness, and so forth. And now here were these five boy balloonists, whose immediate point of fascination was with the girls' mode of flight. There were great waves passing through the Æther, Viridian explained, which a person could catch, and be carried along by, as the sea-wind carries the erne, or as Pacific waves are said to carry the surfers of Hawaii. The girls' wings were

Æther-ærials which sensed in the medium, all but microscopically, a list of variables including weighted light-saturation index, spectral reluctance, and Æther-normalized Reynolds Number. "These are in turn fed back into a calculating device," said Viridian, "which controls our wing parameters, adjusting them 'feather' by 'feather' to maximize Ætheric lift. . . ."

"It would have had to be an Ætherist," Chick whispered to himself.

"Fumes are not the future," declared Viridian. "Burning dead dinosaurs and whatever they ate ain't the answer, Crankshaft Boy."

She immediately began to instruct him in the Ætherodynamics that made it possible for the girls to fly.

"The Æther," Viridian explained, "like the atmosphere around a skyship, may produce lift and drag on the Earth as it moves through space. As long ago as the Michelson-Morley Experiment there's been speculation about a boundary layer."

"Which the planet's irregular surface," Chick began to see then, "mountains and so forth, creates vortices to keep from separating—"

"And we also know that its thickness is proportional to kinematic viscosity, expressed as area per second—making Time inversely proportional to viscosity, and so to the boundary-layer thickness as well."

"But the viscosity of the Æther, like its density, must be negligible. Meaning a very thin boundary layer, accompanied by a considerable dilation of Time."

Darby, who happened to be listening, wandered away at last shaking his head. "Like Sidney and Beatrice Webb around here."

"As well as a very rapid rise," Viridian had continued, "from zero to whatever the speed of the prevailing Æther-wind is. So that to encounter it in its full force, one would not have to venture far from the planetary surface. In our own case, not much higher than rooftop level."

Chick and Viridian would turn out to be the most problematical, or off-and-on-again, of the five pairings. Chick acted sometimes as if his heart were still back at the scenes of previous adventures, and Viridian's day was itself not without lapses into the sentimental pluperfect.

Lindsay Noseworth, the diagnosed gamomaniac, would be hit hardest of all, at no more than the first sidelong smudge of Primula's appearance. "Primula Noseworth," he was soon discovered whispering over and over, "Primula Noseworth . . ." no part of the ship nor moment of the day being exempt from this confounded mooning. The audible equivalent of a sailor's tattoo.

As for Miles, "Oh Glee," she was playfully admonished, "you always were such a goose when it came to the deep ones!" (Miles's spoken feelings, though recorded, were not readily made sense of.)

It was Heartsease, meanwhile, who became fascinated by the somewhat distracted Randolph (her genius for cookery and herbal knowledge, patiently exercised, would eventually cure his dyspepsia).

Blaze and Darby were a furiously passionate "item" right from the beginning, the former mascotte finding himself, for the first time in the company of a woman, not even tongue-tied, no, in fact *dizzyingly aloft,* through aerial resources which appeared to be entirely his own. "Have I lost my common sense," Blaze wondered, "here unchaperoned like this, with the likes of you and all?" Her gaze attending him narrowly but not unkindly, framed by the roof-tiles of her night's lodging spilling away in what might as well be infinite regress, the corroded splendor of the late sky deepening as they stood and, it seemed to Darby, waited, though for what exactly was beyond him. As stoves were lit invisibly beneath their feet, woodsmoke began to seep and blow from the chimney tops, cries of newsboys ascended from the streets below, piercing as song. Arpeggios of bells, each with its own long-cherished name in the local dialect, joined in. Great disks of day-wearied birds tilted and careened above the squares big and small, brushed with penultimate light one moment, shed of it the next.

By morning, with all the girls aboard, the wind had shifted. As Lindsay had confirmed three extra times, it would now take them within a few minutes of arc to their California destination.

That was how they flew northwest and one night looked down and beheld an incalculable expanse of lights, which according to their charts was known as the City of Our Lady, Queen of the Angels. "My heavens," exclaimed Heartsease, "Where on Earth is this?"

"That's sort of the problem," Chick said. "That 'on Earth' part."

While crossing the Continent the boys had expressed wonder at how much more infected with light the night-time terrains passing below them had become—more than anyone could ever remember, as isolated lanterns and skeins of gas-light had given way to electric street-lighting, as if advanced parties of the working-day were progressively invading and settling the unarmed hinterlands of night. But now at last, flying in over southern California and regarding the incandescence which flooded forth from suburban homes and city plazas, athletic fields, movie theatres, rail yards and depots, factory skylights, aerial beacons, streets and boulevards bearing lines of automobile headlights in constant crawl beyond any horizon, they felt themselves in uneasy witness to some final conquest, a triumph over night whose motive none could quite grasp.

"It must have to do with extra work-shifts," Randolph guessed, "increasingly scheduled, that is, beyond the hours of daylight."

"So much additional employment," Lindsay enthused, "as to suggest the further expansion of an already prodigious American economy, is certainly good news for us, considering the hardly negligible fraction of our capital invested therewithin."

"Yep groundhog sweat, misery and early graves," snarled Darby, "that's what keeps us flying around up here in style all right."

"You have certainly been treated well enough, Suckling, by a corporate system any of whose trivial shortcomings with which you still find yourself obliged to quibble must remain, for the rest of us, mercifully obscure if not indeed incomprehensible."

Darby blinked innocently. "Eeyyhh, Noseworth?"

"Don't say it. I am as fond of the subjunctive mood as any, but as the only use to which you ever put it is for a *two-word vulgarism* better left unuttered—"

"Oh. Then how about 'Long live capitalism'? same thing basically, ain't it."

As if enabled by the absorption of a critical quantity of that unrelenting light, Miles spoke, his voice all but breaking beneath some emotion difficult to make out. "Lucifer, son of the morning, bearer of light . . . Prince of Evil."

Lindsay, as Ship's Theological Officer, helpfully began to explain how the early church fathers, in their wish to connect Old and New Testaments at as many points as possible, were trying to correlate Isaiah's epithet for the King of Babylon with Christ's vision, according to Luke, of Satan falling like lightning from heaven. "Complicated further by the ancient astronomers' use of the name Lucifer for Venus when she appears as the morning star—"

"That is etymology," said Miles as politely as he could. "But as for persistence within the human heart, immune to time—"

"Excuse me, what," Darby pretending to raise his hand, ". . . *areyoupeopletalkingabout*?"

Randolph looked up from a chart, and compared it with the crawling lightscape below. "There appears to be an airship facility around Van Nuys that might do the trick. Gentlemen, set the special sky detail."

As it turned out, the check sent by the lawyers bounced and their mailing address, upon investigation, did not exist. The boys found themselves for the moment without employment in a peculiar corner of a planet that might or might not be their own.

"Another damn fool's errand," Darby growled. "When are we gonna learn?"

"You were all in such a hurry," Lindsay replied smugly.

“Think I’ll just wander around today,” Chick said, “and take in the sights.” Around noontime, strolling in Hollywood and finding himself suddenly hungry, he went to stand in line outside a bustling hot-dog emporium called Links, where whom should he run into but his father, “Dick” Counterfly, whom he hadn’t seen since 1892 or thereabouts.

“Great Scott,” exclaimed the elder Counterfly, “ain’t we a long ways from Thick Bush, Alabama.”

“Nearly thirty years.”

“Thought you’d be taller by now.”

“Looks like you’re doing well, sir.”

“Call me Dick, everybody in the world does, even the Chinese. Hell, they’d better. That state of Mississippi deal was the beginning of both our fortunes. See that rig over there?”

“Looks like a Packard.”

“Ain’t she a beauty? Come on, we’ll go for a spin.”

“Dick” was living in a Beaux-Arts mansion out on West Adams with his third wife, Treacle, who was Chick’s age and possibly younger, and seemed unusually attentive to Chick.

“Another gin fizz, Chick?”

“Thanks, already got one,” said Chick, adding, “Treacle,” in a lower voice.

“What’s with the eyelashes, cupcake? You look like you’re old enough to know the score.”

“Get a load of this,” “Dick” motioning them into a dim adjoining room, where a huge piece of machinery, dominated by a rapidly-spinning metallic disk, six feet high and full of round holes in spiraling patterns with a very bright arc light behind it, and a bank of selenium cells that covered one entire wall.

“Dick” went to a panel of switches and palely-lighted gauge faces, and began to crank the contraption up. “Not that I invented any of this really, all the pieces were already out in the market, why that Nipkow scanner there’s been around since 1884. I just happened to see how it could all fit together in a package, you’d say.”

Chick gazed with great scientific curiosity at the shimmering image which appeared on a screen across the room from the spinning disk, as what looked like a tall monkey in a sailor hat with the brim turned down fell out of a palm tree onto a very surprised older man—the skipper of some nautical vessel, to judge by the hat he was wearing.

“I pick this one up every week around this time,” said “Dick,” “though sometimes it seems to come from, well you might think it’s odd, but somewhere not *on* the surface of the Earth so much as—”

"Perpendicular," Chick suggested. He noticed that Treacle was sitting unusually close to him on the sofa, had undone several buttons of her dress, and seemed in an agitated state. And instead of watching the dots of light, revealed faster than the human eye could follow, blinking on and off at different intensities one after the other to create a single framed moving picture, she was watching Chick.

Chick waited until the end of the transmission, whatever it had meant, and excused himself for the evening. Treacle rolled up his necktie and kissed him on the mouth. The next day "Dick" was at the balloon-field in Van Nuys before reveille, gunning the engine of the Packard impatiently.

"Like you to come meet a couple of fellas."

They sped out toward the ocean, and about halfway along the curve of Santa Monica Bay found a complex of galvanized sheds and laboratories, just above the beach, which turned out to be a research facility run by two elderly eccentrics, Roswell Bounce and Merle Rideout.

"Hi, Roswell, what's with the shotgun?"

"Thought you were somebody else."

"Those same heavies, back again, eh?" said "Dick," with a worried expression.

"You mentioned if we ever needed some muscle, there was somebody you could recommend," Merle said.

"And the time is damn sure upon us," Roswell said.

"Yes. Well there's a whiz of a detective downtown," said "Dick," "who'll know just what to do. Got him on retainer myself. Keeps an eye on that Treacle for me."

Chick gave his father a quizzical look. He was about to remark how cheerful and sociable a girl she seemed to be, but somehow thought better of it.

"And if some, say, firearm situation should arise?" muttered Roswell.

"It's his condition," Merle in a stage whisper. "Old-time form of paranoia."

"Better'n goin around thinkin I'm bulletproof."

"Well, packing or not, Lew Basnight's your man." From a dilapidated wallet "Dick" took out a wad of business cards, and flipped through. "Here's his telephone number."

INSIDE THE SHOP, Chick stared in amazement. It was the lab of every boy's dreams! Why, the place even *smelled* scientific—that long-familiar blend of ozone, gutta-percha, solvent chemicals, heated insulation. The shelves and benchtops were crowded with volt-ammeters, rheostats, transformers, arc lamps whole and in pieces, half-used carbons, calcium burners, Oxone tablets, high-tension magnetos, alternators store-bought and home-made, vibrator coils, cut-outs and interruptors, worm drives, Nicol prisms, generating valves, glassblowing torches, Navy surplus Thalofide cells, brand-new Aeolight tubes freshly fallen from the delivery truck, British Blattnerphone components and tons of other stuff Chick had never recalled seeing before.

Merle and Roswell led them to the back of the lab and through triple-locked doors into a small shop space occupied by a mysterious piece of machinery, over whose safety they had been losing some sleep lately, for it had attracted the attention it seemed of some dark criminal enterprise, based, the inventors were all but certain, up in Hollywood.

"See, every photographic subject moves," Roswell explained, "even if it's standing still. It breathes, light bounces off, something. Snapping a photograph is like what the math professors call 'differentiating' an equation of motion—freezing that movement into the very small piece of time it takes the shutter to open and close. So we figured—if shooting a photo is like taking a first derivative, then maybe we could find some way to do the reverse of that, start with the still photo and *integrate* it, recover its complete primitive and release it back into action . . . even back to life . . ."

"We worked at it off and on," Merle said, "but it wasn't till old Lee De Forest added that grid electrode to the Fleming valve that everything began to make sense. Then it seemed clear enough that with a triode valve, an input resistor and a feedback condenser, for instance, you could breadboard a circuit that if you chose your resistance and capacitance right, you could put in a simple alternating voltage onto the grid—call it 'sine of *t*'—and get minus cosine of *t* for an output."

"So that in theory the output," Chick grasped, "can be the indefinite integral of any signal you put on the grid."

"There you go," Roswell nodded. "Better look out for this one, 'Dick.' Any case, electricity and light being pretty much the same thing, just slightly different stretches of the spectrum really, we figured if we could work this integration effect with electricity, then we should also be able to do it using light, should we not?"

"Heck, you've got *my* permission all right," exclaimed 'Dick' Counterfly.

For the professorial of temperament the next step would then've been finding analogies in the world of optics for the De Forest triode, the feedback capacitor, and other physical components of the circuit in question. But with Roswell there was his strikingly advanced case of paranoia querulans to be taken into account. You could see his ears twitching, always a sure sign in him of mental activity, but his mind was not, it had occurred already to Merle, working in anything like a straightforward manner. Fragments of former patent applications, modulated by defectively remembered court appearances, bloomed and streamed kaleidoscopically in and out of his attention. Faces of lawyers he had grown less than fond of, indeed entertained phantasies about murdering, even from years before, swam now distortedly through his thoughts. Not to mention inspiration to be drawn, not always explicably, from the pieces of hardware that kept finding their ways, more and less legally, into the shop. One of the pair of mad inventors would ask, "What the hell we ever gonna do with that," the other would shrug and say, "You never know," and up it would go onto some shelf or into some cabinet, and sure enough, one day they'd need something that would turn infrared light to electricity, or double-refract it at a particular angle of polarization, and there, invisible under a pile of stuff accumulated since, would be the very item.

Merle now had cranked a small gasoline motor-generator into action, brought two carbons together at right angles, and eased them apart again with a blinding arc sizzling between them. He made some lens adjustments. On the wall appeared an enlarged photo of downtown L.A., monochromatic and still. Merle rocked the carbons, turned some knobs, took from a wall safe a brilliant red crystal, brought it over to a platinoid housing and carefully slid it into place. "Lorandite—brought out of Macedonia before the Balkan Wars, pure thallium arsenosulfide, purer quality than you can find anymore." High-vacuum tubes glowed eerily purple. Humming came from two or three sources, not what you'd call in harmony. ". . . Now watch." So smoothly Chick missed the moment, the photo came to life. A horse lifted a hoof. A streetcar emerged from inertia. The clothing of city strollers began to flutter in the breeze.

"Ain't it just the damndest thing you ever saw?" cried "Dick" Counterfly, whose growing familiarity with this rig had only increased his astonishment. One by one over the next half-hour Merle projected other transparencies onto the walls, which pretty soon were covered with scenes from American lives, unquestionably in motion. The combined effect was of a busy population the size of a small city. Inside each frame they were dancing, saloon-fighting, drinking, playing pool, working day jobs, loitering, fucking, strolling, eating in lunchwagons, getting on and off streetcars, dealing pinochle hands, some in black and white, some in color.

In the years since they'd come up with the process, Merle confided, he had begun to understand that he was on a mission to set free the images not just in the photographs he was taking, but in all that came his way, like the prince who with his kiss releases that Sleeping Beauty into wakefulness. One by one, across the land, responsive to his desire, photos trembled, stirred, began to move, at first slowly then accelerating, pedestrians walked away out of the frame, carriages drove along, the horses pulling them shit in the street, bystanders who had their backs turned revealed their faces, streets darkened and gas lamps came on, nights lengthened, stars wheeled, passed, were dissolved in dawn, family gatherings at festive tables were scattered into drunkenness and debris, dignitaries posing for portraits blinked, belched, blew their noses, got up and left the photographer's studio, eventually along with all the other subjects liberated from these photos resumed their lives, though clearly they had moved beyond the range of the lens, as if all the information needed to depict an indefinite future had been there in the initial "snap," at some molecular or atomic fineness of scale whose limit, if any, hadn't yet been reached— "Though you'd think because of the grain-size situation," Roswell pointed out, "that sooner or later we'd've run out of resolution."

"It might be something wrapped in the nature of Time itself," Chick speculated.

"Way beyond me," smiled Roswell, "nothin but old gaffers around here."

"There's a fellow on board my ship, Miles Blundell, who often sees into these matters deeper than most. I'd like to tell him about your invention, if you don't mind."

"Long as he ain't connected with the picture business," said Roswell.

"You'll be sure and look up Detective Basnight now," said "Dick" as they were leaving. "Sometimes all he needs is to make a phone call."

"Shootin somebody'd be better," suggested Roswell with a chirp in his voice.

Walking out through the fog to the Packard, Chick said to his father, "Good thing I never had a snap of you—those fellows could've shown me everything you've been up to all these years."

"Same to you I'm sure, sprout." As they were about to climb in the auto, "Dick," as if it had just occurred to him, said, "Maybe you'd like to drive some?"

"It's embarrassing, but I don't know how."

"Gonna be in L.A. for long, guess you'd better learn." He started the engine. "Teach you if you like. Wouldn't take too long."

Back at the airfield, they found *Inconvenience* in a glare of unaccustomed electrical light frequencies just blossoming into the fragrant desert night. Smells of cooking came from the galley. "Dick" rested his forehead on the steering wheel for a moment. "Guess I should be gettin back to old Treacle."

“Would you like to come on board and have supper, Dad? It’s red beans, shrimps and rice tonight, bayou style. You could meet Viridian—that’s if she’s talking to me again—and later we could take the ship up, go for a little spin over the Basin . . .”

Surprisingly after their years apart his father’s face was not as unreadable as Chick might have expected. “Well. Thought you’re never gonna ask.”

Lew's offices in L.A. were in one of those swank new buildings going up along Broadway, with elevators and electricity throughout, looking into a vast interior court below a domed skylight which admitted blues and golds somehow more intense than the desert-bleached ones you usually saw around town. The outer suite was verdant with dwarf palms and Dieffenbachia, and there were three layers of security to be got past, each featuring a deceptively sylphlike receptionist. These girls also worked at the movie studios up in Hollywood as "stunt" performers whenever a scene, in the wisdom of those insuring the picture, might endanger a star actress obliged, say, to dangle from a skyscraper ledge or drive a roadster back and forth across a railroad track in front of a speeding locomotive. Thetis, Shalimar, and Mezzanine, whose stylish flapper-stenographer turnouts concealed bodies designed for the pleasure of intimates as well as the discomfort of strangers, were all crackerjack drivers, licensed gun owners, and surefooted as burros at the Grand Canyon, knowing how to descend a stairway high-heeled into a hotel ballroom without tripping, though sometimes for fun the madcap Mezzanine liked to do just that, staging shrieking thirty-foot descents just to draw the crowd reaction.

Right down the street was the Pacific Electric Building and its new Coles P.E. Buffet, where Lew liked to grab breakfast, when breakfast happened to be in the cards. When it wasn't, it was usually after a prolonged and hectic night, Lew having taken up what he recognized as serious drinking at an advanced age, around the onset of Prohibition.

Lew had stayed in London as long as he could, but by the time the War was over, Britain, Europe—it seemed all a dream. He could smell those steaks clear across the Atlantic and down that Erie Line, and was dismayed at how long it had taken him to remember that Chicago was home. All that running around. He returned to find that White City Investigations had been bought out by some trust back east and now mostly provided "industrial security," a term for breaking the heads of those either on strike or maybe just thinking about going out, with the ops now all wearing two-tone brown uniforms and packing Colt Automatics. Nate Privett was retired and living in Lincolnwood. Anybody who wanted to see him had to call up his personal secretary and schedule an appointment.

Not that Lew was doing that bad. There was a lot of money from someplace overseas, some said from gambling interests, others insisted it was gun-running, or some extortion racket—the story always came down to how the storyteller felt about Lew.

But all it took was a couple of years in L.A. to turn him into one more old goat of the region with a deep suntan, who'd seen things, taken part in activities, in the toilets of the wealthy, on the back slopes of the dunes of the beach towns, in the shack cities, in high-desert washes, up Hollywood alleyways full of leafy exotics, that made Chicago seem innocent as a playground. He still had faith in his own rough clairvoyance, his aim and speed with a pistol. He drove down to a range near the beach and practiced a lot. Occasionally, ladies here and there around the L.A. Basin, former movie actresses, real-estate agents, badgirls encountered out on various cases, might, out of policy, not mind spending a half hour with him in bed or more commonly upright in some dimly-lit swimming pool, but no, what his alienist Dr. Ghloix called, long-term relationships.

He knew that other lawfolk of his day, those who worked both sides till they'd forgot which they were on, who'd came to rank, some of them, among the baddest of the bad, now, their gray mustaches long shaved away, at peace on this western shore, were getting rich off of real-estate deals only slightly more legit than the train robberies they used to depend on for revenue . . . desperados more modest but once lethal as they come were settled in in little chalet-style houses down in the flats around Pico with their cheery, pie-baking brides, hiring on up the hill as script consultants for the shadow-factories relentlessly turning those wild ancient days into harmless packages of flickering entertainment. Lew had never thought he'd see the day, but out here he found himself saying that every day.

"It seems to be some sort of Negro," announced Thetis. "Again."

"That disapproval, Miss Pomidor?"

She shrugged. “I don’t mind when it’s bootleggers. They know how to act like gentlemen. But these jazz musicians.”

“If it isn’t in that Erno Rapée movie-theme book, she doesn’t want to know,” Shalimar commented. “Mezzanine, now, she’s always out on dates with these fellows.”

“Once you’ve done black,” Mezzanine crooned to a sort of blues melody, “never go back.”

“Mezzanine Perkins!” the girls practicing shocked gasps.

Chester LeStreet had on a luminous gray worsted suit, shirt and display handkerchief in the same vivid shade of fuchsia, ice-cream-colored Homburg hat, hand-painted necktie. Lew, who had had holes in his socks since the weekend, looked around for his sandals and slipped them on.

Chester beamed at him over dark sunglasses with tortoise-shell frames. “Here’s what it is. I play drums in the house band down at the Vertex Club on South Central, maybe you know it?”

“Sure, Tony Tsangarakis’s joint—the Syncopated Strangler case, couple-three years ago. How’s the Greek?”

“Still ain’t back to normal. So much as tap on a temple block, his teeth starts to chattering along.”

“I heard they finally closed the case.”

“Tight as the gates of San Quentin, but now here’s the thing. Miss Jardine Maraca, who was the canary with the band back then?”

“Roommate of one of the victims, as I recall, left town allegedly in fear of her life.”

Chester nodded. “Never heard from since—up till last night anyway. She calls the club long-distance from some motor court up in Santa Barbara with a crazy story about how that other girl, Encarnación, is still alive, she seen her, knows enough not to go yoo-hooing in public, but now somebody’s after her. Tony remembers you from the go-round before, and wonders if you’d like to look into this.”

“Any personal interest here, Mr. LeStreet, if you don’t mind my asking?”

“Just running an errand for the boss.”

“You have a picture of Miss Maraca?”

“Tony gave me this.” The jazz-man reached into a briefcase and handed Lew what seemed to be a publicity shot, with creases and thumbtack holes in it, one of those eight-by-ten glossies you see in lobby displays outside small nightclubs, surrounded by glued-on glitter. Technically she was smiling, but it had that Hollywood rigidity to it that Lew had learned to recognize as fear of somebody else’s power.

"Quite a presentable young woman, Mr. LeStreet."

The musician took off his sunglasses and pretended to study the picture for a minute. "Guess so. Before my time, of course."

"Some of your colleagues around there may still remember her. I'll drop by one of these evenings. First I guess I'll motor up to Santa Barbara. She say where she was staying?"

"Royal Jacaranda Courts, just off the Coast Highway."

"*Oh* yeah, the ol' R.J. . . . well, thanks, and tell the Greek not to worry."

It was in the days just before the earthquake, and Santa Barbara still reflected a lot less light than it was about to under the stucco-and-beam philosophy of the rebuilding to follow. The place for the moment lay dreaming in a darkness of overwatered vegetation, ivy-shrouded suburban ascents into rat-infested pockets of old California money, a relentlessly unacknowledged past. Because of the right-angled piece of local coastline known as the Rincón, the ocean lay to the south of town instead of west, so you had to rotate ninety degrees from everybody else in Southern California to catch the sunset. This angle, according to Scylla, an astrologer of Lew's acquaintance, was the worst of all possible aspects, and doomed the town to reenact endlessly the same cycles of greed and betrayal as in the days of the earliest Barbareños.

The Royal Jacaranda was even more of a wreck than Lew remembered it, and under different management, natch.

A kid who must have been on summer vacation sat painstakingly waxing a ten-foot surfboard which took up most of the space in the office.

"Jardine Maraca. You know when she checked out?"

He looked at the register. "It must've been before I came on."

"Have a gander in the room, if you don't mind."

"For sure." Back to his board. Nice piece of redwood.

At the far end of the courtyard was a Mexican with a hose, chatting with one of the housekeepers. Jardine's room hadn't been made up yet. The bed had been slept on, but not in. Lew made his way through the place, hoping, and not hoping, for surprises. The small chifferobe held only a couple of hairpins and a price tag from the hat department at Capwell's. The shelf over the sink in the bathroom had an empty face-cream jar on it. Lew could see nothing out of the ordinary in either the bowl or the tank of the toilet. But he got an idea. He went down to the office again, flipped a bright new fifty-cent piece to the kid, and asked to use the phone. There was a Filipino hop dealer he knew down on lower State who could gaze into the depths of a toilet bowl the way other scryers might a crystal ball or teacup, and learn the damnedest things, most of them useless, but now and then so illuminative of secrets a subject might think he or she had kept perfectly hidden that there was no way this side of the supernatural to explain it. Cops here and in L.A. respected Emilio's gift enough to allow him discounts on the payoffs required to pursue his career in agricultural goods unmolested.

Emilio picked up on the first ring, but Lew could hardly make him out over the uproar in the background. Lew knew it was probably the missus, but it sounded like an angry mob. Today she and Emilio had been going round and round since about sunrise, and at this point he was more than happy to get out of the house for a while. He showed up at the Royal Jacaranda on an old bicycle, trailed by a nimbus of reefer smoke.

"Thought I'd never have to see *this* place again."

"Oh? Let me guess, some dope delivery went sour. . . ."

"No, this is where we stayed on our honeymoon. Cursed, as far as I'm concerned."

The minute he entered the room, Emilio went all peculiar. "Do me a favor, Lew, take that bedspread and cover up the mirror, O.K.?" He found a towel in the bathroom and did the same with the little mirror over the sink. "They're like fleas sometimes," he muttered, getting down on one knee and carefully lifting the lid of the toilet, "like to jump around. This way it stays focused in one place. . . ."

Lew knew better than to hover. He went outside, leaned against the sunlit stucco, and smoked a Fatima and watched the housekeepers work their way down the line of rooms toward him. Sort of keeping an ear out for Emilio, who had looked—hard to say, nervous or something.

He was at Lew's elbow. "See one of your civilian cigarettes there?"

They stood and smoked and listened to the morning losing its early promise. "Here," Emilio handing over an L.A. address he'd scribbled in some agitation on a picture postcard of the Royal Jacaranda. "That's all that kept showing."

"You're sure."

"Overwhelming, caballero. Don't ask me to go back in and confirm it. And better think twice yourself, Lew."

"Bad, huh?"

"Bad, big . . . many bodies." He threw the cigarette butt into a puddle of hose water the sun hadn't got to yet. "Makes a man appreciate arguing with his old lady, I tell you that."

"Thanks, Emilio. Bill me."

"*Tu mamá.* I'll take cash, right now—I want to start forgetting this soon as I can."

Back at the office, Lew found Thetis in a dither. "You've been getting calls from a crazy person, total panic in his voice, every ten minutes, like he's using an egg timer. Fact, he's due to call again," looking dramatically at her wristwatch, "Just . . . about . . ."

The phone rang. Lew, avuncularly patting Thetis on the shoulder, picked up the receiver.

The panicked voice belonged to Merle Rideout, who lived out at the beach and described himself as an inventor. "Like to come in to your office, but I'm being followed, so any meeting will have to look accidental. You know Sycamore Grove, out on North Figueroa?"

"Used to be a nice place for Iowa girls."

"Still is. Glad we can agree on somethin."

Lew checked out a little 6.35 mm Beretta, just in case.

"Looks like some aggravation in the works, chief," said Shalimar. "You need any muscle along?"

"Nah, just two quick stops to make. But—" He copied the address he'd got from Emilio onto her appointment pad. "In case I don't call in before quitting time, maybe one of you could drive by and have a look. Bring the tommy gun."

Merle had been out here since before the War, and realized at some point that he'd been slowly mutating into a hybrid citrus with no commercial value. One day shortly before the War began over in Europe, he happened to run into Luca Zombini in an electrical shop in Santa Monica. Luca was working up at one of the studios in something called "special photographic effects," mostly glass mattes and so forth, and learning all he could about sound recording.

"Come on over, we'll cook something. Erlys will want to see you, and you can meet all the kids—except for Bria, she's back east pursuing an international banking career, not to mention a number of international bankers."

Erlys's hair was a lot shorter, he noticed, right in style as near as he could tell, with curls falling softly over her forehead. "You're looking about the same as always."

"Better quit flirting with me, I'll have to scream for my husband."

"Whoops."

Trying not to regard Merle as an aging obsessive who didn't smile as much as he should, she filled him in on what she knew of Dally, who was living in London and actually wrote from time to time.

Nunzi came screeching up after a while in a roadster that had seen some determined use, and one by one Merle met the other kids as they drifted in from school.

"You never got married, Merle?"

"Damn," snapping his fingers, "I knew there was somethin I was supposed to do."

She looked down at her toes, brightly revealed in beach sandals. Hummingbirds darted in and out of the bougainvillea. "When we—"

"No, no, no, 'Lys, that would've went on to been a disaster. You know that. Front page, banner headlines, ain't-it-awful follow-ups for years. You got a bargain there with old whatsizname, right place at the right time. Those kids are just aces too, every one. That Nunzi—just get to thinking I know everything there is to know, and . . ." He was smiling, some, finally.

"They're starting to give me a little time off these days," she said. "I get a minute to look in the mirror, it's like meeting somebody I almost know. But," he knew what was coming, "I really miss Dahlia."

"Yeahp. Same here. Me, she needed to get away right when she did, timing couldn't be beat, but still—"

"I don't know how to thank you Merle, she turned out just so—"

"Oh hell she's still only, what, twenty-somethin, got plenty of time yet to git into some extensive evildoin, 'f that's what she wants."

"She's a star of the London stage." Erlys brought out a velveteen album with clippings from English newspapers and magazines, theater programs and publicity photos.

He sat nodding before the images of Miss Dahlia Rideout, surprised she'd kept the name, squeezing his eyes very small, as if in careful scrutiny. "Well, look out, Olga Nethersole," he said in a low voice. "Back away, Mrs. Fiske."

Luca came in with a bag of groceries.

"Evenin Professor," Merle with a quick social smile.

"Somebody'd told me you were coming I'd've let you do the cooking," said Luca.

"I could peel somethin. Carve it up?"

"Most of it's growing out back, come on." They went out the back door and into a sizable garden, full of long green frying peppers, bush-size basil plants, zucchini running all over the place, artichokes with their feathery tops blowing in a wind in today from the desert, eggplants glowing ultraviolet in the shadows, tomatoes looking like the four-color illustrations of themselves that showed up on lugs down at the market. There was a pomegranate tree, and a fig tree, and a lemon tree, all bearing. Luca found the hose and gave everything an evening spray, with his thumb sending a broad fan of water over the whole plot. They got tomatoes and peppers and oregano and some garlic and brought everything back in a straw basket to the kitchen, where Merle found a knife and set about prepping.

"Where's Cici?" Erlys said.

"Had a late call up at the studio." Cici it turned out was playing one of the Li'l Jailbirds, characters in a popular series of one-reel comedies about a gang of reform-school escapees who go around doing good deeds, which at first are always misunderstood as criminal acts by the comical policemen who relentlessly pursue the kids. Cici played the part not of an Italian but a Chinese kid named Dou Ya. The Italian kid, Pippo, was played by a Negro. And so forth. Something to do with orthochromatic film. Cici had developed this private "Chinese" style of jabbering which drove everybody in the house crazy. "Cici, it's a silent movie, you don't have to—"

"Just getting in character, Pop!"

Cici became Merle's favorite of all the kids, though over the years he tried to keep his visits to a considerate level. Didn't want to be anybody's Uncle Merle, and it wasn't really as if time was hanging heavy—though work these days had become more a source of danger than income, which is why he and Roswell finally gave in and decided to hire a private eye.

Never having felt like that he was a citizen of any state in particular, Merle just tended to show up at any state picnic he happened to hear about. No matter which part of the country anybody he met was from, he and his wagon had been through it at least once. Some people even remembered him, or said they did. It was all home.

He wandered now beneath the sycamores, through the cooking smoke, attending calmly to each mid-American face, shrugging on like some old cardigan a nostalgia not his own but in some murky way of use to him. They'd be drinking birch beer and orange juice, eating stuffed peppers they liked to call "mangoes," casseroles of baked beans or macaroni and rat cheese, pineapple upside-down cakes, bread just out of ovens at home and covered in checkered towels. Out here at the Grove, they'd be cooking franks, hamburgers, steaks, and sides of beef over wood fires, slopping on barbecue sauce from time to time, tapping beer kegs, playing horseshoes, shouting at their kids, at each other, at nobody, just to be shouting, particularly if it wasn't raining, which it never seemed to be, and that was one of the big differences for them, no thunder, no cyclones, no hail or snow, the house roofs of Southern California all pitched at shallow angles because there was nothing to shed. . . .

Lew found Merle discussing potato-salad recipes with a bunch of Iowans. "Gettin up early is built into it, you need to have 'em cooked and marinating in oil, vinegar, and mustard for at least three or four hours before you even start thinkin about mayonnaise and spices and all that," whereas other philosophies held add-ins like bacon and celery to be of the essence, or sour cream preferable to mayonnaise, and by now it had turned into quite the lively discussion, with everybody who came wandering into earshot eager to put in a few words of comment, otherwise easygoing wives and mothers, thresher-dinner veterans from way back, getting into screaming matches with roadside-diner cooks who handled easily five hundred pounds of potato salad a day for truck drivers who'd forgot more about job-related eating than seasonal farm laborers ever knew to begin with . . . and everybody with an opinion also seemed to have brought along their own tub of potato salad, and each punctuating his or her argument with a huge forkful of a particular recipe, all but forced into the face of some potato-salad heretic—"Here, just try this, tell me these li'l red-skinned potatoes don't make all the difference." "Hard-boiled eggs are all right 's long as you don't use the whites, just the yolk part, mash it up in with your mayonnaise, not only makes it taste better, it looks better, and if you can find those green peppercorns . . ."

For such a calm-looking fellow, Merle sure took some nervous precautions. After a quickly whispered set of instructions, Lew went back to where he'd parked, drove to a lot near the office, switched cars, went back around the other side of the Grove to pick up Roswell, eventually parked near a P.E. stop, where they boarded the electric and rode the rest of the way to the beach.

Merle and Roswell tried running the situation through for Lew, but it might as well have been Chinese for all he could understand of it. He looked at the rig in question doubtfully.

Then something occurred to him. "Say I had a, just some ordinary photo of somebody, and wanted to know where they were right now and what they were doing . . ."

"Sure," Merle said, "we just dial in the year, date, and time of day we're interested in, it all speeds up, runs through the time between the picture was taken and now in a matter of seconds."

"Then maybe you could help me," Lew said, bringing out the glossy of Jardine Maraca, "you think it'd work on this?"

"Let me just take it in the darkroom a second," Roswell said, "run us a transparent copy, and we'll see what we can see."

What they saw was Jardine, snappily turned out in something shiny and tight, climbing into a Model T and driving east along a recognizable Sunset Boulevard, beneath massive fluted columns with elephants rampant on top and various other gigantic and indeed hallucinatory sets from the movie *Intolerance,* continued almost all the way downtown, took a left up Figueroa, crossed the river, passed Mount Washington and went on through Highland Park to Eagle Rock, made a couple-three turns Lew was able to keep track of, and stopped at last in front of an iron gate in a wall of arroyo stone, with a sign above it reading Carefree Court. Inside among palms and eucalyptus trees were a dozen bungalows in Mission Revival style grouped around a swimming pool with a fountain in it throwing pulses of water into a blurred gray sky. . . .

Jardine sat for a while, as if having a long talk with herself, perhaps about some choice she had to make, which was turning out to be harder than she'd thought.

"AND NOT ONLY can we unfold the future history of these subjects," "Roswell was saying, "we can also reverse the process, to look into their pasts."

"One photograph of a suspicious corpse," it occurred to Lew, "and you could watch who did the deed, catch them in the act?"

"You begin to see why certain interests might feel threatened. All those old long-standing mysteries of the past like, say, the *Times* bombing, all you'd need to do'd be get a shot of First and Broadway where the old building was, run it back to late September 1910 just before the bombing . . ."

"It'll go back that far?"

Roswell and Merle looked at each other.

"You've done it?"

"It was night," Merle a little embarrassed. "They could've been anybody."

". . . only maybe tricky part," said Roswell, "being to find the constant term in the primitive, which differentiation has taken to zero. Usually to look back in the past it's got to be a negative value. But unless we get it right on the nose, there's always the chance that those little folks in the pictures will choose different paths than the originals."

At which point Lew finally remembered bilocation—how in England long ago he had even found himself now and then going off on these forks in the road. Detours from what he still thought of as his official, supposed-to-be life. Since coming back to the States, however, as if they had been no more than vivid dreams, these side-trips had tapered off and presently stopped altogether, and with nobody to talk to about it, Lew had no choice but to take care of day-to-day business and not spend too much time brooding. But here seemed to be those old bilocational powers emerging now once again, only different. "You mean," trying to control a tremor in his voice, gesturing more broadly than he meant to at the breathing image of Jardine, still waiting, "you could watch somebody go on to live a completely different life?"

"Sure, if you wanted to." Roswell giving him a puzzled look that fell just short of annoyed. "But why?"

"Now you've seen the unit in action," said Merle, "let us just give you the rundown on why we asked you in. Some funny things've been happening around here lately. Gorillas out in the alley just standing, smoking, watching. Telephones ring in the middle of the night but nobody's ever on the line. Cars cruise past, closed sedans, smoked-glass windows, very slow, and some of the license-plate numbers show up more than once. And then just out in the course of the day's work, somebody'll pass along a word or two of caution, or concern, never too loud, never allowin their lips to move."

"What it comes down to," said Roswell Bounce, "is we don't want to meet the same melancholy fate as Louis Le Prince, who back in the late '80s had his own system all up and running, basically the same as what the picture business has today, film on reels, sprocket holes, intermittent motion, so forth—one day he climbs on the Paris-Dijon Express and is never heard from again. His wife tries to find out what happened, everybody clams up, seven years later he's legally dead, one or two pieces of his machinery find their way into museums, some of the patents are already on file, but everything else has mysteriously vanished along with ol' Louie."

"And you think somebody actually—"

"Oh, sorry—do you think it's just my P.Q. acting up again? for Pete's sake Mr. Basnight, you've had a long career in gumshoeing, seen your share of the bent and evil, and you must've run into some of these studio big shots by now, what do *you* think?"

"That first they'd try to steal it—bearing in mind that 'theft' as defined in this town often includes the payment of cash, and can even be quite a tidy sum."

"But just makin *it* all disappear," said Roswell, "might not be enough for them."

"What makes you think they've found out anything? Are there records on file? Did you see a lawyer about patent applications?"

"Ha! you ever run into one lawyer you'd trust with a nickel fallen from a blind man's tambourine, why, grab us a flyin pig while you're at it, we'll take 'em both out on tour and make our fortune."

"Seems a little risky, 's all."

"Any ideas on how to proceed?"

"I can post some strong-arm talent outside, but even non-Union like everything else in town, after a while that runs into considerable mazuma—so we should be thinking about longer-term solutions."

"But hell, it's an unlimited scoundrel supply up in 'em studios, every errand boy's a producer waitin to happen, we'll never kill 'em all—"

"I was thinking more of finding you some legal protection."

"We need a miracle we'll wire the Pope," said Roswell.

IT WAS LATE AFTERNOON by the time Lew motored over to the address Emilio had given him. He parked a few doors down from a chalet-style bungalow with a pepper tree in the yard, went up and knocked politely at the front door. And was shocked, or as much as he could be anymore, by the malevolent glamour of the face that so abruptly appeared. Shady side of forty, presentable, but also what he had long come, regretfully, to recognize as haunted. Maybe he ought to've turned and ankled it, but instead he took his hat off all the way and inquired, "This the house that's for rent?"

"Not so far. Should it be, do you think?"

Lew pretended to look in his daybook. "You'd be . . ."

"Mrs. Deuce Kindred." The door screen cast over her face a strange rectilinear mist, which somehow extended to her voice and which for no reason he could figure, thinking about it later, he took as a sexual signal, proceeding to get an erection out on the front porch here and everything— "Did I come to the wrong place?" He watched her eyes flicker down and up.

"Easy to find out."

"The husband home?"

"Come on in." She took a step back and turned, with the beginning of a smile she almost contemptuously would not allow him to see any further stages of, and led him through the olive light of the little front room toward the kitchen. Oh this was going to be sordid as all hell, he knew the feeling by now. At first he had thought it must be him, and some tough-guy sex appeal, but after a while he understood that out on this coast it was nothing personal, it only happened a lot. She wore her stockings rolled just above the knees, flapper style. She paused short of the sociable yellow sunlight ahead of them, pouring into the kitchen just out of reach, and stood in this dimness still with her backside to him, her head tilted, her nape bare beneath the beauty-parlor bob. Lew came ahead, grasped her skirt hem and pulled it all the way up.

"Well. Where'd them step-ins get to?"

"Where do you think?"

"Maybe you want to be down on your hands and knees."

"Just try it, you fucking animal."

"Oh it's like that, huh?"

"You don't mind."

He didn't. This one was sure not about to coöperate, struggling all the way and fairly convincing too, hollering "shameful" this, "brutal" that, "disgusting" eight or ten times, and when they were finished, or Lew was, she wiggled and said, "You ain't fallin asleep back there, I hope." Got up, went on into the kitchen and made coffee. They sat in a little dinette nook, and Lew got around finally to Jardine Maraca and the peculiar reappearance of her roommate Encarnación. . . .

"You've probably heard about these wild parties," Lake said, "that the movie people have out at the beach or up at their mansions in the hills, it's in the scandal sheets all the time."

"Oh, sure, them Hollywood sex orgies."

"I believe it's a soft *g*, but that's the idea. Deuce brought me once or twice, though as he thoughtfully explained, the whole point is not having your wife along. It seems Encarnación was a regular at these affairs until that Syncopated Strangler started tearin up the pea patch, then she disappeared."

"Now I just heard she's surfaced again."

"I thought she was . . ."

"One of the victims, yeahp so'd everybody. You think your husband might've heard anything?"

"That's him pullin in the drive right now, you can ask him."

Deuce stomped in, a cigarette stuck to his lower lip, holding himself in that certain way the little bantamweight fellows have. Lew could see some kind of a shoulder holster with most likely a company-issued Bulldog in it. "Well! what've you two been up to?" beaming more than glaring in Lew's direction. Lew had become a connoisseur of jealous husbands, and this was as close to plain indifferent as he'd seen lately.

"You remember your old sweetie Encarnación," Lake over her shoulder, heading out of the room.

"Nice tits, got strangled out in Santa Monica," Deuce rooting in the icebox, "still dead 's far as I know."

"See, that's the thing—" Lew began.

"Who told you to bother us?" Deuce popping a beer-bottle cap for emphasis.

"Just routine. Long list of names."

"So you're a dick."

"All day."

"I ain't sure I even fucked her, them Mexican spitfires, too much work, don't you think?"

"So it was like you'd only see her at a distance once in a while? Mass of writhing bodies kind of thing?"

"There you go."

"Mind if I ask," Lew nodding in what he hoped was not an offensive way at the firearm under Deuce's jacket, which he had not removed, "what line of work you're in, Mr. Kindred?"

"Security, same 's yourself." Lew kept his eyebrows amiably elevated till Deuce added, "Up at Consequential Pictures."

"Interesting work, I'll bet."

"Be pleasant enough if it wasn't for crazy Anarchists trying to start unions every time a man's back is turned."

"Sure can't have that."

"They want unions up in Frisco it's no sweat off our balls," said Deuce, "but down here, ever since 'em mick bastards bombed the *Times,* it's been open shop, and we aim to keep it that way."

"Standards to maintain."

"You got it."

"Purity."

Drawing from Deuce a displeased squint. "You havin a little fun here, Mr. Basnight? If you're lookin for real sport, get out there in the darkness of night with 'em dago dynamiters all around you. See if that's up your alley."

"Get a lot of them in the picture business, do you?"

"Don't like 'at tone of voice, mister."

"Only one I got. Maybe what you really want to do is direct?"

Mistake. There was Deuce out with his pistol, damn little five-shot and all the chambers Lew could see were full. He'd had a long day, but from the rage in Deuce's face it might not be going to last much longer.

"Yeahp and the scenario goes, he forced his way into my home, officer, made advances to my wife, all I did was act in self-defense."

"Well now Mr. Kindred if I did anything to—"

"Mr. B.? Everything O.K.?"

"What in the hay-ull?" Deuce rolling off of his seat and under the table.

It was Shalimar, and she had remembered to bring the tommy gun.

"Just likes to check up on me," Lew said, "hasn't shot at anybody for, oh for a week anyway."

"Now, dearest, there was that one only yesterday out in Culver City."

"Oh but snookums, she was running so fast you missed her by a mile."

"I'll just let you two, um . . ." Deuce crawling away out onto the patio.

ALL HE'D DROPPED IN FOR really was a beer and a quick shave, and soon enough he was off again, to whatever his smooth-faced evening held. Lake didn't know anymore. She had a baloney sandwich for supper and tried to get something on the radio and then went to the window and sat and waited for the light to drain away over the vast basin hammered all day into a heated quiescence much like her own. She had stopped believing quite so much in cause and effect, having begun to find that what most people took for some continuous reality, one morning paper to the next, had never existed. Often these days she couldn't tell if something was a dream into which she had drifted, or one from which she had just awakened and might not return to. So through the terrible cloudlessness of the long afternoons she passed among dreams, and placed her wagers at the Universal Dream Casino as to which of them should bring her through, and which lead her irreversibly astray.

On the other hand Deuce, when he was in the house, tended to scream a lot. At first Lake took it all literally if not personally, then for years she ignored it, and finally it had occurred to her that in his own way, Deuce must be trying to awaken from his life.

One night he passed from one dream he'd never remember into the middle of another which had been going on all night, a dark swirl of opium haunts, leering foreigners, girls in abbreviated underwear, jazz music full of jangling Chinese fourths. Something exhausting and bloody he came up to close as he dared, and then it was like it was posted. He knew if he went any further he'd be destroyed.

He thought about "getting up" and trying to find somebody to explain what was going on. But he had to be careful because he didn't know if he was still dreaming. There was a woman lying next to him who seemed to be dead. He was alone with a corpse, and understood that he had to've been involved, somehow, even if it was only having failed to prevent what had happened to her. There was blood everywhere, some of it was still wet.

Each time he forced himself to turn and look at her face to see if he knew her, he got distracted. He could hear voices, an inquiry already under way, somewhere in the dwelling, a cylindrical piece of modern Hollywood architecture maybe fifty foot across, three or four stories high, wood floor, a staircase spiraling up the inside of the round stone wall, all the way up, into the dust and shadows where the roof should've been except instead there was a big skylight, with the early light coming through it a dusty rose color.

At first the investigators, some dedicated cadre of Californian youth, only wanted to ask him "a few questions." They never identified themselves by name, or said who they were working for, didn't wear uniforms or carry badges or commissions, but there was no doubting their sincerity. Behind their unshakable politeness Deuce could see they had him figured for the guilty party—hell, so did he. But, not about to run him in just yet, they took their time, followed this routine of their own, this procedure. Without saying it in so many words, they let him know that the body he'd woken up next to wasn't the only one.

"I'm a deputized officer," he kept trying to tell them, but his tongue and vocal cords froze and when he went looking for his deputy's star he couldn't find it.

Every time one of them smiled at him he went cold with fear. They shone with a sinister brilliance, like the high-amperage arc lamps in the studios, while from somewhere invisible, running them, outside the edges of the dream, flowed perhaps unlimited power.

As the questioning got more and more complicated, it was no longer about the crime, the penalty, regrets Deuce might feel, sympathy for the victims—it had come down to his own need to keep his connection with the crime, still unnamed, from ever being revealed. Is how bad it must have been. But there was no way he could ask them for that. And for all he knew the whole town was in on it already. Waiting.

Where were the L.A. police? He listened, hope fading, for sirens, unmuffled motorcycles. Sooner or later a real engine sound in the street would bring this deliverance, and he would find himself released into the pallid shadows and indifferent custody of the day.

LAKE HAS DREAMED more than once of a journey north, always to the same subarctic city and a chill eternal rain. By long-standing custom, young girls of the town borrow babies from mothers, in order to play at birth and parenthood. Their own fertility is so profound that sometimes thinking about a penis is all it takes to get pregnant. So they play their ever-autumnal days away pretending family life. The mothers get some free time, the babies love it.

Running through the town is a great icy river. Sometimes it freezes solid, sometimes it is crowded with miniature icebergs rushing along at terrifying speed among waves often high as those of the sea. There is an uncertainty prevailing here between the worlds above and below the surface of the water. A party of explorers are heading upriver and Lake, joining them, must leave behind a lover or husband, perhaps Deuce, with another woman, for whom he might easily leave her for good. . . . When it comes time to return, it's no longer possible to go back the way they came, and they must detour, day after day, through a great frozen swamp, each moment that passes increasing the chances that he will no longer be in town, that this time he has left her for another . . . there is no one to confide in, the rest of the party are indifferent, they have the details of their mission to preoccupy them . . . sleekly aloof in some foul-weather gear of black oiled tincloth, incapable of sympathy or indeed any human recognition, they ignore her . . . at last she manages to return to the city, and he is still there. The rivalry has all been illusion, they are lovers as ever. . . . Hallelujah.

She wakes briefly. Rain or wind, a sudden light, Deuce in from what he never speaks about, some business, she thinks, up in the hills. . . . The depth of the hour resumes, the darkness and the wind once again moving the branches of the pepper tree in the yard as she slips back again to the northern journey, the gray town now fearful over a child found trapped beneath the ice . . . somehow there are no tools or machinery to break through, the ice must be laboriously melted away with rock salt, brought out onto the frozen surface by convoys of dogsleds . . . day and night the work goes on, the child clearly visible through the melting ice, face up, blurred and waiting, serenely accusatory . . . at last lifted free, though perhaps it is too late now, for she seems very still . . . medical specialists go to work, vigils are set up outside her home . . . churches are filled with townspeople in prayer.

Lake is brought back from a wordless, timeless distraction, perhaps a dream within the dream, forever unrecoverable, into resurrection—the pealing city, the joyous population, shafts of light the color of chrome steel descending on the streets, a gliding view from a high angle, mindfully interrupted for a scene in which the child is reunited with her parents, then resumed to accompany a hymn for choir and orchestra, at first in a minor mode but soon expanding to a major refrain, half a dozen perfect notes, remaining with Lake as she surfaced into the first oblique application of sunlight across the flatlands, an announcement of intention, of weight slowly to increase beyond endurance . . .

Deuce hadn't come in all night. Whatever she expected, or didn't expect from the day, he would not hear it from her. Once she thought they had chosen, together, to resist all penance at the hands of others. To reserve to themselves alone what lay ahead, the dark exceptional fate. Instead she was alone with the sort of recurring dream a long-suffering movie heroine would expect to wake from to find herself pregnant at last.

A DAY OR TWO LATER, Lew went up to Carefree Court. The hour was advanced, the light failing, the air heated by the Santa Ana wind. Palm trees rattled briskly, and the rats in their nests up there hung on for dear life. Lew approached through a twilit courtyard lined with tile-roofed bungalows, stucco archways, and the green of shrubbery deepening as the light went. He could hear sounds of glassware and conversation.

From the swimming pool came sounds of liquid recreation—feminine squeals, deep single-reed utterances from high and low diving-boards. The festivities here this evening were not limited to any one bungalow. Lew chose the nearest, went through the formality of ringing the doorbell, but after waiting a while just walked in, and nobody noticed.

It was a gathering impossible at first to read, even for an old L.A. hand like Lew—society ladies in flapper-rejected outfits from Hamburger's basement, real flappers in extras' costumes—Hebrew headdresses, belly-dancing outfits, bare feet and sandals—in from shooting some biblical extravaganza, sugar daddies tattered and unshaven as street beggars, freeloaders in bespoke suits and sunglasses though the sun had set, Negroes and Filipinos, Mexicans and hillbillies, faces Lew recognized from mug shots, faces that might also have recognized him from tickets long cold he didn't want to be reminded of, and here they were eating enchiladas and hot dogs, drinking orange juice and tequila, smoking cork-tip cigarettes, screaming in each others' faces, displaying scars and tattoos, recalling aloud felonies imagined or planned but seldom committed, cursing Republicans, cursing police federal state and local, cursing the larger corporate trusts, and Lew slowly began to get a handle, for weren't these just the folks that once long ago he'd spent his life chasing, them and their cousins city and country? through brush and up creekbeds and down frozen slaughterhouse alleyways caked with the fat and blood of generations of cattle, worn out his shoes pair after pair until finally seeing the great point, and recognizing in the same instant the ongoing crime that had been his own life—and for achieving this self-clarity, at that time and place a mortal sin, got himself just as unambiguously dynamited.

He gradually understood that what everybody here had in common was having survived some cataclysm none of them spoke about directly—a bombing, a massacre perhaps at the behest of the U.S. government. . . . "No it wasn't Haymarket."

"It wasn't Ludlow. It wasn't the Palmer raids."

"It was and it wasn't." General merriment.

In the center of the turbulence was an elderly gent with a snow-white beard and great snarled eyebrows under a wide-brim black hat he had never been seen to take off by anyone in the room. The light rested on him in an unaccustomed way, as if he were somewhere else, lending his image to the gathering. He reminded Lew of the Tarot card of the hermit with the lantern, an ancient wise-man personage who from time to time had stood near the path Lew thought his life was taking, stood and gazed, and so spooked Lew that he'd done all he could to avoid even a friendly hello. As it turned out he was Virgil Maraca, Jardine's father.

"Sometimes," Virgil was saying, "I like to lose myself in reveries of when the land was free, before it got hijacked by capitalist Christer Republicans for their long-term evil purposes. . . ."

"And what good's that gonna do?" somebody objected. "Just more old-timer's dreaming. Enough of that around. What we need to start doin's go out and kill them, one by one, painfully as possible."

"No argument. Easier for you to contemplate, o' course."

"Startin with the *Times* bomb . . . you'll never convince me Gray Otis himself didn't set it, paid off the McNamaras to take the fall, and Brother Darrow to change the plea. It was all a scheme to destroy union labor in the southern part of this state. Since that fateful December of 1911, the picture business, land development, oil, citrus, every great fortune down here's been either founded or maintained on the basis of starvation wages."

"But twenty employees of the paper were killed in that explosion."

"Twenty or two thousand, what did old Otis care? long as he got this eternal scab's paradise here in return?"

Lew kept a close but sociable eye on Jardine Maraca, passing so smoothly among the guests, smiling, drinking California Champagne from a juice glass, here to visit her father at this reunion of outlaws . . . yet somehow more than everyday déjà vu, the old two-places-at-once condition, kicking up again, he couldn't be sure if he was remembering this now or, worse, *foreseeing* her in some way, so that he had to worry about the possibility that not only might Jardine Maraca be dead but also that it *had not happened* yet. . . . He crept closer. She smelled like cigarette smoke. Sweet Caporals. Intensely, abruptly, she reminded him of Troth, his ex-wife from so long ago.

She looked up, into his eyes, as if issuing a dare. As if, in this unaging and temperate corner of the land, where everything was permitted, she nevertheless would be forbidden.

"I'm supposed to be trying to find you."

"For . . ." If she knew the name, she was reluctant to say it aloud.

"Tony Tsangarakis. The old gang down at the Vertex Club—they're worrying about you."

"You must be smarter than that. How long ago 'd you talk to Tony?"

"Haven't, yet. But a Negro gentleman named LeStreet—"

"Ah . . ." Her face just for an instant might have emptied of hope. But then back came the old publicity-still glaze.

"Chester and Encarnación were married once, for a couple of weeks. It's not that he's a suspect. But he has that history yet to paradiddle his way out of. So as a resource he ain't the first one you'd look to necessarily."

"Well, what can I do to help you out?"

"All taken care of, sorry to say."

"Uh-oh."

"Encarnación only came back for a little while," Jardine said, "just long enough to testify about who it was. A little runt of a studio cop named Deuce Kindred. Police just picked him up for a whole string of orgy-type homicides. One girl, long ago, maybe somebody at the studio could've bought his way out, in return for unquestioning future obedience, but this'll mean a death sentence. Our law-enforcement heroes in L.A. being as bent as any, but only for the lesser felonies."

"You'll be needing a ride out of town at least."

They arranged a time and place but Jardine already had other plans. As the papers told it later, she went out to the airfield at Glendale and stole a barnstormer's Curtis JN and took off, flying low—people at a local fairground remembered seeing her pass overhead, later she was reported following the interurban tracks east, approaching in a carefree spirit electrical power masts, city rooflines, smokestacks, and other dangerous objects, each time zooming skyward at the last moment. She vanished over the desert, creating a powerful shaped silence.

THE NEXT TIME Lew went out to see Merle at the beach, he brought a photograph of Troth, an old silver-gelatin studio portrait. He'd been keeping it in an old alchemy primer, so it had stayed in pretty good shape over the years. Not knowing how to ask, or even what he should ask for.

"Feel like some damn down-and-outer in a story, finds a genie, gets three wishes, maybe you better forget I said anything."

"No. No, it's O.K. I'll make a transparency, we'll put some light through it, see what we've got. Did you want to just go back here, to—looks like about 1890, fact I think I remember that studio in Chicago—or we could send it back even earlier, or . . ."

Merle let it hang there so gently that Lew had scarcely any idea his mind had been read. "What you were saying about sending these pictures off onto different tracks . . . other possibilities . . ."

"That's that constant-term recalibration, or C.T.R., drives Roswell out of the shop and down to the nearest speakeasy, got no patience with that part of it. We're still learning about it, but it seems to be built into the nature of silver somehow. Back when I was still a junior alchemist, passing through What Cheer, Iowa, met up with this old-school spagyrist name of Doddling, who showed me how to get silver to grow just like a tree. Tree of Diana, he called it, goddess of the Moon and all. Damnedest thing. Take some silver, amalgamate it with quicksilver, put it in with just the right amount and strength of nitric acid, wait. Damn if pretty soon it won't start to put out branches, just like a tree only faster, and after a while even leaves."

"Branches," said Lew.

"Right before your eyes—or lens, 'cause you do need some magnification. Doddling said it's because silver is alive. Has its own forks in the road, choices to make just like the rest of us.

"This'll be silent, remember. You won't hear her."

Maybe not . . . but maybe . . .

Amid a technical environment so corrupted by less-than-elevated motives, usually mercenary, for "setting forth against the Enemy Wind" (as early epics of time-travel described it), there must now and then appear one compassionate time-machine story, time travel in the name of love, with no expectation of success, let alone reward.

Now, as if the terrible flood of time had been leapt across in a timeless instant, no more trouble than being switched over to a different track . . . Troth continued to live, in some way more tangible than memory or sorrow, eternally young, while they were still courting, before they fell prey to Time, all in a cascade unstoppable as a spring thaw, what he not that slowly at all understood to be accelerated views of her face and body, of hair lengthening to prodigal fair masses to be then pinned up, and released, and re-piled again and again, woman upon woman settling into the lamplit ends of days full of care, the gingham redoubts of matronhood, the rougings, redefinings, emergences and disguises, dimples and lines and bone realities, each year's face tumbling upon the next in a breathtaking fall. . . .

"But . . . I don't understand. . . . Do you mean that time the streetcar crashed? Or the winter when I had the fever?" Speaking quietly, with downcast eyes, as if all but stupefied by whatever she had come here out of, almost too young for the woman he remembered, innocent as yet of her immortality. The light seemed to have gathered preferentially about her face and golden hair. He imagined himself reaching out to her through dust-crowded shafts of light, not optical so much as temporal light, whatever it was being carried by Time's Æther, cruelly assembled in massless barriers between them. She might not know anymore who he was, what they had been through together. Was that her voice he'd heard? Could she see him from wherever in the mathematical mists she'd journeyed to?

Merle looked up from the controls, touched an invisible hatbrim. "It looks like one of them wonders of science. But having been down your stretch of track myself, I just wish it could be more, 's all."

AND AT THE END of the working day, when all sources of light seemed to have withdrawn as far as they were going to, making shadows as long as they would be and Roswell was off to a circuit of friendly speakeasies, as was his habit most every night, Merle cranked up the Integroscope one more time and took one of the photos he'd kept of Dally, taken when she was about twelve years old, back at Little Hellkite in the San Juans, standing out by the pipeline in the snow, not just smiling for the camera but laughing out loud at something Merle had since tried to remember but couldn't. Maybe someplace hanging in the invisible air was a snowball he'd just thrown at her.

Though it was usually enough to stay in their past together, before she'd left, tonight he decided to bring it all the way up to the present day, on through a high-speed blur of all her time since Telluride and New York and Venice and the War, up to this very evening, except over there in Paris it was morning, and she was just leaving her rooms and going to the train station and riding out to a stop in some *banlieue* where hundreds of feet into the sky abruptly towered the antenna of a million-watt wireless transmitter, some already-forgotten artifact of the War, where he thought he recognized a Béthenod-Latour alternator and beneath the tower a little studio with geraniums at the windows where Dally drank coffee and ate a brioche and sat by a control board while an operator with one of those pointed French mustaches found the coördinates for Los Angeles, and somehow Merle now, tumbling, trembling in a rush of certitude, was on his feet and across the shop, fiddling with the radio receiver, its tubes blooming in an indigo haze, finding the band and frequency, and all at once the image of her silent lips on the wall smoothly glided into synchronization, and her picture was speaking. A distant grown woman's voice propagating through the night Æther clear as if she was in the room. He gazed at her, shaking his head slowly, and she returned the gaze, smiling, speaking without hurry, as if somehow she could see him, too.

Five

Rue du Départ

". . . he would have asked you for my hand," Dally was saying, "being that sort of kid, but we couldn't have reached you even if we knew where you were. . . ."

It would've felt like throwing a bottle in the ocean, except that she knew Merle was there. Even with a fair idea of the odds that he wasn't, given the War and the ocean and the North American continent and a radio spectrum that seemed to expand every time she looked. Somehow the beams emerging far above her were finding their way straight to him, straight and true.

René was smoking Gauloises one after another, studying her through the smoke. He had some unformed notion of her as a spiritual medium, talking to the dead. Clearly an unauthorized use of the equipment, but to tell the truth it was new, and some of it was army parts, and it all tended to drift a bit. These extra unlogged transmissions—and Mademoiselle Rideout must not imagine that she was the only one in Paris so occupied—afforded a way to make introductions, allow the components to clash and partially cancel and learn one another's expectations, seek average values, adapt, slip in to some groove leading to smooth teamwork, power wisely deployed and signals faithfully sent across.

When she was done Dally walked away waving au 'voir with an awkward twirl of her hand behind her, the radio tower in powerful and immediate ascent, like its cousin the Eiffel Tower drastically out of scale with the rest of its neighborhood, and with her head slightly bowed returned to the Métro station. She had no business in this neighborhood beyond calling after Merle across the dimensions. She began to hum the Reynaldo Hahn tune from *Ciboulette* about the suburbanizing of passion, which everybody was humming this season, *"C'est pas Paris, c'est sa banlieue."*

By the time she was back in Montparnasse, she was whistling "J'ai Deux Amants" from the latest Sacha Guitry production.

"'Jour, Dally," called a pretty young woman in trousers.

"'Jour, Jarri."

A group of Americans paused to stare.

"Scyuzay mwah, but ain't you that La Jarretière?"

"Oh, yes, before the . . . War? I used to dance under that name."

"But they say she died—"

"A-and real horribly, too . . ."

The young woman sniffed. "Grand Guignol. They came to see blood. We used the . . . raspberry syrup. My own life was getting complicated . . . death and rebirth as someone else seemed, *just the ticket.* They needed a *succès de scandale,* and I didn't mind. A young beauty destroyed before her time, something the eternally-adolescent male mind could tickle itself with. *Mon Dieu!"* she sang, *"que les hommes sont bêtes!"* in on the tail end of which Dally joined, singing the harmony.

There was a lively musical-comedy scene here in postwar Paris, and after a while Dally had drifted into its, well, *banlieue.* She currently had a small part in *Fossettes l'Enflammeuse,* an operetta of the period by Jean-Raoul Oeuillade—about a type, pretty familiar by now, of hell-raising adolescent seductress or baby vamp who drinks, smokes, uses cocaine, so forth—and staged in New York by famed impresario R. Wilshire Vibe, as *Dimples,* though Dally had taken the time to learn a spot-on impression of the star, Solange St.-Emilion, belting out Fossettes' first big number—

Casse-cou! C'est moi!
Ce'p'ti' j'm'en fou'-la-là!
Casse-cou, mari, tes femmes aussi—
Tous les autres, n'importe quoi!

Dally climbed to her flat just off the rue du Départ and went in the kitchen and made coffee. She had just told Merle the whole story of her life since she'd left him at Telluride, and what a sorry spectacle. . . . She should have been thinking about Merle, but instead for some reason it was Kit now who was on her mind.

Beside the window were shelves with a set of terra-cotta bowls and plates from a shop in Torino, a wedding present she and Kit had given to themselves. The first time she had laid eyes on them, she'd felt immediate contentment. They were glazed in some truly cheerful shade of green—no, more than that, as if the color came from ground-up crystals sensitive to radio waves, able to call back Kit's voice singing "It won't be a stylish marriage . . ." while she thought, This is who we are. We don't have to go worrying about more, and then, out loud, "Well thank heaven you can cook."

They were married in 1915, and went to live in Torino, where Kit got a job working on the Italian bomber aircraft. And then a year or two later came the disaster up at Caporetto, when it looked like the Austrians would just sweep down out of those mountains and keep rolling all the way to Venice. And by then they could neither of them remember why they'd got married, or stayed married, and it was no comfort that nearly everybody else they knew was going through the same kind of misery. They blamed it on the War, of course, and that was true as far as it went. But . . . well, Dally had also gone a little crazy, and did some stupid things. One day she was at the plant when a small phalanx of men in dark suits came out of a metal door, and she recognized one of them as Clive Crouchmas.

Like many before her, Dally had a low tolerance—blamelessly low, considering—for complexos and the work it took to put up with them. And she knew that Clive's demands would be as minimal as a girl could ask. Conjugal bliss? Flings with other men? no problems for Clive. There *was* that awkward business of his having once tried to shop her into white slavery, but both understood that it was perhaps his one moment of genuine blind passion, everybody deserves at least one of those, doesn't he, and at the end of the day Clive was grateful for it, and Dally was semi-sweetly amused.

It wasn't only that Clive had grown older but that in the high-stakes gaming of the life he'd chosen, he had somehow come away with fewer chips, not the night's biggest loser but far short of what he might once have believed was his entitlement. So she wasn't about to wish him too all-out of a disaster.

While his wife got back together with somebody she shouldn't have, Kit was either at the plant or up in the air, and next thing either of them knew, the War was over, Dally was in Paris, and Kit was out in western Ukraine someplace, off on some grand search after she didn't know what. She did know there was fighting still going on out there. He kept sending letters, with different stamps and postmarks each time, and now and then it sounded like he wanted to come back, and she wasn't sure if she wanted him to or not.

This kitchen table was no place to be sitting in the middle of the day. She grabbed a few francs from under one of the green dishes and went out again, just as an airplane flew overhead, muttering serenely to itself. A few blocks to the boulevard and her local café, L'Hémisphère, where she'd discovered that if she only sat at a table outside, before long her life, selections from her life, would repeat themselves in slightly different form, featuring exactly the people she "needed" to see again—as if the notorious café were one of those favored spots that Eastern mystics talked about. Though it might be that the others "needed" to see her as well, sometimes they only passed like ghosts, and looked right at her, and didn't recognize her.

In those days a large American population was forever passing through Paris, changing addresses or lying about them. Some might've been ghosts from the War with unfinished business in the city. But most were the American young, untouched, children with spending money but no idea of what it would or wouldn't buy, come toddling as if down the dark willow-lined approach to some sort of Club Europa of the maimed and gassed and fever-racked, whose members had been initiated by way of war, starvation, and Spanish influenza. Blessedly, there was no telephone at L'Hémisphère, because the owner believed that the instrument was another sort of plague, which would spread through and eventually destroy Montparnasse. Where again would it be possible to leave your note with Octave the barman with such total faith in his character? As soon as the Americans found out there was no telephone, they tended to move on toward the corner of boulevard Raspail and the more famous Dôme, Rotonde, Coupole, and Select.

Sitting here behind a cup of coffee, Dally was able to brood freely about her past, fully confident that in all this rippling interwovenness of desires wise and foolish she would be interrupted at just the right moment, before it got too mopish.

Back when they arrived in Torino, Kit had taken one look and felt right at home. "Can you believe this place? Not a crooked street far's you can see."

Might as well be Denver. The mountains were close, and there was hydroelectric power everywhere. "Well full fuckin circle," is what he muttered to himself, "ain't it."

Kit went to the address Viktor Mulciber had given him in Constantinople and was hired on the spot, and soon was turning his vectorist skills to matters of wing loading, lateral and longitudinal stability, so forth. . . . He ran into one or two familiar faces from Dr. Prandtl's shop at Göttingen, who'd fled Germany out of pacifistic dread at what was coming and comforted themselves that Italian warplanes would only be used against Austria, which was responsible for the War anyway. He was welcomed with a ceremonial shower of beer and the solemn instruction, "Every wing section you'll come across looks just like a circle after a Zhukovsky transformation. Airfoil design's shameful secret. Tell no one."

Based nearby was a small *squadriglia* of Bleriot monoplanes, veterans of the

Italo-Turkish War, in which they had mostly flown reconnaissance over Cyrenaica, with a few proudly displaying bullet holes from the tribesmen's rifle fire. Kit quickly became friendly with the ground crew, who didn't object if he took one up now and then.

One day he and Dally had been having an adult exchange of views about the time she was spending with Clive Crouchmas. Kit had met this bird and didn't like him, though absent a working time machine he didn't see any real way he could deny Dally her past. One more wartime sacrifice, he guessed.

"Come on up with me Dal." His voice suddenly shifting, though just how she couldn't've said.

"Are you crazy?"

"I mean it. I can fix it easy—smuggle you on the ship, time you learned how to fly anyway, you might even get to like it." There was a look of entreaty on his face she failed to register, an unprotected moment she would understand when it was too late.

"The Austrians shoot people down, Kit."

"Not us. Not you and me."

Later she would also recall feeling both sorry for and angry at all his wishful stupidity, and wondered if she'd have done better to lean to the side of pity, even if in the long run pity would only have corroded them sure, more than the rages and constant fights, which at least had some life to them. This time she just shrugged and went into the other room to get dolled up once again for a "dinner engagement" with Crouchmas, at the Cambio, most likely, she thought.

Kit stalked away into town and took refuge as usual at a riverfront bar in I Murazzi, near the Po bridge. His friend Renzo was there already, drinking some vermouth concoction.

On the ground Renzo always struck folks as a little phlegmatic, maybe clinically depressed, not much to say, slept a lot—but in the presence of any sort of airplane he was observed to perk up markedly. As soon as they were taxiing he was all smiles and animation, and by the time the wheels left the ground, his personality had undergone an all but polar shift. He had run through a brisk turnover of *bombardieri,* few of whom lasted more than one mission, many reduced to nervous wrecks long before any targets were even sighted. "I tell you the trouble with just leaning out and looking around for something to drop a bomb on—you don't get the accuracy, plus it isn't going *fast enough* when it hits, you want as much kinetic energy as possible, *vero?*"

Kit squinted. "You're talking about—"

"Una picchiata!"

"What's that?"

"A very steep dive, not like when you go down in a spin, here you'd be *controlling it all the way*—release the bomb as close to target as you can get, then pull up sharply again to get out of the way of the explosion. Think you could figure how to modify *mia bella* Caproni for that?"

"A 'nosedive'? that's insane Renzo, too much stress in all the wrong places, the bracing would snap, control surfaces couldn't take it, the wings would fall off, the engine would either stall or explode—"

"*Si, certo,* but aside from that . . . ?"

Kit was already sketching and scribbling. Renzo trusted him by now. He had already helped replace Renzo's Isotta Franchini engines with four hundred-horsepower Packards and figured how to mount two more Revelli machine guns in the tail and on the underbelly of the aircraft, which was a very large triplane bomber with a five-man crew, affectionately named *Lucrezia,* after the homicidal Borgia heiress.

"Andiamo," Renzo said, standing abruptly. "I'll show you."

"Not in that Caproni," Kit demurred.

"We'll take the SVA."

"That'd be a Warren truss . . . I don't know if it'll—"

"Macchè . . ."

He was right, of course. Once they were in the air, guiding on the single spooky light on top of the Molo Antonelliana, Kit began to see what he was up to here. "Don't suppose we could aim at the Cambio, could we?" Not that they'd still be there, but it seemed a reasonable target.

"Nothing simpler." Renzo banked them over toward the Piazza Carignano. "Hold on, Cowboy!" leaning gleefully on the stick as they went into a steep, stomach-lifting dive.

They were soon going so fast that something happened to time, and maybe they'd slipped for a short interval into the Future, the Future known to Italian Futurists, with events superimposed on one another, and geometry straining irrationally away in all directions including a couple of extra dimensions as they continued hellward, a Hell that could never contain Kit's abducted young wife, to which he could never go to rescue her, which was actually Hell-of-the-future, taken on into its functional equations, stripped and fire-blasted of everything emotional or accidental. . . .

And then Renzo had pulled them up in a shuddering prop-to-tail assault on airframe integrity, and they were sailing above the river as if it was all just a Sunday spin.

Kit could see the appeal. Of course he could. Pure velocity. The incorporation of death into what otherwise would only be a carnival ride.

Dive-bombin in-to the
Ci-ty!
Golly, what fun it
Can be!
Watchin em scat-ter,
Watchin em run,
Hearin em scream when
We fire that gun, my buddy,
We can pull out when
We want to—
We can go zoomin away,
With the ground just so close,
Rushin right up your nose,
We go dive-bombin in-to the day!

"Did you hear that airplane last night?" she said at breakfast.

"Loud, huh? How'd your boyfriend react? Or do I mean not react."

She stared back. "Golly but you're a bastard."

Kit worked off and on at the interesting problem of how to pull a gigantic triplane out of a nosedive, and went up with Renzo for a couple-three more of those *picchiate,* most notably in August of 1917 during a Bolshevik-inspired strike of workers at the weapons factories in Torino.

"Let us hear one of those cowboy screams," suggested Renzo, and Kit complied as they roared steeply down toward a large demonstration. The strikers went scattering like ants in an anthill, caught in the focus of some ray more deadly than sunlight. Kit risked a look over at Renzo, demented even when at rest, and saw that here, approaching the speed of sound, he was being metamorphosed into something else . . . a case of possession. Kit had a velocity-given illumination then. It was all political.

The strike in Torino was crushed without mercy, strikers were killed, wounded, sent into the army, their deferments canceled. Renzo's *picchiata* had been perhaps the first and purest expression in northern Italy of a Certain Word that would not quite exist for another year or two. But somehow like a precognitive murmur, a dreamed voice, it had already provisionally entered Time. "You saw how they broke apart," Renzo said later. "But we did not. We remained single, aimed, unbreakable. *Un vettore, si?*"

"Not if you hadn't pulled us out. If we'd hit—"

"Oh." Renzo refilled his glass. "All that is for the other world."

In October came the disaster at Caporetto, which Renzo blamed on the strikers. "Putting them among the brigades was the worst mistake the Army could have made. Spreading their poisoned lies about peace." He had stopped wearing civilian clothes. He was now in uniform all the time. Eagles seemed to be a prominent motif.

ONE DAY THERE WERE CHILDREN calling up from the street. Dally went to the window. A beautiful woman in a prewar hat stood down there holding the hand of a little girl about five, and with them seemed to be Kit's damn old rogue of a brother Reef, whom she'd last seen stomping his way out of Venice. Shading his eyes from the sun. "That Dahlia?"

They were here as refugees. Most of the fighting was in the northeast, so they had come west to Torino, where Reef had heard Kit was working, from a flier he'd run into in a bar.

"Domenico? What in heck's he been up to, thought he'd be permanently nose-down by now."

"Said you helped him out one time, somethin about he tried to piss out a window on a superior officer—"

"Wasn't the first time, kind of a hobby, don't know how he keeps 'em all straight."

"Listen, before we—"

"Don't," Kit grabbing his brother in a delayed *abrazo*. "Don't. Stay here as long as you need to."

Reef had been working for the Italian army up in a totally unreal Alpscape rigging aerial cableways known in the army as *teleferiche*. "It's the Western Front again, but turned on end—in France they kept trying to outflank each other till there was noplace to go but into the sea. Here us and the Austrians did the same thing only vertical, each army kept trying to get higher ground than the other, till next thing anybody knew, they're all sitting on top of these *very sharp white mountaintops* with their ass freezing in the wind, and noplace to go."

"But into the sky," said Yashmeen.

The wives were getting along just jake, eyeing each other not with any desire or suspicion in particular but compulsively nonetheless, as if there were something which must at any moment be revealed.

"You two studied in Germany together."

"He was in vectors, I was in number theory, we hardly saw each other." The two women, who happened to be in eye-contact, began to smile, in what Reef saw as the beginning of a complicity that might bear some watching.

"But you're the one he fought a duel over."

"*Almost* fought a duel. What did he tell you anyway?"

"I may have exaggerated," Kit said.

"And you're the one he rescued from that army of homicidal Hungarians."

"Not exactly. Kit, I'm beginning to have some doubts, here."

"Yeahp, better watch 'at shit," Reef nodded cackling around a Di Nobili.

To celebrate they all went out to dinner at the Ristorante del Cambio, known locally as "the old lady." Since Kit and Renzo had pretended to dive-bomb the place, Kit had made a point of eating here at least once a week. There had been no veal for years, but despite the shortages Alberto was able to bring them agnolotti, and risotto, and mushroom stew, and tagliarini, and it was truffle season, so some of those showed up as well, almost apologetically. Everybody drank a lot of Nebbiolo. The city was full of acid-yellow light and black and precise shadows back inside the arcades. Searchlights stroked the sky.

One day climbing down out of Renzo's Caproni who should reappear from the olden days but Kit's old Yale classmate Colfax Vibe, who though now in his mid-thirties and officially too old, had hustled his way into the birdmen, as if to make up for his father's purchased deferral fifty years earlier. The U.S. Army Air Service was planning to send about five hundred young pilot candidates over to Italy to train on Capronis, and Colfax was here doing some advance inspection. Except for a little gray at the edges, he showed no other evidence of the years.

'Fax soon had a baseball league active in Torino. He and Kit got in the habit of dropping in to Carpano's for a *punt e mes* once or twice a week. 'Fax had in some very odd and personal way come to terms with Scarsdale's death at the hands of his family's trusted factotum Foley Walker but wouldn't talk about it, any more than he'd act apologetic around Kit.

Faced with Austria's intention to take Venice and the Veneto, Italians resisted so fiercely that at last Kit was shamed into abandoning his engineer's neutrality, and began flying missions, sometimes crewing for Renzo, sometimes alone. For a while he allowed himself to be seduced into the Futurist nosedive, with its æsthetics of blood and explosion.

"You might 's well have stayed in Colorado," Dally said. "Either way you're carryin on that family tradition."

"Beg pardon?" Curious about how far she'd take it.

"Bombs," she said. "Bombs in the family. At least Reef and your Pa put 'em where they'd do some good."

"Austrians," Kit thought he would explain.

"Your brothers-in-arms. They're not the ones need bombing, hell even I know that."

"Then save me."

"What?"

"If I'm such miserable case, help me get back to the right piece of trail at least. You tell me."

She tried. Later she thought she had. But soon enough he had dragged her history with Clive Crouchmas into it again, and she'd fired back with something low-cost about Yashmeen, and it only got louder from there, and salvation was the last thing on anybody's mind.

Next mission he flew, when he got back to the flat afterward, she was gone. *I'm going to Paris. Write to you soon.* Not even her name.

He worried then for weeks, recalling how shaken Dally had been when news came in that the S.S. *Persia* had been torpedoed by a U-boat captain named Max Valentiner, a northern wolf descended into Mediterranean fields, and that among those lost had been Dally's colleague Eleanor Thornton, who had modeled for the Rolls-Royce hood ornament known as the Spirit of Ecstasy. Finally he got a postcard from Paris, with Dally's temporary address, and went back to sleeping at night.

CROSSING A SEA newly perilous and contingent—no longer at the mercy of unknown longitude or unforeseen tempests but of U-boats, the terror of a crossing having now passed from God to the German navy, Reef, Yashmeen, and Ljubica returned to the U.S. pretending to be Italian immigrants. At Ellis Island, Reef, thinking both his English and Italian could get him in trouble whichever he spoke, remained indecisively mute long enough to have a large letter *I,* for Idiot, chalked on his back. Then a few minutes later, somebody in a customs service uniform—Reef never got a good look at his face—came running in out of the great seethe and echo of voices with a wet sponge and erased it again, saving Reef, as he soon discovered, from being sent back to Europe, being that an Idiot at the time was considered likely to become a Public Charge and cost U.S. taxpayers money.

"Wait," Reef said, "who are you?"

"They call me 'The Obliterator.'"

Reef came to think of it as a kindness on the part of some crypto-Anarchist who'd drifted into government work but could still recognize and help out a fellow outlaw. Not that Idiocy couldn't have been a useful cover, or was even that far wrong. They had arrived in the middle of the Red Scare and the Palmer raids, and soon enough began to wonder what they could have been thinking.

They headed west, Reef propelled by his old faith in the westward vector, in finding someplace, some deep penultimate town the capitalist/Christer gridwork hadn't got to quite yet. In a train depot up in Montana during a snowstorm one day, who'd they happen to run into but Frank, Stray, and Jesse, who had the same thing in mind.

"O.K. if we come along?" Reef said.

"Hell yes," Frank and Stray said pretty much together. "Course there is my reputation to worry about," Frank couldn't help adding, "bein seen in your company and so forth."

Jesse didn't look all that surprised but was sure annoyed. "How do you think it feels, comin in bein hit with that?"

"Could've introduced him as your Uncle Reef I guess," Frank said. "But you haven't been that easy to fool lately."

"But what do I even call him? 'Pa' ain't quite right, is it?"

Frank, who really wanted to squeeze the boy in a lengthy embrace, left his hand on Jesse's shoulder awhile. "See, once I would've been all right with just 'Frank,' then you drifted into calling me 'Pa,' and I didn't exactly forbid it 'cause it feels too good to hear it. It does. Maybe you'll see. Meantime you could call him 'sir,' till he gets so uncomfortable with that he'll say, 'Oh, just call me Reef,' or somethin."

Which is how it would work out. Reef would one day be able to pass along pieces of paternal wisdom like how to stack a deck or recognize a company detective, and he and Jesse would have some good days together on streams in the region, though neither was a top-notch fisherman, barely catching enough some days even to keep the dogs happy, but the Umpqua in particular had a way of magically making indifferent anglers into accomplished masters, so helping Reef and Jesse learn their way into companionable silence, which both would come to admit was more than either had hoped for.

Yashmeen, beginning to lose the edges of her all-purpose European accent, one day found herself pregnant again, which both women took as a sign that nothing in their lives all together was about to get too discombobulated by anybody's second thoughts. Especially noting how Reef had begun drifting around in that well-known daze. They had been watching the brothers day to day, alert to signs of buried anger, understanding after a while that they'd been collaborating to the same end. Yashmeen developed a particular affection for Frank and Stray's daughter Ginger and the baby Plebecula. Ljubica and Ginger were about the same age, and hit it off pretty good except for an inevitable kickup now and then. The girls spent hours with the baby, sometimes just gazing at her. Their other gazing was reserved for Jesse, who abruptly found himself with a couple of kid sisters to deal with. Sometimes they would start laughing, and he couldn't help thinking it was at him.

"Not *at,*" both women assured him.

"Ljubica wants to marry you," Yash said, "but don't tell her I told you."

"That'd sure give the Sheriff somethin to think about," Jesse muttered, strangely having trouble knowing what to do with his hands.

"Oh it'll pass," Yash said. "Then look out."

"Your job, really," Stray added, " 'll just be to keep a quiet eye out when they all start showin up at the door with flowers and smellin like hair oil and bay rum and so forth."

"Chores, chores, chores," Jesse snarled contentedly.

FOR A WHILE they were up in the redwoods, and then for a little longer in a town on the Kitsap Peninsula, up in the last corner of the U.S. map, and after this it would have to be Alaska or B.C.

Jesse brought home as an assignment from school "write an essay on What It Means To Be An American."

"Oboy, oboy." Reef had that look on his face, the same look his own father used to get just before heading off for some dynamite-related activities. "Let's see that pencil a minute."

"Already done." What Jesse had ended up writing was,

It means do what they tell you and take what they give you and don't go on strike or their soldiers will shoot you down.

"That's what they call the 'topic sentence'?"

"That's the whole thing."

"Oh."

It came back with a big A+ on it. "Mr. Becker was at the Cour d'Alene back in the olden days. Guess I forgot to mention that."

"We should start our own little republic," Yash said one day. "Secede."

"Yeah but hell," Stray, who never was much of a sigher, would sigh, "em things never work out. Fine idea while the opium supply lasts, but sooner or later plain old personal meanness gets in the way. Somebody runs the well dry, somebody rolls her eyes at the wrong husband—"

"Oh, my," Yashmeen pressing her hands to her bosom as if for palpitations. "No, no, no, we're all way past that, I hope."

A nice long gaze then. Nobody would've said "the wrong wife." Meantime, motherhood and political danger had done little to discourage Yash's desire for other women, though the practical demands of the day would too often keep it in the realm of daydreaming. Stray for her part would remember enjoying a delirious moment or two, usually in city hotel rooms considerably to the east of here, with flushed and trembling younger women pretending to be helpless.

Their moment now would stretch, as if it were awakening after a long snooze someplace. "We about to do something stupid here?" one of them would ask after a while.

"Sure hope so," the other would reply.

"'*Soir,* Dally."

It was Policarpe, an old acquaintance of Kit's once, she gathered, back in Belgium. "Just out licking a few vitrines. You looked about to get lost in thought. Can't have that."

She bought him a cognac. They sat and watched the lighted boulevard. Policarpe worked for a Socialist newspaper. Death had not taken up residence in his eyes but had visited often enough.

"We're in Hell, you know," he said conversationally.

"Everybody thinks we're finally out of there," she said.

A shrug. "The world came to an end in 1914. Like the mindless dead, who don't know they're dead, we are as little aware as they of having been in Hell ever since that terrible August."

"But this"—gesturing round at the blossoming city—"how could this—"

"Illusion. When peace and plenty are once again taken for granted, at your most languorous moment of maximum surrender, the true state of affairs will be borne in upon you. Swiftly and without mercy."

He looked across the street suddenly, reaching for his eyeglasses. "Hallucination, obviously. For a moment I thought I saw your former husband."

In fact he had. Kit had returned to Paris unexpectedly, after some time in Lwów, formerly the metropolis of Galicia, lately the capital of the short-lived West Ukraine Republic.

After Dally had left, and Reef and his family, Kit went on soldiering, or more like engineering, alone, except for an interlude with Dally's friend Fiametta, who had worked at the same hospital. Until one day the War was over, and by then he had run into a strangely possessed algebraist named E. Percy Movay, who was full of news about a fabled group of mathematicians in Lwów, out at the wild frontier of the now-defunct Austro-Hungarian

Empire. Which was how Kit discovered the Scottish Café and the circle of more and less insane who frequented it, and where one night he was presented with a startling implication of Zermelo's Axiom of Choice. It was possible in theory, he was shown beyond a doubt, to take a sphere the size of a pea, cut it apart into several very precisely shaped pieces, and reassemble it into another sphere the size of the sun.

"Because one emits light and the other doesn't, don't you think."

Kit was taken aback. "I don't know."

He spent awhile contemplating this. Zermelo had been a docent at Göttingen when Kit was there and, like Russell, had been preoccupied with the set of all sets that are not members of themselves. He was also notorious around the beer halls for a theory that no expedition could ever reach either of the poles, because the amount of whisky needed was directly proportional to the tangent of the latitude. Polar latitude being 90°, this meant a value approaching infinity—Q.E.D. It didn't surprise Kit much that the peculiar paradox should be traceable in some way back to Zermelo.

"But staggering subsets, fellows—you see what this means don't you? those Indian mystics and Tibetan lamas and so forth were right all along, the world we think we know can be dissected and reassembled into any number of worlds, each as real as 'this' one."

It took Kit awhile to locate the speaker, and was agreeably confounded to see, emerging from behind a gigantic beer stein, the face of Professor Heino Vanderjuice, now strangely youthful, his hair dark again, with a few streaks of gray, his hesitant classroom stoop unbent into a bearing of forthrightness and responsibility.

"Why bless my soul if it isn't Mr. Traverse. You were leaving for Göttingen the last time I saw you."

"It's so good to see you again, sir," Kit embracing him. "Out here."

"Out of the Vibe pocket, I'll bet you mean."

"Well most of all alive and kicking."

"Same goes for me, young fellow." They had another round, left the Scottish Café, and began to stroll down past the University toward Kliński Park. "With so many dead," the Professor reflected after a bit, "it seems disrespectful to them—but I'm glad Scarsdale Vibe is now among their number. Though the company is too good for him. My only regret is that it wasn't I who finally plugged him."

Kit paused in the middle of lighting a cigarette. "Didn't know you'd ever been out gunning for him."

The Professor chuckled. "Had a crack at him once, must've been after you'd left for Germany. Sort of relapse into all-purpose loathing, saw how easily I'd been bought—flattered into thinking myself the equal of Tesla, though of opposite polarity. Beneath Vibe's contempt, though not my own. Furious with myself, more with Vibe, I fetched down my old single-action Navy Colt and got on the morning express to New York. Some vague idea of turning it on myself once I'd done for him. Got to Pearl Street, found a rooftop nearby and settled in to wait. But something curious happened. It had taken me only thirteen steps to climb to where I was, and I saw I was standing not on a roof but on an executioner's scaffold, as if somehow I had already carried out my modest *attentat,* been arrested, tried and condemned for it, and was now awaiting the ultimate penalty. Talk about anomalies in Time!

"It appeared to be somewhere outside New York City, one of those old-time county courthouses with a large gilded dome. A crowd was gathering, a military band was playing marches and airs, children were selling lemonade, American flags, corncobs, hot dogs and so forth. I was plainly visible to all, but no one seemed to be paying me much notice. Then the dome of the courthouse began to lift, or expand skyward, till after a moment I saw it was in fact the spherical gasbag of a giant balloon, rising slowly from behind the dome, where it had been hidden. Sort of that pea-and-sun conjecture again, only different. Of course it was the Chums of Chance, not the first time they'd come to my rescue—though usually it was from professorial inattention, walking off cliffs or into spinning propellers. . . . But this time they had rescued me from my life, from the cheaply-sold and dishonored thing I might have allowed it to become. Young Suckling of course liked to pretend it was nothing—'Eeyynnyyhh, the old coot's telling that one again—that six-gun wasn't even loaded'—but they saved me, nonetheless."

Evening crowds streamed unhurriedly through the park. Somewhere an accordion was playing a jazz-inflected *hopak.* Small boys ran up to pull the braids of girls and run away again, and slightly older couples stood out of the light, embracing. Peacetime.

"The boys are about," Professor Vanderjuice scanning serenely the still-lambent sky. "I usually get a feeling when they are. Maybe you'll meet them. Hitch a ride. They'll take you wherever you want to go."

Further implications of what Kit had begun to think of as the Zermelo Situation continued to arise. "We tell ourselves that Lemberg, Léopol, Lvov, Lviv, and Lwów are all different names for the same city," said E. Percy Movay one night, "but in fact each is a distinct city of its own, with very precise rules of transition from one to the other."

Since Tuva, where he had heard such unaccountably double-jointed singing, in times of perplexity, as other men might routinely curse or absentmindedly reach for their penises or inexplicably begin to weep, Kit had found himself making down in his throat a single low guttural tone, as deep as he could reach, as long as breath would allow. Sometimes he believed that if he got this exactly right it would transport him to "where he should really be," though he had no clear picture of where that was. After he had done this for long enough he began to feel himself enter a distinctly different state of affairs.

One day Professor Vanderjuice vanished. Some claimed to have seen him taken into the sky. Kit went down to the Glowny Dworzec and got on a train headed west, though soon he got off and went across the tracks onto another platform and waited for a train going east, till after a while he was getting on and off trains bound for destinations he was less and less sure of.

It was like the convergence of a complex function. He would come to for brief intervals, and then go back inside a regime of starvation and hallucinating and mental absence. He didn't always know where he was, or—especially unsettling for an old Vectorial hand—which direction he was going. He might drift into consciousness to find he was traveling up the Danube, through the Iron Gates, at the rail of a bouncing little steamer gazing up at the rock walls of the Defile of Kazan, taken inside the roaring of the rapids, as the river, beaten to mist, rose to encompass him, like a god's protective cloak—another time he might all at once be seeing Lake Baikal, or facing some chill boundary at least that pure and uncompromising. The other side of this "Baikal," he understood, was accessible only to those of intrepid spirit. To go there and come back would be like living through the end of the world. From this precise spot along the shoreline it was possible to "see" on the far shore a city, crystalline, redemptive. There was music, mysteriously audible, tonal yet deliberately broken into by dissonances—demanding, as if each note insisted on being attended to. And now and then, in brief periods of lucid return, he found himself thinking about nothing but Dally, aware that they'd separated, but unable to remember why.

After some weeks of this, he began to be visited by a sort of framed shadow suspended in the empty air, a transparent doorway, approaching him at a speed he knew he would not always be able to avoid. At last one day, still hesitant, he decided to approach it—might then, in fright, have lost his balance, and seized all at once as if by gravity, he toppled into the curiously orthogonal opening, exclaiming "What's this," as to the astonishment of onlookers he was turned to shimmering transparency, dwindling into a sort of graceful cone and swept through its point into what appeared to be a tiny or perhaps only distant window of bright plasma. Kit, on the other hand, found that he had remained the same size while the luminous opening began to grow, until it had flowed around and wrapped him in antique rusts and reds, brass gleaming through an interior haze, reassembling until he stood in a quiet hotel room in Paris, with Inner Asian rugs on a wood floor, the smell of tobacco and ganja, and a scholarly old party in a tarboosh and half-glasses bending over a sumptuously-bound stamp album, what collectors called a stockbook, where Kit saw an array of mint, never-hinged, superbly-centered Shambhala postage stamps all with original gum from local trees, issued in complete sets beginning shortly after the Treaty of Berlin (1878), with generic scenes from the Shambhalan countryside, flora and fauna, mountains, waterfalls, gorges providing entry to what the Buddhists called the hidden lands.

The man in the tarboosh turned finally and nodded in a strangely familiar way. "Lord Overlunch. Delighted to meet you."

"What just happened?" Kit feeling dazed. He looked around a little wildly. "I was in Lwów—"

"Excuse me, but you were in Shambhala." He handed Kit the glass and indicated one stamp in particular, whose finely-etched vignette showed a marketplace with a number of human figures, Bactrian camels and horses beneath a lurid sun-and-clouds effect in the sky.

"I like to look at these all carefully with the loupe at least once a week, and today I noticed something different about this ten-dirhan design, and wondered if possibly someone, some rival, had crept in here while I was out and substituted a variant. But of course I found the change immediately, the one face that was missing, your own, I know it well by now, it is, if you don't mind my saying so, the face of an old acquaintance. . . ."

"But I wasn't . . ."

"Well, well. A twin, perhaps."

Lord Overlunch was in town for the Ferrary sale, a major event in the history of the stamp-collecting hobby, at least for a look if not a bid on the Swedish three-skilling yellow.

"And to hunt up a few old faces, don't you know. Since the Spanish Lady passed through, close enough to feel the breeze from her gown, and try not to make out the face behind the black mantilla, one grows compulsive, I fear, about who's aboveground and who below."

"And how'd I get here again?"

"It's the way people reappear these days. The trains are not always running. The switches are not always thrown the right way." He looked at his watch. "Heavens, I'm late. Perhaps you'd like to be my guest this evening at Chez Rosalie. You might enjoy meeting my delightful American friend Miss

Rideout, who was one of the first actually to discover Montparnasse after the war. Some sort of husband in the picture"—and then he gave Kit an unmistakably friendly smile—"very much so indeed, I'm told. Do come along, won't you?"

Couples were out dancing the Hesitation Waltz in the middle of traffic, despite the signs clearly posted forbidding them to. From a nearby nightclub came the *bandoneón*-accompanied strains, ubiquitous in Montparnasse this year, of the melancholy yet catchy tango—

Vege-tariano . . .
No ifs ands or buts—
Eggs and dairy? ah no,
More like roots, and nuts—

Pot roast *prohibido,*
Tenderloin taboo,
why should my heart bleed o-
ver the likes of you?
Never known-to-be
Fond . . .
Of Châteaubriand . . .
Nor particularly close
To chipped beef on toast—steaks and
Chops, ¡a-di-ós!—Vege-

-taria-no . . .
Outcast Argentine,
Never could've gone "*¡O-*
lé!" for that cuisine . . .
Gauchos curse your name,
Still you haunt my brain—
Somehow I'll carry on, oh . . .
Vegetaria-no!

May we imagine for them a vector, passing through the invisible, the "imaginary," the unimaginable, carrying them safely into this postwar Paris where the taxis, battered veterans of the mythic Marne, now carry only lovers and cheerful drunks, and music which cannot be marched to goes on uninterrupted all night, in the bars and *bals musettes* for the dancers who will always be there, and the nights will be dark enough for whatever visions must transpire across them, no longer to be broken into by light displaced from Hell, and the difficulties they find are no more productive of evil than the opening and closing of too many doors, or of too few. A vector through the night into a morning of hosed pavements, birds heard everywhere but unseen, bakery smells, filtered green light, a courtyard still in shade . . .

"LOOK AT 'EM down there."

"All that light."

"All that dancing."

The Garçons de '71 were having their annual convention in Paris. Everybody on the *Inconvenience* was invited. The festivities would be pursued not on the ground but above the City in a great though unseen gathering of skyships.

Their motto was "There, but Invisible."

"The Boys call it the supranational idea," explained Penny Black, wide-eyed and dewy as when she was a girl, recently promoted to admiral of a fleet of skyships after the Bindlestiffs of the Blue had amalgamated with the Garçons de '71, "literally to transcend the old political space, the map-space of two dimensions, by climbing into the third."

"There is, unfortunately," Lindsay was eager to add, "another school of thought which views the third dimension not as an avenue of transcendence but as a means for delivering explosives."

"You can see how marriage has changed him," remarked Primula Noseworth.

"Glad anyhow to see you bunch of no-goods finally coming to your senses," Penny grinned. "Blaze, now, you want to watch out for old Darby here, he's a fast one."

"Who, this slowpoke?" tickling him at a reliable spot among his ribs. "He says I move too fast for him—never at home, always in some kind of trouble, all the rest of that. I told him, read the Agreement."

She referred to the document by which the girls had agreed to join their fortunes with those of *Inconvenience,* only on the understanding that they would always operate independently. They would be frigates, the boys a dreadnought—they would be freebooters and irregulars, the boys Military High Command. The boys would sail along, keeping pretty much to the ship, in an illusion of executive power, and the girls would depart the ship at right angles to its official course to do the adventuring, engaging the Exterior, often at great risk, and returning from their missions like weary commandos to Home Base.

Whereunto everybody had affixed his and her seals, and Miles broke out magnums of 1920 Puisieulx brut.

One day Heartsease discovers that she's expecting a baby, and then, like a canonical part-song, the other girls one by one announce that they are, too.

And on they fly. The ship by now has grown as large as a small city. There are neighborhoods, there are parks. There are slum conditions. It is so big that when people on the ground see it in the sky, they are struck with selective hysterical blindness and end up not seeing it at all.

Its corridors will begin to teem with children of all ages and sizes who run up and down the different decks whooping and hollering. The more serious are learning to fly the ship, others, never cut out for the Sky, are only marking time between visits to the surface, understanding that their destinies will be down in the finite world.

Inconvenience herself is constantly having her engineering updated. As a result of advances in relativity theory, light is incorporated as a source of motive power—though not exactly fuel—and as a carrying medium—though not exactly a vehicle—occupying, rather, a relation to the skyship much like that of the ocean to a surfer on a surfboard—a design principle borrowed from the Æther units that carry the girls to and fro on missions whose details they do not always share fully with "High Command."

As the sails of her destiny can be reefed against too much light, so they may also be spread to catch a favorable darkness. Her ascents are effortless now. It is no longer a matter of gravity—it is an acceptance of sky.

The contracts which the crew have been signing lately, under Darby's grim obsessiveness, grow longer and longer, eventually overflowing the edges of the main table in the mess decks, and occasionally they find themselves engaged to journey very far afield indeed. They return to Earth—unless it is to Counter-Earth—with a form of *mnemonic frostbite,* retaining only awed impressions of a ship exceeding the usual three dimensions, docking, each time precariously, at a series of remote stations high in unmeasured outer space, which together form a road to a destination—both ship and dockage hurtling at speeds that no one wishes to imagine, invisible sources of gravity rolling through like storms, making it possible to fall for distances only astronomers are comfortable with—yet, each time, the *Inconvenience* is brought to safety, in the bright, flowerlike heart of a perfect hyper-hyperboloid that only Miles can see in its entirety.

Pugnax and Ksenija's generations—at least one in every litter will follow a career as a sky-dog—have been joined by those of other dogs, as well as by cats, birds, fish, rodents, and less-terrestrial forms of life. Never sleeping, clamorous as a nonstop feast day, *Inconvenience,* once a vehicle of sky-pilgrimage, has transformed into its own destination, where any wish that can be made is at least addressed, if not always granted. For every wish to come true would mean that in the known Creation, good unsought and uncompensated would have evolved somehow, to become at least more accessible to us. No one aboard *Inconvenience* has yet observed any sign of this. They know—Miles is certain—it is there, like an approaching rainstorm, but invisible. Soon they will see the pressure-gauge begin to fall. They will feel the turn in the wind. They will put on smoked goggles for the glory of what is coming to part the sky. They fly toward grace.